A Dictionary of
English Word Roots

英文字根字典

劉 毅 主編

「英文字根字典」
是全國最完整的背單字字典。

利用「字根」背單字，
能夠舉一反三。

學了「字根」，英文單字
可以增加六倍以上。

序 言

這是一本背單字必備的工具書。我們盡最大的力量,希望所有單字都能查得到。我們把字根、字首、字尾的目錄全部放在前面,想查什麼字根,一目了然。碰到背不下來的單字,就可查閱書後的「索引」,字體儘量加大,讀者可以更快找到。此次修訂,註明常用單字的級數,分 1~7 級,第 1 級最簡單,第 7 級最難。由於 1~6 級是「常用 7000 字」,我們特別以紅字或藍字標示。

字根、字首、字尾很多,如果把它們串聯起來,背起來就非常簡單。例如:

1. auto¦bio¦graphy[4] 〔͵ɔtəbaɪˈɑgrəfɪ 〕 *n.* 自傳(自己一生的紀錄)
   self ¦ *life* ¦*writing*

2. bio¦graphy[4] 〔 baɪˈɑgrəfɪ 〕 *n.* 傳記(別人一生的紀錄)
   life ¦*writing*

3. bio¦logy[4] 〔 baɪˈɑlədʒɪ 〕 *n.* 生物學
   life ¦*study*

4. geo¦logy[7] 〔 dʒiˈɑlədʒɪ 〕 *n.* 地質學
   earth¦*study*

5. geo¦graphy[2] 〔 dʒiˈɑgrəfɪ 〕 *n.* 地理學
   earth¦ *writing*

6. geo¦metry[5] 〔 dʒiˈɑmətrɪ 〕 *n.* 幾何學(古時幾何學測量土地)
   earth¦ 測量

這六個字一起背,是不是很快?像 geology,geography,geometry 這些重要單字不這樣排列,怎麼記得下來?有些字不用「串聯記憶法」,背起來很困難,例如:

cata¦strophe[6] 〔 kəˈtæstrəfɪ 〕 *n.* 大災難(飛機、船、天氣急轉直下
down¦ *turning*　　　　　　　　　都是大災難)

apo¦strophe[7] 〔 əˈpɑstrəfɪ 〕 *n.* 上標點(即 ')
away¦ *turning*(標點想轉離開)

你會了 apostrophe[7],再接著背 catastrophe[6],不是很簡單嗎?接著再背 catalogue[4]〔ˈkætl͵ɔg 〕 *n.* 目錄、category[5] 〔ˈkætə͵gorɪ 〕 *n.* 範圍;種類等,就容易多了。

爲什麼要學英文字根？

1. 不學英文字根，太可怕了！因爲英文單字有 17 萬 1,476 個，
   每個單字有很多的解釋，不學字根，好像單字永遠不夠。

   例如： <u>**cap** | **tain**</u>² 〔ˋkæptən〕 *n.* 船長；機長；隊長；艦長；
   　　　　head | 人　　　　　　　　　　海軍上校；（陸、空）上尉

   　　　因爲艦長的階級是「海軍上校」；陸軍的連長是「上
   　　　尉」；空軍的區隊長是「上尉」，如果不背字根 cap
   　　　（= *head* ），就沒辦法記住這麼多意思。

   再如：capital，一般人只知道「首都」，你知道字根 cap 代表
   head（頭），你才能知道 capital 的所有意思。

   　　　<u>**capit** | **al**</u>³·⁴ 〔ˋkæpət!〕 *n.* 首都；資本；大寫字母
   　　　　head | *n.*

   　　　「頭」是身體中最重要的部份，「首都」是國家最重要
   　　　的城市；「資本；本錢」是做生意最重要的部份；重要
   　　　的字或句首，第一個字母都要用「大寫字母」，你看，
   　　　不是和「頭」一樣重要嗎？英文造字不會亂造，造每一
   　　　個字，都有道理。把根挖起來，才知道它的眞正含意。

2. 學了字根，英文單字可以增加六倍以上。

   學會 captain 以後，就會引申到下面幾個字：

   　　　<u>**chief** | **tain**</u> 〔ˋtʃiftɪn〕 *n.* 首領【當「首長」的人，就是「首領」】
   　　　首長 | 人

   　　　<u>**vill** | **ain**</u>⁵ 〔ˋvɪlən〕 *n.* 土匪【「土匪」通常躲在「村莊」裡】
   　　　village | 人
   　　　村莊

   　　　<u>**chapl** | **ain**</u>⁷ 〔ˋtʃæplɪn〕 *n.* 牧師
   　　　chapel | 人
   　　　教堂

   　　同學在考試時，最感到痛苦的，就是單字量不夠。零零散散
   背，背了後面，前面忘記了，是最大的障礙。利用字根記憶，是
   增加單字最快速的方法。

例如，同學常搞不清楚 preserve 和 reserve 的區別：

pre¦serve[4] 〔 prɪ'zɜv 〕*v.* 保存（保存在以前的狀態）
before¦keep

當名詞用，就是「蜜餞；果醬；保護區；禁獵區」，這個字
不用字根背，怎麼知道這麼多意思？

re¦serve[3] 〔 rɪ'zɜv 〕*v.* 預約；保留；保存（保存到以後再來用）
back¦keep

它的名詞是「儲備物；儲備金」，你如果不用字根，了解單字的
真正意思，你怎麼能分清楚 preserve 和 reserve 呢？字典上這
兩個字都有「保存」的意思，但兩者意義不同。

再如： **ob¦serve**[3] 〔 əb'zɜv 〕*v.* ①觀察 ②遵守
eye¦keep

從這個字的字根意思可以看出，眼睛不停地看，就是「觀察」
或「遵守」。observe 有兩個不同的意思，所以有兩個名詞：
① observation[4] 〔͵ɑbzɚ'veʃən 〕*n.* 觀察
② observance[7] 〔 əb'zɜvəns 〕*n.* 遵守
引申出 observat¦ory[7] 〔 əb'zɜvə͵torɪ 〕*n.* 天文台
　　　　觀察¦地點

　　利用「字根」背單字，能夠舉一反三。每一個英文單字，
往往有很多個意思，例如：impose，字中的 im 表示 on，pose
等於 put，「放在上面」，一般人都知道作「加於」解，如果你
背了這個字的衍生字 imposter[7] 〔 ɪm'pɑstɚ 〕*n.* 騙子；冒充者，
你才會知道，impose 還可當「欺騙」講。同理，compose 這個
字，一般人只知道作「組成」解，如果你背了 composer[4]
〔 kəm'pozɚ 〕*n.* 作曲家，你就會知道，compose 還可當「作
（曲）」解；你背了 composure[7] 〔 kəm'poʒɚ 〕*n.* 平靜，你就會
發現，compose 還有「使平靜；使鎮靜」的意思。

劉毅

如何使用這本字典

I. 凡是對字根、字首、字尾已經有概念的讀者，可以直接看書的頁眉查閱字根或字首。字尾必須查字尾的目錄，如 excursion，可分解成 ex + cur + sion，可以直接翻書，查字根 cur（p.121），也可以查字首 ex（p.680），也可以看字根目錄或字首目錄來查閱。

1. 直接看頁眉查。
2. 查字首目錄。

整個字查「索引」。

1. 直接看頁眉查。
2. 查字根目錄。

1. 直接看頁眉查。
2. 查字根目錄。

整個字查「索引」。

查字尾目錄。

II. 碰到不認識的單字，先翻書末的「索引」。「索引」是按照字母序排列，查「索引」可以發現 important 出現在本字典的第 406 頁。

III. 翻到第 406 頁，找到 important，內容如下：

important[1]〔ɪmˈpɔrtn̩t〕*adj.* 重要的

im	+	port	+	ant
in	+	carry	+	adj.

（古時候房子很小，「**重要的**」東西才搬進來）

IV. 發揮想像力，從字根分析中，我們可以知道 im 表「在裡面」
（= *in*），port 表「攜帶」（= *carry*），而 ant 則是形容詞
字尾，意思是把東西帶到屋內。我們可以想像一下，以前
的人房子小，所以只把重要的東西放在屋子裡，因此這個
字就引申作「重要的」。

V. 舉一反三，了解 important 這個字之後，往前查看它是屬
於哪一個字根分類，結果如下：

458　port = carry（運送） 　　* 拉丁文 *portare*（= *carry*）。

port〔port, pɔrt〕*n.* 舉止；態度；姿勢（表現在身體上的動作）
portable〔'portəbḷ, 'por-〕*adj.* 可攜帶的　　*n.* 可手提之物
portability〔,portə'bɪlɪtɪ〕*n.* 可攜帶性

$\vdots$

import〔*v.* ɪm'pɔrt, -'pɔrt　*n.* 'ɪmpɔrt, -pɔrt〕*v.* 輸入；意含
　　n. 輸入品；涵義；重要性（搬進來）《*im-* = *in-* = in》
importable〔ɪm'pɔrtəbḷ〕*adj.* 可進口的
important〔ɪm'pɔrtṇt〕*adj.* 重要的

> im ＋ port ＋ ant
> ｜　　 ｜　　 ｜
> in ＋ carry ＋ adj.
> 　　　　　　　　（古時候房子很小，「**重要的**」東西
> 　　　　　　　　才搬進來）

importantly〔ɪm'pɔrtṇtlɪ〕*adv.* 重要地
importance〔ɪm'pɔrtṇs〕*n.* 重要；重要性
importation〔,ɪmpor'teʃən, -pɔr-〕*n.* 輸入品；進口
importer〔ɪm'pɔrtɚ〕*n.* 進口商；輸入業者

在查閱的過程中，你可以學會很多跟 port 這個字根有關的
字，以後只要看到 port 出現在單字中，你就會知道這個字
可能跟「攜帶」有關，長久累積下去，你的字根分析能力會
愈來愈強，以後你不需要查字典，也能猜出生字的意義，
這就是「英文字根字典」的妙用。

如何利用字尾背單字

當你看到一個單字，像relative，字尾是ive，通常是形容詞，怎麼變成名詞呢？此時，你查「英文字根字典」p.836，你就可以找出 ive 當作名詞，表「人」的字，加以歸納。

> relat|ive *n.* 親戚【相關的人，就是「親戚」】
> 和～相關　人
>
> nat|ive *n.* 本地人；土人【土人是自然出現的】
> 自然　人
>
> detect|ive *n.* 偵探【偵測的人，就是「偵探」】
> 偵測　人

再如 beggar 這個字，你覺得 ar 很奇怪，你查「英文字根字典」p.826、p.827，你就知道，ar 可以當「人」。

> begg|ar *n.* 乞丐【重複 g 是為了配合發音】
> 乞求　人
>
> burgl|ar *n.* 夜賊【burgle＝竊盜】
> 行竊　人
>
> li|ar *n.* 說謊者【li 源自 lie＝說謊】
> 說謊　人
>
> schol|ar *n.* 學者【在學校的人，通常是「學者」】
> 學校　人
>
> 這四個字，有一個共同特色，都是壞人。你可以運用你的想像力，scholar（學者）如果壞起來，更可怕。

很多人背不下來 stewardess 這個字，如果你知道 stew 是「燉煮」的意思，ard 代表「人」，ess 是陰性字尾，一分析你就知道，stewardess 是「女廚子」，在飛機上幫旅客煮飯的，就是「空中小姐」。其他 ard 表「人」的例子有：

> cow|ard *n.* 懦夫【膽小的人看到母牛就跑】
> 母牛　人
>
> drunk|ard *n.* 醉漢【drunk 是「喝醉的」】
> 喝醉的　人
>
> wiz|ard *n.* 巫師【wiz 源自 wise，古時候聰明
> 聰明的　人　　的人才當巫師】

目　錄

可利用目錄查到字根、字首、字尾的頁碼，一目了然。

▶ 字根（*Root*）

字根目錄

字根目錄

字根目錄

▶ 字首（*Prefix*）

字首目錄

字首目錄

字尾（*Suffix*）

字尾目錄

字　根（Root）

　　英語字根大部分是來自拉丁文。根據這些字
根可了解它們的原義，再配合字首、字尾的活用
組合，對學習英文單字將有莫大的幫助。

1　**ac** , **acr** , **acu** = sour ; sharp（酸的；尖銳的）

* 拉丁文 *acere*（= *be sour*），*acidus*（= *sour*）；*acer* , *acris*
　（= *sharp*），*acuere*（= *sharpen*）。

acid[4]〔'æsɪd〕*adj.* 酸的；酸性的；尖酸刻薄的　*n.* 酸性物質

acidify〔ə'sɪdə,faɪ〕*v.* 酸化；變酸

acidity[7]〔ə'sɪdətɪ〕*n.* 酸味；酸性；酸度

acidize〔'æsə,daɪz〕*v.* 用酸處理；使變酸

acidulate〔ə'sɪdʒə,let〕*v.* 使略帶酸味

　　《拉丁文 *acidulus* = sourish 微酸的》

```
acidul  +  ate
  |         |
sourish  +  v.
```

acidulous〔ə'sɪdʒələs〕*adj.* 微酸的；尖酸刻薄的

acidimeter〔,æsɪ'dɪmətɚ〕*n.* 酸定量器《*meter* 計量器》

acetic〔ə'sitɪk , ə'sɛtɪk〕*adj.* 醋的；酸的

acetify〔ə'sɛtə,faɪ〕*v.*（使）成醋；（使）發酸

acetous〔'æsɪtəs , ə'sitəs〕*adj.* 含醋酸的；產生醋酸的

acerbic[7]〔ə'sɝbɪk〕*adj.* 刻薄的；尖刻的

acerbity〔ə'sɝbətɪ〕*n.* 刻薄；尖刻

acrid[7]〔'ækrɪd〕*adj.* 辛辣的；難聞的

acrimonious[7] 〔͵ækrə'monɪəs 〕*adj.* 辛辣的；尖刻的；劇烈的
《*acrimony* 嚴厲》

```
acri  + moni  + ous
 |        |      |
sharp + state +  adj.
```

acuity[7] 〔 ə'kjuətɪ 〕*n.* 尖銳《*acu* (sharp) + *-ity* (名詞字尾)》
acumen[7] 〔 ə'kjumɪn 〕*n.* 敏銳而正確的判斷力
acute[6] 〔 ə'kjut 〕*adj.* 敏銳的；深刻的；急性的

2 act , ag = act ; drive (行動；驅使)

* 源自於拉丁文 *agere* (= *do* ; *drive*)，過去分詞是 *actus*。
〔變化型〕*ig*。

act[1] 〔 ækt 〕*n.* 行為；法案；一幕　 *v.* 行動；扮演；作用
action[1] 〔'ækʃən 〕*n.* 行動；動作；作用；訴訟；戰鬥
actionable[7] 〔'ækʃənəbl̩ 〕*adj.* 可引起訴訟的；可被控訴的
activate[7] 〔'æktə͵vet 〕*v.* 刺激；使產生活動
activation[7] 〔͵æktə'veʃən 〕*n.* 活化
activator 〔'æktə͵vetɚ 〕*n.* 觸媒；催化劑
active[1] 〔'æktɪv 〕*adj.* 活動的；活躍的；
　能起作用的

```
act + ive
 |     |
act + adj.
```

activity[3] 〔 æk'tɪvətɪ 〕*n.* 活動；活動力
actual[3] 〔'æktʃʊəl 〕*adj.* 眞實的；實際的
actuality[7] 〔͵æktʃʊ'ælətɪ 〕*n.* 現實
actualize 〔'æktʃʊəl͵aɪz 〕*v.* 實現；實行
actually[3] 〔'æktʃʊəlɪ 〕*adv.* 眞實地；實際地
actualist 〔'æktʃʊəlɪst 〕*n.* 現實主義者；現實論者；實際者
《*-ist* 表示人的名詞字尾》
actuate 〔'æktʃʊ͵et 〕*v.* 使活動；使動作；促使

enact[6]〔 ɪn'ækt 〕*v.* 制定為法律；扮演《*en-* = in》

enactment[6]〔 ɪn'æktmənt , ɛn- 〕*n.* (法律之) 創制；法令

```
en  +  act  +  ment
 |       |       |
in  +  act  +   n.
```

exact[2]〔 ɪg'zækt 〕= drive out　*v.* 需要；強索

　　adj. 正確的；精確的；嚴格的《*ex-* = out》

exacting[7]〔 ɪg'zæktɪŋ , ɛg- 〕*adj.* 苛求的；費力的

exaction〔 ɪg'zækʃən 〕*n.* 勒索；榨取；稅

exactitude〔 ɪg'zæktə‚tjud , -‚tud 〕*n.* 正確；精密；嚴正

　　《 *-itude* 抽象名詞字尾》

```
ex  +  act  +  itude
 |       |       |
out  +  act  +   n.
```

exactly[2]〔 ɪg'zæktlɪ 〕*adv.* 正確地

inaction[7]〔 ɪn'ækʃən 〕*n.* 不活動；懶散；怠惰《*in-* = not》

inactive[7]〔 ɪn'æktɪv 〕*adj.* 不活動的；不活潑的；懶惰的

interact[4]〔 *v.* ‚ɪntɚ'ækt *n.* 'ɪntɚ‚ækt 〕*v. , n.* 交互作用；互相影響

　　《*inter-* = between ; among》

react[3]〔 rɪ'ækt 〕*v.* 反動；反作用；起化學反應《*re-* = back》

reactor[7]〔 rɪ'æktɚ 〕*n.* 反動者；起反應者；原子爐

reaction[3]〔 rɪ'ækʃən 〕*n.* 反動；反應；反作用

transact[7]〔 træns'ækt , trænz'ækt 〕*v.* 處理；執行；交易 (行得通)

　　《*trans-* = through》

transaction[6]〔 træns'ækʃən , trænz'ækʃən 〕*n.* 辦理；處理；交易

```
trans  +  act  +  ion
  |        |       |
through  + drive  +  n.
```

agency[4]〔'edʒənsɪ 〕*n.* 動作；力量；代理；經售；代理處；

　　經銷處 (實行；做)

agenda[5] 〔 ə'dʒɛndə 〕 *n.* 議程

agent[4] 〔'edʒənt 〕 *n.* 代理人；代理商；動作者；原動力（做的人）

agile[7] 〔'ædʒəl , -ɪl , -aɪl 〕 *adj.* 活潑的；輕快的；敏捷的

　《 *-ile* 形容詞字尾》

agility[7] 〔 ə'dʒɪlətɪ 〕 *n.* 動作的敏捷；機敏

```
ag  +  il  +  ity
 |      |      |
act  +  adj. +  n.
```

agitate[7] 〔'ædʒə,tet 〕 *v.* 震動；煽動

agitation[7] 〔,ædʒə'teʃən 〕 *n.* 搖動；激動的狀態；煽動

agitator[7] 〔'ædʒə,tetɚ 〕 *n.* 煽動者；遊說者

ambiguous[6] 〔 æm'bɪgjuəs 〕 = driving about　*adj.* 含糊的；
不明確的（躊躇）

```
amb  +   ig  + uous
 |       |      |
about +  drive +  adj.
```

cogent[7] 〔'kodʒənt 〕 = drive together　*adj.* 強有力的；使人信
服的（勸動別人一起去）《*co-* = *com-* = together》

cogitate 〔'kadʒə,tet 〕 *v.* 思考；計畫；設計

cogitable 〔'kadʒətəbl̩ 〕 *adj.* 可思考的；可想像的

exigent[7] 〔'ɛksədʒənt 〕 *adj.* 急切的；緊急的；所需極多的（驅逐
出去）

```
ex  +   ig  + ent
 |       |     |
out +  drive + adj.
```

prodigal[7] 〔'pradɪgl̩ 〕 *adj.* 浪費的；揮霍的　*n.* 浪費者；浪子

　《拉丁文 *prodigere* = drive forth》

3 **acro** = high ; extreme (高的 ; 前端的)

* 希臘文 *akros* (= *extreme* ; *topmost*) 。

acrobat[7] 〔'ækrə,bæt 〕 *n.* 特技表演者
acrogen 〔'ækrədʒən 〕 *n.* 頂生植物《*gen* = produce》
acronym[7] 〔'ækrənɪm 〕 *n.* 頭字語《*acro* (extreme) + *nym* (name)》
acropolis 〔 ə'krɑpəlɪs 〕 *n.* 古希臘城市用以據守的城堡
　　《*acro* (high) + *polis* (city)》

4 **adip** = fat (脂肪)　　* 拉丁文 *adeps* (= *fat*) 。

adipic 〔 ə'dɪpɪk 〕 *adj.* 脂肪的
adipocere 〔'ædəpə,sɪrə 〕 *n.* 屍蠟 (動物屍體在濕處腐爛後產生的
　　軟蠟狀物質)《拉丁文 *cera* = wax》
adipose[7] 〔'ædə,pos 〕 *n.* (動物性) 脂肪　　*adj.* 脂肪 (多) 的
adiposis 〔,ædə'posɪs 〕 *n.* 肥胖症《*-osis* 表示病變狀態的名詞字尾》
adiposity 〔,ædə'pɑsətɪ 〕 *n.* 肥胖症 ; 肥胖

5 **aer** = air (空氣 ; 天空)　　* 希臘文 *aer* , *aero-* (= *air*) 。

aerate[7] 〔'eə,ret 〕 *v.* 加氣於 (液體) ; 使 (土壤等) 通氣
aerial[7] 〔'ɛrɪəl 〕 *adj.* 空氣的 ; 航空的 ; 飛機的
aerify 〔'ɛrə,faɪ 〕 *v.* 在…中充注空氣 ; 使氣化 ; 使蒸發
aerobatics[7] 〔,eərə'bætɪks 〕 *n.* 特技飛行 (表演)

```
aero  +  bat  +  ics
  |        |       |
 air  +  walk  +  n.
```

aerobic[7] 〔,eə'robɪk 〕 *adj.* 有氧運動的 ; 需氧的
　　《*aero* (air) + *b(io)* (life) + *-ic* (形容詞字尾)》

aerobics[7] 〔͵eəˈrobɪks 〕 *n.* 有氧運動

aeronautics 〔͵ɛrəˈnɔtɪks 〕 *n.* 航空學

《*aero* (air) + *naut* (ship) + *-ics* (science)》

aerophotography 〔͵eərofəˈtɑgrəfɪ 〕 *n.* 空中攝影術;空中照

相術《*photography* 攝影術》

```
aero + photo + graph + y
 |       |       |      |
air  + light + write + n.
```

aeroplane[7] 〔ˈɛrə͵plen 〕 *n.* 飛機《*aero* (air) + *plane* (wandering)》

6 **aesthet** = feeling (感覺)

* 希臘文 *aisthanesthai* (= feel) ,*aisthesis* (= feeling) 。

aesthetics[7] 〔 ɛsˈθɛtɪks 〕 *n.* 美學;審美學《*-ics* = science》

aestheticism 〔 ɛsˈθɛtəsɪzm̩ 〕 *n.* 唯美主義

《 *-ism* 表示主義的名詞字尾》

an(a)esthesia 〔͵ænəsˈθiʒə 〕 *n.* 麻醉

```
an + (a)esthes + ia
 |       |        |
not + feeling  + n.
```

an(a)esthetize[7] 〔 əˈnɛsθə͵taɪz 〕 *v.* 使麻醉《 *-ize* 動詞字尾》

syn(a)esthesia 〔͵sɪnəsˈθiʒə 〕 *n.* 共同感覺《*syn-* = same》

7 **(a)estiv** = summer (夏天)

* 拉丁文 *aestas* (= summer) 。

(a)estival 〔ˈɛstəvəl 〕 *adj.* 夏季的

(a)estivate 〔ˈɛstə͵vet 〕 *v.* 夏眠;過夏季

8　**agogue** = leader（領導者）

> * 希臘文 *agein*（= *drive* ; *lead*），*agogos*（= *leader*）。

demagogue[7]〔ˈdɛməˌgɔg〕*n.* 群衆煽動家《*dem* = people》
mystagogue〔ˈmɪstəˌgɑg , -ˌgɔg〕*n.* 引人入密敎者《*myst* = mystery》
pedagogue〔ˈpɛdəˌgɔg〕*n.* 賣弄學問的人；敎師（貶義）《*ped* = child》
synagogue[7]〔ˈsɪnəˌgɔg〕*n.* 猶太敎的會堂；猶太敎會堂之聚會
　《*syn-* = together》

9　**agon** = struggle（掙扎；奮鬥）

> * 希臘文 *agon*（= *contest*），*agonia*（= *struggle*），
> 和 *agogue* 同一字源。

agony[5]〔ˈægənɪ〕*n.* 極大的痛苦（纏繞心頭）
antagonist[7]〔ænˈtægənɪst〕*n.* 敵手；反對者（對立爭鬥的人）
　《*ant-* = *anti-* = against》

ant	+	agon	+	ist
against	+	struggle	+	person

antagonistic[7]〔ænˌtægəˈnɪstɪk〕*adj.* 敵對的；反對的
antagonize[7]〔ænˈtægəˌnaɪz〕*v.* 對抗；反對
protagonist[7]〔proˈtægənɪst〕*n.* 主角；領導者（主要領導人物）
　《*prot-* = *proto-*（first）+ *agonist*（actor）》

10　**agr** = field（田野）

> * 拉丁文 *ager* , *agr-*（= *field*）；希臘文 *agros*（= *field*）。

agrarian〔əˈgrɛrɪən〕*adj.* 土地的；農業的　　*n.* 平均地權論者

agrar	+	ian
field	+	adj., n.

agrestic 〔 əˈgrɛstɪk 〕 *adj.* 農村的;鄉間的

agribusiness 〔ˈægrɪˌbɪznɪs 〕 *n.* 農產企業(業務包括農產品加工
與運銷、農耕用具與肥料的生產等)《*business* 商業》

agriculture[3] 〔ˈægrɪˌkʌltʃɚ 〕 *n.* 農業《*culture* 文化》

agrochemical 〔ˈægrəˌkɛmɪkḷ 〕 *n.* 農業用的化學品(如肥料、
殺蟲劑等) *adj.* 農業化學的《*chemical* 化學製品;化學的》

agrology 〔 əˈgrɑlədʒɪ 〕 *n.* 農業土壤學《*logy* = study》

agronomy 〔 əˈgrɑnəmɪ 〕 *n.* 農藝學;農業經濟學

```
agro  +   nomy
  |         |
field  + management
```

11 **al** = nourish(滋養)

* 拉丁文 *alere*(= *nourish*)。〔變化型〕*ol* , *ul*。

aliment[7] 〔ˈæləmənt 〕 *n.* 營養物;食物;扶養 *v.* 供給營養;扶養

alimental 〔ˌæləˈmɛntḷ 〕 *adj.* 食物的;營養的

alimentary 〔ˌæləˈmɛntərɪ 〕 *adj.* 食物的;營養的;消化的

alimentation 〔ˌæləmɛnˈteʃən 〕 *n.* 營養;扶養

```
ali   + ment + ation
 |        |       |
nourish +  n.  +  n.
```

alimentotherapy 〔ˌæləˈmɛntəˈθɛrəpɪ 〕 *n.* 營養療法;食物療法
《*therapy* 治療法》

alimony[7] 〔ˈæləˌmonɪ 〕 *n.* 贍養費;生活費

adolescence[5] 〔ˌædḷˈɛsns 〕 *n.* 青春期
《*ad-*(to)+ *olesc*(grow up)+ *-ence*(名詞字尾)》

```
ad +  olesc  + ence
 |      |        |
to  + grow up +  n.
```

adolescent[5]〔͵ædḷˈɛsṇt〕*adj.* 青春期的　*n.* 青少年

prolific[7]〔prəˈlɪfɪk〕*adj.* 有生產力的；肥沃的；多產的；豐富的

《*pro-* (forward) + (*o*)*li* (nourish) + -*fic* (形容詞字尾)》

prolificacy〔prəˈlɪfɪkəsɪ〕*n.* 多產；豐富

proliferate[7]〔proˈlɪfəͺret〕*v.* 增生；增加；大量產生

《*fer* = bear (生產)》

proliferous〔proˈlɪfərəs〕*adj.* 細胞增生的；繁殖的；分芽繁殖的

adult[1]〔əˈdʌlt〕*adj.* 成人的；適合成人的　*n.* 成人《*ad-* = to》

adulthood[5]〔əˈdʌlthʊd〕*n.* 成年

adultness〔əˈdʌltnɪs〕*n.* 成熟；老成

12 **alg** = pain (痛苦)　* 希臘文 *algos* (= pain)。

analgesic〔͵ænælˈdʒizɪk〕*n.* 止痛藥　*adj.* 止痛的

neuralgia〔njʊˈrældʒə〕*n.* 神經痛

```
neur + algia
  |       |
nerve + pain
```

nostalgia[7]〔nɑˈstældʒɪə〕*n.* 思鄉病；留戀過去

13 **all** = other (其他的)

* 希臘文 *allos* (= other ; different)。

allegory[7]〔ˈæləͺgorɪ〕*n.* 寓言；諷喻 (用另一種比喻來敘述)

《希臘文 *agoreuein* = speak openly》

allogamy〔əˈlɑgəmɪ〕*n.* 異花授粉；異體受精 (在其他地方結合)

《*gam* = marriage》

allometry〔əˈlɑmətrɪ〕*n.* 異速生長《*metr* = measure》

allomorph〔ˈæləͺmɔrf〕*n.* 語素變體；詞素變體；同質異晶體

(不同的形態)《*morph* = form》

allonym〔'ælənɪm〕*n.*（尤指作家發表作品時使用的）別人的名字；用別人的名字所發表的作品《*onym* = name》

allonymous〔ə'lɑnəməs〕*adj.* 筆名的（其他的名字）

```
all  +  onym  +  ous
 |        |        |
other  +  name  +  adj.
```

allopathy〔ə'lɑpəθɪ〕*n.* 對抗療法（產生和疾病症狀不同的影響）《*path* = disease》

allopatric〔,ælə'pætrɪk〕*adj.* 分布在鄰近不同地區的；分布區不重疊的《希臘文 *patra* = fatherland》

allophone〔'ælə,fon〕*n.* 音位變體（不同的聲音）《*phon* = sound》

14 **alt** = high（高的）　　* 拉丁文 *altus*（= *high*）。

altar[7]〔'ɔltɚ〕*n.* 祭壇（高的地方）

altimeter〔'æltə,mitɚ〕*n.* 高度計《*meter* 計量器》

altitude[5]〔'æltə,tjud〕*n.* 高度；海拔《*-itude* 抽象名詞字尾》

```
alt  +  itude
 |        |
high  +   n.
```

exalt[7]〔ɪg'zɔlt〕*v.* 提高；擢升；使得意；讚揚（高舉）《*ex-* = out；up》

exaltation[7]〔,ɪgzɔl'teʃən，,ɛg-〕*n.*（階級、榮譽等的）提高；狂喜

haughty[7]〔'hɔtɪ〕*adj.* 傲慢的；驕傲的《*haught* = *alt* = high》

15 **alter**，**ali** = other（其他的）

* 拉丁文 *alter*，*alius*（= *other*）。〔變化型〕*altr*。

alter[5]〔'ɔltɚ〕*v.* 改變；更改（變爲其他東西）

alteration[7] 〔͵ɔltə'reʃən 〕 *n.* 變更；更改

altercate[7] 〔'ɔltə͵ket 〕 *v.* 口角；爭論

altercation[7] 〔͵ɔltə'keʃən 〕 *n.* 口角；爭論

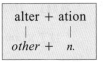

```
alter  +  ation
  |         |
other  +   n.
```

alternate[5] 〔 *adj.* , *n.* 'ɔltə͵nɪt *v.* 'ɔltə͵net 〕

　　adj. 輪流的　 *n.* 交替；輪流；代理者　 *v.* 輪流；交替

alternation 〔͵ɔltə'neʃən 〕 *n.* 交互；交替

alternative[6] 〔 ɔl'tɜnətɪv , æl- 〕 *adj.* 二者擇一的　 *n.* 二者擇一；

　　選擇餘地

alternator 〔'ɔltə͵netə 〕 *n.* 交流發電機

altruism[7] 〔'æltrʊ͵ɪzəm 〕 *n.* 利他主義

　　《 *altru = alter* (other) + *-ism* (表主義的名詞字尾)》

```
altru  +  ism
  |        |
other  +   n.
```

altruistic[7] 〔͵æltrʊ'ɪstɪk 〕 *adj.* 利他主義的

alien[5] 〔'elɪən , 'eljən 〕 *adj.* 外國人的；相反的　 *n.* 外國人 (其他的)

alienable 〔'eljənəb!̩ , 'elɪən- 〕 *adj.* 可讓渡的 (變成他人的東西)

alienate[6] 〔'eljən͵et 〕 *v.* 使疏遠；讓渡

alienation[7] 〔͵elɪən'eʃən 〕 *n.* 疏遠；讓渡

alias[7] 〔'elɪəs 〕 *n.* 別名；化名；假名 (其他名字)

alibi[7] 〔'ælə͵baɪ 〕 *n.* 不在場證明；託辭；藉口 (在其他場所)

　　《 *bi* = place》

adulterate[7] 〔 ə'dʌltə͵ret 〕 *v.* 摻混　 *adj.* 不道德的；墮落的

　　《 *ad-* = to ; *ulter = alter*》

```
ad  +  ulter  +  ate
 |       |        |
to  +  other  +   v.
```

adultery[7] 〔 ə'dʌltərɪ 〕 *n.* 通姦；私通

16 **am** = love (喜愛)

* 拉丁文 *amare* (= *love*)，過去分詞是 *amatus* ; *amicus* (= *friend*)。

amateur[4] 〔ˈæməˌtʃur 〕 *n.* 業餘技藝家；業餘者
(業餘愛好技藝的人)

amatory 〔ˈæməˌtorɪ 〕 *adj.* 戀愛的；色情的

amiable[6] 〔ˈemɪəbḷ 〕 *adj.* 和藹可親的

```
ami  +  able
 |       |
love  +  adj.
```

amicable[7] 〔ˈæmɪkəbḷ 〕 *adj.* 友善的；和平的

amigo[7] 〔əˈmigo 〕 *n.* 朋友

amity 〔ˈæmətɪ 〕 *n.* 友好；和睦

amorist 〔ˈæmərɪst 〕 *n.* 情人；愛情小說作家

amorous[7] 〔ˈæmərəs 〕 *adj.* 多情的；表示愛情的

amour[7] 〔əˈmur 〕 *n.* 戀情

enamo(u)r 〔ɪnˈæmɚ 〕 *v.* 引起愛憐；迷住 《*en-* = in》

paramour 〔ˈpærəˌmur 〕 *n.* 情夫；情婦

enemy[2] 〔ˈɛnəmɪ 〕 *n.* 敵人 (不愛的人) 《*en-* = not ; *em* = *am* = love》

```
en  +  em  +  y
 |      |      |
not  + love  + n.
```

enmity 〔ˈɛnmətɪ 〕 *n.* 敵意；不和；敵對

字根 *ac~avi*

17 **ambul** = walk (走)   * 拉丁文 *ambulare* (= *walk*)。

amble 〔ˈæmbḷ 〕 *v.* 漫步

ambulance[6] 〔ˈæmbjələns 〕 *n.* 救護車

ambulate 〔ˈæmbjəˌlet 〕 *v.* 行走；走動

circumambulate〔͵sɝkəm'æmbjə͵let〕*v.* 繞行；拐彎抹角地說
　《*circum-* = around》

deambulatory〔dɪ'æmbjələ͵torɪ〕*adj.* 走動的；散步的
　n. 迴廊；步道

```
de  + ambul + at(e) +  ory
 |      |       |       |
about + walk  +  v.  + adj., n.
```

perambulator〔pə'æmbjə͵letɚ〕*n.* 漫步者；巡視者
　《*per-*（through）+ *ambul*（walk）+ *-at(e)*（動詞字尾）+ *-or*（person）》

preamble〔'priæmbl̩〕*n.* 序言；開場白《*pre-* = before》

somnambulism〔sɑm'næmbjə͵lɪzəm〕*n.* 夢遊（症）

```
somn + ambul + ism
 |      |      |
sleep + walk + n.
```

【注意】以下單字字源不同，爲方便記憶而歸於此處。

ramble[7]〔'ræmbl̩〕*v. , n.* 漫步

18　**ampl** = large（大的）　* 拉丁文 *amplus*（= *large*）。

ample[5]〔'æmpl̩〕*adj.* 富足的；充分的

ampliate〔'æmplɪ͵et〕*adj.* 廣大的

ampliation〔͵æmplɪ'eʃən〕*n.* 擴大；擴充

amplify[6]〔'æmplə͵faɪ〕*v.* 放大；詳述《*-fy* = make》

amplifier[7]〔'æmplə͵faɪɚ〕*n.* 放大鏡；擴音器

```
ampli +  f(y)  + ier
  |      |       |
large + make  + n.
```

amplitude〔'æmplə͵tjud〕*n.* 廣闊；豐富《*-itude* 抽象名詞字尾》

19 **andr** = man；male（男人；男性）

* 希臘文 *aner*，*andr-*（= *man*；*male*）。

Andrew〔'ændru〕*adj.*【男子名】安德魯

androgen〔'ændrədʒən〕*n.* 雄激素；男性荷爾蒙
　《*andro*（male）+ *gen*（race）》

android[7]〔'ændrɔid〕*adj.* 男性的；雄性的　*n.* 機器人《*-oid* = like》

androecium〔æn'driʃɪəm〕*n.* 雄蕊《希臘文 *oikos* = house》

androgynous〔æn'dradʒənəs〕*adj.* 雙性的；雌雄同體的

andro	+	gyn	+	ous
man	+	woman	+	adj.

Andromeda〔æn'dramɪdə〕*n.* 仙女座；安德洛墨達（希臘神話中，埃塞俄比亞公主，其母誇其貌美而得罪海神波塞頓之妻，致使全國遭到騷擾，本人為救國民毅然獻身，被鎮囚於大石之旁，後為伯修斯（Perseus）救出並娶為妻。）

monandrous〔mə'nændrəs〕*adj.* 具單一雄蕊的；一夫制的
　《*mon-* = *mono-* = single》

polyandry〔ˌpalɪ'ændrɪ〕*n.* 一妻多夫制《*poly-* = many》

20 **anem** = wind（風）　* 希臘文 *anemos*（= *wind*）。

anemochory〔ə'nɛməˌkɔrɪ〕*n.*（植物等的）風力散佈
　《希臘文 *khorein* = move》

anemograph〔ə'nɛməˌgræf〕*n.* 風力自計表；記風儀
　《*graph* = write》

anemography〔ˌænə'magrəfɪ〕*n.* 記風法；風論

anemology〔ˌænə'malədʒɪ〕*n.* 測風學《*logy* = study》

anemophilous〔ˌænə'mafələs〕*adj.* 風媒的；藉風授粉的

21　**ang** = strangle（勒死；窒息）

　　* 拉丁文 *angere*（= *strangle*）。〔變化型〕*anx*。

anger[1]〔'æŋgɚ〕*v.* 激怒　*n.* 憤怒
angry[1]〔'æŋgrɪ〕*adj.* 憤怒的；生氣的
anguish[7]〔'æŋgwɪʃ〕*n.* 身心極度的痛苦
anxiety[4]〔æŋ'zaɪətɪ〕*n.* 憂慮；渴望
anxious[4]〔'æŋkʃəs〕*adj.* 憂慮的；渴望的

22　**angi** = vessel（血管）　　* 希臘文 *angeion*（= *vessel*）。

angiectomy〔,ændʒɪ'ɛktəmɪ〕*n.* 血管切除術

```
angi + ec + tom + y
 |     |    |     |
vessel + out + cut + n.
```

angiogram〔'ændʒɪə,græm〕*n.* 血管造影（照）片《*gram* = write》
angiography〔,ændʒɪ'ɑgrəfɪ〕*n.* 血管造影術《*graph* = write》
angiology〔,ændʒɪ'ɑlədʒɪ〕*n.* 血管淋巴管學；脈管學《*logy* = study》
angioma〔,ændʒɪ'omə〕*n.* 血管瘤；淋巴管瘤《 *-oma* 表示瘤的名詞字尾》
angiopathy〔,ændʒɪ'ɑpəθɪ〕*n.* 血管病；淋巴管病《*path* = disease》
angiotomy〔,ændʒɪ'ɑtəmɪ〕*n.* 血管切開術；血管解剖學
angiocardiogram〔,ændʒɪo'kardɪəgræm〕*n.* 心血管照片
　《*card* = heart》
angiocardiography〔,ændʒɪo,kardɪ'ɑgrəfɪ〕*n.* 心血管造影術

```
angio + cardio + graph + y
  |       |       |      |
vessel + heart + write + n.
```

sporangium〔spə'rændʒɪəm〕*n.* 孢子囊《*spore* 孢子》

23 **angl** = angle（角）

* 拉丁文 *angulus*（= *angle*）。〔變化型〕*angul*。

angle[3]〔'æŋgḷ〕*n.* 角；角度；觀點；方面；角落
  v. 歪曲；作不實的新聞報導
angular[7]〔'æŋgjələ〕*adj.* 有角的；消瘦的；笨拙的
equiangular〔,ikwɪ'æŋgjələ〕*adj.* 等角的《*equi* = equal》
quadrangular〔kwɑd'ræŋgjulə〕*adj.* 四邊形的《*quadr-* = four》

```
quadr + angul + ar
  |        |       |
four   + angle + adj.
```

rectangle[2]〔'rɛktæŋgḷ〕*n.* 長方形；矩形《*rect* = right》
triangle[2]〔'traɪ,æŋgḷ〕*n.* 三角形《*tri-* = three》
triangular[7]〔traɪ'æŋgjələ〕*adj.* 三角形的；三者間的

24 **anim** = breath；mind（呼吸；心）

* 拉丁文 *anima*（= *breath*），*animus*（= *mind*）。

animal[1]〔'ænəmḷ〕*n.* 動物 *adj.* 動物界的；野獸的（有氣息的東西）
animalcule〔,ænə'mælkjul〕*n.* 微生物《*-cule* 表示小的名詞字尾》
animalism〔'ænəmḷ,ɪzəm〕*n.* 獸性；獸性主義；精力
  《*-ism* 表示主義、性質》
animality〔,ænə'mælətɪ〕*n.* 獸性；動物性；動物界
animate[6]〔*adj.* 'ænəmɪt *v.* 'ænə,met〕*adj.* 有生命的；活的
  v. 使活潑；使有生氣

```
anim + ate
  |       |
breath + v.
```

animation[7]〔,ænə'meʃən〕*n.* 興奮；活潑；動畫
animator〔'ænɪ,metə〕*n.* 鼓舞者；卡通片繪製者

animosity[7] 〔ˌænə'mɑsətɪ〕 *n.* 怨恨；憎惡（深映在心頭上的一種感覺）

animus 〔'ænəməs〕 *n.* 惡意；敵意（= *animosity*）

disanimate 〔dɪs'ænəˌmet〕 *v.* 使失去生命；使灰心
   《*dis-* = deprive of》

equanimity 〔ˌikwə'nɪmətɪ〕 *n.* 平靜；鎮定（心裡平衡）

```
equ + anim + ity
 |      |     |
equal + mind + n.
```

inanimate[7] 〔ɪn'ænəmɪt〕 *adj.* 無生命的；無生氣的《*in-* = not》

magnanimity 〔ˌmægnə'nɪmətɪ〕 *n.* 寬大；雅量《*magn* = great》

magnanimous[7] 〔mæg'nænəməs〕 *adj.* 心地高尚的；度量寬大的

reanimate 〔ri'ænəˌmet〕 *v.* 使復活；使恢復生氣；激勵
   《*re-* = again》

```
re + anim + ate
 |     |     |
again + mind + v.
```

unanimity 〔ˌjunə'nɪmətɪ〕 *n.* 全體一致（只有一種心意）
   《*un-* = *uni-* = one》

unanimous[6] 〔ju'nænəməs〕 *adj.* 意見一致的

25   **ann , enn** = year（年）   * 拉丁文 *annus*（= *year*）。

annals 〔'ænl̩z〕 *n.pl.* 年鑑；歷史記載

anniversary[4] 〔ˌænə'vɝsərɪ〕 *n.* 周年；周年紀念（一年巡迴一次）
   《*vers* = turn》

Anno Domini 〔'æno'dɑməˌnaɪ〕 = in the year of our Lord
   耶穌紀元後；西元（略作 A.D.）《拉丁文 *dominus* = lord（主）》

annual[4] 〔'ænjʊəl〕 *adj.* 一年一次的   *n.* 一年生植物；年報；年鑑

annuity 〔ə'njuətɪ〕 *n.* 年金；養老金

biannual[7] 〔 baɪˈænjʊəl 〕 *adj.* 一年兩次的 《*bi-* = two》

```
bi  +  ann  +  ual
|       |      |
two  +  year  +  adj.
```

biennial[7] 〔 baɪˈɛnɪəl 〕 *adj.* 兩年一次的　*n.* 二年生植物

centennial[7] 〔 sɛnˈtɛnɪəl 〕 *adj.* 百年一次的；百年紀念的
　　　n. 百年紀念 《*cent* = hundred》

millennium[7] 〔 məˈlɛnɪəm 〕 *n.* 千年；千禧年

```
mill    +  enn  +  ium
|          |       |
thousand  +  year  +  n.
```

perennial[7] 〔 pəˈrɛnɪəl 〕 *adj.* 四季不斷的；永久的
　　　n. 多年生植物（經過一年）《*per-* = through》

superannuate 〔ˌsupəˈænjuˌet〕 *v.* 認爲年老（病弱）而使退休；
　　給予退休金而使退休；勒令退學（超過年齡）《*super-* = above》

26　anth = flower（花）　　* 希臘文 *anthos*（= *flower*）。

anther 〔ˈænθɚ 〕 *n.* 花藥（雄蕊末端之花粉囊）

anthocyanin 〔ˌænθəˈsaɪənɪn 〕 *n.* 花青素
　　《希臘文 *kuanos* = dark blue》

anthodium 〔 ænˈθodɪəm 〕 *n.* 頭狀花序；總苞

anthography 〔 ænˈθɑgrəfɪ 〕 *n.* 花譜（花的記載）《*graph* = write》

anthology[7] 〔 ænˈθɑlədʒɪ 〕 *n.* 詩集；文選（詩的精華）

```
antho   +  log    +  y
|          |         |
flower  +  gather  +  n.
```

chrysanthemum 〔 krɪsˈænθəməm 〕 *n.* 菊花《*chrys* = gold》

27　anthrop = man（人）　* 希臘文 *anthropos*（= *man*）。

anthropocentric〔,ænθrəpə'sɛntrɪk〕*adj.* 認定人爲宇宙中心的
　《*centr* = center》

anthropography〔,ænθrə'pɑgrəfɪ〕*n.* 人類誌《*graph* = write》

```
anthropo  +  graph  +  y
   |           |        |
  man     +  write  +  n.
```

anthropoid〔'ænθrə,pɔɪd〕*adj.* 似人類的（做成人類的形貌）
　《 *-oid* = 希臘文 *eidos* = form》

anthropology[7]〔,ænθrə'pɑlədʒɪ〕*n.* 人類學《*logy* = study》

anthropomorphic[7]〔,ænθrəpə'mɔrfɪk〕*adj.* 似人型的；
　有人型的（看似人類的形貌）《*morph* = form》

```
anthropo  +  morph  +  ic
   |           |         |
 human    +  form   +  adj.
```

anthropomorphism〔,ænθrəpə'mɔrfɪzəm〕*n.* 擬人論

anthropomorphous〔,ænθrəpə'mɔrfəs〕*adj.* 有人形的；
　擬人論的

misanthrope[7]〔'mɪsən,θrop , 'mɪz-〕*n.* 厭世者
　（= *misanthropist*）《*mis-* = 希臘文 *misein* = hate（憎恨）》

```
mis  +  anthrope
 |         |
hate  +   man
```

misanthropy[7]〔mɪs'ænθrəpɪ〕*n.* 對人類之厭惡

philanthrope〔'fɪlənθrop〕*n.* 慈善家（= *philanthropist*）
　《*phil* = love》

philanthropy[7]〔fə'lænθrəpɪ〕*n.* 博愛；慈善心

字根 ac~avi

28 **apt , ept** = fit (適合的) 　* 拉丁文 *aptus* (= *fit*) 。

apt[5] 〔 æpt 〕 *adj.* 傾向於；適合於
aptitude[6] 〔 ˈæptəˌtjud 〕 *n.* 癖性；才能；適當《 *-itude* 抽象名詞字尾》

```
apt + itude
 |     |
fit  +  n.
```

aptness 〔 ˈæptnɪs 〕 *n.* 適合性；傾向；才能
adapt[4] 〔 əˈdæpt 〕 *v.* 使適合；改編（使適當）《*ad-* = to》
adaptable[7] 〔 əˈdæptəbļ 〕 *adj.* 能適應的；可改編的
adaptation[6] 〔 ˌædəpˈteʃən 〕 *n.* 適應；改編；改編的作品

```
ad + apt + ation
 |    |     |
to + fit +  n.
```

adaptive[7] 〔 əˈdæptɪv 〕 *adj.* 適應的
inapt[7] 〔 ɪnˈæpt 〕 *adj.* 不適宜的；笨拙的《*in-* = not》
inaptitude[7] 〔 ɪnˈæptəˌtjud 〕 *n.* 不適宜；笨拙
inept[7] 〔 ɪnˈɛpt 〕 *adj.* 不適當的；笨拙的；不稱職的
ineptitude[7] 〔 ɪnˈɛptəˌtud , -ˌtjud 〕 *n.* 不適當；笨拙；不稱職

29 **aqua** = water (水) 　* 拉丁文 *aqua* (= *water*) 。

aquacade 〔 ˈækwəˌked 〕 *n.* 水上技藝表演
aqua fortis 〔 ˈækwəˈfɔrtɪs 〕 *n.* 硝酸；硝酸水 (= *nitric acid*)
aquamarine 〔 ˌækwəməˈrin 〕 *n.* 水藍寶石；藍綠色《*marine* = sea》

```
aqua + marine
  |       |
water +  sea
```

aquaplane 〔 ˈækwəˌplen 〕 *n.* 滑水板

aquarium[3]〔əˈkwɛrɪəm〕*n.* 水族館

```
aqua  +  rium
 |        |
water  +  place
```

aquatic[7]〔əˈkwætɪk〕*adj.* 水生的；水的　*n.* 水生植物或動物；
水上運動

aqueduct[7]〔ˈækwɪˌdʌkt〕*n.* 水道；溝渠；導水管《*duct* = lead》

aqueous〔ˈekwɪəs〕*adj.* 水的

aquifer[7]〔ˈækwəfɚ〕*n.* 含水土層《*fer* = carry》

30　**arch** = begin；rule；chief（開始；統治；主要的）

　　* 希臘文 *arkhein*（ = *begin*；*rule*），*arkhi-*（ = *chief*；*first*）。

archaeology[7]〔ˌɑrkɪˈɑlədʒɪ〕*n.* 考古學

archaic[7]〔arˈkeɪk〕*adj.* 古代的；古文的

```
arch  +  aic
 |        |
begin  +  adj.
```

archangel〔ˈɑrkˈendʒəl〕 = chief angel　*n.* 天使長；大天使

archbishop〔ˈɑrtʃˈbɪʃəp〕*n.* 總主教《*bishop* 主教》

archenemy[7]〔ˈɑrtʃˈɛnəmɪ〕 = Satan　*n.* 大敵；魔王；撒旦

archetype[7]〔ˈɑrkəˌtaɪp〕 = the original type　*n.* 原型

architect[5]〔ˈɑrkəˌtɛkt〕 = chief carpenter　*n.* 建築師
　　（木匠的工頭）《*archi*（ chief ）+ *tect*（ builder ）》
　　cf. **technical**（工業的），**texture**（構造）

archives[7]〔ˈɑrkaɪvz〕*n.pl.* 檔案室；檔案

anarchy[7]〔ˈænɚkɪ〕*n.* 無政府狀態；混亂

```
an    +  arch  +  y
 |        |       |
without + ruler  + n.
```

matriarch[7]〔'metrɪˌɑrk〕*n.* 女家長;女族長
monarch[5]〔'mɑnək〕*n.* 君主

```
mon(o) + arch
  |        |
 lone  + ruler
```

oligarchy[7]〔'ɑlɪˌgɑrkɪ〕*n.* 寡頭政治

```
olig + arch + y
 |      |     |
few + ruler + n.
```

patriarch[7]〔'petrɪˌɑrk〕*n.* (男性) 家長;族長;元老

31 **argu** = make clear (解釋清楚)

* 拉丁文 ***arguere*** (= *make clear*) 。

argue[2]〔'ɑrgju〕*v.* 爭論;辯論;提出理由證明
argufy〔'ɑrgjuˌfaɪ〕*v.* (為瑣事) 爭辯不休;對…進行辯論
argute〔ɑr'gjut〕*adj.* 精明的;敏銳的;有洞察力的
counterargument〔'kaʊntəˌɑrgjumənt〕*n.* 反駁;反駁的論點

```
counter +    argu    + ment
  |           |          |
against + make clear +   n.
```

outargue〔aʊt'ɑrgju〕*v.* 在辯論中勝過;駁倒《*out-* = beyond》
unargued〔ʌn'ɑrgjud〕*adj.* 未予反駁的;未經辯論的《*un-* = not》

32 **arm** = weapons (武器)

* 拉丁文 ***arma*** (= *weapons*) , ***armare*** (= *arm*) 。

arms[4]〔ɑrmz〕*n.pl.* 武器;軍械;徽章;圖徽　*v.* 武裝
【注意】與「手臂」之意的 arm 字源不同。

armada〔 ɑrˈmɑdə 〕 *n.* 艦隊《西班牙文 *armada* = fleet (艦隊)》

armament〔ˈɑrməmənt 〕 *n.* 軍備

armed[7]〔 ɑrmd 〕 *adj.* 武裝的；有～裝備的

armistice〔ˈɑrməstɪs 〕 *n.* 休戰 (讓相對的武器豎立起來)《*st* = stand》

```
 armi  +  st  + ice
  |        |     |
weapons + stand + n.
```

armo(u)r[5]〔ˈɑrmɚ 〕 *n.* 甲冑；鐵甲 *v.* 裝甲

armo(u)ry〔ˈɑrmərɪ 〕 *n.* 軍械庫；軍械製造廠；兵工廠
《 *-ry* 表示地點的名詞字尾》

army[1]〔ˈɑrmɪ 〕 *n.* 軍隊；陸軍；群眾

alarm[2]〔 əˈlɑrm 〕 *n.* 驚慌；警報；警鈴 *v.* 使驚慌；警告
（去拿武器）《*al-* = *ad-* = to》

disarm[7]〔 dɪsˈɑrm 〕 *v.* 解除武裝；驅除敵意或懷疑《*dis-* = apart》

disarmament〔 dɪsˈɑrməmənt 〕 *n.* 解除武裝；裁減軍備

33　art = skill；art (技巧；藝術)

*＊拉丁文 **ars** (= *art*；*skill*)。*

art[1]〔 ɑrt 〕 *n.* 藝術；技巧；人工；人文學科；詭計

artful[7]〔ˈɑrtfəl 〕 *adj.* 狡詐的；巧妙的；人爲的；不自然的

artist[2]〔ˈɑrtɪst 〕 *n.* 畫家；藝術家；工藝名家

artistic[4]〔 ɑrˈtɪstɪk 〕 *adj.* 藝術的；藝術家的；藝術性的

artless〔ˈɑrtlɪs 〕 *adj.* 無技巧的；笨拙的；自然的；天眞浪漫的

```
art  +  less
 |       |
art  + without
```

artifact[6]〔ˈɑrtɪˌfækt 〕 *n.* 人工製品；加工品；工藝品《*fact* = make；do》

artificial[4]〔ˌɑrtəˈfɪʃəl 〕 *adj.* 人造的；不自然的；做作的《*fic* = make》

artisan〔ˈɑrtəzn̩ 〕 *n.* 工匠；技工

34　**aster** , **astr** = star（星星）

　　* 希臘文 *aster* , *astron*（= *star*）。

aster〔'æstɚ〕*n.* 紫莞；翠菊（花名）
asterisk[7]〔'æstə,rɪsk〕*n.* 星號
asteroid[7]〔'æstə,rɔɪd〕*n.* 小行星；海星
astral〔'æstrəl〕*adj.* 星的；星形的
astrology[7]〔ə'stralədʒɪ〕*n.* 占星術
astrologer[7]〔ə'stralədʒɚ〕*n.* 占星家
astronaut[5]〔'æstrə,nɔt〕*n.* 太空人
astronomy[5]〔ə'stranəmɪ〕*n.* 天文學

```
astro + nom + y
  |      |     |
star  + law + n.
```

astronomer[5]〔ə'stranəmɚ〕*n.* 天文學家
astrophysics[7]〔,æstro'fɪzɪks〕*n.* 天體物理學
disaster[4]〔dɪz'æstɚ〕*n.* 災難

```
dis  + aster
 |      |
away +  star
```

disastrous[6]〔dɪz'æstrəs〕*adj.* 悲慘的
sterling〔'stɝlɪŋ〕*n.* 純銀《此字可能源自中古英文 *sterre* = star》

35　**athl** = contest；prize（競賽；獎）

　　* 希臘文 *athlos*（= *contest*），*athlon*（= *contest*；*prize*）。

athlete[3]〔'æθlit〕*n.* 運動員
athletics[4]〔æθ'lɛtɪks〕*n.pl.* 運動
decathlon〔dɪ'kæθlan〕*n.* 十項運動《*deca-* = ten》
pentathlon〔pɛn'tæθlən〕*n.* 五項運動《*penta-* = five》

36 **atm** = vapor（蒸氣） * 希臘文 *atmos*（= *vapor*）。

atmology〔æt'mɑlədʒɪ〕 *n.* 水蒸氣學《*logy* = study》
atmometer〔æt'mɑmɪtə〕 *n.* 汽化計；蒸發計《*meter* 計量器》
atmosphere[4]〔'ætməs,fɪr〕 *n.* 大氣；大氣層；氣氛《*sphere* 球體》
atmospherics[7]〔,ætməs'fɛrɪks〕 *n.pl.* 天電；天電干擾
atmospherium〔,ætməs'fɛrɪəm〕 *n.* 雲象儀

37 **audi** = hear（聽）

* 拉丁文 *audire*（= *hear*），*auditus*（= *hearing*）。

audible[7]〔'ɔdəbḷ〕 *adj.* 可聽見的
audience[3]〔'ɔdɪəns〕 *n.* 聽衆；觀衆；正式謁見；覲見
《*-ence* 名詞字尾》

```
audi  +  ence
 |        |
hear  +   n.
```

audio[4]〔'ɔdɪ,o〕 *adj.* 音頻的；聲頻的；聲音的
audiometer〔,ɔdɪ'ɑmətə〕 *n.* 音波計；聽力計
audio-visual[7]〔'ɔdɪo'vɪʒʊəl〕 *adj.* 視聽的《*vis* = see》
audiphone〔'ɔdə,fon〕 *n.* 助聽器《*phone* = sound》
audit[7]〔'ɔdɪt〕 *n.* 查帳 *v.* 旁聽（某課程）
audition[7]〔ɔ'dɪʃən〕 *n.* 聽力；聽覺；試聽 *v.*（作）試聽
auditor[7]〔'ɔdɪtə〕 *n.* 旁聽者；查帳員
auditorial〔,ɔdə'torɪəl〕 *adj.* 聽覺的；查帳員的
auditorium[5]〔,ɔdə'torɪəm〕 *n.* 聽衆席；禮堂
《*-um* 表示地點的名詞字尾》
auditory〔'ɔdə,torɪ〕 *adj.* 聽覺的 *n.* 聽衆（席）
inaudible[7]〔ɪn'ɔdəbḷ〕 *adj.* 聽不見的

```
in  +  audi  +  ble
 |      |        |
not  +  hear  +  adj.
```

字根
ac~avi

obedient[4]〔ə'bidɪənt〕*adj.* 順從的（聽別人說的話）
　《*ob-*（to）+ *edi* = *audire*（hear）+ *-ent*（形容詞字尾）》

```
ob + edi + ent
 |    |     |
to + hear + adj.
```

obey[2]〔o'be〕*v.* 服從；遵守
disobedient[7]〔͵dɪsə'bidɪənt〕*adj.* 不順從的《*dis-* = not》

38　aug = increase；make to grow（增加；使生長）

　　* 拉丁文 *augere*（= *increase*；*make to grow*），過去分詞是 *auctus*。

auction[6]〔'ɔkʃən〕*n.* 拍賣　*v.* 拍賣（漸漸地增加其價值）
auctioneer〔͵ɔkʃən'ɪr〕*n.* 拍賣人　*v.* 拍賣
　《*-eer* 表示人的名詞字尾》

```
auct + ion + eer
 |      |     |
increase + n. + person
```

audacity[7]〔ɔ'dæsətɪ〕*n.* 大膽無畏的精神；膽識；厚顏無恥
augment[7]〔ɔg'mɛnt〕*v.* 增大
augmentative〔ɔg'mɛntətɪv〕*adj.* 增加的；偉大的
august[7]〔ɔ'gʌst〕*adj.* 威嚴的（一直增加到偉大的程度）
author[3]〔'ɔθɚ〕*n.* 創始者；著作者（使事物產生的人）
authority[4]〔ə'θɔrətɪ〕*n.* 權威；權勢；當局；根據（事物產生
　的根源）

```
auth  +  or  + ity
 |        |     |
increase + person + n.
```

authoritative[7]〔ə'θɔrə͵tetɪv〕*adj.* 有權威的
authorize[6]〔'ɔθə͵raɪz〕*v.* 授權；使合法

【注意】以下單字字源不同，爲學習上的方便而納入此處。

authentic[6] 〔ɔ'θɛntɪk 〕 *adj.* 可信的；有根據的；眞正的（作者親筆所寫的）

authenticity[7] 〔,ɔθən'tɪsətɪ , -θɛn- 〕 *n.* 眞實性；確切性

39 aur = ear（耳）　　　* 拉丁文 *auris*（= *ear*）。

aural[7] 〔'ɔrəl 〕 *adj.* 耳的；聽覺的

auricle 〔'ɔrɪkḷ 〕 *n.* 外耳；（心臟的）心耳；耳狀部
　《 *-cle* 表示小的名詞字尾》

auricular 〔 ɔ'rɪkjələ 〕 *adj.* 耳的；（經由）聽覺的；耳語的；耳狀的；心耳的

aurinasal 〔,ɔrɪ'nezḷ 〕 *adj.* 耳鼻的《 *nas* = nose》

```
auri  +  nas  +  al
 |        |       |
ear  +  nose  +  adj.
```

auriscope 〔'ɔrɪˌskop 〕 *n.*（檢查耳朵用的）耳鏡
　《 *scope* 表示「觀察～的器具」》

aurist 〔'ɔrɪst 〕 *n.* 耳科醫生

auscultation 〔,ɔskəl'teʃən 〕 *n.* 聽診《拉丁文 *auscultare* = listen to》

binaural 〔 bɪn'ɔrəl 〕 *adj.*（用）雙耳的；立體迴音的
　《 *bin-* = *bi-* = two》

40 aur = gold（金）　　　* 拉丁文 *aurum*（= *gold*）。

auric 〔'ɔrɪk 〕 *adj.* 金的；含金的；三價金的

auriferous 〔 ɔ'rɪfərəs 〕 *adj.* 產金的；含金的《 *fer* = bear》

aureate 〔'ɔrɪɪt 〕 *adj.* 金（黃）色的；鍍金的；華麗的

aureole 〔'ɔrɪˌol 〕 *n.*（聖像頭部或身體周圍的）光環

41　avi = bird (鳥)　　*拉丁文 *avis* (= bird)。

avian[7] 〔'evɪən〕 *adj.* 鳥類的
aviarist 〔'evɪərɪst〕 *n.* 飛禽飼養家
aviary 〔'evɪ,ɛrɪ〕 *n.* 大鳥籠；鳥舍《 *-ry* 表示地點的名詞字尾》

```
avia  +  ry
 |        |
bird  + place
```

aviate 〔'evɪ,et , 'ævɪ- 〕 *v.* 飛行；航行 (像鳥一樣的)
aviation[6] 〔,evɪ'eʃən〕 *n.* 飛行；航行 (術)
aviator 〔'evɪ,etɚ〕 *n.* 飛機駕駛員
aviatrix 〔,evɪ'etrɪks〕 *n.* 女飛行員《 *trix* = feminine (女性)》
avicide 〔'ævə,saɪd〕 *n.* 殺害鳥類《 *cide* = cut》
aviculture 〔'evɪ,kʌltʃɚ〕 *n.* 鳥類飼養
　　《 *avi* (bird) + *cult* (till 耕種) + *-ure* (名詞字尾)》

```
avi  +  cult  +  ure
 |        |        |
bird  +  till  +   n.
```

auspice[7] 〔'ɔspɪs〕 *n.* 前兆 (以鳥的飛行來預卜吉凶)
　　《 *au* = *avi* (bird) + *spice* = 拉丁文 *specere* (see)》
auspicious[7] 〔ɔ'spɪʃəs〕 *adj.* 幸運的；吉兆的
inauspicious 〔,ɪnɔ'spɪʃəs〕 *adj.* 不幸的；凶兆的《 *in-* = not》

```
in  +  au  +  spic  +  ious
 |      |      |        |
not  + bird +  see  +  adj.
```

augur[7] 〔'ɔgɚ〕 *n.* (古羅馬的) 占卜官　 *v.* 占卜；預言
augural 〔'ɔgjurəl〕 *adj.* 占卜的；預言的
augury 〔'ɔgjərɪ〕 *n.* 占卜；徵兆
inaugurate[7] 〔ɪn'ɔgjə,ret〕 *v.* 舉行就職典禮；創始 (用卜卦算出
　　吉辰)《 *in-* (in) + *augurate* = 拉丁文 *augurare* (augur 占兆)》
inauguration[7] 〔ɪn,ɔgjə'reʃən〕 *n.* 就職 (典禮)；創始

42　**ball** = dance（跳舞）　　* 後期拉丁文 *ballare*（= *dance*）。

ball[1]〔bɔl〕*n.* 舞會
ballad[7]〔'bæləd〕*n.* 民謠
ballet[4]〔bæ'le〕*n.* 芭蕾舞《 *-et* 表示小的名詞字尾》

43　**ban** = proclaim ; forbid（宣布；禁止）

* 日耳曼語 *bannan*（= *proclaim* ; *command* ; *forbid*）。

ban[5]〔bæn〕*v., n.* 禁止
banal[7]〔'benḷ, bə'næl〕*adj.* 陳腐的
bandit[5]〔'bændɪt〕*n.* 強盜；土匪
banish[7]〔'bænɪʃ〕*v.* 放逐《 *-ish* 動詞字尾》
abandon[4]〔ə'bændən〕*v.* 放棄；拋棄《古法文 *bandon* = control》
contraband[7]〔'kɑntrə,bænd〕*n.* 非法買賣；走私貨；違禁品

```
contra  +       band
  |               |
against + legal proclamation
```

44　**band** = bind（捆綁）

* 古斯堪的納維亞語 *band*（= *thin strip that ties or constrains*）。
〔變化型〕*bond*。

band[1]〔bænd〕*n.* 皮帶；帶子；條紋；樂隊　*v.* 聯合；以帶結之
（用來綁縛的東西）
bandage[3]〔'bændɪdʒ〕*n.* 繃帶　*v.* 縛以繃帶
bond[14]〔bɑnd〕*n.* 束縛；債券；契約；保證人　*v.* 抵押；
結合；作保
bond[24]〔bɑnd〕*n.* 同盟；聯盟（團結在一起）
bondage[6]〔'bɑndɪdʒ〕*n.* 奴隸的身份；束縛；囚禁（被束縛住的身份）

bound[5]〔 baʊnd 〕 *adj.* 裝訂好的；必定的；決心的；被束縛的；
駛（飛、開）往～的　*v.* 反彈；限制　*n.* 範圍；界限
boundary[5]〔'baʊndərɪ 〕 *n.* 界線；邊界

45　**bar , barr** = bar（棒子；障礙）

　　* 通俗拉丁文 ***barra*** (= bar) 。

bar[1]〔 bar 〕 *n.* 棒；柵；障礙；律師業；法院；酒館
　　v. 用閂關住；阻礙；飾以條紋　*prep.* 除～之外
barrage[7]〔 bə'raʒ 〕 *n.* 掩護砲火；彈幕；多如彈雨之物
　　v. 佈下彈幕以對抗

```
barr + age
 |      |
bar  +  n.
```

barrel[3]〔'bærəl 〕 *n.* 大桶；槍身　*v.* 裝入桶中（以木棒為材料做成的）
barricade[7]〔,bærə'ked , 'bærə,ked 〕 *n.* 臨時建築的防禦工事；
　　阻擋通路的障礙物　*v.* 設柵防守；阻礙（以棒子來防禦）
barrier[7]〔'bærɪɚ 〕 *n.* 障礙；界線　*v.* 用柵欄圍起來（以柵欄防禦）
barring〔'barɪŋ 〕 *prep.* 除～之外
barrister〔'bærɪstɚ 〕 *n.* 律師
debar〔 dɪ'bar 〕 *v.* 阻止；禁止；排除《*de-* = intensive 加強語氣》
embargo[7]〔 ɪm'bargo 〕 *v.* 禁運；禁止通商；禁止；限制
　　《*em-* = *en-* = in》

```
em + bar + go
 |    |    |
in + bar + go
```

embarrass[4]〔 ɪm'bærəs 〕 *v.* 使困窘；妨礙；使複雜（將棒子放
入其中）
embarrassment[4]〔 ɪm'bærəsmənt 〕 *n.* 困窘
embarrassing[4]〔 ɪm'bærəsɪŋ 〕 *adj.* 令人困窘的

46　**bar** = pressure；weight（壓力；重量）

* 希臘文 *baros*（= *weight*）。

bariatrics〔͵bærɪ'ætrɪks〕 *n.* 肥胖症學

baric〔'bærɪk〕 *adj.*（大）氣壓的

barograph〔'bærə͵græf〕 *n.* 氣壓記錄計《*graph* = write》

barology〔bə'ralədʒɪ〕 *n.* 重力論《*logy* = study》

barometry〔bə'ramɪtrɪ〕 *n.* 氣壓測定法《*metr* = measure》

```
baro  +  metr  +  y
 |         |       |
weight + measure + n.
```

47　**bas** , **bat** = go（去）

* 希臘文 *bainein*（= *go*；*step*），*basis*（= *step* 一步；*pedestal* 基礎）。
〔變化型〕*bet*。

base[1]〔bes〕 *n.* 基礎；基地

basement[2]〔'besmənt〕 *n.* 地下室

basis[2]〔'besɪs〕 *n.* 基礎

basophobia〔͵besə'fobɪə〕 *n.* 步行恐怖（懼怕走動或起立的心理症）
《*baso*（go）+ *phob*（fear）+ *-ia*（condition）》

abasia〔ə'beʒə〕 *n.*（痙攣性）不能步行（症）
《*a-*（not）+ *bas*（go）+ *-ia*（condition）》

acrobat[7]〔'ækrə͵bæt〕 *n.* 表演特技者；賣藝者《*acro* = high》

acrobatic[7]〔͵ækrə'bætɪk〕 *adj.* 賣藝者的

acrobatics〔͵ækrə'bætɪks〕 *n.* 特技；熟練的技巧

aerobatic〔͵eərə'bætɪk〕 *adj.* 飛行技藝的《*aero* = in the air》

```
aero    + bat + ic
  |        |     |
in the air + go + adj.
```

aerobatics〔͵eərə'bætɪks〕 *n.* 高級飛行術；特技飛行（表演）

diabetes[6]〔͵daɪə'bitɪs〕 *n.* 糖尿病《後期拉丁文 *diabetes* = excessive discharge of urine》

48 **bass** = low（低的） * 後期拉丁文 *bassus*（= *low*）。

base[1]〔bes〕 *adj.* 卑鄙的；下等的；劣質的

bass[5]〔bes〕 *n.* 低音部；低音樂器 *adj.* 低音的

basset〔'bæsɪt〕 *n.* 短腿獵犬《法文 *basset* = short》

bassoon〔bə'sun〕 *n.* 低音管

contrabass〔'kɑntrə͵bes〕 *n.* （倍）低音提琴《*contra-* = against》

49 **bat** = beat（打） * 拉丁文 *battere*（= *beat*）。

bat[1]〔bæt〕 *n.* 棒 *v.* 用棒擊

baton[7]〔'bætn̩〕 *n.* 警棍；指揮棒；權杖；司令杖

battalion[7]〔bə'tæljən〕 *n.* 軍隊；大隊；營（加入戰鬥的隊伍）

batter[5]〔'bætɚ〕 *v.* 連擊；敲碎 *n.* 打擊者《*-er* 表示反覆的字尾》

battered[7]〔'bætɚd〕 *adj.* 打扁了的；憔悴的

```
batter + ed
  |       |
beat   + adj.
```

battery[4]〔'bætərɪ〕 *n.* 電池；列砲；砲兵連；毆打

battle[2]〔'bætl̩〕 *n.* 戰鬥；戰爭；勝利 *v.* 作戰（對打）

battlement〔'bætl̩mənt〕 *n.* 城垛；城牆堞口（打的地方）

abate[7]〔ə'bet〕 *v.* 減少；減弱；降低；使緩和（減少打擊）《*a-* = off》

combat[5]〔'kʌmbæt〕 *v.* 格鬥；戰鬥 *n.* 戰鬥；爭鬥（一同對打）

《*com-* = together》

```
com  + bat
  |      |
together + beat
```

combative[7]〔'kɑmbətɪv〕*adj.* 好鬥的
debate[2]〔dɪ'bet〕*v.* 討論 *n.* 討論；辯論（將對方打倒）
  《*de-* = down》

50 bath = deep（深的）   * 希臘文 *bathus*（= *deep*）。

batholith〔'bæθəlɪθ〕*n.* 岩基《*lith* = stone》
bathometer〔bə'θɑmɪtə〕*n.* 水深測量器《*meter* 計量器》
bathos〔'beθɑs〕*n.*【修辭】突降法；陳腐；矯揉造作
bathybic〔bə'θɪbɪk〕*adj.* 深海的；生活於深海的

> bathy + b(io) + ic
> | | |
> *deep* + *life* + *adj.*

bathymetry〔bə'θɪmətrɪ〕*n.*（海洋、湖泊）測深學；海洋生物分布學
bathypelagic〔ˌbæθəpə'lædʒɪk〕*adj.*（尤指深度在 2,000-12,000 英尺之間）深海的《希臘文 *pelagos* = sea》
bathyscaphe〔'bæθəˌskef〕*n.* 探海（潛）艇；深海潛水器
  《希臘文 *skaphe* = skiff（小艇）》
bathysphere〔'bæθɪˌsfɪr〕*n.* 探海球；深海球形潛水器
  《*sphere* 球體》
bathythermograph〔ˌbæθə'θɝməˌgræf〕*n.* 海水測溫儀

> bathy + thermo + graph
> | | |
> *deep* + *heat* + *write*

51 bell = beautiful（美麗的）

  * 拉丁文 *bellus*（= *beautiful*）。

belle〔bɛl〕*n.* 美女；最美的美人

belvedere 〔ˈbɛlvədɪr〕 *n.* （尤指建築物頂層的）觀景樓；瞭望台
《拉丁文 *vedere* = sight》

embellish[7] 〔ɪmˈbɛlɪʃ〕 *v.* 美化；裝飾；潤飾（文章）
《*em-* = *en-*（in）+ *bell*（beautiful）+ *-ish*（動詞字尾）》

```
em  +  bell   + ish
|      |        |
in  + beautiful + v.
```

52 **bell** = war（戰爭）　　* 拉丁文 *bellum*（= *war*）。

antebellum 〔ˈæntɪˈbɛləm〕 *adj.* 戰前的；（特指）美國南北戰爭
之前的《*ante-*（before）+ *bell*（war）+ *-um*（形容詞字尾）》

bellicose 〔ˈbɛləˌkos〕 *adj.* 好戰的；好爭吵的《*-cose* 形容詞字尾》

belligerent[7] 〔bəˈlɪdʒərənt〕 *adj.* 好戰的；好爭吵的；交戰的
《*ger* = carry》

```
belli  +  ger  + ent
|         |       |
war   + carry  + adj.
```

rebel[4] 〔*n.*, *adj.* ˈrɛbḷ *v.* rɪˈbɛl〕 *n.* 叛徒　*adj.* 反叛的　*v.* 反叛
（又引起戰爭）《*re-* = again》

rebellion[6] 〔rɪˈbɛljən〕 *n.* 反叛；反抗

rebellious[7] 〔rɪˈbɛljəs〕 *adj.* 反叛的；難治的；難處理的

rebeldom 〔ˈrɛbḷdəm〕 *n.* 反叛者；暴動地區；叛變《*-dom* = state》

53 **bib** = drink（喝）　　* 拉丁文 *bibere*（= *drink*）。

bib 〔bɪb〕 *n.* 圍兜；（圍裙等的）上部　*v.* 飲（酒）

bibber 〔ˈbɪbɚ〕 *n.* 飲酒者；酒鬼《*-er* 表示人的名詞字尾》

bibulous 〔ˈbɪbjələs〕 *adj.* 好飲酒的；吸水性強的；吸水的

imbibe[7] 〔ɪmˈbaɪb〕 *v.* 喝；飲；吸入（空氣等）；吸收（思想、知識等）《*im-* = *in-* = into》

beverage[6] 〔ˈbɛvərɪdʒ〕 *n.* 飲料《古法文 *beivre* = drink》

54 bibli = book (書) * 希臘文 *biblion*（= book）。

Bible[3] 〔ˈbaɪbḷ〕 *n.* 聖經

bibliofilm 〔ˈbɪblɪəˌfɪlm〕 *n.*（用來拍攝書頁等的）顯微膠片
《*film* 膠捲》

bibliography[7] 〔ˌbɪblɪˈɑgrəfɪ〕 *n.* 參考書目；參考文獻；書目

bibliomancy 〔ˈbɪblɪəˌmænsɪ〕 *n.* 聖經占卜
《*-mancy* = divination（占卜）》

bibliomania 〔ˌbɪblɪəˈmenɪə〕 *n.* 藏書狂

```
biblio +   mania
  |          |
book  +  madness
```

bibliophile 〔ˈbɪblɪəˌfaɪl〕 *n.* 珍藏書籍者

bibliopole 〔ˈbɪblɪəˌpol〕 *n.* 珍本書商；書商《希臘文 *polein* = sell》

bibliopoly 〔ˌbɪblɪˈɑpəlɪ〕 *n.* 珍本書的買賣

bibliotheca 〔ˌbɪblɪəˈθikə〕 *n.* 藏書；藏書室；（藏書者或書商的）書目《希臘文 *theke* = receptacle（貯藏處）》

55 bio = life (生命) * 希臘文 *bios*（= life）。

biochemistry[7] 〔ˌbaɪoˈkɛmɪstrɪ〕 *n.* 生物化學

biodegradable[7] 〔ˌbaɪodɪˈgredəbḷ〕 *adj.* 微生物可分解的

```
bio +   de  + grad + able
 |       |      |      |
life + down + rank +  adj.
```

biogenesis 〔‚baɪoˈdʒɛnəsɪs〕 *n.* 生物發生；生源論
（是一種生物由他種生物演化而成的，而非由無生物演變而成的）

biography[4] 〔baɪˈɑgrəfɪ〕 *n.* 傳記（寫人的一生的東西）
《*graphy* = writing》

biographer[7] 〔baɪˈɑgrəfɚ, bɪ-〕 *n.* 傳記作家

biology[4] 〔baɪˈɑlədʒɪ〕 *n.* 生物學《*logy* = study》

biometry 〔baɪˈɑmətrɪ〕 *n.* 壽命測定；生物統計學
《*met(e)r* = measure（測量）》

biopsy[7] 〔baɪˈɑpsɪ〕 *n.* 活體檢視；活組織切片檢查法

```
bi(o)  +  opsy
 |          |
life   +   sight
```

biosphere[7] 〔ˈbaɪəˌsfɪr〕 *n.* 生物圈；生存範圍

```
bio  +  sphere
 |        |
life  +  globe
```

antibiotic[6] 〔‚æntɪbaɪˈɑtɪk〕 *n.* 抗生素   *adj.* 抗生的
《*anti-* = against》

autobiography[7] 〔‚ɔtəbaɪˈɑgrəfɪ〕 *n.* 自傳（自己的傳記）
《*auto-* = self》

```
auto  +  bio  +  graph  +  y
 |        |        |        |
self  +  life  +  write   +  n.
```

autobiographical[7] 〔‚ɔtəˌbaɪəˈgræfɪkl̩〕 *adj.* 自傳的

symbiotic[7] 〔‚sɪmbaɪˈɑtɪk〕 *adj.* 共生的

```
sym      +  bio  +  tic
 |           |        |
together  +  life  +  adj.
```

56 **blanc** = white (白色)   * 法文 *blanc* (= white) 。

blanch 〔 blæntʃ 〕 *v.* 使變白；漂白 (= *bleach*)；使 (臉等) 變蒼白
blank[2] 〔 blæŋk 〕 *adj.* 空白的；空的 *n.* 空白處
blanket[3] 〔'blæŋkɪt 〕 *n.* 毯子《 *-et* 表示小的名詞字尾》

57 **blast** = bud (芽)   * 希臘文 *blastos* (= bud) 。

blastocyst 〔'blæstəsɪst 〕 *n.* 囊胚《 *cyst* = bladder (囊)》
blastogenesis 〔,blæstə'dʒɛnəsɪs 〕 *n.* 出芽生殖

```
blasto  +  gene  +  (o)sis
  |           |         |
 bud   + produce + condition
```

blastomere 〔'blæstə,mɪr 〕 *n.* 分裂球《 *mer* = part》
blastula 〔'blæstʃulə 〕 *n.* 囊胚《 *-ula* 表示小的名詞字尾》
odontoblast 〔 o'dɑntə,blæst 〕 *n.* 齒胚細胞；成齒質細胞
  《 *odonto* = tooth》

58 **brac** , **brachi** = arm (手臂)

* 希臘文 *brakhion* (= *upper arm*)；拉丁文 *bracchium* (= *arm*)。

brace[5] 〔 bres 〕 *v.* 支撐；振作 *n.* 支撐；支柱；(*pl.*) 牙套
bracelet[4] 〔'breslɪt 〕 *n.* 手鐲《 *-let* 表示小的名詞字尾》
brachium 〔'brekɪəm 〕 *n.* 上臂
brachial 〔'brekɪəl 〕 *adj.* 臂的
brachiate 〔'brekɪɪt 〕 *adj.* 【植物】有交互對枝的；【動物】有臂的
  v. (猴等) 用臂吊盪樹枝前進
brachiopod 〔'brækɪə,pɑd 〕 *n.* 腕足類動物

```
brachio + pod
   |       |
  arm   + foot
```

embrace[5] 〔 ɪmˈbres 〕 *v.* , *n.* 擁抱《*em-* = *en-* = in》

59 **brev** = short (短的)   * 拉丁文 *brevis* (= short) 。

breviate 〔ˈbrivɪˌet 〕 *v.* 摘記；節略
breviary 〔ˈbrivɪˌɛrɪ 〕 *n.* (天主教的) 每日祈禱書
brevity[7] 〔ˈbrɛvətɪ 〕 *n.* 短暫；簡潔
brief[2] 〔 brif 〕 *adj.* 簡短的；短暫的   *n.* 摘要；簡報   *v.* 摘要；作簡報
briefly[2] 〔ˈbriflɪ 〕 *adv.* 簡短地；短暫地
abbreviate[6] 〔 əˈbrivɪˌet 〕 *v.* 使簡單；縮寫《*ab-* = *ad-* = to》

```
ab + brevi + ate
 |      |      |
to  + short  + v.
```

abbreviation[6] 〔 əˌbrivɪˈeʃən 〕 *n.* 縮短；簡寫
abridge[7] 〔 əˈbrɪdʒ 〕 *v.* 縮短；削減
　《*a(b)-* (to) + *bridge* = 拉丁文 *brevis* (short)》
abridg(e)ment 〔 əˈbrɪdʒmənt 〕 *n.* 縮短；削減

60 **bronch** = windpipe (氣管)

　* 希臘文 *bronchos* (= *windpipe*) 。

bronchia 〔ˈbrɑŋkɪə 〕 *n.pl.* 支氣管
bronchial 〔ˈbrɑŋkɪəl 〕 *adj.* 支氣管的
bronchiectasis 〔ˌbrɑŋkɪˈɛktəsɪs 〕 *n.* 支氣管擴張
　《希臘文 *ektasis* = extension》
bronchitis[7] 〔 brɑnˈkaɪtɪs , brɑŋ- 〕 *n.* 支氣管炎
　《 *-itis* = inflammation (發炎)》
bronchoconstriction 〔ˌbrɑŋkokənˈstrɪkʃən 〕 *n.* 支氣管縮小；
　支氣管狹窄《*constriction* 收縮》
bronchography 〔 brɑnˈkɑgrəfɪ 〕 *n.* 支氣管造影術《*graph* = write》

bronchopneumonia 〔ˌbraŋkonjuˈmonjə 〕 *n.* 支氣管肺炎

broncho +	pneumon +	ia
windpipe +	lung +	condition

bronchoscope 〔ˈbraŋkəˌskop 〕 *n.* 支氣管窺鏡

《*scope* 表示「觀察～的器具」》

bronchotomy 〔 braŋˈkatəmɪ 〕 *n.* 支氣管切開術《*tom* = cut》

61 **burs** = bag（袋；囊） * 拉丁文 *bursa*（= *bag*；*purse*）。

bursa 〔ˈbɝsə 〕 *n.* 囊；黏液囊；滑囊

bursar 〔ˈbɝsɚ 〕 *n.*（高等院校、寺院等的）財務主管；司庫；
領取獎學金的學生《*-ar* 表示人的名詞字尾》

disburse[7] 〔 dɪsˈbɝs 〕 *v.* 支出；支付《*dis-* = away》

reimburse[7] 〔ˌriɪmˈbɝs 〕 *v.* 償還；付還（所花的錢）；賠償

re +	im +	burse
again +	in +	bag

purse[2] 〔 pɝs 〕 *n.* 錢包；（女用）手提包

62 **cad**, **cid**, **cas** = fall（落下）

* 拉丁文 *cadere*（= *fall*），*casus*（= *falling*）。〔變化型〕*cid*。

cadaver[7] 〔 kəˈdævɚ, kəˈdevɚ 〕 *n.* 屍體（尤指供解剖用的人屍）

cadaverine 〔 kəˈdævərin 〕 *n.*【生化】屍胺

cadaverous 〔 kəˈdævərəs 〕 *adj.* 像屍體的；蒼白的

cadence[7] 〔ˈkedn̩s 〕 *n.* 韻律；節拍；聲音的抑揚頓挫（聲音落下）

caducous 〔 kəˈdjukəs 〕 *adj.* 短暫的；【植物】（葉子等）早期
脫落的；【動物】（皮、殼等）脫落性的

decadence[7]〔 dɪˋkedns , ˋdɛkədns 〕 *n.* 衰落；墮落（落到下面）

　《*de-* = down》

decadent[7]〔 dɪˋkednt , ˋdɛkə- 〕 *adj.* 頹廢的　　*n.* 頹廢派的藝術家

accident[3]〔ˋæksədənt 〕 *n.* 意外事件；偶發事件（落到身上來）

　《*ac-* = *ad-* = to》

$$ac + cid + ent$$
$$to + fall + n.$$

accidental[4]〔ˏæksəˋdɛntl̩ 〕 *adj.* 偶然的　　*n.* 偶發事件

deciduous〔 dɪˋsɪdʒʊəs 〕 *adj.* 每年落葉的；短暫的（落到下面）

　《*de-* = down》

$$de + cid + uous$$
$$down + fall + adj.$$

incidence[7]〔ˋɪnsədəns 〕 *n.* 落下；影響範圍（落到～上面）

　《*in-* = on》

incident[4]〔ˋɪnsədənt 〕 *adj.* 易於發生的；附帶的　　*n.* 事件

incidental[6]〔ˏɪnsəˋdɛntl̩ 〕 *adj.* 附帶的；偶然的　　*n.* 偶發事件

coincide[6]〔ˏkoɪnˋsaɪd 〕 *v.* 一致；符合；巧合（一起落下）

　《*co-* = *com-* = together》

coincidence[6]〔 koˋɪnsədəns 〕 *n.* 符合；一致；巧合

$$co + in + cid + ence$$
$$together + on + fall + n.$$

coincident〔 koˋɪnsədənt 〕 *adj.* 同時發生的；符合的；巧合的

Occident〔ˋɑksədənt 〕 *n.* 歐美國家；西方國家（太陽落下的方向）

　《*oc-* = *ob-* = toward》　　*cf.* **Orient**（東方國家）

cascade[7]〔 kæsˋked 〕 *n.* 小瀑布　　*v.* 像瀑布般落下（落下的東西）

case[1]〔 kes 〕 *n.* 事件；事情；場合；狀態；訴訟事件；患者；

　【文法】格

　【注意】 表容器的 **case** 是由拉丁文 *capere*（ = receive；hold ）演變而來的。

casual[3]〔ˈkæʒʊəl〕*adj.* 偶然的；臨時的　*n.* 臨時工人；
　臨時收容者

casualty[6]〔ˈkæʒʊəltɪ〕*n.* 意外；因意外而死傷者

occasion[3]〔əˈkeʒən〕*n.* 機會；場合　*v.* 引起；致使
　（落在眼前的事）《*oc-* = *ob-* = before》

```
oc  + cas + ion
 |      |     |
before + fall + n.
```

occasional[4]〔əˈkeʒənḷ〕*adj.* 偶然的；應時的；應景的；臨時的

63　**cal** = heat（熱）　* 拉丁文 *calor*（= heat）。

caldron〔ˈkɔldrən〕*n.*（尤指帶柄的）大鍋

calorie[4]〔ˈkælərɪ〕*n.* 卡路里

calorific〔ˌkæləˈrɪfɪk〕*adj.* 生熱的；產生食物熱卡的
　《*calor*（heat）+ *-if(y)*（make）+ *-ic*（形容詞字尾）》

calorimeter〔ˌkæləˈrɪmətɚ〕*n.* 熱量計

```
calori + meter
  |        |
 heat  + measure
```

calorite〔ˈkæləˌraɪt〕*n.* 耐熱合金
　《*-ite* 表示「具有…的性質」的名詞字尾》

caloricity〔ˌkæləˈrɪsətɪ〕*n.*（人類及熱血動物保持體溫的）生熱力

calorifacient〔kəˌlɑrɪˈfeʃənt〕*adj.*（食物）生熱的；產熱的

```
calori + fac + ient
  |       |      |
 heat + make + adj.
```

nonchalant[7]〔ˈnɑnʃələnt〕*adj.* 漠不關心的；冷淡的（對別人的事
　不熱心）《*non-*（not）+ *chal*（heat）+ *-ant*（形容詞字尾）》

64 **calc** = lime (石灰)   *拉丁文 *calx* , *calc-* (= *lime*)。

calcic 〔'kælsɪk 〕 *adj.* 鈣的;含鈣的

calcify 〔'kælsə,faɪ 〕 *v.* 使成石灰;變成石灰質

calcium[6] 〔'kælsɪəm 〕 *n.* 鈣

calculate[4] 〔'kælkjə,let〕 *v.* 計算;估計;評價 (古時候用小石頭來計數)《*calc* (lime) + *-ul* (表示小的字尾) + *-ate* (動詞字尾)》

```
calc  +  ul  + ate
 |        |     |
lime  + small +  v.
```

calculable 〔'kælkjələbḷ 〕 *adj.* 可計算的;可依賴的

calculation[4] 〔,kælkjə'leʃən 〕 *n.* 計算;預計;謹慎的計劃

calculator[4] 〔'kælkjə,letə 〕 *n.* 計算者;計算機

calculus[7] 〔'kælkjələs 〕 *n.* 微積分;結石
《 *-us* 拉丁名詞字尾,表方法》

chalk[2] 〔tʃɔk 〕 *n.* 白堊;粉筆;粉筆做的記號   *v.* 用粉筆寫

65 **camp** = field (田野;原野)

    *拉丁文 *campus* (= *plain* ; *field*)。

camp[1] 〔kæmp 〕 *n.* 營;營地;營帳   *v.* 露營

campaign[4] 〔kæm'pen 〕 *n.* 戰役;活動   *v.* 發起運動;參加戰役
《 *-aign* 名詞字尾》

campfire[7] 〔'kæmp,faɪr 〕 *n.* 營火;營火會

campsite[7] 〔'kæmp,saɪt 〕 *n.* 露營地;露營預定地

campus[3] 〔'kæmpəs 〕 *n.* 校園;校區

encamp 〔ɪn'kæmp 〕 *v.* 紮營;露營《*en-* = make》

encampment[7] 〔ɪn'kæmpmənt 〕 *n.* 營地;營區;紮營;露營

66 cand = white ; glowing (白色的；光輝的)

* 拉丁文 *candere* (= be white ; shine) ，*candidus* (= white ; glowing) 。

candent (ˈkændənt) adj. 微微閃光的；白熱的
candescence (kænˈdɛsn̩s) n. 白熱
candescent (kænˈdɛsn̩t) adj. 白熱的
candle[2] (ˈkændl̩) n. 蠟燭；燭光《 -le 表示小的名詞字尾》
candid[7] (ˈkændɪd) adj. 坦白的；公正的；率直的《 -id 形容詞字尾》
candidate[4] (ˈkændə,det , ˈkændədɪt) n. 候選人
　　《 -ate 表示人的名詞字尾》　☞ 參照 p.629 ambition 的解說。

```
cand  +  id  +  ate
 |        |      |
white  +  adj.  +  person
```

candidacy[7] (ˈkændɪdəsɪ) n. 候選資格；提名候選
cando(u)r[7] (ˈkændə) n. 坦白；率直；公平；公正
incandescent[7] (,ɪnkənˈdɛsn̩t) adj. 白熱的；極亮的；傑出的
　　《 in- (into) + cand (white) + -escent (形容詞字尾)》

```
in  +  cand  +  escent
 |      |        |
into  +  white  +  adj.
```

incandescence (,ɪnkənˈdɛsn̩s) n. 白熱（狀態）；白熱光

67 cant = sing (唱歌)

* 拉丁文 *canere* (= sing) ，過去分詞是 *cantus*。
　　〔變化型〕*chant , cent*。

cant[7] (kænt) n. 行話；術語；言不由衷之詞
canticle (ˈkæntɪkl̩) n. 教堂禮拜用的頌歌《 -cle 表示小的名詞字尾》
cantor (ˈkæntə) n. （教會的）唱詩班領唱者

descant 〔 dɪˈskænt 〕 *n.* 伴唱；伴奏；歌曲　*v.* 詳述；伴奏；伴唱
《*des-* = *dis-* = apart》

incantation[7] 〔 ˌɪnkænˈteʃən 〕 *n.* 詛咒語；咒文；魔法《*in-* = in；on》

```
in + cant + ation
 |     |      |
in + sing +  n.
```

recant[7] 〔 rɪˈkænt 〕 *v.* 取消己見；放棄信仰《*re-* = back》
chant[5] 〔 tʃænt 〕 *n.* 歌曲；旋律；聖歌；讚美詩　*v.* 單調地說話
enchant[7] 〔 ɪnˈtʃænt 〕 *v.* 蠱惑；施魔法；使迷醉《*en-* = in》
enchantment[7] 〔 ɪnˈtʃæntmənt 〕 *n.* 魅力；蠱惑；施魔法；妖術
accent[4] 〔ˈæksɛnt 〕 *n.* 重音；腔調；音調《*ac-* = *ad-* = to》
accentuate[7] 〔 ækˈsɛntʃʊˌet 〕 *v.* 加重；強調；使更顯明

68　cap , capit = head (頭)

＊ 拉丁文 *caput* , *capit-* (= *head*) 。

cap[1] 〔 kæp 〕 *n.* (無邊的) 帽子
cape[4] 〔 kep 〕 *n.* 岬 (像頭一樣突出來的東西)
capital[3,4] 〔ˈkæpətḷ 〕 *adj.* 與資金有關的；重要的；首都的
　n. 大寫字母；首都；資本
capitalism[4] 〔ˈkæpətḷˌɪzəm 〕 *n.* 資本主義
capitalist[4] 〔ˈkæpətḷɪst 〕 *n.* 資本家
capitalize[7] 〔ˈkæpətḷˌaɪz 〕 *v.* 用大寫字母寫；資本化
capitally 〔ˈkæpətḷɪ 〕 *adv.* 巧妙地；極好地
capitulate[7] 〔 kəˈpɪtʃəˌlet 〕 *v.* (有條件地) 投降
capsize[7] 〔 kæpˈsaɪz 〕 *v.* 使傾覆；傾覆　*n.* 傾覆；顛覆 (捉住船頭)
captain[2] 〔ˈkæptən 〕 *n.* 指揮者；艦長；船長；首領；主將　*v.* 統率
cabbage[2] 〔ˈkæbɪdʒ 〕 *n.* 甘藍菜　*v.* 形成如甘藍菜一樣的頭 (很
大的頭)

decapitate[7] 〔 dɪˈkæpəˌtet 〕 v. 斬首；解雇（把頭切離）《de- = off》

```
de  +  capit  +  ate
 |       |       |
off  +  head  +  v.
```

decapitation 〔 dɪˌkæpəˈteʃən 〕 n. 斬首；解雇
decapitator 〔 dɪˈkæpəˌtetə 〕 n. 斬首者；斷頭機
per capita[7] 〔 pəˈkæpɪtə 〕 adj. 每人的《per 每》
precipitate[7] 〔 prɪˈsɪpəˌtet 〕 v. 突然引起；墜落；使陷於（使頭
　下腳上）《pre- (before) + cipit (head) + -ate (動詞字尾)》
precipitous 〔 prɪˈsɪpətəs 〕 adj. 陡峭的；險峻的；輕率的
recapitulate 〔 ˌrikəˈpɪtʃəˌlet 〕 v. 重述要點

69　cap , cip , cept , ceive = take (拿；捉住)

　　* 拉丁文 capere (= take ; catch) ，過去分詞是 captus。
　　〔變化型〕cip , cept , ceive。

capable[3] 〔ˈkepəbḷ 〕 adj. 有能力的；能幹的；可以～的（能夠取得）
capability[6] 〔ˌkepəˈbɪlətɪ 〕 n. 能力
capacious 〔 kəˈpeʃəs 〕 adj. 容量大的；寬敞的（拿進來許多）
capacity[4] 〔 kəˈpæsətɪ 〕 n. 容量；容積；才能；可能性；資格
　adj. 充其量的；至最高量的
caption[6] 〔ˈkæpʃən 〕 n. 標題；插圖的說明；電影字幕
　v. 加題目（標題、說明、字幕等）（能夠提出的）

```
capt  +  ion
 |        |
take  +   n.
```

captious 〔ˈkæpʃəs 〕 adj. 吹毛求疵的；強辭奪理的
captivate[7] 〔ˈkæptəˌvet 〕 v. 迷惑（把心捉住）
captivating[7] 〔ˈkæptəˌvetɪŋ 〕 adj. 有迷惑力的

captive[6] 〔ˈkæptɪv 〕 *adj.* 被俘的;被迷惑的 *n.* 俘虜;被迷惑者

captivity[6] 〔 kæpˈtɪvətɪ 〕 *n.* 因禁

captor[7] 〔ˈkæptə 〕 *n.* 捕掠者;攻取者

capture[3] 〔ˈkæptʃə 〕 *n.* 捕獲;佔領;捕獲物 *v.* 捕獲;捉住

accept[2] 〔 əkˈsɛpt , æk- 〕 *v.* 接受;同意《*ac-* = *ad-* = to》

acceptable[3] 〔 əkˈsɛptəbḷ , æk- 〕 *adj.* 可接受的;合意的;尚可的

acceptance[4] 〔 əkˈsɛptəns 〕 *n.* 承認;接受;答應

acceptation 〔ˌæksɛpˈteʃən 〕 *n.* 通用的字義;涵義

accepted[7] 〔 əkˈsɛptɪd 〕 *adj.* 一般所接納的

conceive[5] 〔 kənˈsiv 〕 *v.* 想像;以爲;表達;懷孕 (拿走~)

　　《*con-* = with》

```
con  +  ceive
 |        |
with  +  take
```

conceivable[7] 〔 kənˈsivəbḷ 〕 *adj.* 可想像的

concept[4] 〔ˈkɑnsɛpt 〕 *n.* 概念

conception[6] 〔 kənˈsɛpʃən 〕 *n.* 想像力;概念;懷孕

deceive[5] 〔 dɪˈsiv 〕 *v.* 欺騙 (悄悄地拿取) 《*de-* = *dis-* = away》

deceivable 〔 dɪˈsivəbḷ 〕 *adj.* 易受騙的

```
de  +  ceiv  +  able
 |       |        |
away  +  take  +  adj.
```

deceit[7] 〔 dɪˈsit 〕 *n.* 欺騙

deception[7] 〔 dɪˈsɛpʃən 〕 *n.* 欺騙;詭計

deceptive[7] 〔 dɪˈsɛptɪv 〕 *adj.* 虛僞的

except[1] 〔 ɪkˈsɛpt 〕 *v.* 把~除外 *prep.* , *conj.* 除~之外 (取出來)

　　《*ex-* = out》 *cf.* **besides** (除~之外;還有)

exception[4] 〔 ɪkˈsɛpʃən 〕 *n.* 例外;反對;異議

exceptionable 〔 ɪkˈsɛpʃənəbḷ 〕 *adj.* 可反對的;例外的

exceptional[5] 〔 ɪkˈsɛpʃən!〕 *adj.* 例外的；特別的

```
ex  +  cept  +  ion  +  al
│       │      │       │
out  +  take  +  n.  +  adj.
```

inception[7] 〔 ɪnˈsɛpʃən 〕 *n.* 起初；開始；獲得學位（著手；啓程）
  《*in-* = on》

inceptive 〔 ɪnˈsɛptɪv 〕 *adj.* 開始的   *n.* 表始動詞（如 begin、
  start 等）

intercept[7] 〔 ˌɪntəˈsɛpt 〕 *v.* 中途攔截；竊聽（在中間拿取）
  《*inter-* = between》

interception[7] 〔 ˌɪntəˈsɛpʃən 〕 *n.* 奪取；妨礙

```
inter   +  cept  +  ion
  │         │       │
between  +  take  +  n.
```

interceptor 〔 ˌɪntəˈsɛptə 〕 *n.* 攔截者；障礙物

perceive[5] 〔 pəˈsiv 〕 *v.* 感覺；理解（憑感覺取得）《*per-* = through》

percept 〔 ˈpɝsɛpt 〕 *n.* 知覺的對象

perceptible[7] 〔 pəˈsɛptəb! 〕 *adj.* 可知覺的；顯而易見的

perception[6] 〔 pəˈsɛpʃən 〕 *n.* 知覺；理解力

perceptive[7] 〔 pəˈsɛptɪv 〕 *adj.* 知覺的；有洞察力的

```
per      +  cept  +  ive
 │          │       │
through  +  take  +  adj.
```

precept[7] 〔 ˈprisɛpt 〕 *n.* 箴言；教訓；命令書（拿到眾人之前的東西）
  《*pre-* = before》

preceptor 〔 prɪˈsɛptə 〕 *n.* 訓誡者；指導者；教師

receive[1] 〔 rɪˈsiv 〕 *v.* 接受；歡迎；收容；理解（拿到自己這一方）
  《*re-* = back》

receiver[3] 〔 rɪˈsivə 〕 *n.* 收受人；收報機；受話器；聽筒

receivable[7] 〔 rɪ'sivəb！〕 *adj.* 可收到的

```
re + ceiv + able
 |     |      |
back + take + adj.
```

receipt[3] 〔 rɪ'sit 〕 *n.* 收據

receptacle[7] 〔 rɪ'sɛptək！〕 *n.* 容器；花托；插座；貯藏所（收到的東西）

reception[4] 〔 rɪ'sɛpʃən 〕 *n.* 接受；歡迎（會）；容納；接待

receptive[7] 〔 rɪ'sɛptɪv 〕 *adj.* 能接受的

receptor 〔 rɪ'sɛptɚ 〕 *n.* （感受刺激的）神經末梢；感受體

recipient[6] 〔 rɪ'sɪpɪənt 〕 *adj.* 接受的　*n.* 接受者；容器

susceptible[7] 〔 sə'sɛptəb！〕 *adj.* 容易感受的；善感的；感情脆弱的；容易罹患～的（被放到～之下→蒙受）《*sus-* = *sub-* = under》

```
sus  + cept + ible
 |      |      |
under + take + adj.
```

susceptibility[7] 〔 sə,sɛptə'bɪlətɪ 〕 *n.* 感受性；敏銳的感情；容易感受的性質

susceptive 〔 sə'sɛptɪv 〕 *adj.* 能感受的；容許的

anticipate[6] 〔 æn'tɪsə,pet 〕 *v.* 預期；期待；佔先（事先考慮）《*anti-* = before》

```
anti  + cipate
 |       |
before + take
```

anticipation[6] 〔 æn,tɪsə'peʃən 〕 *n.* 預期；期待；佔先

participate[3] 〔 pɚ'tɪsə,pet , par- 〕 *v.* 分享；參與（取得一部分）《*part* = part》

participation[4] 〔 par,tɪsə'peʃən , pɚ- 〕 *n.* 參與；共享

participle[4] 〔 'partəsəp！, 'partsəp！〕 *n.* 分詞（同時進行兩件工作）

emancipate〔 ɪ′mænsə͵pet 〕*v.* 解放；解除；使脫離（把手中的東西拿出來）《*e-* = *ex-*（ out ）+ ***man*** = ***manus***（ hand ）+ ***cipate***（ take ）》

emancipation[7]〔 ɪ͵mænsə′peʃən 〕*n.* 解放

```
e  +  man  +  cipat  +  ion
|       |       |        |
out +  hand  +  take  +  n.
```

70　car = car（車）　　* 拉丁文 *carrus*（ = *four-wheeled cart* ）。

car[1]〔 kɑr 〕*n.* 車；汽車；電車（跑的東西）

career[4]〔 kə′rɪr 〕*n.* 生涯；經歷；職業　*v.* 飛奔（車輛所用的路）

cargo[4]〔′kɑrgo 〕*n.* 貨物（車的貨物）

carry[1]〔′kærɪ 〕*v.* 攜帶；支持；取得；影響；感動（用車搬運）

carriage[3]〔′kærɪdʒ 〕*n.* 運輸；車輛；姿勢；風度（搬運）

《 *-age* 抽象名詞字尾》

```
carri  +  age
  |         |
 car   +   n.
```

carrier[4]〔′kærɪɚ 〕*n.* 運送人；運輸業者；帶菌者；航空母艦

cart[2]〔 kɑrt 〕*n.* 馬車；二輪馬車　*v.* 用車運送

carter〔′kɑrtɚ 〕*n.* 運貨馬車夫

charge[2]〔 tʃɑrdʒ 〕*v.* 裝；充電；命令；控告；突擊　*n.* 充電；負擔；課稅；責任；監督；命令；控告；索價（在車上裝貨）

【解説】 /k/音和/tʃ/音相互變化是常見的現象。出於同一字根，而依發音之不同有不同的拼法和意義的字，稱爲 **doublet**（雙重字；姊妹字）。

【舉例】 arc（弧）– ar*ch*（拱門）

　　　　 *c*adence（韻律）– *ch*ance（機會）

　　　　 *c*amera（照相機）– *ch*amber（室）

　　　　 *c*ard（卡片）– *ch*art（航海圖）

catch（捕捉）– chase（追求）
cavalry（騎兵隊）– chivalry（騎士精神）
canal（運河）– channel（海峽）
cant（術語）– chant（歌）
caress（愛撫）– cherish（珍愛）

discharge[6]〔dɪs'tʃɑrdʒ〕v. 卸下；發射；放出；開除；放電
　　n. 卸貨；發射；放出（物）；放電；免除；履行《**dis-** = away》

chariot[6]〔'tʃærɪət〕n. 古時雙輪戰車；四輪馬車或轎車
　　v. 用雙輪或四輪馬車載運

71　carbo = coal；charcoal（煤；木炭）

　　* 拉丁文 *carbo*（= *charcoal*；*dead or glowing coal*）。

carbon[5]〔'kɑrbən〕n. 碳；複寫紙；碳棒

carbonate〔n. 'kɑrbənɪt , -ˌnet　v. 'kɑrbəˌnet〕n. 碳酸鹽
　　v. 使變為碳酸鹽；使碳化

carboholic〔ˌkɑrbə'hɑlɪk〕n. 愛吃甜食的人《**-(a)holic** 表示「有⋯癖好的人」》

carbohydrate[7]〔ˌkɑrbo'haɪdret〕n. 碳水化合物；醣《**hydr** = water》

carbolic〔kɑr'bɑlɪk〕adj. 用碳製的；煤焦油的

carb	+	ol	+	ic
carbon	+	alcohol	+	adj.

carbide〔'kɑrbaɪd〕n. 碳化物；碳化鈣《**-ide** 表示「化物」》

72　card = heart（心）　　* 希臘文 *kardia*（= *heart*）。

cardiac[7]〔'kɑrdɪˌæk〕adj. 心臟（病）的　　n. 心臟病患者；強心劑

cardiectomy〔ˌkɑrdɪ'ɛktəmɪ〕n. 心部分切除術《**tom** = cut》

cardiogram〔'kɑrdɪəˌgræm〕n. 心電圖《**gram** = write》

cardiology〔ˌkɑrdɪˈɑlədʒɪ〕 *n.* 心臟病學《*logy* = study》

cardiometer〔ˌkɑrdɪˈɑmɪtɚ〕 *n.* 心力測量器；心力計

cardiophobia〔ˌkɑrdɪoˈfobɪə〕 *n.* 心臟病恐怖症《*phob* = fear》

cardiovascular〔ˌkɑrdɪoˈvæskjulɚ〕 *adj.*（病等）心血管的；
　　侵襲心血管的《*vas* = vessel》

cardioverter〔ˌkɑrdɪoˈvɜtɚ〕 *n.* 心律轉變器；復律器《*vert* = turn》

endocarditis〔ˌɛndokɑrˈdaɪtɪs〕 *n.* 心內膜炎

```
endo  +  card  +    itis
  |        |         |
within  +  heart  +  inflammation
```

73　**carn** = flesh（肉）　　* 拉丁文 *caro* , *carn*-（= *flesh*）。

carnage[7]〔ˈkɑrnɪdʒ〕 *n.* 大屠殺（吃肉的時節）

carnal[7]〔ˈkɑrnḷ〕 *adj.* 肉體的；肉慾的

carnalism〔ˈkɑrnḷˌɪzəm〕 *n.* 肉慾主義；享樂主義

carnation[5]〔kɑrˈneʃən〕 *n.* 肉色；淡紅色；康乃馨

carniferous〔kɑrˈnɪfərəs〕 *adj.* 生肉的
　　《 *-iferous* = bearing（產生）》

```
carn  +  iferous
  |        |
flesh  +  bearing
```

carnival[5]〔ˈkɑrnəvḷ〕 *n.* 嘉年華會；狂歡

carnivalesque〔ˌkɑrnəvḷˈɛsk〕 *adj.* 好像過節的；快樂的
　　《 *-esque* = in the manner of（以～風格）》

carnivore[7]〔ˈkɑrnəˌvor〕 *n.* 食肉動物；食蟲植物
　　《*vore* = 拉丁文 *vorare* = devour（吞食）》

carnivorous〔kɑrˈnɪvərəs〕 *adj.* 食肉的；食肉動物的

carrion〔ˈkærɪən〕 *n.* 腐臭的肉；腐敗　*adj.* 腐爛的；腐敗的

discarnate〔dɪsˈkɑrnet〕 *adj.* 無形的《*dis-* = negative（否定）》

incarnate[7] 〔 *adj.* ɪnˈkɑrnɪt　*v.* ɪnˈkɑrnet 〕*adj.* 具有肉體的

　　v. 賦予形體；使具體化；為～之典範（進入肉體之中）《*in-* = in》

```
in + carn + ate
 |     |     |
in + flesh + adj., n.
```

incarnation[7] 〔 ˌɪnkɑrˈneʃən 〕*n.* 賦以形體；化身

74　carp = fruit（果實）　　* 希臘文 *karpos*（= *fruit*）。

carpogenic 〔 ˌkɑrpəˈdʒɛnɪk 〕*adj.* 結果實的《*gen* = produce》
carpology 〔 kɑrˈpɑlədʒɪ 〕*n.* 果實學《*logy* = study》
carpophagous 〔 kɑrˈpɑfəgəs 〕*adj.* 食果實的

```
carpo + phag + ous
  |       |      |
fruit  + eat  + adj.
```

carpophore 〔 ˈkɑrpəˌfor 〕*n.* 心皮柄；子實體
polycarpous 〔 ˌpɑlɪˈkɑrpəs 〕*adj.* 多心皮的《*poly-* = many》

75　cast = throw（投擲）　　* 中古英文 *cast*（= *throw*）。

cast[3] 〔 kæst 〕*v.* 投擲；投射；鑄造；分配角色；脫落

　　n. 投擲；鑄造（物）；分派角色；搭便車
broadcast[2] 〔 ˈbrɔdˌkæst 〕*v.* 廣播；撒播；散布

　　n. 廣播；播種　　*adj.* 廣播的；普遍的
forecast[4] 〔 *v.* forˈkæst　*n.* ˈforˌkæst 〕*v.*, *n.* 預測；預報

　《*fore-* = before》

```
fore + cast
  |     |
before + throw
```

outcast[7] 〔'aʊtˌkæst〕 *n.* 被逐出者；流浪者　*adj.* 被棄的；
無家可歸的

overcast[7] 〔'ovəˌkæst〕 *adj.* 多雲的；陰暗的；憂鬱的　*v.* 使陰暗
《*over-* = above》

telecast[7] 〔'tɛləˌkæst〕 *v.* 以電視播送　*n.* 電視播送《*tele-* = far off》

76　cast , chast = pure（純潔的）

* 拉丁文 *castus*（ = *pure*）；古法文 *chaste*（ = *morally pure*）。

caste[7] 〔kæst〕 *n.* 卡斯德（印度世襲的社會階級，分為僧侶、士族、平
民、奴隸四種階級）；社會地位（排除不同階級）《葡萄牙文 *casta* = race》

castigate 〔'kæstəˌget〕 *v.* 譴責；懲戒；嚴厲批評

```
cast  +      ig    + ate
 |            |       |
pure + compel (to be) + v.
```

chaste[7] 〔tʃest〕 *adj.* 貞潔的；純潔的

chasten 〔'tʃesn̩〕 *v.* 懲戒；使改正；磨練《*-en* 動詞字尾》

chastise[7] 〔tʃæs'taɪz〕 *v.* 懲戒；嚴厲批評《*-ise* 動詞字尾》

unchastity 〔ʌn'tʃæstətɪ〕 *n.* 不貞；不純潔《*un-* = not》

77　caul = stalk（莖）　　　* 拉丁文 *caulis*（ = *stalk* ; *stem*）。

caulescent 〔kɔ'lɛsənt〕 *adj.* 有莖的

cauliflorous 〔ˌkɔlə'florəs〕 *adj.* 在主莖或枝上直接開花結果的

```
cauli +   flor   + ous
  |        |        |
stalk + flower  + adj.
```

cauliflower[7] 〔'kɔləˌflaʊə〕 *n.* 花椰菜

cauliform 〔'kɔləˌfɔrm〕 *adj.* 莖狀的《*form* 形狀》

cauline 〔'kɔlɪn , -aɪn〕 *adj.* 莖的；生於莖上的

78　cause , cuse = reason（理由）

> ＊拉丁文 *causa*（ = *cause* ; *reason* ; *judicial process* ; *lawsuit*）。

cause[1]〔kɔz〕*n.* 原因；理由　*v.* 導致；造成
accuse[4]〔ə'kjuz〕*v.* 指控；控告《*ac-* = *ad-* = to》
excuse[2]〔*v.* ɪk'skjuz　*n.* ɪk'skjus〕*v.* 原諒　*n.* 藉口《*ex-* = out》
recusant〔'rɛkjuznt〕*adj.* 不服從的　*n.* 不服從的人

```
re  +  cus  +  ant
|       |      |
against + reason + adj., n.
```

79　caust , caut = burn（燃燒）

> ＊希臘文 *kaiein*（ = *burn*），*kaustos*（ = *burnt*），
> *kauterion*（ = *branding iron* 烙鐵）。

caustic[7]〔'kɔstɪk〕*n.* 腐蝕劑　*adj.* 腐蝕性的；刻薄的
cautery〔'kɔtərɪ〕*n.* 燒灼；灸；燒灼器
cauterize〔'kɔtə,raɪz〕*v.* 燒灼（傷口）；使（良心、情感等）麻木
holocaust[7]〔'halə,kɔst〕*n.* 大屠殺；大量焚毀《*holo-* = whole》

80　cav = hollow（中空的）　＊拉丁文 *cavus*（ = *hollow*）。

cave[2]〔kev〕*n.* 洞穴　*v.*（使）凹陷
cavern[7]〔'kævən〕*n.* 巨穴；大洞
cavernous[7]〔'kævənəs〕*adj.* 如洞穴的；多洞穴的；凹陷的
cavity[6]〔'kævətɪ〕*n.* 穴；洞；凹處；腔
concave[7]〔kɑn'kev〕*adj.* 凹的；凹面的《*con-* = together》
　cf. **convex**（凸面的）

excavate[7] 〔'ɛkskə,vet 〕v. 挖空；挖掘；挖出《ex- = out》

```
ex +  cav  + ate
 |     |      |
out + hollow +  v.
```

excavation[7] 〔,ɛkskə'veʃən 〕n. 挖掘；發掘
excavator 〔'ɛkskə,vetɚ 〕n. 挖掘者；挖土機

81　cede , ceed , cess = go ; yield (走；讓步)

* 拉丁文 cedere (= go ; yield) ，過去分詞爲 cessus。

abscess[7] 〔'æb,sɛs 〕n. 膿瘡；潰瘍；膿腫《abs- = ab- = away》
accede[7] 〔 æk'sid 〕v. 應允；就職；參加 (向～走去)《ac- = ad- = to》
access[4] 〔'æksɛs 〕n. 接近；通路；入口；附加
accessible[6] 〔 æk'sɛsəbḷ 〕adj. 易接近的；可取得的

```
ac + cess + ible
 |    |      |
to +  go  + adj.
```

accession 〔 æk'sɛʃən , ək- 〕n. 接近；就任；即位；同意；增加
accessory[6] 〔 æk'sɛsərɪ 〕n. 配件　adj. 附加的
antecede 〔,æntə'sid 〕v. 先行；超越 (走向前去)《ante- = before》
antecedence 〔,æntə'sidṇs 〕n. 先行；居先
antecedent 〔,æntə'sidṇt 〕adj. 在先的；在前的　n. 前事；祖先；先行詞；前身
antecessor 〔,æntə'sɛsɚ 〕n. 先行者；前往
cede[7] 〔 sid 〕v. 放棄；割讓
cessation 〔 sɛ'seʃən 〕n. 停止；中斷；斷絕
cession 〔'sɛʃən 〕n. 讓與；割讓；放棄
cessionary 〔'sɛʃən,ɛrɪ 〕n. 受讓人

concede[6]〔kən'sid〕*v.* 容許；勉強承認《*con-* = together》

concession[6]〔kən'sɛʃən〕*n.* 讓步；特許權；租界地

```
con  + cess + ion
 |       |      |
together + yield + n.
```

concessionary〔kən'sɛʃən‚ɛrɪ〕*adj.* 讓步的

concessive〔kən'sɛsɪv〕*adj.* 讓步的

exceed[5]〔ɪk'sid〕*v.* 優於；勝過（越過～向外走去）《*ex-* = out》

exceeding[7]〔ɪk'sidɪŋ〕*adj.* 非常的；過度的

exceedingly[7]〔ɪk'sidɪŋlɪ〕*adv.* 非常地；過度地

excess[5]〔*n.* ɪk'sɛs *adj.* 'ɪksɛs , ɪk'sɛs〕*n.* 過多；過度；超過（額）
　adj. 超過的；多餘的

excessive[6]〔ɪk'sɛsɪv〕*adj.* 過度的

incessant[7]〔ɪn'sɛsn̩t〕*adj.* 不絕的；不斷的（不能放棄）《*in-* = not》

```
in  + cess + ant
 |     |      |
not + yield + adj.
```

intercede[7]〔‚ɪntɚ'sid〕*v.* 說情；從中調停（進入兩者之間）
　《*inter-* = between》

```
inter  + cede
  |        |
between +  go
```

intercession〔‚ɪntɚ'sɛʃən〕*n.* 從中調停；代為求情

intercessor〔‚ɪntɚ'sɛsɚ〕*n.* 仲裁者；調停者

precede[6]〔prɪ'sid〕*v.* 在前；前導；較～優先（走在前面）
　《*pre-* = before》

precedence；**-ency**[7]〔prɪ'sidn̩s(ɪ)〕*n.* 居先；優先權

precedent[6]〔*n.* 'prɛsədənt *adj.* prɪ'sidn̩t〕*n.* 先例；判例
　adj. 在先的

precedented〔'prɛsə,dɛntɪd〕*adj.* 有先例的

preceding[7]〔prɪ'sidɪŋ〕*adj.* 在前的

precession〔pri'sɛʃən , prɪ-〕*n.* 優先

proceed[4]〔prə'sid〕*v.* 繼續進行；進展；著手（去前面）

　　《*pro-* = forward》

```
pro    +  ceed
 |         |
forward +  go
```

proceeding[7]〔prə'sidɪŋ〕*n.* 行動；行為；處置

proceeds[7]〔'prosidz〕*n.pl.* 收入；收益；結果

procedure[7]〔prə'sidʒɚ〕*n.* 程序

process[3]〔'prasɛs〕*n.* 進行；過程；手續；訴訟程序　*v.* 加工；
　　處理；控訴

procession[5]〔prə'sɛʃən〕*n.* 行列　*v.* 排隊前進

processor〔'prasɛsɚ〕*n.* 處理器

recede[7]〔rɪ'sid〕*v.* 後退；向後傾斜；撤退（向後去）《*re-* = back》

```
re   +  cede
 |        |
back +   go
```

recess[7]〔*n.* rɪ'sɛs , 'risɛs　*v.* rɪ'sɛs〕*n.* 休息；放假；深處；凹處
　　v. 隱藏；休會（退居）

recession[6]〔rɪ'sɛʃən〕*n.* 退卻；凹處；蕭條

recessionary〔rɪ'sɛʃən,ɛrɪ〕*adj.* 衰退的

recessive〔rɪ'sɛsɪv〕*adj.* 後退的；隱性的

retrocede〔,rɛtro'sid〕*v.* 歸還；交還（向後走）《*retro-* = backward》

retrocession〔,rɛtro'sɛʃən〕*n.* 後退；交還

secede[7]〔sɪ'sid〕*v.* 脫離；退出（離去）《*se-* = away》

```
se   +  cede
 |        |
away +   go
```

seceder 〔 sɪ'sidɚ 〕 *n.* 脫離者；退出者

secession[7] 〔 si'sɛʃən 〕 *n.* 脫離；退出

secessionism 〔 si'sɛʃən,ɪzəm 〕 *n.* 脫離主義

succeed[2] 〔 sək'sid 〕 *v.* 繼續；繼承；成功（跟在～之後而去）
　　《*suc-* = *sub-* = under》

success[2] 〔 sək'sɛs 〕 *n.* 成功；成功的人或事

successful[2] 〔 sək'sɛsfəl 〕 *adj.* 成功的

$$suc + cess + ful$$
$$under + go + adj.$$

successfully[2] 〔 sək'sɛsfəlɪ 〕 *adv.* 成功地

succession[6] 〔 sək'sɛʃən 〕 *n.* 繼續；繼承；連續

successive[6] 〔 sək'sɛsɪv 〕 *adj.* 連續的

successor[6] 〔 sək'sɛsɚ 〕 *n.* 後繼者；繼承者

82 **cel** = heaven；sky（天國；天空）

　　* 拉丁文 *caelum*（ = *heaven*；*sky*）。

celeste 〔 sə'lɛst 〕 *n.* 天藍色

celestial[7] 〔 sə'lɛstʃəl 〕 *adj.* 天空的；天國的　　*n.* 神仙

ceiling[2] 〔 'silɪŋ 〕 *n.* 天花板

83 **celer** = swift（快速的）　　* 拉丁文 *celer*（ = *swift*）。

celerity 〔 sə'lɛrətɪ 〕 *n.* 敏捷；快速

accelerate[6] 〔 æk'sɛlə,ret 〕 *v.* 加速；促進《*ac-* = *ad-* = to》

acceleration[6] 〔 æk,sɛlə'reʃən 〕 *n.* 加速；促進；加速度

accelerator[7] 〔 æk'sɛlə,retɚ 〕 *n.* 加速者；變速器；加速器；觸媒劑

decelerate[7] 〔 di'sɛlə,ret 〕 *v.* 減速；減緩《*de-* = *dis-* = not》

84 cell = small room；hide（小房間；隱藏）

* 拉丁文 *cella*（= *small room*），*celare*（= *hide*；*conceal*）。

cell[2]〔sɛl〕*n.* 小牢房；單人牢房；（修道院中的）單人小室；
細胞；電池

cellular[7]〔'sɛljələ〕*adj.* 細胞的；多孔的；有網眼的
  《-*ula* 表示小的名詞字尾》

cellulitis〔,sɛlju'laɪtɪs〕*n.* 蜂窩性組織炎《-*itis* = inflammation（發炎）》

intercellular〔,ɪntə'sɛljələ〕*adj.* 細胞間的《*inter-* = between》

multicellular〔,mʌltɪ'sɛljələ〕*adj.* 多細胞的《*multi-* = many》

unicellular〔,junɪ'sɛljələ〕*adj.* 單細胞的《*uni-* = one》

photocell〔'fotə,sɛl〕*n.* 光電池《*photo* = light》

conceal[5]〔kən'sil〕*v.* 隱藏；隱瞞《*con-* = together》

occult[7]〔ə'kʌlt〕*adj.* 難以理解的；神祕的；隱蔽的
  《拉丁文 *occultus* = hidden》

```
oc  +  cult
 |      |
over + cover
```

hell[3]〔hɛl〕*n.* 地獄《*hell* = concealed place》

85 cens = assess（評估）
* 拉丁文 *censere*（= *assess*）。

censor[7]〔'sɛnsə〕*n.*（書刊、報紙、電影等的）審查員
  v. 審查；檢查

censure[7]〔'sɛnʃə〕*n.* 責備；公開譴責　*v.* 責備；譴責

census[7]〔'sɛnsəs〕*n.* 人口調查

recension[7]〔rɪ'sɛnʃən〕*n.* 校訂；校訂本；校訂版

```
re  +  cens  +  ion
 |      |       |
again + assess + n.
```

86 **cent** = hundred (百) * 拉丁文 *centum* (= *hundred*)。

cent[1] 〔 sɛnt 〕 *n.* 一分錢

centenary 〔'sɛntə,nɛrɪ , sɛn'tɛnərɪ 〕 *adj.* 百年的
    n. 一百年；百年紀念《*en* = *ann* = year》

centenarian 〔,sɛntə'nɛrɪən , -'ner- 〕 *adj.* , *n.* 一百歲的 (人)

centennial[7] 〔 sɛn'tɛnɪəl 〕 *adj.* 一百年的；百年一次的
    n. 百年紀念

centigrade[5] 〔'sɛntə,gred 〕 *adj.* 分爲百度的；攝氏的《*grade* 階級》

```
centi  +  grade
  |         |
hundred +  class
```

centimeter[3] 〔'sɛntə,mitɚ 〕 *n.* 公分 (一公尺的百分之一)

centiped(e)[7] 〔'sɛntə,pid 〕 *n.* 蜈蚣 (一百隻腳) 《*ped* = foot》

centuple 〔'sɛntjupḷ 〕 *n.* , *adj.* 一百倍 (的) 《*ple* = fold》

```
centu  +  ple
  |        |
hundred + fold
```

centuplicate 〔 sɛn'tjuplə,ket 〕 *v.* 以百乘之；使成百倍；
    印一百份

century[2] 〔'sɛntʃərɪ 〕 *n.* 百年；一世紀

percent[4] 〔 pɚ'sɛnt 〕 *n.* 百分數；百分比 (每一百) 《*per* 每》

percentage[4] 〔 pɚ'sɛntɪdʒ 〕 *n.* 百分率；部分；手續費

87 **centr** = center (中心) * 拉丁文 *centrum* (= *center*)。

central[2] 〔'sɛntrəl 〕 *adj.* 中央的；中心的；主要的

centralism 〔'sɛntrəl,ɪzəm 〕 *n.* 中央集權主義
    《 *-ism* 表主義的名詞字尾》

centralization[7] 〔,sɛntrəlaɪ'zeʃən 〕 *n.* 集中；中央集權

centrifugal〔sɛnˈtrɪfjʊgḷ〕*adj.* 離心的；利用離心的

《*fugal* = 拉丁文 *fugere* = flee》 *cf.* **fugitive**（逃亡者）

```
centri + fug + al
  │       │     │
center + flee + adj.
```

centripetal〔sɛnˈtrɪpətḷ〕*adj.* 向心的

《*pet* = seek》 *cf.* **petition**（請願）

acentric〔əˈsɛntrɪk〕*adj.* 無中心的；離心的《*a-* = without》

anthropocentric〔͵ænθrəpəˈsɛntrɪk〕*adj.* 認定人爲宇宙中心的；
人類中心主義的《*anthrop(o)* = man》

concentrate[4]〔ˈkɑnsn͵tret , -sɛn-〕*v.* 集中；濃縮；全神貫注

（一起到中心）《*con-* = together》

```
con  + centr + ate
 │       │      │
together + center + v.
```

concentration[4]〔͵kɑnsn͵treʃən , -sɛn-〕*n.* 集中；濃度；專注

decentralize[7]〔diˈsɛntrəl͵aɪz〕*v.* 劃分；分散；疏散

《*de-* = *dis-* = away》

eccentric[7]〔ɪkˈsɛntrɪk〕*adj.* 古怪的；離心的　*n.* 古怪的人；
離心圓（遠離中心的）《*ec-* = *ex-* = out》

eccentricity[7]〔͵ɛksənˈtrɪsətɪ〕*n.* 怪癖性；離心率

heliocentric〔͵hilɪoˈsɛntrɪk〕*adj.* 以太陽爲中心的《*helio* = sun》

88　**cerebr** = brain（腦）　　* 拉丁文 *cerebrum*（= *brain*）。

cerebrum〔ˈsɛrəbrəm〕*n.* 大腦

cerebral[7]〔ˈsɛrəbrəl〕*adj.* 腦的；大腦的；觸動理智的；用腦筋的

cerebrate〔ˈsɛrə͵bret〕*v.* 動腦子；思考

cerebellum〔͵sɛrəˈbɛləm〕n. 小腦

cereb +	ell +	um
brain +	small +	n.

cerebritis〔͵sɛrəˈbraɪtɪs〕n. 腦炎《 *-itis* = inflammation（發炎）》

89　cern , cret = separate（分開）

* 拉丁文 **cernere**（= *separate*；*sift* 選拔；淘汰，*decree* 判定，*observe* 觀察），過去分詞是 **cretus**。

concern[3]〔kənˈsɝn〕v. 與～有關係；關心　n. 關心；關係；公司；憂慮（經過淘汰把相同的東西集合在一起 → 有關係的）《*con-* = together》

concerning[4]〔kənˈsɝnɪŋ〕prep. 關於

concernment〔kənˈsɝnmənt〕n. 事件；事業；重要；關係；關心

discern[7]〔dɪˈzɝn〕v. 看出；辨別；認識（個別分開）《*dis-* = apart》

discernable; **-ible**[7]〔dɪˈzɝnəbḷ〕adj. 可辨別的；可看出的

dis +	cern +	able
apart +	separate +	adj.

discernment〔dɪˈzɝnmənt〕n. 識別；洞察力

discreet[6]〔dɪˈskrit〕adj. 言行謹慎的（個別分出）

discrete[7]〔dɪˈskrit〕adj. 各別的；無連續的；分開的；有區別的（一個二個地分開）

discretion[7]〔dɪˈskrɛʃən〕n. 隨意處理；謹慎

excrete[7]〔ɛkˈskrit, ɪk-〕v. 排泄；分泌（釋放到身體之外）《*ex-* = out》

excrement[7]〔ˈɛkskrɪmənt〕n. 排泄物；糞便

ex +	cre +	ment
out +	separate +	n.

secret[2] 〔ˈsikrɪt 〕 *adj.* 祕密的　　*n.* 祕密；祕訣（被個別區分出來）
　《*se-* = apart》

secretary[2] 〔ˈsɛkrəˌtɛrɪ 〕 *n.* 祕書；〔英〕國務大臣；〔美〕國務卿
　（與祕密有關的人）

```
se  +  cret  +  ary
 |       |       |
apart + separate + person
```

secrete[7] 〔 sɪˈkrit 〕 *v.* 分泌；隱匿；隱藏（個別隔離）《*se-* = apart》

secretion[7] 〔 sɪˈkriʃən 〕 *n.* 隱匿；分泌（物）

secernent 〔 sɪˈsɝnənt 〕 *adj.* 能分泌的　　*n.* 促進分泌之藥

90　　**cert** = sure（確定的）

> * 拉丁文 *certus*（= *certain*），是由前面所說的 *cernere* 而來的，
> 意為「淘汰之後清楚地界定」。

ascertain[7] 〔ˌæsɚˈten 〕 *v.* 確定；探查；探知
　《*a-* = *ad-* = to ; *s* 在此不含有任何特殊意義》

certain[1] 〔ˈsɝtn̩ 〕 *adj.* 確實的；無疑的

certainty[6] 〔ˈsɝtn̩tɪ 〕 *n.* 無疑；確信

certify[6] 〔ˈsɝtəˌfaɪ 〕 *v.* 證明；確信；保證（使明確）《 *-ify* = make》

```
cert  +  ify
 |        |
sure  +  make
```

certifiable[7] 〔ˈsɝtəˌfaɪəbl̩ 〕 *adj.* 可證明的；可確認的；可保證的

certificate[5] 〔 *n.* səˈtɪfəkɪt　*v.* səˈtɪfəˌket 〕 *n.* 證書；執照
　v. 給與證明書；認可

certification[7] 〔ˌsɝtɪfəˈkeʃən 〕 *n.* 證明；保證

certitude[7] 〔ˈsɝtəˌtjud 〕 *n.* 確實之事；確信；確實性
　《 *-itude* 抽象名詞字尾》

concert[3] 〔ˈkɑnsɝt 〕 *n.* 音樂會；一致；和諧《*con-* = together》

disconcert 〔͵dɪskən'sɝt 〕 v. 使驚慌；使不安；破壞；擾亂

　《*dis-* = negative (否定)》

91　**chel** = claw (爪)　　* 希臘文 *khele* (= *claw*) 。

chela 〔'kilə 〕 n. (蟹、蝦等的) 螯；鉗爪

chelate 〔'kilet 〕 adj. 有螯的

chelicera 〔 kə'lɪsərə 〕 n. 螯肢 (節肢動物鉗狀的第一對附器之一)

　《希臘文 *keras* = horn》

cheliferous 〔 kə'lɪfərəs 〕 adj. 帶螯的

$$
\begin{array}{c|c|c}
\text{cheli} + & \text{fer} + & \text{ous} \\
\hline
claw + & carry + & adj.
\end{array}
$$

cheliform 〔'kilə͵fɔrm 〕 n. 螯狀的《*form* 形狀》

cheloid 〔'kilɔɪd 〕 n. 蟹足腫；瘢痕疙瘩《 *-oid* = like》

92　**chem** = chemical (化學的)

　* 後期希臘文 *khemeia* (= *the art of transmutation*) 。

chemical[2] 〔'kɛmɪkḷ 〕 adj. 化學的　 n. 化學藥品

chemist[5] 〔'kɛmɪst 〕 n. 化學家

chemistry[4] 〔'kɛmɪstrɪ 〕 n. 化學

chemiluminescence 〔͵kɛmə͵lumə'nɛsəns 〕 n. 化學發光 (由化學
　反應引起，但不帶來明顯溫度變化)《*lumin* = light》

chemisorb 〔'kɛmə͵sɔrb 〕 v. 用化學方法吸附《*absorb* 吸收》

chemolysis 〔 kɪ'maləsɪs 〕 n. 化學分解

$$
\begin{array}{c|c|c}
\text{chemo} + & \text{lys} + & \text{is} \\
\hline
chemical + & loosen + & n.
\end{array}
$$

chemonuclear〔͵kɛmo'njuklɪr〕*adj.* 核輻射（或核裂變碎片）
誘發化學反應的《*nuclear* 核子的》

chemoreception〔͵kɛmorɪ'sɛpʃən〕*n.* 化學感受（作用）
《*reception* 接受》

chemosmosis〔͵kɛmɑs'mosɪs〕*n.* 化學滲透（作用）
《希臘文 *osmos* = push》

chemosynthesis〔͵kɛmo'sɪnθəsɪs〕*n.* 化學合成《*synthesis* 合成》

chemotropism〔kɪ'mɑtrəpɪzm̩〕*n.* 向化性；向藥性《*trop* = turn》

alchemy[7]〔'ælkəmɪ〕*n.* 煉金術

93   chir , cheir = hand（手）

* 希臘文 *kheir*（= *hand*）。

chirography〔kaɪ'rɑgrəfɪ〕*n.* 書寫；筆跡；書法
《*graphy* = writing》

chiromancy〔'kaɪrə͵mænsɪ〕*n.* 手相術
《 *-mancy* = divination（占卜）》

chiropractic〔͵kaɪrə'præktɪk〕*n.* 脊椎按摩療法《*practice* 實行》

chiropody〔kaɪ'rɑpədɪ〕*n.* 足醫術《*pod* = foot》

chiropteran〔kaɪ'rɑptərən〕*n.* 翼手目動物；蝙蝠

```
chiro + pter + an
  |      |     |
hand + wing +  n.
```

macrocheiria〔'mækro͵kaɪrɪə〕*n.* 巨手《*macro-* = large》

94   chlor = green（綠色）

* 希臘文 *khloros*（= *pale green*）。

chlorate〔'klorɪt, 'klɔr-, -ret〕*n.* 氯酸鹽

chloric〔'klorɪk, 'klɔr-〕*adj.* （含）氯的

chloride〔ˋklɔraɪd，ˋklɔr-，-rɪd〕*n.* 氯化物《*-ide* 表示「化物」》

chlorine[7]〔ˋklɔrin，ˋklɔr-，-rɪn〕*n.* 氯

chlorinate〔ˋklɔrɪ͵net，ˋklɔr-〕*v.* 使氯化；給（水、污水）加氯消毒

chlorocarbon〔͵klɔrəˋkɑrbən，͵klɔr-〕*n.* 氯碳化合物
《*carbon* 碳》

chlorophyl(l)〔ˋklɔrə͵fɪl〕*n.* 葉綠素《*phyll* = leaf》

chlorosis〔kləˋrosɪs〕*n.* 萎黃病；黃化病
《*-osis* 表示病變狀態的名詞字尾》

95 chol = bile（膽汁）　*希臘文 *khole*（= bile）。

cholangitis〔͵kolənˋdʒaɪtɪs〕*n.* 膽管炎

chol +	ang(i) +	itis
bile +	*vessel +*	*inflammation*

cholecystectomy〔͵kaləsɪsˋtɛktəmɪ〕*n.* 膽囊切除術
《*cyst* = bladder（囊）》

cholera[7]〔ˋkalərə〕*n.* 霍亂

choleric[7]〔ˋkalərɪk〕*adj.* 易怒的；暴躁的
　【解說】choler（膽汁），古生理學中四種體液之一，被認爲能促成暴躁脾氣。

cholesterol[6]〔kəˋlɛstə͵rol〕*n.* 膽固醇
　【解說】首先發現於膽石，故名。

chol +	ster(eo) +	ol
bile +	*solid +*	*alcohol*

chololith〔ˋkalə͵lɪθ〕*n.* 膽石（= *gallstone*）《*lith* = stone》

96 **chondr** = grain ; cartilage (細粒；軟骨)

* 希臘文 *khondros* (= grain ; cartilage) 。

chondrify 〔'kɑndrə,faɪ 〕 v. (使) 軟骨化
chondrite 〔'kɑn,draɪt 〕 n. 球粒狀隕石
chondrocranium 〔,kɑndro'krenɪəm 〕 n. 軟骨顱

> chondro + crani + um
> cartilage + skull + n.

chondroma 〔 kɑn'dromə 〕 n. 軟骨瘤《 *-oma* 表示瘤的名詞字尾》
chondrosarcoma 〔,kɑndrosɑr'komə 〕 n. 軟骨肉瘤
　《希臘文 *sarx* = flesh (肉)》
chondrule 〔'kɑndrul 〕 n. 隕石球粒《 *-ule* 表示小的名詞字尾》
mitochondrion 〔,maɪtə'kɑndrɪən 〕 n. 粒線體
　《希臘文 *mitos* = thread (線)》

97 **chor** = dance (跳舞)

* 希臘文 *khoros* (= band of dancers or singers ; dance) ，
　khoreia (= choral dance) 。

choir[5] 〔 kwaɪr 〕 n. 唱詩班
chorus[4] 〔'korəs 〕 n. 合唱；合唱團
choral 〔'kɔrəl 〕 adj. 合唱的；合唱團的
chorister 〔'kɔrɪstə 〕 n. 少年唱詩班團員
chorea 〔 ko'riə 〕 n. 舞蹈症
choreodrama 〔,kɔrɪo'drɑmə 〕 n. 舞蹈劇《 *drama* 戲劇》
choreograph[7] 〔'kɔrɪə,græf 〕 v. 設計舞蹈動作；編舞
　《 *graph* = write》
choreology 〔,kɔrɪ'ɑlədʒɪ 〕 n. 舞譜學《 *logy* = study》
choreopoem 〔'kɔrɪə,po · ɪm 〕 n. 配舞詩劇《 *poem* 詩》

98 chrom = color (顏色) * 希臘文 *khroma* (= *color*)。

chromatic[7] 〔kro'mætɪk〕 *adj.* 彩色的
chromatics 〔kro'mætɪks〕 *n.* 色彩學
chromatin 〔'kromətɪn〕 *n.* (細胞核內的)染色質
chromosome[7] 〔'kromə,som〕 *n.* 染色體

```
chromo + some
   |       |
 color  + body
```

monochromatic[7] 〔,manəkrə'mætɪk〕 *adj.* 單色的

```
mono + chrom + atic
  |      |       |
single + color + adj.
```

polychromatic[7] 〔,palɪkro'mætɪk〕 *adj.* 多色的

```
poly + chrom + atic
  |      |       |
many + color + adj.
```

99 chron = time (時間) * 希臘文 *khronos* (= *time*)。

chronic[6] 〔'kranɪk〕 *adj.* 慢性的;長期的　*n.* 慢性病患者
　(耗費時間的)　*cf.* **acute** (急性的)

```
chron + ic
  |      |
time  + adj.
```

chronicle[7] 〔'kranɪk!〕 *n.* 編年史　*v.* 記事
chronograph 〔'kranə,græf〕 *n.* 記時器《*graph* = write》
chronology[7] 〔krə'nalədʒɪ〕 *n.* 年代紀;年表《*logy* = study》
chronologic(al)[7] 〔,kranə'ladʒɪk(!)〕 *adj.* 按年代順序記載的

chronometer 〔 krə'namətə 〕 *n.* 精密計時器；航海用的經線儀

《*meter* = measure（測量）》

```
chrono +  meter
  |         |
 time   + measure
```

chronometry 〔 krə'namətrɪ 〕 *n.*（科學的）時間測定法
chronoscope 〔'kranə,skop 〕 *n.*（電子用）極微時間測定器

《*scope* 表示「觀察～的器具」》

anachronism 〔 ə'nækrə,nɪzəm 〕 *n.* 時代錯誤（違背時間）

《*ana-* = against》

```
ana  + chron + ism
  |       |       |
against + time  +  n.
```

isochronal 〔 aɪ'sakrənḷ 〕 *adj.* 等時的；同一時間的《*iso-* = equal》
prochronism 〔'prokrənɪzm̩ 〕 *n.* 日期提前（將事件誤記在實際發

生日之前）《*pro-* = before》
synchronize[7] 〔'sɪŋkrə,naɪz 〕 *v.* 同時發生；時間一致《*syn-* = same》
synchronous[7] 〔'sɪŋkrənəs 〕 *adj.* 同時發生的；同時的

100   **chrys** = gold（金黃色）   * 希臘文 *khrusos*（= gold）。

chrysalis 〔'krɪsḷɪs 〕 *n.* 蝶蛹；蟲繭；形成（或轉化）階段

《希臘文 *khrusallis* = golden pupa of a butterfly》
chrysanthemum 〔 krɪs'ænθəməm 〕 *n.* 菊花

```
chrys + anthem + um
  |        |       |
 gold  + flower  +  n.
```

chrysoberyl 〔'krɪsə,bɛrɪl , -əl 〕 *n.* 金綠寶石《*beryl* 綠寶石》
chrysolite 〔'krɪsḷ,aɪt 〕 *n.* 貴橄欖石《 *-lite* 表示「石頭」》
chrysotile 〔'krɪsə,taɪl 〕 *n.* 纖蛇紋石；溫石棉《希臘文 *tilos* = fiber》

101 cide , cise = cut (切割)

* 拉丁文 *caedere* (= *cut*)。〔變化型〕*cise*。

concise[6] 〔 kən'saɪs 〕 *n.* 簡明的；簡潔的；概括的（切短）
《*con-* = with》

concision 〔 kən'sɪʒən 〕 *n.* 簡明；簡潔

decide[1] 〔 dɪ'saɪd 〕 *v.* 決定；解決；裁決（割離 → 下判斷）《*de-* = off》

decision[2] 〔 dɪ'sɪʒən 〕 *n.* 決定；判定；決心

```
de + cis + ion
 |     |    |
off + cut + n.
```

decisive[6] 〔 dɪ'saɪsɪv 〕 *adj.* 決定性的；果決的

excise[7] 〔 ɪk'saɪz 〕 *v.* 切去；刪除《*ex-* = out》

excision 〔 ɪk'sɪʒən , ɛk- 〕 *n.* 削除；除去

germicide 〔 'dʒɝmə,saɪd 〕 *n.* 殺菌劑

herbicide 〔 'hɝbə,saɪd 〕 *n.* 除草藥

homicide[7] 〔 'hɑmə,saɪd 〕 *n.* 殺人者

incise 〔 ɪn'saɪz 〕 *v.* 切割；雕《*in-* = in》

incision[7] 〔 ɪn'sɪʒən 〕 *n.* 切口；切割

incisive[7] 〔 ɪn'saɪsɪv 〕 *adj.* 鋒利的；尖刻的

```
in + cis + ive
 |    |    |
in + cut + adj.
```

incisor 〔 ɪn'saɪzɚ 〕 *n.* 門牙

insecticide[7] 〔 ɪn'sɛktə,saɪd 〕 *n.* 殺蟲劑《*insect* 昆蟲》

matricide 〔 'metrə,saɪd , 'mæ- 〕 *n.* 弒母者
《*matri* = 拉丁文 *mater* = mother》 *cf.* **maternity**（母性）

patricide 〔 'petrɪ,saɪd , 'pæ- 〕 *n.* 弒父者
《*patri* = 拉丁文 *pater* = father》 *cf.* **paternity**（父性）

precise[4]〔prɪ'saɪs〕*adj.* 精確的；考究的；嚴格的（把多餘的東西切掉）《*pre-* = before》

```
pre  +  cise
  |        |
before  +  cut
```

precision[6]〔prɪ'sɪʒən〕*n.* 正確；精確；嚴謹

scissors[2]〔'sɪzəz〕*n.* 剪刀

suicide[3]〔'suə,saɪd〕*v., n.* 自殺（者）（將自己切割）《拉丁文 *su-* = self》

102　cinct = bind；gird（綁；環繞）

* 拉丁文 *cingere*（= *bind*；*gird*），過去分詞是 *cinctus*。

cincture〔'sɪŋktʃə〕*n.* 環繞；腰帶；環繞物；環形地帶
　　v. 束住；環繞

precinct[7]〔'prisɪŋkt〕*n.*（由建築物或圍牆等圍成的）場地；
　　（市鎮中作特定用途的）區域《*pre-* = before》

succinct[7]〔sək'sɪŋkt〕*adj.* 簡潔的；壓縮在小範圍內的
　　《*suc-* = *sub-* = under》

103　circ = circle（圓；環）

* 拉丁文 *circus*（= *circle*；*ring*）。〔變化型〕*circul*。

circle[2]〔'sɝkḷ〕*n.* 圓；圈；週期；範圍　　*v.* 環繞；繞～而行

circular[4]〔'sɝkjələ〕*adj.* 圓的；巡迴的　　*n.* 傳單；廣告；
　　女用的無袖外套

circulate[4]〔'sɝkjə,let〕*v.* 循環；巡迴；傳布（使成圓狀）

circulation[4]〔,sɝkjə'leʃən〕*n.* 循環；流通；通貨；發行數量

circus[3]〔'sɝkəs〕*n.* 馬戲團；圓形競技場

circuit[5]〔'sɝkɪt〕*n.* 周圍；環行；巡迴；電路（到四周）《*it* = go》

encircle[7]〔ɪn'sɝkḷ〕*v.* 環繞；包圍；繞行

semicircle[7]〔'sɛmə,sɝkḷ〕*n.* 半圓形《*semi-* = half》

104 cite = call；urge（召喚；驅策）

*拉丁文 *citare*（= summon 召喚；cause to move）。

cite[5]〔saɪt〕*v.* 引用；召喚

citable〔'saɪtəbḷ〕*adj.* 可引用的

citation[7]〔saɪ'teʃən, sɪ-〕*n.* 引證；傳票

excite[2]〔ɪk'saɪt〕*v.* 刺激；使興奮；招惹（喚出）《*ex-* = out》

excitable[7]〔ɪk'saɪtəbḷ, ɛk-〕*adj.* 易激動的；易興奮的

```
ex  +  cit  +  able
|       |       |
out  +  call  +  adj.
```

excitant〔'ɛksətənt〕*adj.* 興奮的　*n.* 興奮劑

excitement[2]〔ɪk'saɪtmənt〕*n.* 興奮；騷動

incite[7]〔ɪn'saɪt〕*v.* 引起激動；刺激《*in-* = in》

incitement〔ɪn'saɪtmənt〕*n.* 刺激；鼓舞；煽動

recite[4]〔rɪ'saɪt〕*v.* 背誦《*re-* = again》

recital[7]〔rɪ'saɪtḷ〕*n.* 述說；吟誦；獨奏會

recitation〔ˌrɛsə'teʃən〕*n.* 重述；背誦

resuscitate[7]〔rɪ'sʌsəˌtet〕*v.* 使甦醒；使復活；恢復

　《*re-*（again）+ *sus-* = *sub-*（under）+ *cit*（call）+ *-ate*（動詞字尾）》

```
re  +  sus  +  cit  +  ate
|       |       |       |
again  +  under  +  call  +  v.
```

resuscitator〔rɪ'sʌsəˌtetɚ〕*n.* 人工呼吸器；救生員

solicit[7]〔sə'lɪsɪt〕*v.* 懇求；引誘；拉客（完全喚起人心）

　《*soli* = 拉丁文 *sollus* = whole；entire》

solicitation[7]〔səˌlɪsə'teʃən〕*n.* 懇求；誘惑；拉客

solicitor〔sə'lɪsətɚ〕*n.* 懇求者；律師

solicitous〔sə'lɪsɪtəs〕*adj.* 焦慮的；渴望的

solicitude〔sə'lɪsəˌtjud, -ˌtud〕*n.* 焦慮；渴望

105 civi = citizen (公民) * 拉丁文 *civis* (= *citizen*) 。

civic[5] (ˈsɪvɪk) *adj.* 都市的;公民的
civics[7] (ˈsɪvɪks) *n.* 公民學;公民課
civil[3] (ˈsɪvḷ) *adj.* 公民的;民用的;民事的
civilian[4] (səˈvɪljən) *n.* 平民;百姓
civility[7] (səˈvɪlətɪ) *n.* 禮貌
civilize[6] (ˈsɪvḷ͵aɪz) *v.* 使文明;使開化;敎化《 *-ize* 動詞字尾》
civvies (ˈsɪvɪz) *n.pl.* (與軍服相對的) 便服
decivilize (dɪˈsɪvḷ͵aɪz) *v.* 使喪失文明;使淪爲野蠻

```
de  +  civil  +  ize
 |       |       |
down + citizen +  v.
```

106 claim , clam = cry (大叫)

* 拉丁文 *clamare* (= *cry out*) 。

claim[2] (klem) *v.* 要求;主張 *n.* 要求;權利;主張
claimant[7] (ˈklemənt) *n.* 要求者;申請者;索賠者
clamo(u)r[7] (ˈklæmɚ) *n.* 喧鬧;呼喊聲 *v.* 喧鬧;大聲要求或責難
clamorous (ˈklæmərəs) *adj.* 吵鬧的
acclaim[7] (əˈklem) *v.* 歡呼;喝采;稱讚《 *ac-* = *ad-* = to》
acclamation (͵ækləˈmeʃən) *n.* 歡呼;喝采;稱讚

```
ac + clam + ation
 |     |      |
to  + cry  +  n.
```

declaim (dɪˈklem) *v.* 演說;抗辯《*de-* = 加強語氣》
declamation (͵dɛkləˈmeʃən) *n.* 演說;雄辯;雄辯法;朗讀
disclaim[7] (dɪsˈklem) *v.* 否認;放棄;放棄權利
　　《*dis-* = negative (否定)》

exclaim[5] 〔 ɪk'sklem 〕 v. 呼喊《*ex-* = out》

exclamation[7] 〔ˌɛksklə'meʃən 〕 n. 呼喊；感歎（詞）

exclamatory 〔 ɪk'sklæməˌtorɪ , -ˌtɔrɪ 〕 adj. 驚歎的；感歎的

proclaim[7] 〔 pro'klem 〕 v. 宣言；公布；聲明（面向前方呼叫）
《*pro-* = before》

proclamation[7] 〔ˌprɑklə'meʃən 〕 n. 宣言；公布；聲明

```
pro  + clam + ation
 |       |      |
before +  cry  +  n.
```

reclaim[7] 〔 rɪ'klem 〕 v. 矯正；教化；開墾　n. 矯正；教化
（叫回來）《*re-* = back》

reclaimable 〔 rɪ'kleməbḷ 〕 adj. 可挽救的；可矯正的

reclaimant 〔 rɪ'klemənt 〕 n. 矯正者；開墾者

reclamation 〔ˌrɛklə'meʃən 〕 n. 教化；開墾；矯正

107　clar = clear（清楚的；清澈的）

> * 拉丁文 *clarus*（ = *clear* ）。

clarify[4] 〔'klærəˌfaɪ 〕 v. 澄清；使清楚；淨化《 *-ify* = make 》

clarification[7] 〔ˌklærəfə'keʃən 〕 n. 澄清；淨化；說明

clarity[6] 〔'klærətɪ 〕 n. 清澈；清楚

clarion 〔'klærɪən 〕 adj. 嘹亮的　n. 號角；號角聲

declare[4] 〔 dɪ'klɛr 〕 v. 宣佈《*de-* = intensive 加強語氣》

declaration[5] 〔ˌdɛklə'reʃən 〕 n. 宣言

clear[1] 〔 klɪr 〕 adj. 清楚的；清澈的　v. 使清澈；使清楚；清除

clairaudience 〔 klɛr'ɔdɪəns 〕 n. 特別敏銳的聽力《*audi* = hear》

clairvoyance 〔 klɛr'vɔɪəns 〕 n. 千里眼；敏銳的洞察力

```
clair + voy + ance
  |      |      |
clear +  see  +  n.
```

108 **claus**，**close**，**clud**，**clus** = close（關閉）

* 拉丁文 *claudere*（ = *shut*；*close*），過去分詞是 *clausus*。

clause[5]〔klɔz〕*n.* 子句；條款

claustrophobia[7]〔ˌklɔstrə'fobɪə〕*n.* 幽閉恐懼症
《*claustro*（close）+ *phobia*（fear）》

claustrophobic〔ˌklɔstrə'fobɪk〕*adj.*（患）幽閉恐懼症的

claustrophobe〔'klɔstrəˌfob〕*n.* 患幽閉恐懼症的人

close[1]〔*v.* kloz *adj.* klos〕*v.* 關閉；結束　*adj.* 接近的；親近的；
準確的

closet[2]〔'klɑzɪt〕*n.* 壁櫥；小房間；私室（關閉的空間）

closure[6]〔'kloʒ⋗〕*n.* 封閉；封鎖；結尾；終止

disclose[6]〔dɪs'kloz〕*v.* 揭發；洩露《*dis-* = negative（否定）》

disclosure[6]〔dɪs'kloʒ⋗〕*n.* 揭發；洩露

```
dis  +  clos  +  ure
 |        |       |
not  +  shut  +  n.
```

enclose[4]〔ɪn'kloz〕*v.* 圍繞；（隨函）附寄（使成關閉）
《*en-* = cause to be》

conclude[3]〔kən'klud〕*v.* 結束；作結論（共同關閉）
《*con-* = together》

```
con   +  clude
 |         |
together  +  shut
```

conclusion[3]〔kən'kluʒən〕*n.* 結尾；結論；決定；締結

conclusive[7]〔kən'klusɪv〕*adj.* 決定性的

exclude[5]〔ɪk'sklud〕*v.* 拒絕；除外；排除；趕出（關在門外）
《*ex-* = out》

exclusion[7]〔ɪk'skluʒən〕*n.* 排斥；排除；除外

exclusive[6]〔ɪk'sklusɪv〕*adj.* 排外的；獨佔的

include[2] 〔 ɪn'klud 〕 *v.* 包含；包括（關進裡面）《*in-* = in》

inclusion[7] 〔 ɪn'kluʒən 〕 *n.* 包含；包括

inclusive[6] 〔 ɪn'klusɪv 〕 *adj.* 包含在內的

occlude 〔 ə'klud 〕 *v.* 封閉；關閉；吸收

（關閉上面）《*oc-* = *ob-* = over》

```
oc  + clude
|       |
over + shut
```

occlusion 〔 ə'kluʒən 〕 *n.* 閉塞；吸收

preclude[7] 〔 prɪ'klud 〕 *v.* 排除；妨礙；阻止（在前面關閉）

《*pre-* = before》

preclusion 〔 prɪ'kluʒən 〕 *n.* 排除；除外；阻止

recluse[7] 〔 *adj.* rɪ'klus *n.* 'rɛklus , rɪ'klus 〕 *adj.* 隱遁的；隱居的

n. 隱者；隱士（閉居家中）《*re-* = back》

reclusion 〔 rɪ'kluʒən 〕 *n.* 隱遁；遁世；隱士的生活

reclusive[7] 〔 rɪ'klusɪv 〕 *adj.* 隱遁的

seclude[7] 〔 sɪ'klud 〕 *v.* 隱居；隔離；使引退《*se-* = apart》

secluded[7] 〔 sɪ'kludɪd 〕 *adj.* 隔離的；隱居的

```
se  + clud + ed
|       |      |
apart + shut + adj.
```

seclusive 〔 sɪ'klusɪv 〕 *adj.* 喜歡隱居的；隔離性的

seclusion[7] 〔 sɪ'kluʒən 〕 *n.* 隱退；隱居；與世隔絕的場所

cloister 〔 'klɔɪstɚ 〕 *n.* 修道院

cloistral 〔 'klɔɪstrəl 〕 *adj.* 修道院的；隱居的

109　**clin , clim** = bend；slope（彎曲；傾斜）

* 拉丁文 *clinare*（= *bend*；*lean*），*clivus*（= *slope*）；希臘文
klinein（= *slope*；*lean*），*klima*（= *inclination*；*region*），
klimax（= *ladder*）。

acclivous 〔 ə'klaɪvəs 〕 *adj.* 斜坡的；向上傾斜的

《*ac-* = *ad-* = to；up》

decline[6]〔dɪ'klaɪn〕v. 拒絕；衰退；使傾斜　n. 衰退；衰弱；傾斜

（向下彎曲）《de- = down》

declination〔,dɛklə'neʃən〕n. 傾斜；謝絕

declivity〔dɪ'klɪvətɪ〕n. 下傾的斜面　*cf.* **acclivity**（向上的斜坡）

$$\begin{array}{ccc} de & + \; cliv \; + & ity \\ | & | & | \\ down & + \; slope \; + & n. \end{array}$$

declension〔dɪ'klɛnʃən〕n. 傾斜；衰微

incline[6]〔v. ɪn'klaɪn　n. 'ɪnklaɪn〕v. 傾向；傾斜　n. 傾斜

（向～方向彎曲）《in- = towards》

inclination[7]〔,ɪnklə'neʃən〕n. 趨勢；意願；傾斜度

disincline〔,dɪsɪn'klaɪn〕v. 使厭惡；使不感興趣《dis- = not》

disinclination〔,dɪsɪnklə'neʃən〕n. 厭惡

proclivity[7]〔pro'klɪvətɪ〕n. 癖性；傾向；脾氣

recline[7]〔rɪ'klaɪn〕v. 斜倚；橫臥；倚靠；信賴（向後傾倒）

《re- = back》

climax[4]〔'klaɪmæks〕n. 頂點；高潮　v. 到達頂點

anticlimax[7]〔,æntɪ'klaɪmæks〕n. 虎頭蛇尾；突減；令人洩氣的

轉變（高潮的相反）《anti- = against》

climacteric〔klaɪ'mæktərɪk，,klaɪmæk'tɛrɪk〕n., adj.

轉折點（的）；更年期（的）

climate[2]〔'klaɪmɪt〕n. 氣候；（有某種氣候的）地區；風土

climatology〔,klaɪmə'talədʒɪ〕n. 氣候學；風土學《logy = study》

110　coct = cook（烹調）　* 拉丁文 *coquere*（= cook）。

concoct[7]〔kan'kakt〕v. 調製；混合；編造；虛構（一起烹調）

《con- = together》

concoction〔kan'kakʃən〕n. 混合；調製；捏造；虛構

decoct〔dɪ'kakt〕v. 煎（藥）；熬《de- = down》

decoction 〔 dɪˈkɑkʃən 〕 *n.* 煎；熬；藥劑；熬汁
precocious 〔 prɪˈkoʃəs 〕 *adj.* 早熟的；開花結實早的；過早的

```
pre  +  coc  +  ious
 |       |       |
before + cook +  adj.
```

precocity 〔 prɪˈkɑsətɪ 〕 *n.* 早熟；早開；過早

111　coel = hollow（中空的）

　　* 希臘文 *koilos*（= *hollow*）。〔變化型〕*cel*。

coelacanth 〔ˈsilə͵kænθ 〕 *n.* 空棘魚《希臘文 *akantha* = spine》
coelenterate 〔 sɪˈlɛntə͵ret 〕 *n. , adj.* 腔腸動物（的）

```
coel  +  enter  +  ate
 |         |        |
hollow + intestine + n., adj.
```

coelom 〔ˈsiləm 〕 *n.* 體腔（= *celom*）
coelomate 〔ˈsilə͵met 〕 *adj.* 有體腔的　　*n.* 體腔動物
celoscope 〔ˈsilə͵skop 〕 *n.* 腹腔鏡（= *celioscope*）
　　《*scope* 表示「觀察～的器具」》
blastocele 〔ˈblæstə͵sil 〕 *n.* 囊胚腔；分裂腔（= *blastocoel*）
　　《*blast* = bud（芽）》

112　coen , cen = common（共同的）

　　* 希臘文 *koinos*（= *common*）。

cenobite 〔ˈsɛnə͵baɪt 〕 *n.*（修道院）住院修士

```
ceno  + b(io) +  ite
 |       |       |
common + life + person
```

cenogamy 〔 sɪˈnɑgəmɪ 〕 *n.* 共夫共妻制《*gam* = marriage》

cenospecies 〔 ˌsinə'spiʃiz 〕 *n.* 群型種；雜交種《*species* 種類》

coenesthesia 〔 ˌsinɪs'θiʒə 〕 *n.* 普通感覺；存在感覺
《*(a)esthes* = feeling》

coenocyte 〔 'sinəˌsaɪt 〕 *n.* 多核細胞《*cyt* = cell》

coenurus 〔 sɪ'njurəs 〕 *n.* 共尾幼蟲《*ur* = tail》

113　cogn , gnos = know (知道；認識)

* 拉丁文 *cognoscere* (= know) 是由 *co-* (together) +
gnoscere (know) 而來的；希臘文 *gignoskein* (= know)。

cognition[7] 〔 kɑg'nɪʃən 〕 *n.* 認識（力）；認知；知識

cognitive[7] 〔 'kɑgnətɪv 〕 *adj.* 認識的；有認識力的

cognizable 〔 'kɑgnəzəbḷ 〕 *adj.* 可認知的；可知覺的

```
cogniz + able
   |       |
 know  +  adj.
```

cognizance[7] 〔 'kɑgnəzəns 〕 *n.* 認識；認知的範圍；審理權；
指揮權；徽章；標記

cognizant[7] 〔 'kɑgnɪzənt , 'kɑnɪ- 〕 *adj.* 認知的；認識的

incognito[7] 〔 ɪn'kɑgnɪˌto 〕 *adj.* 微行的；匿名的　*adv.* 微行地；
化名地　*n.* 微行者；匿名者 (不為人知)《*in-* = not》

precognition 〔 ˌprikɑg'nɪʃən 〕 *n.* (尤指超感官能力的) 預知
《*pre-* = before》

recognize[3] 〔 'rɛkəgˌnaɪz 〕 *v.* 認識；辨認；承認 (再度知道)
《*re-* = again》

recognizable[7] 〔 'rɛkəgˌnaɪzəbḷ 〕 *adj.* 可被認出的；可被承認的

recognizance 〔 rɪ'kɑgnɪzəns , -'kɑnɪ- 〕 *n.* 保證金；保證書

recognition[4] 〔 ˌrɛkəg'nɪʃən 〕 *n.* 認知；承認；表彰；認識

gnosis 〔 'nosɪs 〕 *n.* 靈知；神秘的直覺

gnostic 〔 'nɑstɪk 〕 *adj.* 有知識的

agnostic[7] 〔 æg'nɑstɪk 〕 *adj.* 不可知論的　*n.* 神不可知論者
《*a-* = not》

```
a  +  gnos  +  tic
|      |        |
not + know + adj., n.
```

diagnose[6] 〔͵daɪəg'nos , -'noz 〕 *v.* 診斷；分析；判斷（通過～而
得知）《*dia-* = through》

```
dia    +  gnose
through + know
```

diagnosis[6] 〔͵daɪəg'nosɪs 〕 *n.* 診斷；審查；分析
prognosis[7] 〔 prɑg'nosɪs 〕 *n.*【醫學】預後（指根據症狀對疾病結果
的預測）；預測（事先知道）《*pro-* = before》

```
pro   +  gnos  +  is
|         |        |
before + know  +  n.
```

prognosticate 〔 prɑg'nɑstɪ͵ket 〕 *v.* 預言；預知；預示
ignore[2] 〔 ɪg'nor , -'nɔr 〕 *v.* 忽視；不理睬《*i-* = *in-* = not》
ignorance[3] 〔'ɪgnərəns 〕 *n.* 無知；不學無術
ignorant[4] 〔'ɪgnərənt 〕 *adj.* 無知的；愚昧的
notorious[6] 〔 no'torɪəs 〕 *adj.* 聲名狼藉的；惡名昭彰的
《中世紀拉丁文 *notus* = known》

114　col = large intestine（大腸）

* 希臘文 *kolon*（ = *large intestine*）。

colic 〔'kɑlɪk 〕 *n. , adj.* 絞痛（的）；急腹痛（的）
colon 〔'kolən 〕 *n.* 結腸
colonic 〔 kə'lɑnɪk 〕 *adj.* 結腸的
colonitis 〔͵kɑlə'naɪtɪs 〕 *n.* 結腸炎《 *-itis* = inflammation（發炎）》

colonoscopy〔ˌkolə'naskəpɪ 〕 *n.* 結腸鏡檢查

```
colono    + scop + y
  |          |     |
large intestine + look + n.
```

colotomy〔 kə'latəmɪ 〕 *n.* 結腸切開術《*tom* = cut》

115   col , cult = till（耕種）

* 拉丁文 *colere*（= *till*；*inhabit*），過去分詞是 *cultus*；
cultivus（= *tilled*）。

colony[3]〔'kalənɪ 〕 *n.* 殖民；殖民地；居留地（耕作的地方）
colonial[5]〔 kə'lonɪəl 〕 *adj.* 殖民地的 *n.* 殖民地居民
colonist[7]〔'kalənɪst 〕 *n.* 殖民地居民；開發殖民地的人
colonize[7]〔'kalə,naɪz 〕 *v.* 殖民；拓殖；建立殖民地
cultivable〔'kʌltəvəbl̩ 〕 *adj.* 可耕種的；可培養的
cultivate[6]〔'kʌltə,vet 〕 *v.* 耕種；栽培；教化；培養

```
cultiv + ate
   |      |
 till   + v.
```

cultivated〔'kʌltə,vetɪd 〕 *adj.* 耕作的；栽植的；有教養的
cultivation[7]〔ˌkʌltə've∫ən 〕 *n.* 耕種；栽培；養殖；修養
culture[2]〔'kʌlt∫ɚ 〕 *n.* 耕種；修養；教養；文化　*v.* 教養；
　培養；耕種
cultural[3]〔'kʌlt∫ərəl 〕 *adj.* 培養的；教養的；文化的；人文的
acculturate〔 ə'kʌlt∫ə,ret 〕 *v.* （使）同化；（使）社會化
　《*ac-* = *ad-* = to》

```
ac + cult + ur(e) + ate
 |    |       |      |
 to + till +  n.   + v.
```

agriculture[3] 〔ˈægrɪˌkʌltʃɚ 〕 *n.* 農業；農藝；農耕（耕耘野地）
《*agri* = 拉丁文 *ager* = field》
agricultural[5] 〔ˌægrɪˈkʌltʃərəl 〕 *adj.* 農業的
apiculture 〔ˈepɪˌkʌltʃɚ 〕 *n.* 養蜂；養蜂業《拉丁文 *apis* = bee》
aquaculture 〔ˈækwəˌkʌltʃɚ 〕 *n.* 飼養或栽培水中動植物

```
aqua  +  cult  +  ure
 |        |        |
water  +  till  +  n.
```

aviculture 〔ˈevɪˌkʌltʃɚ 〕 *n.* 鳥類飼養《*avi* = bird》
floriculture 〔ˈflorɪˌkʌltʃɚ , ˈflɔrɪ- 〕 *n.* 花草栽培；花藝
《拉丁文 *flos* = flower》
pisciculture 〔ˈpɪsɪˌkʌltʃɚ 〕 *n.* 養魚（法）《*pisci* = fish》
sericulture 〔ˈsɛrɪˌkʌltʃɚ 〕 *n.* 養蠶；養蠶業《拉丁文 *sericum* = silk》

116　　coll = neck（脖子；領子）　　* 拉丁文 *collum*（= *neck*）。

collar[3] 〔ˈkɑlɚ 〕 *n.* 衣領；項圈
decollate 〔 dɪˈkɑlet 〕 *v.* 殺⋯的頭；將⋯斬首

```
de    +  coll  +  ate
 |        |        |
away from + neck +  v.
```

white-collar[7] 〔ˈhwaɪtˈkɑlɚ 〕 *adj.* 白領階級的；腦力勞動的
blue-collar[7] 〔ˈbluˈkɑlɚ 〕 *adj.* 藍領階級的；體力勞動的

117　　conch = shell（貝殼）　　* 希臘文 *konkhe*（= *shell*）。

conch 〔 kɑŋk 〕 *n.* 海螺；海螺殼；海螺殼號角
concha 〔ˈkɑŋkə 〕 *n.* （用作服飾或馬具飾的）海螺殼；海螺殼狀物
conchiferous 〔 kɑŋˈkɪfərəs 〕 *adj.* 有貝殼的《*fer* = carry；bear》
conchology 〔 kɑŋˈkɑlədʒɪ 〕 *n.* 貝類學《*logy* = study》

118   copr = dung（糞便）   * 希臘文 *kopros*（= *dung*）。

coprolalia〔ˌkɑprə'leliə〕*n.* 穢褻言語癖《希臘文 *lalein* = talk》

coprolite〔'kɑprəˌlaɪt〕*n.* 糞化石

```
copro +  lite
  |       |
dung  +  stone
```

coprology〔kɑp'rɑlədʒɪ〕*n.* 糞便學；色情文學《*logy* = study》

coprophagous〔kɑp'rɑfəgəs〕*adj.*（甲蟲等）食糞的《*phag* = eat》

coprophilia〔ˌkɑprə'fɪliə〕*n.* 嗜糞癖《*phil* = love》

coprophobia〔ˌkɑprə'fobɪə〕*n.* 恐糞症《*phob* = fear》

119   cord = heart（心）   * 拉丁文 *cor*, *cord-*（= *heart*）。

accord[6]〔ə'kɔrd〕*v.* 使一致；使調和   *n.* 一致；同意；調和
（使想法一致）《*ac-* = *ad-* = to》

accordance[6]〔ə'kɔrdn̩s〕*n.* 一致

according[1]〔ə'kɔrdɪŋ〕*adj.* 一致的；相符的；視～而定的

accordingly[6]〔ə'kɔrdɪŋlɪ〕*adv.* 如前所說；於是

cordial[6]〔'kɔrdʒəl〕*adj.* 誠懇的；友善的；提神的
n. 強心劑；興奮劑

cordiality〔ˌkɔrdʒɪ'ælətɪ〕*n.* 誠懇；熱忱

core[6]〔kor〕*n.*（水果等的）核；物的中心；核心   *v.* 去（果）核

concord〔'kɑnkɔrd, 'kɑŋ-〕*n.* 一致；調和；協定（使同心）
《*con-* = together》

concordance〔kɑn'kɔrdn̩s, kən-〕*n.* 一致；用語索引

concordant〔kɑn'kɔrdn̩t, kən-〕*adj.* 和諧的；一致的

```
con   +  cord  +  ant
 |        |        |
together + heart + adj.
```

courage[2] 〔ˈkɝɪdʒ〕*n.* 勇敢；勇氣

courageous[4] 〔kəˈredʒəs〕*adj.* 勇敢的

discord[7] 〔*v.* dɪsˈkɔrd *n.* ˈdɪskɔrd〕*v.* 不一致；意見不合

　　n. 不一致；不和；不協調的聲音（心意不同）《*dis-* = apart》

discordance 〔dɪsˈkɔrdn̥s〕*n.* 不一致；不和諧

```
dis + cord + ance
 |      |      |
apart + heart + n.
```

discordant 〔dɪsˈkɔrdn̥t〕*adj.* 不一致的；不和諧的；嘈雜的

discourage[4] 〔dɪsˈkɝɪdʒ〕*v.* 使失去勇氣；使氣餒；勸阻；妨礙

　　《*dis-* = away；apart》

discouragement[4] 〔dɪsˈkɝɪdʒmənt〕*n.* 氣餒；沮喪；障礙；阻止

encourage[2] 〔ɪnˈkɝɪdʒ〕*v.* 鼓勵；促進（使有勇氣）

　　《*en-* = cause to be》

encouragement[2] 〔ɪnˈkɝɪdʒmənt〕*n.* 鼓勵；獎勵；促進；激勵物

```
en  + courage + ment
 |       |        |
put in + courage +  n.
```

obcordate 〔ɑbˈkɔrdet〕*adj.* （葉等）倒心臟形的《*ob-* = against》

record[2] 〔*v.* rɪˈkɔrd *n.* ˈrɛkəd〕*v.* 記錄；記載；錄音

　　n. 記錄；唱片；案卷；履歷（記錄下來使能再想起）《*re-* = again》

120　　corp = body（身體）

　　　* 拉丁文 *corpus*，*corpor-*（= body）。

corps[6] 〔kor〕*n.* 軍團；團體

corpse[6] 〔kɔrps〕*n.* 屍體

corporal 〔ˈkɔrpərəl，ˈkɔrprəl〕*adj.* 身體的；肉體的　　*n.* 下士

corporality 〔ˌkɔrpəˈræləti〕*n.* 肉體；有形體

corporate[6] 〔'kɔrpərɪt , 'kɔrprɪt 〕 *adj.* 公司的

corporation[5] 〔ˌkɔrpə'reʃən 〕 *n.* 法人；自治體；團體；公司

```
corpor  +  ation
  |           |
 body   +    n.
```

corporator 〔'kɔrpəˌretɚ 〕 *n.* 公司的股東

corporeal 〔 kɔr'porɪəl , -'pɔr- 〕 *adj.* 肉體的；物質的；具體的

corpulent 〔'kɔrpjələnt 〕 *adj.* 肥胖的；肥大的

corpus 〔'kɔrpəs 〕 *n.* (身) 體；屍體；主體；全集；本金

corpuscle 〔'kɔrpəs!̩ 〕 *n.* 血球；微粒子《 *-cle* 表示小的名詞字尾》

incorporate[7] 〔 *v.* ɪn'kɔrpəˌret *adj.* ɪn'kɔrpərɪt 〕 *v.* 合併；組成
　公司；具體表現　*adj.* 合併的；具體化的；公司 (組織) 的
　《 *in-* = into》

incorporation[7] 〔 ɪnˌkɔrpə'reʃən 〕 *n.* 結合；合併；法人組織；
　公司

corset 〔'kɔrsɪt 〕 *n.* (婦女的) 束腹 (合於體型的東西)

121　**cosm** = universe ; order (宇宙；秩序)

　　* 希臘文 *kosmos* (= order ; universe)，*kosmein* (= arrange)。

cosmetics[6] 〔 kɑz'mɛtɪks 〕 *n.pl.* 化妝品

cosmos[7] 〔'kɑzməs 〕 *n.* (井然有序的) 宇宙；秩序

cosmic[7] 〔'kɑzmɪk 〕 *adj.* 宇宙的；廣大無邊的；和諧的

cosmogony 〔 kɑz'magənɪ 〕 *n.* 宇宙的起源；宇宙開創論
　《 *-gony* = generation (開創)》

cosmonaut 〔'kɑzməˌnɔt 〕 *n.* (蘇俄的) 太空人《 *naut* = sailor》

```
cosmo   +  naut
  |          |
universe +  sailor
```

cosmopolitan[6] 〔͵kɑzmə'pɑlətn̩〕 *adj.* 四海爲家的；世界性的

《*cosmo* (universe) + *polit* = *polis* (city) + *-an* (形容詞字尾)》

microcosm[7] 〔'maɪkrə͵kɑzəm〕 *n.* 小宇宙；人類；縮圖

《*micro-* = small》 *cf.* **macrocosm** (大宇宙；總體)

pancosmism 〔 pæn'kɑzmɪzəm 〕 *n.* 泛宇宙論

《*pan-* (all) + *cosm* (universe) + *-ism* (主義；學說)》

```
pan  +  cosm  + ism
 |        |       |
all  + universe +  n.
```

122 **count** = count (數；計算)

* 拉丁文 *computare* (= *count*)；古法文 *conter* (= *count*)。

count[1] 〔 kaʊnt 〕 *v.* 數；計算；包括；以爲；信賴；有價值

【解說】 中國人從一數到十，會以屈指的方式來算，但美國人的數學比
較不好，他們會先用右手的食指數左手，然後再用左手的食指
數右手。

countdown[7] 〔'kaʊnt͵daʊn 〕 *n.* 倒數計時

counter[4] 〔'kaʊntɚ 〕 *n.* 籌碼；櫃台；計算機

account[3] 〔 ə'kaʊnt 〕 *n.* 報告；記事；原因；考慮；帳戶

v. 說明；引起《*ac-* = *ad-* = to》

```
ac + count
 |     |
to + count
```

accountable[6] 〔 ə'kaʊntəbl̩ 〕 *adj.* 有責任的；可說明的

discount[3] 〔 *v.* 'dɪskaʊnt , dɪs'kaʊnt *n.* 'dɪskaʊnt 〕 *v.* , *n.* 打折扣；
貼現；減少 (除去若干)《*dis-* = exclude》

recount[7] 〔 rɪ'kaʊnt 〕 *v.* 詳述；描述；列舉 (再數一次)《*re-* = again》

123 **cover** = cover（覆蓋）

* 拉丁文 *cooperire*（= *cover completely*）；古法文 *covrir*
（= *cover*）。

cover[1]〔'kʌvɚ〕*v.* 覆蓋；遮蔽；佔（時間或空間）；掩護；通過；
包括；給付；採訪

coverage[6]〔'kʌvərɪdʒ〕*n.* 涵蓋的範圍；保險項目；採訪；
影響範圍

covert[7]〔'kʌvɚt〕*adj.* 暗地的；隱密的 *n.* 庇護所

discover[1]〔dɪ'skʌvɚ〕*v.* 發現（使失去掩蓋）《*dis-* = deprive of》

discovery[3]〔dɪ'skʌvərɪ〕*n.* 發現；發明

```
  dis    + cover + y
   |         |      |
deprive of + cover + n.
```

recover[3]〔rɪ'kʌvɚ〕*v.* 尋回；恢復；補償；痊癒《*re-* = back》

recovery[4]〔rɪ'kʌvərɪ〕*n.* 尋回；恢復；痊癒

uncover[6]〔ʌn'kʌvɚ〕*v.* 移去覆蓋物；洩露；揭露《*un-* 表動作的相反》

124 **cracy , crat** = rule；power（統治；權力）

* 希臘文 *kratos* , *-kratia*（= *rule*；*power*）。

aristocracy[7]〔ˌærə'stɑkrəsɪ〕*n.* 貴族政治；上流社會

```
aristo + cracy
  |        |
 best   + rule
```

autocracy[7]〔ɔ'tɑkrəsɪ〕*n.* 獨裁政治；專制政治《*auto-* = self》

bureaucracy[6]〔bju'rɑkrəsɪ〕*n.* 官僚政治；官僚作風《*bureau* 局》

democracy[3]〔də'mɑkrəsɪ〕*n.* 民主政治；民主主義《*demo* = people》

democrat[5]〔'dɛməˌkræt〕*n.* 信仰民主主義者；（D-）〔美〕民主
黨員

gerontocracy 〔͵dʒɛrən'takrəsɪ〕 *n.* 老人政治

```
geronto + cracy
   |        |
old man  +  rule
```

isocracy 〔aɪ'sakrəsɪ〕 *n.* 平等參政權；平等參政制度《*iso-* = equal》

meritocracy 〔͵mɛrə'takrəsɪ〕 *n.* 英才教育（制）；精英領導階級
《*merit* 優點》

physiocracy 〔͵fɪzɪ'akrəsɪ〕 *n.* 重農主義（指 18 世紀法國古典經濟
學家 Quesnay 創始的經濟學派，其含義是要重視自然經濟法則）；
自然法則政治（指重農主義者倡導的政治體制）《*physio* = nature》

plutocracy 〔plu'takrəsɪ〕 *n.* 富豪統治；財閥政治

```
pluto + cracy
  |       |
wealth +  rule
```

125 crani = skull (頭蓋骨；頭顱)

* 希臘文 ***kranion*** (= *skull*) 。

cranium 〔'krenɪəm〕 *n.* 顱；頭蓋骨

craniocerebral 〔͵krenɪo'sɛrəbrəl〕 *adj.* 顱與腦的

```
cranio + cerebr + al
  |         |      |
skull   +  brain + adj.
```

craniofacial 〔͵krenɪo'feʃəl〕 *adj.* 顱面的《*face* 臉》

craniology 〔͵krenɪ'alədʒɪ〕 *n.* 顱骨學《*logy* = study》

craniometer 〔͵krenɪ'amətɚ〕 *n.* 頭蓋測量器《*meter* 計量器》

craniotomy 〔͵krenɪ'atəmɪ〕 *n.* 顱骨切開術《*tom* = cut》

intracranial 〔͵ɪntrə'krenɪəl〕 *adj.* 頭顱內的；頭蓋骨內的
《*intra-* = within》

pericranium 〔͵pɛrɪ'krenɪəm〕 *n.* 頭骨膜；腦子《*peri-* = around》

126　**cre , cresc** = make ; grow (製造；生長)

> * 拉丁文 *creare* (= *make* ; *produce*)，過去分詞是 *creatus*；
> *crescere* (= *grow*)。〔變化型〕*crease , cret , cru*。

create[2] 〔 krɪˈet 〕 *v.* 創造；創始；製造；致使；封爵
creation[4] 〔 krɪˈeʃən 〕 *n.* 創造；宇宙；萬物；作品；封爵
creative[3] 〔 krɪˈetɪv 〕 *adj.* 有創造力的；創造的
creativity[4] 〔 ˌkrieˈtɪvətɪ 〕 *n.* 創造力
creator[3] 〔 krɪˈetɚ 〕 *n.* 創造者；創始者；(the C-) 造物主
creature[3] 〔 ˈkritʃɚ 〕 *n.* 人；動物

```
creat + ure
  |      |
make  +  n.
```

procreate[7] 〔 ˈprokrɪˌet 〕 *v.* 生育；產生 《*pro-* = forward》
recreate[7] 〔 ˈrɛkrɪˌet 〕 *v.* 消遣；休養；娛樂；恢復精神 《*re-* = again》
re-create[7] 〔 ˌrikrɪˈet 〕 *v.* 重新創造；改造；重做
recreation[4] 〔 ˌrɛkrɪˈeʃən 〕 *n.* 消遣；娛樂；休養
crescendo[7] 〔 krəˈʃɛndo, -ˈsɛn- 〕 *adj. , adv.* 逐漸加強的 (地)；
　逐漸高漲的 (地)　*n.* 漸強音；最高潮
crescent[7] 〔 ˈkrɛsn̩t 〕 *n.* 新月；新月形的東西；回敎勢力
　adj. 新月形的
concrescence 〔 kɑnˈkrɛsəns 〕 *n.* 癒合 《*con-* = *com-* = together》
decrescent 〔 dɪˈkrɛsn̩t 〕 *adj.* 變小的；虧缺的；(月) 下弦的
　《*de-* = down》

```
de  + cresc + ent
 |      |      |
down + grow + adj.
```

decrease[4] 〔 *v.* dɪˈkris　*n.* ˈdikris , dɪˈkris 〕 *v.* 減少　*n.* 減少
　《*de-* = down》
increase[2] 〔 *v.* ɪnˈkris　*n.* ˈɪnkris , ˈɪŋk- 〕 *v.* 增加；增大
　n. 增加；增加量；利益 《*in-* = in》

increment[7] 〔'ɪnkrəmənt 〕 *n.* 增加（量）；增進；盈餘
《*in-* = inside》

```
in   +  cre  + ment
 |       |       |
inside + grow +  n.
```

accretion 〔 ə'kriʃən 〕 *n.* 增大；添加《*ac-* = *ad-* = to》

accrue[7] 〔 ə'kru 〕 *v.* 自然產生；自然增加

concrete[4] 〔 *adj.* , *n.* 'kɑnkrit *v.* kɑn'krit 〕 *adj.* 凝結的；固體的；
具體的 *n.* 混凝土；水泥；具體物 *v.* 舖以水泥；凝固；凝結；
使結合（共同生存 → 緊密的）《*con-* = together》

concretion 〔 kɑn'kriʃən 〕 *n.* 凝結（物）；凝塊；結石；具體化

crew[3] 〔 kru 〕 *n.* （船、飛機的）全體工作人員

recruit[7] 〔 rɪ'krut 〕 *v.* 招募（新兵等）；補充；恢復 *n.* 新兵；
新加入者；初學者（再次成長）

127 **cred** = believe (相信) * 拉丁文 *credere* (= believe)。

credence[7] 〔'kridn̩s 〕 *n.* 相信；信用；證件《 *-ence* 抽象名詞字尾》

credential[7] 〔 krɪ'dɛnʃəl 〕 *n.* 介紹信；（學歷、資格等的）背景

credible[6] 〔'krɛdəbl̩ 〕 *adj.* 可信的；可靠的

```
cred  + ible
 |       |
believe + adj.
```

credibility[6] 〔ˌkrɛdə'bɪlətɪ 〕 *n.* 可信度

credit[3] 〔'krɛdɪt 〕 *n.* 信用；存款；名譽；貸款；學分
v. 信用；信賴；給予學分；歸功於

creditable[7] 〔'krɛdɪtəbl̩ 〕 *adj.* 值得稱讚的；聲譽好的；
可歸功於～的

creditor 〔'krɛdɪtɚ 〕 *n.* 債權人；債主

credo 〔'krido , 'kredo 〕 *n.* 信條；（ the C- ）基督教的使徒信條

credulity〔krə'dulətɪ, -'dju-〕*n.* 輕信

```
credul + ity
  |       |
believe +  n.
```

credulous[7]〔'krɛdʒələs〕*adj.* 輕信的；易受騙的
creed[7]〔krid〕*n.* 信條；（宗教）教條
accredit[7]〔ə'krɛdɪt〕*v.* 譽為；歸功於；信賴；委派；承認合格
　《*ac-* = *ad-* = to》
discredit[7]〔dɪs'krɛdɪt〕*v.* 不信任；懷疑；玷辱　*n.* 不信任；
　懷疑；不名譽；恥辱（遠離信任）《*dis-* = apart》
discreditable〔dɪs'krɛdɪtəbļ〕*adj.* 不名譽的；無信用的；恥辱的
incredulity〔,ɪnkrə'dulətɪ〕*n.* 不信；懷疑

```
in + credul + ity
 |     |      |
not + believe + n.
```

incredulous[7]〔ɪn'krɛdʒələs〕*adj.* 不肯輕信的

```
in + credul + ous
 |     |      |
not + believe + adj.
```

miscreant〔'mɪskrɪənt〕*n.* 惡棍

```
mis  +  cre  + ant
 |       |      |
wrongly + believing + n.
```

128　**cri** = judge（判斷）

　* 希臘文 ***krinein***（= judge），***krites***（= judge），
　krisis（= judgment）。

crisis[2]〔'kraɪsɪs〕*n.* 危機

criterion[6] 〔 kraɪ'tɪrɪən 〕 *n.* 標準；準繩
critic[4] 〔'krɪtɪk 〕 *n.* 批評家；評論家
critical[4] 〔'krɪtɪkl̩ 〕 *adj.* 吹毛求疵的；危急的；重要的；批評的
criticism[4] 〔'krɪtə,sɪzəm 〕 *n.* 吹毛求疵；批評；非難

crit	+ ic	+ ism
judge	+ n.	+ n.

criticize[4] 〔'krɪtə,saɪz 〕 *v.* 批評
hypercritical 〔,haɪpə'krɪtɪkl̩ 〕 *adj.* 苛求的；吹毛求疵的
《 *hyper-* = excessively》
hypocritical[7] 〔,hɪpə'krɪtɪkl̩ 〕 *adj.* 偽善的；矯飾的《 *hypo-* = under》

129　**crim** = crime (罪)

＊ 拉丁文 *crimen* , *crimin-* (= *crime*) 。

crime[2] 〔 kraɪm 〕 *n.* 罪；罪行
criminal[3] 〔'krɪmənl̩ 〕 *n.* 罪犯；犯罪者
criminaloid 〔'krɪmənl̩,ɔɪd 〕 *n.* 有犯罪傾向之人《 *-oid* = like》
criminate 〔'krɪmə,net 〕 *v.* 告發；歸罪；定罪
criminology 〔,krɪmə'nalədʒɪ 〕 *n.* 犯罪學；刑事學《 *logy* = study》
criminologist 〔,krɪmə'nalədʒɪst 〕 *n.* 犯罪學家；刑事學家
incriminate[7] 〔 ɪn'krɪmə,net 〕 *v.* 控告；使有罪；歸咎《 *in-* = in》
recriminate 〔 rɪ'krɪmə,net 〕 *v.* 反控；反責；反唇相譏
《 *re-* = back》

130　**cruc** = cross (十字；交叉)

＊ 拉丁文 *crux* , *cruc-* (= *cross*) 。

crucial[6] 〔'kruʃəl 〕 *adj.* 艱苦的；決定性的；極重要的

cruciate 〔'kruʃɪ,et 〕 *adj.* 有十字形葉或花瓣的；十字形的

crucify[7] 〔'krusə,faɪ 〕 *v.* 釘死在十字架上；壓抑；虐待

```
cruc  +  ify
 |        |
cross + fasten
```

cruciform 〔'krusə,fɔrm 〕 *adj.* 十字形的

crucifix[7] 〔'krusə,fɪks 〕 *n.* 耶穌受難像；十字架

crusade[7] 〔 kru'sed 〕 *n.* 十字軍；改革運動

cruise[6] 〔 kruz 〕 *v.* 巡航；航行；巡邏　*n.* 乘船遊覽

cruiser[6] 〔'kruzɚ 〕 *n.* 巡洋艦；遊覽用遊艇

crux[7] 〔 krʌks 〕 *n.* 關鍵；難題

excruciate[7] 〔 ɪk'skruʃɪ,et 〕 *v.* 施酷刑；拷打；使痛苦

```
ex       +  cruciate
 |            |
thoroughly + cause pain
```

excruciating[7] 〔 ɪk'skruʃɪ,etɪŋ 〕 *adj.* 極痛苦的；非常的

131　cry = cold (冷的)　　* 希臘文 *kruos* (= *icy cold*)。

cryobiology 〔,kraɪobaɪ'alədʒɪ 〕 *n.* 低溫生物學（一門研究低溫對生物影響的學科）《*logy* = study》

cryoconite 〔 kraɪ'akənaɪt 〕 *n.* 冰塵（極地冰雪面上的深色粉塵）《希臘文 *konis* = dust》

cryogen 〔'kraɪədʒən 〕 *n.* 冷劑；冷凍劑（產生低溫的東西）《*gen* = produce》

cryogenics 〔,kraɪə'dʒɛnɪks 〕 *n.* 低溫學

```
'cryo +   gen   + ics
  |        |       |
cold + produce  + n.
```

cryolite〔 'kraɪə,laɪt 〕 *n.* 冰晶石《 *-lite* 表示「石頭」》
cryology〔 kraɪ'ɑlədʒɪ 〕 *n.* 冷藏學；冷凍學
cryometer〔 kraɪ'ɑmətɚ 〕 *n.* 低溫計（內裝酒精，而非水銀）
cryostat〔 'kraɪə,stæt 〕 *n.* 低溫保持器《 *static* 靜止的》
cryosurgery〔,kraɪo's͡ɝdʒərɪ 〕 *n.* 冷凍手術《 *surgery* 手術》
cryotherapy〔,kraɪo'θɛrəpɪ 〕 *n.* 冷凍療法《 *therapy* 治療法》

132　**crypt** = hidden（隱藏的）

* 希臘文 *kruptein*（ = *hide* ），*kruptos*（ = *hidden* ）。

crypt[7]〔 krɪpt 〕 *n.* 地窖
cryptic[7]〔 'krɪptɪk 〕 *adj.* 隱藏的；神秘的

```
crypt  +  ic
  |        |
hidden  +  adj.
```

cryptogram〔 'krɪptə,græm 〕 *n.* 密碼暗號
cryptography〔 krɪp'tɑgrəfɪ 〕 *n.* 密碼法

```
crypto  +  graphy
  |          |
hidden  +  writing
```

cryptographer〔 krɪp'tɑgrəfɚ 〕 *n.* 密碼專家；密碼員
cryptonym〔 'krɪptə,nɪm 〕 *n.* 化名；假名；秘密的名字（隱藏的姓名）《 *onym* = name》

133　**cryst** = crystal（水晶；結晶）

* 希臘文 *krustainein*（ = *freeze* ），*krustallos*（ = *ice* ; *crystal* ）。

crystal[5]〔 'krɪstl̩ 〕 *n.* 水晶；結晶體　*adj.* 水晶（製）的
crystalliferous〔,krɪstə'lɪfərəs 〕 *adj.* 含晶的《 *fer* = bear》

crystallite〔ˈkrɪstəlaɪt〕*n.* 微晶
crystallize[7]〔ˈkrɪstḷ͵aɪz〕*v.* 使結晶；使具體化《 *-ize* 動詞字尾》
crystallography〔͵krɪstḷˈɑgrəfɪ〕*n.* 晶體學

```
crystallo + graph + y
   |          |       |
crystal    + write +  n.
```

crystalloid〔ˈkrɪstḷ͵ɔɪd〕*adj.* 晶狀的；類晶體的　　*n.* 類晶體
《 *-oid* = like 》

134　culp = blame；guilt（責備；罪）

　　* 拉丁文 *culpa*（ = *blame*；*guilt* ）。

culprit[7]〔ˈkʌlprɪt〕*n.* 犯人；罪犯；嫌疑犯
culpable[7]〔ˈkʌlpəbḷ〕*adj.* 該受譴責的
culpability〔͵kʌlpəˈbɪlətɪ〕*n.* 苛責；有罪
exculpate〔ɪkˈskʌlpet〕*v.* 消除疑慮；辯解（使脫罪）《 *ex-* = out 》

```
ex  + culp  + ate
 |     |       |
out + guilt +  n.
```

exculpation〔͵ɛkskʌlˈpeʃən〕*n.* 辯白；申明無罪
inculpate〔ɪnˈkʌlpet〕*v.* 控告；歸罪；指責；連累（使人入罪）
《 *in-* = in；into 》
inculpation〔͵ɪnkʌlˈpeʃən〕*n.* 控告；歸罪；連累；非難；譴責

135　cumb，cub = lie (down)（躺下）

　　* 拉丁文 *-cumbere*，*cubare*（ = *lie down* ）。

cubicle[7]〔ˈkjubɪkḷ〕*n.* 小寢室《 *-cle* 表示小的名詞字尾》
cumber〔ˈkʌmbɚ〕*v.* 阻礙；拖累　*n.* 阻礙；拖累（橫在前方的東西）

cumbersome[7] 〔'kʌmbɚˌsəm 〕*adj.* 笨重的；累贅的
（ = *cumbrous* 〔'kʌmbrəs 〕）《 *-some* 形容詞字尾》

concubine 〔'kɑŋkjʊˌbaɪn 〕*n.* 妾；情婦《*con-* = with》

concubinage 〔 kɑn'kjubənɪdʒ 〕*n.* 納妾；非法同居

decumbence 〔 dɪ'kʌmbəns 〕*n.* 橫臥（的姿勢）（橫於下方）

```
de  +  cumb  +  ence
 |       |        |
down + lie down +  n.
```

decumbent 〔 dɪ'kʌmbənt 〕*adj.* 橫臥的

encumber[7] 〔 ɪn'kʌmbɚ , ɛn- 〕*v.* 阻礙；煩擾；負累；堆滿
（ = *incumber* ）（橫在中間的）《*en-* = in》

encumbrance 〔 ɪn'kʌmbrəns , ɛn- 〕*n.* 阻礙物（ = *incumbrance* ）

incubate[7] 〔'ɪnkjəˌbet 〕*v.* 孵（蛋）；孵化（躺在上面）《*in-* = on》

incubation 〔ˌɪnkjə'beʃən 〕*n.* 孵蛋；孵化；潛伏（期）

incubator 〔'ɪnkjəˌbetɚ 〕*n.* 孵卵器；（早產兒）保育器；
細菌培養器

incubus 〔'ɪnkjəbəs 〕*n.* 夢魘；惡夢；重擔

```
in  +  cub  +  us
 |      |       |
on + lie down +  n.
```
把東西放在躺下來的人身上，
所以是「重擔」。

incumbency[7] 〔 ɪn'kʌmbənsɪ 〕*n.* 任期

incumbent[7] 〔 ɪn'kʌmbənt 〕*adj.* 躺臥的；使負有義務的；現任的
n. 在職者

procumbent 〔 pro'kʌmbənt 〕*adj.* 俯臥的；（植物）匍匐在地上
生長的（橫在前面的）《*pro-* = before》

recumbent 〔 rɪ'kʌmbənt 〕*adj.* 橫臥的；斜靠的；休息的
（橫於後面的）《*re-* = back》

recumbency 〔 rɪ'kʌmbənsɪ 〕*n.* 橫臥

succumb[7] 〔 sə'kʌm 〕*v.* 屈服；屈從；死亡（橫於下方的）
《*suc-* = *sub-* = under》

136 cur , course = run (跑；流動)

* 拉丁文 *currere* (= *run*)，*cursus* (= *running*)。
〔變化型〕*course*。

current[3] 〔ˈkɝənt 〕 *adj.* 現在的；公認的；流傳中的
　　n. 水流；氣流；潮流；傾向；電流
currently[7] 〔ˈkɝəntlɪ 〕 *adv.* 目前；一般
currency[5] 〔ˈkɝənsɪ 〕 *n.* 流通；流傳；通貨；貨幣；流通期間
concur[7] 〔 kənˈkɝ 〕 *v.* 同時發生；協力；贊成 (一起流動)
　　《*con-* = together》

> con<u>cur</u> *v.* 同意 (一起跑)
> con<u>cede</u> *v.* 承認 (一起走) (有勉強意味)

concurrence 〔 kənˈkɝəns 〕 *n.* 同時發生；同意；協力
concurrent[7] 〔 kənˈkɝənt 〕 *adj.* 同時的；協力的；一致的；和諧的
　　n. 競爭者；同心協力者；併發事件
courier[7] 〔ˈkɝɪɚ, ˈkʊrɪɚ 〕 *n.* 導遊
curriculum[5] 〔 kəˈrɪkjələm 〕 *n.* 課程；功課
cursive[7] 〔ˈkɝsɪv 〕 *adj.* 草書的　*n.* 草書；行書
cursor[7] 〔ˈkɝsɚ 〕 *n.* (電腦畫面上的) 游標
cursorial 〔 kɝˈsorɪəl, -ˈsɔr- 〕 *adj.*【動物】(適於) 奔跑的
cursory[7] 〔ˈkɝsərɪ 〕 *adj.* 匆促的；粗略的
decurrent 〔 dɪˈkɝənt 〕 *adj.* (葉等) 從莖下部向上生長的
　　《*de-* = down》
discursive 〔 dɪˈskɝsɪv 〕 *adj.* 散漫的；無層次的 (四處流的)
　　《*dis-* = apart》
excursion[7] 〔 ɪkˈskɝʒən, -ʃən 〕 *n.* 遠足；旅行；遊覽團體；脫離
　　主題 (向外跑出去)《*ex-* = out》

> ex + curs + ion
> | | |
> *out* + *run* + *n.*

excursive 〔 ɪkˈskɝsɪv , ɛk- 〕 *adj.* 漫遊的;散漫的;離題的
（容易走入歧路的）

incur[7] 〔 ɪnˈkɝ 〕 *v.* 遭遇;招致;蒙受（走入災禍之中）《*in-* = into》

incursion 〔 ɪnˈkɝʒən , -ʃən 〕 *n.* 入侵;襲擊;進入;流入
（以～為目標跑進去）

incursive 〔 ɪnˈkɝsɪv 〕 *adj.* 入侵的;來犯的

```
in  + curs + ive
 |      |      |
into +  run + adj.
```

occur[2] 〔 əˈkɝ 〕 *v.* 發生;存在;使想起（在眼前流動）
《*oc-* = *ob-* = before》

occurrence[5] 〔 əˈkɝəns 〕 *n.* 發生;事件

precursor[7] 〔 prɪˈkɝsɚ 〕 *n.* 先驅;先兆;前輩;先進
《*pre-* = before》

```
pre  + curs +   or
 |       |       |
before + run + person
```

recur[6] 〔 rɪˈkɝ 〕 *v.* 重現;再發生;再回到;訴諸《*re-* = back ; again》

recurrence[7] 〔 rɪˈkɝəns 〕 *n.* 再現;再發生;循環

recurrent 〔 rɪˈkɝənt 〕 *adj.* 循環的;再現的;周期性的

succor 〔ˈsʌkɚ 〕 *v.* 救助 *n.* 救助（者）（跑到下面而舉起來）
《*suc-* = *sub-* = under》

transcurrent 〔 trænsˈkɝənt 〕 *adj.* 橫亙的;橫貫的
《*trans-* = across》

```
trans + curr + ent
  |       |      |
across +  run + adj.
```

course[1] 〔 kors , kɔrs 〕 *n.* 過程;路途;行為;課程 *v.* 追趕;奔跑

concourse[7] 〔ˈkɑnkors , ˈkɑŋ- 〕 *n.* 合流;集合;群眾;大道;
車站或公園內的空地（共同流動）《*con-* = together》

discourse[7] 〔 *n.* ˈdɪskors , dɪˈskors *v.* dɪˈskors 〕*n.* 談論；論述；
論文；說教 *v.* 談論；演講（繞著話題走來走去）《*dis-* = apart》

```
dis  +  course
 |         |
apart  +   run
```

intercourse[7] 〔ˈɪntɚˌkors , -ˌkɔrs 〕*n.* 交際；性交；交流（互相
融合）《*inter-* = between》

recourse[7] 〔 rɪˈkors , riˈkɔrs 〕*n.* 求助；請求保護（流回）
《*re-* = back》

137　cur , cure = take care（小心；注意）

　　* 拉丁文 *cura*（= care），*curare*（= take care）。

accurate[3] 〔ˈækjərɪt 〕*adj.* 正確的；準確的（非常小心的）
《*ac-* = *ad-* = to》

accuracy[4] 〔ˈækjərəsɪ 〕*n.* 正確；正確性

```
ac  +   cur     +  acy
 |        |          |
to  + take care  +  n.
```

cure[2] 〔 kjur 〕*n.* 治療（法）；治癒；治療的藥物
　　v. 治療；改正（惡習）；（曬乾或燻製以）保藏（小心地去做）

curer 〔ˈkjurɚ 〕*n.* 治療者；治療器；乾燥食品製造人

curative 〔ˈkjurətɪv 〕*adj.* 治病的

```
cur  +  ative
 |         |
care  +  adj.
```

curious[2] 〔ˈkjurɪəs 〕*adj.* 好奇的；奇妙的；求知的；好管閒事的
　　（非常留心的）

curiosity[4] 〔ˌkjurɪˈasətɪ 〕*n.* 好奇心；求知慾；珍品

curio 〔ˈkjurɪˌo 〕*n.* 古董；珍品

字根 cal~cyt

curate[7] 〔'kjʊrɪt 〕 *n.* (教區的) 副牧師 (在旁邊小心做事的人)

curator[7] 〔 kju'retɚ 〕 *n.* 館長；監護人 (注意全體的人)

manicure[7] 〔'mænɪ͵kjʊr 〕 *v.* 修 (指甲)　　*n.* 修指甲；修指甲師
(= *manicurist*) 《*mani* = hand》

```
mani +  cure
  |       |
hand +  take care
```

pedicure[7] 〔'pɛdɪ͵kjʊr 〕 *n.* 腳病治療；腳病醫生；修腳指甲
《*pedi* = foot》

procure[7] 〔 pro'kjʊr 〕 *v.* 取得；促成；說服 (使轉移注意力)
《*pro-* = for ; in behalf of》

procurable 〔 pro'kjʊrəbḷ 〕 *adj.* 可獲得的

procuration 〔͵prakjə'reʃən 〕 *n.* 代理；獲得；委任狀；佣金

procurator 〔'prakjə͵retɚ 〕 *n.* 代理人

procurement 〔 pro'kjʊrmənt 〕 *n.* 獲得；成就；促成

secure[5] 〔 sɪ'kjʊr 〕 *adj.* 安全的；確實的；堅固的
v. 使安全；擔保；緊閉 (沒有憂慮的) 《*se-* = free from》

security[3] 〔 sɪ'kjʊrətɪ 〕 *n.* 安全；保證；擔保；保證人；抵押品

sinecure 〔'saɪnɪ͵kjʊr 〕 *n.* 閒差

138　**curv** = curved (彎曲的)

* 拉丁文 *curvus* (= *curved*) 。

curve[4] 〔 kɝv 〕 *n.* 曲線；彎曲　*v.* (使) 彎曲；(使) 成曲線

curvy[7] 〔'kɝvɪ 〕 *adj.* 彎彎曲曲的；(多) 轉彎的

curvaceous ; **-ious** 〔 kə'veʃəs 〕 *adj.* 婀娜多姿的；曲線玲瓏的

curvature 〔'kɝvətʃɚ 〕 *n.* 彎曲；(身體器官的) 異常彎曲；曲率

curvifoliate 〔͵kɝvə'folɪɪt 〕 *adj.* 具曲葉的

```
curvi +  foli + ate
  |       |      |
curved +  leaf + adj.
```

curviform 〔'kɜvə,fɔrm 〕 *adj.* 曲線形的《*form* 形狀》

curvilinear 〔,kɜvə'lɪnɪə 〕 *adj.* 曲線的《*line* 線》

139 cuss = strike ; shake (打擊 ; 搖晃)

* 拉丁文 *quatere* (= *strike* ; *shake*) ，過去分詞是 *quassus*。

concuss 〔 kən'kʌs 〕 *v.* 搖動；使（腦）震盪（激烈地搖晃～）

《*con-* = with》

concussion[7] 〔 kən'kʌʃən 〕 *n.* 震動；激動；打擊；衝擊；腦震盪

```
con  +  cuss  +  ion
 |        |       |
together + shake +  n.
```

discuss[2] 〔 dɪ'skʌs 〕 *v.* 討論；商談；議論（打得粉碎）《*dis-* = apart》

discussion[2] 〔 dɪ'skʌʃən 〕 *n.* 討論；議論

percuss 〔 pə'kʌs 〕 *v.* 叩；敲；叩診（徹底敲擊）《*per-* = thoroughly》

percussion[7] 〔 pə'kʌʃən 〕 *n.* 衝擊；衝突；打擊樂器；振動

repercussion[7] 〔,ripə'kʌʃən 〕 *n.* 反應；反射；彈回；回響

《*re-* = back》

quash 〔 kwɑʃ 〕 *v.* 取消；鎮壓（打消）

140 cycl = circle (圓 ; 環)

* 希臘文 *kuklos* (= *circle* ; *ring* ; *wheel*) 。

cycle[3] 〔'saɪkḷ 〕 *n.* 循環；周期；自行車 *v.* 循環；乘自行車

cyclic 〔'saɪklɪk 〕 *adj.* 周期的

cyclist[7] 〔'saɪklɪst 〕 *n.* 騎自行車的人

cyclone 〔'saɪklon 〕 *n.* 旋風；龍捲風；（印度洋上）的颶風

cyclotron 〔'saɪklə,trɑn 〕 *n.* 迴旋加速器（離子加速器的一種）

bicycle[1] 〔'baɪsɪkḷ 〕 *n.* 腳踏車《*bi-* = two》

tricycle[7] 〔'traɪsɪkḷ 〕 *n.* 三輪車 《*tri-* = three》

motorcycle[2] 〔'motə‚saɪkḷ 〕 *n.* 機車

encyclical 〔 ɛn'saɪklɪkḷ 〕 *adj.* 傳閱的；廣為傳布的

encyclop(a)edia[6] 〔 ɪn‚saɪklə'pidɪə 〕 *n.* 百科全書（經過整理的
東西）《*en-* = in》

```
en  +  cyclo  +   pedia
 |        |         |
in  +  circle  +  education
```

recycle[4] 〔 ri'saɪkḷ 〕 *v.* 回收；再利用《*re-* = again》

141 cyst = bladder（膀胱；囊）

* 希臘文 *kustis*（ = *pouch*；*bag*；*bladder*）。

cyst[7] 〔 sɪst 〕 *n.* 包囊；囊腫

cystiform 〔'sɪstɪ‚fɔrm 〕 *adj.* 囊狀的《*form* 形狀》

cystitis 〔 sɪs'taɪtɪs 〕 *n.* 膀胱炎《 *-itis* = inflammation（發炎）》

cystolith 〔'sɪstəlɪθ 〕 *n.* 膀胱結石《*lith* = stone》

cystoma 〔 sɪs'tomə 〕 *n.* 囊瘤《 *-oma* 表示瘤的名詞字尾》

cystoscope 〔'sɪstə‚skop 〕 *n.* 膀胱鏡《*scope* 表示「觀察～的器具」》

142 cyt = cell（細胞）

* 希臘文 *kutos*（ = *vessel*；*container*）。

cytoarchitecture 〔‚saɪto'ɑrkɪ‚tɛktʃɚ 〕 *n.* 細胞結構
《*architecture* 建築》

cytochrome 〔'saɪtə‚krom 〕 *n.* 細胞色素《*chrom* = color》

cytogenesis 〔‚saɪtə'dʒɛnəsɪs 〕 *n.* 細胞發生《*genesis* 誕生》

cytogenetics 〔‚saɪtodʒə'nɛtɪks 〕 *n.* 細胞遺傳學

cytology 〔 saɪ'tɑlədʒɪ 〕 *n.* 細胞學《*logy* = study》

cytopathy 〔 saɪˈtɑpəθɪ 〕 *n.* 細胞病《*path* = disease》

cytopathic 〔ˌsaɪtəˈpæθɪk 〕 *adj.* 細胞病的；引起細胞病變的

```
cyto  +  path  +  ic
 |         |       |
cell  + disease + adj.
```

cytophagy 〔 saɪˈtɑfədʒɪ 〕 *n.* 細胞吞噬作用《*phag* = eat》

143　**dactyl** = finger（手指）

　　* 希臘文 *daktulos* (= *finger*)。

dactyl 〔ˈdæktɪl 〕 *n.* (英詩的) 揚抑抑格；(古典詩的) 長短短格
(將手指的三節比作三個音節)

dactylogram 〔 dækˈtɪləˌgræm 〕 *n.* 指紋《*gram* = write》

dactylography 〔ˌdæktɪˈlɑgrəfɪ 〕 *n.* 指紋學《*graphy* = writing》

dactylology 〔ˌdæktɪˈlɑlədʒɪ 〕 *n.* 指語術

```
dactylo +  log  +  y
   |        |       |
finger  + speak  +  n.
```

pterodactyl 〔ˌtɛrəˈdæktɪl 〕 *n.* 翼手龍《希臘文 *pteron* = wing》

tridactyl 〔 traɪˈdæktɪl 〕 *adj.* 三指的；三趾的《*tri-* = three》

144　**damn** = damage（損害）

　　* 拉丁文 *damnum* (= *damage*；*loss*；*hurt*)。〔變化型〕*demn*。

damage[2] 〔ˈdæmɪdʒ 〕 *n.* 損害

damn[4] 〔 dæm 〕 *v.*, *n.* 咒罵　*interj.* 該死

damnation[7] 〔 dæmˈneʃən 〕 *n.* 指責；罰入地獄

damnify 〔ˈdæmnəˌfaɪ 〕 *v.* 加害；損害

God damn[7] 〔ˈgɑdˈdæm 〕 *n.* 咒罵；詛咒

condemn[5]〔kən'dɛm〕*v.* 譴責

indemnify〔ɪn'dɛmnə,faɪ〕*v.* 賠償；補償；使免負責任

```
in  +  demn  + ify
 |       |       |
not +  damage  +  v.
```

precondemn〔,prikən'dɛm〕*v.*（未經審理或愼重考慮）預定…
有罪《*pre-* = before》

145　deb = owe（欠債）

* 拉丁文 *debere*（= owe）。〔變化型〕*du*。

debt[2]〔dɛt〕*n.* 負債；借款

debtor〔'dɛtɚ〕*n.* 債務人；借主

debit[7]〔'dɛbɪt〕*n.* 借方　*v.* 記入帳戶的借方

debenture〔dɪ'bɛntʃɚ〕*n.* 債券

indebted[7]〔ɪn'dɛtɪd〕*adj.* 負債的；受惠的；感激的《*in-* = in》

```
in  +  debt  +  ed
 |       |       |
in  +  owe  +  adj.
```

due[3]〔dju〕*adj.* 到期的；適當的；預期的；充分的；應得的
n. 應得的東西；正當報酬；會費

duty[2]〔'djutɪ〕*n.* 義務；本分；職務；關稅（應該背負的東西）

dutiful[7]〔'djutɪfəl〕*adj.* 忠實的；盡責的；服從的

146　dei , div = god（神）

* 拉丁文 *deus , divus*（= god）。

deify〔'diə,faɪ〕*v.* 奉爲神；神格化；理想化

deific〔di'ɪfɪk〕*adj.* 予以神化的；使之神聖的；神聖的

deification 〔ˌdiəfə'keʃən 〕 *n.* 神化

deiform 〔'diə,fɔrm 〕 *adj.* 如神的；神性的

deism 〔'diɪzəm 〕 *n.* 理神論；自然神論；自然神敎

【解説】 認爲上帝在創造世界及其法則之後，並未加
以支配的一種理性運動，盛行於十八世紀。

$$de + ism$$
$$god + n.$$

deist 〔'diɪst 〕 *n.* 信奉自然神敎者；理神論者

deity 〔'diətɪ 〕 *n.* 神性；神

divine[4] 〔 də'vaɪn 〕 *adj.* 神的；神聖的

divinity 〔 də'vɪnətɪ 〕 *n.* 神力；（D-）神；神學

divinize 〔'dɪvən,aɪz 〕 *v.* 神聖化

divinization 〔ˌdɪvənə'zeʃən 〕 *n.* 神聖化

147　**dem** = people（民眾）　　* 希臘文 *demos*（= *people*）。

demagogue[7] 〔'dɛmə,gɔg , -,gɑg 〕 *n.* 群眾煽動家《*agogue* = leader》

democracy[3] 〔 də'makrəsɪ 〕 *n.* 民主政治；民主主義《*cracy* = rule》

democrat[5] 〔'dɛmə,kræt 〕 *n.* 信仰民主主義者；（D-）〔美〕民主
黨員

democratic[3] 〔ˌdɛmə'krætɪk 〕 *adj.* 民主政治的；民主主義的

democratism 〔 dɪ'makrətɪzəm 〕 *n.* 民主主義；民主制度

democratize 〔 də'makrə,taɪz 〕 *v.* 民主化；平民化

$$demo + crat + ize$$
$$people + rule + v.$$

demography[7] 〔 dɪ'magrəfɪ 〕 *n.* 人口統計；人口學《*graphy* = writing》

demotic 〔 di'matɪk 〕 *adj.* 民眾的；通俗的

endemic 〔 ɛn'dɛmɪk 〕 *adj.* 地方性的；風土性的　　*n.* 地方病
（所在地的民眾之中）《*en-* = in》

$$en + dem + ic$$
$$in + people + adj.$$

epidemic[6] 〔͵ɛpə'dɛmɪk 〕 *n.* , *adj.* 流行性傳染病（的）（民衆之間的）
《*epi-* = among》

pandemic[7] 〔 pæn'dɛmɪk 〕 *adj.* （疾病）流行全國（全世界）的；
（疾病）流行性的；普遍的《*pan-* = all》

148　**dendr** = tree（樹）　　* 希臘文 *dendron* （ = *tree* ）。

dendrochronology 〔͵dɛndrokrə'nɑlədʒɪ 〕 *n.* 樹木年代學
（一門研究樹木年輪以確定過去事件發生年代的學科）

```
dendro + chrono +   logy
  |         |         |
 tree   +  time  + study of
```

dendroclimatology 〔'dɛndro͵klaɪmə'tɑlədʒɪ 〕 *n.* 樹木氣候學
（分析樹木年輪來研究過去氣候情況）《*climate* 氣候》

dendrogram 〔'dɛndrə͵græm 〕 *n.* 系統樹圖（一種表示親緣關係的
樹狀圖解）《*gram* = write》

dendrology 〔 dɛn'drɑlədʒɪ 〕 *n.* 樹木學

rhododendron 〔͵rodə'dɛndrən 〕 *n.* 杜鵑花
《希臘文 *rhodon* = rose》

149　**dent** = tooth（牙齒）　　* 拉丁文 *dens* , *dent-* （ = *tooth* ）。

dental[6] 〔'dɛntl̩ 〕 *adj.* 牙齒的；齒科的；齒音的

dentate 〔'dɛntet 〕 *adj.* 有牙齒的；鋸齒狀的

```
dent + ate
  |      |
tooth + adj.
```

dentist[2] 〔'dɛntɪst 〕 *n.* 牙科醫生

dentition 〔 dɛn'tɪʃən 〕 *n.* 牙齒的生長；長牙期；齒列

denture 〔'dɛntʃɚ 〕 *n.* 一副牙齒；一副假牙

edentate〔i'dɛntet〕*n.* 貧齒類哺乳動物

　　adj. 無齒的；貧齒類哺乳動物的《*e- = ex- =* out of》

edentulous〔i'dɛntʃələs〕*adj.* 無牙齒的

　　《*e- = ex-* (out of) + *dentul* (tooth) + *-ous* (形容詞字尾)》

```
    e   + dentul + ous
    |       |       |
 out of +  tooth + adj.
```

indent[7]〔ɪn'dɛnt〕*v.* 使成鋸齒狀；把 (每段的首行) 縮格書寫；

　　縮排；訂購　*n.* 正式的訂購單；縮排《*in- = en- =* cause to be》

interdental〔ˌɪntə'dɛntl̩〕*adj.* 在牙齒之間的；將舌尖放在上下

　　牙間而發音的《*inter- =* between》

```
  inter  +  dent  + al
    |        |       |
between +  tooth + adj.
```

150　　**derm** = skin (皮膚)

　　* 希臘文 *derma* (= skin)。〔變化型〕*dermat*。

dermatitis[7]〔ˌdɝmə'taɪtɪs〕*n.* 皮膚炎

```
 dermat +       itis
   |             |
 skin  + inflammation ( 發炎 )
```

dermatology[7]〔ˌdɝmə'talədʒɪ〕*n.* 皮膚病學；皮膚學

dermatologist〔ˌdɝmə'talədʒɪst〕*n.* 皮膚病學家；皮膚科醫師

```
 dermat + olog(y) +   ist
   |        |          |
 skin   + study  + person
```

epidermis[7]〔ˌɛpə'dɝmɪs〕*n.* 表皮；上皮；外皮《*epi- =* upon》

hypoderm〔'haɪpədɝm〕*n.* 皮下結締組織；皮下《*hypo- =* under》

hypodermic 〔ˌhaɪpə'dɝmɪk〕 *adj.* 皮下注射的

```
hypo + derm + ic
  |      |     |
under + skin + adj.
```

pachyderm 〔'pækəˌdɝm〕 *n.* 厚皮動物（象、河馬、犀牛等）；
厚臉皮的人；感覺遲鈍的人《*pachy-* = thick》

taxidermy 〔'tæksəˌdɝmɪ〕 *n.* (動物標本的) 剝製術

xeroderma 〔ˌzɪro'dɝmə〕 *n.* 皮膚乾燥症《*xero* = dry》

151　**dextr** = right；skillful（右邊的；熟練的）

＊拉丁文 *dexter*（= *right*；*skillful*）。

dexter 〔'dɛkstɚ〕 *adj.* 右邊的

dexterity[7] 〔dɛks'tɛrətɪ〕 *n.* 靈巧；熟練

dextral 〔'dɛkstrəl〕 *adj.* 右邊的；(貝殼) 右旋的

dextrose 〔'dɛkstros〕 *n.* 葡萄糖；右旋糖

dextrocardia 〔ˌdɛkstrə'kɑrdɪə〕 *n.* 右位心

```
dextro + card + ia
   |       |     |
right  + heart + n.
```

ambidexterity[7] 〔ˌæmbədɛks'tɛrətɪ〕 *n.* 兩手均靈巧；詭詐
《*ambi-* = both》

152　**dic** = proclaim（宣稱）

＊拉丁文 *dicare*（= *proclaim*；*tell*）。

abdicate[7] 〔'æbdəˌket〕 *v.* 放棄權利；辭職；退位 (宣稱離開某地)
《*ab-* = from》

abdication 〔ˌæbdə'keʃən〕 *n.* 放棄；退位；辭職；棄權

dedicate[6] 〔'dɛdə,ket〕 v. 奉獻;致力;題獻詞於～之上

（宣誓處於對方之下）《 de- = down 》

dedication[6] 〔,dɛdə'keʃən〕 n. 奉獻;獻詞;致力

indicate[2] 〔'ɪndə,ket〕 v. 指示;顯示;表示（向～宣告 → 通知）

in	+	dic	+ ate
towards	+	proclaim	+ v.

indication[4] 〔,ɪndə'keʃən〕 n. 指示;表示;徵候

index[5] 〔'ɪndɛks〕 n. 指針;索引;指數;指標

predicate 〔 n. 'prɛdɪkɪt v. 'prɛdɪ,ket〕 n. 屬性;述詞

v. 斷言;意指（事先宣稱）《 pre- = before 》

pre	+	dic	+ ate
before	+	proclaim	+ n., v.

predication 〔,prɛdɪ'keʃən〕 n. 斷言;斷定;述詞

153 dict = say（說）

* 拉丁文 *dicere*（= *say* ），過去分詞是 *dictus*。〔變化型〕*dit*。

diction[7] 〔'dɪkʃən〕 n. 語法;用字（說法）

dictionary[2] 〔'dɪkʃən,ɛrɪ〕 n. 字典;辭典

《 -ary 表示集合體的名詞字尾 》

dict	+ ion	+ ary
say	+ n.	+ n.

dictate[6] 〔 v. dɪk'tet n. 'dɪktet〕 v. 口授令人筆錄;指定;命令

n. 命令;指令;要求;原則（口說）

dictation[6] 〔 dɪk'teʃən〕 n. 口述;口授;聽寫;命令

dictator[6] 〔 dɪk'tetɚ〕 n. 獨裁者;口授者（發布命令的人）

dictatorial 〔͵dɪktə'torɪəl , -'tɔr- 〕 *adj.* 獨裁的；專橫的

```
dict + ator + ial
 |      |      |
speak +  n.  + adj.
```

dictum 〔'dɪktəm 〕 *n.* 格言；專家的斷言；審判官的意見
《 *-um* 名詞字尾》

benedict 〔'bɛnə͵dɪkt 〕 *n.* 已婚男子

Benedictine 〔͵bɛnə'dɪktɪn 〕 *adj.* 本篤會的　*n.* 本篤會修士

benediction 〔͵bɛnə'dɪkʃən 〕 *n.* 祝福的祈禱；恩賜《 *bene-* = well 》

```
bene + dict + ion
 |      |      |
well +  say  +  n.
```

benedictional 〔͵bɛnə'dɪkʃənəl 〕 *adj.* 使人幸福的

benedictive 〔͵bɛnə'dɪktɪv 〕 *adj.* 賜福的

benedictory 〔͵bɛnə'dɪktərɪ 〕 *adj.* 祝福的

Benedictus 〔͵bɛnɪ'dɪktəs 〕 *n.* 天主教彌撒樂曲

condition[3] 〔kən'dɪʃən 〕 *n.* 條件；狀態　*v.* 使適應；以～爲條件；
　影響；給予補考（一起說 → 補說）《 *con-* = together 》

conditional[7] 〔kən'dɪʃənḷ 〕 *adj.* 附有條件的

conditionable 〔kən'dɪʃənəbḷ 〕 *adj.* 可調節的

contradict[6] 〔͵kɑntrə'dɪkt 〕 *v.* 矛盾；否定；反駁（說反對的話）
　《 *contra-* = against 》

contradiction[6] 〔͵kɑntrə'dɪkʃən 〕 *n.* 矛盾；否定；反駁

contradictious 〔͵kɑntrə'dɪkʃəs 〕 *adj.* 喜爭辯的；矛盾的；
　吹毛求疵的

```
contra + dict + ious
  |        |      |
against +  say  + adj.
```

contradictiously 〔͵kɑntrə'dɪkʃəslɪ 〕 *adv.* 愛反駁地；矛盾地

contradictive〔͵kɑntrə'dɪktɪv〕*adj.* 矛盾的；愛反駁的

contradictorily〔͵kɑntrə'dɪktərəlɪ〕*adv.* 反駁地

edict[7]〔'idɪkt〕*n.* 命令；敕令（說出去）《*e-* = *ex-* = out》

indict[7]〔ɪn'daɪt〕*v.* 控訴；控告；起訴《*in-* = into》

indictable〔ɪn'daɪtəbḷ〕*adj.* 可起訴的

indictee〔͵ɪndaɪt'i〕*n.* 被告

indicter；-or〔ɪn'daɪtɚ〕*n.* 起訴者

indictment[7]〔ɪn'daɪtmənt〕*n.* 起訴

indite〔ɪn'daɪt〕*v.* 著作；撰寫

interdict〔*n.* 'ɪntɚ͵dɪkt *v.* ͵ɪntɚ'dɪkt〕*n.* 禁止；限制

  v. 禁止；限制（插入空檔說話）《*inter-* = between》

interdiction〔͵ɪntɚ'dɪkʃən〕*n.* 禁止；禁治產宣告

interdictory〔͵ɪntɚ'dɪktərɪ〕*adj.* 禁止的

jurisdiction[7]〔͵dʒʊrɪs'dɪkʃən〕*n.* 司法權；管轄權；管轄區域

（說出正義）《*juris* = law》

```
juris + dict + ion
  |      |      |
 law  + say  +  n.
```

jurisdictional〔͵dʒʊrɪs'dɪkʃənḷ〕*adj.* 管轄權的

malediction〔͵mælə'dɪkʃən〕*n.* 詛咒；誹謗（說得很壞）

《*male-* = badly》

maledictory〔͵mælə'dɪktərɪ〕*adj.* 詛咒的；壞話的

predict[4]〔prɪ'dɪkt〕*v.* 預言；預測（事先說）《*pre-* = before》

predictable[7]〔prɪ'dɪktəbḷ〕*adj.* 可預測的

predictably[7]〔prɪ'dɪktəblɪ〕*adv.* 如所預料；不出所料

predictability[7]〔prɪ͵dɪktə'bɪlətɪ〕*n.* 可預測性

prediction[6]〔prɪ'dɪkʃən〕*n.* 預言

predictive〔prɪ'dɪktɪv〕*adj.* 預言的

predictor〔prɪ'dɪktɚ〕*n.* 預測者

valediction〔͵vælə'dɪkʃən〕*n.* 告別；告別辭《*vale-* = farewell》

字根 dactyl~dyn

valedictorian〔ˌvælədɪkˈtorɪən , -ˈtɔr-〕*n.*（畢業典禮時致告別辭的）畢業生代表

vale	+ dict	+ orian
farewell	+ *speak*	+ *n.*

valedictory〔ˌvæləˈdɪktərɪ〕*adj.* 告別的；辭別的
n. 畢業生代表的告別演講；告別演說

verdict[7]〔ˈvɝdɪkt〕*n.* 陪審員的評決；判決；判斷（說出實情）
《***ver*** = true》

vindicate[7]〔ˈvɪndəˌket〕*v.* 辯護；辯解；證明有理由（趁酒興而辯）

vin	+ dic	+ ate
wine	+ *say*	+ *v.*

vindication[7]〔ˌvɪndəˈkeʃən〕*n.* 辯護；證明；用以證明的事實
vindicative〔ˈvɪndəˌketɪv , vɪnˈdɪkətɪv〕*adj.* 辯護的
vindicator〔ˈvɪndəˌketɚ〕*n.* 辯護者
vindicatory〔ˈvɪndəkəˌtorɪ , -tɔrɪ〕*adj.* 辯護的；證明的
vindictive[7]〔vɪnˈdɪktɪv〕*adj.* 懷恨的；報復性的

154 dign = worthy（有價值的）

* 拉丁文 ***dignus***（= *worthy*），***dignari***（= *deem worthy*）。

dignity[4]〔ˈdɪgnətɪ〕*n.* 威嚴；尊嚴；爵位；光榮；居高位（高官）的人（有價值的東西）
dignify[7]〔ˈdɪgnəˌfaɪ〕*v.* 使有威嚴；使高貴《***-ify*** = make》
dignitary〔ˈdɪgnəˌtɛrɪ〕*n.* 高官；貴人；高僧
indignity[7]〔ɪnˈdɪgnətɪ〕*n.* 輕蔑；侮辱；冷落（不承認其價值）

in	+ dign	+ ity
not	+ *worthy*	+ *n.*

indign〔 ɪn'daɪn 〕*adj.* 不值得的；不雅觀的（沒有價值）

indignant[5]〔 ɪn'dɪgnənt 〕*adj.* 憤慨的；不平的（對沒有價值的東西生氣）《*in-* = not》

indignation[6]〔ˌɪndɪg'neʃən 〕*n.* 憤慨；憤憤不平

dainty[7]〔'dentɪ 〕*adj.* 優美的；高雅的；好看的；好吃的
n. 美味的食物

disdain[7]〔 dɪs'den , dɪz- 〕*v.* 輕蔑；鄙視 *n.* 輕蔑；侮蔑
（不承認其價值）《*dis-* = apart》

disdainful[7]〔 dɪs'denfəl , dɪz- 〕*adj.* 輕蔑的；傲慢的

155 divid = divide（分割）

* 拉丁文 *dividere*（= *divide*）。〔變化型〕*divis*。

divide[2]〔 də'vaɪd 〕*v.* 分割；區分；分類；分配 *n.* 分水嶺；分界點

dividend[7]〔'dɪvəˌdɛnd 〕*n.* 被除數；股息；附贈品

division[2]〔 də'vɪʒən 〕*n.* 區分；分割；分配；除法；部分；管區；
（陸軍）師

```
divis  +  ion
  |         |
divide  +  n.
```

divisive[7]〔 də'vaɪsɪv 〕*adj.* 離間的；區分的

divisor〔 də'vaɪzɚ 〕*n.* 除數；約數

divisory〔 də'vaɪzərɪ 〕*adj.* 劃分的；分配的；造成意見不合的

individual[3]〔ˌɪndə'vɪdʒʊəl 〕*adj.* 個體的；個人的；獨特的
n. 個體；個人（不能再分割的）《*in-* = not》

```
in  +  divid  +  ual
 |       |        |
not  +  divide  +  adj.
```

individualism〔ˌɪndə'vɪdʒʊəlˌɪzəm 〕*n.* 個人主義；利己主義

individuality[7] 〔͵ɪndə͵vɪdʒu'ælətɪ 〕 *n.* 個性

indivisible 〔͵ɪndə'vɪzəbḷ 〕 *adj.* 不可分的；不能分裂的；不能整除的 *n.* 極微量；不能分割之物《*in-* = not》

```
in  +  divis  +  ible
 |       |        |
not  +  divide  +  adj.
```

subdivide 〔͵sʌbdə'vaɪd 〕 *v.* 再分；細分（下面再分）《*sub-* = under》

subdivisible[7] 〔͵sʌbdə'vɪzəbḷ 〕 *adj.* 可再分的

156 doc = teach (教導)

> * 拉丁文 *docere*（= teach），*doctor*（= teacher），*doctrina*
> （= teaching）；希臘文 *didaskein*（= teach）。

docent 〔'dosn̩t 〕 *n.* 講師；博物館、畫廊的嚮導兼講解人
《 *-ent* 表示人的名詞字尾》

docile[7] 〔'dɑsḷ , 'dɑsɪl 〕 *adj.* 順從的；可教的（容易教導）
《 *-ile* 形容詞字尾》

docility 〔 dɑ'sɪlətɪ , do- 〕 *n.* 溫順

doctor[1] 〔'dɑktɚ 〕 *n.* 博士；醫師 *v.* 治療；行醫；就醫（教授者）

doctoral 〔'dɑktərəl 〕 *adj.* 博士的；博士學位的；醫生的

```
doct  +   or   +  al
 |        |       |
teach  +  person  +  adj.
```

doctorate 〔'dɑktərɪt 〕 *n.* 博士學位

doctrine[6] 〔'dɑktrɪn 〕 *n.* 教訓；教義；信條；主義（被教導的事）

doctrinal 〔'dɑktrɪnḷ 〕 *adj.* 教義上的；學理上的

doctrinaire 〔͵dɑktrɪ'nɛr 〕 *n.* 純理論家；空論家
《 *-aire* 表示人的名詞字尾》

doctrinarian 〔͵dɑktrɪ'nɛrɪən 〕 *n.* 純理論家；空論家
（ = *doctrinaire* ）

document[5] 〔'dɑkjəmənt 〕 *n.* 證件；文書；公文

documentary[6] 〔͵dɑkjə'mɛntərɪ 〕 *adj.* 文件的；文書上的
　n. 記錄片

```
docu ＋ ment ＋ ary
 │        │       │
teach ＋  n.  ＋ adj., n.
```

documentation[7] 〔͵dɑkjəmɛn'teʃən 〕 *n.* 文書、證件等的提供；
文件、證明的應用

indoctrinate 〔 ɪn'dɑktrɪn͵et 〕 *v.* 灌輸以學說、信仰或主義；
施以思想訓練；教授（使教義進入腦內）《*in-* = into》

```
in ＋ doctrin ＋ ate
 │       │        │
into ＋ teaching ＋ v.
```

indoctrination 〔 ɪn͵dɑktrɪ'neʃən 〕 *n.* （思想、主義的）灌輸

didactic 〔 daɪ'dæktɪk 〕 *adj.* 教訓的；教誨的

didacticism 〔 daɪ'dæktəsɪzəm , dɪ- 〕 *n.* 教訓主義；啓蒙主義

didactics 〔 daɪ'dæktɪks 〕 *n.* 教授法

autodidact 〔͵ɔto'daɪdækt 〕 *n.* 自學自修者（教導自己）《*auto-* = self》

disciple[5] 〔 dɪ'saɪpl̩ 〕 *n.* 門徒；（D-）耶穌十二使徒之一
　《拉丁文 *discere* = learn》

discipline[4] 〔'dɪsəplɪn 〕 *n.* 訓練；風紀；懲罰；規律　*v.* 懲罰；
訓練《拉丁文 *disciplina* = teaching ; learning》

157　**dog , dox** = opinion ; praise（意見；讚美）

　　* 希臘文 *dokein* (= *think* ; *seem good*)，*dogma* (= *opinion* ;
　　belief)，*doxa* (= *opinion* ; *praise*)。

dogma[7] 〔'dɔgmə 〕 *n.* 教條；信條；獨斷

dogmatic 〔 dɔg'mætɪk 〕 *adj.* 教條的；武斷的

dogmatism 〔'dɔgmə͵tɪzəm 〕 *n.* 教條主義；武斷

doxology 〔 dɑks'ɑlədʒɪ 〕 *n.* (基督教的) 頌歌；讚美詩
orthodox 〔'ɔrθə,dɑks 〕 *adj.* 思想正統的；正統的；傳統的；
慣常的 《*ortho-* = straight ; right》

```
ortho  +   dox
  |         |
right  +  opinion
```

paradox[5] 〔'pærə,dɑks 〕 *n.* 似非而是的雋語；自相矛盾的話
(與一般思想相反) 《*para-* = contrary to》
paradoxical 〔,pærə'dɑksɪkl̩ 〕 *adj.* 似非而是的；矛盾的

158 **dol** = grieve ; feel pain (悲傷；覺得痛)

　　　* 拉丁文 *dolere* (= *grieve* ; *feel pain*) 。

dole 〔 dol 〕 *n.* 悲哀；憂愁
doleful 〔'dolfəl 〕 *adj.* 悲傷的；憂鬱的
dolor 〔'dolɚ 〕 *n.* 憂傷；悲痛
dolorous 〔'dɑlərəs , 'do- 〕 *adj.* 憂傷的；悲痛的
condole 〔 kən'dol 〕 *v.* 弔唁；慰問 《*con-* = together》
condolence[7] 〔 kən'doləns 〕 *n.* 弔唁
indolent 〔'ɪndələnt 〕 *adj.* 懶惰的；無痛的

```
in  +   dol    + ent
 |       |        |
not + feel pain + adj.
```

159 **dom** = house (家)　　* 拉丁文 *domus* (= *house*) 。

dome[6] 〔 dom 〕 *n.* 圓頂；如圓頂的東西
domestic[3] 〔 də'mɛstɪk 〕 *adj.* 屬於家的；家務的；馴良的；本國的
domesticate 〔 də'mɛstə,ket 〕 *v.* 使喜歡家庭生活；馴服
domesticity 〔,domɛs'tɪsətɪ 〕 *n.* 家庭生活；家務；家事

domical〔'doməkl̩〕 *adj.* 有圓頂的；圓頂似的

domicile[7]〔'daməsl̩〕 *n.* 家；住所；正式居住地

domiciliate〔,damə'sɪlɪ,et〕 *v.* 定居

semidome〔'sɛmə,dom〕 *n.* 半圓屋頂《*semi-* = half》

160　**dom** , **domin** = rule（統治）

　　* 拉丁文 *dominus*（= *lord* 主人），*dominari*（= *rule*）。

domain[7]〔do'men〕 *n.* 領土；版圖；所有地

dominant[4]〔'damənənt〕 *adj.* 有統治權的；卓越的

dominate[4]〔'damə,net〕 *v.* 支配；統治

domination[7]〔,damə'neʃən〕 *n.* 支配；統治

domineer〔,damə'nɪr〕 *v.* 壓倒；凌駕；作威作福

dominion〔də'mɪnjən〕 *n.* 主權；支配；領土

```
domin + ion
  |      |
 rule  + n.
```

condominium[7]〔,kandə'mɪnɪəm〕 *n.* 共同管轄權

　　《*con-* = *com-* = together》

predominate〔prɪ'damə,net〕 *v.* 佔優勢；掌握主權《*pre-* = before》

```
pre  + domin + ate
 |      |       |
before + rule  + v.
```

predominant[7]〔prɪ'damənənt〕 *adj.* 主要的；有勢力的；傑出的

predominance ; -cy〔prɪ'damənəns(ɪ)〕 *n.* 優越；支配；多數

kingdom[2]〔'kɪŋdəm〕 *n.* 王國；國度；範圍（國王的統治區）

daunt〔dɔnt , dant〕 *v.* 恐嚇；使失去勇氣

　　《拉丁文 *domare* = tame（馴服）》

dauntless〔'dɔntlɪs , 'dant-〕 *adj.* 大膽的；勇敢的

161 **don , dat** = give (給予)

> * 拉丁文 *donum* (= *gift*) ; *dare* (= *give*) ，過去分詞是 *datus*。
> 源自印歐語系的字根 *do-* (= *give*)。〔變化型〕*dos* , *dot* , *dow*。

donate[6] 〔'donet 〕 *v.* 捐贈；贈予

donation[6] 〔 do'neʃən 〕 *n.* 捐贈；捐款

donee 〔 do'ni 〕 *n.* 受贈者《 *-ee* 表示「被動者」》

donor[6] 〔'donə 〕 *n.* 捐贈者

condone[7] 〔 kən'don 〕 *v.* 寬恕；赦免 (完全給予)《 *con-* = wholly》

pardon[2] 〔'pɑrdn̩ 〕 *v.* 寬恕　*n.* 原諒；寬恕 (完全給予)

　《*par-* = *per-* = thoroughly》

$$
\begin{array}{ccc}
\text{par} & + & \text{don} \\
| & & | \\
\textit{thoroughly} & + & \textit{give}
\end{array}
$$

anecdote[6] 〔'ænɪkˌdot 〕 *n.* 軼事；逸事 (沒有被傳到外面的事)

　《*an-* = not ; *ec-* = *ex-* = out》

$$
\begin{array}{ccccc}
\text{an} & + & \text{ec} & + & \text{dote} \\
| & & | & & | \\
\textit{not} & + & \textit{out} & + & \textit{give}
\end{array}
$$

antidote[7] 〔'æntɪˌdot 〕 *n.* 解毒劑 (針對毒藥而給的東西)

　《*anti-* = against》

dose[3] 〔 dos 〕 *n.* 一服藥；一劑藥　*v.* 配藥；服藥 (給予藥品)

dosage[6] 〔'dosɪdʒ 〕 *n.* 配藥；劑量

dower 〔'daʊə 〕 *n.* 寡婦得自亡夫維持生活之財產；嫁妝；天份

　v. 給寡婦應得之財產；賦予

dowry 〔'daʊrɪ 〕 *n.* 嫁妝；天才

endow[7] 〔 ɪn'daʊ 〕 *v.* 捐助；賦予 (給予～)《*en-* = on》

data[2] 〔'detə 〕 *n.pl.* 資料 (單數為 datum 〔'detəm 〕)

date[1] 〔 det 〕 *n.* 日期；約會

dative 〔ˈdetɪv 〕 *n.* 與格（即名詞、代名詞成為間接受詞時的格）
 adj. 與格的

antedate 〔ˈæntɪˌdet , ˌæntɪˈdet 〕 *v.* 比…早發生；在（文件、
 信件）上填寫比實際早的日期《*ante-* = before》

postdate[7] 〔ˌpostˈdet 〕 *v.* 比…晚發生；在（支票、信件、文件）
 上填寫比實際晚的日期《*post-* = after》

outdate[7] 〔 aʊtˈdet 〕 *v.* 使過時

update[5] 〔 ʌpˈdet 〕 *v.* 更新

162　**dorm** = sleep（睡覺）　　　＊拉丁文 *dormire*（ = *sleep* ）。

dormancy 〔ˈdɔrmənsɪ 〕 *n.* 蟄伏；休止

dormant[7] 〔ˈdɔrmənt 〕 *adj.* 蟄伏的；睡眠狀態的；休止的

dormient 〔ˈdɔrmɪənt 〕 *adj.* 睡眠的；蟄伏的

dormition 〔 dɔrˈmɪʃən 〕 *n.* 睡著；睡眠；瀕死；死亡

dormitive 〔ˈdɔrmətɪv 〕 *adj.* 催眠的

dormitory[4,5] 〔ˈdɔrməˌtorɪ 〕 *n.* 宿舍（睡覺的地方）
 《 *-ory* 表示地點的名詞字尾》

dormouse 〔ˈdɔrˌmaʊs 〕 *n.* 冬眠鼠；睡鼠
 《*dor(m)*（ sleep) + *mouse*（ 老鼠)》

163　**dors** = back（背面）　　　＊拉丁文 *dorsum*（ = *back* ）。

dorsad 〔ˈdɔrsæd 〕 *adv.* 向背面

dorsal 〔ˈdɔrsḷ 〕 *adj.* 背（脊）的　　*n.* 背部

endorse[7] 〔 ɪnˈdɔrs 〕 *v.* 簽名於（票據等）的背面；背書；認可
 《*en-* = put on》

endorsement[7] 〔 ɪnˈdɔrsmənt 〕 *n.* 背書；認可

字根 dactyl~dyn

164 **draw** = draw (拉)

> * 古英文 *dragan* (= *drag* ; *draw*)；古英文 *drawen* (= *draw*)。

drawback[6] ('drɔ,bæk) *n.* 缺點；障礙；退還的關稅；退款

drawer[2] (drɔr) *n.* 抽屜；(*pl.*) 內褲 (可拉開的東西)

drawerful ('drɔrfəl) *n.* 一抽屜之量；大量

indrawn ('ɪn'drɔn) *adj.* 內向的《*in-* = into》

outdraw (aut'drɔ) *v.* 比～更能吸引人；拔槍速度快於

　《*out-* = beyond》

overdraw[7] ('ovɚ'drɔ) *v.* 透支；誇張 (拉得過度)《*over-* = excessively》

```
over      + draw
  |           |
excessively + draw
```

redraw (ri'drɔ) *v.* 再起草《*re-* = again》

underdraw (,ʌndɚ'drɔ) *v.* 在～下畫線；不充份地描寫或敘述

　《*under-* = below》

undraw (ʌn'drɔ) *v.* 拉開；扯開；拉回《*un-* 表動作的相反》

withdraw[4] (wɪð'drɔ , wɪθ-) *v.* 收回；撤銷；撤退 (往回拉)

　《*with-* = back》

```
with + draw
  |      |
back + draw
```

165 **dress** = direct ; straighten (針對；糾正)

> * 拉丁文 *dirigere* (= *direct* ; *straighten*)，過去分詞是 *directus*。

dress[2] (drɛs) *v.* 給…穿衣

address[1] (ə'drɛs , 'ædrɛs) *n.* 演講；地址　*v.* 發表演說

　《*ad-* (to) + *dress* (direct)》

overdress ('ovɚ'drɛs) *v.* 使穿著過份講究；使穿得過多

redress〔rɪ'drɛs〕*v.* 改正；矯正

```
    re  +  dress
     |        |
   again + straighten
```

undress[7]〔ʌn'drɛs〕*v.* 脫衣服《*un-* = not》

166 **drom** = run；course (跑；路線)

* 希臘文 *dramein*（= *run*），*dromos*（= *running*；*course*）。

dromometer〔dro'mɑmɪtɚ〕*n.* 速度計《*meter* 計量器》
aerodrome〔'ærə,drom〕*n.* 飛機場 (飛機跑的場所)
　《*aero* = of aircraft》
catadromous〔kə'tædrəməs〕*adj.* (淡水魚等) 為產卵而順流
　入海的《*cata-* = down》
hemodromometer〔,hɛmədro'mɑmɪtɚ〕*n.* 血液流速計
　《*hemo* = blood》

```
   hemo + dromo +  meter
     |       |        |
  blood +  run  + measure
```

hippodrome〔'hɪpə,drom〕*n.* 跑馬場；競技場《*hippo* = horse》
prodrome〔'prodrom〕*n.* 前驅症狀；緒論 (跑在前面)
　《*pro-* = before》
syndrome[7]〔'sɪndrə,mi〕*n.* 綜合症狀；症候群 (一起跑出來的
　症狀)《*syn-* = together》

167 **duce** , **duct** = lead (引導)

* 拉丁文 *ducere*（= *lead*），*ductus*（= *leading*）。

abduct〔æb'dʌkt〕*v.* 綁架；拐走 (帶走)《*ab-* = away》
abduction[7]〔æb'dʌkʃən〕*n.* 綁架；誘拐《*-ion* 名詞字尾》

adduct 〔 ə'dʌkt 〕 *v.* 使內收；併攏（帶至）《*ad-* = to》

conduce 〔 kən'djus 〕 *v.* 助成；貢獻；引起（共同引導）
《*con-* = together》

conducive[7] 〔 kən'djusɪv 〕 *adj.* 有助益的

con　+ duc + ive
｜　　　｜　　｜
together + lead + adj.

conduct[5] 〔 *n.* 'kɑndʌkt *v.* kən'dʌkt 〕 *n.* 行為；處理；引導
v. 領導；指揮；傳導

conductor[4] 〔 kən'dʌktɚ 〕 *n.* 領導者；指揮者；樂團指揮；
〔美〕車掌

deduce[7] 〔 dɪ'djus , -'dus 〕 *v.* 演繹；推論（往下帶）《*de-* = down》

deducible 〔 dɪ'djusəb!　〕 *adj.* 可推知的；可推論的

de　+ duc + ible
｜　　　｜　　｜
down + lead + adj.

deduct[7] 〔 dɪ'dʌkt 〕 *v.* 扣除（往下帶 → 減少）

deduction[7] 〔 dɪ'dʌkʃən 〕 *n.* 減除；扣除

deductive 〔 dɪ'dʌktɪv 〕 *adj.* 推定的；推斷的

duchess 〔 'dʌtʃɪs 〕 *n.* 公爵夫人

ductile 〔 'dʌktɪl 〕 *adj.* 可延展的；柔軟的；溫馴的

ductility 〔 dʌk'tɪlətɪ 〕 *n.* 延展性；柔和；順從

duke 〔 djuk 〕 *n.* 公爵

educate[3] 〔 'ɛdʒə͵ket , -dʒʊ- 〕 *v.* 教育（引出資質）《*e-* = *ex-* = out》

education[2] 〔 ͵ɛdʒə'keʃən , -dʒʊ- 〕 *n.* 教育

e　+ duc + ation
｜　　｜　　｜
out + lead + n.

educe 〔 ɪ'djus , ɪ'dus 〕 *v.* 引出；推斷；分析出

eduction 〔 ɪ'dʌkʃən 〕 *n.* 引出之物；推斷

induce[5] 〔 ɪn'djus 〕 *v.* 引誘；說服；招致（引入）《*in-* = in》

inducement〔 ɪnˈdjusmənt 〕*n.* 勸誘；誘導；引誘物；刺激；動機

```
in + duce + ment
 |     |      |
in + lead  +  n.
```

induct[7]〔 ɪnˈdʌkt 〕*v.* 使正式就職；引入
induction〔 ɪnˈdʌkʃən 〕*n.* 歸納；感應；誘導；序論
inductive〔 ɪnˈdʌktɪv 〕*adj.* 歸納的；感應的；誘導的；序論的
introduce[2]〔 ˌɪntrəˈdjus 〕*v.* 納入；採用；介紹；引進（導入中間）
　《*intro-* = inward》
introduction[3]〔 ˌɪntrəˈdʌkʃən 〕*n.* 介紹；採用；入門
oviduct〔ˈovɪˌdʌkt 〕*n.* 輸卵管《*ovi* = egg》

```
ovi + duct
 |     |
egg + lead
```

produce[2]〔 *n.* ˈprɑdjus *v.* prəˈdjus 〕*n.* 產品；農產品
　v. 製造；產生；提出（向前引導 → 引出）《*pro-* = forward》
producer[2]〔 prəˈdjusɚ 〕*n.* 生產者；電影製片人
product[3]〔ˈprɑdʌkt , ˈprɑdəkt 〕*n.* 產物；結果
production[4]〔 prəˈdʌkʃən 〕*n.* 製造；生產；出示
productive[4]〔 prəˈdʌktɪv 〕*adj.* 多產的；富饒的；富創造力的

```
pro   + duct + ive
 |       |      |
forward + lead + adj.
```

reduce[3]〔 rɪˈdjus 〕*v.* 還原；減少；沖淡；減價（還原）《*re-* = back》
reduced[7]〔 rɪˈdjust 〕*adj.* 減少的；簡化的
reduction[4]〔 rɪˈdʌkʃən 〕*n.* 減少；減少量；縮版；變形
seduce[6]〔 sɪˈdjus 〕*v.* 誘惑；使入歧路；勾引（帶往別處）《*se-* = apart》
seducer[7]〔 sɪˈdjusɚ 〕*n.* 引誘者
seduction[7]〔 sɪˈdʌkʃən 〕*n.* 誘惑；魔力

semiconductor 〔ˌsɛməkən'dʌktə 〕 *n.* 半導體《*semi-* = half》

```
semi +   con   + duct + or
  |       |        |      |
half + together + lead +  n.
```

subdue[7] 〔 səb'dju 〕 *v.* 征服；降低；開墾（往下帶）《*sub-* = under》

superinduce 〔ˌsupərɪn'djus 〕 *v.* 加添；引起《*super-* = over》

traduce 〔 trə'djus 〕 *v.* 詆毀；誹謗；中傷（從一邊引到另一邊）

　　《*tra-* = *trans-* = across》

ventiduct 〔'vɛntɪˌdʌkt 〕 *n.* 通風管；通氣管《*venti* = wind》

viaduct 〔'vaɪəˌdʌkt 〕 *n.* 陸橋；高架橋；棧道《*via* = way ; road》

168　dur = hard；last（堅硬的；持續）

　　* 拉丁文 *durus*（= hard），*durare*（= harden ; last）。

durable[4] 〔'djurəbl̩ 〕 *adj.* 耐久的；持久的

durance 〔'djurəns 〕 *n.* 禁錮；監禁

duration[5] 〔 dju'reʃən 〕 *n.* 持續的時間

duress[7] 〔'djurɪs , dju'rɛs 〕 *n.* 威脅監禁

during[1] 〔'djurɪŋ 〕 *prep.* 在～期間

endure[4] 〔 ɪn'djur 〕 *v.* 持久；耐久；忍耐；忍受（在持續狀態）

　　《*en-* = in》

endurance[6] 〔 ɪn'djurəns 〕 *n.* 忍耐；忍耐力；耐久力

enduring[7] 〔 ɪn'djurɪŋ 〕 *adj.* 耐久的

indurate 〔 *v.* 'ɪndjuˌret *adj.* 'ɪndjurɪt 〕 *v.* 使堅硬；使無感覺；

　　使習慣於　*adj.* 硬化的；無感覺的《*in-* = into》

```
in +  dur  + ate
 |     |      |
into + hard +  v.
```

nondurable 〔 nɑn'djurəbl̩ 〕 *adj.* 不耐久的；不經用的

　　《*non-* = not》

obdurate〔ˋɑbdjərɪt〕 *adj.* 執迷不悟的；倔強的；堅決的（持續
反對）《*ob-* = against》

```
ob  + dur + ate
 |     |     |
against + last + adj.
```

perdure〔pɚˋdjur〕 *v.* 持久；繼續《*per-* = thoroughly》
perdurable〔pɚˋdjurəbḷ〕 *adj.* 持續的；持久的

169   dyn , dynam = power（力量）

希臘文 dynamis（= power）。

dynast〔ˋdaɪnəst〕 *n.* 統治者（尤指世襲者）（擁有力量的人）
《*-ast* 表示人的名詞字尾》
dynastic〔daɪˋnæstɪk〕 *adj.* 朝代的；王朝的

```
dyn  +  ast  +  ic
 |       |      |
power + person + adj.
```

dynasty[4]〔ˋdaɪnəstɪ〕 *n.* 朝代；王朝
dynamic[4]〔daɪˋnæmɪk〕 *adj.* 活動的；精力充沛的；充滿活力的
dynamism〔ˋdaɪnə͵mɪzəm〕 *n.* 物力論（以力及其相互關係來解釋
宇宙）；活力
dynamite[6]〔ˋdaɪnə͵maɪt〕 *n.* 炸藥；能產生不凡效果之人或物
dynamo〔ˋdaɪnə͵mo〕 *n.* 發電機；有活力有個性的人
dynamometer〔͵daɪnəˋmɑmətɚ〕 *n.* 動力計；測力計
《*meter* 計量器》
hydrodynamics〔͵haɪdrodaɪˋnæmɪks〕 *n.* 流體力學
《*hydro* = water》

```
hydro + dynam + ics
  |       |      |
water + power  + n.
```

thermodynamics 〔,θɝmodaɪ'næmɪks 〕 *n.* 熱力學《*thermo* = heat》

170 eco , oec = house (家)   * 希臘文 *oikos* (= house)。

ecology[6] 〔 ɪ'kɑlədʒɪ 〕 *n.* 生態學 (研究生活環境的學問)《*logy* = study》
economy[4] 〔 ɪ'kɑnəmɪ 〕 *n.* 經濟；節約；經濟制度 (處理家務)
economic[4] 〔,ikə'nɑmɪk 〕 *adj.* 經濟學的；經濟上的；實用的
economical[4] 〔,ikə'nɑmɪkḷ 〕 *adj.* 經濟的；節儉的；節省的

```
eco  +  nom   +  ical
 |        |        |
house + manage +  adj.
```

economics[4] 〔,ikə'nɑmɪks 〕 *n.* 經濟學
economist[4] 〔 ɪ'kɑnəmɪst 〕 *n.* 經濟學家；節儉的人
economize[7] 〔 ɪ'kɑnə,maɪz 〕 *v.* 節儉；節約

171 ed = eat (吃)   * 拉丁文 *edere* (= eat)。

edacious 〔 ɪ'deʃəs 〕 *adj.* 貪吃的；狼吞虎嚥的
edible[6] 〔'ɛdəbḷ 〕 *adj.* 可食用的
inedible[7] 〔 ɪn'ɛdəbḷ 〕 *adj.* 不宜食用的；不能吃的《*in-* = not》
obese[7] 〔 o'bis 〕 *adj.* 肥胖的《拉丁文 *obesus* 是 *obedere* 的過去分詞》
obesity[7] 〔 o'bisətɪ 〕 *n.* 肥胖

172 ego = I ; self (我；自己)   * 拉丁文 *ego* (= I)。

ego[5] 〔'igo 〕 *n.* 自我；自尊心
egocentric 〔,igo'sɛntrɪk 〕 *adj.* 自我中心的；利己主義的
egoism 〔'igo,ɪzəm 〕 *n.* 自我主義；利己主義；自私
egoist 〔'igoɪst 〕 *n.* 自我主義者；利己主義者

egomania 〔 ˌigoˈmenɪə 〕 *n.* 利己癖；過分自私；自大狂
　《*mania* = madness (瘋狂)》

```
ego  +  mania
 |        |
self  +  madness
```

egotism 〔ˈigəˌtɪzəm 〕 *n.* 自負；自大；自我吹噓
egotist 〔ˈigətɪst 〕 *n.* 自負者；自大者；自私自利者
egotistic 〔 ˌigəˈtɪstɪk̹ 〕 *adj.* 自我中心的；自以為是的；自私自利的
nonego 〔 nɑnˈigo 〕 *n.* 非我；外界；外物《*non-* = not》
superego 〔 ˌsupɚˈigo 〕 *n.* 超我《*super-* = over》

173　**electr** = electric (電的)

　　＊ 源自希臘文 *elektron* (= *amber* 琥珀)，因為希臘的哲學家
　　泰勒斯做了關於靜電的觀察，他發現琥珀經摩擦後能吸引輕
　　小物質。

electric[3] 〔 ɪˈlɛktrɪk 〕 *adj.* 電的；令人興奮的；刺激的；感動的
electrical[3] 〔 ɪˈlɛktrɪk̹ 〕 *adj.* 電的；與電有關的
electrician[4] 〔 ɪˌlɛkˈtrɪʃən 〕 *n.* 電工；電氣技師；電學家
electricity[3] 〔 ɪˌlɛkˈtrɪsətɪ 〕 *n.* 電；電力；電流；電學
electrify 〔 ɪˈlɛktrəˌfaɪ 〕 *v.* 充電；使帶電；使電化；使感動
electrocute 〔 ɪˈlɛktrəˌkjut 〕 *v.* 施以電刑；誤觸電致死

```
electro  +  (exe)cute
   |            |
electric  +  (out) follow
```

electrochemistry 〔 ɪˌlɛktrəˈkɛmɪstrɪ 〕 *n.* 電化學《*chemistry* 化學》
electrode 〔 ɪˈlɛktrod 〕 *n.* 電極 (電的通路)《*ode* = way》
electrology 〔 ɪˌlɛkˈtrɑlədʒɪ 〕 *n.* 電學《*logy* = study》
electrolysis 〔 ɪˌlɛkˈtrɑləsɪs 〕 *n.* 電解《*lys* = loosen (放鬆；解開)》
electron[6] 〔 ɪˈlɛktrɑn 〕 *n.* 電子
electronics[4] 〔 ɪˌlɛkˈtrɑnɪks 〕 *n.* 電子學

174　empt = take ; buy（拿；買）

> * 拉丁文 *emere*（ = *take* ; *buy* ），過去分詞是 *emptus*。

example[1]〔 ɪgˈzæmpl̩ 〕*n.* 例證；樣本（取出）《*ex-* = out》

exemplar〔 ɪgˈzɛmplɚ , ɛg- 〕*n.* 範本；榜樣

exemplify[7]〔 ɪgˈzɛmpləˌfaɪ , ɛg- 〕*v.* 例證；製作～之正本（做成實例）《*-ify* = make》

exempt[7]〔 ɪgˈzɛmpt , ɛg- 〕*adj.* , *n.* 被免除的（人）
　v. 免除（拿掉；除去）

preempt[7]〔 prɪˈɛmpt 〕*v.* 搶先取得或佔用；預先佔有《*pre-* = before》

```
pre  +  empt
 |       |
before + take
```

prompt[4]〔 prɑmpt 〕*adj.* 迅速的；敏捷的　　*adv.* 迅速地；敏捷地
　v. 鼓動；喚起；激勵（最先去拿）《*pro-* = forward》

promptitude〔ˈprɑmptəˌtjud 〕*n.* 敏捷；機敏《*-itude* 抽象名詞字尾》

promptly[7]〔ˈprɑmptlɪ 〕*adv.* 迅速地；敏捷地

redeem[7]〔 rɪˈdim 〕*v.* 買回；收回；補償（買回）《*red-* = back》

redeemer〔 rɪˈdimɚ 〕*n.* 買回者；拯救者

```
red  +  eem  +  er
 |       |       |
back +  buy  + person
```

redemption[7]〔 rɪˈdɛmpʃən 〕*n.* 贖回；拯救；補償；贖罪

ransom[6]〔ˈrænsəm 〕*n.* 贖金　　*v.* 贖回；補償（把生命買回來）

175　enter = intestine（腸）

> * 希臘文 *enteron*（ = *intestine* ）。

enteritis〔ˌɛntəˈraɪtɪs 〕*n.* 腸炎《*-itis* = inflammation（發炎）》

enterobacteria 〔͵ɛntərobæk'tɪrɪə〕 *n.pl.* 腸細菌《*bacteria* 細菌》

enterobiasis 〔͵ɛntəro'baɪəsɪs〕 *n.* 蟯蟲病

```
        entero  +  b(io)  +    iasis
          |         |           |
      intestine  +  life  +  condition
```

enterology 〔͵ɛntə'rɑlədʒɪ〕 *n.* 腸病學《*logy* = study》

enterostomy 〔͵ɛntə'rɑstəmɪ〕 *n.* 腸造口術《*stom* = mouth》

dysentery 〔'dɪsn͵tɛrɪ〕 *n.* 痢疾；腹瀉《*dys-* = bad》

176　equ = equal（相等的）　　*拉丁文 aequus（= equal）。

equable 〔'ikwəbl̩〕 *adj.* 平靜的；穩定的；一致的；均勻的

equal[1] 〔'ikwəl〕 *adj.* 相同的；平靜的；一致的；能勝任的

　　n. 對手　*v.* 等於；使相等

equalitarian 〔ɪ͵kwɑlə'tɛrɪən〕 *adj.* 平等主義的　*n.* 平等主義者

　《*-arian* 形容詞字尾》

equality[4] 〔ɪ'kwɑlətɪ〕 *n.* 相等；平等

equanimity 〔͵ikwə'nɪmətɪ , ͵ɛkwə-〕 *n.*（心的）平靜

　《*anim* = mind》

```
       equ  +  anim  +  ity
        |        |       |
      equal  +  mind  +  n.
```

equanimous 〔ɪ'kwænɪməs〕 *adj.* 鎮定的；泰然的

equate[5] 〔ɪ'kwet〕 *v.* 使相等；相提並論《*-ate* 動詞字尾》

equation[6] 〔ɪ'kweʒən , -ʃən〕 *n.* 方程式；相等；平衡

equator[6] 〔ɪ'kwetɚ〕 *n.* 赤道（將地球等分的東西）

equilibrium[7] 〔͵ikwə'lɪbrɪəm〕 *n.* 平衡

```
       equi  +  libr  +  ium
        |        |        |
      equal  +  balance  +  n.
```

equinox (ˈikwə͵nɑks, ˈɛkwə-) *n.* 春（秋）分；晝夜平分點
（晝夜等長）《*nox* = night》

```
equi  +  nox
 |        |
equal  +  night
```

equinoctial (͵ikwəˈnɑkʃəl, ͵ɛkwə-) *adj.* 晝夜平分的；春分的；
秋分的；赤道的   *n.* 晝夜平分線

equipoise (ˈikwə͵pɔɪz) *n.* 平衡；平衡力；平衡物；秤錘；砝碼
《*poise* = place》

equiponderate (͵ikwɪˈpɑndə͵ret) *v.* 使（重量、力量、重要
性等）相等或抵消（使重量相等）《*ponder* = weight》

```
equi  +  ponder  +  ate
 |         |         |
equal  +  weight  +  v.
```

equipotential (͵ikwɪpoˈtɛnʃəl) *adj.* 等位的；等勢的；等電位的
《*potential* 位置的；電位的》

equity[7] (ˈɛkwətɪ) *n.* 公正；衡平法

equitable (ˈɛkwɪtəbḷ) *adj.* 公平的；公正的

equivalent[6] (ɪˈkwɪvələnt) *adj.* 相等的；相當的   *n.* 相等物
（價值相等）《*val* = worth（價值）》

equivocal (ɪˈkwɪvəkḷ) *adj.* 模稜兩可的；不確定的；可疑的
（將聲音等分）《*voc* = call》

```
equi  +  voc  +  al
 |        |       |
equal  +  call  +  adj.
```

adequate[4] (ˈædəkwɪt) *adj.* 足夠的；適當的《*ad-* = to》

adequacy (ˈædəkwəsɪ) *n.* 適當；充分；足夠

177 **erg, urg** = work (工作；功)

* 希臘文 *ergon* (= work)；拉丁文 *urgere* (= *press hard*；*push*)。

erg 〔 ɝg 〕 *n.* 爾格 (功的單位)

ergonomics 〔 ˌɝgəˈnɑmɪks 〕 *n.* 人類工程學 (研究如何改善工作
條件，提高工作效率)《*economics* 經濟學》

allergy[5] 〔 ˈæləˌdʒɪ 〕 *n.* 過敏症《*all* = other》

allergic[5] 〔 əˈlɝdʒɪk 〕 *adj.* 過敏的

energetic[3] 〔 ˌɛnəˈdʒɛtɪk 〕 *adj.* 精力充沛的

energize[7] 〔 ˈɛnəˌdʒaɪz 〕 *v.* 激勵

urge[4] 〔 ɝdʒ 〕 *v.* 力勸；催促

chemurgy 〔 ˈkɛmɝdʒɪ 〕 *n.* 農產化學《*chemistry* 化學》

metallurgy 〔 ˈmɛtlˌɝdʒɪ, mɛˈtælədʒɪ 〕 *n.* 冶金術

```
metall + urg  + y
   |      |      |
metal  + work  +  n.
```

thaumaturgy 〔 ˈθɔməˌtɝdʒɪ 〕 *n.* 奇術；魔術；妖法
《希臘文 *thauma* = wonder》

178 **err** = wander；err (流浪；犯錯)

* 拉丁文 *errare* (= *wander*；*err*)。

error[2] 〔 ˈɛrə 〕 *n.* 錯誤；過失

errant 〔 ˈɛrənt 〕 *adj.* 漂泊的；遊俠的；錯誤的；遠離正途的

errancy 〔 ˈɛrənsɪ 〕 *n.* 錯誤

erratic[7] 〔 əˈrætɪk 〕 *adj.* 不穩定的；不確定的；不規律的；奇怪的

erroneous[7] 〔 əˈronɪəs 〕 *adj.* 錯誤的

erratum 〔 ɪˈretəm 〕 *n.* 書寫或印刷中之錯誤；(*pl.*) 勘誤表

aberrant 〔 æb'ɛrənt 〕 *adj.* 偏離常軌的；變態的；異常的
《*ab-* = away》

```
 ab  +   err   + ant
 |        |       |
away + wander + adj.
```

aberrance 〔 æb'ɛrəns 〕 *n.* 偏離常軌；反常
aberration 〔 ˌæbə'reʃən 〕 *n.* 越軌；恍惚；錯亂
inerrant 〔 ɪn'ɛrənt 〕 *adj.* 無錯誤的 《*in-* = not》.
inerratic 〔 ˌɪnɪ'rætɪk 〕 *adj.* 非反覆無常的；有規律的；固定的

179 **erythr** = red（紅色）　　＊希臘文 *eruthros*（= red）。

erythroblast 〔 ɪ'rɪθrəˌblæst 〕 *n.* 成紅血細胞 《*blast* = bud》
erythrocyte 〔 ɪ'rɪθroˌsaɪt 〕 *n.* 紅血球；紅血細胞 《*cyt* = cell》
erythroderma 〔 ɪˌrɪθrə'dʒmə 〕 *n.* 紅膚症 《*derm* = skin》
erythrophyll 〔 ɪ'rɪθroˌfɪl 〕 *n.* 葉紅素 《*phyll* = leaf》
erythropoiesis 〔 ɪˌrɪθropɔɪ'isɪs 〕 *n.* 紅血球生成

```
erythro + poie + sis
   |        |      |
  red   + make +  n.
```

erythema 〔 ˌɛrə'θimə 〕 *n.* 紅斑

180 **ess** = be（存在）

＊拉丁文 *esse*（= be）。〔變化型〕*ent* , *ont*。

essence[6] 〔 'ɛsn̩s 〕 *n.* 本質；要素；精髓
essential[4] 〔 ə'sɛnʃəl 〕 *adj.* 基本的；必要的；精華的　　*n.* 要素
quintessence 〔 kwɪn'tɛsn̩s 〕 *n.* 精髓；第五元素（earth , air , fire , water , aether 五要素中的第五項，即 aether 靈氣）《*quint* = five》

interest[1] 〔'ɪntərɪst , 'ɪntrɪst 〕 *n.* 興趣；嗜好；利益

v. 使感興趣；使熱心（存在於中間）《*inter-* = between》

inter	+	es(s)	+	t
between	+	be	+	n.

interesting[7] 〔'ɪntərɪstɪŋ , -trɪ- 〕 *adj.* 有趣的

disinterested[7] 〔 dɪs'ɪntərəstɪd 〕 *adj.* 公正的

uninterested 〔 ʌn'ɪntərɪstɪd 〕 *adj.* 無關的；冷淡的

absent[2] 〔'æbsn̩t 〕 *adj.* 缺席的；不在的（離開眼前）《*ab-* = away》

present[2] 〔'prɛzn̩t 〕 *adj.* 出席的；現在的　*n.* 現在（在眼前）

pre	+	(es)s	+	ent
before	+	be	+	n., adj.

entity[7] 〔'ɛntətɪ 〕 *n.* 存在；實體

ontogeny 〔 ɑn'tɑdʒənɪ 〕 *n.* 個體發生（學）《*gen* = produce》

ontology 〔 ɑn'tɑlədʒɪ 〕 *n.* 存在論；本體論；實體論《*logy* = study》

sporont 〔'sporənt 〕 *n.* 芽植體；孢子體《希臘文 *spora* = seed》

181　**ethn** = race（種族）　　* 希臘文 *ethnos*（ = race ）。

ethnic[5] 〔'ɛθnɪk 〕 *adj.* 種族的

ethnocentrism 〔,ɛθnə'sɛntrɪzəm 〕 *n.* 民族優越感（以自己的種族為中心）《*centr* = center》

ethnocide 〔'ɛθno,saɪd 〕 *n.* 種族文化滅絕（指對某一種族集團文化的肆意破壞）《*cide* = cut》

ethnography 〔 ɛθ'nɑgrəfɪ 〕 *n.* 人種誌；人種論《*graph* = write》

ethnolinguistics 〔,ɛθnolɪŋ'gwɪstɪks 〕 *n.* 文化語言學（研究語言與文化之間的關係）

ethno	+	lingu	+	ist	+	ics
race	+	language	+	n.	+	n.

ethnology〔εθ'nɑlədʒɪ〕*n.* 人種學《*logy* = study》

ethnomusicology〔ˌεθnoˌmjuzɪ'kɑlədʒɪ〕*n.* 民族音樂學
《*music* 音樂》

ethnopsychology〔ˌεθnəsaɪ'kɑlədʒɪ〕*n.* 民族心理學
《*psychology* 心理學》

182　ev = age（年齡；時代）　　* 拉丁文 *aevum*（= age）。

eternal[5]〔ɪ'tɝnl̩〕*adj.* 永恆的《拉丁文 *aeviternus* = of great age》

coeval〔ko'ivl̩〕*adj.* 同時代的；同年齡的

$$co + ev + al$$
$$equal + age + adj.$$

longeval〔lɑn'dʒivəl〕*adj.* 長壽的

medieval〔ˌmidɪ'ivl̩〕*adj.* 中世紀的；中古時代的《*medi* = middle》

primeval〔praɪ'mivl̩〕*adj.* 原始的；原始時代的；遠古的
《*prim* = first》

183　fa, fess = speak（說）

* 拉丁文 *fari*（= speak），現在分詞是 *fans*；*fabula*（= story）；
fama（= fame 名聲）；*fateri*（= admit），過去分詞是 *fassus*。
全部都是源自於印歐語系的字根 *bha-*（= speak）。

fable[3]〔'febl̩〕*n.* 寓言；傳說；神話；虛構

fabulous[6]〔'fæbjələs〕*adj.* 神話中的；傳說的；荒謬的；
難以置信的

affable〔'æfəbl̩〕*adj.* 和藹可親的；友善的；溫柔的（可以交談的）
《*af-* = *ad-* = to》

affability〔ˌæfə'bɪlətɪ〕*n.* 和藹可親；溫柔；友善

confabulate 〔 kən'fæbjə,let 〕 *v.* 談論；閒談；談心（一起談話）

　　《*con-* = together》

```
con    + fabul + ate
 |         |      |
together + speak + v.
```

ineffable 〔 ɪn'ɛfəbḷ 〕 *adj.* 言語難以形容的；不應說出的

　　《*in-* (not) + *ef-* = *ex-* (out) + *fa* (speak) + *-ble* (able to)》

nefarious 〔 nɪ'færɪəs 〕 *adj.* 凶惡的；邪惡的；無法無天的

　　《*ne-* = not》

preface[6] 〔'prɛfɪs 〕 *n.* 序言；開端　 *v.* 作爲～的序言；開始

　　（寫在前面的話）《*pre-* = before》

prefatory 〔'prɛfə,torɪ 〕 *adj.* 序文的；開場的（事先說的）

　　《*pre-* = before》

fame[4] 〔 fem 〕 *n.* 名聲；名氣；聲望　 *v.* 使有名氣（輿論）

famous[2] 〔'feməs 〕 *adj.* 有名的

infamy[7] 〔'ɪnfəmɪ 〕 *n.* 不名譽；可恥；醜名《*in-* = not》

infamous[7] 〔'ɪnfəməs 〕 *adj.* 可恥的；惡名昭彰的

```
in +  fam + ous
 |     |     |
not + fame + adj.
```

defame 〔 dɪ'fem 〕 *v.* 毀謗；破壞名譽（遠離了名聲）

　　《*de-* = *dis-* = apart》

defamation[7] 〔,dɛfə'meʃən , ,di- 〕 *n.* 誹謗；中傷

defamatory 〔 dɪ'fæmə,torɪ 〕 *adj.* 誹謗的；中傷的

infant[4] 〔'ɪnfənt 〕 *n.* 嬰兒；幼兒　 *adj.* 嬰兒的；幼年的

　　（不會說話的人）《*in-* = not》

infancy 〔'ɪnfənsɪ 〕 *n.* 幼年；初期；未成年

infanticide 〔 ɪn'fæntə,saɪd 〕 *n.* 殺嬰；犯殺嬰罪者《*cide* = cut down》

```
in + fanti  +  cide
 |     |        |
not + speak + cut down
```

infantile〔'ɪnfən͵taɪl , -təl〕*adj.* 嬰兒的；幼稚的；初期的

infantine〔'ɪnfən͵taɪn , -tɪn〕*adj.* 似嬰兒的；幼稚的《*-ine* = like》

fate[3]〔fet〕*n.* 命運；宿命（神的話）

　《拉丁文 *fatum* = thing spoken (by the gods)》

fatal[4]〔'fetl〕*adj.* 致命的；毀滅性的；重大的

confess[4]〔kən'fɛs〕*v.* 承認；自白；聲明（說得很清楚）

　《*con-* = fully》

confession[5]〔kən'fɛʃən〕*n.* 承認；自白

profess[7]〔prə'fɛs〕*v.* 聲稱；公開言明（在衆人之前說）

　《*pro-* = before all ; publicly》

$$
\begin{array}{ccc}
\text{pro} & + & \text{fess} \\
| & & | \\
publicly & + & speak
\end{array}
$$

profession[4]〔prə'fɛʃən〕*n.* 職業；宣佈；表白

professional[4]〔prə'fɛʃənl〕*adj.* 專業的　*n.* 以運動、技藝等
為職業的人

professor[4]〔prə'fɛsɚ〕*n.* 教授

　【解說】　我們一般統稱的「教授」，其實還可以分為許多層級，名稱
　　　　　也各不相同，舉例來說：「（正）教授」是 professor 或 full
　　　　　professor，「副教授」為 associate professor，「助理教授」
　　　　　是 assistant professor，「講師」則是 lecturer，最後就是幫
　　　　　教授改考卷的研究生，也就是「助教」teaching assistant。

184　　**fac** = face（臉；正面）　　*拉丁文 *facies*（ = *face*）。

face[1]〔fes〕*n.* 臉；表面；正面；字面

facial[4]〔'feʃəl〕*adj.* 臉部的；容顏的；表面的

$$
\begin{array}{ccc}
\text{fac} & + & \text{ial} \\
| & & | \\
face & + & adj.
\end{array}
$$

facade[7]〔fə'sɑd〕*n.* 建築物的正面；虛僞或做作的外表

facelift〔'feslɪft〕*v., n.* 爲（建築物、汽車等）作外觀的改善；

整形美容術（使臉能抬起 → 美化）《*lift* 抬起》

facet[7]〔'fæsɪt〕*n.* 小平面；刻面；（事物之）一面

deface[7]〔dɪ'fes〕*v.* 傷毀（外表或美觀）；銷毀；毀滅

（使臉支離破碎）《*de-* = *dis-* = apart》

efface〔ɪ'fes〕*v.* 消除；抹掉；沖淡；使失色《*ef-* = *ex-* = out》

enface〔ɛn'fes〕*v.* 寫（或印、蓋）在（票據、文件等）的面上

《*en-* = on》

foreface〔'fɔrfes〕*n.* 前顏面《*fore-* = before》

ineffaceable〔,ɪnə'fesəbḷ〕*adj.* 不可磨滅的；不能消除的；

不能洗刷的《*in-* = not》

```
in  +  ef  +  face  +  able
 |      |      |        |
not  +  out  +  face  +  adj.
```

interface[7]〔'ɪntə˞,fes〕*n.* 界面；分界面；不同學科之共有事實、

問題、理論《*inter-* = between》

superficial[5]〔,supə˞'fɪʃəl〕*adj.* 表面的；膚淺的；面積的；平方的

《*super-* = above》

```
super  +  fic  +  ial
  |        |       |
above  +  face  +  adj.
```

surface[2]〔's3fɪs〕*n.* 表面；物體之一面或一邊；外表

《*sur-* = *super-* = above》

resurface[7]〔ri's3fɪs〕*v.* 爲⋯鋪設新表面（或路面）；浮上水面；

重新露面《*re-* = again》

subsurface〔sʌb's3fɪs〕*adj.* 表面下的；地表下的；水面下的

n. 地表下土壤；海面下的水層《*sub-* = under》

185 fac , fact , fect , fic
= make ; do (製造；做)

* 拉丁文 *facere* (= *make* ; *do*) ，過去分詞是 *factus*，和英文的 *make, do* 等一樣，是重要動詞。〔變化型〕*fect* , *fic* , *fit* , *feat* , *feit*。

fact[1] 〔 fækt 〕 *n.* 事實；眞相 (成形的事)

factor[3] 〔'fæktɚ 〕 *n.* 因素；原動力　*v.* 分解因數 (構成物)

factory[1] 〔'fæktrɪ , -tərɪ 〕 *n.* 工廠 (製作地)

《 *-ory* 表示場所的名詞字尾》

faction[6] 〔'fækʃən 〕 *n.* 小圈子；小黨派；內訌 (爲做事而造的)

factional 〔'fækʃənḷ 〕 *adj.* 小黨派的；派別間的

factious 〔'fækʃəs 〕 *adj.* 好搞黨派的；好傾軋的

factitious 〔 fæk'tɪʃəs 〕 *adj.* 人爲的；人工的；虛僞的 (特意去做)

factotum 〔 fæk'totəm 〕 *n.* 雜役；佣人 (做每樣事的人)

《 *totum* = everything》

```
fact +  (t)otum
 |        |
 do  +  everything
```

factum 〔'fæktəm 〕 *n.* (法律) 事實

facture 〔'fæktʃɚ 〕 *n.* 製造；製成品

benefactor[7] 〔'bɛnə,fæktɚ , ,bɛnə'fæktɚ 〕 *n.* 施主；恩人 (行善者)

《 *bene-* = well》

malefactor 〔'mælə,fæktɚ 〕 *n.* 罪犯；作惡者 (做壞事的人)

《 *male-* = badly》

manufacture[4] 〔,mænjə'fæktʃɚ 〕 *n.* 製造；製造品

v. 製造；捏造 (用手做)《 *manu* = hand》

putrefacient 〔,pjutrə'feʃənt 〕 *adj.* 腐敗的　*n.* 腐敗劑

《 *putre* = rotten》

```
putre +  fac  + ient
  |       |       |
rotten + make +  adj.
```

facile〔'fæsḷ〕*adj.* 容易的；靈巧的（容易做）

facilitate[6]〔fə'sɪlə‚tet〕*v.* 使容易；使便利（使容易做）

facility[4]〔fə'sɪlətɪ〕*n.* 熟練；靈巧；(*pl.*) 設備

```
fac + il(e) + ity
 │     │      │
 do  + adj. +  n.
```

facsimile[7]〔fæk'sɪməlɪ , -'sɪmə‚li〕*v.* 複製　*n.* 複製；傳眞

　adj. 如複製的（同樣地做）《*simile* = like（像）》

faculty[6]〔'fækḷtɪ〕*n.* 才能；院系；一校的全體教職員

　（做事的人或力）

difficult[1]〔'dɪfə‚kʌlt , -kḷt〕*adj.* 困難的；煩擾的

　（和容易相違的 → 不容易的）《*dif-* = *dis-* = apart》

difficulty[2]〔'dɪfə‚kʌltɪ〕*n.* 困難；障礙

affect[3]〔ə'fɛkt〕*v.* 影響；感動（對～加以推動）《*af-* = *ad-* = to》

affectation〔‚æfɪk'teʃən〕*n.* 假裝；裝腔作勢

```
af + fect + ation
 │    │      │
 to + make +  n.
```

affection[5]〔ə'fɛkʃən〕*n.* 情愛；感情；疾病

affectionate[6]〔ə'fɛkʃənɪt〕*adj.* 摯愛的；親切的

confect〔kən'fɛkt〕*v.* 混合調製；把～做成糖果、蜜餞；湊成

　（一起做）《*con-* = together》

confection〔kən'fɛkʃən〕*n.* 糖果；蜜餞

```
con  + fect + ion
 │      │     │
together + make +  n.
```

confectionary〔kən'fɛkʃən‚ɛrɪ〕*adj.* 糖果的　*n.* 糖果店；糖果

confectionery〔kən'fɛkʃən‚ɛrɪ〕*n.* 糖果糕餅店；糖果店

defect[6]〔dɪ'fɛkt , 'di-〕*n.* 過失；缺點（做法不對 → 不足）

　《*de-* = from》

defection[7] 〔 dɪ'fɛkʃən 〕 *n.* 缺點；過失

effect[2] 〔 ɪ'fɛkt , ə- , ɛ- 〕 *n.* 效果；效力　　*v.* 實現；產生（做出來）
　《*ef-* = *ex-* = out》

effective[2] 〔 ə'fɛktɪv , ɪ'fɛktɪv 〕 *adj.* 有效的；生效的

$$
\begin{array}{ccc}
\text{ef} & +\ \text{fect}\ + & \text{ive} \\
| & | & | \\
out & +\ \ do\ \ + & adj.
\end{array}
$$

effectual 〔 ə'fɛktʃʊəl , ɪ- 〕 *adj.* 有效的

infect[4] 〔 ɪn'fɛkt 〕 *v.* 感染（從中推動）《*in-* = in》

infection[4] 〔 ɪn'fɛkʃən 〕 *n.* 感染；傳染

infectious[6] 〔 ɪn'fɛkʃəs 〕 *adj.* 有傳染性的

disinfect 〔 ˌdɪsɪn'fɛkt 〕 *v.* 消毒；淨化（使不被感染）《*dis-* = not》

perfect[2] 〔 *adj.* 'pɝfɪkt *v.* pɚ'fɛkt 〕 *adj.* 完全的；完美的；無缺的
　v. 改進；改良；完成（做得完整）《*per-* = thoroughly》

perfection[4] 〔 pɚ'fɛkʃən 〕 *n.* 完美；圓滿

imperfect[7] 〔 ɪm'pɝfɪkt 〕 *adj.* 不完全的；有缺點的
　《*im-* = *in-* = not》

$$
\begin{array}{ccc}
\text{im}\ + & \text{per} & +\ \text{fect} \\
| & | & | \\
not\ + & thoroughly & +\ \ do
\end{array}
$$

prefect 〔 'prifɛkt 〕 *n.* 地方官；司令官（站在前頭的人）
　《*pre-* = before》

prefecture 〔 'prifɛktʃɚ 〕 *n.* 縣；地方官之職位或任期

refection 〔 rɪ'fɛkʃən 〕 *n.* 點心；小吃（再做 → 再加餐）
　《*re-* = again》

refectory 〔 rɪ'fɛktərɪ 〕 *n.* 餐廳；膳廳（特指學校或寺院中者）
　《 *-ory* 表示地點的名詞字尾》

$$
\begin{array}{ccc}
\text{re}\ + & \text{fect} & +\ \text{ory} \\
| & | & | \\
again\ + & do & +\ place
\end{array}
$$

deficient[7]〔dɪ'fɪʃənt〕*adj.* 有缺點的；不完全的；缺乏的（不足）

　　《*de-* = *dis-* = apart》

deficiency[4]〔dɪ'fɪʃənsɪ〕*n.* 缺乏；不足

efficacy〔'ɛfəkəsɪ〕*n.* 功效；效力《*ef-* = *ex-* = out》

efficient[3]〔ə'fɪʃənt , ɪ-〕*adj.* 有效率的

efficiency[4]〔ə'fɪʃənsɪ , ɪ-〕*n.* 最經濟的效率；效能

magnificent[4]〔mæg'nɪfəsn̩t〕*adj.* 華麗的；壯觀的；堂皇的

　　《*magn* = great》

```
magn  +  ific  +  ent
 |         |        |
great  +   do   +  adj.
```

magnificence〔mæg'nɪfəsn̩s〕*n.* 華麗；堂皇

proficient[7]〔prə'fɪʃənt〕*adj.* 熟練的　*n.* 專家（做得好 → 進步）

　　《*pro-* = forward》

proficiency[6]〔prə'fɪʃənsɪ〕*n.* 熟練；精通

profit[3]〔'prafɪt〕*n.* 利潤　*v.* 有利；有益（進步）

profitable[4]〔'prafɪtəbl̩〕*adj.* 有利的；有益的

office[1]〔'ɔfɪs , 'afɪs〕*n.* 辦公室；公司；營業所；職責；任務

　　（應該做的事）《*of-* = *ob-* = to》

official[2]〔ə'fɪʃəl〕*adj.* 公務上的；公家的；官方的

　　n. 官吏；公務員

sacrifice[4]〔'sækrə,faɪs , -,faɪz〕*n.* 供奉　*v.* 犧牲；祭祀

　　（做為祝聖的東西）《*sacri* = sacred（神聖的）》

```
sacri  +  fice
  |         |
sacred  +  make
```

suffice[7]〔sə'faɪs , -'faɪz〕*v.* 滿足；足夠（在下面做 → 充滿）

　　《*suf-* = *sub-* = under》

sufficient[3]〔sə'fɪʃənt〕*adj.* 充份的；足夠的　*n.* 足量

affair[2] 〔 ə'fɛr 〕 *n.* 事情；任務；職務；戀情

《古法文 *faire* = 拉丁文 *facere*》

feat[7] 〔 fit 〕 *n.* 功績；事業；表演《fact 的同類字》

defeat[4] 〔 dɪ'fit 〕 *v.* 打敗；破壞；使失敗　　*n.* 失敗《*de-* = down》

feature[3] 〔'fitʃɚ 〕 *n.* 容貌；特徵　　*v.* 以～爲特色（臉的構造）

feasible[6] 〔'fizəbḷ 〕 *adj.* 可實行的；可能的；適合的

counterfeit[7] 〔'kauntɚfɪt 〕 *n., adj.* 假冒（的）；冒牌（的）

　　v. 僞造；模仿；僞裝（做出的東西）《*counter-* = against》

```
af  +  fair
|       |
to  +  make
```

```
counter  +  feit
   |          |
against  +  make
```

forfeit[7] 〔'fɔrfɪt 〕 *n.* 沒收物；罰金；罰鍰　　*adj.* 被沒收的

　　v. 喪失（在外面做 → 失去）《拉丁文 *foris* = out of doors》

forfeiture[7] 〔'fɔrfɪtʃɚ 〕 *n.* 喪失；沒收物；罰金

surfeit 〔's3fɪt 〕 *n.* 過度；過食　　*v.* 飲食過度；使生厭

　　《*sur-* = *super-* = above》

186　**fall , fals** = deceive (欺騙)

* 拉丁文 *fallere* (= *deceive* ; *disappoint*)，過去分詞是 *falsus*。

fail[2] 〔 fel 〕 *v.* 失敗；不及格；未能

fallacy[7] 〔'fæləsɪ 〕 *n.* 謬誤；謬論

fallacious 〔 fə'leʃəs 〕 *adj.* 欺騙的；謬誤的

fallible 〔'fæləbḷ 〕 *adj.* 可能犯錯的

infallible[7] 〔 ɪn'fæləbḷ 〕 *adj.* 絕不會錯的；絕對可靠的《*in-* = not》

false[1] 〔 fɔls 〕 *adj.* 錯的；欺騙的；假的；不實的

falsehood 〔'fɔlshʊd 〕 *n.* 虛假；不實；謊言

　　《 *-hood* 表示性質、狀態的名詞字尾》

falsetto 〔 fɔl'sɛto 〕 *n.* （男歌手的）假聲；假聲歌手　　*adj.* 用假聲

（唱）的　　*adv.* 用假聲

falsify〔'fɔlsə,faɪ〕*v.* 偽造；竄改；說謊

```
fals  +  ify
 |        |
deceive +  v.
```

falsification〔,fɔlsəfə'keʃən〕*n.* 偽造；竄改；說謊；曲解

falsity〔'fɔlsətɪ〕*n.* 錯誤；欺騙

fault[2]〔fɔlt〕*n.* 過錯；缺點　*v.* 做錯

faulty[7]〔'fɔltɪ〕*adj.* 有錯誤的；有缺點的

default[7]〔dɪ'fɔlt〕*n.* 不履行責任；缺席；缺乏　*v.* 怠忽職責；

　缺席《*de-* = intensive（加強語氣）》

187　**fare** = go（去）　*古英文 *faran*（= go）。

fare[3]〔fɛr〕*n.* 車費；乘客；飲食　*v.* 進展；過日子；享受飲食；

　旅行（去的費用）

farewell[4]〔fɛr'wɛl，'fɛr'wɛl〕*v.* 再會　*n.* 告別　*interj.* 再見！

seafaring〔'si,fɛrɪŋ〕*n.*，*adj.* 航海（的）；航海業（的）

thoroughfare〔'θɝo,fɛr〕*n.* 通路；通道（一直走去）

　《*thorough* = 古代是 through 的意思》

```
thorough + fare
   |        |
 through  +  go
```

warfare[6]〔'wɔr,fɛr〕*n.* 戰爭（去打仗）

wayfarer〔'we,fɛrɚ〕*n.*（尤指徒步的）旅行者

welfare[4]〔'wɛl,fɛr，-,fær〕*n.* 福利；幸福（情況進行得很好）

188　**febr** = fever（發燒）　*拉丁文 *febris*（= fever）。

febricity〔fɪ'brɪsətɪ〕*n.* 發燒

febrile〔'fibrəl，'fɛb-〕*adj.* 發燒的；熱病的

febrifacient 〔ˌfɛbrə'feʃənt〕 *n.* 引起發熱之病源；產熱劑

　　adj. 產熱的《*fac* = make》

febrifuge 〔'fɛbrɪˌfjudʒ , -ˌfɪudʒ〕 *n.* 退燒劑；冷飲《*fug* = flee》

189　　**fend** = strike (打擊)

　　* 拉丁文 *fendere* (= *strike*) 。〔變化型〕*fest*。

fend[7] 〔fɛnd〕 *v.* 抵擋；抵禦 (把對方打倒)《defend 的簡形》

fence[2] 〔fɛns〕 *n.* 圍欄；籬笆　　*v.* 防護；閃避；舞劍
　　《defence 的簡形》

defend[4] 〔dɪ'fɛnd〕 *v.* 保護；保衛；辯護 (打倒 → 攻擊是最好的防禦)
　　《*de-* = down》

defendant[7] 〔dɪ'fɛndənt〕 *n.* 被告 (爭辯者)　　*cf.* **plaintiff** (原告)

```
de   +  fend  + ant
 |        |      |
down + strike +  n.
```

defense[4] 〔dɪ'fɛns〕 *n.* 防禦；防護；辯護

defensive[4] 〔dɪ'fɛnsɪv〕 *adj.* 防禦用的；守勢的；自衛的
　　n. 防禦；守勢

offend[4] 〔ə'fɛnd〕 *v.* 冒犯；觸怒；違反 (法律等) (反過來打)
　　《*of-* = *ob-* = against》

offense[4] 〔ə'fɛns〕 *n.* 犯法；觸怒；攻擊

offensive[4] 〔ə'fɛnsɪv〕 *adj.* 無禮的；冒犯的；不快的
　　n. 攻勢；攻擊

```
of    +  fens  + ive
 |        |       |
against + strike + adj.
```

infest[7] 〔ɪn'fɛst〕 *v.* 橫行；騷擾 (打對方)《*in-* = against》

infestation[7] 〔ˌɪnfɛs'teʃən〕 *n.* 橫行；侵擾

manifest[5] ('mænə,fɛst) *adj.* 明白的　*v.* 顯示；表示　*n.* 運貨單

　《*mani* = hand》

manifestation[7] (,mænəfɛs'teʃən) *n.* 顯示；證明；發表

manifesto[7] (,mænə'fɛsto) *n.* 宣言

190　　**fer** = carry ; bear（運送；忍受；結果實）

　　　* 拉丁文 *ferre*（= *carry* ; *bring* ; *bear*）。

ferry[4] ('fɛrɪ) *n.* 渡船；渡口；渡頭　*v.* 以船運（搬運）

ferryboat ('fɛrɪ,bot) *n.* 渡輪

ferriage ('fɛrɪɪdʒ) *n.* 擺渡；渡船業；渡費

fertile[4] ('fɝtl̩) *adj.* 多產的；豐富的；肥沃的（結果）

　cf. **sterile**（不毛的）

fertility[6] (fɝ'tɪlətɪ) *n.* 繁殖力

fertilize[7] ('fɝtl̩,aɪz) *v.* 使肥沃；使豐富

afferent ('æfərənt) *adj.* 傳入的；輸入的；向心性的（向內傳的）

　《*af-* = *ad-* = to》

circumference[7] (sə'kʌmfərəns) *n.* 圓周；周圍

　《*circum-* = around》

confer[6] (kən'fɝ) *v.* 賦予；授與；商議（各自帶來湊在一塊）

　《*con-* = together》

conferee (,kanfə'ri) *n.* 參加會議者

conference[4] ('kanfərəns) *n.* 會議；談判

conferment (kən'fɝmənt) *n.* 授與；頒給（學位、榮譽、

贈品等）

con	+	fer	+	ment
together	+	*carry*	+	*n.*

conferral (kən'fɝrəl) *n.* 授與；商量

conferree (,kanfə'ri) *n.* 參加會議者

conferrer 〔 kənˈfɝ 〕 *n.* 授與者

conifer 〔ˈkɑnəfɚ , ˈkɑn- 〕 *n.* 針葉樹；松柏科植物（結毬果的樹）
《*coni* = cone（毬果）》

coniferous 〔 koˈnɪfərəs 〕 *adj.* 針葉科的；松柏科的

defer[17] 〔 dɪˈfɝ 〕 *v.* 延期；延緩（運送到遠方）《*de-* = *dis-* = apart》

defer[27] 〔 dɪˈfɝ 〕 *v.* 順從；服從（拿到人之下）《*de-* = down》

deferment 〔 dɪˈfɝmənt 〕 *n.* 延期

```
de  +  fer  + ment
 |       |      |
apart + carry +  n.
```

deferrable 〔 dɪˈfɝəbḷ 〕 *adj.* 可延期的

deferral 〔 dɪˈfɝəl 〕 *n.* 延期

deference 〔ˈdɛfərəns 〕 *n.* 服從；敬意

deferent 〔ˈdɛfərənt 〕 *adj.* 恭敬的

deferential[7] 〔ˌdɛfəˈrɛnʃəl 〕 *adj.* 恭敬的

differ[4] 〔ˈdɪfɚ 〕 *v.* 相異；不同（一個個分別搬運）《*dif-* = *dis-* = apart》

difference[2] 〔ˈdɪfərəns 〕 *n.* 相異；差額

different[4] 〔ˈdɪfərənt 〕 *adj.* 不同的；個別的

differentiable 〔ˌdɪfəˈrɛnʃɪəbḷ 〕 *adj.* 可分辨的

differentiability 〔ˌdɪfəˌrɛnʃɪəˈbɪlətɪ 〕 *n.* 可辨性

differential 〔ˌdɪfəˈrɛnʃəl 〕 *adj.* 差別的

differentiate[6] 〔ˌdɪfəˈrɛnʃɪˌet 〕 *v.* 區別；辨別

```
dif  +  fer  + ent + iate
 |       |      |      |
apart + carry + adj. +  v.
```

efferent 〔ˈɛfərənt 〕 *adj.* 傳出的；輸出的；離心的（向外傳的）
《*ef-* = *ex-* = out》

indifferent[5] 〔 ɪnˈdɪfərənt 〕 *adj.* 漠不關心的；冷淡的；中立的
（沒有不同 → 任何一個都相同）《*in-* = not》

infer[6] 〔 ɪnˈfɝ 〕 *v.* 推斷；暗示（把想法引入重心）《*in-* = into》

inferable〔ɪn'fɝəbḷ, 'ɪnfɚ-〕*adj.* 可推知的
inference[6]〔'ɪnfərəns〕*n.* 推斷；推論
inferential〔͵ɪnfə'rɛnʃəl〕*adj.* 推論上的
luminiferous〔͵lumə'nɪfərəs〕*adj.* 發光的；清楚的
　《*lumin* = light》

```
lumin +  ifer  + ous
  |        |       |
light  + carry +  adj.
```

metalliferous〔͵mɛtḷ'ɪfərəs〕*adj.* 含金屬的；產金屬的
　《*metal* 金屬》
odoriferous〔͵odə'rɪfərəs〕*adj.* 芳香的；有香味的《*odor* 香味》
offer[2]〔'ɔfɚ, 'afɚ〕*v.* 提供；奉獻；提議　*n.* 給予；出價；提供
　（拿到近處）《*of-* = *ob-* = near》
offering[6]〔'ɔfərɪŋ〕*n.* 提供
offerings[7]〔'ɔfərɪŋz〕*n.pl.* 捐獻物
offertory〔'ɔfɚ͵torɪ〕*n.* 奉獻儀式；奉獻金
pestiferous〔pɛs'tɪfərəs〕*adj.* 有害的

```
pesti +  fer  + ous
  |       |       |
pest  + carry +  adj.
```

prefer[2]〔prɪ'fɝ〕*v.* 較喜歡；提出；擢陞（運到面前）《*pre-* = before》
preferable[4]〔'prɛfrəbḷ, 'prɛfərə-〕*adj.* 較合意的；較好的

```
pre  +  fer  + able
 |       |       |
before + carry +  adj.
```

preference[5]〔'prɛfərəns〕*n.* 偏愛；選擇；優先
preferential[7]〔͵prɛfə'rɛnʃəl〕*adj.* 優先的；優惠的
preferentialism〔͵prɛfə'rɛnʃəlɪzm̩〕*n.* 優惠主義
preferentialist〔͵prɛfə'rɛnʃəlɪst〕*n.* 優惠主義論者
preferment〔prɪ'fɝmənt〕*n.* 晉升

proffer〔'prɑfɚ〕*v.* 提出　*n.* 提供（運到面前）《*pro-* = before》

refer[4]〔rɪ'fɝ〕*v.* 查詢；歸因；使參考；交給；談到（運回原處）
《*re-* = back》

referable〔'rɛfərəbḷ , rɪ'fɝəbḷ〕*adj.* 可歸因的；可交付的

reference[4]〔'rɛfərəns〕*n.* 指示；參考；諮詢；談到

referendary〔ˌrɛfə'rɛndərɪ〕*n.* 仲裁者

referential〔ˌrɛfə'rɛnʃəl〕*adj.* 參考的；參照的

```
re  +  fer  +  ent  +  ial
|       |       |       |
back + carry +  adj.  +  adj.
```

referral[7]〔rɪ'fɝəl〕*n.* 參考；推薦

somniferous〔sɑm'nɪfərəs〕*adj.* 催眠的；昏昏欲睡的
《*somni* = sleep》

soniferous〔so'nɪfərəs〕*adj.* 傳聲的；發音的《*soni* = sound》

suffer[3]〔'sʌfɚ〕*v.* 蒙受；受苦；受損失（在下面忍受）
《*suf-* = *sub-* = under》

sufferable〔'sʌfərəbḷ〕*adj.* 可忍受的；可容許的

```
suf  +  fer  +  able
|        |       |
under + bear +  adj.
```

sufferance〔'sʌfərəns〕*n.* 容許；容忍；寬容

suffering[7]〔'sʌfərɪŋ〕*n.* 痛苦；苦難

transfer[4]〔*n.* 'trænsfɝ *v.* træns'fɝ〕*v.* 移動；讓渡；轉換
n. 遷移；讓渡；換車（越過～運送）《*trans-* = across》

transferable〔træns'fɝəbḷ〕*adj.* 可轉移的

transferability〔ˌtrænsfɝə'bɪlətɪ〕*n.* 可轉移性

transferor〔træns'fɝɚ〕*n.* 讓渡人

```
trans  +  fer  +  or
|          |       |
across + carry + person
```

transferee〔ˌtrænsfəˈri 〕*n.* 被調任者；受讓人
《 *-ee* 表示「被～的人」》
transference〔 trænsˈfɚəns 〕*n.* 轉移；讓渡
transferential〔 trænsˈfɚənʃəl 〕*adj.* 轉移的；轉讓的

191　**ferr** = iron (鐵)　　* 拉丁文 *ferrum* (= iron) 。

ferrous〔ˈfɛrəs 〕*adj.* 鐵的；含鐵的
ferroalloy〔ˌfɛroˈælɔɪ 〕*n.* 鐵合金《*alloy* 合金》
ferroconcrete〔ˌfɛroˈkɑnkrit , -kɑnˈkrit 〕*n.* 鋼筋混凝土
《*concrete* 混凝土》
ferromagnet〔ˌfɛroˈmægnɪt 〕*n.* 鐵磁物質《*magnet* 磁鐵》
ferriferous〔 fɛˈrɪfərəs 〕*adj.* 產鐵的；含鐵的《*fer* = carry ; bear》

192　**ferv** = boil (沸騰)　　* 拉丁文 *fervere* (= boil) 。

fervid〔ˈfɝvɪd 〕*adj.* 熱情的；激烈的；灼熱的《 *-id* 形容詞字尾》
fervidity〔 fəˈvɪdətɪ 〕*n.* 熱；熱情；熱烈
fervent〔ˈfɝvənt 〕*adj.* 強烈的；熱烈的；白熱的
fervency〔ˈfɝvənsɪ 〕*n.* 熱烈；熱情；熱心
fervor[7]〔ˈfɝvɚ 〕*n.* 熱誠；熱心；白熱
effervescent〔ˌɛfɚˈvɛsn̩t 〕*adj.* 冒泡的；沸騰的；興奮的
《*ef-* = *ex-* (out) + *ferv* (boil) + *-escent* (形容詞字尾)》

ef + ferv + escent
|　　　|　　　|
out + boil +　adj.

perfervid〔 pɚˈfɝvɪd 〕*adj.* 極熱的；灼熱的；熱烈的 (徹底沸騰)
《*per-* = thoroughly》

193 **fest** = festival (節日)

* 拉丁文 *festum* (= *festival*)，複數是 *festa*。

festal 〔'fɛstḷ 〕 *adj.* 節日的；歡樂的；宴樂的
festive[7] 〔'fɛstɪv 〕 *adj.* 節日的；歡樂的；快樂的
festival[2] 〔'fɛstəvḷ 〕 *n.* 節日；慶祝；作樂　 *adj.* 節日的；喜慶的
festivity[7] 〔 fɛs'tɪvətɪ 〕 *n.* 歡宴；作樂；(*pl.*) 慶祝活動
festivous 〔'fɛstəvəs 〕 *adj.* 節日的；歡樂的
festology 〔 fɛs'talədʒɪ 〕 *n.* 討論基督教教會節日的文章

```
fest  +  ology
  |         |
festival  +  study
```

festoon 〔 fɛs'tun 〕 *n.* 裝飾用的花綵　 *v.* 用花綵裝飾；作成花綵

194 **fibr** = fiber (纖維)　　 * 拉丁文 *fibra* (= *fiber*)。

fiber[5] 〔'faɪbɚ 〕 *n.* 纖維
fibril 〔'faɪbrəl 〕 *n.* 小纖維；纖絲；根毛
fibrin 〔'faɪbrɪn 〕 *n.* (血) 纖維蛋白；麩質
fibroblast 〔'faɪbrəblæst 〕 *n.* 成纖維細胞
fibroid 〔'faɪbrɔɪd 〕 *adj.* 纖維性的　 *n.* 纖維瘤；子宮肌瘤
　《 *-oid* = like 》
fibrosis 〔 faɪ'brosɪs 〕 *n.* 纖維變性；纖維化
chondrofibroma 〔ˌkɑndrəfɪ'bromə 〕 *n.* 軟骨纖維瘤
　《 *chondro* = cartilage (軟骨)》

195 **fict** , **fig** = form；shape (形成；形狀)

* 拉丁文 *fingere* (= *form*；*shape*；*feign* 假裝)，過去分詞是
fictus；*figura* (= *form*；*shape*；*figure*)。

fictile 〔'fɪktḷ , -tɪl 〕 *adj.* 可塑性的；陶器的《 *-ile* 形容詞字尾》

fiction[4] 〔'fɪkʃən 〕 n. 小說；想像；虛構（不眞實的假話）

fictional[7] 〔'fɪkʃən̩ 〕 adj. 小說的；想像的；虛構的

fictitious[7] 〔 fɪk'tɪʃəs 〕 adj. 假的；虛構的

fictive 〔'fɪktɪv 〕 adj. 想像的；虛構的

feign[7] 〔 fen 〕 v. 假裝；虛構；杜撰

feint[7] 〔 fent 〕 n. 假裝；偽裝　 v. 假裝；偽裝；騙

figment[7] 〔'fɪgmənt 〕 n. 虛構；想像物

figure[2] 〔'fɪgjɚ , 'fɪgɚ 〕 n. 形狀；數字；圖形；人物；身材
　 v. 演算；表示；加圖案

figuration 〔ˌfɪgjə'reʃən 〕 n. 成形；定形；輪廓

figurative[7] 〔'fɪgjərətɪv 〕 adj. 比喻的；假借的；有文采的

configuration[7] 〔 kən,fɪgjə'reʃən 〕 n. 形狀；外形；輪廓
　《**con-** = wholly》

```
con  +  figur  +  ation
 |        |         |
wholly +  shape  +  n.
```

disfigure[7] 〔 dɪs'fɪgjɚ 〕 v. 破壞（形狀、美觀、價值等）
　（使形狀分離）《**dis-** = apart》

prefigure 〔 pri'fɪgjɚ 〕 v. 預示；預想（事先表示形狀）
　《**pre-** = before》

transfigure 〔 træns'fɪgjɚ 〕 v. 使變形；使變貌；使美化
　（使形狀轉移）《**trans-** = across》

effigy 〔'ɛfədʒɪ 〕 n. 肖像；雕像；畫像（使形狀呈現出來）
　《**ef-** = **ex-** = out》

196　 **fid** = trust（信任）

> * 拉丁文 *fidere*（ = *trust* ），*fides*（ = *faith* ）。

fidelity[6] 〔 faɪ'dɛlətɪ 〕 n. 忠貞；忠誠；精確

fiducial 〔 fɪ'duʃəl , -'dɪu- 〕 adj. 信賴的；有信仰的；信託的

字根
fac~fuse

faith[3] 〔 feθ 〕 *n.* 信仰；信心
faithful[4] 〔'feθfəl 〕 *adj.* 忠實的；忠誠的
bona fide[7] 〔'bonə'faɪdɪ 〕 *adj.* , *adv.* 眞實的（地）；誠實的（地）

```
bona  +  fide
 |        |
good   +  faith
```

confide[7] 〔 kən'faɪd 〕 *v.* 信任；信賴（非常信任）《*con-* = fully》
confidant[7] 〔ˌkɑnfə'dænt , 'kɑnfəˌdænt 〕 *n.* 密友；知己；心腹
　《 *-ant* 表示人的名詞字尾》

```
con   +   fid   +   ant
 |         |         |
fully  +  trust  +  person
```

confidence[4] 〔'kɑnfədəns 〕 *n.* 信任；信心；大膽
confident[3] 〔'kɑnfədənt 〕 *adj.* 自信的；大膽的
confidential[6] 〔ˌkɑnfə'dɛnʃəl 〕 *adj.* 機密的；獲信任的；
　信任他人的
diffidence 〔'dɪfədəns 〕 *n.* 缺乏自信；害羞；謙虛（不能確信）
　《*dif-* = *dis-* = apart》

```
dif   +   fid   +   ence
 |         |         |
apart  +  trust  +   n.
```

diffident 〔'dɪfədənt 〕 *adj.* 羞怯的；無自信的；謙虛的
infidel 〔'ɪnfədḷ 〕 *adj.* 不信教的　*n.* 無宗教信仰的人；異教徒
　《*in-* = not》
infidelity[7] 〔ˌɪnfə'dɛlətɪ 〕 *n.* 無信仰；背信
defy[7] 〔 dɪ'faɪ 〕 *v.* 違抗；公然反抗；蔑視（不相信）
　《*de-* = *dis-* = apart》
defiance[7] 〔 dɪ'faɪəns 〕 *n.* 挑戰；輕視；違抗
defiant[7] 〔 dɪ'faɪənt 〕 *adj.* 大膽反抗的

perfidy 〔'pɝfədɪ 〕 *n.* 背信；不信（遠離信用）

《*per-* = away》

```
per  +  fid  +  y
 |        |       |
away + trust +  n.
```

perfidious 〔 pɚ'fɪdɪəs 〕 *adj.* 背信的；奸詐的

197　**fil** = thread（線）

　　* 拉丁文 ***filum***（ = *thread* ; *spin* 紡織 ）。

file[3] 〔 faɪl 〕 *n.* 文卷檔；檔案；行列　　*v.* 歸檔；排成縱隊
filar 〔'faɪlɚ 〕 *adj.* 線的；絲的
filament 〔'fɪləmənt 〕 *n.* 細絲；纖維；燈絲；花絲
filamentary 〔,fɪlə'mɛntərɪ 〕 *adj.* 絲的；花絲的；如絲的
filiform 〔'fɪlə,fɔrm , 'faɪlə- 〕 *adj.* 絲狀的；纖維狀的
defile 〔 dɪ'faɪl 〕 *n.* 小路；峽道　　*v.* 以縱隊前進；弄髒；褻瀆
　　（ 由山中分出來的路 ）《*de-* = *dis-* = apart》

```
de  +  file
 |        |
apart + thread
```

profile[5] 〔'profaɪl 〕 *n.* 輪廓；側面像；簡要描述　　*v.* 鉤輪廓；
　　畫側面；簡要描述（ 呈現在眼前的線條 ）《*pro-* = forth》
unifilar 〔,junɪ'faɪlɚ 〕 *adj.* 單線的《*uni-* = one》

198　**fili** = son（兒子）　　* 拉丁文 ***filius***（ = *son* ）。

filial 〔'fɪljəl 〕 *adj.* 子女的；孝順的
filiate 〔'fɪlɪ,et 〕 *v.* 確定（ 非婚生子女 ）的父親身份

affiliate[7] 〔 əˈfɪlɪˌet 〕 v. 使緊密聯繫;使隸屬於;判定(非婚生子女)的父親

$$
\begin{array}{ccc}
\text{af} & + \text{ fili } & + \text{ ate} \\
| & | & | \\
to & + son & + v.
\end{array}
$$

disaffiliate 〔 ˌdɪsəˈfɪlɪˌet 〕 v. 使退出;使脫離《*dis-* = away》
filicide 〔ˈfɪləˌsaɪd 〕 n. 殺子(或女)者;殺子(或女)行為
《*cide* = cut》

199　**fin** = end;limit(結束;限制)

* 拉丁文 *finire* (= end; limit),名詞是 *finis*。

fine[11] 〔 faɪn 〕 n., v. 罰款(結束的東西,加以解決的東西)
fine[21] 〔 faɪn 〕 adj. 良好的;卓越的;精巧的
　v. 使精良;精美(被完成)
final[1] 〔ˈfaɪn̩ 〕 adj. 最後的;最終的　　n. 決賽;結局
finale[7] 〔 fɪˈnɑlɪ 〕 n. 終曲;終場
finalist[7] 〔ˈfaɪn̩ˌɪst 〕 n. 決賽選手
finalize[7] 〔ˈfaɪn̩ˌaɪz 〕 v. 完成;做最後決定
finance[4] 〔 fəˈnæns , ˈfaɪnæns 〕 n. 財務;財政;金融
　v. 融通;給予融資(支付的終結)

$$
\begin{array}{cc}
\text{fin} & + \text{ ance} \\
| & | \\
end & + n.
\end{array}
$$

financial[4] 〔 faɪˈnænʃəl , fə- 〕 adj. 財務的;金融的
finish[1] 〔ˈfɪnɪʃ 〕 v. 結束;完成;用盡;終止　　n. 終止;完美
finite[6] 〔ˈfaɪnaɪt 〕 adj. 有限的
finitude 〔ˈfɪnəˌtjud , ˈfaɪnə- 〕 n. 有限;限度
《 *-itude* 抽象名詞字尾》

$$
\begin{array}{cc}
\text{fin} & + \text{ itude} \\
| & | \\
end & + n.
\end{array}
$$

infinite[5] 〔 'ɪnfənɪt 〕 *adj.* 無限的   *n.* 無限《*in-* = not》

infinitesimal[7] 〔 ,ɪnfɪnə'tɛsəm!̩ 〕 *adj.* 無限小的；極微的

    n. 無限小；極微之量《*-esimal* 表示小的形容詞字尾》

```
    in  +  fin  +  it  +  esimal
    |      |      |        |
   not  +  end  + adj. +  adj.
```

infinitive[7] 〔 ɪn'fɪnətɪv 〕 *n.* 不定詞   *adj.* 不定詞的

infinitude 〔 ɪn'fɪnə,tjud 〕 *n.* 無限《*-itude* 抽象名詞字尾》

infinity[7] 〔 ɪn'fɪnətɪ 〕 *n.* 無窮盡；無限大；無量

confine[4] 〔 *n.* 'kɑnfaɪn *v.* kən'faɪn 〕 *n.* 境界；界限   *v.* 限制

    （共有的界限）《*con-* = together》

confinement[7] 〔 kən'faɪnmənt 〕 *n.* 限制；拘留；分娩

```
    con  +  fine  +  ment
    |        |        |
  together + end  +   n.
```

define[3] 〔 dɪ'faɪn 〕 *v.* 下定義；闡釋（定下界限）《*de-* = down》

definite[4] 〔 'dɛfənɪt 〕 *adj.* 明確的

definition[3] 〔 ,dɛfə'nɪʃən 〕 *n.* 明確；定義

definitive[7] 〔 dɪ'fɪnətɪv 〕 *adj.* 確定的；最後的；限定的

indefinite[7] 〔 ɪn'dɛfənɪt 〕 *adj.* 不確定的《*in-* = not》

```
    in  +  de  +  fin  +  ite
    |      |      |       |
   not + down +  end  +  adj.
```

refine[6] 〔 rɪ'faɪn 〕 *v.* 精製；純煉（使再度完成）《*re-* = again》

refined[7] 〔 rɪ'faɪnd 〕 *adj.* 精煉的；文雅的；高尚的

refinement[6] 〔 rɪ'faɪnmənt 〕 *n.* 精煉；文雅；高尚；精美；精巧

200   **firm** = firm（堅固的）   * 拉丁文 *firmus*（= *firm*）。

firm[2] 〔 fɝm 〕 *adj.* 堅固的；穩固的   *v.* 使堅固   *n.* 公司；商店

firmament 〔'fɜməmənt 〕 n. 蒼天；天空（以前被想成堅實不移動的東西）

affirm[6] 〔 ə'fɜm 〕 v. 肯定；斷言（做成堅固的東西）《af- = ad- = to》

affirmative[7] 〔 ə'fɜmətɪv 〕 adj. 肯定的　n. 肯定

cf. **negative**（否定的；否定）

```
af + firm + ative
 |      |      |
to  + firm  +  adj.
```

confirm[2] 〔 kən'fɜm 〕 v. 證實；堅定（做得十分堅固）
《con- = wholly》

confirmation[7] 〔,kɑnfɚ'meʃən 〕 n. 認可；確實；確定

confirmed[7] 〔 kən'fɜmd 〕 adj. 確認的；成習慣的；根深蒂固的

disaffirm[7] 〔,dɪsə'fɜm 〕 v. 抗議；反駁；註銷《dis- = not》

infirm[7] 〔 ɪn'fɜm 〕 adj. 虛弱的；不穩固的（不堅固）《in- = not》

infirmary[7] 〔 ɪn'fɜmərɪ 〕 n. 療養所；醫院
《 -ary 表示場所的名詞字尾》

infirmity 〔 ɪn'fɜmətɪ 〕 n. 虛弱；殘廢；疾病

201　**fix** = fasten（固定）

* 拉丁文 *figere*（= *fasten*），過去分詞是 *fixus*。

fixate[7] 〔'fɪkset 〕 v. 固定；執著

fixation 〔 fɪks'eʃən 〕 n. 固定；執著

fixity 〔'fɪksətɪ 〕 n. 固定（性）；永久性

fixture[7] 〔'fɪkstʃɚ 〕 n. 裝置物（尤指房屋內的附屬裝置）；
固定一職之人

affix 〔 v. ə'fɪks　n. 'æfɪks 〕 v. 固定；黏貼；附加
n. 附加物；字綴（向～固定）《af- = ad- = to》

infix 〔 v. ɪn'fɪks　n. 'ɪn,fɪks 〕 v. 固定；插入；注入
n. 字腰（插於字中）（固定在～裡）《in- = in》

prefix[7]〔 *n.* ˈpriˌfɪks　*v.* priˈfɪks 〕*n.* 字首　*v.* 加字首；置於前
（固定在字根前）《*pre-* = before》

```
 pre  +  fix
  |       |
before + fasten
```

suffix[7]〔 *n.* ˈsʌfɪks　*v.* səˈfɪks , ˈsʌfɪks 〕*n.* 字尾　*v.* 加字尾；附加
（固定在字根後）《*suf-* = *sub-* = under》

transfix〔 trænsˈfɪks 〕*v.* 刺穿；（因驚訝、恐怖等）使發呆
（穿過～而固定）《*trans-* = across》

transfixion〔 trænsˈfɪkʃən 〕*n.* 刺穿；貫穿

```
 trans  +  fix  + ion
   |        |      |
across + fasten +  n.
```

202　**fla** = blow（吹氣）

＊拉丁文 *flare*（= *blow*），過去分詞是 *flatus*。

flavor[3]〔 ˈflevɚ 〕*n.* 口味；風味

flatulent〔 ˈflætʃələnt 〕*adj.* 腸胃脹氣的；空虛的；浮誇的
（吹滿氣體的）

flatulence〔 ˈflætʃələns 〕*n.* 腸胃脹氣；空虛；浮誇

conflate〔 kənˈflet 〕*v.* 匯集在一起；合併（一起吹氣）
《*con-* = together》

conflation〔 kənˈfleʃən 〕*n.* 異文合併（將數種手抄本的異文
合併成一文本）

```
 con   + flat + ion
  |       |      |
together + blow +  n.
```

deflate[7]〔dɪˈflet〕*v.* 放出（球、車胎等）之空氣；削減；緊縮
（使空氣排出）《*de-* = *dis-* = away》

deflation[7]〔dɪˈfleʃən〕*n.* 放出空氣；通貨緊縮

inflate[7]〔ɪnˈflet〕*v.*（灌入氣體）使膨脹；使得意；通貨膨脹
（吹入空氣）《*in-* = into》

inflation[4]〔ɪnˈfleʃən〕*n.* 膨脹；得意；通貨膨脹

reflation〔rɪˈfleʃən〕*n.* 通貨再膨脹《*re-* = again》

203 **flam** , **flagr** = flame ; burn（火焰；燃燒）

> * 拉丁文 *flamma*（= *flame*），動詞是 *flammare*；*flagrare*
> （= *burn*）；*fulgere*（= *shine*）。全部都是源自於印歐語系
> 的字根 *bhel-*（= *shine*；*flash*；*burn*）。

flame[3]〔flem〕*n.* 火焰；燃燒；耀眼之光亮；強烈的情感
v. 焚燒；激動；發出光亮

flammable[7]〔ˈflæməbḷ〕*adj.* 可燃的；易燃的

flamboyant[7]〔flæmˈbɔɪənt〕*adj.* 燦爛的；豔麗的；神氣的
《古法文 *flambe* = flame（燃燒）》

flamingo〔fləˈmɪŋgo〕*n.* 紅鶴；火鶴鳥

aflame〔əˈflem〕*adj.* , *adv.* 燃燒的（地）；熱血沸騰的（地）
《*a-* = on》

inflame〔ɪnˈflem〕*v.* 激起；激動；使紅（腫、熱、發炎等）
（使內部燃燒）《*in-* = in》

inflammable[7]〔ɪnˈflæməbḷ〕*adj.* 易燃的；易激動的；易怒的

```
in + flamm + able
 |     |       |
in + flame + adj.
```

inflammation[7]〔ˌɪnfləˈmeʃən〕*n.* 發炎（處）；激昂；憤怒

inflammatory〔ɪnˈflæməˌtorɪ , -ˌtɔrɪ〕*adj.* 有煽動性的；發炎的

flagrant[7] 〔'flegrənt 〕 *adj.* 惡名昭彰的；極為明顯的

```
flagr + ant
  |      |
burn  + adj.
```

conflagration 〔,kɑnflə'greʃən 〕 *n.* 大火；火災（一起燒起來）

　《*con-* = together》

deflagration 〔,dɛflə'greʃən 〕 *n.* 暴燃（作用）《*de-* = down》

effulgent 〔 ɛ'fʌldʒənt，ɪ- 〕 *adj.* 燦爛的；光輝的（發出光亮）

　《*ef-* = *ex-* = out》

204　**flav** = yellow（黃色）　　* 拉丁文 *flavus*（= *yellow*）。

flavescent 〔 flə'vɛsənt 〕 *adj.* 變成（淡）黃色的；淡黃色的

　《*-escent* = becoming（形容詞字尾）》

flavin 〔'flevɪn，'flævɪn 〕 *n.* 黃素；四羥黃酮醇

flavone 〔'flevon 〕 *n.* 黃酮

flavoprotein 〔,flevo'protin 〕 *n.* 黃素蛋白《*protein* 蛋白質》

riboflavin 〔,raɪbə'flevɪn 〕 *n.* 核黃素《*ribose* 核糖》

205　**flect**，**flex** = bend（彎曲）

　* 拉丁文 *flectere*（= *bend*），過去分詞是 *flexus*。

flexible[4] 〔'flɛksəbḷ 〕 *adj.* 易彎曲的；有彈性的

flexibility[7] 〔,flɛksə'bɪlətɪ 〕 *n.* 彈性；易曲性；適應性

flexion；**flection** 〔'flɛkʃən 〕 *n.* 彎曲；詞尾變化

inflexible 〔 ɪn'flɛksəbḷ 〕 *adj.* 堅硬的；不屈的《*in-* = not》

```
in + flex + ible
 |    |      |
not + bend + adj.
```

inflexibility[7] 〔 ɪn,flɛksə'bɪlətɪ 〕 *n.* 堅硬不屈；不屈性

circumflex 〔'sɝkəm,flɛks 〕 *adj.* 曲折的　*v.* 使彎曲

　　n. 抑揚音符（彎曲周圍）《*circum-* = around》

deflect[7] 〔 dɪ'flɛkt 〕 *v.* 使偏離；使轉向《*de-* = *dis-* = away》

deflection[7] 〔 dɪ'flɛkʃən 〕 *n.* 偏離；偏向

inflect 〔 ɪn'flɛkt 〕 *v.* 使彎曲；使曲折；改變音調《*in-* = into》

inflexion 〔 ɪn'flɛkʃən 〕 *n.* 音調變化；曲折

reflect[4] 〔 rɪ'flɛkt 〕 *v.* 反射；反映；思考（轉回）《*re-* = back》

reflection[4]；**reflexion** 〔 rɪ'flɛkʃən 〕 *n.* 反射；反映；映像；深思

```
re  + flect + ion
 |      |      |
back + bend +  n.
```

reflective[6] 〔 rɪ'flɛktɪv 〕 *adj.* 反射的；深思的

reflex[7] 〔 *v.* rɪ'flɛks *n.*, *adj.* 'riflɛks 〕 *v.* 使折回　*n.* 反射；反照

　　adj. 反射的；不自主的

reflexive 〔 rɪ'flɛksɪv 〕 *adj.* 反射的　　*n.* 反身代名詞

206　flict = strike（打）

　　* 拉丁文 *fligere*（= *strike*），過去分詞是 *flictus*。

afflict[7] 〔 ə'flɪkt 〕 *v.* 使～痛苦（打人）《*af-* = *ad-* = to》

affliction[7] 〔 ə'flɪkʃən 〕 *n.* 痛苦；不幸；災害

afflictive 〔 ə'flɪktɪv 〕 *adj.* 痛苦的；多煩惱的

```
af  + flict + ive
 |      |      |
to + strike + adj.
```

conflict[2] 〔 *v.* kən'flɪkt *n.* 'kɑnflɪkt 〕 *v.* 鬥爭；衝突　*n.* 鬥爭；

　　衝突（對打）《*con-* = together》

inflict[7] 〔 ɪn'flɪkt 〕 *v.* 施加（打擊）；處以（刑罰）（正在打～）

　　《*in-* = upon》

infliction[7] 〔 ɪn'flɪkʃən 〕 *n.* 處罰；痛苦

207 **flor** = flower（花）

> * 拉丁文 *flos*，*flor-*（= *flower*），*florere*（= *bloom* 開花）。

flora〔'florə，'flɔrə〕*n.*（某地或某時代的）植物區系
　　cf. **fauna**（某地或某時代的動物區系）
floral[7]〔'florəl，'flɔrəl〕*adj.* 花的；由花製成的
florist[7]〔'florɪst，'flɔr-，'flɑr-〕*n.* 花匠；經營花卉業者；花店
　　《*-ist* 表示人的名詞字尾》
florescent[7]〔flo'rɛsn̩t〕*adj.* 開花的《*-escent* = becoming（形容詞字尾）》
floret〔'florɪt〕*n.* 小花
floriferous〔flɔ'rɪfərəs〕*adj.* 開花的；多花的《*fer* = bear》

```
flor  +  ifer  +  ous
 |         |        |
flower  +  bear  +  adj.
```

defloration〔ˌdɛflə'reʃən，ˌdiflə-〕*n.* 摘花；蹂躪童貞；摧毀
　　《*de-* = away》
efflorescence〔ˌɛflo'rɛsn̩s，-flɔ-〕*n.* 開花；開花期《*ef-* = *ex-* = out》
flourish[5]〔'flɝɪʃ〕*v.* 茂盛；興隆；裝飾；炫耀（如繁花盛開）
　　《*flour*（flower）+ *-ish*（動詞字尾）》
flourishing[7]〔'flɝɪʃ〕*adj.* 茂盛的；繁榮的
flower[1]〔'flauɚ〕*n.* 花　*v.* 開花
flowery[7]〔'flaurɪ〕*adj.* 百花齊放的；花狀的；絢麗的

208 **flu**，**flux** = flow（流）

> * 拉丁文 *fluere*（= *flow*），過去分詞是 *fluxus*。

fluent[4]〔'fluənt〕*adj.* 流暢的；優雅的（流動的樣子）
fluency[5]〔'fluənsɪ〕*n.* 流暢
fluid[6]〔'fluɪd〕*adj.* 流質的　*n.* 流體
fluidity〔flu'ɪdətɪ〕*n.* 流質；液態；流動狀態

flume[7] 〔 flum 〕 *n.* 峽谷;溝澗;人工水道　*v.* 由水道輸送

flush[4] 〔 flʌʃ 〕 *v.* (臉) 發紅;激流;使興奮

　　n. 臉紅;活力;奔流

fluctuate[7] 〔 ʹflʌktʃʊˏet 〕 *v.* 上下移動;波動

　　《拉丁文 *fluctus* = wave (波)》

flood[2] 〔 flʌd 〕 *v.* 氾濫　*n.* 洪水

```
fluctu + ate
   |      |
 wave  +  v.
```

affluent[7] 〔 ʹæfluənt 〕 *adj.* 豐富的;富裕的;流暢的　*n.* 支流

　　《*af-* = *ad-* = to》

affluence[7] 〔 ʹæfluəns 〕 *n.* 豐富;富裕;流入;湧進

circumfluent 〔 səʹkʌmfluənt 〕 *adj.* 環流的;圍繞的 (流過四周)

　　《*circum-* = around》

circumfluence 〔 səʹkʌmfluəns 〕 *n.* 環流;周流

confluent 〔 ʹkɑnfluənt 〕 *adj.* 合流的;匯集的　*n.* 支流 (共同流)

　　《*con-* = together》

```
con   + flu +  ent
 |       |      |
together + flow + adj.
```

confluence[7] 〔 ʹkɑnfluəns 〕 *n.* 合流;匯流處

effluent[7] 〔 ʹɛfluənt 〕 *adj.* 流出的;放出的　*n.* 流出物;支流

　　(流到外面)《*ef-* = *ex-* = out》

effluence 〔 ʹɛfluəns , -flɪʊ- 〕 *n.* 流出;流出物

```
ef + flu  + ence
 |     |      |
out + flow  +  n.
```

effluvium 〔 ɛʹfluvɪəm , ɪ- 〕 *n.* 臭氣;惡臭

influent 〔 ʹɪnfluənt 〕 *adj.* 流入的　*n.* 支流 (流入其中)《*in-* = into》

influence[2] 〔 ʹɪnfluəns 〕 *n.* 影響力;感化力;權勢　*v.* 影響;改變

influential[4] 〔 ˏɪnfluʹɛnʃəl 〕 *adj.* 有影響力的

influenza[7] 〔 ˏɪnfluʹɛnzə 〕 *n.* 流行性感冒 (= *flu*)

refluent 〔 ʹrɛfluənt 〕 *adj.* 逆流的;倒流的 (逆流的)《*re-* = back》

refluence〔'rɛfluəns〕 n. 逆流；退潮

superfluous〔su'pɝfluəs，sə-〕 adj. 多餘的；不必要的（流過）

　　《*super-* = over》

superfluity〔,supɚ'fluətɪ，,sju-〕 n. 多餘

```
super + flu  + ity
  |      |      |
over  + flow + n.
```

inflow〔'ɪn,flo〕 n. 流入；輸入《*in-* = into》

overflow[5]〔v.,ovɚ'flo n.'ovɚ,flo〕 v. 流出；溢出；氾濫；充溢

　　n. 氾濫；充溢《*over-* = excessively》

reflow〔ri'flo〕 v. 流回；落潮《*re-* = back》

flux〔flʌks〕 n. 漲潮；流出；變遷　　v. 使流出

fluxion〔'flʌkʃən〕 n. 流動；流出；不斷的變化

afflux〔'æflʌks〕 n. 流注；湧流；匯集；充血（流向）《*af-* = *ad-* = to》

conflux〔'kɑnflʌks〕 n. 合流；匯流處；群集（共同流）

　　《*con-* = together》

```
con   + flux
 |       |
together + flow
```

efflux〔'ɛflʌks〕 n. 流出；時光的流逝；終了（流到外面）

　　《*ef-* = *ex-* = out》

influx[7]〔'ɪn,flʌks〕 n. 流入；注入；匯流處；灌輸（流入其中）

　　《*in-* = into》

reflux〔'ri,flʌks〕 n. 逆流；退潮《*re-* = back》

209　**foli** = leaf（葉子）

　　* 拉丁文 *folium*（= *leaf*），複數是 *folia*。

foliage[7]〔'folɪɪdʒ〕 n.【集合名詞】樹或植物的葉子

　　《*-age* 表示集合名詞的字尾》

foliate 〔 *adj.* ˈfolɪɪt *v.* ˈfolɪˏet 〕 *adj.* 有葉的；葉狀的
　　v. 生葉；打成薄片
folio 〔ˈfolɪˏo , ˈfoljo 〕 *n.* 對開張；對開本　*adj.* 對開本的
defoliate 〔 dɪˈfolɪˏet 〕 *v.* 除葉；落葉 (使葉子落下)《*de-* = down》

```
de  +  foli  +  ate
 |       |       |
down  +  leaf  +  v.
```

defoliant 〔 dɪˈfolɪənt 〕 *n.* 脫葉劑；落葉劑
exfoliate 〔 ɛksˈfolɪˏet 〕 *v.* 剝落 (將樹葉剝落)《*ex-* = out》
perfoliate 〔 pɚˈfolɪˏet 〕 *adj.* 抱莖的 (莖穿過葉子生長的)
　　(穿過葉子)《*per-* = through》
portfolio[7] 〔 portˈfolɪˏo 〕 *n.* 紙夾；公事包《*port* = carry》
trifoliate 〔 traɪˈfolɪɪt 〕 *adj.* 三葉的《*tri-* = three》

210　**form** = form (形狀；形式)

　　* 拉丁文 *formare* (= *form*) ，名詞是 *forma*。

form[2] 〔 fɔrm 〕 *n.* 形狀；外貌；形式　*v.* 構成；變成；組織
formal[2] 〔ˈfɔrml̩ 〕 *adj.* 正式的；傳統的；形式上的
formalism 〔ˈfɔrml̩ˏɪzəm 〕 *n.* 形式主義；拘泥形式
formality[7] 〔 fɔrˈmælətɪ 〕 *n.* 拘泥形式；拘禮；正式；儀式
informal[7] 〔 ɪnˈfɔrml̩ 〕 *adj.* 非正式的《*in-* = not》
informality 〔ˏɪnfɔrˈmælətɪ 〕 *n.* 非正式

```
in  +  form  +  al  +  ity
 |      |       |      |
not  +  form  +  adj.  +  n.
```

informally[7] 〔 ɪnˈfɔrməlɪ 〕 *adv.* 非正式地
format[5] 〔ˈfɔrmæt 〕 *n.* 格式
formation[4] 〔 fɔrˈmeʃən 〕 *n.* 構成；組成；構成物

formative〔'fɔrmətɪv〕*adj.* 形成的

formula[4]〔'fɔrmjələ〕*n.* 客套話；公式

formulate[6]〔'fɔrmjə,let〕*v.* 公式化；有系統地述說

conform[6]〔kən'fɔrm〕*v.* 使適合；使順從（做成共同的形狀）

《*con-* = together》

conformable〔kən'fɔrməbl̩〕*adj.* 符合的

conformably〔kən'fɔrməblɪ〕*adv.* 服從地

conformance〔kən'fɔrməns〕*n.* 順從；一致

conformation〔,kɑnfɔr'meʃən〕*n.* 構造；形態；一致

conformist〔kən'fɔrmɪst〕*n.* 遵奉者；順從的人；墨守成規
的人；（C-）英國國教徒

```
con   + form +   ist
 |         |       |
together + form + person
```

conformity〔kən'fɔrmətɪ〕*n.* 相似；一致；遵照

deform[7]〔dɪ'fɔrm〕*v.* 使不成形；使殘廢

《*de-* = *dis-*（put out of）+ *form*（shape）》

deformation〔,difɔr'meʃən〕*n.* 畸形

deformed〔dɪ'fɔrmd〕*adj.* 畸形的

deformity〔dɪ'fɔrmətɪ〕*n.* 畸形；殘廢

```
de    + form + ity
 |        |      |
away  + form + n.
```

inform[3]〔ɪn'fɔrm〕*v.* 通知；告發；訴冤（在心中造形）

《*in-* = into》

informant[7]〔ɪn'fɔrmənt〕*n.* 線民

information[4]〔,ɪnfɚ'meʃən〕*n.* 通知；資料；情報；資訊

informational[7]〔,ɪnfɚ'meʃənl̩〕*adj.* 新聞的

informative[4]〔ɪn'fɔrmətɪv〕*adj.* 提供知識（情報）的；有益的

informed[7] 〔 ɪnˋfɔrmd 〕 *adj.* 有知識的；見聞多的

informer 〔 ɪnˋfɔrmɚ 〕 *n.* 線民

malformation 〔 ͵mælfɔrˋmeʃən 〕 *n.* 畸形 (形狀不佳)

  《 *mal-* = bad 》

perform[3] 〔 pɚˋfɔrm 〕 *v.* 行；做；表演；執行 (完全地造形)

  《 *per-* = thoroughly 》

  【注意】 本字與 form 沒有關聯，而是源自於法語 *fournir* (= furnish ；

      provide) 的形式，為學習上的方便而納入此處。

performable 〔 pɚˋfɔrməbl̩ 〕 *adj.* 可實行的；可完成的

performance[3] 〔 pɚˋfɔrməns 〕 *n.* 履行；行動；表演

per	+	form	+ ance
thoroughly	+	provide	+ n.

performer[5] 〔 pɚˋfɔrmɚ 〕 *n.* 表演者

reform[4] 〔 rɪˋfɔrm 〕 *v.* 改造；改進　*n.* 改革；改善 (再造形)

  《 *re-* = again 》

reformation 〔 ͵rɛfɚˋmeʃən 〕 *n.* 改良；改革；改善

reformational 〔 ͵rɛfɚˋmeʃən̩l 〕 *adj.* 革新的

reformative 〔 rɪˋfɔrmətɪv 〕 *adj.* 改革的

reformatory 〔 rɪˋfɔrmə͵torɪ 〕 *adj.* 改革的　*n.* 感化院

reformed 〔 rɪˋfɔrmd 〕 *adj.* 已改善的；改過自新的

reformer 〔 rɪˋfɔrmɚ 〕 *n.* 改革者

transform[4] 〔 trænsˋfɔrm 〕 *v.* 使變形；改觀 (移轉形狀)

  《 *trans-* = across 》

trans	+ form
across	+ form

transformation[6] 〔 ͵trænsfɚˋmeʃən 〕 *n.* 變形；變換

transformative 〔 trænsˋfɔrmətɪv 〕 *adj.* 變化的

transformer 〔 trænsˋfɔrmɚ 〕 *n.* 變壓器

uniform[2] ('junə,fɔrm) *adj.* 一律的   *n.* 制服
    v. 為～提供制服；使一致（一個形式的）《*uni-* = one》
uniformed ('junə,fɔrmd) *adj.* 穿制服的
uniformity (,junə'fɔrmətɪ) *n.* 一律；相同；一樣
uniformly[7] ('junə,fɔrmlɪ) *adv.* 一樣地
multiform ('mʌltə,fɔrm) *adj.* 多形的；各種的   *n.* 多形的事物
    《*multi-* = many》

211   **fort** = strong (強壯的)   * 拉丁文 *fortis* (= strong)。

fort[4] (fɔrt) *n.* 堡壘；要塞；（北美邊境的）市集（強的地方）
forte[17] (fɔrt) *n.* 長處；擅長
forte[27] ('fɔrtɪ) *adj.* 強音的   *adv.* 強音地   *n.* 強音
fortify[6] ('fɔrtə,faɪ) *v.* 加強；設防（使堅強）《 *-ify* = make》
fortification[7] (,fɔrtəfə'keʃən) *n.* 築城；設防
fortifier ('fɔrtə,faɪɚ) *n.* 強化、鞏固之人或物
fortissimo (fɔr'tɪsə,mo) *n.* (音樂) 最強音   *adj.* 最強音的

```
fort  + issimo
 |        |
strong + utmost
```

fortress[7] ('fɔrtrɪs) *n.* 堡壘
fortitude ('fɔrtə,tjud) *n.* 堅忍；不屈不撓《 *-itude* 抽象名詞字尾》

```
fort  + itude
 |        |
strong +  n.
```

force[1] (fors , fɔrs) *n.* 力量；暴力；影響力；(*pl.*) 軍隊
    v. 強迫；迫使；強行
forcible ('forsəbl̩ , 'fɔrs-) *adj.* 有力的；強行的
comfort[3] ('kʌmfɚt) *v.* 安慰；鼓舞   *n.* 安慰；慰藉；舒適
    《*com-* = wholly》

comfortable[2]〔'kʌmfətəbḷ〕 *adj.* 安逸的；舒適的；愉快的
discomfort[6]〔 dɪs'kʌmfət 〕 *n.* 不舒服；難過　*v.* 使難過；
使不舒服《*dis-* = not》

```
dis  +  com  +  fort
 |       |       |
not  + wholly + strong
```

effort[2]〔'ɛfət 〕 *n.* 努力；奮力（使出力量）《*ef-* = *ex-* = out》
enforce[4]〔 ɪn'fors 〕 *v.* 強行；執行（力量加在～之中）《*en-* = in》
enforcement[4]〔 ɪn'forsmənt , ɛn- 〕 *n.* 強迫；強制；執行
reinforce[6]〔,riɪn'fors 〕= reenforce　*v.* 增援；加強《*re-* = again》
reinforcement[7]〔,riɪn'forsmənt , -'for- 〕 *n.* 增援；加強；
（*pl.*）援兵

```
re  + in + force + ment
 |     |     |       |
again + in + strong +  n.
```

perforce〔 pə'fors , -'fɔrs 〕 *adv.* 不得已地；必須地；強迫地
（憑藉力量）《*per-* = through》

212　**fract , frag** = break（損壞）

* 拉丁文 *frangere* , *frag-*（ = break），過去分詞是 *fractus*。

fraction[5]〔'frækʃən 〕 *n.* 部分；微量；分數（損壞的部分）
fracture[6]〔'fræktʃə 〕 *v.* 裂口；破裂；骨折　*n.* 裂口；破裂
fragile[6]〔'frædʒəl 〕 *adj.* 易碎的；不實在的
fragility〔 fræ'dʒɪlətɪ , frə- 〕 *n.* 脆弱性；虛弱
fragment[6]〔'frægmənt 〕 *n.* 碎片；斷片；破片
fragmentary〔'frægmən,tɛrɪ 〕 *adj.* 片斷的；不完整的

```
frag  + ment + ary
  |      |      |
break +  n.  + adj.
```

fragmentation〔͵frægmən'teʃən〕*n.* 破碎；殘破

frail[6]〔frel〕*adj.* 脆弱的；不堅實的（容易損壞的）

frailty〔'freltɪ〕*n.* 脆弱；意志薄弱

diffract〔dɪ'frækt〕*v.* 分散；使（光線、音波等）繞射（使射開）

《*dif-* = *dis-* = apart》

diffraction〔dɪ'frækʃən〕*n.*（光線、音波等的）繞射

```
dif  +  fract  +  ion
 |        |        |
apart + break  +  n.
```

infract〔ɪn'frækt〕*v.* 侵犯；違反（法律、權利等）（破門而入）

《*in-* = into》

infraction[7]〔ɪn'frækʃən〕*n.* 違反；犯法

refract[7]〔rɪ'frækt〕*v.* 使折射

refractory〔rɪ'fræktərɪ〕*adj.* 難駕馭的；倔強的

```
re  +  fract  +  ory
 |       |        |
back + break  +  adj.
```

refrain[17]〔rɪ'fren〕*n.* 抑制；禁止；詩歌之重疊句（還原）

《*re-* = back》

refrain[27]〔rɪ'fren〕*v.* 抑制；禁止

（出自同一字源而語義不同，為「拉回馬的韁繩」之意）

suffrage〔'sʌfrɪdʒ〕*n.* 投票；贊成；選舉權；參政權

《*suf-* = *sub-* = under》

【解說】美國自 1787 年制憲以來，規定人人都有參政權，但是事實上，
直到 1868 年黑人才獲得參政權，而女性甚至要到 1920 年時，
才眞正擁有參政權。

213 **franc** = free（自由的；免費的）

* 古法文 *franc*（= *free*），*franchir*（= *set free*）。

France[7]〔fræns〕*n.* 法國

frank[2] 〔 fræŋk 〕 *adj.* 坦白的　 *v.* 免費寄送

franchise[7] 〔'fræntʃaɪz 〕 *n.* 參政權；選舉權；特權；經銷權

```
franch  +  ise
  |         |
free   +  make
```

affranchise 〔 ə'fræn,tʃaɪz 〕 *v.* 恢復（奴隸等）自由；解除…的
義務；給予選舉權《*af-* = *ad-* = to》

disfranchise[7] 〔 dɪs'fræntʃaɪz 〕 *v.* 剝奪…選舉權；剝奪…的權力
《*dis-* = deprive of（剝奪）》

enfranchise 〔 ɛn'fræntʃaɪz 〕 *v.* 給…公民權；恢復（奴隸、
農奴等）的自由；免除…的法律義務《*en-* = make》

214　**frater** = brother（兄弟）

* 拉丁文 ***frater***（ = *brother*）。

fraternal[7] 〔 frə't϶nḷ 〕 *adj.* 兄弟的；兄弟會的

fraternity[7] 〔 frə't϶nətɪ 〕 *n.* 兄弟關係；友愛；〔美〕兄弟會；
同行　 *cf.* **sorority**（姐妹會）

fraternize 〔'frætɚ,naɪz 〕 *v.* 親如兄弟；親善

fratricide 〔'frætrə,saɪd , 'frɛtrə- 〕 *n.* 殺兄弟（或姐妹）的行為；
殺兄弟（或姐妹）的人《*cide* = cut》

confraternity 〔,kɑnfrə't϶nətɪ 〕 *n.* 手足之情；（宗敎、慈善事業
等的）團體《*con-* = together》

215　**front** = forehead（前額；前部）

* 拉丁文 ***frons*** , ***front-***（ = *forehead* ; *front*）。

front[1] 〔 frʌnt 〕 *n.* 前面；正面；開頭；前線；陣線
adj. 前面的；正面的

frontier[5] 〔 frʌn'tɪr 〕 *n.* 邊境；邊界　 *adj.* 邊界的

frontlet 〔'frʌntlɪt 〕*n.* 額飾；（鳥類或動物的）前額

《 *-let* 表示小的名詞字尾》

affront[7] 〔 ə'frʌnt 〕*v.* 侮辱；冒犯；泰然面對（面對面）

《 *af-* = *ad-* = to》

confront[5] 〔 kən'frʌnt 〕*v.* 面對；使碰面；對抗；相對

《 *con-* = together》

effrontery 〔 ɪ'frʌntərɪ 〕*n.* 厚顏無恥（使沒有面子）

《 *ef-* = *ex-* = out of》

oceanfront 〔'oʃən,frʌnt 〕*n.* 沿海地帶

riverfront 〔'rɪvɚ,frʌnt 〕*n.* （城鎮的）河邊地區

shorefront 〔'ʃɔr,frʌnt 〕*n.* 沿岸陸地

storefront[7] 〔'stor,frʌnt , 'stɔr- 〕*n.* 商店正面；店面

upfront[7] 〔 ʌp'frʌnt 〕*adj.* 前面的；坦率的；預付的

waterfront[7] 〔'wɔtɚ,frʌnt 〕*n.* 濱水區；碼頭區

---

216 **fug** = flee（逃走）　　* 拉丁文 *fugere*（ = *flee*）。

fugacious 〔 fju'geʃəs 〕*adj.* 早謝的；短暫的；轉眼即逝的

fugitive[7] 〔'fjudʒətɪv 〕*n.* 逃亡者　　*adj.* 逃亡的；瞬間即逝的

febrifuge 〔'fɛbrɪ,fjudʒ , -,fɪudʒ 〕*n.* 退燒劑；冷飲（避熱）

《 *febri* = fever》

lucifugous 〔 lu'sɪfjəgəs 〕*adj.* 避光的；怕光的（逃避光）

《 *luci* = light》

```
luci + fug + ous
  |      |     |
light + flee + adj.
```

refuge[5] 〔'rɛfjudʒ 〕*n.* 避難（所）；保護（逃回安全地）《 *re-* = back》

refugee[4] 〔,rɛfju'dʒi 〕*n.* 避難者；難民《 *-ee* 表示動作的接受者》

subterfuge 〔'sʌbtɚ,fjudʒ 〕*n.* 遁辭；藉口（逃避的手段）

《 *subter* = secretly》

vermifuge 〔'vɝmə,fjudʒ 〕*n.* 驅蟲劑　　*adj.* 用以驅蟲的

（讓蟲逃走之物）《 *vermi* = worm》

217 **fum** = smoke (煙) * 拉丁文 *fumus* (= smoke) 。

fume[5] 〔 fjum 〕 *n.* 煙霧

fumarole 〔 'fjumə,rol 〕 *n.* (火山區的) 噴氣孔
《拉丁文 *fumariolum* = smoke hole》

fumatorium 〔 ,fjumə'torɪəm 〕 *n.* (殺滅植物害蟲等的) 密封
燻蒸室；燻蒸消毒室《 *-ium* 表示地點的名詞字尾》

fumigate 〔 'fjumə,get 〕 *v.* (爲消毒、殺蟲等) 煙燻；蒸燻；
用香薰

```
fum  +  ig  + ate
 |       |      |
smoke + drive + v.
```

perfume[4] 〔 *n.* 'pɝfjum *v.* pə'fjum 〕 *n.* 香水 *v.* 灑香水於
《*per-* = through》

218 **fund** , **found** = base (基礎；底部)

* 拉丁文 *fundus* (= base ; bottom) 。

fund[3] 〔 fʌnd 〕 *n.* 專款；基金 *v.* 儲蓄；爲～備基金

fundamental[4] 〔 ,fʌndə'mɛntḷ 〕 *adj.* 基礎的；根本的；初級的
n. 基本原理

```
funda + ment +  al
  |       |      |
base  +  n.  +  adj.
```

found[3] 〔 faʊnd 〕 *v.* 建立；設立；以～爲根據 (奠定基礎)

foundation[4] 〔 faʊn'deʃən 〕 *n.* 基礎；根據；根基；基金會

founder[4] 〔 'faʊndɚ 〕 *n.* 建立者；設立者

profound[6] 〔 prə'faʊnd 〕 *adj.* 深遠的；深奧的 (到底的)
《*pro-* = forward ; downward》

profundity 〔 prə'fʌndətɪ 〕 *n.* 深奧；奧妙

219　**fuse** = pour (注入；倒入)

＊ 拉丁文 *fundere* (= *pour*)，過去分詞為 *fusus*。
〔變化型〕*found*。

fuse[15] 〔 fjuz 〕*v.* 熔；融合 (為了注入)
fuse[25] 〔 fjuz 〕*n.* 保險絲；導火線　*v.* 裝上保險絲；保險絲燒斷
　【注意】 此字的字源不同，是為了方便起見而收錄於此。

fusible 〔 'fjuzəbl̩ 〕*adj.* 可熔解的；易熔的

```
 fus  +  ible
  |       |
pour  +  adj.
```

fusion[7] 〔 'fjuʒən 〕*n.* 熔解；融合
found[3] 〔 faʊnd 〕*v.* 鑄造 (注入)
foundry 〔 'faʊndrɪ 〕*n.* 鑄造工廠；鑄造法
　《 *-ry* 表示場所的名詞字尾》
confound[7] 〔 kɑn'faʊnd , kən- 〕*v.* 使驚慌；使驚訝；使狼狽
　(共同注入)《 *con-* = together》
refund[6] 〔 *v.* rɪ'fʌnd　*n.* 'ri,fʌnd 〕*v.*, *n.* 退錢；償還《 *re-* = back》
circumfuse 〔 ,sɝkəm'fjuz 〕*v.* 散布；圍繞；充溢
　《 *circum-* = around》

```
circum  +  fuse
   |        |
around  +  pour
```

circumfusion 〔 ,sɝkəm'fjuʒən 〕*n.* 周圍澆灌；散布；圍繞
confuse[3] 〔 kən'fjuz 〕*v.* 使混亂 (共同注入)
confusion[4] 〔 kən'fjuʒən 〕*n.* 混亂；騷亂
diffuse[7] 〔 *v.* dɪ'fjuz　*adj.* dɪ'fjus 〕*v.* 散布；擴散；流布；廣布
　adj. 散布的；擴散的 (注入各處)《 *dif-* = *dis-* = apart》
diffusion 〔 dɪ'fjuʒən 〕*n.* 散布；普及

diffusive〔dɪ'fjusɪv〕*adj.* 散布的；普及的

```
dif  +  fus  +  ive
 |        |       |
apart  +  pour  +  adj.
```

effuse〔ɛ'fjuz , ɪ-〕*v.* 流出；瀉出（流出）《*ef-* = *ex-* = out》
effusion〔ə'fjuʒən , ɪ-〕*n.* 流出；瀉出
effusive〔ɛ'fjusɪv , ɪ-〕*adj.*（感情）洋溢的；熱情奔放的
infuse[7]〔ɪn'fjuz〕*v.* 注入；灌輸（流入）《*in-* = into》
infusion[7]〔ɪn'fjuʒən〕*n.* 注入；灌輸
interfuse〔ˌɪntɚ'fjuz〕*v.* 充滿；散布（注入其間）
　　《*inter-* = between》
perfuse〔pɚ'fjuz〕*v.* 使充滿；撒滿；灑遍（完全注入）
　　《*per-* = thoroughly》
profuse[7]〔prə'fjus〕*adj.* 大量的；浪費的（流出太多）
　　《*pro-* = forth》

```
pro  +  fuse
 |        |
forth  +  pour
```

profusion[7]〔prə'fjuʒən〕*n.* 豐富；大量；浪費
refuse[2]〔rɪ'fjuz〕*v.* 拒絕；謝絕（流回）《*re-* = back》
refusal[4]〔rɪ'fjuzl̩〕*n.* 拒絕；謝絕
suffuse〔sə'fjuz〕*v.* 充盈；布滿（注入下方）《*suf-* = *sub-* = under》

```
suf  +  fuse
 |        |
under  +  pour
```

suffusion〔sə'fjuʒən〕*n.* 充滿；布滿
transfuse〔træns'fjuz〕*v.* 輸入；注射；輸血（從…注入～）
　　《*trans-* = across》
futile[7]〔'fjutl̩ , -tɪl〕*adj.* 無用的；無效的（無用的流入）
refute[5]〔rɪ'fjut〕*v.* 反駁；駁斥（流回 → 說回來）《*re-* = back》

220　**gam** = marriage（婚姻）

　　* 希臘文 *gamos*（= *marriage*）。

bigamy〔'bɪgəmɪ〕*n.* 重婚《*bi-* = two》
bigamist〔'bɪgəmɪst〕*n.* 重婚者
bigamous〔'bɪgəməs〕*adj.* 重婚的
monogamy[7]〔mə'nɑgəmɪ〕*n.* 一夫一妻（制）《*mono-* – single》

mono +	gam	+ y
|	|	|
single +	*marriage* +	*n.*

monogamist[7]〔mə'nɑgəmɪst〕*n.* 行一夫一妻制者
monogamous〔mə'nɑgəməs〕*adj.* 一夫一妻制的
polygamy〔pə'lɪgəmɪ〕*n.* 一夫多妻；一妻多夫；重婚
　《*poly-* = many》
polygamist〔pə'lɪgəmɪst〕*n.* 實行、贊成一夫多妻或一妻多夫者
polygamous〔pə'lɪgəməs〕*adj.* 一夫多妻的；一妻多夫的；
　多配偶的

221　**gastr** = stomach（胃；腹部）

　　* 希臘文 *gaster*（= *stomach*）。

gastric〔'gæstrɪk〕*adj.* 胃的
gastralgia〔gæs'trældʒɪə〕*n.* 胃痛《*alg* = pain》
gastritis〔gæs'traɪtɪs〕*n.* 胃炎《 *-itis* = inflammation（發炎）》
gastroenterology〔ˌgæstroˌɛntə'rɑlədʒɪ〕*n.* 胃腸病學

gastro +	enter	+ ology
|	|	|
stomach +	*intestine* +	*study of*

gastrology〔gæs'trɑlədʒɪ〕*n.* 胃病學

gastronomy 〔 gæs'trɑnəmɪ 〕 *n.* 美食學；（有地區特徵的）烹飪法

```
gastro + nom + y
  |        |     |
stomach + law + n.
```

gastropod 〔'gæstrə,pɑd 〕 *n.* 腹足綱軟體動物《*pod* = foot》
epigastrium 〔,ɛpɪ'gæstrɪəm 〕 *n.* 上腹部《*epi-* = upon》

222　ge = earth（地球；土地）　*希臘文 *ge*（= *earth*）。

apogee 〔'æpə,dʒi 〕 *n.* 遠地點（月球等距離地球最遠的點）；
（權利等的）頂點《*apo-* = away》
geocentric 〔,dʒio'sɛntrɪk 〕 *adj.* 以地球為中心的《*centr* = center》
geography[2] 〔 dʒi'ɑgrəfɪ 〕 *n.* 地理學

```
geo + graphy
 |     |
earth + writing
```

geology[7] 〔 dʒi'ɑlədʒɪ 〕 *n.* 地質學《*logy* = study》
geometry[5] 〔 dʒi'ɑmətrɪ 〕 *n.* 幾何學《*metr* = measure》
geothermal 〔,dʒio'θɝməl 〕 *adj.* 地熱的《*therm* = heat》
perigee 〔'pɛrə,dʒi 〕 *n.* 近地點（月球等距離地球最近之點）

```
peri + gee
 |     |
near + earth
```

223　gen = produce；race（生產；種族）

*拉丁文 *genus*（= *race*），*generare*（= *produce*），*gignere*
（= *bear*；*beget* 生產）；希臘文 *genesis*（= *origin*；*source*）。
在英語中，*gen* 的形式也經常用於「生產；產生」之意，再由
其演變而為「種；種族」等相關意思。

gene[4] 〔 dʒin 〕 *n.* 遺傳因子；基因

genealogy[7] 〔͵dʒɛnɪˈælədʒɪ 〕 *n.* 宗譜；血統；家系學；系圖學
 《*logy* = study》

general[1,2] 〔ˈdʒɛnərəl 〕 *adj.* 一般的；普遍的；概略的；大衆的
 n. 將軍；一般（有關全體）

generality 〔͵dʒɛnəˈrælətɪ 〕 *n.* 一般性；通則；概論

generalize[6] 〔ˈdʒɛnərəl͵aɪz 〕 *v.* 一般化；普遍化

```
gener  +  al  +  ize
  |        |       |
produce + adj. +  v.
```

generate[6] 〔ˈdʒɛnə͵ret 〕 *v.* 產生；發生；造成

generation[4] 〔͵dʒɛnəˈreʃən 〕 *n.* 產生；一代；同一代

generator[6] 〔ˈdʒɛnə͵retɚ 〕 *n.* 發電機；生產者；生殖者

generic[7] 〔 dʒəˈnɛrɪk 〕 *adj.* 屬的；類的

generous[2] 〔ˈdʒɛnərəs 〕 *adj.* 大方的；慷慨的；大量的；豐富的

degenerate[7] 〔 *v.* dɪˈdʒɛnə͵ret *adj.* , *n.* dɪˈdʒɛnərɪt 〕 *v.* 退步；
 落後；退化　*adj.* 退步的；落後的　*n.* 退步之物（種族變得很低）
 《*de-* = down》

```
de  +  gener  +  ate
  |        |        |
down  +  race  +  v.
```

engender[7] 〔 ɪnˈdʒɛndɚ , ɛn- 〕 *v.* 產生；生成（使產生）
 《*en-* = cause to be》

regenerate[7] 〔 rɪˈdʒɛnə͵ret 〕 *v.* 再生；重生（再生）《*re-* = again》

genesis[7] 〔ˈdʒɛnəsɪs 〕 *n.* 創始；（G- ）舊約聖經創世紀

genetics[6] 〔 dʒəˈnɛtɪks 〕 *n.* 遺傳學

genial[7] 〔ˈdʒinjəl 〕 *adj.* 愉快的；和藹的（天生的性情）

abiogenesis 〔͵æbɪəˈdʒɛnɪsɪs 〕 *n.* 自然發生；偶發
 《*a-* (without) + *bio* (life) + *genesis* (創始)》

```
a   +  bio  +  gene  +   sis
  |       |        |         |
without + life + produce + condition
```

biogenesis 〔,baɪo'dʒɛnəsɪs 〕 *n.* 生物發生;生源論

congenial[7] 〔 kən'dʒinjəl 〕 *adj.* 性格相同的;意氣相投的
（共同的性情）《*con-* = together》

endogenous 〔 ɛn'dɑdʒənəs 〕 *adj.* 內部產生的;由內部發展的
（由內產生）《*endo-* = inside》

```
endo  +   gen  + ous
  |        |       |
inside + produce + adj.
```

exogenous 〔 ɛks'ɑdʒɪnəs 〕 *adj.* 外長的;外來的（由外產生）
《*exo-* = outside》

homogeneity 〔,homədʒə'niətɪ , ,hamə- 〕 *n.* 同種;同質;同性
《*homo-* = same》

```
homo  +  gene  + ity
  |        |       |
same + produce + n.
```

indigenous[7] 〔 ɪn'dɪdʒənəs 〕 *adj.* 原產的《*indi-* = within》

genital[7] 〔'dʒɛnətḷ 〕 *adj.* 生殖的　*n.* (*pl.*) 生殖器

anthropogeny 〔,ænθrə'padʒɪnɪ 〕 *n.* 人類起源論《*anthropo* = man》

congenital 〔 kən'dʒɛnətḷ 〕 *adj.* （缺陷）天生的;先天的

pathogenic 〔,pæθə'dʒɛnɪk 〕 *adj.* 致病的;病原的（使人生病的）
《*patho* = disease》

primogenitor 〔,praɪmə'dʒɛnətɚ 〕 *n.* 祖先;始祖（最先出生的人）
《*primo-* = first》

progenitive 〔 pro'dʒɛnətɪv 〕 *adj.* 生殖的《*pro-* = forth》

progenitor 〔 pro'dʒɛnətɚ 〕 *n.* 祖先;前輩（父母之上的人）
《*pro-* = before ; *genitor* 父母親》

progeny 〔'pradʒənɪ 〕 *n.* 子孫;後裔;產物;成果（向前不斷產生）
《*pro-* = forward》

```
pro   + gen(e) + y
  |        |      |
forward + produce + n.
```

schizogenous 〔 skɪˈzɑdʒənəs 〕 *adj.* 分裂生殖的

《*schizo* = split (分裂)》

genius[4] 〔ˈdʒinjəs 〕 *n.* 天才；精靈；守護神 (天生的東西)

ingenious[6] 〔 ɪnˈdʒinjəs 〕 *adj.* 靈敏的；有天才的 (天生的才能)

《*in-* = in》

ingenuous[7] 〔 ɪnˈdʒɛnjʊəs 〕 *adj.* 坦白的；老實的 (天生未經琢磨的)

genocide[7] 〔ˈdʒɛnəˌsaɪd 〕 *n.* 種族滅絕；集體大屠殺 《*cide* = cut》

```
geno + cide
 |      |
race + cut
```

genteel 〔 dʒɛnˈtil 〕 *adj.* 上流的；有禮貌的 (家世好的)

gentile 〔ˈdʒɛntaɪl 〕 *n.* 異邦人；異教徒   *adj.* 異教徒的

gentle[2] 〔ˈdʒɛntḷ 〕 *adj.* 溫和的；文雅的；親切的 (天生好的)

genuine[4] 〔ˈdʒɛnjʊɪn 〕 *adj.* 真正的；真實的 (天生未經琢磨的)

genus 〔ˈdʒinəs 〕 *n.* 種；屬；類 (生下)

eugenics 〔 jʊˈdʒɛnɪks 〕 *n.* 優生學 《*eu-* = well》

```
eu + gen + ics
 |     |     |
well + race + study
```

pregnant[4] 〔ˈprɛgnənt 〕 *adj.* 懷孕的；充滿的 (生產前的情況)

《*pre-* = before》

cognate 〔ˈkɑgnet 〕 *adj.* 同源的；同性質的   *n.* 同源之人、物或字

(共同產生) 《*co-* = *com-* = together》

allergen 〔ˈæləˌdʒɛn 〕 *n.* 過敏原 《*allergy* 過敏症》

antigen 〔ˈæntədʒən 〕 *n.* 抗原 《*anti-* = against》

hydrogen[4] 〔ˈhaɪdrədʒən 〕 *n.* 氫 《*hydro* = water》

nitrogen[7] 〔ˈnaɪtrədʒən 〕 *n.* 氮 《*nitro* = niter (硝石)》

oxygen[4] 〔ˈɑksədʒən 〕 *n.* 氧 《*oxy* = acid (酸)》

224 **ger** = old (老的)

* 希臘文 *geras* (= *old age*)，*geron* (= *old man*)。

geriatrics〔‚dʒɛrɪ'ætrɪks 〕 *n.* 老年醫學；老年保健學
gerontocracy〔‚dʒɛrən'tɑkrəsɪ 〕 *n.* 老人政治《*cracy* = rule》
gerontology〔‚dʒɛrən'tɑlədʒɪ 〕 *n.* 老年醫學；老年學；老人學
gerontophobia〔 dʒə‚rɑntə'fobɪə 〕 *n.* 恐老（症）；憎恨老人

```
geronto + phob + ia
   |        |     |
  old   +  fear +  n.
```

225 **germ** = bud ; seed (芽 ; 種子)

* 拉丁文 *germ* (= *bud* ; *sprout* ; *seed*)。

germ[4]〔 dʒɝm 〕 *n.* 細菌；病菌
germy〔'dʒɝmɪ 〕 *adj.* 充滿細菌的；受細菌感染的
germfree〔'dʒɝm‚fri 〕 *adj.* 無菌的《 *-free* 表示「無⋯的」》
germiculture〔'dʒɝmə‚kʌltʃɚ 〕 *n.* 細菌培養（法）

```
germi + cult + ure
  |       |     |
 seed  + till +  n.
```

germinability〔‚dʒɝmɪnə'bɪlətɪ 〕 *n.* 發芽力《*ability* 能力》
germinal〔'dʒɝmənḷ 〕 *adj.* 幼芽的；初期的；未成熟的
germinant〔'dʒɝmənənt 〕 *adj.* 發芽的：有生長力的
germinate〔'dʒɝmə‚net 〕 *v.* 發芽；產生
germination〔‚dʒɝmə'neʃən 〕 *n.* 發芽；產生
germinative〔'dʒɝmə‚netɪv 〕 *adj.* 發芽的
germule〔'dʒɝmjul 〕 *n.* 小芽；初胚《 *-ule* 表示小的名詞字尾》
ovigerm〔'ovədʒɝm 〕 *n.* 原卵；胚卵《*ovi* = egg》

226　**gest , ger** = carry (攜帶；運送)

　　* 拉丁文 *gerere* (= *carry*)，過去分詞是 *gestus*。

gestate 〔 ˈdʒɛstet 〕 *v.* 懷孕；孕育；醞釀 (計畫)

gestation 〔 dʒɛsˈteʃən 〕 *n.* 懷孕；孕育；發展

gesticulate 〔 dʒɛsˈtɪkjə‚let 〕 *v.* 以動作表達；做表情 (身體運動)

gesture[3] 〔ˈdʒɛstʃɚ 〕 *n.* 手勢；表情；姿勢

congest 〔 kənˈdʒɛst 〕 *v.* 充滿；擁塞；阻塞；充血 (承載在一起)

　　《*con-* = together》

```
con   +  gest
 |        |
together  + carry
```

congestion[7] 〔 kənˈdʒɛstʃən 〕 *n.* 充滿；擁塞；充血

congestive[7] 〔 kənˈdʒɛstɪv 〕 *adj.* 充血的

decongest[7] 〔‚dikənˈdʒɛst 〕 *v.* 緩和…的擁擠；減輕 (瘀血、充血)

　　《*de-* = away》

digest[4] 〔 *v.* daɪˈdʒɛst　*n.* ˈdaɪdʒɛst 〕 *v.* 消化；了解；忍受

　　n. 分類；摘要 (分別搬運 → 分解成塊)《*di-* = *dis-* = apart》

digestible[7] 〔 daɪˈdʒɛstəbl̩ 〕 *adj.* 可消化的；易消化的；可摘要的

digestion[4] 〔 daɪˈdʒɛstʃən 〕 *n.* 消化

digestive[7] 〔 daɪˈdʒɛstɪv 〕 *adj.* (助) 消化的

egest 〔 iˈdʒɛst 〕 *v.* 排泄 (運送出去)《*e-* = *ex-* = out》

egesta 〔 iˈdʒɛstə 〕 *n.pl.* 排泄物

exaggerate[4] 〔 ɪgˈzædʒə‚ret 〕 *v.* 誇張；誇大 (超過程度的)

　　《*ex-* = out》

```
ex  + ag +  ger  + ate
 |     |     |      |
out +  to + carry + v.
```

exaggeration[5] 〔 ɪg‚zædʒəˈreʃən 〕 *n.* 誇張

indigestion[7] 〔‚ɪndəˈdʒɛstʃən ,‚ɪndaɪ- 〕 *n.* 消化不良《*in-* = not》

ingest〔ɪn'dʒɛst〕*v.* 吸收；嚥下（運入）《*in-* = into》

ingesta〔ɪn'dʒɛstə〕*n.pl.* 攝取物

ingestion〔ɪn'dʒɛstʃən〕*n.* 攝取

suggest[3]〔səg'dʒɛst, sə'dʒɛst〕*v.* 使想到；提議；暗示
（拿到～之下）《*sug-* = *sub-* = under》

suggestion[4]〔səg'dʒɛstʃən, sə'dʒɛstʃən〕*n.* 提議；暗示

---

227 glob = ball（球）   * 拉丁文 *globus*（= ball）。

global[3]〔'globḷ〕*adj.* 全球的；球形的

globule〔'glabjul〕*n.* 小球（體）；小滴《*-ule* 表示小的名詞字尾》

globoid〔'globɔɪd〕*adj.* 球形的；近似球形的   *n.* 球形；球形體
《*-oid* = like》

globose〔'globos〕*adj.* 球形的

globular〔'glabjələ〕*adj.* 球形的；全球的；完整的

conglobate〔kan'globet, 'kaŋglo,bet〕*v.* 使成球形

```
con + glob + ate
 |      |      |
with + ball +  v.
```

globefish〔'glob,fɪʃ〕*n.* 河豚

globetrotting〔'glob,tratɪŋ〕*n.* 環球旅行   *adj.* 環球旅行的
《*trot* 快步走》

---

228 gnath = jaw（顎）   * 希臘文 *gnathos*（= jaw）。

gnathic〔'næθɪk〕*adj.* 顎的

gnathion〔'neθɪɑn, 'næθɪ-〕*n.* 頜下點

gnathite〔'ne,θaɪt〕*n.* 顎形附器（節肢動物的一種口器）

gnathitis〔næ'θaɪtɪs〕*n.* 頜炎《*-itis* = inflammation（發炎）》

prognathous〔'pragnəθəs, prag'neθəs〕*adj.* 突顎的
《*pro-* = forward》

229　**gon** = angle（角）　*希臘文 *gonia*（= angle）。

diagonal[7]〔daɪ'æɡənḷ〕*adj.* 對角線的；斜紋的　*n.* 對角線；
斜紋布《*dia-* = across》

goniometry〔͵ɡonɪ'amɪtrɪ〕*n.* 測角（術）

```
gonio  +  metry
  |         |
angle  +  measure
```

trigonometry〔͵trɪɡə'namətrɪ〕*n.* 三角學《*tri-* = three》

pentagon[7]〔'pɛntə͵ɡan〕*n.* 五角形；五邊形《*penta-* = five》

hexagon[7]〔'hɛksə͵ɡan〕*n.* 六角形；六邊形《*hexa-* = six》

octagon[7]〔'aktə͵ɡan〕*n.* 八角形；八邊形《*octa-* = eight》

polygon〔'palɪ͵ɡan〕*n.* 多邊形；多角形《*poly-* = many》

orthogon〔'ɔrθəɡan〕*n.* 矩形；長方形《*ortho-* = straight ; right》

agonic〔e'ɡanɪk〕*adj.* 不成角的；無偏差的

```
a  +  gon  +  ic
|      |       |
not + angle + adj.
```

radiogoniometer〔͵redɪo͵ɡonɪ'amɪtɚ〕*n.* 無線電測向儀
《*radio* 無線電》

230　**gorg** , **gurg** = throat（喉嚨）

*古法文 *gorge*（= throat）；拉丁文 *gurges*（= throat ; whirlpool 漩渦），*gurgulio*（= gullet 咽喉）。

gorge[5]〔ɡɔrdʒ〕*n.* 峽谷；咽喉　*v.* 塞飽；狼吞虎嚥地吃

gorgeous[5]〔'ɡɔrdʒəs〕*adj.* 華麗的；燦爛的；極好的

disgorge〔dɪs'ɡɔrdʒ〕*v.* 吐出；嘔出；被迫交出（非法所得等）
《*dis-* = apart》

engorge〔ɛn'ɡɔrdʒ〕*v.* 大吃；狼吞虎嚥《*en-* = in》

regorge〔rɪˈgɔrdʒ〕v. 吐出；倒流《re- = back》

gurgle〔ˈgɝgl̩〕v. 潺潺地流；發出咯咯聲

ingurgitate〔ɪnˈgɝdʒəˌtet〕v. 狼吞虎嚥；大吃大喝；吞沒

```
in  +  gurgit  +  ate
|        |         |
in  +  throat  +  v.
```

regurgitate[7]〔riˈgɝdʒəˌtet〕v.（液體、氣體等）回流；（人、動物）反胃《re- = back》

231　grad , gress = walk（走）

> * 拉丁文 *gradus*（= *step*；*degree*）；*gradi*（= *walk*），
> 過去分詞是 *gressus*。

grade[2]〔gred〕n. 年級；階級；等級；成績　v. 分級；
分類（一步步）

gradation[7]〔greˈdeʃən〕n. 漸變；階級；等級

gradient[7]〔ˈgrediənt , -djənt〕n. 斜度；坡度

gradual[3]〔ˈgrædʒuəl〕adj. 逐漸的；漸次的

graduate[3]〔v. ˈgrædʒuˌet　n. ˈgrædʒuɪt〕v. 授予學位；畢業
n. 畢業生（學年漸漸晉昇）

```
gradu  +  ate
  |        |
walk   +  n., v.
```

graduation[4]〔ˌgrædʒuˈeʃən〕n. 畢業；分等級

degrade[6]〔dɪˈgred〕v. 降低；降職（階級下降）《de- = down》

degradation〔ˌdɛgrəˈdeʃən〕n. 惡化；退步

```
de   +  grad  +  ation
 |        |         |
down  +  walk  +   n.
```

downgrade[7]〔ˈdaʊnˌgred〕n. 下坡　v. 使降級；使降職

gravigrade〔'grævə,gred〕*adj.* 走路時步伐很重的（走路很重）

　《*gravi* = heavy》

postgraduate〔post'grædʒuɪt , -,et〕*n.* 研究生

　adj. 畢業後繼續研究的（畢業後）《*post-* = after》

retrograde〔'rɛtrə,gred〕*v.* 倒退；退後；退步　*adj.* 倒退的

　（走向後面）《*retro-* = backward》

retro　+　grade
｜　　　　｜
backward + *walk*

undergraduate[5]〔,ʌndɚ'grædʒuɪt , ,et〕*n.* 大學本部學生；大學

　肄業生　*adj.* 大學本部的；肄業生的（還沒畢業）《*under-* = below》

upgrade[6]〔'ʌp'gred〕*v.* 改良；提高　*n.* 增長；改善；上坡

　adj. , adv. 上坡的（地）（階級上升）《*up-* = up》

ingredient[4]〔ɪn'gridɪənt〕*n.* 成份；原料（進入的東西）《*in-* = in》

aggress〔ə'grɛs〕*v.* 侵略；發動攻勢（面向～走去）《*ag-* = *ad-* = to》

aggression[6]〔ə'grɛʃən〕*n.* 侵略；進攻

ag + gress + ion
｜　　｜　　｜
to + *walk* + *n.*

congress[4]〔'kɑngrəs〕*n.* 會議；〔美〕國會（一起去 → 集合）

　《*con-* = together》

　【解說】美國憲法規定「國會」（Congress）為最高立法機構。美國的
　　　　　國會採二院制，由「參議院」（the Senate）和「眾議院」
　　　　　（the House of Representatives）所組成。而台灣的國會則
　　　　　是指「立法院」（Legislative Yuan）。

digress[7]〔daɪ'grɛs〕*v.* 離題（離去）《*di-* = *dis-* = apart》

digressive〔də'grɛsɪv , daɪ-〕*adj.* 離題的；枝節的

di　+　gress + ive
｜　　　｜　　｜
apart + *walk* + *adj.*

egress〔 *n.* 'igrɛs *v.* i'grɛs 〕*n.* 出現 *v.* 出現；出去（走去外面）
《*e-* = *ex-* = out》

ingress〔'ɪngrɛs 〕*n.* 進入（走進）《*in-* = in》

progress[2]〔 *n.* 'prɑgrɛs *v.* prə'grɛs 〕*v.* 進步；進行 *n.* 進步
（走向前）《*pro-* = forward》

progressive[6]〔 prə'grɛsɪv 〕*adj.* 前進的；進步的

regression[7]〔 rɪ'grɛʃən 〕*n.* 退化；退步；回歸（往回走）
《*re-* = back》

retrogress〔'rɛtrə͵grɛs , ͵rɛtrə'grɛs 〕*v.* 後退；倒退（往後走）
《*retro-* = backward》

transgress〔 træns'grɛs 〕*v.* 踰越；違反（越過限度走去）
《*trans-* = across》

232 **gram** , **graph** = write（寫）

* 希臘文 *gramma*（ = *letter*），*graphein*（ = *write*）。

grammar[4]〔'græmɚ 〕*n.* 文法（寫法）

grammarian〔 grə'mɛrɪən 〕*n.* 文法家

barogram〔'bærə͵græm 〕*n.* 氣壓記錄表《*baro* = weight ; pressure》

cryptogram〔'krɪptə͵græm 〕*n.* 密碼；暗號（暗地寫文字）
《*crypto* = hidden》

```
crypto + gram
   |       |
hidden + write
```

diagram[6]〔'daɪə͵græm 〕*n.* 圖表（畫線的東西）《*dia-* = through》

epigram〔'ɛpə͵græm 〕*n.* 雋語；警句（寫在石頭上的東西 → 碑誌）
《*epi-* = upon》

monogram〔'mɑnə͵græm 〕*n.* 花押字（由姓和名第一個字母組合
而成的圖案）《*mono-* = single》

parallelogram〔͵pærə'lɛlə͵græm 〕*n.* 平行四邊形
（對面平行的圖形）《*parallel* 平行的》

program(me)[3]〔'progræm 〕*n.* 節目；計劃；（電腦）程式
（事先書寫的東西）《*pro-* = before》

programmer〔'progræmɚ 〕*n.* 安排節目者；計劃者；規劃
電腦程式者

```
pro  +  gramm  +   er
 |        |         |
before  +  write  + person
```

telegram[4]〔'tɛlə,græm 〕*n.* 電報（從遠方書寫送來的）
《*tele-* = far off》

gramophone〔'græməfon 〕*n.* 留聲機（古時的唱機）
《*phone* = sound》

graph[6]〔 græf，grɑf 〕*n.* 曲線圖；圖表　*v.* 以曲線圖表示

graphic[6]〔'græfɪk 〕*adj.* 圖表的；書寫的；生動的

autograph[6]〔'ɔtə,græf 〕*n.* 親筆（原稿）《*auto-* = self》

biography[4]〔 baɪ'ɑgrəfɪ 〕*n.* 傳記（記錄人的一生）《*bio* = life》

```
bio  +  graph  +  y
 |        |       |
life  +  write  + n.
```

autobiography[4]〔,ɔtəbaɪ'ɑgrəfɪ 〕*n.* 自傳（自己的傳記）

cacography〔 kə'kɑgrəfɪ 〕*n.* 拙劣的書法；錯誤的拼寫
（寫得不好）《*caco* = bad》

calligraphy[5]〔 kə'lɪgrəfɪ 〕*n.* 書法（寫得漂亮）《*calli* = beautiful》

choreography[7]〔,korɪ'ɑgrəfɪ 〕*n.* 舞蹈術；舞蹈（尤指芭蕾舞）

```
choreo  +  graph  +  y
  |          |       |
dance   +   write  + n.
```

dictograph〔'dɪktə,græf 〕*n.*（電話）竊聽器（暗中記下別人說
的話）《*dicto* = speak》

```
dicto  +  graph
  |         |
speak   +  write
```

字根 gam~gyr

geography[2] 〔 dʒiˈɑgrəfɪ 〕 *n.* 地理學 (記錄有關土地的)《*geo* = earth》

hydrography 〔 haɪˈdrɑgrəfɪ 〕 *n.* 水道學；水道測量學
《*hydro* = water》

lexicography 〔ˌlɛksəˈkɑgrəfɪ 〕 *n.* 辭典編纂 (法)
《*lexico(n)* = word》

lithography 〔 lɪˈθɑgrəfɪ 〕 *n.* 石板印刷術《*litho* = stone》

micrography 〔 maɪˈkrɑgrəfɪ 〕 *n.* 顯微鏡製圖；顯微鏡檢查
《*micro-* = small》

```
micro + graph + y
  |       |      |
small  + write + n.
```

monograph 〔ˈmɑnəˌgræf , -ˌgrɑf 〕 *n.* 專論；專文 (單一論述)
《*mono-* = single》

orthography 〔 ɔrˈθɑgrəfɪ 〕 *n.* 正確拼法；拼字法 (寫得正確)
《*ortho-* = right》

phonograph 〔ˈfonəˌgræf 〕 *n.* 留聲機；唱機 (= *gramophone*)

```
phono + graph
  |       |
sound  + write
```

photograph[2] 〔ˈfotəˌgræf 〕 *n.* 照片　*v.* 攝影 (用光來寫的東西)
《*photo* = light》

stenography 〔 stəˈnɑgrəfɪ 〕 *n.* 速寫；速記 (寫得狹窄 → 縮小)
《*steno* = narrow》

telegraph[4] 〔ˈtɛləˌgræf 〕 *n.* 電報；電信　*v.* 打電報
(從遠方書寫送來的)《*tele-* = far off》

topography 〔 toˈpɑgrəfɪ 〕 *n.* 地形學；地誌；地形 (對地方的描寫)
《*topo* = place》

233　**grand** = great (大的)

* 拉丁文 *grandis* (= *big* ; *great*) 。

grand[1] 〔 grænd 〕 *adj.* 偉大的；堂皇的；高貴的；盛大的

grandeur〔'grændʒɚ〕*n.* 偉大；高貴；富麗堂皇

grandiloquent〔græn'dɪləkwənt〕*adj.* 誇大的；詞藻浮誇的
（說大話）《*loqu* = speak》

grandiose〔'grændɪˌos〕*adj.* 宏偉的；堂皇的；浮誇的
《*-ose* 形容詞字尾》

```
grandi + ose
   |      |
 great + adj.
```

grandiosity〔ˌgrændɪ'ɑsətɪ〕*n.* 宏偉；誇大

aggrandize〔'ægrənˌdaɪz , ə'græn-〕*v.* 增大；增加；提高；
擴充（使變大）《*ag-* = *ad-* = to》

aggrandizement〔ə'grændɪzmənt〕*n.* 增大；增加

234　**grat** = please（使高興）

　　* 拉丁文 *gratus*（= *pleasing*），*gratia*（= *favor* ; *grace*）。

grateful[4]〔'gretfəl〕*adj.* 感謝的；感激的（充滿歡喜的）

ungrateful[7]〔ʌn'gretfəl〕*adj.* 不知感激的《*un-* = not》

gratify〔'grætəˌfaɪ〕*v.* 使高興；使滿意（使高興）《*-ify* = make》

gratification[7]〔ˌgrætəfə'keʃən〕*n.* 滿足；令人愉快之事

gratitude[4]〔'grætəˌtjud〕*n.* 感激《*-itude* 抽象名詞字尾》

ingrate〔'ɪngret〕*n.* 忘恩負義的人《*in-* = not》

ingratitude〔ɪn'grætəˌtjud〕*n.* 忘恩負義

```
in + grat + itude
 |     |      |
not + please + n.
```

gratis〔'gretɪs , 'grætɪs〕*adv.* , *adj.* 免費地（的）

gratuitous[7]〔grə'tjuətəs〕*adj.* 沒有報酬的；免費的；無故的

gratuity[7]〔grə'tjuətɪ〕*n.* 小費；禮物；退役慰勞金

gratulate 〔'grætʃʊ‚let〕 v. 歡迎；祝賀；表示欣喜

gratulant 〔'grætʃələnt〕 adj. 欣喜的；祝賀的

grace[4] 〔gres〕 n. 優雅；溫文；仁慈；美德　v. 增光；增色（可喜的）

graceful[4] 〔'gresfəl〕 adj. 優雅的；得體的

gracious[4] 〔'greʃəs〕 adj. 親切的；仁慈的

disgrace[6] 〔dɪs'gres〕 n. 不名譽；恥辱　v. 玷污《dis- = not》

```
dis +  gra  + ce
 |      |      |
not + please + n.
```

agree[1] 〔ə'gri〕 v. 同意；贊成（使對方高興）《a- = ad- = to》

agreeable[4] 〔ə'griəbḷ〕 adj. 令人愉快的

agreement[1] 〔ə'grimənt〕 n. 協定；一致；協調；同意

congratulate[4] 〔kən'grætʃə‚let〕 v. 祝賀；恭賀《con- = together》

congratulation[2] 〔kən‚grætʃə'leʃən〕 n. 祝賀；慶賀；(pl.) 賀詞

ingratiate 〔ɪn'greʃɪ‚et〕 v. 討好；逢迎（使高興向著某人）
　　《in- = toward》

ingratiation 〔ɪn‚greʃɪ'eʃən〕 n. 討好；巴結

235　**grav** = heavy（重的）

> * 拉丁文 **gravis**（= heavy），**gravare**（= make heavy ; cause grief）。〔變化型〕griev。

grave[4] 〔grev〕 adj. 嚴肅的；重大的

gravity[5] 〔'grævətɪ〕 n. 地心引力；萬有引力

gravitate 〔'grævə‚tet〕 v. 吸引；沈澱；沈降

gravitation 〔‚grævə'teʃən〕 n. 引力作用；沈降

gravid 〔'grævɪd〕 adj. 懷孕的（= pregnant）（變重）

gravida 〔'grævɪdə〕 n. 孕婦《 -a = feminine 表示婦女的名詞字尾》

gravimeter 〔grə'vɪmətɚ〕 n. 比重計（= gravity meter）
　　《meter 計量器》

aggravate[7] 〔'ægrə,vet〕 v. (負擔等) 加重；惡化

《 **ag-** = **ad-** = to 》

```
ag  +  grav  + ate
|       |       |
to  + heavy  +  v.
```

aggravation[7] 〔,ægrə'veʃən〕 n. 加重；惡化

grieve[4] 〔 griv 〕 v. 悲傷；傷心 (使心情沈重)

grief[4] 〔 grif 〕 n. 悲傷；憂愁

aggrieve[7] 〔 ə'griv 〕 v. 苦惱《 **ag-** = **ad-** = to 》

236 greg = collect；flock (聚集；群)

* 拉丁文 **grex** (= *flock*) ，**gregare** (= *collect*) 。

gregarious[7] 〔 grɪ'gɛrɪəs 〕 adj. 群居的；合群的 (集合群體)

aggregate 〔 v. 'ægrɪ,get adj., n. 'ægrɪgɪt 〕 v. 合計；集合

adj. 聚合的；總計的   n. 集合；總數 (集合)《 **ag-** = **ad-** = to 》

aggregation 〔,ægrɪ'geʃən〕 n. 集合；集合體

congregate[7] 〔'kɑngrɪ,get〕 v. 集合；聚集 (集聚在一起)

《 **con-** = together 》

congregation 〔,kɑngrɪ'geʃən〕 n. 集合；集會

```
con   +  greg  + ation
|        |        |
together + collect +  n.
```

segregate[7] 〔 v. 'sɛgrɪ,get adj. 'sɛgrəgɪt 〕 v. 隔離；分離

adj. 分離的 (離開群體)《 **se-** = apart 》

segregation[7] 〔,sɛgrɪ'geʃən〕 n. 分離；分開；種族隔離

【解說】美國在 1896-1964 年之間，對黑人是採行所謂的隔離政策
（ **segregation** ），主張自欺欺人的「隔離而平等」，當時的許
多做法都很可笑，像是規定白人坐公車車廂的前半部，黑人坐
後半部，其實這都是一種種族歧視的行為。

egregious 〔ɪˈgridʒəs 〕 *adj.* 非常的；太過的（離開群體）
《*e-* = *ex-* = out》

```
 e  +  greg  +  ious
 |      |       |
out  +  flock  +  adj.
```

237 **gyn** = woman（女人）

* 希臘文 *gune*（= *woman*）。〔變化型〕*gynec*。

gynandromorph 〔 dʒaɪˈnændrə‚mɔrf 〕 *n.* 陰陽人

```
 gyn   +  andro  +  morph
  |         |        |
woman  +  man   +  form
```

gynarchy 〔ˈdʒaɪnɑrkɪ 〕 *n.* 女人政治 《*arch* = rule》
gynecology 〔‚dʒaɪnɪˈkɑlədʒɪ 〕 *n.* 婦科醫學 《*logy* = study》
gynecopathy 〔‚dʒɪnɪˈkɑpəθɪ 〕 *n.* 婦科病 《*path* = disease》
gynephobia 〔‚dʒaɪnɪˈfobɪə 〕 *n.* 恐女症 《*phob* = fear》
gynoecium 〔 dʒaɪˈnisɪəm 〕 *n.* 雌蕊群；雌蕊 《*oec* = house》

238 **gyr** = circle（圓）　　* 希臘文 *guros*（= *circle*）。

gyration 〔 dʒaɪˈreʃən 〕 *n.* 旋轉；迴旋
gyrocompass 〔ˈdʒaɪro‚kʌmpəs 〕 *n.* 迴轉羅盤 《*compass* 羅盤》
gyrodynamics 〔‚dʒaɪrodaɪˈnæmɪks 〕 *n.* 陀螺動力學

```
gyro   +  dynam  +  ics
  |         |        |
circle +  power  +  n.
```

gyrofrequency 〔ˈdʒaɪro‚frikənsɪ 〕 *n.*（電子等的）迴旋頻率
《*frequency* 頻率》

gyrograph 〔ˈdʒaɪrəˌgræf 〕 *n.* 旋轉測度器《*graph* = write》

gyroidal 〔 dʒaɪˈrɔɪdəl 〕 *adj.* 螺旋形的；螺旋形運轉的《 *-oid* = like》

gyroplane 〔ˈdʒaɪrəˌplen 〕 *n.* 旋翼機《*plane* 飛機》

gyroscope 〔ˈdʒaɪrəˌskop 〕 *n.* 陀羅儀；迴轉儀

gyrostabilizer 〔ˌdʒaɪrəˈstebəˌlaɪzə, -ˈstæbə- 〕 *n.* 迴轉穩定器
（利用迴轉儀以減少船或飛機搖晃的裝置）《*stable* 穩定的》

gyrostatics 〔ˌdʒaɪrəˈstætɪks 〕 *n.* 迴旋運動論

```
gyro  +  stat  +  ics
 |        |       |
circle + stand +  n.
```

239　**hab** = have（有）

＊拉丁文 ***habere***（ = *have*；*hold*；*keep* ），***habitare***（ = *live* ）。
〔變化型〕*hibit*。

habit[2] 〔ˈhæbɪt 〕 *n.* 習慣；習性；衣服　*v.* 裝扮（稟賦）

habitual[4] 〔 həˈbɪtʃuəl 〕 *adj.* 習慣的

habitant[7] 〔ˈhæbətənt 〕 *n.* 居民；居住者（有地方 → 居住）

```
habit  +  ant
  |        |
 live  + person
```

habituate 〔 həˈbɪtʃuˌet 〕 *v.* 使習慣

habitude 〔ˈhæbəˌtjud, -tud 〕 *n.* 習慣；習性；氣質；體質
《 *-itude* 抽象名詞字尾》

habitat[6] 〔ˈhæbəˌtæt 〕 *n.* （動植物的）產地；棲息地；居留地

habitation[7] 〔ˌhæbəˈteʃən 〕 *n.* 居住

cohabit[7] 〔 koˈhæbɪt 〕 *v.* 同居（一起住）《*co-* = *con-* = together》

cohabitant 〔 koˈhæbətənt 〕 *n.* 同居者

inhabit[6] 〔 ɪnˈhæbɪt 〕 *v.* 居住（住在裡面）
《*in-* = in》

```
in  +  habit
 |       |
in  +  live
```

字根
hab~ident

inhabitation 〔 ɪnˌhæbəˋteʃən 〕 *n.* 居住
inhabitant[6] 〔 ɪnˋhæbətənt 〕 *n.* 居民

```
in + habit +   ant
 |     |         |
in +  live  + person
```

exhibit[4] 〔 ɪgˋzɪbɪt 〕 *v.* 表現；展示　 *n.* 展覽品（拿出去）《*ex-* = out》
exhibition[3] 〔 ˌɛksəˋbɪʃən 〕 *n.* 表現；博覽會
inhibit[7] 〔 ɪnˋhɪbɪt 〕 *v.* 抑制；禁止；防止（拿在手中 → 抑制）
　《*in-* = in》
inhibition[7] 〔 ˌɪnhɪˋbɪʃən 〕 *n.* 抑制；禁止

```
in + hibit + ion
 |     |       |
in +  have +  n.
```

prohibit[6] 〔 proˋhɪbɪt 〕 *v.* 禁止；阻止（在前面壓制）《*pro-* = before》
prohibition[6] 〔 ˌproəˋbɪʃən 〕 *n.* 禁止；禁令；禁律

240　 hagi = holy（神聖的）　　* 希臘文 *hagios*（= holy）。

hagiarchy 〔 ˋhægɪˌɑrkɪ , ˋhedʒɪ- 〕 *n.* 聖徒統治；神權政治
　《*arch* = rule》
hagiography 〔 ˌhægɪˋɑgrəfɪ , ˌhedʒɪ- 〕 *n.* 聖徒傳記
　《*graph* = write》
hagiolatry 〔 ˌhægɪˋɑlətrɪ , ˌhedʒɪ- 〕 *n.* 聖徒崇拜

```
hagio +  latry
  |        |
holy  + worship
```

hagiology 〔 ˌhægɪˋɑlədʒɪ , ˌhedʒɪ- 〕 *n.* 聖徒文學《*logy* = study》
hagioscope 〔 ˋhægɪəˌskop , ˋhedʒɪ- 〕 *n.* （十字形教堂供人觀看
　神壇之）內壁小窗《*scope* = look》

241　**hal** = breathe（呼吸）

　　* 拉丁文 **halare**（= breathe），**halitus**（= breath）。

exhale[7]〔εks'hel, ɪg'zel〕v. 呼（氣）；呼出；散發《**ex-** = out》
inhale[7]〔ɪn'hel〕v. 吸入《**in-** = in》
halitosis〔,hælə'tosɪs〕n. 口臭《**-osis** 表示病變狀態的名詞字尾》

242　**hal** = salt（鹽）　　* 希臘文 **hals**（= salt）。

halide〔'hælaɪd, 'helaɪd〕n., adj. 鹵化物（的）《**-ide** 表示「化物」》
halobacteria〔,hælobæk'tɪrɪə〕n. 鹽桿菌《**bacteria** 病菌》
halobiotic〔,hælobaɪ'ɑtɪk〕adj. 海洋（生物）的；鹽生的《**bio** = life》
halogen〔'hælədʒən, -dʒɪn〕n. 鹵素（鹵素可以和很多金屬形成鹽類）

```
halo  +  gen
 |        |
salt  +  produce
```

haloid〔'hælɔɪd, 'helɔɪd〕adj. 鹵素的　n. 鹵素之金屬鹽
halophile〔'hælə,faɪl〕n. 適鹽生物；喜鹽生物《**phil** = love》

243　**hap** = luck（運氣）

　　* 古代挪威語 **happ**（= good luck）。

hap〔hæp〕n. 幸運；偶然發生之事
mishap[7]〔'mɪs,hæp, mɪs'hæp〕n. 不幸；災禍；惡運《**mis-** = bad》

```
mis  +  hap
 |       |
bad  +  luck
```

happen[1]〔'hæpən〕v. 發生；偶然發生；碰巧
happening[7]〔'hæpənɪŋ〕n. 事件

haphazard[7]〔 *n.* ′hæp͵hæzə·d *adj.* , *adv.* ′hæp′hæzə·d 〕*n.* 偶然
  adj. , *adv.* 偶然的（地）；隨便的（地）《*hazard* = game of dice》
perhaps[1]〔 pə·′hæps 〕*adv.* 可能；或許（憑藉運氣）《*per-* = through》

244　heli = sun（太陽）　　* 希臘文 *helios*（ = sun）。

heliocentric〔͵hilɪo′sɛntrɪk 〕*adj.* 以太陽為中心的《*centr* = center》
heliogram〔′hilɪo͵græm 〕*n.* 日光反射信號《*gram* = write》
heliograph〔′hilɪo͵græf 〕*n.* 日光反射信號機；太陽照相機；
  日照計《*graph* = write》
helioscope〔′hilɪə͵skop , ′hiljə- 〕*n.* 觀日望遠鏡
  《*scope* 表示「觀察～的器具」》

```
helio + scope
  |        |
 sun  +  look
```

heliotropic〔͵hilɪə′trɑpɪk , -′tropɪk 〕*adj.* 向日性的
  《*trop*(*e*) = turn》
heliotropism〔͵hilɪ′ɑtrəpɪzm̩ 〕*n.* （植物的）向日性
helium〔′hilɪəm 〕*n.* 氦（化學元素，多存於太陽大氣中）

245　helic = spiral（螺旋的）　　* 希臘文 *helix*（ = spiral）。

helix〔′hilɪks 〕*n.* 螺旋線；螺旋飾；耳輪
helical〔′hɛlɪkl̩ 〕*adj.* 螺旋的
helicline〔′hɛlɪ͵klaɪn 〕*n.* 漸升的彎曲坡道；螺旋形彎道

```
helic + (c)line
  |        |
spiral + bend
```

helicograph〔′hɛləko͵græf , -͵grɑf 〕*n.* （畫螺旋曲線用的）螺旋規
  《*graph* = write》

helicoid 〔ˈhɛlɪˌkɔɪd 〕 *n.* 螺旋面   *adj.* 形成螺旋的；具螺紋的；
螺旋面的《 *-oid* = like》

helicopter[4] 〔ˈhɛlɪˌkɑptɚ 〕 *n.* 直昇機（有螺旋狀的翅膀）
《希臘文 *pteron* = wing》

246   **hem** = blood（血）

* 希臘文 *haima*（ = blood）。〔變化型〕 *hemat , em*。

hemal 〔ˈhiməl 〕 *adj.* 血管的；（位於）心臟和大血管一側的

hematic 〔 hiˈmætɪk 〕 *adj.* 血的；補血的   *n.* 補血藥

hematology 〔ˌhiməˈtalədʒɪ 〕 *n.* 血液學《 *logy* = study》

hematothermal 〔ˌhɛmətoˈθɝməl 〕 *adj.*（哺乳動物、鳥等）溫血
的；恆溫的《 *thermal* 熱的》

hematocryal 〔ˌhɛməˈtakrɪəl 〕 *adj.* 冷血的

```
hemato +  cry  +  al
  |          |       |
blood   + cold  + adj.
```

hemophilia 〔ˌhiməˈfɪlɪə 〕 *n.* 血友病

```
hemo + phil +  ia
  |       |       |
blood + love +  n.
```

hemorrhage[7] 〔ˈhɛmərɪdʒ 〕 *n.* 出血《 *rrhage* = burst ; break》

hemorrhoids 〔ˈhɛməˌrɔɪdz 〕 *n.pl.* 痔瘡；痔
《希臘文 *rhoia* = a flowing》

hemostatic 〔ˌhiməˈstætɪk 〕 *adj.* 止血的   *n.* 止血器；止血鉗；
止血劑《 *static* 靜止的》

hematuria 〔ˌhiməˈtjurɪə 〕 *n.* 血尿（症）《 *ur* = urine（尿））

an(a)emia 〔 əˈnimɪə 〕 *n.* 貧血（症）《 *an-* = without》

tox(a)emia 〔 taksˈimɪə 〕 *n.* 毒血症《 *toxic* 有毒的》

ur(a)emia 〔 juˈrimɪə 〕 *n.* 尿毒症

247 hepat = liver (肝)

* 希臘文 *hepar* (= *liver*) 。

hepatic〔hɪˈpætɪk〕*adj.* 肝臟的；肝臟色的

hepatitis〔͵hɛpəˈtaɪtɪs〕*n.* 肝炎《 *-itis* = inflammation (發炎)》

hepatectomy〔͵hɛpəˈtɛktəmɪ〕*n.* 肝切除術《*tom* = cut》

hepatopathy〔͵hɛpəˈtɑpəθɪ〕*n.* 肝病

hepato	+	path	+	y
liver	+	*disease*	+	*n.*

hepatosis〔͵hɛpəˈtosɪs〕*n.* 肝機能病；肝功能障礙

gastrohepatic〔͵gæstrohɪˈpætɪk〕*adj.* 胃肝的《*gastro* = stomach》

248 her = heir (繼承人)

* 拉丁文 *heres* (= *heir*) 。

heir[3]〔ɛr〕*n.* 繼承人 *v.* 繼承

heiress[7]〔ˈɛrɪs〕*n.* 女繼承人

heirloom[7]〔ˈɛrˈlum, -͵lum〕*n.* 傳家寶；祖傳物

（隱約出現之物 → 寶物）《*loom* 隱約出現》

heirship〔ˈɛrʃɪp〕*n.* 繼承人之地位；繼承權

《 *-ship* = state，表示狀態的名詞字尾》

coheir〔koˈɛr〕*n.* 共同繼承人《*co-* = *com-* = together》

co	+	heir
together	+	*heir*

heredity[7]〔həˈrɛdətɪ〕*n.* 遺傳（被繼承的東西）

hereditament〔͵hɛrəˈdɪtəmənt〕*n.* 世襲財產

hereditary[7]〔həˈrɛdə͵tɛrɪ〕*adj.* 世襲的；祖傳的

heritage[6]〔ˈhɛrətɪdʒ〕*n.* 遺產

heritable〔ˈhɛrətəbļ〕*adj.* 可繼承的

inherit[5] 〔 ɪn'hɛrɪt 〕 v. 繼承；延續（財產、權利等）；承受；
遺傳（性質、特性等）《*in-* = in》

inheritance[7] 〔 ɪn'hɛrətəns 〕 n. 繼承；遺傳

```
in +  her  +  it  + ance
 |     |       |       |
in + heir + go  +  n.
```

inheritor 〔 ɪn'hɛrətɚ 〕 n. 繼承人

inheritrix 〔 ɪn'hɛrətrɪks 〕 n. 女性繼承人《*rix* = feminine（女性）》

disinherit 〔,dɪsɪn'hɛrɪt 〕 v. 剝奪繼承權；剝奪人權或特權
《*dis-* = apart ; away》

249　**herb** = grass（草）　* 拉丁文 *herba*（= *grass*）。

herb[5] 〔 ɝb , hɝb 〕 n. 草；草藥

herbage 〔 'ɝbɪdʒ , 'hɝ- 〕 n. 草本植物；草《 *-age* 表示集合名詞的字尾》

herbal[7] 〔 'hɝbl̩ , 'ɝbl̩ 〕 adj. 草本的；草的

herbalism 〔 'hɝbəlɪzəm , 'ɝbə- 〕 n. 草藥學

```
herb  +  al  + ism
 |        |      |
grass  +  adj. +  n.
```

herbalist 〔 'hɝblɪst , 'ɝbl̩- 〕 n. 植物學家；採集植物者；草藥商；
草藥醫生

herbary 〔 'hɝ,bərɪ 〕 n. 草藥園《 *-ary* 表示地點的名詞字尾》

herbicide 〔 'hɝbə,saɪd 〕 n. 除草藥《*cide* = cut》

herbiferous 〔 hɝ'bɪfərəs 〕 adj. 生草的《 *-iferous* = bearing》

```
herb  + ifer  + ous
 |        |       |
grass  + bear  +  adj.
```

herbivore[7] 〔 'hɝbɪ,vor 〕 n. 草食性動物《*vor* = eat》

herbivorous 〔 hɝ'bɪvərəs 〕 adj. 草食的

250 **here , hes** = stick (黏著)

* 拉丁文 *haerere* (= *stick*)。〔變化型〕*hes*。

adhere[7] 〔 əd'hɪr , æd- 〕 *v.* 黏著；附著《*ad-* = to》
adherence[7] 〔 əd'hɪrəns 〕 *n.* 黏著；忠誠
adherent 〔 əd'hɪrənt 〕 *adj.* 黏著的 *n.* 擁護者

```
ad  +  her  + ent
 |      |      |
to  + stick + adj.
```

adhesion 〔 əd'hiʒən , æd- 〕 *n.* 黏附；黏著
adhesive[7] 〔 əd'hisɪv 〕 *adj.* 黏著性的 *n.* 接著劑；膠帶
cohere 〔 ko'hɪr 〕 *v.* 黏著；附著 (黏在一塊)
  《*co-* = *con-* = together》
coherence[7] 〔 ko'hɪrəns 〕 *n.* 一致；連貫

```
co   +  her  + ence
 |       |      |
together + stick +  n.
```

coherent[6] 〔 ko'hɪrənt 〕 *adj.* 一致的；連貫的
cohesion[7] 〔 ko'hiʒən 〕 *n.* 結合；凝聚力
cohesive[7] 〔 ko'hisɪv 〕 *adj.* 有黏著力的；凝聚性的
inhere 〔 ɪn'hɪr 〕 *v.* 存在；固有；具有 (附著於體內)《*in-* = in》
inherence 〔 ɪn'hɪrəns 〕 *n.* 固有；天生；天賦
inherent[6] 〔 ɪn'hɪrənt 〕 *adj.* 固有的；與生俱來的

```
in +  here  + (e)nt
 |     |       |
in + stick  +  adj.
```

inhesion 〔 ɪn'hiʒən 〕 *n.* 固有；天賦 (= *inherence*)
hesitate[3] 〔'hɛzə,tet 〕 *v.* 猶豫；遲疑 (黏著不易分離)
hesitation[4] 〔,hɛzə'teʃən 〕 *n.* 猶豫
hesitant[7] 〔'hɛzətənt 〕 *adj.* 猶豫的

251 **hibern** = winter (冬天)　　* 拉丁文 *hiems* (= *winter*)。

hibernal 〔 haɪˈbɜnḷ 〕 *adj.* 冬季的；寒冷的
hibernate[7] 〔ˈhaɪbə‚net 〕 *v.* 冬眠；過冬
hibernacle 〔ˈhaɪbə‚nækḷ 〕 *n.* 動物冬眠處
hibernaculum 〔‚haɪbəˈnækjələm 〕 *n.* (動物或植物之芽的) 冬眠用之外被；冬芽

252 **hist** = tissue (組織)　　* 希臘文 *histos* (= *web*)。

histiocyte 〔ˈhɪstɪə‚saɪt 〕 *n.* 組織細胞《*cyt* = cell》
histioid 〔ˈhɪstɪɔɪd 〕 *adj.* 組織樣的；蜘蛛網狀的《 *-oid* = like》
histogenesis 〔‚hɪstəˈdʒɛnəsɪs 〕 *n.* 組織發生《*genesis* 誕生》
histology 〔 hɪsˈtalədʒɪ 〕 *n.* 組織學《*logy* = study》
histolysis 〔 hɪsˈtaləsɪs 〕 *n.* 組織溶解

histo +	lys +	is
tissue +	*loosen* +	*n.*

histopathology 〔‚hɪstopəˈθalədʒɪ 〕 *n.* 病理組織學
《*path* = disease》

253 **horr** = tremble (發抖)

* 拉丁文 *horrere* (= *tremble*)。

horrible[3] 〔ˈharəbḷ 〕 *adj.* 可怕的；恐怖的；極厭惡的
horrid 〔ˈhɔrɪd , ˈhar- 〕 *adj.* 可怕的；極可惡的
horrify[4] 〔ˈhɔrə‚faɪ , ˈharə- 〕 *v.* 使驚駭；使戰慄；使恐懼
horrific[7] 〔 hɔˈrɪfɪk , ha- 〕 *adj.* 令人毛骨悚然的；可怖的
horrification 〔‚hɔrəfəˈkeʃən , ‚har- 〕 *n.* 驚駭；戰慄
horror[3] 〔ˈharə 〕 *n.* 恐怖；戰慄；極度憎惡

abhor[7] 〔 əb'hɔr , æb- 〕 v. 憎惡；痛恨 (毛髮豎立地離開)《 ab- = away 》

```
ab  +  hor
|      |
away + tremble
```

abhorrent 〔 əb'hɔrənt , æb- , -'hɑr- 〕 adj. 嫌惡的；令人痛恨的
abhorrence 〔 əb'hɔrəns , æb- , -'hɑr- 〕 n. 憎惡；痛恨；嫌惡的
事情

254 hum = man (人)

* 拉丁文 *humanus* (= *human*) ， *homo* (= *man*) 。
〔變化型〕 *hom* 。

human[1] 〔'hjumən 〕 adj. 人類的 n. 人類
humane[7] 〔 hju'men 〕 adj. 人道的；慈愛的
humanism 〔'hjumən,ɪzəm 〕 n. 人道；人性；人文主義
humanitarian[6] 〔 hju,mænə'tɛrɪən 〕 n.
人道主義者；慈善家 adj. 人道主義的
humanity[4] 〔 hju'mænətɪ 〕 n. 人類；
人性；人道

```
human + ity
|       |
man   + n.
```

humanize 〔'hjumə,naɪz 〕 v. 賦予人性；使成為人；教化
humankind[7] 〔'hjumən,kaɪnd 〕 n. 人類 (= *mankind*)
homicide[7] 〔'hɑmə,saɪd 〕 n. 殺人 (者)《 *cide* = cut 》
homage[7] 〔'hɑmɪdʒ 〕 n. 效忠；臣服；尊敬《 *hom(o)* = man ; servant 》

255 hum = ground (地面)

* 拉丁文 *humus* (= *ground*) 。

humble[2] 〔'hʌmbl̩ 〕 adj. 卑下的；謙遜的；粗陋的
v. 使卑下；貶低 (地位低下的)

humiliate[6] 〔 hju'mɪlɪˌet 〕 v. 使丟臉；屈辱；使羞愧
（將對手按倒在地）

humiliation[7] 〔 hjuˌmɪlɪ'eʃən 〕 n. 丟臉；屈辱

humility[7] 〔 hju'mɪlətɪ 〕 n. 謙卑；謙恭（變得低下）

humus 〔 'hjuməs 〕 n. 腐植土；沃土

exhume 〔 ɪg'zjum , ɪk'sjum 〕 v. 掘出；發掘；使重視
（向地面以外）《*ex-* = out》

```
ex  +  hume
 |       |
out +  ground
```

inhume 〔 ɪn'hjum 〕 v. 埋葬；土葬（送入地裡）《*in-* = into》

posthumous 〔 'pastʃuməs 〕 adj. 死後的；遺著的；死後出版的
（埋葬之後的）《*post-* = after》

256　**hyal** = glass（玻璃）　　* 希臘文 *hualos*（= *glass*）。

hyalite 〔 'haɪəˌlaɪt 〕 n. 玻璃蛋白石《 *-lite* 表示「石頭」》

hyalogen 〔 haɪ'ælədʒən , -ˌgɛn , 'haɪəlo- 〕 n. 透明蛋白原

hyalograph 〔 'haɪəloˌgræf , -ˌgraf 〕 n. 玻璃蝕刻器《*graph* = write》

hyalography 〔ˌhaɪə'lagrəfɪ 〕 n. 玻璃蝕刻術

hyaloid 〔 'haɪəˌlɔɪd 〕 adj. 透明的；玻璃狀的　　n.（眼球的）玻璃
體膜（= *hyaloid membrane*）《 *-oid* = like》

hyaloplasm 〔 'haɪələˌplæzm̩ 〕 n.（細胞的）透明質

```
hyalo  +  plasm
  |         |
glass  +  form
```

257　**hydr** = water（水）　　* 希臘文 *hudor*（= *water*）。

hydrant 〔 'haɪdrənt 〕 n. 給水栓；消防栓

字根 hab~ident

hydrate〔ˈhaɪdret, -drɪt〕*n.* 水化物；氫氧化物 *v.* 使成水化物
hydraulic〔haɪˈdrɔlɪk〕*adj.* 液壓的；油壓的
hydroelectric〔ˌhaɪdro‧ɪˈlɛktrɪk〕*adj.* 水電的；水力發電的
hydrogen[4]〔ˈhaɪdrədʒən, -dʒɪn〕*n.* 氫《*gen* = produce》
hydrogenate〔ˈhaɪdrədʒənˌet, -dʒɪn-〕*v.* 使與氫化合

```
hydro  +   gen   + ate
  |         |        |
water  + produce +  v.
```

hydrography〔haɪˈdrɑgrəfɪ〕*n.* 水道學；水道測量學
    《*graphy* = writing》
hydrolysis〔haɪˈdrɑləsɪs〕*n.* 加水分解；水解作用（用水來分解）
    《*lys* = loosen》
hydrophobia〔ˌhaɪdrəˈfobɪə〕*n.* 恐水症；狂犬病（害怕水）
    《*phob* = fear》
hydroplane〔ˈhaɪdrəˌplen〕*n.* 水上飛機；水上快艇
hydrotherapy〔ˌhaɪdrəˈθɛrəpɪ〕*n.* 水療法（用水治療）
    《*therapy* 治療法》
hydrotropism〔haɪˈdrɑtrəˌpɪzəm〕*n.*（植物）向水性《*trop* = turn》

```
hydro + trop + ism
  |       |      |
water + turn +  n.
```

dehydrate[7]〔diˈhaɪdret〕*v.* 脫水；使變乾（除去水）《*de-* = *dis-* = away》

258　hyet = rain（雨）　* 希臘文 *huetos*（= *rain*）。

hyetal〔ˈhaɪɪtḷ〕*adj.* 雨的；雨量的
hyetograph〔ˈhaɪətəˌgræf, -ˌgrɑf〕*n.* 雨量（分布）圖
    《*graph* = write》
hyetography〔ˌhaɪɪˈtɑgrəfɪ〕*n.* 雨量分布學
hyetology〔ˌhaɪɪˈtɑlədʒɪ〕*n.* 降水學《*logy* = study》
hyetometer〔ˌhaɪɪˈtɑmətɚ〕*n.* 雨量表；雨量器《*meter* 計量器》

259　**hygr** = wet（濕的）　　* 希臘文 *hugros*（= *wet*）。

hygrology〔haɪˈɡrɑlədʒɪ〕*n.* 濕度學
hygrostat〔ˈhaɪɡrəˌstæt〕*n.* 恆濕器；濕度調節器

> hygro　+　stat
> ｜　　　｜
> *wet*　+　*stand*

hygrothermograph〔ˌhaɪɡrəˈθɝməˌɡræf〕*n.* 溫濕計（能同時
記錄溫度和濕度）《*thermo* = heat》

260　**hypno** = sleep（睡覺）　　* 希臘文 *hupnos*（= *sleep*）。

hypnotic[7]〔hɪpˈnɑtɪk〕*adj.* 催眠的；易催眠的
　n.（易）被催眠者；催眠藥
hypnotist〔ˈhɪpnətɪst〕*n.* 施催眠術者
hypnotism〔ˈhɪpnəˌtɪzəm〕*n.* 催眠術；催眠狀態
hypnotize[7]〔ˈhɪpnəˌtaɪz〕*v.* 使進入催眠狀態；使入迷
hypnosis[7]〔hɪpˈnosɪs〕*n.* 催眠狀態；催眠術

> hypno　+　sis
> ｜　　　｜
> *sleep*　+　*n.*

hypnophobia〔ˌhɪpnəˈfobɪə〕*n.* 睡眠恐懼症《*phob* = fear》
hypnotherapy〔ˌhɪpnoˈθɛrəpɪ〕*n.* 催眠療法《*therapy* 治療法》

261　**hyps** = high（高的）　　* 希臘文 *hupsos*（= *height*）。

hypsicephaly〔ˌhɪpsɪˈsɛfəlɪ〕*n.* 尖頭（畸形）
　《希臘文 *kephale* = head》
hypsography〔hɪpˈsɑɡrəfɪ〕*n.* 比較地勢學；測高學；地勢；
　地勢圖；地貌表示法《*graph* = write》
hypsometer〔ˌhɪpˈsɑmɪtɚ〕*n.* 沸點測高計；三角測高儀

262 **hyster** = womb (子宮)

* 希臘文 *hustera* (= womb)。

hysteria[7] 〔 hɪsˈtɪrɪə 〕 *n.* 歇斯底里

【解說】 古代的人認爲，婦女得歇斯底里症是因爲子宮機能失調所引起。

hysterical[6] 〔 hɪsˈtɛrɪkl̩ 〕 *adj.* 歇斯底里的

hysterectomy 〔 ˌhɪstəˈrɛktəmɪ 〕 *n.* 子宮切除 (術) 《 *tom* = cut 》

hysterocatalepsy 〔 ˌhɪstərəˈkætəlɛpsɪ 〕 *n.* 癔病性僵住症
《 *catalepsy* 僵住症 》

263 **icon** = image (形象；偶像)

* 希臘文 *eikon* (= image)。

iconic[7] 〔 aɪˈkɑnɪk 〕 *adj.* 圖像的；偶像的

iconoclast[7] 〔 aɪˈkɑnəˌklæst 〕 *n.* 反對偶像崇拜者；打破傳統信仰
(或習俗) 者

```
icono + clas +   t
  |       |       |
image + break + person
```

iconography 〔 ˌaɪkənˈɑgrəfɪ 〕 *n.* (某一主題的) 圖像記錄；
圖示法；肖像研究 《 *graph* = write 》

iconolatry 〔 ˌaɪkəˈnɑlətrɪ 〕 *n.* 偶像崇拜 《 *latry* = worship 》

iconology 〔 ˌaɪkəˈnɑlədʒɪ 〕 *n.* 圖像學；圖像；象徵手法
《 *logy* = study 》

264 **ident** = the same (相同)

* 拉丁文 *idem* (= the same)。

identic 〔 aɪˈdɛntɪk 〕 *adj.* 措辭相同的；形式相同的

identify[4]〔 aɪˈdɛntəˌfaɪ 〕*v.* 確認；辨識；鑑定《 *-ify* = make》

identification[4]〔 aɪˌdɛntəfəˈkeʃən 〕*n.* 身份證明

identity[3]〔 aɪˈdɛntətɪ 〕*n.* 身份

265　**ideo** = idea（想法）　　　＊希臘文 *idea*（= idea）。

ideogram〔ˈɪdɪəˌgræm , ˈaɪdɪə- 〕*n.* 表意字（如漢字）；表意符號
（如 +, −, =, & ）《 *gram* = write》

ideology[7]〔ˌaɪdɪˈalədʒɪ , ˌɪd- 〕*n.* 意識形態《 *logy* = study》

ideological〔ˌaɪdɪəˈladʒɪkl̩ 〕*adj.* 意識形態的

ideologist〔ˌaɪdɪˈalədʒɪst 〕*n.* 思想理論家；意識形態專家

ideomotor〔ˌaɪdɪəˈmotɚ 〕*adj.*（觀）念（運）動的《 *mot* = move》

266　**idio** = personal；distinct（個人的；獨特的）

＊希臘文 *idios*（= personal；distinct）。

idiographic〔ˌɪdɪəˈgræfɪk 〕*adj.* 個案研究的（研究個人）
《 *graph* = write》

idiom[4]〔ˈɪdɪəm 〕*n.* 某一民族的特別語法；成語；慣用語

idiomatic〔ˌɪdɪəˈmætɪk 〕*adj.* 表現某一語言特性的；慣用的

idiomorphic〔ˌɪdɪəˈmɔrfɪk 〕*adj.* 具有其特有形狀的（形狀獨特）
《 *morph* = form》

idio	+	morph	+	ic
personal	+	*form*	+	*adj.*

idiopathic〔ˌɪdɪəˈpæθɪk 〕*adj.* 自發症的；原發病的（非由他病引
起的）《 *path* = disease；suffering》

idiosyncrasy[7]〔ˌɪdɪəˈsɪnkrəsɪ , -ˈsɪŋ- 〕*n.* 個人心理的特點；
癖性；特質（個人的特質）《 *idio*（ personal ）+ *syn-*（ together ）+
crasy（ mixing ））

267 **idol** = image (形象；偶像)

> * 拉丁文 **idol** (= image)；希臘文 **eidolon** (= phantom)，
> **eidos** (= shape ; form)。

idol[4]〔ˈaɪdḷ〕 n. 偶像；(多神教所崇拜的) 神
idolize[7] 〔ˈaɪdḷ͵aɪz〕 v. 把…當偶像崇拜
idolatry 〔aɪˈdɑlətrɪ〕 n. 偶像崇拜；盲目崇拜《**latry** = worship》
idolum 〔aɪˈdoləm〕 n. 幻象；謬論

268 **ign** = fire (火) * 拉丁文 **ignis** (= fire)。

ignite[7] 〔ɪgˈnaɪt〕 v. 點燃；激起
ignition[7] 〔ɪgˈnɪʃən〕 n. 燃燒；點火裝置
ignitability 〔ɪg͵naɪtəˈbɪlətɪ〕 n. 可燃性《**ability** 能力》
igneous 〔ˈɪgnɪəs〕 adj. (似) 火的；【地質】火成的
ignescent 〔ɪgˈnɛsn̩t〕 adj. (撞擊後) 發出火花的；火爆的
  n. (撞擊後) 發出火花的物質《 **-escent** = becoming (形容詞字尾)》
ignimbrite 〔ˈɪgnɪmbraɪt〕 n. 熔結凝灰岩；熔灰岩

> ign + imbr + ite
> |　　|　　|
> fire + rain + n.

ignitron 〔ɪgˈnaɪtrɑn〕 n. 引燃管《 **-tron** = electron (電子)》
ignis fatuus 〔ˈɪgnɪsˈfætʃʊəs〕 n. 磷火；鬼火；幻想
  《拉丁文 **ignis fatuus** = foolish fire》
reignite 〔͵riɪgˈnaɪt〕 v. 重新點燃；重新激起《 **re-** = again》

269 **insul** = island (島) * 拉丁文 **insula** (= island)。

insular[7] 〔ˈɪnsələ˞〕 adj. 島嶼的；島國根性的；偏狹的
insularity 〔͵ɪnsəˈlærətɪ〕 n. 島國的根性；偏狹

insulate[7] (ˈɪnsəˌlet) v. 隔離；絕緣
insulation[7] (ˌɪnsəˈleʃən) n. 隔離；孤立

```
insul + ation
  |       |
island +  n.
```

insulator (ˈɪnsəˌletɚ, ˈɪnsjʊ-) n. 絕緣體；隔絕物
island[2] (ˈaɪlənd) n. 島；島嶼；島狀物 v. 使成為島；孤立
isle[5] (aɪl) n. 島 v. 使成為島；置於島上
islet[7] (ˈaɪlɪt) n. 小島《 -et 表示小的名詞字尾》
isolate[4] (ˈaɪslˌet, ˈɪs-) v. 使隔離；使孤立

```
isol + ate
  |      |
island +  v.
```

isolation[4] (ˌaɪslˈeʃən, ˌɪsə-) n. 隔離；孤立
peninsula[6] (pəˈnɪnsələ) n. 半島（幾乎成為島的）《pen- = almost》

270 **it** = go (走)   * 拉丁文 ire (= go)，itio (= going)。

itineracy[7] (aɪˈtɪnərəsɪ, ɪ-) n. 巡迴；遊歷（巡迴而行）
itinerant[7] (aɪˈtɪnərənt, ɪ-) adj. 巡迴的；流動的；遊歷的
    n. 巡迴工作者；巡迴傳教士
itinerary[7] (aɪˈtɪnəˌrɛrɪ, ɪ-) n. 旅行路線；旅行計劃
    adj. 旅行的；巡迴的；遊歷的
itinerate[7] (aɪˈtɪnəˌret, ɪ-) v. 巡迴；遊歷
ambit (ˈæmbɪt) n. 周圍；範圍（走過四周）《amb- = ambi- = round》
ambition[3] (æmˈbɪʃən) n. 野心；企圖；抱負；渴望的事物
    （為求取名聲而來回走著）

```
amb + it + ion
 |      |     |
round + go +  n.
```

ambitious[4] (æmˈbɪʃəs) adj. 有野心的；渴望的

circuit[5] 〔 'sɝkɪt 〕 n. 周圍；環行；繞行一周（走過四周）
《*circu-* = *circum-* = around》
circuitous 〔 sə'kjuɪtəs 〕 adj. 迂迴的；繞行的
circuity[7] 〔 sə'kjuətɪ 〕 n. 迂曲；迂迴
coition 〔 ko'ɪʃən 〕 n. 性交（= *coitus*）（一塊兒去）
《*co-* = *com-* = together》
initiate[5] 〔 v. ɪ'nɪʃɪˌet adj. , n. ɪ'nɪʃɪɪt 〕 v. 創始；發起；啓蒙；傳授
祕訣；使入會 adj. 創始的；初期的；啓蒙的；新加入的
n. 初學者；新進者；入會者（走入內部）《*in-* = into》
initiation[7] 〔 ɪˌnɪʃɪ'eʃən 〕 n. 創始；發起

字根 ideo~it

```
in + iti + ation
 |     |     |
into + go +  n.
```

initiative[6] 〔 ɪ'nɪʃɪˌetɪv 〕 n. 起步；初步；主動
adj. 自發的；起初的；率先的
initiator 〔 ɪ'nɪʃɪˌetɚ 〕 n. 創始者；發起人
initial[4] 〔 ɪ'nɪʃəl 〕 adj. 最初的；開始的 n. 姓名的首字母
v. 簽姓名的首字母於～
perish[5] 〔 'pɛrɪʃ 〕 v. 死；毀滅；腐壞（全走光了）《*per-* = thoroughly》
perishable[7] 〔 'pɛrɪʃəbḷ 〕 adj. 易壞的；易死的
sedition 〔 sɪ'dɪʃən 〕 n. 煽動叛亂的言論或行動；暴動；叛亂
（分散人心的話）《*sed-* = *se-* = apart》

```
sed + it + ion
 |    |    |
apart + go +  n.
```

seditionary 〔 sɪ'dɪʃənˌɛrɪ 〕 n. 煽動叛亂者
seditious 〔 sɪ'dɪʃəs 〕 adj. 煽動性的
transit[6] 〔 'trænsɪt , -zɪt 〕 n. 通過；橫斷；變遷 v. 通過；經過；
過境（橫著穿過）《*trans-* = across》

```
trans + it
  |      |
across + go
```

transition[6] 〔 træn'zɪʃən 〕 *n.* 轉移；變遷

transitional 〔 træn'zɪʃənḷ 〕 *adj.* 轉變的；過渡期的

transitive 〔'trænsətɪv 〕 *adj.* 及物的；變遷的；轉移的；中間的
　n. 及物動詞

transitory[7] 〔'trænsə,torɪ , -,tɔrɪ 〕 *adj.* 短暫的；頃刻的

transient[7] 〔'trænʃənt 〕 *adj.* 短暫的；片刻的；易變的
　n. 過境客；短期逗留者

issue[5] 〔'ɪʃu , 'ɪʃju 〕 *v.* 發行　*n.* 發行；議題；（書刊的）期

271　jec t , jac = throw（投擲）

* 拉丁文 *jacere*（ = *throw* ; *cast* ; *lie* 躺 ），*jactare*（ = *toss about* ）。

abject[7] 〔 æb'dʒɛkt , 'æbdʒɛkt 〕 *adj.* 不幸的；可憐的；卑鄙的
　（被丟棄）《*ab-* = away》

abjection 〔 æb'dʒɛkʃən 〕 *n.* 落魄；恥辱

abjectly 〔 æb'dʒɛktlɪ , 'æbdʒɛktlɪ 〕 *adv.* 可憐地

conjecture[7] 〔 kən'dʒɛktʃɚ 〕 *v.* 推想；猜想　*n.* 推測；臆測；推想
　（共同投擲 → 將二者並列而加以推量比較）《*con-* = together》

```
con   +  ject  +  ure
 |        |        |
together + throw +  n.
```

deject 〔 dɪ'dʒɛkt 〕 *v.* 使沮喪；使灰心（投至下方）《*de-* = down》

dejected[7] 〔 dɪ'dʒɛktɪd 〕 *adj.* 沮喪的

dejectedly 〔 dɪ'dʒɛktɪdlɪ 〕 *adv.* 沮喪地

dejection[7] 〔 dɪ'dʒɛkʃən 〕 *n.* 沮喪

eject[7] 〔 ɪ'dʒɛkt 〕 *v.* 噴出；投出；排斥；逐出（向外投）
　《*e-* = *ex-* = out》

ejection[7] 〔 ɪ'dʒɛkʃən , i- 〕 *n.* 噴出；噴出物

ejective[7] 〔 ɪ'dʒɛktɪv 〕 *adj.* 噴出的

ejectment 〔 ɪ'dʒɛktmənt 〕 *n.* 逐出；（租用權之）剝奪

ejector 〔 ɪ'dʒɛktɚ 〕 *n.* 驅逐者；噴射器

inject[6] 〔 ɪn'dʒɛkt 〕 v. 注射；投入；加入（投擲進來）《in- = into》

injectable 〔 ɪn'dʒɛktəbḷ 〕 adj. 可注射的

injection[6] 〔 ɪn'dʒɛkʃən 〕 n. 注射（液）；注入

injector 〔 ɪn'dʒɛktɚ 〕 n. 注射者；噴射器

interject 〔 ˌɪntɚ'dʒɛkt 〕 v. 突然插話；打斷（投入其間）

  《inter- = between》

interjection 〔 ˌɪntɚ'dʒɛkʃən 〕 n. 感歎詞；插入語

```
inter  +  ject  + ion
  |        |       |
between + throw +  n.
```

interjectional 〔 ˌɪntɚ'dʒɛkʃənḷ 〕 adj. 插入的

interjectory 〔 ˌɪntɚ'dʒɛktərɪ 〕 adj. 插入的

object[12] 〔 'ɑbdʒɪkt 〕 n. 物體；目標；目的（被擲於眼前的東西）

  《ob- = before》

object[22] 〔 əb'dʒɛkt 〕 v. 反對；拒絕（投向反對者）《ob- = against》

objection[4] 〔 əb'dʒɛkʃən 〕 n. 反對；異議

objectionable[7] 〔 əb'dʒɛkʃənəbḷ 〕 adj. 會引起反對的；令人討厭的

objectify 〔 əb'dʒɛktəˌfaɪ 〕 v. 使客觀化；使具體化；使物化

objectification 〔 əbˌdʒɛktəfə'keʃən 〕 n. 具體化；物化

objectivate 〔 əb'dʒɛktəˌvet 〕 v. 使客觀化；使具體化

objective[4] 〔 əb'dʒɛktɪv 〕 n. 目標；實體　adj. 實在的；客觀的；
  目標的

objectivity[7] 〔 ˌɑbdʒɛk'tɪvətɪ 〕 n. 客觀性

```
ob   +  ject  + iv(e) + ity
 |       |       |       |
against + throw +  adj.  +  n.
```

objectless 〔 'ɑbdʒɛktlɪs 〕 adj. 無目的的；無受詞的

objector 〔 əb'dʒɛktɚ 〕 n. 反對者

project[2] 〔 v. prə'dʒɛkt　n. 'prɑdʒɛkt 〕 v. 計劃；設計；投影；突出
  n. 計劃；提案；事業（投擲到前方）《pro- = forward》

projectile[7] 〔 prə'dʒɛktḷ , -tɪl 〕 *n.* 拋射物；發射體　*adj.* 投射的；發射的

projection[6] 〔 prə'dʒɛkʃən 〕 *n.* 計劃

projectionist 〔 prə'dʒɛkʃənɪst 〕 *n.* 放映師

projective 〔 prə'dʒɛktɪv 〕 *adj.* 投影的；投射的

projectively 〔 prə'dʒɛktɪvlɪ 〕 *adv.* 投影地

projector[7] 〔 prə'dʒɛktə 〕 *n.* 發起人；設計師；放映機；放映師

reject[2] 〔 rɪ'dʒɛkt 〕 *v.* 拒絕；駁回；捨棄（投擲回去）《*re-* = back》

rejectamenta 〔 rɪˌdʒɛktə'mɛntə 〕 *n.pl.* 廢物

rejectee 〔 rɪˌdʒɛk'ti 〕 *n.* 遭拒絕者

rejecter 〔 rɪ'dʒɛktə 〕 *n.* 拒絕者；拋棄者

rejection[4] 〔 rɪ'dʒɛkʃən 〕 *n.* 拒絕；排洩物

```
re  +  ject  + ion
 |       |       |
back + throw +  n.
```

rejectionist 〔 rɪ'dʒɛkʃənɪst 〕 *adj.* 拒絕承認他人的

rejective 〔 rɪ'dʒɛktɪv 〕 *adj.* 拒絕的

subject[2] 〔 *v.* səb'dʒɛkt　*adj.* , *n.* 'sʌbdʒɪkt 〕 *v.* 使服從；使蒙受；使罹患　*adj.* 從屬的；受支配的；容易罹患～的　*n.* 國民；主詞；主題；科目（投身於～之下）《*sub-* = under》

subjection 〔 səb'dʒɛkʃən 〕 *n.* 隸屬；從屬；服從

subjective[6] 〔 səb'dʒɛktɪv 〕 *adj.* 主觀的；主格的　*n.* 主格

subjectivity 〔 ˌsʌbdʒɛk'tɪvətɪ 〕 *n.* 主觀性

trajectory[7] 〔 trə'dʒɛktərɪ , -trɪ 〕 *n.* 彈道；拋射物的弧形行程（由一端投到另一端的路線）《*tra-* = *trans-* = across》

adjacent[7] 〔 ə'dʒesṇt 〕 *adj.* 近鄰的；毗連的（朝向～投擲）《*ad-* = to》

ejaculate[7] 〔 ɪ'dʒækjuˌlet 〕 *v.* 射出；突然喊叫（投擲出去）

《*e-* = *ex-* = out》

```
e  +  jacul  + ate
 |       |       |
out + throw +  v.
```

ejaculation 〔 ɪˌdʒækjə'leʃən , i- 〕 *n.* 射出；突發的叫聲

interjacent〔͵ɪntɚˈdʒesənt〕*adj.* 在中間的；居間的（被擲於其間）
　《*inter-* = between》

interjacence；**-ency**〔͵ɪntɚˈdʒesəns(ɪ)〕*n.* 在中間

subjacent〔sʌbˈdʒesn̩t〕*adj.* 低下的；下層的（被投往下面）
　《*sub-* = under》

superjacent〔͵supɚˈdʒesn̩t〕*adj.* 在上的《*super-* = above》

272　join , junct , jug = join（加入）

　　* 古法文 *joindre*（= *join*）；拉丁文 *jungere*（= *join*），
　　junctus（= *joined*），*jugum*（= *yoke* 軛）。

join[1]〔dʒɔɪn〕*v.* 連接；加入；聯合

joint[2]〔dʒɔɪnt〕*n.* 關節　*v.* 連接　*adj.* 共同的；共有的

adjoin[7]〔əˈdʒɔɪn〕*v.* 連接；鄰近（與～相連）《*ad-* = to》

conjoin[7]〔kənˈdʒɔɪn〕*v.* 聯合；連接《*con-* = together》

disjoin[7]〔dɪsˈdʒɔɪn〕*v.* 分離；拆散；散開（使失去連接）
　《*dis-* = apart》

```
dis  +  join
 |        |
apart  +  join
```

disjointed[7]〔dɪsˈdʒɔɪntɪd〕*adj.* 脫臼的；雜亂無章的

rejoin[7]〔͵riˈdʒɔɪn〕*v.* 再加入；再結合《*re-* = again》

subjoin[7]〔səbˈdʒɔɪn〕*v.* 補述；增補；添加（在下面加入）
　《*sub-* = under》

junction[7]〔ˈdʒʌŋkʃən〕*n.* 連接；會合處

juncture[7]〔ˈdʒʌŋktʃɚ〕*n.* 連接；時刻；時機

adjunct[7]〔ˈædʒʌŋkt〕*n.* 附屬物；助手；修飾語
　adj. 附屬的；輔助的；臨時的（加上去）《*ad-* = to》

```
ad  +  junct
 |       |
to  +   join
```

adjunction 〔 ə'dʒʌŋkʃən 〕 *n.* 添加；附加
conjunct[7] 〔 kən'dʒʌŋkt 〕 *adj.* 聯合的；結合的（連接在一起）
　《*con-* = together》
conjunction[4] 〔 kən'dʒʌŋkʃən 〕 *n.* 連結；結合；連接詞

> con　+ junct + ion
> ｜　　　｜　　　｜
> *together* + *join* + *n.*

disjunct 〔 dɪs'dʒʌŋkt 〕 *adj.* 分離的；不連續的（不連接的）
　《*dis-* = not》
disjunction[7] 〔 dɪs'dʒʌŋkʃən 〕 *n.* 分離；分裂
injunction[7] 〔 ɪn'dʒʌŋkʃən 〕 *n.* 命令；禁止令（進入連接 → 受約束）
　《*in-* = into》
subjunction 〔 səb'dʒʌŋkʃən 〕 *n.* 增補；添加（在下面加入）
　《*sub-* = under》
subjunctive[7] 〔 səb'dʒʌŋktɪv 〕 *n.* 假設語氣　 *adj.* 假設語氣的
conjugal 〔 'kɑndʒʊɡl̩ 〕 *adj.* 婚姻的；夫妻（間）的（結合在一起的）
　《*con-* = together》

273　**journ** = day（一天）

> *　拉丁文 *dies*（= *day*），*diurnalis*（= *daily*）；
> 　法文 *journee*（= *day*）。

journal[3] 〔 'dʒɝnl̩ 〕 *n.* 日記；日報；雜誌（每天的東西）
journalism[5] 〔 'dʒɝnl̩ˌɪzəm 〕 *n.* 新聞學；新聞雜誌業；報紙雜誌的
　文體；報章雜誌
journey[3] 〔 'dʒɝnɪ 〕 *n.* 旅程；旅行　 *v.* 旅行（一天的旅程）
adjourn[7] 〔 ə'dʒɝn 〕 *v.* 延期《*ad-* = to》

> ad + journ
> ｜　　｜
> *to* + *day*

sojourn 〔 *v.* so'dʒɝn *n.* 'sodʒɝn 〕*v.* 逗留；寄居　*n.* 逗留；寄居
（在歲月之下 → 過日子）《*so-* = *sub-* = under》

diary[2] （'daɪərɪ）*n.* 日記（ =*journal* ）《拉丁文 *dies* = day》

diurnal 〔 daɪ'ɝnḷ 〕*adj.* 一日的；白天的
《拉丁文 *diurnalis* = daily》　*cf.* **nocturnal**（夜的）

274　jud = judge（判斷；審判）

* 拉丁文 *judex*（ =*judge* ），*judicare*（ =*judge* ）。

judge[2] 〔 dʒʌdʒ 〕*v.* 審判；評判；判斷　*n.* 法官；裁判（顯示法律）
《拉丁文 *jus*（ law ）+ *dicare*（ point out ）》

judg(e)ment[2] （'dʒʌdʒmənt ）*n.* 判定；裁判；判斷；意見

ju	+	dg	+ ment
law	+	point out	+ n.

judicatory 〔'dʒudɪkə,torɪ , -,tɔrɪ 〕*adj.* 裁判的；司法的
n. 裁判所；法庭

judicature （'dʒudɪkətʃɚ ）*n.* 裁判；司法官；法院

judicial[7] 〔 dʒu'dɪʃəl 〕*adj.* 司法的；公平的

judiciary 〔 dʒu'dɪʃɪ,ɛrɪ , -'dɪʃərɪ 〕*adj.* 司法的；法官的
n. 司法制度；法官

judicious[7] 〔 dʒu'dɪʃəs 〕*adj.* 明智的；思慮深的（有判斷力）

adjudicate 〔 ə'dʒudɪ,ket 〕*v.* 判決；裁判《*ad-* = to》

ad	+ judic	+ ate
to	+ judge	+ v.

prejudice[6] （'prɛdʒədɪs ）*n.* 偏見；成見；傷害　*v.* 使有偏見；
使有成見；給與損害（事先的判斷）《*pre-* = before》

sub judice 〔 sʌb'dʒudɪsi 〕*adv.* 【拉丁文】在審理中；尚未判決
《*sub-* = under》

275   **jur** = swear (發誓)   * 拉丁文 *jurare* (= *swear*)。

abjure 〔 əb'dʒʊr，æb- 〕 v. 宣誓放棄 (立誓脫離) 《*ab-* = away》

abjuration 〔ˌæbdʒʊ'reʃən 〕 n. 宣誓放棄

adjure 〔 ə'dʒʊr 〕 v. 命令；懇求 (向～發誓) 《*ad-* = to》

adjuration 〔ˌædʒʊ'reʃən 〕 n. 命令；懇求

conjure[1] 〔 kən'dʒʊr 〕 v. 懇求 《*con-* = together》

conjure[2] 〔'kʌndʒɚ，'kɑn- 〕 v. 施魔術；召喚 (靈魂等)
(共同發誓)

conjuration 〔ˌkɑndʒʊ'reʃən 〕 n. 召喚；魔法；懇求

```
con    +  jur   + ation
 |         |        |
together + swear +  n.
```

perjure[7] 〔'pɝdʒɚ 〕 v. 作偽證 《*per-* = over》

perjury[7] 〔'pɝdʒərɪ 〕 n. 偽證 (罪)

276   **just** = law；right (法律；正當的)

* 拉丁文 *jus* (= *law*；*right*)。〔變化型〕*juris*。

just[1] 〔 dʒʌst 〕 *adj.* 正直的；公平的；公正的；精確的
adv. 正巧；剛好；剛才；僅僅

justice[3] 〔'dʒʌstɪs 〕 n. 正義；審判；司法

justify[5] 〔'dʒʌstəˌfaɪ 〕 v. 證明為正當；為～辯護 (使正確)
《 *-ify* = make》

adjust[4] 〔 ə'dʒʌst 〕 v. 調整；調節；適應；調停 (使正確) 《*ad-* = to》

adjustment[4] 〔 ə'dʒʌstmənt 〕 n. 調整；調節

```
ad  + just  + ment
 |      |       |
to  +  law  +   n.
```

injustice[6] 〔 ɪn'dʒʌstɪs 〕 n. 不公正；不公平 《*in-* = not》

unjust[7] 〔 ʌn'dʒʌst 〕 *adj.* 不正的；不當的《*un-* = not》

unjustifiable[7] 〔 ʌn'dʒʌstə‚faɪəbḷ 〕 *adj.* 不合理的；無法接受的；
錯誤的

juridical 〔 dʒʊ'rɪdɪkḷ 〕 *adj.* 裁判（上）的；合法的；法律上的

jurisconsult 〔 ‚dʒʊrɪskən'sʌlt , -'kɑnsʌlt 〕 *n.* 民法學家；國際法
學家；法律學家（思考法律的人）《*consult* = consider》

juris + consult
|　　　|
law + *consider*

jurisdiction[7] 〔 ‚dʒʊrɪs'dɪkʃən 〕 *n.* 司法（權）；司法機關；管轄
（區域）（陳述法律的事物）《*diction* = saying》

jurisprudence 〔 ‚dʒʊrɪs'prudn̩s 〕 *n.* 法律學；法律體系
（有關法律的技術）《*prudence* = skill》

jurist 〔 'dʒʊrɪst 〕 *n.* 法律學者；法律著作家；法學生

jury[5] 〔 'dʒʊrɪ 〕 *n.* 陪審團；評判委員會

【解說】英美的陪審團制度又稱為「人民陪審制」，它和我國的「法官審
理制」是不一樣的。「人民陪審制」是由人民擔任陪審員，來參
與刑事訴訟的審判，通常陪審員只要認定被告是否有罪，至於適
用什麼法律和刑罰，仍由法官決定。

juror 〔 'dʒʊrɚ 〕 *n.* 陪審團之一員；評判員

injure[3] 〔 'ɪndʒɚ 〕 *v.* 傷害；損害；破壞（做不正當的事）《*in-* = not》

in + jure
|　　|
not + *right*

injurious[7] 〔 ɪn'dʒʊrɪəs 〕 *adj.* 有害的

injury[3] 〔 'ɪndʒərɪ 〕 *n.* 傷害；損害；侮辱；無禮

277　juven , jun = young（年輕的）

* 拉丁文 *juvenis*（= *young*），*junior*（= *younger*）。

junior[4] 〔 'dʒunjɚ 〕 *adj.* 年少的；資淺的

juvenescence 〔ˌdʒuvə'nɛsn̩s 〕 *n.* 變年輕；返老還童

> juven + escence
> | |
> *young* + *beginning*

juvenile[5] 〔'dʒuvən̩l , 'dʒuvəˌnaɪl 〕 *adj.* 青少年的；不成熟的
juvenilia 〔ˌdʒuvɪ'nɪlɪə 〕 *n.pl.*（藝術家或作家）少年時代的文藝
作品；適合少年兒童的文藝作品
juvenocracy 〔ˌdʒuvə'nɑkrəsɪ 〕 *n.* 青年政體；青年執政的國家
   《*cracy* = rule》
rejuvenate[7] 〔 rɪ'dʒuvəˌnet 〕 *v.*（使）返老還童；（使）恢復活力
   《*re-* = again》
rejuvenesce 〔 rɪˌdʒuvə'nɛs 〕 *v.*（使）返老還童

278   lab , lep = take ; seize（抓住）

> * 希臘文 *lambanein*（ = *take* ; *seize*），*lepsis*（ = *seizure*）。

syllable[4] 〔'sɪləbl̩ 〕 *n.* 音節   *v.* 分成音節（放在一起唸的音）
   《*syl-* = *syn-* = together》
syllabus[7] 〔'sɪləbəs 〕 *n.* 摘要；概要；教學大綱（抓住所有內容重點）
analeptic 〔ˌænə'lɛptɪk 〕 *adj.* 恢復健康的；強身的
  n. 興奮劑；強壯劑

> ana + lept + ic
> | | |
> *up* + *take* + *adj.*

catalepsy 〔'kætəˌlɛpsɪ , 'kætl̩ˌɛpsɪ 〕 *n.* 僵住症；強直性昏厥
   《*cata-* = down》
epilepsy[7] 〔'ɛpəˌlɛpsɪ 〕 *n.* 癲癇《*epi-* = upon》
narcolepsy 〔'nɑrkəˌlɛpsɪ 〕 *n.* 嗜睡病；發作性睡病
   《*narco* = numbness（麻木）; stupor（昏迷）》
prolepsis 〔 prə'lɛpsɪs 〕 *n.* 預期；預料；預期敘述法；預辯法
   《*pro-* = before》

279 labor = work (工作)

* 拉丁文 *labor* (= *work*) 。

labor[4] ﹝'lebɚ﹞ *n.* 工作；勞動；勞工　*v.* 勞動；努力

laboratory[4] ﹝'læbrə,torɪ , 'læbərə- ﹞ *n.* 實驗室

　《 *-ory* 表示地點的名詞字尾》

labored[7] ﹝'lebəd﹞ *adj.* 痛苦的；困難的；不流暢的

laborer[7] ﹝'lebərɚ﹞ *n.* 勞動者；勞工

laborious ﹝ lə'borɪəs , -'bɔr- ﹞ *adj.* 費力的；艱難的；

　努力的；勤勞的

```
labor  +  ious
  |         |
work   +  adj.
```

belabor[7] ﹝ bɪ'lebɚ ﹞ *v.* 痛擊；嘲弄；辱罵（迫使勞動）《 *be-* = make 》

collaborate[7] ﹝ kə'læbə,ret ﹞ *v.* 合作（一起工作）

　《 *col-* = *com-* = together 》

elaborate[5] ﹝ *v.* ɪ'læbə,ret　*adj.* ɪ'læbrɪt ﹞ *v.* 用心作；苦心經營；

　詳細說明　*adj.* 用心作成的；精巧的；複雜的（努力做出來）

　《 *e-* = *ex-* = out 》

280 lact = milk (牛奶；乳汁)

　* 拉丁文 *lac , lact-* (= *milk*) 。

lactary ﹝'læktərɪ﹞ *adj.* 乳的；產乳白漿汁的

lactase ﹝'læktes﹞ *n.* 乳糖酶

lactate ﹝'læktet﹞ *v.* 分泌乳汁；哺乳

lactometer ﹝ læk'tɑmətɚ ﹞ *n.* 驗乳計；乳汁比重計

```
lacto  +  meter
  |         |
milk   +  measure
```

lactose[7] ﹝'læktos﹞ *n.* 乳糖

ablactation〔͵æblæk'teʃən〕*n.* 斷奶

```
ab  +  lact  +  ation
 |        |       |
away  +  milk  +   n.
```

281   **laps** = slip；glide（滑；滑行）

* 拉丁文 *lapsare*（ = *slip*；*glide* ）。

lapse[7]〔læps〕*n.* 失誤；過失；（小）錯誤

v. 失誤；失足；消失（手滑過）

collapse[4]〔kə'læps〕*v.* 倒塌；崩潰；瓦解；失敗；消沈；頹喪

n. 崩潰；挫折；衰弱；消沈；失敗（一同滑落）

《*col-* = *con-* = together》

collapsible；-able[7]〔kə'læpsəbl̩〕*adj.* 可摺疊的；摺疊式的

（可以折疊的）

```
col   +  laps  +  ible
 |         |        |
together  +  slip  +  adj.
```

elapse[7]〔ɪ'læps〕*v.*（時間）溜走；逝去（時光溜走）

《*e-* = *ex-* = out》

prolapse[7]〔prə'læps〕*v.* 脫垂；脫出　*n.*（身體內部器官之）

脫垂；脫出（向前滑出）《*pro-* = forward》

relapse[7]〔rɪ'læps〕*v.* 回復；復發　*n.* 復發；故態復萌（完全回復）

《*re-* = back》

282   **laryng** = windpipe（氣管）

* 希臘文 *larunx*（ = *the upper windpipe* ）。

laryngal〔lə'rɪŋgəl〕*n.*, *adj.* 喉音（的）

laryngectomy 〔ˌlærɪnˈdʒɛktəmɪ 〕 *n.* 喉頭切除術《*tom* = cut》

laryngitis 〔ˌlærɪnˈdʒaɪtɪs 〕 *n.* 喉炎《 *-itis* = inflammation (發炎)》

laryngology 〔ˌlærɪnˈgɑlədʒɪ 〕 *n.* 喉科學《*logy* = study》

laryngopharynx 〔 ləˌrɪŋgoˈfærɪŋks 〕 *n.* 咽喉《*pharynx* 咽》

laryngoscope 〔 ləˈrɪŋgəˌskop 〕 *n.* 喉鏡

《*scope* 表示「觀察～的器具」》

laryngoscopy 〔ˌlærɪŋˈgɑskəpɪ 〕 *n.* 喉鏡檢查

larynx 〔ˈlærɪŋks 〕 *n.* 喉頭

283　**lat** = bring ; bear (攜帶)

* 拉丁文 *latus* (= *brought* ; *carried* ; *borne*)，是 *ferre* 的
過去分詞。

ablation 〔 æbˈleʃən 〕 *n.* 除去；切除 (搬走)《*ab-* = away》

collate 〔 kɑˈlet 〕 *v.* 對照；校勘 (集合在一起)

《*col-* = *com-* = together》

```
col   +  late
 |         |
together + bring
```

elate[7] 〔 ɪˈlet , i- 〕 *v.* 使興奮　　*adj.* 興奮的；得意的 (將心情表現在外)

《*e-* = *ex-* = out》

illation 〔 ɪˈleʃən 〕 *n.* 推論；結論 (被帶到內部的東西)《*il-* = *in-* = in》

oblate 〔ˈɑblet , əbˈlet 〕 *adj.* 扁圓的《*ob-* = towards》

```
ob   +  late
 |         |
towards + bear
```

prelate 〔ˈprɛlɪt 〕 *n.* 高級教士 (如主教、大主教等) (被帶到前面
位置的人)《*pre-* = before》

prolate 〔ˈprolet 〕 *adj.* 扁長的 (往前拉長)《*pro-* = forth》

relate[3] 〔 rɪˈlet 〕 *v.* 敘述；(使) 有關聯 (還原)《*re-* = back》

字根 lab~lys

relation[2]〔rɪ'leʃən〕*n.* 陳述；關係；親戚

relative[4]〔'rɛlətɪv〕*adj.* 有關係的；相對的　　*n.* 親戚；關係詞

relator〔rɪ'letɚ〕*n.* 陳述者；原告

superlative〔sə'pɝlətɪv , su-〕*adj.* 最高級的；誇張的；超群的

　　n. 最高級的形容詞或副詞；極致（攜帶到界限以外）

　　《*super-* = beyond》

```
super  +  lat  + ive
  |        |      |
beyond + bear + adj.
```

translate[4]〔'trænslet , træns'let〕*v.* 翻譯；解釋；說明（移向別處）

　　《*trans-* = across》

translation[4]〔træns'leʃən〕*n.* 翻譯

translator[4]〔træns'letɚ〕*n.* 翻譯者

ventilate[7]〔'vɛntḷ,et〕*v.* 使通風；以新鮮空氣來淨化～；自由討論

　　（把風帶進來）《*venti* = wind》

```
venti  +  late
  |        |
wind  +  bring
```

ventilation[7]〔,vɛntḷ'eʃən〕*n.* 通風；通風設備；自由討論

delay[2]〔dɪ'le〕*v.* 延期；延緩　　*n.* 耽擱（運往遠處）

　　《*de-* = *dis-* = apart》

284　**lat** = wide（寬的）　　*拉丁文 latus（ = wide）。*

latitude[5]〔'lætə,tjud〕*n.* 緯度；範圍；程度；自由範圍

　　《*-itude* 抽象名詞字尾》

latifoliate〔,lætə'folɪet〕*adj.*【植物】闊葉的

```
lati  +  foli + ate
  |       |      |
wide  + leaf + adj.
```

dilate[7] 〔 daɪˊlet , dɪ- 〕 v. 使擴大;膨脹(向外變寬)
《*di-* = *dis-* = apart》

dilatable 〔 daɪˊletəbḷ , dɪ- 〕 adj. 可膨脹的

dilatation 〔ˌdɪləˊteʃən , ˌdaɪlə- 〕 n. 擴張;膨脹;肥大(症)

285　later = side（邊;側面）

　　* 拉丁文 *latus* , *later-*（= *side*）。

lateral[7] 〔ˊlætərəl 〕 adj. 旁邊的;側面的;側生的
　n. 側面;支線;側生芽

bilateral[7] 〔 baɪˊlætərəl 〕 adj. 兩邊的;雙方的;互惠的《*bi-* = two》

collateral[7] 〔 kəˊlætərəl 〕 adj. 並行的;附帶的
　n. 旁系親屬;附屬品;抵押品(一塊在旁邊)《*col-* = *com-* = together》

```
col   + later + al
 |        |      |
together + side + adj.
```

equilateral 〔ˌikwəˊlætərəl 〕 adj. 等邊的　n. 等邊形;相等的邊
《*equi* = equal》

multilateral 〔ˌmʌltɪˊlætərəl 〕 adj. 多邊的;多國參加的
《*multi-* = many》

quadrilateral 〔ˌkwɑdrəˊlætərəl 〕 adj. 四邊形的;四方面的
　n. 四邊形《*quadri-* = four》

unilateral 〔ˌjunɪˊlætərəl 〕 adj. 單方的;片面的;單獨的
《*uni-* = one》

286　latry = worship（崇拜）

　　* 希臘文 *latreia*（= *worship*）。

bibliolatry 〔ˌbɪblɪˊɑlətrɪ 〕 n. 聖經崇拜;書籍崇拜《*Bible* 聖經》

heliolatry 〔ˌhilɪˊɑlətrɪ 〕 n. 太陽崇拜《*helio* = sun》

字根 lab~lys

necrolatry 〔 nɛ'krɑlətrɪ 〕 n. 死者崇拜

```
necro  +  latry
  |        |
dead body + worship
```

physiolatry 〔ˌfɪzɪ'ɑlətrɪ 〕 n. 自然崇拜《physio = nature》

plutolatry 〔 plu'tɑlətrɪ 〕 n. 財富崇拜；拜金主義

```
pluto  +  latry
  |        |
wealth + worship
```

pyrolatry 〔 paɪ'rɑlətrɪ 〕 n. 拜火；火的崇拜《pyro = fire》

theolatry 〔 θi'ɑlətrɪ 〕 n. 拜神《theo = god》

287　lav , lu = wash（洗）

＊拉丁文 lavare , -luere（= wash）。〔變化型〕lau。

lave 〔 lev 〕 v. 洗濯；沐浴；沖洗

lava[6] 〔'lɑvə , 'lævə 〕 n. 熔岩（沖洗山脊的流體）

lavatory[7] 〔'lævəˌtorɪ 〕 n. 盥洗室；廁所（洗手的地方）
　《 -ory 表示地點的名詞字尾》

lavish[7] 〔'lævɪʃ 〕 v. 浪費；濫用　adj. 豐富的；過多的（如水般地）

```
lav  +  ish
 |       |
wash + adj., v.
```

launder[7] 〔'lɔndɚ , 'lɑn- 〕 v. 洗燙

laundress 〔'lɔndrɪs , 'lɑn- 〕 n. 洗衣婦《 -ess 表示女性的名詞字尾》

laundry[3] 〔'lɔndrɪ , 'lɑn- 〕 n. 洗衣店；送洗的衣物
　《 -ry 表示地點的名詞字尾》

ablution 〔 æb'luʃən , əb- 〕 n. 淨身；齋戒沐浴（洗去身上的髒東西）
　《ab- = away》

deluge (ˈdɛljudʒ) *n.* 大洪水；氾濫；湧到　*v.* 氾濫；湧至；壓倒
《*de-* = *dis-* = away》

dilute[7] (dɪˈlut , daɪ-) *v.* 稀釋；沖淡　*adj.* 稀薄的
《*di-* = *dis-* = apart》

288　lax = loosen (放鬆；解開)

* 拉丁文 *laxare* (= *loosen*) 。

lax[7] (læks) *adj.* 鬆弛的；散漫的；放縱的　*n.* 腹瀉
laxation (lækˈseʃən) *n.* 鬆懈；放縱
laxative (ˈlæksətɪv) *adj.* 通便的；腹瀉的　*n.* 通便劑；瀉藥
laxity (ˈlæksətɪ) *n.* 不嚴謹；放縱
relax[3] (rɪˈlæks) *v.* 放鬆；鬆弛；緩和；減輕《*re-* = back》
relaxation[4] (ˌrilæksˈeʃən) *n.* 鬆弛；放鬆；減輕；休養；娛樂；
精力減退

```
re  +  lax  + ation
|      |       |
back + loosen +  n.
```

release[3] (rɪˈlis) *v.* 解開；釋放；解脫；免除；放棄；發表；發行
n. 解開；釋放；棄權；讓渡；出版物 (放鬆)

289　lect , leg , lig
= choose ; gather ; read (選擇；聚集；讀)

* 拉丁文 *legere* , *-ligere* (= *choose* ; *gather* ; *read*) ，
過去分詞為 *lectus* 。

lectern (ˈlɛktən) *n.* 教堂中的讀經台；桌面傾斜的講台
lection (ˈlɛkʃən) *n.* (於教堂朗讀的) 聖句 (讀)
lecture[4] (ˈlɛktʃə) *n.* 講義；演講　*v.* 演講；教訓；訓誡 (讀)
lecturer[4] (ˈlɛktʃərə) *n.* 演講者；(大學的) 講師

collect[2] 〔kə'lɛkt〕 *v.* 收集；集合；堆積；收款（集合在一起）

《*col-* = *com-* = together》

```
col   +   lect
 |         |
together + gather
```

collection[3] 〔kə'lɛkʃən〕 *n.* 收集；收取；捐款

elect[2] 〔ɪ'lɛkt，ə-〕 *v.* 推舉；選舉　*adj.* 被選舉的（選出）

《*e-* = *ex-* = out》

election[3] 〔ɪ'lɛkʃən〕 *n.* 選舉

electee 〔ɪ,lɛk'ti〕 *n.* 當選人《*-ee* 表示「被～的人」》

elector 〔ɪ'lɛktɚ，ə-〕 *n.* 選舉人；有選舉權者

electorate 〔ɪ'lɛktərɪt，ə-〕 *n.* 選民；選舉團；選區

intellect[6] 〔'ɪntḷ,ɛkt〕 *n.* 智力；理解力（分別是非善惡的能力）

《*intel-* = *inter-* = between》

intellectual[4] 〔,ɪntḷ'ɛktʃʊəl〕 *adj.* 智力的；理智的；有知性的

　　n. 知識份子

neglect[4] 〔nɪ'glɛkt〕 *v.* 疏忽；忽略　*n.* 疏忽；不留心

　　（不緊密 → 鬆懈）《*neg-* = not》

neglectful[7] 〔nɪ'glɛktfəl〕 *adj.* 疏忽的

```
neg +  lect  + ful
 |      |       |
not + gather + adj.
```

recollect 〔,rɛkə'lɛkt〕 *v.* 憶起；記起　〔,rikə'lɛkt〕 *v.* 再聚集

　　（再結合）《*re-* = again》

recollection[7] 〔,rɛkə'lɛkʃən〕 *n.* 記憶（力）；記起；回憶

select[2] 〔sə'lɛkt〕 *v.* 選擇；挑選　*adj.* 挑選出來的；極好的；

　　好挑剔的（選擇分別）《*se-* = apart》

selection[2] 〔sə'lɛkʃən〕 *n.* 選擇；淘汰

```
se  +  lect  + ion
 |      |       |
apart + choose + n.
```

legend[4] 〔'lɛdʒənd 〕 *n.* 傳說 (被誦讀之物)

legendary[6] 〔'lɛdʒənd,ɛrɪ 〕 *adj.* 傳說的；傳奇的　　*n.* 傳奇故事集；
傳奇文學作家

legible[7] 〔'lɛdʒəbļ 〕 *adj.* 易讀的；清楚的；容易察覺的

legion[7] 〔'lidʒən 〕 *n.* 軍隊；軍團；多數 (多數的團體)
　cf. **region** (地區)

diligent[3] 〔'dɪlədʒənt 〕 *adj.* 勤勉的 (很快地選擇區別)
　《*di-* = *dis-* = apart》

```
        di   +   lig   +  ent
        |        |        |
      apart + choose +  adj.
```

diligence[4] 〔'dɪlədʒəns 〕 *n.* 勤勉

elegant[4] 〔'ɛləgənt 〕 *adj.* 優美的；文雅的；高雅的 (被選拔的)
　《*e-* = *ex-* = out》

elegance[7] 〔'ɛləgəns 〕 *n.* 典雅；高雅

eligible[6] 〔'ɛlɪdʒəbļ 〕 *adj.* 合格的；適任的　　*n.* 合格者
　(可被選出的)《*e-* = *ex-* = out》

intelligent[4] 〔 ɪn'tɛlədʒənt 〕 *adj.* 有智力的；聰明的
　(在二者之間作選擇)《*intel-* = *inter-* = between》

intelligence[4] 〔 ɪn'tɛlədʒəns 〕 *n.* 智力；理解力；情報

```
      intel   +   lig   + ence
        |          |        |
     between + choose +   n.
```

intelligible[7] 〔 ɪn'tɛlɪdʒəbļ 〕 *adj.* 易理解的；清楚的

negligent[7] 〔'nɛglədʒənt 〕 *adj.* 疏忽的；忽略的《*neg-* = not》

negligence[7] 〔'nɛglədʒəns 〕 *n.* 疏忽；過失

negligible[7] 〔'nɛglədʒəbļ 〕 *adj.* 可疏忽的；不重要的

sacrilege[7] 〔'sækrəlɪdʒ 〕 *n.* 冒瀆；褻瀆聖物
　(從聖地蒐集來的 → 盜取)《*sacri* = sacred》

290　leg = law（法律）

*　拉丁文 *lex*（= law）。〔變化型〕*legis*。

legal[2]〔'lig!〕*adj.* 法律的；法定的；合法的
legislate〔'lɛdʒɪsˌlet〕*v.* 制定法律；立法（帶來法律）《*late* = bring》
legislation[5]〔ˌlɛdʒɪs'leʃən〕*n.* 立法；【集合名詞】法律
legislative[6]〔'lɛdʒɪsˌletɪv〕*adj.* 立法的；法規規定的　*n.* 立法機關
legislator[6]〔'lɛdʒɪsˌletɚ〕*n.* 立法者；立法委員

```
legis  +  lat  +   or
  |         |        |
 law   +  bring  + person
```

legislature[6]〔'lɛdʒɪsˌletʃɚ〕*n.* 立法機關；立法院
legist〔'lidʒɪst〕*n.* 法律學者
legitimate[6]〔 *adj.* lɪ'dʒɪtəmɪt *v.* lɪ'dʒɪtəˌmet〕*adj.* 合法的；
　正當的；嫡出的；正統的　*v.* 使合法；認爲正當（最具法律性的）
　《*-itim* 表示最高級》
litigate〔'lɪtəˌget〕*v.* 爭訟；爭論《拉丁文 *litem* = lawsuit》
litigation[7]〔ˌlɪtə'geʃən〕*n.* 訴訟

```
lit   + ig + ation
 |        |     |
lawsuit + do +  n.
```

allege[7]〔ə'lɛdʒ〕*v.* 主張；宣稱（宣佈其爲合法者）《*al-* = *ad-* = to》
allegation[7]〔ˌælə'geʃən〕*n.* 主張；陳述；託詞
allegiance[7]〔ə'lidʒəns〕*n.* 忠誠；忠貞《*lawful* → faithful》
privilege[4]〔'prɪvḷɪdʒ〕*n.* 特權　*v.* 給予特權；特許（限於一個人
　的法律）《*privi* = individual》

291　leg = send（派遣）

*　拉丁文 *legare*（= send; *delegate*; *bequeath* 遺贈）。

legate〔 *n.* 'lɛgɪt *v.* lɪ'get〕*n.* 教皇特使；使節；大使　*v.* 遺贈

legation 〔 lɪ'geʃən 〕 *n.* 使節的派遣；公使（館）

legator 〔 lɪ'getə 〕 *n.* 遺贈人；立遺囑人

legatee 〔ˌlɛgə'ti 〕 *n.* 受遺贈者；受遺產者《 *-ee* 表示動作的接受者》

legacy[7] 〔'lɛgəsɪ 〕 *n.* 遺產；繼承物

delegate[5] 〔 *v.* 'dɛləˌget *n.* 'dɛləgɪt 〕 *v.* 派遣（代表）；委派
  n. 代表；使節（任命派遣）《 *de-* = away》

```
de   +      legate
 |            |
away +  send with a commission
```

delegation[5] 〔ˌdɛlə'geʃən 〕 *n.* 代表權的委任；代表團

delegacy 〔'dɛlɪgəsɪ 〕 *n.* 代表權；代表團

relegate[7] 〔'rɛləˌget 〕 *v.* 貶謫；放逐（遣返 → 驅散）
  《 *re-* = back ; away》

relegation[7] 〔ˌrɛlə'geʃən 〕 *n.* 貶謫；驅逐

292　leuc , leuk = white（白色的）

  * 希臘文 *leukos*（ = *white* ）。

leucocyte 〔'lukəˌsaɪt 〕 *n.* 白血球《 *cyt* = cell》

leucoderma 〔ˌlukə'dɝmə 〕 *n.* 白斑病《 *derm* = skin》

leucoma 〔 lu'komə 〕 *n.* 角膜白斑（各種角膜病殘留的白色混濁疤痕）
  《 *-oma* 表示瘤的名詞字尾》

leucopenia 〔ˌlukə'pinɪə 〕 *n.* 白血球減少《希臘文 *penia* = poverty》

leucorrhea 〔ˌlukə'riə 〕 *n.* 白帶

```
leuco  + rrhea
 |         |
white  + flow
```

leuk(a)emia 〔 lu'kimɪə 〕 *n.* 白血病《 *(h)em* = blood》

293　lev = raise；light（提高；輕的）

* 拉丁文 *levare*（= raise），*levis*（= light）。

lever[7]〔'lɛvɚ, 'livɚ〕 *n.* 槓桿；工具　　*v.* 使用槓桿（可輕易舉起的東西）

leverage[7]〔'lɛvərɪdʒ, 'liv-〕 *n.* 槓桿作用；手段；力量

levy[7]〔'lɛvɪ〕 *v.* 徵稅；徵集；扣押　　*n.* 賦稅；徵稅；徵收（徵收）

leviable〔'lɛvɪəbḷ〕 *adj.* 可課稅的

levitate[7]〔'lɛvə,tet〕 *v.* 輕浮；浮於空中

levitation〔,lɛvə'teʃən〕 *n.* 飄浮空中

levity[7]〔'lɛvətɪ〕 *n.* 輕浮；輕率；輕薄（很輕的東西）

alleviate[7]〔ə'livɪ,et〕 *v.* 使緩和；減輕痛苦（使輕鬆）

《*al-* = *ad-* = to》

```
al + levi + ate
 |     |     |
 to + light +  v.
```

alleviation〔ə,livɪ'eʃən〕 *n.* 減輕；緩和

elevate[5]〔'ɛlə,vet〕 *v.* 舉起；提高；鼓舞（舉起來）

《*e-* = *ex-* = out；up》

elevation[7]〔,ɛlə'veʃən〕 *n.* 高地；高度；海拔；上升

elevator[2]〔'ɛlə,vetɚ〕 *n.* 升降運送機；電梯　　*cf.* **escalator**（手扶梯）

relevant[6]〔'rɛləvənt〕 *adj.* 有關的；中肯的（把問題重新提出來探討）

```
re  +  lev  + ant
 |      |      |
again + raise + adj.
```

relevance；-cy[7]〔'rɛləvəns(ɪ)〕 *n.* 適切；中肯

relieve[4]〔rɪ'liv〕 *v.* 減輕；使減少；免除；解救（使痛苦、負擔減輕）

relief[3]〔rɪ'lif〕 *n.* 減輕；救助；救濟；救援；安心

294 **levo** = left (左邊的)　　*拉丁文 *laevus* (= *left*)。

levoglucose 〔ˌlivo'glukos〕 *n.* 左旋葡萄糖
《希臘文 *glukus* = sweet》
levorotation 〔ˌlivoro'teʃən〕 *n.* (向) 左旋 (轉)
《*rotate* 旋轉》
levophobia 〔ˌlivo'fobɪə〕 *n.* 恐左症《*phob* = fear》

295 **liber** = free (自由的)　　*拉丁文 *liber* (= *free*)。

liberal[3] 〔'lɪbərəl〕 *adj.* 慷慨的；寬大的；自由主義的
n. 自由主義者
liberalism 〔'lɪbərəlˌɪzəm〕 *n.* 自由主義；寬宏大量
liberalist 〔'lɪbərəlɪst〕 *n.* 自由主義者
liberality 〔ˌlɪbə'rælətɪ〕 *n.* 慷慨大方；心胸寬大

```
liber + al + ity
  |      |     |
free  + adj. + n.
```

liberalize 〔'lɪbərəlˌaɪz, 'lɪbrəl-〕 *v.* 自由主義化；使寬大
liberalization 〔ˌlɪbərəlaɪ'zeʃən〕 *n.* 自由主義化；寬大

```
liber + al + iz(e) + ation
  |      |     |       |
free  + adj. +  v.   +  n.
```

liberate[6] 〔'lɪbəˌret〕 *v.* 使自由；解放
liberation[6] 〔ˌlɪbə'reʃən〕 *n.* 解放；釋放
liberator 〔'lɪbəˌretɚ〕 *n.* 解放者；釋放者
liberty[3] 〔'lɪbɚtɪ〕 *n.* 自由；自由權；使用權
libertarian 〔ˌlɪbɚ'tɛrɪən〕 *adj.* 自由意志論的　*n.* 自由意志論者
libertine 〔'lɪbɚˌtin〕 *adj.* 自由思想的；放蕩的
n. 自由思想者；放蕩者《*-ine* 形容詞字尾》

296 **liber , libr** = balance ; weigh（平衡；權衡）

* 拉丁文 *libra*（= *scales*），*librare*（= *balance* ; *weigh*）。

Libra[7]〔'laɪbrə〕*n.* 天秤座
libra〔'laɪbrə〕*n.* 磅
deliberate[6]〔*adj.* dɪ'lɪbərɪt *v.* dɪ'lɪbə,ret〕*adj.* 故意的；深思熟慮的
　　v. 仔細考慮（衡量全部的輕重）《*de-* = entirely》
deliberation[7]〔dɪ,lɪbə'reʃən〕*n.* 考慮；審議
deliberative〔dɪ'lɪbə,retɪv〕*adj.* 審議的；考慮過的
equilibrant〔i'kwɪləbrənt〕*n.* 平衡力

```
equi  +  libr  + ant
 |        |       |
equal + balance + adj.
```

equilibrate〔,ikwə'laɪbret , ɪ'kwɪlə,bret〕*v.*（使）平衡
equilibrator〔,ikwɪ'laɪbretə〕*n.* 平衡器

297 **libr** = book（書）

* 拉丁文 *liber* , *libr-*（= *book*）。〔變化型〕*lib*。

library[2]〔'laɪ,brɛrɪ , -brərɪ〕*n.* 圖書館；藏書；書房
　　（收藏書籍的地方）《*-ary* 表示場所的名詞字尾》
librarian[3]〔laɪ'brɛrɪən〕*n.* 圖書館員；圖書館長
libretto〔lɪ'brɛto〕*n.* 歌劇或其他歌曲之詞；歌劇劇本《*-etto* = small》
librettist〔lɪ'brɛtɪst〕*n.* 歌劇、樂劇等劇作家；歌詞作者

```
libr  +  ett  +  ist
 |        |       |
book + small + person
```

libel[7]〔'laɪbḷ〕*n.* 誹謗人之文字、言詞或圖畫；誹謗；諷刺
　　v.（寫或印文字）誹謗；中傷《*-el* = small》
libelous〔'laɪbələs〕*adj.* 誹謗性的

298　lic = be permitted (被允許)

* 拉丁文 *licere* (= *be permitted*) 。

license[4] 〔'laɪsn̩s 〕 *n.* 許可；執照　*v.* 許可
licensee 〔ˌlaɪsn̩'si 〕 *n.* 執照持有者《 *-ee* 表示動作的接受者》
licenser 〔'laɪsənsə·, -sn̩sə· 〕 *n.* 頒發執照者；有權批准執照者
licentiate 〔 laɪ'sɛnʃɪɪt, -ˌet 〕 *n.* 有開業資格者；領得開業執照者
licentious 〔 laɪ'sɛnʃəs 〕 *adj.* 放蕩不拘的；放縱的；不守法則的
illicit[7] 〔 ɪ'lɪsɪt, ɪl'lɪsɪt 〕 *adj.* 違法的；禁止的 (不被允許的)
　　《 *il-* = *in-* = not 》

299　lig = bind (綁)　　* 拉丁文 *ligare* (= *bind*) 。

ligate 〔'laɪget 〕 *v.* 綁；捆；結紮
ligament[7] 〔'lɪgəmənt 〕 *n.* 韌帶；紐帶；聯結物
ligature 〔'lɪgəˌtʃur 〕 *n.* 綁縛之物；結合之物　*v.* 綁；紮
oblige[6] 〔 ə'blaɪdʒ 〕 *v.* 強制；束縛；使感激 (綁住別人)《 *ob-* = to 》
obligate[7] 〔'abləˌget 〕 *v.* 使負義務；使負責；強迫

```
ob  +  lig  +  ate
|      |       |
to  +  bind  +  v.
```

obligation[6] 〔ˌablə'geʃən 〕 *n.* 義務；債務；債券；證券；恩惠
obligatory[7] 〔'ablɪgəˌtorɪ, ə'blɪgəˌtorɪ 〕 *adj.* 義務上的；必須的
religion[3] 〔 rɪ'lɪdʒən 〕 *n.* 宗教 (將自己綁回神身邊)《 *re-* = back 》

```
re  +  lig  +  ion
|      |       |
back + bind  +  n.
```

religious[3] 〔 rɪ'lɪdʒəs 〕 *adj.* 宗教的；信奉宗教的；虔誠的
league[5] 〔 lig 〕 *n.* 同盟；聯盟；盟約　*v.* 同盟；加盟 (繫在一起)
　　《 拉丁文 *ligare* = bind 》

colleague[5]〔'kɑlig〕*n.* 同事《*col-* = *com-* = together》
colligate〔'kɑlɪˌget〕*v.* 綁；束縛

```
col   +  lig  + ate
 |        |      |
together + bind +  v.
```

liable[6]〔'laɪəbl̩〕*adj.* 有～傾向的；易患～的；應負責的（被綁住）
liability[7]〔ˌlaɪə'bɪlətɪ〕*n.* 責任；義務；負擔
ally[5]〔*v.* ə'laɪ *n.* 'ælaɪ〕*v.* 同盟；聯合；結合 *n.* 同盟國；盟友
  （結合在一起）《*al-* = *ad-* (to) + *ly* = 拉丁文 *ligare* (bind)》
alliance[6]〔ə'laɪəns〕*n.* 同盟（國）；聯盟；同盟
allied[7]〔ə'laɪd, 'ælaɪd〕*adj.* 聯盟的；同盟的
rally[5]〔'rælɪ〕*v.* 收集；重整旗鼓；恢復精神
  n. 恢復；集會；長途賽車（再度結合）《*r-* = *re-* = again》

300　**lim , limin** = threshold（門檻；開端）

  * 拉丁文 *limen , limin-*（ = *threshold*）。

limit[2]〔'lɪmɪt〕*n.* , *v.* 限制
limbo[7]〔'lɪmbo〕*n.* (L-)【宗教】地獄的邊境；中間過渡狀態；
  被忘卻的人（或物件）的安置場所；監獄《拉丁文 *limbus* = border》
eliminate[4]〔ɪ'lɪməˌnet〕*v.* 除去（排出界限以外）《*e-* = *ex-* = out》
elimination[7]〔ɪˌlɪmə'neʃən〕*n.* 除去；淘汰；預賽
preliminary[6]〔prɪ'lɪməˌnɛrɪ〕*adj.* 預備的；初步的 *n.* 初步；
  開端《*pre-* = before》（放在門檻之前的 → 開始之前的）

```
pre  +  limin  + ary
 |        |       |
before + threshold + adj.
```

subliminal[7]〔sʌb'lɪmənl̩〕*adj.* 潛意識的；弱得無法感覺到的
  （在產生反應的界限點之下）《*sub-* = under》

301 **lin** = line；flax（線；亞麻）

> * 拉丁文 *linum*（ = *flax*；*linen*），*linea*（ = *string*；*line*）。

linear[7] 〔'lɪnɪɚ 〕 *adj.* 線的；直線的
linen[3] 〔'lɪnɪn 〕 *n.* 亞麻布
lingerie[7] 〔'lænʒəˌri 〕 *n.* 女性內衣褲《古法文 *linge* = linen》
linoleum[7] 〔 lɪ'nolɪəm 〕 *n.* （亞麻）油地氈；油布

```
lin  +  ole  +  um
 |       |       |
flax  +  oil  +  n.
```

linseed 〔'lɪnˌsid 〕 *n.* 亞麻子《*seed* 種子》
baseline[7] 〔'besˌlaɪn 〕 *n.* 基線；底線《*base* 基礎》
coastline[5] 〔'kostˌlaɪn 〕 *n.* 海岸線《*coast* 海岸》
delineate[7] 〔 dɪ'lɪnɪˌet 〕 *v.* （用線）畫出…的輪廓；（用語言
　　文字）描寫《*de-* = completely》
delineation 〔 dɪˌlɪnɪ'eʃən 〕 *n.* 描寫；簡圖
guideline[5] 〔'gaɪdˌlaɪn 〕 *n.* 指導方針《*guide* 引導》
hairline[7] 〔'hɛrˌlaɪn 〕 *n.* 髮際線；細線　*adj.* 極細的
lifeline[7] 〔'laɪfˌlaɪn 〕 *n.* 救生索；生命線
pipeline[6] 〔'paɪpˌlaɪn 〕 *n.* 管線；管道《*pipe* 管子》
sideline[7] 〔'saɪdˌlaɪn 〕 *n.* 界線；副業《*side* 旁邊的》

302 **lingu** = tongue；language（舌頭；語言）

> * 拉丁文 *lingua*（ = *tongue*；*language*）。

lingual 〔'lɪŋgwəl 〕 *adj.* 舌頭的；語言的
linguist[6] 〔'lɪŋgwɪst 〕 *n.* 語言學家；通好幾種外國語言者
linguistic[7] 〔 lɪŋ'gwɪstɪk 〕 *adj.* 語言的；語言學的
linguistics 〔 lɪŋ'gwɪstɪks 〕 *n.* 語言學《*-ics* 表示學問的名詞字尾》

bilingual[7] 〔 baɪˈlɪŋgwəl 〕 *adj.* 兩種語言的;雙語的;能說兩種語言的　　*n.* 能說兩種語言者《*bi-* = two》

```
bi  +  lingu  +  al
 |       |        |
two + language + adj.
```

collingual 〔 kəˈlɪŋgwəl 〕 *adj.* (用)同一種語言的(用同一種語言)
《*col-* = *com-* = with》

monolingual 〔 ˌmɑnəˈlɪŋgwəl 〕 *adj.* , *n.* 僅會一種語言的(人)
《*mono-* = single》

multilingual 〔 ˌmʌltɪˈlɪŋgwəl 〕 *adj.* 用多種語言寫成的;通多種語言的　　*n.* 通多國語言者《*multi-* = many》

```
multi  +  lingu  +  al
  |         |        |
many + language + adj.
```

sublingual 〔 sʌbˈlɪŋgwəl 〕 *adj.* 舌下的《*sub-* = under》

trilingual 〔 traɪˈlɪŋgwəl 〕 *adj.* 三種語言的
　　n. 三種語言寫成的題名或獻詞《*tri-* = three》

language[2] 〔 ˈlæŋgwɪdʒ 〕 *n.* 語言;措辭;語法;術語
《*langu* = *lingu*》

303 **linqu , lict , lip** = leave (離開;遺留)

　　* 拉丁文 *linquere* (= *leave*);希臘文 *leipein* (= *leave*)。

delinquency[7] 〔 dɪˈlɪŋkwənsɪ 〕 *n.* 罪行;不法行爲

```
de  +  linqu  +  ency
 |       |        |
away + leave  +  n.
```

delict 〔 dɪˈlɪkt 〕 *n.* 違法行爲;侵權行爲
《拉丁文 *delictum* 是 *delinquere* 的過去分詞》

relinquish[7] 〔 rɪ'lɪŋkwɪʃ 〕 v. 放棄;廢除

```
re  + linqu + ish
|      |      |
back + leave + v.
```

relic[5] 〔'rɛlɪk 〕 n. (pl.) 遺跡;遺體

relict 〔'rɛlɪkt 〕 adj. 殘存的;遺留的

　　《拉丁文 *relictus* 是 *relinquere* 的過去分詞》

derelict[7] 〔'dɛrə,lɪkt 〕 adj. 被拋棄的;怠忽職務的　　n. 被遺棄者;
疏忽職務者《*de-* = intensive 加強語氣》

eclipse[5] 〔 ɪ'klɪps 〕 n. (日、月) 蝕《*ec-* = *ex-* = out》

ellipsis 〔 ɪ'lɪpsɪs 〕 n. 省略;省略符號《*el-* = *en-* = in》

ellipse 〔 ɪ'lɪps 〕 n. 橢圓

304　**lip** = fat (脂肪)　　* 希臘文 *lipos* (= *fat*)。

lipid 〔'lɪpɪd 〕 n. 脂質

lipochrome 〔'lɪpə,krom 〕 n. 脂色素《*chrom* = color》

lipogenesis 〔,lɪpə'dʒɛnɪsɪs 〕 n. 脂肪生成《*genesis* 誕生》

lipoprotein 〔,lɪpə'protiɪn 〕 n. 脂蛋白《*protein* 蛋白質》

liposoluble 〔,lɪpə'saljəbḷ 〕 adj. 脂溶性的

```
lipo + solu  + ble
|       |       |
fat  + loosen + adj.
```

liposuction 〔'lɪpo,sʌkʃən 〕 n. 抽脂《*suck* 吸》

glycolipid 〔,glaɪkə'lɪpɪd 〕 n. 醣脂類《希臘文 *glukus* = sweet》

305　**liqu** = fluid (液體)　　* 拉丁文 *liquere* (= *fluid*)。

liquate 〔'laɪkwet 〕 v. 熔析

liquefy[7] 〔'lɪkwə,faɪ 〕 v. 使液化;熔解

liquefaction 〔 ˌlɪkwɪˈfækʃən 〕 *n.* 液化；熔解

```
lique + fact + ion
  |       |      |
fluid + make +  n.
```

liquescent 〔 lɪˈkwɛsənt , -snt̩ 〕 *adj.* 液化的；熔解性的
《 *-escent* 形容詞字尾》

liquid[2] 〔ˈlɪkwɪd 〕 *n.* 液體　*adj.* 液體的；明亮的；柔和的；不定的

liquidity[7] 〔 lɪˈkwɪdətɪ 〕 *n.* 流動性；流暢；明亮；流動資產

liquidize 〔ˈlɪkwəˌdaɪz 〕 *v.* 使成液體；使流動

liquor[4] 〔ˈlɪkɚ 〕 *n.* 酒；液體；滷汁；湯藥

306　liter = letter （字母；文字）

*　拉丁文 *littera* (= *letter*)。

literal[6] 〔ˈlɪtərəl 〕 *adj.* 文字的；字母的；逐字的；實際的；精確的

literalism 〔ˈlɪtərəlˌɪzəm 〕 *n.* 寫實主義；直譯主義

literally[7] 〔ˈlɪtərəlɪ 〕 *adv.* 逐字地；字面上地；實在地

literary[4] 〔ˈlɪtəˌrɛrɪ 〕 *adj.* 文學的；著作的；精通文學的

literate[6] 〔ˈlɪtərɪt 〕 *adj.* 能讀和寫的；受過教育的
　n. 能讀和寫者；文人；學者

```
liter + ate
  |      |
letter + adj.
```

literature[4] 〔ˈlɪtərətʃɚ 〕 *n.* 文學；著作；文獻

alliterate 〔 əˈlɪtəˌret 〕 *v.* 押頭韻；用頭韻《*al-* = *ad-* = to》

illiteracy[7] 〔 ɪˈlɪtərəsɪ , ɪlˈlɪ- 〕 *n.* 文盲；無學識《*il-* = *in-* = not》

illiterate 〔 ɪˈlɪtərɪt , ɪlˈlɪ- 〕 *adj.* 不能讀寫的；文盲的；缺乏教育的
　n. 文盲；目不識丁者

obliterate[7] 〔 əˈblɪtəˌret 〕 *v.* 塗抹；擦掉；消滅；毀跡
　（使蓋在文字上面）《*ob-* = over》

preliterate〔pri'litərit〕*adj.* 尚無文字的（文字發明以前）
《*pre-* = before》

```
pre  +  liter  +  ate
 |        |        |
before + letter + adj.
```

subliterary〔sʌb'litə,rɛrɪ〕*adj.* 通俗文學的；二流文學的
（文學層次低）《*sub-* = under》

transliterate〔træns'litə,ret, trænz-〕*v.* 音譯；直譯（按字
面翻譯）《*trans-* = across》

307　**lith** = stone（石頭）　* 希臘文 *lithos*（= *stone*）。

lithic〔'liθik〕*adj.* 石的；結石的；鋰的

lithography〔li'θɑgrəfi〕*n.* 石版印刷術

```
litho  +  graphy
  |         |
stone  +  write
```

lithosphere〔'liθə,sfir〕*n.* 岩石圈《*sphere* 球體》

megalithic〔,mɛgə'liθik〕*adj.* 巨石（造）的；巨石文化時代的
《*mega-* = large》

monolith〔'manḷ,iθ〕*n.* 獨塊巨石；獨石柱（或雕像、碑等）
《*mono-* = single》

neolithic〔,niə'liθik〕*adj.* 新石器時代的

```
neo  +  lith  +  ic
 |       |       |
new  + stone  + adj.
```

paleolithic〔,pelɪə'liθik〕*adj.* 舊石器時代的

```
paleo  +  lith  +  ic
  |        |       |
old   + stone  + adj.
```

308 loc = place（地方）　*拉丁文 locus（=place）。

local[2]〔'lokḷ〕 adj. 場所的；地方的；局部的；每站都停車的
　　n. 當地居民；慢車；地方新聞

locale[7]〔lo'kæl , -'kɑl〕n.（事件的）現場；場所

localism〔'lokḷ͵ɪzəm〕n. 地方性；地方主義；方言

locality[7]〔lo'kælətɪ〕n. 場所；位置；地方

localize[7]〔'lokḷ͵aɪz〕v. 使地方化；限於局部

locate[2]〔'loket , lo'ket〕v. 設於～；位於～

location[4]〔lo'keʃən〕n. 位置；場所；選定位置

locus〔'lokəs〕n.（pl. loci〔'losaɪ〕）所在地；場所；軌跡

allocate[6]〔'ælə͵ket , 'ælo-〕v. 撥出；留下；分配（指定場所）
　　《al- = ad- = to》

```
al  +  loc  +  ate
|       |       |
to  +  place  +  v.
```

collocate〔'kɑlo͵ket〕v. 配置；並列；安置（放在一起）
　　《col- = com- = together》

collocation〔͵kɑlo'keʃən〕n. 安排；佈置；連語

```
col   +  loc  + ation
 |        |       |
together + place +  n.
```

dislocate[7]〔'dɪslo͵ket , dɪs'loket〕v. 使脫臼；使混亂（分開放置）
　　《dis- = apart》

dislocation[7]〔͵dɪslo'keʃən〕n. 脫臼；混亂；斷層

```
dis   +  loc  + ation
 |        |       |
apart + place +  n.
```

mislocate〔mɪs'loket , ͵mɪslo'ket〕v. 放錯；誤置（放錯地方）
　　《mis- = wrong》

relocate[7]〔ri'loket〕*v.* 重新佈置（再度放置）《*re-* = again》

relocation[7]〔,rilo'keʃən〕*n.* 再佈置

translocation〔,trænslo'keʃən〕*n.* 遷移；移動；易位（換位置）
《*trans-* = across》

```
trans + loc + ation
  |       |      |
across + place +  n.
```

lieu[7]〔lɪu , lu〕= place　　***in lieu of*** = in place of～（代之以～）

lieutenant[5]〔lu'tɛnənt , lɪu-〕*n.* 上級代理；副官；陸軍中尉
（代理上司位置者）《*tenant* = holder》

309　log , loqu , locut = speak（説）

* 希臘文 *legein*（= *speak*），*logos*（= *word* ; *speech* ; *thought*）；
拉丁文 *loqui*（= *speak*），過去分詞是 *locutus*。由「説話」
衍生出「語言」、「思想」、「學問」等意思。

catalog(ue)[4]〔'kætḷ,ɔg〕*n.* 目錄　*v.* 編目錄（被仔細述説的東西）
《*cata-* = down ; fully》

decalog(ue)〔'dɛkə,lɔg , -,lɑg〕*n.* 十誡
（= *the Ten Commandments*）《*deca-* = ten》

```
deca + log(ue)
  |       |
 ten +  speak
```

dialog(ue)[3]〔'daɪə,lɔg〕*n.* 對話；會話（二個人之間的言語）
《*dia-* = between》

epilog(ue)[7]〔'ɛpə,lɔg , -,lɑg〕*n.* 結語；收場白（在上面附加的言語）
《*epi-* = upon》

monolog(ue)[7]〔'manḷ,ɔg , -,ɑg〕*n.* 獨白；獨腳戲（獨自一人説）
《*mono-* = alone》

prolog(ue)[7]〔'prolɔg , -lɑg〕*v.* 加上前言　*n.* 前言；開場白
（在前面説話）《*pro-* = before》

travelog(ue) 〔'trævəˌlɔg , -ˌlɑg 〕 *n.* 敘述旅行見聞的演講；
遊記電影

```
trave(l) + log(ue)
   |         |
 travel  +  speak
```

logic[4] 〔'lɑdʒɪk 〕 *n.* 邏輯；理則學
logical[4] 〔'lɑdʒɪkl̩ 〕 *adj.* 邏輯的；合邏輯的
apology[4] 〔 ə'pɑlədʒɪ 〕 *n.* 謝罪；道歉（爲免去罪過而說的話）
《*apo-* = off》
apologize[4] 〔 ə'pɑləˌdʒaɪz 〕 *v.* 道歉；謝罪

```
apo +  log  + ize
 |      |      |
off + speak +  v.
```

apologia 〔ˌæpə'lodʒɪə 〕 *n.* 道歉；（口頭或書面）正式的辯護
apologist 〔 ə'pɑlədʒɪst 〕 *n.* 辯護者；辯解者
apologue 〔'æpəˌlɔg , -ˌlɑg 〕 *n.* 教訓；寓言
analogy[6] 〔 ə'nælədʒɪ 〕 *n.* 類似；相似；類推（與其他東西有關）
《*ana-* = upon》
analogous[7] 〔 ə'næləgəs 〕 *adj.* 類似的；相似的

```
ana +  log  + ous
 |      |      |
upon + speak + adj.
```

eulogy[7] 〔'julədʒɪ 〕 *n.* 頌詞；頌揚 《*eu-* = well》
eulogize 〔'juləˌdʒaɪz 〕 *v.* 稱讚；頌揚
neology 〔 ni'ɑlədʒɪ 〕 *n.* 新語；新說；新義（新的言詞）《*neo-* = new》

```
neo +  log  + y
 |      |     |
new + speak + n.
```

trilogy[7] 〔'trɪlədʒɪ 〕 *n.* 三部曲 《*tri-* = three》

colloquial[6] 〔 kə'lokwɪəl 〕 *adj.* 口語的；談話的；俗語的（一起說）

《*col-* = *com-* = together》

col	+	loqu	+	ial
together	+	*speak*	+	*adj.*

colloquy 〔'kɑləkwɪ 〕 *n.* 談話；會議

eloquent[6] 〔'ɛləkwənt 〕 *adj.* 雄辯的；動人的（滔滔不絕地說）

《*e-* = *ex-* = out》

e	+	loqu	+	ent
out	+	*speak*	+	*adj.*

eloquence[6] 〔'ɛləkwəns 〕 *n.* 雄辯；口才

grandiloquence 〔 græn'dɪləkwəns 〕 *n.* 大話；豪語；誇口

《*grand* = great》

loquacious 〔 lo'kweʃəs 〕 *adj.* 多嘴的；好辯的

loquacity 〔 lo'kwæsətɪ 〕 *n.* 多嘴；饒舌

obloquy 〔'ɑbləkwɪ 〕 *n.* 譴責；責罵；恥辱；毀謗（斥責）

《*ob-* = against》

soliloquy 〔 sə'lɪləkwɪ 〕 *n.* 自言自語；獨白《*sol* = alone》

ventriloquy 〔 vɛn'trɪləkwɪ 〕 *n.* 腹語術《拉丁文 *venter* = belly》

locution[7] 〔 lo'kjuʃən 〕 *n.* 語法；語句；慣用語

allocution 〔,ælə'kjuʃən 〕 *n.* （尤指羅馬教皇的）訓示；訓諭

《*a-* = *ad-* = to》

circumlocution 〔,sɝkəmlo'kjuʃən 〕 *n.* 遁辭；婉轉曲折的說法

（冗長曲折的言詞）《*circum-* = round about》

circum	+	locut	+	ion
round about	+	*speak*	+	*n.*

elocution 〔,ɛlə'kjuʃən 〕 *n.* 演說法；辯論術（表現言詞的方法）

《*e-* = *ex-* = out》

字根 lab~lys

interlocution〔͵ɪntəˌlə'kjuʃən〕*n.* 對話；會談（兩人之間的言詞）

　　《*inter-* = between》

prolocutor〔pro'lakjətɚ〕*n.* 代言人；發言人；議長（代者）

　　《*pro-* = in place of》

310　　logy = study of（～學；～論）

anthropology〔͵ænθrə'palədʒɪ〕*n.* 人類學《*anthropo* = man》

archeology〔͵arkɪ'alədʒɪ〕*n.* 考古學

```
archeo  +  logy
  |         |
ancient + study of
```

astrology[7]〔ə'stralədʒɪ〕*n.* 占星術；占星學《*astro* = star》

biology[4]〔baɪ'alədʒɪ〕*n.* 生物學《*bio* = life》

chronology[7]〔krə'nalədʒɪ〕*n.* 年代學；年代記；年表

　　《*chrono* = time》

embryology〔͵ɛmbrɪ'alədʒɪ〕*n.* 胚胎學；發生學

```
em  +  bryo  +   logy
 |       |        |
in  +  grow  + study of
```

entomology〔͵ɛntə'malədʒɪ〕*n.* 昆蟲學（將昆蟲切成兩部分來研究

　　的學問）《*en-* = in ; *tomo* = cut》

```
en  +  tomo +   logy
 |       |       |
in  +   cut  + study of
```

etymology[7]〔͵ɛtə'malədʒɪ〕*n.* 語源學；語源（研究語言眞義的學問）

　　《*etymo* = meaning of a word（字的意思）》

genealogy〔͵dʒinɪ'ælədʒɪ , ͵dʒɛnɪ-〕*n.* 宗譜；系譜；家系

　　《*genea* = birth ; race ; descent》

geology[7]〔dʒi'alədʒɪ〕*n.* 地質學；地質《*geo* = earth》

meteorology[7] 〔͵mitɪə'rɑlədʒɪ 〕 *n.* 氣象學；氣象
《*meteor* = things in the air (大氣中的現象；流星)》

mineralogy 〔͵mɪnə'ælədʒɪ 〕 *n.* 礦物學 《*minera* = mine》

mythology[6] 〔 mɪ'θɑlədʒɪ 〕 *n.* 神話學 《*myth* 神話》

ornithology 〔͵ɔrnə'θɑlədʒɪ 〕 *n.* 鳥類學；鳥類學的書籍

```
ornitho +   logy
   |          |
 bird   + study of
```

pathology[7] 〔 pə'θɑlədʒɪ 〕 *n.* 病理學 《*patho* = disease》

philology 〔 fɪ'lɑlədʒɪ 〕 *n.* 語言學；文獻學 (喜愛言詞)
《*philo* = love》

phrenology 〔 frɛ'nɑlədʒɪ , frɪ- 〕 *n.* 骨相學
(依骨相讀心的學問) 《*phreno* = mind》

physiology[7] 〔͵fɪzɪ'ɑlədʒɪ 〕 *n.* 生理學 《*physio* 自然；物理》

psychology[4] 〔 saɪ'kɑlədʒɪ 〕 *n.* 心理學 《*psycho* = mind》

theology[7] 〔 θi'ɑlədʒɪ 〕 *n.* 神學 《*theo* = god》

zoology[7] 〔 zo'ɑlədʒɪ 〕 *n.* 動物學 《*zoo* 有關動物的》

311   **long** = long (長的)   * 拉丁文 *longus* (= *long*) 。

longevity[6] 〔 lɑn'dʒɛvətɪ 〕 *n.* 長壽；壽命

longitude[5] 〔'lɑndʒə͵tjud 〕 *n.* 經線；經度 《 *-itude* 抽象名詞字尾》

longitudinal 〔͵lɑndʒə'tjudn̩l , -'tud- 〕 *adj.* 長度的；經度的；縱的

along[1] 〔 ə'lɔŋ 〕 *prep.* 沿著；在～期間   *adv.* 沿著；往前
《*a-* = over against》

belong[1] 〔 bə'lɔŋ 〕 *v.* 屬於 (使成爲長久) 《*be-* = cause to be》

elongate[7] 〔 ɪ'lɔŋget 〕 *v.* 延長；延伸   *adj.* 延長的；細長的
(使變長) 《*e-* = *ex-* = out》

```
e  + long + ate
|      |     |
out + long +  v.
```

elongation〔ɪ͵lɔŋˋgeʃən , ͵ilɔ-〕*n.* 延長；伸長

length²〔lɛŋ(k)θ〕*n.* 長度《*leng*（long）+ *-th*（抽象名詞字尾）》

lengthen³〔ˋlɛŋ(k)θən〕*v.* 加長；延長

lengthy⁶〔ˋlɛŋ(k)θɪ〕*adj.* 冗長的；乏味的

oblong⁵〔ˋablɔŋ〕*adj.* 長方形的；長橢圓形的

　n. 長方形；長橢圓形《*ob-* = toward》

prolong⁵〔prəˋlɔŋ , -ˋlɑŋ〕*v.* 延長（向前延伸）《*pro-* = forward》

prolongate〔prəˋlɔŋget〕*v.* 延長

prolongation〔͵prolɔŋˋgeʃən〕*n.* 延長；延伸

312　**lope** = run（跑）

　　　＊古代冰島語 *hlaupa*（= run；leap）；中古荷蘭語 *lopen*（= run）。

lope〔lop〕*v.* 大步跑；跳躍而行

elope⁷〔ɪˋlop , ə-〕*v.* 私奔；逃走《中古荷蘭語 *ontlopen* = run away》

elopement〔ɪˋlopmənt〕*n.* 私奔

interlope〔͵ɪntəˋlop〕*v.* 無執照營業；干涉他人之事；闖入

　《*inter-* = between》

interloper〔͵ɪntəˋlopə〕*n.*（非法）闖入者；干涉者；無執照
營業者

313　**luc** , **lust** = light（光）

　　　＊拉丁文 *lux*（= light），*lucere*（= shine），*lucidus*（= bright；
　　　clear）；*lustrare*（= enlighten）。

lucent〔ˋlusn̩t〕*adj.* 明亮的；透明的

lucid⁷〔ˋlusɪd , ˋlɪu-〕*adj.* 透明的；清澄的；清醒的

lucidity〔luˋsɪdətɪ , lɪu-〕*n.* 清澄；明晰；明朗；清醒

Lucifer〔ˋlusəfə〕*n.* 金星；撒旦（帶來光亮）《*fer* = bring》

【解説】早期基督教著作中對墮落之前的撒旦的稱呼。

lucifugous 〔 lu'sɪfjəgəs 〕 *adj.* 怕光的；避光的（躲避光線）

《*fug* = flee》

luculent 〔'lukjʊlənt 〕 *adj.* 明晰的；易了解的；鮮明的

elucidate 〔 ɪ'lusə,det , ɪ'lju- 〕 *v.* 闡明；說明（清楚地說出來）

《*e-* = *ex-* = out》

```
e  +  lucid  +  ate
|       |        |
out + clear +  v.
```

noctilucent 〔,nɑktə'lusənt 〕 *adj.* 夜間發光的《*nocti* = night》

pellucid 〔 pə'lusɪd , -'lɪu- 〕 *adj.* 透明的；明瞭的；明晰的

（透過而發亮）《*pel-* = *per-* = through》

translucent 〔 træns'lusn̩t , -'lju- 〕 *adj.* 半透明的

《*trans-* = through》

luster ; **-tre**[7] 〔'lʌstɚ 〕 *n.* 光彩；光澤；光亮毛織品

lustrous[7] 〔'lʌstrəs 〕 *adj.* 光亮的；有光澤的

illustrate[4] 〔'ɪləstret , ɪ'lʌstret 〕 *v.* 舉例說明；圖解（照在～之中）

《*il-* = *in-* = in》

```
il  +  lustr  +  ate
|       |        |
in  + light  +  v.
```

illustration[4] 〔 ɪ,lʌs'treʃən 〕 *n.* 例證；實例；圖解

illustrious 〔 ɪ'lʌstrɪəs 〕 *adj.* 著名的；顯著的；卓越的（閃閃發光）

314 **lud , lus** = play（扮演；遊戲；彈奏）

* 拉丁文 *ludus*（ = *game*），*ludere*（ = *play*）。

allude[7] 〔 ə'lud , ə'lɪud 〕 *v.* 暗指；提及（使浮現某種想法）

《*al-* = *ad-* = to》

allusion[7] 〔 ə'luʒən 〕 *n.* 暗示；提及；引述

collude[7] 〔 kə'lud 〕 *v.* 共謀；串通（一起做）《*col-* = *com-* = together》

delude[7]〔dɪ'lud , -'lɪud〕*v.* 欺騙；迷惑（遊戲；脫離現實）

　《*de-* = off》

delusion[7]〔dɪ'luʒən , -'lɪuʒən〕*n.* 欺瞞；迷惑

```
de  +  lus  +  ion
 |      |       |
off  +  play  +  n.
```

elude[7]〔ɪ'lud , ɪ'ljud〕*v.* 脫逃；躲避（嬉笑著跑出去）

　《*e-* = *ex-* = out》

elusion[7]〔ɪ'luʒən , ɪ'lju-〕*n.* 逃避；迴避

elusive[7]〔ɪ'lusɪv , ɪ'lju-〕*adj.* 逃避的；難以捉摸的

```
e  +  lus  +  ive
|      |       |
out + play  +  adj.
```

illusion[6]〔ɪ'ljuʒən〕*n.* 幻影；幻想；錯覺（在～上面玩耍）

　《*il-* = *in-* = on ; upon》

disillusion[7]〔ˌdɪsɪ'luʒən , -'lju-〕*n.* 幻滅；覺醒

　v. 使幻滅；使醒悟（幻想破滅）《*dis-* = away》

ludicrous[7]〔'ludɪkrəs , 'lɪu-〕*adj.* 滑稽的；可笑的；荒唐的

prelude[7]〔'prɛljud , 'pri-〕*n.* 序幕；前奏曲　*v.* 演奏序曲；做為

　序幕《*pre-* = before》

interlude[7]〔'ɪntɚˌlud , -ˌlɪud〕*n.* 中間時間；間隔之時間；間奏曲

　《*inter-* = between》

postlude〔'postˌlud , -ˌljud〕*n.* 後奏曲；終曲《*post-* = after》

315　**lumin** = light（光）

　　* 拉丁文 *lumen*（= *light*），*luminare*（= *light up*），

　　　和 *luc* , *lust* 同一字源。

luminance〔'lumɪnəns〕*n.* 光線的強度

luminary〔'luməˌnɛrɪ〕*n.* 天體；發光體

luminescence[7] 〔ˌlumə'nɛsn̩s〕 *n.* 螢光；冷光《 *-escence* 名詞字尾》

```
lumin + escence
  │        │
 light  +   n.
```

luminiferous 〔ˌlumə'nɪfərəs〕 *adj.* 發光的（帶光）《*fer* = carry》

luminosity 〔ˌlumə'nɑsətɪ〕 *n.* 光輝；光明；發光物；光度

luminous 〔'lumənəs〕 *adj.* 發光的；有光輝的

illuminate[6] 〔ɪ'lumə‚net，ɪ'lju-〕 *v.* 照明；照亮；說明（照著～）

《*il-* = *in-* = on ; upon》

illumine 〔ɪ'lumɪn，ɪ'lju-〕 *v.* 照亮；照明

relumine 〔rɪ'lumən〕 *v.* 再照明；再點燃（ = *relume*）

《*re-* = again》

316　lys , lyt = loosen（放鬆；解開）

　　* 希臘文 *luein*（ = *loosen*），*lusis*（ = *loosening*）。
　　〔變化型〕*lyt*。

analyse；**-lyze**[4] 〔'æn̩‚aɪz〕 *v.* 分析；分解；解析（放鬆回到原處）

《*ana-* = back》

analysis[4] 〔ə'næləsɪs〕 *n.* 分解；分析；解析

```
ana + lys + is
 │     │     │
back + loosen + n.
```

analytic；**-ical**[6] 〔ˌæn̩'ɪtɪk(l̩)〕 *adj.* 分解的；分析的

electrolyte 〔ɪ'lɛktrə‚laɪt〕 *n.* 電解質；電解液《*electric* 電的》

paralyse；**-lyze**[6] 〔'pærə‚laɪz〕 *v.* 使麻痺；使無能力（鬆弛而脫離）

《*para-* = beside》

paralysis[7] 〔pə'ræləsɪs〕 *n.* 麻痺；中風；無力；無能

palsy 〔'pɔlzɪ〕 *n.* 麻痺；中風；癱瘓　*v.* 使麻痺

317 magn = great（很大的）

* 拉丁文 *magnus*（= great），*major*（= greater），*maximus*
（= greatest）。〔變化型〕*maj*，*max*。

magnanimous[7]〔 mæg'nænəməs 〕*adj.* 心地高尚的；度量寬大的
（心胸寬大）《*anim* = mind》

magnanimity〔͵mægnə'nɪmətɪ 〕*n.* 寬宏大量；高尚；慷慨

magnate〔'mægnet 〕*n.* 大企業家；偉人；巨擘（偉大的人）
《 *-ate* 表示人的名詞字尾》

```
magn  +   ate
 |         |
great  + person
```

magnify[5]〔'mægnə͵faɪ 〕*v.* 放大；擴大；誇張（使寬大）《 *-ify* = make》

magnificent[4]〔 mæg'nɪfəsṇt 〕*adj.* 華麗的；壯觀的；堂皇的
（被做得很大）

magnificence〔 mæg'nɪfəsṇs 〕*n.* 壯麗；堂皇

magnifier〔'mægnə͵faɪɚ 〕*n.* 放大者；放大鏡

magniloquent〔 mæg'nɪləkwənt 〕*adj.* 誇張的；誇大的
（宏大的言詞）《*loqu* = speech》

magniloquence〔 mæg'nɪləkwəns 〕*n.* 誇張；誇大的話

magnitude[6]〔'mægnə͵tjud 〕*n.* 大小；重要；光度
《 *-itude* 抽象名詞字尾》

```
magn + itude
 |       |
great  + n.
```

majesty[5]〔'mædʒɪstɪ , 'mædʒəstɪ 〕*n.* 威嚴；尊嚴；陛下；高貴
（重要的、有威嚴的東西）

majestic[5]〔 mə'dʒɛstɪk 〕*adj.* 高貴的；莊嚴的

major[3]〔'medʒɚ 〕*adj.* 較大的；較多的；成年的；主修的
n. 成年人；主科　*v.* 主修

majority[3]〔 mə'dʒɔrətɪ , -'dʒɑr- 〕*n.* 成年；多數；過半數

maxim[7]〔'mæksɪm〕 *n.* 格言；座右銘（最偉大的眞理）
《*im* = proposition（主張）》

```
   max   +    im
    |          |
 great  +  proposition
```

maximal〔'mæksəməl〕 *adj.* 最大的
maximum[4]〔'mæksəməm〕 *n.* 極大；最大限度；最大數
 adj. 最大的；最高的

318 magnes , magnet
= magnesia；magnet（氧化鎂；磁鐵）

* 希臘文 *Magnesia*，是古代小亞細亞一礦藏豐富的地區。

magnesia〔mæg'niʃə , -ʒə〕 *n.* 氧化鎂
magnesium〔mæg'niʃɪəm , -ʒɪəm〕 *n.* 鎂
magnet[3]〔'mægnɪt〕 *n.* 磁鐵；有吸引力的人（或物）
magnetism[7]〔'mægnə,tɪzəm〕 *n.* 磁性；磁力；吸引力
magnetize〔'mægnə,taɪz〕 *v.*（使）磁化；吸引
magnetoelectric〔mæg,nitoɪ'lɛktrɪk〕 *adj.* 磁電的《*electric* 電的》
magnetophone〔mæg'nitofon〕 *n.* 磁帶錄音機《*phone* = sound》
magnetosphere〔mæg'nito,sfɪr〕 *n.* 磁層《*sphere* 球體》

319 man = stay（停留） * 拉丁文 *manere*（= *stay*）。

manor[7]〔'mænɚ〕 *n.*（英國封建領主的）莊園；（北美殖民時代的）
 永久租地；莊園主宅第；大宗地產
mansion[5]〔'mænʃən〕 *n.* 豪宅；官邸
immanent[7]〔'ɪmənənt〕 *adj.* 內在的
permanent[4]〔'pɝmənənt〕 *adj.* 永久的
《*per-* = through》

```
im + man + ent
 |     |     |
in + stay + adj.
```

remain[3]〔rɪ'men〕*v.* 逗留；依然

```
re  +  main
 |       |
back  +  stay
```

remnant[7]〔'rɛmnənt〕*n.*, *adj.* 殘餘（的）；剩餘（的）
《古法文 *remanant* = remaining》

320　**man** , **manu** = hand（手）

* 拉丁文 *manus*（= *hand*）。

manacle〔'mænəkḷ〕*n.* 手銬；束縛　*v.* 上手銬；束縛
（綁住手的小東西）《 *-cle* = small》

manage[3]〔'mænɪdʒ〕*v.* 處理；經營；管理；設法

management[3]〔'mænɪdʒmənt〕*n.* 經營；管理（人員）；支配；
資方

manager[3]〔'mænɪdʒɚ〕*n.* 經理；管理者

maneuver[7]〔mə'nuvɚ〕*n.* 戰術；策略；手法

manicure[7]〔'mænɪ,kjʊr〕*v.* 修（指甲）　*n.* 修指甲《 *cure* = care》

manifest[5]〔'mænə,fɛst〕*adj.* 明白的　*v.* 顯示；表示　*n.* 運貨單
（用手敲打 → 表示）《 *fest* = strike》

manipulate[6]〔mə'nɪpjə,let〕*v.*（用手）操作；操縱；竄改
《 *pul* = pull》

manipulation[7]〔mə,nɪpjə'leʃən〕*n.* 操作；操縱；竄改

```
mani  +  pul  +  ation
  |        |       |
hand  +  pull  +   n.
```

manner[2]〔'mænɚ〕*n.* 方式；態度；樣子；舉止；（*pl.*）禮貌
《通俗拉丁文 *manuaria* = way of handling something》

manual[4]〔'mænjʊəl〕*adj.* 手的；手工的　*n.* 手冊（用手的）

manufacture[4]〔,mænjə'fæktʃɚ〕*v.* 製造（用手做）《 *fact* = make》

manumit 〔ˌmænjə'mɪt〕v. 解放（奴隸）（由手中釋放出來）
《*mit* = send》

manure[7] 〔mə'njʊr〕n. 肥料　v. 施肥於

manuscript[6] 〔'mænjəˌskrɪpt〕n. 原稿；抄本　*adj.* 手寫的
（用手寫）《*script* = write》

```
manu + script
  |       |
hand  +  write
```

emancipate[7] 〔ɪ'mænsəˌpet〕v. 解放（奴隸）；解除（束縛）
（使被綁住的手鬆綁）
《*e-* = *ex-*（out）+ *man*（hand）+ *cip*（take）+ *-ate*（動詞字尾）》

```
e + man + cip + ate
|    |     |     |
out + hand + take + v.
```

emancipation[7] 〔ɪˌmænsə'peʃən〕n. 解放；解除；解脫

321　mand = order ; entrust（命令；委託）

＊ 拉丁文 *mandare*（= order ; entrust）。〔變化型〕*mend*。

command[3] 〔kə'mænd〕v. 命令；統帥；指揮
n. 命令；指揮；支配《*com-* = together with》

commander[4] 〔kə'mændɚ〕n. 命令者；支配者；司令官

commandment[7] 〔kə'mæn(d)mənt〕n. 戒律；聖誡
the Ten Commandments 摩西的十誡

countermand 〔v. ˌkaʊntɚ'mænd　n. 'kaʊntɚˌmænd〕v. 撤消（命
令）；下令撤消　n. 收回命令（命令的相反）《*counter-* = against》

```
counter + mand
   |        |
against  + order
```

demand[4] 〔 dɪ'mænd 〕 v. 需要；詢問　n. 要求；請求；需要

（命令交付）《 de- = off》

demandable 〔 dɪ'mændəbḷ 〕 adj. 可要求的

demandant 〔 dɪ'mændənt 〕 n. 原告

demander 〔 dɪ'mændɚ 〕 n. 要求者

demanding[7] 〔 dɪ'mændɪŋ 〕 adj. 過分要求的；苛求的；費力的

mandate[7] 〔'mændet 〕 n. 命令；訓令；委託統治　v. 託管

mandatory[7] 〔'mændə,torɪ , -,tɔrɪ 〕 adj. 命令的；受委託統治的；

必須的；強迫性的

remand 〔 rɪ'mænd , -'mɑnd 〕 v. 送回；還押　n. 送還；還押

（命令返回）《 re- = back》

reprimand[7] 〔 n. 'rɛprə,mænd v. ,rɛprə'mænd 〕 n., v. 譴責；懲戒

《拉丁文 reprimenda = (things) to be repressed》

commend[7] 〔 kə'mɛnd 〕 v. 稱讚；推薦；委託（共同委託）

《 com- = together with》

```
com       + mend
 |            |
together with + order
```

commendation[7] 〔,kɑmən'deʃən 〕 n. 稱讚；推薦

recommend[5] 〔,rɛkə'mɛnd 〕 v. 介紹；推薦；勸告（再經一人之手）

《 re- = again》

recommendation[6] 〔,rɛkəmɛn'deʃən 〕 n. 推薦；忠告

322　**mania** = madness（瘋狂）

* 希臘文 mania（ = madness）。

maniac[7] 〔'menɪ,æk 〕 n. 瘋子；入迷的人　adj. 瘋狂的；狂熱的

dipsomania 〔,dɪpsə'menɪə 〕 n. 嗜酒狂；間發性酒狂

《 dipso = thirst（口渴）》

kleptomania〔͵klɛptə'menɪə〕*n.* 偷竊狂；竊盜癖

```
klepto  +  mania
  |          |
steal   +  madness
```

megalomania〔͵mɛgələ'menɪə〕*n.* 誇大狂
《*megalo-* = great》

monomania〔͵mɑnə'menɪə〕*n.* 偏執狂；（對某一事物的）狂熱
《*mono-* = single》

nymphomania〔͵nɪmfə'menɪə〕*n.* 慕男狂；女性色情狂
《*nympho* = bride（新娘）》

pyromania〔͵paɪrə'menɪə〕*n.* 縱火狂《*pyro* = fire》

323   mar , mari = sea（海）

* 拉丁文 *mare*（= *sea*）。

marina[7]〔mə'rinə〕*n.* 小船塢（遊艇、汽艇等的停泊處）

marine[5]〔mə'rin〕*adj.* 海的；海中的；海產的；海運的
n. 航海業；海軍陸戰隊

mariculture〔͵mærə'kʌltʃɚ〕*n.* 海產養殖業《*culture* 養殖》

mariner〔'mærənɚ〕*n.* 船員；水手

maritime〔'mærə͵taɪm〕*adj.* 海的；海事的；海運的

submarine[3]〔*adj.* ͵sʌbmə'rin. 'sʌbmə͵rin〕*adj.* 海底的；
海中的 *n.* 海底動（植）物；潛水艇（海下面的）
《*sub-* = under》

transmarine〔͵trænsmə'rin〕*adj.* 海外的；來自海外的；
橫越海洋的（跨海的）《*trans-* = across》

ultramarine〔͵ʌltrəmə'rin〕*adj.* 海外的；海那邊的；深藍色的
《*ultra-* = beyond》

324　**mark** = mark ; boundary (做記號;邊界)

* 古英文 *mearc* (= *mark* ; *boundary*);中古法文 *marquer*
(= *mark*)。

mark[2] ﹝ mark ﹞ *n.* 符號;分數;標籤　*v.* 記分;做記號;加標籤;
使顯著

marked[7] ﹝ markt ﹞ *adj.* 有記號的;顯著的

markedly[7] ﹝ 'markɪdlɪ ﹞ *adv.* 明顯地;顯著地

marker[7] ﹝ 'markɚ ﹞ *n.* 作記號之人或物;記分員;書籤;籌碼

demarcate ﹝ 'dimar,ket ﹞ *v.* 劃界;區分 (畫下記號) 《*de-* = down》

```
de  + marc + ate
 |      |     |
down + mark +  v.
```

demarcation ﹝ ,dimar'keʃən ﹞ *n.* 定界線;界線;區分

remark[4] ﹝ rɪ'mark ﹞ *v.* 談及;評論;注意　*n.* 評論;注意
(再做記號) 《*re-* = again》

remarkable[4] ﹝ rɪ'markəbḷ ﹞ *adj.* 值得注意的;顯著的

325　**matr** = mother (母親)

* 拉丁文 *mater* (= *mother*)。

maternal[7] ﹝ mə'tɝnḷ ﹞ *adj.* 母親的;似母親的;母系的

maternalism ﹝ mə'tɝnḷ,ɪzəm ﹞ *n.* 母性;母性本能

maternity ﹝ mə'tɝnətɪ ﹞ *n.* 母愛;母性

matriarchy[7] ﹝ 'metrɪ,arkɪ ﹞ *n.* 女家長制;女族長制 《*archy* = rule》

```
matri  + archy
  |        |
mother +  rule
```

matricide ﹝ 'metrə,saɪd , 'mætrə- ﹞ *n.* 弒母;弒母者 (殺了母親)
《*cide* = cut》

matrilineal 〔͵metrɪ'lɪnɪəl, ͵mætrɪ-〕 *adj.* 母系的
《*matri* (mother) + *line* (line 家系) + *-al* (形容詞字尾)》

```
matri  + line + al
  |        |     |
mother + line + adj.
```

matrimony[7] 〔'mætrə͵monɪ〕*n.* 結婚；夫婦關係；婚姻生活
(成爲母親) 《 *-mony* = *-ment* (抽象名詞字尾)》

matrix[7] 〔'metrɪks, 'mæt-〕*n.* 子宮；母體；鑄型；模型；母岩

matron 〔'metrən〕*n.* 年長已婚婦女；護士長；女舍監；保姆

326 **meas , mens** = measure (測量)

* 拉丁文 *metiri* (= *measure*)，過去分詞爲 *mensus*。

measure[2,4] 〔'mɛʒɚ〕*v.* 測量；衡量　*n.* 尺寸；措施

admeasure 〔æd'mɛʒɚ〕*v.* (合適地) 分配給；給予《*ad-* = to》

commeasure 〔kə'mɛʒɚ〕*v.* 與…相等《*com-* = together》

countermeasure 〔'kaʊntɚ͵mɛʒɚ〕*n.* 對抗手段；對策
《*counter-* = *contra-* = against》

immeasurable[7] 〔ɪ'mɛʒərəb!〕*adj.* 不可計量的；無邊無際的

```
im + measur + able
 |     |       |
not + measure + adj.
```

overmeasure 〔'ovɚ͵mɛʒɚ〕*n.* 過量；剩餘量

mensural 〔'mɛnʃʊrəl〕*adj.* (有關) 度量的

commensurate 〔kə'mɛnʃərɪt〕*adj.* 同量的；相稱的

```
com + mensur + ate
 |      |       |
with + measure + adj.
```

dimension[6] 〔də'mɛnʃən〕*n.* 尺寸；規模；次元《*di-* = *dis-* = apart》

immense[5] 〔ɪ'mɛns〕*adj.* 廣大的；巨大的

327 mechan = machine (機器)

* 希臘文 *mechane* (= machine)。

mechanic[4] 〔 məˈkænɪk 〕 *n.* 機械士;技工《 *-ic* 表示人的名詞字尾》
mechanical[4] 〔 məˈkænɪkl̩ 〕 *adj.* 機械的;呆板的;自動的
mechanics[5] 〔 məˈkænɪks 〕 *n.* 機械學;力學;技巧
  《 *-ics* = science ; system》

```
mechan  +   ics
  |          |
machine  + science
```

mechanism[6] 〔 ˈmɛkəˌnɪzəm 〕 *n.* 機械 (裝置);機械論;結構;
  技巧;心理歷程
mechanize[7] 〔 ˈmɛkəˌnaɪz 〕 *v.* 機械化

328 med = heal (治療)   * 拉丁文 *mederi* (= heal)。

medic[7] 〔 ˈmɛdɪk 〕 *n.* 醫生;醫學院學生;醫務兵
  《 *-ic* 表示人的名詞字尾》
medical[3] 〔 ˈmɛdɪkl̩ 〕 *adj.* 醫學的;醫藥的;內科的
  n. 醫生;醫學院學生;體格檢查
medicate[6] 〔 ˈmɛdɪˌket 〕 *v.* 以藥物治療;摻入藥品
medication[6] 〔 ˌmɛdɪˈkeʃən 〕 *n.* 藥物治療;摻入藥品;藥物

```
med  +   ic   + ation
 |        |       |
heal + person  +  n.
```

medicine[2] 〔 ˈmɛdəsn̩ 〕 *n.* 藥;醫學;內科;醫生行業
medicinal[7] 〔 məˈdɪsn̩l̩ 〕 *adj.* 醫藥的;治療的
remedy[4] 〔 ˈrɛmədɪ 〕 *n.* 治療方法;藥物;補救方法
  v. 治療;補救;糾正 (再治療)《 *re-* = again》

remediable 〔 rɪ'midɪəbḷ 〕 *adj.* 可治療的；可補救的；可矯正的

```
re   + medi + able
 |       |      |
again + heal + adj.
```

remedial 〔 rɪ'midɪəl 〕 *adj.* 治療的；補救的；矯正的
irremediable 〔,ɪrɪ'midɪəbḷ , ,ɪrrɪ- 〕 *adj.* 無法治療的；無法補救的
　《*ir-* = *in-* = not》

329　medi = middle (中間的)

　　* 拉丁文 *medius* (= *middle*) 。

medium[3] 〔'midɪəm 〕 *n.* 媒介物；媒體；手段　　*adj.* 中間的
　（在中間的東西）
medial 〔'midɪəl 〕 *adj.* 中間的；普通的；平均的
median[7] 〔'midɪən 〕 *adj.* 中間的　*n.* 中間數字
mediate[5] 〔 *v.* 'midɪ,et　*adj.* 'midɪɪt 〕 *v.* 居中；調停；斡旋
　adj. 中間的；間接的（進入中間）

```
medi + ate
  |      |
middle + adj.
```

mediation[7] 〔,midɪ'eʃən 〕 *n.* 仲裁；調停
mediator 〔'midɪ,etɚ 〕 *n.* 中間人；媒介者；調停仲裁者
mediocre[7] 〔'midɪ,okɚ , ,midɪ'okɚ 〕 *adj.* 平庸的；平凡的
　（位於兩極端之間）《*medi* (middle) + *ocre* (stony mountain)》
medi(a)eval[6] 〔,midɪ'ivḷ , ,mɛdɪ- 〕 *adj.* 中古的　*n.* 中古時代的人
　（中間的時代）《*ev* = age ; time》
Mediterranean[7] 〔,mɛdətə'renɪən 〕 *n.* 地中海　*adj.* 地中海的
　（在土地的正中央）《*terra* = earth》
immediate[3] 〔 ɪ'midɪɪt 〕 *adj.* 直接的；立刻的（沒有間隔）
　《*im-* = *in-* = not》

intermediate[4]（ _v._ ˌɪntɚˈmidɪˌet　_adj._ , _n._ ˌɪntɚˈmidɪɪt ）_v._ 做中間人；干預　_adj._ 中間的　_n._ 中間人（物）（進入二者之中）

《 _inter-_ = between 》

```
inter  +  medi  +   ate
  |        |         |
between + middle + adj., n., v.
```

intermediation（ ˌɪntɚˌmidɪˈeʃən ）_n._ 仲裁；調停

intermediary[7]（ ˌɪntɚˈmidɪˌɛrɪ ）_n._ 中間人；幹旋者

　adj. 中間的；幹旋的《 _-ary_ 表示人或形容詞字尾》

330　**melan** = black（黑色的）

　* 希臘文 _melas_ , _melan-_ （ = black ）。

melancholia[7]（ ˌmɛlənˈkolɪə ）_n._ 憂鬱症

　《 _melan_ （ black ）+ _chol_ （ bile 膽汁 ）+ _-ia_ （ 名詞字尾 ）》

```
melan + chol + ia
  |       |     |
black +  bile + n.
```

【解說】 black bile（黑膽汁），人體四種體液之一，醫藥之父希波克拉底（Hippocrates）視之爲腎或脾的分泌物，並認爲若分泌過多會使人憂鬱。

melancholiac（ ˌmɛlənˈkolɪˌæk ）_n._ 憂鬱症患者

　《 _-iac_ 表示人的名詞字尾》

melancholic（ ˌmɛlənˈkɑlɪk ）_adj._ 憂鬱的；患憂鬱症的

　_n._ 憂鬱症患者

melancholy[6]（ ˈmɛlənˌkɑlɪ ）_adj._ 憂鬱的；悲哀的

　_n._ 憂鬱；悲哀

melanin（ ˈmɛlənɪn ）_n._ 黑色素

melanism（ ˈmɛlənɪzm̩ ）_n._ 黑變病；黑色素過多

melanoma（ ˌmɛləˈnomə ）_n._ 黑素瘤《 _-oma_ = tumor（ 腫瘤 ）》

331 **mell** = honey (蜂蜜；甜蜜)

* 拉丁文 *mel* , *mell-* (= *honey*)；希臘文 *meli* (= *honey*)。

melliferous 〔 məˈlɪfərəs 〕 *adj.* 產蜜的；甜的 《*fer* = bear》
mellifluous 〔 məˈlɪfluəs 〕 *adj.* 聲音甜美的；流暢的

```
melli + flu + ous
  |      |     |
honey + flow + adj.
```

Melissa 〔 məˈlɪsə 〕 *n.* 【女子名】梅利莎
melissa 〔 məˈlɪsə 〕 *n.* 蜜蜂花 《希臘文 *melissa* = honeybee》
molasses 〔 məˈlæsɪz 〕 *n.* 糖蜜
　《後期拉丁文 *mellaceum* = must (葡萄汁)》
marmalade 〔ˈmɑrml͵ed 〕 *n.* 果醬

332 **memor** = remember (記得)

* 拉丁文 *memor* (= *mindful* ; *remembering*)，*memorare*
(= *remind*)。

memorable[4] 〔ˈmɛmərəbl̩ 〕 *adj.* 值得紀念的　*n.* 值得紀念的事物
memorial[4] 〔 məˈmorɪəl , -ˈmɔr- 〕 *n.* 紀念物　*adj.* 紀念的
memory[2] 〔ˈmɛmərɪ 〕 *n.* 記憶力；記憶
memorize[3] 〔ˈmɛmə͵raɪz 〕 *v.* 記於心；背誦；記錄
memorandum[7] 〔͵mɛməˈrændəm 〕 *n.* 備忘錄；便箋 (以備回憶)
　《*memor* (remember) + *-and* = *-end* (be) + *-um* (名詞字尾)》

```
memor  + and + um
  |       |     |
remember + be + n.
```

memoir[7] 〔ˈmɛmwɑr , -wɔr 〕 *n.* (*pl.*) 回憶錄；自傳
memento[7] 〔 mɪˈmɛnto 〕 *n.* 紀念品

commemorate[6]〔kəˈmɛməˌret〕*v.* 紀念；慶祝；表揚

（一起懷念）《*com-* = together》

```
com  +  memor  + ate
 |        |       |
together + remember + v.
```

commemorable〔kəˈmɛmərəbḷ〕*adj.* 值得紀念、慶祝的

commemoration〔kəˌmɛməˈreʃən〕*n.* 紀念；慶祝

remember[1]〔rɪˈmɛmbɚ〕*v.* 記得；記起；問候；饋贈（回想起來）

《*re-* = back》

remembrance[7]〔rɪˈmɛmbrəns〕*n.* 記憶（力）；紀念（物）；

（*pl.*）問候

333　men , mens = month（月）

* 希臘文 *men*（= *month*）；拉丁文 *mensis*（= *month*）。

menopause〔ˈmɛnəˌpɔz〕*n.* 停經；更年期《*pause* 中止》

menology〔mɪˈnɑlədʒɪ〕*n.* 將聖徒和殉道者的生涯按月記錄的

教會曆《希臘文 *logos* = word》

menses〔ˈmɛnsiz〕*n.pl.* 月經

menstruate[7]〔ˈmɛnstruˌet〕*v.* 行經；月經來潮

amenorrhea〔eˌmɛnəˈriə〕*n.* 閉經；無月經《*a-* = not》

```
a  +  meno  + rrhea
|       |       |
not  + month + flow
```

catamenia〔ˌkætəˈminɪə〕*n.pl.* 月經《*cata-* = down》

emmenagogue〔əˈmɛnəgɔg〕*n.* 通經藥

```
em  +  men  + agogue
 |      |       |
in  + month + leader
```

334　**ment** = mind（心智）

*＊ 拉丁文 **mens** , **ment-**（= mind）。*

mental[3]〔'mɛntḷ〕*adj.* 心理的；智力的；精神的
mentalism〔'mɛntḷˌɪzm〕*n.* 唯心論；心理主義
　《 **-ism** = 主義；學說》
mentalist〔'mɛntḷɪst〕*n.* 具心靈感應能力者
　《 **-ist** 表示人的名詞字尾》
mentality[6]〔mɛn'tælətɪ〕*n.* 智力；心理狀態
mention[3]〔'mɛnʃən〕*v.* 提到；述及（使注意）
amentia〔ə'mɛnʃɪə〕*n.* 白痴；精神錯亂（缺乏心智的狀態）
　《**a-** = without》

a	+ ment +	ia
|	|	|
without +	*mind* +	*condition*

comment[4]〔'kɑmɛnt〕*n.* 評論；註解；談論　*v.* 評論；批評；
談論（徹底論及）《**com-** = thoroughly》
commentary[6]〔'kɑmənˌtɛrɪ〕*n.* 註解；評語；紀事
demented[7]〔dɪ'mɛntɪd〕*adj.* 瘋狂的；精神錯亂的（失去心智）
　《**de-** = away》

de	+ ment +	ed
|	|	|
away +	*mind* +	*adj.*

dementia〔dɪ'mɛnʃɪə , -ʃə〕*n.* 痴呆《 **-ia** = condition》
vehement[7]〔'viəmənt , 'vihɪ-〕*adj.* 熱情的；猛烈的；激烈的
（使精神感動）《**vehe** = carry》

vehe	+ ment
|	|
carry +	*mind*

mind[1]〔 maɪnd 〕*n.* 心；意志；精神；理性；智力　*v.* 注意；
關心；介意《古英文 *gemynd* = memory ; thinking》

remind[3]〔 rɪˈmaɪnd 〕*v.* 使想起；提醒（使再想起）《*re-* = again》

reminder[5]〔 rɪˈmaɪndɚ 〕*n.* 提醒者；勾起回憶的人或物

reminiscent[7]〔ˌrɛməˈnɪsn̩t 〕*adj.* 回憶的；喜歡談論往事的；
引起回憶的《*-iscent* 形容詞字尾》

reminiscence[7]〔ˌrɛməˈnɪsn̩s 〕*n.* 回憶；回想；(*pl.*) 回憶錄

335　**mer** = part（部分）　　*希臘文 *meros*（= *part*）。

meroblast〔ˈmɛrəblæst 〕*n.* 部分裂卵；不全裂卵《*blast* = bud》

meroblastic〔ˌmɛrəˈblæstɪk 〕*adj.* (卵) 不全裂的

merohedral〔ˌmɛrəˈhidrəl 〕*adj.* (晶體的) 缺面的；缺面對稱的
《希臘文 *hedron* = side》

meropia〔 məˈropɪə 〕*n.* 半盲

```
mer  +  op  +  ia
 |       |      |
part + sight +  n.
```

polymerous〔 pəˈlɪmərəs 〕*adj.* 由多部分組成的《*poly-* = many》

336　**merc** = trade ; reward（貿易；報酬）

*拉丁文 *mercari*（= *trade*），*merces*（= *reward*），*merx*
（= *merchandise* 商品）。這些字大都來自 *merere*（= *gain* ; *buy*）。

mercantile[7]〔ˈmɝkənˌtil , -ˌtaɪl 〕*adj.* 貿易的；商業的
《*-ile* 形容詞字尾》

mercenary[7]〔ˈmɝsn̩ˌɛrɪ 〕*adj.* 被僱的；圖利的　*n.* 傭兵

mercer〔ˈmɝsɚ 〕*n.* 布商（商人）

merchandise[6]〔ˈmɝtʃənˌdaɪz 〕*n.* 【集合名詞】商品
v. 交易；買賣

merchant[3]〔'mɜtʃənt〕*n.* 商人　*adj.* 商人的；商業的
《 *-ant* 表示人的名詞字尾》

```
merch ＋ ant
  |       |
trade ＋ person
```

market[1] 〔'mɑrkɪt〕*n.* 市場；市集（交易的場所）　*v.* 交易；出售
《 *mark = merc* 》

marketing[7] 〔'mɑrkɪtɪŋ〕*n.* 市場交易；買賣；行銷

mercy[4] 〔'mɜsɪ〕*n.* 慈悲（報酬 → 給予他人的東西）

merciful[7] 〔'mɜsɪfəl〕*adj.* 仁慈的；慈悲的

merciless[7] 〔'mɜsɪlɪs〕*adj.* 不慈悲的；殘忍的

commerce[4] 〔'kɑmɜs〕*n.* 商業；貿易（共同交易）《*com-* = together》

commercial[3] 〔kə'mɜʃəl〕*adj.* 商業的；營利的　*n.* 廣告節目

337　**merg , mers** = sink；dip（沉沒；浸泡）

* 拉丁文 *mergere*（ = *sink*；*dip* ），過去分詞 *mersus*。

merge[6] 〔mɜdʒ〕*v.* 沒入；合併（沉沒）

mergence 〔'mɜdʒəns〕*n.* 沒入；消失

merger[7] 〔'mɜdʒɚ〕*n.* 合併

emerge[4] 〔ɪ'mɜdʒ〕*v.* 出現；露出（從沉沒狀態出來）
《*e-* = *ex-* = out of》

emergence[7] 〔ɪ'mɜdʒəns〕*n.* 出現；露出

emergency[3] 〔ɪ'mɜdʒənsɪ〕*n.* 緊急事件；突發事件（突然出現
的東西）

emergent[7] 〔ɪ'mɜdʒənt〕*adj.* 出現的；緊急的

emersion[7] 〔i'mɜʃən , -ʒən〕*n.* 出現；浮出

```
 e ＋ mers ＋ ion
 |     |      |
out of ＋ sink ＋ n.
```

immerge[7] 〔 ɪ'mɝdʒ 〕 v. 浸入；使陷入（沉沒其中）《*im-* = *in-* = into》
immerse[7] 〔 ɪ'mɝs 〕 v. 浸入；使陷入（ = *immerge*）
immersion[7] 〔 ɪ'mɝʃən 〕 n. 沈入；熱中
submerge[7] 〔 səb'mɝdʒ 〕 v. 浸入水中；淹沒（沉入下面）
　《*sub-* = under》

```
sub   +  merge
 |        |
under  +  sink
```

submergence 〔 səb'mɝdʒəns 〕 n. 潛水；沉沒
submerse[7] 〔 səb'mɝs 〕 v. = submerge
submersion 〔 səb'mɝʃən , -ʒən 〕 n. = submergence
submersible 〔 səb'mɝsəbl̩ 〕 adj. 可潛入水中的　n. 潛水艇

338　**meter , metr** = measure（測量）

　* 希臘文 **metron**（ = *measure*）。

meter[2] 〔 'mitɚ 〕 n. 公尺；測量器　v. 以測量器計量
metric[7] 〔 'mɛtrɪk 〕 adj. 測量的；公制的
metricate 〔 'mɛtrɪ,ket 〕 v. 採用公制
metrology 〔 mɪ'trɑlədʒɪ 〕 n. 度量衡學；度量衡制《*logy* = study》
metronome 〔 'mɛtrə,nom 〕 n. 節拍器（按次序測量）

```
metro   +  nome
  |         |
measure +  regulate
```

aerometer 〔 ,eə'rɑmətɚ 〕 n. 氣量計；氣體比重計《*aero* = air》
anemometer 〔 ,ænə'mɑmətɚ 〕 n. 風速計；測風儀
　《*anemo* = wind》
barometer[6] 〔 bə'rɑmətɚ 〕 n. 氣壓計；晴雨計（測定空氣的重量）
　《*baro* = weight》

centimeter[3] 〔'sɛntə,mitɚ 〕*n.* 公分（百分之一公尺）

《 *centi* = hundredth 》

```
centi  +  meter
  |         |
hundredth + measure
```

chronometer 〔 krə'nɑmətɚ 〕*n.* 航海用的經線儀《 *chrono* = time 》
chronometry 〔 krə'nɑmətrɪ 〕*n.* 測時術；計時法
diameter[6] 〔 daɪ'æmətɚ 〕*n.* 直徑（直徑的長度）《 *dia-* = across 》

```
dia  +  meter
 |        |
across + measure
```

dynamometer 〔,daɪnə'mɑmətɚ 〕*n.* 測力計；功率計

《 *dynamo* = power 》

geometry[5] 〔 dʒi'ɑmətrɪ 〕*n.* 幾何學（測量土地 → 幾何學之先驅）

《 *geo* = earth 》

heliometer 〔,hilɪ'ɑmətɚ 〕*n.* 太陽儀《 *helio* = sun 》
hydrometer 〔 haɪ'drɑmətɚ 〕*n.* （液體）比重計《 *hydro* = water 》
hygrometer 〔 haɪ'grɑmətɚ 〕*n.* 濕度計《 *hygro* = wet 》
odometer 〔 o'dɑmətɚ 〕*n.* （汽車等之）里程表

```
odo +  meter
 |        |
way + measure
```

parameter[7] 〔 pə'ræmətɚ 〕*n.*【數】參數；限制（範圍）

```
para  +  meter
  |         |
alongside + measure
```

perimeter[7] 〔 pə'rɪmətɚ 〕*n.* 周圍；周邊（周圍的長度）《 *peri-* = round 》

```
peri +  meter
 |        |
round + measure
```

seismometer〔saɪz'mɑmətɚ, saɪs-〕*n.* 地震儀《*seismo* = shake》

symmetrical[7]〔sɪ'mɛtrɪkl̩〕*adj.* 對稱的；均勻的

```
sym  +  metr  +  ical
 |        |        |
together + measure + adj.
```

symmetry[6]〔'sɪmɪtrɪ〕*n.* 對稱；調和（都是同樣的長度）
　《*sym-* = together》

thermometer[6]〔θə'mɑmətɚ〕*n.* 溫度計；寒暑表《*thermo* = heat》

trigonometry〔‚trɪgə'nɑmətrɪ〕*n.* 三角法（測量三個角）
　《*tri-* = three ; *gon* = angle（角）》

voltmeter〔'volt‚mitɚ〕*n.* 伏特計；電壓表《*volt* 伏特》

339　**migr** = remove ; wander（移動；流浪）

　　＊拉丁文 migrare（= wander）。

migrate[6]〔'maɪgret〕*v.* 移動；隨季節變化而移居（從某地移動
至某地）

migrant[5]〔'maɪgrənt〕*adj.* 移居的　*n.* 移居者；候鳥

migration[6]〔maɪ'greʃən〕*n.* 移居；移動；移民

migratory[7]〔'maɪgrə‚torɪ, -‚tɔrɪ〕*adj.* 移動的；移居的；
流浪性的

emigrate[6]〔'ɛmə‚gret〕*v.* 移居（他國）（向外移動）
　《*e-* = *ex-* = out》

```
e  +  migr  +  ate
 |      |       |
out + remove +  v.
```

emigrant[6]〔'ɛməgrənt〕*adj.* 移民的　*n.* 移民；僑民

emigration[6]〔‚ɛmə'greʃən〕*n.* 移居；移民

immigrate[4]〔'ɪmə‚gret〕*v.*（自外國）移民（移動過來）
　《*im-* = *in-* = into》

immigrant[4] 〔ˈɪməgrənt , -ˌgrænt 〕 *adj.* 自外移入的
　　n. (自外國移入之) 移民

```
im  +  migr  +  ant
 |       |       |
into + remove + person
```

immigration[4] 〔ˌɪməˈgreʃən 〕 *n.* (自外國) 移居入境
transmigrate 〔 trænsˈmaɪgret , trænz- 〕 *v.* 移居;輪迴
　　(越過界限移動)《*trans-* = across》

```
trans  +  migr  +  ate
  |         |       |
across + remove +  v.
```

transmigrant 〔 trænsˈmaɪgrənt 〕 *adj.* 移居的　　*n.* 移民
transmigration 〔ˌtrænsmaɪˈgreʃən 〕 *n.* 移居;轉生;輪迴

340　milit = soldier;fight (軍人;打仗)

　　　　* 拉丁文 *miles* , *milit-* (= soldier) 。

militant[6] 〔ˈmɪlətənt 〕 *adj.* 好戰的;從事戰鬥的;態度強硬的
　　n. 好戰者;態度強硬者
militancy 〔ˈmɪlətənsɪ 〕 *n.* 好戰;強硬態度;交戰狀態
military[2] 〔ˈmɪləˌtɛrɪ 〕 *adj.* 軍人的;軍事的;戰爭的;好戰的
　　n. 軍隊;【集合名詞】軍人《 *-ary* 形容詞字尾》

```
milit  +  ary
  |        |
soldier + adj.
```

militarize 〔ˈmɪlətəˌraɪz 〕 *v.* 使軍隊化;武裝;使好戰
militarism 〔ˈmɪlətəˌrɪzəm 〕 *n.* 軍國主義;尚武精神
　　《 *-ism* = 主義;學說》
militate 〔ˈmɪləˌtet 〕 *v.* 發生作用;影響

字根 magn~narc

militia[7] 〔 məˈlɪʃə 〕 *n.* 人民自衛隊；民兵部隊；國民軍

demilitarize 〔 diˈmɪlətəˌraɪz 〕 *v.* 廢除軍備；解除軍事控制

（軍事化的相反）《*de-* = negative（否定）》

de +	milit +	ar(y) +	ize
not +	*soldier* +	*adj.* +	*v.*

demilitarization 〔 diˌmɪlətərɪˈzeʃən , -raɪˈze- 〕 *n.* 廢除軍備；
解除軍事控制

remilitarize 〔 riˈmɪlətəˌraɪz 〕 *v.* 重整軍備；再武裝（再度軍事化）
《*re-* = again》

remilitarization 〔ˌrimɪlətərɪˈzeʃən , -raɪˈze- 〕 *n.* 重整軍備；
再武裝

341   **min** = jut ; project（突出）

* 拉丁文 **minere**（ = *jut* ; *project*）。

eminent[7] 〔ˈɛmənənt 〕 *adj.* 卓越的；顯著的（向外面突出 → 展露
頭角）《*e-* = *ex-* = out》

eminence[7] 〔ˈɛmənəns 〕 *n.* 卓越；高地

imminent[7] 〔ˈɪmənənt 〕 *adj.* 迫切的；迫近的（突出於頭部之上）
《*im-* = *in-* = upon ; over》

imminence[7] 〔ˈɪmənəns 〕 *n.* 迫切；迫近

preeminent[7] 〔 prɪˈɛmənənt 〕 *adj.* 優越的；卓越的（比別人先
突出）《*pre-* = before》

pre +	e +	min +	ent
before +	*out* +	*jut* +	*adj.*

preeminence[7] 〔 prɪˈɛmənəns 〕 *n.* 卓越；傑出

prominent[4] 〔ˈprɑmənənt 〕 *adj.* 突出的；顯著的（向前突出）
《*pro-* = forward》

字根 magn~narc

prominence[7] 〔'prɑmənəns 〕 *n.* 突起；顯著；卓越

supereminent 〔,supɚ'ɛmənənt , ,sju- 〕 *adj.* 出類拔萃的；特別崇高的（更加突出）《*super-* = over》

supereminence 〔,supɚ'ɛmənəns , ,sju- 〕 *n.* 出類拔萃；崇高

342 min = small (小的)   * 拉丁文 *minutus* (= small) 。

minify 〔'mɪnə,faɪ 〕 *v.* 縮小；使減少（使變小）《 *-ify* = make》

minification 〔,mɪnəfə'keʃən 〕 *n.* 縮小；減少；削減

minim 〔'mɪnɪm 〕 *n.* 微小；些微

minimal[5] 〔'mɪnɪml̩ 〕 *adj.* 最低限度的

minimize[6] 〔'mɪnə,maɪz 〕 *v.* 減至最少量；貶低

minimum[4] 〔'mɪnəməm 〕 *n.* 最低限度；極小

   《 *-mum* 拉丁文的最高級字尾》 *cf.* **maximum** (極大)

minor[3] 〔'maɪnɚ 〕 *adj.* 較小的   *n.* 未成年者；副科《 *-or* 比較級字尾》

minority[3] 〔 mə'nɔrətɪ , maɪ- 〕 *n.* 少數；未成年

minus[2] 〔'maɪnəs 〕 *n.* 減；缺少   *adj.* 減的；負的   *prep.* 減（使變少）

minuscule[7] 〔 mɪ'nʌskjul 〕 *n.* 小寫字體   *adj.* 小字的；微小的

   《 *-cule* = small》

```
minus + cule
  |       |
small + small
```

minute[11] 〔'mɪnɪt 〕 *n.* 分（六十秒）；片刻   *v.* 量；作～之記錄

   （ 把一小時分成小片段 ）

minute[21] 〔 mə'njut , maɪ- 〕 *adj.* 微細的；精細的（細而小的）

minutia[7] 〔 mɪ'njuʃɪə 〕 *n.* 小節；詳細；細目；瑣事

mince[7] 〔 mɪns 〕 *v.* 切碎；拐彎抹角地說

comminute 〔'kɑmə,njut , -,nut 〕 *v.* 粉碎；弄成粉末；細分

   （ 全部變小 ）《 *com-* = together》

comminution 〔,kɑmə'njuʃən , -'nu- 〕 *n.* 粉碎；磨損

diminish[6]〔dəˈmɪnɪʃ〕 *v.* 減少；縮小（完全縮小）《*di-* = *de-*》

```
di      +  min  + ish
 |          |       |
completely + small + v.
```

diminution〔ˌdɪməˈnjuʃən , -ˈnu-〕 *n.* 減少

diminutive[7]〔dəˈmɪnjətɪv〕 *adj.* 小的；小型的；暱稱的

　n. 表示「小」的語辭；縮小形；暱稱

【注意】以下二字字源不同，為方便而歸於此處。

miniature〔ˈmɪnɪətʃɚ〕 *n.* 縮小物；縮圖；小畫像

　v. 為～作縮影（以紅著色）《拉丁文 *minium* = cinnabar（朱）》

minikin〔ˈmɪnɪkɪn〕 *n.* 微小之物；侏儒　　*adj.* 微小的

　（覺得可愛的東西）《*-kin* 指小東西》

343　　minister = serve（服務）

　　* 拉丁文 *minister*（= *servant*），*ministrare*（= *serve*）。

minister[4]〔ˈmɪnɪstɚ〕 *n.* 牧師；部長；公使　*v.* 服侍；協助

　（小人物 → 僕人）《*-ster* 表示人的名詞字尾》

```
mini  +  ster
 |         |
small + person
```

ministrant〔ˈmɪnɪstrənt〕 *adj.* 服侍的；輔佐的　　*n.* 服侍者；

　輔佐者

ministry[4]〔ˈmɪnɪstrɪ〕 *n.* 教堂牧師；部；部長之職務（任期）；內閣

minstrel〔ˈmɪnstrəl〕 *n.* 吟遊詩人

　《古法文 *menestral* = servant ; entertainer》

administer[6]〔ədˈmɪnəstɚ〕 *v.* 管理；照料（克盡大臣的職務）

　《*ad-* = to》

administration[6]〔ədˌmɪnəˈstreʃən〕 *n.* 管理；行政；政府

administrative[6]〔ədˈmɪnəˌstretɪv〕 *adj.* 管理的；行政的

344　mir = wonder；behold（驚訝地看）

    * 拉丁文 *mirari*（= *wonder*），*mirare*（= *behold*）。

admire[3]〔əd'maɪr〕*v.* 羨慕；敬佩；欣賞（驚訝地瞪大眼睛）
  《*ad-* = at》

admirer[7]〔əd'maɪrə〕*n.* 崇拜者；欣賞者

admiration[4]〔,ædmə'reʃən〕*n.* 欽佩；讚賞

admirable[4]〔'ædmərəbḷ〕*adj.* 令人驚奇的；可敬佩的

```
ad  +  mir  + able
 |      |      |
at  + wonder + adj.
```

miracle[3]〔'mɪrəkḷ〕*n.* 奇蹟；奇事（令人見而驚訝者）

miraculous[6]〔mə'rækjələs〕*adj.* 奇蹟的；神奇的；不可思議的

mirage[7]〔mə'rɑʒ〕*n.* 海市蜃樓；幻想（驚訝地看著的東西）

mirror[2]〔'mɪrə〕*n.* 鏡　*v.* 反映（看的東西）

marvel[5]〔'mɑrvḷ〕*n.* 奇異之事　*v.* 驚異《拉丁文 *mirare* = wonder》

marvel(l)ous[3]〔'mɑrvḷəs〕*adj.* 奇異的；不平常的

345　misc , mix = mix（混合）

    * 拉丁文 *miscere*（= *mix*），過去分詞為 *mixtus*。

miscellaneous[7]〔,mɪsḷ'enɪəs〕*adj.* 各種各樣的；多才多藝的；
  多方面的《拉丁文 *miscellus* = mixed》

miscellanea〔,mɪsḷ'enɪə〕*n.pl.*（尤指文學作品的）雜集；雜錄

miscellany〔'mɪsḷ,enɪ〕*n.* 混合物；大雜燴；文集

miscegenation〔,mɪsɪdʒə'neʃən〕*n.*（白人與黑人的）異族通婚；
  種族混合

```
misce + gen + ation
  |      |      |
 mix  + race +  n.
```

mix[2]〔 mɪks 〕*v.* 混合；調製；混淆

mixer[7]〔'mɪksɚ〕*n.* 混合器；攪拌器；調音器；交際家；調酒用的飲料

mixture[3]〔'mɪkstʃɚ〕*n.* 混合；混合物《 *-ture* 名詞字尾》

admix〔 æd'mɪks , əd- 〕*v.* 混合；摻雜《 *ad-* = to》

admixture〔 æd'mɪkstʃɚ , əd- 〕*n.* 混合；摻雜；混合物

```
ad + mix + ture
 |     |     |
to  + mix +  n.
```

intermix〔,ɪntɚ'mɪks 〕*v.* 混合；交雜；融合（相互混合）
《 *inter-* = among ; between》

intermixture〔,ɪntɚ'mɪkstʃɚ〕*n.* 混合；交雜；融合；混合物

premix〔'pri'mɪks 〕*v.* 預先混合《 *pre-* = before》

346　**mit , miss , mis** = send ; let go（送；釋放）

* 拉丁文 *mittere*（ = *send* ; *throw*），過去分詞為 *missus*。

missile[3]〔'mɪsl̩〕*adj.* 可發射的　*n.* 子彈；飛彈（被投擲）

mission[3]〔'mɪʃən〕*n.* 使命；使節團（奉命被送往）

missionary[6]〔'mɪʃən,ɛrɪ〕*adj.* 傳道的　*n.* 傳道者；傳教士

missive[7]〔'mɪsɪv〕*n.* 公文；（冗長的）信

message[2]〔'mɛsɪdʒ〕*n.* 音信；通信；使命　*v.* 通信；報信
（送給人的東西）

messenger[4]〔'mɛsn̩dʒɚ〕*n.* 使者；報信者；前兆；先驅者（傳送者）

admit[3]〔 əd'mɪt 〕*v.* 承認；允許（送入；移進）《*ad-* = to》

admittance[7]〔 əd'mɪtn̩s 〕*n.* 入場權

admission[4]〔 əd'mɪʃən 〕*n.* 入場、入學許可；承認；告白（被送入）

```
ad + miss + ion
 |     |     |
to  + send +  n.
```

admissive 〔 əd'mɪsɪv 〕 *adj.* 准許進入的；許可的

commit[4] 〔 kə'mɪt 〕 *v.* 委託；犯（罪）（傳送～→委託）

《*com-* = with》

```
        com   +   mit
         │        │        （叫別人帶著一起走，即是「委託」，帶了
     together  +  let go      東西，易見財起意，就會「犯罪」）
```

commitment[6] 〔 kə'mɪtmənt 〕 *n.* 委託；犯罪；禁閉

committee[3] 〔 kə'mɪtɪ 〕 *n.* 委員會（被委任者）《*-ee* 表示「被～的人」》

commission[5] 〔 kə'mɪʃən 〕 *n.* 委任狀；委員會；授權

v. 委任；授權（委任之事）

commissioner[7] 〔 kə'mɪʃənɚ 〕 *n.* 委員；長官

compromise[5] 〔 'kɑmprə,maɪz 〕 *v.* 妥協；危及

n. 妥協（彼此共同約定）《*com-* = together ; *pro-* = forth》

```
     com   +   pro   +  mise
      │        │         │
  together  +  forth  +  send
```

demise[7] 〔 dɪ'maɪz 〕 *v.* 遺贈　*n.* 死亡；繼承（放手）《*de-* = away》

demission 〔 dɪ'mɪʃən 〕 *n.* 辭職

dismiss[4] 〔 dɪs'mɪs 〕 *v.* 解散；開除（零零散散地）；摒除；放棄；

駁回；不受理《*dis-* = apart》

dismissal[7] 〔 dɪs'mɪsl̩ 〕 *n.* 解散；免職；駁回；不受理

```
     dis   +   miss   +   al
      │         │         │
   apart   +   send   +   n.
```

emit[7] 〔 ɪ'mɪt 〕 *v.* 放出；吐露（送出）《*e-* = *ex-* = out》

emitter 〔 ɪ'mɪtɚ 〕 *n.* 發射器

emission[7] 〔 ɪ'mɪʃən 〕 *n.* 發射

emissary[7] 〔 'ɛmə,sɛrɪ 〕 *n.* 密使；間諜（偷偷地送出者）

intermit[7] 〔 ˌɪntɚ'mɪt 〕 *v.* 間歇；中斷（進入其間）《*inter-* = between》

intermittence〔,ɪntɚ'mɪtn̩s〕*n.* 斷續性；間歇性

intermittent[7]〔,ɪntɚ'mɪtn̩t〕*adj.* 斷續的；間歇的　*n.* 間歇熱

```
inter  +  mitt  +  ent
  |        |       |
between  +  send  +  adj.
```

intermission[7]〔,ɪntɚ'mɪʃən〕*n.* 休息時間；暫停

manumit〔,mænjə'mɪt〕*v.* 解放（奴隸）（由手中釋放出來）

《*manu* = hand》

manumission〔,mænjə'mɪʃən，,mænju-〕*n.* 奴隸解放

omit[2]〔o'mɪt，ə'mɪt〕*v.* 遺漏；省略（送走）《*o- = ob- =* away》

omission[7]〔o'mɪʃən〕*n.* 省略；刪除

omissible〔o'mɪsəbl̩〕*adj.* 可省略的；可忽視的

```
o   +  miss  +  ible
 |       |       |
away  +  send  +  adj.
```

omissive〔o'mɪsɪv〕*adj.* 忽略的；省略的

permit[3]〔*v.* pɚ'mɪt　*n.* 'pɝmɪt〕*v.* 許可　*n.* 許可書；證明書

（通過每一關）《*per-* = through》

permittance〔pɚ'mɪtn̩s〕*n.* 許可

permission[3]〔pɚ'mɪʃən〕*n.* 許可

permissive[7]〔pɚ'mɪsɪv〕*adj.* 許可的；寬容的

premise[7]〔*v.* prɪ'maɪz，'prɛmɪs　*n.* 'prɛmɪs〕*v.* 預述；立前提

n. 前提；（*pl.*）房產（置於前面）《*pre-* = before》

pretermit〔,pritɚ'mɪt〕*v.* 忽略；疏忽（飛快地）

《*preter-* = past ; beyond》

pretermission〔,pritɚ'mɪʃən〕*n.* 省略；忽略

```
preter  +  miss  +  ion
  |         |        |
past   +   send   +   n.
```

字根 *magn~narc*

promise[2]〔'promɪs〕*v.* 答應;約定 *n.* 諾言;約定(答應做~)
《*pro-* = forth》

promising[4]〔'promɪsɪŋ〕*adj.* 有前途的;有希望的

promissory〔'promə,sorɪ , -,sɔrɪ〕*adj.* 允諾的;約定的

remiss[7]〔rɪ'mɪs〕*adj.* 疏忽的;無精打采的《*re-* = back》

remit〔rɪ'mɪt〕*v.* 匯寄;匯款;緩和;釋放;赦免;寬恕
(回復本來的狀態)

remittance[7]〔rɪ'mɪtn̩s〕*n.* 匯款

remittee〔rɪmɪ'ti , -'mɪti〕*n.* 受款人《*-ee* 表示「被~的人」》

remitter〔rɪ'mɪtɚ〕*n.* 匯款人;寬恕者《*-er* 表示「做~的人」》

```
re  +  mitt  +  er
 |       |       |
back + send + person
```

remittent〔rɪ'mɪtn̩t〕*adj.* (病熱的)忽重忽輕的 *n.* 弛張熱

remission[7]〔rɪ'mɪʃən〕*n.* 赦免;緩和;減輕

remissive〔rɪ'mɪsɪv〕*adj.* 寬恕的

submit[5]〔səb'mɪt〕*v.* 使服從;使降服;提出;建議(在下面傳遞)
《*sub-* = under》

submitter〔səb'mɪtɚ〕*n.* 屈服者

submission[7]〔səb'mɪʃən〕*n.* 屈服;柔順

submissive[7]〔səb'mɪsɪv〕*adj.* 屈服的;柔順的

```
sub  +  miss  +  ive
 |        |        |
under + send + adj.
```

surmise[7]〔*v.* sɚ'maɪz *n.* 'sɚmaɪz〕*v.* 臆測;猜度 *n.* 臆測;猜度
(投注思考於~之上)《*sur-* = *super-* = upon ; above》

transmit[6]〔træns'mɪt〕*v.* 傳送;傳達(送到對面)《*trans-* = across》

transmitter〔træns'mɪtɚ〕*n.* 傳達者;發話機

transmission[6]〔træns'mɪʃən〕*n.* 送達;讓渡;傳導裝置;轉運

transmissive〔trænz'mɪsɪv〕*adj.* 傳送的;傳染的

347 mod = manner (態度；樣式；方式)

* 拉丁文 *modus* (= *measure* ; *manner* ; *kind* ; *way*)。

mode[5] 〔 mod 〕 *n.* 方法；形式；流行

modal[7] 〔'modḷ〕 *adj.* 樣式的；方式的；形態的

model[2] 〔'madḷ〕 *n.* 模型；模範 *adj.* 模範的 *v.* 塑造；作～之模型

moderate[4] 〔 *adj.* , *n.* 'madərɪt *v.* 'madə,ret 〕 *adj.* 適度的；穩健的；
溫和的 *n.* 穩健的人 *v.* 緩和；主持 (會議) (找出樣式)

moderation[7] 〔,madə'reʃən〕 *n.* 適度；穩健；緩和

moderator[7] 〔'madə,retɚ〕 *n.* 調停者；調整器

modern[2] 〔'madɚn〕 *adj.* 現代的；最近的 *n.* 現代人 (最新樣式的)

```
mod  +  ern
 |       |
manner + adj.
```

modernize[5] 〔'madɚn,aɪz〕 *v.* 使現代化

modest[4] 〔'madɪst〕 *adj.* 謙遜的 (不超越一定的模式)

modesty[4] 〔'madəstɪ〕 *n.* 謙遜

modify[5] 〔'madə,faɪ〕 *v.* 變更；修飾 (為適合模式而加以變更)
《 *-ify* = make 》

```
mod  +  ify
 |       |
manner + make
```

modification[7] 〔,madəfə'keʃən〕 *n.* 變更；修飾

modifier[7] 〔'madə,faɪɚ〕 *n.* 修改的人或物；修飾語

modish 〔'modɪʃ〕 *adj.* 流行的；時髦的《 *-ish* 形容詞字尾》

modulate[7] 〔'madʒə,let〕 *v.* 調整；轉調 (合乎一定的格式)
《 *-ate* 動詞字尾》

modulation[7] 〔,madʒə'leʃən〕 *n.* 調整；轉調

commodity[5]〔kə'madətɪ〕*n.* 商品；貨物（具有各種樣式的）
《*com-* = together》

```
com  + mod + ity
 |       |     |
together + kind + n.
```

commodious〔kə'modɪəs〕*adj.* 便利的；寬敞的；合宜的
commode〔kə'mod〕*n.* 洗臉台；室內的便桶（合乎模式的
便利之物）
accommodate[6]〔ə'kamə,det〕*v.* 給方便；容納；使適應
（使合乎時宜）《*ac-* = *ad-* = to》

```
ac +  com  + mod  + ate
 |      |      |      |
to + together + manner +  v.
```

accommodation[6]〔ə,kamə'deʃən〕*n.* 調節；和解；便利；
（*pl.*）住宿（收容）設備
outmoded〔aut'modɪd〕*adj.* 舊式的；過時的（式樣消失）
《*out-* = out》

348　**mon** = advise；remind（勸告；使想起）

　　* 拉丁文 *monere*（= *advise*；*remind*），過去分詞為 *monitus*。

monition〔mo'nɪʃən〕*n.* 警告；告誡（忠告；勸告）
monitor[4]〔'manətɚ〕*n.* 班長；勸告者；監考員；監視器
　v. 監視；監聽；監控；檢視（勸告的人或物）
monitorship〔'manətɚ,ʃɪp〕*n.* 班長的職務、地位、任期等；監督
　《*-ship* 表性質、作用等的抽象名詞字尾》
monitory〔'manə,torɪ, -,tɔrɪ〕*adj.* 勸告的；訓誡的
monument[4]〔'manjəmənt〕*n.* 紀念碑（像、塔）；遺物
　（使想起的東西）

monumental[7]〔͵mɑnjə'mɛntḷ〕*adj.* 紀念碑的；不朽的

```
monu  +  ment  +  al
  |        |       |
advise  +  n.   + adj.
```

monumentalize〔͵mɑnjʊ'mɛntḷ͵aɪz〕*v.*（以紀念碑等）紀念；
使不朽《*-ize* 動詞字尾》

admonish[7]〔əd'mɑnɪʃ〕*v.* 勸告；警告（忠告；勸告）《*ad-* = to》

```
ad  +  mon  +  ish
 |      |       |
to  + advise +  v.
```

admonition〔͵ædmə'nɪʃən〕*n.* 勸告；警告
admonitor〔əd'mɑnətɚ〕*n.* 勸告者；警告者

```
ad  +  monit  +  or
 |       |        |
to  + advise  +  n.
```

admonitory〔əd'mɑnə͵torɪ , æd- , -͵tɔrɪ〕*adj.* 勸告的；訓誡的；
忠言的
premonish〔pri'mɑnɪʃ〕*v.* 預先警告（先忠告）《*pre-* = before》
premonitory〔prɪ'mɑnə͵torɪ , -͵tɔrɪ〕*adj.* 預先告誡的；前兆的
summon[5]〔'sʌmən〕*v.* 召喚；召集；鼓起（勇氣等）（悄悄地來
加以勸告）《*sum-* = *sub-* = under》

349　**monstr** = show（表示）

> * 拉丁文 *monstrum*（= *portent* 徵兆；*monster*），是由前面
> 所說的 *monere* 而來的；*monstrare*（= *show*）。

monster[2]〔'mɑnstɚ〕*n.* 怪物；惡人（表示物 → 醒目的東西）
monstrous[5]〔'mɑnstrəs〕*adj.* 奇形怪狀的；恐怖的
demonstrate[4]〔'dɛmən͵stret〕*v.* 證明；示範；誇示；表露
（充分地表示）《*de-* = fully》

demonstration[4]〔͵dɛmən'streʃən〕*n.* 表示；論證；示威運動

```
de  +  monstr  +  ation
|        |         |
fully +  show   +  n.
```

demonstrative[7]〔dɪ'mɑnstrətɪv〕*adj.* 表示說明的；論證的；
明確的　*n.* 指示詞

remonstrate〔rɪ'mɑnstret〕*v.* 抗議；忠告（表示反對）
《*re-* = against》

remonstrative〔rɪ'mɑnstrətɪv〕*adj.* 抗議的；忠告的

remonstrance〔rɪ'mɑnstrəns〕*n.* 抗議；諫言

remonstrant〔rɪ'mɑnstrənt〕*adj.* 抗議的；諫言的
n. 抗議者；忠告者

350　mor = custom（習俗）

* 拉丁文 *mos*（= *custom*），複數是 *mores*。

mores〔'mɔriz , 'mor-〕*n.pl.* 風俗；傳統

moral[3]〔'mɔrəl〕*adj.* 道德的；教訓的；精神上的；良心的
n. 教訓；寓意

morale[6]〔mo'ræl , -'rɑl〕*n.* 民心；士氣

moralism〔'mɔrəlɪzm̩〕*n.* 道德主義；倫理主義；教訓；格言
《 *-ism* = 主義；學說》

```
mor  +  al  +  ism
|       |      |
custom + adj. + n.
```

moralist〔'mɔrəlɪst〕*n.* 道德家

morality[6]〔mɔ'rælətɪ〕*n.* 道德；德行；教訓；寓意
《 *-ity* 抽象名詞字尾》

```
mor  +  al  +  ity
|       |      |
custom + adj. + n.
```

moralize〔'mɔrəl,aɪz , 'mɑr- 〕 v. 使道德化；教以道德；教化；
訓話《 *-ize* 動詞字尾》

moralization〔,mɔrəlɪ'zeʃən , -aɪ'ze- 〕 n. 道德化；教化；教訓

amoral[7]〔 e'mɔrəl , -'mɑr- 〕 adj. 與道德無關的；非道德的
　《 *a-* = without》

demoralize[7]〔 dɪ'mɔrəl,aɪz 〕 v. 敗壞道德；使沮喪；使消沈
　《 *de-* = down》

demoralization〔 dɪ,mɔrələ'zeʃən , -,mɑr- , -aɪ'ze- 〕 n. 風俗
敗壞；道德墮落；士氣低落

de + mor + al + iz(e) + ation
down + custom + adj. + v. + n.

immoral[7]〔 ɪ'mɔrəl , ɪm'mɔrəl〕 adj. 不道德的；邪惡的
　《 *im-* = *in-* = not》

unmoral〔 ʌn'mɔrəl , -'mɑr- 〕 adj. 不涉及道德的；不發生道德
問題的（ = *nonmoral* ）

351　　**morph** = form（形狀；形態）

* 希臘文 *morphe*（ = *form* ）。

Morpheus〔'mɔrfɪəs , -fjus 〕 n.（希臘神話）夢之神；睡之神

Morph + eus
form + n.

morphine〔'mɔrfin 〕 n. 嗎啡《*morph-* = Morpheus》

　【解說】注射嗎啡之後，會昏昏欲睡，所以字首是用「（希臘神話）睡
　　　　之神」這個字。

morphology〔 mɔr'fɑlədʒɪ 〕 n. 形態學；地形學；形態；結構
（研究形態的學問）《*logy* = study》

morphological〔,mɔrfə'lɑdʒəkəl 〕 adj. 形態學的；地形學的

amorphous 〔 ə'mɔrfəs 〕 *adj.* 無定形的；無組織的；模糊的

《*a-* = not ; without》

```
    a   + morph + ous
    |       |      |
without +  form  + adj.
```

heteromorphic 〔 ˌhɛtərə'mɔrfɪk 〕 *adj.* 異形的；變形的

（不同形狀）《*hetero-* = different》

isomorphic 〔 ˌaɪsə'mɔrfɪk 〕 *adj.* 同形的；異種同形的

（形狀相同）《*iso-* = equal》

metamorphosis 〔 ˌmɛtə'mɔrfəsɪs 〕 *n.* 蛻變；變形；變態

（形態改變）《*meta-* (change) + *morpho* (form) + *-sis* (process ; act)》

```
  meta   + morpho +   sis
   |         |         |
change  +  form   + process
```

polymorphic 〔 ˌpɑlɪ'mɔrfɪk 〕 *adj.* 多形的；多形態的

（ = *polymorphous* ）《*poly-* = many》

352　mort = death (死亡)

* 拉丁文 *mors* , *mort-* (= *death*) ，*mori* (= *die*) 。

mortal[5] 〔'mɔrtl̩ 〕 *adj.* 不免一死的；人生的　　*n.* 必死的東西；人類

mortality[7] 〔 mɔr'tælətɪ 〕 *n.* 必死的命運；死亡率

mortuary 〔'mɔrtʃuˌɛrɪ 〕 *n.* 停屍間；太平間　　*adj.* 埋葬的；死的

```
mortu  +  ary            im + mort + al
  |        |             |      |     |
death  + place          not + death + adj.
```

immortal[7] 〔 ɪ'mɔrtl̩ 〕 *adj.* 不死的；不滅的；不朽的

《*im-* = *in-* = not》

immortality[7] 〔 ˌɪmɔr'tælətɪ 〕 *n.* 不死；不滅；不朽

mortician 〔 mɔr'tɪʃən 〕 *n.* 殯儀業者

mortify 〔'mɔrtə,faɪ 〕 *v.* 克制；使感到羞辱（使死去；使有想死的念頭）《 *-ify* = make》

mortification 〔,mɔrtəfə'keʃən 〕 *n.* 屈辱；羞辱

morbid[7] 〔'mɔrbɪd 〕 *adj.* 疾病的；不健全的（與死有關的）

morbidity 〔 mɔr'bɪdətɪ 〕 *n.* 病態；不健全

moribund 〔'mɔrə,bʌnd , 'mɑr- , -bənd 〕 *adj.* 將死的；即將消滅的（瀕臨死亡）《*mori* (death) + *bund* (tending toward)》

mori　+　　bund
｜　　　　　｜
death + *tending toward*

mortgage[7] 〔'mɔrgɪdʒ 〕 *n.* 抵押；抵押權　　*v.* 抵押；獻身於（死亡時作的擔保）《 *-gage* = pledge (擔保)》

postmortem 〔,post'mɔrtəm 〕 *adj.* 死後的　　*n.* 驗屍；屍體解剖；事後檢討　*v.* 驗屍《*post-* = after》

353　**mount** = mountain ; ascend (山；上升)

* 古法文 *mont* (= *mountain*) ， *monter* (= *mount ; climb*) ， *amont* (= *upward*) 。

mount[5] 〔 maʊnt 〕 *v.* 上漲；登（山）；騎（馬）；乘

mountain[1] 〔'maʊntn̩ 〕 *n.* 山（可攀登上去之處）《 *-ain* 名詞字尾》

mountainous[4] 〔'maʊntn̩əs 〕 *adj.* 多山的；巨大的

mountainy 〔'maʊntn̩ɪ 〕 *adj.* 居住在山地的

amount[2] 〔 ə'maʊnt 〕 *v.* 共計；等於　　*n.* 總數《*a-* = *ad-* = to》

dismount[7] 〔 dɪs'maʊnt 〕 *v.* 下馬；下車（與登上相反）《*dis-* = negative (否定)》

paramount[7] 〔'pærə,maʊnt 〕 *adj.* 最高的；主要的；卓越的（爬到上面的）《*par-* = *para-* = by》

par　+　amount
｜　　　　｜
by　+　*upward*

remount〔ri'maʊnt〕*v.* 再騎;再搭乘;回溯(再登上)

　　《*re-* = again》

surmount〔sə'maʊnt〕*v.* 戰勝;克服;爬越(山嶺)

　　(爬到~之上)《*sur-* = *super-* = over》

surmountable〔sə'maʊntəbḷ〕*adj.* 可戰勝的;可克服的

montage〔man'taʒ〕*n.* 畫面剪輯;合成畫面(把別張圖貼上去)

montane〔'manten〕*n.* 山地森林　*adj.* 生長在山地森林的

Mont Blanc〔man'blæŋk〕*n.* 白朗峰(阿爾卑斯山脈的最高峰)

cismontane〔sɪs'mantan〕*adj.* 在山脈這一邊的(尤指在阿爾卑斯

　　山脈北側的)《*cis-* = on this side》

Piedmont〔'pidmant〕*n.* 皮得蒙高原(位於美國大西洋岸與阿帕拉

　　契山脈之間)

piedmont〔'pidmant〕*n.*, *adj.* 山麓地區(的)

　　《義大利文 *piede* = foot》

promontory〔'pramən,torɪ, -,tɔrɪ〕*n.* 岬;海角(向前突出的部分)

```
pro   +  mont  + ory
 |          |       |
forward + ascend +  n.
```

tramontane〔trə'mantan〕*adj.*, *n.* 住在山那邊的(人)

　　《*tra-* = *trans-* = across》

354　mov , mot , mob = move(移動)

> * 拉丁文 *movere*(= move),*motio*(= moveing),
> *mobilis*(= movable),*momentum*(= movement)。
> 〔變化型〕*mom* , *mut*。

move[1]〔muv〕*v.* 移動;感動　*n.* 手段;移動

movement[1]〔'muvmənt〕*n.* 運動;動作;移動

movable[2]〔'muvəbḷ〕*adj.* 可動的;動產的　*n.* (*pl.*) 動產;家財

movie[1]〔'muvɪ〕*n.* 電影(此字是 moving picture 的縮略)

remove[3] 〔rɪ'muv〕 *v.* 移去；移動　*n.* 移動；等級（再移動）

《*re-* = again》

removable[7] 〔rɪ'muvəbl̩〕 *adj.* 可移動的；可除去的

```
re   +  mov  + able
 |        |       |
again + move +  adj.
```

removal[6] 〔rɪ'muvl̩〕 *n.* 撤去；除去；罷免

motion[2] 〔'moʃən〕 *n.* 運動；動作　*v.* 以手或頭示意

motivate[4] 〔'motə‚vet〕 *v.* 激發；引發動機

motivation[4] 〔‚motə'veʃən〕 *n.* 引起動機；刺激；誘導

motive[5] 〔'motɪv〕 *adj.* 發動的　*n.* 動機　*v.* 激發；引發動機

motif[7] 〔mo'tif〕 *n.* 主題；主旨

motor[3] 〔'motɚ〕 *n.* 馬達；發動機；汽車　*adj.* 由馬達推動的汽車的

motorize[7] 〔'motə‚raɪz〕 *v.* 裝馬達；機械化

motel[3] 〔mo'tɛl〕 *n.* 汽車旅館《*mo*(*tor*)（汽車）+ (*ho*)*tel*（旅館）》

commotion[7] 〔kə'moʃən〕 *n.* 混亂；暴動（一同引起騷動）

《*com-* = together》

```
com  +  mot  + ion
 |        |      |
together + move + n.
```

demote[7] 〔dɪ'mot〕 *v.* 降低（向下移動）《*de-* = down》

emotion[2] 〔ɪ'moʃən〕 *n.* 感情；情緒（移動出來的東西）

《*e-* = *ex-* = out》

emotional[4] 〔ɪ'moʃənl̩〕 *adj.* 感情的；易受感動的

locomotion[7] 〔‚lokə'moʃən〕 *n.* 移動；運動；運轉；旅行

（由某地移至某地）《*loco*（place）+ *mot*（move）+ -*ion*（名詞字尾）》

locomotive[5] 〔‚lokə'motɪv〕 *n.* 火車頭　*adj.* 移動的；旅行的；

火車頭的

promote[3] 〔 prə'mot 〕 v. 擢陞；促進；創辦 (向前方移動 → 前進)
《*pro-* = forward》

```
pro   +  mote
 |        |
forward + move
```

promoter 〔 prə'motə 〕 n. 贊助者；發起人
promotion[4] 〔 prə'moʃən 〕 n. 擢陞；促進；創立
remote[3] 〔 rɪ'mot 〕 adj. 遙遠的；遠親的 (退到遠處)《*re-* = back》
remoteness 〔 rɪ'motnɪs 〕 n. 遠離；疏遠；偏僻

```
re  + mote + ness
 |     |      |
back + move +  n.
```

mob[3] 〔 mab 〕 n. 暴民；大眾   v. 結群圍攻 (心意容易動搖的)
mobile[3] 〔'mobḷ , 'mobil , -bɪl 〕 adj. 可動的；易變的
《 *-ile* 形容詞字尾》
mobilize[6] 〔'mobḷˌaɪz 〕 v. 流通；動員《 *-ize* 動詞字尾》

```
mob + il(e) + ize
 |      |      |
move +  adj. + v.
```

mobilization 〔ˌmobḷə'zeʃən , -aɪ'ze- 〕 n. 動員；流通
mobillette 〔ˌmobɪ'lɛt 〕 n. 小型機器腳踏車《 *-ette* 表示小的名詞字尾》
mobocracy 〔 mab'akrəsɪ 〕 n. 暴民政治；暴民統治《*mob* 暴民》

```
mobo + cracy
  |      |
mob   + rule
```

automobile[3] 〔'ɔtəməˌbil , ˌɔtə'mobɪl , ˌɔtəmə'bil 〕 n. 汽車
(自己會動)《*auto-* = self》

【解説】 美國人喜歡買大車，例如：Cadillac (凱迪拉克)、Buick (別克)、
Chevrolet (雪佛蘭) 等，他們覺得大車坐起來舒服又安全。

demobilize〔di'mobḷ͵aɪz〕*v.* 遣散；改編（軍隊）；使復原（與動員相反）《*de-* 表示動作的相反》

moment[1]〔'momənt〕*n.* 瞬間；片刻；重要

momentary[7]〔'momən͵tɛrɪ〕*adj.* 瞬間的；刹那的；時時刻刻的

momentous[7]〔mo'mɛntəs〕*adj.* 極重要的

momentum[6]〔mo'mɛntəm〕*n.* 運動量；動力

mutiny[7]〔'mjutn̩ɪ〕*n.* 叛變　*v.* 反抗（反抗行動）

mutinous〔'mjutn̩əs〕*adj.* 反叛的；背叛的

355　**mun** = service（服務）

　　* 拉丁文 ***munus***（= *service performed for the community* ; *duty*），複數是 *munia*。

municipal[6]〔mju'nɪsəpḷ〕*adj.* 市政的；有自治權的；內政的（爲公衆服務的）《*cip* = take》

munificence〔mju'nɪfəsn̩s〕*n.* 慷慨的給與；大方（提供服務）《*fic* = do》

munificent〔mju'nɪfəsn̩t〕*adj.* 慷慨的；大方的

common[1]〔'kɑmən〕*adj.* 共有的；共同的

```
com  +  mon
 |       |
together + duties
```

commune[17]〔*v.* kə'mjun　*n.* 'kɑmjun〕*v.* 親密交談；〔美〕領受聖餐　*n.* 親密的交談《古法文 *comuner* = take common ; share》

commune[27]〔'kɑmjun〕*n.* 市鎮；社區《拉丁文 *communis* = common》

communal[7]〔kə'mjunḷ〕*adj.* 公有的；社區內的

communalize〔kə'mjunḷ͵aɪz〕*v.* 使公有化；使公社化；使集體化

communicate[3]〔kə'mjunə͵ket〕*v.* 傳達；通知；溝通；傳染

communication[4] ﹝ kə,mjunə'keʃən ﹞ *n.* 傳達；溝通；連絡；
通訊設施

communion[7] ﹝ kə'mjunjən ﹞ *n.* 共有；共享；宗教團體；領聖餐禮

```
com  +  mun  +  ion
 |        |       |
together + service +  n.
```

communism[5] ﹝'kɑmju,nɪzəm ﹞ *n.* 共產主義
《 *-ism* 表示主義的名詞字尾》

communist[5] ﹝'kɑmju,nɪst ﹞ *n.* 共產主義者；共產黨員
adj. 共產主義（者）的《 *-ist* 表示人的名詞字尾》

community[4] ﹝ kə'mjunətɪ ﹞ *n.* 社區；團體

immune[6] ﹝ ɪ'mjun ﹞ *adj.* 免疫的；免除的（不必服務）
《 *im-* = *in-* = not》

immunity[7] ﹝ ɪ'mjunətɪ ﹞ *n.* 免疫（性）；免除（稅等）

immunize[7] ﹝'ɪmjə,naɪz ﹞ *v.* 使免疫

356　　**mur** = wall（牆壁）　　*拉丁文 *murus*（= wall）。

mural[7] ﹝'mjʊrəl ﹞ *adj.* 牆上的；壁上的　*n.* 壁畫；壁飾

muralist ﹝'mjʊrəlɪst ﹞ *n.* 壁畫家

extramural ﹝,ɛkstrə'mjʊrəl ﹞ *adj.* 城牆外的；校外的
（大學牆外的）《 *extra-* = outside》

```
extra  +  mur  +  al
  |         |      |
outside  +  wall  +  adj.
```

immure ﹝ ɪ'mjʊr ﹞ *v.* 禁閉；監禁（關在牆內）《 *im-* = *in-* = in》

immurement ﹝ ɪ'mjʊrmənt ﹞ *n.* 監禁；幽居

intramural ﹝,ɪntrə'mjʊrəl ﹞ *adj.* 城牆內的；校內的
《 *intra-* = within》

357　**mut** = change（改變）

* 拉丁文 ***mutare***（= *change*）。

mutable[7]〔'mjutəbḷ〕*adj.* 易變的；無常的

mutability〔ˌmjutə'bɪlətɪ〕*n.* 不定性；易變性

mutate[7]〔'mjutet〕*v.* 變化；【生物】突變《 *-ate* 動詞字尾》

mutation[7]〔mju'teʃən〕*n.* 變化；【生物】突變

mutual[4]〔'mjutʃuəl〕*adj.* 相互的；共同的（彼此調和）

mutuality〔ˌmjutʃu'ælətɪ〕*n.* 相互關係；相互依存

commutate〔'kɑmjuˌtet〕*v.* 轉換（電流的）方向；整流

《*com-* = with》

```
com  +  mut   + ate
 |        |      |
with + change +  v.
```

commutation〔ˌkɑmju'teʃən〕*n.* 轉換；減刑；〔美〕以定期
票通勤

commutator〔'kɑmjuˌtetɚ〕*n.* 整流器；變壓器

commute[5]〔kə'mjut〕*v.* 轉換；減刑；〔美〕買定期票通勤
（能夠變成～）

commuter[5]〔kə'mjutɚ〕*n.* 以定期票通勤者

immutable〔ɪ'mjutəbḷ〕*adj.* 不變的；不能變的

《*im-* = *in-* = not》

```
im  +  mut   + able
 |       |      |
not + change +  adj.
```

permute〔pɚ'mjut〕*v.* 交換；排列（完全地改變）

《*per-* = thoroughly》

permutation〔ˌpɝmjə'teʃən〕*n.* 交換；排列

transmute〔træns'mjut〕*v.* 變形；變質《*trans-* = across》

transmutation〔ˌtrænsmju'teʃən〕*n.* 變形；變質

358 **my** = muscle (肌肉)　　*希臘文 *mus* (= *muscle*)。

myocardial 〔͵maɪə'kardɪəl 〕 *adj.* 心肌的

```
myo  +  card  +  ial
 |        |       |
muscle + heart + adj.
```

myocarditis 〔͵maɪokar'daɪtɪs 〕 *n.* 心肌炎
《 *-itis* = inflammation (發炎)》

myocardium 〔͵maɪə'kardɪəm 〕 *n.* 心肌 (層)

myology 〔 maɪ'alədʒɪ 〕 *n.* 肌肉學;肌肉系統《 *logy* = study》

myoma 〔 maɪ'omə 〕 *n.* 肌瘤《 *-oma* 表示瘤的名詞字尾》

myomalacia 〔͵maɪəmə'leʃɪə 〕 *n.* 肌軟化《希臘文 *malakos* = soft》

359 **myc** = fungus (菌類)　　*希臘文 *mukes* (= *fungus*)。

mycelium 〔 maɪ'silɪəm 〕 *n.* 菌絲體《希臘文 *helos* = nail》

mycology 〔 maɪ'kalədʒɪ 〕 *n.* 黴菌學

mycosis 〔 maɪ'kosɪs 〕 *n.* 黴菌病

mycotoxin 〔͵maɪko'taksɪn 〕 *n.* 黴菌毒素《 *toxin* 毒素》

neomycin 〔͵niə'maɪsɪn 〕 *n.* 新黴素《 *neo-* = new》

360 **myel** = marrow (髓)

*希臘文 *muelos* (= *marrow* ; *spinal cord* 脊髓)。

myelin 〔'maɪəlɪn 〕 *n.* 髓燐脂;髓素

myelitis 〔͵maɪə'laɪtɪs 〕 *n.* 脊髓炎

myelocyte 〔'maɪəlo͵saɪt 〕 *n.* 髓細胞

myeloma 〔͵maɪə'lomə 〕 *n.* 骨髓瘤

poliomyelitis 〔͵polɪo͵maɪə'laɪtɪs 〕 *n.* 脊髓灰質炎;小兒麻痺症
《希臘文 *polios* = gray》

361　myst = mystery（神祕）

> * 拉丁文 *mysticus*；希臘文 *mythos*（ = *mystery*）。

mystagogue〔'mɪstə,gɑg, -,gɔg〕*n.* 引人入密敎者《*agogue* = leader》
mystery[3]〔'mɪst(ə)rɪ〕*n.* 神祕；不可思議《 *-ery* 名詞字尾》

```
myst  +  ery
 |        |
mystery  +  n.
```

mysterious[4]〔mɪs'tɪrɪəs〕*adj.* 神祕性的；不可思議的
mystic[7]〔'mɪstɪk〕*adj.* 神祕的（ = *mystical*）
　n. 神祕家；神祕主義者
mystical[7]〔'mɪstɪkḷ〕*adj.* 神祕的；神祕主義的
mysticism〔'mɪstə,sɪzm̩〕*n.* 神祕主義；神祕論
　《 *-ism* = 主義；理論》
mystify〔'mɪstə,faɪ〕*v.* 使迷惑；神祕化
myth[5]〔mɪθ〕*n.* 神話；傳說；虛構的人（事物）

362　narc = numbness（麻木）

> * 希臘文 *narke*（ = *numbness*；*stupor* 昏迷）。

narcissus〔nɑr'sɪsəs〕*n.* 水仙；（N-）【希臘神話】那西沙斯（愛
　上自己映在水中姿影的美少年，溺死後化爲水仙花）
　【解說】 據傳水仙具有麻醉作用，故名。
narcosis〔nɑr'kosɪs〕*n.* 睡眠狀態；麻醉狀態；昏迷；麻醉作用

```
narco  +  sis
  |        |
numbness + condition
```

narcolepsy〔'nɑrkə,lɛpsɪ〕*n.* 嗜睡病《*lep* = seize（抓住）》
narcotic[7]〔nɑr'kɑtɪk〕*n.* 麻醉劑；致幻毒品　*adj.* 麻醉的；催眠的
narcotize〔'nɑrkə,taɪz〕*v.* 麻醉；使昏迷；麻痹對…的感覺

363 **nas , nar** = nose (鼻子)

> * 拉丁文 *nasus* (= nose) ，*naris* (= nostril 鼻孔) 。

nares〔'neriz〕 *n.pl.* 鼻孔

nasal〔'nezḷ〕 *adj.* 鼻子的；鼻音的　　*n.* 鼻音

nasalize〔'nezḷ,aiz〕 *v.* 使鼻音化；用鼻音說話

nasturtium〔næ'stɜʃəm , nə-〕 *n.* 金蓮花《希臘文 *torquere* = twist》

【解說】因爲它的味道辛辣使人捏鼻，故名。

nostril〔'nɑstrəl , -tril〕 *n.* 鼻孔《古英文 *nosu* = nose》

364 **nat , nasc** = be born (出生；天生)

> * 拉丁文 *nasci* (= be born) ，過去分詞爲 *natus*。

natal[7]〔'netḷ〕 *adj.* 出生的

nation[1]〔'neʃən〕 *n.* 國民；國家；民族 (生而爲者)

national[2]〔'næʃənḷ〕 *adj.* 國民的；國家的　　*n.* 國民

nationality[4]〔,næʃən'æləti〕 *n.* 國籍；國民性

nationalize〔'næʃənḷ,aiz〕 *v.* 使國家化；使成爲國營

nationalization〔,næʃənḷɪ'zeʃən〕 *n.* 國家化；收歸國有

nat	+ ion +	al	+ iz(e) +	ation
born	+ n. +	adj.	+ v. +	n.

native[3]〔'netiv〕 *adj.* 出生地的；本國的；土著的　　*n.* 本地人；土著

naive[5]〔na'iv〕〔法文〕= native　　*adj.* 純眞的；質樸的

nature[1]〔'netʃɚ〕 *n.* 自然；天性；本質 (與生俱來的)

natural[2]〔'nætʃərəl〕 *adj.* 自然的；自然界的；本能的

naturalism〔'nætʃərəl,izəm〕 *n.* 自然主義；自然論

naturalize[7]〔'nætʃərəl,aiz〕 *v.* 使歸化；移植；使自然化；使合理化

naturalization〔,nætʃərəlai'zeʃən〕 *n.* 歸化；移入；自然化

agnate〔'ægnet〕*adj.*, *n.* 父系的（親屬）；同族的（人）

《*ag-* = *ad-* = to》

```
ag  +  nate
|      |
to  +  born
```

agnatic〔æg'nætɪk〕*adj.* 父系親屬的
agnation〔æg'neʃən〕*n.* 父系親屬
cognate〔'kɑgnet〕*adj.* 同族的；同起源的；同性質的（相同來源）

《*cog-* = *com-* = together》

cognation〔kɑg'neʃən〕*n.* 同族；親戚
connate〔'kɑnet〕*adj.* 天賦的；先天性的；（植物）合生的

（與生俱來的）《*con-* = together》

```
con  +  nate
 |       |
together + born
```

connatural〔kə'nætʃərəl〕*adj.* 先天的；同性質的
denature〔di'netʃɚ〕*v.* 改變本性；使變性（與出生時不同）

《*de-* = *dis-* = away》

denaturalize〔di'nætʃ(ə)rəl,aɪz〕*v.* 使不自然；改變～的本性
innate〔ɪn'net〕*adj.* 先天的；本質的（= *inborn*）《*in-* = in》
neonate〔'niə,net〕*n.*（未滿月的）嬰兒（新生兒）《*neo-* = new》
postnatal〔post'netḷ〕*adj.* 出生後的《*post-* = after》
prenatal〔pri'netḷ〕*adj.* 出生前的；胎兒期的《*pre-* = before》
nascence；**-cy**〔'næsəns(ɪ)〕*n.* 誕生；起源
nascent〔'næsṇt〕*adj.* 初生的；初期的
Renaissance[7]〔,rɛnə'zɑns , rɪ'nesṇs〕*n.* 文藝復興（歐洲在十四
世紀至十七世紀的藝術文學之復興運動）；文藝復興時期的藝術、
建築等之形式　*adj.* 文藝復興的（再生）

```
re  +  naiss  +  ance
|        |        |
again + be born +  n.
```

365 nau , nav = ship（船）

> * 希臘文 *naus*（= *ship*），*nautes*（= *sailor*）；
> 拉丁文 *navis*（= *ship*）。

nausea[7]〔'nɔʒə, 'nɔzɪə, 'nɔsɪə〕*n.* 作嘔；噁心

nauseate〔'nɔʒɪ,et, -zɪ,et〕*v.* 使作嘔；厭惡

nauseant〔'nɔʃɪənt〕*adj.* 引起嘔吐的

nauseous[7]〔'nɔʒəs, -zɪəs〕*adj.* 令人作嘔的

nautical[7]〔'nɔtɪkḷ〕*adj.* 船舶的；船員的；航海的

aeronaut〔'ɛrə,nɔt, 'ærə-〕*n.* 飛艇或輕氣球駕駛員；飛艇乘客
（空中航行的人）《*aero* = air》

aeronautics〔,ɛrə'nɔtɪks〕*n.* 航空學；航空術

```
aero + naut +  ics
  |      |      |
air  + ship + science
```

aquanaut〔'ækwə,nɔt〕*n.* 海底（實驗室）工作人員；
（輕裝）潛水員《*aqua* = water》

aquanautics〔,ækwə'nɔtɪks〕*n.*（使用潛水裝備的）水下勘探
與研究

astronaut[5]〔'æstrə,nɔt〕*n.* 太空人（星際航行者）《*astro* = star》

astronautics〔,æstrə'nɔtɪks〕*n.* 太空航行學

oceanaut〔'oʃə,nɔt〕*n.* 潛航員；海底實驗室工作人員

navy[3]〔'nevɪ〕*n.* 海軍；船隊

naval[6]〔'nevḷ〕*adj.* 海軍的；軍艦的

navicert〔'nævɪ,sɝt〕*n.* 航海證明書《*cert* = certification（證明）》

navicular〔nə'vɪkjələ〕*adj.* 船形的（小船狀的）
《*navi*（ship）+ *-cul*（small）+ *-ar*（形容詞字尾）》

```
navi + cul  +  ar
  |     |      |
ship + small + adj.
```

navigate[5] 〔'nævə,get 〕 *v.* 駕駛；航行（使船前進）

　　《*ig* = drive ; *-ate* 動詞字尾》

navigation[6] 〔,nævə'geʃən 〕 *n.* 航海；航空；航海（航空）術

```
nav +  ig  + ation
 |     |       |
ship + drive +  n.
```

navigator 〔'nævə,getɚ 〕 *n.* 航海者；海上探險家；（飛機的）
駕駛員

navigable 〔'nævəgəbḷ 〕 *adj.* 可航行的；適於航行的

circumnavigate 〔,sɝkəm'nævə,get 〕 *v.* 環航（世界）

　　（環繞～航行）《*circum-* = around》

circumnavigation 〔,sɝkəm,nævə'geʃən 〕 *n.* 環航世界一周

366　**necro** = death ; dead（死亡；死的）

　　* 希臘文 *nekros* (= *dead body*)。

necrology 〔 nɛ'krɑlədʒɪ 〕 *n.* 死者名冊；訃聞（死亡通知）

　　《*logy* = speaking》

necromancy 〔'nɛkrə,mænsɪ 〕 *n.* 巫術；通靈術

　　（召亡靈以占卜未來）《 *-mancy* = divination（預言；占卜）》

```
necro + mancy
  |       |
death + divination
```

necromancer 〔'nɛkrə,mænsɚ 〕 *n.* 巫術師；通靈者

necropolis 〔 nɛ'krɑpəlɪs , nɪ- 〕 *n.* （古代都市的）大墳場；
公共墓地（死人城）《*polis* = city》

necropsy 〔'nɛkrɑpsɪ 〕 *n.* 驗屍；屍體解剖

　　《*necro* (death) + *(o)ps* (visible) + *-y* (名詞字尾)》

necrosis 〔 nɛ'krosɪs 〕 *n.* 壞死；壞疽《 *-sis* = condition》

necrophobia 〔,nɛkrə'fobɪə 〕 *n.* 死亡恐怖（害怕死亡）《*phob* = fear》

necrotomy 〔 nɛ'krɑtəmɪ 〕 *n.* 屍體解剖（切開死人）

《*necro* (death) + *tom* (cut) + *-y* (名詞字尾)》

```
necro + tom + y
  |      |    |
death + cut + n.
```

367　**nect** = bind (綁)

＊ 拉丁文 *nectere* (= bind) 。〔變化型〕*nex*。

connect[3] 〔 kə'nɛkt 〕 *v.* 連接；聯繫；接通；使有關（連在一起）

《*con-* = together》

connection[3] 〔 kə'nɛkʃən 〕 *n.* 連接；關係；聯想；親戚

connective[7] 〔 kə'nɛktɪv 〕 *adj.* 連接的；聯合的

```
con  + nect + ive
 |      |      |
together + bind + adj.
```

connector[7] 〔 kə'nɛktɚ 〕 *n.* 連接的人或物；連接器

disconnect[4] 〔 ˌdɪskə'nɛkt 〕 *v.* 使分離；脫離；斷絕《*dis-* = apart》

disconnected[7] 〔 ˌdɪskə'nɛktɪd 〕 *adj.* 分離的；不連貫的

interconnect[7] 〔 ˌɪntɚkə'nɛkt 〕 *v.* (使) 彼此連接 (聯繫)

（互相連接）《*inter-* = between》

```
inter  +   con   + nect
  |         |        |
between + together + bind
```

interconnection 〔 ˌɪntɚkə'nɛkʃən 〕 *n.* 彼此連接 (聯繫)

annex[7] 〔 *v.* ə'nɛks　*n.* 'ænɛks 〕 *v.* 附加；合併；併吞

　　n. 附屬物；附件（向～連接）《*an-* = *ad-* = to》

annexation 〔 ˌænɛks'eʃən 〕 *n.* 附加物；附件；合併

nexus 〔 'nɛksəs 〕 *n.* 連結；連繫；聯絡；關係《 *-us* 拉丁名詞字尾》

368   **neg** = deny (否認)   * 拉丁文 *negare* (= *deny*) 。

negate 〔 'nɪget , nɪ'get 〕 *v.* 否定；否認

negation 〔 nɪ'geʃən 〕 *n.* 否定；否認

negative[2] 〔 'nɛgətɪv 〕 *adj.* 否定的；消極的；【數學】負的

     n. 否定；拒絕；【數學】負數

neglect[4] 〔 nɪ'glɛkt 〕 *v.* 忽視；怠慢   *n.* 忽視；怠慢 (拒絕集合)

     《 *lect* = gather 》

neglectable[7] 〔 nɪ'glɛktəbl̩ 〕 *adj.* 可以忽視的；微不足道的

neglectful[7] 〔 nɪ'glɛktfəl 〕 *adj.* 疏忽的；不小心的

negligence[7] 〔 'nɛglədʒəns 〕 *n.* 怠慢；不注意 《 *lig* = *lect* = gather 》

```
neg  +  lig   +  ence
 |        |         |
deny  + gather  +  n.
```

negligible[7] 〔 'nɛglədʒəbl̩ 〕 *adj.* 可忽略的；無關緊要的

negotiate[4] 〔 nɪ'goʃɪ,et 〕 *v.* 交涉；談判；商議 《 *oti* = leisure (閒暇)》

     cf. **otiose** (〔 'otɪ,os 〕 *adj.* 閒散的；多餘的)

negotiation[6] 〔 nɪ,goʃɪ'eʃən 〕 *n.* 交涉；商議

negatron 〔 'nɛgə,trɑn 〕 *n.* 陰電子 (= *negative electron*)

abnegate 〔 'æbnɪ,get 〕 *v.* 放棄 (權力)；克制 (慾望) (否認

     權力 → 放棄權力；否認慾望 → 克制慾望)   *n.* 叛教者；變節者

     adj. 叛教的；變節的 (否定而分離) 《 *ab-* = from；negate (否認)》

```
ab  +  neg  +  ate
 |       |       |
from + deny  + n., adj.
```

renegade[7] 〔 'rɛnɪ,ged 〕 *n.* 叛教者；叛徒   *adj.* 叛教的；背叛的

     v. 叛教；變節 (再次否定)

     《 *re-* (again) + *neg* (deny) + *-ade* (表示人的名詞字尾)》

renege 〔 rɪ'nɪg , -'nig 〕 *v.* 違背諾言；食言

369 nerv , neur = nerve (神經)

* 拉丁文 *nervus* (= *nerve*) ；希臘文 *neuron* (= *nerve*) 。

neural 〔'njʊrəl , 'nʊrəl 〕 *adj.* 神經 (系統) 的；神經中樞的
neuralgia 〔 njʊ'rældʒə 〕 *n.* 神經痛
　　《*neur* (nerve) + *alg* (pain) + -*ia* (condition)》
neurasthenia 〔,njʊrəs'θinɪə , ,nʊ- 〕 *n.* 神經衰弱
　　《*neur* (nerve) + *a-* (without) + *sthen* (strength) + -*ia* (condition)》

```
neur  +   a   +  sthen  +   ia
 |        |        |         |
nerve + without + strength + condition
```

neuritis 〔 njʊ'raɪtɪs , nʊ- 〕 *n.* 神經炎 《 -*itis* = inflammation (發炎)》
neurobiology 〔,njʊrobaɪ'aːlədʒɪ 〕 *n.* 神經生物學《*biology* 生物學》
neurochemistry 〔,njʊro'kɛmɪstrɪ 〕 *n.* 神經化學《*chemistry* 化學》
neurology 〔 njʊ'raːlədʒɪ 〕 *n.* 神經 (病) 學《*logy* = science ; study》

```
neuro  +  logy
  |         |
nerve  +  study
```

neurological[7] 〔,njʊrə'laːdʒɪkəl 〕 *adj.* 神經學的
neurosis 〔 njʊ'rosɪs , nʊ- 〕 *n.* 神經病；精神官能病
　　《 -*sis* = condition》
neurotic[7] 〔 njʊ'raːtɪk 〕 *adj.* 患神經病的；過於神經質的
　　n. 神經病患者
nervous[3] 〔'nɝvəs 〕 *adj.* 神經的；緊張的；神經質的
enervate 〔'ɛnɚˌvet 〕 *v.* 使衰弱；使失去活力 (使神經失效)
　　《*e-* = *ex-* (out) + *nerv* (nerve) + -*ate* (動詞字尾)》

```
 e  +  nerv  +  ate
 |      |        |
out  +  nerve  +  v.
```

innervate 〔 ɪ'nɝvet , 'ɪnɚˌvet 〕 *v.* 使神經分布於～；使神經活動
　　(使神經發生功用)《*in-* = in》

unnerve 〔 ʌn'nɝv 〕 *v.* 抽取神經；嚇壞；使失去勇氣

（使沒有神經）《*un-* 表示動作的相反》

370　**neutr** = neither (兩者皆不)

　　* 拉丁文 ***neuter*** (= *neither*)。

neuter 〔'njutɚ 〕 *adj.* 中性的；無性的；中立的

　n. 中性字；中性；中性生物　*v.* 去勢；使中和

neutral[6] 〔'njutrəl 〕 *adj.* 中立的；中性的　*n.* 中立國；中立者

　（兩者都不介入）

neutralism 〔'njutrəlɪzm̩ 〕 *n.* 中立主義；中立政策；中立

　《 *-ism* = 主義》

neutralist 〔'njutrəlɪst , 'nu- 〕 *n.* 中立主義者

　adj. 遵行、主張中立主義的《 *-ist* 表示人的名詞字尾》

neutrality 〔 nju'træləti 〕 *n.* 中立；中性

neutralize 〔'njutrəl͵aɪz 〕 *v.* 使中立；中和

neutron 〔'njutrɑn , 'nu- 〕 *n.* 中子

371　**nihil** = nothing (什麼也沒有)

　　* 拉丁文 ***nihil*** (= *nothing*)。

nihil 〔'naɪhɪl 〕 *n.* 無；虛無；無價值之物

nihilism 〔'naɪəl͵ɪzəm 〕 *n.* 虛無主義；虛無論；無政府主義

nihilist 〔'naɪəlɪst 〕 *n.* 虛無論者；無政府主義者

nihilistic 〔͵naɪə'lɪstɪk 〕 *adj.* 虛無論（者）的；虛無主義（者）的

nihility 〔 naɪ'hɪləti 〕 *n.* 虛無；無

annihilate 〔 ə'naɪə͵let 〕 *v.* 消滅（使變成無）《*an-* = *ad-* = to》

```
an ＋ nihil ＋ ate
 │      │       │
to ＋ nothing ＋ v.
```

annihilation〔ə,naɪə'leʃən〕*n.* 消滅；毀滅
annihilator〔ə'naɪə,letə〕*n.* 消滅者；消滅物

372　nitr = niter（硝石）　　＊希臘文 *nitron*（= *niter*）。

nitrate〔'naɪtret〕*n.* 硝酸鹽　*v.* 用硝酸處理；使硝化
nitrous〔'naɪtrəs〕*adj.* 含氮的；亞硝酸的
nitrobenzene〔,naɪtrə'bɛnzin〕*n.* 硝基苯《*benzene* 苯》
nitrogen〔'naɪtrədʒən〕*n.* 氮《*gen* = produce》
nitroglycerin〔,naɪtrə'glɪsrɪn , -sərɪn〕*n.* 硝化甘油（炸藥的原料）
　　《*glycerin* 甘油》

373　noc = harm（傷害）

　　＊拉丁文 *nocere*（= *harm*）。〔變化型〕*nox*。

nocent〔'nosənt〕*adj.* 有害的
nocuous〔'nakjuəs〕*adj.* 有害的；有毒的
noxious〔'nakʃəs〕*adj.* 有害的；有毒的
innocent[3]〔'ɪnəsn̩t〕*adj.* 無罪的；無害的；無邪的；無知的
　　（沒有傷害）《*in-* = not》

```
in ＋ noc ＋ ent
 │     │      │
not ＋ harm ＋ adj.
```

innocence[4]〔'ɪnəsn̩s〕*n.* 無罪；天眞無邪；無知
innocency〔'ɪnəsənsɪ , 'ɪnəsn̩sɪ〕*n.* 天眞行爲
　　《*-ency* 表行爲、性質》
innocuity〔ɪ'nakjuətɪ〕*n.* 無害；無害的事情
obnoxious[7]〔əb'nakʃəs , ab-〕*adj.* 令人不悅的；討厭的；可憎的
　　（對～有害）《*ob-* = toward》

374　**noct** = night（夜晚）

* 拉丁文 *nox* , *noct-*（ = *night*）。

noctambulant〔nɑkˈtæmbjələnt〕*adj.* 夜間步行的；夢遊的
　（夜間行走）《*ambul* = walk》

noctambulism〔nɑkˈtæmbjəˌlɪzəm〕*n.* 夢遊症

noctambulist〔nɑkˈtæmbjəlɪst〕*n.* 夢遊者

noctilucent〔ˌnɑktəˈlusənt〕*adj.* 夜間發光的《*luc* = light》

```
nocti  +  luc  +  ent
  |         |       |
night  +  light  +  adj.
```

nocturnal[7]〔nɑkˈtɝnəl , -n̩〕*adj.* 夜晚的；夜間活動的；夜行性的
　（夜間活動）《*turn* = turn》

nocturne〔ˈnɑktɝn〕*n.* 夜曲；夢幻曲；夜景畫

noctivagant〔nɑkˈtɪvəgənt〕*adj.* 夜遊的；夜行的
　（夜晚到處遊蕩）

```
nocti  +  vag  +  ant
  |         |       |
night  +  wander  +  adj.
```

equinox〔ˈikwəˌnɑks , ˈɛkwə-〕*n.* 春（秋）分；晝夜平分點
　（晝夜等長）《*equi* = equal》

equinoctial〔ˌikwəˈnɑkʃəl , ˌɛkwə-〕*adj.* 晝夜平分的；
　春（秋）分的

375　**nom** = law（法則）

* 希臘文 *nemein*（ = *manage*），*nomos*（ = *law*）。

anomie〔ˈænəmɪ〕*n.* 社會之紊亂（沒有法則）《*a-* = without》

antinomy〔ænˈtɪnəmɪ〕*n.* 二律相悖；矛盾《*anti-* = against》

astronomical 〔͵æstrə'nɑmɪkl̩〕 *adj.* 天文學的；極大的

```
astro + nom + ical
  |      |      |
star  + law  + adj.
```

autonomy[6] 〔ɔ'tɑnəmɪ〕 *n.* 自治權；自治區《*auto-* = self》
Deuteronomy 〔͵djutə'rɑnəmɪ〕 *n.* 【聖經】申命記
economy[4] 〔ɪ'kɑnəmɪ〕 *n.* 經濟；節儉

```
eco  +  nom  + y
 |       |      |
house + manage + n.
```

heteronomy 〔͵hɛtə'rɑnəmɪ〕 *n.* 受制於人；他律
《*hetero-* = other》

376　　**nom** , **nomin** = name (名字)

* 拉丁文 *nomen* , *nomin-* (= name) 。

nominal[7] 〔'nɑmənl̩〕 *adj.* 名字的；名義上的；象徵性的
nominalism 〔'nɑmənl̩ɪzm̩〕 *n.* 唯名論
　cf. **realism** (實體論；實在論)
nominate[5] 〔'nɑmə͵net〕 *v.* 提名；任命；指派
nomination[6] 〔͵nɑmə'neʃən〕 *n.* 提名；任命
nominative 〔'nɑmənətɪv〕 *adj.* 提名的；任命的；主格的　*n.* 主格
nominator 〔'nɑmə͵netɚ〕 *n.* 提名者；任命者；推薦者
nominee[6] 〔͵nɑmə'ni〕 *n.* 被提名者；被任命者《 *-ee* 表動作的接受者》
binomial 〔baɪ'nomɪəl〕 *n.* , *adj.* 【數】二項式 (的)；【生物】雙
　名 (的) (指由兩個詞組成的物種名稱)《*bi-* = two》

```
bi  + nom  + ial
 |     |      |
two + name + adj.
```

denominate 〔 *v.* dɪˋnɑmə͵net *adj.* dɪˋnɑmənɪt 〕 *v.* 命名；取名
  adj. 有名稱的；具體的（定下名字）《*de-* = down》

```
de   + nomin + ate
 |        |      |
down +  name  +  v.
```

denomination 〔 dɪ͵nɑməˋneʃən 〕 *n.* 命名；名稱；派別；
  （重量、長度、貨幣等之）單位
denominational 〔 dɪ͵nɑməˋneʃənl̩ 〕 *adj.* 派別的；教派的
denominative 〔 dɪˋnɑmə͵netɪv , -nətɪv 〕 *adj.* 命名的；有名稱的
denominator 〔 dɪˋnɑmə͵netɚ 〕 *n.* 命名者；分母；共同點
ignominy 〔ˋɪgnə͵mɪnɪ 〕 *n.* 不名譽；羞恥；可恥的行為
  《*ig-* = *in-* = not》

```
ig + nomin + y
 |     |     |
not + name  + n.
```

ignominious 〔͵ɪgnəˋmɪnɪəs 〕 *adj.* 不名譽的；可恥的；屈辱的
misnomer 〔 mɪsˋnomɚ 〕 *n.* 名字、名詞的誤用；錯誤的名詞
  《*mis-* = wrong》

```
mis  + nom + er
 |      |     |
wrong + name + n.
```

polynomial 〔͵pɑlɪˋnomɪəl 〕 *n.* , *adj.*【數】多項式（的）；
  【生物】多詞學名（的）《*poly-* = many》
renown 〔 rɪˋnaʊn 〕 *n.* 名望；聲譽（再三出現的名字）
  《*re-*（again）+ *nown* = *nomin*（name）》

377   **norm** = rule；norm（規則；標準）

    * 拉丁文 ***norma***（= *rule* ; *norm*）。

norm[6]〔 nɔrm 〕 *n.* 標準；模範

normal[3] (ˈnɔrml̩) *adj.* 正常的；正規的　*n.* 常態；標準；正常的人

normalize (ˈnɔrml̩͵aɪz) *v.* 標準化；正常化；常態化

　《 *-ize* = make 》

normalization (͵nɔrml̩əˈzeʃən , -aɪˈze-) *n.* 標準化；正常化

normality (nɔrˈmælətɪ) *n.* 標準；正常狀態

```
norm + al + ity
  |     |    |
norm + adj. + n.
```

normally[7] (ˈnɔrml̩ɪ) *adv.* 正常地；標準地；常態地

normative (ˈnɔrmətɪv) *adj.* 合於規範的；規範的

abnormal[6] (æbˈnɔrml̩) *adj.* 不正常的；變態的；畸形的

　（偏離正常）《 *ab-* = away 》

abnormality (͵æbnɔrˈmælətɪ) *n.* 變態；反常；畸形

enormity (ɪˈnɔrmətɪ) *n.* 廣大；極惡；暴行（超出規則之外）

　《 *e-* = *ex-* = out of 》

```
e   + norm + ity
 |     |      |
out of + rule + n.
```

enormous[4] (ɪˈnɔrməs) *adj.* 巨大的；極惡的

subnormal (sʌbˈnɔrml̩) *adj.* 正常以下的；智力低於正常的

　n. 智力低於常人者（低於一般標準）《 *sub-* = under 》

supernormal (͵supəˈnɔrml̩ , ͵sju-) *adj.* 異常的；非凡的

　（超過一般標準）《 *super-* = over 》

378　**not** = mark（標示；記號）

　　　　* 拉丁文 *nota* (= mark)，*notare* (= mark)。

note[1] (not) *n.* 符號；筆記；音符　*v.* 注意；加以注解

noted[7] (ˈnotɪd) *adj.* 著名的；顯著的；有音譜的

nota bene (ˈnotəˈbinɪ) = mark well = 注意（簡作 **N.B.** ）

notable[5] 〔'notəbḷ〕 *adj.* 著名的　*n.* 名人

```
not  +  able
 |        |
mark  +  adj.
```

notary 〔'notərɪ〕 *n.* 公證人（記錄下來的人）

notarial 〔no'tɛrɪəl , -'tær- , -'ter-〕 *adj.* 公證的；公證人的

notarize 〔'notə,raɪz〕 *v.* 公證；公證人證明

notarization 〔,notəraɪ'zeʃən〕 *n.* 公證

notandum 〔no'tændəm〕 *n.* 備忘錄；備忘錄記載之事（記下要做的事）《*not*（mark）+ *-and* = *-end*（be）+ *-um*（a thing）》

```
not  +  and  +  um
 |        |       |
mark  +  be   +  thing
```

notation[7] 〔no'teʃən〕 *n.* 符號法；記數法；記譜法

notice[1] 〔'notɪs〕 *n.* 公告；注意　*v.* 注目；通知（爲了提示的標幟）

noticeable[5] 〔'notɪsəbḷ〕 *adj.* 引人注目的；顯著的

notify[5] 〔'notə,faɪ〕 *v.* 公告；通知《*-ify* = make》

notification[7] 〔,notəfə'keʃən〕 *n.* 通知；通知書

notion[5] 〔'noʃən〕 *n.* 概念；意見（應該記住的想法）

notorious[6] 〔no'torɪəs〕 *adj.* 聲名狼藉的；惡名昭彰的

annotate[7] 〔'æno,tet〕 *v.* 註解；評註（加以標明）《*an-* = *ad-* = to》

```
an  +  not  +  ate
 |       |       |
to  +  mark  +  v.
```

annotation 〔,æno'teʃən〕 *n.* 註解；評註

connote 〔kə'not〕 *v.* 暗示；含意；包涵（標示在一起 → 含意）
《*con-* = together》

connotation 〔,kɑnə'teʃən〕 *n.* 含意；暗示

```
con    +  not  +  ation
 |          |        |
together + mark  +   n.
```

connotative 〔 ˈkɑnəˌtetɪv , kəˈnotətɪv 〕 *adj.* 暗示的；含蓄的

denote 〔 dɪˈnot 〕 *v.* 表示；指示（記載於下方）

《*de-* = down》

denotation 〔ˌdinoˈteʃən 〕 *n.* 表示；指示；名稱；意義

end-note 〔ˈɛndˌnot 〕 *n.* （書末或章節末的）尾註

footnote[7] 〔ˈfʊtˌnot 〕 *n.* 注釋

---

379 nounce , nunci = report (報告)

* 拉丁文 ***nuntiare*** (= *report* ; *give a message*)。

announce[3] 〔 əˈnaʊns 〕 *v.* 宣布；發表；通知（向大眾報告）

《*an-* = *ad-* = to》

announcement[3] 〔 əˈnaʊnsmənt 〕 *n.* 宣布；布告；發表；通知

```
an + nounce + ment
 |      |        |
to  + report  +  n.
```

annunciate 〔 əˈnʌnʃɪˌet 〕 *v.* 佈告；告知

annunciation 〔 əˌnʌnsɪˈeʃən 〕 *n.* 通知；佈告

denounce[6] 〔 dɪˈnaʊns 〕 *v.* 公開指責；當眾責罵（報以強硬的姿態）

《*de-* = down ; fully》

denunciation 〔 dɪˌnʌnsɪˈeʃən 〕 *n.* 告發；警告

```
de  + nunci + ation
 |      |       |
down + report +  n.
```

enunciate 〔 ɪˈnʌnsɪˌet , -ʃɪ- 〕 *v.* 發音；宣布；發表（報告出來）

《*e-* = *ex-* = out》

enunciation 〔 ɪˌnʌnsɪˈeʃən , -ʃɪ- 〕 *n.* 發音；宣布；發表

pronounce[2] 〔 prəˈnaʊns 〕 *v.* 宣告；發音（表明）

《*pro-* = forth》

pronouncement 〔 prəˈnaʊnsmənt 〕 *n.* 宣告；發表

pronunciation[4]〔 prə͵nʌnsɪ'eʃən 〕 *n.* 發音 (法)

```
pro  +  nunci  +  ation
 |        |        |
forth +  report  +  n.
```

renounce[7]〔 rɪ'naʊns 〕 *v.* 放棄；否認 (倒回去說 → 不接受)
　《*re-* = back》
renouncement〔 rɪ'naʊnsmənt 〕 *n.* 放棄；否認
renunciation〔 rɪ͵nʌnsɪ'eʃən 〕 *n.* 放棄；否認

380　**nov** = new (新的)

　　* 拉丁文 *novus* , *novellus* (= *new*) 。

nova〔 'novə 〕 *n.* 【天文】新星
novation〔 no'veʃən 〕 *n.* 【法律】(債務、契約等的) 更替
novel[2]〔 'navḷ 〕 *adj.* 新奇的　 *n.* 小說
novelette〔 ͵navḷ'ɛt 〕 *n.* 短篇或中篇小說《*-ette* = small》
novelist[3]〔 'navḷɪst 〕 *n.* 小說家
novelty[7]〔 'navḷtɪ 〕 *n.* 新奇；新鮮
novice[5]〔 'navɪs 〕 *n.* 初學者；新手；見習修行者《*-ice* 表示行為者》
novity〔 'navətɪ 〕 *n.* 新奇；新鮮 (= *novelty*)
novitiate〔 no'vɪʃɪɪt 〕 *n.* 見習期間；新手 (充滿新鮮感的時期)
　　《*noviti* (novity) + *-ate* (名詞字尾)》

```
noviti  +  ate
  |         |
novity  +   n.
```

innovate[7]〔 'ɪnə͵vet 〕 *v.* 改革；革新 (導入新觀念)《*in-* = in》
innovation[6]〔 ͵ɪnə'veʃən 〕 *n.* 革新；新制度
innovator[7]〔 'ɪnə͵vetɚ 〕 *n.* 革新者；改革者
renovate[7]〔 'rɛnə͵vet 〕 *v.* 修復；革新 (重新修訂)《*re-* = again》
renovation[7]〔 ͵rɛnə'veʃən 〕 *n.* 革新；修補

381 **nucle** = nut (核果)

> * 希臘文 *nux* (= *nut*)，*nucleus* (= *kernel* 核心)。

nucleus[5] 〔'njuklɪəs 〕 *n.* 核心；細胞核
nuclear[4] 〔'njuklɪɚ 〕 *adj.* 核的；核子的；細胞核的
nucleonics 〔,njuklɪ'ɑnɪks 〕 *n.* 核子學《 *-ics* = science》
nucleoprotein 〔,njuklɪə'protiɪn 〕 *n.* 核蛋白質《*protein* 蛋白質》
enucleate 〔 ɪ'njuklɪ,et 〕 *v.* 除去細胞核；摘出 (腫瘤等)
　　adj. 無細胞核的《*e-* = *ex-* = out》

382 **nul** = nothing (什麼也沒有)

> * 拉丁文 *nullus* (= *not any*)。〔變化型〕*null*。

null[7] 〔 nʌl 〕 *adj.* 無效的；無意義的；無的；零的
nullify 〔'nʌlə,faɪ 〕 *v.* 使無效；取消；使無意義；抵消《 *-ify* = make》
nullification 〔,nʌləfə'keʃən 〕 *n.* 無效；取消；作廢

null	+	ific	+	ation
nothing	+	make	+	n.

nullity 〔'nʌlətɪ 〕 *n.* 無效；作廢；無
annul[7] 〔 ə'nʌl 〕 *v.* 取消；作廢 (使變成無)《*an-* = *ad-* = to》
annulment 〔 ə'nʌlmənt 〕 *n.* 取消；廢止；無效

383 **numer** = number；count (數字；計算)

> * 拉丁文 *numerus* (= *number*)，*numerare* (= *count*)。

number[1] 〔'nʌmbɚ 〕 *n.* 數字；數目；一些　*v.* 數；含有；數目達到
numberless 〔'nʌmbɚlɪs 〕 *adj.* 無數的；很多的 (= *innumerable*)
numberable 〔'nʌmbərəbḷ 〕 *adj.* 可數的；可計算的

numerable〔'njumərəbḷ , 'nu- 〕*adj.* 可數的；可計算的

numeral〔'njumərəl 〕*n.* 數字　*adj.* 數字的

numerate〔'njumə‚ret 〕*v.* 數；計算；讀（數）

```
numer + ate
  |       |
count  +  v.
```

numerator〔'njumə‚retɚ 〕*n.* 計算者；（分數的）分子

　cf. **denominator**（分母）

numerical〔 nju'mɛrɪkḷ 〕*adj.* 數字的；以數字表示的

numerous[4]〔'njumərəs 〕*adj.* 數目眾多的

enumerate〔 ɪ'njumə‚ret 〕*v.* 計算；數；列舉（計算出來）

　《*e-* = *ex-* = out》

enumeration〔 ɪ‚njumə'reʃən , ɪ‚nu- 〕*n.* 計算；列舉；目錄

innumerable〔 ɪ'njumərəbḷ , ɪn'nju- , -'nu- 〕*adj.* 無數的；

　數不清的（不能數的）《*in-* = not》

```
in + numer + able
 |     |       |
not + count + adj.
```

supernumerary〔‚supɚ'njumə‚rɛrɪ , -'nu- , ‚sju- 〕*n.* 冗員；臨時

　雇員；臨時演員　*adj.* 額外的；多餘的；臨時雇的（超出正常數目）

　《*super-*（over）+ *numer*（number）+ *-ary*（表示人的名詞字尾）》

384　**nutri** = nourish（滋養）

　* 拉丁文 *nutrire*（= *nourish*）。

nutrient[6]〔'njutrɪənt , 'nu- 〕*adj.* 營養的；滋養的　*n.* 滋養物；

　營養物

nutriment〔'njutrəmənt , 'nu- 〕*n.* 營養品；食物；幫助生長之物

nutrition[6]〔 nju'trɪʃən 〕*n.* 營養；食物；營養學

nutritious[6]〔nju'trɪʃəs〕*adj.* 滋養的；營養的

nutritive〔'njutrətɪv，'nu-〕*adj.* 營養的；關於營養的；滋養的

innutrition〔͵ɪnju'trɪʃən，͵ɪnnju-，-nu-〕*n.* 營養不良（失調）
（不營養）《*in-* = not》

malnutrition[7]〔͵mælnju'trɪʃən〕*n.* 營養不足；營養不良（失調）
（營養差）《*mal-* = bad》

385 ocul = eye（眼睛）　　　* 拉丁文 *oculus*（ = eye）。

ocular〔'ɑkjələ〕*adj.* 眼睛的；視覺的；像眼睛的
n.（望遠鏡、顯微鏡等的）接目鏡

ocularly〔'ɑkjələlɪ〕*adv.* 視覺地；眼睛地

oculist〔'ɑkjəlɪst〕*n.* 眼科醫師

oculomotor〔͵ɑkjʊlə'motə〕*adj.* 使眼球動的；動眼的
《*motor* = move》

```
oculo + motor
  |       |
 eye  +  move
```

binocular[6]〔baɪ'nɑkjələ，bɪ-〕*adj.* 雙眼並用的　*n.*（*pl.*）雙筒望
遠鏡（用兩眼）《*bi-* = two》

inoculate〔ɪn'ɑkjə͵let〕*v.* 預防注射；攪入；灌輸（將芽狀物種入
體內 → 接種）《*in-*（in）+ *ocul*（eye；bud 芽）+ *-ate*（動詞字尾）》

```
in + ocul + ate
 |     |     |
in +  eye +  v.
```

inoculation〔ɪn͵ɑkjə'leʃən〕*n.* 預防注射；接種疫苗；灌輸

monocular〔mə'nɑkjələ〕*adj.* 單眼的；單眼用的
n. 單眼鏡（只用一眼）《*mon-* = *mono-* = single》

386　od , hod = way（路）　　* 希臘文 *hodos*（= way）。

anode〔'ænod〕 *n.* 陽極；正極《*an-* = *ana-* = up》
cathode〔'kæθod〕 *n.* 陰極《*cat-* = *cata-* = down》
episode[6]〔'ɛpə,sod〕 *n.*（人生的）一段經歷；插曲；連續劇的一集

> ep(i) ＋ is ＋ ode
> |　　　｜　　｜
> *besides* ＋ *into* ＋ *way*

exodus[7]〔'ɛksədəs〕 *n.*（成群的）外出；（大批人的）移居國外；
（E-）出埃及記《*ex-* = out》
method[2]〔'mɛθəd〕 *n.* 方法《*met-* = *meta-* = after》
odograph〔'odə,græf〕 *n.*（車輛等的）里程計；記步器
《*graph* = write》
odometer〔o'dɑmətɚ〕 *n.*（車輛等的）里程計《*meter* = measure》
periodic〔,pɪrɪ'ɑdɪk〕 *adj.* 周期性的；間歇性的

> peri ＋ od ＋ ic
> |　　　｜　　｜
> *round* ＋ *way* ＋ *adj.*

synod〔'sɪnəd〕 *n.* 教會會議；教會法院《*syn-* = together》

387　od , ol = smell（氣味；聞）

* 拉丁文 *odor*（= smell），*olere*（= emit a smell）。

odor[5]〔'odɚ〕 *n.* 氣味；臭氣
deodorize〔di'odə,raɪz〕 *v.* 除去…的臭味《*de-* = away》
malodorous〔mæl'odərəs〕 *adj.* 有惡臭的《*mal-* = bad》
olfaction〔ɑl'fækʃən〕 *n.* 嗅覺《拉丁文 *olfacere* = smell》

> ol 　＋ fact ＋ ion
> |　　　　｜　　｜
> *emit a smell* ＋ *make* ＋ *n.*

olfactory〔ɑlˈfæktərɪ〕*adj.* 嗅覺的

redolent〔ˈrɛdḷənt〕*adj.* 芳香的;氣味強烈的;充滿…氣氛的
《*red-* = *re-* = intensive 加強語氣》

ozone[5]〔ˈozon , oˈzon〕*n.* 臭氧《希臘文 *ozein* = smell》

388　**od** = song(歌曲;詩歌)

* 希臘文 *aeidein*(= *sing*),*oide*(= *song*)。

ode〔od〕*n.* 頌詩;賦

epode〔ˈɛpod〕*n.* 長短句相間的抒情詩體;(古希臘抒情頌詩的)
第三節(即最後一節)

```
ep  +  od  + e
 |      |     |
after + sing + n.
```

palinode〔ˈpælɪˌnod〕*n.*(取消或放棄舊作中某些內容的)翻案
詩;(蘇格蘭法律中的)正式撤回

```
palin +  od  + e
  |      |     |
back  + song + n.
```

comedy[4]〔ˈkɑmədɪ〕*n.* 喜劇《希臘文 *komos* = revel(狂歡)》

tragedy[4]〔ˈtrædʒədɪ〕*n.* 悲劇;不幸《希臘文 *tragos* = goat》

【解說】緣於伯羅奔尼撒人的「羊人劇」(satyr play)對古典希臘悲
劇的影響。

melody[2]〔ˈmɛlədɪ〕*n.* 旋律;曲調;歌曲《希臘文 *melos* = song》

monody〔ˈmɑnədɪ〕*n.*(希臘悲劇的)獨唱頌歌;輓歌;哀歌
《*mon-* = *mono-* = single》

parody[7]〔ˈpærədɪ〕*n.* 諷刺詩文　*v.* 拙劣地模仿
《*par-* = *para-* = beside》

prosody〔ˈprɑsədɪ〕*n.* 詩體學;(特定的)詩體《*pros-* = to》

psalmodic〔sæl'mɑdɪk〕*adj.* 唱讚美詩的；有讚美詩風格的
　《*psalm* 讚美詩》

rhapsody〔'ræpsədɪ〕*n.* 狂想曲；狂熱讚詞；（現代的）狂詩
　《希臘文 *rhapsoidia* = verse composition》

```
rhaps +  od  + y
  |       |    |
stitch + song + n.
```

threnody〔'θrɛnədɪ〕*n.* 輓歌；哀歌；哀悼
　《希臘文 *threnos* = dirge（輓歌；哀歌）》

389　**onym** = name（名字）　* 希臘文 *onoma*（= *name*）。

onomatopoeia〔ˌɑnəˌmætə'piə〕*n.* 擬聲詞；聲喻法
　（用聲音表達名稱）《*poeia* = make》

acronym[7]〔'ækrənɪm〕*n.* 頭字語（由數個字開頭字母組成之字）
　《*acro* = extreme（前端的）》

anonym〔'ænəˌnɪm〕*n.* 匿名者；假名（沒有姓名的）
　《*an-* = without》

anonymous[6]〔ə'nɑnəməs〕*adj.* 不知名的；匿名的

```
an    + onym + ous
 |       |     |
without + name + adj.
```

antonym[6]〔'æntəˌnɪm〕*n.* 反義字（相反的名稱）
　《*ant-* = *anti-* = against》

autonym〔'ɔtənɪm〕*n.* 眞名；本名（自己的名字）
　《*aut-* = *auto-* = self》　*cf.* **pseudonym**（假名；筆名）

homonym〔'hɑməˌnɪm〕*n.* 同音異義字；同名異人
　（名稱相同，但是內容不一樣）《*homo-* = same》

```
homo + nym
  |     |
same + name
```

matronymic〔ˌmætrə'nɪmɪk〕*adj.* 出自母親或女性祖先之名的；

母姓的（＝*metronymic*） *n.* 取自母親或女性祖先之名

《*matr* = mother》

metonymy〔mə'tɑnəmɪ〕*n.* 換喻（如：將 king 改稱為 the crown）

（改變名稱）《*met-* = *meta-* = change》

```
met  +  onym  +  y
 |        |       |
change + name +  n.
```

paronym〔'pærənɪm〕*n.* 同源字（在旁邊的另一名稱）

《*par-* = *para-* = beside》

patronymic〔ˌpætrə'nɪmɪk〕*adj.* 取自父（祖）名的

n. 取自父（祖）名之名字《*patr* = father》

pseudonym[7]〔'sjudn̩ˌɪm〕*n.* 假名；筆名（不實的名稱）

《*pseudo* = false》

synonym[6]〔'sɪnəˌnɪm〕*n.* 同義字（相同的名稱）《*syn-* = same》

390　**OO , OV** = egg（蛋；卵）

* 希臘文 *oion*（＝*egg*）；拉丁文 *ovum*（＝*egg*）。

oogenesis〔ˌoə'dʒɛnəsɪs〕*n.* 卵生成《*genesis* 誕生》

oogonium〔ˌoə'gonɪəm〕*n.* 卵原細胞；卵囊

```
oo  +  gon  +  ium
 |       |       |
egg + seed  +  n.
```

oology〔o'ɑlədʒɪ〕*n.* 鳥卵學《*logy* = study》

oval[4]〔'ovl̩〕*adj.* 橢圓形的　*n.* 橢圓形；橢圓形跑道

oviduct〔'ovɪˌdʌkt〕*n.* 輸卵管

```
ovi  +  duct
 |       |
egg +  lead
```

ovulation 〔͵ovjuˈleʃən 〕 *n.* 排卵

ovum 〔ˈovəm 〕 *n.* 卵；卵細胞

biovular 〔 baɪˈovjələ 〕 *adj.* 雙卵性的；雙卵性雙胞胎特有的

　　《*bi-* = two》

monovular 〔 manˈovjələ 〕 *adj.* 單卵的；單卵雙胞胎特有的

　　《*mon-* = *mono-* = single》

391　　**oper** = work (工作)

　　* 拉丁文 *opus* (= work) ，*operari* (= work) 。

opus[7] 〔ˈopəs 〕 *n.* 作品；作品編號

opera[4] 〔ˈapərə 〕 *n.* 歌劇；歌劇院 (寫作的結果)《 *-a* 名詞字尾》

operable[7] 〔ˈapərəbl̩ , ˈaprə- 〕 *adj.* 可實行的；可動手術的

operant 〔ˈapərənt 〕 *adj.* 工作的；發生作用的

　　n. 工作的人或物；發生作用的人或物

operate[2] 〔ˈapə͵ret 〕 *v.* 動作；操作；產生；生效；動手術

```
oper + ate
 |      |
work +  v.
```

operatic 〔͵apəˈrætɪk 〕 *adj.* 歌劇的；歌劇式的

operation[4] 〔͵apəˈreʃən 〕 *n.* 工作；動作；管理；手術；

　　(*pl.*) 軍事行動；數學運算

operational[6] 〔͵apəˈreʃənl̩ 〕 *adj.* 可使用的；作戰的；現役的

operative[7] 〔ˈapə͵retɪv , ˈapərətɪv 〕 *adj.* 動作的；工作的；

　　有效的；手術的

operator[3] 〔ˈapə͵retə 〕 *n.* 工作者；接線生；施行手術者

cooperate[4] 〔 koˈapə͵ret 〕 *v.* 合作；協力 (一起工作)

　　《*co-* = *com-* = together》

```
co    + oper + ate
 |       |      |
together + work +  v.
```

cooperation[4] 〔 ko͵apə'reʃən 〕 *n.* 合作；協力；合作社
cooperative[4] 〔 ko'apə͵retɪv 〕 *adj.* 合作的；願意合作的　*n.* 合作社
cooperator 〔 ko'apə͵retə 〕 *n.* 合作者

392　ophthalm = eye (眼睛)

　　* 希臘文 *ophthalmos* (= *eye*) 。

ophthalmia 〔 af'θælmɪə 〕 *n.* 眼炎
ophthalmic 〔 af'θælmɪk 〕 *adj.* 眼的；患眼炎的
ophthalmology 〔͵afθæl'malədʒɪ 〕 *n.* 眼科學《*logy* = study》
ophthalmologist 〔͵afθæl'malədʒɪst 〕 *n.* 眼科醫師
ophthalmometer 〔͵afθæl'mamətə 〕 *n.* 眼膜曲率計《*meter* 計量器》
ophthalmoplegia 〔 af͵θælmə'plidʒɪə 〕 *n.* 眼肌癱瘓；眼肌麻痺

> ophthalmo　+　pleg　+　ia
> 　　|　　　　　|　　　　|
> 　eye　+ paralysis + condition

ophthalmoscope 〔 af'θælmə͵skop 〕 *n.* 檢目鏡；檢眼器
　　《*scope* 表示「觀察～的器具」》
ophthalmotomy 〔͵afθæl'matəmɪ 〕 *n.* 眼球切開術《*tom* = cut》

393　opt = eye；sight (眼睛；視力)

　　* 希臘文 *ops* (= *eye*)，*opsis* (= *sight*)，*optos* (= *visible*) 。

optic 〔'aptɪk 〕 *adj.* 眼睛的；視覺的
optical[7] 〔'aptɪkl̩ 〕 *adj.* 眼的；視覺的；幫助視力的；光學的
optician 〔 ap'tɪʃən 〕 *n.* 眼鏡和光學儀器製造者；眼鏡和光學儀器
　　販賣商《 *-ian* 表示人的名詞字尾》
optics 〔'aptɪks 〕 *n.* 光學《 *-ics* = science》
optometer 〔 ap'tamətə 〕 *n.* 視力計；視力檢定器《*meter* 計量器》

optometrist〔ɑp'tɑmətrɪst〕*n.* 驗光醫師；配鏡師

```
opto  +  metr  +   ist
  |        |        |
sight + measure + person
```

optometry〔ɑp'tɑmətrɪ〕*n.* 驗光；視力檢定
biopsy〔baɪ'ɑpsɪ〕*n.* 活體檢視；活組織切片檢查法《*bio* = life》
hyperopia〔ˌhaɪpə'opɪə〕= far sight　*n.* 遠視
　《*hyper-* (far) + *op* (sight) + *-ia* (condition)》
myopia〔maɪ'opɪə〕= short sight　*n.* 近視；缺乏遠見
　《*my-* = short》
myopic〔maɪ'ɑpɪk〕*adj.* 近視的；缺乏遠見的

394　opt = choose (選擇)

　　* 拉丁文 *optare* (= *choose* ; *wish*)。

opt[7]〔ɑpt〕*v.* 選擇
optative〔'ɑptətɪv〕*adj.* 表願望的　*n.* 【文法】祈願語氣
option[6]〔'ɑpʃən〕*n.* 選擇 (權)
optional[6]〔'ɑpʃən!〕*adj.* 可選擇的；隨意的　*n.* 選修科目

```
opt   + ion +  al
  |       |     |
choose +  n.  + adj.
```

adopt[3]〔ə'dɑpt〕*v.* 採用；收養 (選擇~)《*ad-* = to》
adoptable[7]〔ə'dɑptəb!〕*adj.* 可採用的；可收養的
adoptee〔əˌdɑp'ti〕*n.* 被收養者《*-ee* 表示「被~的人」》
adopter〔ə'dɑptə〕*n.* 採用者；養父母
adoption[7]〔ə'dɑpʃən〕*n.* 採用；收養

【解說】領養小孩在美國非常普遍。但他們領養小孩並不是為了要有人繼
　　　承香火，而是為了讓家裡熱鬧一點，豐富家庭生活。他們對於領
　　　養不同種族，以及殘障兒童的意願，相對來說也比較高。

adoptive[7]〔əˋdɑptɪv〕*adj.* 收養關係的
co-opt[7]〔koˋɑpt〕*v.* 將…選爲新成員《*co-* = *com-* = together》

395　**optim** = best（最佳的）

　　* 拉丁文 *optimus*（= *best*）。

optimism[5]〔ˋɑptəˌmɪzəm〕*n.* 樂觀主義（往最好的方向想）
　　《*-ism* 表示主義的名詞字尾》　*cf.* **pessimism**（悲觀主義）
optimist[7]〔ˋɑptəmɪst〕*n.* 樂觀主義者《*-ist* 表示人的名詞字尾》
optimize[7]〔ˋɑptəˌmaɪz〕*v.* 表示樂觀；使發揮最大作用
optimum[7]〔ˋɑptəməm〕*n.*（成長的）最佳條件　*adj.* 最適宜的

396　**ora** = speak；pray（説；禱告）

　　* 拉丁文 *orare*（= *speak*；*pray*）。

oral[4]〔ˋɔrəl〕*adj.* 口頭的；口述的　*n.* 口試《*-al* 形容詞字尾》
orate〔ˋoret，ˋɔret，oˋret〕*v.* 演說
oration〔oˋreʃən，əˋreʃən〕*n.* 演說
orator〔ˋɔrətɚ，ˋɑrətɚ〕*n.* 演說者
oratorical〔ˌɔrəˋtɔrɪkl̩〕*adj.* 演說的；修辭的
oratorio〔ˌɔrəˋtorɪo，ˌɑr-〕*n.* 神劇（以基督教《聖經》故事爲主題）
oratory〔ˋɔrəˌtorɪ〕*n.* 演說術；修辭
　　《拉丁文 *oratoria* = public speaking》
oratrix〔ˋɔrətrɪks〕*n.* 女性演說家《*trix* = feminine（女性的）》

```
ora  +  trix
 |        |
speak + feminine
```

oracle〔ˋɔrəkl̩〕*n.* 神諭；神命；神使；神的啓示（神口中説出的話）
oracular〔ɔˋrækjələ〕*adj.* 神諭的；獨斷的

adoration〔͵ædə'reʃən〕*n.* 崇拜；愛慕（希望和～說話）《*ad-* = to》

inexorable〔ɪn'ɛksərəbḷ〕*adj.* 無情的；不爲所動的；不能改變的（不能說出的）《*in-*（not）+ *ex-*（out）+ *ora*（speak）+ *-(a)ble*（形容詞字尾）》

```
in  +  ex  +  ora   + (a)ble
 |      |      |         |
not  + out + speak  +  adj.
```

inexorability〔ɪn͵ɛksərə'bɪlətɪ〕*n.* 無情；嚴密性

peroral〔pə'rɔrəl〕*adj.* 經口的（經過口的）《*per-* = through》

perorate〔'pɛrə͵ret〕*v.* 作冗長的演說；做結論（從頭到尾地說）

peroration〔͵pɛro'reʃən〕*n.*（演說之）結論；精彩的演說

397　**ordin** = order（秩序；命令）

*　拉丁文 *ordo*（= order），*ordinare*（= arrange）。

order[1]〔'ɔrdɚ〕*n.* 順序；有秩序；規則；命令；訂貨單；點菜　*v.* 整頓；命令；訂貨；點菜

orderly[6]〔'ɔrdɚlɪ〕*adj.* 有秩序的；規矩的　*adv.* 根據規定地；有條不紊地

ordinal〔'ɔrdṇəl〕*adj.* 順序的　*n.* 序數（= *ordinal number*）

ordinance〔'ɔrdṇəns , 'ɔrdnəns〕*n.* 法令；條例；習慣；習俗

```
ordin + ance
  |      |
order  +  n.
```

ordinary[2]〔'ɔrdṇ͵ɛrɪ , 'ɔrdnɛrɪ〕*adj.* 普通的；正常的；一般的；平凡的（秩序中的）

ordinarily[7]〔'ɔrdṇ͵ɛrɪlɪ , 'ɔrdnɛrɪlɪ , ͵ɔrd'nɛrəlɪ〕*adv.* 通常；普通地

ordinate〔'ɔrdṇ͵et , 'ɔrdṇɪt〕*n.*【數學】縱座標

cf. **abscissa**（橫座標）

ordination〔͵ɔrdn̩'eʃən〕*n.* 聖職的任命（儀式）；法令的頒布；整頓；排列

ordinee〔͵ɔrdə'ni〕*n.* 新任教會執事《*-ee* 表示動作的接受者》

coordinate[6]〔*v.* ko'ɔrdn̩͵et *adj.*, *n.* ko'ɔrdn̩ɪt〕*v.* 使同等；協調　*adj.* 同等的；對等的　*n.* 同等的人或物（使處於同一次序）

《*co-* = *com-* = with》

```
co  + ordin + ate
 |      |      |
with + order +  v.
```

coordination[7]〔ko͵ɔrdn̩'eʃən〕*n.* 同等；協調

coordinative[7]〔ko'ɔrdn̩͵etɪv〕*adj.* 同等的；協調的

coordinator[7]〔ko'ɔrdə͵netɚ〕*n.* 同等的人或物；協調者

disorder[4]〔dɪs'ɔrdɚ〕*n.* 無秩序；混亂；騷動；疾病　*v.* 使紊亂；致病（沒有秩序）《*dis-* = away》

extraordinary[4]〔ɪk'strɔrdn̩͵ɛrɪ, ͵ɛkstrə'ɔr-〕*adj.* 非常的；特別的；特任的；臨時的（超出平常的）《*extra-* = beyond》

```
extra  + ordin + ary
  |        |      |
beyond + order + adj.
```

extraordinarily[7]〔ɪk'strɔrdn̩͵ɛrɪlɪ, ͵ɛkstrə'ɔr-〕*adv.* 特別地；非常地

inordinate[7]〔ɪn'ɔrdn̩ɪt〕*adj.* 無節制的；不規則的；過度的（無次序的）《*in-* = not》

primordial〔praɪ'mɔrdɪəl〕*adj.* 原始的；最初的；根本的　*n.* 原始物；根本（最初階段）《*prim* = primary》

```
prim  + ordi + al
  |      |     |
primary + order + adj.
```

subordinate[6]〔*v.* sə'bɔrdn̩͵et *adj.*, *n.* sə'bɔrdn̩ɪt〕*v.* 使居下位；使服從　*adj.* 下級的；次要的；附屬的　*n.* 屬下；附屬物（在下的次序）《*sub-* = under》

subordination〔sə,bɔrdn̩'eʃən〕*n.* 下位；次要；隸屬；服從

subordinative〔sə'bɔrdə,netɪv , -nətɪv〕*adj.* 從屬的；附屬的

398　ori = rise ; begin（上升；開始）

* 拉丁文 *oriri*（= *rise* ; *begin* ; *be born*）。〔變化型〕*ort*。

orient[5]〔*n.* 'ɔrɪ,ɛnt　*adj.* 'orɪənt　*v.* 'orɪ,ɛnt〕*n.* 東方；（the O~）東方諸國（太陽昇上來的地方）　*adj.* 東方的　*v.* 使（建築物等）朝東

Oriental[5]〔,ori'ɛntl̩〕*adj.* 東方諸國的　*n.* 東方人

　　cf. **Occidental**（西洋的；西洋人）

orientate〔'orɪɛn,tet , ,orɪ'ɛntet , 'ɔr- , ,ɔr-〕*v.* 使向東；使定方位；使適應新環境

orientation[7]〔,orɪɛn'teʃən〕*n.*（建築物等的）朝東；指導；定位

origin[3]〔'ɔrədʒɪn〕*n.* 起源；出處（事物的開端）

original[3]〔ə'rɪdʒənl̩〕*adj.* 最初的；最早的　*n.* 原文；原物

originality[6]〔ə,rɪdʒə'næləti〕*n.* 創造力；創意

```
origin   +  al  + ity
  |          |      |
beginning  + adj. + n.
```

originate[6]〔ə'rɪdʒə,net〕*v.* 創始；發明

originative[7]〔ə'rɪdʒə,netɪv〕*adj.* 獨創的

originator〔ə'rɪdʒə,netɚ〕*n.* 創始者；發起人

aboriginal[6]〔,æbə'rɪdʒənl̩〕*adj.* 原始的；土著的　*n.* 原始居民；土人（始於最初的）《*ab-* = from》

abortion[5]〔ə'bɔrʃən〕*n.* 流產；墮胎（錯誤的出生）《*ab-* = amiss》

　　【解說】美國自 1973 年開始讓「墮胎、人工流產」合法化，但爭議性仍很大，贊成「選擇權」（pro-choice）的人士，主張婦女對自己的身體有自主權；贊成「生命權」（pro-life）的人士，主張未出生的嬰兒有活著的權利。然而，英國早在 1967 年就已經通過墮胎合法化了。

disorient[7]〔dɪsˈɔrɪˌɛnt , -ˈor- 〕v. 使失去方位；使偏歪；使迷惑
（使離開東方）《**dis-** = away》

disorientate〔dɪsˈɔrɪɛnˌtet 〕v. = disorient

```
    dis  + orient + ate
     |       |       |
   away + rising +  v.
```

disorientation[7]〔dɪsˌɔrɪɛnˈteʃən 〕n. 失去方向；偏歪

reorient[7]〔v. riˈɔrɪɛnt , -ˈor-　adj. riˈɔrɪənt , -ˈor- 〕v. 再改方向；
再定方位；再適應　　adj. 再改方向的《**re-** = again》

reorientate〔riˈɔrɪɛnˌtet 〕v. = reorient

reorientation〔riˌɔrɪɛnˈteʃən 〕n. 再改方向；再定方位；再適應

399　　orn = decorate（裝飾）

　　* 拉丁文 ***ornare***（ = *decorate* ）。

ornament[5]〔n. ˈɔrnəmənt　v. ˈɔrnəˌmɛnt 〕n. 裝飾（品）；增光彩
的人或物　v. 裝飾

ornamental[7]〔ˌɔrnəˈmɛntḷ 〕adj. 裝飾品的；裝飾的　　n. 裝飾物

```
   orna   + ment + al
     |        |      |
 decorate +  n.  + adj.
```

ornamentalist〔ˌɔrnəˈmɛntḷɪst 〕n. 裝飾家；設計家

ornamentation〔ˌɔrnəmɛnˈteʃən , -mən- 〕n. 裝飾；修飾；
【集合名詞】裝飾品

ornate〔ɔrˈnet 〕adj. 裝飾華麗的；（文體）華麗不實的；
注重修辭的《 **-ate** 形容詞字尾》

```
   orn    + ate
    |        |
 decorate + adj.
```

adorn[7]〔əˈdɔrn 〕v. 裝飾（向～裝飾）《**ad-** = to》

adornment〔əˈdɔrnmənt 〕n. 裝飾；裝飾品

400　oscill = swing（搖擺）

＊拉丁文 *oscillare*（= *swing*）。

oscillate[7]〔'ɑsḷ,et〕*v.* 擺動；猶豫；上下波動
oscillogram〔ə'sɪlə,græm〕*n.* 波形圖《*gram* = write》
oscillometer〔,ɑsɪ'lɑmɪtɚ〕*n.* 示波計（一種測量船隻橫搖角或
　縱搖角的儀器）《*meter* 計量器》
oscilloscope〔ə'sɪlə,skop〕*n.* 示波器《*scope* 表示「觀察～的器具」》

401　oss , oste = bone（骨頭）

＊拉丁文 *os* , *oss-*（= *bone*）；希臘文 *osteon*（= *bone*）。

osseous〔'ɑsɪəs〕*adj.* 骨的；骨狀的；由骨構成的
ossicle〔'ɑsɪkḷ〕*n.* 小骨《*-cle* = small》
ossify〔'ɑsə,faɪ〕*v.* 骨化；硬化；僵化；使冷酷無情《*-ify* = make》
ossification〔,ɑsəfə'keʃən〕*n.* 骨化；硬化；遲鈍化；冷淡化
ossuary〔'ɑsjʊ,ɛrɪ , 'ɑʃjʊ-〕*n.* 藏骨堂；骨罐；骨甕（納骨處）
　《*-ary* 表示場所的名詞字尾》

```
ossu  +  ary
 |         |
bone  +  place
```

osteoarthritis〔,ɑstɪoɑr'θraɪtɪs〕*n.* 骨關節炎《*arthritis* 關節炎》
osteoblast〔'ɑstɪəblæst〕*n.* 造骨細胞；成骨細胞（骨頭的芽）
　《希臘文 *blastos* = bud（芽）》

```
osteo  +  blast
  |         |
 bone  +  bud
```

osteology〔,ɑstɪ'ɑlədʒɪ〕*n.* 骨學；骨結構《*logy* = study》
osteological〔,ɑstɪə'lɑdʒɪkḷ〕*adj.* 骨學的；骨結構的
osteologist〔,ɑstɪ'ɑlədʒɪst〕*n.* 骨學專家

osteomyelitis 〔͵ɑstɪə͵maɪə'laɪtɪs 〕 *n.* 骨髓炎《*myelitis* 脊髓炎》
osteopathist 〔͵ɑstɪ'ɑpəθɪst 〕 *n.* 整骨醫生
(= *osteopath* ('ɑstɪə͵pæθ 〕)《*path* = disease》
osteopathy 〔͵ɑstɪ'ɑpəθɪ 〕 *n.* 整骨療法

402　oxy = sharp ; acid (強烈的 ; 酸的)

* 希臘文 *oxus* (= *sharp* ; *acid*)。

oxygen[4] ('ɑksədʒən 〕 *n.* 氧《*gen* = produce》
oxidant ('ɑksədənt 〕 *n.* 氧化劑
oxide ('ɑksaɪd 〕 *n.* 氧化物《 *-ide* 表示「化物」》
oxidize ('ɑksə͵daɪz 〕 *v.* (使) 氧化 ;(使) 生鏽
paroxysm ('pærəks͵ɪzəm 〕 *n.* 發作 ;(感情等的) 突發
《*par-* = *para-* = beyond》

403　pac = peace (和平)

* 拉丁文 *pax* , *pacem* (= *peace*) ; 古法文 *pais* (= *peace*)。

pacify[7] ('pæsə͵faɪ 〕 *v.* 使平靜 ; 安撫 ; 使恢復和平《 *-ify* = make》
pacific[5] 〔 pə'sɪfɪk 〕 *adj.* 和平的 ; 愛好和平的 ; 平靜的

pac	+	if(y)	+	ic
|		|		|
peace	+	*make*	+	*adj.*

pacificate 〔 pə'sɪfə͵ket 〕 *v.* = pacify
pacification 〔͵pæsəfə'keʃən 〕 *n.* 講和 ; 和解 ; 安撫
pacifier ('pæsə͵faɪɚ 〕 *n.* 撫慰者 ; 調停者 ;〔美〕(嬰兒的) 奶嘴
pacifism ('pæsə͵fɪzəm 〕 *n.* 和平主義《 *-ism* 表示主義的名詞字尾》
pacifist[7] ('pæsəfɪst 〕 *n.* 和平主義者
appease[7] 〔 ə'piz 〕 *v.* 撫慰 ; 平息 ; 緩和《*ap-* = *ad-* = to》

404　**pact** = agree ; fasten（同意；繫緊）

* 拉丁文 *pacisci*（ = *agree* ），*pangere*（ = *fasten* ）。

pact[6]〔 pækt 〕*n.* 協定；公約；協議
compact[5]〔 *n.* ˈkɑmpækt *v.*, *adj.* kəmˈpækt 〕*n.* 協定；契約；粉盒；
　小型汽車　*v.* 結緊；固結　*adj.* 結實的；緊密的；簡潔的
　（緊密地結合在一起）《 *com-* = together 》
compactly〔 kəmˈpæktlɪ 〕*adv.* 緊密地；簡潔地；結實地
compactness〔 kəmˈpæktnɪs 〕*n.* 緊密；結實；（面積等之）小

com	+	pact	+	ness
together	+	fasten	+	*n.*

compactor〔 kəmˈpæktɚ 〕*n.* 壓土機
impact[4]〔 *n.* ˈɪmpækt　*v.* ɪmˈpækt 〕*n.* 衝擊；撞擊力；影響
　v. 擠入；壓緊；撞擊；發生影響《拉丁文 *impingere* = push against 》
impacted〔 ɪmˈpæktɪd , -tɛd 〕*adj.* 壓緊的；嵌入的
impaction〔 ɪmˈpækʃən 〕*n.* 壓緊；嵌入

405　**pan** = bread（麵包）　　* 拉丁文 *panis*（ = *bread* ）。

panada〔 pəˈnɑdə 〕*n.* 麵包粥（以麵包加糖、牛奶、調味料等煮成）；
　麵糊（拌餡、作醬或煮湯用）
pantry[7]〔ˈpæntrɪ 〕*n.*（家庭的）食品儲存室；（餐館等的）餐具室；
　配膳室《 *-try* 表示場所的名詞字尾 》
company[2]〔ˈkʌmpənɪ 〕*n.* 交誼；夥伴（一起吃飯、用膳）
　《 *com-* = together 》
companion[4]〔 kəmˈpænjən 〕*n.* 夥伴；同行者

com	+	pan	+	ion
together	+	bread	+	*n.*

companionship[6] 〔kəm'pænjənʃɪp〕*n.* 交誼;交往
《 *-ship* 抽象名詞字尾》
accompany[4] 〔ə'kʌmpənɪ〕*v.* 伴隨(跟隨其後)
《 *ac-* = *ad-* = to 》

406 **par** = appear (出現)

* 拉丁文 ***parere*** (= *appear* ; *come in sight*) 。

appear[1] 〔ə'pɪr〕*v.* 出現;呈現《 *ap-* = *ad-* = to 》
appearance[2] 〔ə'pɪrəns〕*n.* 出現;外觀
apparent[3] 〔ə'pærənt , ə'pɛrənt〕*adj.* 明白的;明顯的

```
ap  +  par  + ent
 |      |      |
 to +  appear + adj.
```

apparition 〔,æpə'rɪʃən〕*n.* 幽靈;妖怪
transparent[5] 〔træns'pɛrənt〕*adj.* 透明的;率直的
(穿過而看得見)《 *trans-* = through 》

407 **par** = bear (生)

* 拉丁文 ***parere*** (= *bear* ; *give birth to*) 。〔變化型〕*part*。

parent[1] 〔'pɛrənt , 'pærənt , 'perənt〕*n.* 父;母;(*pl.*) 雙親;
根源《 *-ent* 表示人的名詞字尾》
parental[7] 〔pə'rɛntl̩〕*adj.* 父親的;母親的;父母的;雙親的
parentage 〔'pɛrəntɪdʒ〕*n.* 父或母的地位或狀態;出身;家系
《 *-age* 抽象名詞字尾》
parturient 〔pɑr'tjʊrɪənt〕*adj.* 臨盆的;分娩的;(意念、發現
等) 即將產生的 *n.* 產婦《拉丁文 ***parturire*** = be in labor (分娩中)》
parturition 〔,pɑrtjʊ'rɪʃən〕*n.* 生產;分娩

biparous ('bɪpərəs) *adj.* 雙生的;二枝的;二軸的

（一次生兩個）《*bi-* = two》

```
bi  +  par  +  ous
 |      |      |
two  +  bear  +  adj.
```

multiparous (mʌl'tɪpərəs) *adj.* 多產的;一胎多子的

（一次生很多）《*multi-* = many》

oviparous (o'vɪpərəs) *adj.* 卵生的;產卵的《*ovi* = egg》

uniparous (ju'nɪpərəs) *adj.* 一胎一卵或一子的;單梗的

（一次生一個）《*uni-* = one》

viviparous (vaɪ'vɪpərəs) *adj.* 胎生的;母體發芽的

《*vivi* = alive》

408 **par** = equal（相等的）　　* 拉丁文 *par*（= equal）。

par[7] (pɑr) *n.* 同地位;同程度

parity ('pærətɪ) *n.* 等價;同等

compare[2] (kəm'pɛr) *v.* 比較;匹敵;比喻（把～放在一起）

《*com-* = together》

comparable[6] ('kɑmpərəbḷ) *adj.* 可比較的;可匹敵的

```
com  +  par  +  able
 |       |       |
together + equal + adj.
```

comparability[7] (ˌkɑmpərə'bɪlətɪ) *n.* 可相比;相似

comparative[6] (kəm'pærətɪv) *adj.* 比較的;比較而言的

n. 比較級

comparison[3] (kəm'pærəsṇ) *n.* 比較;比擬;相似

disparate[7] ('dɪspərɪt) *adj.* 不同的;不相似的;異類的

《*dis-* = apart》

disparity (dɪs'pærətɪ) *n.* 不同;不等

imparity[7] 〔 ɪmˈpærətɪ 〕 *n.* 不同;不等;不平衡;差異

《*im-* = *in-* = not》

```
im  +  par  +  ity
 |       |      |
not + equal +  n.
```

pair[1] 〔 pɛr 〕 *n.* 一對;一雙 *v.* 成雙;成對(二個同等的東西)

peer[4] 〔 pɪr 〕 *n.* 上院議員;貴族;同輩(居於同等地位者)

　　v. 與~匹敵;凝視;細看;出現

peerage 〔ˈpɪrɪdʒ 〕 *n.*【集合名詞】貴族;貴族階級

peerless[7] 〔ˈpɪrlɪs 〕 *adj.* 無比的;無雙的(沒有相同的兩樣東西)

umpire[5] 〔ˈʌmpaɪr 〕 *n.* 裁定人;裁判(棒球、板球運動的裁判)

　　v. 審判(不在同立場的人) *cf.* **referee**(籃球、足球、排球、拳擊、

摔角等運動的裁判)

409　**par** = prepare(準備)

　　* 拉丁文 *parare*(= *prepare*;*make ready*)。

pare[7] 〔 pær 〕 *v.* 剝去(外皮)(為了準備)

parade[3] 〔 pəˈred 〕 *n.* 行列;遊行隊伍 *v.* 列隊行進(使準備齊全的)

【解說】 美國人很喜歡以遊行來慶祝節日,例如:復活節遊行(**Easter**
parade)、聖誕節遊行等。遊行時一定會有樂隊(marching
bands)、鼓號、花車(float)等,有時候政治人物還會出來
揮揮手。

apparatus[7] 〔ˌæpəˈretəs , ˌæpəˈrætəs 〕 *n.* 儀器;裝置(準備好的
設施)

prepare[1] 〔 prɪˈpɛr 〕 *v.* 準備;預備(事先加以準備)《*pre-* = before》

preparation[3] 〔ˌprɛpəˈreʃən 〕 *n.* 準備;預備

```
pre  +  par   + ation
 |        |       |
before + prepare +  n.
```

preparatory 〔 prɪˈpærəˌtorɪ 〕 *adj.* 準備的;預備的 *n.* 預備學校

字根 pact~radi

repair³〔rɪ'pɛr〕*v.* 修繕；修理 *n.* 修繕；修補（再整理）
　《*re-* = again》
reparable〔'rɛpərəbḷ〕*adj.* 可修理的；可補救的；可補償的

```
re   +   par   + able
 |         |        |
again + make ready + adj.
```

reparation〔,rɛpə're∫ən〕*n.* 賠償
reparative〔rɪ'pærətɪv〕*adj.* 修理的；賠償的
separate²〔*v.* 'sɛpə,ret *adj.*, *n.* 'sɛpərɪt〕*v.* 分離；隔開
　adj. 分離的 *n.* 抽印本；單行本（另外準備）《*se-* = apart》
separation³〔,sɛpə're∫ən〕*n.* 分離；分開

410　**part** = part（部分；分開）

> * 拉丁文 *pars*, *partem*（= *part* 部分），*partire*（= *part* 分開）。

part¹〔part〕*n.* 部分；要素 *v.* 分開；排出
partage〔par'taʒ〕*n.* 部分；分配；區分
parting〔'partɪŋ〕*n.* 別離；死去 *adj.* 離別的；臨別的
partake⁷〔pɚ'tek〕*v.* 分擔；分享；參與（抽取一部分→擔任一部分）

```
par(t) + take
  |        |
part  +  take
```

partial⁴〔'par∫əl〕*adj.* 一部分的；偏袒的
partiality⁷〔par'∫ælətɪ, ,par∫ɪ'ælətɪ〕*n.* 偏袒；偏見；偏愛
partible〔'partəbḷ〕*adj.* 可分的
participate³〔pɚ'tɪsə,pet〕*v.* 參與；分享（擔任一部分）《*cip* = take》

```
parti + cip + ate
  |      |      |
part  + take +  v.
```

participant⁵〔pɚ'tɪsəpənt〕*n.* 參與者；共享者 *adj.* 參與的；
　共享的

participation[4] 〔 par͵tɪsə'peʃən , pə- 〕 *n.* 參加；共享

participator 〔 par'tɪsə͵petə , pə- 〕 *n.* 分享者；參與者；參加者

participle[4] 〔'partəsəpḷ 〕 *n.* 分詞 (具有形容詞與動詞兩個性質的詞類)

particle[5] 〔'partɪkḷ 〕 *n.* 分子；(微) 粒子 (細微的部分)

《 *-cle* 表示小的名詞字尾》

```
parti +  cle
  |       |
part  +   n.
```

particular[2] 〔 pə'tɪkjələ , pə- , par- 〕 *adj.* 單獨的；獨有的；
特別的；講究的；詳細的

particularity[7] 〔 pə͵tɪkjə'lærətɪ , par- 〕 *n.* 特別；特質；講究；
詳細

particulate 〔 par'tɪkjəlet , -lɪt 〕 *adj.* 微粒狀的　　*n.* 微粒狀物質

```
parti +  cul  + ate
  |       |      |
part  + small + adj.
```

partisan 〔'partəzn 〕 *n.* 同黨者；游擊隊　　*adj.* 黨派的；游擊隊的
(偏向同一邊的人)

partition[7] 〔 par'tɪʃən , pə- 〕 *n.* 分割；分配　　*v.* 分割；分配
(分成幾個部分)

partitioner 〔 par'tɪʃənə 〕 *n.* 瓜分者；分割者

partner[2] 〔'partnə 〕 *n.* 分擔者；夥伴；共同協力者；舞伴

partnership[4] 〔'partnə͵ʃɪp 〕 *n.* 合夥；合作《 *-ship* 抽象名詞字尾》

apart[3] 〔 ə'part 〕 *adv.* 分開地；遠離地 (分離)《 *a-* = *ad-* = to》

apartment[2] 〔 ə'partmənt 〕 *n.* 公寓；房間；公寓式房屋

```
a +  part + ment
|     |      |
to + part +  n.
```

compart 〔 kəm'part 〕 *v.* 分隔 (分成幾個部分)《 *com-* = with》

compartment[7] 〔 kəm'partmənt 〕 *n.* 區劃；隔間

counterpart[6] 〔'kaʊntɚ,pɑrt 〕 *n.* 副本;相對的人或物;極相似的人或物《*counter-* = opposite (相對的)》

depart[4] 〔 dɪ'pɑrt 〕 *v.* 離開;出發;違反;放棄;死 (分開)
《*de-* = *dis-* = apart》

department[2] 〔 dɪ'pɑrtmənt 〕 *n.* 部門;部;院;系;科
(分開了的東西)

departure[4] 〔 dɪ'pɑrtʃɚ 〕 *n.* 離開;出發;違反;新行動或新方針的開始

```
de  +  part  +  ure
 |       |       |
apart + part +  n.
```

forepart 〔'for,pɑrt 〕 *n.* 前部;(時間的) 前段《*fore-* = before》

impart[7] 〔 ɪm'pɑrt 〕 *v.* 分給;傳授 (給予各部分)《*im-* = *in-* = in;on》

impartation 〔,ɪmpɑr'teʃən 〕 *n.* 分與;傳授

```
im  +  part  +  ation
 |       |       |
in  +  part  +   n.
```

impartial[7] 〔 ɪm'pɑrʃəl 〕 *adj.* 公平的;光明正大的 (不偏向某一部分)《*im-* = *in-* = not》

impartiality 〔,ɪmpɑr'ʃælətɪ 〕 *n.* 不偏不倚;光明正大

impartment 〔 ɪm'pɑrtmənt 〕 *n.* 分給;分給物;傳授;告知
(= *impartation*)

parcel[3] 〔'pɑrsl̩ 〕 *n.* 包裹   *v.* 分成數份;分配 (小的部分)
《 *-cel* 表示小的名詞字尾》

portion[3] 〔'porʃən , 'pɔr- 〕 *n.* 部分;一份   *v.* 分割;分配

apportion 〔 ə'porʃən , ə'pɔr- 〕 *v.* 分派;分配;分攤
(分成小部分)《*ap-* = *ad-* = to》

```
ap  +  port  +  ion
 |       |       |
to  +  part  +   v.
```

proportion[5] 〔 prə'porʃən , -'por- 〕 *n.* 比例；均衡；部分

　v. 使均衡；使相稱；均分《*pro-* = forward》

proportional 〔 prə'porʃən! , -'por- 〕 *adj.* 成比例的；比例的；

　相稱的

proportionate 〔 prə'porʃənɪt , -'por- 〕 *adj.* = proportional

disproportion[7] 〔 ˌdɪsprə'porʃən 〕 *n.* 不相稱；不均衡

　v. 使不均衡；使不相稱《*dis-* = not》

411　pass = pass（通過）

　　*　拉丁文 *passus*（ = *step* ; *pace*）；古法文 *passer*（ = *pass*）。

pass[1] 〔 pæs , pɑs 〕 *v.* 通過；經過；傳遞；使及格；度過

　n. 經過；及格；通行證；隘口；傳球

passage[3] 〔 'pæsɪdʒ 〕 *n.* 通道；走廊；經過；（文章或演講的）一段

```
pass  +  age
 |        |
pass  +   n.
```

passenger[2] 〔 'pæsn̩dʒɚ 〕 *n.* 乘客；旅客；不生產分子

passerby[7] 〔 'pæsɚ'baɪ , 'pɑs- 〕 *n.* 過路人；行人（從旁邊經過的人）

passover 〔 'pæsˌovɚ 〕 *n.* 踰越節獻祭之羊；耶穌基督；

　（P-）踰越節《*over* 越過》

　【解說】猶太人的節慶，大約在三月底、四月初的時候。

passport[3] 〔 'pæsˌport , -ˌport 〕 *n.* 護照；達成目的的手段

　（通過出入口的證明）《*port* = gate》

```
pass  +  port
 |        |
pass  +  gate
```

password[3] 〔 'pæsˌwɝd 〕 *n.* 密碼；口令

pastime[5] 〔 'pæsˌtaɪm , 'pɑs- 〕 *n.* 娛樂；消遣（消磨時間）

bypass[7]〔'baɪˌpæs〕*n.* 旁道；旁路　*v.* 設旁道；繞道；規避；
越級（報告等）（走旁邊的路）《*by* 旁邊》

compass[5]〔'kʌmpəs〕*n.* 範圍；繞道；指南針；(*pl.*) 圓規
v. 環行；包圍；瞭解（完全通過）《*com-* = thoroughly》

```
com    + pass
 |        |
thoroughly + pass
```

impasse[7]〔ɪm'pæs , 'ɪmpæs〕*n.* 僵局；死巷；死路（無法通過）
《*im-* = *in-* = not》

impassable〔ɪm'pæsəbḷ〕*adj.* 不能通行的

overpass[2]〔*v.* ˌovɚ'pæs , -'pɑs　*n.* 'ovɚˌpæs , -ˌpɑs〕*v.* 越過；
超越；違反　*n.* 天橋；陸橋（從上面經過）《*over-* = above》

repass〔ri'pæs , -'pɑs〕*v.* 再通過；再經過《*re-* = again》

surpass[6]〔sɚ'pæs , -'pɑs〕*v.* 超越；勝過；凌駕（超過）
《*sur-* = *super-* = over》

```
sur + pass
 |      |
over + pass
```

trespass[6]〔'trɛspəs〕*v.* 侵入；侵犯；觸犯　*n.* 侵入；侵犯
（擅自穿過）《*tres-* = *trans-* = across》

trespasser〔'trɛspəsɚ〕*n.* 侵害者；不法侵入者；侵佔他人土地者

underpass[4]〔'ʌndɚˌpæs , -ˌpɑs〕*n.* 地下之通路（尤指鐵、公路）；
地下道（從下面通過）《*under-* = under》

412　pat , pass = suffer（遭受）

> * 拉丁文 *pati*（= *suffer*；*endure*），過去分詞為 *passus*。

patient[2]〔'peʃənt〕*adj.* 忍耐的；容忍的　*n.* 患者；病人
（受到極深刻的痛苦）

patience[3]〔'peʃəns〕*n.* 忍耐；耐心

impatient[7] 〔 ɪm'peʃənt 〕 *adj.* 不耐煩的；不能忍受的（無法忍受的）

inpatient[7] 〔'ɪn,peʃənt 〕 *n.* 住院病人

outpatient[7] 〔'aʊt,peʃənt 〕 *n.* 門診病人

compatible[6] 〔 kəm'pætəbl 〕 *adj.* 能共處的；能相容的

（能一起容忍的）《*com-* = together》

```
com  +  pat  +  ible
 |        |       |
together + suffer + adj.
```

compatibility[7] 〔 kəm,pætə'bɪlətɪ 〕 *n.* 相容；和諧共處；適合

incompatible[7] 〔,ɪnkəm'pætəbl 〕 *adj.* 勢不兩立的；矛盾的

《*in-* = not》

passion[3] 〔'pæʃən 〕 *n.* 熱情；熱愛　　*v.* 表露感情（受到刺激而

悸動的心情）

passionate[5] 〔'pæʃənɪt 〕 *adj.* 熱烈的；熱情的

passive[4] 〔'pæsɪv 〕 *adj.* 消極的；被動的　　*n.* 被動語態（接受）

passivism 〔'pæsə,vɪzm̩ 〕 *n.* 被動主義；消極主義；消極抵抗

《 *-ism* 表示主義的名詞字尾》

compassion[5] 〔 kəm'pæʃən 〕 *n.* 同情；憐憫（生出同樣的心情）

《*com-* = together》

```
com  +  pass  +  ion
 |        |        |
together + suffer  +  n.
```

compassionate[5] 〔 *adj.* kəm'pæʃənɪt *v.* kəm'pæʃənet 〕 *adj.*

同情的；憐憫的　　*v.* 同情；憐憫

dispassion 〔 dɪs'pæʃən 〕 *n.* 冷淡；冷靜；公平；不動感情

（不帶感情）《*dis-* = not》

dispassionate 〔 dɪs'pæʃənɪt 〕 *adj.* 不動感情的；公平的；冷靜的

impassible 〔 ɪm'pæsəbl 〕 *adj.* 不覺得痛苦的；無知覺的；

無動於衷的 《*im-* = *in-* = not》

impassibility 〔,ɪmpæsə'bɪlətɪ , ɪm,pæs- 〕 *n.* 無知覺；無動於衷

impassion 〔 ɪmˈpæʃən 〕 *v.* 使感動；激起～的熱情（注入感情）
《 *im-* = *in-* = into》

impassionate 〔 ɪmˈpæʃənɪt 〕 *adj.* 充滿熱情的；激昂的；熱烈的
（ = *impassioned* ）

```
im  + passion + ate
 |       |       |
into + passion + adj.
```

impassioned 〔 ɪmˈpæʃənd 〕 *adj.* 充滿熱情的；慷慨激昂的
impassive 〔 ɪmˈpæsɪv 〕 *adj.* 毫無感情的；鎮靜的；麻木的；
靜止的《 *im-* = *in-* = not》

413   **path** = feeling ; suffering ; disease
（感覺；痛苦；疾病）

* 希臘文 ***pathos*** (= *suffering* ; *feeling* ; *emotion* ; *disease*) 。

pathos 〔ˈpeθɑs 〕 *n.* 哀愁；悲哀（心中深刻接受者）
pathetic[6] 〔 pəˈθɛtɪk 〕 *adj.* 哀憐的；悲慘的
pathogeny 〔 pəˈθɑdʒɪnɪ 〕 *n.* 病原（論）（產生痛苦）
pathology 〔 pəˈθɑlədʒɪ 〕 *n.* 病理學（病痛之學）
antipathy 〔 ænˈtɪpəθɪ 〕 *n.* 反感；嫌惡《 *anti-* = against》

```
anti  + path  + y
 |       |      |
against + feeling + n.
```

antipathetic 〔 ænˌtɪpəˈθɛtɪk , ˌæntɪpə- 〕 *adj.* 令人厭惡的；
天生嫌惡的
apathy[7] 〔ˈæpəθɪ 〕 *n.* 缺乏感情；冷淡；漠不關心（沒有感覺）
《 *a-* = without》
apathetic 〔 ˌæpəˈθɛtɪk 〕 *adj.* 冷淡的；無動於衷的；缺乏感情的
empathy[7] 〔ˈɛmpəθɪ 〕 *n.* （心理）感情移入；神入

```
em + path  + y
 |     |      |
in  + feeling + n.
```

字根 pact~radi

neuropathy〔nʊˈrɑpəθɪ, nju-〕*n.* 神經系疾病《*neuro* = nerve》

psychopathic〔ˌsaɪkəˈpæθɪk〕*adj.* 精神病的；精神錯亂的

psychopathy〔saɪˈkɑpəθɪ〕*n.* 精神病；精神變態

《*psycho*（mind）+ *pathy*（disease）》

```
psycho +  path  + y
   |        |      |
 mind   + disease + n.
```

sympathetic[4]〔ˌsɪmpəˈθɛtɪk〕*adj.* 同情的；同感的；和諧的

（有共同感覺的）《*sym-* = *syn-* = together》

sympathize[5]〔ˈsɪmpəˌθaɪz〕*v.* 同情；有同感；同意

sympathy[4]〔ˈsɪmpəθɪ〕*n.* 同感；同情

414　**patr** = father（父親）　* 拉丁文 *pater*（= *father*）。

paternal[7]〔pəˈtɝnḷ〕*adj.* 父親的；仁慈的

paternity〔pəˈtɝnətɪ〕*n.* 父系；父權

patriarch[7]〔ˈpetrɪˌɑrk〕*n.* 家長；族長（管理家族的父輩）

《*arch* = rule》

patrician〔pəˈtrɪʃən〕*n.* 貴族　*adj.* 貴族的；出身高貴的

patricide〔ˈpætrɪˌsaɪd, ˈpetrɪ-〕*n.* 弒父者；弒父罪（殺了父親）

《*cide* = cut》

patrilineal〔ˌpætrɪˈlɪnɪəl〕*adj.* 父系的

《*patri*（father）+ *line*（線；系）+ *-al*（形容詞字尾）》

```
patri + line + al
  |       |     |
father + line + adj.
```

patrimony〔ˈpætrəˌmonɪ〕*n.* 世襲財產（接續父親的人）

patriot[5]〔ˈpetrɪət〕*n.* 愛國者（愛祖先之國的人）

patriotic[6]〔ˌpetrɪˈɑtɪk〕*adj.* 愛國的；有愛國心的

patriotism〔ˈpetrɪətɪzəm〕*n.* 愛國心

patron[5] 〔'petrən〕 *n.* 保護者；資助人（立於如同父親地位者）

patronage[7] 〔'petrənɪdʒ〕 *n.* 保護；援助

patronize[7] 〔'petrən,aɪz〕 *v.* 照顧；光顧；資助；保護

compatriot 〔kəm'petrɪət〕 *n.* 同胞　*adj.* 同國的（同祖國的人）

　《*com-* = with》

expatriate 〔ɛks'petrɪ,et〕 *v.* 驅逐；放逐（被送出祖先的國家）

　《*ex-* = out》

```
ex  +  patri  +  ate
|         |        |
out  +  father  +  v.
```

repatriate 〔ri'petrɪ,et〕 *v.* 遣返（回到祖先的國家）

　《*re-* = back》

repatriation 〔,ripetrɪ'eʃən〕 *n.* 遣返

415　ped = child（小孩）　　* 希臘文 *pais* , *paid-*（= *child*）。

pedagogue 〔'pɛdə,gɑg , -,gɔg〕 *n.* 小學教師（常含蔑視之意）；
愛賣弄學問的人《*agogue* = leader》

pedagogic 〔,pɛdə'gɑdʒɪk , -'gɔdʒɪk〕 *adj.*（小學）教師的；
教學的；教學法的《*agog* = lead ; *-ic* 形容詞字尾》

```
ped  +  agog  +  ic
 |        |       |
child  +  lead  +  adj.
```

pedagogy 〔'pɛdə,godʒɪ , -,gɑdʒɪ〕 *n.* 教學；教學法《*-y* 名詞字尾》

pedant 〔'pɛdn̩t〕 *n.* 腐儒；愛賣弄學問的人

　《*-ant* 表示人的名詞字尾》

pedantic 〔pɪ'dæntɪk〕 *adj.* 好賣弄學問的；迂腐的

pedantry 〔'pɛdn̩trɪ〕 *n.* 賣弄學問；迂腐《*-ry* 名詞字尾》

pediatrician 〔,pidɪə'trɪʃən , ,pɛdɪ-〕 *n.* 小兒科醫生

　《*iatr* = healing ; *-ician* 表示人的名詞字尾》

pediatrics 〔ˌpidɪˈætrɪks , ˌpɛdɪ- 〕 *n.* 小兒科《 *-ics* = science》

```
ped  +  iatr  +  ics
 |        |       |
child + healing + science
```

pedophilia 〔ˌpidəˈfɪlɪə 〕 *n.* 戀童症（以兒童爲對象之色情狂）
《 *pedo* (child) + *phil* (love) + *-ia* (表示病名的字尾)》

416 **ped** = foot (腳)　　＊拉丁文 *pes* , *ped-* (= *foot*) 。

pedal[4] 〔ˈpɛdḷ 〕 *adj.* 腳的　*n.* 踏板　*v.* 踩踏板而行
pedate 〔ˈpɛdet 〕 *adj.* 有足的；足狀的《 *-ate* 形容詞字尾》
peddle[6] 〔ˈpɛdḷ 〕 *v.* 沿街叫賣
peddler[5] 〔ˈpɛdlɚ 〕 *n.* 小販
pedestal 〔ˈpɛdɪstḷ 〕 *n.* 台；座；基礎　*v.* 置於高臺上
　（成爲根部的地方）《 *stal* = stall (台)》
pedestrian[6] 〔 pəˈdɛstrɪən 〕 *adj.* 徒步的；散文體的；單調的
　n. 行人（走路去）
pedicab 〔ˈpɛdɪkæb 〕 *n.* 三輪車（用腳踩的計程車）《 *cab* = taxi》

```
pedi + cab
 |      |
foot + taxi
```

pedicure[7] 〔ˈpɛdɪkˌjʊr 〕 *n.* 腳病治療；腳病醫生；修腳指甲
pedigree[7] 〔ˈpɛdəˌgri 〕 *n.* 家譜；出身（族譜的樹狀圖呈鶴爪狀）
　《古法文 *pie de grue* = crane's foot》
pedometer 〔 pɪˈdɑmətɚ , pɛdˈɑmə- 〕 *n.* 計程器
　《 *meter* 計量器》
biped 〔ˈbaɪpɛd 〕 *n.* 二足動物　*adj.* 二足的《 *bi-* = two》
centipede[7] 〔ˈsɛntəˌpid 〕 *n.* 蜈蚣（一百隻腳）《 *centi* = hundred》
multiped 〔ˈmʌltəˌpɛd 〕 *adj.* 多足的　*n.* 多足動物（ = *multipede*）
　《 *multi-* = many》

quadruped〔'kwɑdrə,pɛd〕*n.* 四足獸　*adj.* 四足的
　《*quadru-* = four》

expedite[7]〔'ɛkspɪ,daɪt〕*v.* 使加速　*adj.* 無阻礙的
　（從束縛物中抽出腳）《*ex-* = out》

expedition[6]〔,ɛkspɪ'dɪʃən〕*n.* 遠征（隊）；探險（隊）（使足向外）

```
ex  +  pedi  +  tion
 |       |       |
out  +  foot  +  n.
```

expeditionary〔,ɛkspɪ'dɪʃən,ɛrɪ〕*adj.* 遠征的；探險的
　n. 遠征隊員；探險隊員

expeditious〔,ɛkspɪ'dɪʃəs〕*adj.* 迅速的；敏捷的

expedient[7]〔ɪk'spidɪənt〕*adj.* 便宜的；方便的　*n.* 手段；辦法
　（有助於行進的）

expedience；**-ency**〔ɪk'spidɪəns(ɪ)〕*n.* 便宜；方便

impede[7]〔ɪm'pid〕*v.* 妨礙；阻礙（纏住兩腳的）《*im-* = *in-* = in》

impediment〔ɪm'pɛdəmənt〕*n.* 障礙；語言障礙

417　ped = ground（土地；土壤）

　* 希臘文 *pedon*（= *ground*；*earth*）。

pedalfer〔pɪ'dælfɚ〕*n.* 淋餘土；鐵鋁土

```
ped   +    al    +  fer(r)
 |          |         |
ground + aluminum +  iron
```

pedocal〔'pɛdəkæl〕*n.* 鈣層土《*calcium* 鈣》

pedograph〔'pɛdə,græf〕*n.* 紙上（印下的）腳印

pedology〔pɪ'dɑlədʒɪ〕*n.* 土壤學《*logy* = study》

pedosphere〔'pɛdəs,fɪr〕*n.* （地球的）土壤圈《*sphere* 球體》

418 **pel , puls** = drive (驅動 ; 驅趕)

* 拉丁文 *pellere* (= *push* ; *drive*) ，過去分詞為 *pulsus*。

pulse[5] 〔 pʌls 〕 *n.* 脈搏 ; 律動   *v.* 搏動 ; 鼓動 (促使血液流通的振動)

pulsar 〔 'pʌlsɑr , -sɚ 〕 *n.* 【天文學】脈衝星

pulsate[7] 〔 'pʌlset 〕 *v.* 鼓動 ; 脈動

pulsatile 〔 'pʌlsətḷ , -tɪl 〕 *adj.* 脈動的 ; 悸動的 ; 打擊 (樂器等) 的
  n. 打擊樂器《 *-ile* 形容詞字尾》

pulsation 〔 pʌl'seʃən 〕 *n.* 鼓動 ; 脈動

```
puls  +  at(e)  +  ion
 |         |        |
drive  +   v.   +   n.
```

pulsometer 〔 pʌl'samətɚ 〕 *n.* 脈搏計

compel[5] 〔 kəm'pɛl 〕 *v.* 強迫 ; 迫使 (促使去做)《 *com-* = with》

compellable 〔 kəm'pɛləbḷ 〕 *adj.* 強迫的

compellent 〔 kəm'pɛlənt 〕 *adj.* 引人注目的

compeller 〔 kəm'pɛlɚ 〕 *n.* 強迫者 ; 強制者

compelling[7] 〔 kəm'pɛlɪŋ 〕 *adj.* 強烈的 ; 令人信服的

compulsion[7] 〔 kəm'pʌlʃən 〕 *n.* 強制

compulsive[7] 〔 kəm'pʌlsɪv 〕 *adj.* 強制的 ; 強迫的 ; 禁不住的

compulsory[7] 〔 kəm'pʌlsərɪ 〕 *adj.* 強制的

```
com  +  puls  +  ory
 |        |       |
with  +  drive  + adj.
```

dispel[7] 〔 dɪ'spɛl 〕 *v.* 卸除 ; 驅散 (趕走)(驅散)《 *dis-* = apart ; away》

dispellent 〔 dɪ'spɛlənt 〕 *adj.* 分散的

expel[6] 〔 ɪk'spɛl 〕 *v.* 驅逐 ; 逐出 (驅逐在外)《 *ex-* = out》

expellant ; -lent 〔 ɪk'spɛlənt , ɛk- 〕 *adj.* 有驅逐力的
  n. 驅除劑 ; 排毒劑

expellee 〔 ˌɛkspɛ'li 〕 *n.* 被逐出者 ; 被開除者

expeller 〔 ɛk'spɛlə 〕 *n.* 驅逐者；開除者

expulse 〔 ɪk'spʌls 〕 *v.* 驅逐

expulsion[7] 〔 ɪk'spʌlʃən 〕 *n.* 放逐；驅逐

expulsive 〔 ɪk'spʌlsɪv 〕 *adj.* 驅逐的；開除的

impel[7] 〔 ɪm'pɛl 〕 *v.* 推進（驅策往前方去）《*im-* = *in-* = on ; forward》

impellent 〔 ɪm'pɛlənt 〕 *adj.* 推進的　*n.* 推進力

impeller 〔 ɪm'pɛlə 〕 *n.* 推動者；（渦輪）葉片

impulse[5] 〔 'ɪmpʌls 〕 *n.* 推進；衝動；刺激

impulsion 〔 ɪm'pʌlʃən 〕 *n.* 推進；衝動；刺激

```
im  +  puls  +  ion
 |       |        |
on  +  drive  +   n.
```

impulsive[7] 〔 ɪm'pʌlsɪv 〕 *adj.* 衝動的；易衝動的

propel[6] 〔 prə'pɛl 〕 *v.* 推進；促進（驅策到前面去）《*pro-* = forward》

propellant；-lent 〔 prə'pɛlənt 〕 *adj.* 推進的　*n.* 推動者

propeller[6] 〔 prə'pɛlə 〕 *n.* 推動者；螺旋槳

```
pro   +  pell  +  er
 |         |        |
forward  + drive  + n.
```

propulsion 〔 prə'pʌlʃən 〕 *n.* 推進（力）；衝動

propulsive 〔 prə'pʌlsɪv 〕 *adj.* 推進的；有推動力的

propulsor 〔 prə'pʌlsə 〕 *n.* 推進物；推進燃料

repel[7] 〔 rɪ'pɛl 〕 *v.* 逐退；驅逐（驅逐返回）《*re-* = back》

repellence 〔 rɪ'pɛləns 〕 *n.* 抵抗性

repellent[7] 〔 rɪ'pɛlənt 〕 *adj.* 擊退的　*n.* 驅蟲劑

```
re   +  pell  +  ent
 |        |        |
back  + drive  +  adj.
```

repeller 〔 rɪ'pɛlə 〕 *n.* 擊退者；抵制者

repelling 〔 rɪ'pɛlɪŋ 〕 *adj.* 令人厭惡的

repulse〔rɪ'pʌls〕v. 擊退；拒絕　n. 擊退；拒絕

repulsion[7]〔rɪ'pʌlʃən〕n. 擊退；嫌惡；排斥作用

repulsive[7]〔rɪ'pʌlsɪv〕adj. 令人厭惡的；討厭的

peal〔pil〕v. 鳴響　n. 響聲（使其發出聲音）

appeal[3]〔ə'pil〕v. 懇求；訴諸　n. 吸引力（跑入～地方）
《 *ap-* = *ad-* = to 》

appealing[7]〔ə'pilɪŋ〕adj. 懇求的；令人心動的《 *-ing* 形容詞字尾》

appellant〔ə'pɛlənt〕adj. 上訴的　n. 上訴者

```
ap  +  pell  +  ant
 |      |       |
to  +  drive + adj., n.
```

appellate〔ə'pɛlɪt〕adj. 上訴的

appellation〔͵æpə'leʃən〕n. 名稱；稱呼

appellative〔ə'pɛlətɪv , -lɪtɪv〕adj. 名稱的；命名的
n. 名稱；通稱

appellee〔͵æpə'li〕n. 被上訴者

appellor〔ə'pɛlɔr , ͵æpə'lɔr〕n. 上訴者

repeal[7]〔rɪ'pil〕v. 撤銷；撤回　n. 撤銷；廢止（驅使回復）
《 *re-* = back 》

419 pen , pun = punish（處罰）

* 拉丁文 *poena*（ = *punishment* ）， *punire*（ = *punish* ）。

penal〔'pinl̩ , -nəl〕adj. 刑罰的；應受處罰的

penalize[7]〔'pinl̩͵aɪz , 'pɛnl̩-〕v. 宣告有罪；規定應罰

penalty[4]〔'pɛnl̩tɪ〕n. 刑罰；罰金

punish[2]〔'pʌnɪʃ〕v. 處罰；刑罰

punishment[2]〔'pʌnɪʃmənt〕n. 處罰；刑罰

punitive〔'pjunətɪv〕adj. 處罰的；刑罰的

impunity〔ɪm'pjunətɪ〕n. 不受懲罰；免受傷害《 *im-* = *in-* = not 》

【注意】以下的字字源不同，爲方便而歸於此處。

repent[7] 〔 rɪ'pɛnt 〕 v. 懊悔；悔悟（不斷地感到抱歉）

《*re-* (again) + *pent* (make sorry)》

repentance 〔 rɪ'pɛntəns 〕 n. 後悔；悔恨

repentant 〔 rɪ'pɛntənt 〕 adj. 後悔的；遺憾的

penance 〔'pɛnəns 〕 n. 後悔　v. 懲罰

penitence 〔'pɛnətəns 〕 n. 後悔；悔悟

penitent 〔'pɛnətənt 〕 adj. 後悔的《拉丁文 *paenitere* = repent》

《*penit* (repent) + *-ent* (形容詞字尾)》

penitentiary 〔,pɛnə'tɛnʃərɪ 〕 n. 感化院；監獄　adj. 後悔的；

應予懲罰的（使其反悔的地方）《*-ary* 表示場所的字尾》

420　pend , pens , pond
= hang；weigh；pay（懸掛；衡量；付錢）

> * 拉丁文 *pendere* (= *hang*；*weigh*；*pay*)，過去分詞爲 *pensus*；
> *pondus* (= *weight*)，*ponderare* (= *weigh*；*consider*)。

pend 〔 pɛnd 〕 v. 懸掛；使懸而未決

pendant；**-ent** 〔'pɛndənt 〕 n. 垂飾；耳環（垂下來的東西）

adj. 下垂的；懸垂的

pendency 〔'pɛndənsɪ 〕 n. 未決定

pendentive 〔 pɛn'dɛntɪv 〕 n.【建築】三角穹窿

pending[7] 〔'pɛndɪŋ 〕 adj. 未決定的；待解決的

pendular 〔'pɛndjələ 〕 adj. 鐘擺運動的；擺動的

pendulous 〔'pɛndʒələs 〕 adj. 下垂的；搖擺的；動盪不定的

```
pend + ulous
  |       |
hang +  adj.
```

pendulum 〔'pɛndʒələm 〕 n. 鐘擺（往下垂吊的東西）

append 〔 ə'pɛnd 〕 v. 附添；增加（懸掛上去）《*ap-* = *ad-* = to》

appendage[7] 〔 ə'pɛndɪdʒ 〕 *n.* 附屬物；下屬《 *-age* 名詞字尾》

```
ap  +  pend  +  age
 |      |       |
to  +  hang  +  n.
```

appendant 〔 ə'pɛndənt 〕 *adj.* 添加的；附屬的　*n.* 附屬物

appendicular 〔 ,æpən'dɪkjələ 〕 *adj.* 附屬物的；四肢的

appendix[7] 〔 ə'pɛndɪks 〕 *n.* 附錄；盲腸

appendicitis 〔 ə,pɛndə'saɪtɪs 〕 *n.* 盲腸炎；闌尾炎
　《 *-itis* = inflammation (發炎)》

compend 〔'kɑmpɛnd 〕 *n.* 概略（懸掛在一起）《 *com-* = together》

compendious 〔 kəm'pɛndɪəs 〕 *adj.* 簡潔的；摘要的

compendiously 〔 kəm'pɛndɪəslɪ 〕 *adv.* 簡潔地；摘要地

compendium 〔 kəm'pɛndɪəm 〕 *n.* 概略；手冊《 *-um* 名詞字尾》

```
com  +  pendi  +  um
 |        |       |
together + weighed + n.
```

depend[2] 〔 dɪ'pɛnd 〕 *v.* 依靠；依賴（垂掛於）《 *de-* = down》

dependable[4] 〔 dɪ'pɛndəbḷ 〕 *adj.* 可靠的

dependably 〔 dɪ'pɛndəblɪ 〕 *adv.* 可靠地

dependability 〔 dɪ,pɛndə'bɪlətɪ 〕 *n.* 可靠性；可信任

dependant；-ent[4] 〔 dɪ'pɛndənt 〕 *n.* 隨員；家眷　*adj.* 依賴的；
　從屬的（依賴者）

dependence[7] 〔 dɪ'pɛndəns 〕 *n.* 依靠；信任

dependency[7] 〔 dɪ'pɛndənsɪ 〕 *n.* 依賴；信任；附屬物；屬地

expend[7] 〔 ɪk'spɛnd 〕 *v.* 花費（計算出來）《 *ex-* = out》

expendable[7] 〔 ɪk'spɛndəbḷ 〕 *adj.* 可消耗的；可拋棄的

expending[7] 〔 ɪk'spɛndɪŋ 〕 *n.* 支出

expenditure[7] 〔 ɪk'spɛndɪtʃə 〕 *n.* 消費；經費

expense[3] 〔 ɪk'spɛns 〕 *n.* 費用；消費；～費

expensive[2] 〔 ɪk'spɛnsɪv 〕 *adj.* 昂貴的

expensively[7] 〔 ɪk'spɛnsɪvlɪ 〕 *adv.* 昂貴地

impend 〔 ɪm'pɛnd 〕 *v.* 逼近；迫近（懸在上面）《*im-* = *in-* = on》

impendence；-ency 〔 ɪm'pɛndəns(ɪ) 〕 *n.* 來臨

impending[7] 〔 ɪm'pɛndɪŋ 〕 *adj.* 可能發生的；即將舉行的

```
im  +  pend  +  ing
 |      |       |
on  +  hang  +  adj.
```

independence[2] 〔 ˌɪndɪ'pɛndəns 〕 *n.* 獨立；自主（不依賴）
　《*in-* = not》

independency 〔 ˌɪndɪ'pɛndənsɪ 〕 *n.* 獨立國；獨立

independent[2] 〔 ˌɪndɪ'pɛndənt 〕 *adj.* 獨立的；不依賴他人的；
　自主的

```
in  +  de   +  pend  +  ent
 |      |       |        |
not + down  +  hang  +  adj.
```

interdependence 〔 ˌɪntɚdɪ'pɛndəns 〕 *n.* 相互依賴（彼此依賴）
　《*inter-* = mutual》

interdependent 〔 ˌɪntɚdɪ'pɛndənt 〕 *adj.* 相互依賴的

perpend 〔 *v.* pɚ'pɛnd *n.* 'pɝpənd 〕 *v.* 仔細考慮；注意（徹底地
　衡量）　　*n.* 貫石（貫穿牆壁露出二端之石）《*per-* = thoroughly》

```
per      +  pend
 |           |
thoroughly + hang
```

perpendicular[7] 〔 ˌpɝpən'dɪkjələ 〕 *adj.* 垂直的；直立的
　n. 垂直線；垂直面；直立（直接懸垂而下）《*per-* = through》

perpendicularity 〔 ˌpɝpənˌdɪkjə'lærətɪ 〕 *n.* 垂直

perpendicularly 〔 ˌpɝpən'dɪkjələlɪ 〕 *adv.* 垂直地

spend[1] 〔 spɛnd 〕 *v.* 花費；耗用（計量分開）《*s-* = *dis-* = apart》

spendable 〔 'spɛndəbl̩ 〕 *adj.* 可花費的

spender 〔 'spɛndɚ 〕 *n.* 揮霍者

spending[7] 〔 'spɛndɪŋ 〕 *n.* 開銷；花費

stipend 〔 'staɪpɛnd 〕 *n.* 薪水；津貼；退休金

　《拉丁文 *stips* = small payment》

stipendiary 〔 staɪ'pɛndɪˌɛrɪ 〕 *adj.* 有薪水的　*n.* 支領薪水的人

suspend[5] 〔 sə'spɛnd 〕 *v.* 懸掛；暫停營業 (垂吊而下)

　《*sus-* = *sub-* = under》

suspenders 〔 sə'spɛndəz 〕 *n.pl.* 背帶；吊帶

suspense[6] 〔 sə'spɛns 〕 *n.* 未定 (狀態)；懸念；擔心；懸疑

suspensible 〔 sə'spɛnsəbl̩ 〕 *adj.* 可懸掛的；可懸浮的

suspension[6] 〔 sə'spɛnʃən 〕 *n.* 懸吊；中止；停職；休學

suspensive 〔 sə'spɛnsɪv 〕 *adj.* 未決定的；懸念的

```
sus   + pens + ive
 |        |      |
under + hang + adj.
```

suspensively 〔 sə'spɛnsɪvlɪ 〕 *adv.* 未決定地；暫停地

suspensor 〔 sə'spɛnsə 〕 *n.* 懸吊繃帶

suspensory 〔 sə'spɛnsərɪ 〕 *adj.* 懸吊的；中止的　*n.* 懸垂肌

pensile 〔 'pɛnsl̩ 〕 *adj.* 懸垂的

pension[6] 〔 'pɛnʃən 〕 *n.* 年金；退休金　*v.* 給予養老金 (計算給予金錢)

pensioner 〔 'pɛnʃənə 〕 *n.* 領養老金的人

pensive[7] 〔 'pɛnsɪv 〕 *adj.* 思考的；憂鬱的　*cf.* **pensee** (〔 pɑ'se 〕 冥想錄)

compensate[6] 〔 'kɑmpənˌset 〕 *v.* 償還；補償

　(把兩個東西放在一起比較 → 然後彌補不足的)　《*com-* = together》

```
com   + pens + ate
 |        |      |
together + weigh + v.
```

compensation[6] 〔 ˌkɑmpən'seʃən 〕 *n.* 補償；賠償

dispense[5] 〔 dɪ'spɛns 〕 *v.* 分配；實施；免除；配 (藥)

　(分稱於秤的兩端)　《*dis-* = apart》

dispensable[6] 〔 dɪˈspɛnsəbḷ 〕 *adj.* 能分配的；可有可無的

```
dis  +  pens  +  able
 |        |       |
apart  +  weigh  +  adj.
```

indispensable[5] 〔 ˌɪndɪsˈpɛnsəbḷ 〕 *adj.* 不可或缺的；不可避免的

　《*in-* = not》

dispensary 〔 dɪˈspɛnsərɪ 〕 *n.* 藥局；藥房（將藥分配於秤兩端的地方）

　《 *-ary* 表示場所的名詞字尾》

dispenser[7] 〔 dɪsˈpɛnsɚ 〕 *n.* 藥劑師

dispensation 〔 ˌdɪspənˈseʃən 〕 *n.* 分配；處方；天道

prepense 〔 prɪˈpɛns 〕 *adj.* 預謀的；蓄意的（事先把秤懸起來）

　《*pre-* = before》

propensity[7] 〔 prəˈpɛnsətɪ 〕 *n.* 傾向；癖好（向前方垂下 → 傾向）

　《*pro-* = forward》

recompense 〔ˈrɛkəmˌpɛns 〕 *v.* 報酬；賠償　　*n.* 報酬；賠償

　（償還回來）《*re-* = back》

poise[7] 〔 pɔɪz 〕 *n.* 均衡；鎮定　　*v.* 使均衡（平均重量）

　《古法文 *pois* = weight ; balance》

counterpoise 〔ˈkaʊntɚˌpɔɪz 〕 *n.* 平均；均衡　　*v.* 使平衡；使均衡

　（秤另一端的重量）《*counter-* = against》

```
counter  +  poise
  |           |
against  +  weight
```

ponder[6] 〔ˈpɑndɚ 〕 *v.* 熟慮；深思（在心裡衡量）

ponderable 〔ˈpɑndərəbḷ 〕 *adj.* 可估計的；可深慮的

　n. 可考慮的事物

ponderous 〔ˈpɑndərəs 〕 *adj.* 沈重的；沈悶的

preponderate 〔 prɪˈpɑndəˌret 〕 *v.* 數目超過；重量勝過

　（超出重量）《*pre-* = before ; in excess》

preponderant 〔 prɪˈpɑndərənt , -drən- 〕 *adj.* 佔優勢的；主要的

421 **pept** , **peps** = digest (消化)

> * 希臘文 ***peptein*** (= *digest*) ，***pepsis*** (= *digestion*) 。

pepsin 〔 'pɛpsɪn 〕 *n.* 胃液素
peptic 〔 'pɛptɪk 〕 *adj.* 消化性的；促進消化的；胃液素的
　n. 消化性物質；促進消化物質
dyspepsia 〔 dɪ'spɛpʃə 〕 *n.* 消化不良《*dys-* = bad》
eupepsia 〔 ju'pɛpʃə 〕 *n.* 消化良好《*eu-* = well》
eupeptic 〔 ju'pɛptɪk 〕 *adj.* 消化良好的

422 **per** = try (試驗)

> * 拉丁文 ***periri*** (= *go through* 通過 ; *try* 試驗 ; *experience* 經歷) ;
> 希臘文 ***peira*** (= *trial* ; *experiment*) 。

peril[5] 〔 'pɛrəl 〕 *n.* 危險；冒險　*v.* 處於險境 (似乎可以通過的試煉)
perilous 〔 'pɛrələs 〕 *adj.* 危險的；冒險的
empirical 〔 ɛm'pɪrɪkl̩ 〕 *adj.* 憑經驗的；經驗主義的；依據實驗或
　觀察的 (在試驗中)《*em-* = *en-* = in》
empiricism 〔 ɛm'pɪrə,sɪzəm 〕 *n.* 經驗主義；經驗論
　《*-ism* = 主義；理論》

em +	pir	+ ic +	ism
in +	*experiment* +	*adj.* +	*n.*

empiricist 〔 ɛm'pɪrəsɪst 〕 *n.* 經驗主義者；實證主義者
　《*-ist* 表示人的名詞字尾》
experience[2] 〔 ɪk'spɪrɪəns 〕 *v.* 經驗；經歷　*n.* 經驗；體驗
　(充分地去體驗)《*ex-* = fully》
experiment[3] 〔 ɪk'spɛrəmənt 〕 *n.* 實驗　*v.* 實驗 (充分地試過)
experimental[4] 〔 ɪk,spɛrə'mɛntl̩ 〕 *adj.* 實驗的；實驗用的
experimentation 〔 ɪk,spɛrəmɛn'teʃən 〕 *n.* 實驗；試驗

字根 pact~radi

expert[2]〔 *n.* ˈɛkspɝt *adj.* ɪkˈspɝt, ˈɛkspɝt 〕*n.* 專家 *adj.* 熟練的；老練的（累積豐富經驗的人）

expertise[6]〔ˌɛkspəˈtiz 〕*n.* 專門技術；專門知識；專家之見

imperil[7]〔 ɪmˈpɛrəl 〕*v.* 危及；使陷於危險（置於危險之中）
《*im-* = *in-* = into》

423　pet, petit = seek（尋求）

* 拉丁文 *petere*（= *seek*；*strive*），過去分詞是 *pettius*。
〔變化型〕*peat*。

petition[7]〔 pəˈtɪʃən 〕*n.* 請願；陳情　*v.* 請求；陳請（求取；祈願）

petitionary〔 pəˈtɪʃəˌnɛrɪ 〕*adj.* 請願的；請求的

petitioner〔 pəˈtɪʃənɚ 〕*n.* 請願者；訴願人；（離婚訴訟的）原告

```
petit + ion +   er
  |      |       |
seek +  n.  + person
```

appetite[2]〔ˈæpəˌtaɪt 〕*n.* 食慾；慾望（欲求的情緒）《*ap-* = *ad-* = to》

appetitive〔ˈæpəˌtaɪtɪv 〕*adj.* 增進食慾的；食慾上的

appetizer[7]〔ˈæpəˌtaɪzɚ 〕*n.* 開胃的食物

appetizing〔ˈæpəˌtaɪzɪŋ 〕*adj.* 開胃的；促進食慾的；引起慾望的
《*-ing* 形容詞字尾》

appetent〔ˈæpətənt 〕*adj.* 欲求的；渴望的

```
ap + pet + ent
 |    |     |
to + seek + adj.
```

compete[3]〔 kəmˈpit 〕*v.* 競爭（一起尋求一樣東西 → 爭奪）
《*com-* = together》

competition[4]〔ˌkɑmpəˈtɪʃən 〕*n.* 競爭

competitive[4]〔 kəmˈpɛtətɪv 〕*adj.* 競爭的；競爭激烈的；有競爭力的

competitor[4] 〔 kəm'pɛtətɚ 〕 *n.* 競爭者
competence[6] 〔'kɑmpətəns 〕 *n.* 資產；能力；資格（非常適於競爭）
competent[6] 〔'kɑmpətənt 〕 *adj.* 能幹的；勝任的
incompetent[7] 〔 ɪn'kɑmpətənt 〕 *adj.* 無能力的；不能勝任的
　　《*in-* = not》

```
in  +  com  +  pet  +  ent
 |       |      |      |
not + together + strive + adj.
```

impetus[7] 〔'ɪmpətəs 〕 *n.* 刺激；衝力（為爭取而激起的動力）
　　《*im-* = *in-* = on ; upon》
impetuous 〔 ɪm'pɛtʃʊəs 〕 *adj.* 猛烈的；衝動的
repeat[2] 〔 rɪ'pit 〕 *v.* 重複；跟著說　*n.* 重複；重播節目《*re-* = again》
repetition[4] 〔,rɛpɪ'tɪʃən 〕 *n.* 重複；模仿
centripetal 〔 sɛn'trɪpətḷ 〕 *adj.* 向心的；利用向心力的（求取中心）
　　《*centri* = center》　*cf.* **centrifugal**（離心的；離心力的）

424　petr = rock（岩石）　　*希臘文 petra（= rock）。

petrify[7] 〔'pɛtrə,faɪ 〕 *v.* 使石化；（因恐懼等而）嚇呆
（使變成石頭）《 *-ify* = make》
petrification 〔,pɛtrəfə'keʃən 〕 *n.* 石化；化石；嚇呆
（= *petrifaction* ）
petrochemistry 〔,pɛtro'kɛmɪstrɪ 〕 *n.* 石油化學；岩石化學
　　《*chemistry* 化學》
petrography 〔 pi'trɑgrəfɪ 〕 *n.* 岩石記載學；岩石分類
（記載岩石）《*graphy* = writing》
petroleum[6] 〔 pə'trolɪəm 〕 *n.* 石油《*petr*（stone）+ *oleum*（oil）》

```
petr  +  oleum
 |        |
stone  +  oil
```

petroliferous 〔,pɛtrə'lɪfərəs 〕 *adj.* 出產石油的
（生產石油）《*petrol*（oil）+ *-iferous*（bearing 生產）》

petrology 〔 pɪˈtrɑlədʒɪ 〕 *n.* 岩石學（研究岩石的學問）《*logy* = study》

petrologist 〔 pɪˈtrɑlədʒɪst 〕 *n.* 岩石學家

425 phag = eat (吃)   * 希臘文 *phagein* (= eat)。

anthropophagous 〔ˌænθrəˈpɑfəgəs 〕 *adj.* 食人肉的

《*anthropo* = man》

esophagus 〔 iˈsɑfəgəs 〕 *n.* 食道

eso	+	phag	+	us
carry	+	eat	+	n.

necrophagous 〔 nɛˈkrɑfəgəs 〕 *adj.* 食屍的；食腐肉的

《希臘文 *nekros* = dead body》

sarcophagous 〔 sɑrˈkɑfəgəs 〕 *n.* 石棺

【解說】 此字源自希臘文 *sarx*（flesh 肉）+ *phagein*（eat），早期的
石棺是由石灰石造成，石灰石被認爲能使屍體快速腐爛。

zoophagous 〔 zoˈɑfəgəs 〕 *adj.* 食動物的；食肉的《*zoo* = animal》

426 phan = appear；show (出現；顯現)

* 希臘文 *phainein* (= show)，*phainesthai* (= appear)。
〔變化型〕*phen* , *fan* , *phas*。

phantasm 〔ˈfæntæzəm 〕 *n.* 幻想；幽靈（浮在眼前的東西）

phantom[7] 〔ˈfæntəm 〕 *n.* 幻影；幽靈；虛無飄渺的事；有名無實
的人或物　*adj.* 虛幻的；若鬼的；虛無飄渺的；捉摸不定的

diaphanous 〔 daɪˈæfənəs 〕 *adj.* 透明的；半透明的；模糊不清的

（能看透的）《*dia-* = through》

dia	+	phan	+	ous
through	+	show	+	adj.

phenomenon[4] 〔 fə'namə,nan 〕 *n.* 現象；特殊的人；特殊事物
（顯現出來的東西）

phenomenal[7] 〔 fə'namən! 〕 *adj.* 現象的；非凡的

fantasy[4] 〔'fæntəsɪ , 'fæntəzɪ 〕 *n.* 幻想；白日夢；幻想曲

fantasia 〔 fæn'teʒɪə , -ʒə , -zɪə 〕 *n.* 幻想曲

fantastic[4]；**-tical** 〔 fæn'tæstɪk(!) 〕 *adj.* 空想的；怪誕的

fancy[3] 〔'fænsɪ 〕 = fantasy 的縮寫　*n.* 想像；喜歡
v. 空想；喜歡；想像　*adj.* 精緻的

fancied 〔'fænsɪd 〕 *adj.* 想像的；幻想的

fanciful[7] 〔'fænsɪfəl 〕 *adj.* 富於幻想的；異想天開的；奇異的；
想像的

phase[6] 〔 fez 〕 *n.* 方面；階段；時期　*v.* 使配合；分段實施
（眼睛所能看到的情況）

emphasize[3] 〔'ɛmfə,saɪz 〕 *v.* 強調（明白地表示）《*em-* = *en-* = in》

emphasis[4] 〔'ɛmfəsɪs 〕 *n.* 強調

emphatic[6] 〔 ɪm'fætɪk 〕 *adj.* 強調的；有力的

427　pharmac = drug（藥）

* 希臘文 *pharmakon*（= *drug*）。

pharmacy[6] 〔'farməsɪ 〕 *n.* 藥房；藥劑學

pharmacist[6] 〔'farməsɪst 〕 *n.* 藥劑師

pharmaceutical 〔,farmə'sutɪk! 〕 *adj.* 配藥的；製藥的；
藥（劑）師的；藥（物）的　*n.* 藥物

pharmacodynamic 〔,farməkodaɪ'næmɪk 〕 *adj.* 藥效的

pharmaco	+	dynam	+	ic
drug	+	power	+	adj.

pharmacology 〔,farmə'kalədʒɪ 〕 *n.* 藥理學；藥物學《*logy* = study》

pharmacop(o)eia 〔,farməkə'piə 〕 *n.* 處方書；藥典（調藥時需要
看的東西）《希臘文 *poiein* = make》

428 **pharyng** = throat（喉嚨；咽喉）

* 希臘文 *pharunx*（= *throat*）。

pharyngeal〔ˌfærɪnˈdʒiəl〕*adj.* 咽的

pharyngectomy〔ˌfærɪnˈdʒɛktəmɪ〕*n.* 咽頭切除術《*tom* = cut》

pharyngitis〔ˌfærɪnˈdʒaɪtɪs〕*n.* 咽炎《 *-itis* = inflammation（發炎）》

pharyngocele〔fəˈrɪŋgəsil〕*n.* 咽突出；咽囊腫
  《希臘文 *kele* = tumor（腫瘤）》

pharyngonasal〔fəˌrɪŋgoˈnezḷ〕*adj.* 咽鼻的《*nasal* 鼻子的》

pharynx〔ˈfærɪŋks〕*n.* 咽

429 **phe , phas** = speak（說）

* 希臘文 *phanai*（= *speak*），*phasis*（= *utterance*），
  pheme（= *speech*）。

aphasia〔əˈfeʒə〕*n.* 失語症；無語言能力《*a-* = without》

blaspheme〔blæsˈfim〕*v.* 褻瀆（神祇）；咒罵（說別人的壞話）
  《希臘文 *blapsis* = evil》

euphemism〔ˈjufəˌmɪzəm〕*n.* 婉言；委婉的說法
  （聽來舒服的說法）《*eu-* = well》

prophecy〔ˈprɑfəsɪ〕*n.* 預言；預言的事物（事先說出）
  《*pro-* = before》

prophesy[7]〔ˈprɑfəˌsaɪ〕*v.* 預言；（代神）發言

prophet[5]〔ˈprɑfɪt〕*n.* 預言者；預言家

430 **phil** = love（愛）   * 希臘文 *philein*（= *love*）。

philanthropy[7]〔fəˈlænθrəpɪ〕*n.* 慈善；善行；慈善事業
  《*anthrop* = man》

philanthropic〔ˌfɪlənˈθrɑpɪk〕*adj.* 慈善的；博愛的

philanthropist〔fə'lænθrəpɪst〕*n.* 慈善家；博愛主義者

```
phil + anthrop + ist
 |       |        |
love  + human  +  n.
```

philharmonic〔,fɪlə'manɪk , fɪlhar'm- 〕*adj.* 愛好音樂的
n. 愛樂協會《*phil* (love) + *harmon* (agreement) + *-ic* (形容詞字尾)》

philodendron〔,fɪlə'dɛndrən 〕*n.* 黃蘗

```
philo + dendr + on
 |       |      |
love  + tree  + n.
```

philosophy[4]〔fə'lɑsəfɪ 〕*n.* 哲學
《*philo* (love) + *soph* (wisdom) + *-y* (名詞字尾)》

bibliophile〔'bɪlɪə,faɪl , -fɪl 〕*n.* 珍愛書籍者；藏書家
《*biblio* (book) + *phile* (love)》

431　phobia = fear (恐懼)　* 希臘文 *phobos* (= *fear*)。

phobia[7]〔'fobɪə 〕*n.* 恐懼症

acrophobia〔,ækrə'fobɪə 〕*n.* 懼高症；高空恐懼症
《*acro* = high》

claustrophobia〔,klɔstrə'fobɪə 〕*n.* 幽閉恐懼症

```
claustro + phobia
   |         |
close    +  fear
```

hydrophobia〔,haɪdrə'fobɪə 〕*n.* 狂犬病；恐水症
《*hydro* = water》

photophobia〔,fotə'fobɪə 〕*n.* 畏光症《*photo* = light》

xenophobia〔,zɛnə'fobɪə 〕*n.* 仇視外國人；恐懼外國人
《*xeno* = foreign》

432   phon = sound（聲音）   * 希臘文 *phone*（= *sound*）。

phoneme（'fonim）*n.* 音素；音位

phonemics（fo'nimɪks）*n.* 音位學《*-ics* = science》

phonetic（fo'nɛtɪk , fə- ）*adj.* 語音的；語音學的；表示發音的

phonetician（,fonə'tɪʃən）*n.* 語音學家

phonetics（fo'nɛtɪks , fə- ）*n.* 語音學

phonic（'fɑnɪk , 'fonɪk）*adj.* 音的；語音的；發音上的

phonics（'fonɪks , 'fɑnɪks）*n.* 聲學；利用語音學的敎授法

phonogenic（,fonə'dʒɛnɪk）*adj.* 產生良好音響的（產生聲音）
  《*gen* = produce》

```
phono  +  gen   +  ic
  |         |        |
sound  +  produce + adj.
```

phonogram（'fonə,græm）*n.* （速記用的）表音符號；標音符號；
  形聲字《*gram* = write》

phonograph（'fonə,græf）*n.* 留聲機；唱機（記錄聲音的東西）
  《*graph* = write》

phonography（fo'nɑgrəfɪ）*n.* 表音速記法；表音拼字法
  （聲音的記錄）《*graphy* = writing》

```
phono  + graphy
  |        |
sound  + writing
```

phonology（fo'nɑlədʒɪ）*n.* 音韻學；語音學（指語音的歷史
  研究）《*logy* = study》

phonometer（fo'nɑmətɚ）*n.* 音波測定器《*meter* 計量器》

phonophile（'fonə,faɪl）*n.* 唱片愛好者；音響愛好者
  《*phile* = love》

phonovision（,fonə'vɪʒən）*n.* 電話電視；有線電視
  （= *phonevision*）

cacophony 〔kæ'kɑfənɪ, kə- 〕 *n.* 不調和的聲音；刺耳的聲音

《*caco-* = bad》　　*cf.* **euphony**（悅耳的聲音；諧音）

```
caco + phon + y
  |      |      |
 bad + sound + n.
```

cacophonous〔kæ'kɑfənəs, kə- 〕 *adj.* 不調和的；刺耳的

euphony〔'jufənɪ 〕 *n.* 諧音；悅耳之音

《*eu-* = well（和「u」的發音相同）》

euphonious〔ju'fonɪəs 〕 *adj.* 悅耳的；好聽的

```
eu  + phon + ious
 |      |      |
well + sound + adj.
```

gramophone〔'græmə,fon 〕 *n.*〔英〕留聲機

(=〔美〕*phonograph*)《*gram(o)* = write》

homophone〔'hɑmə,fon 〕 *n.* 同音異形異義字（聲音相同）

《*homo-* = same》

interphone〔'ɪntɚ,fon 〕 *n.* 內部電話；內線電話；對講機

(= *intercom*)（互通聲音）《*inter-* = mutual》

megaphone〔'mɛgə,fon 〕 *n.* 傳聲筒；擴音器（將聲音放大的東西）

《*mega-* = large》

microphone[3]〔'maɪkrə,fon 〕 *n.* 擴音器；麥克風

（把小的聲音變大的東西）《*micro-* = small》

saxophone[7]〔'sæksə,fon 〕 *n.* 薩克斯風（由比利時樂器研究者

Adolphe Sax 所發明，故以他的名字命名）

symphony[4]〔'sɪmfənɪ 〕 *n.* 交響樂；色彩的協調（一同響起）

《*sym-* = together》

telephone[2]〔'tɛlə,fon 〕 *n.* 電話　　*v.* 打電話《*tele-* = far off》

xylophone〔'zaɪlə,fon 〕 *n.* 木琴《*xylo* = wood》

```
xylo + phone
  |      |
wood + sound
```

433　**photo** = light（光）

* 希臘文 *phos* , *phot-*（ = *light* ）。

photochemistry〔ˌfotəˈkɛmɪstrɪ〕*n.* 光化學
《*chemistry* 化學》

photochromic〔ˌfotəˈkramɪk〕*adj.* 可逆光變色的
《*chrom* = color》

photocomposition〔ˌfotoˌkampəˈzɪʃən〕*n.* 照相打字排版
《*composition* 排字》

```
photo  +   com   + pos + ition
  |         |        |      |
light  + together + put  +  n.
```

photoconduction〔ˌfotokənˈdʌkʃən〕*n.* 光電導
《*conduction* 傳導》

photocopy[7]〔ˈfotəˌkapɪ〕*v.* , *n.* 影印（本）

photocopier〔ˌfotoˈkapɪɚ〕*n.* 影印機

photocurrent〔ˈfotoˌkʌrənt〕*n.* 光電流《*current* 電流》

photodetector〔ˈfotədɪˈtɛktɚ〕*n.* 光偵測器
《*detector* 偵測器》

photoelectric〔ˌfoto·ɪˈlɛktrɪk〕*adj.* 光電的；光電照相裝置的
《*electric* 電的》

photogenic[7]〔ˌfotəˈdʒɛnɪk〕*adj.* 發光性的；適合拍照的；
上鏡頭的（產生光的）《*gen* = produce》

```
photo  +  gen   + ic
  |        |       |
light  + produce + adj.
```

photograph[2]〔ˈfotəˌgræf〕*n.* 照片；相片　*v.* 照相；攝影；
呈現在照片上（利用光來記錄）《*graph* = write》

photographer[2]〔fəˈtagrəfɚ〕*n.* 照相師；攝影師

photography[4]〔fəˈtagrəfɪ〕*n.* 照相術；攝影術

photometer 〔 fo'tɑmətɚ 〕 *n.* 光度計;測光器《*meter* 計量器》

photophobia 〔 ,fotə'fobɪə 〕 *n.* 畏光;晝盲;懼光症(害怕光)
  《*phob* = fear》

```
photo + phob + ia
  |      |     |
light + fear + n.
```

photoprint 〔'fotə,prɪnt 〕 *n.* 照相印刷

photosensitive 〔 ,fotə'sɛnsətɪv 〕 *adj.* 感光性的(對光敏感)
  《*sensitive* 敏感的》

```
photo + sensit + ive
  |       |       |
light + feel  + adj.
```

photosynthesis 〔 ,fotə'sɪnθəsɪs 〕 *n.* 光合作用;光合成
  (利用光來合成)《*synthesis* 合成》

phototherapy 〔 ,fotə'θɛrəpɪ 〕 *n.* 光線療法(用光治療)
  《*therapy* 治療》

phototube 〔'fotə,tjub 〕 *n.* 光電管《*tube* 管》

telephoto 〔'tɛlə,foto 〕 *n.* 遠距攝影照片   *adj.* 用望遠鏡攝影的

```
tele + photo
  |      |
far  + light
```

phosphorus 〔'fɑsfərəs 〕 *n.* 磷(單質磷在空氣中會自燃而發光)
  《希臘文 *pherein* = carry》

434 phren = mind (心;精神)

  * 希臘文 *phren* (= *mind*) 。

phrenic 〔'frɛnɪk 〕 *adj.* 膈的;精神上的

phrenitis 〔 frɪ'naɪtɪs 〕 *n.* 膈炎;腦炎;精神錯亂
  《 *-itis* = inflammation (發炎)》

phrenology〔frɛ'nɑlədʒɪ〕*n.* 顱相學《*logy* = study》

schizophrenia〔͵skɪtsə'frinə, ͵skɪzə-〕*n.* 精神分裂症

```
schizo + phren + ia
  |        |     |
split  +  mind + n.
```

frantic[5]〔'fræntɪk〕*adj.* 發狂似的

frenetic〔frə'nɛtɪk〕*adj.* 發狂似的；狂熱的；精神錯亂的；
精神病的　*n.* 瘋子

435　**phyl** = race（種族）　　* 希臘文 *phulon*（= *race*）。

phylon〔'faɪlɑn〕*n.*（有血統關係的）種族

phylogeny〔faɪ'lɑdʒənɪ〕*n.* 種系發生；無形事物發展史
　　《*gen* = produce》

phylum〔'faɪləm〕*n.*（動物分類上的）門；語系

436　**phyll** = leaf（葉子）　　* 希臘文 *phullon*（= *leaf*）。

phyllode〔'fɪlod〕*n.* 葉狀柄《 *-ode* = like》

phylloid〔'fɪlɔɪd〕*adj.* 葉狀的《 *-oid* = like》

phyllome〔'fɪlom〕*n.* 葉狀器官；葉原體

phyllophagous〔fə'lɑfəgəs〕*adj.* 食葉的

```
phyllo + phag + ous
  |        |     |
leaf   +  eat  + adj.
```

phyllopod〔'fɪlə͵pɑd〕*adj.* 葉足亞綱甲殼動物的；有葉狀足的
　　n. 葉足亞綱甲殼動物《*pod* = foot》

字根 pact~radi

字根 pact~radi

437   physi = nature (自然)

* 希臘文 *phusis* (= *nature*)，*phusikos* (= *of nature*)。

physic 〔'fɪzɪk 〕 *n.* 藥劑 (尤指瀉藥)；醫術；醫學
　　v. 給…用藥；給…服瀉藥；治癒
physical[4] 〔'fɪzɪkl̩ 〕 *adj.* 物質的；物理學的；身體的
physician[4] 〔 fə'zɪʃən 〕 *n.* 內科醫師
physicist[4] 〔'fɪzəsɪst 〕 *n.* 物理學家
physiocracy 〔,fɪzɪ'akrəsɪ 〕 *n.* 重農主義；自然法則政治
　　《*cracy* = rule》
physiognomy 〔,fɪzɪ'agnəmɪ 〕 *n.* 面貌；觀相術；(事物的) 外貌

```
physio + gnom + y
  |        |     |
nature + know + n.
```

physiography 〔,fɪzɪ'agrəfɪ 〕 *n.* 自然地理學；地文學；地貌學
　　《*graphy* = writing》
physiology[7] 〔,fɪzɪ'alədʒɪ 〕 *n.* 生理學；生理機能 《*logy* = study》

438   phyt = plant (植物)　　* 希臘文 *phuton* (= *plant*)。

phytogenesis 〔,faɪto'dʒɛnəsɪs 〕 *n.* 植物發生；植物進化
　　《*genesis* 誕生》
phytography 〔 faɪ'tagrəfɪ 〕 *n.* 記述植物學；植物分類學
　　《*graphy* = writing》
phytology 〔 faɪ'talədʒɪ 〕 *n.* 植物學 《*logy* = study》
phytophagous 〔 faɪ'tafəgəs 〕 *adj.* 食植物的

```
phyto + phag + ous
  |       |     |
plant + eat  + adj.
```

phytotoxin 〔,faɪtə'taksɪn 〕 *n.* 植物毒素 《*toxin* 毒素》

439 **pict** = paint (繪畫)

＊拉丁文 pingere（＝paint），過去分詞為 pictus。〔變化型〕pig。

pictograph[7] （'pɪktə,græf , -,grɑf ）n. 象形文字（以圖形寫下的東西）

pictorial[7] （ pɪk'torɪəl , -'tɔr- ）adj. 圖畫的；用圖畫說明的

pictorialize[7] （ pɪk'torɪəl,aɪz ）v. 使圖畫化

picture[1] （'pɪktʃə ）n. 畫；照片；肖像　v. 畫；生動描述

```
    pict + ure
     |      |
   paint +  n.
```

picturesque[6] （,pɪktʃə'rɛsk ）adj. 如畫的；栩栩如生的

《 *-esque* = in the manner of（以～風格）》

depict[6] （ dɪ'pɪkt ）v. 描寫；敘述（詳細描述）《*de-* = down ; fully》

depiction[7] （ dɪ'pɪkʃən ）n. 描寫；敘述

pigment[7] （'pɪgmənt ）n. 顏料；色素

pigmental （ pɪg'mɛntl̩ ）adj. （有）顏料的；（有）色素的

440 **pil** = hair (毛髮)　＊拉丁文 *pilus*（＝hair）。

pilous （'paɪləs ）adj. 多軟毛的；由毛髮組成的；多髮狀的

pily （'paɪlɪ ）adj. （尤指某些狗的皮毛）有絨毛的；絨毛狀的

caterpillar[3] （'kætə,pɪlə , -tə- ）n. 毛蟲

《法國北部的古法文 *catepelose* = hairy cat》

depilate （'dɛpə,let ）v. 除毛；使脫毛

```
    de + pil + ate
     |     |    |
  away + hair + v.
```

depilatory （ dɪ'pɪlə,torɪ ）adj. 有脫毛效果的　n. 除毛劑

horripilation （ hɑ,rɪpə'leʃən ）n. （因受冷或驚恐等而引起的）

毛髮豎立；雞皮疙瘩《拉丁文 *horrere* = bristle（豎立）》

441 **plac** = please（取悅）

* 拉丁文 *placere*（= *please*）。〔變化型〕*pleas*。

placate[7]〔'pleket〕 *v.* 安慰；撫慰；安撫

placable〔'plekəbl̩〕 *adj.* 可安撫的；溫和的；寬容的

placability〔,plekə'bılətı〕 *n.* 易安撫；溫和；寬容

placatory〔'plekə,torı, -,tɔrı〕 *adj.* 撫慰的；懷柔的

placebo[7]〔plə'sibo〕 *n.* 安慰劑；（無害的）假藥

placid[7]〔'plæsıd〕 *adj.* 平穩的；安靜的；沈著的
《 *-id* 形容詞字尾》

placidity〔plæ'sıdətı〕 *n.* 平穩；安靜；沈著

```
plac  +  id  + ity
 |        |     |
please + adj. +  n.
```

complacent[7]〔kəm'plesn̩t〕 *adj.* 自滿的；得意的（完全被取悅）
《*com-* = thoroughly》

complacency[7]〔kəm'plesn̩sı〕 *n.* 自滿；得意

implacable〔ım'plekəbl̩, -'plæk-〕 *adj.* 難平息的；難和解的；
殘忍的；無情的（不能安撫的）《*im-* = *in-* = not》

```
im  +  plac  + able
 |      |       |
not + please + adj.
```

please[1]〔pliz〕 *v.* 取悅；使高興；喜歡；願意；請

pleased[7]〔plizd〕 *adj.* 高興的；滿意的；愉快的

pleasing[7]〔'plizıŋ〕 *adj.* 愉快的；令人喜歡的；可愛的

pleasant[2]〔'plɛzn̩t〕 *adj.* 愉快的；快活的；友善的

pleasantry〔'plɛzn̩trı〕 *n.* 詼諧；幽默；開玩笑
《 *-ry* 名詞字尾》

pleasure[2]〔'plɛʒɚ〕 *n.* 快樂；樂趣；享樂；願望；愛好

字根 pact~radi

complaisance〔 kəmˊplezn̩s 〕 *n.* 慇懃；彬彬有禮；親切（徹底地取悅）《*com-* (thoroughly) + *plais* (please) + *-ance* (名詞字尾)》

com	+	plais	+	ance
thoroughly	+	*please*	+	*n.*

complaisant〔 kəmˊpleznt 〕 *adj.* 慇懃的；彬彬有禮的；親切的
displease[6]〔 dɪsˊpliz 〕 *v.* 使不快；使厭煩；觸怒（使不高興）
　《*dis-* = not》
displeasing[7]〔 dɪsˊplizɪŋ 〕 *adj.* 不愉快的
displeasure[7]〔 dɪsˊplɛʒ⼂ 〕 *n.* 不愉快；不滿；生氣
unpleasant[7]〔 ʌnˊplɛznt 〕 *adj.* 令人不愉快的；討厭的《*un-* = not》

442 **plagi** = oblique（斜的）

> * 希臘文 *plagios* (= *oblique*)。

plagiocephalic〔 ˌpledʒɪəsəˊfælɪk 〕 *adj.* 斜頭（畸形）的
　《希臘文 *kephale* = head》
plagiocephalism〔 ˌpledʒɪəˊsɛfəlɪzm̩ 〕 *n.* 斜頭（畸形）
plagioclase〔 ˊpledʒɪəˌkles 〕 *n.* 斜長岩
plagiotropic〔 ˌpledʒɪəˊtrɑpɪk 〕 *n.*【植物】斜向（性）的

plagio	+	trop	+	ic
oblique	+	*turn*	+	*adj.*

plagiotropism〔 ˌpledʒɪˊɑtrəˌpɪzm̩ 〕 *n.*【植物】斜向性

443 **plain** = beat the breast（搥胸悲痛）

> * 拉丁文 *plangere* (= *beat one's breast*)，過去分詞為 *planctus*。
> 〔變化型〕*plaint*。

plaint〔 plent 〕 *n.* 抱怨；悲嘆；控訴

plaintiff[7]〔ˈplentɪf〕*n.* 原告　*cf.* **defendant**（被告）

plaintive[7]〔ˈplentɪv〕*adj.* 悲傷的；哀怨的；哭訴的

plaintiveness〔ˈplentɪvnɪs〕*n.* 悲傷；哀怨；哭訴

complain[2]〔kəmˈplen〕*v.* 抱怨；發牢騷；控訴（一起搥胸）

《*com-* = together》

complainant[7]〔kəmˈplenənt〕*n.* 控訴人；原告（= *plaintiff*）

《*-ant* 表示人的名詞字尾》

```
com    +    plain    + ant
 |           |          |
together + beat the breast +  n.
```

complaint[3]〔kəmˈplent〕*n.* 抱怨；牢騷；控訴；疾病

《*-t* 名詞字尾》

444　**plan** = flat（平的）　　* 拉丁文 *planus*（= *flat* ; *clear*）。

plain[2]〔plen〕*adj.* 明白的；簡單的；平凡的　*n.* 平原

plane[17]〔plen〕*n.* 平面；水平；飛機　*adj.* 平的；平坦的

plane[27]〔plen〕*n.* 刨刀　*v.* 刨平

planish〔ˈplænɪʃ〕*v.* 打平；壓平；輾平；磨光《*-ish* 動詞字尾》

explain[2]〔ɪkˈsplen〕*v.* 解釋；說明（把話攤開來說）

《*ex-* = out》

explanation[4]〔ˌɛkspləˈneʃən〕*n.* 解釋；說明

445　**plant** = plant（植物；種植）

* 拉丁文 *planta*（= *plant*）。

plant[1]〔plænt〕*n.* 植物；工廠；設備　*v.* 種植；設置；灌輸

plantation[5]〔plænˈteʃən〕*n.* 種植地；造林地；移民；殖民（地）

planter〔ˈplæntɚ〕*n.* 種植者；耕作者；農場主人；播種機

plantlet〔ˈplæntlɪt〕*n.* 小植物；樹苗《*-let* = small》

implant[7] 〔 ɪm'plænt 〕 *v.* 移植（器官等）；灌輸（思想等）；
種植；插入（種植進去）《*im- = in-* = into》

```
im + plant
 |     |
into + plant
```

implantation[7] 〔 ,ɪmplæn'teʃən 〕 *n.* 移植；灌輸；插入；種植
transplant[6] 〔 træns'plænt 〕 *v.* 移植；使移居；可移植
（由這裡移到那裡種植）《*trans-* = across》
transplantable 〔 træns'plæntəbḷ 〕 *adj.* 可移植的
transplantation 〔,trænsplæn'teʃən 〕 *n.* 移植；移植物；
移居；移民

446 **plas** = form（形成）

* 希臘文 *plassein*（ = *mold* ; *form* ），*plasma*（ = *something
molded* ）。

plasma[7] 〔'plæzmə 〕 *n.* 漿；血漿；原生質
plaster[7] 〔'plæstɚ 〕 *n.* 灰泥；熟石膏；膏藥　*v.* 塗灰泥於；掩飾；
塗膏藥於
plastic[3] 〔'plæstɪk 〕 *adj.* 塑膠的；整形的　*n.* 塑膠（製品）
autoplastic 〔,ɔtə'plæstɪk 〕 *adj.* 自體移植的

```
auto + plast + ic
  |      |      |
self  + form + adj.
```

ectoplasm 〔'ɛktə,plæzəm 〕 *n.* 外質（指細胞基質外部的膠化區）
《*ecto-* = outside》
metaplasm 〔'mɛtə,plæzəm 〕 *n.* 後成質；詞形變異
《*meta-* = after》
paraplasm 〔'pærə,plæzm̩ 〕 *n.* 副質《*para-* = beside》
protoplasm 〔'protə,plæzəm 〕 *n.* 原生質《*proto-* = first》

447 plaud = strike ; clap (打擊；拍手)

* 拉丁文 *plaudere* (= *strike* ; *clap*) 。〔變化型〕*plode*。

applaud[5] 〔 ə'plɔd 〕 *v.* 鼓掌；稱讚 (一起拍手)《*ap-* = *ad-* = to ; together》

applaudable 〔 ə'plɔdəbḷ 〕 *adj.* 值得稱讚的

applause[5] 〔 ə'plɔz 〕 *n.* 鼓掌；稱讚

applausive 〔 ə'plɔsɪv 〕 *adj.* 喝采的；讚揚的

```
ap   + plaus + ive
 |       |      |
together + clap + adj.
```

plaudit 〔'plɔdɪt 〕 *n.* (通常用 *pl.*) 鼓掌；嘉許

plausible[7] 〔'plɔzəbḷ 〕 *adj.* 似合理的；似真實的 (幾乎令人不禁鼓掌的)

plausibility 〔,plɔzə'bɪlətɪ 〕 *n.* 似合理；似真

explode[3] 〔 ɪk'splod 〕 *v.* 爆炸；發作 (拍著手把演員自舞台逐出)
《*ex-* = out》

explosion[4] 〔 ɪk'sploʒən 〕 *n.* 爆發；爆炸聲

```
ex + plos + ion
 |     |     |
out + clap + n.
```

explosive[4] 〔 ɪk'splosɪv 〕 *adj.* 易爆炸的   *n.* 爆炸物；爆發音

implode[7] 〔 ɪm'plod 〕 *v.* 在內部破裂；爆炸 (向內爆炸)
《*im-* = *in-* = into》

448 ple , plei = more (更多的)

* 希臘文 *pleon* , *pleion* (= *more*) 。

pleochroism 〔,plɪ'akroɪzəm 〕 *n.* (晶體等的) 多色性

```
pleo + chro  + ism
 |      |       |
many + color +  n.
```

pleonasm〔'pliə͵næzəm〕*n.* 冗言；贅語
pleonastic〔͵pliə'næstɪk〕*adj.* 冗言的；贅語的
pleionexia〔͵plaɪə'nɛksɪə〕*n.* 貪婪癖；貪氧性（血紅素與氧結合
過份牢固）

449　**plen，plet** = fill；full（使充滿；充滿的）

　　* 拉丁文 *plere*（= *fill*），*plenus*（= *full*）。
　　〔變化型〕*plet，ple，pli，ply*。

plenary〔'plinərɪ，'plɛnərɪ〕*adj.* 完全的；絕對的；全體出席的
（充滿了 → 沒有缺點的）
plenipotentiary〔͵plɛnəpə'tɛnʃərɪ，-ʃɪ͵ɛrɪ〕*adj.* 有全權的
　n. 全權大使（儲備所有的力量）《*potent* = powerful》

```
pleni +  potent  + iary
  |        |         |
full  + powerful +  adj.
```

plenitude[7]〔'plɛnə͵tjud，-͵tud〕*n.* 充足；豐饒《*-itude* 抽象名詞字尾》
plenty[3]〔'plɛntɪ〕*n.* 豐富；充分　*adj.* 豐富的　*adv.* 十分；充分
plenteous〔'plɛntɪəs〕*adj.*【詩】豐饒的；豐富的（= *plentiful*）

```
plent + eous
  |       |
fill  +  adj.
```

plentiful[4]〔'plɛntɪfəl〕*adj.* 豐富的；很多的；充分的
plenum〔'plinəm〕*n.* 充滿物質的空間；高壓狀態；充實；
　全體會議（完全充滿）《*-um* 抽象名詞字尾》
complete[2]〔kəm'plit〕*v.* 完成；使完成　*adj.* 完全的；完美的；
　絕對的（以~裝滿）《*com-* = together；with》

```
com + plete
 |      |
with +  fill
```

completeness 〔 kəm'plitnɪs 〕 n. 完全；完成

completion[7] 〔 kəm'pliʃən 〕 n. 完成；圓滿

complement[6] 〔 n. 'kampləmənt v. 'komplə,mɛnt 〕 n. 補語；
補充物 v. 補充；補足（補滿；填滿）

complementary[7] 〔,komplə'mɛntərɪ 〕 adj. 補充的；補足的；
互補的

comply[7] 〔 kəm'plaɪ 〕 v. 應允；同意（滿足對方的要求）

compliance[7] 〔 kəm'plaɪəns 〕 n. 應允；順從

compliant[7] 〔 kəm'plaɪənt 〕 adj. 應允的；順從的

compliment[5] 〔 n. 'kampləmənt v. 'komplə,mɛnt 〕 n. 恭維；
稱讚；(pl.) 問候；道賀 v. 稱讚；道賀（使對方滿足的東西）

complimentary[7] 〔,komplə'mɛntərɪ 〕 adj. 讚美的；恭維的

```
com + pli + ment + ary
 │     │      │      │
with + fill +  n.  + adj.
```

deplete[7] 〔 dɪ'plit 〕 v. 用盡；【醫】放血（使空虛）
《 de- = away 》

expletive[7] 〔 'ɛksplɪtɪv 〕 adj. 僅有文法功用而無實際意義的
n. 虛字；助詞；咒罵詞（充滿於外 → 附加的）《 ex- = out 》

implement[6] 〔 n. 'ɪmpləmənt v. 'ɪmplə,mɛnt 〕 n. 工具；
器具；手段 v. (以工具) 供給；實現（充滿於家中的東西）
《 im- = in- = in 》

impletion[7] 〔 ɪm'pliʃən 〕 n. 充滿；充實

```
im + plet + ion
 │    │      │
in + fill +  n.
```

replenish[7] 〔 rɪ'plɛnɪʃ 〕 v. (再) 裝滿；補充《 re- = again 》

replenishment 〔 rɪ'plɛnɪʃmənt 〕 n. 補充；補給；補給品

replete[7] 〔 rɪ'plit 〕 adj. 充滿的；飽足的

repletion 〔 rɪ'pliʃən 〕 n. 充滿；飽食

supply[2] 〔 sə'plaɪ 〕 v. 補充；供給 n. 補充；供給；(pl.) 生活必需品；國家之支出 (充塞其下) 《 *sup-* = *sub-* = under 》

```
sup  +  ply
 |       |
under +  fill
```

supple[7] 〔 'sʌpl̩ 〕 adj. 柔軟的；敏捷的；順從的；奉承的

supplement[6] 〔 n. 'sʌpləmənt v. 'sʌplə,mɛnt 〕 n. 補充物；補遺；附刊 v. 增補；補充

supplemental[7] 〔 ,sʌplə'mɛntl̩ 〕 adj. 補充的；補遺的；增補的

supplementary[7] 〔 ,sʌplə'mɛntərɪ 〕 adj. 補充的；補遺的；增補的

supplier[7] 〔 sə'plaɪɚ 〕 n. 供應者

accomplish[4] 〔 ə'kamplɪʃ 〕 v. 完成；達成 《 *ac-* = *ad-* = to 》

accomplishment[4] 〔 ə'kamplɪʃmənt 〕 n. 完成；成就；(pl.) 技藝；才能

450 plex , plic , ply = fold (摺疊)

* 拉丁文 *-plex* (= *-fold*) ，*plicare* (= *fold* ; *twist*)；古法文 *plier* (= *fold*) 。〔變化型〕*ple* , *pli* , *ploit* , *ploy* , *play* 。

ply[7] 〔 plaɪ 〕 n. 層；重；傾向 v. 經常從事於；忙於 (折返 → 反覆去做)

pliable[7] 〔 'plaɪəbl̩ 〕 adj. 易曲折的；柔軟的；順從的 (= *pliant* 〔 'plaɪənt 〕) (可曲折的)

pliers[7] 〔 'plaɪɚz 〕 n.pl. 鉗子 (使彎曲的工具)

apply[2] 〔 ə'plaɪ 〕 v. 應用；專心；申請；塗；敷 (重疊於其上) 《 *ad-* = to 》

appliance[4] 〔 ə'plaɪəns 〕 n. 工具；應用 (物)

```
ap  +  pli  +  ance
 |      |       |
to  +  fold  +  n.
```

applicable[6] 〔ˈæplɪkəbḷ〕*adj.* 適合的

applicability 〔͵æplɪkəˈbɪlətɪ〕*n.* 適合性

applicant[4] 〔ˈæpləkənt〕*n.* 申請者；求職者

application[4] 〔͵æpləˈkeʃən〕*n.* 應用；申請；塗敷物

applied[7] 〔əˈplaɪd〕*adj.* 應用的

imply[4] 〔ɪmˈplaɪ〕*v.* 暗指；意味（重疊其中）《*im-* = *in-* = in》

implicate[7] 〔ˈɪmplɪ͵ket〕*v.* 牽連；暗示

```
im + plic + ate
 |     |     |
in + fold +  v.
```

implication[6] 〔͵ɪmplɪˈkeʃən〕*n.* 暗示；牽連

implicit[6] 〔ɪmˈplɪsɪt〕*adj.* 含蓄的；暗含的

reply[2] 〔rɪˈplaɪ〕*v.* 答覆；反應　*n.* 答覆；回答（反覆）
　《*re-* = back》

replica[7] 〔ˈrɛplɪkə〕*n.* 複製；摹寫品

replicate[7] 〔ˈrɛplɪ͵ket〕*v.* 折疊；複製；臨摹

replication[7] 〔͵rɛpləˈkeʃən〕*n.* 折轉；複製品；回聲；答覆

complicate[4] 〔*v.* ˈkamplə͵ket *adj.* ˈkampləkɪt〕*v.* 使複雜
　adj. 組成的；複雜的（重疊在一塊）《*com-* = together》

```
com  + plic + ate
 |      |     |
together + fold +  v.
```

complicated[7] 〔ˈkamplə͵ketɪd〕*adj.* 複雜的；難以理解的

complication[6] 〔͵kampləˈkeʃən〕*n.* 複雜的狀態；紛擾

complicity[7] 〔kəmˈplɪsətɪ〕*n.* 共謀；共犯；串通

complex[3] 〔*adj.* kəmˈplɛks *n.* ˈkamplɛks〕*adj.* 複合的；錯綜的
　n. 複合物

complexion[6] 〔kəmˈplɛkʃən〕*n.* 膚色；外觀（複合的東西）

complexity[6] 〔kəmˈplɛksətɪ〕*n.* 錯綜；複雜

explicate[7] 〔ˈɛksplɪ͵ket〕*v.* 解說；說明（向外疊 → 開）《*ex-* = out》

explicable[7]〔'ɛksplɪkəbḷ〕*adj.* 可說明的；可解釋的

```
ex  +  plic  +  able
 |       |       |
out  +  fold  +  adj.
```

explication[7]〔,ɛksplɪ'keʃən〕*n.* 描述；說明

explicit[6]〔ɪk'splɪsɪt〕*adj.* 明白的；明確的

exploit[6]〔*n.* 'ɛksplɔɪt *v.* ɪk'splɔɪt〕*n.* 功績；偉業
　v. 開發；剝削；利用（公諸於衆人之前的行爲）

exploitation[7]〔,ɛksplɔɪ'teʃən〕*n.* 開發；剝削；利用

perplex[7]〔pɚ'plɛks〕*v.* 使困窘；使混亂（完全捲入）
　《*per-* = thoroughly》

perplexed[7]〔pɚ'plɛkst〕*adj.* 困惑的；混亂的

```
per      +  plex  +  ed
 |           |       |
thoroughly  +  twist  +  adj.
```

perplexity〔pɚ'plɛksətɪ〕*n.* 困惑；混亂；複雜

supplicate〔'sʌplɪ,ket〕*v.* 懇求；祈禱（把身體向下彎曲）
　《*sup-* = *sub-* = under》

supplication〔,sʌplɪ'keʃən〕*n.* 懇求

supplicant〔'sʌplɪkənt〕*n.* 懇求者

suppliance〔'sʌplɪəns〕*n.* 懇求

suppliant〔'sʌplɪənt〕*n.* 懇求者；請願者　*adj.* 懇求的；請願的

deploy[7]〔dɪ'plɔɪ〕*v.* 部署；展開（將重疊的東西分散）
　《*de-* = *dis-* = apart》

```
de     +  ploy
 |         |
apart  +  fold
```

deployer〔dɪ'plɔɪɚ〕*n.* 部署者；調度者

deployment[7]〔dɪ'plɔɪmənt〕*n.* 部署；展開

display[2]〔dɪ'sple〕*v.* 展示；陳列　*n.* 陳列；展覽《*dis-* = apart》

employ[3]〔ɪmˈplɔɪ〕*v.* 雇用；使用；使從事
　n. 雇用（捲入工作之中）《*em-* = *in-* = in》

employee[3]〔ɪmˈplɔɪ‧i , ˌɛmplɔɪˈi〕*n.* 受雇者；員工；職員
　《*-ee* 表示「被～的人」》

employer[3]〔ɪmˈplɔɪɚ〕*n.* 雇主；老板

employment[3]〔ɪmˈplɔɪmənt〕*n.* 雇用；職業；工作；使用

```
em  +  ploy  +  ment
 |       |        |
 in  +  fold  +   n.
```

simple[1]〔ˈsɪmpḷ〕*adj.* 簡單的；樸素的；單純的（只有一層的）
　《*sim-* = 拉丁文 *singuli* = one by one》

simpleton[7]〔ˈsɪmpḷtən〕*n.* 愚人；蠢貨

simplicity[6]〔sɪmˈplɪsətɪ〕*n.* 簡單；樸素；單純

simplify[6]〔ˈsɪmpləˌfaɪ〕*v.* 使簡單；使單純《*-fy* = make》

duple〔ˈdjupḷ〕*adj.* 加倍的；雙重的；二拍子的（重覆兩次）
　《*du-* = two》

duplex[7]〔ˈdjuplɛks , ˈdu-〕*adj.* 雙重的；二倍的

```
du  +  plex
 |      |
two  +  fold
```

duplicate[7]〔*v.* ˈdjupləˌket *adj.* , *n.* ˈdjupləkɪt〕*v.* 複製；加倍；重複
　adj. 副的；雙重的　*n.* 副本；複製物

duplication[7]〔ˌdjupləˈkeʃən〕*n.* 複製（品）

duplicator〔ˈdjupləˌketɚ〕*n.* 複寫器；複本製作人

duplicity[7]〔djuˈplɪsətɪ〕*n.* 口是心非；言行不一

diploma[4]〔dɪˈplomə〕*n.* 文憑；畢業證書　*v.* 給予學位證書
　（折成二層的紙）《*di-* = double》

diplomat[4]〔ˈdɪpləˌmæt〕*n.* 外交官

diplomate〔ˈdɪpləˌmet〕*n.* 專科醫生

diplomatic[6]〔ˌdɪpləˈmætɪk〕*adj.* 外交的；有外交手腕的

diplomacy[6]〔dɪˈploməsɪ〕*n.* 外交手腕；權謀

diplomatist〔dɪ'plomətɪst〕*n.* 外交家（= *diplomat*）

triple[5]〔'trɪpḷ〕*adj.* 三倍的；三重的　*v.* 使成三倍（重複三次的）
《*tri-* = three》

triplex〔'trɪplɛks，'traɪ-〕*adj.* 三倍的；三重的

triplicate〔*v.* 'trɪplə,ket *adj.*，*n.* 'trɪpləkɪt〕*v.* 使成三倍
adj. 三倍的；三重的　*n.* 完全相同的三物之一

```
tri  + plic + ate
 |      |      |
three + fold +  v.
```

triplication〔,trɪplə'keʃən〕*n.* 分成三份；三重

triplicity〔trɪ'plɪsətɪ〕*n.* 三倍；三重；三個一組

quadruple[7]〔'kwɑdrupḷ，kwɑd'rupḷ〕*v.* 使成四倍　*adj.* 四重的；
四倍的　*n.* 四倍；四重（重複四次的）《*quadru-* = four》

quadruplicate〔*v.* kwɑd'ruplɪ,ket *adj.*，*n.* kwɑd'ruplɪkɪt〕*v.*
使成四倍；四次反覆　*adj.* 四倍的；四重的　*n.* 相同四份文件之一

multiple[4]〔'mʌltəpḷ〕*adj.* 複合的；多重的　*n.* 倍數《*multi-* = many》

multiplex〔'mʌltə,plɛks〕*adj.* 多樣的；複合的

multiply[2]〔'mʌltə,plaɪ〕*v.* 增加；乘

```
multi + ply
  |      |
many  + fold
```

multiplicity〔,mʌltə'plɪsətɪ〕*n.* 多樣；重複

multiplicate〔'mʌltəplɪ,ket〕*adj.* 多重的

multiplication[7]〔,mʌltəplə'keʃən〕*n.* 增加；增殖；乘法

multiplicative〔'mʌltəplɪ,ketɪv〕*adj.* 有增殖力的；乘法的

plait〔plet，plæt〕*n.* 髮辮；褶　*v.* 編成辮；摺疊

pleach〔plitʃ〕*v.* 編結（樹枝等）

pleat〔plit〕*n.*（衣服上的）褶　*v.* 將～打褶

plight[6]〔plaɪt〕*n.* 情勢；困境（疊起來）；誓約；婚約
v. 宣誓；保證

451 plore = cry (流淚；大叫)

* 拉丁文 *plorare* (= *weep* ; *cry out*) 。

deplore 〔 dɪ'plor 〕 *v.* 悲痛；深感遺憾 (流許多眼淚)
《*de-* = fully》

deplorable[7] 〔 dɪ'plorəbḷ , -'plɔr- 〕 *adj.* 悲哀的；可嘆的

explore[4] 〔 ɪk'splor , -'splɔr 〕 *v.* 探險；探究 (看到所要尋找的
目標時會大叫)《*ex-* = out》

exploration[6] 〔,ɛksplə'reʃən 〕 *n.* 探險；探究

explorer[7] 〔 ɪk'splorɚ 〕 *n.* 探險者

implore[7] 〔 ɪm'plor , -'plɔr 〕 *v.* 懇求；哀求 (流著眼淚央求)
《*im-* = *in-* = into》

imploration 〔,ɪmplə'reʃən 〕 *n.* 哀求；懇求

452 plus , plur = more (更多的)

* 拉丁文 *plus* , *plur-* (= *more*) 。

plus[2] 〔 plʌs 〕 *prep.* 加上　 *adj.* 加的；正的　 *n.* 加號；正號

plural[4] 〔'plʊrəl 〕 *n.* , *adj.* 複數 (的)

plurality 〔 plʊ'rælətɪ 〕 *n.* 複數；多數；過半數

surplus[6] 〔's3plʌs 〕 *n.* , *adj.* 過剩 (的)；剩餘 (的)
《*sur-* = *super-* = over》

453 pneum , pneumon = breathe ; lung (呼吸；肺)

* 希臘文 *pnein* (= *blow* ; *breathe*) , *pneumon* (= *lung*) 。

pneuma 〔'njumə 〕 *n.* 元氣；精神；神靈；聖靈

pneumatic 〔 nju'mætɪk 〕 *adj.* 充氣的；空氣的；氣體的

pneumatology 〔ˌnjuməˈtalədʒɪ 〕 *n.* 氣體（治療）學；靈物學；聖靈論《*logy* = study》

pneumatometer 〔ˌnjuməˈtamətɚ 〕 *n.* 呼吸氣量測定器；肺活量計《*meter* 計量器》

pneumatophore 〔 njuˈmætəˌfor 〕 *n.*（植物）出水通氣根；（動物）氣包囊；浮囊

```
pneumato  +  phore
   |            |
 breath   +  carry
```

pneumonia[6] 〔 njuˈmonjə 〕 *n.* 肺炎
pneumothorax 〔ˌnjuməˈθɔræks 〕 *n.* 氣胸《*thorax* 胸腔》

454　**pod , pus** = foot (腳)

* 希臘文 *pous*（= *foot*），*-podos*（= *footed*）。

podiatry 〔 poˈdaɪətrɪ 〕 *n.* 足病學《希臘文 *iatreia* = healing》
podiatrist 〔 poˈdaɪətrɪst 〕 *n.* 〔美〕足病醫生
podium[7] 〔ˈpodɪəm 〕 *n.* 講台；樂隊指揮台
antipodal 〔 ænˈtɪpədl̩ 〕 *adj.* 對蹠的；在地球上的正反兩側的；正相反的《*anti-* = against》
arthropod 〔ˈarθrəˌpad 〕 *n. , adj.* 節肢動物（的）
　《希臘文 *arthron* = joint》
bipod 〔ˈbaɪˌpad 〕 *n.* 兩腳架《*bi-* = two》
decapod 〔ˈdɛkəˌpad 〕 *n.* 十腳類動物（如龍蝦等）《*deca-* = ten》
hexapod 〔ˈhɛksəˌpad 〕 *n.* 昆蟲；有六足的節肢動物
　adj. 具六足的；昆蟲的《*hexa-* = six》
octopus[5] 〔ˈaktəpəs 〕 *n.* 章魚《*octo-* = eight》
tripod[7] 〔ˈtraɪpad 〕 *n.* 三腳架；三腳凳；三腳桌《*tri-* = three》
unipod 〔ˈjunɪˌpad 〕 *n.* 獨腳架　*adj.* 獨腳的《*uni-* = one》

455 **pol** = axis (軸)

* 希臘文 *polos* (= *axis*) 。

pole[3] ﹝ pol ﹞ *n.* (南、北) 極
polar[5] ﹝ 'polə ﹞ *adj.* 極地的
polarity[7] ﹝ po'lærətɪ ﹞ *n.* (兩) 極性；極端
polarize ﹝ 'polə,raɪz ﹞ *v.* (使) 極化；(使) 兩極化
polarimeter ﹝ ,polə'rɪmətə ﹞ *n.* 偏振計《*meter* 計量器》
polariscope ﹝ po'lærə,skop ﹞ *n.* 偏光儀《*scope* = look》

456 **polis , polit**
= city ; government (城市 ; 政府)

* 希臘文 *polis* (= *city* ; *state*) ，*polites* (= *citizen*) ，
politeia (= *government*) 。

acropolis ﹝ ə'krɑpəlɪs ﹞ *n.* 衛城 (古希臘城市的衛城，通常建在
山丘上)《*acro* = high》
cosmopolis ﹝ kɑz'mɑpəlɪs ﹞ *n.* 國際都市 (具有世界重要性的都市)
《*cosmo* = world》
cosmopolitan[6] ﹝ ,kɑzmə'pɑlətn̩ ﹞ *adj.* 四海為家的；世界主義的；
世界性的　*n.* 四海為家的人；世界主義者

cosmo	+	polit	+	an
universe	+	city	+	adj., n.

megalopolis ﹝ ,mɛgə'lɑpəlɪs ﹞ *n.* 大都會區 (大都市)
《*megalo-* = great》
megalopolitan ﹝ ,mɛgəlo'pɑlətn̩ ﹞ *adj., n.* 大都會區的 (居民)
metropolis ﹝ mə'trɑplɪs ﹞ *n.* 首都；主要都市；中心都市
(母親都市)《*metro* = mother》
metropolitan[6] ﹝ ,mɛtrə'pɑlətn̩ ﹞ *adj., n.* 首都的 (人)；
大都市的 (人)

necropolis〔nɛ'krapəlɪs，nɪ-〕*n.* 大墓地（死者的都市）
　《*necro* = death》
polity〔'palətɪ〕*n.* 政治型態；政體；國家
politic〔'palə,tɪk〕*adj.* 明智的；有智慮的；策略性的；政治的
political[3]〔pə'lɪtɪk!〕*adj.* 政治的；政治上的
politician[3]〔,palə'tɪʃən〕*n.* 政治家；政客；從政者
politics[3]〔'palə,tɪks〕*n.* 政治；政治學；政見；政策《*-ics* = science》

```
polit    +    ics
  |            |
government + science
```

police[1]〔pə'lɪs〕*n.* 警察；警方；治安隊（維持國家治安的人）
policy[2]〔'paləsɪ〕*n.* 政策；方針；策略；明智
impolitic[7]〔ɪm'palə,tɪk〕*adj.* 不智的；失策的《*im-* = *in-* = not》

457　popul = people（民眾）

　* 拉丁文 *populus*（= *people*）。〔變化型〕*publ*。

populace[7]〔'papjəlɪs，-ləs〕*n.* 大眾；民眾
popular[2,3]〔'papjələ〕*adj.* 民眾的；受歡迎的
popularity[4]〔,papjə'lærətɪ〕*n.* 聲望；流行

```
popul + ar + ity
  |      |    |
people + adj. + n.
```

popularize[7]〔'papjələ,raɪz〕*v.* 使大眾化；使普及
populate[6]〔'papjə,let〕*v.* 居住於；殖民於
population[2]〔,papjə'leʃən〕*n.* 人口；人口數
populous[7]〔'papjələs〕*adj.* 人口稠密的

```
popul + ous
  |      |
people + adj.
```

public[1] 〔ˈpʌblɪk〕 *adj.* 公衆的；公共的　*n.* 大衆

publicity[4] 〔pʌbˈlɪsətɪ〕 *n.* 出風頭；公開；廣告

publicize[5] 〔ˈpʌblɪˌsaɪz〕 *v.* 發表；宣揚

publish[4] 〔ˈpʌblɪʃ〕 *v.* 公開；出版

publication[4] 〔ˌpʌblɪˈkeʃən〕 *n.* 發表；出版（物）

depopulate〔dɪˈpɑpjəˌlet〕 *v.* 使人口減少（人離去）《*de-* = away》

```
de  + popul + ate
 |      |      |
away + people +  v.
```

depopulation〔ˌdipɑpjəˈleʃən〕 *n.* 人口減少

overpopulated[7] 〔ˌovɚˈpɑpjəˌletɪd〕 *adj.* 人口過多的（人口太多）
　《*over-* = too much》

overpopulation[7] 〔ˈovɚˌpɑpjəˈleʃən〕 *n.* 人口過多

republic[3] 〔rɪˈpʌblɪk〕 *n.* 共和國（人民的東西）
　《*re* = 拉丁文 *res* = thing》

republican[5] 〔rɪˈpʌblɪkən〕 *adj.* 共和國的；共和政體的；
　（R-）共和黨的　*n.* 共和主義者；（R-）共和黨員

```
re  + publ  + ic  +  an
 |     |       |      |
thing + people + adj. + person
```

republish〔riˈpʌblɪʃ〕 *v.* 再頒佈；再版《*re-* = again》

republication〔ˌripʌblɪˈkeʃən〕 *n.* 再版；再發表

underpopulated〔ˌʌndɚˈpɑpjəˌletɪd〕 *adj.* 人口稀少的
　（人口不足）《*under-* = insufficient》

458　**port** = carry（運送）　　* 拉丁文 *portare*（= *carry*）。

port[2] 〔port, pɔrt〕 *n.* 舉止；態度；姿勢（表現在身體上的動作）

portable[4] 〔ˈportəbl̩, ˈpɔr-〕 *adj.* 可攜帶的　*n.* 可手提之物

portability〔ˌportəˈbɪlətɪ〕 *n.* 可攜帶性

portage〔ˈportɪdʒ , ˈpɔr- 〕*n.* 搬運；（兩水路間的）陸運

```
port ＋ age
 |      |
carry ＋ n.
```

portative〔ˈportətɪv 〕*adj.* 可攜帶的

portamento〔ˌportəˈmɛnto 〕*n.* 滑音

porter[4]〔ˈportɚ , ˈpɔr- 〕*n.* 腳夫；挑夫；侍者

portfolio[7]〔 portˈfolɪˌo 〕*n.* 紙夾；公事包（搬運紙的東西）
　　《*folio* 對摺紙；對開紙》

portly〔ˈportlɪ , ˈpɔrt- 〕*adj.* 肥胖的；莊嚴的（身體的搬運）

comport[7]〔 kəmˈport , -ˈpɔrt 〕*v.* 舉止；相稱（搬動身體）
　　《*com-* = with》

comportable〔 kəmˈpɔrtəbḷ 〕*adj.* 合適的

comportably〔 kəmˈpɔrtəblɪ 〕*adv.* 合適地

comportment〔 kəmˈportmənt , -ˈpɔrt- 〕*n.* 舉動；態度

```
com ＋ port ＋ ment
 |      |      |
with ＋ carry ＋ n.
```

deport[7]〔 dɪˈport , -ˈpɔrt 〕*v.* 舉止；放逐（搬走）
　　《*de-* = down ; away》

deportee〔ˌdiporˈti , -pɔr- 〕*n.* 被放逐者《 *-ee* 表示「被～的人」》

deportation[7]〔ˌdiporˈteʃən , -pɔr- 〕*n.* 充軍；放逐

deportment〔 dɪˈportmənt , -ˈpɔrt- 〕*n.* 風度；態度

disport〔 dɪˈsport , -ˈspɔrt 〕*v.* 嬉戲；展示　*n.* 娛樂；嬉戲
　　（將自己運離工作）《*dis-* = apart》

```
dis ＋ port
 |      |
apart ＋ carry
```

export[3]〔 *v.* ɪksˈport , ˈɛksport *n.* ˈɛksport 〕*v.* 輸出；外銷
　　n. 輸出品（搬出去）《*ex-* = out》

字根 pact~radi

exportable〔ɛks'portəbḷ〕*adj.* 可出口的

exportation〔͵ɛkspor'teʃən〕*n.* 出口

exporter〔ɪk'sportɚ〕*n.* 出口商；輸出業者

import[3]〔*v.* ɪm'port , -'port *n.* 'ɪmport , -port〕*v.* 輸入；意含
　n. 輸入品；涵義；重要性（搬進來）《*im-* = *in-* = in》

importable〔ɪm'portəbḷ〕*adj.* 可進口的

important[1]〔ɪm'portṇt〕*adj.* 重要的

```
im  +  port  + ant
 |      |      |
 in  + carry  + adj.
```
（古時候房子很小，「**重要的**」東西
才搬進來）

importantly[7]〔ɪm'portṇtlɪ〕*adv.* 重要地

importance[2]〔ɪm'portṇs〕*n.* 重要；重要性

importation〔͵ɪmpor'teʃən , -por-〕*n.* 輸入品；進口

importer〔ɪm'portɚ〕*n.* 進口商；輸入業者

purport[7]〔*n.* 'pɝport *v.* pɚ'port , 'pɝport〕*n.* 主旨；意義
　v. 意指；聲稱（搬到前方）《*pur-* = *pro-* = forward》

purported[7]〔pɚ'portɪd〕*adj.* 傳聞的

purportedly[7]〔pɚ'portɪdlɪ〕*adv.* 據說

report[1]〔rɪ'port〕*v.* 報告；報導；控告　*n.* 報告；傳聞
　《*re-* = back》

reportable〔rɪ'portəbḷ〕*adj.* 可報導的；值得報導的

reportage〔rɪ'portɪdʒ , -'por-〕*n.* 報導的文章；報告文學

```
re  +  port  + age
 |      |      |
back + carry  + n.
```

reportedly[7]〔rɪ'portɪdlɪ〕*adv.* 據說

reporting[7]〔rɪ'portɪŋ〕*n.* 新聞報導

reportorial〔͵rɛpɚ'torɪəl〕*adj.* 記者的；報告的

sport[1]〔sport , spɔrt〕= disport 的縮寫　*n.* 遊戲；玩笑；運動會
　adj. 運動的　*v.* 遊戲

sportful〔'sportfəl〕*adj.* 鬧著玩的

sporting[7]〔'sportɪŋ〕*adj.* 運動的

sportingly〔'sportɪŋlɪ〕*adv.* 在運動方面；有氣度地

sportive〔'sportɪv〕*adj.* 喜歡玩的；開玩笑的；愉快的

sportively〔'sportɪvlɪ〕*adv.* 開玩笑地；愉快地

sporty[7]〔'sportɪ, 'spor-〕*adj.* 像運動員的；華麗的；輕浮的

support[2]〔sə'port, -'pɔrt〕*v.* 支持；贍養　*n.* 支持；贍養

　（搬上去 → 拿上去）《*sup-* = *sub-* = up》

supportable[7]〔sə'portəbḷ, -'pɔrt-〕*adj.* 可支持的；可扶養的

```
sup  +  port  +  able
 |        |        |
 up  +  carry  +  adj.
```

supportably〔sə'portəblɪ〕*adv.* 可支持地；可忍受地

supportability〔sə,portə'bɪlətɪ〕*n.* 支持度；容忍度

supporter〔sə'portɚ, -'pɔr-〕*n.* 支持者；贊助者

supportive[7]〔sə'pɔrtɪv〕*adj.* 支持的

supportless〔sə'pɔrtlɪs〕*adj.* 無支持的

transport[3]〔*v.* træns'port, -'pɔrt　*n.* 'trænsport, -pɔrt〕

　v. 運送；放逐　*n.* 輸送（搬到對面）《*trans-* = across》

transportable〔træns'portəbḷ〕*adj.* 可運輸的

transportation[4]〔,trænspɚ'teʃən〕*n.* 運輸；運輸工具；放逐

transporter〔træns'portɚ〕*n.* 運輸者

459　**port** = gate；harbor（大門；港口）

　*＊拉丁文 **porta**（= gate），**portus**（= port；harbor）。*

port[2]〔port, pɔrt〕*n.*（城牆的）門；港口；砲門；城門

　（進入船內的門）

portal[7]〔'portḷ, 'pɔr-〕*n.* 正門；入口

portcullis 〔 port'kʌlɪs , pɔr- 〕 *n.* 古代城堡可升降的鐵閘門

porter[4] 〔'pɔrtɚ , 'pɔr- 〕 *n.* 門房；看門人

portico 〔'pɔrtɪ͵ko , 'pɔr- 〕 *n.* 門廊；柱廊

porch[5] 〔 portʃ , pɔrtʃ 〕 *n.* 門廊；走廊

importune 〔͵ɪmpɚ'tjun , -'tun , ɪm'pɔrtʃən 〕 *v.* 一再地要求；
不斷地請求（不能進港 → 強要進港）《*im-* = *in-* = not》

importunate 〔 ɪm'pɔrtʃənɪt 〕 *adj.* 煩人的；糾纏不休的
《*-ate* 形容詞字尾》

```
im + portun + ate
 |      |       |
not +  port  + adj.
```

importunity 〔͵ɪmpɚ'tjunətɪ 〕 *n.* 糾纏不休；強求

opportune[7] 〔͵ɑpɚ'tjun 〕 *adj.* 合宜的；及時的（靠近港口的）
《*op-* = *ob-* = near》

opportunism[7] 〔͵ɑpɚ'tjunɪzəm 〕 *n.* 機會主義

opportunist[7] 〔͵ɑpɚ'tjunɪst 〕 *n.* 機會主義者；投機者

opportunity[3] 〔͵ɑpɚ'tjunətɪ 〕 *n.* 機會；時機

passport[3] 〔'pæs͵port , -͵pɔrt 〕 *n.* 護照；手段（通過港口時
必要的東西）

460   **pos** , **pon** = place；put（放）

* 古法文 *poser*（= *place*；*set*；*put*）；拉丁文 *ponere*（= *place*；
put），過去分詞為 *positus*。*pausare*（= *pause*），由「停止」
演變成「使休息」。〔變化型〕*pound*。

pose[2] 〔 poz 〕 *n.* 姿勢；態度　*v.* 作姿態；假裝（放置的狀態）

posit[7] 〔'pɑzɪt 〕 *v.* 放置；假定

position[1] 〔 pə'zɪʃən 〕 *n.* 位置；姿勢；職位　*v.* 安放；放置

positive[2] 〔'pɑzətɪv 〕 *adj.* 確實的；積極的；陽性的
n. 實在；正數；陽極（訂下的位置）

post[12] 〔 post 〕 *n.* 職位；崗位 *v.* 安置；駐紮（被訂下的位置）

post[22] 〔 post 〕 *n.* 郵政；郵件 *v.* 郵寄

postage[3] 〔'postɪdʒ 〕 *n.* 郵費；郵資《 *-age* 抽象名詞字尾》

postal[7] 〔'postḷ 〕 *adj.* 郵政的；郵局的

posture[6] 〔'pastʃծ 〕 *n.* 姿勢；心境 *v.* 擺～姿勢；裝作～的樣子
（放置身體的方法）

```
post + ure
 |     |
put  +  n.
```

apposite 〔'æpəzɪt 〕 *adj.* 適當的；適切的（正適合放置的）
《 *ap-* = *ad-* = to》

apposition 〔͵æpə'zɪʃən 〕 *n.* 並置；同位格

```
ap + posit + ion
 |     |      |
to  + put  +  n.
```

component[6] 〔 kəm'ponənt 〕 *adj.* 組成的 *n.* 成分
（被放置在一起）《 *com-* = together》

compose[4] 〔 kəm'poz 〕 *v.* 組成；構成；作曲；寫作；排（字）；
使平靜；使鎮靜（放在一起）《 *com-* = together》

composedly 〔 kəm'pozɪdlɪ 〕 *adv.* 鎮靜地；泰然自若地

composer[4] 〔 kəm'pozծ 〕 *n.* 作曲家；作曲者

composite[7] 〔 kəm'pazɪt 〕 *adj.* 混合成的 *n.* 合成物

compositor 〔 kəm'pazɪtծ 〕 *n.* 排字工人

composition[4] 〔͵kampə'zɪʃən 〕 *n.* 組成；作文；作曲；
混合物；布局

compost[7] 〔'kampost 〕 *n.* 混合肥料；混合物

composure[7] 〔 kəm'poʒծ 〕 *n.* 冷靜；沈著；鎮定

```
com  + pos + ure
 |      |     |
together + put +  n.
```

compound[5] 〔 *n.*, *adj.* ˈkɑmpaʊnd *v.* kəmˈpaʊnd 〕*v.* 調和；調解；
妥協　*adj.* 合成的；複合的　*n.* 複合字；混合物；化合物
（放在一起）

decompose[7] 〔 ˌdikəmˈpoz 〕*v.* （使）分解；（使）腐敗
（使組成好的分開）《*de-* = *dis-* = apart》

depose[7] 〔 dɪˈpoz 〕*v.* 免職；【法律】作證（從位置上離去）
《*de-* = *dis-* = from；away》

deposit[3] 〔 dɪˈpɑzɪt 〕*n.* 沈澱物；存款；押金　*v.* 放下；沈澱；
存（錢）（被置於下方的東西）《*de-* = down》

deposition[7] 〔 ˌdɛpəˈzɪʃən 〕*n.* 免職；【法律】宣誓證言；沈澱（物）

depositor 〔 dɪˈpɑzɪtɚ 〕*n.* 存款者；沈澱器

depository 〔 dɪˈpɑzəˌtorɪ, -ˌtɔrɪ 〕*n.* 倉庫；受託者
《 *-ory* 表示場所的名詞字尾》

discompose 〔 ˌdɪskəmˈpoz 〕*v.* 使不安；使慌亂《*dis-* = apart》

discomposure 〔 ˌdɪskəmˈpoʒɚ 〕*n.* 不安；慌亂

dispose[5] 〔 dɪˈspoz 〕*v.* 陳列；佈置（個別分開放置）《*dis-* = apart》

```
dis  +  pose
 |        |
apart  +  put
```

disposable[6] 〔 dɪˈspozəbḷ 〕*adj.* 用完即丟的；可任意處置的

disposal[6] 〔 dɪˈspozḷ 〕*n.* 處置；支配使用；廚餘處理機

【解說】 **Disposal** 是美國廚房很普通的小家電，安裝在廚房的「水槽」
（sink）裡，只要一按開關，內部的刀片便會高速旋轉，將菜
梗、小骨頭全部絞碎，然後排入下水道。

disposition[7] 〔 ˌdɪspəˈzɪʃən 〕*n.* 佈置；排列；配置；意向；性情

exponent[7] 〔 ɪkˈsponənt 〕*adj.* 說明的　*n.* 解說者；代表物
（置於其外 → 顯示）《*ex-* = out》

```
ex  +  pon  +  ent
 |       |      |
out  +  put  +  adj., n.
```

expose[4] 〔 ɪk'spoz 〕 v. 暴露；展覽；遺棄（置於外部）《*ex-* = out》

exposure[4] 〔 ɪk'spoʒɚ 〕 n. 暴露；揭露；遺棄

```
ex + pos + ure
 |     |     |
out + put +  n.
```

exposition[7] 〔ˌɛkspə'zɪʃən 〕 n. 博覽會；說明（安置於外以明白表示）

expositor 〔 ɪk'spɑzɪtɚ 〕 n. 解釋者；註解者

expound[7] 〔 ɪk'spaʊnd 〕 v. 解釋；詳細說明

impose[5] 〔 ɪm'poz 〕 v. 課稅；強使；加（負擔、懲罰）於

（置於～之上）《*im-* = *in-* = on》

imposer 〔 ɪm'pozɚ 〕 n. 徵收者；課徵者；強制實行者

imposing[6] 〔 ɪm'pozɪŋ 〕 adj. 堂皇的；威風的；宏偉的

```
im + pos + ing
 |    |     |
on + put + adj.
```

imposition[7] 〔ˌɪmpə'zɪʃən 〕 n. 徵稅；負擔；欺騙

impostor[7] 〔 ɪm'pɑstɚ 〕 n. 騙子；冒名頂替者

imposture[7] 〔 ɪm'pɑstʃɚ 〕 n. 欺騙；詐欺；詐欺行為

imposturous 〔 ɪm'pɑstʃərəs 〕 adj. 欺騙的

indispose[7] 〔ˌɪndɪ'spoz 〕 v. 使不適當；使身體不適；使厭惡

（不在適當位置）《*in-* = not ; *dis-* = apart》

indisposed[7] 〔ˌɪndɪ'spozd 〕 adj. 不願意的

indisposition 〔ˌɪndɪspə'zɪʃən 〕 n. 不舒服；小病；不願意；嫌惡

interpose[7] 〔ˌɪntɚ'poz 〕 v. 插入；提出；調停；干涉（置於其間）

《*inter-* = between》

interposal 〔ˌɪntɚ'pozl̩ 〕 n. 插入；介入

interposer 〔ˌɪntɚ'pozɚ 〕 n. 插入者

interposition 〔ˌɪntɚpə'zɪʃən 〕 n. 介入；仲裁

juxtapose[7] 〔ˌdʒʌkstə'poz 〕 v. 並排；並列；並置（放在旁邊）

《*juxta* = beside》

opponent[5]〔əˋpɑnənt〕*adj.* 對立的　*n.* 對手；敵手
（置身於反對的立場）《*op-* = *ob-* = against》

oppose[4]〔əˋpoz〕*v.* 反對；相反；以～對抗（處於相反的）
《*op-* = *ob-* = against》

```
op    + pose
 |       |
against + put
```

opposite[3]〔ˋɑpəzɪt〕*adj.* 相對的；反對的　*n.* 相反的人或物
adv. 在對面地　*prep.* 在～對面

opposition[6]〔͵ɑpəˋzɪʃən〕*n.* 反對；對立；反對黨

postpone[3]〔postˋpon〕*v.* 延擱（置於其後）《*post-* = after》

```
post + pone
 |      |
after + put
```

postponement[3]〔postˋponmənt〕*n.* 延擱；拖延；延期
（提出來的人）《*pro-* = forward》

predispose[7]〔͵pridɪsˋpoz〕*v.* 使傾向；使偏愛；使易患
（事先安置）《*pre-* = before》

predisposition[7]〔͵pridɪspəˋzɪʃən〕*n.* 傾向；偏好；體質

preposition[4]〔͵prɛpəˋzɪʃən〕*n.* 介系詞；介詞（放在名詞前面）

```
pre   + pos + ition
 |       |      |
before + put +  n.
```

prepositional〔͵prɛpəˋzɪʃənḷ〕*adj.* 介系詞的；介詞的

prepositive〔prɪˋpɑzətɪv〕*adj.*【文法】前置的

proponent[7]〔prəˋponənt〕*n.* 提議者；擁護者；支持者

propose[2]〔prəˋpoz〕*v.* 提議；計劃（放在前面）《*pro-* = before》

proposal[3]〔prəˋpozḷ〕*n.* 提議；計畫

```
pro   + pos + al
 |       |     |
before + put + n.
```

proposition[7]〔ˌprɑpəˈzɪʃən〕*n.* 提議；命題；定理

purpose[1]〔ˈpɝpəs〕*n.* 目的；意圖；決心　*v.* 意圖；打算
（置於前端的醒目物品）《*pur-* = *pro-* = before》

repose[17]〔rɪˈpoz〕*v.* 休息；安眠　*n.* 休息；安靜《*re-* = again》

repose[27]〔rɪˈpoz〕*v.* 置；放

reposal〔rɪˈpozl̩，-zəl〕*n.* 安臥；信賴

reposeful〔rɪˈpozfl̩〕*adj.* 休息的；平靜的；沈著的

```
re  + pose + ful
 |     |      |
again +  put + adj.
```

reposer〔rɪˈpozɚ〕*n.* 安息者

reposit〔rɪˈpɑzɪt〕*v.* 貯藏；保存（放回來）《*re-* = back》

reposition[7]〔ˌripəˈzɪʃən〕*v.* 重新佈署（軍隊等）

repository〔rɪˈpɑzəˌtorɪ，-ˌtɔrɪ〕*n.* 貯藏器（所）；容器；
寶庫；靈骨塔；埋葬地（放置地點）《 *-ory* 表示場所的名詞字尾》

superimpose[7]〔ˌsupərɪmˈpoz〕*v.* 置於～上；重疊；添加
（放在上面）《*super-* = above；*im-* = *in-* = on》

```
super + im + pose
  |      |     |
above +  on + put
```

superimposition〔ˌsupɚˌɪmpəˈzɪʃən〕*n.* 重疊

superpose〔ˌsupɚˈpoz，ˌsju-〕*v.* 置於～上；重疊

superposition〔ˌsupɚpəˈzɪʃən，ˌsju-〕*n.* 重合

suppose[3]〔səˈpoz〕*v.* 想像；假定（置於其下）《*sup-* = *sub-* = under》

supposedly[7]〔səˈpozɪdlɪ〕*adv.* 想像上；或許；恐怕

supposition〔ˌsʌpəˈzɪʃən〕*n.* 假定；推測

presuppose〔ˌprisəˈpoz〕*v.* 預先假定；以～爲前提；成爲必要
（事先假定）《*pre-* = before》

```
pre  + sup  + pose
 |      |      |
before + under + put
```

presupposition 〔͵prɪsʌpə'zɪʃən 〕 *n.* 假定；推測；前提；先決條件
transpose[7] 〔 træns'poz 〕 *v.* 改換～之位置或順序《*trans-* = across》
transposition 〔͵trænspə'zɪʃən 〕 *n.* 轉換；調換
pause[3] 〔 pɔz 〕 *n.* 休止（符）；躊躇；斷句　*v.* 中止；躊躇

461　pot , poss = be able ; power（能夠；力量）

> * 拉丁文 ***posse*** (= be able)，***potis*** (= powerful ; able)。

possible[1] 〔'pɑsəbḷ 〕 *adj.* 可能的
potent[7] 〔'potṇt 〕 *adj.* 強而有力的；有效的
potence ; -cy[7] 〔'potṇs(ɪ) 〕 *n.* 潛力；效能；勢力
potentate 〔'potṇ͵tet 〕 *n.* 有權勢者；君主；統治者《 *-ate* 表「人」》
potential[5] 〔 pə'tɛnʃəl 〕 *adj.* 可能的；潛在的　*n.* 可能性；潛力
potentiality 〔 pə͵tɛnʃɪ'ælətɪ 〕 *n.* 可能性；潛力
potentialize 〔 pə'tɛnʃəl͵aɪz 〕 *v.* 使有潛力
potentiate 〔 pə'tɛnʃɪ͵et 〕 *v.* 賦予力量；強化《 *-iate* = make》

```
potent  +  iate
  |          |
powerful  +  make
```

impotent[7] 〔'ɪmpətənt 〕 *adj.* 無力的；虛弱的；陽萎的
　n. 虛弱者；衰老者；不能行房者《*im-* = *in-* = not》
impotence ; -cy[7] 〔'ɪmpətəns(ɪ) 〕 *n.* 無力；虛弱；陽萎
omnipotent[7] 〔 ɑm'nɪpətənt 〕 *adj.* 全能的（具備所有的力量）
　《*omni-* = all》

```
omni  +  pot   + ent
  |        |       |
 all   + power +  adj.
```

omnipotence[7] 〔 ɑm'nɪpətəns 〕 *n.* 全能
prepotent 〔 prɪ'potṇt 〕 *adj.* 非常優勢的；優生的（比別人先有力）
　《*pre-* = before》

462　pot , pos = drink (喝)

* 拉丁文 *potare* (= *drink*)；希臘文 *posis* (= *drinking*)。

potable[7] 〔'potəbḷ 〕 *adj.* 適於飲用的
potation 〔 po'teʃən 〕 *n.* (酒類) 飲料
potion[7] 〔'poʃən 〕 *n.* (毒藥或靈藥等藥水的) 一服；一劑
poison[2] 〔'pɔɪzn̩ 〕 *n.* 毒藥
potbelly[7] 〔'pat,bɛlɪ 〕 *n.* 肥大的肚子；大腹便便的人《*belly* 肚子》
pothouse 〔'pat,haʊs 〕 *n.* 旅店；小酒館
potvalor 〔'pat,vælɚ 〕 *n.* 酒後之勇《*valor* 勇氣》
compotation 〔,kampə'teʃən 〕 *n.* 同飲；共飲

```
com  +  pot  +  ation
 |        |       |
together + drink +  n.
```

compotator 〔'kampə,tetɚ 〕 *n.* 酒友
symposium 〔 sɪm'pozɪəm 〕 *n.* 古希臘宴會後的餘興；座談會；
　論文集《*sym-* = *syn-* = together》

【解説】 古代的希臘人流行在喝飯後酒的時候，同時進行知識方面的
　　　　討論。哲人柏拉圖曾在對話篇 the Symposium 中提到這種
　　　　場合中的探討。現在，symposium 仍然具有就一個問題交
　　　　換各種意見，並加以記錄的意思。

463　prec = pray (祈禱)

* 拉丁文 *prex* (= *prayer*)，*precari* (= *pray*)。

precarious[7] 〔 prɪ'kɛrɪəs 〕 *adj.* 不可靠的；不安定的；危險的；
　不穩定的 (必須祈禱的)
precariousness 〔 prɪ'kɛrɪəsnɪs 〕 *n.* 不安定；危險
precatory 〔'prɛkə,torɪ , -,tɔrɪ 〕 *adj.* 懇求的；請求的
deprecate[7] 〔'dɛprə,ket 〕 *v.* 駁斥；反對；輕視 (祈禱能去除)
　《*de-* = *dis-* = away》

deprecation[7] 〔͵dɛprə'keʃən〕 *n.* 反對；不贊成
deprecative 〔'dɛprə͵ketɪv〕 *adj.* 反對的；不贊成的；辯解的

```
de  + prec + ative
 |      |      |
away + pray  + adj.
```

deprecatory 〔'dɛprəkə͵torɪ〕 *adj.* 反對的；不贊成的；辯解的
imprecate 〔'ɪmprɪ͵ket〕 *v.* 祈求（降禍）；詛咒（祈禱災禍降臨）
《*im-* = *in-* = into》
imprecation 〔͵ɪmprɪ'keʃən〕 *n.* 祈求（降禍）；詛咒；咒語
imprecatory 〔'ɪmprɪkə͵tɔrɪ , -͵torɪ〕 *adj.* 詛咒的

464 **preci** = price（價格）   * 拉丁文 *pretium*（= *price*）。

precious[3] 〔'prɛʃəs〕 *adj.* 貴重的；寶貴的；過分講究的；非常的
preciosity 〔͵prɛʃɪ'asətɪ , ͵prɛsɪ-〕 *n.* 過分講究；挑剔
preciousness 〔'prɛʃəsnɪs〕 *n.* 貴重；寶貴
appreciate[3] 〔ə'priʃɪ͵et〕 *v.* 重視；賞識；欣賞；感激；瞭解；
升值（對~有好評價）《*ap-* = *ad-* = to》
appreciable 〔ə'priʃɪəbḷ〕 *adj.* 可看見的；可感知的；可察覺到的
appreciably 〔ə'priʃɪəblɪ〕 *adv.* 可感知地；有幾分可辨地
appreciation[4] 〔ə͵priʃɪ'eʃən〕 *n.* 重視；鑑賞（力）；評價；
感激；升值

```
ap + preci + at(e) + ion
 |     |       |      |
to + price  +  v.  +  n.
```

appreciative[7] 〔ə'priʃɪ͵etɪv〕 *adj.* 有鑑賞力的；感激的
appreciator 〔ə'priʃɪ͵etɚ〕 *n.* 鑑賞者；賞識者
depreciate 〔dɪ'priʃɪ͵et〕 *v.* 減價；貶值；輕視（降低~的價值）
《*de-* = down》
depreciation 〔dɪ͵priʃɪ'eʃən〕 *n.* 跌價；貶值；輕視

depreciatory 〔 dɪˈpriʃɪəˌtorɪ , -ˌtɔrɪ 〕 *adj.* 貶值的；輕視的

```
de  + preci + at(e) + ory
|      |       |       |
down + price +  v.   + adj.
```

praise[2] 〔 prez 〕 *v., n.* 稱讚；讚美；讚頌（有價值）
　《*prais* = *preci* = price》
appraise[7] 〔 əˈprez 〕 *v.* 估價；鑑定；評估（對～定價值）
　《*ap-* = *ad-* = to》
appraisal[7] 〔 əˈprezḷ 〕 *n.* 估價；鑑定《*-al* 名詞字尾》

465　**pred** = prey；plunder（獵物；掠奪）

　　＊ 拉丁文 *praeda*（= *prey*；*plunder*）。

predacious 〔 prɪˈdeʃəs 〕 *adj.* 捕食性的；食肉的
predator[7] 〔ˈprɛdətɚ 〕 *n.* 掠奪者；捕食動物；肉食動物
predatory[7] 〔ˈprɛdəˌtorɪ , -ˌtɔrɪ 〕 *adj.* 掠奪的；捕食性的；肉食的

```
preda  + tory
|        |
plunder + adj.
```

prey[5] 〔 pre 〕 *n.* 獵物；掠食；犧牲者　*v.* 捕食；掠奪（捕獲物）
depredate 〔ˈdɛprɪˌdet 〕 *v.* 劫掠；蹂躪；掠奪《*de-* = down》
depredation 〔ˌdɛprɪˈdeʃən 〕 *n.* 掠奪（的行為）；劫掠；
　破壞的痕跡

466　**prehend** , **pris** = seize（抓住）

　　＊ 拉丁文 *prendere* , *prehendere*（= *take*；*seize*），*prendere*
　　是 *prehendere* 的簡型；古法文 *pris*（= *taken*）。

prehensile 〔 prɪˈhɛnsḷ 〕 *adj.* 適於抓握的；
　有理解力的（能抓住的）《*-ile* 形容詞字尾》

```
prehens + ile
|         |
seize   + adj.
```

prehension〔 prɪˈhɛnʃən 〕 *n.* 捕捉；領會；理解

apprehend[7]〔͵æprɪˈhɛnd 〕 *v.* 逮捕；理解；憂懼（捕捉）

《*ap-* = *ad-* = to》

apprehensible〔͵æprɪˈhɛnsəbḷ 〕 *adj.* 可理解的

```
ap + prehens + ible
 |      |        |
to  +  seize  + adj.
```

apprehension[7]〔͵æprɪˈhɛnʃən 〕 *n.* 逮捕；理解力；恐懼；憂慮

apprehensive[7]〔͵æprɪˈhɛnsɪv 〕 *adj.* 憂鬱的；敏悟的；有知覺的

apprentice〔 əˈprɛntɪs 〕 *n.* 學徒　*v.* 使爲學徒（捉來做徒弟）

apprenticeship[7]〔 əˈprɛntɪs͵ʃɪp 〕 *n.* 學徒的身份；學徒的期限

《*-ship* 表示性質、狀態的抽象名詞字尾》

comprehend[5]〔͵kɑmprɪˈhɛnd 〕 *v.* 了解；領悟；包含（捉住～）

《*com-* = with》

```
com + prehend
 |       |
with  + seize
```

comprehensible〔͵kɑmprɪˈhɛnsəbḷ 〕 *adj.* 能理解的

comprehension[5]〔͵kɑmprɪˈhɛnʃən 〕 *n.* 理解（力）；包括

comprehensive[6]〔͵kɑmprɪˈhɛnsɪv 〕 *adj.* 廣博的；有理解力的

misapprehend〔͵mɪsæprɪˈhɛnd 〕 *v.* 誤解（錯誤理解）

《*mis-* = wrong》

misapprehension〔͵mɪsæprɪˈhɛnʃən 〕 *n.* 誤解

reprehend〔͵rɛprɪˈhɛnd 〕 *v.* 責難；申斥（逮捕帶回）

《*re-* = back》

```
re + prehend
 |       |
back  + seize
```

reprehensible〔͵rɛprɪˈhɛnsəbḷ 〕 *adj.* 應受譴責的；應受責難的

reprehension〔͵rɛprɪˈhɛnʃən 〕 *n.* 非難；譴責

prison[2] 〔'prɪzn̩〕*n.* 監獄；監禁　*v.* 囚禁（安置所捉犯人的地方）

prisoner[2] 〔'prɪznɚ，'prɪzn̩ɚ〕*n.* 囚犯；俘虜

imprison[6] 〔 ɪm'prɪzn̩ 〕*v.* 下獄；收押；禁錮（進入牢獄之中）

　《*im-* = *in-* = in》

imprisonment[6] 〔 ɪm'prɪzn̩mənt 〕*n.* 監禁；下獄；禁錮

apprise[7] 〔 ə'praɪz 〕*v.* 報告；通知（取消息給～）

　《*ap-* = *ad-* = to》

comprise[6]；**-prize** 〔 kəm'praɪz 〕*v.* 包括；由～構成（一起收入）

　《*com-* = together》

enterprise[5] 〔'ɛntɚ͵praɪz 〕*n.* 企業；進取心（把事業掌握在手中）

　《*enter-* = among》

enterprising[7] 〔'ɛntɚ͵praɪzɪŋ 〕*adj.* 有進取心的

```
enter  +  pris  +  ing
  |        |        |
among  +  seize  +  adj.
```

reprisal 〔 rɪ'praɪzl̩ 〕*n.* 報復；報復性劫掠（收回來）《*re-* = back》

surprise[1] 〔 sə'praɪz 〕*v.* 使驚訝；突擊　*n.* 驚訝；奇襲；意外之事

　（為捉～而攻於其上）《*sur-* = *super-* = above；upon》

surprisingly[7] 〔 sə'praɪzɪŋlɪ 〕*adv.* 令人驚訝地

prize[2] 〔 praɪz 〕*n.* 獎品；戰利品（從敵方取得的物品，競賽後

　取得之物）　*v.* 擄獲（以下的意思是從 price「價格」而來的）

　adj. 值得給獎的　*v.* 珍視；估價

467　**press** = press（壓）　* 拉丁文 *pressare*（= *press*）。

press[2] 〔 prɛs 〕*v.* 壓；壓平；逼迫；堅持　*n.* 緊急；印刷；群眾；

　新聞界

pressing[7] 〔'prɛsɪŋ 〕*adj.* 急迫的；強求的

pressure[3] 〔'prɛʃɚ 〕*n.* 壓力；困厄；急迫

pressurize[7] 〔'prɛʃə͵raɪz 〕*v.* 施壓；逼迫

compress[7] 〔 kəm'prɛs 〕 *v.* 壓縮；鎮壓（壓在一起）
《*com-* = together》

compressed 〔 kəm'prɛst 〕 *adj.* 壓縮的；壓緊的

compressible 〔 kəm'prɛsəbḷ 〕 *adj.* 可壓縮的

compression[7] 〔 kəm'prɛʃən 〕 *n.* 壓縮；壓榨

```
com    + press + ion
 |         |       |
together + press +  n.
```

compressive 〔 kəm'prɛsɪv 〕 *adj.* 有壓縮力的；壓榨的

compressor 〔 kəm'prɛsɚ 〕 *n.* 壓縮機

depress[4] 〔 dɪ'prɛs 〕 *v.* 壓下；使沮喪；使蕭條（壓往下方）
《*de-* = down》

depressant 〔 dɪ'prɛsṇt 〕 *adj.* 有鎮靜作用的　*n.* 鎮靜劑

```
de    + press + ant
 |        |       |
down  + press + adj., n.
```

depressed[7] 〔 dɪ'prɛst 〕 *adj.* 沮喪的；受壓制的；不景氣的

depressing[7] 〔 dɪ'prɛsɪŋ 〕 *adj.* 沈悶的；令人沮喪的

depression[4] 〔 dɪ'prɛʃən 〕 *n.* 降低；沮喪；不景氣；低氣壓

depressive 〔 dɪ'prɛsɪv 〕 *adj.* 憂鬱的；抑鬱的

depressor 〔 dɪ'prɛsɚ 〕 *n.* 壓抑者；壓板

express[2] 〔 ɪk'sprɛs 〕 *v.* 表達；擠出；快遞　*adj.* 確定的；
　特別的；快速的（壓擠出來）《*ex-* = out》

expressage 〔 ɛks'prɛsɪdʒ , ɪks- 〕 *n.* 快遞；捷運業

expressible 〔 ɪk'sprɛsəbḷ 〕 *adj.* 可表達的

expression[3] 〔 ɪk'sprɛʃən 〕 *n.* 表現；表情；措辭

expressionism 〔 ɪk'sprɛʃənˌɪzəm 〕 *n.* 表現主義；表現派
　《*-ism* = 主義；學說》

expressionist 〔 ɪk'sprɛʃənɪst 〕 *n.* 表現派藝術家
　adj. 表現派的

expressive[3] 〔 ɪkˈsprɛsɪv 〕 *adj.* 表現的；意味深長的

```
ex + press + ive
 |     |      |
out + press + adj.
```

expressly[7] 〔 ɪkˈsprɛslɪ 〕 *adv.* 明白地；顯然地；專誠地
expresso[7] 〔 ɪkˈsprɛso 〕 *n.* 濃縮咖啡（用蒸汽加壓煮出）
impress[3] 〔 *v.* ɪmˈprɛs *n.* ˈɪmprɛs 〕 *v.* 使印象深刻；銘記；蓋印
　n. 印象；蓋印（押附於心上）《*im-* = *in-* = on》
impressible 〔 ɪmˈprɛsəbḷ 〕 *adj.* 易受影響的
impression[4] 〔 ɪmˈprɛʃən 〕 *n.* 印象；意念；蓋印
impressionable[7] 〔 ɪmˈprɛʃənəbḷ 〕 *adj.* 易受感動的；易受影響的

```
im + press + ion + able
 |     |      |      |
on + press +  n.  + adj.
```

impressionism 〔 ɪmˈprɛʃənˌɪzəm 〕 *n.* 印象主義；印象派
impressionist 〔 ɪmˈprɛʃənɪst 〕 *n.* 印象主義者；印象派藝術家
impressive[3] 〔 ɪmˈprɛsɪv 〕 *adj.* 感人的；給人深刻印象的
oppress[6] 〔 əˈprɛs 〕 *v.* 壓迫；壓抑（對～施加壓力）
　《*op-* = *ob-* = against》

```
op   + press
 |      |
against + press
```

oppression[6] 〔 əˈprɛʃən 〕 *n.* 壓迫；鬱悶
oppressive[7] 〔 əˈprɛsɪv 〕 *adj.* 壓迫的；抑鬱的
oppressor 〔 əˈprɛsɚ 〕 *n.* 壓迫者；暴虐者
repress[6] 〔 rɪˈprɛs 〕 *v.* 鎮壓；抑制（壓迫回來）《*re-* = back》
repression 〔 rɪˈprɛʃən 〕 *n.* 鎮壓；抑制
repressible 〔 rɪˈprɛsəbḷ 〕 *adj.* 可鎮壓的；可抑制的
repressive 〔 rɪˈprɛsɪv 〕 *adj.* 抑制的；鎮壓的
repressor 〔 rɪˈprɛsɚ 〕 *n.* 抑制者；鎮壓者

suppress[5] 〔 sə'prɛs 〕*v.* 鎮壓；抑制；隱瞞；禁止出版（壓往下方）
《*sup-* = *sub-* = under》

suppressible 〔 sə'prɛsəbḷ 〕*adj.* 可鎮壓的；可抑制的；
可隱瞞的；可禁止的

```
sup  + press + ible
  |      |       |
under + press + adj.
```

suppression 〔 sə'prɛʃən 〕*n.* 鎮壓；抑制；禁止出版
suppressive[7] 〔 sə'prɛsɪv 〕*adj.* 鎮壓的；抑制的
suppressor 〔 sə'prɛsɚ 〕*n.* 鎮壓者；抑制者；隱蔽者；禁止者

468 prim , prin = first（第一的）

* 拉丁文 *primus*（= *first*）。〔變化型〕*prin* , *prem*。

prime[4] 〔 praɪm 〕*adj.* 首要的；第一的；最初的　*n.* 最初部分；
初期；全盛期；春天　*v.* 上火藥；倒水於抽水機中；塗底漆；使起動
primer 〔'prɪmɚ 〕*n.* 初級讀本　〔'praɪmɚ 〕*n.* 導火線；裝火藥者
prim(a)eval 〔 praɪ'mivḷ 〕*adj.* 原始時代的；太古的
（最早的時期）《*ev* = age》
primitive[4] 〔'prɪmətɪv 〕*adj.* 原始的；創始的　*n.* 原始人
primitivism 〔'prɪmətɪv͵ɪzəm 〕*n.* 原始社會崇拜主義；原始方法；
原始作風
primogenitor 〔͵praɪmə'dʒɛnətɚ 〕*n.* 祖先；始祖
《*genitor* = 生產的人 → 雙親》

```
primo + genitor
  |        |
first  + parents
```

primogeniture 〔͵praɪmə'dʒɛnətʃɚ 〕*n.* 長子的身份；長子繼承制
（最先出生的）
primordial 〔 praɪ'mɔrdɪəl 〕*adj.* 原始的；最初的；根本的
（最先開始的）《*ordial* = 拉丁文 *ordiri* = begin》

primordium〔praɪˈmɔrdɪəm〕*n.* 原始細胞《*-um* 名詞字尾》

```
prim + ordi + um
  |      |      |
first + begin + n.
```

primrose〔ˈprɪmˌroz〕*n.* 櫻草；淡黃色　*adj.* 櫻草的；
淡黃色的；歡樂的（最早的薔薇 → 早春開放的花）

primus〔ˈpraɪməs〕*adj.* 第一的；首位的；最年長的

primacy〔ˈpraɪməsɪ〕*n.* 首位；首要

prima donna〔ˈpriməˈdɑnə〕*n.* 歌劇中第一女主角；首席女歌星
《義大利文 *donna* = lady》

primal[7]〔ˈpraɪml̩〕*adj.* 最初的；主要的；原始的

primary[3]〔ˈpraɪˌmɛrɪ, -mərɪ〕*adj.* 第一的；初級的；根本的
n. 原色；初選

primarily[7]〔ˈpraɪˌmɛrəlɪ〕*adv.* 主要地；首要地；首先地

primate[7]〔ˈpraɪmet〕*n.* 主教；總主教；靈長類；領袖；
階級或地位最高者《 *-ate* 表示人的名詞字尾》

prince[2]〔prɪns〕*n.* 王子；諸侯（坐於首席者）《 *-ce* = take》

principal[2]〔ˈprɪnsəpl̩〕*adj.* 重要的；首要的　*n.* 首長；主犯；
資本；校長

```
prin + cip +   al
  |     |       |
first + take + adj., n.
```

principle[2]〔ˈprɪnsəpl̩〕*n.* 原則；主義（第一的東西）

premier[6]〔*adj.* ˈprimɪɚ *n.* prɪˈmɪr〕*adj.* 首要的　*n.* 首相；
國務總理

469　**priv** = individual；deprive（個人的；剝奪）

　＊ 拉丁文 *privus*（ = *individual*），*privare*（ = *deprive*），
　過去分詞是 *privatus*。

private[2]〔ˈpraɪvɪt〕*adj.* 私人的；祕密的；私立的

privacy[4]〔'praɪvəsɪ〕*n.* 隱居；獨處；祕密；私事；隱私

privately[7]〔'praɪvɪtlɪ〕*adv.* 私下地；不公開地

privation〔praɪ'veʃən〕*n.* 匱乏；窮困

privatism〔'praɪvətɪzm̩〕*n.* 個人主義；利己主義《*-ism* = 主義》

privative〔'prɪvətɪv〕*adj.* 缺乏的；剝奪的

privatize〔'praɪvə,taɪz〕*v.* 使民營化；使私有化

privilege[4]〔'prɪvl̩ɪdʒ〕*n.* 特權；恩典；特殊利益
（限於一個人的法律）《*leg* = law》

```
privi   + lege
  |         |
individual + law
```

privileged[7]〔'prɪvl̩ɪdʒd〕*adj.* 特權的；有特殊利益的

privy[7]〔'prɪvɪ〕*adj.* 私下知情的；私有的；君主私有或私用的
n.【法律】當事人；關係人

privily〔'prɪvəlɪ〕*adv.* 私下地；祕密地

privity〔'prɪvətɪ〕*n.* 參與祕密；暗中參與；默契

deprive[6]〔dɪ'praɪv〕*v.* 剝奪；使喪失（從～奪走）
《*de-* = *dis-* = from》

deprived〔dɪ'praɪvd〕*adj.* 被剝奪的；貧窮的；貧困的

deprivation〔,dɛprɪ'veʃən〕*n.* 剝奪；褫奪公權；損失

underprivileged[7]〔'ʌndɚ'prɪvəlɪdʒd〕*adj.* 貧困的；社會地位
低下的

470　**prob** = test（試驗）

* 拉丁文 *probare*（= *test* ; *try* ; *prove*）。〔變化型〕*prov*。

prove[1]〔pruv〕*v.* 試驗；證明；表現

proof[3]〔pruf〕*n.* 證明；證據；考驗　*adj.* 試驗過的；防～的
v. 使（布）防水

probable[3]〔'prɑbəbḷ〕*adj.* 可能的；或有的（可能證明的）

probably[7]〔'prɑbəblɪ〕*adv.* 或許；大概

probability[7]〔,prɑbə'bɪlətɪ〕*n.* 可能性；機會；或然率
（有可能的事）

probate〔'probet〕*n.* 經認證的遺囑　*v.* 認證（遺囑）

probation[7]〔pro'beʃən〕*n.* 試驗；檢定；緩刑（進行測試）

probationary〔pro'beʃən,ɛrɪ〕*adj.* 試用的；試驗的；
試用期間的

```
prob + ation + ary
  |      |       |
test  +  n.   + adj.
```

probationer〔pro'beʃənɚ〕*n.* 練習生；試讀生；被試用者；
見習者

probative〔'probətɪv , 'prɑb-〕*adj.* 試驗的；提供證據的

probe[7]〔prob〕*n.* 探針；調查　*v.* 探察；以探針探察（檢查傷痛
的工具）

probing〔'probɪŋ〕*adj.* 試探的；探查的；深入的

probity〔'probətɪ , 'prɑ-〕*n.*（經過試煉證明的）誠正；正直廉潔

approbate〔'æprə,bet〕*v.* 通過；認可；核准；嘉許
（向～試驗後同意）《*ap-* = *ad-* = to》

approbation〔,æprə'beʃən〕*n.* 許可；認可；核准；嘉許

```
ap + prob + at(e) + ion
 |    |       |       |
to + test  +  v.   +  n.
```

approbative〔'æpro,betɪv〕*adj.* 許可的；認可的；核准的；嘉許的

approbatory〔ə'probə,torɪ〕*adj.* 許可的；認可的；核准的；
嘉許的

approve[3]〔ə'pruv〕*v.* 贊成；同意；核准；證明為《*ap-* = *ad-* = to》

approvable〔ə'pruvəbḷ〕*adj.* 可贊成的；可核准的

approval[4]〔ə'pruvḷ〕*n.* 贊成；批准

disapprove[6] 〔͵dɪsə'pruv〕 *v.* 不贊成；不准許；非難《*dis-* = not》

```
dis  +  ap  +  prove
 |       |       |
not  +  to   +  test
```

disapproval[7] 〔͵dɪsə'pruvḷ〕 *n.* 不承認；不贊成

disprove[7] 〔dɪs'pruv〕 *v.* 反證；證明爲僞（證明相反）
《*dis-* = apart；away》

disproof 〔dɪs'pruf〕 *n.* 反證；反駁

improve[2] 〔ɪm'pruv〕 *v.* 改良；改善；進步（可以產生好處的）
《古法文 *prou* = profit（利益）》

improvement[2] 〔ɪm'pruvmənt〕 *n.* 改良；改善；進步

reprobate 〔'rɛprə͵bet〕 *v.* 斥責；拒絕　*adj.* 墮落的；放蕩的
　n. 無賴漢；墮落者《*re-* = opposite》

```
re    +      prob      + ate
 |            |            |
opposite + prove to be worthy + v.
```

reprobation 〔͵rɛprə'beʃən〕 *n.* 指責；【神學】遺棄

reprove 〔rɪ'pruv〕 *v.* 譴責；責罵

reproof 〔rɪ'pruf〕 *n.* 譴責；斥責

reprieve[7] 〔rɪ'priv〕 *v.* 緩刑；暫時救出　*n.* 緩刑；暫時解脫

471 **propr** = one's own（自己的）

* 拉丁文 *proprius*（ = one's own）。

proper[3] 〔'prɑpɚ〕 *adj.* 適當的；高尚的；特有的

property[3] 〔'prɑpɚtɪ〕 *n.* 財產；所有物；所有權；性質；特性

propriety[7] 〔prə'praɪətɪ〕 *n.* 適當；禮節；(*pl.*) 行爲規範

```
propri + ety
  |       |
proper +  n.
```

字根 pact~radi

proprietary[7]〔 prəˈpraɪəˌtɛrɪ 〕*adj.* 有財產的；所有權的；
獨佔的；專賣的　*n.* 所有者；所有權
proprietor[7]〔 prəˈpraɪətə 〕*n.* 所有者；經營者；房東
proprietorial〔 prəˌpraɪəˈtorɪəl 〕*adj.* 所有的；所有權的
proprietorship〔 prəˈpraɪətəˌʃɪp 〕*n.* 所有權
　《 *-ship* 抽象名詞字尾》
appropriate[4]〔 *adj.* əˈproprɪɪt *v.* əˈproprɪˌet 〕*adj.* 適合的；
適當的；專屬的　*v.* 擅用；據爲己有；撥款（使變成自己的）
《 *ap-* = *ad-* = to》

> ap　+　propri　+　ate
> 　│　　　　│　　　　│
> *to*　+　*one's own*　+　*adj.*

appropriation〔 əˌproprɪˈeʃən 〕*n.* 據爲己有；擅用；撥款
appropriator〔 əˈproprɪˌetə 〕*n.* 擅用者；佔用者
expropriate〔 ɛksˈproprɪˌet 〕*v.* 沒收；徵用（土地）
（使失去所有權）《 *ex-* = out》

> ex　+　propri　+　ate
> 　│　　　　│　　　│
> *out*　+　*one's own*　+　*v.*

expropriation〔 ɛksˌproprɪˈeʃən 〕*n.*（土地）徵用；徵收
impropriety〔 ˌɪmprəˈpraɪətɪ 〕*n.* 不適當；不正當的行爲；
錯誤的詞句《 *im-* = *in-* = not》

> im　+　propri　+　ety
> 　│　　　　│　　　│
> *not*　+　*proper*　+　*n.*

misappropriate〔 ˌmɪsəˈproprɪˌet 〕*v.* 誤用；侵佔；盜用
（不當地使用）《 *mis-* = wrong》
misappropriation〔 ˌmɪsəˌproprɪˈeʃən 〕*n.* 私吞；霸佔；濫用

472　prox , proach = near（接近的）

> * 拉丁文 *prope*（= *near*），*proximus*（= *nearest*）。
> 〔變化型〕*proach*。

proximal〔'prɑksəml̩〕*adj.* 最近的；接近身體中心的
proximity[7]〔prɑk'sɪmətɪ〕*n.* 接近；近似
approximate[6]〔*adj.* ə'prɑksəmɪt *v.* ə'prɑksə,met〕*adj.* 近似的；
　大概的　*v.* 接近（向～接近）《*ap-* = *ad-*（to）+ *proximate*（nearest）》

> ```
> ap + proxim + ate
>  |     |      |
> to + nearest + adj.
> ```

approximately[7]〔ə'prɑksəmɪtlɪ〕*adv.* 大概；近乎
approach[3]〔ə'protʃ〕*v.* 接近；近似　*n.* 接近；方法；步驟；通路
　（向～靠近）《*ap-* = *ad-* = to》
approachable[7]〔ə'protʃəbl̩〕*adj.* 可接近的；易親近的

> ```
> ap + proach + able
>  |     |      |
> to + near  + adj.
> ```

approachability〔ə,protʃə'bɪlətɪ〕*n.* 可接近性；易接近；可親
reproach[7]〔rɪ'protʃ〕*v.* 譴責；責備（再次接近）《*re-* = again》
reproachful〔rɪ'protʃfl̩〕*adj.* 責備的；表示譴責的
reproaching〔rɪ'protʃɪŋ〕*adj.* 責備的；譴責的

473　psych = soul；mind（靈魂；心智）

> * 希臘文 *psukhe*（= *soul*；*mind*）。〔變化型〕*psycho*。

psyche[7]〔'saɪkɪ〕*n.* 靈魂；精神
psychedelic〔,saɪkɪ'dɛlɪk〕*adj.* 使產生幻覺的
psychiatry[7]〔saɪ'kaɪətrɪ〕*n.* 精神病治療法；精神病學
　《*iatr* = healing；*-y* 名詞字尾》

psychiatric〔͵saɪkɪ'ætrɪk〕*adj.* 精神病的；精神病治療的
《 *-ic* 形容詞字尾》

psychiatrist〔saɪ'kaɪətrɪst〕*n.* 精神病醫師；精神病學家
《 *-ist* 表示人的名詞字尾》

```
psych +   iatr   +   ist
  |         |          |
soul  + healing + person
```

psychic[7]〔'saɪkɪk〕*adj.* 靈魂的；精神上的；心靈的

psychics〔'saɪkɪks〕*n.* 心靈研究；心靈哲學；心理學《 *-ics* = science》

psychoanalysis〔͵saɪkoə'næləsɪs〕*n.* 心理分析；精神分析
《*analysis* 分析》

psychoanalyze〔͵saɪko'ænḷͺaɪz〕*v.* 以心理分析法診斷與治療

psycholinguistics〔͵saɪkolɪŋ'gwɪstɪks〕*n.* 心理語言學
《*linguistics* 語言學》

```
psycho + linguist + ics
   |         |        |
 soul  + tongue  +  n.
```

psychology[4]〔saɪ'kɑlədʒɪ〕*n.* 心理學《*logy* = study》

psychological[4]〔͵saɪkə'lɑdʒɪkḷ〕*adj.* 心理上的；心理學的

psychologist[4]〔saɪ'kɑlədʒɪst〕*n.* 心理學家

psychologize〔saɪ'kɑlə͵dʒaɪz〕*v.* 研究心理學；從心理學上分析

psychoneurosis〔͵saɪkonju'rosɪs〕*n.* 心理性神經病；精神神
經症《*neurosis* 神經病》

psychopath〔'saɪkə͵pæθ〕*n.* 精神病患者《*path* = disease》

psychopathy〔saɪ'kɑpəθɪ〕*n.* 精神病

```
psycho +  path   + y
   |         |       |
 soul  + disease +  n.
```

psychosis〔saɪ'kosɪs〕*n.* 精神病；精神異常《 *-sis* = condition》

psychosomatic〔͵saɪkəso'mætɪk〕*adj.* 精神與身體的；
身心關係的《*somat* = body》

474 **pto** = fall (落下)　　*希臘文 piptein (= fall)。

Ptolemaic 〔,tɑləˈme‧ɪk 〕 *adj.* 托勒密的；托勒密天動說的；
托勒密王朝的
ptomaine 〔ˈtomen 〕 *n.* 屍鹼；屍毒
ptosis 〔ˈtosɪs 〕 *n.* 上瞼下垂；下垂
nephroptosis 〔,nɛfrəpˈtosɪs 〕 *n.* 腎下垂《希臘文 *nephros* = kidney》
symptom[6] 〔ˈsɪmptəm 〕 *n.* 症狀《*sym-* = *syn-* = together》

475 **pud** = be ashamed (感到羞恥)

　　* 拉丁文 *pudere* (= be ashamed)。

pudency 〔ˈpjudn̩sɪ 〕 *n.* 謙虛；拘謹；羞怯；靦腆
pudenda 〔 pjuˈdɛndə 〕 *n.pl.* (尤指女性的) 外生殖器；外陰
pudicity 〔 pjuˈdɪsətɪ 〕 *n.* 謙虛；貞節；純潔
impudent[7] 〔ˈɪmpjədənt 〕 *adj.* 厚顏無恥的；無禮的《*im-* = *in-* = not》
impudicity 〔,ɪmpjəˈdɪsətɪ 〕 *n.* 無恥；不謙恭
repudiate 〔 rɪˈpjudɪ,et 〕 *v.* 拒絕；否認；聲明與…脫離關係

re	+	pudi	+	ate
back , away	+	be ashamed	+	v.

476 **pugn** = fight (打架；爭吵)

　　* 拉丁文 *pugnus* (= fist) , *pugnare* (= fight)。

pugnacious[7] 〔 pʌgˈneʃəs 〕 *adj.* 好鬥的；愛吵架的
《 *-acious* 形容詞字尾》
pugnacity 〔 pʌgˈnæsətɪ 〕 *n.* 好鬥；愛吵架
impugn 〔 ɪmˈpjun 〕 *v.* 指責；非難；駁斥 (使置於鬥爭中)
《*im-* = *in-* = into》
impugnable 〔 ɪmˈpjunəbl̩ 〕 *adj.* 可非難的；可指責的；可駁斥的

impugnment〔ɪm'pjunmənt〕*n.* 攻擊;非難;駁斥;指責

inexpugnable〔,ɪnɪks'pʌgnəbḷ〕*adj.* 難攻陷的;難征服的;
難推翻的(無法擊敗的)《*in-* = not;*ex-* = out》

$$in + ex + pugn + able$$
$$not + out + fight + adj.$$

repugnance;-ancy〔rɪ'pʌgnəns(ɪ)〕*n.* 嫌惡;厭棄;矛盾
(反對 → 嫌惡)《*re-* = against》

repugnant[7]〔rɪ'pʌgnənt〕*adj.* 討厭的;矛盾的;敵對的

pugilism〔'pjudʒə,lɪzəm〕*n.* 拳擊《拉丁文 *pugil* = boxer》

pugilist〔'pjudʒəlɪst〕*n.* 拳擊手

pugilistic〔,pjudʒə'lɪstɪk〕*adj.* 拳擊的

477　**pung,punct** = prick(刺)

* 拉丁文 *pungere*(= *prick*),過去分詞是 *punctus*,
由「穿刺」引申為「(突出之)點」的意思。

pungent[7]〔'pʌndʒənt〕*adj.* 刺激性的;辛辣的

pungency〔'pʌndʒənsɪ〕*n.* 刺激;辛辣;劇烈;敏銳

punctate〔'pʌŋktet〕*adj.* 有斑點的

punctilio〔pʌŋk'tɪlɪ,o〕*n.* 細節;拘泥形式(突出的小點)

punctilious〔pʌŋk'tɪlɪəs〕*adj.* 留心細節的;拘泥形式的
(拘泥於小節的)

punctual[6]〔'pʌŋktʃuəl〕*adj.* 守時的;仔細的(守住時間上的一點)

punctuality[7]〔,pʌŋktʃu'ælətɪ〕*n.* 準時;迅速

$$punct + ual + ity$$
$$prick + adj. + n.$$

punctuate[7]〔'pʌŋktʃu,et〕*v.* 加標點於;加重(加上點)

punctuation[7]〔,pʌŋktʃu'eʃən〕*n.* 標點;標點法

puncture[7]（'pʌŋktʃɚ）*n.* 孔；洞　*v.* 有破孔；穿孔；刺穿
（穿透開孔）

acupuncture[7]（*n.* 'ækju͵pʌŋktʃɚ *v.* ͵ækjʊ'pʌŋktʃɚ）*n. , v.* 針灸
《*acu* = sharp》

compunction（kəm'pʌŋkʃən）*n.* 追悔；良心不安（刺穿心靈）
《*com-* = with》

compunctious（kəm'pʌŋkʃəs）*adj.* 懊悔的；良心不安的

expunge（ɪk'spʌndʒ , ɛk-）*v.* 刪去；除去（刺穿出去）《*ex-* = out》

expunction（ɪk'spʌŋkʃən）*n.* 刪除

```
ex  +  punct  +  ion
 |        |        |
out  +  prick  +   n.
```

venipuncture（͵vɛnə'pʌŋktʃɚ）*n.* 靜脈穿刺《*vein* 靜脈》

pounce[7]（paʊns）*n.* 猛禽之爪；急襲；猛撲　*v.* 飛撲；以利爪抓住

punch[3]（pʌntʃ）*n.* 打洞器；拳打　*v.* 拳擊；打洞（刺穿開孔的東西）

poignant[7]（'pɔɪnənt , 'pɔɪnjənt）*adj.* 尖刻的；痛切的；辛辣的
（似乎能夠刺穿的）

point[1]（pɔɪnt）*n.* 點；地點；目的；時刻　*v.* 使銳利；指示

appoint[4]（ə'pɔɪnt）*v.* 任命；指定；約定（指定表明一點）

appointee（ə͵pɔɪn'ti , ͵æpɔɪn'ti）*n.* 被任命者

appointer（ə'pɔɪntɚ）*n.* 任命者

appointment[4]（ə'pɔɪntmənt）*n.* 約定（會面）；任命；指定
　cf. **promise**（諾言；約定）

```
ap  +  point  +  ment
 |        |        |
to  +  prick  +    n.
```

【解說】美國人非常重視約定，做什麼事都要事先預約，假如沒有事
先約好，就登門拜訪他人，會被視爲不禮貌的行爲。他們連
看病都要先約好時間，否則醫師無法當場做門診。

disappoint[3]（͵dɪsə'pɔɪnt）*v.* 使失望；使受挫折（遠離指定者）
《*dis-* = apart ; away》

disappointment[3]（͵dɪsə'pɔɪntmənt）*n.* 失望；挫折

478　pur = pure（純粹的）　　* 拉丁文 *purus*（= *pure*；*clean*）。

pure[3] 〔 pjʊr 〕 *adj.* 純粹的；單純的；純潔的；完全的
purify[6] 〔'pjʊrə,faɪ 〕 *v.* 淨化；洗除罪惡；精煉（使清潔）《 *-ify* = make》
purification[7] 〔,pjʊrəfə'keʃən 〕 *n.* 淨化；精煉；洗罪

```
pur  +  ific  + ation
 |        |       |
pure + make  +   n.
```

purism 〔'pjʊrɪzəm 〕 *n.*（語言等的）純粹主義；修辭癖《 *-ism* = 主義》
puritan 〔'pjʊrətn̩ 〕 *n.* 嚴謹的人；（P-）清教徒
　　adj. 生活嚴肅的；（P-）清教徒的

```
pur  +  it(y) +   an
 |        |        |
pure +   n.  + person
```

puritanic；**-ical** 〔,pjʊrə'tænɪk(l̩) 〕 *adj.* 像清教徒的；嚴謹的；
　　嚴格的
purity[6] 〔'pjʊrətɪ 〕 *n.* 純潔；天真無邪；純粹
impure[7] 〔 ɪm'pjʊr 〕 *adj.* 不純潔的；不純的；不道德的；複雜的
　　《 *im-* = *in-* = not》
impurity[7] 〔 ɪm'pjʊrətɪ 〕 *n.* 不潔；不純；不貞潔；混雜物

479　purg = purify（淨化）

　　* 拉丁文 *purgare*（= *purify*；*purge*）。

purge[7] 〔 pɝdʒ 〕 *v.* 使清淨；洗罪；整肅；通腸；使瀉
purgation 〔 pɝ'geʃən 〕 *n.* 洗罪；淨化；（吃瀉藥）淨腸
purgative 〔'pɝgətɪv 〕 *n.* 瀉藥　 *adj.* 淨化的；通便的
purgatory 〔'pɝgə,torɪ 〕 *n.* 煉獄；（暫時的）受難；暫時受苦之地
purgee 〔 pɝ'dʒi 〕 *n.* 被整肅者《 *-ee* 表示「被～的人」》
purger 〔'pɝdʒɚ 〕 *n.* 清除者；洗滌者；整肅者；瀉藥

compurgation 〔͵kɑmpɝ'geʃən〕 *n.* 根據數人之證詞對嫌犯作無罪之判決（共同使其無罪）《*com-* = together》

```
com  + purg + ation
 |       |      |
together + purify +  n.
```

expurgate 〔 ɪk'spɝget 〕 *v.* 刪除；修訂（使潔淨）《*ex-* = out》

expurgation 〔͵ɛkspɝ'geʃən〕 *n.* 刪除；修訂

expurgator 〔'ɛkspɝ͵getɚ 〕 *n.* 刪除者；修訂者

expurgatory 〔 ɛks'pɝgə͵torɪ 〕 *adj.* 刪除的

unexpurgated 〔͵ʌnɛks'pɝgetɪd〕 *adj.* 未經刪除的；完全的《*un-* = not》

480　**pute** = think；prune（想；修剪）

　　* 拉丁文 *putare*（= *think*；*count*；*prune*）。

amputate[7] 〔'æmpjə͵tet , -pjʊ- 〕 *v.* 切斷；減除（使周圍清爽）《*am-* = *ambi-* = about》

```
am + put + ate
 |    |     |
about + prune +  v.
```

compute[5] 〔 kəm'pjut 〕 *v.* 計算；估計（和數字一起考慮）《*com-* = together》

computer[2] 〔 kəm'pjutɚ 〕 *n.* 電子計算機；電腦

computerese 〔 kəm͵pjutə'riz 〕 *n.* 電腦語言；電腦用語（和電腦相關的用語）《 *-ese* = related to》

```
com  + puter +   ese
 |       |        |
together + think + related to
```

computerize[5] 〔 kəm'pjutə͵raɪz 〕 *v.* 使電腦化

computation 〔͵kɑmpjʊ'teʃən〕 *n.* 計算；算法

depute〔 dɪ'pjut 〕*v.* 委託（某人）為代理（把想法置於其下
→ 委任於人）《*de-* = down》

deputation〔ˌdɛpjə'teʃən 〕*n.* 代理者；代表團
（不用自己想，有人代理）

```
de   +  put  + ation
 |       |      |
away + think +  n.
```

deputy[6]〔'dɛpjətɪ 〕*n.* 代理人；（從前法國等的）議員

dispute[4]〔 dɪ'spjut 〕*v.* 爭論；辯論；反抗　*n.* 辯論；爭論
（改變其想法）《*dis-* = apart》

disputable〔 dɪ'spjutəbl̩ 〕*adj.* 有爭論餘地的；未確定的

disputation〔ˌdɪspjʊ'teʃən 〕*n.* 爭辯；爭論

disputatious〔ˌdɪspjʊ'teʃəs 〕*adj.* 好爭論的；引起爭論的

impute〔 ɪm'pjut 〕*v.* 歸（咎）於（認為是～的罪）《*im-* = *in-* = in》

imputation〔ˌɪmpjʊ'teʃən 〕*n.* 歸罪；責難

indisputable〔ˌɪndɪ'spjutəbl̩ 〕*adj.* 不容置辯的；無容懷疑的；
明白的；確實的（不需爭論的）《*in-* = not》

```
in  +  dis  + put  + able
 |      |      |      |
not + apart + think + adj.
```

putative〔'pjutətɪv 〕*adj.* 推定的；假定的；想像的（用想的）

repute〔 rɪ'pjut 〕*v.* 認為；視為　*n.* 聲望；名譽《*re-* = again》

reputation[4]〔ˌrɛpjə'teʃən 〕*n.* 名譽；聲望

reputable〔'rɛpjətəbl̩ 〕*adj.* 有聲望的；名譽好的

disreputable〔 dɪs'rɛpjətəbl̩ 〕*adj.* 名譽不好的；可恥的；
不體面的（名譽佳的相反）《*dis-* = negative（否定）》

```
dis     +  re  + put  + able
 |          |     |      |
negative + again + think + adj.
```

disrepute〔ˌdɪsrɪ'pjut 〕*n.* 不名譽；不受歡迎

481　**pyr** = fire (火)　*希臘文 pur (= fire)。

pyre 〔 paɪr 〕 *n.* (火葬用的) 柴堆
pyroconductivity 〔 ˌpaɪroˌkɑndʌk'tɪvətɪ 〕 *n.* 高溫導電性
　《*conduct* 引導》
pyrogenic 〔 ˌpaɪrə'dʒɛnɪk 〕 *adj.* 由熱引起的；火成的
　《*gen* = produce》
pyrography 〔 paɪ'rɑgrəfɪ 〕 *n.* 烙畫術；烙出之畫《*graph* = write》
pyromaniac[7] 〔 ˌpaɪrə'menɪˌæk 〕 *n.* 有縱火狂的人
pyrotechnics 〔 ˌpaɪrə'tɛknɪks 〕 *n.* 煙火；軍用煙火 (指照明彈、
　煙霧彈等)

482　**quer** = complain (抱怨)

　　*拉丁文 queri (= complain)。

quarrel[3] 〔 'kwɔrəl , 'kwɑr- 〕 *n.* , *v.* 爭論；爭吵
quarreler 〔 'kwɔrələ , 'kwɑr- 〕 *n.* 爭吵者；好爭論者
quarrelsome[6] 〔 'kwɔrəlsəm , 'kwɑr- 〕 *adj.* 愛爭吵的
querimonious 〔 ˌkwɪrɪ'monɪəs 〕 *adj.* 愛埋怨的；常常訴苦的
querulous 〔 'kwɛrələs 〕 *adj.* 愛抱怨的；吹毛求疵的；易怒的

483　**quer** , **quest** , **quir** , **quisit**
　　= seek ; ask (尋求；問)

　　　*拉丁文 quaerere (= seek ; gain ; ask)，過去分詞為 quaesitus。

query[6] 〔 'kwɪrɪ 〕 *v.* 質問；詢問　*n.* 質問 (尋求答案)
quest[5] 〔 kwɛst 〕 *n.* 探詢；探求 (物)　*v.* 搜尋
question[1] 〔 'kwɛstʃən 〕 *n.* 疑問；問題　*v.* 詢問；懷疑
questionable[7] 〔 'kwɛstʃənəbl̩ 〕 *adj.* 引起爭論的；可疑的

questionnaire[6] 〔͵kwɛstʃən'ɛr 〕 *n.* 問卷調查《 *-aire* 名詞字尾》

```
quest  +  tionn  +  aire
  |        |         |
seek   +   n.   +    n.
```

acquire[4] 〔 ə'kwaɪr 〕 *v.* 獲得；習得（求得；取得）《*ac-* = *ad-* = to》
acquirement 〔 ə'kwaɪrmənt 〕 *n.* 獲得；學識
acquisition[6] 〔͵ækwə'zɪʃən 〕 *n.* 獲得（物）
acquisitive 〔 ə'kwɪzətɪv 〕 *adj.* 想獲得的；貪得的
conquer[4] 〔'kɔŋkɚ 〕 *v.* 征服；得勝（完全求得）《*con-* = wholly》
conqueror[7] 〔'kɑŋkərɚ 〕 *n.* 征服者；勝利者
conquest[6] 〔'kɑŋkwɛst 〕 *n.* 征服；戰利品
disquisition 〔͵dɪskwə'zɪʃən 〕 *n.* 論文；專論（尋求分成細部的
　東西）《*dis-* = apart》
exquisite[6] 〔'ɛkskwɪzɪt , ɪk's- 〕 *adj.* 精美的；纖美的；高尚的
　（被求取的 → 選拔出來的）《*ex-* = out》

```
ex  +  quis  +  ite
 |       |       |
out +   seek  +  adj.
```

inquire[5] ; **enquire** 〔 ɪn'kwaɪr 〕 *v.* 詢問；調查（深入尋求）
　《*in-* , *en-* = into》
inquiry[6] 〔 ɪn'kwaɪrɪ 〕 *n.* 詢問；問題；調查
inquest 〔'ɪnkwɛst 〕 *n.* 審訊；驗屍
inquisition 〔͵ɪnkwə'zɪʃən 〕 *n.* 調查；審訊
inquisitive[7] 〔 ɪn'kwɪzətɪv 〕 *adj.* 好奇的；好問的
perquisite 〔'pɝkwəzɪt 〕 *n.* 額外補貼；賞錢；犒賞；臨時津貼
　（完全求得的東西）《*per-* = thoroughly》
require[2] 〔 rɪ'kwaɪr 〕 *v.* 需要；要求（再度尋求）《*re-* = again》
requirement[2] 〔 rɪ'kwaɪrmənt 〕 *n.* 需要的事物；要求的事物；
　必要條件

```
re   +  quire  +  ment
 |        |         |
again +  seek  +    n.
```

requisite〔ˈrɛkwəzɪt〕*adj.* 必須的　*n.* 必需品

prerequisite[7]〔priˈrɛkwəzɪt〕*n.* 首要的事物；必備的事物
（事先必須準備的東西）《*pre-* = before》

requisition〔ˌrɛkwəˈzɪʃən〕*n.* 請求；要求；徵用
v. 徵用；徵收

request[3]〔rɪˈkwɛst〕*n.* 請求；需要　*v.* 請求；要求

sequester〔sɪˈkwɛstɚ〕*v.* 退隱；扣押；沒收（尋求離開）
《*se-* = apart》

484　**qui** = quiet；rest（安靜的；靜止）

> * 拉丁文 *quies*（ = *quiet*；*rest*）；*quiescere*（ = *rest*），
> 過去分詞是 *quietus*。

quiet[1]〔ˈkwaɪət〕*adj.* 安靜的；靜止的；鎮靜的　*n.* 安靜；平靜；
鎮靜　*v.* 使安靜；使鎮定

quietness〔ˈkwaɪətnɪs〕*n.* 寂靜；鎮定

quietude〔ˈkwaɪəˌtjud〕*n.* 安靜；平靜；鎮靜《*-(t)ude* 名詞字尾》

quietus〔kwaɪˈitəs〕*n.* （債務的）償清；生命的終止；最後的一擊
《*-us* 名詞字尾》

disquiet〔dɪsˈkwaɪət〕*v.* 使不安；使憂慮　*n.* 不安；憂慮
《*dis-* = deprive of》

inquietude〔ɪnˈkwaɪəˌtjud〕*n.* （身心的）不安；動搖；焦慮
《*in-* = not》

```
in  +  quiet  +  (t)ude
 |       |         |
not  +  rest   +    n.
```

unquiet〔ʌnˈkwaɪət〕*adj.* 不安的；心神不寧的；紛擾的
《*un-* = not》

quiescence〔kwaɪˈɛsn̩s〕*n.* 寂靜；安靜；靜止

quiescent〔kwaɪˈɛsn̩t〕*adj.* 安靜的；不動的

acquiesce[7] 〔 ˌækwɪˈɛs 〕 *n.* 默許;勉強同意 (安靜不說話)

《 *ac-* = *ad-* = to 》

```
ac  +  qui  + esce
|       |       |
to  + quiet  +  n.
```

acquiescence 〔 ˌækwɪˈɛsn̩s 〕 *n.* 默許;默認;順從
acquiescent 〔 ˌækwɪˈɛsn̩t 〕 *adj.* 默許的;默認的;順從的

485   quit = free ; release (自由的;釋放)

* 古法文 *quite* (= *free* ; *clear*) ,*quite* (= *release*) 。

quit[2] 〔 kwɪt 〕 *v.* 停止;放棄;辭職;離開
quittance 〔 ˈkwɪtn̩s 〕 *n.* 免除;赦免;收據;報答
quitter 〔 ˈkwɪtɚ 〕 *n.* 怕事者;懦夫;遇困難即罷手者
acquit[7] 〔 əˈkwɪt 〕 *v.* 宣告無罪;開釋;免除;還清 (債務等)

(使自由)《 *ac-* = *ad-* = to 》

acquittal 〔 əˈkwɪtl̩ 〕 *n.* 履行;盡責;付清;償還;開釋;不起訴

```
ac  + quitt +  al
|       |       |
to  +  free  +  n.
```

requite 〔 rɪˈkwaɪt 〕 *v.* 報答;酬謝;報復 (免除了又回來)

《 *re-* = back 》

requital 〔 rɪˈkwaɪtl̩ 〕 *n.* 報答;回報;報復
unrequited 〔 ˌʌnrɪˈkwaɪtɪd 〕 *adj.* 無回報的;無報復的《 *un-* = not 》

486   radi = ray (光線)   * 拉丁文 *radius* (= *ray*) 。

radium 〔 ˈredɪəm 〕 *n.* 鐳《 *-um* 拉丁字尾 》
radius[5] 〔 ˈredɪəs 〕 *n.* 半徑;範圍 (由中心所發的光能到達的範圍)
radial 〔 ˈredɪəl 〕 *adj.* 半徑的;放射狀的 (能夠發出光線的)

radiate[6] 〔'redɪ,et 〕 *v.* 發射；放出；輻射出　　*adj.* 發光的；輻射狀的

radiation[6] 〔,redɪ'eʃən 〕 *n.* 輻射；放射；輻射能

radiative 〔'redɪ,etɪv 〕 *adj.* 放射的；輻射的

radiator[6] 〔'redɪ,etɚ 〕 *n.* 發光體；放熱體；放熱器

radiant[6] 〔'redɪənt 〕 *adj.* 發光的；放熱的；輻射的　　*n.* 光點；輻射點

```
radi + ant
 |     |
ray  + adj.
```

radiance；**-ancy** 〔'redɪəns(ɪ) , -djəns(ɪ) 〕 *n.* 閃爍；發光

radio[1] 〔'redɪ,o 〕 *n.* 無線電報；無線電話；無線電廣播；收音機

radioactive[7] 〔,redɪo'æktɪv 〕 *adj.* 有輻射能的；放射性的

（主動輻射的）《*active* 主動的》

```
radio + act + ive
  |      |     |
ray   + act + adj.
```

radioactivity 〔,redɪo,æk'tɪvətɪ 〕 *n.* 放射性；放射現象

radiology 〔,redɪ'ɑlədʒɪ 〕 *n.* 放射學；應用輻射學；放射線科

《*logy* = study》

radiotelephone 〔,redɪo'tɛləfon 〕 *n.* 無線電話（機）

《*telephone* 電話機》

irradiate 〔 ɪ'redɪ,et 〕 *v.* 照耀；發出；照射（將光線投射在～上）

《*ir-* = *in-* = on》

```
ir + radi + ate
 |    |      |
on + ray  + v.
```

irradiation 〔,ɪredɪ'eʃən , ɪ,re- 〕 *n.* 發光；光線；照射

irradiant 〔 ɪ'redɪənt 〕 *adj.* 發光的；燦爛的

irradiance 〔 ɪ'redɪəns 〕 *n.* 發光；光輝；燦爛

487　**radic** = root（根）　* 拉丁文 *radix*（= root）。

radical[6]〔ˈrædɪkḷ〕adj. 根本的；急進的；【數學】根的
　n. 急進分子；【數學】根號（從根本的）
radicalism〔ˈrædɪkḷˌɪzm̩〕n. 急進；急進主義《-ism = 主義》
radicalize〔ˈrædɪkḷˌaɪz〕v. 使激進；使激烈化
radicalization〔ˌrædɪkḷaɪˈzeʃən〕n. 激進化；激烈化
radicand〔ˈrædəˌkænd〕n.【數學】被開方數（根號內的數字）
　《-and = -end = inside》
radicle〔ˈrædɪkḷ〕n.（植物的）小根；幼根《-le 表示小的字尾》

```
radic  +  le
  |       |
root   +  small
```

radish[5]〔ˈrædɪʃ〕n. 紅蘿蔔（很大的根部）
radix〔ˈredɪks〕n. 根；基數；詞根（屬於根本的）
deradicalize〔diˈrædɪkḷˌaɪz〕v. 使不急進（激進的相反）
　《de- = dis- = negative（否定）》

```
de    + radic +  al  + ize
 |        |      |      |
negative + root + adj. + v.
```

eradicate[7]〔ɪˈrædɪˌket〕v. 根除；撲滅（從根部拔起）《e- = ex- = out》
eradicable〔ɪˈrædɪkəbḷ〕adj. 可根絕的；可拔去的
eradication〔ɪˌrædɪˈkeʃən〕n. 根除；撲滅
eradicator〔ɪˈrædɪˌketɚ〕n. 除草器；根絕者

488　**rap** = snatch（奪取）

　* 拉丁文 *rapere*（= snatch 奪取；seize 抓住）；古法文 *ravir*
　（= seize）。〔變化型〕rav。

rape[7]〔rep〕n., v. 搶劫；破壞；強姦（勉強奪取）
rapist[7]〔ˈrepɪst〕n. 強姦者《-ist 表示人的名詞字尾》

rapacious〔rəˊpeʃəs〕adj. 強奪的；貪婪的

rapacity〔rəˊpæsətɪ〕n. 搶奪；貪婪；貪吃

rapid[2]〔ˊræpɪd〕adj. 迅速的；急促的　n.pl. 急灘；湍流（搶奪時的姿態）

rapidity〔rəˊpɪdətɪ〕n. 迅速；急促

```
rap  + id + ity
 |      |     |
snatch + adj. + n.
```

rapt〔ræpt〕adj. 狂喜的；恍惚迷離的（已被攫取的心靈）

rapture[7]〔ˊræptʃɚ〕n. 狂喜；恍惚

enrapt〔ɛnˊræpt〕adj. 狂喜的；神魂顛倒的《en- = make》

enrapture〔ɪnˊræptʃɚ, ɛn-〕v. 使狂喜；使恍惚

rapturous〔ˊræptʃərəs〕adj. 狂喜的

raptorial〔ræpˊtorɪəl, -ˊtɔr-〕adj. 猛禽類的　n. 猛禽（強取獵物的）

```
rapt  + or + ial
 |       |     |
snatch + n. + adj.
```

ravage[6]〔ˊrævɪdʒ〕v. 蹂躪；破壞　n. 蹂躪；破壞（搶奪而去）

raven[7]〔ˊrævən〕v. 捕食；掠奪（搶奪）

ravening〔ˊrævənɪŋ〕adj. 貪婪而飢餓的《-ing 形容詞字尾》

ravish[7]〔ˊrævɪʃ〕v. 強奪；強姦；使銷魂（搶奪）

ravishment〔ˊrævɪʃmənt〕n. 強奪；強姦；狂喜

489　ras , rad = scrape（刮掉；擦去）

* 拉丁文 *radere*（= scrape），過去分詞是 *rasus*。
〔變化型〕*raz , rasc*。

abrade〔əˊbred〕v. 擦掉；擦傷；磨損（刮掉）《ab- = away》

abradant〔əˊbredənt〕adj. 研磨用的；有磨擦性的（= *abrasive*）

abrase〔 ə'brez 〕v. 擦去；刮掉

abrasion〔 ə'breʒən 〕n. 磨擦；擦傷；磨損；剝蝕

abrasive[7]〔 ə'bresɪv 〕adj. 研磨的；磨擦的　n. 研磨料

erase[7]〔 ɪ'res 〕v. 擦掉；抹去；消除（從～中擦去）《e- = ex- = out of》

```
  e   +  rase
  |      |
out of + scrape
```

eras(e)able〔 ɪ'rezəbḷ 〕adj. 可擦掉的；可抹去的

eraser[2]〔 ɪ'resɚ 〕n. 橡皮擦；板擦

erasure〔 ɪ'reʒɚ 〕n. 抹去；擦掉《-ure 抽象名詞字尾》

raze[7]〔 rez 〕v.（從記憶中）消逝；忘卻；摧毀

razor[3]〔 'rezɚ 〕n. 剃刀；刮鬍刀

rascal[5]〔 'ræskḷ 〕n. 流氓；惡棍

rascality〔 ræs'kæləti 〕n. 流氓行為；壞事

rasp〔 ræsp 〕n. 粗銼刀；粗銼聲；刺耳聲　v. 用粗銼刀銼；
　發出刺耳聲《古代高地德語 raspon = scrape》

raspy〔 'ræspɪ 〕adj. 刺耳的；粗糙的

490　**rat** = reckon；reason（斷定；推理）

　　* 拉丁文 **reri**（ = *reckon*；*reason* ），**ratio**（ = *reckoning* ）。
　　〔變化型〕*ratio*。

ratify〔 'rætə,faɪ 〕v. 批准《-ify 動詞字尾》

ratio[5]〔 'reʃo 〕n. 比率；比例

ratiocinate〔 ,ræʃɪ'ɑsṇ,et 〕v. 推論；推理（試著找出理由）
　　《cin = 拉丁文 conari = try》

ratiocination〔 ,ræʃɪ,ɑsṇ'eʃən 〕n. 推理；推論；推斷

```
ratio  + cin + at(e) + ion
  |       |      |      |
reason + try  +  v.  +  n.
```

字根 radic~rur

ration[7] 〔'reʃən 〕 n. 定額；定量；配給（量）；配額食物
rational[6] 〔'ræʃənḷ 〕 adj. 理性的；講道理的；合理的
rationale 〔ˌræʃə'næl 〕 n. 理論；理論基礎；原理
rationalism 〔'ræʃənḷˌɪzəm 〕 n. 唯理論；理性主義《 -ism = 主義》
rationalist 〔'ræʃənḷɪst 〕 n. 唯理論者；理性主義者
rationality 〔ˌræʃə'nælətɪ 〕 n. 理性；合理
rationalize 〔'ræʃənḷˌaɪz 〕 v. 使合於理性；使合理化；
用理論來說明

```
ratio  +  nal  +  ize
  |        |       |
reason  +  adj.  +  v.
```

rationalization 〔ˌræʃənəlɪ'zeʃən 〕 n. 合理化；【數學】有理化
irrational[7] 〔 ɪ'ræʃənḷ 〕 adj. 不合理的；無理性的
《 ir- = in- = not》
irrationality 〔 ɪˌræʃə'nælətɪ 〕 n. 不合理；無理性；無知

491   rect = right；straight（正確的；直的）

* 拉丁文 *rectus*（ = right；straight）。

rectal 〔'rɛktḷ 〕 adj. 直腸的
rectangle[2] 〔'rɛktæŋgḷ 〕 n. 矩形（正確的角 → 直角）《*angle* 角》
rectify[7] 〔'rɛktəˌfaɪ 〕 v. 修正；矯正；精餾；整流（使正確）
《 -ify = make》

```
rect  +  ify
  |       |
right  +  make
```

rectifiable 〔'rɛktəˌfaɪəbḷ 〕 adj. 可修正的；可精餾的；可整流的
rectifier 〔'rɛktəˌfaɪɚ 〕 n. 修正者；矯正器；整流器；精餾器
rectilineal 〔ˌrɛktə'lɪnɪəl 〕 adj. 成直線的（完全筆直的）

rectitude〔'rɛktə,tjud , -tud〕n. 誠實;正直(正確的事物)
《 *-itude* 抽象名詞字尾》

```
rect  +  itude
 |         |
right  +   n.
```

rector〔'rɛktɚ〕n.(英美聖公會的)教區牧師;(天主教耶穌會的)神學院院長;(某些學校的)校長(矯正人心的人)

rectum〔'rɛktəm〕= straight intestine n. 直腸《 *-um* 拉丁字尾》

correct[1]〔kə'rɛkt〕v. 改正;校正;醫治 adj. 正確的;適當的(改正~)《*cor-* = *con-* = with》

correction[7]〔kə'rɛkʃən〕n. 改正;修正

correctitude〔kə'rɛktə,tjud〕n. 品行端正;適宜

```
cor  +  rect  +  itude
 |        |        |
with  +  right  +  n.
```

corrective〔kə'rɛktɪv〕adj. 改正的;矯正的;(藥)中和的

corrector〔kə'rɛktɚ〕n. 改正者;矯正者;中和劑

direct[1]〔də'rɛkt , daɪ-〕v. 指導;指引 adj. 直接的;坦白的
《*di-* = *dis-* = apart》

direction[2]〔də'rɛkʃən , daɪ-〕n. 指導;說明;方向

directive[7]〔də'rɛktɪv〕adj. 指揮的;指導的

```
di  +  rect  +  ive
 |       |       |
apart  +  straight  +  adj.
```

director[2]〔də'rɛktɚ , daɪ-〕n. 管理者;指揮者;導演

directory[6]〔də'rɛktərɪ , daɪ-〕n. 人名住址簿;指南 adj. 指導的

erect[5]〔ɪ'rɛkt〕v. 建立;豎立 adj. 直立的;豎起的(筆直向上的)
《*e-* = *ex-* = out;up》

erectile〔ɪ'rɛktɪl〕adj. 可建立的;勃起性的《 *-ile* 形容詞字尾》

```
e  +  rect  +  ile
|       |       |
out , up  +  straight  +  adj.
```

erection[7] 〔 ɪˋrɛkʃən 〕 *n.* (使) 直立；豎立；建築物

erectness 〔 ɪˋrɛktnɪs 〕 *n.* 垂直

erector 〔 ɪˋrɛktɚ 〕 *n.* 建立者；設立者

escort[5] 〔 *n.* ˋɛskɔrt *v.* ɪˋskɔrt 〕 *n.* 護衛；護花使者　*v.* 護衛；護航
　（ 中途完全不出差錯地直接送到 ）《*es-* = *ex-* = out》

incorrect[7] 〔 ͵ɪnkəˋrɛkt 〕 *adj.* 不正確的；錯誤的

indirect[7] 〔 ͵ɪndəˋrɛkt 〕 *adj.* 間接的；迂迴的

492　**reg** = king；rule（國王；統治）

　　　　　* 拉丁文 *rex*（ = *king* ），*regere*（ = *rule* ）。

regal[7] 〔 ˋrigḷ 〕 *adj.* 帝王的；華麗的

regalia 〔 rɪˋgelɪə , -ljə 〕 *n.* 王權；王權的標幟

regality 〔 riˋgælətɪ 〕 *n.* 王權；王土

regent 〔 ˋridʒənt 〕 *n., adj.* 攝政（ 的 ）（ 代替國王統治的 ）

regency 〔 ˋridʒənsɪ 〕 *n.* 攝政職位；攝政政治（ 期間 ）

regicide 〔 ˋrɛdʒə͵saɪd 〕 *n.* 弒君；弒君者（ 殺掉國王 ）《*cide* = cut》

```
regi + cide
 |      |
king + cut
```

regime[6] 〔 rɪˋʒim 〕 *n.* 政體；體制

regiment[7] 〔 ˋrɛdʒəmənt 〕 *n.* 統治；（ 軍 ）團

Regina 〔 rɪˋdʒaɪnə 〕 *n.* 女王《 *-a* 拉丁文的女性名詞字尾》

Regius 〔 ˋridʒɪəs 〕 *adj.* 國王的

region[2] 〔 ˋridʒən 〕 *n.* 區域；領域（ 統治的地區 ）

realm[5] 〔 rɛlm 〕 *n.* 王國；領域（ 國王統治的地區 ）

```
reg + ion
 |     |
rule + n.
```

regnal 〔 ˋrɛgnəl 〕 *adj.* 國的；朝的；國王的

regnant 〔 ˋrɛgnənt 〕 *adj.* 統治的；流行的

reign[5] 〔 ren 〕 *n.* 統治（ 時代 ）　*v.* 統治；盛行

regular[2] 〔'rɛgjələ˞〕*adj.* 有規則的；定期的；正常的；正規的
　　n. 正規兵；老顧客（完全受支配的）

regularity[7] 〔ˌrɛgjə'lærətɪ〕*n.* 規則；定期

regulate[4] 〔'rɛgjəˌlet〕*v.* 管理；規定；調整

regulation[4] 〔ˌrɛgjə'leʃən〕*n.* 規定；條例　　*adj.* 標準的；正規的

irregular[7] 〔ɪ'rɛgjələ˞〕*adj.* 不規則的；不合常規的《*ir-* = *in-* = not》

```
ir  +  regul  +  ar
│        │        │
not  +  rule  +  adj.
```

royal[2] 〔'rɔɪəl〕*adj.* 王室的；皇家的；莊嚴的

royalty[6] 〔'rɔɪəltɪ〕*n.* 王族；王國；上演稅；版稅

rigid[5] 〔'rɪdʒɪd〕*adj.* 嚴格的；僵硬的（如王者一般嚴屬的）

```
rig  +  id
│        │
rule  +  adj.
```

rigidity 〔rɪ'dʒɪdətɪ〕*n.* 堅硬；剛直；嚴格

rigo(u)r 〔'rɪgə˞〕*n.* 嚴格；嚴酷；嚴密

rigo(u)rous[6] 〔'rɪgərəs〕*adj.* 嚴格的；嚴屬的；嚴密的

493　　**ren** = kidney（腎）　　* 拉丁文 *renes*（= *kidneys*）。

renal 〔'rinl̩〕*adj.* 腎臟的；關於腎臟的

adrenal 〔æd'rinl̩〕*adj.* 腎上腺的　　*n.* 腎上腺《*ad-* = near》

adrenalin[7] 〔æd'rɛnl̩ɪn〕*n.* 腎上腺素

adrenalectomy 〔əˌdrinə'lɛktəmɪ〕*n.* 腎上腺切除術《*tom* = cut》

adrenergic 〔ˌædrə'nɝdʒɪk〕*adj.* 腎上腺素的；（藥理作用）類似
　　腎上腺素的《*erg* = work》

adrenochrome 〔ə'drinəˌkrom〕*n.* 腎上腺素紅《*chrom* = color》

adrenocortical 〔əˌdrino'kɔrtəkəl〕*adj.* 腎上腺皮質的
　　《拉丁文 *cortex* = outer layer》

494 rept = creep (爬行)

* 拉丁文 *repere*（= *creep*），過去分詞為 *reptus*。

reptant〔'rɛptənt〕*adj.* 匍匐的；爬行的；蔓延的

reptile[5]〔'rɛptḷ〕*adj.* 卑鄙的；爬行的 *n.* 卑鄙的人；爬蟲類
（在地上爬的）

reptilian〔rɛp'tɪlɪən〕*adj.* 爬蟲類的；卑鄙的 *n.* 爬蟲類

surreptitious[7]〔,sɝəp'tɪʃəs〕*adj.* 祕密的；偷偷的；鬼祟的
（從下面爬過去 → 偷偷爬過去）《*sur- = sub- =* under》

495 rhin = nose (鼻子)

* 希臘文 *rhis* , *rhin*（= *nose*）。

rhinitis〔raɪ'naɪtɪs〕*n.* 鼻炎《 *-itis =* inflammation（發炎）》

rhinoceros[5]〔raɪ'nɑsərəs〕*n.* 犀牛

```
rhino  +  ceros
  |         |
nose   +   horn
```

rhinology〔raɪ'nɑlədʒɪ〕*n.* 鼻科學《*logy =* study》

rhinoplasty〔'raɪnə,plæstɪ〕*n.* 鼻成形術《*plas =* form》

rhinoscope〔'raɪnə,skop〕*n.* 鼻鏡《*scope* 表示「觀察～的器具」》

496 rhiz = root (根)

* 希臘文 *rhiza*（= *root*）。

rhizogenesis〔,raɪzə'dʒɛnəsɪs〕*n.* 生根；根之生長

rhizoma〔raɪ'zomə〕*n.* 根莖

rhizomatic〔,raɪzə'mætɪk〕*adj.* 根莖的；如根莖的；地下莖狀的

rhizophagous〔raɪ'zɑfəgəs〕*adj.* 以根為食的；吃根的
《*phag =* eat》

rhizopod〔'raɪzə,pɑd〕*n.* 根足類動物《*pod =* foot》

497　**rid , ris** = laugh（笑）

> * 拉丁文 *ridere*（= *laugh*），過去分詞為 *risus*。

ridicule[6]〔ˈrɪdɪˌkjul〕*n. , v.* 譏笑；嘲弄

ridiculous[5]〔rɪˈdɪkjələs〕*adj.* 可笑的；荒謬的

risible〔ˈrɪzəbḷ〕*adj.* 能笑的；愛笑的；可笑的

risibility〔ˌrɪzəˈbɪlətɪ〕*n.* 笑的能力；笑的傾向與性質

deride〔dɪˈraɪd〕*v.* 嘲笑；愚弄（不懷好意地笑）《*de-* = *dis-* = away》

```
de  +  ride
 |      |
away +  laugh
```

derision[7]〔dɪˈrɪʒən〕*n.* 嘲笑；愚弄；笑柄

derisive〔dɪˈraɪsɪv〕*adj.* 嘲笑的；愚弄的；可笑的

derisory〔dɪˈraɪsərɪ〕*adj.* 嘲笑的；愚弄的；可笑的（= *derisive*）

498　**rip , riv** = stream；bank（河流；河岸）

> * 拉丁文 *rivus*（= *stream*），*ripa*（= *bank*）。

riparian〔rɪˈpɛrɪən〕*adj.* 河岸（上）的　*n.* 河岸土地所有人；
河邊居民

river[1]〔ˈrɪvɚ〕*n.* 河流

arrive[2]〔əˈraɪv〕*v.* 抵達（到岸邊）《*ar-* = *ad-* = to》

derive[6]〔dəˈraɪv〕*v.* 獲得；起源（從河裡引水）《*de-* = off》

derivation〔ˌdɛrəˈveʃən〕*n.* 引申；起源；衍生物

```
de +  riv  + ation
 |     |      |
off + river +  n.
```

rival[5]〔ˈraɪvḷ〕*n.* 對手；敵手　*adj.* 競爭的　*v.* 與…競爭
《拉丁文 *rivalis* 的意思是「共用同一條河流的人」》

outrival〔aʊtˈraɪvḷ〕*v.* 在競爭中勝過（對手）《*out-* = beyond》

499 rob = strong（強壯的）

> * 拉丁文 *robur*（= *oak*；*strength*），*roborare*（= *make strong*）。

robust[5]〔ro'bʌst〕*adj.* 強健的；堅定的；堅固耐用的
roborant〔'rɑbərənt〕*adj.* 使身體強壯的；增強體力的
  n. 強壯劑
corroborate[7]〔kə'rɑbə,ret〕*v.* 確認；證實（完全鞏固）
  《*cor-* = *com-* = wholly》

$$
\begin{array}{ccc}
\text{cor} & + \text{robor} + & \text{ate} \\
| & | & | \\
wholly & + strong + & v.
\end{array}
$$

corroboration〔kə,rɑbə'reʃən〕*n.* 證實；進一步的證據
corroborative〔kə'rɑbə,retɪv〕*adj.* 使更加確鑿的；
  確證（性）的

500 rode , ros = gnaw（咬）

> * 拉丁文 *rodere*（= *gnaw*）。〔變化型〕*ros*。

rodent[7]〔'rodn̩t〕*n.* 齧齒類　*adj.* 齧齒類動物的；咬的；嚙的
rodenticide〔ro'dɛntə,saɪd〕*n.* 滅鼠藥《*cide* = cut》

$$
\begin{array}{ccc}
\text{rod} & + \text{ent} + & \text{icide} \\
| & | & | \\
gnaw & + n. + & cut
\end{array}
$$

corrode[7]〔kə'rod〕*v.* 腐蝕；侵蝕（徹底地咬）
  《*cor-* = *com-* = thoroughly》
corrosion[7]〔kə'roʒən〕*n.* 腐蝕；侵蝕；（心神的）損傷

$$
\begin{array}{ccc}
\text{cor} & + \text{ros} + & \text{ion} \\
| & | & | \\
thoroughly & + gnaw + & n.
\end{array}
$$

corrosive〔kə'rosɪv〕*adj.* 腐蝕的；侵蝕的　*n.* 腐蝕性物質

erode[6] 〔 ɪˈrod 〕 *v.* 腐蝕；侵蝕（咬去，咬掉）《*e-* = *ex-* = out》

erosion[7] 〔 ɪˈroʒən 〕 *n.* 腐蝕；侵蝕；沖蝕

erosive 〔 ɪˈrosɪv 〕 *adj.* 腐蝕的；侵蝕的

501　**rog** = ask（詢問；要求）　　* 拉丁文 *rogare*（= *ask*）。

rogation 〔 roˈgeʃən 〕 *n.* 法案（的提出）；祈禱；祈願

abrogate 〔ˈæbrəˌget 〕 *v.* 廢止；取消（要求除去）《*ab-* = away》

abrogation 〔ˌæbrəˈgeʃən 〕 *n.* 廢止；取消

arrogance[7] 〔ˈærəgəns 〕 *n.* 傲慢；自大（無禮地向別人要求）

　　《*ar-* = *ad-* = to》

```
ar  +  rog  +  ance
|       |       |
to  +  ask  +   n.
```

arrogant[6] 〔ˈærəgənt 〕 *adj.* 傲慢的；自大的

arrogate 〔ˈærəˌget 〕 *v.* 僭越；霸佔

arrogation 〔ˌærəˈgeʃən 〕 *n.* 霸佔；越權；橫暴

derogate 〔ˈdɛrəˌget 〕 *v.* 貶損；減損（要求下來）《*de-* = down》

derogatory 〔 dɪˈragəˌtori , -ˌtɔrɪ 〕 *adj.* 毀損（名譽）的；貶抑的

interrogate[7] 〔 ɪnˈtɛrəˌget 〕 *v.* 訊問；審問；質問（在～之間問）

　　《*inter-* = between》

```
inter  +  rog  +  ate
  |        |       |
between +  ask  +   v.
```

interrogation[7] 〔 ɪnˌtɛrəˈgeʃən 〕 *n.* 訊問；審問；質問；疑問

interrogative 〔ˌɪntəˈragətɪv 〕 *adj.* 疑惑的；疑問的　 *n.* 疑問詞

interrogator 〔 ɪnˈtɛrəˌgetɚ 〕 *n.* 訊問者；質詢者

interrogatory 〔ˌɪntəˈragəˌtori 〕 *adj.* 質問的；疑問的

prerogative 〔 prɪˈragətɪv 〕 *n.* 特權；帝王的特權　 *adj.* 有特權的

　　（先要求）《*pre-* = before》

502 roll , rol = roll (滾動)   * 古法文 *rolle* (= *roll*) 。

roll[1] 〔 rol 〕 *v.* 滾動　 *n.* 轉動；卷軸；名冊；一卷

role[2] 〔 rol 〕 *n.* 角色；職責（演員的腳本寫在羊皮紙卷上）

rollback[7] 〔'rol,bæk 〕 *n.* (物價、利率等的) 回降；擊退；回滾

control[2] 〔 kən'trol 〕 *v., n.* 控制；管理（核帳時要比對帳冊上的記錄）
　　《*contr(a)-* = against》

controller[2] 〔 kən'trolə 〕 *n.* 管理者；審計員

enrol(l)[5] 〔 ɪn'rol 〕 *v.* 登記；參加（記在名冊中）《*en-* = in》

logroll 〔'lɔg,rol 〕 *v.* 相互吹捧；互投贊成票促使（法案等）通過
　　（互相幫對方滾木頭蓋房子）《*log* 圓木》

503 rot = wheel ; turn (輪子；旋轉)

　　　　* 拉丁文 *rota* (= *wheel*)，*rotare* (= *turn*)。

rota 〔'rotə 〕 *n.* 〔英〕勤務輪值（表）

rotary 〔'rotərɪ 〕 *adj.* 旋轉的；輪流的

rotate[6] 〔'rotet 〕 *v.* 旋轉；循環；交替

rotation[6] 〔 ro'teʃən 〕 *n.* 旋轉；循環；輪流

rotational 〔 ro'teʃənḷ 〕 *adj.* 旋轉的；輪流的；交替的；循環的

```
rot  + ation + al
 |       |      |
wheel +  n.  + adj.
```

rotator 〔 ro'tetə 〕 *n.* 旋轉者；迴轉機

rotatory 〔'rotə,torɪ 〕 *adj.* 旋轉的；迴轉的；循環的

rotor[7] 〔'rotə 〕 *n.* 旋轉輪；旋轉翼

rotund 〔 ro'tʌnd 〕 *adj.* 圓胖的；聲音宏亮的（像輪子一樣）
　　《*-und* = like》

```
rot  + und
 |      |
wheel + like
```

字根 radic~rur

rotunda〔roˈtʌndə〕*n.*（有圓頂的）圓形建築物；圓廳

rotundity〔roˈtʌndətɪ〕*n.* 圓形；（聲音）宏亮

dextrorotatory〔ˌdɛkstrəˈrotəˌtɔrɪ〕*adj.* 右旋的
  《*dextro* = right hand》

levorotatory〔ˌlivoˈrotəˌtɔrɪ〕*adj.* 左旋的《*levo* = left hand》

roulette[7]〔ruˈlɛt〕*n.* 輪盤賭；（滾壓騎縫線或騎縫孔的）滾輪
  《*-ette* 表示小的名詞字尾》

504　rrhea = flow（流）

　*希臘文 **rhein**（= *flow*），**rhoia**（= *a flowing*）。

rheometer〔riˈɑmətɚ〕*n.* 流變計；血流速度計；電流計
  《*meter* 計量器》

rheostat〔ˈriəˌstæt〕*n.* 變阻器

catarrh〔kəˈtɑr〕*n.* 卡他；黏膜炎《*cata-* = down》

diarrhea[7]〔ˌdaɪəˈriə〕*n.* 腹瀉《*dia-* = through》

gonorrhea〔ˌgɑnəˈriə〕*n.* 淋病《希臘文 *gonos* = seed（種子）》

　【解說】　原認為此病排出膿液中含精子，故名。

hemorrhoids[7]〔ˈhɛməˌrɔɪdz〕*n.pl.* 痔瘡《*hemo* = blood》

menorrhea〔ˌmɛnəˈriə〕*n.* 月經；月經過多

```
meno  +  rrhea
  |        |
month  +  flow
```

pyorrhea〔ˌpaɪəˈriə〕*n.* 膿溢；牙槽膿溢《希臘文 *puon* = pus（膿）》

505　rud = crude（天然的；粗糙的）

　*拉丁文 **rudis**（= *crude*；*unlearned*）。

rude[2]〔rud〕*adj.* 無禮的；粗暴的；粗陋的；野蠻的

rudiment〔ˈrudəmənt〕*n.*（*pl.*）基礎；初步
rudimental〔͵rudəˈmɛntl̩〕*adj.* 基本的；早期的；未發展的
　（ = *rudimentary*）

```
rudi  +  ment  +  al
 |        |        |
crude  +   n.   +  adj.
```

rudimentary[7]〔͵rudəˈmɛntərɪ〕*adj.* 基本的；初期的；未發展的
erudite〔ˈɛrʊ͵daɪt〕*adj.* 博學的；飽學的（脫離無知狀態）
　《*e-* = *ex-* = out；*-ite* 形容詞字尾》
erudition〔͵ɛrʊˈdɪʃən〕*n.* 學識；博學；飽學

506　**rupt** = break（破裂）　* 拉丁文 *rumpere*（ = *break*）。

rupture[7]〔ˈrʌptʃɚ〕*n.* 破裂；絕交　*v.* 破裂；斷絕
abrupt[5]〔əˈbrʌpt〕*adj.* 突然的；出其不意的（突然破裂的）
abruption〔əˈbrʌpʃən〕*n.* 突然裂開

```
ab  +  rupt  +  ion
 |      |        |
off  + break  +  n.
```

bankrupt[4]〔ˈbæŋkrʌpt〕*n.* 破產者　*adj.* 破產的　*v.* 使破產
　（銀行倒閉的）
bankruptcy[7]〔ˈbæŋkrʌptsɪ, -rəptsɪ〕*n.* 破產；倒閉；（聲望、
　地位等的）喪失
corrupt[5]〔kəˈrʌpt〕*adj.* 腐敗的；貪污的　*v.* 使腐敗；使墮落
　（完全受損）《*cor-* = *com-* = wholly》
corruption[6]〔kəˈrʌpʃən〕*n.* 腐化；墮落；貪污
disrupt[7]〔dɪsˈrʌpt〕*v.* 使破裂；使中斷
　（破裂分散）《*dis-* = apart》
disruption[7]〔dɪsˈrʌpʃən〕*n.* 分裂；中斷

```
dis  +  rupt
 |       |
apart  + break
```

erupt[5] 〔 ɪ'rʌpt 〕 v. 爆發；噴出；出疹；長牙（破殼而出）
《*e-* = *ex-* = out》

eruption[6] 〔 ɪ'rʌpʃən 〕 n. 爆發；出疹；噴出；長牙

incorrupt 〔 ˌɪnkə'rʌpt 〕 adj. 不腐敗的；清廉的《*in-* = not》

incorruptible 〔 ˌɪnkə'rʌptəbḷ 〕 adj. 廉潔的；不貪污受賄的

```
in  +  cor  +  rupt  +  ible
 |      |       |       |
not + wholly + break +  adj.
```

interrupt[3] 〔 ˌɪntə'rʌpt 〕 v. 打斷；妨礙；插嘴（割入其間的）
《*inter-* = between》

interruption[4] 〔 ˌɪntə'rʌpʃən 〕 n. 打岔；中斷

irrupt 〔 ɪ'rʌpt 〕 v. 突然衝入；闖入（破除界限進入其中）
《*ir-* = *in-* = in》

irruption 〔 ɪ'rʌpʃən 〕 n. 衝入；闖入；侵入

route[4] 〔 rut , raʊt 〕 n. 道路；路線（樹林的裂口）

routine[3] 〔 ru'tin 〕 n. 例行公事；慣例；常規　 adj. 日常的；
慣例的；例行的（事情的脈絡）

507　**rur , rus** = country（鄉下）

* 拉丁文 *rus , rur-*（ = *open land ; country*）。

rural[4] 〔 'rʊrəl 〕 adj. 鄉村的；農村的；有關農業的

rurality 〔 rʊ'ræləti 〕 n. 田園生活；田園風味

ruralize 〔 'rʊrəlˌaɪz 〕 v. 田園化；農村化；過田園生活

```
rur    +  al  +  ize
 |         |      |
country  + adj. +  v.
```

rustic[7] 〔 'rʌstɪk 〕 adj. 鄉村的；農村的；樸素的；粗野的

rusticate 〔 'rʌstɪˌket 〕 v. 去鄉村；過鄉村生活

rustication 〔 ˌrʌstɪ'keʃən 〕 n. 送往鄉間；鄉居生活；停學（處分）

rusticity 〔 rʌs'tɪsəti 〕 n. 田園風味；田園生活；粗野；質樸

508 sacr , sanct = sacred (神聖的)

* 拉丁文 **sacer** (= sacred) ，**sacrare** (= make sacred) ；
sancire (= make sacred) ，**sanctus** (= holy) 。
〔變化型〕secr 。

sacred[5] 〔'sekrɪd 〕*adj.* 神聖的；不可侵犯的

sacrifice[4] 〔'sækrə,faɪs , -,faɪz 〕*n.* 犧牲；獻身　*v.* 犧牲；獻祭
（ 成爲神聖的東西 ）《*ifice* = make》

```
sacr  +  ifice
  |        |
sacred  +  make
```

sacrilege[7] 〔'sækrəlɪdʒ 〕*n.* 褻瀆神聖（ 由聖地奪取 ）《*lege* = gather》

sacrilegious 〔,sækrɪ'lɪdʒəs 〕*adj.* 褻瀆神聖的；盜竊聖物的

sacrosanct 〔'sækro,sæŋkt 〕*adj.* 神聖不可侵犯的 (比神聖更
神聖的)

sacrament 〔'sækrəmənt 〕*n.* 聖禮；聖餐；象徵

sacramental 〔,sækrə'mɛntḷ 〕*adj.* 聖禮的；聖餐的；神聖的；
象徵的

saint[5] 〔 sent 〕*n.* 聖徒；聖者　*v.* 列爲聖徒

sanctify 〔'sæŋktə,faɪ 〕*v.* 使神聖；使聖潔（ 成爲神聖）《 *-ify* = make》

```
sanct  +  ify
  |        |
sacred  +  make
```

sanctification 〔,sæŋktəfə'keʃən 〕*n.* 神聖化

sanctimony 〔'sæŋktə,monɪ 〕*n.* 僞裝的神聖氣槪；僞裝的虔誠

sanctimonious 〔,sæŋktə'monɪəs 〕*adj.* 僞裝神聖的；僞裝虔誠的

sanction[6] 〔'sæŋkʃən 〕*n.* 批准；制裁　*v.* 批准；授權（ 神聖的裁奪 ）

sanctity 〔'sæŋktətɪ 〕*n.* 神聖；神聖之物（ 神聖之事 ）

sanctuary[6] 〔'sæŋktʃu,ɛrɪ 〕*n.* 神殿；庇護（ 所 ）；聖堂
（ 神聖的場所 ）《 *-ary* 表示場所的名詞字尾》

consecrate 〔'kɑnsɪ,kret 〕 *v.* 奉爲神聖；供獻（使神聖）

《*con-* = with》

```
con  +  secr  + ate
 |       |       |
with  + sucred  + v.
```

consecration 〔,kɑnsɪ'kreʃən 〕 *n.* 貢獻；聖職授任；奉爲神聖

desecrate 〔'dɛsɪ,kret 〕 *v.* 褻瀆；污辱（脫離神聖）

《*de-* = *dis-* = away》

desecration 〔,dɛsɪ'kreʃən 〕 *n.* 褻瀆神聖

execrate 〔'ɛksɪ,kret 〕 *v.* 咒罵；憎惡（不屬神聖的東西）《*ex-* = out》

```
ex  +  ecr  + ate
 |      |      |
out  + sacred + v.
```

execration 〔,ɛksɪ'kreʃən 〕 *n.* 詛咒；憎惡；被詛咒的人或物

execrable 〔'ɛksɪkrəbḷ 〕 *adj.* 討厭的；可恨的；非常差的

obsecrate 〔'ɑbsɪ,kret 〕 *v.* 懇求；籲請（因爲是神聖的）

《*ob-* = on account of》

obsecration 〔,ɑbsɪ'kreʃən 〕 *n.* 懇求；請願

---

509 sal = salt（鹽）   * 拉丁文 *sal*（ = *salt*）。

salad[2] 〔'sæləd 〕 *n.* 沙拉；生菜食品；涼拌食品

salary[4] 〔'sælərɪ 〕 *n.* 薪水（源於古羅馬發鹽給士兵做爲薪餉）

salaried 〔'sælərɪd 〕 *adj.* 支領薪水的；有薪水的

salify 〔'sælə,faɪ 〕 *v.* 使有鹽；使和鹽化合

saliferous 〔 sə'lɪfərəs 〕 *adj.* 含鹽的；產鹽的《 *-ferous* = bearing》

saline[7] 〔'selaɪn 〕 *adj.* 鹽的；含鹽的；鹹的《 *-ine* 形容詞字尾》

salina 〔 sə'laɪnə 〕 *n.* 鹽水湖；鹽沼《 *-a* 名詞字尾》

```
sal  + in(e) + a
 |      |       |
salt  + adj.  + n.
```

salinity〔 sə'lɪnətɪ 〕*n.* 鹽分；鹽度

salinize〔'sælə,naɪz 〕*v.*（使土）鹽分過多；使鹽漬化

salt[1]〔 sɔlt 〕*n.* 鹽；食鹽；提神物；刺激　*adj.* 鹹的；食鹽的　*v.* 加鹽；用鹽醃

salted〔'sɔltɪd 〕*adj.* 鹽醃的；鹹的；老練的；經驗豐富的

salter〔'sɔltə 〕*n.* 製鹽業者；鹽商；製鹽工人；醃漬業者

saltern〔'sɔltən 〕*n.* 鹽田；製鹽場《 *-ern* 表示場所的名詞字尾》

```
salt  +  ern
 |        |
salt  +  place
```

desalt〔 di'sɔlt 〕*v.* 脫鹽；淡化（海水、鹽水）（除去鹽分）
《 *de-* = *dis-* = away》

desalination〔 di,sælə'neʃən 〕*n.* 除鹽作用；脫鹽

510　**sal , sil , sult** = leap（跳）

　　* 拉丁文 ***salire***（ = *leap*）。〔變化型〕*sil , sult*。

salient〔'selɪənt 〕*adj.* 顯著的；突出的；跳躍的　*n.* 突出部分

salience ; -ency〔'selɪəns(ɪ) 〕*n.* 突出（部分）；特徵

sally〔'sælɪ 〕*n.* 突擊；突發；遠足旅行　*v.* 突擊；出發旅行
（跳出去）

salmon[5]〔'sæmən 〕*n.* 鮭；橙紅色（飛魚）

saltant〔'sæltənt 〕*adj.* 跳舞的；跳躍的

saltation〔 sæl'teʃən 〕*n.* 跳躍；突變；跳舞

assail[7]〔 ə'sel 〕*v.* 攻擊；責罵（猛撲上去）《 *as-* = *ad-* = to》

assault[5]〔 ə'sɔlt 〕*n. , v.* 攻擊；襲擊；肉搏

desultory〔'dɛsḷ,torɪ , -,tɔrɪ 〕*adj.* 無秩序的；散漫的（跳離開來）
《 *de-* = off》

```
de  +  sult  +  ory
 |       |       |
off  +  leap  +  adj.
```

exult〔 ɪg'zʌlt , ɛg- 〕*v.* 狂喜;歡騰(超出歡喜的範圍)

《*ex-* = out》

exultation〔 ͵ɛgzʌl'teʃən , ͵ɛksʌl- 〕*n.* 狂喜;歡騰

insult[4]〔 *v.* ɪn'sʌlt *n.* 'ɪnsʌlt 〕*v.* 侮辱   *n.* 傲慢無禮;侮辱

(猛撲上去)《*in-* = on》

in + sult
on + leap

resile〔 rɪ'zaɪl 〕*v.* 跳回;彈回;退縮(跳回來)《*re-* = back》

resilient[7]〔 rɪ'zɪlɪənt 〕*adj.* 有彈性的;活潑的

resilience;**-ency**〔 rɪ'zɪlɪəns(ɪ) 〕*n.* 彈性;輕快

result[2]〔 rɪ'zʌlt 〕*v.* 產生;終歸   *n.* 結果;效果

(反轉過來發生影響)《*re-* = back》

511 salut , san = health (健康)

> * 拉丁文 *sanare*(= *heal* 治療),過去分詞是 *sanatus*;
> *sanus*(= *healthy*),*sanitas*(= *health*);*salus* , *salut-*
> (= *health*),*salutare*(= *greet*)。〔變化型〕*salub*。

salute[5]〔 sə'lut 〕*v. , n.* 敬禮;致敬(祈求對方的健康)

salutatory〔 sə'lutə͵torɪ , -͵tɔrɪ 〕*n. , adj.* 致敬(的);

祝賀(的)

salutation〔 ͵sæljə'teʃən 〕*n.* 致意;敬禮

salutary〔 'sæljə͵tɛrɪ 〕*adj.* 有益的;有益健康的

salubrious〔 sə'lubrɪəs , sə'lju- 〕*adj.* 有益健康的

salubrity〔 sə'lubrətɪ 〕*n.* 有益健康

sane[6]〔 sen 〕*adj.* 神志清明的;健全的

sanity[7]〔 'sænətɪ 〕*n.* 心智健全;穩健

insane[7]〔 ɪn'sen 〕*adj.* 瘋狂的;患精神病的(精神不健全的)

《*in-* = not》

insanity[7] 〔ɪnˈsænətɪ〕 *n.* 瘋狂；神經錯亂

```
in  +  san  +  ity
|       |       |
not + health +  n.
```

sanative〔ˈsænətɪv〕 *adj.* 治療疾病的；有益健康的

sanatory〔ˈsænəˌtorɪ , -ˌtɔrɪ〕 *adj.* 有益健康的；治療的
（治療後回復健康）

sanatorium〔ˌsænəˈtorɪəm , -ˈtɔr-〕 *n.* 療養院
（＝〔美〕*sanitarium*〔ˌsænəˈtɛrɪəm〕）（治療疾病的地方）
《-*um* 表示場所的名詞字尾》

```
sanat + ori + um
|        |      |
heal  + adj. +  n.
```

sanitary[7] 〔ˈsænəˌtɛrɪ〕 *adj.* 衛生的（對健康有益的）

sanitate〔ˈsænətet〕 *v.* 使合衛生；添置衛生設備

sanitation[6] 〔ˌsænəˈteʃən〕 *n.* 衛生設備

sanitarian〔ˌsænəˈtɛrɪən , -ˈter-〕 *adj.* 衛生的 *n.* 衛生學家

insanitary〔ɪnˈsænəˌtɛrɪ〕 *adj.* 不衛生的《*in-* ＝ not》

512 sanguin ＝ blood（血）

*拉丁文 *sanguis* , *sanguin-*（＝ *blood*）。

sanguine〔ˈsæŋgwɪn〕 *adj.* 多血的；紅潤的；快活的；樂觀的
《-*ine* 形容詞字尾》

```
sangu + ine
|        |
blood + adj.
```

sanguinary〔ˈsæŋgwɪnˌɛrɪ〕 *adj.* 血腥的；嗜血的；殘暴的

sanguineous〔sæŋˈgwɪnɪəs〕 *adj.* 血的；血紅色的；多血的；
樂天的

sanguinity 〔 sæŋ'gwɪnətɪ 〕 *n.* 紅潤;快活;樂觀

consanguine 〔 kən'sæŋgwɪn 〕 *adj.* 同血緣的;同血親的;同族的

（相同血緣）《*con-* = together》

consanguinity 〔 ˌkɑnsæŋ'gwɪnətɪ 〕 *n.* 血親（關係）;血緣;親族

ensanguine 〔 ɛn'sæŋgwɪn 〕 *v.* 血染;血濺（使一片血淋淋）

《*en-* = make into》

513 sap = be wise;taste（聰明;品嚐）

* 拉丁文 *sapere*（= *be wise*;*taste*）。〔變化型〕*sip*,*sag*。

sapid 〔'sæpɪd 〕 *adj.* 美味的;有趣味的

sapient 〔'sepɪənt 〕 *adj.* 賢明的;睿智的;自以為聰明的

n. （史前的）智人

insipid[7] 〔 ɪn'sɪpɪd 〕 *adj.* 淡而無味的;枯燥無味的

```
in + sip + id
 |     |    |
not + taste + adj.
```

insipient 〔 ɪn'sɪpɪənt 〕 *adj.* 愚蠢的

sage[7] 〔 sedʒ 〕 *adj.* 賢明的 *n.* 聖人;聖賢

514 sat = enough（足夠的）

* 拉丁文 *satis*（= *enough*），*satiare*（= *fill full*;*satisfy*），
satur（= *sated* 膩的;*full*）。

sate[7] 〔 set 〕 *v.* 使充分滿足;使膩

satiate 〔 *v.* 'seʃɪˌet *adj.* 'seʃɪɪt 〕 *v.* 使飽;使滿足

adj. 滿足的;飽足的

satiation 〔 ˌseʃɪ'eʃən 〕 *n.* 飽滿

satiable 〔'seʃɪəbḷ,'seʃə- 〕 *adj.* 可使飽的

satiety 〔 sə'taɪətɪ,sæ- 〕 *n.* 生膩;飽滿

insatiable[7] 〔 ɪnˈseʃɪəbḷ 〕 *adj.* 不知足的；貪的《*in-* = not》

```
in  +  sati  +  able
|       |        |
not  +  full  +  adj.
```

insatiability 〔 ɪnˌseʃɪəˈbɪlətɪ , -ˌseʃə- 〕 *n.* 貪慾

insatiate 〔 ɪnˈseʃɪɪt 〕 *adj.* 不知足的

satire[7] 〔 ˈsætaɪr 〕 *n.* 諷刺；譏刺（偶爾在盛於各色盤中的菜餚中加入反胃的東西）

satisfy[2] 〔 ˈsætɪsˌfaɪ 〕 *v.* 使滿足；償還《 *-fy* = make》

satisfaction[4] 〔 ˌsætɪsˈfækʃən 〕 *n.* 滿足；償還

satisfactory[3] 〔 ˌsætɪsˈfæktərɪ 〕 *adj.* 滿意的；圓滿的

dissatisfy 〔 dɪsˈsætɪsˌfaɪ 〕 *v.* 使不滿足；使不滿意《*dis-* = not》

```
dis  +  satis  +  fy
|        |         |
not  +  full   +  v.
```

dissatisfaction[7] 〔 ˌdɪssætɪsˈfækʃən 〕 *n.* 不滿；不平

dissatisfactory 〔 ˌdɪssætɪsˈfæktərɪ 〕 *adj.* 令人不滿的；不能令人滿意的

saturate[7] 〔 *v.* ˈsætʃəˌret *adj.* ˈsætʃərɪt 〕 *v.* 浸；飽和；滲透 *adj.* 飽和的（滿出來）

saturation[7] 〔 ˌsætʃəˈreʃən 〕 *n.* 浸透；飽和

soil[1] 〔 sɔɪl 〕 *v.* 以青草餵（牛馬）（使家畜飽足）

515　**scal** = ladder（梯子）　* 拉丁文 *scala*（ = ladder ）。

scale[3] 〔 skel 〕 *v.* 用梯子攀登；爬越　*n.* 音階；比例尺；規模；尺；尺上的刻度

scalable 〔 ˈskeləbḷ 〕 *adj.* 可攀登的

scalar 〔 ˈskelɚ 〕 *adj.* 梯狀的；分等級的

escalade〔͵ɛskə'led〕*v.* 用梯攀登

escalate[6]〔'ɛskə͵let〕*v.*（使）逐步上升；（使）逐步增強；
（使）逐步擴大；乘自動扶梯爬登

escalator[4]〔'ɛskə͵letɚ〕*n.* 電扶梯

【解說】在美國搭電扶梯時，大家都會自動往右邊靠，好讓趕時間的
人走左邊。台灣的百貨公司也都設有電扶梯（**escalator**）和
電梯（**elevator**），要直接前往高樓層的人，就會搭乘電梯，
而想要一層一層逛的人，則會搭電扶梯。

de-escalate〔di'ɛskə͵let〕*v.* 逐步降低；逐步縮小《*de-* = down》

516 scend = climb（爬；攀登）

* 拉丁文 *scandere*（= *climb*）。〔變化型〕*scens , scent*。

scan[5]〔skæn〕*v.* 審訊；按韻律吟誦（詩）（一步一步往上爬）

scansion〔'skænʃən〕*n.* 詩之韻律分析

ascend[5]〔ə'sɛnd〕*v.* 上升；攀登《*a-* = *ad-* = to》

ascent[7]〔ə'sɛnt〕*n.* 攀登；上升

ascensive〔ə'sɛnsɪv〕*adj.* 上升的；進步的

```
 a  +  scens  +  ive
 |       |        |
 to  +  climb  +  adj.
```

ascension〔ə'sɛnʃən〕*n.* 上升；（the A-）耶穌的升天

ascendant；**-ent**[7]〔ə'sɛndənt〕*adj.* 上升的；優勢的　*n.* 優勢；祖先

ascendancy；**-ency**〔ə'sɛndənsɪ〕*n.* 主權；優越

descend[6]〔dɪ'sɛnd〕*v.* 下降；傳下來；突襲《*de-* = down》

descent[6]〔dɪ'sɛnt〕*n.* 降下；遺傳；襲擊

descendant[6]〔dɪ'sɛndənt〕*n.* 後裔（延著家譜而下）

condescend[7]〔͵kɑndɪ'sɛnd〕*v.* 屈尊；降低身分；特別親切對待
（和對方一起下降）《*con-* = together》

condescension〔͵kɑndɪ'sɛnʃən〕*n.* 謙卑；屈從

transcend[7] 〔 træn'sɛnd 〕 v. 超越；凌駕（攀越）《**trans-** = beyond》

```
tran(s) + scend
  |          |
beyond  +  climb
```

transcendent〔 træn'sɛndənt 〕 adj. 超凡的；卓越的
transcendence；**-ency**〔 træn'sɛndəns(ɪ) 〕 n. 超凡；卓越
transcendental〔,trænsɛn'dɛntl̩ 〕 adj. 卓越的；形而上學的；
超自然的

517　schiz = split（分裂）　* 希臘文 *skhizein*（ = *split* ）。

schism〔'sɪzəm 〕 n. 分裂；派別
schist〔 ʃɪst 〕 n. 片岩
schizogenesis〔,skɪzə'dʒɛnəsɪs 〕 n. 分裂生殖《**gen** = produce》
schizophrenia〔,skɪtsə'frinə , ,skɪzə- 〕 n. 精神分裂症
《**phren** = mind》

518　sci = know（知道）

* 拉丁文 *scire*（ = *know* ），*scientia*（ = *knowledge* ）。

science[2]〔'saɪəns 〕 n. 科學；學術（得知的東西）
scientific[3]〔,saɪən'tɪfɪk 〕 adj. 科學的；合乎科學的
scientist[2]〔'saɪəntɪst 〕 n. 科學家
sciolism〔'saɪə,lɪzəm 〕 n. 一知半解
sciolist〔'saɪəlɪst 〕 n. 一知半解者
conscience[4]〔'kɑnʃəns 〕 n. 良心（知道罪惡的心）《**con-** = with》

```
con + sci + ence
 |     |     |
with + know + n.
```

conscientious[6]〔,kɑnʃɪ'ɛnʃəs 〕 adj. 本著良心行事的；謹慎的

conscious[3] 〔'kɑnʃəs〕 *adj.* 有意識的；知覺的（知道～）

consciousness[7] 〔'kɑnʃəsnɪs〕 *n.* 知覺；意識

subconscious[7] 〔sʌb'kɑnʃəs〕 *adj.* 潛意識的；下意識的

《*sub-* = under》

```
sub  + con + sci  + ous
 |      |     |      |
under + with + know + adj.
```

unconscious[7] 〔ʌn'kɑnʃəs〕 *adj.* 無意識的；昏迷的；未察覺的

《*un-* = not》

nescient 〔'nɛʃənt, 'nɛʃɪənt〕 *adj.* 無知的；不可知的 《*ne-* = not》

```
ne + sci  + ent
 |     |      |
not + know + adj.
```

nescience 〔'nɛʃəns, 'nɛʃɪəns〕 *n.* 無知；不可知論

omniscient[7] 〔ɑm'nɪʃənt〕 *adj.* 全知的（完全了解的）

《*omni-* = all》

omniscience 〔ɑm'nɪʃəns〕 *n.* 全知；無所不知；（the O-）上帝

```
omni + sci  + ence
  |     |       |
 all + know +  n.
```

prescient 〔'prɛʃənt, 'pri-〕 *adj.* 預知的；先見的 《*pre-* = before》

prescience 〔'prɛʃəns, 'pri-〕 *n.* 預知；先見

prescientific 〔ˌprisaɪən'tɪfɪk〕 *adj.* 科學文明以前的；近代科學以前的

---

519 **scler** = hard（硬的）　　*希臘文 *skleros*（= hard）。

sclera 〔'sklɪrə〕 *n.* （眼球之）鞏膜

sclerenchyma 〔sklɪ'rɛŋkɪmə〕 *n.* 【植物】厚壁組織

《*parenchyma* 薄壁組織》

字根 sacr～surge

scleroderma 〔ˌsklɪrəˈdɝmə 〕 *n.* 硬皮病《*derma* = skin》

scleroid 〔ˈsklɪrɔɪd 〕 *adj.* 硬的；硬質的

sclerosis 〔 sklɪˈrosɪs 〕 *n.* (動脈等的) 硬化 (症)

《 *-osis* 表示病變狀態的名詞字尾》

520 scop = look (看) * 希臘文 *skopein* (= *look*) 。

scope[6] 〔 skop 〕 *n.* 範圍；視野 (眼睛所見的範圍)

horoscope[7] 〔ˈhɔrəˌskop 〕 *n.* 占星術

stereoscope 〔ˈstɛrɪəˌskop , ˈstɪrɪ- 〕 *n.*
立體鏡 (一種觀看立體相片或圖畫的光學儀器)

```
horo  +  scope
  |         |
hour  +   look
```

tachistoscope 〔 təˈkɪstəˌskop 〕 *n.* 速讀訓練機

```
tachisto  +  scope
   |           |
 fast    +    look
```

521 scrib , script = write (寫)

* 拉丁文 *scribere* (= *write*) ，過去分詞爲 *scriptus* 。

scribe 〔 skraɪb 〕 *n.* 書記；抄寫者；作家 (書寫的人)

scribble[7] 〔ˈskrɪbl̩ 〕 *v.* 潦草書寫；亂寫 *n.* 潦草書寫；胡書亂寫

scribbler 〔ˈskrɪblɚ 〕 *n.* 三流作家

scribbling 〔ˈskrɪblɪŋ 〕 *n.* 亂寫

scrip 〔 skrɪp 〕 *n.* 臨時股票；證券；代用紙幣 (寫下的文件)

script[6] 〔 skrɪpt 〕 *n.* 手跡；腳本；正本

scripture 〔ˈskrɪptʃɚ 〕 *n.* 經文；經典；聖經 (被寫下的東西)

```
script  +  ure
  |         |
write  +    n.
```

scrivener 〔ˈskrɪvənɚ 〕 *n.* 代書人

字根 sacr~surge

ascribe 〔 ə'skraɪb 〕 *v.* 歸因於～（寫於～）《*a-* = *ad-* = to》

ascription 〔 ə'skrɪpʃən 〕 *n.* 歸因

ascriptive 〔 ə'skrɪptɪv 〕 *adj.* 可歸因的

circumscribe[7] 〔 ˌsɝkəm'skraɪb 〕 *v.* 劃界線；限制（寫上範圍）

《*circum-* = round》

```
circum + scribe
  |        |
round  +  write
```

circumscription 〔 ˌsɝkəm'skrɪpʃən 〕 *n.* 限制；界限內區域

conscribe 〔 kən'skraɪb 〕 *v.* 徵服兵役（一起寫下姓名）

《*con-* = together》

conscript 〔 *adj.* , *n.* 'kɑnskrɪpt *v.* kən'skrɪpt 〕 *adj.* 徵召的

n. 徵兵　*v.* 徵召（服兵役）

conscription 〔 kən'skrɪpʃən 〕 *n.* 徵兵

```
con    + script + ion
  |        |       |
together + write +  n.
```

conscriptive 〔 kən'skrɪptɪv 〕 *adj.* 徵兵的

describe[2] 〔 dɪ'skraɪb 〕 *v.* 描寫；形容（寫得很詳細）

《*de-* = down ; fully》

describer 〔 dɪ'skraɪbɚ 〕 *n.* 敘述者

description[3] 〔 dɪ'skrɪpʃən 〕 *n.* 描寫；種類

descriptive[5] 〔 dɪ'skrɪptɪv 〕 *adj.* 描寫的；記述的

indescribable[7] 〔 ˌɪndɪ'skraɪbəbl̩ 〕 *adj.* 不能言傳的；難以形容的

《*in-* = not》

```
in +  de  + scrib + able
 |    |      |       |
not + down + write + adj.
```

inscribe[7] 〔 ɪn'skraɪb 〕 *v.* 題記；銘刻；登記（寫於～之上）

《*in-* = upon》

inscriber〔 ɪn'skraɪbɚ 〕*n.* 銘刻者

inscription[7]〔 ɪn'skrɪpʃən 〕*n.* 題名；題獻

inscriptive〔 ɪn'skrɪptɪv 〕*adj.* 銘刻的

manuscript[6]〔'mænjə,skrɪpt 〕*adj.* 手寫的　*n.* 原稿；抄本
（用手寫的）《*manu* = hand》

nondescript[7]〔'nɑndɪ,skrɪpt 〕*adj.* 難以形容的；難以分類的
n. 難以分類或名狀的人或物

```
non  +  de  + script
 |      |      |
not  + down + write
```

postscript〔'pos·skrɪpt , 'post- 〕*n.*（信件中）附筆；再啓
（簡寫爲 P.S.）（加寫於後面的）《*post-* = after》

prescribe[6]〔 prɪ'skraɪb 〕*v.* 規定；開藥方（事先寫好的）
《*pre-* = before》

prescript〔'priskrɪpt 〕*n.* 命令；規定

prescription[6]〔 prɪ'skrɪpʃən 〕*n.* 規定；處方

prescriptive〔 prɪ'skrɪptɪv 〕*adj.* 規定的；慣例的

proscribe[7]〔 pro'skraɪb 〕*v.* 摒棄於法律保護之外；放逐；禁止
（把罪犯的名字公佈出來）《*pro-* = forth ; publicly》

proscriber〔 pro'skraɪbɚ 〕*n.* 禁止者

proscription〔 pro'skrɪpʃən 〕*n.* 禁止；放逐

proscriptive〔 pro'skrɪptɪv 〕*adj.* 禁止的

rescript〔'riskrɪpt 〕*n.* 敕令；詔書；副本《*re-* = back》

subscribe[6]〔 səb'skraɪb 〕*v.* 捐助；簽署；訂購（寫在下面）
《*sub-* = under》

subscriber〔 səb'skraɪbɚ 〕*n.* 捐助者；署名者；訂購者

```
sub  + scrib +   er
 |      |        |
under + write + person
```

subscript〔'sʌbskrɪpt 〕*n.* 寫於下面的數字或文字
adj. 寫於下邊的

subscription[6] 〔 səb'skrɪpʃən 〕 *n.* 署名；捐款；訂閱
subscriptive 〔 səb'skrɪptɪv 〕 *adj.* 訂購的
superscribe 〔 ͵supɚ'skraɪb , ͵sju- 〕 *v.* 將（名字等）寫在
　某物上面（寫在上面）《*super-* = above》
superscript 〔 'supɚ͵skrɪpt 〕 *n.* 寫在上面的文字
superscription 〔 ͵supɚ'skrɪpʃən , ͵sju- 〕 *n.* 題字；銘刻
transcribe[7] 〔 træn'skraɪb 〕 *v.* 謄寫；錄音；樂曲改編（轉寫）
　《*trans-* = across ; over》
transcriber 〔 træn'skraɪbɚ 〕 *n.* 抄寫員
transcribable 〔 træn'skraɪbəbḷ 〕 *adj.* 可抄寫的；可轉譯的
transcript[6] 〔 'træn͵skrɪpt 〕 *n.* 副本；謄本；成績單
transcription[7] 〔 træn'skrɪpʃən 〕 *n.* 抄寫；錄音；刊印
transcriptional 〔 træn'skrɪpʃənḷ 〕 *adj.* 抄寫的；改編的

522　**scut** = shield（盾）　　* 拉丁文 *scutum*（= *shield*）。

scutage 〔 'skjutɪdʒ 〕 *n.* 免服兵役稅
scutate 〔 'skjutet 〕 *adj.* 具盾片的；具大鱗的；盾形的
scutcheon 〔 'skʌtʃən 〕 *n.*（裝飾性）鎖孔銅蓋
scutiform 〔 'skjutɪ͵fɔrm 〕 *adj.* 盾狀的《*form* 形狀》
escutcheon 〔 ɪ'skʌtʃən 〕 *n.* 飾有紋章的盾；鎖眼蓋
squire 〔 skwaɪr 〕 *n.* , *v.* 護衛《古法文 *escuier* = shield carrier》

523　**sect** = cut（切割）

　　* 拉丁文 *secare*（= *cut*），過去分詞為 *sectus*。

sect[7] 〔 sɛkt 〕 *n.* 宗派；教派；分派；派系
sectarian 〔 sɛk'tɛrɪən 〕 *adj.* 宗派的；派系的；學派的；黨派心強的
　n. 黨派或宗派心強的人
sectary 〔 'sɛktərɪ 〕 *n.* 同屬一宗派的人

sectile〔'sɛktɪl〕*adj.*（礦物）可截斷的《*-ile* 形容詞字尾》

```
sect + ile
 |      |
cut  + adj.
```

section[2]〔'sɛkʃən〕*n.* 部分；區域；部門；段落；斷面
　v. 區分；劃分

sectional〔'sɛkʃənl̩〕*adj.* 部分的；部門的；段落的；斷面的

sectionalism〔'sɛkʃənl̩,ɪzəm〕*n.* 地方主義；地方偏見；
　地域觀念；派系主義

sectionalize〔'sɛkʃənə,laɪz〕*v.* 分成小部分；區分

bisect[7]〔baɪ'sɛkt〕*v.* 平分；分為二等分（切割成兩部分）
　《*bi-* = two》

bisection〔baɪ'sɛkʃən〕*n.* 平分；二等分

dissect[7]〔dɪ'sɛkt〕*v.* 解剖；切開；詳細研究（切割開來）
　《*dis-* = apart》

dissection〔dɪ'sɛkʃən〕*n.* 解剖；切開；詳細研究或分析

```
dis  + sect + ion
 |       |      |
apart + cut  + n.
```

dissector〔dɪ'sɛktɚ〕*n.* 解剖者；解剖器具

insect[2]〔'ɪnsɛkt〕*n.* 昆蟲；微賤的人（軀體分割成一節一節）
　《*in-* = into》

insectarium〔,ɪnsɛk'tɛrɪəm〕*n.* 昆蟲飼養所；昆蟲館
　（= *insectary*）（飼養昆蟲的地方）《*-arium* 表示場所的名詞字尾》

```
insect + arium
   |       |
  昆蟲   + place
```

insecticide[7]〔ɪn'sɛktə,saɪd〕*n.* 殺蟲劑（殺昆蟲的東西）《*cide* = cut》

insectivore〔ɪn'sɛktə,vor〕*n.* 食蟲動物；食蟲植物《*vor* = eat》

insectivorous〔,ɪnsɛk'tɪv(ə)rəs〕*adj.* 食蟲的；食蟲類的

intersect[7] 〔͵ɪntɚˋsɛkt 〕 v. 橫斷；交叉（交互切割）《*inter-* = between》

intersection[6] 〔͵ɪntɚˋsɛkʃən 〕 n. 橫斷；交叉；

（道路的）交叉點；交點

```
inter + sect + ion
  |      |      |
between + cut +  n.
```

transect 〔 trænˋsɛkt 〕 v. 橫切；橫斷；截斷（從這端切到那端）

《*tran(s)-* = across》

transection 〔 trænˋsɛkʃən 〕 n. 橫切面；橫斷面

vivisect 〔͵vɪvəˋsɛkt 〕 v. 活體解剖（切割活的東西）《*vivi* = alive》

vivisection 〔͵vɪvəˋsɛkʃən 〕 n. 活體解剖

secant 〔ˋsikənt , ˋsikænt 〕 adj. 分割的；交割的 n. 正割；割線

segment[5] 〔ˋsɛgmənt 〕 n. 部分；分節；斷片 v. （使）分裂

《*seg* = cut》

524 sed , sid , sess = sit（坐）

* 拉丁文 *sedere*（= *sit*）。〔變化型〕*sid* , *sess*。

sedate[7] 〔 sɪˋdet 〕 adj. 安詳的；肅靜的（穩定地坐著）

sedative[7] 〔ˋsɛdətɪv 〕 adj. 鎮定的 n. 鎮定劑（使坐下）

sedentary[7] 〔ˋsɛdn͵tɛrɪ 〕 adj. 慣於久坐的；不活動的；定居的；

不遷徙的 n. 慣於久坐的人

sediment[7] 〔ˋsɛdəmənt 〕 n. 沈澱物；沖積物 v. 沈澱（沉積於底部的）

sedimentation 〔͵sɛdəmənˋteʃən 〕 n. 沈澱（作用）

sedulous 〔ˋsɛdʒələs 〕 adj. 勤勉的；努力不懈的（一直坐著工作）

```
sed + ulous
 |     |
sit +  adj.
```

sessile 〔ˋsɛsḷ , -ɪl 〕 adj. 固定的（坐著不能動）

session[6] 〔ˋsɛʃən 〕 n. 開會（期）；開庭（期）（坐在會議席上的）

assess[6] 〔 ə'sɛs 〕 v. 評估；評定；課（稅或其他費用）
（使坐下 → 訂定）《**as-** = **ad-** = to》

assessor 〔 ə'sɛsɚ 〕 n. 估稅員；顧問

```
as  +  sess  +   or
 |      |        |
to  +  sit  +  person
```

assiduous 〔 ə'sɪdʒʊəs 〕 adj. 勤勉的（面對桌子坐著）《**as-** = **ad-** = to》
assiduity 〔 ˌæsə'djuətɪ , -'du- 〕 n. 勤勉
dissidence 〔 'dɪsədəns 〕 n. 異議《**dis-** = apart》

```
dis  +  sid  +  ence
 |       |       |
apart  +  sit  +  n.
```

dissident[6] 〔 'dɪsədənt 〕 adj. , n. 意見不同的（人）；持異議的（人）
（分開坐著的）
insidious[7] 〔 ɪn'sɪdɪəs 〕 adj. 陰險的；狡猾的（隱匿坐於其內者）
《**in-** = in》
obsess[7] 〔 əb'sɛs 〕 v. （魔鬼、妄想等）縈擾；纏擾；困擾《**ob-** = against》
obsession[7] 〔 əb'sɛʃən 〕 n. 縈擾；著迷；妄想
obsessive[7] 〔 əb'sɛsɪv 〕 adj. 妄想的；（恐懼等）盤據於心的

```
ob  +  sess  +  ive
 |       |       |
against  +  sit  +  adj.
```

possess[4] 〔 pə'zɛs 〕 v. 擁有；（惡魔等）纏附；克制
《**pos** = 拉丁文 **potis** = able》

possessed 〔 pə'zɛst 〕 adj. 著魔的；瘋狂的；鎮定的
possession[4] 〔 pə'zɛʃən 〕 n. 持有；（pl.）財產；著魔
dispossess 〔 ˌdɪspə'zɛs 〕 v. 奪取；霸佔；逐出；剝奪
（使擁有的東西失去）《**dis-** = away》
prepossess 〔 ˌpripə'zɛs 〕 v. 使人抱持（感情、觀念）；使有好
印象；（感情、觀念）盤據心頭（事先擁有）《**pre-** = before》

repossess〔͵ripə'zɛs〕*v.* 再取得；收回；復有（再次擁有）
　《*re-* = again》
preside[6]〔prɪ'zaɪd〕*v.* 開會做主席；管理（坐在前面）《*pre-* = before》

```
pre  +  side
 |       |
before +  sit
```

president[2]〔'prɛzədənt〕*n.* 總統；會長；（大學）校長（坐於首
　席的人）
presidency[6]〔'prɛzədənsɪ〕*n.* 總統的職位；總統的任期
presidential[6]〔͵prɛzə'dɛnʃəl〕*adj.* 總統的；統轄的；支配的
presidium〔prɪ'sɪdɪəm〕*n.* 常務委員會；主席團《*-ium* 表集合名詞》
reside[5]〔rɪ'zaɪd〕*v.* 居住；存在（返回坐下）《*re-* = back》
residence[5]〔'rɛzədəns〕*n.* 居住（期間）；住宅

```
re  +  sid  +  ence
 |       |       |
back  +  sit  +   n.
```

resident[5]〔'rɛzədənt〕*adj.* 居住的；居留的；定居的
　n. 居住者；駐外代表
residential[6]〔͵rɛzə'dɛnʃəl〕*adj.* 住宅的；居住用的；與居住有關的
residual[7]〔rɪ'zɪdʒʊəl〕*adj.* 剩餘的；殘留的　*n.* 剩餘；殘留物
　（殘留置於後頭的）
residue[7]〔'rɛzə͵dju，-͵du〕*n.* 殘餘；餘產
subside[7]〔səb'saɪd〕*v.* 降落；下沈；（暴風雨）平息（坐在下方）
　《*sub-* = under》
subsidence〔səb'saɪdn̩s，'sʌbsədəns〕*n.* 沈澱；陷下；平息
subsidize[7]〔'sʌbsə͵daɪz〕*v.* 補助；資助；津貼（置於後面加以援助）
　《*sub-* = under；behind》

```
sub  +  sid  +  ize
 |       |       |
behind +  sit  +   v.
```

subsidy[7]〔ˈsʌbsədɪ〕*n.* 津貼；補助金
subsidiary[7]〔səbˈsɪdɪ͵ɛrɪ〕*adj.* 輔助的；補助的
supersede〔͵supɚˈsid，͵sju-〕*v.* 代替；更換；免職；廢止
（坐在首位）《*super-* = above》

```
super  +  sede
  |        |
above  +   sit
```

supersession〔͵supɚˈsɛʃən，͵sju-〕*n.* 代替；廢棄
siege[6]〔sidʒ〕*n.* 圍攻；圍城（兵士坐於城的四周）
besiege[6]〔bɪˈsidʒ〕*v.* 圍攻；困惱《*be-* = make》
consult[4]〔kənˈsʌlt〕*v.* 請教；參考；查閱（坐在一起）
《*con-* = together》
consultant[4]〔kənˈsʌltənt〕*n.* 諮詢者；顧問

```
con    +  sult  +  ant
  |         |        |
together + sit  + person
```

consultation[6]〔͵kɑnslˈteʃən〕*n.* 請教；參考；調查
exile[5]〔ˈɛgzaɪl，ˈɛksaɪl，*v. also* ɪgˈzaɪl〕*n.，v.* 放逐；流放
（使坐於外面）《*ex-* = out》

525　semin = seed（種子）

* 拉丁文 *semen*，*semin-*（= *seed*）。

seminal[7]〔ˈsɛmənl〕*adj.* 精液的；種子的；生殖的；如種子般的；
有潛力的
seminar[6]〔ˈsɛmə͵nɑr〕*n.* 研討會；討論式的課程
seminary〔ˈsɛmə͵nɛrɪ〕*n.*（罪惡等的）溫床；神學院；學校
（尤指私立女子學校）（孕育種子之處）《*-ary* 表示場所的名詞字尾》

semination 〔,sɛmə'neʃən 〕 *n.* 播種；接種；傳播

```
semin + ation
  |       |
seed  +   n.
```

seminiferous 〔,sɛmə'nɪfərəs 〕 *adj.* 產生精子的；產生精液的；
輸精的（產生種子）《 *-(i)ferous* = bearing 》

disseminate 〔 dɪ'sɛmə,net 〕 *v.* 傳播；使普及；散布（散播種子）
《 *dis-* = apart 》

dissemination 〔 dɪ,sɛmə'neʃən 〕 *n.* 傳播；普及；散布

```
dis  + semin + ation
 |       |       |
apart +  seed  +  n.
```

disseminator 〔 dɪ'sɛmə,netɚ 〕 *n.* 傳播者；散布者

inseminate[7] 〔 ɪn'sɛmə,net 〕 *v.* 使受精；播種；灌輸（使種子進入）
《 *in-* = into 》

insemination 〔 ɪn,sɛmə'neʃən 〕 *n.* 受精；播種

526　sen = old（老的）　＊拉丁文 *senex*（ = old ）。

senate[7] 〔'sɛnɪt 〕 *n.* 參議院；議會；元老院；評議會
（由具有權威的人所組成）《 *senatus* = council of elders 》

senator[6] 〔'sɛnɪtɚ 〕 *n.* 參議員；元老院議員；評議員

senatorial 〔,sɛnə'torɪəl , -'tɔr- 〕 *adj.* 參議院的；參議員的；
元老院的；元老院議員的

senescent 〔 sə'nɛsn̩t 〕 *adj.* 老朽的；衰老的（變老的）
《 *-escent* = becoming 》

senescence 〔 sə'nɛsn̩s 〕 *n.* 老朽；衰老

senile[7] 〔'sinaɪl 〕 *adj.* 衰老的；老邁的；高齡的
（老年的）《 *-ile* 形容詞字尾 》

senility[7] 〔 sə'nɪlətɪ 〕 *n.* 老邁；衰老

```
sen + ile
 |     |
old + adj.
```

senior[4]〔'sinjə〕*adj.* 年長的；資深的；上級的；最高年級的
　　n. 年長者；資深者；最高年級學生（比較老的）
　　《 *-ior* 形容詞字尾，表比較》
seniority[7]〔 sin'jɔrətɪ〕*n.* 年長；資深；年資

527　sens , sent = feel（感覺到）

　　* 拉丁文 *sentire*（= *feel* ; *perceive*），過去分詞爲 *sensus*。

sense[1]〔 sɛns 〕*n.* 感官；知覺；意義；判斷力　　*v.* 覺得；感知
sensibility[7]〔,sɛnsə'bɪlətɪ〕*n.* 感覺；感性；情感
sensible[3]〔'sɛnsəbḷ〕*adj.* 明理的；可感覺的

```
sens + ible
  |      |
feel  + adj.
```

sensitive[3]〔'sɛnsətɪv〕*adj.* 敏感的；過敏的；易感光的
sensitivity[5]〔,sɛnsə'tɪvətɪ〕*n.* 敏感；感受性；感度；感光度
sensitize〔'sɛnsə,taɪz〕*v.* 使敏感
sensor[7]〔'sɛnsə〕*n.* 探測設備；敏感裝置；感覺器官
sensorium〔 sɛn'sorɪəm , -'sɔr-〕*n.* 感覺中樞
sensory[7]〔'sɛnsərɪ〕*adj.* 感覺的；感覺器官的

```
sens + ory
  |      |
feel  + adj.
```

sensual[7]〔'sɛnʃʊəl〕*adj.* 肉體上的；官能的
sensualism〔'sɛnʃʊə,lɪzəm〕*n.* 肉慾主義；官能主義
　　《 *-ism* 表示主義的名詞字尾》
sensualist〔'sɛnʃʊəlɪst〕*n.* 好色者；官能主義者
sensuality[7]〔,sɛnʃʊ'ælətɪ〕*n.* 官能性；喜愛感官享受；好色
sensualize〔'sɛnʃʊə,laɪz〕*v.* 使沉溺於酒色；使色情化；使荒淫

sensuous〔'sɛnʃʊəs〕*adj.* 感覺的；感官的

sensate〔'sɛnset〕*adj.* 有感覺的；可感覺的

sensation[5]〔sɛn'seʃən〕*n.* 感覺；感動

sensational[7]〔sɛn'seʃənḷ〕*adj.* 令人激動的；感動的

```
sens  +  ation  +  al
 |         |        |
feel  +    n.    + adj.
```

sensationalize〔sɛn'seʃənə,laɪz〕*v.* 渲染；使聳人聽聞

sentient〔'sɛnʃ(ɪ)ənt〕*adj.* 有知覺的；有感覺的；敏感的；意識的

sentience〔'sɛnʃ(ɪ)əns〕*n.* 感覺；知覺力；感性

sentiment[5]〔'sɛntəmənt〕*n.* 情緒；感情；傷感

sentimental[6]〔,sɛntə'mɛntḷ〕*adj.* 感情的；感傷的

sentimentality〔,sɛntəmɛn'tælətɪ〕*n.* 多愁善感；感傷

sentence[1]〔'sɛntəns〕*n.* 宣判；句子　*v.* 宣判；判決

　（有感而發的東西）

sentential〔sɛn'tɛnʃəl〕*adj.* 句子的；判決的

sententious〔sɛn'tɛnʃəs〕*adj.* 警句多的；簡潔的

assent[7]〔ə'sɛnt〕*v.* 同意　*n.* 贊同；同意（感覺對方的心情）

　《*as-* = *ad-* = to》

```
as  +  sent
 |       |
to  +  feel
```

assentient〔ə'sɛnʃənt〕*adj.* 同意的　　*n.* 贊同者

assentation〔,æsɛn'teʃən〕*n.* 迎合；附和

consent[5]〔kən'sɛnt〕*n.* , *v.* 同意（共同地感覺）《*con-* = together》

consentient〔kən'sɛnʃənt , -ʃɪənt〕*adj.* 一致的；同意的

```
con    +  sent +  ient
 |         |       |
together + feel + adj.
```

consentaneous 〔ˌkɑnsɛnˈtenɪəs〕 *adj.* 相合的；一致的

consensus[6] 〔kənˈsɛnsəs〕 *n.* 一致；輿論

dissent[7] 〔dɪˈsɛnt〕 *v.* 持異議　*n.* 異議（產生別的感覺）《*dis-* = apart》

dissenter 〔dɪˈsɛntɚ〕 *n.* 持異議的人；反對者

dissentient 〔dɪˈsɛnʃənt〕 *adj., n.* 持異議的（人）

dissension 〔dɪˈsɛnʃən〕 *n.* 衝突；意見不合

extrasensory 〔ˌɛkstrəˈsɛnsərɪ〕 *adj.* 知覺外的；超感覺的
（超越感官的）《*extra-* = beyond》

insensate 〔ɪnˈsɛnset, -sɪt〕 *adj.* 無感覺的；愚鈍的；無情的
《*in-* = not》

insensible 〔ɪnˈsɛnsəbḷ〕 *adj.* 無感覺的；失去意識的；未察覺的

```
in + sens + ible
 |     |      |
not + feel + adj.
```

insensitive[7] 〔ɪnˈsɛnsətɪv〕 *adj.* 感覺遲鈍的；無感覺的

nonsense[4] 〔ˈnɑnsɛns〕 *n.* 無意義的話；愚蠢的行為（沒有意義）

presentiment 〔prɪˈzɛntəmənt〕 *n.* 預感；預覺（事先的感覺）
《*pre-* = before》

resent[5] 〔rɪˈzɛnt〕 *v.* 憤恨（再次感覺 → 怒氣油然而生）《*re-* = again》

resentful[7] 〔rɪˈzɛntfəl〕 *adj.* 憤慨的

resentment[5] 〔rɪˈzɛntmənt〕 *n.* 憤恨

scent[5] 〔sɛnt〕 *v.* 嗅出；聞出；察覺　*n.* 氣味；香（味）；嗅覺
（用鼻子感覺）

528　sequ , secut , sue = follow（跟隨）

* 拉丁文 *sequi*（= *follow*），過去分詞是 *secutus*；
英法語 *suer*（= *follow after*）。

sequacious 〔sɪˈkweʃəs〕 *adj.* 順從的；卑屈的；合乎邏輯的
（願意跟隨的）

sequel[7] 〔'sikwəl 〕 *n.* 結果；續篇（接續者）

sequence[6] 〔'sikwəns 〕 *n.* 連續；序列；結果

```
sequ  +  ence
 |        |
follow +  n.
```

sequent 〔'sikwənt 〕 *adj.* 連續的；結果的　*n.* 結果

sequential[7] 〔 sɪ'kwɛnʃəl 〕 *adj.* 隨之而來的；連續的；結果的

consequence[4] 〔'kɑnsə,kwɛns 〕 *n.* 結果；重要

（一同繼續 → 繼於其後的事）《*con-* = together》

consequent[4] 〔'kɑnsə,kwɛnt 〕 *adj.* 由～而起的；（在理論上）必

然的　*n.* 結果；影響

consequential[7] 〔,kɑnsə'kwɛnʃəl 〕 *adj.* 結果的；重要的；自大的

obsequious 〔 əb'sikwɪəs 〕 *adj.* 逢迎的；諂媚的（緊黏在後面的）

《*ob-* = near》

```
ob  +  sequ  +  ious
 |       |        |
near +  follow +  adj.
```

subsequence 〔'sʌbsɪ,kwɛns 〕 *n.* 後來；繼起（繼於後面的東西）

《*sub-* = under》

subsequent[6] 〔'sʌbsɪ,kwɛnt 〕 *adj.* 後來的；繼起的

consecution 〔,kɑnsɪ'kjuʃən 〕 *n.* 連續；一致（一起承接）

《*con-* = together》

consecutive[7] 〔 kən'sɛkjətɪv 〕 *adj.* 連續的；表示結果的

```
con   +  secut  +  ive
 |        |          |
together +  follow +  adj.
```

execute[5] 〔'ɛksɪ,kjut 〕 *v.* 實施；執行；處死

（繼續向外行去 → 到處行得通的）《*ex-* = out》

execution[6] 〔,ɛksɪ'kjuʃən 〕 *n.* 履行；執行死刑；實現

executive[5] 〔 ɪɡˋzɛkjʊtɪv 〕 *adj.* 行政的；實行的　*n.* 行政官；
執行部門

executor 〔 ɪɡˋzɛkjətɚ 〕 *n.* 指定遺囑執行人　〔ˋɛksɪͺkjutɚ 〕 *n.*
執行者

persecute[7] 〔ˋpɝsɪͺkjut 〕 *v.* 迫害；困惑

persecution[7] 〔ͺpɝsɪˋkjuʃən 〕 *n.* 迫害

```
per   +  secut  + ion
 |         |        |
through + follow +  n.
```

prosecute[6] 〔ˋprɑsɪͺkjut 〕 *v.* 實行；告發（事先進行手續）
《**pro-** = forth》

prosecution[6] 〔ͺprɑsɪˋkjuʃən 〕 *n.* 進行；起訴；原告

prosecutor[7] 〔ˋprɑsɪͺkjutɚ 〕 *n.* 原告；檢察官

sue[7] 〔 su , sɪu 〕 *v.* 控告；請求（跟著轉）

【解說】 美國是個人民很愛提起訴訟的國家，幾乎任何事都可以告上
　　　　法院。甚至出現過自己告自己，因自己不慎傷害自己，而要
　　　　求保險公司理賠的案件。法院最終判決本人勝訴，並要求保
　　　　險公司理賠。

ensue[7] 〔 ɛnˋsju 〕 *v.* 隨後發生；結果（繼續～）《**en-** = **in-** = upon》

pursue[3] 〔 pɚˋsu , -ˋsɪu 〕 *v.* 追捕；繼續；追求；照～而行
（繼續向前進）《**pur-** = **pro-** = forth》

pursuance 〔 pɚˋsuəns , -ˋsju- 〕 *n.* 追求；從事

```
pur  +  su   + ance
 |       |       |
forth + follow +  n.
```

pursuit[4] 〔 pɚˋsut , -ˋsjut 〕 *n.* 追捕；追求；職業

suit[2] 〔 sut , sjut 〕 *v.* 適合於；適應　*n.* 一套；一組；請求；訴訟
（繼續做下去 → 使合於）《古法文 *sieute* = set of things》

suitable[3] 〔ˋsutəbḷ , ˋsɪu- , ˋsju- 〕 *adj.* 適當的

suite[6] 〔 swit 〕 *n.* 隨員；一組；組曲；套房（跟從者）

529 sert = join ; put (結合 ; 放)

* 拉丁文 *serere* (= *join* ; *put*) ，過去分詞爲 *sertus*。

series[5] 〔'sɪrɪz , 'siriz , 'sɪrɪz , 'sirɪz 〕 *n.* 連續；系列；叢書
（結合的東西）

serial[7] 〔'sɪrɪəl 〕 *adj.* 連載的；連續的；排成系列的
n. 連載小說；連續劇

seriate 〔 *v.* 'sɪrɪ,et *adj.* 'sɪrɪɪt 〕 *v.* 按順序排列
adj. 順序的；連續的

serried 〔'sɛrɪd 〕 *adj.* 擁擠的；密集的（使團結）

assert[6] 〔 ə's3t 〕 *v.* 斷言；辯護；堅持主張（自己的權利、意見）
《*as-* = *ad-* = to》

assertion[7] 〔 ə's3ʃən 〕 *n.* 斷言；主張；辯護

```
as  +  sert  +  ion
 |      |       |
to  +  join  +  n.
```

assertive[7] 〔 ə's3tɪv 〕 *adj.* 斷定的

concert[3] 〔 *n.* 'kɑns3t *v.* kən's3t 〕 *n.* 音樂會；一致；和諧
v. 協議進行（團結在一起）《*con-* = together》

desert[2] 〔 *adj.* , *n.* 'dɛzɚt *v.* dɪ'z3t 〕 *adj.* 不毛的；沙漠的 *n.* 沙漠
v. 放棄；遺棄（脫離相結合）《*de-* = off》

deserted[7] 〔 dɪ'z3tɪd 〕 *adj.* 荒蕪的；爲人所棄的

desertion[7] 〔 dɪ'z3ʃən 〕 *n.* 背棄；擅離職守

dissertation 〔,dɪsɚ'teʃən 〕 *n.* （學位）論文
（離開群體 → 個別分開詳細論述）《*dis-* = apart》

```
dis   +  sert  +  ation
 |        |        |
apart  +  join  +  n.
```

【解說】 要拿到博士學位（**doctoral degree**），最重要的就是要寫
博士論文（**dissertation**），來證明自己學有所成。

exert⁶〔 ɪgˈzɜt 〕v. 運用；施行（使出力量於外）《*ex-* = out》
exertion⁷〔 ɪgˈzɜʃən 〕n. 努力；費力；運用
insert⁴〔 ɪnˈsɜt 〕v. 插入；嵌入　n. 插入物（置於其中）《*in-* = into》
insertion⁷〔 ɪnˈsɜʃən 〕n. 插入（物）；嵌入
reassert⁷〔 ˌriəˈsɜt 〕v. 重作斷言；再申明《*re-* = again》
reassertion〔 ˌriəˈsɜʃən 〕n. 重作斷言；再申明

530　　serv = serve；keep（服務；保存）

＊拉丁文 *servire*（ = *serve* ），*servare*（ = *keep* ; *protect* ）。

serve¹〔 sɜv 〕v. 服務；供應；侍候；備餐
　n.（網球等的）開球；發球
server⁵〔ˈsɜvɚ 〕n. 侍者
servant²〔ˈsɜvənt 〕n. 僕人；公務員
service¹〔ˈsɜvɪs 〕n. 貢獻；業務；助益；服務
servile〔ˈsɜvl̩, -vɪl 〕adj. 奴隸的；卑屈的（服務）《*-ile* 形容詞字尾》
servility〔 sɚˈvɪlətɪ 〕n. 奴隸狀態；奴性；卑屈
servitude〔ˈsɜvəˌtjud 〕n. 奴役；苦役

serv ＋ itude
　|　　　|
serve ＋ n.

serf〔 sɜf 〕n. 農奴；奴隸（服侍者）
serfdom〔ˈsɜfdəm 〕n. 農奴的身分；農奴制《*-dom* = state》
sergeant⁵〔ˈsɑrdʒənt 〕n. 中士；警官（服侍者）
conserve⁵〔 v. kənˈsɜv　n. kənˈsɜv , ˈkɑnsɜv 〕v. 保存；節省
　n. 保存；保全；(*pl.*) 蜜餞（共同保有）《*con-* = together》
conservable〔 kənˈsɜvəbl̩ 〕adj. 可保存的；可節省的
conservancy〔 kənˈsɜvənsɪ 〕n. 保護；管理
conservation⁶〔ˌkɑnsɚˈveʃən 〕n. 保存；保護（林）

conservative[4]〔kən'sɝvətɪv〕*adj.* 保存的；保守的；謹慎的
n. 保守者；（C-）保守黨員

```
con    + serv + ative
 |        |      |
together + keep +  adj.
```

conservator〔kən'sɝvətɚ〕*n.* 保護者；文物保護員

conservatory[7]〔kən'sɝvə,torɪ, -,tɔrɪ〕*n.* 溫室；音樂學校
（保存地）《 *-ory* 表示場所的名詞字尾》

deserve[4]〔dɪ'zɝv〕*v.* 應得（賞罰）（加強服務）《 *de-* = fully》

deserved[7]〔dɪ'zɝvd〕*adj.* 應得的

deservedly〔dɪ'zɝvɪdlɪ〕*adv.* 應得地；當然地

disserve〔dɪs'sɝv〕*v.* 虐待；傷害（遠離問候）《 *dis-* = apart》

disservice[7]〔dɪs'sɝvɪs〕*n.* 損害；傷害；虐待

observe[3]〔əb'zɝv〕*v.* 遵守；觀察；注意（保留在眼前 → 觀察）
《 *ob-* = to》

observance[7]〔əb'zɝvəns〕*n.* 遵守；儀式

```
ob + serv + ance
 |    |      |
 to + keep +  n.
```

observation[4]〔,ɑbzɚ'veʃən〕*n.* 觀察力；注意；評論

observatory[7]〔əb'zɝvə,torɪ〕*n.* 天文台；氣象台；瞭望台
《 *-ory* 表示場所的名詞字尾》

preserve[4]〔prɪ'zɝv〕*v.* 保存；保管；醃（蔬菜）　*n.* 保護；保存；
（ *pl.* ）蜜餞；動物飼養場（保持在以前的狀態 → 保存）《 *pre-* = before》

```
pre  + serve
 |      |
before + keep
```

preservation[4]〔,prɛzɚ'veʃən〕*n.* 保存；保護

preservationist〔,prɛzɚ'veʃənɪst〕*n.* 保護者

preservative[7]〔prɪ'zɝvətɪv〕*adj.* 保存的　*n.* 防腐劑；保護物

reserve³〔rɪ'zɝv〕*v.* 保留；預訂；延期 *n.* 貯藏物；預備部隊；
謹慎；節制（保留到以後再來用）《*re-* = back》

reserved⁷〔rɪ'zɝvd〕*adj.* 保留的；預訂的（不使自己顯露）

reservation⁴〔ˌrɛzə'veʃən〕*n.* 保留（條件）；預定

```
re  + serv + ation
 |      |       |
back + keep +   n.
```

reservoir⁶〔'rɛzəˌvɔr , -ˌvwɔr , -ˌvwɑr〕*n.* 貯水池；水庫 *v.* 蓄積

subserve〔səb'sɝv〕*v.* 裨益於；有助於（服務於下部）
《*sub-* = under》

subservience〔səb'sɝvɪəns〕*n.* 卑屈；從屬；有益

subserviency〔səb'sɝvɪənsɪ〕*n.* 卑屈；有益

subservient⁷〔səb'sɝvɪənt〕*adj.* 卑屈的；有裨益的；從屬的

531 sign = mark（記號）

* 拉丁文 *signare*（= *mark*）， *signum*（= *mark* ; *token* 標記）。

sign²〔saɪn〕*n.* 記號；徵兆 *v.* 簽字；做手勢；表示

signal³〔'sɪɡnl̩〕*n.* 信號；動機 *v.* 向～作信號；表示
  adj. 信號的；顯著的

signally〔'sɪɡnl̩ɪ〕*adv.* 顯著地；非常地

signalize〔'sɪɡnəˌlaɪz〕*v.* 使著名；顯示

signatory〔'sɪɡnəˌtorɪ , -ˌtɔrɪ〕*adj.* 簽字的 *n.* 簽署者；簽約國

signature⁴〔'sɪɡnətʃə〕*n.* 簽字；記號

signee〔saɪ'ni〕*n.* 簽署者

signer〔'saɪnə〕*n.* 簽名者

signet〔'sɪɡnɪt〕*n.* 印章；圖章

signify⁶〔'sɪɡnəˌfaɪ〕*v.* 表示；有重要性
  （作出信號）《*-ify* = make》

```
sign + ify
 |      |
mark + make
```

significant[3] 〔 sɪɡˋnɪfəkənt 〕 *adj.* 有意義的；重大的；暗示的

significance[4] 〔 sɪɡˋnɪfəkəns 〕 *n.* 重要；意義

signification 〔 ͵sɪɡnɪfəˋkeʃən 〕 *n.* 意味；意義；表示；表明

significative 〔 sɪɡˋnɪfə͵ketɪv 〕 *adj.* 意味深長的；表示～的

assign[4] 〔 əˋsaɪn 〕 *v.* 分配；指派；讓渡（按照指示訂定）

《*as-* = *ad-* = to》

assignable 〔 əˋsaɪnəbḷ 〕 *adj.* 可指派的；可認定的

assignation 〔 ͵æsɪɡˋneʃən 〕 *n.* 指定；讓渡；約會；歸因

assignee 〔 ə͵saɪˋni , ͵æsəˋni 〕 *n.* 受讓人；受託者

《 *-ee* 表示「被～的人」》

assigner 〔 əˋsaɪnɚ 〕 *n.* 分配人；指定人

assignment[4] 〔 əˋsaɪnmənt 〕 *n.* 分派；讓渡；指定的工作

```
as  +  sign  +  ment
|       |        |
to  +  mark  +   n.
```

cosign[7] 〔 ͵koˋsaɪn 〕 *v.* 連署《*co-* = *com-* = together》

cosignatory 〔 koˋsɪɡnə͵torɪ 〕 *adj.* 連署的　*n.* 連署人；連署國

consign[7] 〔 kənˋsaɪn 〕 *v.* 交付；委託（共同簽署）

《*con-* = together》

consignable 〔 kənˋsaɪnəbḷ 〕 *adj.* 可委託的；可交付的

consignation 〔 ͵kɑnsɪɡˋneʃən 〕 *n.* 委託；託送

consignee 〔 ͵kɑnsaɪˋni , -sɪˋni 〕 *n.* 受託者；收貨人；承銷人

consigner ; -or 〔 kənˋsaɪnɚ 〕 *n.* 委託者；寄貨人；貨主

```
con   +  sign  +   er
|         |         |
together  +  mark  + person
```

consignment[7] 〔 kənˋsaɪnmənt 〕 *n.* （貨物的）委託

countersign 〔 ˋkaʊntɚ͵saɪn 〕 *v.* 連署；副署；承認

n. 對答暗號；口令；連署；副署《*counter-* = *contra-* = against》

countersignature 〔 ͵kaʊntɚˋsɪɡnətʃɚ 〕 *n.* 副署；連署

design² 〔 dɪˈzaɪn 〕 v. 設計；作圖案；打算　　n. 圖案；設計；意圖（在計劃上作記號）《*de-* = down》

designed⁷ 〔 dɪˈzaɪnd 〕 adj. 有計劃的；故意的

designedly 〔 dɪˈzaɪnɪdlɪ 〕 adv. 故意地

designer³ 〔 dɪˈzaɪnɚ 〕 n. 設計家；陰謀者

designate⁶ 〔 v. ˈdɛzɪgˌnet　adj. ˈdɛzɪgnɪt 〕 v. 指出；指定；命名　adj. 指派好的；選定的

designation⁷ 〔ˌdɛzɪgˈneʃən , ˌdɛs- 〕 n. 指示；指標；名稱

```
de  +  sign  +  ation
 |       |        |
down +  mark  +   n.
```

designator 〔ˈdɛzɪgˌnetɚ 〕 n. 指定者

ensign⁷ 〔ˈɛnsaɪn , ˈɛnsn̩ 〕 n. 旗；軍旗；旗手；徽章（有記號在上面）《*en-* = *in-* = on》

insignia⁷ 〔 ɪnˈsɪgnɪə 〕 n.pl. 標誌；徽章（上面有記號）《*in-* = on；*-ia* 複數名詞字尾》

resign⁴ 〔 rɪˈzaɪn 〕 v. 辭職；順從；委託（再度簽署 → 辭職時的署名）《*re-* = again》

resigned⁷ 〔 rɪˈzaɪnd 〕 adj. 順從的；聽天由命的

resignedly 〔 rɪˈzaɪnɪdlɪ 〕 adv. 認命地

resignation⁴ 〔ˌrɛzɪgˈneʃən , ˌrɛs- 〕 n. 辭呈；順從

undersign 〔ˌʌndɚˈsaɪn 〕 v. 在（信或文件等）的末尾簽名

532　simil , simul , sembl
=like；same（類似的；相同的）

* 拉丁文 *similis*（= like），*simul*（= together；at the same time）。〔變化型〕*sembl*。

simile⁷ 〔ˈsɪməˌli 〕 n. 直喻；明喻（類似的東西）

similar² 〔ˈsɪmələ 〕 adj. 類似的；同樣的　　n. 類似物

similarity[3] 〔͵sɪmə'lærətɪ〕*n.* 類似；類似點；相似處

similitude〔 sə'mɪlə͵tjud , -͵tud 〕*n.* 類似；比喻；相似的人或物
《 *-itude* 抽象名詞字尾》

```
simil + itude
  |       |
 like  +  n.
```

simulate[7] 〔'sɪmjə͵let 〕*v.* 假裝；扮演；類似　*adj.* 僞裝的；模擬的

simulant〔'sɪmjʊlənt 〕*adj.* 假裝的；模擬的

simultaneous[6]〔͵saɪml̩'tenɪəs , ͵sɪm- , -njəs 〕*adj.* 同時發生的；
同時的；同時存在的《 *-taneous* 形容詞字尾》

```
simul + taneous
  |        |
 same  +   adj.
```

simultaneity〔͵saɪml̩tə'niətɪ , ͵sɪml̩- 〕*n.* 同時存在；
同時發生；同時

simulcast〔'saɪml̩͵kæst , 'sɪml̩- 〕*v. , n.* (無線電和電視) 聯播
《*simul(taneous)* + *(broad)cast* (播送)》

assimilate[7]〔 ə'sɪml̩͵et 〕*v.* 同化；理解 (使成爲相同)
《*as-* = *ad-* = to》

assimilation〔 ə͵sɪml̩'eʃən 〕*n.* 同化 (作用)

dissimilate[7]〔 dɪ'sɪmə͵let 〕*v.* (使) 異化；(使) 變得不同
(使不相同)《*dis-* = not》

```
dis + simil + ate
 |      |      |
not + same  +  v.
```

dissimulate〔 dɪ'sɪmjə͵let 〕*v.* 掩飾；假裝《*dis-* 表示加強語氣》

semblance[7]〔'sɛmbləns 〕*n.* 相似；外觀

assemble[4]〔 ə'sɛmbl̩ 〕*v.* 聚集；集合 (集合志同道合者)
《*as-* = *ad-* = to》

assemblage〔ə'sɛmblɪdʒ〕*n.* 集合；集合物；集團；裝配
《 *-age* 抽象名詞字尾》

```
as  +  sembl  +  age
 |       |        |
to  +  same   +   n.
```

assembly[4]〔ə'sɛmblɪ〕*n.* 會合；集會；(A-)(美國州議會的) 下院
disassemble[7]〔͵dɪsə'sɛmbl̩〕*v.* 拆卸；分解
dissemble〔dɪ'sɛmbl̩〕*v.* 掩飾；隱藏；假裝 (使變得不像)
《*dis-* = not》
facsimile[7]〔fæk'sɪməlɪ〕*n.* 複製；無線電傳眞；傳眞照片
　v. 複製 (做成相同 → 複製)《*fac* = make》

```
fac  +  simile
 |        |
make  +  same
```

resemble[4]〔rɪ'zɛmbl̩〕*v.* 相似 (再看感覺也相同)《*re-* = again》
resemblance[6]〔rɪ'zɛmbləns〕*n.* 相似；形象
verisimilar〔͵vɛrə'sɪmələ〕*adj.* 像是眞實的；可能的 (像眞的)
《*ver(i)* = true》
verisimilitude〔͵vɛrəsə'mɪlə͵tjud〕*n.* 似眞；好像眞實；逼眞

533　**sinu** = curve (彎曲)

　　* 拉丁文 *sinus* (= *curve* ; *hollow* 洞)。

sinuate〔'sɪnju͵et , -ɪt〕*adj.* 彎曲的；波狀的
sinuation〔͵sɪnju'eʃən〕*n.* 曲折
sinuous〔'sɪnjuəs〕*adj.* 彎曲的；蜿蜒的；迂迴的；乖僻的

```
sinu  +  ous
 |        |
curve  +  adj.
```

sinuosity〔͵sɪnju'ɑsətɪ〕*n.* 彎曲；蜿蜒

sinus〔ˈsaɪnəs〕*n.* 竇；靜脈竇；凹處；彎曲；廔管

sinusitis〔ˌsaɪnəˈsaɪtɪs〕*n.* 靜脈竇炎《 *-itis* = inflammation（發炎）》

insinuate[7]〔ɪnˈsɪnjʊˌet〕*v.* 暗示；暗諷；迂迴地說（拐彎抹角地進入）《*in-* = into》

insinuation〔ɪnˌsɪnjʊˈeʃən〕*n.* 暗示；巧妙巴結

insinuative〔ɪnˈsɪnjʊˌetɪv〕*adj.* 暗示的；巧妙巴結的

534　**sist** = stand（站）

　　* 拉丁文 *sistere*（ = *take a stand*；*cause to stand*）。

assist[3]〔əˈsɪst〕*v.* 出席；幫助（站在一旁）《*as-* = *ad-* = to》

assistance[4]〔əˈsɪstəns〕*n.* 幫助

assistant[2]〔əˈsɪstənt〕*adj.* 幫助的　*n.* 助手

```
as  +  sist  +  ant
 |      |       |
to  +  stand  + adj., n.
```

assistantship〔əˈsɪstəntˌʃɪp〕*n.* 研究生助教獎學金

consist[4]〔kənˈsɪst〕*v.* 組成；存在；相容（站在一起）
　《*con-* = together》

consistent[4]〔kənˈsɪstənt〕*adj.* 一致的；經常不變的

consistence；-ency[7]〔kənˈsɪstəns(ɪ)〕*n.*（言行）一致；
　堅固；濃度

desist[7]〔dɪˈzɪst〕*v.* 停止；斷念（離去；走開）《*de-* = away》

exist[2]〔ɪgˈzɪst〕*v.* 存在；發生；活著（繼續站著）《*ex-* = out；forth》

existence[3]〔ɪgˈzɪstəns〕*n.* 存在；生存；實在

```
ex  +  ist  +  ence
 |      |       |
out  + stand  +  n.
```

existent[7]〔ɪgˈzɪstənt，ɛg-〕*adj.* 現存的；現行的；目前的

existential[7]〔ˌɛgzɪsˈtɛnʃəl〕*adj.* 存在主義的

existentialism 〔͵ɛgzɪs'tɛnʃəlɪzm̩ 〕 *n.* 存在主義

existentialist 〔͵ɛgzɪs'tɛnʃəlɪst 〕 *n.* 存在主義者

insist[2] 〔 ɪn'sɪst 〕 *v.* 強調；堅持（站在～之上不動）《*in-* = on》

insistent[7] 〔 ɪn'sɪstənt 〕 *adj.* 堅持的；強求的；顯著的

insistence[6]；**-ency** 〔 ɪn'sɪstəns(ɪ) 〕 *n.* 堅持；強調

persist[5] 〔 pɚ'zɪst , -'sɪst 〕 *v.* 堅持；固執（始終屹立）《*per-* = through》

persistent[6] 〔 pɚ'sɪstənt , -'zɪst- 〕 *adj.* 固執的；堅持的；持續性的

persistence[6]；**-ency** 〔 pɚ'sɪstəns(ɪ) , -'zɪst- 〕 *n.* 堅持；固執；持續

```
per   +  sist  + ence
 |        |        |
through + stand +   n.
```

resist[3] 〔 rɪ'zɪst 〕 *v.* 抵抗；對抗；忍住　*n.* 防染劑；絕緣塗料
（站在反方向）《*re-* = back ; against》

resistant[6] 〔 rɪ'zɪstənt 〕 *adj.* 抵抗的；有抵抗力的；有耐力的

resistance[4] 〔 rɪ'zɪstəns 〕 *n.* 抵抗（力）；地下組織

resister 〔 rɪ'zɪstɚ 〕 *n.* 抵抗者

resistible 〔 rɪ'zɪstəbl̩ 〕 *adj.* 可抵抗的

resistibility 〔 rɪ͵zɪstə'bɪlətɪ 〕 *n.* 抵抗力

resistive 〔 rɪ'zɪstɪv 〕 *adj.* 有抵抗力的

resistiveness 〔 rɪ'zɪstɪvnɪs 〕 *n.* 抵抗力

resistivity 〔͵rizɪs'tɪvətɪ 〕 *n.* 抵抗力

resistless 〔 rɪ'zɪstlɪs 〕 *adj.* 無法抵抗的

irresistible[7] 〔͵ɪrɪ'zɪstəbl̩ 〕 *adj.* 無法抵抗的；無法抗拒的
《*ir-* = *in-* = not》

subsist 〔 səb'sɪst 〕 *v.* 生存；生活；過日子；存在；供養；給與
糧食（站在下面）《*sub-* = under》

```
sub  +  sist
 |       |
under + stand
```

subsistence；**-ency**[7] 〔 səb'sɪstəns(ɪ) 〕 *n.* 生活；生存；生計

535　smith = worker（工人）　*源自古英文。

blacksmith[5]〔'blæk,smɪθ〕 n. 鐵匠　cf. **whitesmith**（錫匠；銀匠）
goldsmith[7]〔'gold,smɪθ〕 n. 金匠
gunsmith[7]〔'gʌn,smɪθ〕 n. 槍砲工人
locksmith[7]〔'lɑk,smɪθ〕 n. 鎖匠
swordsmith[7]〔'sord,smɪθ〕 n. 製造或修理刀劍之工匠
wordsmith[7]〔'wɜd,smɪθ〕 n. 語言專家；以寫作維生的人

536　soci = companion；join（同伴；結合）

*拉丁文 *socius*（ = *companion* ），*sociare*（ = *join* ）。

sociable[6]〔'soʃəbḷ〕 adj. 好交際的；社交性的；聯誼的
sociability〔,soʃə'bɪlətɪ〕 n. 好交際；交際性；友善
social[2]〔'soʃəl〕 adj. 社會的；社交的；有關社會地位的；群居的
socialism[6]〔'soʃəl,ɪzəm〕 n. 社會主義；社會主義運動
socialist[6]〔'soʃəlɪst〕 n. 社會主義者；社會黨黨員
socialite[7]〔'soʃə,laɪt〕 n. 社會名流《 *-ite* 表示人的名詞字尾》

soci	+	al	+	ite
companion	+	adj.	+	person

socialize[6]〔'soʃə,laɪz〕 v. 使社會化；使社會主義化
socialization[7]〔,soʃəlɪ'zeʃən〕 n. 社會化；社會主義化
society[2]〔sə'saɪətɪ〕 n. 社會；協會；社交界；交際
sociology[6]〔,soʃɪ'ɑlədʒɪ〕 n. 社會學《 *ology* = study》

soci	+	ology
companion	+	study

sociological〔,soʃɪə'lɑdʒɪkḷ〕 adj. 社會學的；社會問題的
sociologist〔,soʃɪ'ɑlədʒɪst〕 n. 社會學家

associate[4]〔 *v.* ə'soʃɪ,et *n.* ə'soʃɪɪt 〕*v.* 聯想;結交　*n.* 同伴;準會員
　　adj. 同伴的;準~（向~結交）《*as-* = *ad-* = to》

associable〔 ə'soʃɪəbḷ 〕*adj.* 可聯想的;聯想得到的

```
as + soci + able
 |     |      |
to + join + adj.
```

associated[7]〔 ə'soʃɪ,etɪd 〕*adj.* 聯合的;有關聯的;聯想的
association[4]〔 ə,sosɪ'eʃən 〕*n.* 協會;團體;交際;交往;聯想
associative〔 ə'soʃɪ,etɪv 〕*adj.* 聯合的;聯想的
consociate〔 *v.* kən'soʃɪ,et *adj.* kən'soʃɪɪt , -,et 〕*v.*（使）聯合
　　（與~一起結交）　*adj.* = associate《*con-* = together》
consociation〔 kən,soʃɪ'eʃən 〕*n.* 聯合;聯盟
dissociate[7]〔 dɪ'soʃɪ,et 〕*v.* 分開;使脫離;分裂（不結交）
　　《*dis-* = not》

```
dis + soci + ate
 |     |      |
not + join + v.
```

dissociable〔 dɪ'soʃɪəbḷ , -'soʃəbḷ 〕*adj.* 可分離的;孤僻的
dissociation〔 dɪ,soʃɪ'eʃən 〕*n.* 分離;分裂

537　**sol** = alone（單獨的）

　　* 拉丁文 *solus*（ = *alone*）。

sole[5]〔 sol 〕*adj.* 唯一的;專用的
solely[7]〔'solɪ 〕*adv.* 單獨地;僅僅;完全地
solitary[5]〔'salə,tɛrɪ 〕*adj.* 孤獨的;唯一的　*n.* 獨居者（只有一人的）
solitude[6]〔'salə,tjud 〕*n.* 孤獨;荒僻之地;獨居

```
sol  + itude
 |      |
alone + n.
```

solo⁵〔'solo〕n. 獨唱（曲）；獨奏（曲）　adj. 單獨的

soloist⁷〔'so͵lo‧ɪst〕n. 獨唱者；獨奏者

soliloquy⁷〔sə'lɪləkwɪ〕n. 獨白（獨自一人說的話）

《*loquy* = speech》

console⁵〔kən'sol〕v. 安慰（共同表示獨身的寂寞）

```
con  +  sole
 |       |
wholly + alone
```

consolation⁶〔͵kɑnsə'leʃən〕n. 安慰；慰藉

solace⁷〔'sɑlɪs , -əs〕n. 安慰；慰藉　v. 安慰；減輕（悲傷）

desolate⁷〔adj. 'dɛsḷɪt　v. 'dɛsḷ͵et〕v. 使荒蕪；使悲傷；遺棄

adj. 荒涼的；荒廢的（完全陷於寂寞無助）《*de-* = fully》

desolation⁷〔͵dɛsḷ'eʃən〕n. 荒廢；悲哀

```
de  +  sol  + ation
 |      |       |
fully + alone +  n.
```

538　sol = sun（太陽）　　*拉丁文 *sol*（= *sun*）。

solar⁴〔'solɚ〕adj. 太陽的；與太陽有關的

solarium〔so'lɛrɪəm〕n. 日光浴室；日晷儀

《*-arium* 表示場所的名詞字尾》

```
sol + arium
 |     |
sun +  n.
```

solarize〔'solə͵raɪz〕v. 使暴露於日光下；使感光；安裝利用
太陽能的設備

solarization〔͵soləraɪ'zeʃən〕n. 曝曬

solstice[7] 〔ˈsɑlstɪs〕 *n.* 【天文】至日；至（太陽向南或向北離赤道最遠的時候）

circumsolar 〔ˌsɝkəmˈsolɚ〕 *adj.* 環日的；繞太陽轉的（環繞太陽）

《*circum-* = around》

extrasolar 〔ˌɛkstrəˈsolɚ〕 *adj.* 太陽系外的（超越太陽）

《*extra-* = beyond》

```
extra  +  sol  +  ar
  |        |       |
beyond  +  sun  +  adj.
```

insolate 〔ˈɪnsoˌlet〕 *v.* 曝曬於陽光（放在陽光中）《*in-* = in》

insolation 〔ˌɪnsoˈleʃən〕 *n.* 曝曬於陽光；中暑；日照（率）

parasol 〔ˈpærəˌsɔl〕 *n.* 陽傘（預防太陽照射）《*para-* = against》

```
para   +  sol
  |        |
against +  sun
```

subsolar 〔sʌbˈsolɚ〕 *adj.* 太陽下的；日下的（太陽底下）

《*sub-* = under》

turnsole 〔ˈtɝnˌsol〕 *n.* 向陽性植物（隨太陽轉）

539   solid = solid（堅固的）

> * 拉丁文 *solidus*（= *solid* ; *firm*），與 *sollus*（= *whole*）有關。
> 〔變化型〕*sold*。

solid[3] 〔ˈsɑlɪd〕 *adj.* 堅實的；固體的；一致的   *n.* 固體；固體物質（完全結合成一整體）

solidity 〔səˈlɪdətɪ〕 *n.* 固體性；體積；實質

solidarity[6] 〔ˌsɑləˈdærətɪ〕 *n.* 團結一致

solidify[7] 〔səˈlɪdəˌfaɪ〕 *v.* 使凝固；團結一致（結合成為一體）

《*-ify* = make》

consolidate[7]〔kən'salə,det〕*v.* 鞏固；強化；結合（完全結合成
一體）《*con-* = wholly》

consolidation[7]〔kən,salə'deʃən〕*n.* 鞏固；強化；團結

solder〔'sadɚ〕*n.* 焊劑；接合物　*v.* 焊接

soldier[2]〔'soldʒɚ〕*n.* 軍人；士兵

solemn[5]〔'saləm〕*adj.* 嚴肅的；莊重的；嚴重的
《拉丁文 *sollemnis* = formal》

solemnity〔sə'lɛmnətɪ〕*n.* 莊嚴；嚴肅；儀式

540　solv , solut = loosen（鬆開）

* 拉丁文 *solvere*（= *loosen*），過去分詞為 *solutus*。
〔變化型〕*solu*。

solve[2]〔salv〕*v.* 解決；溶解

soluble[7]〔'saljəbḷ〕*adj.* 可溶解的；可解決的

solute〔'saljut , 'soljut , 'solut〕*n.* 溶質

solution[2]〔sə'luʃən , -'lju-〕*n.* 解決；溶解；溶液

solvable[7]〔'salvəbḷ〕*adj.* 可解決的；可溶解的

solvent[7]〔'salvənt〕*adj.* 有溶解力的；能償還的　*n.* 溶劑；溶媒

absolve[7]〔æb'salv , əb- , -'zalv〕*v.* 赦免；解除（鬆綁放出）
《*ab-* = away》

```
ab  +  solve
 |       |
away + loosen
```

absolution〔,æbsə'luʃən , -sḷ'juʃən〕*n.* 赦免；免除

absolute[4]〔'æbsə,lut〕*adj.* 絕對的；無條件的（鬆懈解放的 → 不受
約束的）

dissolve[6]〔dɪ'zalv〕*v.* 溶解；解散（分解開來）《*dis-* = apart》

dissoluble〔dɪ'saljəbḷ〕*adj.* 可溶解的；可解散的

dissolution[7]〔,dɪsə'luʃən , -sḷ'juʃən〕*n.* 溶解；解除

dissolute〔'dɪsə,lut , 'dɪsə,ljut〕 *adj.* 放蕩的（放鬆懈怠的心情）

```
dis  +  solute
 |        |
apart  +  loosen
```

dissolvable〔dɪ'zɑlvəbḷ〕 *adj.* 可解除的；可溶解的
dissolvent〔dɪ'zɑlvənt〕 *adj.* 有溶解力的　*n.* 溶劑
insolvable〔ɪn'sɑlvəbḷ〕 *adj.* 無法解決的《*in-* = not》
insolvency[7]〔ɪn'sɑlvənsɪ〕 *n.* 無力清償債務；破產

```
in  +  solv   +  ency
 |       |        |
not  +  loosen  +  n.
```

insolvent[7]〔ɪn'sɑlvənt〕 *adj.* 無力清償債務的；破產的
resolve[4]〔rɪ'zɑlv〕 *v.* 分解；決定；解決；議決　*n.* 決心
（鬆解使回復原狀）《*re-* = back ; again》
resolvable〔rɪ'zɑlvəbḷ〕 *adj.* 可分解的；可解決的
resolvent〔rɪ'zɑlvənt〕 *adj.* 分解的；溶解的　*n.* 溶劑；消腫藥
resolute[6]〔'rɛzə,lut , 'rɛzḷ,jut〕 *adj.* 堅決的；勇敢的；斷然的
resolution[4]〔,rɛzə'ljuʃən , -zḷ'juʃən〕 *n.* 決心；決議（案）；解決

541　somn = sleep（睡）　* 拉丁文 *somnus*（= *sleep*）。

somnambulate〔sɑm'næmbjə,let〕 *v.* 夢遊（睡眠時走動）
《*ambul* = walk》

```
somn  +  ambul  +  ate
  |        |        |
sleep  +  walk   +  v.
```

somnambulism〔sɑm'næmbjə,lɪzəm〕 *n.* 夢遊症
（= *sleepwalking*）《 *-ism* 表示「疾病」》
somnambulist〔sɑm'næmbjəlɪst〕 *n.* 夢遊症患者
somniferous〔sɑm'nɪfərəs〕 *adj.* 催眠的；想睡的（產生睡眠欲望）
《 *-ferous* = causing》

字根
sacr~surge

somniloquy 〔 sɑm'nɪləkwɪ 〕 *n.* 夢話；說夢話（睡眠中說的話）

《*loquy* = speech》

somnolent 〔'sɑmnələnt 〕 *adj.* 想睡的；催眠的

somnolence 〔'sɑmnələns 〕 *n.* 昏昏欲睡；嗜睡狀態

insomnia[7] 〔 ɪn'sɑmnɪə 〕 *n.* 失眠；失眠症（睡不著）《*in-* = not》

insomniac[7] 〔 ɪn'sɑmnɪæk 〕 *adj.* 失眠症的；令人失眠的

n. 失眠症患者

542　son = sound（聲音）　　* 拉丁文 *sonus*（= *sound*）。

sonant 〔'sonənt 〕 *adj.* 有聲音的；有聲的

sonance 〔'sonəns 〕 *n.* 有聲音的性質或狀態；有聲

sonar[7] 〔'sonɑr 〕 *n.* 聲納（利用聲波的反射探測水中障礙物或海底狀況

的裝置）

sonata[7] 〔 sə'nɑtə 〕 *n.* 奏鳴曲

sonic[7] 〔'sɑnɪk 〕 *adj.* 音的；音波的；音速的

soniferous 〔 so'nɪfərəs 〕 *adj.* 發出聲音的；傳聲的（產生聲音）

《 *-ferous* = causing》

```
soni  +  ferous
 |         |
sound  +  causing
```

sonnet[7] 〔'sɑnɪt 〕 *n.* 十四行詩《 *-et* 表示小的名詞字尾》

sonorous 〔 sə'norəs , -'nɔr- 〕 *adj.* 響亮的；鏗鏘的

sonority 〔 sə'nɔrətɪ 〕 *n.* 響亮；鳴響

assonant 〔'æsənənt 〕 *adj.* 諧音的《*as-* = *ad-* = to》

assonance 〔'æsənəns 〕 *n.* 諧音；（詩的）半諧音

consonant[4] 〔'kɑnsənənt 〕 *n.* 子音　　*adj.* 一致的；和諧的

（一起發出的聲音）《*con-* = together》

```
con  +  son  +  ant
 |       |       |
together + sound + adj.
```

consonance[7] 〔'kɑnsənəns〕 *n.* 一致；和諧

dissonant[7] 〔'dɪsənənt〕 *adj.* 不和諧的；不一致的（聲音分散）

《*dis-* = apart》

dissonance[7] 〔'dɪsənəns〕 *n.* 不和諧的聲音；不一致

resonant[7] 〔'rɛznənt〕 *adj.* 響亮的；產生共鳴的（有回聲）

《*re-* = back》

resonance[7] 〔'rɛznəns〕 *n.* 響亮；共鳴；回響

resonate[7] 〔'rɛzə,net〕 *v.* 共鳴；共振

re	+	son	+	ate
back	+	*sound*	+	*v.*

resonator 〔'rɛzə,netɚ〕 *n.* 共鳴器；共鳴體；共振器

subsonic[7] 〔sʌb'sɑnɪk〕 *adj.* 低於音速的（速度比聲音低）

《*sub-* = under》

supersonic[6] 〔,supɚ'sɑnɪk〕 *adj.* 超音速的；超音波的 *n.* 超音波
（速度超越聲音）《*super-* = over》

super	+	son	+	ic
over	+	*sound*	+	*adj.*

ultrasonic[7] 〔,ʌltrə'sɑnɪk〕 *adj.* 超音波的；超音速的

《*ultra-* = beyond》

unison[7] 〔'junəsn̩ , -zn̩〕 *n.* 和諧；一致（單獨一種聲音）《*uni-* = one》

unisonant 〔ju'nɪsənənt〕 *adj.* 同音的；和諧的；一致的

unisonous 〔ju'nɪsənəs〕 *adj.* = unisonant

543　soph = wise；wisdom（聰明的；智慧）

* 希臘文 *sophos*（= wise），*sophia*（= wisdom）。

sophism 〔'sɑfɪzəm〕 *n.* 詭辯；似是而非的理論（聰明的言論）

《*-ism* 表示性質的名詞字尾》

sophist〔'safɪst〕*n.* 詭辯家;詭辯學者

sophistic〔sə'fɪstɪk〕*adj.* 詭辯的

```
soph  +  ist   +  ic
 |        |        |
wise  + person  + adj.
```

sophisticate〔sə'fɪstɪ,ket〕*v.* 使世故;複雜化　*n.* 世故的人
（會詭辯）

sophisticated[6]〔sə'fɪstɪ,ketɪd〕*adj.* 世故的;極有素養的;複雜的

sophistication[7]〔sə,fɪstɪ'keʃən〕*n.* 世故;良好教養;複雜

sophistry〔'safɪstrɪ〕*n.* 詭辯;詭辯法

sophomore[4]〔'safm̩,or , -,ɔr〕*n.*（大學、高中的）二年級學生
（一半聰明,一半愚笨）《拉丁文 *sophos*（wise）+ *moros*（foolish）》

cf. **freshman**（一年級學生）,**junior**（三年級學生）,**senior**（四年級學生）

```
sopho  +  more
  |         |
wise   + foolish
```

sophomoric〔,safə'mɔrɪk〕*adj.* 二年級學生的;一知半解的;
膚淺的

philosophy[4]〔fə'lasəfɪ〕*n.* 哲學;人生觀;冷靜（愛好智慧）
《*philo* = love》

philosopher[4]〔fə'lasəfɚ〕*n.* 哲學家;冷靜達觀者

philosophic;**-ical**[4]〔,fɪlə'safɪk(l̩)〕*adj.* 哲學的;達觀的

544　　sort = kind（種類）

　　* 拉丁文 *sors* , *sort-*（= *lot* 籤 ; *fate* 命運）;古法文 *sorte*（= *kind*）。

sort[2]〔sɔrt〕*n.* 種類　*v.* 分類;整理;揀選

sorter〔'sɔrtɚ〕*n.* 分類者;整理者;揀選者

assort[7]〔ə'sɔrt〕*v.* 分類;配合;符合;交往（按種類分）
《*as-* = *ad-* = to》

assorted[7] 〔 ə'sɔrtɪd 〕 *adj.* 各色俱備的；什錦的；相配的

assortment[7] 〔 ə'sɔrtmənt 〕 *n.* 分類；各色齊備；什錦

```
as + sort + ment
 |     |      |
to + kind +   n.
```

consort[7] 〔 *n.* 'kɑnsɔrt *v.* kən'sɔrt 〕 *n.* 配偶；隨航的船隻
v. 交往；一致；符合（同類）《*con-* = with》

consortium 〔 kən'sɔrʃɪəm 〕 *n.* 國際財團；國際性集團；協會
《 *-ium* 名詞字尾》

```
con + sort + ium
 |     |      |
with + kind +  n.
```

resort[15] 〔 ˌri'sɔrt 〕 *v.* 再分類；重新分類（再次按種類分）
《*re-* = again》

resort[25] 〔 rɪ'zɔrt 〕 *v.* 常去；訴諸   *n.* 遊樂地；訴諸
《*re-* = back ; *sort* = come out》

545　spec , spect , spic = see ; look (看)

＊ 拉丁文 *specere* (= see ; look) ，*spectare* (= watch)。
〔變化型〕*spic*。

species[4] 〔 'spiʃɪz , -ʃiz 〕 *n.* 種類（外觀相同的整體）

special[1] 〔 'spɛʃəl 〕 *adj.* 特別的；專門的；臨時的
n. 特別的人（物）；特派員；專送信函；特電；號外；特刊

specialist[5] 〔 'spɛʃəlɪst 〕 *n.* 專家；專科醫師

```
spec + ial + ist
 |      |     |
see + adj. + person
```

speciality[6] 〔 ˌspɛʃɪ'ælətɪ 〕 *n.* 專門；專攻；特色；名產

specialize[6] 〔'spɛʃəl,aɪz 〕 *v.* 使專門化；專攻

specimen[5] 〔'spɛsəmən 〕 *n.* 樣品；標本（專門展示的東西）

spice[3] 〔 spaɪs 〕 *n.* 香料；趣味；風味　*v.* 加以香料（混雜在一起的東西）

specify[6] 〔'spɛsə,faɪ 〕 *v.* 指定；詳細記載（使特殊）《 *-ify* = make》

```
spec  +  ify
 |        |
see   +  make
```

specific[3] 〔 spɪ'sɪfɪk 〕 *adj.* 特別的；明確的　*n.* 特效藥

specious[7] 〔'spiʃəs 〕 *adj.* 似是而非的；華而不實的

spectacle[5] 〔'spɛktəkḷ 〕 *n.* 景象；壯觀；(*pl.*) 眼鏡（用來看的東西）

spectacular[6] 〔 spɛk'tækjələ 〕 *adj.* 供人觀看的；壯觀的　*n.* 豪華電視節目

spectator[5] 〔'spɛktetə, spɛk'tetə 〕 *n.* 旁觀者

```
spect  +  at(e)  +   or
 |          |         |
see    +   v.    + person
```

spectral[7] 〔'spɛktrəl 〕 *adj.* 幽靈的；可怕的；光譜的（看得見的東西）

spectre; **-ter** 〔'spɛktə 〕 *n.* 幽靈；鬼

spectrum[6] 〔'spɛktrəm 〕 *n.* 光譜（閉上眼睛之後還能看見的東西）

specular 〔'spɛkjələ 〕 *adj.* 如鏡的；反射的

speculate[6] 〔'spɛkjə,let 〕 *v.* 思索；投機；推測（用心眼來看）

speculation[7] 〔,spɛkjə'leʃən 〕 *n.* 思索；投機；推想

speculator[7] 〔'spɛkjə,letə 〕 *n.* 投機者；思想家

speculum 〔'spɛkjələm 〕 *n.* 檢查鏡；反射鏡（用來看的儀器）
《 *-um* 名詞字尾》

```
specul  +  um
  |         |
see    +    n.
```

auspice[7] 〔'ɔspɪs 〕 *n.* 前兆；吉兆；保護（看鳥而算出吉兆）
《*au* = *avi* = bird》

conspicuous[7] 〔 kən'spɪkjuəs 〕 *adj.* 顯著的；引人注目的
（能夠完全看清楚）《*con-* = thoroughly》

con	+ spic + uous
thoroughly	+ see + adj.

frontispiece 〔'frʌntɪs‚pis , 'frɑn- 〕 *n.* （書籍的）卷首插圖；
（門窗頂上的）三角楣飾（能夠在前面看到者）

perspicuous 〔 pə'spɪkjuəs 〕 *adj.* 明白的；明顯的（清楚地看到）
《*per-* = through》

perspicacious 〔‚pɝspɪ'keʃəs 〕 *adj.* 眼光銳利的；明察的

transpicuous 〔 træn'spɪkjuəs 〕 *adj.* 透明的（看穿；看透）
《*tran(s)-* = through》

tran	+ spic + uous
through	+ see + adj.

despise[5] 〔 dɪ'spaɪz 〕 *v.* 輕蔑（鄙視）《*de-* = down》

despicable[7] 〔'dɛspɪkəbļ 〕 *adj.* 可鄙的；卑劣的

despite[4] 〔 dɪ'spaɪt 〕 *n.* 侮辱；輕蔑　*prep.* 不顧；縱使

aspect[4] 〔'æspɛkt 〕 *n.* 外觀；形勢；容貌；方面（看～）
《*a-* = *ad-* = to ; at》

circumspect[7] 〔'sɝkəm‚spɛkt 〕 *adj.* 慎重的（看清楚四周）
《*circum-* = round》

circum	+ spect
round	+ see

conspectus 〔 kən'spɛktəs 〕 *n.* 概觀；摘要；大綱（整個一起看）
《*con-* = together ; *-us* 名詞字尾》

expect[2] 〔 ɪk'spɛkt 〕 *v.* 預期；期待（等待著向外看去）《*ex-* = out》

expectant[7] 〔 ɪk'spɛktənt 〕 *adj.* 期待的；懷孕的

```
ex  +  pect  +  ant
|       |       |
out  +  see  +  adj.
```

expectancy[7] 〔 ɪk'spɛktənsɪ 〕 *n.* 期待；預期；可能性；將來的指望
expectation[3] 〔 ,ɛkspɛk'teʃən 〕 *n.* 期望；預料；可能性
inspect[3] 〔 ɪn'spɛkt 〕 *v.* 檢查；查閱（窺視內部）《*in-* = into》
inspection[4] 〔 ɪn'spɛkʃən 〕 *n.* 檢查；視察；檢閱
inspector[3] 〔 ɪn'spɛktɚ 〕 *n.* 檢查員；巡視員（官）
introspect[7] 〔 ,ɪntrə'spɛkt 〕 *v.* 內省（看到心靈內部）

```
intro  +  spect
  |         |
within  +  look
```

introspection[7] 〔 ,ɪntrə'spɛkʃən 〕 *n.* 內省；反省《*-ion* 名詞字尾》
perspective[6] 〔 pɚ'spɛktɪv 〕 *n.* 透視法；前景；前途；正確的眼光
　　adj. 透視的（直視無礙）《*per-* = through》

```
per    +  spect  +  ive
 |         |        |
through  +  see  +  adj.
```

prospect[7] 〔 'prɑspɛkt 〕 *n.* 期望；景色；眺望　　*v.* 探採（金礦等）；
　　探勘；尋找（看前方）《*pro-* = forward》
prospective[7] 〔 prə'spɛktɪv 〕 *adj.* 預期的；未來的；有希望的
respect[2] 〔 rɪ'spɛkt 〕 *v.* 尊敬；重視；顧慮　　*n.* 敬重；關心；
　　（*pl.*）敬意（一再注視）《*re-* = again》
respectable[4] 〔 rɪ'spɛktəbl̩ 〕 *adj.* 可尊敬的；有聲望的；相當好的
　　（應受尊重的）

```
re     +  spect  +  able
 |         |        |
again  +  see  +  adj.
```

respectful[4] 〔 rɪˈspɛktfəl 〕 *adj.* 表示尊敬的（充滿尊敬之意）

respective[6] 〔 rɪˈspɛktɪv 〕 *adj.* 各別的（有關各自的）

retrospect[7] 〔ˈrɛtrəˌspɛkt 〕 *v.* 回顧　*n.* 回顧；追憶（向後看）
《*retro-* = backward》

retrospective[7] 〔ˌrɛtrəˈspɛktɪv 〕 *adj.* 回顧的；回想的

```
retro    + spect + ive
  |          |       |
backward +  see  +  adj.
```

suspect[3] 〔 *v.* səˈspɛkt *n.*, *adj.* ˈsʌspɛkt 〕 *v.* 猜想；懷疑　*n.* 嫌疑犯
adj. 可疑的（猜疑外表之下的東西）《*sus-* = *sub-* = under》

suspicion[3] 〔 səˈspɪʃən 〕 *n.* 懷疑；嫌疑

suspicious[4] 〔 səˈspɪʃəs 〕 *adj.* 可疑的

spy[3] 〔 spaɪ 〕 *v.* 偵察；窺察　*n.* 間諜；偵探（視察）
《古法文 *espier* = watch》

espy[7] 〔 əˈspaɪ 〕 *v.* 看出；探出《*e-* 是由於發音的需要而添加的》

espionage[7] 〔ˈɛspɪənɪdʒ, əˈspaɪənɪdʒ 〕 *n.* 間諜活動

espial 〔 ɪˈspaɪəl, ɛ- 〕 *n.* 偵察；監視

字根 *sacr~surge*

546　**sper** = hope（希望）　* 拉丁文 *sperare*（= hope）。

desperado[7] 〔ˌdɛspəˈredo 〕 *n.* 亡命之徒；暴徒（絕望的人）
《*de-* = deprive of；*-ado* 表「人」》

```
de       + sper  + ado
  |          |       |
deprive of + hope + person
```

desperate[4] 〔ˈdɛspərɪt 〕 *adj.* 絕望的；自暴自棄的；拼命的

desperately[7] 〔ˈdɛspərɪtlɪ 〕 *adv.* 絕望地；自暴自棄地；拼命地

desperation[7] 〔ˌdɛspəˈreʃən 〕 *n.* 絕望；自暴自棄；拼命

despair[5] 〔 dɪˈspɛr 〕 *n.* 絕望；令人失望的人或物　*v.* 絕望；斷念
（失去希望）《*spair* = *sper* = hope》

despairing 〔 dɪˈspɛrɪŋ 〕 *adj.* 絕望的

prosper[4] 〔ˈprɑspɚ 〕 = be favorable　*v.* 繁榮；成功
（有希望往前進）《*pro-* = forward》

prosperity[4] 〔 prɑsˈpɛrətɪ 〕 *n.* 繁榮；成功；幸運

prosperous[4] 〔ˈprɑspərəs 〕 *adj.* 繁榮的；成功的

547　**spers** = scatter（散布）

* 拉丁文 *spargere*（= *scatter*），過去分詞是 *sparsus*。

asperse 〔 əˈspɝs 〕 *v.* 誹謗；中傷（對～散布謠言）
《*a(s)-* = *ad-* = to》

aspersion[7] 〔 əˈspɝʒən 〕 *n.* 誹謗；中傷

disperse[6] 〔 dɪˈspɝs 〕 *v.* 使分散；驅散；消散；散布（四處散播）
《*di-* = *dis-* = apart》

dispersal[7] 〔 dɪˈspɝsḷ 〕 *n.* 分散；消散

dispersed 〔 dɪˈspɝst 〕 *adj.* 零零散散的；稀疏的

```
di   +  spers  +  ed
 |        |        |
apart + scatter + adj.
```

dispersion[7] 〔 dɪˈspɝʃən 〕 *n.* 分散；散布；消散

dispersive 〔 dɪˈspɝsɪv 〕 *adj.* 散布性的；分散的

intersperse 〔ˌɪntɚˈspɝs 〕 *v.* 散布；散置；點綴（在～之間撒）
《*inter-* = between》

```
inter   +  sperse
  |          |
between + scatter
```

interspersion 〔ˌɪntɚˈspɝʃən 〕 *n.* 散布；散置；點綴

sparse[7] 〔 spɑrs 〕 *adj.* 稀少的；稀疏的

sparsity 〔ˈspɑrsətɪ 〕 *n.* 稀疏；稀少；稀薄

548　spher = ball（球）

> * 希臘文 *sphaira*（= *ball*）；拉丁文 *sphaera*（= *ball*）。

sphere[6]〔sfɪr〕*n.* 球；球體；天體；範圍；地位
spherical〔'sfɛrɪkl̩〕*adj.* 球狀的；天體的
sphericity〔sfɪ'rɪsətɪ〕*n.* 球狀；球形
spherics〔'sfɛrɪks〕*n.* 球面幾何學；球面三角學《 *-ics* = science》
spheroid〔'sfɪrɔɪd〕*n.* 橢圓體（形狀類似球的物體）
　《 *-oid* = resembling（相似的）》
spherometer〔sfɪ'rɑmətɚ〕*n.* 球面計；測球體（測量球體的儀器）
　《 *meter* = measure》

```
sphero  +   meter
  |          |
 ball   +  measure
```

spherule〔'sfɛrul〕*n.* 小球；小球體（小的球）《 *-ule* = small》
atmosphere[4]〔'ætməs,fɪr〕*n.* 大氣；大氣層；氣氛（地球四周的
　氣體）《 *atmo(s)* = vapor》

```
atmo  +  sphere
 |         |
vapor  +  ball
```

atmospheric；**-ical**〔,ætməs'fɛrɪk(l̩)〕*adj.* 大氣的；利用大氣的
hemisphere[6]〔'hɛməs,fɪr〕*n.* 半球；範圍；領域《 *hemi-* = half》
hemispheric；**-ical**〔,hɛmə'sfɛrɪk(l̩)〕*adj.* 半球狀的

549　spir = breathe（呼吸）

> * 拉丁文 *spirare*（= *breathe*）。

spirit[2]〔'spɪrɪt〕*n.* 精神；靈魂；心靈；幽靈；酒精
　（呼吸 → 生命的根源）

dispirit〔 dɪ'spɪrɪt 〕 *v.* 使氣餒；使沮喪（使精神喪失）
《*di-* = *dis-* = deprive of》

inspirit〔 ɪn'spɪrɪt 〕 *v.* 激勵；鼓舞（注入精神）《*in-* = into》

```
in + spirit
 |     |
into + breathe
```

spirited[7]〔'spɪrɪtɪd 〕 *adj.* 有精神的；熱烈的

spiritless〔'spɪrɪtlɪs 〕 *adj.* 無精打采的

spiritual[4]〔'spɪrɪtʃʊəl 〕 *adj.* 精神上的；神聖的

spiritualism〔'spɪrɪtʃʊəlˌɪzəm 〕 *n.* 招魂說

spiritualist〔'spɪrɪtʃʊəlɪst 〕 *n.* 靈媒

spirituality[7]〔ˌspɪrɪtʃʊ'ælətɪ 〕 *n.* 靈性

spiritualize〔'spɪrɪtʃʊəlˌaɪz 〕 *v.* 使精神化；使高尚

spirituel〔ˌspɪrɪtʃʊ'ɛl 〕 *adj.* 高雅的；活潑的

spirituous〔'spɪrɪtʃʊəs 〕 *adj.* 含酒精的

spiracle〔'spaɪrəkl̩ , 'spɪ- 〕 *n.* 通氣孔（呼吸的通道）

spirant〔'spaɪrənt 〕 *n.* , *adj.* 摩擦音（的）

sprite[7]〔 spraɪt 〕 *n.* 小精靈《古法文 *esprit* = spirit》

sprightly〔'spraɪtlɪ 〕 *adj.* 活潑的；愉快的

esprit[7]〔 ɛ'spri 〕 *n.* 精神

aspire[7]〔 ə'spaɪr 〕 *v.* 渴望；立志（對～吐氣）《*a-* = *ad-* = to》

aspirant[7]〔'æspərənt 〕 *n.* 渴望者　*adj.* 野心勃勃的

aspiration[7]〔ˌæspə'reʃən 〕 *n.* 呼吸；渴望

aspirational〔ˌæspə'reʃənl̩ 〕 *adj.* 有抱負的

aspiring[7]〔 ə'spaɪrɪŋ 〕 *adj.* 有抱負的

aspirate〔 *v.* 'æspəˌret *n.* , *adj.* 'æspərɪt 〕 *v.* 將…發成送氣音；
（用吸引器）抽吸（體腔中的液體）　*n.* 送氣音；抽出物
adj. 送氣音的

conspire[7]〔 kən'spaɪr 〕 *v.* 密謀；協力（一起呼吸，一鼻子出氣
→ 密謀）《*con-* = together》

conspiracy[6] 〔 kən'spɪrəsɪ 〕 *n.* 密謀；謀叛

```
con    +   spir   + acy
 |          |        |
together + breathe +  n.
```

conspirator[7] 〔 kən'spɪrətɚ 〕 *n.* 密謀者；謀叛者
conspiratorial 〔 kən,spɪrə'torɪəl 〕 *adj.* 陰謀的
expire[6] 〔 ɪk'spaɪr 〕 *v.* 呼氣；期滿；熄滅 (吐出氣)《*ex-* = out》
expiration[6] 〔 ,ɛkspə'reʃən 〕 *n.* 呼出；期滿
expiratory 〔 ɪk'spaɪrə,torɪ 〕 *adj.* 吐氣的
expiry[7] 〔 ɪk'spaɪrɪ , 'ɛkspərɪ 〕 *n.* 終止；期滿《*-y* 名詞字尾》
inspire[4] 〔 ɪn'spaɪr 〕 *v.* 鼓舞；激起；給與靈感 (吹入生氣)
　　《*in-* = into》
inspired[7] 〔 ɪn'spaɪrd 〕 *adj.* 極好的
inspiration[4] 〔 ,ɪnspə'reʃən 〕 *n.* 靈感；吸氣；鼓勵 (者)
inspirational[7] 〔 ,ɪnspə'reʃənl̩ 〕 *adj.* 啓發靈感的；鼓舞人心的
inspirator 〔 'ɪnspə,retɚ 〕 *n.* 激勵者
inspiring[7] 〔 ɪn'spaɪrɪŋ 〕 *adj.* 激勵人心的；啓發靈感的
perspire[7] 〔 pɚ'spaɪr 〕 *v.* 流汗 (透過皮膚呼吸)
　　《*per-* = through》
perspirable 〔 pɚ'spaɪrəbl̩ 〕 *adj.* 可排汗的
perspiration[7] 〔 ,pɝspə'reʃən 〕 *n.* 流汗；汗

```
per    +  spir   + ation
 |          |         |
through + breathe +   n.
```

perspiratory 〔 pɚ'spaɪrə,torɪ 〕 *adj.* 排汗的
respire[7] 〔 rɪ'spaɪr 〕 *v.* 呼吸 (恢復呼吸)《*re-* = back》
respirable 〔 'rɛspərəbl̩ 〕 *adj.* 適合呼吸的
respiration[7] 〔 ,rɛspə'reʃən 〕 *n.* 呼吸；呼吸作用
respirator[7] 〔 'rɛspə,retɚ 〕 *n.* (紗布) 口罩；防毒面具；
　　人工呼吸器

respiratory 〔 rɪ'spaɪrə,torɪ 〕 *adj.* 呼吸的；呼吸作用的

```
re  +  spira  + tory
 |        |       |
back + breathe + adj.
```

suspire 〔 sə'spaɪr 〕 *v.* 嘆氣；渴望（下面的呼吸）
　　《*sus-* = *sub-* = under》
suspiration 〔 ,sʌspə'reʃən 〕 *n.* 嘆息
transpire[7] 〔 træn'spaɪr 〕 *v.* 排出；洩露；發散（氣息穿透）
　　《*tran(s)-* = through》
transpirable 〔 træn'spaɪrəbḷ 〕 *adj.* 可蒸發的
transpiration 〔 ,trænspə'reʃən 〕 *n.* 蒸發；發散
transpirational 〔 ,trænspə'reʃənḷ 〕 *adj.* 蒸發的

550　splend = shine（發光）

　　* 拉丁文 *splendere*（= *shine*）。

splendent 〔 'splɛndənt 〕 *adj.* 光亮的；燦爛的；出色的
splendid[4] 〔 'splɛndɪd 〕 *adj.* 光輝的；壯麗的；卓越的；極好的
　　《*-id* 形容詞字尾》
splendiferous 〔 splɛn'dɪfərəs 〕 *adj.* 壯麗的；出色的；極好的
　　（發光的）《*-ferous* = bearing》
splendo(u)r 〔 'splɛndɚ 〕 *n.* 光輝；壯麗；卓越
　　《*-o(u)r* 抽象名詞字尾》

```
splend  +  o(u)r
  |          |
shine   +    n.
```

resplendent[7] 〔 rɪ'splɛndənt 〕 *adj.* 絢爛的；華麗的（徹底照耀）
　　《*re-* = thoroughly》
resplendence 〔 rɪ'splɛndəns 〕 *n.* 光輝；華麗

551 spond , spons = promise (保證)

* 拉丁文 *spondere* (= *promise*)，過去分詞為 *sponsus*。

sponsor[6] 〔'spɑnsə 〕 *n.* 保證人；教父（母）；贊助者
  v. 贊助；主辦；主持（約定保證的人）
sponsion 〔'spɑnʃən 〕 *n.* 保證
spouse[6] 〔 spaʊz , spaʊs 〕 *n.* 配偶（許下諾言的人）
despond 〔 dɪ'spɑnd 〕 *v.* 沮喪（停止束縛）《*de-* = *dis-* = away》
despondent[7] 〔 dɪ'spɑndənt 〕 *adj.* 沮喪的；失望的

```
de  +  spond  +  ent
 |        |        |
away + promise + adj.
```

despondence；**-ency** 〔 dɪs'pɑndəns(ɪ) 〕 *n.* 意氣消沈
respond[3] 〔 rɪ'spɑnd 〕 *v.* 回答；反應；負責（應允約定）《*re-* = back》
response[3] 〔 rɪ'spɑns 〕 *n.* 回答；反應

```
re  +  sponse
 |       |
back + promise
```

responsible[2] 〔 rɪ'spɑnsəbḷ 〕 *adj.* 負責任的；可信賴的
  （可以遵守允諾的）
responsibility[3] 〔 rɪ,spɑnsə'bɪlətɪ 〕 *n.* 責任；負擔
responsive[7] 〔 rɪ'spɑnsɪv 〕 *adj.* 有反應的；回答的；易感動的；
  敏感的
correspond[4] 〔 ,kɔrə'spɑnd 〕 *v.* 符合；相稱；通信（一起同聲回答）
  《*cor-* = *com-* = together》

```
cor  +  re  +  spond
 |       |       |
together + back + promise
```

correspondent[6] 〔 ,kɔrə'spɑndənt 〕 *adj.* 一致的；相當的
  n. 通信者；相稱者；通訊記者

correspondence[5] 〔,kɔrə'spɑndəns 〕 *n.* 一致；相稱；通信；信件

correspondingly 〔,kɔrə'spɑndɪŋlɪ 〕 *adv.* 同樣地；相應地

transponder 〔 træns'pɑndɚ 〕 *n.* (自動) 應答機

　　《*trans*(*mit*) (傳送) + (*res*)*pond* + *-er*》

552　st(a), stit, stitu(t)
= stand；set up (站；設立)

　　* 拉丁文 *stare* (= *stand*)，*statuere* (= *set up*；*put*)；
　　希臘文 *esthn* (= *I stood*)；梵文 *stha* (= *stand*) 之類的
　　例子不勝枚舉。"*st-*" 有 "*stand*" 之意，源自於印歐語系的
　　字根 *sta-* (= *stand*)，英語中的 "*-st-*" 多由「站立」的基
　　本意思，衍生出來有「靜止」、「持續」、「固定」、
　　「隱忍順從」之意，是非常重要的一個字根。

stable[3] 〔'stebl̩ 〕 *adj.* 堅固的；穩定的　*n.* 馬廄 (馬所站立的地點)
　　v. 居於廄中 (站立著)

stabilize[6] 〔'stebl̩,aɪz 〕 *v.* 使穩定

stabilization 〔,steblə'zeʃən 〕 *n.* 穩定；安定

stability[6] 〔 stə'bɪlətɪ 〕 *n.* 穩定；耐久性

stage[2] 〔 stedʒ 〕 *n.* 舞台；階段；時期　*v.* 表演；上演 (站著的東西)

stance[7] 〔 stæns 〕 *n.* 姿勢；態度；立場

```
stan  +  ce
 |        |
stand  +  n.
```

stanch 〔 stæntʃ, stɑntʃ 〕 *v.* 〔美〕止 (血)；使 (傷口) 止血

stanchion 〔'stænʃən 〕 *n.* 支柱　*v.* 給…裝支柱

stasis[7] 〔'stesɪs 〕 *n.* 瘀血；停滯

state[1] 〔 stet 〕 *n.* 狀態；威嚴；州；國家　*adj.* 國家的；州的
　　v. 說；陳述 (站著的狀態)

stately 〔'stetlɪ 〕 *adj.* 威嚴的；堂皇的

statement[1] 〔'stetmənt 〕 *n.* 陳述；聲明書

statesman[5] 〔'stetsmən 〕 *n.* 政治家

static[7] 〔'stætɪk 〕 *adj.* 靜止的；靜態的（一直站著的）

station[1] 〔'steʃən 〕 *n.* 位置；臺；火車站（一直站立的場所）

stationary[6] 〔'steʃən,ɛrɪ 〕 *adj.* 固定的；不變的

sta	+ tion	+ ary
stand +	*n.* +	*adj.*

stationer 〔'steʃənɚ 〕 *n.* 文具商（握有市場以出售書籍的人）

stationery[6] 〔'steʃən,ɛrɪ 〕 *n.* 文具；信紙

statist 〔'stetɪst 〕 *n.* 統計學家（描述國家所處狀態的人）

statistics[5] 〔 stə'tɪstɪks 〕 *n.* 統計（表）；統計學

statue[3] 〔'stætʃʊ 〕 *n.* 雕像；鑄像（立著的東西）

stature[6] 〔'stætʃɚ 〕 *n.* 身材（站著時的高度）

stat	+ ure
stand +	*n.*

status[4] 〔'stetəs 〕 *n.* 狀態；身分；地位（站著的狀態）

statute[7] 〔'stætʃʊt 〕 *n.* 法令；法規；規則

estate[5] 〔 ə'stet 〕 *n.* 地產；財產

stead 〔 stɛd 〕 *n.* 位置；利益；代替（站立處）

steady[3] 〔'stɛdɪ 〕 *adj.* 穩定的；沈著的　*v.* 使穩定；沈著（穩固地站立著）

steadfast[7] 〔'stɛd,fæst , -fə- 〕 *adj.* 堅定的；不移的（穩穩地站立著）

apostasy 〔 ə'pɑstəsɪ 〕 *n.* 脫黨；背教；變節（背對背分別站立）

《*apo-* = away from》

apo	+ sta	+ sy
away +	*stand* +	*n.*

apostate〔ə'pɑstet〕*n.* 脫黨者；背教者；變節者

circumstance[4]〔'sɝkəm‚stæns〕*n.* 情況；境遇；細節（站立在
周圍）《*circum-* = around》

```
circum  +   stan   +  ce
  |           |         |
around  +  stand   +  n.
```

circumstantial[7]〔‚sɝkəm'stænʃəl〕*adj.* 不重要的；詳細的

circumstantiate〔‚sɝkəm'stænʃɪ‚et〕*v.* 詳細說明

constant[3]〔'kɑnstənt〕*adj.* 不變的；不斷的；忠貞的 *n.* 常數
（始終不變地站在一塊）《*con-* = together》

constancy〔'kɑnstənsɪ〕*n.* 不變；堅定；忠誠

contrast[4]〔*n.* 'kɑntræst *v.* kən'træst〕*n.* 對照；反襯
v. 對比；對照（立於反面者）《*contra-* = against》

destine[7]〔'dɛstɪn〕*v.* 指定；命運注定（站立在命運之下）
《*de-* = down》

destiny[5]〔'dɛstənɪ〕*n.* 命運；宿命

destination[5]〔‚dɛstə'neʃən〕*n.* 目的（地）（被指定前往的地方）

distant[2]〔'dɪstənt〕*adj.* 遠離的；冷淡的（遠遠地站立著）
《*di(s)-* = apart》

```
di  +  st  + ant
 |      |      |
apart + stand + adj.
```

distance[2]〔'dɪstəns〕*n.* 距離；疏遠 *v.* 使遠離

ecstasy[6]〔'ɛkstəsɪ〕*n.* 狂喜；恍惚（立於理性之外）
《*ec-* = *ex-* = out》

ecstatic[7]〔ɪk'stætɪk, ɛk-〕*adj.* 狂喜的；出神的

establish[4]〔ə'stæblɪʃ〕*v.* 設立；制定《*e-* 在此無特殊意義》

establishment[4]〔ə'stæblɪʃmənt〕*n.* 設立；制定；（設立的
醫院、學校和工廠等）建築物

字根 sacr~surge

extant[7]〔ɪkˈstænt, ˈɛkstənt〕*adj.* 現存的（直到現在站著的）
《*ex-* = out》

instant[2]〔ˈɪnstənt〕*adj.* 立刻的；緊急的；本月的 *n.* 頃刻；剎那
（即刻站到近處的）《*in-* = upon ; near》

instance[2]〔ˈɪnstəns〕*n.* 建議；實例；訴訟程序 *v.* 示例證明
（緊迫的東西）

instantaneous[7]〔ˌɪnstənˈtenɪəs〕*adj.* 即時的；即時發生的

metastasis〔məˈtæstəsɪs〕*n.* 變形；新陳代謝；急轉（改變
原來的狀態）《*meta-* =「變化」之意》

obstacle[4]〔ˈɑbstəkḷ〕*n.* 障礙；妨礙物（站在反對立場）
《*ob-* = over ; against》

```
      ob   +   sta   +   cle
      |         |         |
   against  +  stand  +   n.
```

obstetric；**-ical**〔əbˈstɛtrɪk(ḷ), ɑb-〕*adj.* 產科的
（站在產婦之旁）《*ob-* = near》

obstinate[5]〔ˈɑbstənɪt〕*adj.* 固執的；難控制的 *n.* 固執的人
（立於反對立場）《*ob-* = over ; against》

obstinacy[7]〔ˈɑbstənəsɪ〕*n.* 倔強；頑固

solstice[7]〔ˈsɑlstɪs〕*n.* 至日（太陽離赤道最北或最北的時間）；
最高點（太陽靜止的那一點）《*sol* = sun》

substance[3]〔ˈsʌbstəns〕*n.* 物質；實質；主旨（立於表象之下）
《*sub-* = under》

substantial[5]〔səbˈstænʃəl〕*adj.* 實在的；堅實的；重大的
n.（*pl.*）本質；要點

```
      sub   +   stant   +   ial
       |          |          |
     under  +   stand   +   adj.
```

substantiate[7]〔səbˈstænʃɪˌet〕*v.* 使實體化；證實；證明

transubstantiate〔͵trænsəb'stænʃ͵et〕*v.* (使)變質;【宗教】
(使)化體(指聖餐的麵包和葡萄酒變爲耶穌的身體和血)
《*trans-* = across》

transubstantiation〔͵trænsəb͵stænʃɪ'eʃən〕*n.* 變質;【宗教】
聖餐變體

restore[4]〔rɪ'stor , -'stɔr〕*v.* 歸還;使復位;修補《*re-* = back ; again》

restoration[6]〔͵rɛstə'reʃən〕*n.* 恢復;復位

restorative〔rɪ'storətɪv , -'stɔr-〕*adj.* (精神等)回復的
n. 興奮劑

system[3]〔'sɪstəm〕*n.* 系統;組織;制度(站在一塊)
《*sy(s)-* = *syn-* = together》

constitute[4]〔'kɑnstə͵tjut〕*v.* 組成;任命;設立(站在一塊兒)
《*con-* = together》

constituent[6]〔kən'stɪtʃuənt〕*adj.* 構成的;有選舉權的
n. 成分;選民

constitution[4]〔͵kɑnstə'tjuʃən〕*n.* 構成;體格;性情;憲法

```
con  +  stitut  +  ion
 |        |        |
together + stand  +  n.
```

【解說】 全世界最早的「成文憲法」(written constitution),就是美
國憲法。憲法是國家的根本大法,所以要通過修憲案的門檻
非常高,在台灣必須有四分之三的立法委員出席,然後出席
者之中,需有四分之三的人同意,修憲案才能通過。

constitutional[5]〔͵kɑnstə'tjuʃənḷ〕*adj.* 體質的;生來的;憲法的

constitutionalism〔kɑnstə'tjuʃənḷ͵ɪzəm〕*n.* 立憲主義

constitutionalist〔͵kɑnstə'tjuʃənḷɪst〕*n.* 立憲主義者;憲法擁護者

constitutionality〔͵kɑnstə͵tjuʃən'ælətɪ〕*n.* 符合憲法

constitutive〔'kɑnstə͵tjutɪv〕*adj.* 組成的;基本的

destitute[7]〔'dɛstə͵tjut〕*adj.* 窮困的(離開衣食而生存)《*de-* = away》

destitution[7]〔͵dɛstə'tjuʃən〕*n.* 貧困;缺乏;不足

institute[5] 〔'ɪnstə,tjut 〕 *v.* 創立；制定；著手（引起；建立）

n. 協會；學會；研究所；講習會（被設立的東西）《*in-* = up》

institution[6] 〔,ɪnstə'tjuʃən 〕 *n.* 設立；制定；慣例；機構

institutional[7] 〔,ɪnstə'tjuʃənl̩ 〕 *adj.* 機構的

prostitute[7] 〔'prɑstə,tjut 〕 *v.* 賣身　*adj.* 賣身的；只圖金錢的

n. 娼妓；出賣節操的人（為了出賣身體而站在眾人之前）

《*pro-* = forth》

prostitution[7] 〔,prɑstə'tjuʃən 〕 *n.* 賣淫；濫用

```
pro  +  stitut  +  ion
 |        |         |
forth  +  stand  +  n.
```

restitute 〔'rɛstə,tjut , -tut 〕 *v.* 使恢復原狀；賠償損失（還原到原

有的狀態）《*re-* = back》

restitution[7] 〔,rɛstə'tjuʃən 〕 *n.* 賠償；復舊；恢復；復位

substitute[5] 〔'sʌbstə,tjut 〕 *v.* 代替　*n.* 代替者（物）；代用品；

代用字　*adj.* 代理的；代用的《*sub-* = under ; in place of》

```
sub  +  stitute
 |        |
under  +  stand
```

substitution[6] 〔,sʌbstə'tjuʃən 〕 *n.* 代替；取代

superstition[5] 〔,supɚ'stɪʃən 〕 *n.* 迷信（呆立於令人震驚害怕的事物

旁邊）《*super-* = above ; near》

【解說】 中國人迷信，但其實西方人也一樣迷信。比如大家都聽過的，
打破鏡子會倒楣三年，或者十三號星期五之類的。其中也有些
蠻有趣的，像午夜時撥打七個九，電話會接通到地獄。這個迷
信大概貝爾（發明電話的人）出生以前還沒有吧。

superstitious[6] 〔,supɚ'stɪʃəs 〕 *adj.* 迷信的

```
super  +  stit  +  ious
  |        |        |
above  +  stand  +  adj.
```

553 **stall** = place (地方)

* 古英文 *steall* (= *place for standing*)；中世紀拉丁文 *stallum*
(= *stall ; place*)；義大利文 *stallo* (= *stall ; place*)。

stall[5] 〔 stɔl 〕 *n.* (劇院) 正廳前排座位；攤位 (站立的場所)
　 v. (飛機) 失速下降；藉故拖延
forestall[7] 〔 fɔr'stɔl , fɔr 〕 *v.* 先發制人；壟斷 (先佔一步)
　《*fore-* = before》
install[4] 〔 ɪn'stɔl 〕 *v.* 裝設；安置 (放置其中)《*in-* = in》
installation[6] 〔 ˏɪnstə'leʃən 〕 *n.* 裝設；裝置
instal(l)ment[6] 〔 ɪn'stɔlmənt 〕 *n.* 分期付款 (支付設備的款額)

554 **stell** = star (星星)　　* 拉丁文 *stella* (= *star*)。

stellar[7] 〔'stɛlɚ 〕 *adj.* 星星的；多星的；如星的；主要的
stellate 〔'stɛlɪt , -let 〕 *adj.* 星狀的；放射狀的
stelliform 〔'stɛlɪˏfɔrm 〕 *adj.* 星形的；放射狀的
stellular 〔'stɛljʊlɚ 〕 *adj.* 小星形的；星星花紋的
　《 *-ul(e)* = small ; *-ar* 形容詞字尾》

stell	+	ul	+	ar
star	+	small	+	adj.

constellate 〔'kɑnstəˏlet 〕 *v.* 成群聚集；成群地閃耀；形成星座；
　以群星裝飾 (像星星般聚在一起)《*con-* = together》

con	+	stell	+	ate
together	+	star	+	v.

constellation[7] 〔ˏkɑnstə'leʃən 〕 *n.* 星座；星群
interstellar[7] 〔ˏɪntɚ'stɛlɚ 〕 *adj.* 星際的 (星球之間的)
　《*inter-* = between ; among》

555　**steno** = narrow（窄的）

　　* 希臘文 *stenos*（= *narrow*）。

stenography[7]〔 stə'nɑgrəfɪ 〕 *n.* 速記；速記法《*graphy* = writing》
stenographer〔 stə'nɑgrəfɚ 〕 *n.* 〔美〕速記員
stenophyllous〔,stɛnə'fɪləs 〕 *adj.* 狹葉的

```
steno  + phyll + ous
  |        |       |
narrow +  leaf  + adj.
```

stenosis〔 stɪ'nosɪs 〕 *n.* 狹窄症

556　**stereo** = solid（固體的；立體的）

　　* 希臘文 *stereos*（= *solid*）。

stereo[3]〔'stɛrɪo 〕 *n.* 立體音響；立體聲　*adj.* 立體聲的
stereograph〔'stɛrɪə,græf 〕 *n.* 立體照片；立體畫《*graph* = write》
stereoscope〔'stɛrɪə,skop 〕 *n.* 體視鏡（一種觀看立體相片或圖畫的光學儀器）《*scope* = look》
stereotype[5]〔'stɛrɪə,taɪp 〕 *n.* 鉛版印刷；刻板印象《*type* 類型》

557　**stig**, **sting**, **stinct** = prick（刺）

　　* 拉丁文 *stigare*, *stinguere*（= *prick*）。〔變化型〕*stinct*。

sting[3]〔 stɪŋ 〕 *v.* 刺；螫；刺激　*n.* 刺傷；痛苦；刺激（物）
stingy[4]〔'stɪndʒɪ 〕 *adj.* 吝嗇的；小氣的；缺乏的
distinguish[4]〔 dɪ'stɪŋgwɪʃ 〕 *v.* 區別；使顯著（明顯地區別）
　　《*di(s)-* = apart》

```
di   + stingu + ish
 |       |       |
apart +  prick  + v.
```

distinguished[4]〔dɪ'stɪŋgwɪʃt〕*adj.* 著名的；卓越的
distinct[4]〔dɪ'stɪŋkt〕*adj.* 分別的；清楚的（清楚地分別）
distinction[5]〔dɪ'stɪŋkʃən〕*n.* 差別；卓越；特性
distinctive[5]〔dɪ'stɪŋktɪv〕*adj.* 表示差異的；差別性的；獨特的
extinguish[7]〔ɪk'stɪŋgwɪʃ〕*v.*（火）熄滅；消滅；使沈默（消滅）
　　《*ex-* = out》
extinguisher[7]〔ɪk'stɪŋgwɪʃɚ〕*n.* 滅火器；消滅者
extinct[5]〔ɪk'stɪŋkt〕*adj.* 滅種的；熄滅的
extinction[7]〔ɪk'stɪŋkʃən〕*n.* 熄滅；消滅；滅絕
instinct[4]〔'ɪnstɪŋkt〕*n.* 本能；直覺（內部興起的東西）《*in-* = in ; on》
instinctive[7]〔ɪn'stɪŋktɪv〕*adj.* 本能的；直覺的
instigate[7]〔'ɪnstə,get〕*v.* 鼓動；煽動（刺入）《*in-* = in ; on》
instigation[7]〔,ɪnstə'geʃən〕*n.* 敎唆；煽動

字根 sacr~surge

in +	stig	+ ation
in +	prick	+ n.

instigator[7]〔'ɪnstə,getɚ〕*n.* 煽動者
stimulate[6]〔'stɪmjə,let〕*v.* 刺激；鼓勵；激勵（刺人；戳人）
　　《拉丁文 *stimulus* = spur（刺激）》
stimulant[7]〔'stɪmjələnt〕*n.* 興奮劑；刺激（物）　*adj.* 刺激性的
stimulation[6]〔,stɪmjə'leʃən〕*n.* 刺激；激勵
stimulus[6]〔'stɪmjələs〕*n.* 刺激（物）；激勵
stigma[7]〔'stɪgmə〕*n.* 恥辱；紅斑；氣孔（被加上記號的）
　　《希臘文 *stigma* = mark ; puncture》
stigmatic〔stɪg'mætɪk〕*adj.* 恥辱的；氣孔的

558　**still** = drop（滴下）　*拉丁文 *stilla*（ = drop）。

distill[7]〔dɪ'stɪl〕*v.* 蒸餾；（使）滴下（使一滴滴分別落下）
　　《*di-* = *dis-* = apart》

distillate (ˈdɪstḷɪt, -ˌet) *n.* 蒸餾物；精華
distillation[7] (ˌdɪstḷˈeʃən) *n.* 蒸餾；蒸餾法；蒸餾物
distiller (dɪˈstɪlɚ) *n.* 蒸餾酒製造業者；蒸餾器
distillery[7] (dɪˈstɪlərɪ) *n.* 蒸餾酒製造廠《*-ery* 表示場所的名詞字尾》

```
di  +  still  +  ery
 |       |       |
apart + drop +  n.
```

instill[7] (ɪnˈstɪl) *v.* 逐漸灌輸；徐徐滴入（慢慢滴進去）《*in-* = into》
instillation (ˌɪnstɪˈleʃən) *n.* 灌輸；點滴（法）
instillment (ɪnˈstɪlmənt) *n.* = instillation

559 **stom** = mouth (嘴)

* 希臘文 *stoma* , *stomat-* (= *mouth*)。

stomach[2] (ˈstʌmək) *n.* 胃；肚子；腹部
stomachic[7] (stoˈmækɪk) *adj.* 胃的　*n.* 健胃劑
stomatology (ˌstoməˈtalədʒɪ) *n.* 口腔學《*ology* = study》
colostomy (kəˈlastəmɪ) *n.* 結腸造口術《*colon* 結腸》
peristome (ˈpɛrɪˌstom) *n.* （蘚類的）孢蒴齒；（無脊椎動物的）
　　圍口部；口緣《*peri-* = around》

560 **ston** = stone (石頭)　　　* 古英文 *stan* (= *stone*)。

stony (ˈstonɪ) *adj.* 石（頭）的；多石的；鐵石心腸的
capstone (ˈkæpˌston) *n.* 壓頂石；頂點《*cap* = head》
gravestone[7] (ˈgrevˌston) *n.* 墓碑《*grave* 墳墓》
hailstone[7] (ˈhelˌston) *n.* 雹塊《*hail* 冰雹》
milestone[5] (ˈmaɪlˌston) *n.* 里程碑《*mile* 英哩》
millstone (ˈmɪlˌston) *n.* 石磨；重擔《*mill* 磨粉機》
rubstone (ˈrʌbˌston) *n.* 磨刀石《*rub* 磨光》
touchstone[7] (ˈtʌtʃˌston) *n.* 試金石；檢驗標準《*touch* 觸摸》

561　**strat** = army（軍隊）

* 希臘文 *stratos*（= *army*），*strategos*（= *general* 將軍）。

stratagem〔'strætədʒəm〕*n.* 策略；計謀；詭計

```
strat  +  ag  +  em
  |        |      |
army  +  lead  +  n.
```

strategy[3]〔'strætədʒɪ〕*n.* 戰略；策略
strategic[6]〔strə'tidʒɪk〕*adj.* 戰略（上）的
stratocracy〔strə'tɑkrəsɪ〕*n.* 軍人統治《*cracy* = rule》

562　**strat** = spread（展開）

* 拉丁文 *sternere*（= *extend*；*spread*），過去分詞是 *stratus*。

stratum[7]〔'stretəm〕*n.*【地質】地層；層；階層；階級
stratus〔'stretəs〕*n.* 層雲
stratify[7]〔'strætə,faɪ〕*v.* 使分層；使形成階層《*-ify* = make》
stratification〔,strætəfə'keʃən〕*n.* 階層的形成；【地質】層理
stratocumulus〔,stretə'kjumjʊləs〕*n.* 層積雲《*cumulus* 積雲》
stratosphere[7]〔'strætə,sfɪr〕*n.*【氣象】同溫層；平流層
　《*sphere* 球體》
prostrate[7]〔'prɑstret〕*adj.* 俯伏的；降伏的；筋疲力盡的
　v. 使平臥；使筋疲力盡（攤在前面）《*pro-* = before》
street[1]〔strit〕*n.* 街；街道（鋪上去的路）

563　**string**, **strict** = draw tight（拉緊）

* 拉丁文 *stringere*（= *draw tight*；*compress*），過去分詞為
　strictus（和 *strong* 有關係）。〔變化型〕*strain*, *stress*。

string[2]〔strɪŋ〕*n.* 帶；細繩；一串；弦　*v.* 收緊；上弦；成串
　（用來綑綁的東西）

stringent[7]〔 'strɪndʒənt 〕 *adj.* 嚴格的；緊迫的（被緊綁住）

stringency〔 'strɪndʒənsɪ 〕 *n.* 嚴格；迫切；手頭很緊

string	+	ency
draw tight	+	*n.*

straight[2] 〔 stret 〕 *adj.* 直立的；正直的　　*n.* 直線　　*adv.* 直接地；坦白地（完全張開）

strain[5] 〔 stren 〕 *v.* 拉緊；濫用；努力　　*n.* 努力；緊張；壓力

strait[5] 〔 stret 〕 *adj.* 狹窄的　　*n.* 海峽；狹窄處（拉緊）

straiten〔 'stretn̩ 〕 *v.* 使困苦；使窘迫《 *-en* = make 》

strangle[6] 〔 'stræŋg̩l 〕 *v.* 勒死；使窒息（綁著）

strang	+	le
draw tight	+	*v.*

strangulate〔 'stræŋgjə,let 〕 *v.* 絞扼；勒死

stress[2] 〔 strɛs 〕 *n.* 壓迫；重要；緊張；重音　　*v.* 著重；強調（拉緊）

stretch[2] 〔 strɛtʃ 〕 *v.* 伸張；拉緊；誇張　　*n.* 伸展；寬闊的空間；一口氣（緊張）

strict[2] 〔 strɪkt 〕 *adj.* 嚴密的；嚴格的（使緊張）

strictness〔 'strɪktnɪs 〕 *n.* 嚴格；嚴密

stricture〔 'strɪktʃɚ 〕 *n.* 非難；約束；狹窄

astringent[7] 〔 ə'strɪndʒənt 〕 *adj.* 收斂性的；嚴酷的

　　n. 收斂劑（拉緊）《 *a-* = *ad-* = to 》

a	+	string	+	ent
to	+	*draw tight*	+	*adj.*

astringency〔 ə'strɪndʒənsɪ 〕 *n.* 收斂性；嚴酷

astrict〔 ə'strɪkt 〕 *v.* 束縛；緊束

astriction〔 ə'strɪkʃən 〕 *n.* 約束；便秘

constringe〔 kən'strɪndʒ 〕*v.* 緊縮；壓縮（綁在一塊）
　《*con-* = together》
constrain[7]〔 kən'stren 〕*v.* 強迫；拘禁
constrained〔 kən'strend 〕*adj.* 強迫的；有束縛感的
constraint[7]〔 kən'strent 〕*n.* 強迫；束縛《 *-t* 名詞字尾》

```
con   +   strain   + t
 |          |         |
together + draw tight + n.
```

constrict[7]〔 kən'strɪkt 〕*v.* 收緊
constriction[7]〔 kən'strɪkʃən 〕*n.* 收縮；壓縮
constrictive[7]〔 kən'strɪktɪv 〕*adj.* 收縮性的；緊縮的
constrictor[7]〔 kən'strɪktə 〕*n.* 能緊縮之物；括約肌
distrain〔 dɪ'stren 〕*v.* 強制執行（拉開；拉走）《*di(s)-* = apart》
distrainee〔ˌdɪstre'ni 〕*n.* 財物被扣押者《 *-ee* 表示「被～的人」》

```
di(s) +   strain   +   ee
 |          |           |
apart + draw tight + person
```

distrainer；**-or**〔 dɪ'strenə 〕*n.* 扣押者
distraint〔 dɪ'strent 〕*n.* 扣押財物
distress[5]〔 dɪ'strɛs 〕*v.* 使痛苦；迫使　*n.* 痛苦；憂愁；窮困
　（強行拉走）
distressful〔 dɪ'strɛsfəl 〕*adj.* 痛苦的；窮困的；悲慘的
district[4]〔 'dɪstrɪkt 〕*n.* 行政區；地域（被拉開的部分）
overstrain〔 *v.* ˌovə'stren *n.* 'ovəˌstren 〕*v.* 使過度緊張；
　工作過度　*n.* 過度緊張；過勞（拉得太緊）《*over-* = too much》

```
over   +   strain
 |           |
too much + draw tight
```

restrain[5]〔 rɪ'stren 〕*v.* 抑制；監禁（拉回原處）

restraint[6]〔 rɪ'strent 〕 n. 抑制；監禁
restrict[3] 〔 rɪ'strɪkt 〕 v. 限制；約束

```
re   +   strict
|         |
back + draw tight
```

restriction[4] 〔 rɪ'strɪkʃən 〕 n. 限制；約束
restrictive[7] 〔 rɪ'strɪktɪv 〕 adj. 限制的；拘束的

564 stroph = turn (轉動)

* 希臘文 strephein (= twist ; turn) 。〔變化型〕strept。

anastrophe 〔 ə'næstrəfɪ 〕 n. 詞語倒裝法《ana- = back》
apostrophe[7] 〔 ə'pɑstrəfɪ 〕 n. 撇號；上標點 (即 ')
《apo- = away》
boustrophedon 〔,bustrə'fidn̩ 〕 n. 牛耕式轉行書寫法 (一種
古代書寫法，由右至左，再由左至右互錯成行，古埃及語、古希臘
語等曾用過這種書寫方法)

```
bou + strophe + don
|        |        |
ox  +  turn   +  n.
```

catastrophe[6] 〔 kə'tæstrəfɪ 〕 n. 大災難《cata- = down》
catastrophic[7] 〔,kætə'strɑfɪk 〕 adj. 大災難的
ecocatastrophe 〔,ɛkokə'tæstrəfɪ , ,iko- 〕 n. (環境污染造成的)
大規模或世界性的生態災難《ecology 生態學》
strephosymbolia 〔,strɛfosɪm'balɪə 〕 n. 識字困難 (一種兒童
視覺病，其特徵爲將形狀相似之字母互相混淆，如 b-d、q-p) ；
視像倒反《symbol 符號》
streptococcus 〔,strɛptə'kakəs 〕 n. 鏈球菌《coccus 球菌》

565　**stru , struct** = build（建造）

> * 拉丁文 *struere*（ = *build* ），過去分詞爲 *structus*，
> 原意爲「重疊」。

structure[3]（'strʌktʃ⋅ ）*n.* 構造（物）；結構
structural[5]（'strʌktʃərəl ）*adj.* 構造上的；結構上的
construct[4]（ kən'strʌkt ）*v.* 組成；構成；建築《*con-* = together》
construction[4]（ kən'strʌkʃən ）*n.* 建築（物）；構造；解釋
reconstruct[7]（ˌrikən'strʌkt ）*v.* 重建；改造《*re-* = again》

re	+	con	+	struct
again	+	*together*	+	*build*

reconstruction[7]（ˌrikən'strʌkʃən ）*n.* 重建（物）；改造（物）
construe[7]（ kən'stru ）*v.* 分析；解釋　*n.* 解釋；推斷（組合成意義）
destroy[3]（ dɪ'strɔɪ ）*v.* 破壞；毀滅；殺戮（使建築物倒下）
　《*de-* = down》
destruct[7]（ dɪ'strʌkt ）*v.* 破壞；炸毀
destructible[7]（ dɪ'strʌktəbl̩ ）*adj.* 可破壞的；可毀滅的
destruction[4]（ dɪ'strʌkʃən ）*n.* 破壞；毀滅
destructive[5]（ dɪ'strʌktɪv ）*adj.* 破壞的；有害的

de	+	struct	+	ive
down	+	*build*	+	*adj.*

instruct[4]（ ɪn'strʌkt ）*v.* 教授；指導；通知（構建於心中）
　《*in-* = into》
instruction[3]（ ɪn'strʌkʃən ）*n.* 教授；教導
instructive[7]（ ɪn'strʌktɪv ）*adj.* 有益的；教訓的
instructor[4]（ ɪn'strʌktɚ ）*n.* 教師；指導者；教練；（大學的）講師
　cf. **assistant professor**（助教）, **associate professor**（副教授）, **professor**
　　（教授）

instrument[2] (ˈɪnstrəmənt) *n.* 工具；器具；樂器 (建設必需的工具)

instrumental[7] (ˌɪnstrəˈmɛntļ , -stru-) *adj.* 有幫助的；樂器的

instrumentality (ˌɪnstrəmɛnˈtælətɪ , -stru-) *n.* 媒介；助力；
工具

misconstrue[7] (ˌmɪskənˈstru , mɪsˈkɑn-) *v.* 誤解 (錯誤的解釋)
《*mis-* = wrongly》

```
   mis   +  con  + strue
    |        |       |
 wrongly + together + build
```

misconstruction (ˌmɪskənˈstrʌkʃən) *n.* 曲解；誤解

obstruct[7] (əbˈstrʌkt) *v.* 阻隔；妨礙 (重疊妨礙物品)
《*ob-* = against》

obstruction[7] (əbˈstrʌkʃən) *n.* 障礙 (物)；封鎖

obstructive[7] (əbˈstrʌktɪv) *adj.* 妨礙的

```
   ob   + struct + ive
    |       |       |
 against + build + adj.
```

substructure (sʌbˈstrʌktʃ⯑) *n.* 下層結構；基礎工程；地基
《*sub-* = under》

superstructure (ˈsupⱥˌstrʌktʃⱥ , ˈsju-) *n.* 上層構造；上層
建築物 《*super-* = above》

566　suade , suas = advise (勸告)

* 拉丁文 *suadere* (= *advise*)，過去分詞為 *suasus*。

suasion (ˈsweʒən) *n.* 勸說；勸誘

suasive (ˈswesɪv) *adj.* 有說服力的

dissuade[6] (dɪˈswed) *v.* 勸阻；阻止 (勸告不要做~)
《*dis-* = apart》

dissuasion[7] 〔dɪ'sweʒən〕 *n.* 諫言;勸止

  cf. **persuasion**(說服;勸告)

```
dis + suas + ion
 |     |      |
apart + advise + n.
```

dissuasive[7] 〔dɪ'swesɪv〕 *adj.* 勸阻的
persuade[3] 〔pɚ'swed〕 *v.* 說服;使相信(充分的勸告)
  《*per-* = thoroughly》
persuasion[4] 〔pɚ'sweʒən〕 *n.* 說服;勸誘;信念
persuasible 〔pɚ'swesəbḷ〕 *adj.* 可說服的
persuasive[4] 〔pɚ'swesɪv〕 *adj.* 能勸誘的   *n.* 動機;誘因

567   sume , sumpt = take(拿)

  * 拉丁文 *sumere*(= *take*),過去分詞為 *sumptus*。

sumptuary 〔'sʌmptʃʊˏɛrɪ〕 *adj.* 節省費用的;抑制奢侈的
sumptuous[7] 〔'sʌmptʃʊəs〕 *adj.* 奢侈的;費用大的(拿走許多錢)
assume[4] 〔ə'sjum〕 *v.* 假定;擔任;假裝;僭越(拿取衣服、外表、
  他人物品、想法)《*as-* = *ad-* = to》
assuming[7] 〔ə'sjumɪŋ , ə'sum-〕 *adj.* 傲慢的;僭越的
assumption[6] 〔ə'sʌmpʃən〕 *n.* 假定;擔任;傲慢;僭越

```
as + sumpt + ion
 |     |      |
to + take + n.
```

assumptive 〔ə'sʌmptɪv〕 *adj.* 假定的;假裝的;僭越的
consume[4] 〔kən'sum , -'sjum〕 *v.* 消耗;消費;浪費
  (完全取用耗盡)《*con-* = wholly》
consumer[4] 〔kən'sumɚ , -'sjumɚ〕 *n.* 消費者

```
con + sum + er
 |     |     |
wholly + take + person
```

consumerism 〔 kənˈsumə͵rɪzəm 〕 *n.* 保護消費者主義
《 *-ism* = 主義》

consumption[6] 〔 kənˈsʌmpʃən 〕 *n.* 消耗；肺病

consumptive 〔 kənˈsʌmptɪv 〕 *adj.* 消耗的；消費的；肺病的
n. 肺病患者

presume[6] 〔 prɪˈzum 〕 *v.* 假定；推測；冒昧 (比別人先拿)
《*pre-* = before》

presumable[7] 〔 prɪˈzuməbḷ , -ˈzɪum- 〕 *adj.* 可假定的

presuming[7] 〔 prɪˈzumɪŋ 〕 *adj.* 推測的

presumption[7] 〔 prɪˈzʌmpʃən 〕 *n.* 推定；傲慢；僭越

presumptive[7] 〔 prɪˈzʌmptɪv 〕 *adj.* 假定的

presumptuous[7] 〔 prɪˈzʌmptʃʊəs 〕 *adj.* 僭越的；無顧忌的

pre	+	sumptu	+	ous
before	+	*take*	+	*adj.*

reassume[7] 〔͵riəˈsjum 〕 *v.* 再承擔；重新假定；再開始說
《*re-* = again》

resume[5] 〔 rɪˈzum , -ˈzɪum , -ˈzjum 〕 *v.* 重新開始；繼續；重獲
(再度取得) 《*re-* = back ; again》

resume[5] 〔͵rɛzʊˈme 〕 *n.* 摘要；履歷表

resumption[7] 〔 rɪˈzʌmpʃən 〕 *n.* 重新開始；繼續

resumptive[7] 〔 rɪˈzʌmptɪv 〕 *adj.* 概要的；再開始的

unassuming[7] 〔͵ʌnəˈsumɪŋ 〕 *adj.* 謙虛的；不矯揉造作的《*un-* = not》

568   **summ** = sum ; highest (總數；最高的)

* 拉丁文 *summa* (= *sum*) ，*summus* (= *highest*) 。

summary[3] 〔ˈsʌmərɪ 〕 *n.* 摘要；概要   *adj.* 摘要的；即刻的
(綜合看來)

summarily[7] 〔ˈsʌmərəlɪ 〕 *adv.* 簡略地；扼要地；即刻

summarize[4] 〔ˈsʌmə͵raɪz 〕 *v.* 扼要地說；概述

summarization〔͵sʌmərɪ'zeʃən , -raɪ- 〕*n.* 概述
summation〔 sʌm'eʃən 〕*n.* 加法；合計；總括（算總數）
summit[3]〔'sʌmɪt 〕*n.* 頂點；顛峰；高階層（最高點）
consummate[7]〔 *v.* 'kɑnsə͵met *adj.* kən'sʌmɪt 〕*v.* 完成
　adj. 完全的；圓滿的（一起達到頂點）《*con-* = together》

```
con  +  summ  +  ate
 |        |       |
together + highest +  v.
```

consummation〔͵kɑnsə'meʃən 〕*n.* 完成；達成
consummatory〔 kən'sʌmə͵tɔrɪ 〕*adj.* 完成的；實現的

569　sur = sure；secure（確定的；安全的）

　　* 拉丁文 *securus*（ = *secure* ）；古法文 *seur*（ = *secure* ）。

assure[7]〔 ə'ʃʊr 〕*v.* 保證；使確信（朝向安全）《*as-* = *ad-* = to》
assured[7]〔 ə'ʃʊrd 〕*adj.* 確實的；有保證的；確信的

```
as +  sur  +  ed
 |     |       |
to +  sure  +  adj.
```

assurance[4]〔 ə'ʃʊrəns 〕*n.* 保證；確信；信心；無恥
assuring[7]〔 ə'ʃʊrɪŋ 〕*adj.* 保證的；令人確信的
ensure[7]〔 ɪn'ʃʊr 〕*v.* 確保；保護；保證（使確定）《*en-* = cause to be》
insure[5]〔 ɪn'ʃʊr 〕*v.* 保險；投保（使進入安全狀態）《*in-* = into》
insurable[7]〔 ɪn'ʃʊrəbl̩ 〕*adj.* 應保險的；可保險的
insurance[4]〔 ɪn'ʃʊrəns 〕*n.* 保險；保險單；保險費；保險金

```
in +  sur  +  ance
 |     |       |
into + sure  +  n.
```

insurant[7]〔 ɪn'ʃʊrənt 〕*n.* 投保人；被保險人
insurer[7]〔 ɪn'ʃʊrɚ 〕*n.* 保險業者；保證人

reassure[7] 〔͵riə'ʃʊr 〕 v. 使安心；再保證 《*re-* = again》
reassurance[7] 〔͵riə'ʃʊrəns 〕 n. 安心；確信；再保證
reassuring[7] 〔͵riə'ʃʊrɪŋ 〕 adj. 使安心的；可靠的
reinsure 〔͵riɪn'ʃʊr 〕 v. 再投保
reinsurance 〔͵riɪn'ʃʊrəns 〕 n. 再投保

570 surge = rise (上升；起立)

字根 sacr~surge

* 拉丁文 *surgere* (= *rise*)，過去分詞為 *surrectus*；
古法文 *sourse* (= *rising* ; *beginning*)。〔變化型〕*surrect*。

surge[5] 〔 sɝdʒ 〕 v. (海水、情感等的) 起伏；澎湃　n. 巨浪；洶湧
　(湧起；隆起)
surgy 〔'sɝdʒɪ 〕 adj. 如大浪的；澎湃的
insurgency[7] 〔 ɪn'sɝdʒənsɪ 〕 n. 暴動 《*in-* = against》
insurgent[7] 〔 ɪn'sɝdʒənt 〕 adj. 暴動的；衝擊的；造反的；反抗的
　n. 暴動者；叛徒；反抗者；反對派 (蜂湧到~)
insurrection[7] 〔͵ɪnsə'rɛkʃən 〕 n. 暴動；造反

in	+	surrect	+	ion
against	+	rise	+	n.

resurge[7] 〔 rɪ'sɝdʒ 〕 v. 復活；再起 (再次站起來) 《*re-* = again》
resurgence[7] 〔 rɪ'sɝdʒəns 〕 n. 復活；再起
resurgent[7] 〔 rɪ'sɝdʒənt 〕 adj. 復活的；再起的　n. 再起者；復活者
resurrect[7] 〔͵rɛzə'rɛkt 〕 v. 恢復；復興；挖出；使復活；使重新流行
resurrection[7] 〔͵rɛzə'rɛkʃən 〕 n. (the R~) 耶穌的復活；恢復；
　發掘屍體；重新喚醒；重新啓用
source[2] 〔 sors 〕 n. 泉源；來源 (湧上來的源地)
resource[3] 〔 rɪ'sors , 'risors 〕 n. (常用 pl.) 資源；來源；策略
　(接踵而至的東西) 《*re-* = again》
resourceful[7] 〔 rɪ'sorsfəl , -'sɔrs- 〕 adj. 富於機智的；多資源的

571　**tac** = silent (沉默的)

> * 拉丁文 *tacere* (= *silent*)，過去分詞是 *tacitus*。〔變化型〕*tic*。

tacit[7] 〔'tæsɪt 〕*adj.* 無言的；沉默的
taciturn 〔'tæsə,tɝn 〕*adj.* 沉默寡言的
taciturnity 〔,tæsə'tɝnətɪ 〕*n.* 沉默寡言
reticence[7] 〔'rɛtəsn̩s 〕*n.* 緘默；保守

```
 re   +  tic  + ence
  |        |      |
again + silent +  n.
```

reticent[7] 〔'rɛtəsn̩t 〕*adj.* 緘默的；保守的；謹慎的 (一再沉默)
　《*re-* = again》

572　**tail** = cut (裁剪；切割)　　* 古法文 *taillier* (= *cut*)。

tailor[3] 〔'telɚ 〕*n.* 裁縫師　*v.* 縫製 (衣服)
tailoring 〔'telərɪŋ 〕*n.* 裁縫業；裁縫的技術
curtail[7] 〔 kɝ'tel , kə- 〕*v.* 縮減；剝奪《拉丁文 *curtus* = cut short》
curtailment 〔 kɝ'telmənt 〕*n.* 縮減；削減
detail[3] 〔'ditel , dɪ'tel 〕*n.* 詳情；細節；瑣事
　v. 詳述；派遣 (切割成一片一片)

```
de  + tail
 |      |
apart + cut
```

　《*de-* = *dis-* = apart》
detailed[7] 〔 dɪ'teld ,'diteld 〕*adj.* 詳細的
entail[7] 〔 ɪn'tel 〕*v.* 使負擔；使需要；限定繼承 (使負責切割)
　《*en-* = into》
entailment 〔 ɪn'telmənt 〕*n.* (不動產的) 繼承人限定
retail[16] 〔'ritel 〕*n.* , *v.* 零售　*adj.* 零售的　*adv.* 以零售價格
　(再切 → 分得更小去販賣)《*re-* = again》
retail[26] 〔'ritel , rɪ'tel 〕*v.* 轉述
retailer 〔'ritelɚ 〕*n.* 零售商　〔 rɪ'telɚ 〕*n.* 傳播謠言的人

573 **tang , tact** = touch (接觸)

> * 拉丁文 *tangere* (= touch) ，過去分詞為 *tactus*，源自印歐
> 語系的字根 *tag-* (= touch ; handle) 。〔變化型〕*ting*。

tangency 〔'tændʒənsɪ 〕 *n.* 接觸

tangent[7] 〔'tændʒənt 〕 *adj.* 接觸的；相切的

　　n. 切線 (面) ；正切

tangible[7] 〔'tændʒəbḷ 〕 *adj.* 可觸知的；確實的；實質的

　　n.pl. 有形資產

tact[6] 〔 tækt 〕 *n.* 機智；圓滑；觸摸 (接觸之巧妙手法)

tactful[7] 〔'tæktfəl 〕 *adj.* 機智的；圓滑的；老練的

tactile 〔'tæktɪl 〕 *adj.* 有觸覺的《 *-ile* 形容詞字尾》

tactility 〔 tæk'tɪlətɪ 〕 *n.* 感觸性；觸感

tactual 〔'tæktʃuəl 〕 *adj.* 觸覺的

contact[2] 〔'kɑntækt 〕 *n.* 接觸；聯繫　*v.* 發生接觸 (接合在一起)

　　《 *con-* = together 》

```
con   +  tact
 |        |
together + touch
```

contagion 〔 kən'tedʒən 〕 *n.* 接觸傳染；傳染病；道德敗壞
　　(接觸感染)

contagious[5] 〔 kən'tedʒəs 〕 *adj.* 接觸傳染的

contiguity 〔ˌkɑntə'gjuətɪ 〕 *n.* 接觸；接近

contiguous[7] 〔 kən'tɪgjuəs 〕 *adj.* 接觸的；鄰近的

contingency[7] 〔 kən'tɪndʒənsɪ 〕 *n.* 偶然性；意外事故

contingent[7] 〔 kən'tɪndʒənt 〕 *adj.* 偶發的；有條件的；備用的

　　n. 意外之事 (偶然地接觸)

```
con   +  ting  + ent
 |        |       |
together + touch + adj.
```

intact[6]〔 ɪnˈtækt 〕*adj.* 完整的；原封不動的；未受損的

（未經接觸 → 完整）《*in-* = not》

intangible[7]〔 ɪnˈtændʒəbl̩ 〕*adj.* 不可觸摸的；非實體的；含糊的

integer〔ˈɪntədʒɚ 〕*n.* 整數；整體（沒有被碰觸 → 沒有被損壞）

integral[7]〔ˈɪntəgrəl 〕*adj.* 必要的；整數的；積分的

　n. 整數；積分；完整物

integrant〔ˈɪntəgrənt 〕*adj.* 構成整體的　*n.* 成分

integrate[6]〔ˈɪntəˌgret 〕*v.* 使完全；求～之積分

```
in  +  tegr  +  ate
 |        |       |
not  +  touch  +  v.
```

integration[6]〔ˌɪntəˈgreʃən 〕*n.* 完成；積分法

integrity[6]〔 ɪnˈtɛgrətɪ 〕*n.* 正直；完整

attain[6]〔 əˈten 〕*v.* 達到；成就；得到（用手碰到目標物）

　《*at-* = *ad-* = to》

attainment[6]〔 əˈtenmənt 〕*n.* 達到；(*pl.*) 學識

attaint〔 əˈtent 〕*v.* 羞辱；喪失公權或財產　*n.* 污點（接觸

病菌、污物）

taint[7]〔 tent 〕*v.* 受感染；腐敗　*n.* 污點；腐敗；墮落

574　**tax** , **tact** = arrange（排列）

* 希臘文 *tassein*（= *arrange*），*taxis*（= *arrangement*）。

〔變化型〕*tact*。

taxidermy[7]〔ˈtæksəˌdɝmɪ 〕*n.*（動物標本的）剝製術《*derm* = skin》

taxidermist〔ˈtæksəˌdɝmɪst 〕*n.*（動物標本的）剝製師

taxonomy〔 tæksˈɑnəmɪ 〕*n.* 分類學；（動植物）分類系統

```
taxo       +  nomy
 |             |
arrangement  +  method
```

taxonomist〔 tæks'ɑnəmɪst 〕 *n.* 分類學家

syntax 〔'sɪntæks 〕 *n.* 句法;語法;句子結構 (分析)

《*syn-* = together》

tactics[6] 〔'tæktɪks 〕 *n.* 戰術

```
tact      +   ics
 |             |
arrangement + science
```

tactician 〔 tæk'tɪʃən 〕 *n.* 戰術家;策略家

575 techn = art ; skill (藝術;技巧)

* 希臘文 *tekhne* (= *art* ; *skill*) 。

technics 〔'tɛknɪks 〕 *n.* 工藝學;技術;技巧《 *-ics* = science》

technical[3] 〔'tɛknɪkḷ 〕 *adj.* 技術的;專門的;工業的

technicality[7] 〔ˌtɛknɪ'kælətɪ 〕 *n.* 專門性;專門的事項;專門用語

technically 〔'tɛknɪkḷɪ 〕 *adv.* 專門地;技術上地

technician[4] 〔 tɛk'nɪʃən 〕 *n.* 技術員;專家;技巧純熟的人

```
techn + ic  +   ian
 |       |        |
skill  + adj. + person
```

technique[3] 〔 tɛk'nik 〕 *n.* 技巧;技術;方法 (= 〔美〕 *technic*)

《 *-ique* 名詞字尾》

technocracy 〔 tɛk'nɑkrəsɪ 〕 *n.* 科技主義;科技專家政治

(用科技來治理國家)《 *cracy* = rule》

technocrat 〔'tɛknəˌkræt 〕 *n.* 科技主義者;專家治國論者

《 *crat* = ruler》

```
techno + crat
  |        |
skill   + ruler
```

technological[4] 〔 ˌtɛknəˈlɑdʒɪkḷ 〕 *adj.* 科學技術的

technologist 〔 tɛkˈnɑlədʒɪst 〕 *n.* 科技專家

technology[3] 〔 tɛkˈnɑlədʒɪ 〕 *n.* 科學技術；專門用語《*logy* = study》

technophobia 〔 ˌtɛknəˈfobɪə 〕 *n.* 技術恐懼（指對技術對社會及環境造成不良影響的恐懼）《*phob* = fear》

pyrotechnic 〔 ˌpaɪrəˈtɛknɪk 〕 *adj.* 煙火（製造術）的；燦爛的；天花亂墜的《*pyro* = fire》

576 tect = builder（建築者）

* 希臘文 *tekton*（= *builder*）。

tectology 〔 tɛkˈtɑlədʒɪ 〕 *n.*【生物】組織形態學；組織構造學《*logy* = study》

tectonic 〔 tɛkˈtɑnɪk 〕 *adj.* 建築的；構造的；地殼構造（上）的

architect[5] 〔 ˈɑrkəˌtɛkt 〕 *n.* 建築師《*archi* = chief》

architectonic 〔 ˌɑrkɪtɛkˈtɑnɪk 〕 *adj.* 建築上的；結構嚴謹合理的；知識系統化的

577 tect , teg = cover（覆蓋）

* 拉丁文 *tegere*（= *cover*），過去分詞爲 *tectus*。

detect[2] 〔 dɪˈtɛkt 〕 *v.* 發現；查明；探獲（拿走遮蔽物）《*de-* = away from》

detectaphone 〔 dɪˈtɛktəˌfon 〕 *n.* 監聽器；竊聽器《*phone* = sound》

de	+ tecta	+ phone
away from	+ *cover*	+ *sound*

detection[7] 〔 dɪˈtɛkʃən 〕 *n.* 探出；查知

detective[4] 〔 dɪˈtɛktɪv 〕 *n.* 偵探 *adj.* 偵探的（找尋發掘的人）

detector[7] 〔 dɪ'tɛktɚ 〕 n. 發現者；檢測器

```
de      + tect  + or
|         |        |
away from + cover +  n.
```

protect[2] 〔 prə'tɛkt 〕 v. 保護；防護（遮蔽於前方）
《*pro-* = before》

protection[3] 〔 prə'tɛkʃən 〕 n. 保護（者）；防護

protectionism 〔 prə'tɛkʃənˌɪzəm 〕 n. 保護貿易主義；保護政策
《 *-ism* = 主義 》

protectionist 〔 prə'tɛkʃənɪst 〕 n. 保護貿易論者

protective[3] 〔 prə'tɛktɪv 〕 adj. 保護的；防護的

protector[7] 〔 prə'tɛktɚ 〕 n. 擁護者；保護者；保護裝置；支援者

protege 〔'protəˌʒe , ˌprotə'ʒe 〕 n. 受保護者；子民
《 *-e* 表示男性行爲接受者 》

```
pro    + teg   +   e
|        |         |
before + cover + person
```

protegee[7] 〔'protəˌʒe , ˌprotə'ʒe 〕 n. 女性被保護人
《 *-ee* 表示女性行爲接受者 》

tegument 〔'tɛgjəmənt 〕 n. 外皮；外殼

578   temper = mix properly（適當地混合）

* 拉丁文 *temperare*（ = *mix properly*；*moderate*；*regulate*），
和拉丁文 *tempus* 有關，原爲「合於時間的」。

temper[3] 〔'tɛmpɚ 〕 v. 緩和；調劑；鍛鍊   n. 氣質；性情；脾氣

temperament[6] 〔'tɛmprəmənt , -pərə- 〕 n. 體質；氣質；【音樂】
平均律（被認爲是人體內四種液體比率而訂出的）

temperamental[7] 〔ˌtɛmpərə'mɛntl̩ 〕 adj. 氣質的；神經質的；
易怒的

temperance[7] 〔'tɛmprəns 〕 *n.* 自制；禁酒（適度的控制）
temperate[7] 〔'tɛmprɪt 〕 *adj.* 有節制的；適度的；溫和的
temperature[2] 〔'tɛmprətʃə 〕 *n.* 溫度；體溫

```
temper  + at(e) +  ure
  |          |       |
moderate +  adj.  +  n.
```

tempered[7] 〔'tɛmpəd 〕 *adj.* 有氣質的；溫和的；已調節的；
淬鍊過的
tempersome 〔'tɛmpəsəm 〕 *adj.* 暴怒的
　《*-some* 形容詞字尾，表示「具有～性質」》
attemper 〔 ə'tɛmpə 〕 *v.* 緩和；調節；鍛鍊《*at-* = *ad-* = to》
distemper[7] 〔 dɪs'tɛmpə 〕 *n.* 犬熱病；失調；情緒不好；
不安；騷動（不適當的）《*dis-* = apart》

579　**tempor** = time（時間；時代）

> ＊拉丁文 *tempus*（ = *time*；*season*）。

tempo[5] 〔'tɛmpo 〕 *n.* 速度；節奏
temporal[7] 〔'tɛmpərəl 〕 *adj.* 現世的；世俗的；暫時的
n. (*pl.*) 俗事
temporary[3] 〔'tɛmpə,rɛrɪ 〕 *adj.* 一時的；臨時的
temporize 〔'tɛmpə,raɪz 〕 *v.* 順應潮流；妥協（合於時間動向的）
tempest[6] 〔'tɛmpɪst 〕 *n.* 暴風雨；騷亂（時節所帶來的東西）
contemporary[5] 〔 kən'tɛmpə,rɛrɪ 〕 *adj.* 同時代的；現代的；
當代的　*n.* 同時代的人（時代相同的）《*con-* = together》

```
con     + tempor  +  ary
 |           |         |
together +  time   + adj., n.
```

contemporaneity 〔 kən,tɛmpərə'niətɪ 〕 *n.* 同時代性

contemporaneous 〔 kənˌtɛmpə'renɪəs 〕 *adj.* 同時代的；
屬同一時期的

contretemps 〔'kɑntrəˌtɑŋ 〕 *n.* 不巧發生的意外事件；令人尷尬
的事（發生在不對的時間）《*contre-* = *contra-* = against》

extempore 〔 ɪk'stɛmpərɪ , -ˌri 〕 *adj.* 即席的　*adv.* 臨時地；
即席地《拉丁文 *ex tempore* = at the moment》

extemporaneous 〔 ɛkˌstɛmpə'renɪəs 〕 *adj.* 即席的；無準備的

extemporize 〔 ɪk'stɛmpəˌraɪz , ɛk- 〕 *v.* 即席演說；隨意演奏
或演唱

extemporization 〔 ɪkˌstɛmpərə'zeʃən 〕 *n.* 即席作成；即席之作

580　**tempt** = try（嘗試）

> * 拉丁文 *temptare* , *tentare*（= *handle* ; *touch* ; *try*），表示
> 「（用手）碰觸以實驗」的意思。〔變化型〕*tent*。

tempt[5] 〔 tɛmpt 〕 *v.* 勸誘；勾引（試試心志的強弱）

temptation[5] 〔 tɛmp'teʃən 〕 *n.* 誘惑

tempter 〔'tɛmptɚ 〕 *n.* 誘惑者；誘惑物

tempting[7] 〔'tɛmptɪŋ 〕 *adj.* 誘惑性的；令人心動的

temptress 〔'tɛmptrɪs 〕 *n.* 誘人的女性《 *-ess* 表示女性的名詞字尾》

attempt[3] 〔 ə'tɛmpt 〕 *v.* 嘗試；攻擊　*n.* 嘗試；攻擊
《*at-* = *ad-* = to》

```
at + tempt
 |      |
to  +  try
```

attempted[7] 〔 ə'tɛmptɪd 〕 *adj.* 意圖的；未遂的

tentacle[7] 〔'tɛntəkḷ 〕 *n.* 觸角；觸鬚（作爲碰觸試探的東西）

tentation 〔 tɛn'teʃən 〕 *n.* 試驗調整

tentative[5] 〔'tɛntətɪv 〕 *adj.* 試驗性的；暫時的；猶豫的　*n.* 試驗

581 **ten , tin , tain** = hold ; keep (握住 ; 維持)

* 拉丁文 *tenere* (= hold ; keep) 。〔變化型〕*tin* , *tain*。

tenable[7] 〔'tɛnəbḷ 〕*adj.* 可守的；可維持的

tenacious[7] 〔 tɪ'neʃəs 〕*adj.* 固執的；黏性強的 (緊緊握住不放)

tenacity[7] 〔 tɪ'næsətɪ 〕*n.* 黏性強；固執

tenancy[7] 〔'tɛnənsɪ 〕*n.* 租地；租屋；租用 (期間)

tenant[5] 〔'tɛnənt 〕*n.* 佃戶；房客；居住者 (擁有者)

　　v. (土地、房屋等) 租賃；居住

tendril 〔'tɛndrɪl 〕*n.* (植物的) 卷鬚 (緊緊抓住的東西)

tenement 〔'tɛnəmənt 〕*n.* 住宅；合租房屋

tenet[7] 〔'tɛnɪt , 'tinɪt 〕*n.* 信條；教條；主義 (緊緊保護的東西)

tenor[7] 〔'tɛnɚ 〕*n.* 要旨；男高音；次中音 (被涵蓋的東西)

tenure[7] 〔'tɛnjɚ 〕*n.* 保有 (權)；保有期間；保有的條件或形式

```
ten  +  ure
 |        |
hold  +   n.
```

abstain[7] 〔 əb'sten , æb- 〕*v.* 戒除；棄權 (從～放手)《*abs-* = from》

abstention 〔 æb'stɛnʃən , əb- 〕*n.* 自制；戒除；棄權

abstinence[7] 〔'æbstənəns 〕*n.* 禁食；禁酒；禁慾

abstinent[7] 〔'æbstənənt 〕*adj.* 節制的；禁慾的

appertain[7] 〔ˌæpɚ'ten 〕*v.* 與～有關；屬於 (完全持有)

　　《*ap-* = *ad-* = to ; *per-* = thoroughly》

```
ap  +   per    +  tain
 |       |          |
to  + thoroughly + hold
```

contain[2] 〔 kən'ten 〕*v.* 包含；容納；容忍 (保護～)《*con-* = with》

container[4] 〔 kən'tenɚ 〕*n.* 容器；貨櫃

containerized 〔 kən'tenəˌraɪzd 〕*adj.* 用貨櫃運送的

containment[7] 〔 kən'tenmənt 〕*n.* 包含；抑制；牽制；圍堵

content[14]〔'kɑntɛnt , kən'tɛnt 〕*n.* 內容;目錄;容積
content[24] 〔 kən'tɛnt 〕*n.* 滿足 *adj.* 滿足的 *v.* 使滿足
contented[7] 〔 kən'tɛntɪd 〕*adj.* 滿足的
contentment[4] 〔 kən'tɛntmənt 〕*n.* 滿足

```
con  +  tent  +  ment
 |        |        |
with  +  hold  +   n.
```

continence[7] 〔'kɑntənəns 〕*n.* 自制;節欲
continent[3] 〔'kɑntənənt 〕*adj.* 自制的;節欲的(壓制)
 n. 洲;大陸
continental[5] 〔,kɑntə'nɛntl̩ 〕*adj.* 大陸的;大陸性的
continue[1] 〔 kən'tɪnjʊ 〕*v.* 繼續;延期(繼續保持~)
continual[4] 〔 kən'tɪnjʊəl 〕*adj.* 連續的;頻繁的

```
con  +  tinu  +  al
 |        |       |
with  +  hold  +  adj.
```

continuance 〔 kən'tɪnjʊəns 〕*n.* 連續;續篇
continuation[7] 〔 kən,tɪnjʊ'eʃən 〕*n.* 連續;續篇
continuity[5] 〔,kɑntə'njuətɪ 〕*n.* 連續;電影分景劇本
continuous[4] 〔 kən'tɪnjʊəs 〕*adj.* 不斷的;連續的
countenance[7] 〔'kɑʊntənəns 〕*n.* 表情;容貌;贊成;沉著(包含
 於臉上的東西) *v.* 贊許;贊助《*coun-* = *con-* = together》

```
coun  +  ten  +  ance
  |       |       |
together + hold  +  n.
```

detain[6] 〔 dɪ'ten 〕*v.* 阻止;扣押(隔離於另一處)《*de-* = away》
detainee[7] 〔 dɪ,te'ni 〕*n.* 被扣留者;未判決的囚犯
 《*-ee* 表示「被~的人」》
detainer 〔 dɪ'tenɚ 〕*n.* 非法侵佔(他人的所有物);繼續監禁令
detention[7] 〔 dɪ'tɛnʃən 〕*n.* 監禁;拘留;延遲

entertain[4]〔͵ɛntɚˋten〕*v.* 使娛樂；款待；懷抱（希望等）

（接入其中）《*enter-* = *inter-* = among》

entertainer[7]〔͵ɛntɚˋtenɚ〕*n.* 接待者；表演娛樂節目者

```
enter  +  tain  +   er
  |         |        |
among  +  hold  +  person
```

entertainingly〔͵ɛntɚˋtenɪŋlɪ〕*adv.* 有趣地

entertainment[4]〔͵ɛntɚˋtenmənt〕*n.* 娛樂；招待

impertinent[7]〔ɪmˋpɝtṇənt〕*adj.* 不適當的；不切題的；魯莽的

《*im-* = *in-* = not；*per-* = thoroughly》

impertinence；-ency〔ɪmˋpɝtṇəns(ɪ)〕*n.* 不切題；無關係；魯莽

lieutenant[5]〔luˋtɛnənt，lɪu-，lɛf-〕*n.* 副官；陸軍中尉；少尉；

海軍上尉；中尉（代替保衛地點者）《*lieu* = place》

maintain[2]〔menˋten，mən-〕*v.* 保持；贍養；主張（保有於手掌中）

《*main* = *manus* = hand》

maintainable〔menˋtenəbḷ〕*adj.* 可維持的

maintainer〔menˋtenɚ〕*n.* 養護者

maintenance[5]〔ˋmentənəns，-tɪn-〕*n.* 支持；維持；生活費用

```
main  +  ten  + ance
  |        |       |
hand  +  hold  +   n.
```

obtain[4]〔əbˋten〕*v.* 獲得；流行（存在於自己身邊）《*ob-* = near》

pertain[7]〔pɚˋten〕*v.* 屬於；有關；適合（完全有關的）

《*per-* = thoroughly》

pertinence；-ency[7]〔ˋpɝtṇəns(ɪ)〕*n.* 恰當；切題；直接的關係

pertinent[7]〔ˋpɝtṇənt〕*adj.* 切題的；有關係的　*n.*（常用 *pl.*）附屬物

pertinacious〔͵pɝtṇˋeʃəs〕*adj.* 執拗的；頑強的

pertinaciousness〔͵pɝtṇˋeʃəsnɪs〕*n.* 固執

pertinacity〔͵pɝtṇˋæsətɪ〕*n.* 執拗；固執

retain[4]〔rɪˋten〕*v.* 保留；維持；雇用（保留在後方）《*re-* = back》

rein[6] 〔 ren 〕 *n.* 韁繩；牽制　　*v.* (以韁繩) 駕馭；控制
（ 保留住馬的東西 ）

retention[7] 〔 rɪ'tɛnʃən 〕 *n.* 保持；記憶 (力)；拘留

```
re  + tent + ion
 |      |      |
back + hold +  n.
```

retentive[7] 〔 rɪ'tɛntɪv 〕 *adj.* 保持的；記性好的
retinue[7] 〔'rɛtn̩,ju , -,nu 〕 *n.* 侍從；隨員 (存於其後 → 跟隨)
sustain[5] 〔 sə'sten 〕 *v.* 支撐；維持；忍耐 (從下面舉起)

　　《*sus-* = *sub-* = up from below》

sustainable[7] 〔 sə'stenəbl̩ 〕 *adj.* 可支撐的；可持續的；可忍耐的

```
sus          + tain + able
 |              |      |
up from below + hold + adj.
```

sustainability[7] 〔 sə,stenə'bɪlətɪ 〕 *n.* 持續性
sustainer 〔 sə'stenɚ 〕 *n.* 支持者
sustainment 〔 sə'stenmənt 〕 *n.* 支持；維持
sustenance[7] 〔'sʌstənəns 〕 *n.* 營養物；維持；扶助
sustentation 〔,sʌstɛn'teʃən 〕 *n.* 支持；扶助；糧食

582 tend , tens , tent = stretch (伸展)

　　* 拉丁文 *tendere* (= *stretch* ; *extend*)，過去分詞為
　　tensus , *tentus*。

tend[13] 〔 tɛnd 〕 *v.* 易於；有助於；通向 (伸展往某一方)
tend[23] 〔 tɛnd 〕 *v.* 服侍；看管；照料
tendance[7] 〔'tɛndəns 〕 *n.* 照料；看護
tendency[4] 〔'tɛndənsɪ 〕 *n.* 趨勢；傾向；癖性 (傾向；面向)

```
tend   + ency
 |        |
stretch +  n.
```

tendentious〔tɛnˈdɛnʃəs〕*adj.* 有特定傾向的；宣傳性的

tender[3]〔ˈtɛndɚ〕*adj.* 柔軟的；親切的；善感的（易於伸展的）

　n. 招標；建議（伸出來）　*v.* 提出；提供

tendon[7]〔ˈtɛndən〕*n.* 腱（緊拉著的東西）《*-on* 名詞字尾》

tense[4]〔tɛns〕*adj.* 緊張的　*v.* 變為緊張

tensile[7]〔ˈtɛnsl̩, -sɪl〕*adj.* 伸張的；張力的《*-ile* 形容詞字尾》

tension[4]〔ˈtɛnʃən〕*n.* 緊張；張力；壓力　*v.* 緊張

tensity〔ˈtɛnsətɪ〕*n.* 緊張；緊張度

tensive〔ˈtɛnsɪv〕*adj.* 緊張的

tent[2]〔tɛnt〕*n.* 天幕；帳篷（張開的東西）　*v.* 住於帳篷中

attend[2]〔əˈtɛnd〕*v.* 出席；照顧；侍候；參加（周圍充滿氣息）

　《*at-* = *ad-* = to》

attendance[5]〔əˈtɛndəns〕*n.* 出席；侍候

```
at  +  tend  + ance
|       |       |
to + stretch +  n.
```

attendant[6]〔əˈtɛndənt〕*n.* 侍者；陪從；出席人

　adj. 陪從的；附隨的；出席的

attender〔əˈtɛndɚ〕*n.* 出席者

attention[2]〔əˈtɛnʃən〕*n.* 注意；(*pl.*) 慇懃；款待

attentional〔əˈtɛnʃənl̩〕*adj.* 注意的

attentive[7]〔əˈtɛntɪv〕*adj.* 專注的；慇懃的；關懷的

contend[5]〔kənˈtɛnd〕*v.* 爭鬥；辯論；主張（彼此競爭）

　《*con-* = together》

```
con   +   tend
|          |
together + stretch
```

contender[7]〔kənˈtɛndɚ〕*n.* 競爭者

contention[7]〔kənˈtɛnʃən〕*n.* 辯論；競爭

contentious[7]（kən'tɛnʃəs）*adj.* 好爭論的；愛爭辯的；
足以引起爭論的

distend[7]（dɪ'stɛnd）*v.* 擴張；膨脹（分開擴散）《*dis-* = apart》

distensible（dɪ'stɛnsəbḷ）*adj.* 會膨脹的

```
dis  +  tens  +  ible
 |        |        |
apart + stretch + adj.
```

distensibility（dɪs,tɛnsə'bɪlətɪ）*n.* 膨脹性；擴張

distension（dɪ'stɛnʃən）*n.* 膨脹；延伸

extend[4]（ɪk'stɛnd）*v.* 伸展；擴大；給予（向外張開擴大）
《*ex-* = out》

extensible（ɪk'stɛnsəbḷ）*adj.* 可伸展的；可擴大的

extensile（ɛk'stɛnsɪl）*adj.* 可伸出的；可伸長的《*-ile* 形容詞字尾》

extension[5]（ɪk'stɛnʃən）*n.* 擴充；伸展；（電話）分機

extensity（ɛk'stɛnsətɪ）*n.* 擴張性

extensive[5]（ɪk'stɛnsɪv）*adj.* 廣闊的；大規模的；粗放的

extensor（ɪk'stɛnsɚ）*n.* 伸肌

extent[4]（ɪk'stɛnt）*n.* 程度；範圍

hypertension[7]（,haɪpɚ'tɛnʃən）*n.* 高血壓（症）《*hyper-* = over》

```
hyper  +  tens  +  ion
  |         |        |
 over  + stretch +  n.
```

intend[4]（ɪn'tɛnd）*v.* 意欲；存心；設計（把心志伸展至～）
《*in-* = towards》

intended[7]（ɪn'tɛndɪd）*adj.* 故意的；有計劃的；未婚的
n. 未婚夫（妻）

intendance（ɪn'tɛndəns）*n.* 監督；管理（部）（心志所向）

intendant（ɪn'tɛndənt）*n.* 管理者；監督官

intendment（ɪn'tɛndmənt）*n.*（法的）眞意；正確的解釋

intense[4]（ɪn'tɛns）*adj.* 強烈的；熱情的；緊張的（集中心志的）

字根 tac~umbr

intensify[4] 〔 ɪnˈtɛnsəˌfaɪ 〕 v. 劇烈；加強《 *-ify* = make》

```
in   +  tens  +  ify
 |        |        |
towards + stretch + make
```

intensification 〔 ɪnˌtɛnsəfəˈkeʃən 〕 n. 強烈；激烈化；增大

intension 〔 ɪnˈtɛnʃən 〕 n. 緊張；強度；內涵

intensity[4] 〔 ɪnˈtɛnsətɪ 〕 n. 強度；強烈

intensive[4] 〔 ɪnˈtɛnsɪv 〕 adj. 激烈的；精深的；密集的；強調的

intent[5] 〔 ɪnˈtɛnt 〕 n. 意圖；意向　adj. 專注的

intention[4] 〔 ɪnˈtɛnʃən 〕 n. 意圖；意義；概念

intentional[7] 〔 ɪnˈtɛnʃənḷ 〕 adj. 有意的；企圖的

intentionally[7] 〔 ɪnˈtɛnʃənḷɪ 〕 adv. 故意地

ostensible[7] 〔 ɑsˈtɛnsəbḷ 〕 adj. 假裝的；可公開的（前面貼滿的）
　《 *os-* = before》

```
os   +  tens  +  ible
 |        |        |
before + stretch + adj.
```

ostensive 〔 ɑsˈtɛnsɪv 〕 adj. 明示的；表面的

ostentation 〔 ˌɑstənˈteʃən 〕 n. 虛飾；誇耀

ostentatious 〔 ˌɑstənˈteʃəs , -tɛn- 〕 adj. 誇張的；虛飾的

portend[7] 〔 porˈtɛnd , pɔr- 〕 v. 預示；預兆（向前擴張 → 指明表示）
　《 *por-* = *pro-* = forward》

portent 〔 ˈportɛnt , ˈpɔr- 〕 n. 預兆；徵兆

portentous 〔 porˈtɛntəs , pɔr- 〕 adj. 不祥的；驚人的；非常的

```
por   +  tent  +  ous
 |        |        |
towards + stretch + adj.
```

portentously 〔 pɔrˈtɛntəslɪ 〕 adv. 有預兆地

portentousness 〔 pɔrˈtɛntəsnɪs 〕 n. 預兆

pretend[3] 〔 prɪˈtɛnd 〕 v. 假裝；要求（向前伸張開來）《 *pre-* = before》

pretence；**-se**[7]〔prɪ'tɛns〕*n.* 藉口；偽裝；要求
pretension[7]〔prɪ'tɛnʃən〕*n.* 權利；矯飾；要求
pretentious[7]〔prɪ'tɛnʃəs〕*adj.* 矯飾的；驕傲的
subtend〔səb'tɛnd〕*v.*（弦、三角形的邊）正對（弧、角）
　《*sub-* = under》
superintend〔‚suprɪn'tɛnd〕*v.* 監督；管理（向~之上伸展注意力）
　《*super-* = above》

```
super  +  in   +  tend
  |        |       |
above + towards + stretch
```

superintendence〔‚suprɪn'tɛndəns〕*n.* 監督；管理
superintendent[7]〔‚suprɪn'tɛndənt〕*n.* 監督者；管理者；督學

583　**tenu** = thin（薄的）　* 拉丁文 *tenuis*（= *thin*）。

tenuity〔tɛn'juətɪ，tɪ'nɪuətɪ〕*n.* 細；稀薄；貧乏
tenuous[7]〔'tɛnjuəs〕*adj.* 細的；稀薄的；薄弱的
attenuate[7]〔*v.* ə'tɛnju‚et *adj.* ə'tɛnjuɪt〕*v.* 使稀薄；減弱；減少
　adj. 稀薄的；細的；薄的；弱的《*at-* = *ad-* = to》
attenuation〔ə‚tɛnju'eʃən〕*n.* 細小；薄弱；減弱
extenuate[7]〔ɪk'stɛnju‚et〕*v.* 減輕；掩飾；使人原諒《*ex-* = out》
extenuation〔ɪk‚stɛnju'eʃən〕*n.* 減輕；藉口

584　**terg** = back（背部）　* 拉丁文 *tergum*（= *back*）。

tergum〔'tɝgəm〕*n.*【動物】背甲；【昆蟲】背板
tergal〔'tɝgəl〕*adj.*【動物】背甲的；背板的
tergiversate〔'tɝdʒɪvɚ‚set〕*v.* 改變立場；背叛；支吾；搪塞

```
tergi + vers + ate
  |      |      |
back  + turn +  v.
```

585 term = end ; limit (末端；界限)

*拉丁文 **terminus** (= end ; boundary ; limit)。*

term[2] 〔t₃m〕*n.* 期限；期間；學期；術語；(*pl.*) 措辭；交誼
v. 命名；稱為

terminable[7] 〔't₃mɪnəbḷ〕*adj.* 有期限的；可終結的

```
termin  +  able
  |         |
limit    +  adj.
```

terminal[5] 〔't₃mənḷ〕*adj.* 末端的；終點的；定期的 *n.* 末端；終點

terminate[6] 〔*v.* 't₃mə,net *adj.* 't₃mənɪt〕*v.* 終結；限定；期滿
adj. 有限的

termination[7] 〔,t₃mə'neʃən〕*n.* 結束；末端；字尾

terminative[7] 〔't₃mə,netɪv , -nətɪv〕*adj.* 終結的；決定性的

terminator[7] 〔't₃mə,netɚ〕*n.* 終結者

terminology[7] 〔,t₃mə'nɑlədʒɪ〕*n.* 術語；專門名詞 (術語之學)

```
termin   +  ology
  |           |
boundary  +  study
```

terminus 〔't₃mənəs〕*n.* 終點；起點

conterminous 〔kɑn't₃mənəs , kən-〕*adj.* 毗鄰的；有共同
邊界的 (有同一界限)《**con-** = together》

determine[3] 〔dɪ't₃mɪn〕*v.* 決心；確定；測定 (定出清楚的界限)
《**de-** = down ; fully》

determinable 〔dɪ't₃mɪnəbḷ〕*adj.* 可確定的；可決定的

determinant 〔dɪ't₃mənənt〕*adj.* 決定的 *n.* 決定因素

determinate[7] 〔dɪ't₃mənɪt〕*adj.* 限定的；明確的；堅決的

```
de   +  termin  +  ate
 |         |         |
down  +  limit   +  adj.
```

determination[4] 〔dɪ,t₃mə'neʃən〕*n.* 決心；測定；判決

determined[7]〔dɪˈtɜmɪnd〕*adj.* 堅決的；已決定的

determiner〔dɪˈtɜmɪnɚ〕*n.* 限定詞；決定因素

determinism〔dɪˈtɜmɪnˌɪzəm〕*n.* 決定論；宿命論

《 *-ism* = 主義；理論》

determinist〔dɪˈtɜmɪnɪst〕*n.* 決定論者；宿命論者

exterminate[7]〔ɪkˈstɜməˌnet〕*v.* 消滅；消除

（向界限以外 → 成爲虛無狀態）《*ex-* = out》

extermination[7]〔ɪkˌstɜməˈneʃən〕*n.* 根絕；消滅

```
ex  +  termin  +  ation
│         │         │
out +   limit   +   n.
```

exterminator[7]〔ɪkˈstɜməˌnetɚ〕*n.* 根絕者；殺蟲劑

predeterminate〔ˌpridɪˈtɜmənɪt , -net〕*adj.* 預先決定的

v. 注定；預定（事前被決定的）《*pre-* = before》

predetermination[7]〔ˌpridɪˌtɜməˈneʃən〕*n.* 預先決定

586 **terr** = earth（地球；土地） 　　*拉丁文 *terra*（= earth）。

terrace[5]〔ˈtɛrɪs , -əs〕*n.* 梯田；台地；陽台；（話劇等之）舞台

（高而平坦的地方） *v.* 使成梯形地

terrain[7]〔tɛˈren〕*n.* 地形；地勢

terramycin〔ˌtɛrəˈmaɪsɪn〕*n.* 土黴素《*mycin* = fungus（黴菌）》

terraqueous〔tɛˈrekwɪəs〕*adj.* 由水與陸地合成的

《拉丁文 *aqua* = water》

```
terr  +  aqu  +  eous
│         │        │
earth +  water +  adj.
```

terrene〔tɛˈrin〕*adj.* 地球的；陸地的；現世的

terrestrial[7]〔təˈrɛstrɪəl〕*adj.* 陸地的；現世的　*n.* 地球人

territory[3]〔ˈtɛrəˌtorɪ , -ˌtɔrɪ〕*n.* 領土；土地；領域

territorial[7]〔ˌtɛrəˈtorɪəl〕*adj.* 領土的；土地的

exterritorial 〔,ɛkstɛrə'torɪəl 〕 *adj.* 治外法權的
（ = *extraterritorial*）（領土之外的）《*ex-* = out》
extraterrestrial[7] 〔,ɛkstrətə'rɛstrɪəl 〕 *adj.* 地球外的；大氣層
外的；宇宙的（地球之外的）《*extra-* = beyond》
extraterritorial 〔,ɛkstrə,tɛrə'torɪəl 〕 *adj.* 治外法權的
inter 〔 ɪn'tɝ 〕 *v.* 埋葬（向地裡去）《*in-* = into》

```
in  +  ter
 |      |
into + earth
```

interment[7] 〔 ɪn'tɝmənt 〕 *n.* 埋葬；葬禮
disinter[7] 〔,dɪsɪn'tɝ 〕 *v.* 挖出；使顯現（與埋葬相反）《*dis-* = contrary》
disinterment 〔,dɪsɪn'tɝmənt 〕 *n.* 發掘
Mediterranean[7] 〔,mɛdətə'renɪən 〕 *adj.* 地中海的；陸地包圍的
n. 地中海（在陸地之中的）《*medi* = middle》
subterranean[7] 〔,sʌbtə'renɪən 〕 *adj.* 地下的；祕密的
n. 穴居人；地下洞穴（在陸地之下的）《*sub-* = under》

587 **terr** = frighten（使驚嚇）

* 拉丁文 *terrere*（ = *frighten*）。

terrible[2] 〔'tɛrəbl̩ 〕 *adj.* 可怕的；嚴重的；非常的；差勁的
terrify[4] 〔'tɛrə,faɪ 〕 *v.* 使害怕；驚嚇
terrific[2] 〔 tə'rɪfɪk 〕 *adj.* 非常的；極好的
terror[4] 〔'tɛrɚ 〕 *n.* 恐怖；恐怖的原因；可怕的人或物
terrorism[7] 〔'tɛrə,rɪzəm 〕 *n.* 恐怖主義；恐怖行為；恐怖狀態
《*-ism* = 主義；狀態》

```
terr  + or + ism
 |       |    |
frighten + n. + n.
```

terrorist[7] 〔'tɛrərɪst 〕 *n.* 恐怖主義者；恐怖分子
terrorize[7] 〔'tɛrə,raɪz 〕 *v.* 使恐怖；脅迫；實施恐怖統治

deter[6] 〔 dɪˈtɝ 〕 v. 妨礙；阻止；使斷念《*de-* = *dis-* 表加強語氣》

deterrent[7] 〔 dɪˈtɝrənt 〕 *adj.* 妨礙的；遏阻的　*n.* 阻礙物

deterrence[7] 〔 dɪˈtɛrəns 〕 *n.* 阻止；遏阻；阻礙物

588　**test** = witness（證明）　*拉丁文 testis（= witness）。*

test[2] 〔 tɛst 〕 *n.* 試驗；考驗　*v.* 試驗；分析

【解説】 字源有異，但為了方便起見歸入此處。原意是試探「金的
性質」而使用的土製壺。

testament[7] 〔ˈtɛstəmənt 〕 *n.* 遺囑；聖約書（成為證據者）

testamentary 〔ˌtɛstəˈmɛntərɪ 〕 *adj.* 遺囑的；舊約（新約）聖經的

```
testa  + ment + ary
  |        |      |
witness +  n.  + adj.
```

testate 〔ˈtɛstet 〕 *adj.* 留有遺囑的　*n.* 留有遺囑的死者

testator 〔ˈtɛstetɚ, tɛsˈtetɚ 〕 *n.* 立遺囑的人

testatrix 〔 tɛsˈtetrɪks 〕 *n.* 女性立遺囑者《*rix* = feminine（女性）》

testify[7] 〔ˈtɛstəˌfaɪ 〕 *v.* 證明；表明（作證）《 *-ify* = make》

```
test  +  ify
  |       |
witness + make
```

testimony[7] 〔ˈtɛstəˌmonɪ 〕 *n.* 證言；口供；證實

testimonial[7] 〔ˌtɛstəˈmonɪəl 〕 *n.* 證明書；獎狀；感謝狀
　adj. 證明的；褒揚的；感謝的

attest[7] 〔 əˈtɛst 〕 *v.* 證明；證實《*at-* = *ad-* = to》

attestation 〔ˌætɛsˈteʃən 〕 *n.* 證明（書）；證據

attester ; -or 〔 əˈtɛstɚ 〕 *n.* 證人

```
at +  test  +  er
 |      |       |
to + witness + person
```

contest[4]〔*v.* kən'tɛst *n.* 'kɑntɛst 〕*v.* 爭取；駁斥；競爭
　n. 競爭；比賽（一起拿出證據加以爭論）《*con-* = together》

contestant[6]〔kən'tɛstənt 〕*n.*（比賽會場的）競爭者；選手

contestation〔,kɑntɛs'teʃən 〕*n.* 爭論；競爭；論點

detest[7]〔dɪ'tɛst 〕*v.* 深惡；憎惡（因叫出神明來作充分證明而被憎惡）
　《*de-* = down；fully》

detestable〔dɪ'tɛstəbḷ 〕*adj.* 極可惡的

detestation〔,ditɛs'teʃən 〕*n.* 深惡；厭惡

```
de    +   test   + ation
 |          |        |
down  + witness  +   n.
```

protest[4]〔*n.* 'protɛst *v.* prə'tɛst 〕*v.* 堅決聲明；抗議　*n.* 抗議；
　聲明（在衆人之前提出反面證據）《*pro-* = before；publicly》

protestant〔'prɑtɪstənt 〕*n.* 抗議者；（P-）新教徒
　adj. 提出異議的；（P-）新教徒的

protestation〔,prɑtəs'teʃən 〕*n.* 聲明；抗議

589　text = weave（編織）

　　＊拉丁文 *texere*（= *weave*），過去分詞是 *textus*。

text[3]〔tɛkst 〕*n.* 正文；原文（被編織的）

textile[6]〔'tɛkstḷ，-tɪl，-taɪl 〕*adj.* 織物的　*n.* 織物（的原料）

textual[7]〔'tɛkstʃʊəl 〕*adj.* 本文的；原文的

texture[6]〔'tɛkstʃɚ 〕*n.* 織法；質地；組織；構造

textural〔'tɛkstʃərəl 〕*adj.* 織地的；組織上的

context[4]〔'kɑntɛkst 〕*n.* 上下文；某事的前後關聯
　（使和本文在一起的）《*con-* = together》

```
text  +  ure
 |        |
weave +   n.
```

```
con    +   text
 |          |
together + weave
```

contextual〔kən'tɛkstʃʊəl〕*adj.* 上下文的；依前後關係的
contexture〔kən'tɛkstʃɚ, kɑn-〕*n.* 組織；構造（共同織成）
intertexture〔ˌɪntɚ'tɛkstʃɚ〕*n.* 編織；編織物（交互編織）
　《*inter-* = between》
pretext[7]〔'pritɛkst〕*n.* 藉口（眼前所編織的話）《*pre-* = before》
subtle[6]〔'sʌtḷ〕*adj.* 陰險的；微妙的；敏銳的（織法的精細）
　《*sub-* = beneath ; closely》
subtlety[7]〔'sʌtḷtɪ〕*n.* 敏銳；細微；陰險；微妙；精細
tissue[3]〔'tɪʃʊ〕*n.*【生理】組織《古法文 *tistre* = weave》

590　the(o) = god（神）　* 希臘文 *theos*（= god）。

theism〔'θiɪzəm〕*n.* 有神論；一神教《*-ism* = 主義；理論》
theist〔'θiɪst〕*n.* 有神論者；一神論者
theocracy〔θi'ɑkrəsɪ〕*n.* 神權政治；神權政體（由神統治）
　《*cracy* = rule》
theocrat〔'θiəˌkræt〕*n.* 神權政治家；神權主義者《*crat* = ruler》
theocratic〔ˌθiə'krætɪk〕*adj.* 神權（主義）的
theology[7]〔θi'ɑlədʒɪ〕*n.* 神學《*logy* = study》

```
theo  +  logy
 |        |
god   +  study
```

theologian〔ˌθiə'lodʒən〕*n.* 神學者；神學家
theological〔ˌθiə'lɑdʒɪkḷ〕*adj.* 神學的；神學上的
theologize〔θi'ɑləˌdʒaɪz〕*v.* 以神學的方式處理
apotheosis〔əˌpɑθɪ'osɪs, ˌæpə'θiəsɪs〕*n.* 神聖化；尊崇爲神；
　頌揚（使與神相關）《*apo-* = related to ; *-sis* = condition》
apotheosize〔ə'pɑθɪəˌsaɪz, ˌæpə'θiəˌsaɪz〕*v.* 奉爲神聖；
　尊崇爲神；頌揚

atheism[7] 〔'eθɪ‚ɪzəm 〕 *n.* 無神論 《*a-* = without》

```
   a   +  the + ism
   |       |     |
without + god +  n.
```

atheist 〔'eθɪɪst 〕 *n.* 無神論者
atheistic[7] 〔‚eθɪ'ɪstɪk 〕 *adj.* 無神論（者）的
monotheism 〔'manəθi‚ɪzəm 〕 *n.* 一神敎；一神論
《*mono-* = single》

monotheist 〔'manə‚θiɪst 〕 *n.* 一神敎信徒；一神論者

```
mono  + the +    ist
  |      |        |
single + god + person
```

pantheism 〔'pænθi‚ɪzəm 〕 *n.* 泛神論；多神敎 《*pan-* = all》
pantheist 〔'pænθiɪst 〕 *n.* 泛神論者
pantheon 〔'pænθɪ‚an 〕 *n.* 萬神殿；偉人祠；（一國人民所
信仰的）諸神《*-on* 名詞字尾》

```
pan + the + on
 |     |     |
all + god +  n.
```

polytheism 〔'paləθi‚ɪzəm 〕 *n.* 多神敎；多神論《*poly-* = many》
polytheist 〔'palə‚θiɪst 〕 *n.* 多神敎徒；多神論者

591　therap = cure（治療）

* 希臘文 *therapeuein*（ = *cure* ; *treat*）。

therapy[6] 〔'θɛrəpɪ 〕 *n.* 治療法
therapeutic[7] 〔‚θɛrə'pjutɪk 〕 *adj.* 治療的；有療效的
chemotherapy[7] 〔‚kɛmo'θɛrəpɪ 〕 *n.* 化學療法《*chemistry* 化學》
heliotherapy 〔‚hilɪo'θɛrəpɪ 〕 *n.* 日光療法《*helio* = sun》

hydrotherapy 〔͵haɪdrə'θɛrəpɪ 〕 *n.* 水療法（用水治療）
《*hydro* = water》

hypnotherapy 〔͵hɪpno'θɛrəpɪ 〕 *n.* 催眠療法《*hypno* = sleep》

physiotherapy 〔͵fɪzɪo'θɛrəpɪ 〕 *n.* 物理療法《*physics* 物理學》

psychotherapy[7] 〔͵saɪko'θɛrəpɪ 〕 *n.* 心理療法；精神療法
《*psychology* 心理學》

psychotherapist[7] 〔͵saɪko'θɛrəpɪst 〕 *n.* 精神治療醫師

radiotherapy 〔'redɪo'θɛrəpɪ 〕 *n.* X 光治療法；放射線治療法
《*radio* = ray（光線）》

592 **therm** = heat（熱）   * 希臘文 *therme*（= heat）。

thermal[7] 〔'θɝml̩ 〕 *adj.* 熱的；溫泉的

thermos[7] 〔'θɝməs 〕 *n.* 熱水瓶

thermostat[7] 〔'θɝmə͵stæt 〕 *n.* 自動調溫器；恆溫器

diathermy 〔'daɪə͵θɝmɪ 〕 *n.* 透熱療法；透熱電療機《*dia-* = through》

dia	+ therm	+ y
through	+ heat	+ n.

geothermic 〔͵dʒio'θɝmɪk 〕 *adj.* 地熱的《*geo* = earth》

593 **thes , thet** = place；put（放）

> * 希臘文 *tithenai*（= place；put），*thesis*（= placing）。
> 〔變化型〕*thet*。

thesis[7] 〔'θisɪs 〕 *n.* 論文；主題；命題；論點（將意見放進去）
《 -(*s*)*is* 名詞字尾》

antithesis[7] 〔 æn'tɪθəsɪs 〕 *n.* 對照；正相反的事物；對句
（放在對立的位置）《*anti-* = against》

antithetic ; -ical 〔͵æntə'θɛtɪk(l̩) 〕 *adj.* 相反的；對照的；對句的

hypothesis[7]〔haɪˈpɑθəsɪs〕*n.* 假設；假定；前提（放在下面）
《*hypo-* = under》

```
hypo  +  thesis
 |         |
under  +  place
```

hypothesize[7]〔haɪˈpɑθəˌsaɪz〕*v.* 作假設；假定
hypothetic；**-ical**[7]〔ˌhaɪpəˈθɛtɪk(l̩)〕*adj.* 假設的；假定的
parenthesis[7]〔pəˈrɛnθəsɪs〕*n.* 插入句；圓括弧（放進句子中）
《*par(a)-* = beside；*en-* = in》
parenthesize[7]〔pəˈrɛnθəˌsaɪz〕*v.* 置於括弧內；加入插句
parenthetic；**-ical**〔ˌpærənˈθɛtɪk(l̩)〕*adj.* 插入句的；附帶說明的
synthesis[7]〔ˈsɪnθəsɪs〕*n.* 綜合；合成；綜合體（放在一起）
《*syn-* = together》

```
syn    +  thes  +   (s)is
 |          |         |
together  +  put  +  condition
```

synthesize[7]〔ˈsɪnθəˌsaɪz〕*v.* 綜合；合成
synthetic[6]；**-ical**〔sɪnˈθɛtɪk(l̩)〕*adj.* 綜合的；合成的

594　**tim** = fear（恐懼）　　＊拉丁文 *timere*（= *fear*）。

timid[4]〔ˈtɪmɪd〕*adj.* 膽小的；怯懦的《*-id* 形容詞字尾》
timidity〔tɪˈmɪdətɪ〕*n.* 膽小；怯懦
timorous〔ˈtɪmərəs〕*adj.* 膽小的；畏怯的
intimidate[6]〔ɪnˈtɪməˌdet〕*v.* 威嚇；脅迫；恐嚇（使害怕）
《*in-* = make》

```
in   +  tim  +  id  +  ate
 |        |       |      |
make  +  fear  +  adj.  +  v.
```

intimidation[7]〔ɪnˌtɪməˈdeʃən〕*n.* 威嚇；脅迫
intimidator〔ɪnˈtɪməˌdetɚ〕*n.* 威嚇者；脅迫者

595 **tom** = cut（切割）

* 希臘文 *temnein*（ = *cut* ），*tomos*（ = *cutting* ）。

tome〔 tom 〕*n.* 大本書；大冊書；（大部著作的）一冊

atom[4]〔'ætəm 〕*n.* 原子《*a-* = not》

anatomy[7]〔ə'nætəmɪ 〕*n.* 解剖學《*ana-* = up》

autotomy[7]〔ɔ'tatəmɪ 〕*n.* 自割（當蝦、海盤車、蜥蜴等動物遭到
攻擊時，腳、爪、尾等會自動脫落的反射作用）《*auto-* = self》

entomology〔ˌɛntə'malədʒɪ 〕*n.* 昆蟲學

$$
\begin{array}{ccc}
\text{en} + & \text{tom} + & \text{ology} \\
| & | & | \\
in + & cut + & study\ of
\end{array}
$$

epitome[7]〔ɪ'pɪtəmɪ 〕*n.* 典型；縮影《*epi-* = into》

anthropotomy〔ˌænθrə'patəmɪ 〕*n.* 人體解剖（學）
《*anthropo* = man》

appendectomy[7]〔ˌæpən'dɛktəmɪ 〕*n.* 盲腸切除（術）

$$
\begin{array}{cccc}
\text{append} + & \text{ec} + & \text{tom} + & \text{y} \\
| & | & | & | \\
appendix + & out + & cut + & n.
\end{array}
$$

hysterotomy〔ˌhɪstə'ratəmɪ 〕*n.* 剖腹產術；子宮切開術
《*hystero* = womb（子宮）》

laparotomy〔ˌlæpə'ratəmɪ 〕*n.* 剖腹術
《希臘文 *lapara* = flank（側腹）》

vasectomy〔væs'ɛktəmɪ 〕*n.* 輸精管切除術
《*vas* = vessel（管）》

596 **ton** = tone（語調）

* 希臘文 *tonos*（ = *tone* ）；拉丁文 *tonus*（ = *tone* ）。

tone[1]〔 ton 〕*n.* 音色；語調；風格；色調　*v.* 調和

tonal 〔'tonḷ〕 *adj.* 音色的；音調的；色調的

```
ton  +  al
 |       |
tone  +  adj.
```

tonality 〔to'næləti〕 *n.* 音調；色調

tonetics 〔to'nɛtiks〕 *n.* 聲調學《 *-ics* = science》

atonal[7] 〔e'tonḷ, æ-〕 *adj.* 無調的；不成調的（沒有音調）

《*a-* = without》

atonality 〔ˌeto'næləti〕 *n.* 無調性

atonic 〔ə'tɑnɪk, e-, æ-〕 *adj.* 無重音的；輕聲的

```
a    +  ton  +  ic
 |        |       |
without  +  tone  +  adj.
```

baritone[7] 〔'bærəˌton〕 *n., adj.* 男中音（的）

《希臘文 *barus* = heavy》

diatonic[7] 〔ˌdaɪə'tɑnɪk〕 *adj.* 全音階的（各種音調都有）

《*dia-* = through》

intone[7] 〔ɪn'ton〕 *v.* 吟詠；詠唱；加上抑揚（唱出音調）

《*in-* = into》

intonation[4] 〔ˌɪnto'neʃən〕 *n.* 詠唱；抑揚；音調；語調

monotone[7] 〔'mɑnəˌton〕 *n.* 單調；無變化《*mono-* = single》

```
mono  +  tone
  |        |
single  +  tone
```

monotonous[6] 〔mə'nɑtn̩əs〕 *adj.* 單調的；無變化的；無聊的

monotony[6] 〔mə'nɑtn̩ɪ〕 *n.* 單調；無變化；乏味

overtone[7] 〔'ovɚˌton〕 *n.* 泛音；弦外之音；暗示《*over-* = beyond》

semitone 〔'sɛməˌton〕 *n.* 半音；半音程《*semi-* = half》

undertone[7] 〔'ʌndɚˌton〕 *n.* 低聲；淡色；含意；暗流；

潛在因素；市場動向《*under-* = under》

597 **ton** = thunder（打雷） *拉丁文 *tonare*（= *thunder*）。

astonish[5]〔ə'stɑnɪʃ〕*v.* 使驚訝（晴天霹靂）
《*as-* = *ex-* = out》

detonate[7]〔'dɛtə,net〕*v.*（使）爆裂；（使）爆炸（如打雷般）
《*de-* = down》

detonation〔,dɛtə'neʃən〕*n.* 爆炸；爆炸聲

detonator〔'dɛtə,netɚ〕*n.* 雷管；炸藥

stun[5]〔stʌn〕*v.* 使目瞪口呆；把…擊昏

598 **top** = place（地方） *希臘文 *topos*（= *place*）。

topocentric〔,tɑpə'sɛntrɪk〕*adj.* 以地面上的某點為中心
（測定）的；地面點的《*centr* = center》

topography[7]〔to'pɑgrəfɪ〕*n.* 地形學；地誌；地形
（對地方的描寫）《*graph* = write》

topology〔to'pɑlədʒɪ〕*n.* 地勢學《*logy* = study》

toponym〔'tɑpə,nɪm〕*n.* 地名；以地名而命之名

```
 top  + onym
  |       |
place + name
```

toponymy〔tə'pɑnəmɪ〕*n.* 地名學

isotope[7]〔'aɪsə,top〕*n.* 同位素《*iso-* = equal》

599 **tor** , **tort** = twist（扭曲）

*拉丁文 *torquere*（= *twist*），過去分詞為 *tortus*。

torch[5]〔tɔrtʃ〕*n.* 火炬；（知識、文化的）光（搓繩浸泡在瀝青中）

torment[5]〔*n.* 'tɔrmɛnt *v.* tɔr'mɛnt〕*n.* 痛苦；煩惱
v. 加以拷問；使痛苦

torsion〔ˈtɔrʃən〕 *n.* 扭轉

torture[5]〔ˈtɔrtʃɚ〕 *n.* 拷問；痛苦；打擊

　　v. 使受痛苦；折磨；曲解（扭打身體）

```
tort  +  ure
 |        |
twist  +  n.
```

torturer〔ˈtɔrtʃərɚ〕 *n.* 拷問者；折磨者

torturous〔ˈtɔrtʃərəs〕 *adj.* 使痛苦的

tortuous[7]〔ˈtɔrtʃʊəs〕 *adj.* 彎曲的；歪曲的；不正直的

tortoise[3]〔ˈtɔrtəs , -tɪs〕 *n.* 龜（腳部彎曲的動物）

contort[7]〔kənˈtɔrt〕 *v.* 扭歪；歪曲（扭在一塊兒）

　　《*con-* = together》

contortion[7]〔kənˈtɔrʃən〕 *n.* 扭歪；彎曲

```
con   +  tort  +  ion
 |        |        |
together + twist +  n.
```

contortionist[7]〔kənˈtɔrʃənɪst〕 *n.* 雜技表演者（能將身體任意

　　扭轉的人）

distort[6]〔dɪsˈtɔrt〕 *v.* 扭曲；曲解《*dis-* = apart》

distortion[7]〔dɪsˈtɔrʃən〕 *n.* 變形；曲解

distortionist〔dɪsˈtɔrʃənɪst〕 *n.* 漫畫家

extort[7]〔ɪkˈstɔrt , ɛk-〕 *v.* 勒索；強索（擰出）《*ex-* = out》

extortion[7]〔ɪkˈstɔrʃən , ɛk-〕 *n.* 強取；勒索

retort[5]〔rɪˈtɔrt〕 *v.* 反駁；反擊　 *n.* 反駁（扭轉回來）《*re-* = back》

retortion〔rɪˈtɔrʃən〕 *n.* 返回；折回；報復

600　 **tour** = turn（轉）

　　* 拉丁文 *tornare*（= turn in a lathe），*tornus*（= lathe 旋盤）。

　　〔變化型〕*torn , tourn , turn*。

tour[2]〔tʊr〕 *n.* 漫遊；旅行　 *v.* 遊歷；巡迴演出

tourism[3]〔ˈtʊrɪzm̩〕 *n.* 觀光事業；觀光旅行；【集合用法】觀光客

tourist[3]〔ˈtʊrɪst〕 *n.* 觀光客

tournament[5] 〔'tɝnəmənt , 'tʊr- 〕 *n.*（中古騎士的）馬上比武
（大會）；錦標賽（馬兒迅速轉變方向）

attorney[7] 〔 ə'tɝnɪ 〕 *n.* 代理人；律師（代替者）《*at- = ad- =* to》

```
at + torne + y
|     |      |
to + turn  + n.
```

contour[7] 〔'kɑntʊr 〕 *n.* 輪廓；外形界線   *v.* 畫地形線（一起繞一圈）
《*con- =* together》

detour[7] 〔'ditʊr , dɪ'tʊr 〕 *n.* 繞道；改道   *v.* 繞道而行
《*de- = dis- =* away》

turn[1] 〔 tɝn 〕 *v.* 轉動；翻動；轉向；轉變   *n.* 轉動；輪流

turnaround[7] 〔'tɝnə,raʊnd 〕 *n.* 轉變《*around* 環繞》

return[1] 〔 rɪ'tɝn 〕 *v. , n.* 返回；回報；恢復；回答（轉回）
《*re- =* back》

字根 tac~umbr

601 **tox** = poison（毒藥）   * 拉丁文 *toxicum*（*= poison*）。

toxic[5] 〔'tɑksɪk 〕 *adj.* 有毒的；中毒的

toxicant 〔'tɑksɪkənt 〕 *adj.* 有毒的   *n.* 毒物；毒藥

toxicity 〔 tɑks'ɪsətɪ 〕 *n.* 毒性

toxicology[7] 〔,tɑksɪ'kɑlədʒɪ 〕 *n.* 毒物學《*ology =* study》

toxicologist 〔,tɑksɪ'kɑlədʒɪst 〕 *n.* 毒物學家

toxin[7] 〔'tɑksɪn 〕 *n.* 毒素

antitoxic 〔,æntɪ'tɑksɪk 〕 *adj.* 抗毒素的；抗毒性的（對抗毒素）
《*anti- =* against》

```
anti  +  tox   + ic
|        |       |
against + poison + adj.
```

antitoxin 〔,æntɪ'tɑksɪn 〕 *n.* 抗毒素

detoxify 〔 di'tɑksə,faɪ 〕 *v.* 解毒（去除毒素）《*de- = dis- =* away》

endotoxin〔͵ɛndo'taksɪn〕*n.*（病原菌內的）內毒素（內在的毒）
　　《*endo-* = inside》

intoxicate[7]〔ɪn'taksə͵ket〕*v.* 使醉；使陶醉；使中毒（中毒）
　　《*in-* = into》

```
in  +  tox  +  ic  +  ate
 |      |      |      |
into + poison + adj. + v.
```

intoxicant〔ɪn'taksəkənt〕*adj.* 醉人的　*n.* 麻醉劑；
　　醉人的東西；酒類飲料
intoxicated[7]〔ɪn'taksə͵ketɪd〕*adj.* 醉的；歡天喜地的
intoxication[7]〔ɪn͵taksə'keʃən〕*n.* 醉；陶醉；中毒

602　　tract = draw（拉；畫）

　　＊拉丁文 *trahere*（= *draw*），過去分詞爲 *tractus*；
　　　tractare（= *handle*）。〔變化型〕*treat*。

trace[3]〔tres〕*v.* 回溯；追蹤；描繪　*n.* 足跡；痕跡；描繪
track[2]〔træk〕*n.* 足跡；軌道；線路　*v.* 追蹤
trackage〔'trækɪdʒ〕*n.*【集合用法】鐵路軌道；鐵路的使用權
　　《*-age* 抽象名詞字尾》
tract[7]〔trækt〕*n.* 區域；（討論宗教、政治問題的宣傳用）小册子
　　（走路的範圍）
tractable〔'træktəbḷ〕*adj.* 溫順的；馴良的；易處理的（可能拉回的）

```
tract + able
  |      |
draw  + adj.
```

traction[7]〔'trækʃən〕*n.* 牽引（力）；牽引機（拉扯）
tractive〔'træktɪv〕*adj.* 曳引的；牽引的
tractor[7]〔'træktɚ〕*n.* 牽引機；牽引者
trail[3]〔trel〕*v.* 拖；拉；追蹤；尾隨　*n.* 蹤跡；小徑

trailer[7] 〔'trelɚ 〕 *n.* 跟隨在後的人（物）；電影預告片

train[1] 〔 tren 〕 *v.* 教養；訓練（使人延展）　*n.* 列車；行列；導火線
（拉成一線的東西）

trait[6] 〔 tret 〕 *n.* 特性；特點（拉線）

treat[5,2] 〔 trit 〕 *v.* 對待；治療；處理　*n.* 款待（處理問題、人、事態）

treatment[5] 〔'tritmənt 〕 *n.* 待遇；治療；處理

```
treat  +  ment
  |         |
draw   +   n.
```

treatise 〔'tritɪs 〕 *n.* 論文（論述的東西）

treaty[5] 〔'tritɪ 〕 *n.* 條約；談判

abstract[4] 〔 *adj.* 'æbstrækt , æb'strækt　*v.* æb'strækt　*n.* 'æbstrækt 〕
adj. 抽象的；理論的　*v.* 抽去；摘要；使抽象化　*n.* 摘要；抽象
（從～拉走）《 *abs-* = from 》

abstracted 〔 æb'stræktɪd 〕 *adj.* 心不在焉的

abstractedly 〔 æb'stræktɪdlɪ 〕 *adv.* 心不在焉地

abstraction[6] 〔 æb'strækʃən , əb- 〕 *n.* 抽象（觀念）；心不在焉

```
abs  +  tract  +  ion
 |        |        |
from  +  draw  +   n.
```

abstractionism 〔 æb'strækʃən͵ɪzəm 〕 *n.* 抽象派；抽象主義

abstractionist 〔 æb'strækʃənɪst 〕 *n.* 抽象派畫家

abstractive 〔 æb'stræktɪv 〕 *adj.* 抽象的

attract[3] 〔 ə'trækt 〕 *v.* 吸引；招引（吸引）《 *at-* = *ad-* = to 》

attractable 〔 ə'træktəbḷ 〕 *adj.* 可被吸引的

attraction[4] 〔 ə'trækʃən 〕 *n.* 吸引力；誘惑力；引力

attractive[3] 〔 ə'træktɪv 〕 *adj.* 嫵媚的；動人的；有吸引力的

```
at  +  tract  +  ive
 |       |        |
to  +  draw  +   adj.
```

attractively〔əˈtræktɪvlɪ〕*adv.* 吸引人地

attractor〔əˈtræktə〕*n.* 有吸引力的人或物

contract[3]〔*v.* kənˈtrækt *n.* ˈkɑntrækt〕*v.* 締結；訂立；收縮；
  感染 *n.* 合同；婚約（彼此吸引）《*con-* = together》

contracted[7]〔kənˈtræktɪd〕*adj.* 收縮的；狹窄的

contractible[7]〔kənˈtræktəbḷ〕*adj.* 可收縮的；收縮性的

contractibility〔kən,træktəˈbɪlətɪ〕*n.* 可收縮性

contractile〔kənˈtræktḷ, -tɪl〕*adj.* 有收縮性的

contraction[7]〔kənˈtrækʃən〕*n.* 收縮；（貸款、資金等）緊縮

contractive〔kənˈtræktɪv〕*adj.* 有收縮性的

contractor[6]〔kənˈtræktə, ˈkɑntræktə〕*n.* 立契約者；承包商；
  收縮肌

con	+	tract	+	or
together	+	draw	+	person

contractual[7]〔kənˈtræktʃʊəl〕*adj.* 契約（上）的

contracture〔kənˈtræktʃə〕*n.* 攣縮

detract[7]〔dɪˈtrækt〕*v.* 減損；降低《*de-* = *dis-* = away》

detraction〔dɪˈtrækʃən〕*n.* 減除；誹謗

detractive〔dɪˈtræktɪv〕*adj.* 貶低的

detractor[7]〔dɪˈtræktə〕*n.* 誹謗者

distract[6]〔dɪˈstrækt〕*v.* 分心；困擾；使輕鬆（拉往別的方向）
  《*dis-* = apart》

distracted[7]〔dɪˈstræktɪd〕*adj.* 分心的

distractedly〔dɪˈstræktɪdlɪ〕*adv.* 心煩意亂地

distractible〔dɪˈstræktəbḷ〕*adj.* 容易分心的

distracting[7]〔dɪˈstræktɪŋ〕*adj.* 令人分心的

distraction[6]〔dɪˈstrækʃən〕*n.* 分心；狂亂

distractive〔dɪˈstræktɪv〕*adj.* 分散注意力的

extract[6]〔*v.* ɪkˈstrækt *n.* ˈɛkstrækt〕*v.* 摘取；抽出；吸取
  n. 選粹；摘取物（抽出來）《*ex-* = out》

extractable〔 ɪk'stræktəb!〕*adj.* 可萃取的；可摘錄的
extraction[7]〔 ɪk'strækʃən 〕*n.* 抽出；拔取；抽出物；選粹

```
ex + tract + ion
 │     │      │
out + draw +  n.
```

extractive〔 ɪk'stræktɪv 〕*adj.* 萃取的
extractor〔 ɛk'stræktɚ 〕*n.* 抽出者；選取者；抽出器
intractable[7]〔 ɪn'træktəb!〕*adj.* 不聽話的；難駕馭的；倔強的；
　難處理的《*in-* = not》
protract[7]〔 pro'trækt 〕*v.* 延長；伸張（向前方拉伸）《*pro-* = forth》
protractile〔 pro'træktɪl 〕*adj.* 伸出的；可伸長的
protraction[7]〔 pro'trækʃən 〕*n.* 拖延；延長；伸長；製圖
protractor〔 pro'træktɚ 〕*n.* 使延長的人或物；量角器；伸肌
retrace[7]〔 rɪ'tres 〕*v.* 折回；追溯；回顧《*re-* = back》
retract[7]〔 rɪ'trækt 〕*v.* 縮回；收回（往後拉）《*re-* = back》

```
re  + tract
 │      │
back + draw
```

retractable[7]〔 rɪ'træktəb!〕*adj.* 可撤回的；可收縮的
retractile〔 rɪ'trækt! , -tɪl 〕*adj.* 收縮自如的；可縮進去的
retractility〔ˌritræk'tɪlətɪ 〕*n.* 伸縮性；伸縮能力
retraction[7]〔 rɪ'trækʃən 〕*n.* 縮回；收回
retractive〔 rɪ'træktɪv 〕*adj.* 可收回的
retractor〔 rɪ'træktɚ 〕*n.* 伸縮裝置；縮回者
subtract[2]〔 səb'trækt 〕*v.* 減去；扣除（往下拉）《*sub-* = under》

```
sub  + tract
 │      │
under + draw
```

subtraction[7]〔 səb'trækʃən 〕*n.* 減去；扣除；減法
subtractive〔 səb'træktɪv 〕*adj.* 減法的

subtractively〔səb'træktɪvlɪ〕*adv.* 減法地
entreat〔ɪn'trit〕*v.* 懇求；乞求（吸引人心）《*en-* = in》
entreaty〔ɪn'tritɪ〕*n.* 懇求；乞求
maltreat〔mæl'trit〕*v.* 虐待（報以惡行）《*mal-* = badly》
portray[4]〔por'tre , pɔr-〕*v.* 畫像；描繪（向前畫 → 描繪）
　《*por-* = *pro-* = forward》

```
   por   +  tray
    |        |
 forward +  draw
```

portrait[3]〔'portret , 'pɔr- , -trɪt〕*n.* 肖像；描寫
retreat[4]〔rɪ'trit〕*v.* 撤回；退卻　*n.* 撤退；退隱；避難所
　（向後拉）《*re-* = back》
subtrahend〔'sʌbtrə,hɛnd〕*n.* 減數
　《*subtrah* = *subtract* = draw；*-end* 名詞字尾》　　*cf.* **minuend**（被減數）

603　**tribut** = pay；bestow（給予；贈與）

　　　* 拉丁文 *tribuere*（= assign；pay；bestow），過去分詞為 *tributus*。

tribute[5]〔'trɪbjut〕*n.* 貢金；貢物；貢獻（贈與之物）
tributary〔'trɪbjə,tɛrɪ〕*adj.* 納貢的；支流的　*n.* 屬國；支流
attribute[7]〔*v.* ə'trɪbjut　*n.* 'ætrə,bjut〕*v.*（性質、原因等）歸於；
　諉於　*n.* 性質；品性；象徵（使歸屬於～）《*at-* = *ad-* = to》
attribution〔,ætrə'bjuʃən〕*n.* 歸因；歸屬；職權
attributive〔ə'trɪbjətɪv〕*adj.* 歸屬的　*n.* 修飾語
contribute[4]〔kən'trɪbjut〕*v.* 捐助；貢獻；促成（給予分配的份兒）
　《*con-* = together》

```
   con   +  tribute
    |         |
together +  bestow
```

contribution[4]〔,kɑntrə'bjuʃən〕*n.* 捐助；貢獻；投稿
contributor[7]〔kən'trɪbjətɚ〕*n.* 捐助者；貢獻者；投稿人

distribute[4]〔 dɪ'strɪbjʊt 〕 v. 分配；分發；散佈；分類（分配給予）
《**dis-** = apart》
distribution[4]〔,dɪstrə'bjuʃən 〕 n. 分配；分類；頒發；分布
retribution[7]〔,rɛtrə'bjuʃən 〕 n. 報應；罰；報復《**re-** = back》
retributive〔 rɪ'trɪbjətɪv 〕; **-tory**〔 -,torɪ 〕 adj. 報應的；報償的

604　**trich** = hair（毛髮）　　　* 希臘文 **thrix**（ = hair）。

trichiasis〔 trɪ'kaɪəsɪs 〕 n. 倒睫
trichina〔 trɪ'kaɪnə 〕 n. 旋毛蟲
trichinosis〔,trɪkə'nosɪs 〕 n. 旋毛蟲病
trichogen〔'trɪkədʒən 〕 n. 毛原細胞《**gen** = produce》
trichoid〔'trɪkɔɪd 〕 adj. 毛狀的；像毛的《**-oid** = like》
trichology〔 trɪ'kɑlədʒɪ 〕 n. 毛髮學《**logy** = study》
trichomycosis〔,trɪkəmaɪ'kosɪs 〕 n. 毛髮菌病；髮癬菌病
《**mycosis** 黴菌病》

605　**trit** = rub（摩擦）

* 拉丁文 **terere**（ = rub ; wear down），過去分詞為 **tritus**。

trite[7]〔 traɪt 〕 adj. 陳腐的
attrition[7]〔 ə'trɪʃən 〕 n. 摩擦；磨損《**at-** = **ad-** = to》
contrite[7]〔'kɑntraɪt , kən'traɪt 〕 adj. 悔罪的；痛悔的（內心受折磨）
《**con-** = together》
detriment[7]〔'dɛtrəmənt 〕 n. 損害（磨損）《**de-** = away》
detrimental[7]〔,dɛtrə'mɛntl̩ 〕 adj. 有害的；不利的

de	+	tri	+	ment	+	al
apart	+	rub	+	n.	+	adj.

detrition〔 dɪ'trɪʃən 〕 n. 磨損（作用）；消耗
detritus〔 dɪ'traɪtəs 〕 n. 岩碎；碎石

字根 tac~umbr

606　**trop** = turn（轉）　*希臘文 *tropos*（= *turn*）。

tropic[6]〔'trɑpɪk〕*n.* 回歸線；熱帶地方　　*adj.* 熱帶的（太陽到此往回轉）

tropical[3]〔'trɑpɪkḷ〕*adj.* 熱帶（地方）的；熱帶性的

tropism〔'tropɪzəm〕*n.*（對刺激的）向性；屈性

heliotrope〔'hiljə,trop〕*n.* 天芥菜屬植物（向陽而開淡紫色花的植物）（跟著太陽轉）《*helio* = sun》

heliotropism〔,hilɪ'ɑtrəpɪzm̩〕*n.* 向日性；屈光性

hydrotropism（haɪ'drɑtrə,pɪzəm）*n.* 向水性（跟著水走）
　　《*hydro* = water》

subtropical[7]（sʌb'trɑpɪkḷ）*adj.* 亞熱帶的
　　《*sub-* = secondary（次；亞）》

subtropics（sʌb'trɑpɪks）*n.pl.* 亞熱帶地方

trophy[6]〔'trofɪ〕*n.* 戰利品；獎品（代表敵人的戰敗）
　　《希臘文 *trope* = turning ; defeat of the enemy》

607　**troph** = nourish（滋養）

　　*希臘文 *trophe*（= *nourishment*）。

trophic〔'trɑfɪk〕*adj.* 營養的；有關營養（作用）的

trophoblast〔'trɑfə,blæst〕*n.*（胚胎）滋養層《*blast* = bud（芽）》

trophogenic〔,trɑfə'dʒɛnɪk〕*adj.* 營養生成的《*gen* = produce》

trophology（tro'fɑlədʒɪ）*n.* 營養學《*logy* = study》

trophoplasm〔'trɑfə,plæzm̩〕*n.* 營養質《*plas* = form》

atrophy[7]〔'ætrəfɪ〕*n.*, *v.* 萎縮；衰退（沒有營養）《*a-* = not》

```
a  +  troph  +  y
|       |       |
not +  nourish  +  n.
```

hypertrophy（haɪ'pɝtrəfɪ）*n.* 肥胖；異常發達（過度營養）
　　《*hyper-* = beyond》

608　**trud** , **trus** = thrust ; push（插入；推）

　　* 拉丁文 *trudere*（ = *thrust* ; *push* ; *urge* ），過去分詞爲 *trusus*。

abstruse〔 æb'strus , əb- 〕*adj.* 難解的；深奧的（推向別處
　　→ 隱蔽不清楚）《*abs-* = away》

detrude〔 dɪ'trud 〕*v.* 推出；推下（推倒）《*de-* = down》

extrude[7]〔 ɪk'strud , ɛk- 〕*v.* 逼出；擠出；逐出（推到外面）
　　《*ex-* = out》

extrusion〔 ɪk'struʒən 〕*n.* 擠出；壓出

```
ex  +  trus  +  ion
|       |       |
out  +  push  +  n.
```

extrusive〔 ɪk'strusɪv 〕*adj.* 壓出的；噴出的

intrude[6]〔 ɪn'trud 〕*v.* 闖入；侵擾（推擠進來）《*in-* = into》

intruder[6]〔 ɪn'trudɚ 〕*n.* 闖入者

intrusion[7]〔 ɪn'truʒən 〕*n.* 闖入；侵擾

intrusive[7]〔 ɪn'trusɪv 〕*adj.* 闖入的；干擾的

obtrude[7]〔 əb'trud 〕*v.* 強迫接受；闖進（不請自來）《*ob-* = against》

obtrusion[7]〔 əb'truʒən 〕*n.* 強迫接受；莽撞

obtrusive[7]〔 əb'trusɪv 〕*adj.* 強迫人的；突出的

```
ob  +  trus  +  ive
|       |       |
against + push  +  adj.
```

obtrusiveness〔 əb'trusɪvnɪs 〕*n.* 莽撞；突出

protrude[7]〔 pro'trud 〕*v.* 伸出；吐出（向前突出）《*pro-* = forth》

protrudent〔 pro'trudənt 〕*adj.* 突出的

protrusion[7]〔 pro'truʒən 〕*n.* 突出；伸出

protrusile〔 pro'trusɪl 〕*adj.* 可突出的；可伸出的

```
pro  +  trus  +  ile
|       |       |
forth + push  +  adj.
```

protrusive〔 proˈtrusɪv 〕*adj.* 突出的；伸出的

threat[3]〔 θrɛt 〕*n.* 恐嚇；威脅；惡兆（推擠壓迫）
　《拉丁文 ***trudere*** = push》

threaten[3]〔ˈθrɛtn̩ 〕*v.* 恐嚇；威脅；即將來臨

thrust[5]〔 θrʌst 〕*v.* 插入；力推；擠進　　*n.* 刺；攻擊

609　**tuber** = swelling（膨脹）

* 拉丁文 ***tuber***（ = lump ; bump ; swelling ）。

tubercle〔ˈtjubəkl̩，ˈtu- 〕*n.* 小結節；結核《 *-cle* 表示小的名詞字尾》

tuberous〔ˈtjubərəs，tu- 〕*adj.* 有結節的；結節狀的；塊莖狀的

tuberculosis[7]〔 tjuˌbɝkjəˈlosɪs，ˈtu- 〕*n.* 結核（病）；肺結核

```
tuber  +  cul  +  osis
  |         |       |
swelling + small +  n.
```

protuberance〔 proˈtjubərəns，-ˈtu- 〕*n.* 突起；瘤（向前膨脹）
　《*pro-* = forward》

610　**tum** = swell（膨脹）

* 拉丁文 ***tumere***（ = swell ），***tumultus***（ = disturbance ）。

tumefy〔ˈtjuməˌfaɪ，ˈtu- 〕*v.*（使）腫脹；（使）脹大
　《 *-efy* 動詞字尾》

tumefaction〔ˌtjuməˈfækʃən，ˌtu- 〕*n.* 腫脹；腫大；腫脹的部分

tumescent〔 tjuˈmɛsn̩t 〕*adj.* 腫脹的；腫大的《 *-escent* = becoming》

tumescence〔 tjuˈmɛsn̩s 〕*n.* 腫脹

tumid〔ˈtjumɪd，ˈtu- 〕*adj.* 腫脹的；浮誇的《 *-id* 形容詞字尾》

tumidity〔 tjuˈmɪdətɪ，tu- 〕*n.* 腫脹；誇張

```
tum  +  id  +  ity
 |       |      |
swell + adj. +  n.
```

tumo(u)r⁶ 〔'tjumə , 'tumə 〕 *n.* 腫瘤

tumo(u)rous 〔'tjumərəs 〕 *adj.* (似) 腫瘤的

tumult⁷ 〔'tjumʌlt , 'tu- 〕 *n.* 喧囂；騷動；激動 (情緒的膨脹)

tumultuary 〔 tju'mʌltʃʊ,ɛrɪ , tu- 〕 *adj.* 喧囂的；混亂的；無秩序的

tumultuous⁷ 〔 tju'mʌltʃʊəs , tu- 〕 *adj.* 喧囂的；激動的

contumacious 〔,kɑntju'meʃəs 〕 *adj.* 抗拒的；堅不服從的 (桀傲
　不馴的)《*con-* (together) + 拉丁文 *tumere* (swell ; be proud)》

contumacy 〔'kɑntjuməsɪ , 'kɑntu- 〕 *n.* 抗拒；不服從

contumely 〔'kɑntjuməlɪ , 'kɑntu- 〕 *n.* 傲慢無禮；侮辱

611　　**turb** = disturb (擾亂)

> * 拉丁文 **turbare** (= *disturb*) ，**turba** (= *crowd ; turmoil*) ，
> 　原意是「分散群體」。

turbid 〔'tɝbɪd 〕 *adj.* 混濁不清的；濃密的

turbidity 〔 tɝ'bɪdətɪ 〕 *n.* 混濁；混亂

turbulent⁷ 〔'tɝbjələnt 〕 *adj.* 狂暴的；動亂的；騷動的

turbulence ; -ency⁷ 〔'tɝbjələns(ɪ) 〕 *n.* 動亂；騷動

turmoil⁶ 〔'tɝmɔɪl 〕 *n.* 騷動；混亂

disturb⁴ 〔 dɪ'stɝb 〕 *v.* 攪亂；妨礙；打擾 (打散群體)《*dis-* = apart》

disturbance⁶ 〔 dɪ'stɝbəns 〕 *n.* 擾亂；騷動

perturb⁷ 〔 pə'tɝb 〕 *v.* 使心煩意亂；擾亂 (完全攪亂)
　《*per-* = thoroughly》

per	+	turb
|		|
thoroughly	+	*disturb*

perturbation 〔,pɝtə'beʃən 〕 *n.* 擾亂；煩惱

imperturbable 〔,ɪmpə'tɝbəbḷ 〕 *adj.* 沉著的；冷靜的
　(不會被攪亂)《*im-* = *in-* = not》

trouble¹ 〔'trʌbḷ 〕 *v.* 煩惱；麻煩；憂慮　　*n.* 煩惱；困難；麻煩

troublesome⁴ 〔'trʌbḷsəm 〕 *adj.* 困難的；麻煩的

troublous 〔'trʌbləs 〕 *adj.* 使人苦惱的；不安的

612　typh = fever（發燒）

* 希臘文 *tuphein*（= *smoke* 冒煙），*tuphos*（= *fever*；*smoke*）。

typhus〔'taɪfəs〕 *n.* 斑疹傷寒
typhoid〔'taɪfɔɪd〕 *adj.* 傷寒的　*n.* 傷寒《*-oid* = like》
adenotyphus〔ˌædɪnə'taɪfəs〕 *n.* 淋巴腺型傷寒
　　《希臘文 *aden* = gland（腺）》

613　ultim = last（最後的）　　* 拉丁文 *ultimus*（= *last*）。

ultima〔'ʌltəmə〕 *n.* 尾音節；末音節
ultimate[6]〔'ʌltəmɪt〕 *adj.* 最後的；結局的；根本的
ultimately[7]〔'ʌltəmɪtlɪ〕 *adv.* 最後；終於
ultimatum[7]〔ˌʌltə'metəm〕 *n.* 最後通牒《*-um* 名詞字尾》

> ultimat ＋ um
> 　｜　　　　｜
> *last*　＋　*n.*

ultimo〔'ʌltəˌmo〕 = in the last month　*adj.* 上個月的（略作 ult.）
penultimate〔pɪ'nʌltəmɪt〕 *n.*, *adj.* 由字尾倒數第二音節（的）
　　（幾乎最後一個）《*pen-* = almost》
antepenultimate〔ˌæntɪpɪ'nʌltəmɪt〕 *n.*, *adj.* 倒數第三音節（的）
　　（= *antepenult*）（倒數第二個的前一個）《*ante-* = before》

614　umbr = shadow（陰影）

* 拉丁文 *umbra*（= *shade*；*shadow*）。

umbra〔'ʌmbrə〕 *n.*（太陽黑子的）中央黑暗部分；本影（日蝕
　時地球或月球的影子）
umbrage〔'ʌmbrɪdʒ〕 *n.* 陰影；不快；憤怒

umbrageous〔 ʌm'bredʒəs 〕 *adj.* 多蔭的；成蔭的；易怒的

umbral〔'ʌmbrəl 〕 *adj.* 陰影的；成蔭的

umbrella² 〔 ʌm'brɛlə 〕 *n.* 傘；傘狀物；保護（遮有小陰影之物）
《 *-ella* 名詞字尾，表示「小」》

adumbrate〔 æd'ʌmbret , 'ædəm,bret 〕 *v.* 勾畫輪廓；暗示；
用陰影遮蔽（使有陰影）《 *ad-* = to》

```
ad  +  umbr  +  ate
 |       |       |
to  +  shadow  +  v.
```

adumbration〔,ædʌm'breʃən 〕 *n.* 勾畫；暗示；蔭蔽

adumbrative〔 æd'ʌmbrətɪv 〕 *adj.* 隱約顯示的；輕描淡寫的；
籠統預示的

penumbra〔 pɪ'nʌmbrə 〕 *n.* （日蝕、月蝕的）半影部；（太陽
黑子周圍的）半影（幾乎成為影子）《 *pen-* = almost》

somber⁷〔'sɑmbɚ 〕 *adj.* 微暗的；暗色的；陰沉的（在陰影下）
《 *so-* = *sub-* (under) + (*u*)*mber* = *umbr* (shadow)》

615 **und** = wave（波浪）　　* 拉丁文 *unda* (= *wave*)。

undulate〔'ʌndjə,let 〕 *v.* 波動；起伏
《拉丁文 *undula* = wavelet (小浪；漣漪)》

abound⁶〔 ə'baʊnd 〕 *v.* 充滿；大量存在《 *ab-* = from》

abundant⁵〔 ə'bʌndənt 〕 *adj.* 豐富的；充足的

inundate⁷〔 ɪn'ʌndet 〕 *v.* 氾濫；使充滿（水湧到上面）
《 *in-* = onto》

```
in  +  und  +  ate
 |      |      |
onto  + wave  +  v.
```

redundant⁶〔 rɪ'dʌndənt 〕 *adj.* 多餘的；冗贅的；豐富的
（不斷起伏波動）《 *red-* = *re-* = again》

616　**ur** = tail（尾巴）　　*希臘文 *oura*（= *tail*）。

uropod〔'jʊrə,pɑd〕*n.*（甲殼類、節足類動物的）尾足；腹足

```
uro + pod
 |     |
tail + foot
```

uropygium〔,jʊrə'paɪdʒɪəm〕*n.*（鳥的）尾部（長尾羽的部分）
《希臘文 *puge* = buttocks（臀部）》

urostyle〔'jʊrə,staɪl〕*n.* 尾杆骨《希臘文 *stulos* = pillar（柱子）》

anurous[7]〔ə'njʊrəs〕*adj.* 無尾的《*an-* = without》

squirrel[2]〔'skwɝəl〕*n.* 松鼠；松鼠的毛皮《希臘文 *skia* = shadow》

617　**ur** = urine（尿）

*拉丁文 *urina*（= *urine*）；希臘文 *ouron*（= *urine*）。

urine[6]〔'jʊrɪn〕*n.* 尿

urinal〔'jʊrənl̩〕*n.* 尿壺；（男用）小便池

urinate[7]〔'jʊrə,net〕*v.* 排尿；小便

urethra〔ju'riθrə〕*n.* 尿道

urology[7]〔ju'rɑlədʒɪ〕*n.* 泌尿學《*logy* = study》

urogenital〔,jʊrə'dʒɛnətl̩〕*adj.* 泌尿生殖器的《*genital* 生殖的》

uroscopy〔ju'rɑskəpɪ〕*n.* 驗尿（查看尿液）《*scop* = look》

618　**urb** = city（城市）　　*拉丁文 *urbs*（= *city*）。

urban[4]〔'ɝbən〕*adj.* 都市的；都市特有的

urbane[7]〔ɝ'ben〕*adj.* 都市風格的；文雅的；有禮貌的（有都市性質的）

urbanism〔'ɝbənɪzm̩〕*n.* 都市生活（研究）；（人口的）集中都市

urbanite〔'ɝbən‚aɪt〕*n.* 都市生活者《*-ite* 表示人的名詞字尾》

```
urb  +  an  +  ite
 |       |      |
city  +  adj. + person
```

urbanity〔ɝ'bænətɪ〕*n.* 都市風尚；文雅；(*pl.*) 禮節
urbanize〔'ɝbən‚aɪz〕*v.* 使都市化；使文雅
urbanization〔‚ɝbənɪ'zeʃən〕*n.* 都市化
urbanology〔‚ɝbə'nalədʒɪ〕*n.* 都市學；都市研究《*ology* = study》
urbanologist〔‚ɝbə'nalədʒɪst〕*n.* 都市問題專家；都市研究專家
conurbation〔‚kanɚ'beʃən〕*n.* 集合城市；都市集團
　　（聚集在一起的城市）《*con-* = together》
exurb〔'ɛksɝb〕*n.* 郊外周圍地區（城市之外）《*ex-* = out》

```
ex  +  urb
 |      |
out  + city
```

exurban〔ɛk'sɝbən〕*adj.* 郊外周圍地區的
exurbia〔'ɛksəbɪə〕*n.*【集合名詞】郊外周圍住宅地區《*-ia* 名詞字尾》
interurban〔‚ɪntɚ'ɝbən〕*adj.* 都市間的　　*n.* 都市間的鐵路
　　（電車、巴士等）（都市間）《*inter-* = between》
suburb[3]〔'sʌbɝb〕*n.* 市郊；近郊；郊區（城市附近）《*sub-* = near》
suburban[6]〔sə'bɝbən〕*adj.* 市郊的；郊區的　　*n.* 郊區居民
suburbanite〔sə'bɝbən‚aɪt〕*n.* 郊區居民《*-ite* 表示人的名詞字尾》
suburbia[7]〔sə'bɝbɪə〕*n.*【集合名詞】郊區；郊區居民

619　**us , ut** = use（使用）

　　* 拉丁文 *uti*（= *use*），過去分詞為 *usus*。

use[1]〔*v.* juz *n.* jus〕*v.* 利用；實行　　*n.* 用法；利用；用途
usage[4]〔'jusɪdʒ〕*n.* 使用；用法；習慣；習俗
usance〔'juzn̩s〕*n.*【商】支付匯票的習慣期限

useful[1] 〔'jusfəl 〕 *adj.* 有用的；有益的
useless[7] 〔'juslɪs 〕 *adj.* 無用的；無效的
usual[2] 〔'juʒʊəl 〕 *adj.* 經常的（一直延用的）
usufruct 〔'juzjʊ,frʌkt , 'jusju- 〕 *n.* 收益權；使用權（可任意使用）
　《*fruct* = full enjoyment (充分享有)》

```
usu  +    frʌct
 |         |
use  +  full enjoyment
```

usufructuary 〔,juzjʊ'frʌktʃʊ,ɛrɪ 〕 *adj.* 使用權的　 *n.* 使用權者
usurp[7] 〔 jʊ'zɝp 〕 *v.* 簒奪；霸佔（爲了取來自己使用）
usurpation 〔,juzɚ'peʃən 〕 *n.* 簒位；霸佔
usury 〔'juʒərɪ 〕 *n.* 高利貸（利用金錢所生的巨額利息）《 *-ry* 名詞字尾》
usurer 〔'juʒərɚ 〕 *n.* 放高利貸者
usurious 〔 ju'ʒʊrɪəs 〕 *adj.* 高利貸的；高利的
utensil[6] 〔 ju'tɛnsḷ 〕 *n.* 器皿；用具（日常用品）
utile 〔'jutɪl 〕 *adj.* 實用的；有用的
utilize[6] 〔'jutḷ,aɪz 〕 *v.* 利用

```
ut  + ile
 |     |
use + adj.
```

utilization[7] 〔,jutḷə'zeʃən 〕 *n.* 利用
utility[6] 〔 ju'tɪlətɪ 〕 *n.* 有用；效用
utilitarian[7] 〔,jutɪlə'tɛrɪən , ju,tɪlə- 〕 *n.* 功利主義者
　 adj. 功利主義的
abuse[6] 〔 *v.* ə'bjuz *n.* ə'bjus 〕 *v.* 濫用；虐待　 *n.* 濫用；虐待；惡習
　（離開了正確的用法）《 *ab-* = from》
abusive[7] 〔 ə'bjusɪv 〕 *adj.* 妄用的
disabuse 〔,dɪsə'bjuz 〕 *v.* 解惑；釋疑（使不濫用）《 *dis-* = not》

```
dis +  ab  + use
 |      |      |
not + from + use
```

disuse[7] 〔 *n.* dɪs'jus *v.* dɪs'juz 〕 *n.* , *v.* 廢棄；不用
disused 〔,dɪs'juzd 〕 *adj.* 不再使用的；廢棄的

inutile〔ɪn'jutɪl〕*adj.* 無用的；無益的《*in-* = not》

inutility〔,ɪnju'tɪlətɪ〕*n.* 無用；無益的人或物

misuse[7]〔*n.* mɪs'jus *v.* mɪs'juz〕*n., v.* 誤用；濫用；虐待（錯誤使用）
《*mis-* = wrongly》

misusage〔mɪs'jusɪdʒ, -'juz-〕*n.* 誤用；虐待

```
mis   + us + age
 |       |     |
wrongly + use +  n.
```

peruse[7]〔pə'ruz〕*v.* 精讀（讀盡全書）《*per-* = through》

perusal[7]〔pə'ruzḷ〕*n.* 詳察；精讀

620 vac , van , void = empty（空的）

> * 拉丁文 *vacare*（= be empty），*vanus*（= empty）；
> 古法文 *voide*（= empty）。

vacant[3]〔'vekənt〕*adj.* 空的；空缺的；閒暇的

vacancy[5]〔'vekənsɪ〕*n.* 空職；空虛；空閒

vacate[7]〔'veket〕*v.* 使出缺；撤離（使空虛）

vacation[2]〔ve'keʃən, və-〕*n.* 休假；空出　*v.* 度假

vacationist〔ve'keʃənɪst〕*n.* 休假者；度假的人

vacuum[5]〔'vækjuəm〕*n.* 真空；空間

vacuity〔væ'kjuətɪ, və-〕*n.* 空虛；茫然

vacuous[7]〔'vækjuəs〕*adj.* 空虛的；愚蠢的；閒散的

evacuate[6]〔ɪ'vækju,et〕*v.* 撤退；疏散；排泄（使空虛）
《*e-* = *ex-* = out》

```
e + vacu + ate
|    |      |
out + empty + v.
```

vain[4]〔ven〕*adj.* 無效的；空虛的（沒有內容的）

vanity[5]〔'vænətɪ〕*n.* 空虛；虛榮（心）

vanish[3] 〔'vænɪʃ 〕 v. 消失；消滅（變成空虛）

evanesce 〔,ɛvə'nɛs 〕 v. 逐漸消失（出去而消失）《e- = ex- = out》

```
e  +  van  +  esce
|      |        |
out + empty  +  v.
```

evanescence 〔,ɛvə'nɛsns 〕 n. 逐漸消失

evanescent 〔,ɛvə'nɛsnt 〕 adj. 易消散的；暫時的

void[7] 〔 vɔɪd 〕 adj. 無效的；空的；缺乏的　n. 空虛；空處
　v. 使無效；排泄

voidance 〔'vɔɪdns 〕 n. 放棄；無效；排泄

avoid[2] 〔 ə'vɔɪd 〕 v. 避免（出去外面而使空虛）《a- = ex- = out》

```
a  +  void
|      |
out + empty
```

avoidance[7] 〔 ə'vɔɪdns 〕 n. 迴避；取消

devoid[7] 〔 dɪ'vɔɪd 〕 adj. 缺乏的（拿走而變爲空虛）《de- = dis- = apart》

inevitable[6] 〔 ɪn'ɛvətəbḷ 〕 adj. 不可避免的《in- = not ; e- = ex- = out》
　《in- (not) + 拉丁文 evitare (avoid)》

vainglorious 〔 ven'glorɪəs 〕 adj. 自負的；虛榮心強的
　《vain (empty) + glor (glory) + -ious (形容詞字尾)》

621　vade, vas = go (走)　　* 拉丁文 vadere (= go)。

evade[7] 〔 ɪ'ved 〕 v. 逃避；閃避（逃避在外面）《e- = ex- = out》

evasion[7] 〔 ɪ'veʒən 〕 n. 逃避；藉口

evasive[7] 〔 ɪ'vesɪv 〕 adj. 逃避的；難以捉摸的

invade[4] 〔 ɪn'ved 〕 v. 侵略；侵襲（進來）《in- = into》

```
in  +  vade
|       |
into +  go
```

invader[7] 〔 ɪn'vedɚ 〕 *n.* 侵略者；侵害者

invasion[4] 〔 ɪn'veʒən 〕 *n.* 侵略；侵害

invasive[7] 〔 ɪn'vesɪv 〕 *adj.* 侵入的；侵略性的

pervade[7] 〔 pɚ'ved 〕 *v.* 遍布；瀰漫（直接穿過）《*per-* = through》

pervasion 〔 pɚ'veʒən 〕 *n.* 遍布；瀰漫

wade[5] 〔 wed 〕 *v.* 跋涉；艱苦進行　*n.* 跋涉（特別指在水中行走）

waddle 〔 'wɑdḷ 〕 *v.* 蹣跚而行　*n.* 搖擺而行

622　**vag** = wander (流浪)

　* 拉丁文 *vagus* (= *wandering*) ，*vagari* (= *wander*) 。

vagabond 〔 'væɡə,bɑnd 〕 *adj.* 流浪的；無賴的
　n. 無賴；流浪者　*v.* 流浪

vagabondage 〔 'væɡə,bɑndɪdʒ 〕 *n.* 流浪生活；流浪癖；
　【集合名詞】流浪者《 *-age* 名詞字尾》

vagary 〔 və'ɡɛrɪ , ve- , -'ɡerɪ 〕 *n.* 妄想；狂妄行為（心情之漫遊）

vagarious 〔 və'ɡɛrɪəs 〕 *adj.* 奇特的；古怪的

vagrancy[7] 〔 'veɡrənsɪ 〕 *n.* 流浪；漂泊

vagrant[7] 〔 'veɡrənt 〕 *n.* 流浪漢；無賴　*adj.* 流浪的；無賴的

vague[5] 〔 veɡ 〕 *adj.* 含糊的；茫然的

divagate 〔 'daɪvə,ɡet 〕 *v.* 徘徊；入歧途；離題（因漫遊而迷失）
　《 *di-* = *dis-* = away》

```
di   +   vag   + ate
 |         |        |
away  +  wander  +  v.
```

divagation 〔 ,daɪvə'ɡeʃən 〕 *n.* 入歧途；離題

extravagant[7] 〔 ɪk'strævəɡənt 〕 *adj.* 奢侈的；放縱的
　（越過限度的浪擲）《 *extra-* = beyond》

extravagance[7] 〔 ɪk'strævəɡəns 〕 *n.* 奢侈；浪費；放縱

extravaganza[7] 〔 ɪk,strævə'ɡænzə , ɛk- 〕 *n.* 狂想曲（劇）；狂言

623　**val** , **vail** = strong；worth（強壯的；有價值的）

* 拉丁文 ***valere***（ = be strong ; be worth ）。

valence〔'veləns〕 *n.* 原子價

valiant[6]〔'væljənt〕 *adj.* 勇敢的；英勇的（強壯勇敢的）

valid[6]〔'vælɪd〕 *adj.* 有效的；正確的；健康的（有效力的）

validate[7]〔'vælə,det〕 *v.* 使有法律效力；確認

validation[7]〔,vælə'deʃən〕 *n.* 確認

validity[6]〔və'lɪdətɪ〕 *n.* 效力；確實性；正當

```
val   + id + ity
 |       |     |
strong + adj. + n.
```

valo(u)r[7]〔'vælɚ〕 *n.* 勇氣；勇猛

valo(u)rous〔'vælərəs〕 *adj.* 勇敢的

value[2]〔'væljʊ〕 *n.* 價值；估價　*v.* 估價；評價；尊重

valuable[3]〔'væljʊəb̩l〕 *adj.* 有價值的；可計算價值的

　　n. (*pl.*) 貴重物品；珠寶

valuation〔,væljʊ'eʃən〕 *n.* 評價；估價

avail[7]〔ə'vel〕 *v.* 有用；有利；有效　*n.* 利益；效用

　　（能給予價值）《*a-* = *ad-* = to》

available[3]〔ə'veləb̩l〕 *adj.* 可利用的；近便的；有效力的

```
a + vail  + able
|    |       |
to + worth + adj.
```

convalesce〔,kɑnvə'lɛs〕 *v.* (病後) 恢復健康；漸癒

　　（一起變強壯）《*con-* = together》

convalescence[7]〔,kɑnvə'lɛsn̩s〕 *n.* 康復；康復期

convalescent〔,kɑnvə'lɛsn̩t〕 *adj.* 逐漸康復的　*n.* 康復中的病人

countervail〔͵kaʊntɚˋvel〕*v.* 抵消；補償；對抗（對抗的強度）
《*counter-* = *contra-* = against》

```
counter  +  vail
   |          |
against  +  strong
```

devaluate〔di'væljʊ͵et〕*v.* 減低～的價值；貶值（價值降低）
《*de-* = down》

devaluation〔͵divæljʊ'eʃən〕*n.* 貶值

evaluate[4]〔ɪ'væljʊ͵et〕*v.* 評價；估計；求值（評估價值）
《*e-* = *ex-* = out》

equivalent[6]〔ɪ'kwɪvələnt〕*adj.* 相等的；相當的
n. 等量；相等物（價值相等）《*equi* = equal》

invalid[7]〔'ɪnvəlɪd〕*adj.* 有病的；殘廢的　*n.* 病人；殘兵
v. 使殘廢；使病弱；使退後　*adj.*〔ɪn'vælɪd〕無效的；薄弱的
（不強壯的）《*in-* = not》

```
in  +  val  +  id
 |      |      |
not + strong + adj.
```

invalidate〔ɪn'vælə͵det〕*v.* 使無價值；使無效

invalidity〔͵ɪnvə'lɪdətɪ〕*n.* 無價值；無效

invaluable[6]〔ɪn'væljəbḷ〕*adj.* 無法估價的；非常珍貴的
cf. **valueless**（無價值的）

multivalent〔͵mʌltə'velənt, mʌl'tɪvə-〕*adj.* 多原子價的
《*multi-* = many》

prevail[5]〔prɪ'vel〕*v.* 流行；佔優勢；戰勝（過於強大）
《*pre-* = before；excessively》

```
pre      +  vail
 |           |
excessively + strong
```

prevalent[7]〔'prɛvələnt 〕 *adj.* 普遍的；流行的
prevalence ; -ency[7] 〔'prɛvələns(ɪ) 〕 *n.* 普遍
prevailing[7] 〔 prɪ'velɪŋ 〕 *adj.* 普及的；流行的；優勢的
undervalue 〔'ʌndə'væljʊ 〕 *v.* 低估；輕視（看低～的價值）
  《*under-* = under》
undervaluation 〔ˌʌndəˌvæljʊ'eʃən 〕 *n.* 低估；輕視

624　**var(i)** = diverse ; change（不同的；變化）

  * 拉丁文 *variare*（ = *change* ），*varius*（ = *various* ; *diverse* ）。

vary[3] 〔'vɛrɪ 〕 *v.* 改變；不同
variable[6] 〔'vɛrɪəbl̩ 〕 *adj.* 易變的；可變動的　　*n.* 易變化的東西
variability[7] 〔ˌvɛrɪə'bɪlətɪ 〕 *n.* 易變；可變性
variance[7] 〔'vɛrɪəns 〕 *n.* 變化；差異；不和；衝突
variant[7] 〔'vɛrɪənt 〕 *adj.* 相異的；不同的；易變的　　*n.* 變形；異形
variation[6] 〔ˌvɛrɪ'eʃən 〕 *n.* 變化
varicolored 〔'vɛrɪˌkʌləd 〕 *adj.* 雜色的；五顏六色的
varied[7] 〔'vɛrɪd 〕 *adj.* 種種的；有變化的
variegate 〔'vɛrɪˌget 〕 *v.* 使成雜色；使有變化（驅使其變化）
  《*eg* = 拉丁文 *agere* = drive》

vari	+	eg	+	ate
change	+	*drive*	+	*v.*

variegated 〔'vɛrɪˌgetɪd 〕 *adj.* 雜色的；有變化的
variegation 〔ˌvɛrɪ'geʃən 〕 *n.* 雜色；斑駁
variety[3] 〔 və'raɪətɪ 〕 *n.* 變化；多樣性；種類
variform 〔'vɛrɪˌfɔrm 〕 *adj.* 有多種形態的；形形色色的
variometer 〔ˌvɛrɪ'ɑmətə 〕 *n.* 磁力偏差計《*meter* 計量器》

625 vas = vessel (血管)

* 拉丁文 *vas* (= *vessel*)。

vascular 〔'væskjələ 〕 *adj.* 脈管的；血管的

vasoactive 〔ˌvezo'æktɪv 〕 *adj.* (尤指在血管的舒張或收縮方面)
作用於血管的《*active* 能起作用的》

vasoconstriction 〔ˌvæsokən'strɪkʃən 〕 *n.* 血管收縮
《*constrict* 收緊》

vasoconstrictor 〔ˌvæsokən'strɪktə 〕 *n.* 血管收縮神經；
血管收縮劑

vasodilation 〔ˌvezodaɪ'leʃən 〕 *n.* 血管舒張《*dilate* 擴大》

vasospasm 〔'vezoˌspæzəm 〕 *n.* 血管痙攣《*spasm* 痙攣》

626 veh , vect = carry (運送；傳達)

* 拉丁文 *vehere* (= *carry*)，過去分詞為 *vexus*；
vector (= *carrier*)。〔變化型〕*vex*。

vehement[7] 〔'viəmənt 〕 *adj.* 激烈的；感情強烈的

```
vehe  +  ment
 |         |
carry  +  mind
```

vehicle[3] 〔'viɪkḷ 〕 *n.* 車輛；傳播媒介《 *-cle* 表示小的名詞字尾》

vection 〔'vɛkʃən 〕 *n.* (病原體的) 媒介過程

vector[7] 〔'vɛktə 〕 *n.*【數學】向量；航線；帶菌生物；病毒媒介昆蟲
(如蚊、蠅等)

advection 〔 æd'vɛkʃən 〕 *n.* 平流《*ad-* = to》

convection[7] 〔 kən'vɛkʃən 〕 *n.* 對流《*con-* = together》

invective[7] 〔 ɪn'vɛktɪv 〕 *n. , adj.* 痛罵 (的)；辱罵 (的)；
猛烈抨擊 (的)《*in-* = in》

vex[7] 〔 vɛks 〕 *v.* 使苦惱；煩擾

convex[7] 〔'kɑnvɛks 〕 *adj.* 凸面的 *n.* 凸透鏡

627   veloc = fast（快的）

* 拉丁文 *velox* , *veloc-*（ = *fast*）。

velocity[7]〔vəˈlɑsətɪ〕 *n.* 迅速；速度

velocimeter〔ˌvɛləˈsɪmətə〕 *n.* 速度計《*meter* 計量器》

velocipede〔vəˈlɑsəˌpid〕 *n.* 腳蹬車（自行車的前身，一種用
雙腳踩地朝前推進的兩輪車或三輪車）；〔美〕兒童用三輪車
《*ped* = foot》

velodrome〔ˈviləˌdrom〕 *n.*（自行車或摩托車的）賽車場
（競速的場所）《希臘文 *dromos* = racecourse（跑道）》

628   velop = wrap（包；裹）

* 古法文 *veloper*（ = *wrap up*）。

develop[2]〔dɪˈvɛləp〕 *v.* 發展；開發；揭露；顯示（將包裹打開）
《*de-* = *dis-* = apart》

development[2]〔dɪˈvɛləpmənt〕 *n.* 發展；開發；【攝影】顯影

envelop[7]〔ɪnˈvɛləp〕 *v.* 包裝；圍繞；掩藏（包起來）《*en-* = in》

envelope[2]〔ˈɛnvəˌlop , ˈɑn- , ɪnˈvɛləp〕 *n.* 信封；封套
（作包裝用的）

envelopment〔ɪnˈvɛləpmənt , ɛn-〕 *n.* 包封；包封物；包紙

629   ven , vent = come（來）

* 拉丁文 *venire*（ = *come*）。

advent[7]〔ˈædvɛnt〕 *n.*（A-）耶穌降臨；到來（來到）《*ad-* = to》

adventitious[7]〔ˌædvɛnˈtɪʃəs , ˌædvən-〕 *adj.* 偶然的；外來的；
偶發的

adventive〔ædˈvɛntɪv〕 *adj.*（動植物）外來的；非本土的
n. 外來的動植物（從外而來的）

adventure[3] 〔 əd'vɛntʃɚ 〕 n. 冒險；奇遇；投機　v. 冒險嘗試
（來到危險的地方）

```
ad  +  vent  +  ure
|        |        |
to  +  come  +  n.
```

adventurous[7] 〔 əd'vɛntʃərəs 〕 adj. 冒險的；大膽的；危險的
venture[5] 〔'vɛntʃɚ 〕 = adventure 的縮寫
venturous 〔'vɛntʃərəs 〕 adj. 大膽的；冒險性的；危險的
venturesome[7] 〔'vɛntʃɚsəm 〕 adj. 冒險的；危險的；大膽的
　　《 -some 形容詞字尾，表示「具有～性質」》
misadventure[7] 〔,mɪsəd'vɛntʃɚ 〕 n. 不幸；災難（不好的遭遇）
　　《 mis- = bad》

```
mis  +  ad  +  vent  +  ure
|       |       |        |
bad  +  to  +  come  +  n.
```

circumvent[7] 〔,sɝkəm'vɛnt 〕 v. 勝過；規避；繞行（從周圍來）
　　《 circum- = around》
circumvention 〔,sɝkəm'vɛnʃən 〕 n. 阻遏；繞行
contravene[7] 〔,kɑntrə'vin 〕 v. 違反；反駁；牴觸（來對抗）
　　《 contra- = against》
contravention 〔,kɑntrə'vɛnʃən 〕 n. 違反；違反的行為；反駁
convene[7] 〔 kən'vin 〕 v. 集合；召集（一同齊聚而來）
　　《 con- = together》
convention[4] 〔 kən'vɛnʃən 〕 n. 召集；會議；協定；習俗
conventional[4] 〔 kən'vɛnʃənḷ 〕 adj. 傳統的；陳舊的；協定的

```
con  +  vent  +  ion  +  al
|        |       |      |
together  +  come  +  n.  +  adj.
```

conventioneer 〔 kən,vɛnʃən'ɪr 〕 n. 大會或會議的出席者
　　《 -eer 表示人的名詞字尾》

convenient[2]〔kən'vinjənt〕 *adj.* 便利的；方便的

（集合在一起對什麼都方便）

convenience[4]〔kən'vinjəns〕 *n.* 方便；便利的事物；〔英〕廁所

event[2]〔ɪ'vɛnt〕 *n.* 事件；結果；成果；（競賽）項目

（發生而來的東西）《*e-* = *ex-* = out》

eventful[7]〔ɪ'vɛntfəl〕 *adj.* 多事的；重要的

eventual[4]〔ɪ'vɛntʃuəl〕 *adj.* 結果的；最後的；可能的

eventuate〔ɪ'vɛntʃu,et〕 *v.* 結果；終歸

invent[2]〔ɪn'vɛnt〕 *v.* 發明；虛構（來到某物之上 → 想到）《*in-* = upon》

invention[4]〔ɪn'vɛnʃən〕 *n.* 發明；發明物；發明的才能；

虛構的故事

```
 in  + vent + ion
  |      |     |
upon + come +  n.
```

inventor[3]〔ɪn'vɛntɚ〕 *n.* 發明者

inventory[6]〔'ɪnvən,torɪ , -,tɔrɪ〕 *n.* 目錄；庫存品

v. 將～登入目錄；盤點

prevent[3]〔prɪ'vɛnt〕 *v.* 阻礙；防止；預防（阻擋往前去的路）

《*pre-* = before》

prevention[4]〔prɪ'vɛnʃən〕 *n.* 防止；預防

```
 pre  + vent + ion
  |      |      |
before + come +  n.
```

preventive[6]〔prɪ'vɛntɪv〕 *adj.* 預防的　　*n.* 預防方法；預防藥

intervene[6]〔,ɪntɚ'vin〕 *v.* 介入；干涉；調停（來到其間）

《*inter-* = between》

intervention[6]〔,ɪntɚ'vɛnʃən〕 *n.* 介入；干涉；調停

intervenient〔,ɪntɚ'vinjənt〕 *adj.* 介於中間的；居間的

supervene〔,supɚ'vin , ,sju-〕 *v.* 接著來；附帶發生；併發

（跟著到上面來）《*super-* = over ; upon》

supervention 〔,supɚˈvɛnʃən , ,sju- 〕 *n.* 續發；併發；附加

```
super + vent + ion
  |      |      |
upon  + come +  n.
```

venue[7] 〔ˈvɛnju 〕 *n.* 會場；舉辦地點；審判地點

avenue[3] 〔ˈævə,nju 〕 *n.* (對) 大街；兩邊有樹的通道；方法；途徑
(到~的道路) 《*a-* = *ad-* = to》

revenue[6] 〔ˈrɛvə,nju 〕 *n.* 歲入；(*pl.*) 收入總額；國稅局
(再次回來的金錢) 《*re-* = back》

souvenir[4] 〔ˈsuvə,nɪr 〕 *n.* 紀念品；紀念物 (接近心靈而來 → 想出)
《*sou-* = *sub-* = under ; near》

630 venge = avenge (報仇)

* 古法文 *vengier* (= *avenge*) 。

vengeance[7] 〔ˈvɛndʒəns 〕 *n.* 復仇；報復
vengeful[7] 〔ˈvɛndʒfəl 〕 *adj.* 復仇的；復仇心重的
avenge[7] 〔 əˈvɛndʒ 〕 *v.* 復仇；報復 (對~報仇) 《*a-* = *ad-* = to》
avenger 〔 əˈvɛndʒɚ 〕 *n.* 復仇者

```
a + veng(e) +  er
|      |       |
to + avenge + person
```

revenge[4] 〔 rɪˈvɛndʒ 〕 *v.* , *n.* 報仇；報復 (再報仇) 《*re-* = again》
revengeful 〔 rɪˈvɛndʒfəl 〕 *adj.* 充滿復仇心的；懷恨的

631 vent = wind (風) * 拉丁文 *ventus* (= *wind*) 。

vent[7] 〔 vɛnt 〕 *n.* 孔；通風孔；出口；吐露 *v.* 鑽孔於；發洩
ventage 〔ˈvɛntɪdʒ 〕 *n.* 出口；發洩口
venter 〔ˈvɛntɚ 〕 *n.* 腹；胃；子宮
venthole 〔ˈvɛnt,hol 〕 *n.* 通氣孔

ventilate[7]〔'vɛntl̩.et〕v. 使通風；以空氣淨化；公開討論
ventilation[7]〔.vɛntl̩'eʃən〕n. 通風；通風設備；自由討論
ventilator〔'vɛntl̩.etɚ〕n. 通風設備；氣窗

632 **ver** = true (真實的；確實的)

＊ 拉丁文 *verus*（= *true*）。

very[1,4]〔'vɛrɪ〕adj. 真正的；同一的　adv. 非常地；很
veridical〔vɪ'rɪdɪk̩l〕= true speaking　adj. 真實的；真正的
《*dic* = speak》
verify[7]〔'vɛrə.faɪ〕v. 證明；鑑定；【法律】作證 (表示真實的事物)
《*-ify* = make》
verifiable〔'vɛrə.faɪəb̩l〕adj. 可證明的；可確證的
verification[7]〔.vɛrəfɪ'keʃən〕n. 證明；鑑定；確認
verily〔'vɛrəlɪ〕adv. 真正地；真實地
verisimilar〔.vɛrə'sɪmələ〕adj. 像是真實的；可能的
(看起來像真的一樣)《*simil* = like》

```
veri  +  simil  +  ar
 |        |        |
true  +  like   + adj.
```

verisimilitude〔.vɛrəsə'mɪlə.tjud , -.tud〕n. 逼真；逼真的事物
verity〔'vɛrətɪ〕n. 真實；真理
veritable〔'vɛrətəb̩l〕adj. 真實的；實在的
veracious〔və'reʃəs〕adj. 誠實的；真實的
veracity[7]〔və'ræsətɪ〕n. 誠實；精確；真實性
verdict[7]〔'vɝdɪkt〕n. (陪審團的) 判決；判斷 (實在的言詞)
《*dict* = saying》

```
ver  +  dict
 |       |
true +  saying
```

aver[7]〔ə'vɝ〕v. 斷言；【法律】證明；辨明《*a-* = *ad-* = to》

633 **verb** = word (字 ; 詞)

* 拉丁文 *verbum* (= *word*) 。

verb[4] 〔 vɝb 〕 *n.* 動詞

verbal[5] 〔'vɝbḷ 〕 *adj.* 言辭的;口頭的;逐字的;動詞的
 n. 動狀詞

verbalism 〔'vɝbḷ͵ɪzm̩ 〕 *n.* 語言的表現;拘泥字句;冗長;套語

verbalist 〔'vɝbḷɪst 〕 *n.* 善用言辭的人;拘泥字句的人

verbality 〔 vɚ'bælətɪ 〕 *n.* 冗詞;語言的表達;動詞的特性

verbalize 〔'vɝbḷ͵aɪz 〕 *v.* 用言語表達;作動詞用;嘮叨

verbatim 〔 vɚ'betɪm 〕 *adj.* 逐字的　*adv.* 逐字地
 《 *-atim* 形容詞字尾,表示「以～方式」》

```
verb  +  atim
 |         |
word  +   adj.
```

verbiage 〔'vɝbɪɪdʒ 〕 *n.* 冗詞;廢話;措辭
 《 *-age* 抽象名詞字尾》

verbify 〔'vɝbə͵faɪ 〕 *v.* 用做動詞;使 (名詞等) 動詞化

verbose[7] 〔 vɚ'bos 〕 *adj.* 冗長的;嘮叨的 (用太多詞語)
 《 *-ose* 形容詞字尾》

verbosity 〔 vɚ'bɑsətɪ 〕 *n.* 冗長;嘮叨

adverb[4] 〔'ædvɝb 〕 *n.* 副詞 (修飾動詞) 《*ad-* = to》

adverbial 〔 əd'vɝbɪəl , æd- 〕 *adj.* 副詞的;副詞性的

```
ad  +  verb  +  ial
 |        |       |
to  +  word  +  adj.
```

proverb[4] 〔'prɑvɝb 〕 *n.* 諺語;格言;人盡皆知的人或事物
 (以前的詞語) 《*pro-* = before》

proverbial[7] 〔 prə'vɝbɪəl 〕 *adj.* 諺語的;聞名的

634 verg = incline (傾向；傾斜)

* 拉丁文 *vergere* (= *incline*) 。

verge[6] 〔 vɝdʒ 〕 *n.* 邊緣 *v.* 臨接；傾向；瀕臨
converge[7] 〔 kən'vɝdʒ 〕 *v.* 集中於一點；使趨於同一目標
　（ 朝相同方向傾斜 ）《*con-* = together》
convergence[7] 〔 kən'vɝdʒəns 〕 *n.* 匯合；聚合
convergent 〔 kən'vɝdʒənt 〕 *adj.* 集中於一點的
diverge[7] 〔 də'vɝdʒ , daɪ- 〕 *v.* 分歧；差異；逸出 (正軌)
　（ 傾斜分開 ）《*di-* = *dis-* = apart》
divergence；-**ency**[7] 〔 də'vɝdʒəns(ɪ) , daɪ- 〕 *n.* 分歧；不和；逸出
divergent 〔 də'vɝdʒənt , daɪ- 〕 *adj.* 分歧的；差異的

635 verm = worm (蟲)　　* 拉丁文 *vermis* (= *worm*) 。

vermicelli 〔 ‚vɝmə'sɛlɪ 〕 *n.* 一種硬而脆的細麵條
vermicide 〔 'vɝmə‚saɪd 〕 *n.* 殺蠕蟲劑；殺腸蟲藥《*cide* = cut》
vermicular 〔 vɝ'mɪkjələ 〕 *adj.* 蠕蟲狀的；蠕動的
vermiform 〔 'vɝmə‚fɔrm 〕 *adj.* 蠕蟲形的《*form* 形狀》
vermin 〔 'vɝmɪn 〕 *n.* 害蟲；歹徒
verminous 〔 'vɝmɪnəs 〕 *adj.* 長蟲的；因害蟲引起的；令人討厭的
vermivorous 〔 vɝ'mɪvərəs 〕 *adj.* (鳥等) 食蟲的

vermi	+	vor	+	ous
worm	+	eat	+	adj.

636 vers , vert = turn (轉移；使轉變；轉向)

* 拉丁文 *vertere* (= *turn*) ，過去分詞為 *versus*。

verse[3] 〔 vɝs 〕 *n.* 詩；韻文；(聖經的) 一小節；詩節
　adj. 詩的；以詩寫成的 (變為新的格式)

versed〔vɝst〕*adj.* 韻文的；精通的；熟練的

versify〔'vɝsəˌfaɪ〕*v.* 作詩；以詩記述；將（散文）改寫成韻文
《 *-ify* = make 》

versification〔ˌvɝsəfə'keʃən〕*n.* 作詩；作詩法；詩學

version[6]〔'vɝʒən , 'vɝʃən〕*n.* 翻譯；譯本；版本；改寫本；陳述
說法；變體（轉換成別國語言）

versatile[6]〔'vɝsətɪl , -taɪl〕*adj.* 多才多藝的；多方面的
《 *-ile* 形容詞字尾 》

```
versat + ile
  |       |
turn  +  adj.
```

versus[5]〔'vɝsəs〕*prep.* ⋯對⋯；⋯與⋯對比（兩者轉往相反方向）

vertebra[7]〔'vɝtəbrə〕*n.* 脊椎（讓身體轉動的部位）

vertebrate〔'vɝtəˌbret〕*adj.* 有脊椎的　*n.* 脊椎動物

vertex〔'vɝtɛks〕*n.* 頂點；【天文】天頂；【解剖】頭頂；
【數學】頂點（上昇物往下轉變的那一點）

vertical[5]〔'vɝtɪkḷ〕*adj.* 天頂的；頂點的；垂直的；直立的
n. 垂直線；垂直面

vertigo〔'vɝtɪˌgo〕*n.* 暈眩；頭暈（眼睛轉動）

vertiginous〔vɝ'tɪdʒənəs〕*adj.* 令人暈眩的；旋轉的

vortex〔'vɔrtɛks〕*n.* 漩渦；旋風（迴旋的東西）

adverse[7]〔'ædvɝs , əd'vɝs〕*adj.* 逆的；反對的；不利的；敵對的
（轉過身來面對～）《 *ad-* = to 》

adversary[7]〔'ædvəˌsɛrɪ〕*n.* 對手；仇敵；（A-）魔王；撒旦
（反對者）

```
ad + vers + ary
 |     |      |
to  + turn +  n.
```

adversity[7]〔əd'vɝsətɪ〕*n.* 逆境；不幸；災難

advert[7]〔əd'vɝt , æd-〕*v.* 談及；述及；注意（把注意力轉向～）

advertence；-ency〔əd'vɜtns(I)〕*n.* 論及；注意

advertise[3]；**-tize**〔'ædvə͵taɪz，͵ædvə'taɪz〕*v.* 登廣告；通知
（引起個人注意～）

advertiser[5]〔'ædvə͵taɪzə͵，͵ædvə'taɪzə〕*n.* 刊登廣告者；
廣告客戶

advertisement[3]；**-tize-**〔͵ædvə'taɪzmənt，əd'vɜtɪzmənt〕
n. 廣告；宣傳

animadvert〔͵ænəmæd'vɜt〕*v.* 批評；非難（把心轉向）
《*anim* = mind》

```
anim + ad + vert
 |     |     |
mind + to + turn
```

anniversary[4]〔͵ænə'vɜsərɪ〕*n.* 周年；周年紀念　*adj.* 年年的；
每年的（每年回來的）《*anni* = year》

avert[7]〔ə'vɜt〕*v.* 防止；避開（面向他方）《*a-* = *abs-* = away》

averse[7]〔ə'vɜs〕*adj.* 嫌惡的；反對的；不願意的（迴避的態度）

aversion[7]〔ə'vɜʒən，-ʃən〕*n.* 嫌惡；嫌惡的事物；討厭的人

controvert〔'kɑntrə͵vɜt，͵kɑntrə'vɜt〕*v.* 否認；反駁；辯論
（面向反面）《*contro-* = *contra-* = against》

controversy[6]〔'kɑntrə͵vɜsɪ〕*n.* 爭論；辯論

controversial[6]〔͵kɑntrə'vɜʃəl〕*adj.* 引起爭論的；好爭論的

```
contro + vers + ial
  |       |      |
against + turn + adj.
```

converse[4]〔*v.*，*adj.* kən'vɜs　*n.* 'kɑnvɜs〕*v.* 談話　*adj.* 倒轉的；
方向或行動相反的　*n.* 相反的事物（面對面的）
《*con-* = together》

conversant〔'kɑnvəsnt，kən'vɜsnt〕*adj.* 親近的；精通的；
熟識的

conversation[2]〔͵kɑnvə'seʃən〕*n.* 談話；會話

convert[5] 〔 *v.* kənˈvɝt　*n.* ˈkɑnvɝt 〕 *v.* 轉變；兌換；改變宗教信仰
n. 改變宗教信仰或意見的人（一起改變）

```
con  + vert
 |       |
together + turn
```

convertible[7] 〔 kənˈvɝtəbḷ 〕 *adj.* 可以改變的；可兌換的；
可使改變信仰的

conversion[5] 〔 kənˈvɝʃən , -ʒən 〕 *n.* 轉換；變換；信仰的改變

divers 〔ˈdaɪvɚz 〕 *adj.* 不同的；種種的（個別離開）《 *di-* = *dis-* = apart 》

diverse[6] 〔 dəˈvɝs , daɪ- 〕 *adj.* 不同的；互異的；種種的；有變化的

diversify[6] 〔 dəˈvɝsəˌfaɪ , daɪ- 〕 *v.* 使變化；使多樣化《 *-ify* = make 》

```
di  + vers + ify
 |      |      |
apart + turn + make
```

diversity[6] 〔 dəˈvɝsətɪ , daɪ- 〕 *n.* 多樣性

divert[6] 〔 dəˈvɝt , daɪ- 〕 *v.* 使轉向；轉移（注意力）；娛樂
（離開向著其他方向）

diversion[6] 〔 dəˈvɝʒən , daɪ- , -ʃən 〕 *n.* 轉向；娛樂

divorce[4] 〔 dəˈvors , -ˈvɔrs 〕 *n.* , *v.* 離婚；分離

evert 〔 iˈvɝt 〕 *v.* 外翻；翻轉（向著外面）《 *e-* = *ex-* = out 》

```
e + vert
|    |
out + turn
```

extrovert[7] 〔ˈɛkstroˌvɝt 〕 *n.* 外向的人　*v.* 使外向（轉向外面）
《 *extro-* = *extra-* = outside 》

inadvertent[7] 〔ˌɪnədˈvɝtṇt 〕 *adj.* 不注意的；疏忽的
《 *in-* = not ; *ad-* = to 》

inadvertence ; -ency 〔ˌɪnədˈvɝtṇs(ɪ) 〕 *n.* 不注意；疏忽

introvert[7] 〔 *v.* ˌɪntrəˈvɝt　*n.* ˈɪntrəˌvɝt 〕 *v.* 使內向；使內省
n. 內向的人（向著內部）《 *intro-* = within 》

introversion 〔ˌɪntrəˈvɝʃən, -ʒən〕 *n.* 內向（型）；
（器官）內傾；內轉

invert[7] 〔ɪnˈvɝt〕 *v.* 顛倒；前後倒置（將下部向上）《*in-* = up》

inverse[7] 〔ɪnˈvɝs, ˈɪnvɝs〕 *adj.* 逆的；反的　*n.* 逆反；倒轉之物

inversion[7] 〔ɪnˈvɝʃən, -ʒən〕 *n.* 倒轉；【文法】倒裝法

```
in + vers + ion
 |     |      |
up + turn +  n.
```

malversation 〔ˌmælvɚˈseʃən〕 *n.* （公務員的）貪污；受賄
（將身體轉向壞處）《*mal-* = badly》

obvert 〔əbˈvɝt, ab-〕 *v.* 將～的正面轉向；【邏輯】反換（命題）
（面對～方向）《*ob-* = towards》

obverse 〔*adj.* əbˈvɝs, ˈabvɝs *n.* ˈabvɝs〕 *adj.* 正面的；相對的
n. （貨幣等的）正面；前面（彼此面面相對）

obversion 〔abˈvɝʃən〕 *n.* 轉向；【邏輯】命題之反換；換質
（如將 "All men are mortal." 改爲 "No men are immortal."）

pervert[7] 〔*v.* pɚˈvɝt *n.* ˈpɝvɝt〕 *v.* 曲解；誤解；誤用
n. 墮落的人；性變態者（把背對著正直的道路）《*per-* = thoroughly》

```
per     + vert
 |         |
thoroughly + turn
```

perversion[7] 〔pɚˈvɝʒən, -ʃən〕 *n.* 曲解；誤解；變態

perverse[7] 〔pɚˈvɝs〕 *adj.* 剛愎的；任性的

perversity 〔pɚˈvɝsətɪ〕 *n.* 邪惡；剛愎

retrovert 〔ˌrɛtrəˈvɝt〕 *v.* 使向後彎曲；使後屈（轉向後面）
《*retro-* = backward》

retroversion 〔ˌrɛtrəˈvɝʃən〕 *n.* 向後彎曲；後屈

```
retro   + vers + ion
 |          |     |
backward + turn + n.
```

revert[7] 〔 rɪˈvɝt 〕 v. 回到（原話題）；恢復（原狀）；歸屬（還原）
　《*re-* = back》

reversion 〔 rɪˈvɝʒən , -ˈvɝʃ- 〕 n. 歸屬權；倒退

reverse[5] 〔 rɪˈvɝs 〕 adj. 顛倒的；相反的　　n. 顛倒；背面；逆運；
　不幸　v. 逆行；顛倒（向著後面）

reversal[7] 〔 rɪˈvɝsəl , -sḷ 〕 n. 顛倒

reversible[7] 〔 rɪˈvɝsəbḷ 〕 adj. 可顛倒的；可翻轉的；可推翻的

subvert[7] 〔 səbˈvɝt 〕 v. 顛覆；破壞（從下翻轉過來）
　《*sub-* = under》

```
 sub  +  vert
  |       |
under  +  turn
```

subversion[7] 〔 səbˈvɝʃən , -ʒən 〕 n. 顛覆；破壞

subversive[7] 〔 səbˈvɝsɪv 〕 adj. 顛覆的；破壞的

tergiversation 〔ˌtɝdʒəvɚˈseʃən 〕 n. 變節；規避；支吾其詞
　（背向對著）《*tergi* = back》

transverse 〔 trænsˈvɝs , trænz- 〕 adj. 橫的；橫斷的
　n. 橫斷物；橫軸（完全指向橫向者）《*trans-* = across》

```
trans  +  verse
  |        |
across  +  turn
```

transversal 〔 trænsˈvɝsḷ , trænz- 〕 adj. 橫斷的
　n. 橫斷線；截線

traverse[7] 〔 v. ˈtrævɚs , trəˈvɝs n. ˈtrævɚs , -ɝs 〕 v. 橫過；反對；
　詳細討論　n. 橫斷（路）.；橫木《*tra-* = *trans-* = across》

universe[3] 〔ˈjunəˌvɝs 〕 n. 宇宙；全世界；全人類
　（把萬物合成一體）《*uni-* = one》

universal[4] 〔ˌjunəˈvɝsḷ 〕 adj. 全世界的；一般的；宇宙的

university[4] 〔ˌjunəˈvɝsətɪ 〕 n. 大學；大學的校舍
　（把幾個學院合成一體）

637　vest = clothe；garment（穿衣；衣服）

*拉丁文 *vestis*（ = *garment*；*clothing*），*vestire*（ = *clothe*）。

vest[3]〔vɛst〕*n.* 背心　*v.* 授與；歸屬

vestment〔'vɛstmənt〕*n.* 衣服

vesture〔'vɛstʃɚ〕*n.*【集合名詞】衣服；覆蓋物

　《 *-ure* 表示集合名詞》

divest[7]〔də'vɛst, daɪ-〕*v.* 脫掉；剝奪；使放棄（使衣服脫離身體）

　《 *di-* = *dis-* = apart》

```
di  +  vest
 |       |
apart + clothe
```

divestiture〔də'vɛstətʃɚ, daɪ-〕*n.* 脫衣；剝奪

divestment〔də'vɛstmənt, daɪ-〕*n.* = divestiture

invest[4]〔ɪn'vɛst〕*v.* 投資；使穿上；授與（進入衣服內）

　《 *in-* = in》

investment[4]〔ɪn'vɛstmənt〕*n.* 投資；資金

investor[7]〔ɪn'vɛstɚ〕*n.* 投資者

638　vi，via，voy = way（路）

*拉丁文 *via*（ = *way*）。〔變化型〕*vey*，*voy*。

via[5]〔'vaɪə〕*prep.* 經由（ = *by way of*）

viaduct[7]〔'vaɪə,dʌkt〕*n.* 高架橋；陸橋（引導道路跨越山谷河流）

　《 *duct* = lead》

voyage[4]〔'vɔɪ·ɪdʒ〕*n.* 航海；航行　*v.* 航海；航行（走過）

convey[4]〔kən've〕*v.* 運輸；傳達；讓與（使歸於同道）

　《 *con-* = together》

conveyance[7]〔kən'veəns〕*n.* 搬運；傳達；讓與（證書）

convoy[7]〔kən'vɔɪ〕*v., n.* 護送；護衛；護航（走同一條路）

deviate[7] 〔'divɪ,et 〕 v. 脫軌;脫離;違背 (從路線上離開)
n. 離經叛道者;性格異常者;性變態者　adj. 不正常的;異常的
《 *de-* = *dis-* = away from 》

```
 de    +  vi  + ate
  |        |      |
away from + way  +  v.
```

deviant[7] 〔'divɪənt 〕 adj. 脫軌的　n. 脫軌的事物;不正常者
(= *deviate*)

deviation[7] 〔,divɪ'eʃən 〕 n. 脫軌;偏差;航線變更

devious[7] 〔'divɪəs 〕 adj. 繞道的;不正當的 (離開路線的)

envoy[7] 〔'ɛnvɔɪ 〕 n. 全權公使;使者 (放在路上 → 派遣)
《 *en-* = on 》

invoice[7] 〔'ɪnvɔɪs 〕 n., v. (開) 發票 (放在路上的 → 贈送)
《 *in-* = on 》

```
in  +  vo  + ice
 |      |     |
on  + way  +  n.
```

obviate 〔'ɑbvɪ,et 〕 v. 避免;防止 (在路上毀壞 → 不能通行)
《 *ob-* = against 》

obvious[3] 〔'ɑbvɪəs 〕 adj. 明白的;顯然的 (橫臥靠近路面處 → 被人
看見) 《 *ob-* = near 》

pervious 〔'pɝvɪəs 〕 adj. (水) 可浸透的;(光線) 可透過的
(穿越道路) 《 *per-* = through 》

impervious[7] 〔 ɪm'pɝvɪəs 〕 adj. 透不過的;不受影響的
《 *im-* = *in-* = not 》

previous[3] 〔'privɪəs 〕 adj. 在前的;先前的 (走到前面的道路)
《 *pre-* = before 》

```
pre   +  vi  + ous
  |       |      |
before + way  + adj.
```

trivia[7] 〔ˈtrɪvɪə〕*n.pl.* 瑣事（三條路 → 買東西的婦女們碰面交談的
好地方 → 內容大致沒有趣味）《*tri-* = three》

trivial[6] 〔ˈtrɪvɪəl〕*adj.* 不重要的；瑣碎的　*n.*（常用 *pl.*）普通的
事物

triviality 〔ˌtrɪvɪˈælətɪ〕*n.* 瑣事；平凡；平凡的事物

639　**vic , vice** = substitution（代理）

> * 拉丁文 *vicis*（= *change*；*interchange*；*substitution*）。
> 〔變化型〕*vis*。

vicar 〔ˈvɪkɚ〕*n.* 教區牧師；代理人

vicarious[7] 〔vaɪˈkɛrɪəs〕*adj.* 替代別人的；代理的

vice-chairman 〔ˈvaɪsˈtʃɛrmən〕*n.* 副會長；副議長；副委員長

vice-chancellor 〔ˈvaɪsˈtʃænsəlɚ〕*n.* 大學副校長；副大法官

【解說】 **chancel** 原是指格子，**chancellor** 則是指看守圍欄的人，也就
是在圍欄後工作的人，之後引申爲貴族、大使館或國王的秘
書、大臣，在美國此字表示法院的首席法官，或是某些大學
的校長。

vice-consul 〔ˈvaɪsˈkɑnsḷ〕*n.* 副領事

vice-governor 〔ˈvaɪsˈgʌvɚnɚ〕*n.* 副州長；副總督

vice-minister 〔ˈvaɪsˈmɪnɪstɚ〕*n.* 副部長；次長

vice-president[3] 〔ˈvaɪsˈprɛzədənt〕*n.* 副總統

vice-principal 〔ˈvaɪsˈprɪnsəpḷ〕*n.* 副校長

vice-regent 〔ˈvaɪsˈridʒənt〕*n.* 副攝政；副執政

viscount 〔ˈvaɪkaʊnt〕*n.* 子爵（代理的伯爵）

> 《*vis* = *vice*（in place of）+ *count*（伯爵）》

vis	+	count
|		|
in place of	+	*companion*

640 **vict , vinc** = conquer (征服)

> * 拉丁文 *vincere* (= *conquer*) ，過去分詞為 *victus*。
> 〔變化型〕 *vanqu*。

victor[6] 〔'vɪktɚ 〕 *n.*, *adj.* 勝利者 (的)

victorious[6] 〔 vɪk'torɪəs, -rjəs 〕 *adj.* 勝利的；戰勝的

victory[2] 〔'vɪktərɪ, 'vɪktrɪ 〕 *n.* 勝利；戰勝

vanquish 〔'væŋkwɪʃ 〕 *v.* 征服；擊敗

invincible[7] 〔 ɪn'vɪnsəbḷ 〕 *adj.* 不可征服的；難以克服的 《*in-* = not》

in +	vinc +	ible
not +	conquer +	adj.

convince[4] 〔 kən'vɪns 〕 *v.* 使信服；說服 (完全征服對方)
《*con-* = thoroughly》

convincible 〔 kən'vɪnsəbḷ 〕 *adj.* 可使相信的；可說服的

convincing[7] 〔 kən'vɪnsɪŋ 〕 *adj.* 令人信服的

conviction[6] 〔 kən'vɪkʃən 〕 *n.* 信念；信服；判罪

convict[5] 〔 *v.* kən'vɪkt *n.* 'kɑnvɪkt 〕 *v.* 證明有罪；宣告有罪
n. 罪犯 (使其深知有罪)

evict[7] 〔 ɪ'vɪkt 〕 *v.* 逐出；趕出；收回 (征服出去) 《*e-* = *ex-* = out》

evince 〔 ɪ'vɪns 〕 *v.* 表明；顯示出；喚起 (幾乎不殘留任何疑問的
全然了解) 《*e-* = *ex-* = out ; fully》

641 **vid , vis** = see (看見)

> * 拉丁文 *videre* (= *see*) ，過去分詞為 *visus*。

video[2] 〔'vɪdɪ,o 〕 *n.* 電視；錄影；錄影帶 *adj.* 電視的；錄影的

visa[5] 〔'vizə 〕 *n.* 簽證 *v.* 給予簽證 (出示的證件) 《 *-a* 名詞字尾》

visage 〔'vɪzɪdʒ 〕 *n.* 容貌；外觀 (外貌)

visible[3] 〔'vɪzəbḷ 〕 *adj.* 可見的；顯而易見的

vision[3]〔'vɪʒən〕 n. 幻想；夢想；視力；美景；洞察力

　v. 在夢中顯現；夢見（眼睛能看到的）

visionary[7]〔'vɪʒən‚ɛrɪ〕 adj. 幻想的；不實際的；空想的

　n. 幻想家；夢想家

```
vis + ion + ary
 |     |     |
see +  n. + adj.
```

visit[1]〔'vɪzɪt〕 v. 視察；訪問；參觀　n. 訪問；參觀；作客（去看）

visitant〔'vɪzətənt〕 n. 訪問者；幽靈；候鳥

visitation〔‚vɪzə'teʃən〕 n. 視察；訪問；天譴

visitor[2]〔'vɪzɪtɚ〕 n. 訪客；觀光客；住客

visor[7]〔'vaɪzɚ〕 n. （頭盔的）面甲；護面；（帽子的）帽簷；

　（汽車的）遮陽板

vista[7]〔'vɪstə〕 n. 遠景；回想；展望

visual[4]〔'vɪʒʊəl〕 adj. 視覺的；可見的；真實的

visualize[6]〔'vɪʒʊəl‚aɪz〕 v. 想像；想見；使可見；使顯現

advise[3]〔əd'vaɪz〕 v. 忠告；通知（糾正別人的行為）《ad- = to》

```
ad + vise
 |    |
to +  see
```

advisement〔əd'vaɪzmənt〕 n. 熟慮

adviser[3]; **-or**〔əd'vaɪzɚ〕 n. 勸告者；顧問；指導教授；導師

advisory[7]〔əd'vaɪzərɪ〕 adj. 顧問的；勸告的；供諮詢的

advice[3]〔əd'vaɪs〕 n. 忠告；通知

devise[4]〔dɪ'vaɪz〕 v. 設計；發明；遺贈（不動產）　n. 遺贈的財產

　（辨別 → 計畫）《de- = dis- = apart》

device[4]〔dɪ'vaɪs〕 n. 發明物；圖案；策略；裝置

envisage〔ɛn'vɪzɪdʒ〕 v. 正視；面對；想像（使看見）《en- = make》

```
en  + vis + age
 |     |     |
make + see +  v.
```

envision[7] 〔 ɛn'vɪʒən 〕 *n. , v.* 想像；默想

envy[3] 〔'ɛnvɪ 〕 *n.* 羨慕；嫉妒　*v.* 羨慕；嫉妒 (看見～而羨慕)
　《*en-* = on》

envious[4] 〔'ɛnvɪəs 〕 *adj.* 羨慕的；嫉妒的

invidious 〔 ɪn'vɪdɪəs 〕 *adj.* 招人猜忌的；招嫉妒的；惹人反感的
　(看到～而嫉妒)《*in-* = on》

```
in  +  vid  +  ious
 |       |       |
on  +  see  +  adj.
```

evident[4] 〔'ɛvədənt 〕 *adj.* 明白的；顯然的 (看著外面)
　《*e-* = *ex-* = out》

evidence[4] 〔'ɛvədəns 〕 *n.* 證據；(法庭) 證詞　*v.* 顯示；證明

improvise[7] 〔'ɪmprə,vaɪz , ,ɪmprə'vaɪz 〕 *v.* 即席賦 (詩) ；
　即席演奏；即席而作 (事先並沒有看到 → 沒有事先準備的)
　《*im-* = *in-* = not ; *pro-* = before》

invisible[7] 〔 ɪn'vɪzəbḷ 〕 *adj.* 看不見的；難分辨的《*in-* = not》

previse 〔 prɪ'vaɪz 〕 *v.* 預知；預見 (預先看見)《*pre-* = before》

```
pre   +  vise
 |         |
before  +  see
```

prevision 〔 prɪ'vɪʒən 〕 *n.* 先見；預知；預感

provide[2] 〔 prə'vaɪd 〕 *v.* 供給；預備 (預先看見)《*pro-* = before》

provident 〔'pravədənt 〕 *adj.* 先見之明的；預知的

providential 〔,pravə'dɛnʃəl 〕 *adj.* 神的；神意的；幸運的

providence[7] 〔'pravədəns 〕 *n.* 節約；慎重；(P-) 上帝的保佑

```
pro    +  vid  +  ence
 |         |       |
before  +  see  +   n.
```

provision[7] 〔 prə'vɪʒən 〕 *n.* 供應；準備；設備；條款　*v.* 供以食物

provisory 〔 prə'vaɪzərɪ 〕 *adj.* 附有條件的；臨時的；暫定的

prudent[7]〔ˈprudn̩t〕*adj.* 謹慎的；節儉的（仔細地看著前面）
　《*pru-* = *pro-* = before》

prudence〔ˈprudn̩s〕*n.* 慎重；節儉

prudential〔pruˈdɛnʃəl〕*adj.* 慎重的；細心的
　n.（*pl.*）慎重考慮；慎重考慮過的事

purvey[7]〔pɚˈve〕*v.* 供給；供應（事先看見）《*pur-* = *pro-* = before》

```
pur  +  vey
 |       |
before + see
```

purveyance〔pɚˈveəns〕*n.* 供應

purveyor[7]〔pɚˈveɚ〕*n.* 供應者

revise[4]〔rɪˈvaɪz〕*v.* 校訂；改訂　*n.* 校訂；改訂（版）（改正）
　《*re-* = again》

revision[4]〔rɪˈvɪʒən〕*n.* 校正；改訂（本）

supervise[5]〔ˌsupɚˈvaɪz〕*v.* 監督；指導；管理（從上往下看）
　《*super-* = above》

supervision[6]〔ˌsupɚˈvɪʒən〕*n.* 監督；指導；管理

```
super  +  vis  +  ion
  |        |       |
above  +  see  +  n.
```

supervisor[5]〔ˌsupɚˈvaɪzɚ〕*n.* 監督者；管理人

supervisory[7]〔ˌsupɚˈvaɪzərɪ〕*adj.* 監督（者）的；管理（人）的

surveillance[7]〔sɚˈveləns〕*n.* 監視；看守《*veil* = see》

surveillant〔sɚˈvelənt〕*adj.* 監視的；監督的　*n.* 監視者；監督者

survey[3]〔*v.* sɚˈve　*n.* ˈsɝve , sɚˈve〕*v.* 觀察；測量；視察
　n. 眺望；測量（圖）；視察（從上往下看）《*sur-* = *super-* = over》

surveyor[7]〔sɚˈveɚ〕*n.* 監督者；鑑定人；測量員

```
sur  +  vey  +   or
 |       |       |
over  + see  + person
```

televise[7] 〔'tɛləˌvaɪz 〕 *v.* 用電視播送；播映（看遠處傳來的物體）

《*tele-* = far off》

television[2] 〔'tɛləˌvɪʒən 〕 *n.* 電視；電視機

interview[2] 〔'ɪntəˌvju 〕 *n., v.* 面談；會見；訪問（彼此見面）

《*inter-* = between》

interviewee 〔ˌɪntəvju'i 〕 *n.* 被面試者；受訪者

《 *-ee* 表示「被～的人」》

interviewer 〔'ɪntəˌvjuə 〕 *n.* 面試者；訪問者

purview 〔'pɝvju 〕 *n.* 範圍；權限；視界（能看透的部分）

《*pur-* = *per-* = through》

review[2] 〔 rɪ'vju 〕 *v., n.* 再調查；複習；回顧；評論；檢閱

（反覆再看）《*re-* = again》

---

642   vig , veg = lively（活潑的；充滿活力的）

* 拉丁文 *vigere*（= be lively），*vigil*（= *awake*），
vigilia（= *watch*）。由「沒有睡」引申爲「通宵值
夜」、「進行活動而未眠」之意。

vigil[7] 〔'vɪdʒəl 〕 *n.* 徹夜不眠；守夜（通宵未睡之狀態）

vigilance[7] 〔'vɪdʒələns 〕 *n.* 警戒；不眠（症）

vigilant[7] 〔'vɪdʒələnt 〕 *adj.* 警醒的；警戒的

vigo(u)r[5] 〔'vɪgə 〕 *n.* 活力；精力；元氣（生活、活動的力量）

vigorous[5] 〔'vɪgərəs 〕 *adj.* 活潑的；強健的；精力充沛的

invigorate[7] 〔 ɪn'vɪgəˌret 〕 *v.* 使強壯；鼓舞；激勵

（注入活力）《*in-* = in》

in	+	vig	+	or	+	ate
in	+	*lively*	+	*n.*	+	*v.*

invigoration 〔 ɪnˌvɪgə'reʃən 〕 *n.* 激勵；鼓舞

invigorator 〔 ɪn'vɪgəˌretə 〕 *n.* 激勵者；補藥

vegetate〔'vɛdʒə,tet〕*v.* 像植物般地生長和生活；茫茫然地過日子

　《拉丁文 ***vegetare*** = enliven》

vegetation[5]〔,vɛdʒə'teʃən〕*n.* 植物；草木；單調貧乏的生活

vegetable[1]〔'vɛdʒətəbḷ〕*n., adj.* 植物（的）；蔬菜（的）

　（生長出來的東西）

643　vit = life（生命）　＊拉丁文 *vita*（= *life*）。

viable[7]〔'vaɪəbḷ〕*adj.* 能生存的；可實行的《法文 *vie* = life》

vital[4]〔'vaɪtḷ〕*adj.* 生命的；致命的；不可缺的

vitality[6]〔vaɪ'tælətɪ〕*n.* 活力；生氣；生動

vitalize〔'vaɪtḷ,aɪz〕*v.* 賦予生命；使有生機

vitamin(e)[3]〔'vaɪtəmɪn〕*n.* 維他命；維生素（維持生命的物質）

　《***-amin(e)*** 名詞字尾，表示「物質」》

avitaminosis〔e,vaɪtəmɪn'osɪs〕*n.* 維生素缺乏症

　《***a-*** = without；***-osis*** = condition》

```
    a    + vit + amin +  osis
    |       |      |       |
 without + life +  n.  + condition
```

devitalize〔di'vaɪtḷ,aɪz〕*v.* 奪去～的生命或活力（使喪失生命）

　《***de-*** = ***dis-*** = away》

revitalize[7]〔ri'vaɪtḷ,aɪz〕*v.* 使恢復元氣；使復活；使復興

　（再賦予生命）《***re-*** = again》

644　viv = live（生活；生存）

　＊拉丁文 *vivere*（= *live*），過去分詞爲 *victus*；*vivus*（= *alive*）。

victual〔'vɪtḷ〕*n.*（*pl.*）食物；食品（保持生命的東西）

　v. 供以食物；儲備食物

victual(l)er〔'vɪtḷɚ，'vɪtlɚ〕*n.* 糧食供應者；運糧船

viand（'vaɪənd）*n.* 食品；（*pl.*）食糧；食物

viva（'vivə）*interj.* 歡呼聲　*n.* 歡呼聲

vivacious[7]（vaɪ'veʃəs , vɪ- ）*adj.* 活潑的；快活的

```
viv  +  acious
 |        |
live  +   adj.
```

vivacity（vaɪ'væsətɪ , vɪ- ）*n.* 活潑；（色彩）鮮明

vivarium（vaɪ'vɛrɪəm , -'ver- ）*n.*（作成自然生息狀態的）動物飼養所或植物栽培所《*-arium* 表示場所的名詞字尾》

vivid[3]（'vɪvɪd）*adj.* 鮮明的；閃耀的；活潑的；生動的

vivify（'vɪvə‚faɪ）*v.* 賦予生命；使活潑；使生動《*-fy* = make》

vivisect（‚vɪvə'sɛkt , 'vɪvə‚sɛkt）*v.*（動物）活體解剖（將活的物體切開分成幾部分）《*sect* = cut》

vivisection（‚vɪvə'sɛkʃən）*n.* 活體解剖

convivial（kən'vɪvɪəl）*adj.* 歡宴的；快樂的（樂於共同生存）《*con-* = together》

revive[5]（rɪ'vaɪv）*v.* 復活；甦醒；重演（再活過來）《*re-* = again》

revival[6]（rɪ'vaɪvl̩）*n.* 回復；甦醒；（R- ）文藝復興

revivify（rɪ'vɪvə‚faɪ）*v.* 使復活；使振作；使還原

revivification（rɪ‚vɪvəfə'keʃən）*n.* 恢復氣力；還原

reviviscence（‚rɛvɪ'vɪsn̩s）*n.* 復活；甦醒

survive[2]（sə'vaɪv）*v.* 繼續存在；較～活得長久（生存得勝於其他東西）《*sur-* = *super-* = above》

```
sur  +  vive
 |       |
above +  live
```

survival[3]（sə'vaɪvl̩）*n.* 殘存；殘存的人（物）；遺物；遺風

survivor[3]（sə'vaɪvɚ）*n.* 殘存者；生存者；遺族；遺物

645   **voc , voke** = voice ; call (聲音 ; 喊叫)

* 拉丁文 ***vox*** (= *voice*) ，***vocare*** (= *call*) 。

vocal[6] 〔'vokl̩〕 *adj.* 聲的；聲音的   *n.* 聲音

vocalist[7] 〔'vokl̩ɪst〕 *n.* 聲樂家；歌手

vocalize 〔'vokl̩,aɪz〕 *v.* 出聲；說；喊叫

vocable 〔'vokəbl̩〕 *n.* 字；單字 (由聲音構成的)

vocabulary[2] 〔 və'kæbjə,lɛrɪ , vo- 〕 *n.* 用語範圍；字彙
　《 *-ary* 表示「整體；群體」》

vocation[6] 〔 vo'keʃən 〕 *n.* 天職；職業 (奉命喚出神明的職業)
　cf. **vacation** (假期)

vociferate 〔 vo'sɪfə,ret 〕 *v.* 大聲喊叫；吼叫 (使聲音能傳送
　至遠處) 《*fer* = carry》

```
voci  +  fer  +  ate
 |        |       |
voice + carry +  v.
```

vociferous 〔 vo'sɪfərəs 〕 *adj.* 大聲喊的；喧嘩的；嘈雜的

vouch[7] 〔 vautʃ 〕 *v.* 保證；擔保 (發出聲音大聲說)

advocate[6] 〔 *v.* 'ædvə,ket *n.* 'ædvəkɪt 〕 *v.* 主張；提倡
　n. 擁護者；提倡者；替人說情者 (為人與主義吶喊)

advocacy[7] 〔'ædvəkəsɪ〕 *n.* 提倡；辯護；擁護

avocation 〔,ævə'keʃən〕 *n.* 副業；嗜好 (非正式職業)
　《*a-* = not》

```
 a  +  voc  + ation
 |      |       |
not + voice +  n.
```

avouch 〔 ə'vautʃ 〕 *v.* 保證；承認；斷言

avow[7] 〔 ə'vau 〕 *v.* 公開承認；坦白承認

convoke 〔 kən'vok 〕 *v.* 召集 (會議) (呼喊使集合在一起)
　《*con-* = together》

convocation 〔,kɑnvə'keʃən 〕 *n.* 召集;集會;會議

```
con   + voc + ation
 |       |      |
together + call +  n.
```

equivocal[7] 〔 ɪ'kwɪvəkḷ 〕 *adj.* 意義不明顯的;模稜兩可的
（無論何者都是一樣的說法 → 無法決定是何者）《*equi* = equal》

equivocate[7] 〔 ɪ'kwɪvə,ket 〕 *v.* 含糊其辭;閃躲（一種曖昧不清的說法）

```
equi + voc + ate
 |      |     |
equal + voice +  v.
```

equivoke;**-voque** 〔'ɛkwə,vok , 'ikwə- 〕 *n.* 雙關語;
模稜兩可的說法;含糊的辭語

evoke[7] 〔 ɪ'vok 〕 *v.* 喚起;使追憶到（喚出外面）《*e-* = *ex-* = out》

evocation 〔,ɛvo'keʃən 〕 *n.* 召喚;喚起

invoke[7] 〔 ɪn'vok 〕 *v.* 祈求;求助於（大聲呼喚神明）《*in-* = on》

invocation 〔,ɪnvə'keʃən 〕 *n.* 祈求;祈願

```
in + voc + ation
 |     |     |
on + call +  n.
```

multivocal 〔 mʌl'tɪvəkḷ 〕 *adj.* 喧嘩的;多義的;曖昧的
（許多聲音）《*multi-* = many》

provoke[6] 〔 prə'vok 〕 *v.* 刺激;引起;激起（衝到前面吶喊 → 引出）
《*pro-* = forth》

provoking 〔 prə'vokɪŋ 〕 *adj.* 刺激的;煽動的;惱人的

provocation[7] 〔,prɑvə'keʃən 〕 *n.* 刺激;挑撥

revoke[7] 〔 rɪ'vok 〕 *v.* 取消;使無效（叫喚回來）《*re-* = back》

revocation 〔,rɛvə'keʃən 〕 *n.* 取消;癈止

irrevocable[7] 〔 ɪ'rɛvəkəbḷ 〕 *adj.* 不能取消的;不能變更的
《*ir-* = *in-* = not》

646　vol = fly（飛）

＊拉丁文 *volare*（= *fly*），*volitare*（= *flit* 輕快地飛）。

volant〔'volənt〕*adj.* 飛的；能飛的；敏捷的

volatile[7]〔'valətḷ〕*adj.* 揮發性的；（人等）善變的；暴躁的
《*-ile* 形容詞字尾》

volatilize〔'valətḷ,aɪz〕*v.*（使）揮發

```
volat + il(e) + ize
  |       |      |
 fly  +  adj. +  v.
```

volitant〔'valɪtənt〕*adj.* 飛行的；快速的

647　vol = will（意志；意願）

＊拉丁文 *velle*（= *wish*），*voluntas*（= *will*）。

voluntary[4]〔'valən,tɛrɪ〕*adj.* 自願的；自發的；故意的
n. 自發的行動；自願的行為

involuntary[7]〔ɪn'valən,tɛrɪ〕*adj.* 非本意的；無心的；不隨意的
《*in-* = not》

```
in  + volunt + ary
 |      |       |
not +  will  + adj.
```

volunteer[4]〔,valən'tɪr〕*n.* 志願者；義勇兵　*v.* 自願；自願效勞；
自願投軍

voluptuous[7]〔və'lʌptʃuəs〕*adj.* 色情的；奢侈逸樂的
（把快樂附加在身上）

volition[7]〔vo'lɪʃən〕*n.* 意欲；意志（力）

volitional〔vo'lɪʃənḷ〕*adj.* 意志的；意欲的

benevolence[7]〔bə'nɛvələns〕*n.* 慈善（心）；博愛（爲善的意志）
　《*bene-* = good》

```
bene  +  vol  +  ence
 |        |       |
good  +  will  +  n.
```

malevolence[7]〔mə'lɛvələns〕*n.* 惡意（惡意的心志）《*male-* = ill》

648　volve , volut = roll（滾動；捲）

　　＊拉丁文 *volvere*（= *roll* ; *turn about*），過去分詞爲 *volutus*。

voluble〔'valjəbḷ〕*adj.*（植物）纏繞的；口若懸河的；多言的
　（易於回轉的）

volume[3]〔'valjəm〕*n.* 書籍；卷冊；體積；音量（捲起來的東西）

volumeter[7]〔və'lumətɚ〕*n.* 體積計；容積計《*meter* 計量器》

voluminous〔və'lumənəs , -'lju-〕*adj.* 冊數很多的；大部頭的；
　（作家）多產的

volute〔və'lut , və'lɪut〕*n.* 渦形；渦形物

volution〔və'ljuʃən〕*n.* 旋轉；渦形；螺環

circumvolute〔sɚ'kʌmvə,ljut〕*v.* 纏繞；迂迴（繞在周圍）
　《*circum-* = around》

convolve〔kən'valv〕*v.* 捲；盤；旋繞（繞在一起）
　《*con-* = together》

```
con   +  volve
 |         |
together + roll
```

convoluted[7]〔'kanvə,lutɪd〕*adj.* 纏繞的；錯雜的

convolution〔,kanvə'luʃən〕*n.* 盤繞；迴旋

devolve[7]〔dɪ'valv〕*v.* 傳下；移交（向下傳遞）《*de-* = down》

devolution〔,dɛvə'luʃən , -vḷ'juʃən〕*n.* 傳下；移交；退化

evolve⁶〔ɪ'vɑlv〕v. 發展;進化(向外回轉)《e- = ex- = out》

```
e  + volve
|      |
out +  roll
```

evolution⁶〔͵ɛvə'luʃən , -'lju- 〕n. 展開;進化;進化論
evolutionism〔͵ɛvə'luʃənɪzəm 〕n. 進化論
evolutionist〔͵ɛvə'luʃənɪst 〕n. 進化論者
involve⁴〔ɪn'vɑlv〕v. 包括;牽涉;專心於(捲入其中)《in- = into》

```
in  + volve
|       |
into +  roll
```

involvement⁴〔ɪn'vɑlvmənt 〕n. 包含;牽涉;捲入
involute〔'ɪnvə͵ljut , -͵lut 〕adj. 內捲的;紛亂的;複雜的
involution〔͵ɪnvə'luʃən , -'lju- 〕n. 捲入;複雜;退化
revolve⁵〔rɪ'vɑlv〕v. 考慮;熟思;周轉;循環(使改變其想法)
  《re- = back ; again》
revolver⁷〔rɪ'vɑlvɚ 〕n. 連發手槍;左輪
revolution⁴〔͵rɛvə'luʃən 〕n. 公轉;革命(情勢的回轉)
revolutionary⁴〔͵rɛvə'luʃən͵ɛrɪ 〕adj. 革命的;革命性的
  n. 革命者
revolt⁵〔rɪ'volt 〕v. 背叛;起反感 n. 反抗;叛變;嫌惡(背對著)
  《re- = back》

649 **vor** = eat (吃)   * 拉丁文 *vorare* (= *devour* ; *eat*) 。

voracious⁷〔vo'reʃəs 〕adj. 狼吞虎嚥的;貪婪的
voracity〔və'ræsətɪ 〕n. 貪食;暴食;貪婪
carnivore⁷〔'kɑrnə͵vor , -͵vɔr 〕n. 食肉動物;食蟲植物
  《carni = flesh》

carnivorous[7] 〔 kɑr'nɪvərəs 〕 *adj.* 肉食性的

devour[5] 〔 dɪ'vaʊr 〕 *v.* 吞食；毀滅；貪婪地看（吃下去）

《*de-* = down ; *vour* = *vor* = eat》

devouringly 〔 dɪ'vaʊrɪŋlɪ 〕 *adv.* 貪婪地；吞噬般地

granivorous 〔 grə'nɪvərəs 〕 *adj.* 食穀類的《*gran* = grain》

```
grani  +  vor  +  ous
  |        |       |
grain  +  eat  +  adj.
```

herbivore[7] 〔'hɝbə,vɔr 〕 *n.* 食草動物《*herb* = grass》

herbivorous 〔 hɝ'bɪvərəs 〕 *adj.* 草食性的

insectivore 〔 ɪn'sɛktə,vɔr 〕 *n.* 食蟲動物；食蟲植物《*insect* 昆蟲》

insectivorous 〔,ɪnsɛk'tɪvərəs 〕 *adj.* 食蟲的

omnivore 〔'ɑmnəvɔr , -vor 〕 *n.* 雜食動物（什麼都吃）《*omni-* = all》

```
omni  +  vore
  |        |
 all   +  eat
```

omnivorous[7] 〔 ɑm'nɪvərəs 〕 *adj.* 雜食的；無所不讀的

piscivorous 〔 pɪ'sɪvərəs 〕 *adj.* 食魚的《*pisci* = fish》

650　**vulcan** = Vulcan（火與鍛冶之神）

* 拉丁文 *Volcanus*（ = *Vulcan*），Vulcan 是羅馬神話中的火
與鍛冶之神，相當於希臘神話中的 Hephaestus。

volcano[4] 〔 vɑl'keno 〕 *n.* 火山

volcanic[7] 〔 vɑl'kænɪk 〕 *adj.* 火山的

vulcanian 〔 vʌl'kenɪən 〕 *adj.* 鍛冶的；火山的；火山爆發的；
火山作用的

vulcanite 〔'vʌlkən,aɪt 〕 *n. , adj.* 硬質橡膠（的）

vulcanize 〔'vʌlkən,aɪz 〕 *v.* 使硫化；使硬化

651 vulg = common people (普通平民)

* 拉丁文 *vulgus*（ = *common people* ）。

vulgar[6]〔 'vʌlgɚ 〕 *adj.* 粗俗的
vulgarize〔 'vʌlgə,raɪz 〕 *v.* 使粗俗化；使通俗化
vulgarian〔 vʌl'gɛrɪən 〕 *n.* 粗俗的富人；暴發戶
divulge[7]〔 də'vʌldʒ 〕 *v.* 洩露；揭發

```
  di    +    vulge
  |          |
apart  +  common people
```

652 vulse = pluck (拉出；拔出)

* 拉丁文 *vellere*（ = *pluck* ），過去分詞為 *vulsus*。

avulsion〔 ə'vʌlʃən 〕 *n.* 撕裂；扯開；裂片
　《*a-* = *ab-* = from》
convulse〔 kən'vʌls 〕 *v.* 震動；痙攣；抽搐（引起~）
　《*con-* = with》
convulsion〔 kən'vʌlʃən 〕 *n.* 變動；動亂；痙攣；(*pl.*) 大笑
convulsive〔 kən'vʌlsɪv 〕 *adj.* 痙攣的；騷動的
evulsion〔 ɪ'vʌlʃən 〕 *n.* 拔出；拔去（拉出；拔出）
　《*e-* = *ex-* = out》
revulsion[7]〔 rɪ'vʌlʃən 〕 *n.* 劇變；拉回；厭惡；誘導法（拉回）
　《*re-* = back》
revulsive〔 rɪ'vʌlsɪv 〕 *adj.* 誘導的　 *n.* 誘導劑；誘導器具

```
 re   +  vuls  +  ive
 |        |        |
back  +  pluck  +  adj.
```

653 war = aware (知道的;察覺到的)

* 古英文 *wær* (= *aware*;*cautious*) 。

wary[5] ('wɛrɪ) *adj.* 小心的;謹慎的
aware[3] (ə'wɛr) *adj.* 知道的;注意到的
beware[5] (bɪ'wɛr) *v.* 小心;提防
unaware[7] (,ʌnə'wɛr) *adj.* 不知道的;未察覺到的 《*un-* = not》

654 wright = worker (工人)

* 古英文 *wyrcan* (= *work*),*wryhta* (= *worker*) 。

cartwright ('kart,raɪt) *n.* 車匠;修車工 《*cart* 貨車》
playwright[5] ('ple,raɪt) *n.* 劇作家 《*play* 戲劇》
shipwright ('ʃɪp,raɪt) *n.* 造船工人;修船者 《*ship* 船》
wheelwright ('hwil,raɪt) *n.* 車輪 (或車輛) 修造工
　《*wheel* 車輪》
wrought (rɔt) *adj.* 精製的;精緻的

655 xen = foreign (外國的)

* 希臘文 *xenos* (= *foreign*;*strange*) 。

xenogamy (zə'nagəmɪ) *n.* 異花受粉 (和別的花結合)
　《*gam* = marriage》
xenogeneic (,zɛnədʒɛ'nɪɪk) *adj.* 異種的 (外來的品種)

```
xeno  + gene + ic
 |       |     |
foreign + race + adj.
```

xenon ('zɛnɑn) *n.* 氙 (一種稀有氣體元素)
xenophile ('zɛnə,faɪl) *n.* 喜愛外國 (人) 的人 《*phil* = love》

656 xer = dry （乾的） * 希臘文 *xeros* （= *dry*）。

xerography 〔 zɪ'rɑgrəfɪ 〕 *n.* 靜電印刷；乾印術 《*graph* = write》
xerophagy 〔 zɪ'rɑfədʒɪ 〕 *n.* 乾齋（以乾物爲食品之齋）《*phag* = eat》
xerophilous 〔 zɪ'rɑfələs 〕 *adj.* （適合）生長在乾熱地區的

```
xero + phil + ous
 |      |      |
dry  + love + adj.
```

xerophyte 〔'zɪrə,faɪt 〕 *n.* 耐旱植物 《*phyt* = plant》
xerox[6] 〔'zɪrɑks 〕 *n.* 全錄式影印　*v.* 用全錄影印法影印

657 xyl = wood （木頭） * 希臘文 *xylon* （= *wood*）。

xylem 〔'zaɪlɛm 〕 *n.* 【植物】木質部
xylograph 〔'zaɪlə,græf 〕 *n.* 木刻版；（木）版畫 《*graph* = write》
xylography 〔 zaɪ'lɑgrəfɪ 〕 *n.* 木刻術；木刻版印刷術；
（木）版畫印畫法
xyloma 〔 zaɪ'lomə 〕 *n.* 木瘤；樹癭 《 *-oma* 表示瘤的名詞字尾》
xylophagan 〔 zaɪ'lɑfəgən 〕 *n.* 食木蟲；蝕木蟲

```
xylo + phag + an
 |      |      |
wood + eat  + n.
```

658 zo = animal （動物） * 希臘文 *zoion* （= *animal*）。

zoo[1] 〔 zu 〕 *n.* 動物園
zooid 〔'zoɔɪd 〕 *adj.* 動物的；似動物的　*n.* 游動孢子；游動精子；
（無性生殖產生的）個體 《 *-oid* = like》
zoology[7] 〔 zo'ɑlədʒɪ 〕 *n.* 動物學 《*ology* = study》
cainozoic 〔,kaɪnə'zoɪk 〕 *n.*, *adj.* 【地質】新生代（的）
《希臘文 *kainos* = new》

epizoon〔͵ɛpɪˊzoɑn〕*n.* 體表寄生蟲；外寄生蟲（指寄生在其他動物身體表面的動物）《*epi-* = upon》

protozoan〔͵protəˊzoən〕*n., adj.* 原生動物（的）

```
proto  +   zo   +  an
  |         |        |
first  + animal + n., adj.
```

659　zyg = yoke (結合)　　* 希臘文 *zugon* (= *yoke*) 。

zygosis〔zaɪˊgosɪs〕*n.* 接合

zygote〔ˊzaɪgot〕*n.* 受精卵；接合體

zygodactyl〔͵zaɪgəˊdæktɪl〕【鳥類】*adj.* 對趾的　*n.* 對趾鳥

```
zygo  + dactyl
  |        |
yoke  + finger
```

heterozygous〔͵hɛtərəˊzaɪgəs〕*adj.* 雜合的；異型接合的
《*hetero-* = different》

homozygous〔͵homəˊzaɪgəs〕*adj.* 純合的；同型接合的
《*homo-* = same》

660　zym = leaven (酵母)　　* 希臘文 *zume* (= *leaven*) 。

zyme〔zaɪm〕*n.* 酶；病菌

zymology〔zaɪˊmɑlədʒɪ〕*n.* 酶學；發酵學《*ology* = study》

zymosis〔zaɪˊmosɪs〕*n.* 發酵；發酵病；傳染病

zymurgy〔ˊzaɪmɝdʒɪ〕*n.* 釀造學

```
zym   +  urg  +  y
  |        |       |
leaven + work  +  n.
```

enzyme[7]〔ˊɛnzaɪm〕*n.* 酵素；酶《*en-* = in》

字 首 (Prefix)

字首的機能，主要是限定字根的意思，或確定字根的方向，和字的意思有很重要的關聯。

1 **a-** = in；on   * 表示「在～之中」或「在～之上」。

aback[7] 〔 ə'bæk 〕 *adv.* 向後地 (= *backwards*)

abaft 〔 ə'bæft 〕 *adv.* 在船尾

abed 〔 ə'bɛd 〕 *adv.* 在床上

ablaze[7] 〔 ə'blez 〕 *adv.* , *adj.* 著火；發光的

a	+	blaze
on	+	*fire*

aboard[3] 〔 ə'bord , ə'bɔrd 〕 *adv.* 在船上；在飛機上；在汽車上 (= *on board*)

abreast[7] 〔 ə'brɛst 〕 *adv.* 並肩

abroad[2] 〔 ə'brɔd 〕 *adv.* 在國外；遠；廣

across[1] 〔 ə'krɔs 〕 *adv.* , *prep.* 橫過

afar[7] 〔 ə'fɑr 〕 *adv.* 遙遠地

afloat[7] 〔 ə'flot 〕 *adj.* , *adv.* (在水上或空中) 漂浮的 (地)；流傳甚廣的 (地)；(在經濟上) 應付自如的 (地)

afoot[7] 〔 ə'fut 〕 *adj.* , *adv.* 徒步的 (地)

aground[7] 〔 ə'graund 〕 *adv.* , *adj.* (船) 擱淺

ahead[1] 〔 ə'hɛd 〕 *adv.* 在前地；在～之先 《*a-* (on) + *head* (head)》

a	+	head
on	+	head

alive[2] 〔 ə'laɪv 〕 *adj.* 活的；活動的；活潑的；有效的

aloof[7] 〔 ə'luf 〕 *adv.* 遠離；躲開 《*loof* = *luff* (讓船逆風而行)》

amid⁴〔ə'mɪd〕*prep.* 在其中

　　《*a-*（on）+ *mid*（middle）》

among¹〔ə'mʌŋ〕*prep.* 在～之中

around¹〔ə'raʊnd〕*adv.*, *prep.* 環繞

asleep²〔ə'slip〕*adj.*, *adv.* 睡著的（地）

astir〔ə'stɝ〕*adj.* 動起來的；轟動的

astride⁷〔ə'straɪd〕*prep.* 跨騎；在兩旁

away¹〔ə'we〕*adv.* 在遠方；離去

```
a  +  mid
|     |
on + middle
```

2 **a-** = intensive　　* 作為加強語氣用，表示動作的開始或結束。

abide⁵〔ə'baɪd〕*v.* 居留；遵守；等待

alike²〔ə'laɪk〕*adj.*, *adv.* 相似的（地）；同樣的（地）

aloud²〔ə'laʊd〕*adv.* 大聲地

amaze³〔ə'mez〕*v.* 使吃驚；使驚愕

　　《*a-*（intensive）+ *maze*（confused）》

```
a   +  maze
|      |
intensive + confused
```

arise⁴〔ə'raɪz〕*v.* 起來；上升

arouse⁴〔ə'raʊz〕*v.* 喚起；激起

ashamed⁴〔ə'ʃemd〕*adj.* 羞恥的；慚愧的

athirst〔ə'θɝst〕*adj.* 渴望的《*a-*（intensive）+ *thirst*（dry）》

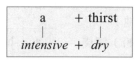

```
a   +  thirst
|      |
intensive + dry
```

await⁴〔ə'wet〕*v.* 等候；期待

awake³〔ə'wek〕*v.* 叫醒；醒來；使覺醒；喚起　*adj.* 醒著的；

　警覺的　*cf.* **awaken**（叫醒；使覺醒；喚起）

3 a- , an- = not ; without　　*〔變化型〕am-。

abasia 〔 ə'beʒə 〕 *n.* 不能步行症
　《*a-* (not) + *basia* (step)》

abiosis 〔 ˌæbɪ'osɪs 〕 *n.* 無生命狀態
　《*a-* (without) + *biosis* (way of living)》

abyss[7] 〔 ə'bɪs 〕 *n.* 深淵;深坑;地獄 (無底的)
　《*a-* (without) + *byss* (bottom)》

achromatic 〔 ˌækrə'mætɪk 〕 = colorless　*adj.* 無色的
　《*a-* (without) + *chromat* (color) + *-ic* (形容詞字尾)》
　cf. **chromatic** (顏色的;色彩的)

```
     a     + chromat +  ic
     |         |        |
  without +  color   + adj.
```

adamant[7] 〔 'ædəˌmənt 〕 *adj.* 堅硬的;固執的
　《*a-* (not) + *damant* (conquer)》

Amazon[7] 〔 'æməˌzn̩ 〕 *n.* 希臘神話中的女戰士;(the～) 亞馬遜河
　《*a-* (without) + *mazon* (breast 乳房)》

　【解說】希臘的傳說中,有一個使希臘軍隊大感頭疼的女性兵團,她們
　　　　　把妨礙自己拉弓的右乳房切除,希臘人依照這個傳說造了這個
　　　　　字。1541 年時,西班牙的探險家 Orellana,對住在當時稱為
　　　　　Rio Santa Maria dela 河流域部族中女性的勇猛善戰,感到印
　　　　　象深刻,因此將此河川命名為 **the Amazon**。

ambrosia[7] 〔 æm'broʒɪə 〕 *n.* 神的食物;味美的食物 (非人間的)
　《*am-* = *a-* (not) + *brosia* (mortal)》

amnesty[7] 〔 'æmˌnɛstɪ 〕 *n.* 大赦;特赦 (尤指政治犯)
　(沒有記憶 → 忘了罪惡)　《*a-* (not) + *mnesty* (remember)》
　cf. **amnesia** (健忘症;記憶喪失)

```
    a  +  mnesty
    |       |
   not + remember
```

amoral[7] 〔 eˈmɔrəl , -ˈmɑr- 〕 *adj.* 非道德的；與道德無關的
　《*a-* (without) + *moral* (道德的)》

an(a)emia[7] 〔 əˈnimɪə 〕 = want of blood 　 *n.* 貧血症
　《*an-* (without) + *aem* (blood) + *-ia* (表示病名的字尾)》

an(a)esthetic[7] 〔 ˌænəsˈθɛtɪk 〕 *n.* 麻醉劑　　*adj.* 麻醉的 (無知覺的)
　《*an-* (not) + *aesthetic* (perceptive)》　 *cf.* **aesthetic** (審美的)

anarchy[7] 〔ˈænəkɪ 〕 *n.* 無政府 (狀態)
　《*an-* (without) + *arch* (ruler) + *-y* (名詞字尾)》　 *cf.* **monarch** (君主)

```
an   + arch + y
 |      |     |
without + ruler + n.
```

anecdote[6] 〔ˈænɪkˌdot 〕 = not given out = a story in private life
　 n. 軼事 (未被發表的話)
　《*an-* (not) + *ec-* = *ex-* (out) + *dote* (given)》

```
an +  ec  + dote
 |     |     |
not +  out + given
```

anodyne 〔ˈænəˌdaɪn 〕 *adj.* 止痛的　　 *n.* 止痛藥
　《*an-* (without) + *odyne* (pain)》

```
an    + odyne
 |       |
without + pain
```

anomaly[7] 〔 əˈnɑməlɪ 〕 *n.* 反常；例外
　《*an-* (not) + *(h)omal* (even 相等的) + *-y* (名詞字尾)》

apathy[7] 〔ˈæpəθɪ 〕 = want of feeling　 *n.* 冷淡；漠不關心
　《*a-* (without) + *pathy* (feeling)》

aphasia 〔 əˈfeʒə 〕 *n.* 失語症；無語言能力
　《*a-* (without) + *phas* (speak) + *-ia* (表示病名的字尾)》

asocial[7] 〔 eˈsoʃəl 〕 *adj.* 不善社交的；利己的；不合群的
　《*a-* (not) + *social* (社會的)》

asylum[6] 〔 əˈsaɪləm 〕 *n.* 避難所；庇護所；救濟院（沒有逮捕權力的地方）《*a-* (without) + *syl* (right of seizure) + *-um* (表示地點的字尾)》

```
  a    +    syl    +   um
  |         |          |
without + right of seizure + place
```

asymmetric[7] 〔 ͵esɪˈmɛtrɪk 〕 *adj.* 不對稱的
《*a-* (not) + *sym-* (together) + *metric* (measure)》

asymmetry[7] 〔 əˈsɪmɪtrɪ 〕 *n.* 不對稱；不均勻
《*a-* (not) + *sym-* (together) + *metry* (measuring)》

atheism[7] 〔ˈeθɪ͵ɪzəm 〕 *n.* 無神論
《*a-* (without) + *the* (god) + *-ism* (表主義、學說的字尾)》

```
  a   +  the + ism
  |        |     |
without + god +  n.
```

atom[4] 〔ˈætəm 〕 *n.* 原子；極少量的東西（不能再分割的東西）
《*a-* (not) + *tom* (cut ; divide)》

atypical[7] 〔 eˈtɪpɪkḷ 〕 *adj.* 非典型的；反常的；不規則的
《*a-* (not) + *typical* (典型的)》

4　**ab-** = from ; away from ; off

*〔變化型〕a- , abs- (c 和 t 之前) , adv- , av- 。

abaxial 〔 æbˈæksɪəl 〕 *adj.* 離開軸的；不在軸上的
《*ab-* (away) + *ax* (axis 軸) + *-ial* (形容詞字尾)》

abdicate[7] 〔ˈæbdə͵ket 〕 *v.* 放棄權利；讓位；辭職（宣布離開）
《*ab-* (from) + *dicate* (proclaim 發表宣言)》

abduce[7] 〔 æbˈdjus 〕 *v.* 使外旋；外展
《*ab-* (away) + *duce* (lead)》

abduct[7] 〔 æbˈdʌkt , əb- 〕 *v.* 綁架；誘拐
《*ab-* (away) + *duct* (lead)》

abject[7] 〔 æb'dʒɛkt , 'æbdʒɛkt 〕 *adj.* 卑鄙的；可憐的（扔掉；拋棄）

《*ab-* (away) + *ject* (throw)》

```
ab  +  ject
|       |
away +  throw
```

abnormal[6] 〔 æb'nɔrml̩ 〕 *adj.* 變態的；不正常的（離開標準）

《*ab-* (away from) + *norm* (rule) + *-al* (形容詞字尾)》

abominate[7] 〔 ə'bɑmə,net 〕 *v.* 痛恨；厭惡（有前兆而離開）

《*ab-* (away) + *omin* (omen 前兆) + *-ate* (動詞字尾)》

```
ab  +  omin  +  ate
|        |        |
away +  omen  +  v.
```

abrade 〔 ə'bred 〕 *v.* 摩擦；擦傷；折磨

《*ab-* (away) + *rade* (scrape)》

abrupt[5] 〔 ə'brʌpt 〕 *adj.* 突然的；唐突的（突然破碎）

《*ab-* (off) + *rupt* (break)》

abscess[7] 〔 'æb,sɛs 〕 *n.* 膿瘡；潰瘍（離身體而去）

《*abs-* (away) + *cess* (go)》

abscond[7] 〔 æb'skɑnd 〕 *v.* 潛逃；逃亡（隱藏起來）

《*ab-* (away) + *scond* (conceal)》

```
ab  +  scond
|        |
away +  conceal
```

absolve[7] 〔 æb'sɑlv 〕 *v.* 免（罪）；赦免（釋放）

《*ab-* (away) + *solve* (loosen 解開)》

absorb[4] 〔 əb'sɔrb 〕 *v.* 吸收；併吞；使全神貫注

《*ab-* (off) + *sorb* (suck up)》

abstain[7] 〔 əb'sten 〕 *v.* 戒絕（從～抽身）

《*abs-* = *ab-* (from) + *tain* (hold)》

abstract[4] 〔 *v.* æb'strækt *n. , adj.* 'æbstrækt 〕 *v.* 抽出；抽去；提煉；
摘要　*adj.* 抽象的　*n.* 抽象（拔出）

《*abs-* = *ab-*（from）+ *tract*（draw）》

abstruse〔 æb'strus 〕 *adj.* 難解的

《*abs-* = *ab-*（away）+ *truse*（thrust 插入）》

abuse[6] 〔 ə'bjuz 〕 *v.* 濫用；妄用（不合乎正確用法）

《*ab-*（from）+ *use*（use）》

advance[2] 〔 əd'væns 〕 *v. , n.* 前進《*adv-* = *ab-*（from）+ *ance*（before）》

advantage[3] 〔 əd'væntɪdʒ 〕 *n.* 利益；優勢；優點　*v.* 有利於；
有助於《*ad-* = *ab-*（from）+ *vant*（before）+ *-age*（名詞字尾）》

avaunt〔 ə'vɔnt , ə'vɑnt 〕 *interj.* 走開

《*av-* = *ab-*（from）+ *aunt*（before）》

avert[7] 〔 ə'vɝt 〕 *v.* 避開；移轉《*a-* = *ab-*（away）+ *vert*（turn）》

avocation〔,ævə'keʃən 〕 *n.* 副業；嗜好

《*a-* = *ab-*（away from）+ *vocation*（工作）》

5　**ad-** = at；for；to

* 表示「方向、變化、完成、增加、開始」，或只表「加強」的重
要字首。〔變化型〕藉著後面字首的同化作用，而有以下的變化：
a- , ab- , ac- , af- , ag- , al- , an- , ap- , ar- , as- , at- 。

abandon[4] 〔 ə'bændən 〕 = at one's disposal　*v.* 放棄；捨棄

《*a-* = *ad-*（to）+ *bandon*（control）》　*cf.* **ban**（禁止）

abase[7] 〔 ə'bes 〕 *v.* 貶抑；降低（職位、階級等）（走向更低的位置）

《*a-* = *ad-*（to）+ *base*（lower）》

```
a  +  base
|     |
to +  lower
```

abate[7] 〔 ə'bet 〕 *v.* 減少；減輕；降低《*a-* = *ad-*（to）+ *bate*（beat 打）》

abbreviate[6] 〔 ə'brivɪ,et 〕 *v.* 縮短；縮寫

《*ab-* = *ad-*（to）+ *brevi*（brief；short）+ *-ate*（動詞字尾）》

abeyance〔ə'beəns〕*n.* 終止；暫緩

《*a-* = *ad-*（at）+ *bey*（wait 等待）+ *-ance*（名詞字尾）》

```
a  +  bey  +  ance
|      |       |
to  +  wait  +  n.
```

abridge[7]〔ə'brɪdʒ〕*v.* 縮短；刪節（文字或語言）

《*a-* = *ad-*（to）+ *bridge*（short）》

abut[7]〔ə'bʌt〕*v.* 鄰接；接近；接觸；緊靠

《*a-* = *ad-*（to）+ *but*（end）》

accede[7]〔æk'sid〕*v.* 允諾；同意；就職

《*ac-* = *ad-*（to）+ *cede*（go；come）》

accelerate[6]〔æk'sɛlə,ret〕*v.* 加速；促進

《*ac-* = *ad-*（to）+ *celer*（quick）+ *-ate*（動詞字尾）》

```
ac  +  celer  +  ate
|       |        |
to  +  quick  +  v.
```

accept[2]〔ək'sɛpt〕*v.* 領受；接受《*ac-* = *ad-*（to）+ *cept*（take）》

acclimate[7]〔ə'klaɪmɪt〕*v.* 使服水土；使適應新環境

《*ac-* = *ad-*（to）+ *climate*（氣候）》

accomplice[7]〔ə'kɑmplɪs〕*n.* 從犯；同謀者

《*ac-* = *ad-*（to）+ *com-*（together）+ *plice*（fold）》

```
ac  +   com    +  plice
|        |          |
to  +  together  +  fold
```

accost[7]〔ə'kɔst〕*v.* 向人打招呼；搭訕（朝著肋骨 → 接近人）

《*ac-* = *ad-*（to）+ *cost*（rib 肋骨）》

accumulate[6]〔ə'kjumjə,let〕*v.* 堆積；積聚

《*ac-* = *ad-*（to）+ *cumulate*（heap up）》

accuse[4]〔ə'kjuz〕*v.* 控告《*ac-* = *ad-*（to）+ *cuse*（lawsuit；reason）》

accustom[5]〔ə'kʌstəm〕*v.* 使習慣《*ac-* = *ad-*（to）+ *custom*（習慣）》

achieve[3] 〔 ə'tʃiv 〕 v. 完成；實現 《*a-* (to) + *chieve* (chief)》

acknowledge[5] 〔 ək'nɑlɪdʒ 〕 v. 承認；答謝

《*ac-* = *ad-* (to) + *know* (know) + *-ledge* (名詞字尾)》

```
ac  +  know  +  ledge
|       |        |
to  +  know  +   n.
```

acquaint[4] 〔 ə'kwent 〕 v. 告知；使熟識

《*ac-* = *ad-* (to) + *quaint* (know)》

acquire[4] 〔 ə'kwaɪr 〕 v. 獲得 《*ac-* = *ad-* (to) + *quire* (seek)》

cf. **inquire** (探問；詢問)，**require** (需求；要求)

adapt[4] 〔 ə'dæpt 〕 v. 使適合；使適應 (使恰當)

《*ad-* (to) + *apt* (fit)》

addict[5] 〔 ə'dɪkt 〕 v. 使耽溺；使熱中 (如~所言)

《*ad-* (to) + *dict* (say)》

address[1] 〔 ə'drɛs 〕 n. 演講；住址　v. 發表演說

《*ad-* (to) + *dress* (direct)》

adduce[7] 〔 ə'djus , ə'dus 〕 v. 引證；舉出例證

《*ad-* (to) + *duce* (lead)》

adept[7] 〔 ə'dɛpt 〕 *adj.* 熟練的 《*ad-* (to) + *ept* (grasp)》

adhere[7] 〔 əd'hɪr 〕 v. 黏著；附著 《*ad-* (to) + *here* (stick 黏貼)》

```
ad  +  here
|       |
to  +  stick
```

adjudge 〔 ə'dʒʌdʒ 〕 v. 判決；認為 《*ad-* (to) + *judge* (判定)》

admire[3] 〔 əd'maɪr 〕 v. 讚賞 《*ad-* (at) + *mire* (wonder)》

adorn[7] 〔 ə'dɔrn 〕 v. 裝飾 《*ad-* (to) + *orn* (decorate 裝飾)》

advent[7] 〔 'ædvɛnt 〕 n. 到來；來臨；(A-) 耶穌降臨

《*ad-* (to) + *vent* (come)》

adverse[7] 〔 əd'vɝs , 'ædvɝs 〕 *adj.* 逆的；反對的；不利的 (轉過身來)

《*ad-* (to) + *verse* (turn)》

advocate[6] 〔 *v.* ˈædvə͵ket *n.* ˈædvəkɪt 〕*v.* 擁護；主張；倡導
n. 提倡者；倡導者；擁護者；替人辯護者
《*ad-* (to) + *voc* (call) + *-ate* (動詞字尾)》

```
ad + voc + ate
 |     |     |
to  + call +  v.
```

affiliate[7] 〔 əˈfɪlɪ͵et 〕*v.* 聯合；使有密切關係；收為養子
(使成為兒子)《*af-* = *ad-* (to) + *fili* (son) + *-ate* (動詞字尾)》

affirm[6] 〔 əˈfɝm 〕*v.* 確認；斷言 (使堅固)
《*af-* = *ad-* (to) + *firm* (堅固的)》

afflict[7] 〔 əˈflɪkt 〕*v.* 使痛苦 (打倒)
《*af-* = *ad-* (to) + *flict* (strike)》　*cf.* **conflict** (爭鬥；戰鬥)

affront[7] 〔 əˈfrʌnt 〕*v.* 侮辱；冒犯　*n.* 侮辱 (指著額頭)
《*af-* = *ad-* (to) + *front* (forehead)》

```
af +  front
 |      |
to + forehead
```

aggress[7] 〔 əˈgrɛs 〕*v.* 侵略；進攻 (走向~)
《*ag-* = *ad-* (to) + *gress* (walk)》　*cf.* **progress** (進步；進展)

aggrieve[7] 〔 əˈgriv 〕*v.* 使苦惱 (重壓)
《*ag-* = *ad-* (to) + *grieve* (weight down)》

align[7] 〔 əˈlaɪn 〕*v.* 排成直線；使合作 (成行)
《*a-* = *ad-* (to) + *lign* (line)》

allay[7] 〔 əˈle 〕*v.* 使鎮靜；緩和 (痛苦、恐懼等) (使躺下來)
《*al-* = *ad-* (to) + *lay* (cause to lie)》

allocate[6] 〔 ˈæləˌket 〕*v.* 定位置；部署 (訂定地點)
《*al-* = *ad-* (to) + *locate* (place)》

allot[7] 〔 əˈlɑt 〕*v.* 分配；指派；分配~作某種用途
《*al-* = *ad-* (to) + *lot* (share)》

```
al +  lot
 |     |
to + share
```

allow[1] 〔 ə'laʊ 〕 v. 允許《*al-* = *ad-* (to) + *low* (praise)》

alloy[7] 〔 v. ə'lɔɪ n. 'ælɔɪ , ə'lɔɪ 〕 v. 使成合金；貶低；損害

　　 n. 合金；雜質（綁在一起 → 混合）《*al-* = *ad-* (to) + *loy* = *lig* (bind)》

```
al  +  loy
 |      |
to  +  bind
```

allude[7] 〔 ə'lud 〕 v. 提及（表露想法）《*al-* = *ad-* (to) + *lude* (play)》

allure[7] 〔 ə'lʊr , ə'lɪʊr 〕 v. 引誘；誘惑　 n. 誘惑（力）

　　《*al-* = *ad-* (to) + *lure* (誘惑)》

amass[7] 〔 ə'mæs 〕 v. 積聚《*a-* = *ad-* (to) + *mass* (mass 一團)》

ameliorate[7] 〔 ə'miljə,ret 〕 v. 改善；修正

　　《*a-* = *ad-* (to) + *melior* (better) + *-ate* (動詞字尾)》

```
a  +  melior  +  ate
 |       |        |
to  +  better  +  v.
```

amenable[7] 〔 ə'minəbḷ , -'mɛn- 〕 adj. 順從的；有順從義務的

　　《*a-* = *ad-* (to) + *men* (lead) + *-able* (形容詞字尾)》

amount[2] 〔 ə'maʊnt 〕 v. 總計；共達　　 n. 總數；總額

　　《*a-* = *ad-* (to) + *mount* (mountain 山)》

annex[7] 〔 ə'nɛks 〕 v. 附加；合併（結合）

　　《*an-* = *ad-* (to) + *nex* (bind)》

annihilate[7] 〔 ə'naɪə,let 〕 v. 消滅（使無）

　　《*an-* = *ad-* (to) + *nihil* (nothing) + *-ate* (動詞字尾)》

　　 cf. **nihil**（虛無）， **nihilism**（虛無主義）

```
an  +  nihil  +  ate
 |       |        |
to  +  nothing  +  v.
```

appall[7] 〔 ə'pɔl 〕 v. 使驚駭《*ap-* = *ad-* (to) + *pall* (grow pale)》

appease[7] 〔 ə'piz 〕 v. 撫慰（人）；平息（憤怒）；緩和（情緒）

　　（使平靜）《*ap-* = *ad-* (to) + *pease* (peace)》

append[7]〔 ə'pɛnd 〕 *v.* 附加；增補（佩帶～；懸掛～）

《*ap-* = *ad-* (to) + *pend* (hang)》

appertain[7]〔͵æpɚ'ten 〕 *v.* 屬於；關連（完全掌握）

《*ap-* = *ad-* (to) + *per-* (thoroughly) + *tain* (hold)》

```
ap +  per   + tain
|      |       |
to + thoroughly + hold
```

apply[2]〔 ə'plaɪ 〕 *v.* 應用；申請；敷塗（重合）

《*ap-* = *ad-* (to) + *ply* (fold)》

appraise[7]〔 ə'prez 〕 *v.* 評價；估量；鑑定（朝向～確定價值）

《*ap-* = *ad-* (to) + *praise* (price)》

apprise[7]〔 ə'praɪz 〕 *v.* 通知；告知（取消息給～）

《*ap-* = *ad-* (to) + *prise* (seize)》

approbate〔'æprə͵bet 〕 *v.* 批准；許可；認可（向～證明）

《*ap-* = *ad-* (to) + *prob* (prove) + *-ate* (動詞字尾)》

```
ap + prob + ate
|     |      |
to + prove + v.
```

arrange[2]〔 ə'rendʒ 〕 *v.* 安排；整理；商定；準備（向～排列）

《*ar-* = *ad-* (to) + *range* (rank)》

arrest[2]〔 ə'rɛst 〕 *v. , n.* 逮捕；阻止；妨礙（使站住）

《*ar-* = *ad-* (to) + *re-* (back) + *st* (stand)》

arrogant[6]〔'ærəgənt 〕 *adj.* 傲慢的；自大的（厚著臉皮要求時的態度）

《*ar-* = *ad-* (to) + *rog* (ask) + *-ant* (形容詞字尾)》

```
ar + rog + ant
|     |     |
to + ask + adj.
```

ascertain[7]〔͵æsɚ'ten 〕 *v.* 探知；確定

《*as-* = *ad-* (to) + *certain* (sure)》

asset[5]〔'æsɛt 〕 *n.* 有價值的東西 《*as-* = *ad-* (to) + *set* (enough)》

assert[6] 〔 ə'sɝt 〕 *v.* 主張；斷言（結合自己的權利）

《*as-* = *ad-* (to) + *sert* (join or bind together)》　*cf.* **series**（連續）

assuage[7] 〔 ə'swedʒ 〕 *v.* 緩和；減輕；平息（使舒服）

《*as-* = *ad-* (to) + *suage* (agreeable)》

assume[4] 〔 ə'sjum 〕 *v.* 假定；擔任；承擔；採用；假裝；霸佔；

承繼（他人的債務）《*as-* = *ad-* (to) + *sume* (take)》

```
as  +  sume
 |      |
to  +  take
```

attach[4] 〔 ə'tætʃ 〕 *v.* 附上；（使）附屬；使迷戀

《*at-* = *ad-* (to) + *tach* (stake 拴)》

attain[6] 〔 ə'ten 〕 *v.* 達到；成就；完成《*at-* = *ad-* (to) + *tain* (touch)》

attest[7] 〔 ə'tɛst 〕 *v.* 證明；表明；使宣誓；爲～作證

《*at-* = *ad-* (to) + *test* (witness 證人)》

attire[7] 〔 ə'taɪr 〕 *v.* 穿衣；盛裝

《*at-* = *ad-* (to) + *tire* (dress)》

```
at  +  tire
 |      |
to  +  dress
```

attract[3] 〔 ə'trækt 〕 *v.* 吸引；引誘

《*at-* = *ad-* (to) + *tract* (draw)》

attune[7] 〔 ə'tun , ə'tjun 〕 *v.* 調音；使調和；使適應（使音調和諧）

《*at-* = *ad-* (to) + *tune* (tone 音調)》

avenge[7] 〔 ə'vɛndʒ 〕 *v.* 爲～報仇《*a-* = *ad-* (to) + *venge* (revenge 復仇)》

```
a  +  venge
 |      |
to  +  revenge
```

avenue[3] 〔 'ævəˌnju 〕 *n.* 大街；林蔭大道《*a-* = *ad-* (to) + *venue* (come)》

avow[7] 〔 ə'vaʊ 〕 *v.* 公開承認；坦白承認

《*a-* = *ad-* (to) + *vow* (call 發出聲音)》

　cf. **avouch**（承認），**advocate**（提倡；主張）

```
a  +  vow
 |      |
to  +  call
```

6　**al-** = all

almighty[7] 〔 ɔl'maɪtɪ 〕= all-powerful　*adj.* 萬能的
almost[1] 〔'ɔl,most 〕= nearly　*adv.* 差不多；幾乎
alone[1] 〔 ə'lon 〕= quite by oneself　*adj. , adv.* 單獨的；單獨地
always[1] 〔'ɔlwez 〕= all the way　*adv.* 永遠；總是

7　**ambi-** = about ; around ; on both sides

＊拉丁文 *ambo*，表示「二者」、「周圍」。〔變化型〕amb-。

ambidextrous[7] 〔,æmbə'dɛkstrəs 〕 *adj.* 兩手都很靈巧的 (雙手都像右手一樣)　*cf.* **dexter** (右側的)，**dexterity** (靈敏)，**dexterous** (靈敏的)
《*ambi-* (both) + *dext(e)r* (the right hand) + *-ous* (形容詞字尾)》
ambience[7] 〔'æmbɪəns 〕= environment　*n.* 周圍；環境

amb	+	i(t)	+	ence
around	+	go	+	*n.*

ambient[7] 〔'æmbɪənt 〕 *adj.* 周圍的 (繞行)
《*amb-* = *ambi-* (around) + *i(t)* (go) + *-ent* (形容詞字尾)》
ambiguity[6] 〔,æmbɪ'gjuətɪ 〕 *n.* 兩種或兩種以上的意義；曖昧

amb	+	igu	+	ity
both	+	drive	+	*n.*

ambiguous[6] 〔 æm'bɪgjuəs 〕= driving about　*adj.* 含糊的；不明確的 (踟躕)
《*amb-* = *ambi-* (about) + *ig* (drive) + *-uous* (形容詞字尾)》

amb	+	ig	+	uous
about	+	drive	+	*adj.*

ambition[3] 〔 æm'bɪʃən 〕 *n.* 野心；雄心（走來走去）

《*amb-* = *ambi-*（ about ）+ *it*（ go ）+ *-ion*（ 名詞字尾 ）》

$$\begin{array}{ccc} amb & + \ it \ + & ion \\ | & | & | \\ about & + \ go \ + & n. \end{array}$$

【解說】 以前這個字只用於政客。想求取官位的人，總是穿著白衣，到處
奔走演說，以求得選票。因此「到處走動」（ **ambire** ）就代表
「渴望權勢」的意思，後來漸漸也用於英文的一般情況中。此外
「候選人」（ **candidate** ）是「白的」（ **candid** ）「人」（ **ate** ）
的意思。

ambivalent[7] 〔 æm'bɪvələnt 〕 *adj.* 含有矛盾心情的；猶疑不決的
（ 兩種衝突的情緒 ）《*ambi-*（ both ）+ *val*（ strong ）+ *-ent*（ 形容詞字尾 ）》

8 amphi- = around ; on both sides

* 希臘文 *amphi*，和 ambi- 具有相同的意義。

amphibian[7] 〔 æm'fɪbɪən 〕 *adj.* 水陸兩棲的　　*n.* 兩棲類（ 生活在水
中和陸上 ）《*amphi-*（ on both sides ）+ *bi*（ life ）+ *-an*（ 形容詞字尾 ）》

amphibiology 〔 æm,fɪbɪ'ɑlədʒɪ 〕 *n.* 兩棲生物學（ 研究兩棲生物的
學問 ）《*amphi-*（ on both sides ）+ *bio*（ life ）+ *logy*（ study ）》

amphitheater[7] 〔'æmfə,θɪətə 〕 = round theater　　*n.* 圓形劇場

9 ana- = up ; back ; again

* 希臘文 *ana*，表示「向上」、「向後」、「再」的意思。
〔變化型〕an-。

anabaptist 〔,ænə'bæptɪst 〕 = one who baptizes again
n. 再洗禮派教徒（ 再洗禮 ）

anabiosis 〔,ænəbaɪ'osɪs 〕 *n.* 回復知覺；復活
《*ana-*（ again ）+ *bio*（ life ）+ *-sis*（ 名詞字尾 ）》

anabolism〔ə'næbḷͺɪzəm〕 *n.* 合成代謝
　《*ana-* (up) + *bol* (throw) + *-ism* (名詞字尾)》

anachronism[7]〔ə'nækrəͺnɪzəm〕 *n.* 時代錯誤 (時代變遷)
　《*ana-* (sometimes used in the sense of "against") + *chron* (time) +
　-ism (名詞字尾)》

```
ana  +  logy
 |        |
upon  + statement
```

analogy[6]〔ə'nælədʒɪ〕 *n.* 相似；類似 (言詞相關者)
　《*ana-* (upon) + *logy* (statement)》

anamnesis〔ͺænæm'nisɪs〕 *n.* (尤指對前世生活的) 回憶；既往症
　《*ana-* (back) + *mne* (remember) + *-sis* (名詞字尾)》

anamorphosis〔ͺænə'mɔrfəsɪs〕 *n.* 失眞圖像；【植物】畸形
發育；漸變；(昆蟲的) 增節變態
　《*ana-* (up) + *morpho* (form) + *-sis* (名詞字尾)》

anatomy[7]〔ə'nætəmɪ〕 *n.* 解剖學 《*ana-* (up) + *tomy* (cut)》

10　**ante-** = before (與 post- 相反)

　　* 拉丁文 *ante*，表示時間或空間上的「在前」。
　　〔變化型〕anti- , ant- , anci- , an-。

ante[7]〔'æntɪ〕 *n.* (看過手中的牌而未發新牌前所下的) 賭注
antecedent[7]〔ͺæntə'sidn̩t〕 *adj.* 在先的　　*n.* 先行詞
　《*ante-* (before) + *ced* (go) + *-ent* (形容詞字尾)》
antechamber〔'æntɪͺtʃembɚ〕 = anteroom　　*n.* 來賓接待室
antedate[7]〔ͺæntɪ'det〕 = date before　　*n.* 提前的日期
　v. 較～先發生或存在
antediluvian〔ͺæntɪdɪ'luvɪən〕 *adj.* 洪水時代以前的；太古的
　《*ante-* (before) + *diluv* (flood) + *-ian* (形容詞字尾)》

```
ante  + diluv +  ian
 |        |       |
before + flood + adj.
```

antemeridian 〔,æntɪmə'rɪdɪən 〕= before noon　*adj.* 上午的；
　午前的《*ante-*（ before ）+ *meri*（ middle ）+ *dian*（ day ）》
　cf. **postmeridian**（ 下午的；午後的 ）

```
ante  +  meri  + dian
 |        |       |
before + middle + day
```

antenuptial 〔,æntɪ'nʌpʃəl 〕*adj.* 婚前的
　《*ante-*（ before ）+ *nuptial*（ wedding ）》

anterior[7] 〔 æn'tɪrɪɚ 〕ante 的比較級 = more in front　*adj.* 前面的
　cf. **posterior**（ 後面的 ）

anteroom 〔'æntɪ,rum 〕*n.*（ 通入正室之 ）前廳；接待室

```
ante  +  room
 |        |
before +  room
```

anticipate[6] 〔 æn'tɪsə,pet 〕*v.* 預期；預想；希望（ 先拿 ）
　《*anti-*（ beforehand ）+ *cipate*（ take ）》

ancient[2] 〔'enʃənt 〕*adj.* 古代的　*n.* 老人；古人

ancestor[4] 〔'ænsɛstɚ 〕= forefather　*n.* 祖先（ 走在前面的人 ）
　《*an-* = *ante-*（ before ）+ *ces*（ go ）+ *-tor*（ 名詞字尾 ）》
　cf. **posterity**（ 後代 ）

11　**anti-** = against；opposite to（ 與 pro- 相反 ）

　＊希臘文 *anti*，表示「相反」、「抵抗」的意思。〔變化型〕ant-。

antibiotic[6] 〔,æntɪbaɪ'atɪk 〕*n.* 抗生素　*adj.* 抗生的；抗菌的

```
anti  +  bio  +  tic
  |       |        |
against + life + adj., n.
```

anticancer 〔,æntɪ'kænsɚ 〕*adj.* 抗癌的《*cancer* 癌症》

anti-communist 〔,æntɪ'kamjunɪst 〕*adj.* 反共的

anticorrosive 〔,æntɪkə'rosɪv 〕 *adj.* 防腐的《*corrosive* 腐壞的》

antinuclear 〔,æntɪ'njuklɪɚ 〕 *adj.* 反核能的《*nuclear* 核子的》

antipathy[7] 〔 æn'tɪpəθɪ 〕 *n.* 反感（對立的感情）
　　《*anti-* (against) + *pathy* (feeling)》　*cf.* **sympathy** (同情)

antiphonal 〔 æn'tɪfənl̩ 〕 *adj.* 交互輪唱的　*n.* 唱和詩歌集

```
anti  +  phon  +  al
 |        |        |
against + sound + adj., n.
```

antipodes 〔 æn'tɪpə,diz 〕 *n.pl.* 對蹠地（地球上正反相對的兩
　　個地點）

```
anti  +  podes
 |        |
opposite + foot
```

antiseptic[7] 〔,æntə'sɛptɪk 〕 *adj.* 防腐的　*n.* 防腐劑（防止腐爛）
　　《*anti-* (against) + *sept* (putrid 腐爛的) + *-ic* (形容詞兼名詞字尾)》

```
anti  +  sept  +  ic
 |        |        |
against + putrid + adj., n.
```

antisocial[7] 〔,æntɪ'soʃəl 〕 *adj.* 不善社交的；違反社會制度的

antithesis[7] 〔 æn'tɪθəsɪs 〕 *n.* 對照；對比；正相反（設於對面的東西）
　　《*anti-* (against) + *thesis* (setting ; placing)》

antiwar[7] 〔,æntɪ'wɔr 〕 *adj.* 反戰的《*war* 戰爭》

antarctic[6] 〔 ænt'ɑrktɪk 〕 *adj.* 南極的　*n.* 南極地區（北極的相反）
　　《*ant-* = *anti-* (opposite to) + *arctic* (北極)》

Antarctica[7] 〔 ænt'ɑrktɪkə 〕 *n.* 南極洲

```
Ant  +  arctica
 |        |
opposite + arctic
```

antonym[6] 〔'æntə,nɪm 〕 *n.* 反義字（對立的名稱）
　　《*ant-* = *anti-* (opposite) + *onym* (name)》　*cf.* **synonym** (同義字)

12 apo- = from ; away ; off *〔變化型〕ap-。

apogee[7] 〔'æpə,dʒi〕 *n.* 遠地點（月球或人造衛星在其軌道上離地球最遠的一點）；巔峰；頂點《*apo-*（away）+ *gee*（earth）》

apology[4] 〔ə'palədʒɪ〕 *n.* 道歉《*apo-*（off）+ *logy*（speech）》

apostle 〔ə'pasḷ〕 *n.* 使徒（耶穌的十二門徒之一）
《*apo-*（away）+ *stle*（send）》

aphelion 〔æ'filɪən〕 *n.* 遠日點（行星或彗星軌道上與太陽相距最遠的點）《*ap-*（away）+ *hel*（sun）+ *-ion*（名詞字尾）》

13 auto- = self

*希臘文 *autos*，表示「自己」。〔變化型〕auth-。

autobiography[4] 〔,ɔtəbaɪ'agrəfɪ〕 *n.* 自傳（描寫自己生活的東西）
《*auto-*（self）+ *bio*（life）+ *graphy*（writing）》

autocracy[7] 〔ɔ'takrəsɪ〕 *n.* 專制政治《*auto-*（self）+ *cracy*（rule）》
cf. **democracy**（民主政治）

autocrat[7] 〔'ɔtə,kræt〕 *n.* 獨裁者；專制君主

```
auto + crat
  |     |
self  + rule
```

autocratic[7] 〔,ɔtə'krætɪk〕 *adj.* 獨裁的；專制的
《*auto-*（self）+ *crat*（rule）+ *-ic*（形容詞字尾）》

autogamy 〔ɔ'tagəmɪ〕 *n.*（植物）自花受粉；（動物）自體生殖
《*auto-*（self）+ *gamy*（marriage）》

autogenous 〔ɔ'tadʒənəs〕 *adj.* 自生的；單性生殖的（自己出生的）
《*auto-*（self）+ *gen*（born）+ *-ous*（形容詞字尾）》

```
auto + gen + ous
  |     |     |
self + born + adj.
```

autoinfection 〔͵oto · ɪn'fɛkʃən 〕 *n.* 自體感染（在自己體內起作用）
《*auto-*（self）+ *in-*（in）+ *fect*（act）+ *-ion*（名詞字尾）》

```
auto + in + fect + ion
 |     |     |      |
self  + in + act +  n.
```

automate[7] 〔'ɔtə͵met 〕 *v.* 使自動化《*auto-*（self）+ *mate*（think）》
automatic[3] 〔͵ɔtə'mætɪk 〕 *adj.* 自動的

```
auto +   mat   + ic
 |        |       |
self  + thinking + adj.
```

automation[7] 〔͵ɔtə'meʃən 〕 *n.* 自動控制；自動操作
《*auto-*（self）+ *mat*（thinking）+ *-ion*（名詞字尾）》
automaton[7] 〔ɔ'tɑmə͵tɑn 〕 *n.* 自動機械裝置

```
auto +   mat   + on
 |        |       |
self  + thinking + n.
```

autonomy[6] 〔ɔ'tɑnəmɪ 〕 = self-government　*n.* 自治權；自治區
autonym[7] 〔'ɔtənɪm 〕 *n.* 眞名　*adj.* 本名的（自己的名字）
《*auto-*（self）+ *onym*（name）》
cf. **antonym**（反義字），**synonym**（同義字）
autopsy[7] 〔'ɔtɑpsɪ 〕 *n.* 驗屍；分析；實地觀察　*v.* 解剖
《*aut(o)-*（self）+ *opsy*（sight）》

```
aut(o) + opsy
 |        |
self   + sight
```

autotomy[7] 〔ɔ'tɑtəmɪ 〕 *n.* 自割（動物在遭受攻擊時會自行切除身體
的一部分）《*auto-*（self）+ *tom*（cut）+ *-y*（名詞字尾）》
authentic[6] 〔ɔ'θɛntɪk 〕 = one who does things with his own
hands　*adj.* 可信的；可靠的；眞正的（是自己親手做的）
《*aut-* = *auto-*（self）+ *hent*（doer）+ *-ic*（形容詞字尾）》

14　**be-** = make　　* 把形容詞、名詞給動詞化。

becalm〔 bɪˋkɑm 〕*v.* 使不動《*be-* + *calm* (安靜的)》
befool[7]〔 bɪˋful 〕*v.* 愚弄《*be-* + *fool* (傻人)》
befoul[7]〔 bɪˋfaʊl 〕*v.* 污染《*be-* + *foul* (dirty)》

```
be  +  foul
|        |
make + dirty
```

befriend[7]〔 bɪˋfrɛnd 〕*v.* 對待～如朋友；照顧；協助
　《*be-* + *friend* (朋友)》
beguile[7]〔 bɪˋgaɪl 〕*v.* 欺騙 (籌畫奸計)《*be-* + *guile* (wile 奸計)》

```
be  +  guile
|        |
make + wile
```

belittle[7]〔 bɪˋlɪtl̩ 〕*v.* 貶低；輕視《*be-* + *little* (卑微的)》
benumb[7]〔 bɪˋnʌm 〕*v.* 使麻木《*be-* + *numb* (無感覺的)》
betroth[7]〔 bɪˋtrɔθ 〕*v.* 許配 (宣布眞相)《*be-* + *troth* (truth 眞實)》

15　**be-** = cover with
　　* 表示「覆蓋」，多加在名詞之前，形成及物動詞。

becloud〔 bɪˋklaʊd 〕*v.* 蒙蔽；使變得黑暗《*be-* + *cloud* (雲)》
bedew〔 bɪˋdju 〕*v.* 沾濕《*be-* + *dew* (露)》
befog〔 bɪˋfɑg 〕*v.* 被霧籠罩；使模糊；迷惑《*be-* + *fog* (霧)》
bestar〔 bɪˋstar 〕*v.* 佈滿星星《*be-* + *star* (星)》

16　**be-** = upon　　* 表示「在～之上」。

become[1]〔 bɪˋkʌm 〕 = come upon　*v.* 變爲；成爲
befall[7]〔 bɪˋfɔl 〕 = fall upon　*v.* 降臨；遭遇

behold[7] 〔 bɪˈhold 〕= hold upon　*v.* 看見《*be-* + *hold* (hold)》

```
be   +  hold
 |        |
upon  +  hold
```

bemoan[7] 〔 bɪˈmon 〕= moan upon　*v.* 悲悼；慟哭

bemuse[7] 〔 bɪˈmjuz 〕= muse upon　*v.* 使沉思；使困惑

beset 〔 bɪˈsɛt 〕= set upon　*v.* 包圍；圍困

bespeak 〔 bɪˈspik 〕= speak upon　*v.* 預定；預先要求

bestow[7] 〔 bɪˈsto 〕*v.* 把～給予《*be-* + *stow* (put)》

```
be   +  stow
 |        |
upon  +  put
```

betide 〔 bɪˈtaɪd 〕*v.* 降臨；發生《*be-* + *tide* (happen)》

betray[6] 〔 bɪˈtre 〕*v.* 背叛《*be-* + *tray* (hand over)》

17　be- = by　* 表示「在～旁邊」。

because[1] 〔 bɪˈkɔz 〕*conj.* 因為《*be-* + *cause* (理由)》

before[1] 〔 bɪˈfɔr 〕*prep.* , *adv.* 在前；以前《*be-* + *fore* (在前的)》

behalf[5] 〔 bɪˈhæf 〕*n.* 方面；支持；贊成《*be-* + *half* (side)》

```
be  +  half
 |       |
by  +  side
```

behind[1] 〔 bɪˈhaɪnd 〕*prep.* 在～後面；落後《*be-* + *hind* (在後的)》

below[1] 〔 bəˈlo 〕*prep.* , *adv.* 在～下面《*be-* + *low* (下面的)》

beneath[3] 〔 bɪˈniθ 〕*prep.* 在～下面《*be-* + *neath* (down)》

bequeath[7] 〔 bɪˈkwɪð 〕*v.* 遺贈；遺留 (根據遺言)
　　《*be-* + *queath* (saying)》

```
be  +  queath
 |        |
by  +  saying
```

beside[1] 〔 bɪ'saɪd 〕 *prep.* 在旁；在～邊《*be-* + *side* (邊)》

between[1] 〔 bɪ'twin 〕 *prep.* , *adv.* 在～中間《*be-* + *tween* (two)》

beyond[2] 〔 bɪ'jɑnd 〕 *prep.* 越過；超過《*be-* + *yond* (yonder ; across)》

18　be- = intensive (加強語氣)

bedeck 〔 bɪ'dɛk 〕 *v.* 裝飾；使美麗《*be-* + *deck* (裝飾)》

bedrench 〔 bɪ'drɛntʃ 〕 *v.* 使濕透

befit[7] 〔 bɪ'fɪt 〕 *v.* 適當；合適《*be-* + *fit* (適合)》

befuddle[7] 〔 bɪ'fʌdl̩ 〕 *v.* 使酒醉昏迷；使迷惑《*be-* + *fuddle* (灌醉)》

begird 〔 bɪ'gɝd 〕 *v.* 捲繞；包圍《*be-* + *gird* (圍繞)》

beloved[5] 〔 bɪ'lʌvd 〕 *adj.* 所愛的　*n.* 所愛的人

bereave[7] 〔 bə'riv 〕 *v.* 奪去；使喪失《*be-* + *reave* (rob)》

```
    be    + reave
    |        |
intensive + rob
```

besiege[6] 〔 bɪ'sidʒ 〕 *v.* 包圍；圍攻；湧至《*be-* + *siege* (包圍)》

besmear[7] 〔 bɪ'smɪr 〕 *v.* 抹遍；塗遍《*be-* + *smear* (塗)》

bethink 〔 bɪ'θɪŋk 〕 *v.* 思考；考慮；想起《*be-* + *think* (思考)》

bewail[7] 〔 bɪ'wel 〕 *v.* 哀悼；悲傷《*be-* + *wail* (woe 悲痛)》

```
    be    + wail
    |        |
intensive + woe
```

19　bene- = well ; good (與 male- 相反)

   * 表示「很好」。〔同義詞〕bon- = bonus = good。

benediction[7] 〔ˌbɛnə'dɪkʃən 〕 *n.* 祝禱；祝福；(飯前的) 感恩禱告
《*bene-* (well) + *dict* (say) + *-ion* (名詞字尾)》

benefaction[7] 〔͵bɛnəˈfækʃən 〕*n.* 恩惠;施惠;捐助 (行善)
《*bene-* (well) + *fact* (do) + *-ion* (名詞字尾)》

```
bene + fact + ion
 |      |      |
well  +  do  +  n.
```

benefactor[7] 〔͵bɛnəˈfæktɚ 〕*n.* 施主;恩人;捐助人 (行善者)
《*bene-* (well) + *factor* (doer)》

beneficence 〔 bɪˈnɛfəsn̩s 〕*n.* 恩惠;施與
《*bene-* (good) + *fic* (do) + *-ence* (名詞字尾)》

beneficial[5] 〔͵bɛnəˈfɪʃəl 〕*adj.* 有益的
《*bene-* (well) + *fic* (do) + *-ial* (形容詞字尾)》

```
bene + fic + ial
 |      |     |
well  +  do  +  adj.
```

beneficiary[7] 〔͵bɛnəˈfɪʃərɪ 〕*n.* 受益人;受惠者
《*bene-* (well) + *fic* (do) + *-iary* (表示人的字尾)》

```
bene + fic +  iary
 |      |      |
well  +  do  + person
```

benefit[3] 〔ˈbɛnəfɪt 〕*n.* 利益 *v.* 有益於

benevolent[7] 〔 bəˈnɛvələnt 〕*adj.* 慈善的
《*bene-* (good) + *vol* (wish) + *-ent* (形容詞字尾)》
cf. **voluntary** (自願的)

```
bene +  vol  + ent
 |      |      |
good + wish + adj.
```

benign[7] 〔 bɪˈnaɪn 〕*adj.* (人) 和藹可親的;(氣候等) 溫和的;
(病等) 良性的《*beni-* (well) + *gn* = *gen* (produce)》

benignant 〔 bɪˈnɪgnənt 〕*adj.* 親切的;溫和的;良性的
《*beni-* (well) + *gn* = *gen* (produce) + *-ant* (形容詞字尾)》

bonus[5] 〔'bonəs 〕 *n.* 獎金;紅利（賜予之物）

【解說】 **bonus** 這個字是來自拉丁文,是「好」的意思。獎金、紅利是大家都覺得好的東西。在台灣的百貨公司,每逢週年慶時,常常會有買兩千送兩百的活動,那兩百元的部分,就是購物的 bonus。

boon[7] 〔 bun 〕 *n.* 恩惠;恩賜;恩物
bounteous 〔'baʊntɪəs 〕 *adj.* = bountiful
bountiful[7] 〔'baʊntəfəl 〕 *adj.* 慷慨的;大方的;豐富的
bounty[7] 〔'baʊntɪ 〕 *n.* 慷慨;獎勵金

20 **bi-** = double;two   *〔變化型〕bin-。

bicameral[7] 〔 baɪ'kæmərəl 〕 *adj.* （議會）兩院制的
《 *bi-* (two) + *camer* (chamber) + *-al* (形容詞字尾)》
bicentennial[7] 〔,baɪsɛn'tɛnɪəl 〕 *n.* 兩百周年紀念日

```
bi  +  cent  + enn  + ial
 |      |        |      |
two + hundred + year +  n.
```

bicolored[7] 〔'baɪ,kʌləd 〕 *adj.* 二色的
bicuspid[7] 〔 baɪ'kʌspɪd 〕 *n.* 前臼齒

```
bi  + cuspid
 |      |
two + point
```

biennial[7] 〔 baɪ'ɛnɪəl 〕 *adj.* 二年一次的
《 *bi-* (two) + *enn* (year) + *-ial* (形容詞字尾)》
bifurcated 〔'baɪfə,ketɪd , baɪ'fɜketɪd 〕 *adj.* 分叉的
《 *bi-* (two) + *furcat* (fork 分叉) + *-ed* (形容詞字尾)》

```
bi  + furcat + ed
 |      |       |
two + fork  + adj.
```

bigamy[7]〔ˈbɪgəmɪ〕*n.* 重婚《*bi-*（double）+ *gamy*（marriage）》
　　cf. **monogamy**（一夫一妻制）

bilingual[7]〔baɪˈlɪŋgwəl〕*adj.* 兩種語言的；雙語的
　　《*bi-*（two）+ *lingu*（language）+ *-al*（形容詞字尾））》

```
bi  +  lingu  +  al
 |       |        |
two + language + adj.
```

bimonthly[7]〔baɪˈmʌnθlɪ〕*adj.* 兩個月一次的；一個月兩次的

binocular[6]〔baɪˈnɑkjələ〕*adj.* 雙眼並用的　*n.* 雙目望遠鏡或
　顯微鏡《*bin-*（two）+ *ocul*（eye）+ *-ar*（形容詞字尾）》
　　cf. **ocular**（眼睛的），**oculist**（眼科醫生）

bipartisan[7]〔baɪˈpɑrtəzn̩〕*adj.* 兩黨的

```
bi  +  parti  +  san
 |       |        |
two +  party  +  man
```

bipod[7]〔ˈbaɪˌpɑd〕*n.* 兩腳架《*bi-*（two）+ *pod*（foot）》

bipolar[7]〔baɪˈpolə〕*adj.* 有兩極的

bisexual[7]〔baɪˈsɛkʃuəl〕*adj.* 兩性的

biweekly[7]〔baɪˈwiklɪ〕*adj.* , *adv.* 隔週的（地）；一週兩次的（地）

21　by- = secondary ; beside

by-election〔ˈbaɪɪˌlɛkʃən〕*n.* 補選（附帶的選舉）
　　《*by-*（secondary）+ *election*（選舉）》

bygone[7]〔ˈbaɪˌgɔn〕*adj.* 過去的　*n.* 過去的事
　　《*by-*（secondary）+ *gone*（過去的）》

byline[7]〔ˈbaɪˌlaɪn〕*n.*（報刊文章開頭的）作者署名行
　　《*by-* + *line*（線））》

bypass[7]〔ˈbaɪˌpæs〕*n.* 環外通路；（心）血管繞道手術　*v.* 繞道
　　《*by-*（beside）+ *pass*（經過）》

bypath 〔'baɪˌpæθ 〕 *n.* 旁道；（學科的）次要分支
　　《*by-*（ secondary ）+ *path*（ 小路 ）》

byproduct[7] 〔'baɪˌprɑdəkt 〕 *n.* 副產品；（意想不到的）結果；
　　副作用《*by-*（ secondary ）+ *product*（ 產品 ）》

bystander[7] 〔'baɪˌstændɚ 〕 *n.* 旁觀者（一旁的站立者）
　　《*by-*（ beside ）+ *stander*（ 站立者 ）》

byword[7] 〔'baɪˌwɝd 〕 *n.* 俗語；諺語；（某種特點的）代名詞；笑柄
　　《*by-* + *word*（ 字 ）》

22 caco- = bad

cacodemon 〔ˌkækə'dimən 〕 *n.* 惡魔；壞人
　　《*caco-*（ bad ）+ *demon*（ 惡魔 ）》

cacography 〔 kə'kɑgrəfɪ 〕 *n.* 拙劣的書寫；錯誤的拼寫
　　《*caco-*（ bad ）+ *graphy*（ writing ）》

cacophony[7] 〔 kə'kɑfənɪ 〕 *n.* 刺耳的聲音
　　《*caco-*（ bad ）+ *phony*（ sound ）》

23 cata- = down ; downwards ; fully

　　* 希臘文 *kata*，表示「向下」、「完全」。〔變化型〕cat-。

cataclysm[7] 〔'kætəˌklɪzəm 〕 *n.* 洪水；（政治上等的）大變動
　　（沖刷而下）《*cata-*（ down ）+ *clysm*（ wash ）》

catacomb[7] 〔'kætəˌkom 〕 *n.* 地下墓穴
　　《*cata-*（ down ）+ *comb*（ hollow ）》

catadromous 〔 kə'tædrəməs 〕 *adj.*（ 魚 ）為產卵而順流入海的
　　（順流而下）《*cata-*（ down ）+ *drom*（ run ）+ *-ous*（ 形容詞字尾 ）》

```
cata  +  drom  +  ous
 │        │       │
down  +  run   +  adj.
```

catalog(ue)[4] 〔ˈkætḷ͵ɔg〕 n. 目錄　v. 編列目錄（描寫得很詳細）
《*cata-*（ fully ）+ *logue*（ say ; tell ）》

```
cata  +  logue
 |         |
down  +   say
```

catalyst[7] 〔ˈkætḷɪst〕 n. 催化劑；觸媒（使釋放出來）
《*cata-*（ down ）+ *lys*（ loosen ）+ *-t*（ 名詞字尾 ）》

catapult[7] 〔ˈkætə͵pʌlt〕 n. 彈弓　v. 彈出（高飛後落下）
《*cata-*（ down ）+ *pult*（ brandish 揮；舞動 ）》

cataract[7] 〔ˈkætə͵rækt〕 = rushing down　n. 大瀑布；洪流
（破碎轟然落下）《*cata-*（ down ）+ *ract*（ break ）》

catastasis 〔kəˈtæstəsɪs〕 n. 戲劇之高潮
《*cata-*（ down ）+ *sta*（ stand ）+ *-sis*（ condition ）》

catastrophe[6] 〔kəˈtæstrəfɪ〕 = turning down　n. 異常的災禍；
大災難（面臨惡運）《*cata-*（ down ）+ *strophe*（ turning ）》

```
cata  +  strophe
 |         |
down  +  turning
```

catatonia 〔͵kætəˈtonɪə〕 n. 緊張症《*cata-*（ down ）+ *tonia*（ tension ）》
category[5] 〔ˈkætə͵gorɪ〕 n. 類；種；部門（當作一集體 → 看成一個
集體）《*cat-*（ down ）+ *egory*（ assembly 會議 ）》

24　circum- = around ; round about

* 拉丁文 *circum*，表示「環繞」、「在～周圍」。
〔變化型〕circu-。

circumambulate 〔͵sɝkəmˈæmbjə͵let〕 v. 巡行；繞行
《*circum-*（ around ）+ *ambulate*（ walk ）》
circumcise[7] 〔ˈsɝkəm͵saɪz〕 v. 行割禮；割除包皮（割掉周圍）
《*circum-*（ around ）+ *cise*（ cut ）》

circumference[7] 〔 səˈkʌmfərəns 〕 *n.* 圓周；周圍

《*circum-* (around) + *fer* (carry) + *-ence* (名詞字尾)》

```
circum +  fer  + ence
   |       |      |
around + carry +  n.
```

circumfuse 〔ˌsɝkəmˈfjuz 〕 *v.* 周圍灌溉 (液體)；散佈

《*circum-* (around) + *fuse* (pour)》

circumjacent 〔ˌsɝkəmˈdʒesṇt 〕 *adj.* 周圍的

《*circum-* (around) + *jac* (throw) + *-ent* (形容詞字尾)》

circumlocution 〔ˌsɝkəmloˈkjuʃən 〕 *n.* 迂迴累贅的陳述

《*circum-* (around) + *locut* (speak) + *-ion* (名詞字尾)》

```
circum + locut + ion
   |       |      |
around + speak +  n.
```

circumlunar 〔ˌsɝkəmˈlunɚ 〕 *adj.* 環繞月球的

《*circum-* (around) + *lun* (moon) + *-ar* (形容詞字尾)》

```
circum +  lun  + ar
   |       |      |
around + moon + adj.
```

circumnavigate[7] 〔ˌsɝkəmˈnævəˌget 〕 *v.* 環遊 (世界)

《*circum-* (around) + *navigate* (sail)》

circumpolar 〔ˌsɝkəmˈpolɚ 〕 *adj.* 圍繞極地的；極地附近的

《*circum-* (around) + *pol* (axis of a sphere 球體的軸) + *-ar* (形容詞字尾)》

circumspect[7] 〔ˈsɝkəmˌspɛkt 〕 *adj.* 慎重的 (仔細地看看周圍)

《*circum-* (around) + *spect* (look)》

circumstance[4] 〔ˈsɝkəmˌstæns 〕 *n.* 環境；情況 (周圍的東西)

《*circum-* (around) + *stan* (stand) + *-ce* (名詞字尾)》

circuit[5] 〔ˈsɝkɪt 〕 *n.* 一圈；一周；周圍；電路；回路 (繞行)

《*circu-* = *circum-* (around) + *it* (go)》

25 cis- = on this side

> * 拉丁文 *cis*，表示「在…這一邊的」、「繼…之後的」、
> 「順（式）」之意。

cisalpine〔sɪs'ælpaɪn〕*adj.* 在阿爾卑斯山脈南側的（即靠羅馬
這一邊的）《*cis-*（on this side）+ *Alpine*（阿爾卑斯山的）》

cisatlantic〔ˌsɪsət'læntɪk〕*adj.*（就說話的人的位置而言）在大
西洋這一邊的《*cis-*（on this side）+ *Atlantic*（大西洋的）》

cislunar〔sɪs'lunə〕*adj.* 在月球與地球之間的；在月球這一邊的
（指面向地球這一邊的）《*cis-*（on this side）+ *lunar*（月亮的）》

cistron〔'sɪstrɑn〕*n.*（遺傳）順反子
《*cis-*（on this side）+ *tr-* = *trans-*（across）+ *-on*（名詞字尾）》

26 com- = together；with；wholly

> * 拉丁文 *cum*（= *with*），表示「與」、「合」、「共」、「全」
> 之意。〔變化型〕co-, col-, comb-, con-, cor-, coun-。

combat[5]〔'kɑmbæt〕*v., n.* 戰鬥；爭鬥（彼此對打）
《*com-*（together）+ *bat*（beat）》

combine[3]〔kəm'baɪn〕*v.* 聯合；結合（把兩件事結合起來）
《*com-*（together）+ *bine*（two）》

```
com   +  bine
 |        |
together +  two
```

comfort[3]〔'kʌmfət〕*v.* 安慰　*n.* 安慰；慰藉
《*com-*（together）+ *fort*（strong）》

commemorate[6]〔kə'mɛməˌret〕*v.* 紀念；慶祝
《*com-*（together）+ *memorate*（remind）》

commence[6]〔kə'mɛns〕*v.* 開始《*com-*（together）+ *mence*（initiate）》

commend[7]〔kə'mɛnd〕*v.* 稱讚（把～交到某人手上）
《*com-*（together）+ *mend*（put into the hands of）》

commensal 〔 kəˈmɛnsəl 〕 *adj.* 共餐的；共生的　　*n.* 共生動植物
（同餐桌的）《*com-* (together) + *mens* (table) + *-al* (形容詞字尾)》
cf. **parasite** (寄生物)

```
com  + mens +  al
 |       |      |
together + table + adj.
```

commensurate[7] 〔 kəˈmɛnʃərɪt , -ˈmɛnsə- 〕 *adj.* 同量的；相稱的；
平衡的《*com-* (together) + *mensur* (measure) + *-ate* (形容詞字尾)》

commingle[7] 〔 kəˈmɪŋgl̩ 〕 *v.* 混合；混雜
《*com-* (together) + *mingle* (混合)》

commiserate[7] 〔 kəˈmɪzəˌret 〕 *v.* 同情；憐憫 (一起受難)
《*com-* (together) + *miser* (misery) + *-ate* (動詞字尾)》

commotion[7] 〔 kəˈmoʃən 〕 *n.* 騷動；暴動 (一起行動)
《*com-* (together) + *mot* (move) + *-ion* (名詞字尾)》

```
com  + mot + ion
 |      |      |
together + move + n.
```

commute[5] 〔 kəˈmjut 〕 *v.* 通勤；變換；減刑
《*com-* (together) + *mute* (change)》

compatriot[7] 〔 kəmˈpetrɪət 〕 *n.* 同胞 (同愛祖國的人)
《*com-* (together) + *patri* (father) + *-ot* (表示人的名詞字尾)》

```
com  + patri +  ot
 |       |       |
together + father + person
```

compile[6] 〔 kəmˈpaɪl 〕 *v.* 編輯；聚集 (財富等) (彙集在一起)
《*com-* (together) + *pile* (heap 堆)》

compose[4] 〔 kəmˈpoz 〕 *v.* 組成；構成；作曲；寫作；排 (字)；
使平靜；使鎮靜 (放在一起)《*com-* (together) + *pose* (place)》

coadjutor 〔 ˌkoəˈdʒutɚ 〕 *n.* 助手；夥伴
《*co-* (together) + *adjut* (help) + *-or* (表示人的名詞字尾)》

coadunate〔 ko'ædʒunɪt 〕*adj.* 連生的；聯合的；統一的

《*co-*（together）+ *ad-*（to）+ *unate*（unite）》

```
    co   + ad + unate
    |      |     |
together + to  + unite
```

coalesce[7]〔͵koə'lɛs 〕*v.* 合併；聯合；癒合（一起成長）

《*co-* = *com-*（together）+ *alesce*（grow up）》

coalition[7]〔͵koə'lɪʃən 〕*n.* 聯合；聯盟

《*co-* = *com-*（together）+ *alition* = *alesce*（grow up）》

coeducation[7]〔͵koɛdʒə'keʃən 〕*n.* 男女合校的教育

《*co-* = *com-*（together）+ *education*（教育）》

coequal[7]〔 ko'ikwəl 〕*adj.* 相等的　*n.* 相等的人或物

《*co-*（together）+ *equal*（平等的）》

coerce[7]〔 ko'ɝs 〕*v.* 強迫；壓迫（一起約束）

《*co-* = *com-*（together）+ *erce*（restrain 限制）》

coeval〔 ko'ivl̩ 〕*adj.* 同時代的　*n.* 同時代的人或物

《*co-* = *com-*（together）+ *ev*（age）+ *-al*（形容詞字尾）》

```
   co   + ev + al
   |      |    |
together + age + adj.
```

coexist[7]〔͵ko‧ɪg'zɪst 〕*v.* 同時存在；共存（共同存在）

《*co-* = *com-*（together）+ *ex*（out）+ *(s)ist*（stand）》

cognomen〔 kɑg'nomən 〕*n.* 名字《*cog-*（together）+ *nomen*（name）》

cohabitation[7]〔 ko͵hæbə'teʃən 〕*n.* 同居；共同生活（共同居住）

《*co-* = *com-*（together）+ *habit*（live）+ *-ation*（名詞字尾）》

```
   co   + habit + ation
   |       |       |
together + live  +  n.
```

cohere[7]〔 ko'hɪr 〕*v.* 黏著；凝聚；一致；協調；連貫（黏在一起）

《*co-* = *com-*（together）+ *here*（stick 黏貼）》

coincide[6] 〔ˏkoɪnˈsaɪd 〕 *v.* 與～一致；符合（一起掉下來）

  《*co-* = *com-* (together) + *incide* (fall upon)》

collaborate[7] 〔 kəˈlæbəˏret 〕 *v.* 合作

  《*col-* = *com-* (together) + *labor* (work) + *-ate* (動詞字尾)》

```
col    + labor + ate
 |         |      |
together + work + v.
```

collapse[4] 〔 kəˈlæps 〕 *n.* 倒塌　*v.* 使倒塌（一起滑落）

  《*col-* = *com-* (together) + *lapse* (glide down)》

colleague[5] 〔ˈkɑlig 〕 *n.* 同事；同僚（共同選出的人）

  《*col-* = *com-* (together) + *league* (choose)》

collide[6] 〔 kəˈlaɪd 〕 *v.* 碰撞；互撞（一起打）

  《*col-* = *com-* (together) + *lide* (strike ; dash)》

collimate 〔ˈkɑləˏmet 〕 *v.* 對準；調節

  《*col-* = *com-* (together) + *limate* (make straight)》

collinear 〔 kəˈlɪnɪɚ 〕 *adj.* 在同一直線上的

  《*col-* = *com-* (together) + *line* (line) + *-ar* (形容詞字尾)》

```
col    + line + ar
 |        |     |
together + line + adj.
```

collusion[7] 〔 kəˈluʒən 〕 *n.* 共謀；串通；勾結（一起扮演）

  《*col-* = *com-* (together) + *lus* (play) + *-ion* (名詞字尾)》

```
col    + lus + ion
 |       |     |
together + play + n.
```

combustion[7] 〔 kəmˈbʌstʃən 〕 *n.* 燃燒（完全燃燒）

  《*com-* (wholly) + *bust* (burn) + *-ion* (名詞字尾)》

concave[7] 〔 *adj.* kɑnˈkev *n.* ˈkɑnkev 〕 *adj.* 凹面的；凹陷的

  n. 凹透鏡《*con-* = *com-* (together) + *cave* (hollow 中空的)》

  cf. **convex**（凸面的；凸透鏡）

conceit[6] 〔kən'sit〕*n.* 自負；自大；奇思幻想（一手全包）

　《*con-* = *com-* (together) + *ceit* = *ceive* (take)》

concentrate[4] 〔'kɑnsn̩,tret , -sɛn-〕*v.* 集中；專心（一起到中心）

　《*con-* = *com-* (together) + *centr* (center) + *-ate* (動詞字尾)》

con	+	centr	+	ate
together	+	*center*	+	*v.*

conclave[7] 〔'kɑnklev〕*n.* 祕密會議

　《*con-* = *com-* (with) + *clave* (key)》

conclude[3] 〔kən'klud〕*v.* 結束；使完畢；下結論（一起關閉）

　《*con-* = *com-* (together) + *clude* (shut)》

　cf. **exclude** (除去；除外)，**include** (包含在內)

concoct[7] 〔kɑn'kɑkt〕*v.* 調製；編造；策畫

　《*con-* = *com-* (together) + *coct* (cook)》

concord[7] 〔'kɑnkɔrd , 'kɑŋ-〕*n.* 和諧；一致；同意（同心）

　《*con-* = *com-* (together) + *cord* (heart)》　*cf.* **cordial** (熱誠的)

concourse[7] 〔'kɑnkors , 'kɑŋ-〕*n.* 匯合；合流；集合（一起流走）

　《*con-* = *com-* (together) + *course* (run)》

　cf. **concur** (意見一致)，**current** (水流或氣流)

con	+	course
together	+	*run*

condemn[5] 〔kən'dɛm〕*v.* 反對；責難

　《*con-* = *com-* (together) + *demn* (harm)》

condense[6] 〔kən'dɛns〕*v.* 濃縮；使簡潔（使濃）

　《*con-* = *com-* (together) + *dense* (make thick)》

condescend[7] 〔,kɑndɪ'sɛnd〕*v.* 屈尊；俯就；降低身份

　《*con-* = *com-* (together) + *descend* (下降)》

condole[7] 〔kən'dol〕*v.* 安慰；同情；哀悼（分擔悲傷）

　《*con-* = *com-* (together) + *dole* (grief)》

confederate[7] 〔 *adj.* , *n.* kənˈfɛdərɪt *v.* kənˈfɛdə͵ret 〕 *adj.* 同盟的；
共謀的　*n.* 同盟者；共謀者　*v.* 同盟；共謀
《*con-* = *com-* (together) + *feder* (league 聯盟) + *-ate* (形容詞兼名詞、
動詞字尾)》

```
con  +  feder  +  ate
 |        |         |
together + league + adj., n., v.
```

confer[6] 〔 kənˈfɝ 〕 *v.* 賜予；頒給 (一起帶來)
《*con-* = *com-* (together) + *fer* (bear ; carry)》

configuration[7] 〔 kən͵fɪgjəˈreʃən 〕 *n.* 外型；輪廓；地勢 (整個形狀)
《*con-* = *com-* (wholly) + *figur* (form) + *-ation* (名詞字尾)》

```
con  +  figur  +  ation
 |        |         |
wholly + form  +   n.
```

confiscate[7] 〔ˈkɑnfɪs͵ket 〕 *v.* 沒收；充公 (全部收入國庫)
《*con-* = *com-* (wholly) + *fisc* (treasury) + *-ate* (動詞字尾)》

confront[5] 〔 kənˈfrʌnt 〕 *v.* 面臨；使面對；對照 (面對面)
《*con-* = *com-* (with) + *front* (forehead)》

confute[7] 〔 kənˈfjut 〕 *v.* 駁倒；證明錯誤
《*con-* = *com-* (together) + *fute* (beat)》

congeal[7] 〔 kənˈdʒil 〕 *v.* (使) 凍僵；凝結 (凍結)
《*con-* = *com-* (together) + *geal* (freeze)》

congenial[7] 〔 kənˈdʒinjəl 〕 *adj.* 氣質相似的；意氣投合的 (共同
的氣質)　《*con-* = *com* = together》

```
con  +    geni    +  al
 |          |          |
together + inborn nature + adj.
```

conglomerate[7] 〔 kənˈglɑmə͵ret 〕 *v.* 聚結成塊 (線團糾結在一起)
《*con-* = *com-* (together) + *glomer* (ball of yarn 線團) + *-ate* (動詞
字尾)》

conjugate[7]〔 *v.* ˈkɑndʒəˌget *adj.* , *n.* ˈkɑndʒʊˌget 〕*v.* 結合
adj. 結合的　*n.* 同源詞
《*con-* = *com-*（ together ）+ *jug*（ join ）+ *-ate*（ 動詞字尾 ）》

conjunction[4]〔 kənˈdʒʌŋkʃən 〕*n.* 結合；連接；連接詞（ 連接起來 ）
《*con-* = *com-*（ together ）+ *junct*（ join ）+ *-ion*（ 名詞字尾 ）》

```
con   + junct + ion
 |        |       |
together + join  +  n.
```

consent[5]〔 kənˈsɛnt 〕*v.* , *n.* 准許；同意（ 共同的感情 ）
《*con-* = *com-*（ together ）+ *sent*（ feel ）》
cf. **sense**（ 感覺 ）, **sentiment**（ 感情 ）

constipate[7]〔ˈkɑnstəˌpet 〕*v.* 使便祕；使呆滯；約束；限制
《*con-* = *com-*（ together ）+ *stip*（ cram 塞滿 ）+ *-ate*（ 動詞字尾 ）》

```
con   + stip  + ate
 |        |      |
together + cram +  v.
```

consume[4]〔 kənˈsum , -ˈsjum 〕*v.* 消耗；消費；耗盡（ 完全拿走 ）
《*con-* = *com-*（ wholly ）+ *sume*（ take ）》

contaminate[5]〔 kənˈtæməˌnet 〕*v.* 弄髒；污染（ 一起接觸 ）
《*con-* = *com-*（ together ）+ *tamin*（ touch ）+ *-ate*（ 動詞字尾 ）》

contemplate[5]〔ˈkɑntəmˌplet 〕*v.* 默想；考慮
《*con-* = *com-*（ wholly ）+ *template*（ temple ）》

cooperate[4]〔 koˈɑpəˌret 〕*v.* 合作（ 一起工作 ）
《*co-* = *com-*（ together ）+ *operate*（ work ）》

correct[1]〔 kəˈrɛkt 〕*v.* 修正　*adj.* 正確的（ 使完全正確 ）
《*cor-* = *com-*（ thoroughly ）+ *rect*（ right ）》

correlate[7]〔ˈkɔrəˌlet 〕*v.* 相關連；使互相關連（ 一起帶回 ）
《*cor-* = *com-*（ together ）+ *re-*（ back ）+ *late*（ bring ）》

corrugate[7]〔ˈkɔrəˌget 〕*v.*（ 使 ）起皺；（ 使 ）成波狀（ 產生皺紋 ）
《*cor-* = *com-*（ together ）+ *rug*（ wrinkle ）+ *-ate*（ 動詞字尾 ）》

corrupt[5]〔 kəˈrʌpt 〕*adj.* 腐敗的；貪污的　*v.* 使腐敗；使墮落
（ 一起弄壞 ）《*cor-* = *com-*（ together ）+ *rupt*（ break ）》

council[4] 〔'kaʊnsḷ 〕 *n.* 會議（共同召集）

《*coun-* = *com-* (together) + *cil* (call)》

counsel[5] 〔'kaʊnsḷ 〕 *n.* 商議；商量；忠告（共同提出）

《*coun-* = *com-* (together) + *sel* (take)》

27　contra- = against（反對；逆）

*〔變化型〕contro- , counter-。

contraband[7] 〔'kɑntrə,bænd 〕 *n.* 走私（品）

contradict[6] 〔,kɑntrə'dɪkt 〕 *v.* 否認；反駁（說相對的話）

《*contra-* (against) + *dict* (speak)》

contradistinction 〔,kɑntrədɪ'stɪŋkʃən 〕 *n.* 對比

contraindicate[7] 〔,kɑntrə'ɪndə,ket 〕 *v.* （病徵）顯示（某種治療方法或處理）不當

contrary[4] 〔'kɑntrɛrɪ 〕 *adj.* 相反的；不利的　*n.* 相反（的事物）

adv. 相反地《 *contra-* (against) + *-(a)ry* (形容詞字尾)》

```
contra + (a)ry
   |       |
against + adj.
```

contrast[4] 〔 *n.* 'kɑntræst *v.* kən'træst 〕 *n.* 對照　*v.* 對比

《*contra-* (against) + *st* (stand)》

contravene[7] 〔,kɑntrə'vin 〕 *v.* 違反；牴觸（對立）

《*contra-* (against) + *vene* (come)》

controversy[6] 〔'kɑntrə,vɝsɪ 〕 *n.* 爭論

```
contro + vers + y
   |       |     |
against + adj. + n.
```

controvert[7] 〔'kɑntrə,vɝt , ,kɑntrə'vɝt 〕 *v.* 辯駁；否認（反對而轉過身來）《*contro-* = *contra-* (against) + *vert* (turn)》

counter[4] 〔'kaʊntɚ 〕 *adj.* 相反的　*adv.* 相反地　*v.* 反對；對抗

《*counter-* = *contra-* (against)》

counteract[7] 〔͵kaʊntɚ'ækt 〕 *v.* 抵消；消除 (相對的作用)
《*counter-* = *contra-* (against) + *act* (act)》

counterattack[7] 〔 *v.* ͵kaʊntərə'tæk *n.* 'kaʊntərə͵tæk 〕 *v.* , *n.* 反攻；
反擊《*counter-* = *contra-* (against) + *at-* (to) + *tack* (stake 拴)》

```
counter + at + tack
   |       |    |
against +  to + stake
```

counterbalance[7] 〔 *n.* 'kaʊntɚ͵bæləns *v.* ͵kaʊntɚ'bæləns 〕 *n.*
平衡力；對抗力 *v.* 使平衡；抵消《*balance* 均衡；抵消》

counterfeit[7] 〔'kaʊntɚfɪt 〕 *n.* 偽造品 *adv.* 假冒的 *v.* 偽造
(違法去做)《*counter-* = *contra-* (against) + *feit* (make)》

```
counter + feit
   |       |
against +  make
```

countermand[7] 〔͵kaʊntɚ'mænd 〕 *v.* 撤回；取消
《*counter-* (against) + *mand* (command)》

countermeasure[7] 〔'kaʊntɚ͵mɛʒɚ 〕 *n.* 對策《*measure* 手段》

counterpart[6] 〔'kaʊntɚ͵part 〕 *n.* 相對的人或物；極相似的人或物
《*counter-* (matching 相對的) + *part* (part)》

counterpoint[7] 〔'kaʊntɚ͵pɔɪnt 〕 *n.* 對應物；(音樂) 對位法

countersign[7] 〔'kaʊntɚ͵saɪn 〕 *n.* 口令；答號

counterspy[7] 〔'kaʊntɚ͵spaɪ 〕 *n.* 反間諜

counterstroke 〔'kaʊntɚ͵strok 〕 *n.* 還擊

28　de- = down ; downward

* 由「往下」之意衍生為「分離、否定、加強」，是很重要的字首。

debase[7] 〔 dɪ'bes 〕 *v.* 貶低；降格；貶值 (往低處降)
《*de-* (down) + *base* (low)》

debate[2] 〔 dɪˈbet 〕 v., n. 討論；辯論（打倒）

《 *de-* (down) + *bate* (beat)》

debris[7] 〔ˈdebri 〕 n. 殘骸；垃圾；碎片；岩屑

《 *de-* (down) + *bris* (break)》

decadence[7] 〔 dɪˈkedṇs , ˈdɛkədəns 〕 n. 衰落；墮落；頹廢（落下）

《 *de-* (down) + *cadence* (falling)》

decapitate[7] 〔 dɪˈkæpə͵tet 〕 v. 斬首；砍頭（頭和身體分開）

《 *de-* (down ; off) + *capit* (head) + *-ate* (動詞字尾)》

```
de     + capit + ate
|         |       |
down , off + head  +  v.
```

decay[5] 〔 dɪˈke 〕 v., n. 衰落；衰微；腐爛（落下）

《 *de-* (down) + *cay* (fall)》

decease[7] 〔 dɪˈsis 〕 v., n. 死亡（走了）《 *de-* (from ; away) + *cease* (go)》

deceive[5] 〔 dɪˈsiv 〕 v. 欺騙（拿走）《 *de-* (from ; away) + *ceive* (take)》

decide[1] 〔 dɪˈsaɪd 〕 v. 決定；決心；決意（割開）

《 *de-* (off) + *cide* (cut)》 *cf.* **suicide** (自殺)

```
de + cide
|     |
off + cut
```

decipher[7] 〔 dɪˈsaɪfɚ 〕 v. 譯（密碼）成普通文字 n. 解碼

《 *de-* (off) + *cipher* (暗號)》

declaim[7] 〔 dɪˈklem 〕 v. 辯解；高聲朗讀（高喊）

《 *de-* (fully) + *claim* (cry out)》

declare[4] 〔 dɪˈklɛr 〕 v. 宣告；斷言（十分清楚）

《 *de-* (fully) + *clare* (clear)》

decrepit[7] 〔 dɪˈkrɛpɪt 〕 adj. 衰老的；老朽的；破舊的（破裂倒塌）

《 *de-* (down) + *crepit* (crack)》

```
de + crepit
|     |
down + crack
```

decry[7] 〔 dɪ'kraɪ 〕 v. 責難；貶抑

deduce[7] 〔 dɪ'djus , -'dus 〕 v. 演繹；推論（帶領往下走）
　《*de-*（ down ）+ *duce*（ lead ）》

defect[6] 〔 dɪ'fɛkt , 'difɛkt 〕 n. 過失；缺點（沒有做好）
　《*de-*（ down ; from ）+ *fect*（ do ; make ）》

defer[7] 〔 dɪ'fɝ 〕 v. 服從；順從（把自己往下帶）
　《*de-*（ down ）+ *fer*（ carry ）》

deflate[7] 〔 dɪ'flet 〕 v. 排出空氣；通貨緊縮（放氣）
　《*de-*（ down ）+ *flate*（ blow ）》　*cf.* **inflate**（ 使膨脹；使通貨膨脹 ）

deflower[7] 〔 dɪ'flaʊ⅗ 〕 v. 摧毀～之花；奪去（婦女）之貞節（奪花）
　《*de-*（ from ; away ）+ *flower*（ flower ）》

deform[7] 〔 dɪ'fɔrm 〕 v. 使殘廢；使醜（奪走了美麗）
　《*de-*（ away ）+ *form*（ beauty ; form ）》

```
    de  + form
    |      |
   down + form
```

delinquency[7] 〔 dɪ'lɪŋkwənsɪ 〕 n. 怠忽職守；犯罪；過失
　（ 離開本務 ）《*de-*（ away ; from ）+ *linqu*（ leave ）+ *-ency*（ 名詞字尾 ）》

```
    de      + linqu + ency
    |          |        |
  away , from + leave  +  n.
```

deluge[7] 〔'dɛljudʒ 〕 n. 大洪水；豪雨；氾濫　 v. 使氾濫；（ 洪水般 ）
湧到（ 將財物沖刷走 ）《*de-*（ away ）+ *luge*（ wash ）》

demarcation[7] 〔ˌdimɑr'keʃən 〕 n. 界限；劃分；區分（下標記）
　《*de-*（ down ）+ *marc* = *mark*（ mark ）+ *-ation*（ 名詞字尾 ）》

```
    de  + marc + ation
    |      |       |
   down + mark  +  n.
```

demerit[7] 〔 di'mɛrɪt 〕 n. 過失；短處（優點的相反）
　《*de-*（ negative 否定 ）+ *merit*（ 優點 ）》

demolish[7] 〔 dɪ'mɑlɪʃ 〕 *v.* 拆除;毀壞;推翻

《拉丁文 *demoliri* = pull down》

demonstrate[4] 〔'dɛmən,stret 〕 *v.* 證明;(用標本或實驗)示範

(表示得很清楚)《*de-* (fully) + *monstrate* (show)》

denigrate[7] 〔'dɛnə,gret 〕 *v.* 塗黑;玷辱

《*de-* (intensive) + *nigr* (black) + *-ate* (動詞字尾)》

depict[6] 〔 dɪ'pɪkt 〕 *v.* 描畫;描寫(描繪得很充分)

《*de-* (down;fully) + *pict* (paint)》 *cf.* **picture** (繪畫)

depurate[7] 〔 dɪ'pjʊret 〕 *v.* 使淨化;精煉

《*de-* (intensive) + *pur* (pure) + *-ate* (動詞字尾)》

```
de    + pur  + ate
 |        |      |
intensive + pure +  v.
```

deprave[7] 〔 dɪ'prev 〕 *v.* 使墮落;使腐敗

《*de-* (down) + *prave* (crooked)》

derelict[7] 〔'dɛrə,lɪkt 〕 *adj.* 被拋棄的;不負責的;怠忽職守的

n. 遺棄物;社會棄兒;無家可歸的窮人;疏忽職守者

《*de-* (down) + *relict* (relinquish 放棄)》

desiccate[7] 〔'dɛsə,ket 〕 *v.* 使乾燥;使脫水;使(感情或智力)枯竭

《*de-* (intensive) + *sicc* (dry) + *-ate* (動詞字尾)》

despise[5] 〔 dɪ'spaɪz 〕 *v.* 輕視;蔑視(往下看)

《*de-* (down) + *spise* (look)》

despoil[7] 〔 dɪ'spɔɪl 〕 *v.* 奪取;掠奪(奪走)

《*de-* (away) + *spoil* (strip 剝奪)》

detail[3] 〔 *v.* dɪ'tel *n.* 'ditel 〕 *v.* 詳述 *n.* 細節(切得很細)

《*de-* (fully) + *tail* (cut)》 *cf.* **tailor** (縫製;裁縫)

detain[6] 〔 dɪ'ten 〕 *v.* 拘留;扣押;使延遲(保持隔離)

《*de-* (from;away) + *tain* (hold)》

```
de      + tain
 |          |
from , away + hold
```

dethrone[7]〔dɪ'θron〕v. 廢黜（王）；推翻（退位）

《*de-*（down）+ *throne*（王位）》

devastate[7]〔'dɛvəs,tet〕v. 使荒廢；毀滅（變成完全的荒地）

《*de-*（fully）+ *vast*（waste）+ *-ate*（動詞字尾）》

devour[5]〔dɪ'vaur〕v. 吞食；毀滅；貪婪地看（盡量吃）

《*de-*（fully）+ *vour*（eat）》

29　de- = apart；away；from

＊表示「分離、除去」的意思。為字首 dis- 的變化型。

debark[7]〔dɪ'bɑrk〕v. 登陸（離開船）《*de-* = *dis-*（apart）+ *bark*（ship）》

cf. **bark**（帆船），**barque**（船），**barge**（平底載貨船）

debauch[7]〔dɪ'bɔtʃ〕v. 使誤入歧途《*de-* = *dis-*（away）+ *bauch*（beam）》

debouch〔dɪ'buʃ〕v. 出發；流出；出現

《*de-* = *dis-*（away）+ *bouch*（move）》

decamp[7]〔dɪ'kæmp〕v. 秘密而匆忙地移居；逃亡；撤營

（離開戰場）《*de-* = *dis-*（apart）+ *camp*（field）》

decode[7]〔di'kod〕v. 譯解

《*de-* = *dis-*（apart）+ *code*（密碼）》　*cf.* **encode**（譯為密碼）

decorticate[7]〔di'kɔrtə,ket〕v. 除去外皮

《*de-* = *dis-*（from）+ *cortic*（bark 樹皮）+ *-ate*（動詞字尾）》

```
de  + cortic + ate
 |      |       |
from + bark  + v.
```

deface[7]〔dɪ'fes〕v. 損壞（外表或美觀）；塗掉；註銷

《*de-* = *dis-*（apart）+ *face*（face）》

defalcate〔dɪ'fælket〕v. 盜用公款

《*de-* = *dis-*（apart）+ *falc*（sickle 鐮刀）+ *-ate*（動詞字尾）》

```
de  + falc   + ate
 |      |       |
apart + sickle + v.
```

defer[7] 〔 dɪˈfɝ 〕 *v.* 延緩；延期 《*de-* = *dis-* (apart) + *fer* (carry)》

deficit[7] 〔ˈdɛfəsɪt 〕 *n.* 不足額；赤字
　《*de-* = *dis-* (apart) + *fic* (do) + *-it* (名詞字尾)》

defraud[7] 〔 dɪˈfrɔd 〕 *v.* 詐取 《*de-* = *dis-* (from) + *fraud* (cheat)》

defrost[7] 〔 diˈfrɔst 〕 *v.* 去冰或霜 (分開霜)
　《*de-* = *dis-* (apart) + *frost* (霜)》

defy[7] 〔 dɪˈfaɪ 〕 *v.* 不服從；公然反抗 (遠離信賴)
　《*de-* = *dis-* (apart) + *fy* (trust)》

dehydrate[7] 〔 diˈhaɪdret 〕 *v.* 脫水
　《*de-* = *dis-* (apart) + *hydr(o)* (water) + *-ate* (動詞字尾)》
　cf. **hydrogen** (氫)

```
de  +  hydr  +  ate
 |        |      |
apart + water +  v.
```

demur[7] 〔 dɪˈmɝ 〕 *v.* 躊躇；猶豫 《*de-* = *dis-* (from) + *mur* (delay)》

denude 〔 dɪˈnjud , -ˈnud 〕 *v.* 使裸露；剝奪 (使裸露)
　《*de-* = *dis-* (apart) + *nude* (uncovered)》

derange[7] 〔 dɪˈrendʒ 〕 *v.* 使錯亂；擾亂
　《*de-* = *dis-* (apart) + *range* (order)》

descant 〔 dɛsˈkænt 〕 *v.* 詳述　*n.* 詳述；伴唱 (唱出來)
　《*des-* = *dis-* (apart) + *cant* (sing)》

```
des  +  cant
 |       |
apart + sing
```

detach[6] 〔 dɪˈtætʃ 〕 *v.* 解開；分離；派遣 (拴的相反)
　《*de-* = *dis-* (opposite 否定) + *tach* (stake 拴)》

detour[7] 〔ˈditʊr , dɪˈtʊr 〕 *n.* 改道；繞道　*v.* 繞道而行 (分離；迴轉)
　《*de-* = *dis-* (apart) + *tour* (turn)》

devoid[7] 〔 dɪˈvɔɪd 〕 *adj.* 缺乏的；沒有的；空的；無的
　《*de-* = *dis-* (from) + *void* (empty)》

devote[4] 〔 dɪˈvot 〕 *v.* 專心從事；獻身於；致力於；奉獻
　《*de-* = *dis-* (from) + *vote* (vow)》

30　**deca-** = ten

> * 希臘文 *deka*，拉丁文 *decem*，表示「十」。而 deci- 是表示「十分之一」的意思。

decade[3]〔'dɛked , dɛk'ed 〕= a company of ten
　n. 十年；由十所構成的一組

decagon〔'dɛkə͵gɑn , -gən 〕*n.* 十角型；十邊形
　《*deca-* (ten) + *gon* (angle)》

decalogue〔'dɛkə͵lɔg , -͵lɑg 〕= the Ten Commandments
　n. 十誡《*deca-* (ten) + *logue* (speech)》

```
deca + logue
  |      |
 ten  + speech
```

decameron〔 dɪ'kæmərən 〕*n.* 十日談（義大利 Boccaccio 所著，包括一百個故事）《*deca-* (ten) + *meron* (day)》

decapod〔'dɛkə͵pɑd 〕*n.* 十腳類動物（如龍蝦等）
　《*deca-* (ten) + *pod* (foot)》

```
deca + pod
  |     |
 ten  + foot
```

December[1]〔 dɪ'sɛmbɚ 〕*n.* 十二月

　【解說】凱撒之前的羅馬曆是以三月（March）為始，共有十個月。當時的十月稱為 **December**。後來雖加上一月（January）、二月（February）而成十二個月，但其餘各月的名稱並沒有改變，只是往後順延二個月，乃稱十二月為 **December**，其餘以此類推：October（八月→十月）。

decigram〔'dɛsə͵græm 〕*n.* 公釐（十分之一公克）
　《*deci-* (tenth) + *gram* (公克)》

deciliter ; -tre〔'dɛsə͵litɚ 〕*n.* 公合（十分之一公升）
　《*deci-* (tenth) + *liter* ; *-tre* (公升)》

decimal[7] 〔'dɛsəml̩ 〕*n.*, *adj.* 十進制（的）；小數（的）
《*decim-*（ tithe 十分之一）+ *-al*（形容詞字尾)》
cf. **decimal point**（小數點）

decimeter〔'dɛsə,mitə 〕= 1/10 meter = 10 cm　*n.* 公寸
（十分之一公尺）

31　demi- = half

* 在古法文中 *demi* 就代表「一半」的意思。

demigod[7]〔'dɛmə,gɑd 〕*n.* 半神半人（神和人所生的後代）

demilune〔'dɛmɪ,lun 〕*n.* 新月；新月形堡壘；（唾液腺中之）半鉤月形粒狀體　*adj.* 半月狀的

demitasse〔'dɛmə,tæs , -,tɑs 〕*n.* （餐後用的）小咖啡杯；一小杯黑咖啡《*demi-*（ half ）+ *tasse*（ cup)》

demivolt〔'dɛmɪ,volt 〕*n.* （騎馬時的）半騰空轉彎

32　di- , diplo- = double ; twice

* 希臘文 *dis*，表示「雙」、「二倍」；*diploos*（= *double*）是由 *di-* + *-ploos*（ *-fold*）而來的。

dichromatic〔,daɪkro'mætɪk 〕*adj.* 二色的
《*di-*（ double ）+ *chromat*（ color ）+ *-ic*（形容詞字尾)》

dilemma[6]〔 də'lɛmə , daɪ- 〕*n.* 左右爲難的情況（在兩項假設之間）
《*di-*（ double ）+ *lemma*（ assumption)》

dioxide[7]〔 daɪ'ɑksaɪd , -ɪd 〕*n.* 二氧化物
《*di-*（ double ）+ *oxide*（氧化物)》

diphthong[7]〔'dɪfθɔŋ 〕*n.* 雙母音（如 au 等)
《*di-*（ double ）+ *phthong*（ sound)》

diplegia〔 daɪ'plidʒɪə 〕*n.* 兩側麻痹；兩側癱瘓
《*di-*（ double ）+ *pleg*（ stroke 中風 ）+ *-ia*（表示病症的字尾)》

diploblastic 〔͵dɪploˈblæstɪk 〕 *adj.* 雙胚層的
《*diplo-* (double) + *blast* (bud) + *-ic* (形容詞字尾)》

diplococcus 〔͵dɪploˈkɑkəs 〕 *n.* 雙球菌
《*diplo-* (double) + *coccus* (球菌)》

diploid 〔ˈdɪplɔɪd 〕 *adj.* 倍數的；具兩套染色體的　 *n.* 具兩套染色體之細胞

diploma[4] 〔 dɪˈplomə 〕 = paper folded double　 *n.* 文憑；畢業證書；獎狀 (對折的紙)《*di-* (double) + *plo* (fold) + *-ma* (名詞字尾)》

【解說】 高中以下的畢業學位，不能叫作 **degree**，要用 **diploma** 這個字。

33　**dia-** = across ; between ; through

　　* 希臘文 *dia*，和 di- 有密切關係，表示「穿越」、「在兩者之間」的意思。

diacritical[7] 〔͵daɪəˈkrɪtɪk!〕 *adj.* 區別的 (分隔兩者的)
《*dia-* (between) + *crit* (separate) + *-ical* (形容詞字尾)》

diagnosis[6] 〔͵daɪəgˈnosɪs 〕 *n.* 診斷 (知道兩者的不同)
《*dia-* (between) + *gnosis* (knowledge)》　 *cf.* **ignorant** (無知的)

diagonal[7] 〔 daɪˈægən!〕 *adj.* 斜的　 *n.* 對角線
《*dia-* (through ; across) + *gon* (angle) + *-al* (形容詞字尾)》

dia	+ gon + al
through , across	+ *angle* + *adj.*

diagram[6] 〔ˈdaɪə͵græm 〕 *n.* 圖樣；圖表
《*dia-* (through) + *gram* (write)》

dialect[5] 〔ˈdaɪəlɛkt 〕 *n.* 方言；同語系的語言 (特別選用的言詞)
《*dia-* (between) + *lect* (choose)》

dialog(ue)[3] 〔ˈdaɪə͵lɔg 〕 *n.* 對話 (兩人之間的話)
《*dia-* (between) + *logue* (speech)》　 *cf.* **monolog(ue)** (獨白)

diameter[6] 〔 daɪˈæmətɚ 〕 *n.* 直徑 (直接測量)
《*dia-* (through) + *meter* (measure)》

diaphanous[7]〔daɪˈæfənəs〕*adj.* 透明的

```
dia   + phan + ous
 |       |      |
through + show + adj.
```

diatribe[7]〔ˈdaɪəˌtraɪb〕*n.* 痛責；猛烈的抨擊；譴責（摩擦使產生衝突）《*dia-*（between）+ *tribe*（rub）》

34　dicho- = in two

　* 希臘文 *dikha*，表示「成兩半」、「對分」的意思。
　〔變化型〕dich-。

dichasium〔daɪˈkezɪəm〕*n.*【植物】二歧聚傘花序

dichogamy〔daɪˈkɑgəmɪ〕*n.* 雌雄蕊異時成熟

dichotomy[7]〔daɪˈkɑtəmɪ〕*n.* 分裂；二分法；叉狀分枝；弦月
　《*dicho-*（in two）+ *tom*（cut）+ *-y*（名詞字尾）》

dichotomous〔daɪˈkɑtəməs〕*adj.* 分成兩個的；叉狀分枝的

35　dis- = apart；away；not

　* dis-是由拉丁文 duo = two 的變化形 duis 衍生而來的，原本是
　「一分爲二」的意思，乃是由「分離」引申爲「除去」、「剝
　奪」、「反對」、「否定」，尤其是加強語氣的重要字首。
　〔變化型〕de-, des-, di-, dif-, s-。

disable[6]〔dɪsˈebl̩〕*v.* 使無能力；使殘廢（剝奪能力）
　《*dis-*（deprive of 剝奪）+ *able*（capability）》

```
dis    + able
 |        |
deprive of + ability
```

disadvantage[4]〔ˌdɪsədˈvæntɪdʒ〕*n.* 不利；缺點；損失
　《*dis-*（negative 否定）+ *advantage*（利益；優點）》

disagree[2] 〔͵dɪsə'gri 〕 v. 意見不合；不一致；不符合

　《*dis-* (not) + *agree* (同意；符合)》

disallow[7] 〔͵dɪsə'laʊ 〕 v. 不允許；拒絕

disannul 〔͵dɪsə'nʌl 〕 v. 取消；廢棄 (使無)

　《*dis-* (intensive) + *an-* = *ad-* (to) + *nul* (nothing)》

```
   dis    + an +   nul
    |        |      |
intensive + to + nothing
```

disappear[2] 〔͵dɪsə'pɪr 〕 v. 不見；消失

　《*dis-* (not) + *ap-* = *ad-* (to) + *pear* (come forth)》

disapprove[6] 〔͵dɪsə'pruv 〕 v. 不贊成；反對 (不願向～證明)

　《*dis-* (not) + *ap-* = *ad-* (to) + *prove* (prove)》

```
   dis    + ap + prove
    |        |      |
intensive + to + prove
```

disarray[7] 〔͵dɪsə're 〕 v., n. 紊亂；無秩序 《*dis-* (not) + *array* (排列)》

disaster[4] 〔 dɪz'æstɚ 〕 n. 災禍；不幸

```
dis + aster
 |      |
not + star
```

disavow[7] 〔͵dɪsə'vaʊ 〕 v. 不承認；否認；拒絕接受

　《*dis-* (not) + *a-* = *ad-* (to) + *vow* (call)》

disband[7] 〔 dɪs'bænd 〕 v. 解散 (軍隊) (把團體分散)

　《*dis-* (apart) + *band* (band together)》

disbelieve[7] 〔͵dɪsbə'liv 〕 v. 不相信 《*dis-* (negative) + *believe*》

discard[5] 〔 v. dɪs'kɑrd　n. 'dɪskɑrd 〕 v. 拋棄；丟掉　　n. 被棄的人

　或物 (擲出無用的紙牌) 《*dis-* (apart) + *card* (paper)》

discern[7] 〔 dɪ'zɝn , -'sɝn 〕 v. 辨別；認出 (一個一個分開)

　《*dis-* (apart) + *cern* (separate)》

discolor[7] 〔 dɪs'kʌlɚ 〕 v. 使變色 《*dis-* (away) + *color* (為～著色)》

disconsolate[7] 〔 dɪs'kɑnsl̩ɪt 〕 *adj.* 哀傷的；憂鬱的（不能安慰的）

　　《*dis-* (not) + *consol* (console 安慰) + *-ate* (形容詞字尾)》

```
dis  +  consol  + ate
 |        |        |
not  +  console  + adj.
```

discontent[7] 〔 ˌdɪskən'tɛnt 〕 *adj.* 不滿意的

　　《*dis-* (not) + *con-* (together) + *tent* (hold)》

discontinue[7] 〔 ˌdɪskən'tɪnjʊ 〕 *v.* 中止；停止（不持續）

　　《*dis-* (not) + *con-* = *com-* (wholly) + *tinue* (hold)》

```
dis  +  con   + tinue
 |       |       |
not  + wholly + hold
```

discord[7] 〔 *v.* dɪs'kɔrd　*n.* 'dɪskɔrd 〕 *v.* 不一致；不合　*n.* 不一致；
意見不合（心離開了）《*dis-* (apart) + *cord* (heart)》

cf. **concord** (和諧)

discourage[4] 〔 dɪs'kɝɪdʒ 〕 *v.* 使氣餒；使沮喪；使打消念頭
（剝奪勇氣）《*dis-* (deprive of) + *courage* (勇氣)》

discourse[7] 〔 dɪ'skors 〕 = run about　*n.* 談話；論述；演講
v. 談論；演講（在話題間流連）《*dis-* (apart) + *course* (run)》

```
dis  + course
 |       |
apart +  run
```

discredit[7] 〔 dɪs'krɛdɪt 〕 *v.* 懷疑

```
dis  + credit
 |       |
not  + believe
```

discreet[6] 〔 dɪ'skrit 〕 *adj.* 言行謹慎的；小心的（一個個分開）

　　《*dis-* (apart) + *creet* (separate)》

discrepancy[7] 〔 dɪ'skrɛpənsɪ 〕 *n.* 矛盾；不一致；不符（意見分歧）

　　《*dis-* (apart) + *crep* (crack) + *-ancy* (名詞字尾)》

discrete[7] 〔 dɪ'skrit 〕 *adj.* 個別的；不連續的（個別分開）

《*dis-*（apart）+ *crete*（separate）》

discriminate[5] 〔 dɪ'skrɪmə,net 〕 *v.* 歧視；區別待遇（在～之間

造成空間）《*dis-*（apart）+ *crimin*（space）+ *-ate*（動詞字尾）》

```
dis  +  crimin  +  ate
 |         |        |
apart  +  space  +  v.
```

disease[3] 〔 dɪ'ziz 〕 *n.* 疾病（離開安樂）《*dis-*（apart）+ *ease*》

disembark[7] 〔,dɪsɪm'bɑrk 〕 *v.* 卸貨；登陸；下船（不在船上）

《*dis-*（not）+ *em-* = *in-*（in）+ *bark*（ship）》

disembogue 〔,dɪsɛm'bog 〕 *v.* 注入；流入

《*dis-*（apart）+ *em-*（in）+ *bogue*（mouth）》

```
dis  +  em  +  bogue
 |       |       |
apart  +  in  +  mouth
```

disenchant[7] 〔,dɪsɪn'tʃænt 〕 *v.* 使醒悟；使不再著迷

《*dis-*（apart）+ *enchant*（bewitch）》

disfavor[7] 〔 dɪs'fevɚ 〕 *n.* 不贊成；討厭；失寵《*dis-*（not）+ *favor*》

disfigure[7] 〔 dɪs'fɪgjɚ 〕 = deform   *v.* 破壞（美觀、形狀、價值等）

《*dis-*（apart；away）+ *figure*（form）》

disfranchise[7] 〔 dɪs'fræntʃaɪz 〕 *v.* 褫奪公權

《*dis-*（deprive of）+ *franchise*（公民權）》   *cf.* **enfranchise**（給與公民權）

disgorge[7] 〔 dɪs'gɔrdʒ 〕 *v.* 吐出；流出；（河川把水）注入

（從喉嚨中噴出）《*dis-*（apart）+ *gorge*（throat）》

```
dis  +  gorge
 |        |
apart  +  throat
```

disguise[4] 〔 dɪs'gaɪz 〕 *v.*, *n.* 改裝；假扮；偽裝（改變做法）

《*dis-*（apart）+ *guise*（manner；fashion）》

disgust[4] 〔 dɪs'gʌst 〕 *n.*, *v.* 厭惡；使嫌惡（不能品味）

《*dis-*（apart）+ *gust*（taste）》   *cf.* **gust**（味；風味）

dishearten[7] 〔 dɪs'hɑrtn̩ 〕 v. 使沮喪；使氣餒 (心碎)

《 *dis-* (apart) + *heart* (heart) + *-en* (動詞字尾)》

dishevel[7] 〔 dɪ'ʃɛvl̩ 〕 v. 使 (髮等) 散亂《 *di(s)-* (apart) + *shevel* (hair)》

dishonest[2] 〔 dɪs'ɑnɪst 〕 adj. 不誠實的《 *dis-* (not) + *honest* (honor)》

disillusion[7] 〔 ˌdɪsɪ'luʒən 〕 v. 使幻想破滅

《 *dis-* (apart) + *illusion* (幻想)》

disincline[7] 〔 ˌdɪsɪn'klaɪn 〕 v. 使厭惡；使不感興趣 (不向～方向彎曲)

《 *dis-* (not) + *in-* (towards) + *cline* (bend)》

disintegrate[7] 〔 dɪs'ɪntəˌgret 〕 v. (使) 崩潰；(使) 分解；(使)

瓦解 (使不完整)《 *dis-* (not) + *integr* (whole) + *-ate* (動詞字尾)》

```
dis  +  in  +  tegr  + ate
 |       |      |        |
not  +  not  + touch  +  v.
```

dislodge[7] 〔 dɪs'lɑdʒ 〕 v. 驅逐；逐出《 *dis-* (apart) + *lodge* (暫住)》

dismay[6] 〔 dɪs'me 〕 n. 驚慌；絕望 v. 使驚慌；使絕望；使氣餒

《 *dis-* (intensive) + *may* (frighten)》

dismember[7] 〔 dɪs'mɛmbɚ 〕 v. 割斷四肢；使四分五裂 (把四肢個

別分開)《 *dis-* (apart) + *member* (limb 四肢)》

dismiss[4] 〔 dɪs'mɪs 〕 = send away v. 解散；使告退；開除

《 *dis-* (away) + *miss* (send)》

cf. **missile** (投射出的武器，如飛彈、火箭等)

disparate[7] 〔 'dɪspərɪt 〕 adj. 不同的

```
dis  +  par  + ate
 |       |       |
not  + equal  + adj.
```

dispersion[7] 〔 dɪ'spɝʃən , -ʒən 〕 n. 散佈；分散；離散

《 *dis-* (apart) + *(s)pers* (scatter) + *-ion* (名詞字尾)》

```
dis  + (s)pers + ion
 |       |        |
apart + scatter +  n.
```

displace[6] 〔 dɪs'ples 〕*v.* 取代;移動;免職;撤換(使喪失位置)
《*dis-* (deprive of) + *place* (place)》

display[2] 〔 dɪ'sple 〕*v. , n.* 展示;展覽;陳列(將重疊的東西伸展開
來使能看到)《*dis-* (apart) + *play* (fold)》

dispose[5] 〔 dɪ'spoz 〕*v.* 排列;陳列;處置(個別放置)
《*dis-* (apart) + *pose* (place)》

disregard[6] 〔͵dɪsrɪ'gɑrd 〕*v. , n.* 忽視;不理(不再看一眼)
《*dis-* (not) + *re-* (again) + *gard* = *guard* (watch)》

dis	+	re	+	gard
not	+	again	+	watch

disrupt[7] 〔 dɪs'rʌpt 〕*v.* 使分裂;使中斷(破裂分離)
《*dis-* (apart) + *rupt* (break ; brust)》

dissect[7] 〔 dɪ'sɛkt 〕*v.* 解剖;分析

dis	+	sect
away	+	cut

dissent[7] 〔 dɪ'sɛnt 〕*v.* 不同意《*dis-* (away) + *sent* (think)》

dissipate[7] 〔'dɪsə͵pet 〕*v.* 驅散;揮霍(丟開來)
《*dis-* (apart) + *sip* (throw) + *-ate* (動詞字尾)》

dis	+	sip	+	ate
apart	+	throw	+	v.

dissolve[6] 〔 dɪ'zɑlv 〕*v.* 溶解;解散;解除(放鬆成為個體)
《*dis-* (apart) + *solve* (loosen)》

distract[6] 〔 dɪ'strækt 〕*v.* 分心;轉移(意向);困擾(拉開)
《*dis-* (apart) + *tract* (draw)》

distribute[4] 〔 dɪ'strɪbjut 〕*v.* 分配;分發;散布(個別給予)
《*dis-* (apart) + *tribute* (give)》

despatch[7] 〔 dɪ'spætʃ 〕*v. , n.* 派遣;速辦(= *dispatch*)(急忙搬
運事物)《*des-* = *dis-* (intensive) + *patch* (hasten)》

dessert[2] 〔 dɪ'zɝt 〕 *n.* 餐後的甜點（最後的食物）

《*des-* = *dis-* (apart ; away) + *sert* (serve)》

digest[4] 〔 *v.* də'dʒɛst , daɪ- *n.* 'daɪdʒɛst 〕 *v.* 消化；了解；領悟
n. 摘要；分類（整齊地分開、運送）

《*di-* = *dis-* (apart) + *gest* (carry)》

dilapidate[7] 〔 də'læpə,det 〕 *v.* (使) 荒廢；(使) 破損（石頭四散）

《*di-* = *dis-* (apart) + *lapid* (stone) + *-ate* (動詞字尾)》

```
di  + lapid + ate
|      |      |
apart + stone + v.
```

dilute[7] 〔 dɪ'lut , daɪ- 〕 *v.* 沖淡；稀釋　*adj.* 淡的；稀薄的（沖淡）

《*di-* = *dis-* (apart) + *lute* (wash)》

dimension[6] 〔 də'mɛnʃən 〕 *n.* 尺寸（長、寬、高）；規模；次元

《*di-* = *dis-* (apart) + *mension* (measure)》

diminish[6] 〔 də'mɪnɪʃ 〕 *v.* 減少；縮小（使變小）

《*di-* = *dis-* (intensive) + *mini* (small) + *-sh* (動詞字尾)》

differ[4] 〔'dɪfɚ 〕 *v.* 相異；不同；意見不合（個別搬運）

《*dif-* = *dis-* (apart) + *fer* (carry)》

difficult[1] 〔'dɪfəkl̩t 〕 *adj.* 困難的（不容易）

《*dif-* = *dis-* (apart) + *ficult* (easy)》

cf. **facile** (輕而易舉的)，**facilitate** (使容易)

diffident[7] 〔'dɪfədənt 〕 *adj.* 羞怯的；缺乏自信的；謙虛的（對自己
不信賴 ）《*dif-* = *dis-* (apart) + *fid* (trust) + *-ent* (形容詞字尾)》

```
dif  + fid + ent
|      |     |
apart + trust + adj.
```

diffuse[7] 〔 dɪ'fjuz 〕 *v.* 流布；傳播；散布（注入各處）

《*dif-* = *dis-* (apart) + *fuse* (pour)》

diverge[7] 〔 də'vɝdʒ , daɪ- 〕 *v.* 分歧；差異（傾斜分開）

《*di-* = *dis-* (apart) + *verge* (bend)》

diverse[6] 〔 dəˈvɝs 〕 *adj.* 多種的；不同的

```
di  +  verse
|       |
away + turn
```

divert[6] 〔 dəˈvɝt 〕 *v.* 轉移；娛樂

spend[1] 〔 spɛnd 〕 *v.* 花用；耗費（一點點分開放在秤上量）
　《*s-* (dis- 的簡型) + *pend* (weigh)》

stain[5] 〔 sten 〕 *v.* 污染　*n.* 污點（脫離了本來的顏色）
　《*s-* (dis- 的簡型) + *tain* (dye 染色)》

字首 deca-~e-

36　**duo-** = double ; two

　* 〔變化型〕do- , dou- , du- 。

duodecimal〔ˌdjuəˈdɛsəml̩ , ˌduə- 〕 *adj.* 十二進位法的
　n. 十二進位法《*duo-* (two) + *decimal* (十進位)》

duologue〔ˈdjuəˌlɔg 〕 *n.* 對話；（限於兩人之）對話劇
　《*duo-* (two) + *logue* (speech)》

dodecagon〔 doˈdɛkəˌgɑn , -gən 〕 *n.* 十二角形；十二邊形
　《*do-* = *duo-* (two) + *deca-* (ten) + *gon* (angle)》

```
do  +  deca  +  gon
|       |        |
two +  ten  +  angle
```

dozen[4] 〔ˈdʌzn̩ 〕 *n.* 一打；十二個《*do-* = *duo-* (two) + *zen* (ten)》

double[2] 〔ˈdʌbl̩ 〕 *adj.* 雙重的　*adv.* 加倍地　*n.* 二倍　*v.* 使加倍
　《*dou-* = *duo-* (two) + *ble* (fold)》

doubt[2] 〔 daʊt 〕 *v.* 懷疑；猶疑　*n.* 懷疑（有兩種想法）

dual[6] 〔ˈdjuəl , ˈduəl 〕 *adj.* 二重的；兩層的
　《*du-* = *duo-* (two) + *-al* (形容詞字尾)》

dubious[6] 〔ˈdjubɪəs , ˈdu- 〕 = moving in two directions
　adj. 懷疑的；可疑的；曖昧不明的（向兩個方向行動）

duel[7] 〔ˈdjuəl 〕= a combat between two　*n.*, *v.* 決鬥

duet(t)[7] 〔 djuˈɛt , du- 〕= a piece of music for two
n. 二部合唱；二重奏

duplex[7] 〔ˈdjuplɛks , ˈdu- 〕*adj.* 雙重的；二倍的
《*du-* = *duo-* (two) + *plex* (fold)》

du	+	plex
|		|
two	+	*fold*

duplicate[7] 〔ˈdjupləkɪt 〕*adj.* 完全相同的；複製的（雙重）
《*du-* = *duo-* (two) + *plic* (fold) + *-ate* (形容詞字尾)》

du	+	plic	+	ate
|		|		|
two	+	*fold*	+	*adj.*

duplicity[7] 〔 djuˈplɪsətɪ 〕*n.* 口是心非；不誠實；欺騙
《*du-* = *duo-* (two) + *plic* (fold) + *-ity* (名詞字尾)》

37　**dys-** = bad

dyscalculia 〔ˌdɪskælˈkjulɪə 〕*n.* (腦傷或疾病所致的) 計算障礙
《*dys-* (bad) + *calcul*(*ate*) (計算) + *-ia* (表示病症的字尾)》

dyschronous 〔ˈdɪskrənəs 〕*adj.* 不合時的
《*dys-* (bad) + *chron* (time) + *-ous* (形容詞字尾)》

dysfunction[7] 〔 dɪsˈfʌŋkʃən 〕*n.* (身體器官的) 機能障礙
《*dys-* (bad) + *function* (功能)》

dysgenics 〔 dɪsˈdʒɛnɪks 〕*n.* 劣生學；種族退化學
《*dys-* (bad) + *gen* (bear) + *-ics* (表示學問的字尾)》

dysgraphia 〔 dɪsˈgræfɪə 〕*n.* (大腦受傷等引起的) 書寫困難
《*dys-* (bad) + *graph* (write) + *-ia* (表示病症的字尾)》

dyslexia[7] 〔 dɪsˈlɛksɪə 〕*n.* 誦讀困難
《*dys-* (bad) + *lex* (speech) + *-ia* (表示病症的字尾)》

dysmenorrhea 〔ˌdɪsmɛnəˈriə 〕 *n.* 痛經
　《*dys-* (bad) + *meno* (month) + *rrhea* (flow)》

dyspepsia 〔 dɪˈspɛpʃə 〕 *n.* 消化不良 (= *indigestion*)
　《*dys-* (bad) + *peps* (digest) + *-ia* (表示病症的字尾)》

dysphasia 〔 dɪsˈfeʒə , -ʒɪə 〕 *n.* 言語困難
　《*dys-* (bad) + *phas* (speak) + *-ia* (表示病症的字尾)》

dystopia[7] 〔 dɪsˈtopɪə 〕 *n.* (想像的) 反烏托邦；悲慘的社會
　《*dys-* (bad) + *(u)topia* (烏托邦；夢想的社會)》

dystrophy 〔ˈdɪstrəfɪ 〕 *n.* 營養不良；營養障礙
　《*dys-* (bad) + *troph* (nourish) + *-y* (名詞字尾)》

dysuria 〔 dɪsˈjʊrɪə 〕 *n.* 排尿困難；排尿疼痛
　《*dys-* (bad) + *ur* (urine 尿) + *-ia* (表示病症的字尾)》

38　e-

* 這個字首沒有特別的意義，只是為了聲音的考量，而加在 s 音
之前。

escalade[7] 〔ˌɛskəˈled 〕 *v.* 用梯攀登 (城牆)　　*n.* 雲梯攻城法
　《*scale* = ladder》

escort[5] 〔 *n.* ˈɛskɔrt *v.* ɪˈskɔrt 〕 *n.* 護送者；護衛隊　　*v.* 護送；護航
　《*scort* = guide》

especial[7] 〔 əˈspɛʃəl 〕 *adj.* 特別的；特殊的

espouse[7] 〔 ɪˈspaʊz 〕 *v.* 嫁；娶；採取；贊助《*a spouse* = a wife》

espy[7] 〔 əˈspaɪ 〕 *v.* 看出；探出

Esquire[7] 〔 əˈskwaɪr 〕 = a gentleman　　*n.* 先生 (放在男人姓名後的
尊稱)

establish[4] 〔 əˈstæblɪʃ 〕 *v.* 建立；設立；證實
　《*e-* + *stabli* (firm) + *-sh* (動詞字尾)》

estrange[7] 〔 əˈstrendʒ 〕 *v.* 使疏遠；遠離《*e-* + *strange* (foreign)》

evaporate[7] 〔 ɪˈvæpəˌret 〕 *v.* 蒸發；消失；使脫水
　《*e-* + *vapor* (steam) + *-ate* (動詞字尾)》

39 ecto- = outside

ectoblast〔'εktə‚blæst〕*n.* 外胚層；外膜
《*ecto-*（outside）+ *blast*（bud）》

ectoparasite〔‚εktə'pærə‚saɪt〕*n.* 體表寄生蟲；外寄生物
《*ecto-*（outside）+ *parasite*（寄生蟲）》

ectoplasm〔'εktə‚plæzəm〕*n.* 細胞膜
《*ecto-*（outside）+ *plasm*（form）》

40 en- = at ; in ; into ; near ; on

* 從「在中間」之意演變成「進入某種狀態，使成為～」等，把表
示 make 之意的名詞、形容詞變為及物動詞。〔變化型〕el- , em-。

enact[6]〔ɪn'ækt〕*v.* 制定為法律（做法律）《*act* 法令》

enamo(u)r[7]〔ɪn'æmɚ〕*v.* 使喜愛；迷住
《*en-*（in）+ *amour*（love）》

encase[7]〔ɪn'kes , εn'kes〕= put into a case *v.* 裝於箱；包圍

enchase[7]〔εn'tʃes〕*v.* 鑲嵌《*en-*（in）+ *chase*（frame）》

```
en + chase
 |     |
in  + frame
```

enclose[4]〔ɪn'kloz〕= close in *v.* 圍繞；附寄；包含

encompass[7]〔ɪn'kʌmpəs〕*v.* 圍繞；包圍；包含（完全進入）
《*en-*（in）+ *com-*（wholly）+ *pass*（pass）》

```
en +  com  + pass
 |     |      |
in + wholly + pass
```

encounter[4]〔ɪn'kaʊntɚ〕*v. , n.* 對抗；遭遇（進入衝突狀態）
《*en-*（in）+ *counter-* = *contra-*（against）》

encourage[2]〔ɪn'kɝɪdʒ〕= give courage to *v.* 鼓勵；促進；助長

encroach[7] 〔 ɪn'krotʃ 〕 *v.* 侵佔；侵略；侵蝕

《*en-* (in) + *croach* (hook)》

encumber[7] 〔 ɪn'kʌmbɚ , ɛn- 〕 *v.* 妨害；阻礙 (加入障礙物)

《*en-* (in) + *cumber* (obstacle)》　*cf.* **cumber** (阻礙)

endeavo(u)r[5] 〔 ɪn'dɛvɚ 〕 *v.* , *n.* 努力；竭力 (在本分中)

《*en-* (in) + *deavour* (duty)》

endorse[7] 〔 ɪn'dɔrs , ɛn- 〕 *v.* 簽名於 (票據等) 的背面；背書

(寫在背面) 《*en-* (put on) + *dorse* (back)》

energy[2] 〔'ɛnɚdʒɪ 〕 *n.* 精力；活力；能力；能量 (讓人能夠工作)

《*en-* (into) + *erg* (work) + *-y* (名詞字尾)》

```
en  +  erg  +  y
 |      |      |
into + work +  n.
```

enfold[7] 〔 ɪn'fold 〕 = enclose ; embrace　*v.* 包裹；擁抱

engage[3] 〔 ɪn'gedʒ 〕 *v.* 雇用；從事；訂婚；答應 (保證會去做)

《*en-* (in) + *gage* (pledge 保證)》

engorge[7] 〔 ɛn'gɔrdʒ 〕 *v.* 狼吞虎嚥 《*en-* (in) + *gorge* (throat)》

engrave[7] 〔 ɪn'grev 〕 *v.* 雕刻；銘記心上 (刻在內部)

《*en-* (in) + *grave* (cut)》

```
en  +  grave
 |       |
in  +   cut
```

engross[7] 〔 ɪn'gros 〕 *v.* 使全神貫注 《*en-* (in) + *gross* (large)》

enhance[6] 〔 ɪn'hæns 〕 *v.* 增加；提高 《*en-* (in) + *hance* (high)》

enjoin[7] 〔 ɪn'dʒɔɪn 〕 *v.* 吩咐；命令；要求 (使加入 → 使聽命)

《*en-* (in) + *join*》

enlarge[4] 〔 ɪn'lɑrdʒ 〕 = make large　*v.* 擴大；增加；擴充

enlighten[6] 〔 ɪn'laɪtn̩ 〕 = give light to　*v.* 啟迪；開導；教化

enlist[7] 〔 ɪn'lɪst 〕 = list in　*v.* (使) 入伍；協助；支持 (列入名單)

enliven[7] 〔 ɪn'laɪvən 〕 = make active　*v.* 使活潑；使有生氣

字首 ecto-~extra-

enrage[7]〔ɪn'redʒ, ɛn-〕*v.* 激怒；使暴怒（進入生氣之中）

《***rage*** 盛怒》

enrapture[7]〔ɪn'ræptʃɚ〕*v.* 使狂喜；使著迷

《***en-*** (in) + ***rapt*** (seize) + ***-ure*** (動詞字尾)》

en	+ rapt	+ ure
in	+ *seize*	+ *v.*

enrich[6]〔ɪn'rɪtʃ〕= make rich　*v.* 使富裕；使肥沃；充實

ensemble[7]〔ɑn'sɑmbl̩〕*n.* 全體《***en-*** (at) + ***semble*** (at the same time)》

enshrine[7]〔ɪn'ʃraɪn〕= put into a shrine　*v.* 奉祀；珍藏；銘記

enshroud[7]〔ɛn'ʃraʊd〕*v.* 掩蓋；遮蔽（放在衣服中）

《***en-*** (in) + ***shroud*** (garment)》

en	+ shroud
in	+ *garment*

enslave[7]〔ɪn'slev, ɛn-〕= make a slave to　*v.* 奴役

ensnare[7]〔ɛn'snɛr〕= put into a snare　*v.* 誘惑；陷害

entangle[7]〔ɪn'tæŋgl̩〕*v.* 使糾纏；牽連；使陷入

《***en-*** (intensive) + ***tangle*** (使糾纏)》

enthrall[7]〔ɪn'θrɔl〕*v.* 迷惑；迷住；奴役（使～成爲奴隸）

《***en-*** (intensive) + ***thrall*** (slave)》

en	+ thrall
intensive	+ *slave*

entitle[5]〔ɪn'taɪtl̩〕= give a title to

v. 定（著作或人的）名稱；使有資格

entomb[7]〔ɪn'tum〕= place in a tomb　*v.* 埋葬；安放墓中

entrench[7]〔ɪn'trɛntʃ〕= put into a trench

v. 以壕溝圍繞；堅持（主張等）；確立（慣例等）

entrust[7]〔ɪn'trʌst〕= give trust to　*v.* 委託；託付（信任）

envelop[7] 〔 ɪnˈvɛləp 〕= wrap in　*v.* 包裝；圍繞

《*en-* (in) + *velop* (wrap)》

envelope[2] 〔ˈɛnvəˌlop , ɪnˈvɛləp 〕*n.* 信封；封套；封袋

environment[2] 〔 ɪnˈvaɪrənmənt 〕*n.* 環境；周圍情況（環繞在周圍）

《*en-* (in) + *viron* (circuit 周圍) + *-ment* (名詞字尾)》

```
en  +  viron  +  ment
 |       |        |
in  +  circuit  +  n.
```

ellipsis[7] 〔 ɪˈlɪpsɪs 〕*n.* 省略法；省略符號

《*el-* = *en-* (in) + *lipsis* (leave)》

embank[7] 〔 ɪmˈbæŋk 〕*v.* 築堤；築（鐵路）的路基

embark[6] 〔 ɪmˈbɑrk 〕*v.* 乘船；搭載《*em-* = *en-* (in) + *bark* (ship)》

```
em  +  bark
 |      |
in  +  ship
```

embarrass[4] 〔 ɪmˈbærəs 〕*v.* 使困窘（干涉）《*bar* 阻塞》

embattle[7] 〔 ɛmˈbætl̩ 〕*v.* 備戰；設防《*em-* = *en-* (in) + *battle* (beat)》

embed[7] 〔 ɪmˈbɛd 〕= put in a bed　*v.* 埋入；深留（於內心）

embellish[7] 〔 ɪmˈbɛlɪʃ 〕*v.* 裝飾；布置（使成美好狀態）

《*em-* = *en-* (in) + *bell* (beautiful) + *-ish* (動詞字尾)》

```
em  +   bell    +  ish
 |       |          |
in  +  beautiful  +  v.
```

embezzle[7] 〔 ɪmˈbɛzl̩ 〕*v.* 盜用《*em-* = *en-* (in) + *bezzle* (destroy)》

emblem[7] 〔ˈɛmbləm 〕*n.* 象徵；標記；徽章

《*em-* = *en-* (in) + *blem* (throw)》

```
em  +  blem
 |      |
in  +  throw
```

embody[7] 〔 ɪmˈbɑdɪ 〕= make into a body　*v.* 使具體化

embrace[5] 〔 ɪmˈbres 〕 *v.*, *n.* 擁抱 (在雙臂之中)

　《*em-* = *en-* (in) + *brace* (two arms)》

　cf. **brace** (緊縛或支撐的東西)，**bracelet** (手鐲)

embroider[7] 〔 ɪmˈbrɔɪdɚ 〕 *v.* 刺繡；修飾

　《*em-* = *en-* (in) + *broider* (刺繡)》

emplace[7] 〔 ɛmˈples 〕 = put in position　*v.* 放置

empower[7] 〔 ɪmˈpaʊɚ 〕 = give power to　*v.* 授權給；使能

41　　**endo-** = within

endocarp 〔ˈɛndoˌkɑrp 〕 *n.* 內果皮 (指果皮的內層)

　《*endo-* (within) + *carp* (fruit)》

endocrine[7] 〔ˈɛndoˌkraɪn 〕 *adj.* 內分泌的　*n.* 內分泌腺；激素

　《*endo-* (within) + *crine* (separate)》

endoderm 〔ˈɛndoˌdɝm 〕 *n.* 內胚層 《*endo-* (within) + *derm* (skin)》

endogamy 〔 ɛnˈdɑgəmɪ 〕 *n.* 同族結婚

　《*endo-* (within) + *gamy* (marriage)》

endometrium 〔ˌɛndoˈmitrɪəm 〕 *n.* 子宮內膜

　《*endo-* (within) + *metr* (womb 子宮) + *-ium* (名詞字尾)》

endometritis 〔ˌɛndomɪˈtraɪtɪs 〕 *n.* 子宮內膜炎

　《*endo-* (within) + *metr* (womb 子宮) + *-itis* (表示發炎的字尾)》

endoscope 〔ˈɛndəˌskop 〕 *n.* 內視鏡；內診鏡

　《*endo-* (within) + *scope* (look)》

42　　**ennea-** = nine　　* 希臘文 *ennea*，表示「九」。

ennead 〔ˈɛnɪˌæd 〕 *n.* 九個一組

enneagon 〔ˈɛnɪəˌgɑn 〕 *n.* 九邊形；九角形

　《*ennea-* (nine) + *gon* (angle)》

enneahedron 〔ˌɛnɪəˈhidrən 〕 *n.* 九面體

　《*ennea-* (nine) + *hedr* (side) + *-on* (名詞字尾)》

43　ento- = within

entoblast 〔'ɛntə,blæst 〕 *n.* 內胚層

entocranial 〔,ɛntə'kreniəl 〕 *adj.* 顱內的
《*ento-* (within) + *crani* (skull 頭顱) + *-al* (形容詞字尾)》

entoderm 〔'ɛntə,dɝm 〕 *n.* 內胚層

entogastric 〔,ɛntə'gæstrɪk 〕 *adj.* 胃內的
《*ento-* (within) + *gastr* (stomach) + *-ic* (形容詞字尾)》

entozoic 〔,ɛntə'zoɪk 〕 *adj.* 內寄生的
《*ento-* (within) + *zo* (animal) + *-ic* (形容詞字尾)》

44　eo- = dawn (黎明；開始)

Eocene 〔'iə,sin 〕 *n.* 始新世　　*adj.* 始新世的
《*eo-* (dawn) + *cene* (new)》

eohippus 〔,io'hɪpəs 〕 *n.* 始祖馬　《*eo-* (dawn) + *hippus* (horse)》

eolith 〔'iə,lɪθ 〕 *n.* 原始石器　《*eo-* (dawn) + *lith* (stone)》

45　epi- = among ; besides ; to ; upon

＊表示「在～之上」或「在～之中」。〔變化型〕ep-。

epic[7] 〔'ɛpɪk 〕 *n.* , *adj.* 敘事詩 (的)　《*epi-* (upon) + *c* = *cus* (narrative)》

epicene[7] 〔'ɛpə,sin 〕 *adj.* 兼具兩性特徵的；通性的
《*epi-* (upon) + *cene* (common)》

epicenter[7] 〔'ɛpɪ,sɛntɚ 〕 *n.* 震源

epidemic[6] 〔,ɛpə'dɛmɪk 〕 *adj.* 傳染性的　　*n.* 流行性傳染病
《*epi-* (among) + *dem* (people) + *-ic* (形容詞字尾)》

epi	+	dem	+	ic
|		|		|
among	+	*people*	+	*adj.*

epigram[7] 〔ˈɛpəˌɡræm〕 *n.* 雋語;警句;諷刺短詩(加寫上去的東西)
　《*epi-* (upon) + *gram* (write)》

epigraph[7] 〔ˈɛpəˌɡræf, -ˌɡrɑf〕 *n.* 碑文;墓誌銘(碑上寫的東西)
　《*epi-* (upon) + *graph* (write)》

epilog(ue)[7] 〔ˈɛpəˌlɔɡ, -ˌlɑɡ〕 *n.* (文學作品的) 結語;(戲劇中的)
收場白《*epi-* (upon) + *logue* (speech)》　*cf.* **prolog(ue)** (開場白)

```
epi + logue
 |      |
upon + speech
```

Epiphany[7] 〔ɪˈpɪfənɪ〕 *n.* 主顯節(基督教紀念耶穌基督向世人顯現
的日子,時間爲每年的一月六日)《*epi-* (upon) + *phany* (show)》

episode[6] 〔ˈɛpəˌsod, -ˌzod〕 *n.* (人生、小說或詩歌中的) 插曲
(從旁邊插入的東西)《*epi-* (besides) + *sode* (coming in)》

epistle 〔ɪˈpɪsḷ〕 *n.* 書信 (尤指正式冗長而帶有教訓意味的信)
(被通知~的東西)《*epi-* (to) + *stle* (send)》

```
epi + stle
 |     |
to + send
```

epitaph[7] 〔ˈɛpəˌtæf〕 *n.* 墓誌銘《*epi-* (upon) + *taph* (tomb)》

epithet[7] 〔ˈɛpəˌθɛt〕 *n.* 表示特性的修飾語;綽號;別稱
(加在某人身上的東西)《*epi-* (upon) + *thet* (put)》

epitome[7] 〔ɪˈpɪtəmɪ〕 *n.* 梗概;摘要;縮影;典型 (切割修剪而成)
　《*epi-* (upon) + *tome* (cut)》

ephemeral[7] 〔əˈfɛmərəl〕 *adj.* 短暫的;朝生暮死的 (只有一天
的壽命)《*ep-* = *epi-* (upon) + *hemer* (day) + *-al* (形容詞字尾)》

```
ep + hemer + al
 |     |      |
upon + day + adj.
```

epoch[7] 〔ˈɛpək〕 *n.* 紀元;劃時代的事;(地質) 期;紀
　《*ep-* = *epi-* (upon) + *och* (hold)》

eponym〔ˈɛpəˌnɪm〕n. 人名名稱（指某時代、理論、藥品等的名稱是根據代表性人物或其發明者的名字而命名）

《**ep-** = **epi-**（upon）+ **onym**（name）》

46 **eso-** = within

esoteric[7]〔ˌɛsəˈtɛrɪk〕adj. 秘傳的；深奧的

《希臘文 **esoterikos** = inner》

esotropia〔ˌɛsoˈtropɪə〕n.【醫】內斜視

《**eso-**（within）+ **trop**（turn）+ **-ia**（表示病症的字尾）》

47 **eu-** = well

　　* 希臘文 **eu**，表示「良好」。〔變化型〕ev-。

eugenics[7]〔juˈdʒɛnɪks〕n. 優生學

《**eu-**（well）+ **gen**（bear）+ **-ics**（表示學問的字尾）》

eulogy[7]〔ˈjulədʒɪ〕n. 頌辭；頌德文

《**eu-**（well）+ **logy**（speak）》

eupepsia〔juˈpɛpʃə, -ʃɪə〕n. 消化良好

《**eu-**（well）+ **peps**（digest 消化）+ **-ia**（condition）》

cf. **dyspepsia**（消化不良）

eu +	peps +	ia
well +	*digest* +	*condition*

euphemism[7]〔ˈjufəˌmɪzəm〕n. 委婉的說法（使好聽）

《**eu-**（well）+ **phem**（speak）+ **-ism**（名詞字尾）》

euphony〔ˈjufənɪ〕= a pleasing sound　n. 諧音；悅耳之音

《**eu-**（well）+ **phony**（sound）》

euphoria[7]〔juˈforɪə〕n. 心情愉快

《**eu-**（well）+ **phor**（bear）+ **-ia**（condition）》

字首 ecto-～extra-

euthanasia[7] 〔͵juθə'neʒə , -ʒɪə 〕= easy death　*n.* 安樂死
《*eu-* (well) + *thanas* (die) + *-ia* (表有關醫學的字尾)》

euthenics 〔 ju'θɛnɪks 〕 *n.* 優境學 (研究通過改善環境來改良人種
的學科) 《*eu-* (well) + *then* (swell + *-ics* (science)》

Eutopia 〔 ju'topɪə 〕 *n.* 烏托邦
《*eu-* (well) + *top* (place) + *-ia* (condition)》

$$eu + top + ia$$
$$well + place + condition$$

eutrophic 〔 ju'trɑfɪk 〕 *adj.* 營養正常的；(湖泊等) 富含養份的
《*eu-* (well) + *troph* (food) + *-ic* (形容詞字尾)》

evangel[7] 〔 ɪ'vændʒəl 〕= good news　*n.* 福音；佳音；指導原則
《*ev-* = *eu-* (well) + *angel* (tidings 消息)》

48 **eury-** = wide

* 希臘文 *eurus*，表示「寬」、「廣」。

eurybath 〔'jurɪ͵bæθ 〕 *n.* (可在水中各種不同深度生存的) 廣深性
水生生物 《*eury-* (wide) + *bath* (deep)》

eurycephalic 〔͵jurəsə'fælɪk 〕 *adj.* 頭部寬大的
《*eury-* (wide) + *cephal* (head) + *-ic* (形容詞字尾)》

eurygnathic 〔͵jurɪg'næθɪk 〕 *adj.* 闊頜的
《*eury-* (wide) + *gnath* (jaw 顎) + *-ic* (形容詞字尾)》

euryphagous 〔 ju'rɪfəgəs 〕 *adj.* 廣食性的 (指能吃各種食物生存的)
《*eury-* (wide) + *phag* (eat) + *-ous* (形容詞字尾)》

eurythermal 〔͵jurə'θɜmḷ 〕 *adj.* 廣溫性的
《*eury-* (wide) + *therm* (heat) + *-al* (形容詞字尾)》

eurytopic 〔͵jurɪ'tɑpɪk 〕 *adj.* 廣適應性的
《*eury-* (wide) + *top* (place) + *-ic* (形容詞字尾)》

49 **ex-** = fully ; out of

* 表示「出自」或「超出」、「完全」。

〔變化型〕a- , e- , ec- , ef- , es- , iss- , s- 。

exacerbate[7] 〔 ɪgˈzæsə͵bet , ɪkˈsæs- 〕 v. 使惡化；加劇；激怒
（使不高興）《 *ex-* (out) + *acerb* (sharp) + *-ate* (動詞字尾)》

```
ex  +  acerb  +  ate
 |       |        |
fully  +  sharp  +  v.
```

exact[2] 〔 ɪgˈzækt 〕 v. 需要；強索   adj. 正確的；精確的（跑出去）
《 *ex-* (out) + *act* (drive)》

exaggerate[4] 〔 ɪgˈzædʒə͵ret 〕 v. 誇大；誇張（向外擴張）
《 *ex-* (out) + *ag-* = *ad-* (to) + *gerate* (carry)》

```
ex  +  ag  +  gerate
 |      |       |
out  +  to  +  carry
```

example[1] 〔 ɪgˈzæmpl̩ 〕 n. 例證；實例 《 *ex-* (out) + *ample* (take)》

exasperate[7] 〔 ɪgˈzæspə͵ret , ɛg- 〕 v. 激怒；激起（使非常粗暴）
《 *ex-* (fully) + *asper* (rough) + *-ate* (動詞字尾)》

exceed[5] 〔 ɪkˈsid 〕 v. 超過；越過（越過後走向外面）
《 *ex-* (out) + *ceed* (go)》

excel[5] 〔 ɪkˈsɛl 〕 v. 優於；勝過；擅長（脫穎而出）
《 *ex-* (out) + *cel* (rise)》

except[1] 〔 ɪkˈsɛpt 〕 v. 把～除外   prep. , conj. 除～之外（拿往別處）
《 *ex-* (out) + *cept* (take)》

excerpt[6] 〔 ˈɛksɝpt 〕 n. 摘錄；選粹   v. 摘錄（挑選出來）
《 *ex-* (out) + *cerpt* (pick)》

```
ex  +  cerpt
 |       |
out  +  pick
```

exchange[3] 〔 ɪks'tʃendʒ 〕 *v.* 交換；交易；互換（完全變換）

　《*ex-* (fully) + *change*》

exclude[5] 〔 ɪk'sklud 〕 *v.* 拒絕；除去；除外（關在門外）

　《*ex-* (out) + *clude* (shut)》　*cf.* **include**（包括）

excoriate[7] 〔 ɪk'skɔrɪˌet 〕 *v.* 脫皮

　《*ex-* (out) + *cori* (skin) + *-ate* (動詞字尾)》

```
ex + cori + ate
 |     |     |
out + skin +  v.
```

excruciate[7] 〔 ɪk'skruʃɪˌet 〕 *v.* 折磨；拷打；使痛苦（背負十字架）

　《*ex-* (out) + *cruci* (cross) + *-ate* (動詞字尾)》

excuse[2] 〔 *v.* ɪk'skjuz　*n.* ɪk'skjus 〕 *v.* 原諒　*n.* 藉口

　《*ex-* (out) + *cuse* (cause)》

execute[5] 〔'ɛksɪˌkjut 〕 *v.* 實現；執行（繼續向外走）

　《*ex-* (out) + *ecute* (follow)》

```
ex + ecute
 |     |
out + follow
```

exempt[7] 〔 ɪg'zɛmpt , ɛg- 〕 *v.* 免除　*n.* 被免除義務者

　adj. 被免除的（除去）《*ex-* (out) + *empt* (take)》

exercise[2] 〔'ɛksəˌsaɪz 〕 *n.* , *v.* 運動；練習

　《*ex-* (out) + *ercise* (enclose)》

exert[6] 〔 ɪg'zɝt 〕 *v.* 運用；施行（拿出所有的力量）

　《*ex-* (out) + *ert* (put together)》

exhale[7] 〔 ɛks'hel , ɪg'zel 〕 *v.* 呼出；呼（氣）；發出（氣、煙、味等）

　（吐氣）《*ex-* (out) + *hale* (breathe)》　*cf.* **inhale**（吸入）

exhaust[4] 〔 ɪg'zɔst , ɛg- 〕 *v.* 用盡；耗盡　*n.* 廢棄（牽出）

　《*ex-* (out) + *haust* (draw)》

exhibit[4] 〔 ɪg'zɪbɪt 〕 *v.* 顯示；陳列　*n.* 展覽品；陳列品

　（用手捧出來）《*ex-* (out) + *hibit* (have)》　*cf.* **habit**（習慣）

exhilarate[7] 〔 ɪgˋzɪləˌret 〕 *v.* 使興高采烈；使快活（使高興）
《*ex-*（out）+ *hilar*（glad）+ *-ate*（動詞字尾）》

```
ex + hilar + ate
 |      |      |
out + glad +  v.
```

exhort[7] 〔 ɪgˋzɔrt 〕 *v.* 勸告；力勸
《*ex-*（out）+ *hort*（urge）》

exhume[7] 〔 ɪgˋzjum, ɪkˋsjum 〕 *v.* 掘出（屍體）；掘（墓）
（挖出地面）《*ex-*（out）+ *hume*（ground）》
cf. **inhume**（埋葬），**humble**（卑下的）

exit[3] 〔ˋɛgzɪt, ˋɛksɪt 〕 *n.* 出口；退路（走到外面）
《*ex-*（out）+ *it*（go）》

exonerate[7] 〔 ɪgˋzɑnəˌret 〕 *v.* 免罪；免除（義務等）（免去負擔）
《*ex-*（out）+ *oner*（burden）+ *-ate*（動詞字尾）》

```
ex +  oner  + ate
 |      |      |
out + burden +  v.
```

exorbitant[7] 〔 ɪgˋzɔrbətənt 〕 *adj.* 過分的
《*ex-*（out）+ *orbit*（track）+ *-ant*（形容詞字尾）》

exorcise[7] 〔ˋɛksɔrˌsaɪz 〕 *v.* 驅除（妖魔等）；驅邪；拔除
（立誓驅除）《*ex-*（out）+ *orc*（oath）+ *-ise*（動詞字尾）》

```
ex +  orc  + ise
 |      |      |
out + oath +  v.
```

expand[4] 〔 ɪkˋspænd 〕 *v.* 擴張；擴大；膨脹（向外擴展）
《*ex-*（out）+ *pand*（spread）》

expect[2] 〔 ɪkˋspɛkt 〕 *v.* 預期；期待（等得不耐煩而向外張望）
《*ex-*（out）+ *pect*（look）》

expel[6] 〔 ɪkˋspɛl 〕 *v.* 驅除；逐出；開除（趕到外面）
《*ex-*（out）+ *pel*（drive）》

expiate[7] 〔'ɛkspɪˌet 〕 *v.* 補償；為～而受罰；避免；躲開

《*ex-* (fully) + *pi* (appease 撫慰) + *-ate* (動詞字尾)》

```
ex  +   pi  + ate
 |       |      |
fully + appease +  v.
```

expire[6] 〔 ɪk'spaɪr 〕 *v.* 期滿；熄滅；死亡 (吐氣)

《*ex-* (out) + *pire* (breathe)》　　*cf.* **inspire** (鼓舞)

explicit[6] 〔 ɪk'splɪsɪt 〕 *adj.* 明確的 (向外摺疊 → 表現在外)

《*ex-* (out) + *plicit* (folded)》　　*cf.* **implicit** (暗含的)

expose[4] 〔 ɪk'spoz 〕 *v.* 暴露；展覽；陳列 (放在外面)

《*ex-* (out) + *pose* (place)》

expound[7] 〔 ɪk'spaʊnd 〕 *v.* 解釋；說明 (置於外面)

《*ex-* (out) + *pound* (put)》　　*cf.* **exponent** (說明者)

```
ex + pound
 |     |
out +  put
```

exquisite[6] 〔'ɛkskwɪzɪt , ɪk's- 〕 *adj.* 精美的；極度的 (被要求)

《*ex-* (out) + *quisite* (sought)》　　*cf.* **query** (質問)，**quest** (探求)

exsiccate[7] 〔'ɛksɪˌket 〕 *v.* 弄乾

《*ex-* (out) + *sicc* (dry) + *-ate* (動詞字尾)》

```
ex + sicc + ate
 |     |     |
out +  dry  +  v.
```

exterior[5] 〔 ɪk'stɪrɪɚ 〕 *adj.* 外面的；外部的　　*n.* 外面；外表

《*exter-* (out) + *-ior* (表比較級的字尾)》

exterminate[7] 〔 ɪk'stɝməˌnet 〕 *v.* 消滅；消除 (向界限以外)

《*ex-* (out ; beyond) + *termin* (boundary) + *-ate* (動詞字尾)》

cf. **term** (術語；期限；條件)

external[5] 〔 ɪk'stɝnḷ 〕 *adj.* 外部的；外面的

《*extern-* (out) + *-al* (形容詞字尾)》

extinguish[7] 〔 ɪk'stɪŋgwɪʃ 〕 v. 熄滅；撲滅；滅絕（戳刺而消失）

《**ex-**（ out ）+ **(s)tingu**（ prick ）+ **-ish**（ 動詞字尾 ）》

extirpate[7] 〔'ɛkstɚˌpet , ɪk'stɝpet 〕 v. 根除；根絕（連根拔除）

《**ex-**（ out ）+ **tirp** = **strip**（ root ）+ **-ate**（ 動詞字尾 ）》

```
ex  +  tirp  +  ate
 |       |       |
out  +  root  +  v.
```

extol[7] 〔 ɪk'stɑl , -'stol 〕 v. 讚揚；激賞（高舉）

《**ex-**（ fully ）+ **tol**（ raise ）》

extort[7] 〔 ɪk'stɔrt , ɛk- 〕 v. 勒索；敲詐；強求（扭出）

《**ex-**（ out ）+ **tort**（ twist ）》　 cf. **torsion**（扭轉），**torture**（拷問）

extradite[7] 〔'ɛkstrəˌdaɪt 〕 v. 引渡（逃犯或囚犯等）

《**ex-**（ out ）+ **tradite**（ surrender 引渡 ）》

```
ex  +  tradite
 |       |
out  +  surrender
```

extricate[7] 〔'ɛkstrɪˌket 〕 v. 救出；使解脫（衝出障礙）

《**ex-**（ out ）+ **tric**（ obstacle ）+ **-ate**（ 動詞字尾 ）》

extrinsic[7] 〔 ɛk'strɪnsɪk 〕 = outward　 adj. 非固有的；外在的

extrude[7] 〔 ɪk'strud , ɛk- 〕 v. 逼出；擠出；逐出（擠出）

《**ex-**（ out ）+ **trude**（ thrust ）》　 cf. **intrude**（ 闖入；侵擾 ）

exuberant[7] 〔 ɪg'zjubərənt 〕 adj. 豐富的；繁茂的；充滿活力的

《**ex-**（ out ）+ **uber**（ fruitful ）+ **-ant**（ 形容詞字尾 ）》

```
ex  +  uber  +  ant
 |       |       |
out  +  fruitful  +  adj.
```

exude[7] 〔 ɪg'zjud , -'zud 〕 v. （ 使 ）滲出；（ 使 ）發散（流汗）

《**ex-**（ out ）+ **ude** = **sude**（ sweat ）》

abash[7] 〔 ə'bæʃ 〕 v. 使羞愧；使臉紅（極度驚訝）

《**a-** = **ex-**（ extremely ）+ **bash**（ express astonishment ）》

alight[7] 〔 ə'laɪt 〕 v. 由車上或馬上下來

《 *a-* = *ex-* (out) + *light* (dismount)》

amend[7] 〔 ə'mɛnd 〕 v. 修正；改善 (表露出缺點)

《 *a-* = *ex-* (out) + *mend* (fault)》

avoid[2] 〔 ə'vɔɪd 〕 v. 避免；宣佈無效

《 *a-* = *ex-* (out) + *void* (empty 空的)》

ebullient[7] 〔 ɪ'bʌljənt 〕 adj. 沸騰的；熱情奔放的；活力充沛的

(沸騰)《 *e-* = *ex-* (out) + *bull* (boil) + *-ient* (形容詞字尾)》

edit[3] 〔'ɛdɪt 〕 = give out = publish v. 編輯

《 *e-* = *ex-* (out) + *dit* (give)》

educate[3] 〔'ɛdʒə,ket , -dʒʊ- 〕 v. 教育 (導出才能)

《 *e-* = *ex-* (out) + *ducate* (lead)》

effeminate[7] 〔 adj. ə'fɛmənɪt v. ə'fɛmənet 〕 adj. 柔弱的 v. 使柔弱

《 *ef-* = *ex-* (out) + *feminate* (woman)》

egress[7] 〔 n. 'igrɛs v. i'grɛs 〕 n. 出去；出現；出口 v. 出現；出去

(走出來)《 *e-* = *ex-* (out) + *gress* (go ; walk)》 cf. **progress** (進步)

```
e  + gress
|     |
out +  go
```

eject[7] 〔 ɪ'dʒɛkt , i- 〕 v. 噴出；投出 (投出)

《 *e-* = *ex-* (out) + *ject* (throw)》

elaborate[5] 〔 adj. ɪ'læbərɪt v. ɪ'læbə,ret 〕 adj. 精巧的；複雜的

v. 用心地做；苦心經營 (被給予許多工作)

《 *e-* = *ex-* (fully) + *labor* (work) + *-ate* (動詞字尾)》

```
e  + labor + ate
|     |      |
out + work +  v.
```

elapse[7] 〔 ɪ'læps 〕 v. (時間) 溜走 (滑行)

《 *e-* = *ex-* (away) + *lapse* (glide)》 cf. **collapse** (倒塌)

elect[2] 〔 ɪ'lɛkt , ə- 〕 v. 選舉 adj. 選出的 (選出)

《 *e-* = *ex-* (out) + *lect* (choose)》 cf. **collect** (收集)

elicit[7] 〔 ɪˈlɪsɪt 〕 v. 誘出；引出《*e-* = *ex-* (out) + *licit* (entice)》

elide 〔 ɪˈlaɪd 〕 v. 省略；刪除（除去）

《*e-* = *ex-* (out) + *lide* (strike)》

eliminate[4] 〔 ɪˈlɪməˌnet 〕 v. 除去；淘汰（排出界限以外）

《*e-* = *ex-* (out) + *limin* (threshold 門檻；界限) + *-ate* (動詞字尾)》

cf. **limit**（界限）

```
e  +  limin  + ate
|      |        |
out + threshold +  v.
```

elite[6] 〔 ɪˈlit , eˈlit 〕 n. 優秀分子；精英（挑選出來者）

《*elite* = *elect* (choose out)》

elocution[7] 〔 ˌɛləˈkjuʃən 〕 n. 辯論術；演說術（說話的方法）

《*e-* = *ex-* (out) + *locut* (speak) + *-ion* (名詞字尾)》

cf. **eloquent**（雄辯的）

```
e  + locut + ion
|     |       |
out + speak +  n.
```

elope[7] 〔 ɪˈlop , ə- 〕 v. 私奔；逃亡（逃跑）

《*e-* = *ex-* (out) + *lope* (run)》

emaciate[7] 〔 ɪˈmeʃɪˌet 〕 v. 使消瘦；使憔悴（使變瘦）

《*e-* = *ex-* (out) + *maci* (lean 瘦的) + *-ate* (動詞字尾)》

emanate[7] 〔 ˈɛməˌnet 〕 v.（光、熱、香氣等）發出；發散（流出來）

《*e-* = *ex-* (out) + *man* (flow) + *-ate* (動詞字尾)》

emancipate[7] 〔 ɪˈmænsəˌpet 〕 v. 解放；解除（束縛）（把手中的東西拿出來）《*e-* = *ex-* (out) + *man* = *manus* (hand) + *cipate* (take)》

```
e  + man + cipate
|     |      |
out + hand + take
```

erudite[7] 〔 ˈɛruˌdaɪt 〕 adj. 博學的；有學識的（脫離無知的狀態）

《*e-* = *ex-* (out) + *rud* (unlearned 未受敎育的) + *-ite* (形容詞字尾)》

eruption[6] 〔 ɪˈrʌpʃən 〕 *n.* (火山) 爆發；噴出（破裂而出）

《 *e-* = *ex-* (out) + *rupt* (break) + *-ion* (名詞字尾)》 *cf.* **rupture** (破裂)

```
e  +  rupt  +  ion
|       |        |
out +  break  +  n.
```

event[2] 〔 ɪˈvɛnt 〕 *n.* 事件；結果（發生的事）

《 *e-* = *ex-* (out) + *vent* (come)》

evident[4] 〔ˈɛvədənt 〕 *adj.* 明顯的（可由外看見的）

《 *e-* = *ex-* (out) + *vid* (see) + *-ent* (形容詞字尾)》 *cf.* **vision** (視力)

evince[7] 〔 ɪˈvɪns 〕 *v.* 表明（大勝 → 毫無疑問的）

《 *e-* = *ex-* (fully) + *vince* (conquer)》 *cf.* **convince** (說服)

evoke[7] 〔 ɪˈvok 〕 *v.* 喚起；引起

《 *e-* = *ex-* (out) + *voke* (call)》 *cf.* **vocation** (職業)

eccentric[6] 〔 ɪkˈsɛntrɪk , ɛk- 〕 *adj.* 古怪的；怪癖的 *n.* 古怪的人

(脫離中心的)《 *ec-* = *ex-* (out) + *centr* (center) + *-ic* (形容詞字尾)》

```
ec  +  centr  +  ic
|        |        |
out +  center  +  adj.
```

eclipse[5] 〔 ɪˈklɪps 〕 *n.* (日、月) 蝕；（名聲等）喪失；衰落

v. 蝕；遮掩；使晦暗《 *ec-* = *ex-* (out) + *lipse* (leave)》

ecstasy[6] 〔ˈɛkstəsɪ 〕 *n.* 狂喜；恍惚；出神（在應立足的地方

之外 → 忘我）《 *e-* = *ex-* (out) + *stasy* (standing)》

efface[7] 〔 ɪˈfes , ɛ- 〕 *v.* 塗抹；消除；沖淡（在表面以外）

《 *ef-* = *ex-* (out) + *face* (表面)》

effete[7] 〔 ɛˈfit , ɪ- 〕 *adj.* 筋疲力竭的；衰弱的；無生產力的

(沒有生產力)《 *ef-* = *ex-* (out) + *fete* (productive)》

effort[2] 〔ˈɛfət 〕 *n.* 努力（的結果）（力量外放）

《 *ef-* = *ex-* (out) + *fort* (force)》

```
ef  +  fort
|       |
out +  force
```

effuse[7] 〔 ɛ'fjuz , ɪ- 〕 *v.* 流出；瀉出；散佈 (流出)

　《*ef-* = *ex-* (out) + *fuse* (pour)》

　cf. **confuse** (使混亂)，**diffuse** (傳播)，**refuse** (拒絕)

escape[3] 〔 ə'skep , ɪ- 〕 = out of one's cape　*v.* , *n.* 逃脫；逃走

　(迅速脫掉外套)《*cape* 無袖的短外套 》

sample[2] 〔'sæmpl 〕 *n.* 樣品；樣本　*v.* 取樣品 (拿出)

　《*s-* = *ex-* (out) + *ample* (take)》

50　**exo-** = outside

exotic[6] 〔 ɪg'zɑtɪk 〕 = outward ; foreign　*adj.* 外國產的　*n.* 舶來品

exoatmosphere 〔,ɛkso'ætməs,fɪr 〕 *n.* 外大氣層

　《*exo-* (outside) + *atmosphere* (大氣層)》

exobiology 〔,ɛksəbaɪ'alədʒɪ 〕 *n.* 外空生物學 (生物學之一分支，

　探索地球外存在生物的可能性)《*exo-* (outside) + *biology* (生物學)》

exocardia 〔,ɛkso'kardɪə 〕 *n.* 異位心

　《*exo-* (outside) + *cardia* (heart)》

exogamy 〔 ɛks'agəmɪ 〕 *n.* 異族結婚

　《*exo-* (outside) + *gam* (marriage) + *-y* (名詞字尾)》

exopathic 〔,ɛksə'pæθɪk 〕 *adj.* 病因在體外的

　《*exo-* (outside) + *path* (disease) + *-ic* (形容詞字尾)》

exotoxin 〔,ɛksə'taksɪn 〕 *n.* 外毒素 《*exo-* (outside) + *toxin* (毒素)》

51　**extra-** = beyond

　* 拉丁文 *exter*，一般多加在形容詞之前，表示「在～之外」、

　　「超出」之意。

extra[2] 〔'ɛkstrə 〕 = beyond what is necessary　*adj.* 額外的；

　特別的　*n.* 額外的事物或人員

extracurricular[6] 〔,ɛkstrəkə'rɪkjələ 〕 *adj.* 課外的 (課程以外的)

　《*extra-* (beyond) + *curri* (run) + *-cular* (形容詞字尾)》

extrajudicial[7]〔,ɛkstrədʒu'dɪʃəl 〕 *adj.* 法庭外的；與訴訟無關的
（司法之外的）《*extra-* (beyond) + *judic* (judge) + *-ial* (形容詞字尾)》

extramural〔,ɛkstrə'mjʊrəl 〕 *adj.* 校外的；城牆外的 (牆外的)
《*extra-* (beyond) + *mur* (wall) + *-al* (形容詞字尾)》

```
extra  +  mur  +  al
  |         |      |
beyond  +  wall  +  adj.
```

extraordinary[4]〔 ɪk'strɔrdn̩,ɛrɪ 〕 = beyond ordinary
adj. 非常的；特別的；驚人的；臨時的

extrasensory[7]〔,ɛkstrə'sɛnsərɪ 〕 *adj.* 知覺外的；超感覺的 (感覺
之外的)《*extra-* (beyond) + *sens* (feel) + *-ory* (形容詞字尾)》

```
extra  +  sens  +  ory
  |         |       |
beyond  +  feel  +  adj.
```

extravagant[7]〔 ɪk'strævəgənt 〕 *adj.* 奢侈的；過度的 (悠遊於界限
之外)《*extra-* (beyond) + *vag* (wander) + *-ant* (形容詞字尾)》
cf. **vagabond** (流浪者)，**vagary** (妄想)

extravasate〔 ɛk'strævə,set 〕 *v.* 使流出
《*extra-* (beyond) + *vas* (vessel) + *-ate* (動詞字尾)》

extreme[3]〔 ɪk'strim 〕 *adj.* 極端的；過度的；非常的
《*extr-* = *extra-* (beyond) + *-eme* (形容詞字尾)》

extremity[7]〔 ɪk'strɛmətɪ 〕 *n.* 極端；困境；極端手段

52　for- = away from

* 由「分離」之意引申為「禁止」、「除外」等的否定意思，或為
「破壞」及「強迫」的意思。

forbear[7]〔 fɔr'bɛr 〕 = refrain from　*v.* 自制；避免
forbid[4]〔 fə'bɪd 〕 = bid away from　*v.* 禁止；不許 (從～分離)
foreclose[7]〔 fɔr'kloz 〕 = exclude　*v.* 排除；妨礙

forget[1] ﹝ fə'gɛt ﹞= get away from　*v.* 忘記；忽略（已遠離～）

forgive[2] ﹝ fə'gɪv ﹞= give away　*v.* 原諒（就此作罷）

forgo[7] ﹝ fɔr'go ﹞= pass over　*v.* 棄絕；拋棄；放棄（經過）

forsake[6] ﹝ fə'sek ﹞ *v.* 遺棄；革除（努力脫離）

   《*for-*（ away from ）+ *sake*（ strive ）》

```
       for    +  sake
        |         |
    away from + strive
```

forswear[7] ﹝ fɔr'swɛr ﹞= deny an oath　*v.* 誓絕；戒絕；放棄

53　**fore-** = before　　* 表示「在～之前」。〔變化型〕for-。

forearm[7] ﹝'for͵arm , 'fɔr- ﹞ *n.* 前臂（肘至腕的部分）

forebear[7] ﹝'for͵bɛr , 'fɔr- ﹞= ancestor　*n.* 祖先

forebode[7] ﹝ for͵bod ﹞ *v.* 預示；預兆

foredoom ﹝ for'dum , fɔr- ﹞ *v.* 預先注定《*doom* 命運》

forefather[7] ﹝'for͵faðə , 'fɔr- ﹞ *n.* 祖先；祖宗

forefinger[7] ﹝'for͵fɪŋgə , 'fɔr- ﹞ *n.* 食指

forefront[7] ﹝'for͵frʌnt , 'fɔr- ﹞ *n.* 最前面；最前線

foregoing[7] ﹝ for'go · ɪŋ , fɔr- ﹞ *adj.* 前面的；前述的

foregone[7] ﹝ for'gɔn , fɔr- ﹞ *adj.* 先前的；既往的

foreground[7] ﹝'for͵graʊnd , 'fɔr- ﹞ *n.* 前景

forehead[3] ﹝'fɔrɪd , 'fɔr͵hɛd ﹞ *n.* 前額；前部

foreknowledge[7] ﹝'for͵nɑlɪdʒ ﹞ *n.* 預知；先知

```
    fore  +  know  +  ledge
     |        |         |
   before +  know  +   n.
```

foreman[7] ﹝'formən , 'fɔr- ﹞ *n.* 工頭；領班（站在前面的男子）

foremost[7] ﹝'for͵most , 'fɔr- ﹞ *adj.* 最先的；首要的　*adv.* 首先

forerun[7] ﹝ for'rʌn , fɔr- ﹞ *v.* 為～之先驅；超越

foresee[6] 〔 for'si , fɔr- 〕 *v.* 先見；預知
foreshadow[7] 〔 for'ʃædo , fɔr- 〕 *v.* 預示；預兆
foresight[7] 〔'for,saɪt , 'fɔr- 〕 *n.* 先見之明；遠見；深謀遠慮
foretaste[7] 〔'for,test , 'fɔr- 〕 *n.* 預嚐；先試
foretell[7] 〔 for'tɛl , fɔr- 〕 *v.* 預言；預測
forethought[7] 〔'for,θɔt , 'fɔr- 〕 *n.* 事先的考慮；預籌
foretime[7] 〔'for,taɪm , 'fɔr- 〕 *n.* 往昔
forewarn[7] 〔 for'wɔrn , fɔr- 〕 *v.* 預先警告
foreword[7] 〔'for,wɝd , 'fɔr- 〕 *n.* 前言；引言；序
former[2] 〔'fɔrmɚ 〕 *adj.* 以前的；前者的
forward[2] 〔'fɔrwɚd 〕 *adj.* 向前的；前部的　*adv.* 前面地；向前面
　　n. 前鋒　*v.* 轉遞；轉寄

54　**forth-** = towards　*表示「向前」。

forthcoming[6] 〔'forθ'kʌmɪŋ , 'fɔrθ- 〕 *adj.* 即將出現的；
　　需要時即有的
forthright[7] 〔,forθ'raɪt , 'forθ,raɪt 〕 *adj.* 坦白的；直率的
　　adv. 一往直前地　*n.* 直路
forthwith[7] 〔 forθ'wɪθ , -'wɪð 〕 *adv.* 立刻；不猶豫地

55　**hecto-** = hundred　*希臘文 hekaton，表示「百」。

hectare[7] 〔'hɛktɛr 〕 *n.* 公頃（一百公畝）
hectogram 〔'hɛktə,græm 〕 *n.* 公兩（一百公克）
hectograph 〔'hɛktə,græf 〕 *n.* 膠版印刷
hectoliter ; **-tre** 〔'hɛktə,litɚ 〕 *n.* 公石（一百公升）
hectometer ; **-tre**[7] 〔'hɛktə,mitɚ 〕 *n.* 百公尺；公引
hecatomb 〔'hɛkə,tom , -,tum 〕 *n.*（古希臘和羅馬的）大獻祭
　　（祭獻公牛一百頭）；大犧牲；大屠殺《希臘文 *bous* = ox》

56 hemi- = half　　* 希臘文 *hemi*，表示「一半」。

hemicrania (ˌhɛmɪˈkrenɪə) *n.* 偏頭痛
《*hemi-* (half) + *crania* (頭蓋骨)》
hemicycle (ˈhɛməˌsaɪkl̩) *n.* 半圓 (形)
hemiplegic (ˌhɛmɪˈplidʒɪk) *adj.* 半身不遂的
《*hemi-* (half) + *pleg* (stroke 中風) + *-ic* (形容詞字尾)》
hemisphere[6] (ˈhɛməsˌfɪr) *n.* 半球 《*hemi-* (half) + *sphere* (ball)》

57 hendeca- = eleven　　* 希臘文 *hendeka*，表示「十一」。

hendecagon (hɛnˈdɛkəˌgɑn) *n.* 十一角形；十一邊形
《*hendeca-* (eleven) + *gon* (angle) 》
hendecahedron (hɛnˌdɛkəˈhidʒrən) *n.* 十一面體
《*hendeca-* (eleven) + *hedr* (side) + *-on* (名詞字尾)》
hendecasyllable (ˌhɛndɛkəˈsɪləbl̩) *n.* 含有十一個音節的詩行
(或詞) 《*hendeca-* (eleven) + *syllable* (音節)》
hendecasyllabic (ˌhɛdɛkəsɪˈlæbɪk) *adj.* 含有十一個音節的

58 hepta- = seven　　* 希臘文 *hepta*，表示「七」。

heptachord (ˈhɛptəˌkɔrd) *n.* 七聲音階；(古希臘) 七弦樂器
《*hepta-* (seven) + *chord* (heart)》
heptagon (ˈhɛptəˌgɑn) *n.* 七邊形；七角形
《*hepta-* (seven) + *gon* (angle)》
heptahedron (ˌhɛptəˈhidrən) *n.* 七面體
《*hepta-* (seven) + *hedr* (side) + *-on* (名詞字尾)》
heptameter (hɛpˈtæmətɚ) *n.* 七音步 (的詩)
《*hepta-* (seven) + *meter* (音步)》
heptarchy (ˈhɛptɑrkɪ) *n.* 七頭政治；(H-) (英國的) 七王國
《*hept-* (seven) + *arch* (rule) + *-y* (名詞字尾)》

59 hetero- = other ; different

* 源自於希臘文 *heteros*，表示「另一的」、「不同的」。

heteroclite 〔'hɛtərə,klaɪt 〕 *n.* 不規則詞類　*adj.* 不規則變化的
《*hetero-* (other) + *clite* (declension 語尾變化)》

heterocyclic 〔,hɛtərə'saɪklɪk 〕 *adj.* 雜環的
《*hetero-* (other) + *cycl* (circle) + *-ic* (形容詞字尾)》

```
hetero + cycl + ic
  |       |     |
other + circle + adj.
```

heterodont 〔,hɛtərə'dɔnt 〕 *adj.* 異形齒的
《*heter(o)-* (other) + *odont* (tooth)》

heterodox 〔'hɛtərə,dɑks , 'hɛtrə- 〕 = of strange opinion
adj. 異端的 《*hetero-* (other) + *dox* (opinion)》　*cf.* **orthodox** (正統的)

heterogeneous[7] 〔,hɛtərə'dʒɪnɪəs , -njəs 〕 *adj.* 不同的；異類的；
龐雜的 (其他種類的)《*hetero-* (other) + *gene* (kind 種類) + *-ous*
(形容詞字尾)》

```
hetero + gene + ous
  |       |      |
other + kind + adj.
```

heteronym 〔'hɛtərə,nɪm 〕 *n.* 同拼法異音異義字 (拼法相同而名
稱不同的東西)《*hetero-* (other) + *(o)nym* (name)》

heterosexual[5] 〔,hɛtərə'sɛkʃʊəl 〕 *adj.* , *n.* 異性戀的 (人)
cf. **homosexual** (同性戀的人)

60 hexa- = six　* 希臘文 *hex*，表示「六」。

hexad 〔'hɛksæd 〕 *n.* 六之數；六個一組
hexagon[7] 〔'hɛksə,gɑn 〕 *n.* 六角形 《*hexa-* (six) + *gon* (angle)》
hexagram[7] 〔'hɛksə,græm 〕 *n.* 六角星形；六線形

hexameter[7] 〔 hɛks'æmətə 〕 *n.* 六音步（的詩）（以六來測量）
《 *hexa-*（ six ）+ *meter*（ measure ）》
hexangular 〔 hɛks'æŋgjələ 〕 *adj.*（有）六角的
hexapod 〔'hɛksə,pɑd 〕 *adj.*（有）六足的　　*n.* 六足類；昆蟲類
《 *hexa-*（ six ）+ *pod*（ foot ）》

61　holo- = whole

holocaust[7] 〔'hɑlə,kɔst 〕 *n.* 大屠殺；全部燒死
《 *holo-*（ whole ）+ *caust*（ burn ）》
Holocene[7] 〔'hɑlə,sin 〕 *n.* 全新世　　*adj.* 全新世的
《 *holo-*（ whole ）+ *cene*（ new ）》
hologram[7] 〔'hɑlə,græm 〕 *n.* 全息圖《 *holo-*（ whole ）+ *gram*（ mark ）》
holograph[7] 〔'hɑlə,græf 〕 *n.* 親筆文書　　*adj.* 親筆的
《 *holo-*（ whole ）+ *graph*（ write ）》
holoscopic 〔,hɑlə'skɑpɪk 〕 *adj.* 綜觀全局的
《 *holo-*（ whole ）+ *scop*（ look ）+ *-ic*（ 形容詞字尾 ）》

62　homo- = same（與 hetero- 相反）

　　* 希臘文 *homos*，表示「相同」。

homocentric[7] 〔,homə'sɛntrɪk 〕 *adj.* 同心的；共心的（相同中心的）
《 *homo-*（ same ）+ *centr*（ center ）+ *-ic*（ 形容詞字尾 ）》
homodont 〔,homə'dant 〕 *adj.* 同形齒的
《 *hom(o)-*（ same ）+ *odont*（ tooth ）》
homogeneous[7] 〔,homə'dʒɪnɪəs 〕 *adj.* 同類的；相似的
（相同種類的）《 *homo-*（ same ）+ *gene*（ kind ）+ *-ous*（ 形容詞字尾 ）》
　　cf. **heterogeneous**（異類的）

homo	+	gene	+	ous
|		|		|
same	+	*kind*	+	*adj.*

homogenize[7] 〔 hoˋmɑdʒəˏnaɪz 〕 v. 使均質

```
homo + gen(e) + ize
  |       |       |
same  +  kind  +  v.
```

homograph 〔ˋhɑməˏgræf 〕 n. 同形異義字（同形）
《 **homo-**（ same ）+ **graph**（ write ）》

homologate 〔 həˋmɑləˏget 〕 v. 贊同；確認
《 **homo-**（ same ）+ **logate**（ speak ）》

homologous[7] 〔 hoˋmɑləgəs 〕 = saying the same *adj.* 相同的；
對應的《 **homo-**（ same ）+ **log**（ saying ）+ **-ous**（ 形容詞字尾 ）》

```
homo  +  log   + ous
  |       |       |
same  + saying +  adj.
```

homonym[7] 〔ˋhɑməˏnɪm 〕 n. 同音異義字（同名）
《 **homo-**（ same ）+ **(o)nym**（ name ）》
cf. **synonym**（ 同義字 ），**heteronym**（ 同拼法異音異義字 ）

homophile 〔ˋhɑməˏfaɪl 〕 = homosexual n. 同性戀者
（ 喜愛同性 ）《 **homo-**（ same ）+ **phile**（ love ）》

homophone[7] 〔ˋhɑməˏfon 〕 n. 同音異形異義字（同音）
《 **homo-**（ same ）+ **phone**（ sound ）》

homosexual[5] 〔ˏhɑməˋsɛkʃʊəl 〕 adj. , n. 同性戀的（ 人 ）

63　**homo-** = human（ 人類 ）

homage[7] 〔ˋhɑmɪdʒ 〕 n. 尊敬
homicide[7] 〔ˋhɑməˏsaɪd 〕 n. 殺人
Homo sapiens[7] 〔ˋhomoˋsepɪˏɛnz 〕 n. 人類

```
homi + cide
  |      |
human + kill
```

```
Homo + sapiens
  |       |
human +  wise
```

64　hyper- = above ; beyond

> * 源自於希臘文 *huper*，表示「超出」、「高於」、「過度」。

hyperacidity[7] 〔,haɪpərə'sɪdətɪ〕 *n.* 胃酸過多症《*acid* 酸》

hyperactive[7] 〔,haɪpɚ'æktɪv〕 *adj.* 極度活躍的；過分積極的
《*active* 活動的；積極的》

hyperbaton 〔haɪ'pɝbətɑn〕 *n.* 倒置法
《*hyper-* (beyond) + *baton* (step)》

hyperbole[7] 〔haɪ'pɝbə,li , -lɪ〕 *n.* 誇張法（擲向遠處）
《*hyper-* (beyond) + *bole* (throw)》

hyperborean 〔,haɪpɚ'borɪən , -'bɔr-〕 *adj. , n.* 極北的（住民）
（甚至超越北風的）
《*hyper-* (beyond) + *bore(as)* (north wind) + *-an* (形容詞字尾)》

```
hyper  +  bore(as)  +  an
  |         |         |
beyond  +  north wind  +  adj.
```

hypercritical[7] 〔,haɪpɚ'krɪtɪkḷ〕 *adj.* 吹毛求疵的

hypercriticism 〔,haɪpɚ'krɪtə,sɪzm̩〕 *n.* 嚴苛的批評；吹毛求疵
《*criticism* 批評》

hyperinflation[7] 〔'haɪpɚɪn,fleʃən〕 *n.* 超級通貨膨脹（過度膨脹）
《*hyper-* (beyond) + *in-* (into) + *flat* (blow) + *-ion* (名詞字尾)》

hypermilitant[7] 〔,haɪpɚ'mɪlətənt〕 *adj.* 極端好戰的
《*militant* 好戰的》

hyperopia 〔,haɪpɚ'opɪə〕 = far sight　*n.* 遠視
《*hyper-* (beyond) + *op* (eyesight) + *-ia* (condition)》
cf. **myopia** (近視)

```
hyper  +   op   +   ia
  |        |        |
beyond  +  eyesight  +  condition
```

hyperpiesia 〔,haɪpəpaɪ'iʒə〕 *n.* 原發性高血壓
《*hyper-* (beyond) + *pies* (pressure) + *-ia* (condition)》

字首 for~hypo-

hypersensitive[7] 〔͵haɪpɚ'sɛnsətɪv 〕 *adj.* 過度敏感的
《*sensitive* 敏感的》

hypersonic[7] 〔͵haɪpɚ'sɑnɪk 〕 *adj.* 超音速的（超越聲音的）
《*hyper-* (beyond) + *son* (sound) + *-ic* (形容詞字尾)》

hypertension[7] 〔'haɪpɚ'tɛnʃən 〕 *n.* 高血壓《*tension* 壓力》

65 hypo- = under (與 hyper- 相反)

* 希臘文 *hupo*，表示「在～之下」、「低於」，與 *hyper-* 相反。

hypocrisy[6] 〔hɪ'pɑkrəsɪ 〕 = the playing of a part on the stage
n. 偽善；矯飾（在舞台上演戲 → 裝模作樣）

hypogastric 〔͵haɪpə'gæstrɪk 〕 *adj.* 下腹部的（胃下面的）
《*hypo-* (under) + *gastr* (stomach) + *-ic* (形容詞字尾)》

hypostasis 〔haɪ'pɑstəsɪs , hɪ- 〕 *n.* 基礎；本質（在表象之下的）
《*hypo-* (under) + *stasis* (placing ; standing)》

hypotension[7] 〔͵haɪpə'tɛnʃən 〕 *n.* 低血壓《*tension* 壓力》

hypothecate 〔haɪ'pɑθə͵ket 〕 *v.* 抵押；擔保（壓在箱子下）
《*hypo-* (under) + *thec* (case) + *-ate* (動詞字尾)》

hypo	+	thec	+	ate
under	+	case	+	v.

hypothermia[7] 〔͵haɪpə'θɝmɪə 〕 *n.* 低體溫（低溫）
《*hypo-* (under) + *therm* (heat) + *-ia* (condition)》

hypo	+	therm	+	ia
under	+	heat	+	condition

hypothesis[7] 〔haɪ'pɑθəsɪs 〕 *n.* 假說；假設（作為基礎）
《*hypo-* (under) + *thesis* (placed)》

hypothetical[7] 〔͵haɪpə'θɛtɪkḷ 〕 *adj.* 不確定的；假設的

66　in- = in；into；on　*〔變化型〕il-, im-, ir-。

inbeing〔ˈɪnˌbiɪŋ〕n. 內在；本質；本性

inborn[7]〔ˈɪnˌbɔrn〕adj. 天生的；天賦的

inbreathe[7]〔ɪnˈbrið〕= inhale　v. 吸入；吸進
　　《*in-* (into) + *breathe* (呼吸)》

incarcerate[7]〔ɪnˈkɑrsəˌret〕v. 拘留；監禁 (關進牢房)
　　《*in-* (into) + *carcer* (cell) + *-ate* (動詞字尾)》

incarnate[7]〔v. ɪnˈkɑrnet　adj. ɪnˈkɑrnɪt〕v. 賦以形體；使具體化
　　adj. 具有肉體的；化身的 (進入肉體的)　《*in-* (in) + *carn* (flesh 肉體)
　　+ *-ate* (動詞字尾)》　cf. **carnival** (嘉年華會)

```
in + carn + ate
 |     |     |
in + flesh +  v.
```

incense[5]〔ɪnˈsɛns〕= cause to burn　v. 使大發雷霆；激怒
　　(使燃燒起來)

incentive[6]〔ɪnˈsɛntɪv〕adj. 刺激的　n. 刺激；誘因；動機
　　《*in-* (in) + *cent* = *cant* (sing) + *-ive* (形容詞兼名詞字尾)》

inceptive〔ɪnˈsɛptɪv〕adj. 開始的；起初的 (開始；著手)
　　《*in-* (on) + *cept* (take) + *-ive* (形容詞字尾)》

```
in + cept + ive
 |     |     |
on + take + adj.
```

incident[4]〔ˈɪnsədənt〕adj. 易於發生的；附帶的　n. 事件；附帶
　　事件 (由上面飄落)　《*in-* (on) + *cid* (fall) + *-ent* (形容詞字尾)》

incinerate[7]〔ɪnˈsɪnəˌret〕v. 燒成灰；焚化；火葬
　　《*in-* (in) + *ciner* (ashes) + *-ate* (動詞字尾)》

incipient[7]〔ɪnˈsɪpɪənt〕= inceptive　adj. 剛開始的；初期的
　　《*in-* (on) + *cipi* (take) + *-ent* (形容詞字尾)》

```
in + cipi + ent
 |     |     |
on + take + adj.
```

incise[7]〔ɪn'saɪz〕*v.* 切;割《*in-*(in)+ *cise*(cut)》

incline[6]〔ɪn'klaɪn〕*v.* 愛好;傾向(向~靠過去)

《*in-*(towards)+ *cline*(lean)》

cf. **decline**(使傾斜),**recline**(斜倚;橫臥)

include[2]〔ɪn'klud〕*v.* 包含在內(關在裡面)

《*in-*(in)+ *clude*(shut)》 *cf.* **exclude**(除外)

income[2]〔'ɪn,kʌm〕*n.* 收入;所得(進來的東西)

increase[2]〔*v.* ɪn'kris *n.* 'ɪnkris〕*v., n.* 增加;增多

《*in-*(in)+ *crease*(grow)》 *cf.* **decrease**(減少)

incriminate[7]〔ɪn'krɪmə,net〕*v.* 使有罪;控告(使入罪)

《*in-*(into)+ *crimin*(crime)+ *-ate*(動詞字尾)》

```
in + crimin + ate
 |      |       |
into + crime  +  v.
```

incur[7]〔ɪn'kɝ〕*v.* 遭遇;陷於(流向~)

《*in-*(upon)+ *cur*(run)》 *cf.* **current**(水流)

incurve[7]〔*n.* 'ɪn,kɝv *v.* ɪn'kɝv〕*n.* 彎曲;(棒球)內曲球

v. 使內曲(往內彎)

individual[3]〔,ɪndə'vɪdʒʊəl〕*n.* 個人;個體 *adj.* 個別的;單獨的

《*in-*(in)+ *dividu*(divide)+ *-al*(名詞字尾)》

```
in + dividu + al
 |      |      |
in + divide  + n.
```

indoor[3]〔'ɪn,dor〕*adj.* 室內的 *cf.* **outdoor**(戶外的)

induce[5]〔ɪn'djus〕*v.* 引誘;說服;招致(導向~)

《*in-*(towards)+ *duce*(lead)》

indulge[5]〔ɪn'dʌldʒ〕*v.* 放任;縱容;耽於;熱中(對~很順從)

《*in-*(towards)+ *dulge*(kind 溫和的)》

infatuate[7]〔ɪn'fætʃʊ,et〕*v.* 使迷戀;使糊塗(使變成傻瓜)

《*in-*(in)+ *fatu*(foolish)+ *-ate*(動詞字尾)》

infect[4] 〔 ɪn'fɛkt 〕 = put in　*v.* 傳染（進入病菌）

《*in-*（in）+ *fect*（make；put）》

infiltrate[7] 〔 ɪn'fɪltret 〕 *v.*（使）滲透；（使）潛入

《*in-*（in）+ *filtrate*（過濾；滲透）》

inflame[7] 〔 ɪn'flem 〕 *v.* 激動；激起；使紅腫；使發炎

《*in-*（in）+ *flame*（火燄）》

inflate[7] 〔 ɪn'flet 〕 *v.* 使膨脹；使得意；使物價上漲

（吹進去 → 使膨脹）《*in-*（in）+ *flate*（blow）》

influence[2] 〔'ɪnfluəns 〕 *n.* 影響；感化（力）；權力；有勢力者

v. 影響《*in-*（in）+ *flu*（flow）+ *-ence*（名詞字尾）》　*cf.* **fluid**（流體）

```
in +  flu  + ence
 |      |      |
in + flow  +  n.
```

infringe[7] 〔 ɪn'frɪndʒ 〕 = break in　*v.* 違反；觸犯；侵害

《*in-*（in）+ *fringe*（break）》

infuriate[7] 〔 ɪn'fjurɪˌet 〕 *v.* 激怒（使生氣）

《*in-*（in）+ *furi*（fury）+ *-ate*（動詞字尾）》

```
in + furi + ate
 |     |     |
in + fury +  v.
```

infuse[7] 〔 ɪn'fjuz 〕 *v.* 注入；灌輸《*in-*（into）+ *fuse*（pour）》

cf. **effuse**（流出；散布）

ingrained[7] 〔 ɪn'grend 〕 *adj.* 根深蒂固的；徹底的（天性中的）

《*in-*（in）+ *grain*（天性）+ *-ed*（形容詞字尾）》

```
in + grain + ed
 |     |      |
in + nature + adj.
```

inhale[7] 〔 ɪn'hel 〕 *v.* 吸入《*in-*（in）+ *hale*（breathe）》

cf. **exhale**（呼出）

inherit[5] 〔 ɪn'hɛrɪt 〕 *v.* 繼承《*in-*（in）+ *herit*（繼承）》

cf. **hereditary**（遺傳的），**heritage**（遺產），**heir**（繼承人）

inhibit[7] 〔 ɪnˈhɪbɪt 〕 *v.* 抑制（持著 → 壓制）

《*in-*（in）+ *hibit*（have）》　*cf.* **habit**（習慣）

inject[6] 〔 ɪnˈdʒɛkt 〕 *v.* 注射；投入；加入《*in-*（into）+ *ject*（throw）》

injunction[7] 〔 ɪnˈdʒʌŋkʃən 〕 *n.* 命令；指示；強制令（把人結合
起來的東西）《*in-*（in）+ *junct*（join）+ *-ion*（名詞字尾）》

```
in + junct + ion
 |     |      |
in + join  +  n.
```

inland[5] 〔ˈɪnlənd 〕 *adj.* 內陸的；國內的　*n.* 內地；腹地
adv. 在內地

inlet[7] 〔ˈɪnˌlɛt 〕 *n.* 港灣；入口（海水進入之處）

innate[7] 〔 ɪˈnet, ɪnˈnet 〕 = inborn　*adj.* 天生的；天賦的

《*in-*（in）+ *nate*（be born）》　*cf.* **native**（自然的；生來的）

innovate[7] 〔ˈɪnəˌvet 〕 *v.* 改革；革新

《*in-*（in）+ *nov*（new）+ *-ate*（動詞字尾）》　*cf.* **novel**（新奇的；小說）

```
in + nov + ate
 |    |     |
in + new +  v.
```

inquire[5] 〔 ɪnˈkwaɪr 〕 *v.* 調查；詢問（探求）

《*in-*（into）+ *quire*（search）》

inroad[7] 〔ˈɪnˌrod 〕 *n.* 侵略；侵害；損害（進入敵人的道路）

inrush 〔ˈɪnˌrʌʃ 〕 = rushing in　*n.* 湧入；流入

inscribe[7] 〔 ɪnˈskraɪb 〕 *v.* 題記；刻銘《*in-*（upon）+ *scribe*（write）》

```
in  + scribe
 |      |
upon + write
```

insect[2] 〔ˈɪnsɛkt 〕 *n.* 昆蟲（被切入 → 昆蟲身上的縫隙）

《*in-*（into）+ *sect*（cut）》　*cf.* **section**（切斷；部分）

insert[4] 〔 ɪnˈsɝt 〕 *v.* 插入；崁入　*n.* 插入的東西（加在裡面）

《*in-*（into）+ *sert*（join）》

inshore[7] 〔 *adj.* ˈɪnˌʃor *adv.* ˈɪnˈʃor 〕 *adj.* 近海岸的　　*adv.* 向海岸地
　《*in-* (towards) + *shore* (海岸)》

insight[6] 〔 ˈɪnˌsaɪt 〕= the power of seeing into　*n.* 洞察力；見識

inspect[3] 〔 ɪnˈspɛkt 〕*v.* 檢查；檢閱 (看到內部)
　《*in-* (in) + *spect* (look)》

inspirit[7] 〔 ɪnˈspɪrɪt 〕= give spirit to　*v.* 激勵；鼓舞 (使有精神)

instead[3] 〔 ɪnˈstɛd 〕*adv.* 代替；更換《*in-* (in) + *stead* (place)》

intake[7] 〔ˈɪnˌtek 〕*n.* 入口；攝取 (量) (拿進去的地方)

intoxicate[7] 〔 ɪnˈtɑksəˌket 〕*v.* 使醉；使陶醉；使中毒 (中毒)
　《*in-* (into) + *toxic* (poison 毒) + *-ate* (動詞字尾)》

```
in + toxic  + ate
 |     |       |
into + poison + v.
```

intricate[7] 〔ˈɪntrəkɪt 〕*adj.* 錯綜複雜的；難了解的 (遭遇阻礙之物)
　《*in-* (in) + *tric* (obstacle 妨礙) + *-ate* (形容詞字尾)》

intrigue[7] 〔 ɪnˈtrig 〕*n.* 陰謀　*v.* 陰謀對付；引起～的興趣
　(使遭遇阻礙)《*in-* (in) + *trigue* = *tric* (obstacle)》

intuition[5] 〔ˌɪntjʊˈɪʃən 〕*n.* 直覺；直覺力 (有洞察力)
　《*in-* (in) + *tuit* (watch) + *-ion* (名詞字尾)》

```
in +  tuit  + ion
 |     |       |
in +  watch +  n.
```

inundation[7] 〔ˌɪnʌnˈdeʃən 〕*n.* 氾濫；洪水；如洪水般湧到
　(大水湧入)《*in-* (in) + *und* (wave) + *-ation* (名詞字尾)》

```
in +  und  + ation
 |     |       |
in +  wave +   n.
```

inure[7] 〔 ɪnˈjʊr 〕*v.* 使習慣於 (經常練習)《*in-* (in) + *ure* (practice)》

invade[4] 〔 ɪnˈved 〕*v.* 侵犯；侵略
　《*in-* (into) + *vade* (go)》　*cf.* **wade** (跋涉)

inveigle[7] 〔 ɪn'vigḷ , -'vegḷ 〕 v. 誘騙；誘惑 (使人眼盲)

《*in-* (in) + *veigle* (blind)》

invest[4] 〔 ɪn'vɛst 〕 v. 籠罩；投資；花費 (進入衣服內)

《*in-* (in) + *vest* (clothe)》

investigate[3] 〔 ɪn'vɛstə,get 〕 v. 調查；研究 (追蹤進入)

《*in-* (in) + *vestigate* (trace 追蹤)》

involve[4] 〔 ɪn'vɑlv 〕 v. 包括；影響；牽涉 (捲入其中)

《*in-* (in) + *volve* (roll)》

illation[7] 〔 ɪ'leʃən 〕 = inference n. 推論；結論 (帶入內部)

《*il-* = *in-* (in) + *lat* (bring) + *-ion* (名詞字尾)》

```
il +   lat  + ion
 |      |      |
in + bring +  n.
```

illuminate[6] 〔 ɪ'lumə,net , ɪ'lju- 〕 = enlighten ; light up

v. 照亮；闡釋；說明 (光線照在～上)

《*il-* = *in-* (on ; upon) + *lumin* (light) + *-ate* (動詞字尾)》

cf. **luminary** (發光體)

```
il    + lumin + ate
 |        |      |
on , upon + light +  v.
```

illusion[6] 〔 ɪ'ljuʒən 〕 n. 幻影；幻想；錯覺 (耽溺於玩樂中)

《*il-* = *in-* (in) + *lus* (play ; jest) + *-ion* (名詞字尾)》

illustrate[4] 〔'ɪləstret , ɪ'lʌstret 〕 = throw light upon

v. 舉例說明；作圖解 (光線照在～上)

《*il-* = *in-* (upon) + *lustr* (light) + *-ate* (動詞字尾)》 *cf.* **luster** (光澤)

imbibe[7] 〔 ɪm'baɪb 〕 v. 喝；吸收；攝取 (喝進去)

《*im-* = *in-* (in) + *bibe* (drink)》

immanent[7] 〔'ɪmənənt 〕 adj. 內在的；內在性的 (在裡面的)

《*im-* = *in-* (in) + *man* (remain) + *-ent* (形容詞字尾)》

```
im +  man  + ent
 |     |      |
in + remain + adj.
```

immerge[7] 〔 ɪˈmɝdʒ 〕 *v.* 浸；沈入（沈入其中）
　《*im-* = *in-* (into) + *merge* (sink)》　*cf.* **emerge**（出現）

immigrate[4] 〔ˈɪməˌgret 〕 *v.* (使)（自外國）移民（信步而入）
　《*im-* = *in-* (into) + *migrate* (wander)》　*cf.* **emigrate** 遷居（他國）

immolate[7] 〔ˈɪməˌlet 〕 *v.* 犧牲；宰殺作祭品
　《*im-* = *in-* (on) + *molate* (sacrificial meal)》

impair[7] 〔 ɪmˈpɛr 〕 *v.* 損害；傷害（使更糟）
　《*im-* = *in-* (make) + *pair* (worse)》

impale[7] 〔 ɪmˈpel 〕 *v.* 刺住；刺穿；處以刺刑（用竹竿穿過）
　《*im-* = *in-* (into) + *pale* (pole)》

impart[7] 〔 ɪmˈpɑrt 〕 = give a part of　*v.* 傳授；告知
　《*im-* = *in-* (on ; upon) + *part* (share 分配)》

impeach[7] 〔 ɪmˈpitʃ 〕 *v.* 告發；彈劾；責難；懷疑（使上腳鐐）
　《*im-* = *in-* (on ; upon) + *peach* = *pedic* (fetter 腳鐐)》

```
        im   + peach
        |       |
     on , upon + fetter
```

impediment[7] 〔 ɪmˈpɛdəmənt 〕 *n.* 妨礙；阻礙（踏入）
　《*im-* = *in-* (in) + *pedi* (foot) + *-ment* (名詞字尾)》

```
     im + pedi + ment
     |     |      |
     in + foot +  n.
```

impenetrate[7] 〔 ɪmˈpɛnɪˌtret 〕 *v.* 透入；穿入
　《*im-* = *in-* (into) + *penetrate* (pierce 穿透)》

impersonate[7] 〔 ɪmˈpɝsn̩ˌet 〕 *v.* 扮演；模擬
　《*im-* = *in-* (in) + *person* + *-ate* (動詞字尾)》

impinge[7] 〔 ɪmˈpɪndʒ 〕 *v.* 撞擊；侵犯（擊打）
　《*im-* = *in-* (in) + *pinge* (strike)》

implant[7] 〔 ɪmˈplænt 〕 = plant in　*v.* 灌輸；移植（器官等）
（種入腦海中）

implement[6] 〔'ɪmpləmənt 〕 *n.* 工具；器具（充滿其中）

《*im-* = *in-* (in) + *ple* (fill) + *-ment* (名詞字尾)》

```
im + ple + ment
|     |     |
in + fill +  n.
```

implicate[7] 〔'ɪmplɪ͵ket 〕 *v.* 牽連；暗示；使糾結（輾轉而入）

《*im-* = *in-* (in) + *plicate* (fold)》 *cf.* **explicate** (說明；解說)

imply[4] 〔 ɪm'plaɪ 〕 *v.* 包含；暗示（折疊於其中）

《*im-* = *in-* (in) + *ply* (fold)》

import[3] 〔 *v.* ɪm'port *n.* 'ɪmport 〕 *v.* 輸入；含～的意思

n. 輸入；意義；重要性（搬入）

《*im-* = *in-* (in) + *port* (carry)》 *cf.* **export** (輸出)

impose[5] 〔 ɪm'poz 〕 *v.* 課（稅）；強加（置於其上）

《*im-* = *in-* (on ; upon) + *pose* (place)》

impound[7] 〔 ɪm'paund 〕 *v.* 關在欄中；監禁；貯（水）（圍在某地）

《*im-* = *in-* (in) + *pound* (place)》

impoverish[7] 〔 ɪm'pɑvərɪʃ 〕 = make poor *v.* 使貧乏；使變虛弱

《*im-* = *in-* (in) + *pover* (poor) + *-ish* (動詞字尾)》

```
im + pover + ish
|     |       |
in + poor  +  v.
```

imprecate[7] 〔'ɪmprɪ͵ket 〕 *v.* 祈求降禍；詛咒（祈禱降禍給某人）

《*im-* = *in-* (on ; upon) + *prec* (pray) + *-ate* (動詞字尾)》

```
im + prec + ate
|     |      |
on + pray +  v.
```

impregnate[7] 〔 ɪm'prɛgnet 〕 = make pregnant

v. 使懷孕；灌輸（使成為產前狀態）

《*im-* = *in-* (in) + *pregn* (be before a birth) + *-ate* (動詞字尾)》

imprint[7] 〔 ɪm'prɪnt 〕 = print on *v.* 加戳記；使留下印象；使銘記

imprison[6] 〔 ɪmˈprɪzn̩ 〕= put in prison　*v.* 下獄；監禁

irradiate[7] 〔 ɪˈrediˌet 〕= throw rays of light upon　*v.* 照射；
用放射線處理《*ir-* = *in-* (on) + *radi* (ray 光線) + *-ate* (動詞字尾)》

```
ir  +  radi  +  ate
 |      |      |
on  +  ray  +  v.
```

irrigate[7] 〔ˈɪrəˌget 〕*v.* 灌溉；灌注 (使～濕潤)
《*ir-* = *in-* (upon) + *rigate* (wet)》

irruption[7] 〔 ɪˈrʌpʃən 〕*n.* 侵入；闖入 (破～而入)
《*ir-* = *in-* (in) + *rupt* (burst) + *-ion* (名詞字尾)》

67　**in-** = negative；not (否定)

*〔變化型〕en- , i- , il- , im- , ir-。

inaccessible[7] 〔ˌɪnəkˈsɛsəbl̩ 〕*adj.* 不能親近的；不能得到的
《*in-* (not) + *accessible* (可接近的)》

inaccurate[7] 〔 ɪnˈækjərɪt 〕*adj.* 不準確的
《*in-* (not) + *accurate* (準確的)》

inadequate[7] 〔 ɪnˈædəkwɪt 〕*adj.* 不適切的；不充分的
《*in-* (not) + *adequate* (適切的)》

```
in  +  ad  +  equ   +  ate
 |     |      |        |
not  +  to  +  equal  +  adj.
```

inappropriate[7] 〔ˌɪnəˈproprɪɪt 〕*adj.* 不合宜的
《*in-* (not) + *appropriate* (合宜的)》

inaudible[7] 〔 ɪnˈɔdəbl̩ 〕*adj.* 聽不見的
《*in-* (not) + *audible* (聽得見的)》

incapable[7] 〔 ɪnˈkepəbl̩ 〕*adj.* 不能的《*in-* (not) + *capable* (有能力的)》

incautious 〔 ɪnˈkɔʃəs 〕*adj.* 不注意的；輕率的
《*in-* (not) + *cautious* (謹慎的)》

incest[7] 〔'ɪnsɛst 〕 *n.* 亂倫《*in-* (not) + *cest* (chaste 貞潔的)》

```
in  +  cest
|      |
not + chaste
```

inclement[7] 〔 ɪn'klɛmənt 〕 *adj.* 嚴寒的；殘酷的

```
in  +  clement
|      |
not +  mild
```

incoherent[7] 〔,ɪnko'hɪrənt 〕 *adj.* 無條理的；不協調的
《*in-* (not) + *coherent* (調和的)》

incommode[7] 〔,ɪnkə'mod 〕 *v.* 使不舒服；擾亂；阻礙
《*in-* (not) + *commode* (方便的)》

incomparable[7] 〔 ɪn'kɑmpərəbl̩ 〕 *adj.* 不能比較的；舉世無雙的
《*in-* (not) + *comparable* (可比較的)》

```
in  +  com   +  par  + able
|      |         |      |
not + together + equal + adj.
```

inconsistent[7] 〔,ɪnkən'sɪstənt 〕 *adj.* 矛盾的；不合的
《*in-* (not) + *consistent* (一致的)》

inconstant[7] 〔 ɪn'kɑnstənt 〕 *adj.* 無常的；多變的
《*in-* (not) + *constant* (不變的)》

inconvenient[7] 〔,ɪnkən'vinjənt 〕 *adj.* 不方便的；打擾的
《*in-* (not) + *convenient* (方便的)》

indecisive[7] 〔,ɪndɪ'saɪsɪv 〕 *adj.* 缺乏決心的；優柔寡斷的
《*in-* (not) + *decisive* (決定的)》

indigestion[7] 〔,ɪndaɪ'dʒɛstʃən 〕 *n.* 消化不良
《*in-* (not) + *digestion* (消化)》

```
in  +  di   +  gest  + ion
|      |        |       |
not + apart + carry  + n.
```

indiscreet[7] 〔͵ɪndɪ'skrit〕*adj.* 不穩重的;輕率的

《*in-* (not) + *discreet* (謹慎的)》

indispensable[5] 〔͵ɪndɪs'pɛnsəbļ〕*adj.* 不可缺少的

《*in-* (not) + *dispensable* (不重要的)》

indolent[7] 〔'ɪndələnt〕*adj.* 懶惰的;怠惰的

《*in-* (not) + *dolent* (feel pain)》

ineffective[7] 〔͵ɪnə'fɛktɪv〕*adj.* 沒有效果的;不能起作用的

《*in-* (not) + *effective* (有效果的)》

inefficient[7] 〔͵ɪnə'fɪʃənt〕*adj.* 無效率的;不稱職的

《*in-* (not) + *efficient* (有效率的)》

```
in + ef + fici + ent
 |    |     |     |
not + out + do + adj.
```

inequality[7] 〔͵ɪnɪ'kwɑlətɪ〕*n.* 不平等

《*in-* (not) + *equality* (平等)》

infallible[7] 〔ɪn'fæləbļ〕*adj.* 絕對無誤的;絕對可靠的;肯定有效的

《*in-* (not) + *fallible* (可能犯錯的)》

infamous[7] 〔'ɪnfəməs〕= notorious　*adj.* 惡名昭彰的;聲名狼藉的

《*in-* (not) + *famous* (有名的)》

inflexible[7] 〔ɪn'flɛksəbļ〕*adj.* 不能彎曲的;欠缺彈性的

```
in + flex + ible
 |    |      |
not + bend + adj.
```

infrequent[7] 〔ɪn'frikwənt〕*adj.* 稀少的;罕見的

《*in-* (not) + *frequent* (頻繁的)》

innutrition 〔͵ɪnju'trɪʃən〕*n.* 營養不良

《*in-* (not) + *nutrition* (營養)》

insane[7] 〔ɪn'sen〕*adj.* 瘋狂的

《*in-* (not) + *sane* (神智清楚的)》

insecure[7] 〔͵ɪnsɪ'kjʊr〕*adj.* 不安全的;有危險的

《*in-* (not) + *secure* (安全的)》

insensitive[7]〔 ɪnˈsɛnsətɪv 〕 *adj.* 感覺遲鈍的

insignificant[7]〔ˌɪnsɪgˈnɪfəkənt 〕 *adj.* 不重要的；無意義的；
微小的《*in-* (not) + *significant* (有意義的；重要的)》

> | in | + | sign | + | ific | + | ant |
> |---|---|---|---|---|---|---|
> | | | \| | | \| | | \| |
> | *not* | + | *mark* | + | *make* | + | *adj.* |

insufficient[7]〔ˌɪnsəˈfɪʃənt 〕 *adj.* 不充足的；能力不足的
《*in-* (not) + *sufficient* (足夠的)》

insuperable〔 ɪnˈsupərəbḷ 〕 *adj.* 不能克服的

> | in | + | super | + | able |
> |---|---|---|---|---|
> | | | \| | | \| |
> | *not* | + | *over* | + | *adj.* |

intangible[7]〔 ɪnˈtændʒəbḷ 〕 *adj.* 無形的；無法捉摸的

> | in | + | tang | + | ible |
> |---|---|---|---|---|
> | | | \| | | \| |
> | *not* | + | *touch* | + | *adj.* |

invaluable[6]〔 ɪnˈvæljəbḷ 〕 *adj.* 無價的；非常珍貴的 (無法評價的)
《*in-* (not) + *valuable* (有價值的)》 *cf.* **valueless** (沒有價值的)

invisible[7]〔 ɪnˈvɪzəbḷ 〕 *adj.* 看不見的

invulnerable[7]〔 ɪnˈvʌlnərəbḷ 〕 *adj.* 不會受傷害的；無懈可擊的
《*in-* (not) + *vulnerable* (易受傷害的)》

enemy[2]〔ˈɛnəmɪ 〕 *n.* 敵人 (不是朋友)
《*en-* = *in-* (not) + *emy* (friend)》 *cf.* **amicable** (友善的)

> | en | + | emy |
> |---|---|---|
> | \| | | \| |
> | *not* | + | *friend* |

ignoble[7]〔 ɪgˈnobḷ 〕 *adj.* 卑賤的；下流的
《*i-* = *in-* (not) + *gnoble* (noble)》

ignominy[7]〔ˈɪgnəˌmɪnɪ 〕 *n.* 不名譽 (不名譽的)
《*i-* = *in-* (not) + *gnominy* (something by which one is known 名聲)》

ignorant[4] 〔ˈɪgnərənt〕 adj. 無知的；愚昧的；不知道的
　《i- = in- (not) + gnor (know) + -ant (形容詞字尾)》

```
 i  + gnor  + ant
 |     |       |
not + know  + adj.
```

illegal[7] 〔ɪˈligḷ〕 adj. 非法的《il- = in- (not) + legal (合法的)》

illegible[7] 〔ɪˈlɛdʒəbḷ〕 adj. 難讀的；難辨認的

illegitimate[7] 〔ˌɪlɪˈdʒɪtəmɪt〕 adj. 違法的；私生的
　《il- = in- (not) + legitimate (合法的)》

illiberal[7] 〔ɪˈlɪbərəl〕 adj. 心胸狹窄的；吝嗇的
　《il- = in- (not) + liberal (大方的；寬大的)》

illicit[7] 〔ɪˈlɪsɪt〕 adj. 違法的；不合法的
　《il- = in- (not) + licit (合法的)》

illiterate[7] 〔ɪˈlɪtərɪt〕 adj. , n. 未受教育的 (人)；不會讀寫的 (人)
　《il- = in- (not) + literate (能讀能寫的)》

illogical[7] 〔ɪˈlɑdʒɪkḷ〕 adj. 不合常理的；不合邏輯的
　《il- = in- (not) + logical (合理的)》

imbecile[7] 〔ɪmˈbəsḷ〕 n. 弱智者；極愚蠢的人　adj. 低能的；愚蠢的
　(沒有幕僚支持)《im- = in- (without) + becile (staff 幕僚)》

immaculate[7] 〔ɪˈmækjəlɪt〕 = spotless　adj. 潔淨的；無瑕的
　(沒有斑點的)《im- = in- (not) + maculate (be spotted)》

```
im + maculate
 |      |
not + be spotted
```

immaterial[7] 〔ˌɪməˈtɪrɪəl〕 adj. 非物質的；不重要的
　《im- = in- (not) + material (物質的)》

immature[7] 〔ˌɪməˈtjʊr〕 adj. 未成熟的
　《im- = in- (not) + mature (成熟的)》

immeasurable[7] 〔ɪˈmɛʒərəbḷ〕 adj. 不能測量的
　《im- = in- (not) + measurable (可測得的)》

immediate[3] 〔 ɪˈmidɪɪt 〕 *adj.* 直接的;即刻的(沒有間隔的)

《*im-* = *in-* (not) + *mediate* (middle)》　*cf.* **medium** (媒體)

immense[5] 〔 ɪˈmɛns 〕 *adj.* 無邊的(無法測知的)

《*im-* = *in-* (not) + *mense* (measure)》　*cf.* **mete** (分配)

```
im  +  mense
|        |
not  +  measure
```

immobile[7] 〔 ɪmˈmobɪl 〕 *adj.* 不動的;固定的;靜止的

《*im-* = *in-* (not) + *mobile* (move)》

immodest[7] 〔 ɪˈmɑdɪst 〕 *adj.* 無禮的;放肆的;不端莊的

《*im-* = *in-* (not) + *modest* (有禮的)》

immortal[7] 〔 ɪˈmɔrtl̩ 〕 *adj.* 不朽的;永世的　*n.* 不朽人物;神

《*im-* = *in-* (not) + *mortal* (必死的)》

immutable[7] 〔 ɪˈmjutəbl̩ 〕 *adj.* 不變的;永恒的

《*im-* = *in-* (not) + *mutable* (changeable)》

impalpable 〔 ɪmˈpælpəbl̩ 〕 *adj.* 觸摸不到的;感覺不到的;

難理解的《*im-* = *in-* (not) + *palpable* (可觸知的)》

```
im  +  palp  +  able
|        |        |
not  +  touch  +  adj.
```

imparity[7] 〔 ɪmˈpærətɪ 〕 *n.* 不等;不平衡

《*im-* = *in-* (not) + *parity* (平等)》　*cf.* **par** (同等)

impartial[7] 〔 ɪmˈpɑrʃəl 〕 *adj.* 公平的;不偏不倚的

《*im-* = *in-* (not) + *partial* (不公平的)》

impeccable[7] 〔 ɪmˈpɛkəbl̩ 〕 *adj.* 完美的;純潔的

《*im-* = *in-* (not) + *pecc* (sin 犯罪) + *-able* (形容詞字尾)》

impecunious 〔 ˌɪmpɪˈkjunɪəs 〕 *adj.* 沒有錢的;貧窮的

《*im-* = *in-* (without) + *pecun* (money) + *-ious* (形容詞字尾)》

```
im    +  pecun  +  ious
|          |         |
without  +  money  +  adj.
```

impenetrable[7] 〔 ɪm'pɛnətrəbl̩ 〕 *adj.* 不能穿過的；不可理解的
 《*im-* = *in-* (not) + *penetrable* (可貫穿的)》

impenitent 〔 ɪm'pɛnətənt 〕 *adj.* , *n.* 不悔悟的 (人)
 《*im-* = *in-* (not) + *penitent* (悔悟的)》

impertinent[7] 〔 ɪm'pɝtn̩ənt 〕 *adj.* 不相干的；魯莽的；不適宜的
 《*im-* = *in-* (not) + *pertinent* (適切的)》

```
im  +   per    +  tin  + ent
 |       |         |      |
not + thoroughly + hold + adj.
```

impious 〔'ɪmpɪəs 〕 *adj.* 不敬的；不虔誠的
 《*im-* = *in-* (not) + *pious* (虔誠的)》

implacable[7] 〔 ɪm'plekəbl̩ 〕 *adj.* 難和解的；難平息的
 《*im-* = *in-* (not) + *placable* (溫和的)》

impolite[7] 〔,ɪmpə'laɪt 〕 *adj.* 不客氣的；無禮的
 《*im-* = *in-* (not) + *polite* (禮貌的)》

impotent[7] 〔'ɪmpətənt 〕 *adj.* 無力的；無助的
 《*im-* = *in-* (not) + *potent* (強有力的)》

impractical[7] 〔 ɪm'præktɪkl̩ 〕 *adj.* 不切實際的；空想的
 《*im-* = *in-* (not) + *practical* (實際的)》

imprecise[7] 〔,ɪmprɪ'saɪz 〕 *adj.* 不準確的；不明確的；模糊不清的
 《*im-* = *in-* (not) + *precise* (正確的)》

```
in  +  pre  + cise
 |      |       |
not + before + cut
```

字首 in-～iso-

imprudent[7] 〔 ɪm'prudn̩t 〕 *adj.* 不謹慎的；不加思慮的
 《*im-* = *in-* (not) + *prudent* (謹慎的)》

impunity[7] 〔 ɪm'pjunətɪ 〕 *n.* 免除 (懲罰、損失、傷害等)

```
im +  pun  + ity
 |     |      |
not + punish + n.
```

irrational[7] 〔 ɪˈræʃən̩ 〕 *adj.* 不合理的　*n.* 無理數
　《*ir-* = *in-* (not) + *rational* (理性的)》

ir	+	rat	+ ion +	al
not	+	*reason*	+ *n.*	+ *adj.*

irredeemable[7] 〔ˌɪrɪˈdiməb̩ 〕 *adj.* 不能挽救的；不能恢復的
　《*ir-* = *in-* (not) + *redeemable* (可買回的)》

irregular[7] 〔 ɪˈrɛgjələ 〕 *adj.* 不規則的；不整齊的；不一致的
　《*ir-* = *in-* (not) + *regular* (規則的)》

irrelative[7] 〔 ɪˈrɛlətɪv 〕 *adj.* 無關係的；不相干的
　《*ir-* = *in-* (not) + *relative* (相關的)》

ir	+	re	+	lat	+	ive
not	+	*back*	+	*bring*	+	*adj.*

irrelevant[7] 〔 ɪˈrɛləvənt 〕 *adj.* 不適切的；離題的
　《*ir-* = *in-* (not) + *relevant* (切題的)》

irreligious 〔ˌɪrɪˈlɪdʒəs 〕 *adj.* 不虔誠的；無信仰的
　《*ir-* = *in-* (not) + *religious* (虔誠的；宗教的)》

irresistible[7] 〔ˌɪrɪˈzɪstəb̩ 〕 *adj.* 不能抵抗的；無法抗拒的
　《*ir-* = *in-* (not) + *resistible* (可抗拒的)》

irresolute[7] 〔 ɪˈrɛzəˌlut , -ˈrɛzl̩ˌjut 〕 *adj.* 不果斷的；猶豫不決的
　《*ir-* = *in-* (not) + *resolute* (果斷的；堅決的)》

irresponsible[7] 〔ˌɪrɪˈspɑnsəb̩ 〕 *adj.* 不須負責任的
　《*ir-* = *in-* (not) + *responsible* (應負責任的)》

68　**infra-** = below

infracostal 〔ˌɪnfrəˈkɑstl̩ , -ˈkɔs- 〕 *adj.* (位於) 肋骨下的
　《*infra-* (below) + *costa* (肋骨) + *-(a)l* (形容詞字尾)》

infrahuman 〔ˌɪnfrəˈhjumən 〕 *adj.* (在進化程度上) 低於人類的；
　似人類的；類人猿的　*n.* 低於人類的動物；類人動物
　《*infra-* (below) + *human* (人類)》

infrared[7]〔͵ɪnfrə'rɛd〕*adj.* 紅外線的　*n.* 紅外線
　《*infra-* (below) + *red* (紅色)》

infrasonic[7]〔͵ɪnfrə'sɑnɪk〕*adj.* (聲波) 頻率低於聽覺範圍的；
人類聽覺聽不到的
　《*infra-* (below) + *son* (sound) + *-ic* (形容詞字尾)》

infrastructure[7]〔'ɪnfrə͵strʌktʃɚ〕*n.* 基礎建設
　《*infra-* (below) + *structure* (結構；建築物)》

69　**inter-** = between；among

　　*〔變化型〕enter- , intel-。

intercede[7]〔͵ɪntɚ'sid〕*v.* 求情；調停

inter	+	cede
between	+	go

intercept[7]〔͵ɪntɚ'sɛpt〕*v.* 中途攔截；截獲；阻止 (在中間抓到)
　《*inter-* (between) + *cept* (catch)》

interchange[7]〔͵ɪntɚ'tʃendʒ〕*v.* 交換；輪替
　《*inter-* (between) + *change*》

intercollegiate[7]〔͵ɪntɚkə'lidʒɪɪt〕*adj.* 大學間的；學院間的

interfere[4]〔͵ɪntɚ'fɪr〕*v.* 牴觸；干涉 (彼此對打)
　《*inter-* (between) + *fere* (strike)》

inter	+	fere
between	+	strike

interfuse〔͵ɪntɚ'fjuz〕*v.* 使混合；瀰漫 (注入兩者之間)
　《*inter-* (between) + *fuse* (pour)》

interim[7]〔'ɪntərɪm〕*n.* 中間時期　*adj.* 中間的；暫時的；臨時的

interior[5]〔ɪn'tɪrɪɚ〕*adj.* 內部的；內陸的；國內的
　n. 內部；內陸；室內《*inter-* (among) + *-ior* (表比較級的字尾)》

interjacent〔,ɪntəˈdʒesənt 〕= lying between *adj.* 在中間的；居間的《*inter-*(between)+ *jac* (lie)+ *-ent* (形容詞字尾)》

```
inter  + jac + ent
  |        |     |
between + lie + adj.
```

interject[7]〔,ɪntəˈdʒɛkt 〕*v.* 突然插入（言詞等）

interlace[7]〔,ɪntəˈles 〕*v.*（使）交織；（使）組合（把兩者編織起來）
《*inter-*(between)+ *lace* (編織)》

interlude[7]〔ˈɪntəˌlud 〕*v.* 間奏（曲）；中間
《*inter-*(between)+ *lude* (play)》 *cf.* **prelude** (前奏曲)

intermediary[7]〔,ɪntəˈmidɪˌɛrɪ 〕*n.* 介紹人；講解人

intermingle[7]〔,ɪntəˈmɪŋgḷ 〕*v.* 混合；攙雜
《*inter-*(between)+ *mingle* (混合)》

intermission[7]〔,ɪntəˈmɪʃən 〕*n.* 中斷；中場休息

intermit[7]〔,ɪntəˈmɪt 〕*v.* 暫停；中止；間歇（進入間隙）
《*inter-*(between)+ *mit* (send)》

intermittent[7]〔,ɪntəˈmɪtṇt 〕*adj.* 間歇性的；斷續的

```
inter  + mitt + ent
  |        |      |
between + send + adj.
```

intermix[7]〔,ɪntəˈmɪks 〕*v.* 混合；混雜
《*inter-*(between)+ *mix* (mix)》

international[2]〔,ɪntəˈnæʃənḷ 〕*adj.* 國際的；國際性的
（國與國之間）《*inter-*(between)+ *national* (國家的)》

internecine〔,ɪntəˈnisɪn 〕*adj.* 殘殺的；血腥的；兩敗俱傷的
《*inter-*(between)+ *necine* (kill)》

interpellate〔 ɪnˈtɝpɪˌlet 〕*v.* 質詢（議會中）
《*inter-*(between)+ *pell* (urge)+ *-ate* (動詞字尾)》

```
inter  + pell + ate
  |        |      |
between + urge +  v.
```

interplay[7] 〔'ɪntɚ͵ple〕*n.* 相互作用（在彼此間作用）

《*inter-*（between）+ *play*（play）》

interpolate〔ɪn'tɝpə͵let〕*v.* 加添字句；竄改（在其中潤飾）

《*inter-*（between）+ *pol*（polish）+ *-ate*（動詞字尾）》

```
    inter  +  pol   + ate
      |        |       |
  between + polish +  v.
```

interpose〔͵ɪntɚ'poz〕*v.* 使介入；置於～之間；調停

《*inter-*（between）+ *pose*（put）》

interpret[4]〔ɪn'tɝprɪt〕*v.* 解釋；闡明；口譯（在兩者間確定價值）

《*inter-*（between）+ *pret* = *prec*（price）》

```
    inter  +  pret
      |        |
  between +  price
```

interrelate[7]〔͵ɪntɚrɪ'let〕*v.* 使相互聯繫

《*inter-*（between）+ *re-*（back）+ *late*（bring）》

interrupt[3]〔͵ɪntə'rʌpt〕*v.* 中斷；妨礙（決裂）

《*inter-*（between）+ *rupt*（break）》

intersect[7]〔͵ɪntɚ'sɛkt〕*v.* 貫穿；相交（從中切過）

《*inter-*（between）+ *sect*（cut）》

intersperse[7]〔͵ɪntɚ'spɝs〕*v.* 散置；點綴

《*inter-*（between）+ *sperse*（scatter）》

interstate[7]〔͵ɪntɚ'stet , 'ɪntɚ͵stet〕*adj.* 州際的

interstellar[7]〔͵ɪntɚ'stɛlɚ〕*adj.* 星際的

《*inter-*（between）+ *stellar*（star）》

interstice[7]〔ɪn'tɝstɪs〕*n.* 空隙；裂縫（站在兩者之間）

《*inter-*（between）+ *stice* = *sist*（stand）》

```
    inter  +  stice
      |        |
  between +  stand
```

interval[6] 〔'ɪntəvl̩〕 *n.* 間隔；距離；差異（在牆與牆之間）

　《*inter-*（between）+ *val*（wall）》

intervene[6] 〔͵ɪntə'vin〕 *v.* 介於其間；介入；干涉；調停

　《*inter-*（between）+ *vene*（come）》

intertwine[7] 〔͵ɪntə'twaɪn〕 *v.* 糾纏；纏繞；交織

　《*inter-*（between）+ *twine*（纏繞）》

interurban[7] 〔͵ɪntə'ɝbən〕 *adj.* 城市間的

interweave[7] 〔͵ɪntə'wiv〕 *v.* 交織；混合

　《*inter-*（between）+ *weave*（編織）》

enterprise[5] 〔'ɛntəˏpraɪz〕 *n.* 事業；企業；進取心（在許多東西

之中拿到）　《*enter-* = *inter-*（among）+ *prise*（take in hand）》

cf. **prize**（獎品；戰利品）

```
enter  +   prise
  |          |
among + take in hand
```

entertain[4] 〔͵ɛntə'ten〕 *v.* 款待；使娛樂（保持關係）

　《*enter-* = *inter-*（among）+ *tain*（hold）》

intellect[6] 〔'ɪntl̩ˏɛkt〕 *n.* 知性；智力；理解力；知識份子

（從中選取的能力）　《*intel-*（between）+ *lect*（choose）》

intelligence[4] 〔ɪn'tɛlədʒəns〕 *n.* 智力；理解力；情報

　《*intel-* = *inter-*（between）+ *ligence*（choose）》

70　**intra- , intro-**
　　= inward；within（與 extra- 相反）

intramural[7] 〔͵ɪntrə'mjʊrəl〕 *adj.* 校內的

```
intra  + mur + al
  |        |    |
within + wall + adj.
```

intraoffice[7] 〔͵ɪntrə'ɔfɪs〕 *adj.* 公司內的；公司各部門之間的

intraparty 〔'ɪntrə'pɑrtɪ 〕 *adj.* 黨內的

intrapersonal[7] 〔'ɪntrə'pɝsən! 〕 *adj.* 個人頭腦中的；內心的

   cf. **interpersonal** (人與人之間的；人際關係的)

intra-school[7] 〔'ɪntrə'skul 〕 *adj.* 校內的

intravenous[7] 〔,ɪntrə'vinəs 〕 *adj.* 靜脈內的；靜脈注射的

   《 *intra-* (within) + *ven* (vein 靜脈) + *-ous* (形容詞字尾)》

```
intra  +  ven  +  ous
  |        |       |
within  +  vein  +  adj.
```

introduce[2] 〔,ɪntrə'djus 〕 *v.* 推薦；介紹；引導

   《 *intro-* (inward) + *duce* (lead)》

intromit[7] 〔,ɪntrə'mɪt 〕 *v.* 進入；干涉

   《 *intro-* (within) + *mit* (send)》

introspect[7] 〔,ɪntrə'spɛkt 〕 *v.* 內省 (看內部)

   《 *intro-* (within) + *spect* (look)》

introspective[7] 〔,ɪntrə'spɛktɪv 〕 *adj.* 內省的 (看內部)

```
intro  +  spect  +  ive
  |         |        |
within  +  look   +  adj.
```

introvert[7] 〔 *v.* ,ɪntrə'vɝt *n.* 'ɪntrə,vɝt 〕 *v.* 使內向；使內省

   n. 內向的人《 *intro-* (within) + *vert* (turn)》

71 **iso-** = equal (相等的)   * 希臘文 *isos*。

isobar 〔'aɪsə,bɑr 〕 *n.* 等壓線《 *iso-* (equal) + *bar* (pressure)》

isochronal 〔 aɪ'sɑkrən! 〕 *adj.* 同一時間的；等時 (性) 的

   《 *iso-* (equal) + *chron* (time) + *-al* (形容詞字尾)》

```
iso  +  chron  +  al
 |        |        |
equal  +  time  +  adj.
```

isogloss〔ˈaɪsəˌglɑs〕*n.* 等語線（同一語言特徵之地區境界線）

　　《*iso-*（equal）+ *gloss*（language）》

isogonic〔ˌaɪsəˈgɑnɪk〕*adj.* 等偏角的

　　《*iso-*（equal）+ *gon*（angle）+ *-ic*（形容詞字尾）》

isomer〔ˈaɪsəmɚ〕*n.*（同質）異構體

　　《*iso-*（equal）+ *mer*（part）》

isometric；**-rical**[7]〔ˌaɪsəˈmɛtrɪk(l̩)〕*adj.* 等大（等積、等容量、等

　　角）的《*iso-*（equal）+ *metr* = *meter*（measure）+ *-ic(al)*（形容詞字尾）》

```
iso  +  metr  +  ic(al)
 |        |        |
equal + measure + adj.
```

isosceles〔aɪˈsɑsl̩ˌiz〕*adj.* 等腰的《*iso-*（equal）+ *sceles*（leg）》

isotherm〔ˈaɪsəˌθɝm〕*n.* 等溫線《*iso-*（equal）+ *therm*（heat）》

isotope[7]〔ˈaɪsəˌtop〕*n.* 同位素《*iso-*（equal）+ *tope*（place）》

72　**kilo-** = thousand　　* 希臘文 *khilioi*，表示「千」。

kilobyte[7]〔ˈkɪləˌbaɪt〕*n.*（電腦）千位元組《*byte* 電腦位元組》

kilocalorie〔ˈkɪləˌkælərɪ〕*n.* 大卡（一千卡）

　　《*calorie* 熱量單位，卡路里》

kilocycle〔ˈkɪləˌsaɪkl̩〕*n.* 千周（頻率單位）

kilogram[3]〔ˈkɪləˌgræm〕*n.* 公斤（一千公克）

kilohertz[7]〔ˈkɪləˌhɝts〕*n.* 千赫《*hertz* 赫，周波數單位》

```
kilo   +  hertz
 |         |
thousand + unit
```

kiloliter；**-tre**[7]〔ˈkɪləˌlitɚ〕*n.* 公秉（一千公升）

kilometer[3]；**-tre**〔ˈkɪləˌmitɚ〕*n.* 公里（一千公尺）

kiloton[7]〔ˈkɪləˌtʌn〕*n.* 千噸

kilovolt[7]〔ˈkɪləˌvolt〕*n.* 千伏特

kilowatt[7]〔ˈkɪləˌwat〕*n.* 千瓦（電力單位）

73　macro- = large ; long　　* 希臘文 *makros*。

macroanalysis〔ˌmækroə'næləsɪs 〕 *n.* 巨量分析 (應用於經濟理論)
《*analysis* 分析》　*cf.* **microanalysis** (微量分析)

macrobiotics[7]〔ˌmækrobaɪ'atɪks 〕 *n.* 延年益壽的飲食法
(研究長壽的學問)《*macro-* (long) + *bio* (life) + *-tics* (study)》

macrocosm[7]〔'mækrəˌkazəm 〕 *n.* 大宇宙；總體
《*macro-* (large) + *cosm* (universe)》　*cf.* **microcosm** (小宇宙；縮圖)

```
macro  +  cosm
  |         |
large  +  universe
```

macroeconomics[7]〔'mækrəˌikə'namɪks 〕 *n.* 總體經濟學；宏觀
經濟學《*economics* 經濟學》
cf. **microeconomics** (個體經濟學；微觀經濟學)

macro-engineering[7]〔'mækroˌɛndʒə'nɪrɪŋ 〕 *n.* 大規模工程計畫
的研究《*engineering* 工程學》

macrometeorology[7]〔ˌmækroˌmitiə'ralədʒɪ 〕 *n.* 巨氣象學
(研究廣大區域內氣候之科學)《*meteorology* 氣象學》

macromolecule[7]〔ˌmækro'maləˌkjul 〕 *n.* 巨大分子；高分子
《*molecule* 分子》

macroscopic; **-ical**[7]〔ˌmækrə'skapɪk(l̩) 〕 *adj.* 肉眼可見的；
巨視的《*macro-* (large) + *scop* (look) + *-ic(al)* (形容詞字尾)》

74　mal(e)- = badly ; ill (與 bene- 相反)

* 拉丁文 *male*，表示「不舒服」。

maladjustment[7]〔ˌmælə'dʒʌstmənt 〕 *n.* 調節不良；適應不良
《*mal-* (badly) + *adjustment* (調節)》

maladministration〔ˌmælədˌmɪnə'streʃən 〕 *n.* 經營不善；惡政
《*mal-* (badly) + *administration* (管理)》

maladroit[7] 〔͵mælə'drɔɪt 〕 *adj.* 愚鈍的

《*mal-* (badly) + *adroit* (巧妙的)》

```
mal  +  a  + droit
 |       |      |
badly  +  to  + right
```

malady[7] 〔'mælədɪ 〕 = be kept badly   *n.* 疾病；缺點 (不好的狀態)

《*mal-* (badly) + *ady* (held ; kept)》

malaise[7] 〔 mæ'lez 〕 *n.* 不適；小病；微恙 (不舒服)

《*mal-* (ill) + *aise* (comfort)》

malapropism[7] 〔'mæləprɑp͵ɪzəm 〕 *n.* 文字之滑稽或怪誕的誤用；
被誤用的字

```
mal  +    aprop      + ism
 |         |           |
badly + to the purpose +  n.
```

malaria[6] 〔 mə'lɛrɪə 〕 *n.* 瘧疾；瘴氣

```
mal  + aria
 |      |
badly  + air
```

malcontent[7] 〔'mælkən͵tɛnt 〕 *n.* 不滿者；不滿分子   *adj.* 不滿的

《*mal-* (badly) + *content* (滿足；滿足的)》

malediction[7] 〔͵mælə'dɪkʃən 〕 *n.* 詛咒；誹謗 (說壞話)

《*male-* (badly) + *dict* (speak) + *-ion* (名詞字尾)》

```
male  + dict  + ion
 |       |       |
badly + speak  +  n.
```

malefactor[7] 〔'mælə͵fæktɚ 〕 = an evil-doer   *n.* 犯罪者；惡徒

(做壞事的人) 《*male-* (badly) + *factor* (doer)》

cf. **benefactor** (恩人)

maleficent[7] 〔 mə'lɛfəsn̩t 〕 *adj.* 有害的；邪惡的；惡行的

《*male-* (badly) + *fic* (do) + *-ent* (形容詞字尾)》

malevolent[7] 〔 mə'lɛvələnt 〕 *adj.* 惡意的（懷有惡意的）

《*male-*（ badly ）+ *vol*（ wish ）+ *-ent*（ 形容詞字尾 ）》

cf. **benevolent**（ 慈善的 ），**voluntary**（ 自願的 ）

malfeasance[7] 〔ˌmæl'fizn̩s 〕 *n.*（ 公務員的 ）不法行為；瀆職

《*mal-*（ badly ）+ *feas*（ do ）+ *-ance*（ 名詞字尾 ）》

```
mal  +  feas  +  ance
 |        |        |
badly  +  do   +   n.
```

malformation[7] 〔ˌmælfɔr'meʃən 〕 *n.* 奇形怪狀；畸形（ 形狀不好 ）

《*mal-*（ badly ）+ *form*（ form ）+ *-ation*（ 名詞字尾 ）》

malfunction[7] 〔 mæl'fʌŋkʃən 〕 *n.* 機能不全；故障　*v.* 故障

（ 功能失常 ）《*mal-*（ badly ）+ *function*（ 功能 ）》

```
mal  +  funct  +  ion
 |        |        |
bad  +  perform  +  n.
```

malice[7] 〔'mælɪs 〕 = badness ; ill will　*n.* 惡意；預謀

malicious[7] 〔 mə'lɪʃəs 〕 *adj.* 懷惡意的；心毒的

```
mal  +  ici  +  ous
 |       |       |
badly  +  n.  +  adj.
```

malign[7] 〔 mə'laɪn 〕 *adj.* 有害的；惡性的；惡意的　*v.* 誹謗；中傷

（ 產生惡意 ）《*mali-*（ badly ）+ *gn* = *gen*（ produce ）》

malignant[7] 〔 mə'lɪgnənt 〕 *adj.* 惡性的；惡意的；有害的（ 做出壞

東西的 ）《*mali-*（ bad ）+ *gn* = *gen*（ produce ）+ *-ant*（ 形容詞字尾 ）》

cf. **benignant**（ 仁慈的；有利的 ）

malinger[7] 〔 mə'lɪŋgɚ 〕 *v.* 裝病（ 將瘦誇大為病 ）

《*mal-*（ badly ）+ (*l*)*inger*（ thin ）》

malnourished[7] 〔ˌmæl'nɝɪʃt 〕 *adj.* 營養失調的；營養不良的

（ 營養不好的 ）《*mal-*（ badly ）+ *nourished*（ 營養的 ）》

malnutrition[7]〔͵mælnju'trɪʃən〕*n.* 營養失調；營養不良

《*mal-*（bad）+ *nutrition*（營養）》

maltreat[7]〔mæl'trit〕*v.* 虐待

75　**mega-** = large；million

> * 希臘文 *megas*，表示「巨大的」、「百萬」。〔變化型〕megalo-。

megabyte[7]〔'mɛgə͵baɪt〕*n.*（電腦）百萬位元組

《*mega-*（million）+ *byte*（電腦位元組）》

megahertz[7]〔'mɛgə͵hɝts〕*n.* 兆赫

megalith〔'mɛgə͵lɪθ〕*n.*（史前時期的）巨石

《*mega-*（large）+ *lith*（stone）》

```
mega  +  lith
 |        |
large  +  stone
```

megalomania[7]〔͵mɛgələ'menɪə〕*n.* 妄想自大狂（幻想誇大的疾病）

《*megalo-*（large）+ *mania*（insanity 精神錯亂）》

megalopolitan〔͵mɛgəlo'pɑlətən〕*adj.* 大都市的

《*megalo-*（large）+ *polit*（city）+ *-an*（形容詞字尾）》

```
megalo  +  polit  +  an
  |          |        |
large   +   city  +  adj.
```

megaphone[7]〔'mɛgə͵fon〕*n.* 擴音器；傳聲筒（使聲音擴大）

《*mega-*（large）+ *phone*（sound）》

megaron〔'mɛgərɑn〕*n.* 中央大廳《*mega-*（large）+ *ron*（place）》

```
mega  +  ron
 |        |
large  +  place
```

megaton[7]〔'mɛgə͵tʌn〕*n.* 一百萬噸《*mega-*（million）+ *ton*（噸）》

megavolt[7]〔'mɛgə͵volt〕*n.* 百萬伏特《*mega-*（million）+ *volt*（伏特）》

megawatt[7]〔'mɛgə͵wɑt〕*n.* 百萬瓦特《*mega-*（million）+ *watt*（瓦特）》

76　**meso-** = middle

　　* 希臘文 *mesos*，表示「中間的」。〔變化型〕mes-。

mesarch〔'mɛzɑrk〕*adj.*【植物】中始式的；【生物】中生演替的
　　《*mes-* (middle) + *arch* (beginning)》

mesencephalon〔،mɛsɛn'sɛfə،lɑn〕*n.* 中腦
　　《*mes-* (middle) + *en-* (in) + *cephal* (head) + *-on* (名詞字尾)》

mesoblast〔'mɛsə،blæst〕*n.* 中胚層《*meso-* (middle) + *blast* (bud)》

mesocarp〔'mɛsə،kɑrp〕*n.* 中果皮《*meso-* (middle) + *carp* (fruit)》

mesoderm〔'mɛsə،dɝm〕*n.* 中胚層《*meso-* (middle) + *derm* (skin)》

mesoglea〔،mɛso'gliə〕*n.* 中膠層《*meso-* (middle) + *glea* (glue 膠)》

mesomorphic〔،mɛsə'mɔrfɪk〕*adj.* 體育型體質的；中胚層體型的
　　《*meso-* (middle) + *morph* (form) + *-ic* (形容詞字尾)》

Mesopotamia[7]〔،mɛsəpə'temɪə , -'temjə〕*n.* 美索不達米亞
　　(亦稱兩河流域，在亞洲西南部底格里斯河和幼發拉底河兩河之間)
　　《*meso-* (middle) + *potam* (river) + *-ia* (名詞字尾)》

77　**meta-** = after ; among ; with

　　* 希臘文 *meta*，一般表「變化」之意，主要用在科學用語。

metabolism[7]〔mə'tæbḷɪzəm〕*n.* 新陳代謝 (在～之後投入)
　　《*meta-* (after) + *bol* (throw) + *-ism* (名詞字尾)》

metagenesis〔،mɛtə'dʒɛnəsɪs〕*n.* 世代交替
　　《*meta-* (change) + *genesis* (創世)》

metamorphosis[7]〔،mɛtə'mɔrfəsɪs〕= transformation　*n.* 蛻變；
變形；(昆蟲等之) 變態《*meta-* (change) + *morphosis* (formation)》

```
meta  +  morphosis
  |            |
change  +  formation
```

metaphor[6]〔'mɛtəfɚ〕*n.* 隱喻《*meta-* (change) + *phor* (carry)》

metaphysical[7] 〔͵mɛtə'fɪzɪk!〕*adj.* 形而上（學）的；非物質的；
極抽象的《*meta-*（after）+ *physic(s)*（物理學）+ *-al*（形容詞字尾）》

```
meta  +  phys  +   ic(s)  +   al
  |        |         |         |
change + nature + science +  adj.
```

metastasis〔mə'tæstəsɪs〕*n.* 變形；轉移；新陳代謝；
（話題之）急轉《*meta-*（change）+ *stasis*（position）》

metathesis〔mə'tæθəsɪs〕*n.* 音位轉變
《*meta-*（change）+ *thesis*（place）》

```
meta  + thesis
  |       |
change + place
```

meteor[7]〔'mitɪɚ〕*n.* 大氣現象；流星；隕石
《*met-* = *meta-*（among）+ *eor*（anything suspended 空中的懸浮物）》

metonymy〔mə'tɑnəmɪ〕*n.* 換喻
《*met-* = *meta-*（change）+ *onym*（name）+ *-y*（名詞字尾）》
cf. **antonym**（反義字），**synonym**（同義字）

method[2]〔'mɛθəd〕*n.* 方法；體系；秩序（跟隨其後而去）
《*meth-* = *meta-*（after）+ *od*（way））》

78　micro- = small

　　* 希臘文 *mikros*，表示「小的」。

microanalysis[7]〔͵maɪkroə'næləsɪs〕*n.* 微量分析《*analysis* 分析》
microbe[7]〔'maɪkrob〕= a small living thing　*n.* 微生物；細菌
《*micro-*（small）+ *be*（life））》
microbiology[7]〔͵maɪkrobaɪ'ɑlədʒɪ〕*n.* 微生物學《*biology* 生物學》

```
micro + bio +  logy
  |      |       |
small + life + studying
```

microcosm[7] 〔'maɪkrəˌkazəm 〕 *n.* 小宇宙；縮圖
《 *micro-* (small) + *cosm* (universe)》

microeconomics[7] 〔ˌmaɪkrəˌɛkə'namɪks 〕 *n.* 個體經濟學；
微觀經濟學《 *economics* 經濟學 》
cf. **macroeconomics** (總體經濟學；宏觀經濟學)

microfiche 〔'maɪkrəˌfiʃ 〕 *n.* 縮微膠片

```
micro  +    fiche
  |          |
small  +  index card
```

micrometeorology[7] 〔ˌmaɪkroˌmitɪə'ralədʒɪ 〕 *n.* 微氣象學
《 *meteorology* 氣象學 》

```
micro  +    meteor      +  ology
  |           |              |
small  +  things in the air  +  studying
```

micrometer[7] 〔 maɪ'kramətɚ 〕 *n.* (顯微鏡、望遠鏡用的) 測微計

```
micro  +  meter
  |         |
small  +  measure
```

microphone[3] 〔'maɪkrəˌfon 〕 *n.* 擴音器；麥克風 (使聲音由小變大)
《 *micro-* (small) + *phone* (sound)》

microscope[4] 〔'maɪkrəˌskop 〕 *n.* 顯微鏡 (觀察小東西之物)
《 *micro-* (small) + *scope* (look)》

microwave[3] 〔'maɪkrəˌwev 〕 *n.* 微波《 *wave* 波 》

79 **milli-** = thousand ; thousandth

millibar[7] 〔'mɪlɪˌbar 〕 *n.* 毫巴 (壓力單位，巴的千分之一)
《 *milli-* (thousandth) + *bar* (pressure)》

milligram[7] 〔'mɪləˌgræm 〕 *n.* 毫克 (千分之一公克)

milliliter ; -**tre**[7] 〔'mɪləˌlitɚ 〕 *n.* 公撮 (千分之一公升)

millimeter ; -tre[7]〔'mɪlə,mitɚ 〕 *n.* 毫米；公釐（千分之一公尺）

millennial[7] 〔 mə'lɛnɪəl 〕 *adj.* 千年的；千年期間的

《 *mill(e)-* (thousand) + *enn* (year) + *-ial* (形容詞字尾)》

```
mill(e)  +  enn  +  ial
   |          |       |
thousand  +  year  +  adj.
```

millepede[7] 〔'mɪlə,pid 〕 = millipede　　*n.* 馬陸；千足蟲

《 *mille-* (thousand) + *pede* (foot)》

millepore[7] 〔'mɪlɪ,por , -,pɔr 〕 *n.* 千孔蟲（一種有許多小孔的珊瑚）

《 *mille-* (thousand) + *pore* (opening)》

80 **mis-** = bad(ly) ; ill ; wrong(ly)

* 一般是以帶有「貶抑」的語氣表示「錯誤」，但也可單表「否定」。

misaddress 〔,mɪsə'drɛs 〕 *v.* 用錯稱呼；寄錯（信件）

misadjustment 〔,mɪsə'dʒʌstmənt 〕 *n.* 調整不妥；失調

misadvise[7] 〔,mɪsəd'vaɪz 〕 *v.* 給予錯誤的勸告

```
mis  +  ad  +  vise
 |        |       |
wrong  +  to  +  see
```

misapply[7] 〔,mɪsə'plaɪ 〕 *v.* 誤用

misapprehend[7] 〔,mɪsæprɪ'hɛnd 〕 *v.* 誤解；想錯

《 *apprehend* 了解 》

misarrange[7] 〔,mɪsə'rendʒ 〕 *v.* 排列錯誤；安排不妥當

misbegotten[7] 〔,mɪsbɪ'gɑtn̩ 〕 *adj.* 私生的

《 *mis-* (wrongly) + *be* (intensive) + *gotten* (get)》

```
mis   +   be   +  gotten
 |         |         |
wrongly + intensive + get
```

misbehave[7] 〔,mɪsbɪ'hev 〕 *v.* 行為不檢 《 *behave* 行為；舉止》

misbelief[7] 〔ˌmɪsbə'lif 〕 *n.* 錯誤的想法；異教的信仰

mischance[7] 〔 mɪs'tʃæns 〕 *n.* 不幸；壞運

mischief[4] 〔'mɪstʃɪf 〕 = an ill result *n.* 災害

misconceive[7] 〔ˌmɪskən'siv 〕 *v.* 誤解；誤認

```
mis  + con + ceive
 |       |      |
wrong + with + take
```

misconduct[7] 〔 *n.* mɪs'kɑndʌkt *v.* ˌmɪskən'dʌkt 〕 *n.*, *v.* 行為不檢
《*conduct* 行為》

miscreant[7] 〔'mɪskrɪənt 〕 *adj.* 道德敗壞的；邪惡的
《*mis-* (bad) + *creant* (believe)》

```
mis + creant
 |      |
bad + believe
```

misdate[7] 〔 mɪs'det 〕 *v.* 填錯日期；誤記日期 *n.* 錯誤的日期

misdeed[7] 〔 mɪs'did 〕 *n.* 惡行；罪行

misdirect[7] 〔ˌmɪsdə'rɛkt 〕 *v.* 指錯方向；錯用；指示錯誤

misfortune[4] 〔 mɪs'fɔrtʃən 〕 *n.* 不幸；災難

misgive[7] 〔 mɪs'gɪv 〕 *v.* 使懷疑；使焦慮

mislead[4] 〔 mɪs'lid 〕 *v.* 誤導；使誤解；使迷離

misplace[7] 〔 mɪs'ples 〕 *v.* 錯置；誤放

mispronounce[7] 〔ˌmɪsprə'naʊns 〕 *v.* 發錯音
《*pronounce* 發音》

misspend[7] 〔 mɪs'spɛnd 〕 *v.* 濫用；亂花；浪費

mistake[1] 〔 mə'stek 〕 *n.* 錯誤
《*mis-* (wrongly) + *take* (get)》

misstate[7] 〔 mɪs'stet 〕 *v.* 錯誤陳述

misstep[7] 〔 mɪs'stɛp 〕 *n.* 失足；過失；失策

mistrust[7] 〔 mɪs'trʌst 〕 *n.*, *v.* 不信任；懷疑

misunderstand[4] 〔'mɪsʌndɚ'stænd 〕 *v.* 誤解

81　**miso-** = hate

misanthropy[7]〔 mɪs'ænθrəpɪ 〕 *n.* 憎惡世人；厭世
　《*mis-* (hate) + *anthropy* (man)》
misogamy[7]〔 mɪ'sagəmɪ 〕 *n.* 厭惡結婚；厭婚症
　《*miso-* (hate) + *gamy* (marriage)》
misogynist[7]〔 mɪ'sadʒənɪst 〕 = woman hater　*n.* 厭惡女人的男人
　《*miso-* (hate) + *gyn* (woman) + *-ist* (表人的名詞字尾)》
misogyny[7]〔 mɪ'sadʒənɪ 〕 *n.* 厭惡女性；厭女症
　《*miso-* (hate) + *gyny* (woman)》
misology〔 mɪ'sal*ə*gɪ 〕 *n.* 厭惡辯論《*miso-* (hate) + *logy* (speech)》
misoneism〔ˌmɪsə'niɪzm̩ 〕 *n.* 討厭新事物；厭新症
　《*miso-* (hate) + *ne* (new) + *-ism* (名詞字尾)》

82　**mono-** = alone ; single ; sole

*表示「單一」。〔變化型〕mon-。

monochrome[7]〔 'manəˌkrom 〕 *n.* 單色畫　*adj.* 單色的
　《*mono-* (single) + *chrome* (color)》　*cf.* **achromatic** (無色的)
monocracy〔 mo'nakrəsɪ 〕 *n.* 獨裁政治 (= *autocracy*)
　《*mono-* (alone) + *cracy* (rule)》
monocycle[7]〔 'manəˌsaɪkl̩ 〕 *n.* 單輪車
　《*mono-* (single) + *cycle* (circle)》
monogamy[7]〔 mə'nagəmɪ 〕 *n.* 一夫一妻制；一夫一妻
　《*mono-* (alone) + *gamy* (marriage)》　*cf.* **polygamy** (一夫多妻)

```
mono  +  gamy
 |         |
alone  +  marriage
```

monoglot〔 'manəˌglat 〕 *adj.* , *n.* 只通一種語言的 (人)
　(= *monolingual*) (單一語言)
　《*mono-* (single) + *glot* (language)》

monogram[7] 〔'mɑnə͵græm 〕*n.* 組合文字；花押字（將姓名的首字母組成圖案）（以第一個字母寫成的）

《*mono-*（ single ）+ *gram*（ write ）》

monolatry 〔 mə'nɑlətrɪ 〕*n.* 一神崇拜

《*mono-*（ single ）+ *latry*（ worship ）》

monolingual 〔͵mɑnə'lɪŋgwəl 〕*adj. , n.* 只用一種語言的（ 人 ）（ 單一語言 ）《*mono-*（ single ）+ *lingu*（ language ）+ *-al*（ 形容詞字尾 ）》

```
mono  +  lingu   +  al
 |         |         |
single +  language +  adj.
```

monolog(ue)[7] 〔'mɑnl͵ɔg 〕*n.* 獨白；獨角戲（ = *soliloquy* ）

《*mono-*（ alone ）+ *logue*（ spoke ）》

monopoly[6] 〔 mə'nɑpl̩ɪ 〕*n.* 獨占；專賣權

《*mono-*（ sole ）+ *poly*（ sell ）》

monopolize[7] 〔 mə'nɑpl̩͵aɪz 〕*v.* 獨占；壟斷（ 獨家販賣 ）

《*mono-*（ single ）+ *pol*（ sell ）+ *-ize*（ 動詞字尾 ）》

monosyllable[7] 〔'mɑnə͵sɪləbl̩ 〕*n.* 單音節；單音節字

《*mono-*（ single ）+ *syllable*（ 音節 ）》

monotheism[7] 〔'mɑnəθi͵ɪzəm 〕*n.* 一神教；一神論

《*mono-*（ single ）+ *the*（ god ）+ *-ism*（ 表主義的名詞字尾 ）》

cf. **polytheism**（ 多神教；多神論 ）

monotonous[6] 〔 mə'nɑtn̩əs 〕*adj.* 單調的；無變化的

《*mono-*（ single ）+ *ton*（ tone ）+ *-ous*（ 形容詞字尾 ）》

```
mono  +  ton  +  ous
 |        |        |
single +  tone  +  adj.
```

monotony[6] 〔 mə'nɑtn̩ɪ 〕*n.* 單調；無變化；乏味

《*mono-*（ single ）+ *ton*（ tone ）+ *-y*（ 名詞字尾 ）》

monarch[5] 〔'mɑnə˞k 〕*n.* 帝王；統治者

《*mon-* = *mono-*（ alone ）+ *arch*（ rule ）》

monk[3] 〔 mʌŋk 〕= solitary　*n.* 修道士；僧人　*cf.* **nun**（ 修女 ）

83 mult(i)- = many ; much

* 拉丁文 *multus*，表示「多的」。

multichannel[7] 〔͵mʌltɪ'tʃænḷ 〕*adj.* 多頻道的；多通道的
　《*multi-* (many) + *channel* (電路；波段)》

multicolor[7] 〔͵mʌltɪ'kʌlɚ 〕*n.* 多種顏色
　《*multi-* (many) + *color* (color)》

multicultural[7] 〔͵mʌltɪ'kʌltʃərəl 〕*adj.* 多種文化的

multifarious 〔͵mʌltə'fɛrɪəs 〕*adj.* 各式各樣的；五花八門的
　(說得很多) 《*multi-* (much) + *fari* (speak) + *-ous* (形容詞字尾)》

```
multi  +  fari  +  ous
  |        |        |
much   +  speak  +  adj.
```

multiform[7] 〔'mʌltə͵fɔrm 〕*adj.* 各種形式的；多種的
　《*multi-* (many) + *form* (form)》

multilingual[7] 〔͵mʌltɪ'lɪŋgwəl 〕*adj.* 使用多種語言的
　《*multi-* (many) + *lingu* (language) + *-al* (形容詞字尾)》

multimedia[7] 〔͵mʌltɪ'midɪə 〕*adj.* 多媒體的

multiparous 〔 mʌl'tɪpərəs 〕*adj.* 一產多胎的；多產的 (一胎
生很多的) 《*multi-* (many) + *par* (bear) + *-ous* (形容詞字尾)》

```
multi  +  par  +  ous
  |       |       |
many   +  bear  +  adj.
```

multiply[2] 〔'mʌltə͵plaɪ 〕*v.* 增加；繁殖；乘 (許多東西重疊在一起)
　《*multi-* (much) + *ply* (fold)》

multipurpose[7] 〔͵mʌltɪ'pɝpəs 〕*adj.* 多目標的；用途廣的 (許多
置於前端的醒目物品)
　《*multi-* (many) + *pur-* = *pro-* (before) + *pose* (put)》

multitude[7] 〔'mʌltə͵tjud 〕*n.* 多數；群眾；民眾
　《*mult-* (many ; much) + *-itude* (名詞字尾)》

multivalence 〔ˌmʌltəˈveləns , mʌlˈtɪvə- 〕 *n.* 多原子價 (許多價值)
《*multi-* (many ; much) + *val* (worth) + *-ence* (名詞字尾)》

multi	+	val	+	ence
many , much	+	*worth*	+	*n.*

multivocal 〔 mʌlˈtɪvəkl̩ 〕 *adj.* 表多種意義的 (擁有許多聲音)
《*multi-* (many) + *voc* (voice) + *-al* (形容詞字尾)》

multocular 〔 mʌlˈtɑkjələ˞ 〕 *adj.* 多眼的
《*mult-* (many) + *ocul* (eye) + *-ar* (形容詞字尾)》
cf. **ocular** (眼睛的) ， **oculist** (眼科醫生)

84 **myria-** = countless ; ten thousand

* 表示「很多」、「萬」。

myriad[7] 〔ˈmɪrɪəd 〕 *n.* 無數；無數的人 (或物)   *adj.* 無數的；
各種各樣都有的；包羅萬象的

myriameter 〔ˈmɪrɪəˌmitə˞ 〕 *n.* 一萬公尺；十公里

myriapod 〔ˈmɪrɪəˌpɑd 〕 *n.* 多足類動物   *adj.* 多足類的

myriorama 〔ˌmɪrɪəˈrɑmə 〕 *n.* 萬景畫 (由多個部分組合而成，
各個部分可以變換組合方式，形成種種不同的畫面)

85 **nano-** = dwarf

* 希臘文 *nanos*，表示「矮小」、「十億分之一」。
〔變化型〕nanno-。

nanoid 〔ˈnenɔɪd , ˈnænɔɪd 〕 *adj.* 矮小的

nanoatom 〔ˈnenɔˌætəm 〕 *n.* 毫微原子
《*nano-* (dwarf) + *atom* (原子)》

nanocephalia 〔ˌnænəsəˈfelɪə 〕 *n.* 頭小畸型；小頭
《*nano-* (dwarf) + *cephal* (head) + *-ia* (名詞字尾)》

nanomelus 〔nɛ'nɑmələs 〕 *n.* 肢小畸胎
《*nano-* (dwarf) + *melus* (limb 四肢)》

nanometer[7] 〔'næno,mitɚ 〕 *n.* 奈米 (十億分之一米)

nanosecond[7] 〔'næno,sɛkənd 〕 *n.* 十億分之一秒

nannofossil 〔'nɛnɔ,fɑsḷ 〕 *n.* 微化石 《*nano-* (dwarf) + *fossil* (化石)》

nannoplankton 〔'nɛnɔ,plæŋtən 〕 *n.* 微型浮游生物
《*nano-* (dwarf) + *plankton* (浮游生物)》

86 **ne-** = negative ; not (否定)

* 表示「非」、「不」。〔變化型〕na-, n-, neg-。

nefarious[7] 〔nɪ'fɛrɪəs 〕 *adj.* 不正的；極惡的 (違背神的言詞)
《*ne-* (not) + *fari* (speak) + *-ous* (形容詞字尾)》 *cf.* **fate** (命運)

nescience 〔'nɛʃəns 〕 *n.* 無知；不知；不可知論 (= *ignorance*)
《*ne-* (not) + *science* (knowing)》 *cf.* **science** (科學)

```
ne + science
 |      |
not + knowing
```

neuter[7] 〔'njutɚ 〕 *adj.* 中性的；中立的；無性的 (非二者之一)
《*ne-* (not) + *uter* (whether of the two 二者中任一)》

naught[7] 〔 nɔt 〕 = nothing *n.* 零；無 《*na-* (not) + *ught* (thing)》

```
na + ught
 |    |
not + thing
```

nay[7] 〔 ne 〕 = no *adv.* 否；不 *n.* 否定；拒絕；禁止

neither[2] 〔'niðɚ 〕 *adv.*, *conj.*, *adj.*, *pron.* 既非；皆不；兩者都不
《*n-* (not) + *either*》

never[1] 〔'nɛvɚ 〕 *adv.* 絕不 《*n-* (not) + *ever*》

none[2] 〔 nʌn 〕 *pron.*, *adj.*, *adv.* 毫無；無人；無物；毫不
《*n-* (not) + *one*》

null[7] 〔 nʌl 〕= not any　*adj.* 無效的；無意義的

　《*n-* (not) + *ull* (any)》

```
n  +  ull
|      |
not  +  any
```

negotiate[4] 〔 nɪˈgoʃɪˌet 〕*v.* 交涉；協定；商議（沒有閒暇）

　《*neg-* = *ne-* (not) + *oti* (leisure) + *-ate* (動詞字尾)》

　cf. **otiose**（懶惰的），**otiosity**（怠惰）

87　　**neo-** = new　　* 希臘文 *neos*，表示「新」。

neoclassicism[7] 〔 ˌnioˈklæsəˌsɪzm̩ 〕*n.* 新古典主義

　《*classicism* 古典主義 》

neocolonialism[7] 〔 ˌniokəˈlonɪəˌlɪzəm 〕*n.* 新殖民地主義

　《*colonialism* 殖民主義 》

```
neo  +  colon  +  ial  +  ism
 |        |        |       |
new  +   till   +  adj. +  n.
```

neofascism[7] 〔 ˌnioˈfæʃɪzm̩ 〕*n.* 新法西斯主義《*fascism* 法西斯主義 》

neoglacial[7] 〔 ˌnioˈgleʃəl 〕*n.* 新冰河時期《*neo-* (new) + *glacial* (ice)》

neoimpressionism[7] 〔 ˌnio · ɪmˈprɛʃənˌɪzəm 〕*n.* 新印象主義

　《*impressionism* 印象主義 》

neolithic[7] 〔 ˌniəˈlɪθɪk 〕*adj.* 新石器時代的

　《*neo-* (new) + *lith* (stone) + *-ic* (形容詞字尾)》

```
neo  +  lith  +  ic
 |       |       |
new  +  stone +  adj.
```

neologism[7] 〔 niˈɑləˌdʒɪzəm 〕*n.* 新字；新字義；使用新字（使用
　新言詞）《*neo-* (new) + *log* (speak) + *-ism* (表理論的的名詞字尾)》

neon[6] 〔 ˈniɑn 〕*n.* 氖

neonatal[7]〔͵nio'netḷ〕= newly-born　*adj.* 初生的

《*neo-* (new) + *nat* (born) + *-al* (形容詞字尾)》

```
neo + nat + al
 |     |     |
new + born + adj.
```

neophyte[7] 〔'niə͵faɪt 〕*n.* 新入教者；新手；初學者 (= *beginner*)

《*neo-* (new) + *phyte* (plant)》

neorealism[7] 〔͵nio'riəl͵ɪzəm 〕*n.* 新寫實主義《*realism* 寫實主義 》

neoromanticism[7] 〔͵nioro'mæntə͵sɪzəm 〕*n.* 新浪漫主義

《*romanticism* 浪漫主義 》

88 **non-** = not

* 表示「非」、「無」。通常用在名詞、形容詞、副詞之前。

nonaggression[7] 〔͵nanə'grɛʃən 〕*n.* 不侵略；不侵犯 (不向~走去)

《*non-* (not) + *ag-* = *ad-* (to) + *gress* (walk) + *-ion* (名詞字尾)》

nonaligned[7] 〔͵nanə'laɪnd 〕*adj.* 不結盟的；中立的 (不成行的)

《*non-* (not) + *a-* = *ad-* (to) + *lign* (line) + *-ed* (形容詞字尾)》

```
non + a + lign + ed
 |    |    |      |
not + to + line + adj.
```

nonallergic[7] 〔͵nanə'lɝdʒɪk 〕*adj.* 非過敏性的

《*non-* (not) + *all* (other) + *erg* (action) + *-ic* (形容詞字尾)》

nonchalant[7] 〔'nanʃələnt 〕*adj.* 冷漠的；無動於衷的

《*non-* (not) + *chal* (care for) + *-ant* (形容詞字尾)》

noncombatant[7] 〔 nan'kambətənt 〕*n. , adj.* 非戰鬥人員 (的)

(不一起對打)《*non-* (not) + *com-* (together) + *bat* (beat) +

-ant (名詞兼形容詞字尾)》

```
non + com    + bat + ant
 |     |        |     |
not + together + beat + n., adj.
```

noncombustible[7]〔ˌnɑnkəm'bʌstəbḷ〕*adj.* 非易燃的；不燃性的
《*non-*（ not ）+ *comb-* = *com-*（ together ）+ *ust*（ burn ）+ *-ible*（ 形容詞
字尾)》

noncommittal[7]〔ˌnɑnkə'mɪtḷ〕*adj.* 不明確的；含糊的（傳遞不清楚）
《*non-*（ not ）+ *com-*（ with ）+ *mitt*（ send ）+ *-al*（ 形容詞字尾)》

```
non  +  com  +  mitt  +  al
 |       |       |       |
not  +  with  +  send  +  adj.
```

nonconductor[7]〔ˌnɑnkən'dʌktɚ〕*n.* 絕緣體
《*non-*（ not ）+ *con-*（ together ）+ *duct*（ lead ）+ *-or*（ 名詞字尾)》

nonconformity[7]〔ˌnɑnkən'fɔrmətɪ〕*n.* 不順從；不一致；
非國敎主義（ 形狀不同 ）
《*non-*（ not ）+ *con-*（ together ）+ *form*（ form ）+ *-ity*（ 名詞字尾)》

noncooperation[7]〔ˌnɑnkoˌɑpə'reʃən〕*n.* 不合作（ 不一起工作 ）
《*non-*（ not ）+ *co-* = *com-*（ together ）+ *operat*（ work ）+ *-ion*（ 名詞字尾)》

nondurable[7]〔nɑn'djʊrəbḷ〕*adj.* 不耐久的；不經用的（ 不持久的 ）
《*non-*（ not ）+ *dur*（ lasting ）+ *-able*（ 形容詞字尾)》

```
non  +  dur   +  able
 |       |        |
not  +  lasting  +  adj.
```

nonentity[7]〔nɑn'ɛntətɪ〕*n.* 不存在；不存在之物；不足取的人
或物（ 不存在 ）《*non-*（ not ）+ *entity*（ being)》

nonessential[7]〔ˌnɑnə'sɛnʃəl〕*adj.*, *n.* 非本質的（ 事物 ）；
不重要的（ 事物或人 ）
《*non-*（ not ）+ *essent*（ 本質 ）+ *-ial*（ 形容詞兼名詞字尾)》

nonmember[7]〔nɑn'mɛmbɚ〕*n.* 非會員；非黨員
《*non-*（ not ）+ *member*（ 會員)》

nonpareil[7]〔ˌnɑnpə'rɛl〕*adj.* 無比的；無雙的
《*non-*（ not ）+ *pareil*（ equal)》

nonpartisan[7]〔 nɑnˈpɑrtəzn̩ 〕 *adj.* 無黨派的；客觀的；無偏袒的（不偏向一邊的）《*non-*（not）+ *part*（part）+ *is*（same）+ *-an*（形容詞字尾）》

```
non  +  part  +  is   +  an
 |       |        |       |
not  +  part  +  same  +  adj.
```

nonproductive[7]〔 ˌnɑnprəˈdʌktɪv 〕 *adj.* 不生產的；無生產力的；非生產性的《*non-*（not）+ *pro-*（forward）+ *duct*（lead）+ *-ive*（形容詞字尾）》

nonsectarian〔 ˌnɑnsɛkˈtɛrɪən 〕 *adj.* 無宗派的；不屬於任何宗派的（不分派的）《*non-*（not）+ *sect*（cut）+ *-arian*（形容詞字尾）》

```
non  +  sect  +  arian
 |       |        |
not  +  cut   +  adj.
```

nonstop[7]〔ˈnɑnˈstɑp 〕 *adj.* 不停的；直達的《*non-*（not）+ *stop*（停止）》
nonverbal[7]〔 ˌnɑnˈvɝbl̩ 〕 *adj.* 不使用文字的；非語文的《*non-*（not）+ *verb*（word）+ *-al*（形容詞字尾）》

89 novem- , non- = nine

* 拉丁文 *novem*，表示「九」，序數為 *nonus*（= *ninth*）。

November[1]〔 noˈvɛmbɚ 〕 *n.* 十一月　☞ 見 p.658 December 解說。
novena〔 noˈvinə 〕 *n.*（天主教）連續九天的祈禱式
nonary〔ˈnonərɪ 〕 *adj.* 九進的　*n.* 九個一組《*nona-*（nine）+ *-ry*》
nonagon〔ˈnɑnəˌgɑn 〕 *n.* 九邊形；九角形《*nona-*（nine）+ *gon*（angle）》

90 ob- = at ; against ; before ; near ; over ; towards

*〔變化型〕o- , oc- , of- , op- , os- 。

obdurate〔ˈɑbdjərɪt, -də-〕*adj.* 頑固的；執拗的；冷酷的

（頑固地反對）《*ob-*（against）+ *dur*（hard）+ *-ate*（形容詞字尾）》

```
ob   + dur  + ate
 |       |       |
against + hard + adj.
```

obedient[4]〔əˈbidɪənt〕*adj.* 服從的（傾聽他人所言）

《*ob-*（在此處無意義）+ *edi*（hear）+ *-ent*（形容詞字尾）》

cf. **audience**（聽眾）

obese[7]〔oˈbis〕*adj.* 過度肥胖的《*ob-*（over）+ *ese*（eat）》

obfuscate[7]〔ɑbˈfʌsket, ˈɑbfəsˌket〕*v.* 使暗淡；使困惑

（使整面黑暗）《*ob-*（over）+ *fuscate*（darken）》

obituary[7]〔əˈbɪtʃʊˌɛrɪ, o-〕*n.* 訃聞　*adj.* 死亡的（近於死亡）

《*ob-*（near）+ *it*（go）+ *-uary*（名詞字尾）》

object[2]〔*v.* əbˈdʒɛkt *n.* ˈɑbdʒɪkt〕*v.* 反對；拒絕　*n.* 物體；目的；

對象（對～投擲東西）《*ob-*（towards ; against）+ *ject*（throw）》

objurgate〔ˈɑbdʒɚˌget, əbˈdʒɝget〕*v.* 責罵；譴責（咒罵）

《*ob-*（against）+ *jurg*（scold）+ *-ate*（動詞字尾）》

```
ob   + jurg + ate
 |       |      |
against + scold + v.
```

oblige[6]〔əˈblaɪdʒ〕*v.* 強制；施於；加於（綁住）

《*ob-*（to）+ *lige*（bind）》

oblique[7]〔əˈblik〕*adj.* 斜的；歪的；不正的　*v.* 歪斜；傾斜

（向～彎曲）《*ob-*（towards）+ *lique*（bent）》

oblivion[7]〔əˈblɪvɪən〕*n.* 湮沒；遺忘；赦免

《*ob-*（over）+ *liv*（smooth）+ *-ion*（名詞字尾）》

```
ob  +  liv  + ion
 |       |      |
over + smooth + n.
```

oblong[5]〔ˈɑblɔŋ〕*n.* , *adj.* 長方形（的）《*ob-*（across ; over）+ *long*》

obscene[7] 〔 əb'sin 〕 *adj.* 猥褻的；淫亂的；令人不悅的（向著污穢）

《*ob-* (towards) + *scene* (filth 污穢)》

obscure[6] 〔 əb'skjur 〕 *adj.* 不清楚的；隱藏的；不著名的

v. 使暗；使不分明（覆蓋住全部）《*ob-* (over) + *scure* (covered)》

obstacle[4] 〔'ɑbstəkḷ 〕 *n.* 障礙物（立在路上的東西）

《*ob-* (over against) + *sta* (stand) + *-cle* (表示事物的名詞字尾)》

```
   ob     +  sta  + cle
   |          |      |
over against + stand +  n.
```

obstinate[5] 〔'ɑbstənɪt 〕 *adj.* 固執的；難醫治的（難以忍受的）

《*ob-* (over against) + *stinate* (cause to stand)》

obstruct[7] 〔 əb'strʌkt 〕 *v.* 阻隔；遮蔽；妨害（爲反對而築）

《*ob-* (over against) + *struct* (build)》 *cf.* **structure** (構造)

obtain[4] 〔 əb'ten 〕 *v.* 獲得；流行（在身邊的）

《*ob-* (near ; close to) + *tain* (hold)》 *cf.* **tenable** (守得住的)

obtund 〔 ɑb'tʌnd 〕 *v.* 使（機能）變鈍；使（痛苦）緩和

《*ob-* (against) + *tund* (strike)》

obvious[3] 〔'ɑbvɪəs 〕 *adj.* 明白的；一目了然的（橫放在路上的 → 醒

目的）《*ob-* (near) + *vi* = *via* (way) + *-ous* (形容詞字尾)》

omit[2] 〔 o'mɪt 〕 = let go *v.* 略去；遺漏；疏忽（使去）

《*o-* = *ob-* (在此處無意義) + *mit* (send)》 *cf.* **mission** (派遣；使節團)

occasion[3] 〔 ə'keʒən 〕 *n.* 機會；場合；原因；事件 *v.* 引起

（落在眼前）《*oc-* = *ob-* (before) + *cas* (fall) + *-ion* (名詞字尾)》

```
  oc   + cas + ion
  |       |     |
before + fall +  n.
```

occult[7] 〔 ə'kʌlt 〕 *adj.* 神祕的；難以理解的；超自然的（覆蓋起來）

《*oc-* = *ob-* (over) + *cult* (cover)》

occupy[4] 〔'ɑkjəˌpaɪ 〕 *v.* 占有；占領；使忙碌；占據（補捉～）

《*oc-* = *ob-* (at) + *cupy* (seize)》 *cf.* **captive** (俘虜)

occur[2] 〔 ə'kɝ 〕 v. 被想起；發生；存在（流向～）

　《oc- = ob- (towards) + cur (run)》　cf. **current**（水流）

offend[4] 〔 ə'fɛnd 〕 v. 冒犯；使不悅（打擊～）

　《of- = ob- (against) + fend (strike)》

offer[2] 〔'ɔfɚ 〕 v. 呈贈；奉獻；提出；表示　n. 提供；提議；企圖

　（拿到前面）《of- = ob- (near) + fer (carry)》

opponent[5] 〔 ə'ponənt 〕 adj. 相對的；敵對的　n. 敵對者（因反對

而設置）《op- = ob- (against) + pon (place) + -ent (形容詞字尾)》

cf. **oppose**（反對）

```
op    +  pon  +  ent
 |        |       |
against + place + adj.
```

oppress[6] 〔 ə'prɛs 〕= press against　v. 鎮壓；壓迫（壓制）

　《op- = ob- (against) + press》

ostentation[7] 〔ˌɑstən'teʃən 〕 n. 誇張（在前面展示）

　《os- = ob- (before) + tent (stretch) + -ation (名詞字尾)》

91　octa- = eight　＊希臘文 *okto*。〔變化型〕octo-。

octagon[7] 〔'ɑktəˌgɑn 〕 n. 八角形

　《octa- (eight) + gon (angle；corner 角)》

octahedron 〔ˌɑktə'hidrən 〕 n. 八面體

　《octa- (eight) + hedr (side) + -on (名詞字尾)》

```
octa  +  hedr  +  on
 |        |       |
eight  +  side  +  n.
```

octave[7] 〔'ɑktev 〕 n. (音樂) 第八音；一個音階；(宗敎) 從節日

起第八天；十四行詩中的起首八行；八個一組

octavo 〔 ɑk'tevo 〕 n. 八開本；八開本的書　adj. 八開的

October[1] 〔 ɑk'tobɚ 〕 n. 十月　☞ 見 p.658 December 解說。

octodecimo 〔͵ɑkto′dɛsə͵mo 〕*n.* 十八開本

　　《*octo-*（eight）+ *decimo*（ten）》

```
octo + decimo
  |       |
eight +  ten
```

octopus[5] 〔′ɑktəpəs 〕*n.* 章魚；強有力且能為害的組織（八隻腳）

　　《*octo-*（eight）+ *pus*（foot）》

```
octo + pus
  |      |
eight + foot
```

octosyllable 〔′ɑktə͵sɪləbḷ 〕*n.* 八音節字；八音節的詩句

　　《*octo-*（eight）+ *syllable*（音節）》

octuple 〔′ɑktʊpḷ 〕*adj.* 八倍的　*n.* 八倍　*v.* 變成八倍

　　（重覆八次的）《*octu-* = *octo-*（eight）+ *ple*（fold）》

92　oligo- = few

　　* 表示「少」、「缺乏」。〔變化型〕olig-。

oligemia 〔͵ɑlə′gimɪə 〕*n.* 血量減少

　　《*olig-*（few）+ *em*（blood）+ *-ia*（表示病症的字尾）》

oligocarpous 〔͵ɑləgo′kɑrpəs 〕*adj.* 幾乎沒有果實的；果實不多的

　　《*olig-*（few）+ *carp*（fruit）+ *-ous*（形容詞字尾）》

oligochrome 〔′ɑləgo͵krom 〕*adj.*（裝飾物等）只用少數顏色的

　　n. 只用少數顏色的圖案《*olig-*（few）+ *chrome*（color）》

oligophagous 〔͵ɑlə′gɑfəgəs 〕*adj.* 寡食性的；狹食性的

　　《*olig-*（few）+ *phag*（eat）+ *-ous*（形容詞字尾）》

oligophrenia 〔͵ɑləgo′frinɪə 〕*n.* 智力發育不全；精神幼稚

　　《*olig-*（few）+ *phren*（mind）+ *-ia*（表示病症的字尾）》

oligopoly 〔͵ɑlə′gɑpəlɪ 〕*n.* 寡頭賣主壟斷

　　《*olig-*（few）+（*mono*）*poly*（獨占）》

oligotrophic〔ˌɑləgoˈtrɑfɪk〕*adj.*（湖泊、池塘等）貧營養的
《*olig-*（few）+ *troph*（nourish）+ *-ic*（形容詞字尾）》

93　omni- = all

　　* 希臘文 *omnis*，表示「全部」。

omnibus[7]〔ˈɑmnəˌbʌs〕*n.* 公共汽車；精選集　*adj.* 綜合的

omnicompetent〔ˌɑmnɪˈkɑmpɪtənt〕*adj.* 有全權的
《*omni-*（all）+ *competent*（能幹的）》

omnifarious〔ˌɑmnəˈfɛrɪəs〕*adj.* 種種的；各色各樣的（談論所有的事）《*omni-*（all）+ *fari*（speak）+ *-ous*（形容詞字尾）》

```
omni  +  fari  + ous
 |         |       |
all   +  speak  + adj.
```

omnipotent[7]〔amˈnɪpətənt〕*adj.* 全能的　　*n.* 全能者
《*omni-*（all）+ *pot*（power）+ *-ent*（形容詞兼名詞字尾）》

omnipresent[7]〔ˌɑmnɪˈprɛznt〕*adj.* 無處不存在的；普遍的

omniscient[7]〔amˈnɪʃənt〕= all-knowing　*adj.* 無所不知的
《*omni-*（all）+ *scient*（knowing）》　*cf.* **science**（科學）

omnivorous[7]〔amˈnɪvərəs〕*adj.* 雜食的
《*omni-*（all）+ *vor*（eat）+ *-ous*（形容詞字尾）》
cf. **voracious**（飲食過量的）

94　ortho- = straight ; right

　　* 希臘文 *orthos*，表示「直（向）的」、「正（確）的」。

orthodontist[7]〔ˌɔrθəˈdɑntɪst〕*n.* 矯正牙齒的牙醫

```
ortho   + dont  +  ist
  |         |        |
straight + tooth + person
```

orthodox[7] 〔'ɔrθə,dɑks 〕 *adj.* 正統的；公認的；傳統的；慣常的；

（ O～ ）東正教的　　 *n.* 正統派；（ O～ ）東正教教徒（思想正確的）

《*ortho-* (right) + *dox* (opinion)》

orthodoxy 〔'ɔrθə,dɑksɪ 〕 *n.* 正統；信守正統學說；正教

orthogonal 〔 ɔr'θɑgənəl , -nḷ 〕 *adj.* 直角的；正交的；矩形的

《*ortho-* (right) + *gon* (angle) + *-al* (形容詞字尾)》

```
ortho +  gon  +  al
  |       |       |
right  + angle +  adj.
```

orthography 〔 ɔr'θɑgrəfɪ 〕 *n.* 正確拼字；拼字法；正投影法

（ 拼法正確 ）《*ortho-* (right) + *graphy* (writing)》

orthographer 〔 ɔr'θɑgrəfɚ 〕 *n.* 拼字正確的人；拼字學者

(= *orthographist*)

orthographic 〔,ɔrθə'græfɪk 〕 *adj.* 拼字正確的；拼字的；

正投影的

orthop(a)edic[7] 〔,ɔrθə'pidɪk 〕 *adj.* 整形外科的；矯正手術的

（ 使小孩容貌端正 ）《*ortho-* (right) + *p(a)ed* (child) + *-ic* (形容詞字尾)》

```
ortho + p(a)ed +  ic
  |       |       |
right  + child  + adj.
```

orthop(a)edics[7] 〔,ɔrθə'pidɪks 〕 *n.* 整形外科；矯正手術；整形術

《 *-ics* = science》

orthop(a)edist 〔,ɔrθə'pidɪst 〕 *n.* 整形外科醫生

orthopsychiatry 〔,ɔrθosaɪ'kaɪətrɪ 〕 *n.* 精神衛生學；矯治精神

醫學（ 矯正精神的醫學 ）《*psychiatry* 精神醫學》

orthoptic 〔 ɔr'θɑptɪk 〕 *adj.* 兩眼斜視矯正的；視軸矯正的

（ 往直的看 ）《*ortho* (straight) + *(o)pt* (eye ; sight) + *-ic* (形容詞字尾)》

```
ortho + (o)pt +  ic
  |       |       |
right  +  eye  + adj.
```

95　**out-** = beyond；out

* 由「向外」引申而爲「超越」、「勝過」的意思。

outargue[7]〔aʊt'ɑrgjʊ〕*v.* 在辯論中勝過～

outbreak[6]〔'aʊt,brek〕= break out（爆發）的名詞　*n.* 爆發；暴動

【解說】將動詞片語～out 的順序倒過來構成一個單字，而成爲原片語的
名詞型的例子很多，以下舉出一些：

cast out（趕出去）→ outcast（流浪者）
come out（出現）→ outcome（結果）
cry out（高聲呼叫）→ outcry（叫喊；抗議）
fit out（裝備）→ outfit（裝備；用具）
flow out（流出）→ outflow（流出；流出量）
go out（外出）→ outgo（外出；支出）
lay out（用錢）→ outlay（支出；花費）
let out（放出）→ outlet（出口；放出）
look out（小心；警戒）→ outlook（展望；見解；瞭望）
pour out（流出）→ outpour（流出；流出物）
put out（出產）→ output（出產；產品；產量）
set out（出發；開始）→ outset（著手；最初）

outdo[5]〔aʊt'du〕*v.* 凌駕；勝過（勝過）

outdoor[3]〔'aʊt,dor〕*adj.* 戶外的

outface[7]〔aʊt'fes〕*v.* 勇敢地面對；嚇倒；輕視

outgrow[7]〔aʊt'gro〕*v.* 長得大過；比～長得更大；因長大而脫離
（成長超越）

outlandish[7]〔aʊt'lændɪʃ〕*adj.* 異國風味的；異樣的
（外面的土地的）

outlaw[6]〔'aʊt,lɔ〕*n.* 被放逐者；罪犯；惡徒　*v.* 使成爲非法
（在法律之外）

outlay[7]〔'aʊt,le〕*n.* 花費；開銷；支出
（在外面花的錢）《*out-*（out）+ *lay*（spend）》

out	+	lay
out	+	*spend*

outline[3] 〔'aʊt,laɪn〕 n. 外型；輪廓；概要 v. 描述要點；
畫～的輪廓（外面的線）

outlive[7] 〔aʊt'lɪv〕 v. 生存得比～更久（= survive）（存活下去）

outmatch[7] 〔aʊt'mætʃ〕 v. 勝過；擊敗；超過

outnumber[6] 〔aʊt'nʌmbɚ〕 v. 數目勝過～

outpace[7] 〔aʊt'pes〕 v. 追過；比～跑得快；勝過（速度超過）

outrage[6] 〔'aʊt,rɛdʒ〕 n. 暴行 v. 凌辱（踰矩的）

《 **outr-** = **ultra-** (beyond) + **-age** (名詞字尾)》

```
outr  +  age
 |        |
beyond  +  n.
```

outrun[7] 〔aʊt'rʌn〕 v. 跑得較快；追過

outshine[7] 〔aʊt'ʃaɪn〕 v. 比～更亮；勝過；使～失色（比～更亮）

outside[1] 〔'aʊt'saɪd〕 n. 外面 adj. 在外的 adv. 外面地

outspoken[7] 〔'aʊt'spokən〕 adj. 坦白的；直言無諱的

outstanding[4] 〔'aʊt'stændɪŋ〕 adj. 著名的；顯著的；突出的

outweigh[7] 〔aʊt'we〕 v. 比～更重；優於；勝過

outwit[7] 〔aʊt'wɪt〕 v. 以機智勝過（在才智上取勝）

96 over- = above ; across ; beyond

* 從「覆蓋」、「超越」、「勝過」引申爲「過度」、「太過」之意。

overact[7] 〔'ovɚ'ækt〕 v. 動作過度

overbear[7] 〔,ovɚ'bɛr〕 v. 壓倒；克服；鎮壓

overblow[7] 〔,ovɚ'blo〕 v. 吹散；吹過

overboard[7] 〔'ovɚ,bord〕 adv. 在船外

《 **over-** (beyond) + **board** (side of ship)》

```
over  +  board
 |        |
beyond  +  side of ship
```

overbridge[7] ﹝'ovɚ͵brɪdʒ﹞ *n.* ﹝英﹞天橋；陸橋
(= ﹝美﹞ *overpass*)

overburden[7] ﹝'ovɚ'bɝdn̩﹞ *v.* 使負擔過重

overcast[7] ﹝'ovɚ͵kæst﹞ *adj.* (天空) 陰暗的；陰沉的　*v.* 使陰暗

overcloud[7] ﹝͵ovɚ'klaʊd﹞ *v.* 以雲遮蔽；使憂鬱

overcoat[3] ﹝'ovɚ͵kot﹞ *n.* 大衣；外套

overcome[4] ﹝͵ovɚ'kʌm﹞ *v.* 擊敗；壓倒

overcredulous ﹝'ovɚ'krɛdʒʊləs﹞ *adj.* 過度輕信的

over	+	cred	+	ulous
too much	+	believe	+	adj.

overcrowd[7] ﹝͵ovɚ'kraʊd﹞ *v.* 過度擁擠

overcrust[7] ﹝͵ovɚ'krʌst﹞ *v.* 以外皮或外殼包覆

overdo[5] ﹝'ovɚ'du﹞ *v.* 過分；過度烹煮

overdraw[7] ﹝'ovɚ͵drɔ﹞ *v.* 透支；誇張

overdrink ﹝͵ovɚ'drɪŋk﹞ *v.* 飲酒過量

overdue[7] ﹝'ovɚ'dju﹞ *adj.* 過期的；遲到的
《 *over-* (beyond) + *due* (adequate)》

over	+	due
beyond	+	adequate

overeat[5] ﹝'ovɚ'it﹞ *v.* 吃得過多

overestimate[7] ﹝'ovɚ'ɛstə͵met﹞ *v.* 對～估計過高；高估

over	+	estim	+	ate
beyond	+	value	+	v.

overflow[5] ﹝ *v.* ͵ovɚ'flo　*n.* 'ovɚ͵flo ﹞ *v.* 溢出；氾濫；充滿
n. 氾濫；過剩

overhang[7] ﹝͵ovɚ'hæŋ﹞ *v.* 懸垂；突出；迫近 (懸於～之上)

overhaul[7]（ *v.* ˏovɚˋhɔl *n.* ˋovɚˏhɔl ）*v. , n.* 徹底分解；分解檢查
（把零件拖出來檢查）

```
over  + haul
 |       |
beyond + draw
```

overhear[5]（ˏovɚˋhɪr ）*v.* 偶然聽到；偷聽；竊聽（越過~聽到）

overlap[6]（ *v.* ˏovɚˋlæp *n.* ˋovɚˏlæp ）*v. , n.* 部分重疊（互搭在~之上）

overlay[7]（ *v.* ˏovɚˋle *n.* ˋovɚˏle ）*v.* 覆蓋；塗上；壓倒 *n.* 覆蓋物

overload[7]（ *v.* ˏovɚˋlod *n.* ˋovɚˏlod ）*v. , n.* 超載；過度負荷

overlook[4]（ˏovɚˋluk ）*v.* 俯視；監視；看漏（越過~往下看）

overnight[4]（ˋovɚˋnaɪt ）*adv.* 整夜；通宵；一夜之間
 adj. 夜裡的；一夜的

overpay[7]（ˋovɚˋpe ）*v.* 報酬過多

overpeopled[7]（ˏovɚˋpipl̩d ）*adj.* 人口過剩的

```
over   + people + (e)d
  |        |        |
too much + people + adj.
```

overpower[7]（ˏovɚˋpauɚ ）*v.* 打敗；克服；壓倒（力量超越）

overrate[7]（ˋovɚˋret ）*v.* 估計過高

overrule[7]（ˏovɚˋrul ）*v.* 否決；駁回；宣佈~無效

overseas[2]（ *adj.* ˋovɚˋsiz *adv.* ˏovɚˋsiz ）*adj. , adv.* 海外的（地）

oversee[7]（ˏovɚˋsi ）*v.* 監督；管理；指導

oversight[7]（ˋovɚˏsaɪt ）*n.* 疏忽；看漏；監督；看管

oversleep[5]（ˋovɚˋslip ）*v.* 睡過頭；睡眠過久

overtake[4]（ˏovɚˋtek ）*v.* 追及；趕上；使突然遭遇

overthrow[4]（ˏovɚˋθro ）*v.* 推翻；打倒；使瓦解

overtime[7]（ *n. , adj. , adv.* ˋovɚˏtaɪm *v.* ˏovɚˋtaɪm ）*n.* 加班；加班
 時間 *adj. , adv.* 加班的（地）；超時的（地） *v.* 使超過時間

overturn[6]（ *v.* ˏovɚˋtɝn *n.* ˋovɚˏtɝn ）*v. , n.* 推翻；傾覆；顛覆

overwhelm[5]（ˏovɚˋhwɛlm ）*v.* 使不安；壓倒；傾覆

97 **paleo-** = old
*希臘文 *palaios*，表示「古代的」、「舊的」。

paleoanthropology 〔ˌpelɪoˌænθrəˈpalədʒɪ 〕 *n.* 古人類學
  《*paleo-* (old) + *anthropology* (人類學)》

paleobotany 〔ˌpelɪəˈbɑtn̩ɪ 〕 *n.* 古植物學
  《*paleo-* (old) + *botany* (植物學)》

paleogeology 〔ˌpelɪodʒɪˈɑlədʒɪ 〕 *n.* 古地質學
  《*paleo-* (old) + *geology* (地質學)》

paleography 〔ˌpelɪˈɑgrəfɪ 〕 *n.* 古文書學；古字體
  《*paleo-* (old) + *graph* (write) + *-y* (名詞字尾)》

paleontology[7] 〔ˌpelɪɑnˈtɑlədʒɪ 〕 *n.* 古生物學
  《*pale-* (old) + *ont* (be 存在) + *ology* (study)》

Paleozoic[7] 〔ˌpelɪəˈzo · ɪk 〕 *n.* , *adj.* 古生代 (的)
  《*paleo-* (old) + *zo* (animal) + *-ic* (形容詞字尾)》

98 **pan(to)-** = all

panacea[7] 〔ˌpænəˈsiə 〕 = all-healing   *n.* 萬靈藥
  《*pan-* (all) + *acea* (cure ; remedy 治療)》

panchromatic 〔ˌpænkroˈmætɪk 〕 *adj.* 全色的；易於感受各色
  之光的 《*pan-* (all) + *chromat* (color) + *-ic* (形容詞字尾)》
  cf. **chromatic** (色彩的)

pan	+	chromat	+	ic
all	+	color	+	adj.

pandemonium[7] 〔ˌpændɪˈmonɪəm 〕 *n.* 地獄的首都；群鬼的宮殿；
  騷亂 《*pan-* (all) + *demon* (惡魔) + *-ium* (表示場所的名詞字尾)》

panoply 〔ˈpænəplɪ 〕 *n.* 全副甲冑；全副裝備；華麗的衣飾
  《*pan-* (all) + *opl* (weapon) + *-y* (名詞字尾)》

pan	+	opl	+	y
all	+	weapon	+	n.

panorama[7] 〔ˌpænəˈræmə〕 n. 全景；全圖；範圍（整體的外觀）
《*pan-*（ all ）+ *orama*（ view ）》

pantheism[7] 〔ˈpænθiˌɪzəm〕 n. 泛神論
《*pan-*（ all ）+ *the*（ god ）+ *-ism*（ 表示主義的字尾 ）》
cf. **atheism**（ 無神論 ）

pantheon[7] 〔ˈpænθɪˌɑn〕 n. 萬神殿；偉人祠；（ 一國人民所信仰
的 ）諸神《*pan-*（ all ）+ *the*（ god ）+ *-on*（ 希臘字尾 ）》

pantomime[7] 〔ˈpæntəˌmaɪm〕 n. 默劇 *v.* 打手勢（ 完全模仿他人
的人 ）《*panto-*（ all ）+ *mime*（ imitator 模仿者 ）》 *cf.* **mimic**（ 模擬的 ）

99　para- = against ; beside ; beyond ; contrary

*〔變化型〕par- , pa-。

parable[7] 〔ˈpærəbl̩〕 n. 比喻；寓言（ 抛向旁邊 ）
《*para-*（ beside ）+ *ble*（ throw ）》

parachute[4] 〔ˈpærəˌʃut〕 n. 降落傘（ 防止掉落的東西 ）
《*para-*（ against ）+ *chute*（ fall ）》

```
para  + chute
 |       |
against +  fall
```

paraclete 〔ˈpærəˌklit〕 n. 辯護者；安慰者（ 站在旁邊呼喚 ）
《*para-*（ beside ）+ *clete*（ call ）》

paradigm[7] 〔ˈpærəˌdaɪm〕 n. 範例；典型；詞類變化表
（ 在旁邊的例子 ）《*para-*（ beside ）+ *digm*（ example ）》

```
para  + digm
 |       |
beside + example
```

paradox[5] 〔ˈpærəˌdɑks〕 n. 矛盾

```
para  + dox
 |      |
beside + opinion
```

paragon[7] 〔'pærə͵gɑn 〕 *n.* 傑出典範；完人

《*par-* = *para-* (beyond) + *agon* (sharpen 使敏銳)》

paragraph[4] 〔'pærə͵græf 〕 *n.* (文章等) 段、節；新聞的一節；
短評　*v.* 把 (文章) 分段；寫短評 (爲了表示意義的一致，在字
裡行間加上的符號) 《*para-* (beside) + *graph* (write)》

```
para  +  graph
 |         |
beside  +  write
```

parhelion 〔 pɑr'hilɪən 〕 *n.* 幻日 (出現於日暈上的光點)

《*par-* = *para-* (beside) + *hel* (sun) + *-ion* (名詞字尾)》

parallel[5] 〔'pærə͵lɛl 〕 = side by side　*adj.* 平行的；相似的
n. 平行線；並列；類似；比較　*v.* 比較 (在彼此的旁邊)

《*par-* = *para-* (beside) + *allel* (one another)》

parallelogram[7] 〔͵pærə'lɛlə͵græm 〕 *n.* 平行四邊形 (畫成平行)

《*parallel* (平行的) + *ogram* (write)》

paralogism 〔 pə'rælədʒɪzm̩ 〕 *n.* 謬誤推理 (違反理論的)

《*para-* (contrary to) + *logism* (理論)》

paralyze[6] 〔'pærə͵laɪz 〕 *v.* 使麻痺；使不活動 (鬆弛而脫離)

《*para-* (beside) + *lyze* (loosen)》

paranoid[7] 〔'pærənɔɪd 〕 *n.* 偏執狂患者　*adj.* 偏執狂的
(心智不正常)　《*para-* (beside) + *noid* (mind)》

paraphrase[7] 〔'pærə͵frez 〕 *n.* 意譯　*v.* 意譯；釋義 (用別的說法)

《*para-* (beside) + *phrase* (speak)》

paraplegia 〔͵pærə'plidʒɪə 〕 *n.* 半身不遂 (近乎麻痺)

《*para-* (beside) + *pleg* (paralysis 麻痺) + *-ia* (condition)》

```
para  +  pleg     +    ia
 |        |             |
beside + paralysis + condition
```

parasite[7] 〔'pærə͵saɪt 〕 *n.* 寄生蟲；依人爲生者 (靠近食物旁邊)

《*para-* (beside) + *site* (food)》

parasol[7] 〔'pærə,sɔl 〕 *n.* 陽傘（防止太陽的熱）

　《*para-*（against）+ *sol*（sun）》　*cf.* **solar**（太陽的）

paratyphoid 〔,pærə'taıfɔıd 〕 *n.*, *adj.* 副傷寒（的）（近乎傷寒）

　《*para-*（beside）+ *typhoid*（傷寒）》

parenthesis[7] 〔 pə'rɛnθəsıs 〕 *n.* 插入句；圓括弧（放入其中）

　《*par-* = *para-*（beside）+ *en-*（in）+ *thesis*（put）》

```
par   + en + thesis
 |       |     |
beside + in +  put
```

parody[7] 〔'pærədı 〕 *n.* 諷刺詩文　*v.* 拙劣地模仿（別的唱法）

　《*par-* = *para-*（beside）+ *od*（song）+ *-y*（名詞字尾）》

palsy〔'pɔlzı 〕 *n.* 中風　*v.* 使麻痺（鬆弛而脫離）

　《*pa-* = *para-*（beside）+ *lsy*（loosen）》

100　**pen-** = almost　　* 拉丁文 *paene*，表示「幾乎」、「近於」。

peninsula[6] 〔 pə'nınsələ 〕 *n.* 半島（幾乎是島）

　《*pen-*（almost）+ *insula*（island）》

```
pen   + insula
 |        |
almost + island
```

penultimate[7] 〔 pı'nʌltəmıt 〕 *adj.* 倒數第二的（幾近於最後）

　《*pen-*（almost）+ *ultimate*（last）》

penumbra 〔 pı'nʌmbrə 〕 *n.*（日蝕、月蝕的）半影部；（太陽黑

點周圍的）半影（幾乎是影子）《*pen-*（almost）+ *umbra*（shadow）》

cf. **umbrella**（傘）

101　**penta-** = five　　* 希臘文 *pente*，表示「五」。

pentachord 〔'pɛntə,kɔrd 〕 *n.* 五絃琴《*penta-*（five）+ *chord*（string）》

pentagon[7] 〔'pɛntə,gɑn 〕 *n.* 五角形《*penta-* (five) + *gon* (angle)》

cf. **the Pentagon** (美國國防部五角大廈，位於維吉尼亞州的阿靈頓)

pentagram[7] 〔'pɛntə,græm 〕 *n.* 星形《*penta-* (five) + *gram* (write)》

pentahedron 〔,pɛntə'hidrən 〕 *n.* 五面體

《*penta-* (five) + *hedr* (side) + *-on* (名詞字尾)》

```
penta  +  hedr  +  on
  |         |       |
 five   +  side  +  n.
```

pentamerous 〔 pɛn'tæmərəs 〕 *adj.* 五個 (相等的) 部分組成的

《*penta-* (five) + *mer* (part) + *-ous* (形容詞字尾)》

pentameter 〔 pɛn'tæmətɚ 〕 *adj.* , *n.* 五音步的 (詩行)

《*penta-* (five) + *meter* (measure)》

pentarchy 〔'pɛntɑrkɪ 〕 *n.* 五頭政治；五國聯盟

《*pent-* = *penta-* (five) + *archy* (rule)》 *cf.* **monarchy** (君主政治)

```
pent  +  archy
  |        |
 five  +  rule
```

102　per- = away ; thoroughly ; through

* 表示「完全、徹底、遠離」。〔變化型〕par- , pel- , pil- 。

perambulate 〔 pə'æmbjə,let 〕 *v.* 巡行；巡迴；漫步 (步行穿過)

《*per-* (through) + *ambul* (walk) + *-ate* (動詞字尾)》

perceive[5] 〔 pɚ'siv 〕 *v.* 感覺；知覺 (完全接受 → 用心抓住)

《*per-* (thoroughly) + *ceive* (take)》

percolate[7] 〔'pɝkə,let 〕 *v.* (使) 過濾；(使) 滲透

《*per-* (through) + *col* (filter 過濾) + *-ate* (動詞字尾)》

```
per    +  col   +  ate
 |         |        |
through + filter +  v.
```

perception[6] 〔 pə'sɛpʃən 〕 *n.* 知覺;感受

percussion[7] 〔 pə'kʌʃən 〕 *n.* 衝擊;敲打 (徹底地敲打)

　《*per-* (thoroughly) + *cuss* (strike) + *-ion* (名詞字尾)》

perdition[7] 〔 pə'dɪʃən 〕 *n.* 浩劫;惡報;毀滅;地獄

　《*per-* (away) + *dit* (give) + *-ion* (名詞字尾)》

peremptory[7] 〔 pə'rɛmptərɪ 〕 *adj.* 斷然的;強制的;
絕對的;專橫的 (完全持有的)

　《*per-* (thoroughly) + *empt* (take) + *-ory* (形容詞字尾)》

```
per     + empt + ory
 |          |      |
thoroughly + take + adj.
```

perennial[7] 〔 pə'rɛnɪəl 〕 *adj.* 永久的;終年無間斷的 (終年的)

　《*per-* (through) + *enn* (year) + *-ial* (形容詞字尾)》

perfect[2] 〔 'pɝfɪkt 〕 *adj.* 無缺的;完美的 (做得很好)

　《*per-* (thoroughly) + *fect* (make)》

```
per     + fect
 |         |
thoroughly + make
```

perfidy 〔 'pɝfədɪ 〕 *n.* 背信;不誠實 (遠離別人的信賴)

　《*per-* (away from) + *fidy* (faith)》

perforate[7] 〔 'pɝfə,ret 〕 *v.* 穿孔;打洞;貫穿 (穿孔)

　《*per-* (through) + *for* (opening) + *-ate* (動詞字尾)》

perform[3] 〔 pə'fɔrm 〕 *v.* 實行;履行 (完全供給)

　《*per-* (thoroughly) + *form* (provide ; furnish)》

perfume[4] 〔 *n.* 'pɝfjum *v.* pə'fjum 〕 *n.* 芳香;香料;香水
v. 使香;灑香水於 (像煙一樣地飄)

　《*per-* (through) + *fume* (smoke)》

perfunctory[7] 〔 pə'fʌŋktərɪ 〕 *adj.* 敷衍的;表面的;草率的
(草率地做) 《*per-* (away) + *funct* (perform) + *-ory* (形容詞字尾)》

perish[5] 〔ˈpɛrɪʃ〕 *v.* 死；毀滅（完全離去）

　　《*per-*（thoroughly）+ *ish*（go）》

permanent[4] 〔ˈpɝmənənt〕 *adj.* 永久的；不變的；耐久的；常設的

　　（一直存在的）《*per-*（through）+ *man*（remain）+ *-ent*（形容詞字尾）》

```
per  +  man  + ent
 |       |      |
through + remain + adj.
```

permeate[7] 〔ˈpɝmɪˌet〕 *v.* 滲透；充滿；普及；普遍（滑行穿過）

　　《*per-*（through）+ *me*（glide）+ *-ate*（動詞字尾）》

permit[3] 〔pɚˈmɪt〕 *v.* 許可（通行無阻）

　　《*per-*（through）+ *mit*（send）》　*cf.* **mission**（任務）

pernicious[7] 〔pɚˈnɪʃəs〕 *adj.* 有害的；有毒的；致命的；惡性的

　　（完全殺害的）《*per-*（thoroughly）+ *nic*（kill）+ *-ious*（形容詞字尾）》

```
per    + nic + ious
 |        |     |
thoroughly + kill + adj.
```

perpendicular[7] 〔ˌpɝpənˈdɪkjəlɚ〕 *adj.* 垂直的；直立的

　　n. 垂直面；直立（直直垂下）

　　《*per-*（through）+ *pendicu*（weigh）+ *-lar*（形容詞字尾）》

　　cf. **pendant**（垂飾）

perpetual[7] 〔pɚˈpɛtʃuəl〕 *adj.* 永遠的；永久的；終身的（一直

　　尋求下去）《*per-*（throughout）+ *pet*（seek）+ *-ual*（形容詞字尾）》

　　cf. **petition**（祈禱）

```
per     + pet + ual
 |         |     |
throughout + seek + adj.
```

perplex[7] 〔pɚˈplɛks〕 *v.* 使困擾；使迷惑（完全編入）

　　《*per-*（thoroughly）+ *plex*（plait 編成辮）》

persecute[7] 〔ˈpɝsɪˌkjut〕 *v.* 迫害；困惑；煩擾（窮追不捨）

　　《*per-*（continually）+ *secute*（follow）》　*cf.* **sequence**（順序）

persevere[6] 〔͵pɝsə'vɪr 〕*v.* 堅忍（徹底地嚴格）
《*per-*（ thoroughly ）+ *severe*（ strict ）》

```
 per    + severe
  |         |
thoroughly + strict
```

persist[5] 〔 pɚ'sɪst 〕*v.* 固執；持久（一直站著）
《*per-*（ through ）+ *sist*（ cause to stand still 堅定地站著 ）》

perspective[6] 〔 pɚ'spɛktɪv 〕*adj.* 透視的　*n.* 透視法；透視畫；
遠景；前途（一直看到遠處）
《*per-*（ through ）+ *spect*（ see ）+ *-ive*（ 形容詞字尾 ）》

perspicuity[7] 〔͵pɝspɪ'kjuətɪ 〕*n.* 清楚；明晰

```
 per   + spicu + ity
  |        |      |
through + look  +  n.
```

perspiration[7] 〔͵pɝspə'reʃən 〕*n.* 流汗；汗（透過皮膚呼吸）
《*per-*（ through ）+ *spir*（ breathe ）+ *-ation*（ 名詞字尾 ）》　*cf.* **spirit**（ 精神 ）

```
 per    +  spir  + ation
  |         |        |
through + breathe +   n.
```

perspire[7] 〔 pɚ'spaɪr 〕*v.* 流汗

```
 per    +  spire
  |         |
through + breathe
```

persuade[3] 〔 pɚ'swed 〕*v.* 說服；使相信（徹底地忠告）
《*per-*（ thoroughly ）+ *suade*（ advise ）》　*cf.* **suasion**（ 勸說 ）

pertinent[7] 〔'pɝtn̩ənt 〕*adj.* 切題的；中肯的；有關係的
（ 牢牢地握住 ）《*per-*（ thoroughly ）+ *tin*（ hold ）+ *-ent*（ 形容詞字尾 ）》
cf. **tenable**（ 可守的 ）

```
 per      +  tin  + ent
  |          |      |
thoroughly + hold + adj.
```

peruse[7]〔 pə'ruz 〕*v.* 精讀；細讀（完全地使用）

　《*per-*（ thoroughly ）+ *use*》

pervade[7]〔 pɚ'ved 〕*v.* 遍及；瀰漫；走遍（一直走過去）

　《*per-*（ through ）+ *vade*（ go ）》　*cf.* **wade**（ 跋涉 ）

pervasive[7]〔 pɚ'vesɪv 〕*adj.* 遍佈的；瀰漫的

pervert[7]〔 *v.* pɚ'vɝt　*n.* 'pɝvɝt 〕*v.* 引入邪路；誤用；曲解

　n. 入邪道的人；性變態者（完全轉移方向）

　《*per-*（ thoroughly ）+ *vert*（ turn ）》

parboil[7]〔'par,bɔɪl 〕*v.* 使熱度過高；煮成半熟

　《*par-* = *per-*（ thoroughly ）+ *boil*》

　【解說】本來應是「完全煮熟」的意思，但是後來字型演變成《part +

　　　　　boil》，因此成為「煮了一部分→半熟」之意。

pardon[2]〔'pardn̩ 〕*v. , n.* 原諒（完全給與）

　《*par-* = *per-*（ thoroughly ）+ *don*（ give ）》　*cf.* **donation**（ 贈與 ）

```
┌─────────────────────────┐
│   par    +  don          │
│    |         |           │
│ thoroughly + give        │
└─────────────────────────┘
```

pellucid〔 pə'lusɪd 〕*adj.* 透明的；明瞭的（透過~而發亮）

　《*pel-* = *per-*（ through ）+ *lucid*（ shine ）》　*cf.* **lucid**（ 透明的 ）

pilgrim[4]〔'pɪlgrɪm 〕= passing a（ foreign ）country

　n. 朝聖者；香客；旅人《*pil-* = *per-*（ through ）+ *grim*（ land ; country ）》

103　**peri-** = around ; round about

　　　　* 表示「周圍」、「環繞」。

pericardium〔,pɛrɪ'kardɪəm 〕*n.* 心包；心囊（心臟周圍的東西）

　《*peri-*（ around ）+ *card*（ heart ）+ *-ium*（ 名詞字尾 ）》

```
┌────────────────────────────┐
│  peri  +  card  +  ium      │
│    |        |       |       │
│ around + heart  +  n.       │
└────────────────────────────┘
```

pericarp 〔'pɛrɪ,kɑrp 〕 *n.* 果皮（水果周圍）
  《*peri-* (around) + *carp* (fruit)》

pericope[7] 〔 pə'rɪkə,pi 〕 *n.* 摘錄；選段《*peri-* (around) + *cope* (cut)》

periderm 〔'pɛrɪdʒm 〕 *n.* 外皮（周圍的皮）
  《*peri-* (around) + *derm* (skin)》

perigee[7] 〔'pɛrə,dʒi 〕 *n.* 近地點（月球或人造衛星在軌道上最接近地
  球之點）《*peri-* (around) + *gee* (earth)》 *cf.* **apogee**（遠地點）

perihelion 〔,pɛrɪ'hiliən 〕 *n.* 近日點（太陽系的天體最接近太陽的
  位置）《*peri-* (around) + *heli* (sun) + *-on* (名詞字尾)》
  cf. **aphelion**（遠日點）

$$
\begin{array}{ccccc}
\text{peri} & + & \text{heli} & + & \text{on} \\
| & & | & & | \\
around & + & sun & + & n.
\end{array}
$$

perilune 〔'pɛrə,lun 〕 *n.* 近月點（月亮周圍）
  《*peri-* (around) + *lune* (moon)》

perimeter[7] 〔 pə'rɪmətɚ 〕 *n.* 周圍；周長；周邊（測量周圍）
  《*peri-* (around) + *meter* (measure)》

period[2] 〔'pɪrɪəd 〕 *n.* 周期；期間；時代；完結；句點（繞一周
  的時間）《*peri-* (round) + *od* (way)》 *cf.* **Exodus**（出埃及記）

peripatetic 〔,pɛrəpə'tɛtɪk 〕 *adj.* 到處漫游的；四處走走的
  《*peri-* (around) + *patet* (walk) + *-ic* (形容詞字尾)》

periphery[7] 〔 pə'rɪfərɪ 〕 *n.* 周圍；外圍；表面；（神經的）末梢
  （傳到周圍）《*peri-* (around) + *pher* (carry) + *-y* (名詞字尾)》

$$
\begin{array}{ccccc}
\text{peri} & + & \text{pher} & + & \text{y} \\
| & & | & & | \\
around & + & carry & + & n.
\end{array}
$$

periphrase[7] 〔'pɛrɪ,frez 〕 *v.* 拐彎抹角地說（繞著彎說話）
  《*peri-* (round) + *phrase* (speak)》

periscope[7] 〔'pɛrə,skop 〕 *n.* 潛望鏡（環視四周）
  《*peri-* (around) + *scope* (look)》

104 **poly-** = many * 希臘文 *polus*，表示「眾多」。

polyandry〔͵palɪˈændrɪ〕*n.* 一妻多夫制
　　《*poly-*（many）+ *andry*（a man）》

polycentric〔͵palɪˈsɛntrɪk〕*adj.* 多中心的；多元論的
　　《*poly-*（many）+ *centr*（center）+ *-ic*（形容詞字尾）》

polychrome〔ˈpalɪ͵krom〕*n. , adj.* 多色（的）；多色印刷（的）
　　《*poly-*（many）+ *chrome*（color）》

polydomous〔pəˈlɪdəməs〕*adj.* 多巢的
　　《*poly-*（many）+ *dom*（house）+ *-ous*（形容詞字尾）》

```
poly  +  dom  +  ous
 |        |       |
many  +  house +  adj.
```

polygamy[7]〔pəˈlɪgəmɪ〕*n.* 一夫多妻
　　《*poly-*（many）+ *gamy*（marriage）》　*cf.* **monogamy**（一夫一妻制）

polyglot[7]〔ˈpalɪ͵glat〕*adj. , n.* 通曉數種語言的（人）
　　《*poly-*（many）+ *glot*（language ; tongue）》　*cf.* **glottis**（喉門）

polygon[7]〔ˈpalɪ͵gan〕*n.* 多角形；多邊形《*poly-*（many）+ *gon*（angle）》

polygraph[7]〔ˈpalɪ͵græf〕*n.* 多產作家；測謊器；複寫儀
　　《*poly-*（many）+ *graph*（write）》

polyhedron〔͵palɪˈhidrən〕*n.* 多面體
　　《*poly-*（many）+ *hedr*（side）+ *-on*（名詞字尾）》

```
poly  +  hedr  +  on
 |        |        |
many  +  side  +  n.
```

polymath[7]〔ˈpalɪ͵mæθ〕*n.* 博學者　*adj.* 博學的
　　《*poly-*（many）+ *math*（learn）》

polymorphous〔͵palɪˈmɔrfəs〕*adj.* 多形的；多形態的
　　《*poly-*（many）+ *morph*（form）+ *-ous*（形容詞字尾）》

```
poly  +  morph  +  ous
 |        |         |
many  +  form   +  adj.
```

polyphonic[7] 〔͵pɑlɪˈfɑnɪk 〕 *adj.* 多音的；多聲合成的；複調的

《*poly-* (many) + *phon* (sound) + *-ic* (形容詞字尾)》

polyphony[7] 〔 pəˈlɪfənɪ 〕 *n.* 多音；多聲曲

《*poly-* (many) + *phony* (sound)》

polysyllable[7] 〔ˈpɑləͺsɪləbḷ 〕 *n.* (三個音節以上的) 多音節字

《*poly-* (many) + *syllable* (音節)》

polytechnic 〔͵pɑləˈtɛknɪk 〕 *n.* 工藝學校　*adj.* 各種工藝的

polytheism[7] 〔ˈpɑləθiͺɪzəm 〕 *n.* 多神論；多神敎

《*poly-* (many) + *the* (god) + *-ism* (表示主義的名詞字尾)》

105　**post-** = after；behind (與 ante- 相反)

* 表示「在後」。

postbellum 〔 postˈbɛləm 〕 *adj.* 戰後的；【美】南北戰爭後的

《*post-* (after) + *bell* (war) + *-um* (形容詞字尾)》

cf. **antebellum** (戰前的)

```
post + bell + um
 |      |     |
after + war + adj.
```

postdate[7] 〔͵postˈdet 〕 *v.* 把日期填遲

postdoctoral[7] 〔 postˈdɑktərəl 〕 *adj.* 取得博士學位後的 (研究的)

《*post-* (after) + *doctor* (博士) + *-al* (形容詞字尾)》

posterior[7] 〔 pɑsˈtɪrɪɚ 〕 *adj.* 後部的；位於後面的

posterity[7] 〔 pɑsˈtɛrətɪ 〕 *n.* 子孫；後裔 (後繼者)

postern[7] 〔ˈpostɚn 〕 *n.* 後門；側門　*adj.* 後面的；在後的

《*post-* (after) + *-ern* (形容詞兼名詞字尾)》

postface 〔ˈpɑstͺfes 〕 *n.* 跋；後記 《*post-* (after) + *face* (speak)》

postgraduate[7] 〔 postˈgrædʒuɪt 〕 *adj.* 大學畢業後的；研究所的

n. 研究生 (畢業後繼續研究) 《*post-* (after) + *graduate* (畢業)》

posthumous[7]〔'pɑstʃʊməs〕*adj.* 死後出版的；遺腹的；死後的（人死埋入土中之後的）《*post-* (after) + *humous* (ground)》

```
post  +  humous
 |         |
after  +  ground
```

posthumously[7]〔'pɑstʃʊməslɪ〕*adv.* 死後地
《*post-* (after) + *hum* (ground) + *-ous* (形容詞字尾) + *-ly* (副詞字尾)》

```
post  +  humous  +  ly
 |         |         |
after  +  ground  +  adj.
```

postlude〔'post͵lud , -͵ljud〕*n.* 後奏 (曲) (在戲劇的後面)
《*post-* (after) + *lude* (play)》 *cf.* **prelude** (前奏曲)

postmeridian〔͵postmə'rɪdɪən〕*adj.* 午後的
《*post-* (after) + *meri* (middle) + *dian* (day)》

```
post  +  meri  +  dian
 |        |        |
after  +  middle  +  day
```

postmortem[7]〔͵post'mɔrtəm〕*adj.* 死後的 *n.* 驗屍
《*post-* (after) + *mortem* (death)》 *cf.* **mortal** (不免一死的)

postnatal[7]〔post'netl̩〕*adj.* 出生後的；產後的
《*post-* (after) + *nat* (born) + *-al* (形容詞字尾)》

```
post  +  nat  +  al
 |        |       |
after  +  born  +  adj.
```

postnuptial〔post'nʌpʃəl〕*adj.* 婚後的
《*post-* (after) + *nuptial* (wedding)》

postpone[3]〔post'pon〕*v.* 延期 (置於其後)
《*post-* (after) + *pone* (put)》 *cf.* **component** (成分)

postpose〔post'poz〕*v.* (形容詞等) 後置《*post-* (after) + *pose* (put)》

postscript[7]〔'post͵skrɪpt〕*n.* (信件中的) 附筆；(本文的) 後記
(略作 p.s.) 《*post-* (after) + *script* (write)》 *cf.* **script** (筆跡)

106　pre- = before

preadolescent[7] 〔͵priædə'lɛsn̩t 〕 *adj.* 青春前期的
　《*pre-* (before) + *ad-* (to) + *olesc* (grow up) + *-ent* (形容詞字尾)》
preamble[7] 〔'priæmbl̩ , prɪ'æmbl̩ 〕 *n.* (條約、憲法等之) 前文；
　導言《*pre-* (before) + *amble* (walk)》
precaution[5] 〔 prɪ'kɔʃən 〕 *n., v.* 預防 (事前的準備)　*cf.* **caution** (小心)

```
pre  +  caut  + ion
 |       |       |
before + beware +  n.
```

precede[6] 〔 pri'sid , prɪ- 〕 *v.* 在前；在先；高於 (走向前頭)
　《*pre-* (before) + *cede* (go)》
precept[7] 〔'prisɛpt 〕 *n.* 命令；教訓；箴言；令狀 (事先取得)
　《*pre-* (before) + *cept* (take)》　　*cf.* **capture** (捕獲)
precinct[7] 〔'prisɪŋkt 〕 *n.* 周圍；範圍；附近；警察管區
　(事先限定的地方)《*pre-* (before) + *cinct* (surruond)》

```
pre  +  cinct
 |       |
before + surround
```

precipice[7] 〔'prɛsəpɪs 〕 *n.* 懸崖；生死關頭 (以頭在先 → 倒栽)
　《*pre-* (before) + *cipice* = *caput* (head)》　　*cf.* **capital** (首都)
preclude[7] 〔 prɪ'klud 〕 *v.* 阻止；排除；妨礙 (在眼前關閉)
　《*pre-* (in front) + *clude* (shut)》　　*cf.* **exclude** (排除)，**include** (包含)
precocious[7] 〔 prɪ'koʃəs 〕 *adj.* 過早的；早熟的 (在時機到來之前
　成熟)《*pre-* (before) + *coc* (cook ; ripen) + *-ious* (形容詞字尾)》

```
pre  +  coc  + ious
 |       |      |
before + cook +  adj.
```

predecessor[6] 〔'prɛdɪ͵sɛsɚ 〕 *n.* 前任；祖先 (先前離去的人)
　《*pre-* (before) + *de-* (away) + *cess* (go) + *-or* (表示人的名詞字尾)》
　cf. **successor** (後繼者)

predict[4] 〔 prɪ'dɪkt 〕 v. 預言；預知（事先說）

　《**pre-**（ before ）+ **dict**（ say ）》

predilection[7] 〔,pridḷ'ɛkʃən 〕 n. 偏愛；偏好（事先選好）

　《**pre-**（ before ）+ **dilection**（ choose out from others ）》

preexist[7] 〔,priɪg'zɪst 〕 v. 先存在（之前就存在）

prefabricate[7] 〔 pri'fæbrə,ket 〕 v. 預先建造；預先製造（先做）

　《**pre-**（ before ）+ **fabricate**（ construct ）》　　cf. **fabric**（ 構造；織物 ）

```
      pre   +   fabric   +  ate
       |          |          |
    before  +  construct  +  v.
```

preface[6] 〔'prɛfɪs 〕 n. 序文；前言；開場白　v. 作序；寫前言；

開始（事先說的話）《**pre-**（ before ）+ **face**（ speak ）》

prefer[2] 〔 prɪ'fɝ 〕 v. 較喜歡；提出；偏愛（搬到前面）

　《**pre-**（ before ）+ **fer**（ carry ）》

pregnant[4] 〔'prɛgnənt 〕 adj. 懷孕的；含蓄的；重要的（產前狀態）

　《**pre-**（ before ）+ **gnant**（ bear 生產 ）》

```
      pre   +   gnant
       |          |
    before  +   bear
```

prehistoric[5] 〔,priɪs'tɔrɪk 〕 adj. 史前的

prejudice[6] 〔'prɛdʒədɪs 〕 n. 偏見　v. 含有成見（事先的判斷）

　《**pre-**（ before ）+ **judice**（ judgement ）》　　cf. **judicial**（ 司法的；公正的 ）

prelect[7] 〔 prɪ'lɛkt 〕 v. 演講；講課《**pre-**（ before ）+ **lect**（ read ）》

prelife[7] 〔 prɪ'laɪf 〕 n. 前世

prelude[7] 〔'prɛljud 〕 n. 前奏曲　v. 為～之前奏（戲劇前面的部分）

　《**pre-**（ before ）+ **lude**（ play ）》

　cf. **interlude**（ 間奏曲 ），**postlude**（ 後奏曲 ）

premature[6] 〔,primə'tjur 〕 adj. 未成熟的；過早的（成熟之前的）

premium[7] 〔'primɪəm 〕 n. 額外費用；獎金；佣金；保險費

（事先收取的費用）《**pre-**（ before ）+ **mium**（ take ）》

preoccupy[7] 〔 pri'ɑkjə,paɪ 〕*v.* 使凝神於；盤據（心頭）；預佔
（事先佔有）

prepare[1] 〔 prɪ'pɛr 〕*v.* 準備；調製（事先準備）
 《*pre-* (before) + *pare* (get ready)》

preponderate[7] 〔 prɪ'pɑndə,ret 〕*v.* 重量勝過；數目超過；
力量大過；佔優勢（事先衡量）
 《*pre-* (before) + *ponder* (weigh) + *-ate* (動詞字尾)》

字首 paleo~pseudo-

```
pre   + ponder + ate
 |        |       |
before  + weigh +  v.
```

preposterous[7] 〔 prɪ'pɑstərəs 〕*adj.* 荒謬的；可笑的；不合理的（前
前後後反反覆覆）《*pre-* (before) + *poster* (after) + *-ous* (形容詞字尾)》

prerequisite[7] 〔 pri'rɛkwəzɪt 〕*adj.* 必須預先具備的
 n. 首要的事物

presage[7] 〔 *n.* 'prɛsɪdʒ *v.* prɪ'sedʒ 〕*n.* 前兆；預感 *v.* 預示；
預知；預言（事先感受到）《*pre-* (before) + *sage* (perceive)》

```
pre   +  sage
 |        |
before + perceive
```

prescribe[6] 〔 prɪ'skraɪb 〕*v.* 規定；開藥方（事先寫）
 《*pre-* (before) + *scribe* (write)》

present[2] 〔'prɛznt 〕*adj.* 出席的；現在的 *n.* 現在（在眼前）
 《*pre-* (before) + *sent* (being 存在)》 *cf.* **absent** (缺席的；不在的)

preserve[4] 〔 prɪ'zɝv 〕*v.* 保存（保持在以前的狀態）
 《*pre-* (before) + *serve* (keep)》

```
pre   + serve
 |       |
before + keep
```

preside[6] 〔 prɪ'zaɪd 〕*v.* 管理；開會時擔任主席（坐在前面）
 《*pre-* (before) + *side* (sit)》

prestige[6] 〔'prɛstɪdʒ 〕 *n.* 聲望；影響力

《*pre-* (before) + *stige* (bind)》

presume[6] 〔 prɪ'zum 〕 *v.* 假定；推測；敢於；佔便宜 (先拿)

《*pre-* (before) + *sume* (take)》

pretend[3] 〔 prɪ'tɛnd 〕 *v.* 假裝；主張；聲稱；嘗試 (展開在面前看)

《*pre-* (before) + *tend* (stretch ; spread)》

pretext[7] 〔 *n.* 'pritɛkst *v.* pri'tɛkst 〕 *n.* 藉口；託詞　　*v.* 以～為藉口

《*pre-* (before) + *text* (weave)》

```
pre  +  text
 |        |
before + weave
```

prevail[5] 〔 prɪ'vel 〕 *v.* 盛行；流行；佔優勢；戰勝；有效 (向前伸展

勢力) 《*pre-* (before) + *vail* (be strong)》　*cf.* **valiant** (勇敢的)

prevent[3] 〔 prɪ'vɛnt 〕 *v.* 預防；防止 (來到面前)

《*pre-* (before) + *vent* (come)》　　*cf.* **advent** (來臨)

```
pre  +  vent
 |        |
before + come
```

preview[5] 〔'pri,vju 〕 *v.*, *n.* 試映；試演；預展；預告 (片)

(事先看) 《*pre-* (before) + *view* (see)》

previous[3] 〔'privɪəs 〕 *adj.* 以前的；先前的 (前面的路的)

《*pre-* (before) + *vi* = *via* (way) + *-ous* (形容詞字尾)》

107　**pro-** = before ; for ; forth ; forward

＊原本是相當於英語 for 的拉丁文字首，可以用 for 的意思推

想。由「為了～」而產生「代替～」、「贊成～的」、「偏

愛」等意思；或由「向～」演變為「向前」、「事先」、

「公開地」、「因應～」之意。

〔變化型〕pur-, pr- (pro 的簡型)，拉丁文的 *pro* 在古代

法文中是 *pur* (現代法文 **pour** = 英文 **for**)。

pro-American[7] 〔͵proə'mɛrɪkən 〕 *adj.* 親美的

  《*pro-* (for) + *American* (American)》

problem[1] 〔'prɑbləm 〕 *n.* 問題 (向前投擲)

  《*pro-* (forward) + *blem* (casting)》

proceed[4] 〔 prə'sid 〕 *v.* 繼續進行；開始 (往前)

  《*pro-* (before) + *ceed* (go)》   *cf.* **precede** (先行)

proclaim[7] 〔 pro'klem 〕 *v.* 宣言；公布；聲明 (在衆人之前喊叫)

  《*pro-* (before) + *claim* (cry aloud)》   *cf.* **clamour** (喧鬧)

procure[7] 〔 pro'kjur 〕 *v.* 取得；獲得；說服 (爲了～而負起照顧之責)

  《*pro-* (for ; in behalf of) + *cure* (take care of)》

prodigal[7] 〔'prɑdɪgḷ 〕 *adj.* 浪費的；不吝惜的   *n.* 浪費者 (向前

追趕 → 不斷付出)《*prod-* (forth) + *ig* (drive) + *-al* (形容詞字尾)》

cf. **agent** (代理人；動作者)；原動力)

produce[2] 〔 *v.* prə'djus   *n.* 'prɑdjus 〕 *v.* 製造；出產   *n.* 農產品

(向前引出)《*pro-* (forward) + *duce* (lead)》

```
pro    + duce
 |         |
forward + lead
```

profane[7] 〔 prə'fen 〕 = outside of the temple   *adj.* 非神聖的；

不敬的；凡俗的；異教的   *v.* 玷污 (神殿之外)

  《*pro-* (before) + *fane* (temple 寺廟；神殿)》   *cf.* **fane** (神殿)

profess[7] 〔 prə'fɛs 〕 *v.* 聲稱；明言；執業；教授；信奉 (公開承認)

  《*pro-* (before all ; publicly) + *fess* (acknowledge 承認)》

cf. **confess** (招認)

proficient[7] 〔 prə'fɪʃənt 〕 *adj.* 精通的   *n.* 專家 (往前做 → 進步)

  《*pro-* (forward) + *fici* (make) + *-ent* (形容詞字尾)》

```
pro    + fici  + ent
 |         |       |
forward + make  + adj.
```

profit[3] 〔'prɑfɪt 〕*n.* 利益　*v.* 有利（前進；進步）

《*pro-* (before) + *fit* (make)》　*cf.* **fact**（事實）

profligate[7] 〔'prɑfləgɪt 〕*adj.* 放蕩的；揮霍的　*n.* 放蕩者；浪子

（ 不顧一切往前衝 ）《*pro-* (forward) + *flig* (drive) + *-ate* (形容詞字尾)》

```
pro   +  flig +  ate
 |         |      |
forward + drive + adj.
```

profound[6] 〔 prə'faʊnd 〕*adj.* 深遠的；深奧的；低的（ 地下深處 ）

《*pro-* (forward → downward) + *found* (ground ; bottom)》

cf. **found**（創立），**fund**（基金）

profuse[7] 〔 prə'fjus 〕*adj.* 浪費的；豐富的；很多的（ 倒出 ）

《*pro-* (forth) + *fuse* (pour)》

progeria 〔 pro'dʒɪrɪə 〕*n.* 早衰；（ 兒童 ）早衰症

《*pro-* (forward) + *geria* (old age)》

```
pro   +  geria
 |         |
forward + old age
```

prognosis[7] 〔 prɑg'nosɪs 〕*n.* 預後（ 根據症狀對疾病結果的預測 ）；

預測《*pro-* (before) + *gnosis* (know)》

program(me)[3] 〔'progræm 〕= a public notice in writing

n. 節目單；節目；計畫；程式　*v.* 排～之節目單；擬～之計畫

（ 公開寫的通告 ）《*pro-* (before) + *gram* (writing)》

progress[2] 〔 *n.* 'progrɛs *v.* prə'grɛs 〕*n.* 進行；進步；發達

v. 進步；前進（ 向前進 ）《*pro-* (forward) + *gress* (walk)》

cf. **retrogress**（退化）

```
pro   +  gress
 |         |
forward + walk
```

prohibit[6] 〔 pro'hɪbɪt 〕*v.* 禁止；阻止（ 保持在～之前 → 阻礙去路 ）

《*pro-* (before) + *hibit* (have ; hold)》　*cf.* **habit**（習慣）

project[2] 〔 *v.* prə'dʒɛkt *n.* 'pradʒɛkt 〕*v.* 發射;突出;投影;計畫;
表達 *n.* 計畫;提案;事業（向前投擲）
《*pro-* (forward) + *ject* (throw)》

```
pro  +  ject
 |        |
forward + throw
```

prolix 〔'prolɪks 〕*adj.* 冗長的《*pro-* (forward) + *lix* (flow)》

prolog(ue)[7] 〔'prolɔg , -lag 〕*n.* 序言;開場白 *v.* 為～之序言或
序幕（前面的話）《*pro-* (before) + *logue* (speech)》

prolong[5] 〔 prə'lɔŋ , -'laŋ 〕*v.* 延長（向前一直延伸）
《*pro-* (forward ; onward) + *long*》

promenade[7] 〔ˌpramə'ned 〕*n.* 散步;遊行 *v.* 散步（往前進）
《*pro-* (forward) + *menade* (drive on)》 *cf.* **menace**（威脅）

prominent[4] 〔'pramənənt 〕*adj.* 突出的;顯著的（向前突出）
《*pro-* (forth) + *min* (jut 突出) + *-ent* (形容詞字尾)》
cf. **eminent**（卓越的）

```
pro + min + ent
 |     |     |
forth + jut + adj.
```

promiscuous[7] 〔 prə'mɪskjuəs 〕*adj.* 混雜的;雜交的;不加選擇的
（先混合）《*pro-* (before) + *misc* (mix) + *-uous* (形容詞字尾)》

promise[2] 〔'pramɪs 〕*n.* 諾言;約定 *v.* 答應（置於前方）
《*pro-* (forth) + *mise* (send)》 *cf.* **mission**（任務）

promote[3] 〔 prə'mot 〕*v.* 升遷;支援;提倡;促進;創辦
（向前移動）《*pro-* (toward) + *mote* (move)》
cf. **move**（移動），**motion**（動作）

promulgate[7] 〔 prə'mʌlget 〕*v.* 公布;頒布;傳播;散播（在大眾
前公告）《*pro-* (before) + *mulg* = *vulg* (people) + *-ate* (動詞字尾)》

```
pro  +  mulg  +  ate
 |        |       |
before + people + v.
```

pronoun[4] 〔'pronaʊn〕*n.* 代名詞（代替名詞）

　《*pro-*（ instead of ）+ *noun*》

pronounce[2] 〔 prə'naʊns 〕*v.* 宣告；斷言；宣稱；發音（向前告知）

　《*pro-*（ forth ）+ *nounce*（ tell ）》　*cf.* **announce**（宣佈）

propel[6] 〔 prə'pɛl 〕*v.* 推進；促進；鼓勵（向前馳去）

　《*pro-*（ forward ）+ *pel*（ drive ）》　*cf.* **pulse**（脈搏）

```
pro  +  pel
 |       |
forward + drive
```

prophecy[7] 〔'prɑfəsɪ 〕*n.* 預言（事先說）

　《*pro-*（ before ）+ *phe* = *phemi*（ speak ）+ *-cy*（ 名詞字尾 ）》

　cf. **euphemism**（委婉的說法）

propitious[7] 〔 prə'pɪʃəs 〕*adj.* 有利的；吉兆的；慈悲的；順遂的

　（向前尋求）《*pro-*（ forward ）+ *pit* = *pet*（ seek ）+ *-ious*（ 形容詞字尾 ）》

proportion[5] 〔 prə'porʃən 〕*n.* 均衡；相稱；比率；關係；調和；

　比例　*v.* 使均衡；使相稱（與部分有關）

　《*pro-*（ in relation to 相關 ）+ *portion*（ 部分 ）》

propose[2] 〔 prə'poz 〕*v.* 提議；推薦（置於前方）

　《*pro-*（ before ）+ *pose*（ put ）》

```
pro  +  pose
 |       |
before + put
```

propound 〔 prə'paʊnd 〕*v.* 提出；提議（放到前面）

　《*pro-*（ before ）+ *pound*（ place ）》

prorogue 〔 pro'rog 〕*v.* 休會；閉會（公開請求）

　《*pro-*（ publicly ）+ *rogue*（ ask ）》　*cf.* **arrogant**（自大的）

prosecute[6] 〔'prɑsɪ,kjut 〕*v.* 實行；進行；告發；起訴（跟隨～往

　前進）《*pro-*（ before ）+ *secute*（ follow ）》　*cf.* **sequence**（繼續；順序）

```
pro  +  secute
 |       |
before + follow
```

prospect[5] 〔'prɑspɛkt 〕 *n.* 眺望處；景色；期望 *v.* 探勘
（眺望前方）《*pro-* (before) + *spect* (look)》

prospectus[7] 〔 prə'spɛktəs , prɑ- 〕 *n.* (即將出版之新作品等的)
內容說明書；(創辦學校醫院、企業等之) 計劃書；發起書
《*pro-* (forward) + *spect* (look) + *-us* (名詞字尾)》

prostitute[7] 〔'prɑstə‚tjut 〕 *n.* 娼妓；為賺錢而做壞事的人
v. 賣身；濫用 (像物品般公諸於眾人之前)
《*pro-* (forth) + *stitute* (place)》

```
pro + stitute
 |       |
forth + place
```

protect[2] 〔 prə'tɛkt 〕 *v.* 防護；保護 (在前面遮蔽)
《*pro-* (before) + *tect* (cover)》

protest[4] 〔 *v.* prə'tɛst *n.* 'protɛst 〕 *v.* 抗議；反對；斷言 *n.* 抗議
(公開作證)《*pro-* (publicly) + *test* (bear witness 作證)》
cf. testify (證明)

protrude[7] 〔 pro'trud 〕 *v.* 突出；伸出；凸出 (向前突出)
《*pro-* (forth) + *trude* (thrust 伸)》 *cf.* **intrude** (侵入)

```
pro + trude
 |      |
forth + thrust
```

provenance[7] 〔'prɑvənəns 〕 *n.* 起源；出處；由來
《*pro-* (forth) + *ven* (come) + *-ance* (名詞字尾)》

provide[2] 〔 prə'vaɪd 〕 *v.* 提供；規定；預備 (先看見)
《*pro-* (before) + *vide* (see)》 *cf.* **vision** (幻像)

provoke[6] 〔 prə'vok 〕 *v.* 激怒；引起；刺激 (向前大聲呼喊)
《*pro-* (forth) + *voke* (call)》 *cf.* **vocation** (職業)

```
pro + voke
 |      |
forth + call
```

purchase[5]〔'pɝtʃəs〕*v.* 獲得；購買　*n.* 購買；購得之物；收益

（追求～）《*pur-* = *pro-*（for）+ *chase*（追）》　*cf.* **pursue**（追求）

purport[7]〔*n.* 'pɝport *v.* pə·'port〕*n.* 主旨；要旨；目的

v. 聲稱；意指；意謂（根據搬運的東西）

《*pur-* = *pro-*（according to）+ *port*（carry）》

```
 ●   pur    +  port
       |        |
   according to + carry
```

purpose[1]〔'pɝpəs〕*n.* 目的；意向；宗旨；決心　*v.* 計畫；意欲

（置於前方）《*pur-* = *pro-*（before）+ *pose*（put）》

pursue[3]〔pə·'su〕*v.* 追捕；追擊；繼續；追求；糾纏；實行

（跟隨前進）《*pur-* = *pro-*（forth）+ *sue*（follow）》

cf. **prosecute**（實行），**sue**（求婚；控告）

purvey[7]〔pə·'ve〕*v.* 供應；供給（事先看到）

《*pur-* = *pro-*（before）+ *vey*（see）》　*cf.* **survey**（測量）

proffer[7]〔'prɑfə·〕*v.*, *n.* 提供（向前提出）

《*pr-* = *pro-*（before）+ *offer*》

prudent[7]〔'prudn̩t〕*adj.* 謹慎的；慎重的（看見前端）

108　**prot(o)-** = first

* pro- 的最高級。由「最～的」引申為「最初的」、「原始的」、
「原型的」等意思。

protocol[7]〔'protə͵kɑl〕*n.* 草約；條約草案；議定書　*v.* 擬定草案

（最先黏上的）《*proto-*（first）+ *col*（glue 膠水）》

```
  proto + col
    |      |
  first  + glue
```

protomartyr〔͵proto'mɑrtə·〕*n.* 最初的殉道者

《*proto-*（first）+ *martyr*（殉道者）》

protoplasm〔'protə͵plæzəm〕*n.* 原生質
　《*proto-*（ first ）+ *plasm*（ something formed 形成的東西)》

protoplast〔'protə͵plæst〕*n.* 原人；初成物；原物；原生質體
　《*proto-*（ first ）+ *plast*（ something formed 形成的東西)》

prototype[7]〔'protə͵taɪp〕= the original type　*n.* 原型；模範

protozoa[7]〔͵protə'zoə〕*n.pl.* 原生動物
　《*proto-*（ first ）+ *zoa*（ animal)》

protozoan[7]〔͵protə'zoən〕*n.*, *adj.* 原生動物（的）
　《*proto-*（ first ）+ *zo*（ animal ）+ *-an*（ 形容詞兼名詞字尾)》

```
proto +  zo  +  an
  |       |      |
first + animal + adj., n.
```

protozoology〔͵protəzo'a/ələdʒɪ〕*n.* 原生動物學（ 研究原始動物的
學問 ）　《*proto-*（ first ）+ *zo*（ animal) + *ology*（ study)》

109　**pseudo-** = false　　* 希臘文 *pseudes*，表示「假的」。

pseudo[7]〔'sjudo〕= false　*adj.* 假的；偽的

pseudocarp〔'sjudəkɑrp〕*n.* 假果；附果
　《*pseudo-*（ false ）+ *carp*（ fruit)》

pseudoclassic〔͵sjudə'klæsɪk , ͵su-〕*adj.* 擬古的

pseudoclassicism〔͵sjudə'klæsəsɪzm̩〕*n.* 擬古典主義；
　偽古典主義《*classicism* 古典主義》

pseudology〔sju'dalədʒɪ〕*n.* 說謊；捏造；虛構
　《*pseudo-*（ fake ）+ *logy*（ word)》

pseudomorph〔'sjudəmɔrf〕*n.* 假象
　《*pseudo-*（ false ）+ *morph*（ form)》

```
pseudo + morph
  |        |
false  +  form
```

pseudomyopia〔͵sudəmaɪˈopɪə〕 *n.* 假性近視《*myopia* 近視》

pseudonym[7]〔ˈsjudn̩͵ɪm〕 *n.* 假名；筆名

　　《*pseud(o)-* (false) + *onym* (name)》

pseudopod〔ˈsjudə͵pad〕 *n.* (變形蟲等的) 假足；偽足

　　(= *pseudopodium*)　《*pseudo-* (false) + *pod* (foot)》

pseudoscience〔͵sjudoˈsaɪəns〕 *n.* 擬似科學；假科學

110　quadr- , quart- = four

　　　* 拉丁文 *quattuor*，表示「四」，序數為 *quartus* (= *fourth*)。

quadrennial〔kwadˈrɛnɪəl〕 *adj.* 每四年一次的；四年間的

　　《*quadr-* (four) + *enn* (year) + *-ial* (形容詞字尾)》

```
quadr  +  enn  +  ial
  |         |       |
four  +  year  +  adj.
```

quadricentennial〔͵kwadrɪsɛnˈtɛnɪəl〕 *n.* , *adj.* 四百周年紀念 (的)

　　《*quadri-* (four) + *cent* (hundred) + *enn* (year) + *-ial* (形容詞字尾)》

quadrilingual〔͵kwadrɪˈlɪŋgwəl〕 *adj.* (用) 四國語言的

　　《*quadri-* (four) + *lingu* (language) + *-al* (形容詞字尾)》

```
quadri  +   lingu   +  al
  |           |          |
four   +  language  +  adj.
```

quadripartite〔͵kwadrɪˈpartaɪt〕 *adj.* 分成四組的；由四部分所

　　組成的《*quadri-* (four) + *part* (part) + *-ite* (形容詞字尾)》

quadriplegia[7]〔͵kwadrəˈplidʒɪə〕 *n.* 四肢麻痺

　　《*quadri-* (four) + *pleg* (paralysis 麻痺) + *-ia* (condition)》

quadrisyllable〔ˈkwadrə͵sɪləbl̩〕 *n.* 四音節字

　　《*quadri-* (four) + *syllable* (音節)》

quadruped〔ˈkwadrə͵pɛd〕 *n.* 四足獸　 *adj.* 有四足的

　　《*quadru-* (fourfold) + *ped* (foot)》

quadruple〔ˋkwɑdrʊpḷ, kwɑdˊrʊpḷ〕*adj.* 四倍的　*n.* 四倍
v. 使成四倍；變成四倍《*quadru-* (four times) + *ple* (fold)》
quarter[2]〔ˋkwɔrtɚ〕*n.* 四分之一；十五分鐘；二角五分
quarterly[7]〔ˋkwɔrtɚlɪ〕*adj. , adv.* 一年發行四次的（地）；
每季的（地）　*n.* 季刊
quarterfinal[7]〔͵kwɔrtɚˋfaɪnḷ〕*n. , adj.* 四分之一決賽（的）；
複賽（的）
quartet[7]〔kwɔrˊtɛt〕*n.* 四重唱（奏）；四重唱（奏）曲；
四重唱（奏）樂團；四個一組

111　quasi- = as if

* 拉丁文 *quasi*，表示「類似」、「半」、「準」。

quasi-cholera〔ˋkwɑsɪˋkɑlərə〕*n.* 疑似霍亂
quasi-contract〔ˋkwɑsɪˋkɑntrækt〕*n.* 準契約
quasi-judicial[7]〔ˋkwɑsɪdʒuˊdɪʃəl〕*adj.* 準司法的
quasi-official[7]〔ˋkwɑsɪəˊfɪʃəl〕*adj.* 半官方的
quasi-war[7]〔ˋkwɑsɪˋwɔr〕*n.* 準戰爭

112　quinqu- , quint- = five

* 拉丁文 *quinque*，表示「五」，序數為 *quintus* (= *fifth*)。

quinquelateral〔͵kwɪnkɪˊlætərəl〕*adj.* 五邊的
《*quinque-* (five) + *later* (side) + *-al* (形容詞字尾)》
quinquennial〔kwɪnˊkwɛnɪəl〕*adj.* 每五年（發生或出現）一次
的；（持續）五年的　*n.* 每五年發生一次的事；五周年紀念
《*quinqu-* (five) + *enn* (year) + *-ial* (形容詞字尾)》
quint〔kwɪnt〕*n.* 五胞胎之一；五個一組
quintessence[7]〔kwɪnˊtɛsn̩s〕*n.* 精髓；第五元素
《*quint-* (five) + *essence* (要素)》

quintet[7] 〔 kwɪn'tɛt 〕 *n.* 五重唱（奏）；五重唱（奏）曲；五重唱
（奏）樂團；五個一組

quintuple[7] 〔'kwɪntjʊpḷ 〕 *adj.* 五倍的　*n.* 五倍　*v.* 使成五倍
　《*quintu-*（five）+ *ple*（fold）》

113　re- = again ; back

　　* 表示「再次」、「反覆」。〔變化型〕red- , ren-。

rebate[7] 〔 *n.* 'ribet *v.* rɪ'bet , 'ribet 〕 *n.* 折扣；退款　*v.* 予以折扣；
予以回扣（價格再往下降）《*re-*（again）+ *bate*（beat）》

rebel[4] 〔 *v.* rɪ'bɛl *adj.* , *n.* 'rɛbḷ 〕 *v.* 謀反；反叛　*adj.* 謀反的；反叛的
n. 叛徒（又引起戰爭）《*re-*（again）+ *bel*（war）》
　cf. **belligerent**（交戰中的）

```
re  + bel
|      |
again + war
```

rebirth[7] 〔 ri'bɝθ 〕 *n.* 重生；再生；新生

rebound[7] 〔 *v.* rɪ'baʊnd *n.* 'ri,baʊnd 〕 *v.* , *n.* 彈回；跳回；回響
（跳回）《*re-*（back）+ *bound*（jump）》

rebuke[7] 〔 rɪ'bjuk 〕 *v.* , *n.* 叱責；非難（再打）
　《*re-*（again）+ *buke*（beat）》

rebut[7] 〔 rɪ'bʌt 〕 *v.* 反駁；舉出反證（反推回來）
　《*re-*（back）+ *but*（push）》

recalcitrant[7] 〔 rɪ'kælsɪtrənt 〕 *adj.* , *n.* 頑強的（人）；
不服從的（人）；固執的（人）（反踢回去）
　《*re-*（back）+ *calcitr*（kick）+ *-ant*（形容詞字尾）》

```
re  + calcitr + ant
|       |       |
back +  kick  + adj.
```

recall[4] 〔 *v.* rɪˈkɔl *n.* ˈriˌkɔl 〕*v.* 記起；召回；取消；撤回
n. 回憶；撤回；罷免（喚回）《**re-**（back）+ **call**》

recant[7] 〔 rɪˈkænt 〕*v.* 取消主張；撤回聲明（唱歌反對）
《**re-**（back）+ **cant**（sing））》

recapitulate[7] 〔 ˌrikəˈpɪtʃəˌlet 〕*v.* 重覆要點；摘要而言；概述
（再提要點）《**re-**（again）+ **capit**（head）+ **-ulate**（動詞字尾））》

```
re  + capit + ulate
 |      |      |
again + head +  v.
```

recede[7] 〔 rɪˈsid 〕*v.* 後退；撤回；降低（往後退）
《**re-**（back）+ **cede**（go））》

receive[1] 〔 rɪˈsiv 〕*v.* 接受；收留；收到；歡迎；容納（拿到自己的
地方）《**re-**（back）+ **ceive**（take））》

reciprocate[7] 〔 rɪˈsɪprəˌket 〕*v.* 交換；回報；報答（有來有往）

recite[4] 〔 rɪˈsaɪt 〕*v.* 背誦；詳述（再次誦讀）
《**re-**（again）+ **cite**（呼叫））》

reclaim[7] 〔 rɪˈklem 〕*v.* 糾正（某人的）錯誤；教化；開拓；馴服；
取回 *n.* 矯正；教化（反覆叫喊）
《**re-**（back；again）+ **claim**（cry out））》 *cf.* **clamour**（喧鬧）

```
re  + claim
 |      |
again + cry out
```

recline[7] 〔 rɪˈklaɪn 〕*v.* 斜倚；橫臥；憑依（往後靠）
《**re-**（back）+ **cline**（lean））》

recognize[3] 〔 ˈrɛkəgˌnaɪz 〕*v.* 承認；認得（再確認原來已知者）
《**re-**（again）+ **cognize**（know））》 *cf.* **cognizance**（認知）

recoil[7] 〔 rɪˈkɔɪl 〕*v.* 退卻；彈回；起反應 *n.* 跳回；反作用；
後座力（向後退下）《**re-**（back）+ **coil**（hinder part 後部））》

reconcile[6] 〔 ˈrɛkənˌsaɪl 〕*v.* 和解；復交；調停；使一致（使得再度
和諧）《**re-**（again）+ **concile**（使和諧））》 *cf.* **conciliate**（和好）

recondite[7] 〔'rɛkən,daɪt , rɪ'kɑndaɪt 〕 *adj.* 深奧的；難解的；
隱藏的；祕密的（隱藏起來的）
《*re-*（back）+ *cond*（hide）+ *-ite*（形容詞字尾）》

```
re  + cond + ite
|      |      |
back + hide + adj.
```

reconnaissance[7] 〔rɪ'kɑnəsəns 〕 *n.* 偵察；調查；勘察（再度探知）
《*re-*（again）+ *connaiss*（know）+ *-ance*（名詞字尾）》

record[2] 〔*v.* rɪ'kɔrd *n.* 'rɛkəd 〕 *v.* 記錄　*n.* 記錄；唱片；前科
（再度在心上）《*re-*（again）+ *cord*（heart）》　*cf.* **cordial**（熱心的）

recoup[7] 〔rɪ'kup 〕 *v.* 彌補；償還；扣留《*re-*（back）+ *coup*（cut）》

recreation[4] 〔,rɛkrɪ'eʃən 〕 *n.* 娛樂；消遣；休養（為了再產生活力）
《*re-*（again）+ *creat(e)*（produce）+ *-ion*（名詞字尾）》

```
re  + creat(e) + ion
|       |         |
again + produce + n.
```

recruit[6] 〔rɪ'krut 〕 *v.* 招募（新兵等）；補充；恢復　*n.* 新兵；
新加入者；初學者（再次成長）《*re-*（again）+ *cruit*（grow）》

recuperate[7] 〔rɪ'kjupə,ret 〕 *v.* 恢復；休養
《*re-*（back）+ *cuper*（gain）+ *-ate*（動詞字尾）》

```
re  + cuper + ate
|      |      |
back + gain + v.
```

recur[6] 〔rɪ'kɝ 〕 *v.* 重現；再回到；再發生（流回源頭）
《*re-*（back）+ *cur*（run）》　*cf.* **current**（水流）

recycle[4] 〔ri'saɪkḷ 〕 *v.* 回收；再利用《*re-*（again）+ *cycle*（循環）》

redress[7] 〔rɪ'drɛs 〕 *v., n.* 修正；改正；平反；補救
《*re-*（back）+ *dress*（set up）》

reduce[3] 〔rɪ'djus 〕 *v.* 減少；降低；打折扣；減弱；恢復；使變形；
使簡化；節食（引導回歸）《*re-*（back）+ *duce*（lead）》

redundant[6] 〔 rɪ'dʌndənt 〕 *adj.* 多餘的；冗贅的；豐富的

（不斷起伏波動）《**red-**（again）+ **und**（wave）+ **-ant**（形容詞字尾））》

```
red  +  und  +  ant
 |       |       |
again +  wave  +  adj.
```

reduplicate[7] 〔 *v.* rɪ'djuplə͵ket *adj.* rɪ'djupləkɪt 〕 *v.* 加倍；重複

adj. 加倍的；重複的

《**re-**（again）+ **duplic**（double）+ **-ate**（動詞兼形容詞字尾））》

refer[4] 〔 rɪ'fɝ 〕 *v.* 指；稱（為）；言及；參考（運回）

《**re-**（back）+ **fer**（bear；carry））》

reflect[4] 〔 rɪ'flɛkt 〕 *v.* 反射；反映；表達；考慮（曲折而回）

《**re-**（back）+ **flect**（bend））》 *cf.* **flexible**（有彈性的）

```
re   +  flect
 |       |
back +  bend
```

reform[4] 〔 rɪ'fɔrm 〕 *v.* 改革；改正；矯正 *n.* 改革；改正

（重新造型）《**re-**（again）+ **form**》

refraction[7] 〔 rɪ'frækʃən 〕 *n.* 折射；折射作用（折回）

《**re-**（back）+ **fract**（break）+ **-ion**（名詞字尾））》

```
re   +  fract  +  ion
 |        |        |
back +  break  +   n.
```

refresh[4] 〔 rɪ'frɛʃ 〕 *v.* 使恢復精神；恢復（記憶）

（使再度涼爽）《**re-**（again）+ **fresh**》

refrigerator[2] 〔 rɪ'frɪdʒə͵retɚ 〕 *n.* 冰箱；冷藏庫（使再冷卻）

《**re-**（again）+ **frigerat(e)**（cool）+ **-or**（表示物品的名詞字尾））》

cf. **frigid**（寒冷的）

refuge[5] 〔 'rɛfjudʒ 〕 *n.* 避難（所）；保護；隱蔽所；救護所（逃回）

《**re-**（back）+ **fuge**（flee 逃脫））》 *cf.* **fugitive**（逃亡者；短暫的）

refund[6] 〔 *v.* rɪˈfʌnd *n.* ˈriˌfʌnd 〕 *v.* , *n.* 退錢；償還
《*re-* (back) + *fund* (pour)》

refurbish[7] 〔 riˈfɝbɪʃ 〕 *v.* 整修；刷新 (使光亮如新)
《*re-* (again) + *furbish* (make bright)》

refuse[2] 〔 rɪˈfjuz 〕 *v.* 拒絕 (流回 → 不被容的)
《*re-* (back) + *fuse* (pour)》

regard[2] 〔 rɪˈgɑrd 〕 *v.* 認爲；考慮；看待
《*re-* (back) + *gard* (watch over)》

register[4] 〔 ˈrɛdʒɪstɚ 〕 *v.* 登記；註册 《*re-* (again) + *gister* (bear)》

```
 re  +  gister
  |       |
again  +  bear
```

regress[7] 〔 *v.* rɪˈgrɛs *n.* ˈrigrɛs 〕 *v.* 後退；退回　　*n.* 後退；回歸；
退步 (向後行走) 《*re-* (back) + *gress* (walk)》　　*cf.* **progress** (進步)

regurgitate[7] 〔 riˈgɝdʒəˌtet 〕 *v.* (使) 回流；反胃
《*re-* (back) + *gurgit* (flood) + *-ate* (動詞字尾)》

```
 re  + gurgit + ate
  |      |       |
back  + flood  +  v.
```

rehabilitate[7] 〔 ˌrihəˈbɪləˌtet 〕 *v.* 恢復；修復
《*re-* (back) + *habilit* (make suitable) + *-ate* (動詞字尾)》

rehearse[4] 〔 rɪˈhɝs 〕 *v.* 預演；排演；細說；詳述
(反覆耙平土壤 → 公演前反覆練習)《*re-* (again) + *hearse* (harrow 耙)》

reimburse[7] 〔 ˌriɪmˈbɝs 〕 *v.* 償還；付還；退款；賠償
(重新放入錢包)《*re-* (again) + *im-* = *in-* (in) + *burse* (bag)》

```
 re  +  im  + burse
  |      |      |
again  +  in  +  bag
```

reinforce[6] 〔 ˌriɪnˈfors , -ˈfɔrs 〕 *v.* 增強；加強；增援；增兵
(使更強壯有力)《*re-* (again) + *in-* (in) + *force* (strong)》

reiterate[7] 〔 ri'ɪtə,ret 〕 *v.* 反覆地說或做；重述；重申（一再重覆）
《*re-* (again) + *iterate* (repeat)》

reject[2] 〔 rɪ'dʒɛkt 〕 *v.* 拒絕；駁斥；丟棄（擲回）
《*re-* (back) + *ject* (throw)》

rejuvenate[7] 〔 rɪ'dʒuvə,net 〕 *v.* （使）返老還童；（使）恢復活力
（使再度年輕）《*re-* (again) + *juven* (young) + *-ate* (動詞字尾)》

```
re    + juven + ate
|        |       |
again + young +  v.
```

relax[3] 〔 rɪ'læks 〕 *v.* 放鬆；鬆弛；鬆懈（鬆弛成原來的狀態）
《*re-* (back) + *lax* (loosen)》

relevant[6] 〔'rɛləvənt 〕 *adj.* 有關的；切題的；中肯的（再舉起
→ 有力量去做）《*re-* (again) + *lev* (raise) + *-ant* (形容詞字尾)》
cf. **levitate**（減輕）

```
re    + lev + ant
|        |     |
again + raise + adj.
```

relic[5] 〔'rɛlɪk 〕 *n.* 遺物；遺跡；遺風；紀念物（留下來的東西）
《*re-* (back) + *lic* (leave)》

relieve[4] 〔 rɪ'liv 〕 *v.* 減輕；免除；使放心；解救（使再站起來）
《*re-* (again) + *lieve* (raise)》　*cf.* **lever**（槓桿）

relinquish[7] 〔 rɪ'lɪŋkwɪʃ 〕 *v.* 放棄；讓與；鬆手；放手（留下）
《*re-* (back) + *linquish* (leave)》

reluctant[4] 〔 rɪ'lʌktənt 〕 *adj.* 不情願的；勉強的；難處理的；
頑抗的（不願努力）《*re-* (back ; against) + *luct* (struggle) +
-ant (形容詞字尾)》

```
re    + luct   + ant
|        |        |
back + struggle + adj.
```

remain[3] 〔 rɪ'men 〕 *v.* 依然；逗留《*re-* (back) + *main* (stay)》

remedy[4] 〔ˈrɛmədɪ 〕 *n.* 治療法；藥物；補救方法

v. 治癒；修理；糾正《*re-* (again) + *medy* (heal 治癒)》

cf. **medical** (醫學的)

reminiscence[7] 〔ˌrɛməˈnɪsn̩s 〕 *n.* 回想；追憶；引人回憶的事物；

(*pl.*) 回憶錄 (再次想起)

《*re-* (again) + *minisc* (remember) + *-ence* (名詞字尾)》

```
re   +  minisc  + ence
 |        |         |
again + remember +  n.
```

remit[7] 〔rɪˈmɪt 〕 *v.* 匯款；緩和；減輕；赦免；重審 (原樣送回)

《*re-* (back) + *mit* (send)》

remonstrate[7] 〔rɪˈmɑnstret 〕 *v.* 忠告；規勸；抗議 (表示相反

的意見) 《*re-* (against) + *monstrate* (show)》   *cf.* **monster** (怪物)

remorse[7] 〔rɪˈmɔrs 〕 *n.* 悔恨；懊悔 (再咬)

《*re-* (again) + *morse* (bite)》

remunerate[7] 〔rɪˈmjunəˌret 〕 *v.* 報答；報酬 (回贈對方)

《*re-* (back) + *muner* (give) + *-ate* (動詞字尾)》

```
re   + muner + ate
 |       |       |
back +  give  +  v.
```

renew[3] 〔rɪˈnju 〕 *v.* 更新；換新；恢復；重訂 (再成為新的)

renounce[7] 〔rɪˈnaʊns 〕 *v.* 放棄；否認 (收回消息)

《*re-* (back) + *nounce* (bring a message)》

repast[7] 〔rɪˈpæst 〕 *n.* 食物；菜餚；餐 (再次餵食)

《*re-* (again) + *past* (feed)》

repeat[2] 〔rɪˈpit 〕 *v.* 重複；跟著說   *n.* 重複；重播 (再次請求)

《*re-* (again) + *peat* (seek)》   *cf.* **petition** (祈願；懇求)

repel[7] 〔rɪˈpɛl 〕 *v.* 驅逐；拒絕；排斥 (追回)

《*re-* (back) + *pel* (drive)》   *cf.* **pulse** (脈搏)

repent[7] 〔 rɪˈpɛnt 〕 *v.* 後悔（再次後悔）

《*re-* (again) + *pent* (make sorry)》　*cf.* **penitent**（後悔的）

```
re  +  pent
 |      |
again + make sorry
```

replace[3] 〔 rɪˈples 〕 *v.* 取代；代替；放回《*re-* (back) + *place* (put)》

reply[2] 〔 rɪˈplaɪ 〕 *v.* 回答；反應　*n.* 回答（疊回）

《*re-* (back) + *ply* (fold)》

report[1] 〔 rɪˈport 〕 *v.* 報告；報導；通知　*n.* 報導；報告；紀錄

（拿回）《*re-* (back) + *port* (carry)》

reprisal[7] 〔 rɪˈpraɪzl̩ 〕 *n.* 報復；復仇（取回）

《*re-* (back) + *pris* (take) + *-al* (名詞字尾)》

```
re  + pris + al
 |     |     |
back + take + n.
```

reproach[7] 〔 rɪˈprotʃ 〕 *v.* 責備　*n.* 非難；譴責；不名譽；恥辱

（再向前進）《*re-* (again) + *proach* (nearer)》　*cf.* **propinquity**（近處）

repudiate[7] 〔 rɪˈpjudɪˌet 〕 *v.* 拒絕；否認；駁斥

《*re-* (back) + *pudi* (be ashamed) + *-ate* (動詞字尾)》

repugnant[7] 〔 rɪˈpʌgnənt 〕 *adj.* 討厭的；矛盾的；不一致的；

敵對的（敵對的）《*re-* (back) + *pugn* (fight) + *-ant* (形容詞字尾)》

```
re  + pugn + ant
 |     |      |
back + fight + adj.
```

repute[7] 〔 rɪˈpjut 〕 *v.* 被認爲　*n.* 名聲（重新考慮）

《*re-* (again) + *pute* (think)》　*cf.* **compute**（計算）

require[3] 〔 rɪˈkwaɪr 〕 *v.* 要求；需要（再次請求）

《*re-* (again) + *quire* (seek)》　*cf.* **quest**（探求）

requite[7] 〔 rɪˈkwaɪt 〕 *v.* 回報；報答；報復（免除了又回來）

《*re-* (back) + *quite* (release)》

rescind[7]〔rɪˈsɪnd〕*v.* 廢止；使無效；取消（再剪）
《*re-*（again）+ *scind*（cut））》

rescue[4]〔ˈrɛskjʊ〕*v.* 拯救；援助（將某人拉出危險地，回到安全地方）
《*re-*（back）+ *scue*（pull away））》

research[4]〔rɪˈsɝtʃ , ˈrisɝtʃ〕*v.* , *n.* 研究；調查（一再探求）
《*re-*（again）+ *search*（go round））》

```
re  +  search
 |        |
again + go round
```

resemble[4]〔rɪˈzɛmbḷ〕*v.* 像（再次看到相同的東西）
《*re-*（again）+ *semble*（imitate 模仿））》 *cf.* **similar**（類似的）

```
re  +  semble
 |        |
again + imitate
```

resist[3]〔rɪˈzɪst〕*v.* 抵抗；抗拒；忍住 *n.* 防銹劑；防腐劑
（站在～對面）《*re-*（back；against）+ *sist*（stand））》

respect[2]〔rɪˈspɛkt〕*v.* 尊敬；顧慮；重視；關於
n. 尊敬；關心；方面；顧慮（反覆張望）
《*re-*（back）+ *spect*（look））》

resplendent[7]〔rɪˈsplɛndənt〕*adj.* 絢爛的；華麗的；閃耀的
（更加閃亮的）《*re-*（again）+ *splend*（shine）+ *-ent*（形容詞字尾））》

```
re  + splend + ent
 |       |       |
again + shine + adj.
```

restore[4]〔rɪˈstor〕*v.* 恢復；重建；修補；使復原（再次建立）
《*re-*（again）+ *store*（establish））》

restrain[5]〔rɪˈstren〕*v.* 抑制；限制（再次拉緊）
《*re-*（again）+ *strain*（draw tight））》 *cf.* **stringent**（嚴格的）

resume[5]〔rɪˈzum , -ˈzjum〕*v.* 重新開始；繼續；重獲；再取
（再拿起）《*re-*（again）+ *sume*（take））》 *cf.* **assume**（假定；擔任）

resurrection[7]〔͵rɛzə'rɛkʃən〕*n.* 復活；恢復；(the R-) 耶穌復活（再站起來）《*re-* (again) + *surrect* = *surgere* (rise) + *-ion* (名詞字尾)》
cf. **resurgence** (復活)

```
re   + surrect + ion
 |        |        |
again +  rise   +  n.
```

retaliate[7]〔rɪ'tælɪ͵et〕*v.* 報復；復仇
《*re-* (back) + *tali* (talion 報復) + *-ate* (動詞字尾)》

retard[7]〔rɪ'tɑrd〕*v.*, *n.* 阻礙；妨礙；遲滯
《*re-* (back) + *tard* (slow)》

reticent[7]〔'rɛtəsn̩t〕*adj.* 沈默寡言的；保守的；謹慎的（一再沈默的）《*re-* (again) + *tic* (silent) + *-ent* (形容詞字尾)》

```
re   + tic   + ent
 |       |       |
again + silent + adj.
```

retire[4]〔rɪ'taɪr〕*v.* 退休；隱退；告退；就寢；撤退 (拉回)
《*re-* (back) + *tire* (draw)》

retort[5]〔rɪ'tɔrt〕*v.* 反駁；反擊　*n.* 反駁；蒸餾器 (扭轉回來)
《*re-* (back) + *tort* (twist)》　*cf.* **torsion** (扭轉)

retract[7]〔rɪ'trækt〕*v.* 縮回；收回；撤回 (拉回)
《*re-* (back) + *tract* (draw)》

retrench[7]〔rɪ'trɛntʃ〕*v.* 節約；縮減 (開支等)；刪除；省略（削減）《*re-* (back) + *trench* (cut)》

```
re   + trench
 |       |
back +  cut
```

retrieve[6]〔rɪ'triv〕*v.* 尋回；恢復；更正；補償；挽回 (再次發現)
《*re-* (again) + *trieve* (find)》

reunion[4]〔ri'junjən〕*n.* 重聚；團圓；再結合；懇親會（再成為一體）《*re-* (again) + *un-* (one) + *-ion* (名詞字尾)》

reveal³〔rɪˈvil〕*v.* 顯示;洩露;顯出(取下面紗)

　　《*re-*(back)+ *veal*(veil))》

revenue⁶〔ˈrɛvəˌnju〕*n.* 收入總額;歲入(回到金庫的東西)

　　《*re-*(back)+ *venue*(come))》

reverberate⁷〔rɪˈvɝbəˌret〕*v.* 起回聲;回響;反射(使再振動)

　　《*re-*(again)+ *verber*(beat)+ *-ate*(動詞字尾))》

```
┌──────────────────────────┐
│   re  + verber + ate     │
│   |       |       |      │
│  again +  beat  +  v.    │
└──────────────────────────┘
```

revere⁷〔rɪˈvɪr〕*v.* 尊敬;崇敬(敬畏)《*re-*(back)+ *vere*(fear))》

revise⁴〔rɪˈvaɪz〕*v.* 校訂;改訂　*n.* 校訂;改訂(版)(再看一次)

　　《*re-*(again)+ *vise*(see))》　*cf.* **vision**(幻像)

revive⁵〔rɪˈvaɪv〕*v.* 甦醒;復活;重振;振興(再活)

　　《*re-*(again)+ *vive*(live))》　*cf.* **vivid**(生動的)

```
┌──────────────────────┐
│   re  + vive         │
│   |      |           │
│  again + live        │
└──────────────────────┘
```

revoke⁷〔rɪˈvok〕*v.* 取消;廢止;宣告無效(叫回)

　　《*re-*(back)+ *voke*(call))》　*cf.* **voice**(聲音)

revolt⁵〔rɪˈvolt〕*v.* 叛亂;嫌惡　*n.* 叛亂;變節(反轉)

　　《*re-*(back)+ *volt*(roll))》

reward⁴〔rɪˈwɔrd〕*n.*, *v.* 報酬;報答《*re-*(back)+ *ward*(care for))》

redeem⁷〔rɪˈdim〕*v.* 買回;收回;贖回;履行;補償(買回)

　　《*red-*(back)+ 拉丁文 *emere*(buy))》

```
┌──────────────────────┐
│   red  + eem         │
│   |       |          │
│  again +  buy        │
└──────────────────────┘
```

redintegrate〔rɪˈdɪntəˌgret〕*v.* 使再完整;重建;更新

　　(使再完全)《*red-*(again)+ *integr*(whole)+ *-ate*(動詞字尾))》

　　cf. **integral**(整體)

render[6] 〔'rɛndə 〕 v. 致使；報答；翻譯；給與；放棄（回贈）
《**ren-** (back) + **der** (give)》

114　**retro-** = backward　　* 拉丁文 *retro*，表示「向後」。

retroact[7] 〔,rɛtro'ækt 〕 v. 反動；反作用；溯及既往（作用回來）
《**retro-** (backward) + **act** (act)》

retroflex[7] 〔'rɛtrə,flɛks 〕 adj. 反曲的；翻轉的；捲舌的（往後彎）
《**retro-** (backward) + **flex** (bend)》

```
retro   +  flex
  |          |
backward + bend
```

retrograde[7] 〔'rɛtrə,gred 〕 v. 後退；倒退；退化；退步
adj. 後退的；退化的（向後走）
《**retro-** (backward) + **grade** (go)》　 cf. **grade** (等級；年級)

retrospect[7] 〔'rɛtrə,spɛkt 〕 v., n. 回顧（回頭看）
《**retro-** (backward) + **spect** (look)》

115　**se-** = apart；away　　* 拉丁文 *sed*，表示「分離」。

secede[7] 〔 sɪ'sid 〕 v. 脫離；退出（離去）
《**se-** (apart) + **cede** (go)》

seclude[7] 〔 sɪ'klud 〕 v. 隔離；使隱居（分開關閉）
《**se-** (apart) + **clude** (shut)》

secret[2] 〔'sikrɪt 〕 adj. 祕密的　 n. 祕密；祕訣（和其他東西分開）
《**se-** (apart) + **cret** (separate)》

```
se   +  cret
 |        |
apart + separate
```

secrete[7] 〔 sɪ'krit 〕 v. 分泌（分離）《**se-** (apart) + **crete** (separate)》

secure[5]〔 sɪ'kjʊr 〕*adj.* 安全的；確定的；無慮的　*v.* 使安全；擔保
（沒有顧慮）《*se-* (free from) + *cure* (care)》

seduce[6]〔 sɪ'djus 〕*v.* 引誘；使入歧途；勾引（帶到另一處）
《*se-* (apart) + *duce* (lead)》

segregate[7]〔'sɛgrɪˌget 〕*v.* 隔離；分離（離群）
《*se-* (apart) + *greg* (flock 群) + *-ate* (動詞字尾)》
cf. **gregarious**（群居的）

```
se  + greg + ate
|      |      |
apart + flock +  v.
```

select[2]〔 sə'lɛkt 〕*v.* 選擇；挑選　*adj.* 精選的；挑剔的（選擇劃分）
《*se-* (apart) + *lect* (choose)》　*cf.* **elect**（選舉）

separate[2]〔 *v.* 'sɛpəˌret *adj.* 'sɛpərɪt 〕*v.* 使分開；分居；隔開
adj. 分離的；各別的；單獨的（另外準備）
《*se-* (apart) + *par* (prepare) + *-ate* (動詞字尾)》

```
se  +  par  + ate
|       |      |
apart + prepare +  v.
```

sequester[7]〔 sɪ'kwɛstɚ 〕*v.* 使退隱；暫時扣押；沒收（尋求分開）
《*se-* (apart) + *quest* (seek) + *-er* (動詞字尾)》

sever[7]〔'sɛvɚ 〕*v.* 切斷；斷絕；終止；區別　*cf.* **several**（幾個的）

116　semi- = half

semiannual[7]〔ˌsɛmɪ'ænjʊəl 〕*adj.* 半年的；每半年的
《*semi-* (half) + *annu* (year) + *-al* (形容詞字尾)》

```
semi + annu + al
|      |      |
half + year +  adj.
```

semicircle[7]〔'sɛməˌsɝkl̩ 〕*n.* 半圓形

semicolon[7] 〔'sɛmə,kolən 〕 *n.* 分號（；）
　《*semi-*（ half ）+ *colon*（ 冒號)》

semiconductor[7] 〔,sɛməkən'dʌktɚ 〕 *n.* 半導體
　《*semi-*（ half ）+ *conductor*（ 導體)》

semiconscious[7] 〔,sɛmə'kanʃəs 〕 *adj.* 半意識的
　《*semi-*（ half ）+ *conscious*（ aware)》

```
semi + conscious
 |       |
half  +  aware
```

semidiameter 〔,sɛmɪdaɪ'æmətɚ 〕 = radius　*n.* 半徑
　《*semi-*（ half ）+ *diameter*（ 直徑)》

semifinal[7] 〔,sɛmə'faɪnḷ 〕 *n.* , *adj.* 準決賽（ 的 ）
　《*semi-*（ half ）+ *final*（ 最終的；決定的)》

semimonthly[7] 〔,sɛmə'mʌnθlɪ 〕 *adj.* , *adv.* 每半月的（ 地 ）；每月兩
　次的（ 地 ）　*n.* 半月刊　*cf.* **bimonthly**（ 兩個月一次的（ 地 ）；雙月刊)

semiofficial[7] 〔,sɛmɪə'fɪʃəl 〕 *adj.* 半官方的；半正式的

semiprofessional[7] 〔,sɛməprə'fɛʃənḷ 〕 *adj.* , *n.* 半職業性的（ 人 ）
　《*semi-*（ half ）+ *professional*（ 專業的；從事專門職業的人)》

semitropical[7] 〔,sɛmə'trapɪkḷ 〕 *adj.* 亞熱帶的

117　**sept-** = seven

　＊拉丁文 *septem*，表示「七」。〔變化型〕septi-。

septangle 〔'sɛp,tæŋgḷ 〕 *n.* 七角形《*sept-*（ seven ）+ *angle*（ 角)》
September[1] 〔sɛp'tɛmbɚ 〕 *n.* 九月　☞ 見 p.658 December 解說。
septempartite 〔,sɛptɛm'partaɪt 〕 *adj.* 分成七部分的
　《*septem-*（ seven ）+ *part*（ part ）+ *-ite*（ 形容詞字尾)》

```
septem + part + ite
  |        |      |
seven  +  part +  adj.
```

septenary〔'sɛptə,nɛrɪ〕*adj.* 七的；七年一次的

　n. 七個一組；七年間

septennial〔sɛp'tɛnɪəl〕*adj.* 連續七年的；七年一次的

　《*sept-*（ seven ）+ *enn*（ year ）+ *-ial*（ 形容詞字尾 ）》

septilateral〔,sɛptɪ'lætərəl〕*adj.* 七邊的

　《*septi-*（ seven ）+ *later*（ side ）+ *-al*（ 形容詞字尾 ）》

septisyllable〔,sɛptə'sɪləbl̩〕*n.* 七音節字

　《*septi-*（ seven ）+ *syllable*（ 音節 ）》

118　sesqui- = one-and-one-half

sesquicentennial[7]〔,sɛskwɪsɛn'tɛnɪəl〕*adj.* 一百五十年的；

　一百五十周年紀念的　*n.* 一百五十周年紀念

　《*sesqui-*（ one-and-one-half ）+ *centennial*（ 百年紀念的 ）》

sesquihora〔,sɛskwɪ'horə〕*n.* 一小時半

　《*sesqui-*（ one-and-one-half ）+ *hora*（ hour ）》

sesquipedalian〔,sɛskwɪpə'delɪən〕*adj.* 一英尺半長的；

　（ 詞 ）很長的；愛用長詞的　*n.* 很長的詞；音節很多的詞

　《*sesqui-*（ one-and-one-half ）+ *ped*（ foot ）+ *-alian*（ 形容詞字尾 ）》

119　sex- = six

sexcentenary〔sɛks'sɛntɪ,nɛrɪ〕*n. , adj.* 六百（ 的 ）；

　六百周年紀念（ 的 ）《*sex-*（ six ）+ *cent*（ hundred ）+ *en*（ year ）

　+ *-ary*（ 形容詞兼名詞字尾 ）》

sex	+	cent	+	en	+	ary
six	+	hundred	+	year	+	adj., n.

sexennial〔sɛks'ɛnɪəl〕*adj.* 連續六年的；六年一次的

　《*sex-*（ six ）+ *enn*（ year ）+ *-ial*（ 形容詞字尾 ）》

sexpartite 〔 sɛks'pɑrtaɪt 〕 *adj.* 分成六部分的

《*sex-* (six) + *part* (part) + *-ite* (形容詞字尾)》

```
sex  +  part  +  ite
 |       |       |
six  +  part  +  adj.
```

sextuple[7] 〔'sɛkstjʊpl̩ 〕 *adj.* 六重的；六倍的　　*n.* 六倍　　*v.* 使成六倍

120　step- = orphaned

　　* 表示「成爲孤兒的」，之後引申爲「同父異母的」、「繼的」。

stepbrother[7] 〔'stɛp،brʌðɚ 〕 *n.* 異父 (異母) 兄弟

　　cf. **half brother** (同父異母或同母異父兄弟)

stepchild[3] 〔'stɛp،tʃaɪld 〕 *n.* 夫或妻前次婚姻所生之子女

stepdaughter[7] 〔'stɛp،dɔtɚ 〕 *n.* 夫或妻前次婚姻所生之女；繼女

stepfather[3] 〔'stɛp،fɑðɚ 〕 *n.* 繼父；後父

stepmother[3] 〔'stɛp،mʌðɚ 〕 *n.* 繼母；後母

stepparent[7] 〔'stɛp،pɛrənt 〕 *n.* 繼父或繼母

stepsister[7] 〔'stɛp،sɪstɚ 〕 *n.* 異父 (異母) 姊妹

　　cf. **half sister** (同父異母或同母異父姊妹)

stepson[7] 〔'stɛp،sʌn 〕 *n.* 夫或妻前次婚姻所生之子

121　sub- = under

　　* sub- 是由 sup- 演變而來的，其比較級爲 super，最高級是
　　supreme。sub- 原爲高的意思，如 super，supreme 是指「以
　　上；極度；超越」之意。依照 sub- 本來的意思「高」演變而
　　來的字有 **sublime** (崇高的；使崇高)。
　　〔變化型〕suc- , suf- , sug- , sum- , sup- , sur- , sus-。

subaudition 〔،sʌbɔ'dɪʃən 〕 *n.* 心領神會；言外之意

《*sub-* (under) + *audit* (hear) + *-ion* (名詞字尾)》

subcelestial 〔͵sʌbsə′lɛstʃəl 〕 *adj.* 天頂下的；世俗的

《*sub-* (under) + *celest* (heaven) + *-ial* (形容詞字尾)》

```
sub  +  celest  +  ial
 |        |         |
under  +  heaven  +  adj.
```

subconscious[7] 〔 sʌb′kɑnʃəs 〕 *adj.* 潛意識的　*n.* 潛意識

《*sub-* (under) + *conscious* (aware)》

subculture[7] 〔′sʌb͵kʌltʃɚ 〕 *n.* 次文化

subcutaneous 〔͵sʌbkju′tenɪəs 〕 *adj.* 皮下的；存在於皮下的

《*sub-* (under) + *cut* (skin) + *-aneous* (形容詞字尾)》

```
sub  +  cut  +  aneous
 |       |        |
under  + skin  +  adj.
```

subdivide[7] 〔͵sʌbdə′vaɪd 〕 *v.* 再分；細分

《*sub-* (under) + *divide* (divide)》

subdue[7] 〔 səb′dju 〕 *v.* 壓制；減弱；征服 (置於其下)

《*sub-* (under) + *due* (put)》

```
sub  +  due
 |       |
under  + put
```

subhead[7] 〔′sʌb͵hɛd 〕 *n.* 副標題

subjacent 〔 sʌb′dʒesn̩t 〕 *adj.* 在下的；位於下面的；成為基礎的

(投擲在下面)《*sub-* (under) + *jac* (throw) + *-ent* (形容詞字尾)》

subject[2] 〔 *v.* səb′dʒɛkt　*adj.* , *n.* ′sʌbdʒɪkt 〕 *v.* 使服從；使蒙受；提出

adj. 受制於；服從的；易受；聽從；依照　*n.* 學科；主題；主詞；

臣民 (往下投擲)《*sub-* (under) + *ject* (throw)》

subjugate[7] 〔′səbdʒə͵get 〕 *v.* 征服；使服從；使隸屬

(使加入～之下)《*sub-* (under) + *jug* (join) + *-ate* (動詞字尾)》

subjunctive[7]〔 sʌb'dʒʌŋktɪv 〕*adj.* 假設語氣的；假設法的
《*sub-*（ under ）+ *junct*（ join ）+ *-ive*（ 形容詞字尾 ）》

```
sub  +  junct  +  ive
 |        |       |
under  +  join  +  adj.
```

sublet[7]〔 sʌb'lɛt 〕*v.* 轉租；轉包《*sub-*（ under ）+ *let*（ rent ）》

sublime[7]〔 sə'blaɪm 〕*adj.* 莊嚴的；崇高的；雄偉的；壯麗的；
卓越的（ 達到門楣的高度 ）《*sub-*（ up to ）+ *lime*（ lintel 門楣 ）》

submarine[3]〔 *adj.* ˌsʌbmə'rin *n.* 'sʌbməˌrin 〕*adj.* 海面下的
n. 潛水艇《*sub-*（ under ）+ *marine*（ sea ）》　*cf.* **mariner**（ 水手 ）

submerge[7]〔 səb'mɝdʒ 〕*v.* 置於水中；淹沒；遮覆；埋沒
（ 浸泡其下 ）《*sub-*（ under ）+ *merge*（ dip ）》　*cf.* **emerge**（ 出現；浮出 ）

```
sub  +  merge
 |        |
under  +  dip
```

submit[5]〔 səb'mɪt 〕*v.* 屈服；提出；主張
《*sub-*（ under ）+ *mit*（ send ）》

suborn〔 sə'bɔrn 〕*v.* 教唆；買通；收買
《*sub-*（ under ）+ *orn*（ furnish ）》

subpoena[7]〔 sə'pinə 〕*n.* 傳票　*v.* 傳喚
《*sub-*（ under ）+ *poena*（ punishment ）》

```
sub  +  poena
 |        |
under  +  punishment
```

sub rosa〔 sʌb'rozə 〕*adv.* 祕密地；機密地
《*sub-*（ under ）+ *rosa*（ rose ）》

subscribe[6]〔 səb'skraɪb 〕*v.* 訂閱；簽名；簽署；捐助；同意
（ 寫於下方 ）《*sub-*（ under ）+ *scribe*（ write ）》　*cf.* **scribe**（ 抄寫員 ）

subside[7]〔 səb'saɪd 〕*v.*（ 熱病、憤怒、暴風等 ）平息；降落；
下沈；坐下（ 掉入下方 ）《*sub-*（ under ）+ *side*（ settle ）》

subsist[7]〔 səb'sɪst 〕v. 存在；維持生活；居住；位於（立於下方）
《*sub-* (under) + *sist* (stand)》

substance[3]〔'sʌbstəns 〕n. 物質；實體；實質；本質（立於表相之下方的東西）《*sub-* (under) + *stan* (stand) + *-ce* (名詞字尾)》

substitute[5]〔'sʌbstə,tjut 〕v. 代替；取代；替換　n. 代理者；代用品　adj. 代替的；代理的（代替～而設置）
《*sub-* (under ; in place of 取代) + *stitute* (place)》
cf. **constitute** (構成)

subsume[7]〔 səb'sum 〕v. 包含；包括（納入～下）
《*sub-* (under) + *sume* (take)》

```
sub  +  sume
 |        |
under  +  take
```

subterfuge[7]〔'sʌbtɚ,fjudʒ 〕n. 遁辭；藉口；詭計（藉～來逃避）
《*subter-* (under) + *fuge* (flee)》

subtitle[7]〔'sʌb,taɪtl̩ 〕n. 副標題；翻譯字幕；說明字幕（在下面的標題）《*sub-* (under) + *title* (標題)》

suburb[3]〔'sʌbɝb 〕n. 郊區；市郊（接近都市）
《*sub-* (under ; near) + *urb* (town ; city)》　cf. **urban** (都市的)

```
sub  +  urb
 |        |
under  +  city
```

【解說】　在大都市的近郊，通常會有一些住宅區，住在那裡的人多半是白天在城裡上班的中產階級，因爲他們的經濟能力不錯，所以郊區的房子通常比較漂亮，比較安全。

subway[2]〔'sʌb,we 〕n.〔美〕地下鐵；〔英〕地下道
（ =〔美〕*underpass* ）（在地下的道路）《*sub-* (under) + *way*》

【解說】　美國的地下鐵叫作 **subway**，英國則是叫作 **underground** 或 **tube**。台灣有大眾捷運系統（**MRT**），捷運的路線有些是在地下，有些是在地面上，而在地下的部分其實就跟地下鐵很類似。

succeed[2] 〔 səkˈsid 〕 *v.* 成功；繼續；繼承（跟隨～去）

　《*suc-* = *sub-*（ under ）+ *ceed*（ go ）》

succinct[7] 〔 səkˈsɪŋkt 〕 *adj.* 簡潔的；簡明的（綁起來置於其下）

　《*suc-* = *sub-*（ under ）+ *cinct*（ bind ）》

```
suc  +  cinct
 |        |
under  +  bind
```

suffer[3] 〔 ˈsʌfɚ 〕 *v.* 受苦；忍受

　《*suf-* = *sub-*（ under ）+ *fer*（ bear ）》

suffice[7] 〔 səˈfaɪs 〕 *v.* 足夠；使滿足；合格（做了置於其下 → 補充）

　《*suf-* = *sub-*（ under ）+ *fice*（ make ）》

suffocate[6] 〔 ˈsʌfəˌket 〕 *v.* 使窒息；悶死（置於喉嚨之下）

　《*suf-* = *sub-*（ under ）+ *foc* = *fauc*（ gullet 咽喉 ）+ *-ate*（ 動詞字尾 ）》

　cf. **faucet**（ 水龍頭 ）

```
suf  +  foc  +  ate
 |       |       |
under + gullet +  v.
```

suffuse[7] 〔 səˈfjuz 〕 *v.* 充滿；佈滿（流往下方）

　《*suf-* = *sub-*（ under ）+ *fuse*（ pour ）》

suggest[3] 〔 səˈdʒɛst , səgˈdʒɛst 〕 *v.* 建議；使想到；促成；提出；

　使聯想；暗示（搬到下方）《*sug-* = *sub-*（ under ）+ *gest*（ carry ）》

summon[5] 〔 ˈsʌmən 〕 *v.*（ 證人的 ）傳喚；傳召；召集；鼓起（勇氣 ）

　（ 叫出來暗中勸告 ）《*sum-* = *sub-*（ under ）+ *mon*（ advise ）》

　cf. **monition**（ 警告 ）

support[2] 〔 səˈport 〕 *v.* 支持；支撐；幫助；維持；支援

　n. 援助；贊成；支持；後援者；支持物（搬到下面 → 支持 ）

　《*sup-* = *sub-*（ under ）+ *port*（ carry ）》

suppress[5] 〔 səˈprɛs 〕 *v.* 鎮壓；扣留（往下壓 ）

　《*sup-* = *sub-*（ under ）+ *press*（ 壓 ）》

suppurate〔'sʌpjəˌret〕v. 化膿；生膿；出膿（底下發臭）

　　《**sup-** = **sub-**（under）+ **pur**（foul matter）+ **-ate**（動詞字尾））

```
    sup   +   pur    + ate
     |         |        |
   under + foul matter +  v.
```

surrogate[7]〔'sɝəgɪt〕n. 代理；代理人；代用品（要求代替）

　　《**sur-** = **sub-**（under）+ **rog**（ask）+ **-ate**（名詞字尾））

susceptible[7]〔sə'sɛptəbl̞〕adj. 易受影響的；易被感染的（在下面

接受）《**sus-** = **sub-**（under）+ **cept**（take）+ **-ible**（形容詞字尾））

suspect[3]〔v. sə'spɛkt adj., n. 'sʌspɛkt〕v. 懷疑

adj. 令人懷疑的　　n. 嫌疑犯；被懷疑之人（看下面）

　　《**sus-** = **sub-**（under）+ **(s)pect**（look））

sustain[5]〔sə'sten〕v. 維持；供應；抵擋；遭受；忍耐（在下面擁有）

　　《**sus-** = **sub-**（under）+ **tain**（hold）） cf. **tenable**（可守的）

122　super- = above；over

> * 表示「在～之上」、「過分」。
>
> 〔變化型〕supra-, sopra-, sover-, sur-。

superabundant〔ˌsupərə'bʌndənt〕adj. 過多的；過剩的；

有餘的（過度充足的）《**super-**（above）+ **abundant**（充足的））

superb[6]〔su'pɝb〕adj. 上等的；豪華的；壯麗的（比其他好）

supercharge[7]〔ˌsupɚ'tʃɑrdʒ, ˌsju-〕v. 以增壓器增加（引擎等的）

馬力；過度苛責（增加負荷）《**super-**（above）+ **charge**（load））

supercilious[7]〔ˌsupɚ'sɪlɪəs〕adj. 自大的；傲慢的；目空一切的

（高於眼皮的）《**super-**（above）+ **cili**（eyelid 眼皮）+ **-ous**（形容詞

字尾））

```
   super  +  cili  + ous
     |         |      |
   above  + eyelid + adj.
```

superconscious 〔ˌsupɚˈkanʃəs 〕 *adj.* 超意識的
《*super-*（ over ）+ *conscious*（ aware ）》

superficial[5] 〔ˌsupɚˈfɪʃəl 〕 *adj.* 表面的；表皮的；膚淺的
（臉上的）《*super-*（ above ）+ *fici*（ face ）+ *-al*（ 形容詞字尾 ）》

```
super + fici + al
  |      |     |
above + face + adj.
```

superfluous[7] 〔suˈpɝfluəs 〕 *adj.* 多餘的（越過~而流）
《*super-*（ over ）+ *flu*（ flow ）+ *-ous*（ 形容詞字尾 ）》
cf. **fluent**（ 流暢的 ）

superimpose[7] 〔ˌsupɚɪmˈpoz 〕 *v.* 置於~之上；重疊；添加
（置於~之上）《*super-*（ over ）+ *im-*（ in ）+ *pose*（ put ）》

```
super + im + pose
  |     |     |
over + in + put
```

superintend 〔ˌsuprɪnˈtɛnd 〕 *v.* 監督；管理（在~之上警戒）
《*super-*（ over；above ）+ *intend*（ attend to ）》

superior[3] 〔 səˈpɪriɚ 〕 *adj.* 較好的；優秀的；佔優勢的
n. 上司；長輩；優秀的人（較上面的）
《*super-*（ above ）+ *-ior*（ 表比較級的字尾 ）》

supermarket[2] 〔ˈsupɚˌmarkɪt 〕 *n.* 超級市場

supernal 〔 suˈpɝn̩l 〕 *adj.* 天上的；神聖的；在上的；高的
（在上的）《*supern-*（ above ）+ *-al*（ 形容詞字尾 ）》

supernatural[7] 〔ˌsupɚˈnætʃrəl 〕 *adj.*, *n.* 超自然的（事物）；
不可思議的（事物）（超越自然）

supernumerary 〔ˌsupɚˈnjuməˌrɛrɪ 〕 *adj.* 額外的；多餘的
n. 冗員；臨時演員（超過原定數量）
《*super-*（ over ）+ *numer*（ number ）+ *-ary*（ 形容詞字尾 ）》

```
super + numer + ary
  |       |      |
over + number + adj.
```

superscribe 〔ˌsupɚˈskraɪb〕 v. 書寫姓名、住址於（信件、包裹）
之外面（寫在上面）《*super-*（ above ）+ *scribe*（ write ）》

supersonic[6] 〔ˌsupɚˈsɑnɪk〕 adj. 超音速的（超過音速）
《*super-*（ over ）+ *son*（ sound ）+ *-ic*（ 形容詞字尾 ）》

superstition[5] 〔ˌsupɚˈstɪʃən〕 n. 迷信（呆立～於之上）
《*super-*（ above ）+ *stit*（ stand ）+ *-ion*（ 名詞字尾 ）》

```
super  +  stit  + ion
  |         |       |
above  +  stand  +  n.
```

superstructure 〔ˈsupɚˌstrʌktʃɚ〕 n. 上部構造；上層結構；
上位概念（地基上的）建築物（在上面的結構）
《*super-*（ above ）+ *struct*（ build ）+ *-ure*（ 名詞字尾 ）》

supervene 〔ˌsupɚˈvin〕 v. 附帶發生；接著來；併發（到～之上）
《*super-*（ over ; upon ; near ）+ *vene*（ come ）》　*cf.* **venture**（ 冒險 ）

supervise[5] 〔ˌsupɚˈvaɪz〕 v. 監督（ = *superintend* ）
《*super-*（ above ）+ *vise*（ see ）》

```
super  +  vise
  |         |
above  +  see
```

supreme[5] 〔səˈprim〕 adj. 最高的；至尊的；無上的；最重要的；
最後的（在最上面的）《*sup(e)r-*（ above ）+ *-eme*（ 表最高級的字尾 ）》

supremacy[7] 〔səˈprɛməsɪ〕 n. 最高；至尊；主權；優越
《*suprem(e)*（ highest ）+ *-acy*（ 名詞字尾 ）》

supranational 〔ˌsuprəˈnæʃənḷ〕 adj. 超國家的；超民族的
《*supra-*（ above ）+ *national*（ 國家的 ）》

supraorbital 〔ˌsuprəˈɔrbɪtḷ〕 adj. 眼窩上的
《*supra-*（ above ）+ *orbital*（ 眼窩的 ）》

suprarenal 〔ˌsuprəˈrinəl〕 n. , adj. 腎上腺（的）
《*supra-*（ above ）+ *ren*（ kidney ）+ *-al*（ 名詞兼形容詞字尾 ）》

soprano[7] 〔səˈpræno〕 n. 女高音；女高音歌手

sovereign[5] 〔'sɑvrɪn 〕= supreme ; chief ; principal

　　n. 君主；最高統治者　　*adj.* 至高的；有主權的

surcharge[7] 〔 *n.* 'sɝˏtʃɑrdʒ *v.* sɝ'tʃɑrdʒ 〕*n., v.* 超載；索取額外費

　　用；充電過度（超過負荷）《*sur-* = *super-* (over) + *charge* (load)》

```
sur  +  charge
 |        |
over  +  load
```

surface[2] 〔'sɝfɪs 〕*n.* 表面；外面　　*adj.* 表面的　　*v.* 舖（路面）；

　　浮出水面（臉上）《*sur-* = *super-* (above) + *face*》

surfeit[7] 〔'sɝfɪt 〕*n.* 過食；過飲；過多；過剩　　*v.* 過食；過飲

　　（做太多）《*sur-* = *super-* (over) + *feit* (do)》

surmise[7] 〔 *n.* 'sɝmaɪz *v.* sɚ'maɪz 〕*n.* 推測；猜度；臆度　　*v.* 推測；

　　臆度（置於上方）《*sur-* = *super-* (upon ; above) + *mise* (send)》

surmount[7] 〔 sɚ'maʊnt 〕*v.* 戰勝；克服；爬越；置於上面

　　（升到～之上）《*sur-* = *super-* (over) + *mount* (ascend)》

```
sur  +  mount
 |        |
over  +  ascend
```

surname[7] 〔'sɝˏnem 〕*n.* 姓；別號；綽號（加到名字上的稱號）

　　《*sur-* = *super-* (over) + *name*》

surpass[6] 〔 sɚ'pæs 〕= pass over　　*v.* 凌駕；超越；勝過；

　　非～所能勝任（越過～）

surplus[6] 〔'sɝplʌs 〕*n., adj.* 過剩（的）；剩餘（的）（多於需要的）

　　《*sur-* = *super-* (above) + *plus* (more)》

```
sur  +  plus
 |        |
above  +  more
```

surrender[4] 〔 sə'rɛndɚ 〕*v.* 投降；耽於；縱於；屈服於　　*n.* 投降；

　　降服；放棄（傳到～的手上）《*sur-* = *super-* (upon) + *render* (給與)》

surround[3] 〔 sə'raund 〕 v. 包圍；環繞；圍繞 (圍在～上)

《 *sur-* = *super-* (over) + *round* (round)》

surveillance[7] 〔 sə·'veləns 〕 = watch over　　 n. 監視；看守；監督

《 *sur-* = *super-* (over) + *veill* (watch) + *-ance* (名詞字尾)》

```
sur  + veill + ance
 |       |       |
over + watch +  n.
```

survey[3] 〔 v. sə·'ve n. 'sɝve 〕 v. 勘察；調查；測量；眺望；概述

　　 n. 視察；調查；眺望 (看上方) 《 *sur-* = *super-* (over) + *vey* (see)》

survive[2] 〔 sə·'vaɪv 〕 v. 生命較～爲長；殘存 (勝過～而生存)

《 *sur-* = *super-* (above) + *vive* (live)》　　 *cf.* **victuals** (食品)

123   **syn-** = with；together

> * 表示「在～之上」或「在～之中」。相當於拉丁文 *co-* 的
> 字首，表示「一起」、「同時」、「相似」之意。
> 〔變化型〕sy- , syl- , sym-。

synchronism 〔'sɪŋkrə,nɪzəm 〕 n. 同時發生；同時性；併發；

對照歷史年表 (同時做的事)

《 *syn-* (together) + *chron* (time) + *-ism* (名詞字尾)》

```
syn   + chron + ism
 |        |      |
together + time +  n.
```

syndicate[7] 〔 n. 'sɪndɪkɪt v. 'sɪndɪ,ket 〕 n. 企業組合；集團

　　 v. 組織成集團 (根據法律共同組成) 《 *syn-* (together) + *dicate* (justice)》

syndrome[7] 〔'sɪndrə,mi 〕 n. 症候群；綜合症狀；習慣；習性

　　 (一起出現的病症) 《 *syn-* (together) + *drome* (run)》

```
syn   + drome
 |       |
together + run
```

synergistic 〔͵sɪnɚˈdʒɪstɪk〕 *adj.* 協力合作的；產生增強劑作用的

```
syn   +  erg  + istic
 |        |       |
together + work +  adj.
```

synergy[7] 〔ˈsɪnɚdʒɪ〕 *n.* 協同作用；增效作用；協力
  《*syn-* (together) + *ergy* (work)》

synonym[6] 〔ˈsɪnəͺnɪm〕 *n.* 同義字 (意思相同的名字)
  《*syn-* (together) + *onym* (name)》 *cf.* **antonym** (反義字)

synopsis[7] 〔sɪˈnɑpsɪs〕 *n.* 大意；要略；綱領 (全部一起看)
  《*syn-* (together) + *opsis* (seeing ; sight)》 *cf.* **optics** (光學)

syntax[7] 〔ˈsɪntæks〕 *n.* 句子構造；造句法 (共同排定順序)
  《*syn-* (together) + *tax* (order)》 *cf.* **tactics** (戰術；策略)

synthesis[7] 〔ˈsɪnθəsɪs〕 *n.* 綜合；合成 (放置在一起)
  《*syn-* (together) + *thesis* (putting)》

system[3] 〔ˈsɪstəm〕 *n.* 系統；組織；體系；秩序；制度；方法
  (站在一起的事物)
  《*sy-* = *syn-* (together) + *ste* (stand) + *-m* (名詞字尾 = -ment)》

```
sy   +  ste  + m
 |        |     |
together + stand + n.
```

syllepsis 〔sɪˈlɛpsɪs〕 *n.* 【文法】兼用法；【修飾】雙敘法 (一起
  使用) 《*syl-* = *syn-* (together) + *lep* (take) + *-sis* (名詞字尾)》

syllogism 〔ˈsɪləͺdʒɪzəm〕 *n.* 三段論法；演繹法 (一起推論)
  《*syl-* = *syn-* (together) + *logism* (reasoning 推論)》
  cf. **logic** (邏輯；理則學)

symbiosis[7] 〔͵sɪmbaɪˈosɪs〕 *n.* 共生；共棲；共存 (一起生活)
  《*sym-* = *syn-* (together) + *bio* (life) + *-sis* (名詞字尾)》

```
sym   + bio + sis
 |        |     |
together + life +  n.
```

symbol[2] 〔'sɪmbḷ〕 *n.* 象徵;符號;記號(共同投擲 → 總是和～在一起)《*sym-* = *syn-* (together) + *bol* (throw)》

symmetry[6] 〔'sɪmɪtrɪ〕 *n.* 對稱;勻稱;調和;相稱(共有的法度 → 同樣的法度)《*sym-* = *syn-* (together) + *metry* (measure)》

sympathy[4] 〔'sɪmpəθɪ〕 *n.* 同情;同感;共鳴;憐憫;贊同(共有的感情)《*sym-* = *syn-* (together) + *pathy* (feeling)》

　　cf. **antipathy** (反感),**pathos** (哀愁)

symphony[4] 〔'sɪmfənɪ〕 *n.* 交響樂;聲音的協調;諧音;色彩的協調《*sym-* = *syn-* (together) + *phony* (sound)》　　*cf.* **phonetic** (語音的)

symptom[6] 〔'sɪmptəm〕 *n.* 症狀;徵候;徵兆(和病一起降臨身體的東西 → 有病才出現的東西)《*sym-* = *syn-* (together) + *ptom* (fall)》

124　tele- = far off　　* 希臘文 *tele*,表示「遠距離」。

telecommunication[7] 〔ˌtɛləkəˌmjunə'keʃən〕 *n.* 電信學;遠距離通信(從遠處交流)《*tele-* (far off) + *com-* (together) + *municat* (make public) + *-ion* (名詞字尾)》

```
tele  +  com   +  municat  +  ion
 |         |         |          |
far off + together + make public + n.
```

telegram[4] 〔'tɛləˌgræm〕 *n.* 電報(從遠方寫來)
　《*tele-* (far off) + *gram* (writing)》

telegraph[4] 〔'tɛləˌgræf〕 *n.* 電訊;電報機　*v.* 打電報;以電報傳達(從遠處寫來)《*tele-* (far off) + *graph* (writing)》

telemetry 〔tə'lɛmətrɪ〕 *n.* 遙感勘測
　《*tele-* (far off) + *metry* (measure)》

telepathy[7] 〔tə'lɛpəθɪ〕 *n.* 心電感應;傳心術(從遠處傳來的感覺)《*tele-* (far off) + *pathy* (feeling)》

```
tele  +  pathy
 |         |
far off + feeling
```

telephone[2] 〔'tɛləˌfon 〕 *n.* 電話 　*v.* 打電話（從遠處傳來的聲音）
　《*tele-* (far off) + *phone* (sound)》

telescope[4] 〔'tɛləˌskop 〕 *n.* 望遠鏡（看遠處的東西）
　《*tele-* (far off) + *scope* (look)》

teletypewriter 〔ˌtɛlə'taɪpˌraɪtɚ 〕 *n.* 打字電報機
　《*tele-* (far off) + *typewriter* (typewriter)》

teleview 〔'tɛləˌvju 〕 *v.* 看電視；用電視機收看（看遠處傳來的映像）
　《*tele-* (far off) + *view* (see)》

television[2] 〔'tɛləˌvɪʒən 〕 *n.* 電視（機）（遠處物體的映像）
　《*tele-* (far off) + *vision* (映像)》

Telstar 〔'tɛlˌstɑr 〕 *n.* 通信衛星《*tel(e)-* (far off) + *star* (star)》

125　ter- = three　　* 拉丁文 *ter*，表示「三」。

tercet 〔'tɝsɪt , tɝ'sɛt 〕 *n.* 同韻三行詩節；三連音

ternary 〔'tɝnərɪ 〕 *adj.* 由三部分組成的；第三的；三元的

tertian 〔'tɝʃən 〕 *adj.* 【醫學】每三日發作的　*n.* 隔日熱

tertiary[7] 〔'tɝʃɪˌɛrɪ , -ʃərɪ 〕 *adj.* 第三的；【醫學】第三期的

tercentenary 〔 tɝ'sɛntəˌnɛrɪ 〕 *n.* 三百周年紀念（或慶典）
　adj. 三百年的；三百周年的；三百周年紀念的
　《*ter-* (three) + *centennial* (百年紀念的)》

tercentennial 〔ˌtɝsɛn'tɛnɪəl 〕 *n.* , *adj.* = tercentenary

126　tetra- = four

* 希臘文 *tettares*，表示「四」。

tetrachord 〔'tɛtrəˌkɔrd 〕 *n.* 四音音階；一種古代的四絃琴
　《*tetra-* (four) + *chord* (string)》

tetragon 〔'tɛtrəˌɡɑn 〕 *n.* 四角形；方形建築
　《*tetra-* (four) + *gon* (angle)》

tetrahedron 〔͵tɛtrə'hidrən 〕 *n.* 四面體

《*tetra-* (four) + *hedr* (side) + *-on* (名詞字尾)》

```
tetra + hedr + on
  |      |      |
four  + side +  n.
```

tetralogy 〔 tɛ'trælədʒɪ 〕 *n.* 四聯劇；四部曲

《*tetra-* (four) + *logy* (word)》

tetrarch 〔'titrɑrk 〕 = a governor of a fourth part of a province

n. (古羅馬帝國) 一州的四分之一的領主《*tetra-* (four) + *arch* (rule)》

tetrastich 〔'tɛtrə͵stɪk 〕 *n.* 四行詩《*tetra-* (four) + *stich* (line)》

tetrasyllable 〔͵tɛtrə'sɪləbḷ 〕 *n.* 四音節字

《*tetra-* (four) + *syllable* (音節)》

127   **trans-** = beyond；across；over

* 拉丁文 *trans*，表示「超越」、「通過」。

〔變化型〕tra- , tran- , tres-。

transaction[6] 〔 træns'ækʃən 〕 *n.* 交易；辦理；處理；執行；事項

(不斷推進事物)《*trans-* (across) + *act* (drive) + *-ion* (名詞字尾)》

cf. **agent** (代理人)，**agile** (敏捷的)

```
trans +  act  + ion
  |      |      |
across + drive +  n.
```

transcalent 〔 træns'kelənt 〕 *adj.* 傳熱的

《*trans-* (across) + *cal* (be hot) + *-ent* (形容詞字尾)》

transduce[7] 〔 træns'djus 〕 *v.* 將 (能量等) 轉換 (使變化)

《*trans-* (across) + *duce* (lead)》

transfer[4] 〔 *v.* træns'fɝ *n.* 'trænsfɝ 〕 *v.* 轉移；調職；轉車；

轉學；轉帳   *n.* 遷移；調職；轉帳 (越過～搬運)

《*trans-* (across) + *fer* (carry)》

transfigure[7] 〔 træns'fɪgjɚ 〕 *v.* 使變形；使改觀 (移動形狀 → 改變)
《*trans-* (across) + *figure* (形狀)》

transform[4] 〔 træns'fɔrm 〕 *v.* 使轉變

transfuse[7] 〔 træns'fjuz 〕 *v.* (從一容器) 倒於 (另一容器)；輸血；
灌輸 (倒入) 《*trans-* (across) + *fuse* (pour)》   *cf.* **infuse** (注入)

```
trans + fuse
  |      |
across + pour
```

transfusion[7] 〔 træns'fjuʒən 〕 *n.* 輸血；注入
《*trans-* (across) + *fus* (pour) + *-ion* (名詞字尾)》

transgress[7] 〔 træns'grɛs 〕 *v.* 違反 (法律)；踰越 (限度)；
(在道德上) 犯罪《*trans-* (across) + *gress* (walk)》
cf. **grade** (階級)

transient[7] 〔'trænʃənt 〕 *adj.* 瞬間的；短暫的；過境的

transit[6] 〔'trænsɪt 〕 *n.* 通過；運送；搬運；通行 *v.* 通過；過境
(走向對岸)《*trans-* (across) + *it* (go)》   *cf.* **itinerant** (巡迴的)

transitory[7] 〔'trænsə,torɪ 〕 *adj.* 短暫的；一時的

translate[4] 〔 træns'let 〕 *v.* 翻譯；移動；變爲；解釋；說明
(被搬到對面)《*trans-* (across) + *late* (carried)》

translucent[7] 〔 træns'lusn̩t 〕 *adj.* 半透明的

```
trans + luc + ent
  |      |     |
across + shine + adj.
```

transmit[6] 〔 træns'mɪt 〕 *v.* 傳送；傳達；傳播 (送到對面)
《*trans-* (across) + *mit* (send)》

transmute[7] 〔 træns'mjut 〕 *v.* 使變形；使變質 (完全改變)
《*trans-* (across) + *mute* (change)》   *cf.* **mutable** (易變的)

```
trans + mute
  |      |
across + change
```

transparent[5]〔træns'pɛrənt〕*adj.* 透明的；明白的（透過～看到）

《*trans-*（through）+ *parent*（appear））》 *cf.* **apparent**（明白的）

transport[3]〔*v.* træns'port *n.* 'trænsport〕*v.* 輸送；運送

n. 運輸；運輸機（船）（搬到對面）

《*trans-*（across）+ *port*（carry））》 *cf.* **portable**（可攜帶的）

transship[7]〔træns'ʃɪp〕*v.* 轉運；轉乘《*trans-*（across）+ *ship*（運送））》

transverse[7]〔træns'vɝs〕*adj.* 橫貫的

```
trans + verse
  |       |
across +  turn
```

tradition[2]〔trə'dɪʃən〕*n.* 傳統；傳說；因襲（給與對面 → 傳遞）

《*tra-* = *trans-*（across）+ *dit*（give）+ *-ion*（名詞字尾））》

```
tra + dit + ion
 |     |     |
across + give + n.
```

traitor[5]〔'tretɚ〕*n.* 賣國賊；背信者（把東西給敵方的人）

《拉丁文 *traditor* = *tra-*（across）+ *(d)it*（give）+ *-or*（表示人的名詞字尾））》

traverse[7]〔'trævɚs〕*v.* 經過；橫過；橫貫；反對；仔細檢查

n. 橫貫；橫亙之物（轉變方向而越過）

《*tra-* = *trans-*（across）+ *verse*（turn））》

```
tra + verse
 |      |
across + turn
```

tranquil[6]〔'træŋkwɪl〕*adj.* 平靜的；安靜的（靜止於其上）

《*tran-* = *trans-*（beyond）+ *quil*（rest））》

transcend[7]〔træn'sɛnd〕*v.* 超越；凌駕（超越～攀登）

《*tran-* = *trans-*（beyond）+ *scend*（climb））》

cf. **ascend**（上升），**descend**（下降）

transcribe[7]〔træn'skraɪb〕*v.* 抄寫；刊印；改編（轉寫於）

《*tran-* = *trans-*（across；over）+ *scribe*（write））》 *cf.* **describe**（描述）

transpire[7] 〔 træn'spaɪr 〕 v. 排出；發散；蒸發；洩露；爲人所知
（透過皮膚呼吸）《*tran-* = *trans-* (through) + *spire* (breathe)》

```
tran   +  spire
 |         |
through +  breathe
```

transude 〔 træn'sud 〕 v. (使) 滲出
《*tran-* = *trans-* (across) + *sude* (sweat)》

travesty[7] 〔'trævɪstɪ 〕 n. (嚴肅作品的) 滑稽化；詼諧化；曲解
（刻意裝扮以引人嘲笑）
《*tra-* = *trans-* (across) + *vest* (dress) + *-y* (名詞字尾)》

```
tra   +  vest  + y
 |        |       |
across + dress  + n.
```

trespass[6] 〔'trɛspəs 〕 n., v. 侵入；違背；侵害 (越過境界通行)
《*tres-* = *trans-* (across) + *pass*》

128 tri- = three ; threefold

* 拉丁文 *tres*，表示「三」、「三次」。

triangle[2] 〔'traɪ͵æŋgḷ 〕 n. 三角形；三個所組成的一組；
（男女的）三角關係《*tri-* (three) + *angle* (角)》

tribe[3] 〔 traɪb 〕 n. 部落；種族；一群人
《*tri-* (three) + *be* = 拉丁文 *bus* (family)》

【解說】古時位在羅馬的三個種族 the Ramnes, Tities, Luceres 中任
何一省均稱爲 **tribe**，此種稱法遂沿用至今。

tribune[7] 〔'trɪbjun 〕 = the chief of a tribe n. 護民官；
民衆的保護人；講壇

tricar[7] 〔'traɪ͵kɑr 〕 n. 機動三輪車

trichord[7] 〔'traɪ͵kɔrd 〕 n. 三絃樂器；三絃琴
《*tri-* (three) + *chord* (string)》

tricycle[7]〔'traɪsɪk!〕 *n.* 三輪車

trident[7]〔'traɪdn̩t〕 *n.* 三叉戟

triennial[7]〔traɪ'ɛnɪəl〕 *adj.* 每三年一次的

```
tri  +  enn  +  ial
 |       |      |
three + year +  adj.
```

trigonometry[7]〔ˌtrɪgə'nɑmətrɪ〕 *n.* 三角學（三角法則）
《*tri-* (three) + *gono* (angle) + *metry* (measure)》

```
tri  + gono +  metry
 |      |        |
three + angle + measure
```

trilateral[7]〔traɪ'lætərəl〕 *adj.* 有三邊的　*n.* 三邊形；三角形
《*tri-* (three) + *later* (side) + *-al* (形容詞字尾)》

trilogy[7]〔'trɪlədʒɪ〕 *n.*(戲劇、小說、歌劇等的) 三部曲

trimester[7]〔traɪ'mɛstɚ〕 *n.* 三個月期間；三月一期
《*tri-* (three) + *mester* (month)》

trio[7]〔'trio〕 *n.* 三重奏；三個一組

tripartite〔traɪ'partaɪt , 'trɪpɚˌtaɪt〕 *adj.* 分成三部分的；三者
間的；一式三份的《*tri-* (three) + *part* (part) + *-ite* (形容詞字尾)》

```
tri  + part + ite
 |      |      |
three + part + adj.
```

triple[5]〔'trɪp!〕 *adj.* 三倍的；三部的　*n.* 三倍　*v.* 使成三倍
(重疊三個)《*tri-* (three) + *ple* (fold)》

tripod[7]〔'traɪpad〕 *n.* 三腳架；三腳凳；三腳桌
《*tri-* (three) + *pod* (foot)》

trisection〔traɪ'sɛkʃən〕 *n.* 三部分；三等份 (分成三份)
《*tri-* (three) + *sect* (cut) + *-ion* (名詞字尾)》

```
tri  + sect + ion
 |      |      |
three + cut +  n.
```

trisyllable 〔 trɪ'sɪləbl̩, traɪ- 〕 *n.* 三音節字
　《*tri-* (three) + *syllable* (音節)》

triunity 〔 traɪ'junətɪ 〕 *n.* 三位一體；三人一組
　《*tri-* (three) + *unity* (一體)》

trivia[7] 〔'trɪvɪə 〕 *n.pl.* 瑣事

```
tri  +  via
 |       |
three +  way
```

trivial[6] 〔'trɪvɪəl 〕 *adj.* 不重要的；瑣碎的；無趣的；平常的
　《*tri-* (three) + *vi(a)* (way) + *-al* (形容詞字尾)》　*cf.* **trifle** (瑣事)
　【解説】這個字的意思有兩種說法，①由「合三條路的地方」變成「各方向的聚集之處」→「各處都有的」→「平凡的」②集合三條路的岔口，是購物回來的女性必定會合而談天的地方，而她們的談話內容大多「很無聊」由此而引申出此一字義。

129 **twi-** = two ＊表示「二」、「二倍」。

twice[1] 〔 twaɪs 〕 *adv.* 二度；二回；二倍

twig[3] 〔 twɪg 〕 *n.* 嫩枝；末梢

twilight[6] 〔'twaɪˌlaɪt 〕 *n.* 微光；(日出前) 微明；薄暮；黃昏
（明暗二者間的光）

```
twi  +  light
 |       |
two  +  light
```

twill 〔 twɪl 〕 *n.* 斜紋布　*v.* 織成斜紋 (織兩次的)

twin[3] 〔 twɪn 〕 *n.* 雙胞胎之一；一對雙胞胎　*adj.* 雙胞胎的；成對的

twine[7] 〔 twaɪn 〕 *v.* 編結；編織；纏繞；盤繞　*n.* 合股線；細繩；編織；盤繞（聚集二者）

twist[3] 〔 twɪst 〕 *v.* 捲纏；扭曲；使變形；盤旋；曲解　*n.* 線；繩；扭曲；彎折；偏差；技巧（二個編在一起）

130　ultra- = beyond

*拉丁文 *ulter*，表示「在～之外」、「超越」。

ultra[7]〔ˈʌltrə〕*adj.* 極端的；過度的　*n.* 極端主義者

ultramarine〔͵ʌltrəməˈrin〕*adj.* 海外的；深藍色的
n. 群青（一種顏料）；深藍色《*ultra-* (beyond) + *marine* (sea)》

ultramodern[7]〔͵ʌltrəˈmɑdən〕*adj.* 極端現代的

ultramontane〔͵ʌltrəˈmɑnten〕*adj. , n.* 阿爾卑斯山南方的
（人）；義大利的（人）《*ultra-* (beyond) + *mont* (mountain)
+ *-ane* = *-an* (形容詞兼名詞字尾)》

ultramundane〔͵ʌltrəˈmʌnden〕*adj.* 世界之外的；
太陽系以外的；另一個世界的
《*ultra-* (beyond) + *mund* (world) + *-ane* (形容詞字尾)》

```
ultra  +  mund  +  ane
  |         |        |
beyond  +  world  +  adj.
```

ultrared〔͵ʌltrəˈrɛd〕*adj.* 紅外（線）的

ultrashort〔͵ʌltrəˈʃɔrt〕*adj.* 超短波的

ultrasonic[7]〔͵ʌltrəˈsɑnɪk〕= supersonic　*adj.* 超音波的
《*ultra-* (beyond) + *son* (sound) + *-ic* (形容詞字尾)》

```
ultra  +  son  +  ic
  |        |       |
beyond  +  sound  +  adj.
```

ultratropical〔͵ʌltrəˈtrɑpɪk!〕*adj.* 熱帶以外的；較熱帶更熱的

ultraviolet[7]〔͵ʌltrəˈvaɪəlɪt〕*adj.* 紫外（線）的

131　un- = not

*接於名詞、形容詞、副詞前，表「否定」之意。

unabashed[7]〔͵ʌnəˈbæʃt〕*adj.* 不羞赧的；臉皮厚的；不知恥的
《*un-* (not) + *abashed* (羞赧的)》

unabridged[7]〔͵ʌnə'brɪdʒd〕*adj.* 未刪節的；完整的

《*un-*（not）+ *abridged*（刪節的）》

unalterable〔ʌn'ɔltərəb!〕*adj.* 不能改變的；不變的

《*un-*（not）+ *alterable*（可改變的）》

unambiguous[7]〔͵ʌnæm'bɪgjʊəs〕*adj.* 明白的

《*un-*（not）+ *ambiguous*（含糊的）》

unambitious[7]〔͵ʌnæm'bɪʃəs〕*adj.* 無野心的；不顯眼的；質樸的

《*un-*（not）+ *ambitious*（有野心的）》

```
un  +  amb  +  it  +  ious
|       |       |      |
not + round +  go  +  adj.
```

unapproachable[7]〔͵ʌnə'protʃəb!〕*adj.* 不易接近的；冷淡的；

無與倫比的《*un-*（not）+ *approachable*（易接近的；可親近的）》

unartistic[7]〔͵ʌnɑr'tɪstɪk〕*adj.* 與藝術無關的；非藝術的

《*un-*（not）+ *artistic*（藝術的；藝術性的）》

unashamed[7]〔͵ʌnə'ʃemd〕*adj.* 不羞恥的；不知恥的；厚臉皮的

《*un-*（not）+ *ashamed*（羞恥的；慚愧的）》

unattainable[7]〔͵ʌnə'tenəb!〕*adj.* 難到達的

《*un-*（not）+ *attainable*（可到達的）》

```
un  +  at  +  tain  +  able
|       |       |        |
not +  to  +  hold  +  adj.
```

unattended[7]〔͵ʌnə'tɛndɪd〕*adj.* 被忽視的；無隨員的；

無伴的；無人照顧的

《*un-*（not）+ *attend*（照顧；服侍；注意）+ *-ed*（形容詞字尾）》

```
un  +  at  +  tend  +  ed
|       |       |       |
not +  to  + stretch + adj.
```

unattractive[7]〔͵ʌnə'træktɪv〕*adj.* 不吸引人的

《*un-*（not）+ *attractive*（吸引人的）》

unavailable[7] 〔ˌʌnəˈveləbḷ 〕 *adj.* 不可獲得的；達不到的；
不能利用的《*un-* (not) + *available* (可用的)》

unauthorized[7] 〔 ʌnˈɔθəˌraɪzd 〕 *adj.* 未經授權的；未經公認的
《*un-* (not) + *authorized* (經授權的；公認的)》

unaware[7] 〔ˌʌnəˈwɛr 〕 *adj.* 未察覺到的；不知道的
《*un-* (not) + *aware* (察覺的；知道的)》

unbecoming[7] 〔ˌʌnbɪˈkʌmɪŋ 〕 *adj.* 不合適的
《*un-* (not) + *becoming* (合適的)》

unbelief 〔ˌʌnbɪˈlif 〕 *n.* 懷疑；不信仰上帝
《*un-* (not) + *belief* (信仰)》

unbiased[7] 〔 ʌnˈbaɪəst 〕 *adj.* 無偏見的；不偏不倚的；公平的
《*un-* (not) + *biased* (有偏見的)》

unblemished[7] 〔 ʌnˈblɛmɪʃt 〕 *adj.* 無污點的；潔白的
《*un-* (not) + *blemish* (injure) + *-ed* (形容詞字尾)》

```
un + blemish + ed
 |      |       |
not + injure + adj.
```

uncanny[7] 〔 ʌnˈkænɪ 〕 *adj.* 奇怪的；神祕的；不尋常的
《*un-* (not) + *canny* (靈敏的；小心的)》

uncertainty[7] 〔 ʌnˈsɝtṇtɪ 〕 *n.* 不確實；疑點；不可靠
《*un-* (not) + *certainty* (確實)》

unchangeable[7] 〔 ʌnˈtʃendʒəbḷ 〕 *adj.* 不變的
《*un-* (not) + *changeable* (易變的)》

```
un + change + able
 |     |       |
not + change + adj.
```

unchaste[7] 〔 ʌnˈtʃest 〕 *adj.* 淫蕩的；不貞的；無貞操的
《*un-* (not) + *chaste* (貞操的)》

uncivilized[7] 〔 ʌnˈsɪvḷˌaɪzd 〕 *adj.* 未開化的；野蠻的
《*un-* (not) + *civilized* (開化的；文明的)》

uncomely[7] 〔 ʌnˈkʌmlɪ 〕 *adj.* 不優美的
　《*un-* (not) + *comely* (悅目的)》

uncomfortable[7] 〔 ʌnˈkʌmfətəbl̩ 〕 *adj.* 不舒適的；不安的；
　不愉快的《*un-* (not) + *comfortable* (舒適的；輕鬆的)》

un +	com +	fort +	able
not +	wholly +	strong +	adj.

uncommitted[7] 〔 ˌʌnkəˈmɪtɪd 〕 *adj.* 未邃的；中立的
　《*un-* (not) + *committed* (介入的)》

unconditional[7] 〔 ˌʌnkənˈdɪʃənəl 〕 *adj.* 無條件的；無限制的
　《*un-* (not) + *conditional* (有條件的；有約束的)》

unconformity[7] 〔 ˌʌnkənˈfɔrmətɪ 〕 *n.* 不一致
　《*un-* (not) + *conformity* (一致)》

uncongenial[7] 〔 ˌʌnkənˈdʒinjəl 〕 *adj.* 不協調的；不適合的
　《*un-* (not) + *congenial* (協調的)》

unconscious[7] 〔 ʌnˈkɑnʃəs 〕 *adj.* 無意識的；未察覺的；失去意識的
　《*un-* (not) + *conscious* (有意識的；察覺的)》

un +	con +	sci +	ous
not +	with +	know +	adj.

uncontrollable[7] 〔 ˌʌnkənˈtroləbl̩ 〕 *adj.* 難控制的；無法管束的
　《*un-* (not) + *controllable* (可控制的)》

uncourteous[7] 〔 ʌnˈkɝtɪəs 〕 *adj.* 不知禮儀的；粗魯的
　《*un-* (not) + *courteous* (有禮貌的)》

un +	court +	eous
not +	enclosure +	adj.

uncultivated[7] 〔 ʌnˈkʌltəˌvetɪd 〕 *adj.* 無教養的；未開化的
　《*un-* (not) + *cultivated* (有教養的)》

undecided[7] 〔 ˌʌndɪˈsaɪdɪd 〕 *adj.* 未決定的；不果斷的；模糊的
　《*un-* (not) + *decided* (果斷的；明確的)》

undefined[7] 〔͵ʌndɪˈfaɪnd 〕 *adj.* 未下定義的；不明確的
《*un-* (not) + *define* (下定義) + *-(e)d* (形容詞字尾)》

```
un +  de  + fine + (e)d
 |     |      |      |
not + down + end +  adj.
```

undeniable[7] 〔͵ʌndɪˈnaɪəbḷ 〕 *adj.* 不可否認的；無可爭辯的
《*un-* (not) + *deniable* (否認的)》

undescribable[7] 〔͵ʌndɪˈskraɪbəbḷ 〕 *adj.* 筆墨難以形容的
《*un-* (not) + *describable* (可描寫的)》

undesirable[7] 〔͵ʌndɪˈzaɪrəbḷ 〕 *adj.* 不宜的；不受歡迎的；
惹人厭的《*un-* (not) + *desirable* (合意的；喜歡的)》

undetermined[7] 〔͵ʌndɪˈtɝmɪnd 〕 *adj.* 未決定的；不明確的；
不堅決的《*un-* (not) + *determined* (決定的)》

```
un +  de  + termin  + ed
 |     |       |       |
not + down + boundary + adj.
```

undue[7] 〔 ʌnˈdju 〕 *adj.* 過度的；不適當的；未到期限的
《*un-* (not) + *due* (適當的；到期的)》

uneasy[7] 〔 ʌnˈizɪ 〕 *adj.* 不安的；焦慮的《*un-* (not) + *easy* (輕鬆的)》

unemployed[7] 〔͵ʌnɪmˈplɔɪd 〕 *adj.* 失業的；未被僱用的
《*un-* (not) + *employed* (受僱的)》

unequal[7] 〔 ʌnˈikwəl 〕 *adj.* 不等的；不公平的；不能勝任的
《*un-* (not) + *equal* (相等的)》

unexhausted[7] 〔͵ʌnɪgˈzɔstɪd 〕 *adj.* 未用完的
《*un-* (not) + *exhausted* (疲倦的)》

```
un + ex + haust + ed
 |    |     |      |
not + out + draw + adj.
```

unfair[7] 〔 ʌnˈfɛr 〕 *adj.* 不公平的；不正當的
《*un-* (not) + *fair* (公平的；正當的)》

字首 ultra-~with-

unfamiliar[7] 〔͵ʌnfə'mɪljɚ〕 *adj.* 不熟悉的

《*un-* (not) + *familiar* (熟悉的)》

un	+	famili	+	ar
not	+	family	+	adj.

unfeasible[7] 〔ʌn'fizəbl̩〕 *adj.* 不可行的；無法實行的

《*un-* (not) + *feasible* (可行的)》

unfeigned[7] 〔ʌn'fend〕 *adj.* 不虛假的；眞實的；誠實的

《*un-* (not) + *feigned* (虛假的)》

unfinished[7] 〔ʌn'fɪnɪʃt〕 *adj.* 未完成的；未潤飾的；粗糙的

《*un-* (not) + *finished* (完成的)》

unfortunate[7] 〔ʌn'fɔrtʃənɪt〕 *adj.* 不幸的

《*un-* (not) + *fortun* (chance) + *-ate* (形容詞字尾)》

un	+	fortun	+	ate
not	+	chance	+	adj.

unfriendly[7] 〔ʌn'frɛndlɪ〕 *adj.* 不友善的；含有敵意的

《*un-* (not) + *friendly* (友善的)》

ungenerous[7] 〔ʌn'dʒɛnərəs〕 *adj.* 度量狹窄的；吝嗇的

《*un-* (not) + *generous* (寬大的)》

un	+	gener	+	ous
not	+	race	+	adj.

unhealthy[7] 〔ʌn'hɛlθɪ〕 *adj.* 不健康的；不衛生的；不道德的

《*un-* (not) + *healthy* (健康的)》

unheard[7] 〔ʌn'hɝd〕 *adj.* 未被聽見的；不被理睬的

《*un-* (not) + *heard* (聽到的)》

unimaginative[7] 〔͵ʌnɪ'mædʒɪnətɪv〕 *adj.* 缺乏想像力的

《*un-* (not) + *imaginative* (富想像力的)》

uninhabited[7] 〔͵ʌnɪn'hæbɪtɪd〕 *adj.* 無人居住的

《*un-* (not) + *inhabited* (有居民的)》

unintentional[7] 〔͵ʌnɪn'tɛnʃənl 〕*adj.* 不是故意的；不知不覺的；
無心的《*un-*（ not ）+ *intentional*（ 故意的 ）》

un +	in +	tent +	ion +	al
not +	towards +	stretch +	n. +	adj.

unknowingly[7] 〔 ʌn'noɪŋlɪ 〕*adv.* 無知地；未察覺地
《*un-*（ not ）+ *knowingly*（ 故意地 ）》

unknown[7] 〔 ʌn'non 〕*adj.* 未知的；不明的；不知名的
《*un-*（ not ）+ *known*（ 有名的 ）》

unlicensed[7] 〔 ʌn'laɪsn̩st 〕*adj.* 無執照的；未經當局許可的
《*un-*（ not ）+ *licensed*（ 有執照的 ）》

unmanned[7] 〔 ʌn'mænd 〕*adj.* 無人的；自動操縱的
《*un-*（ not ）+ *manned*（ 有人操縱的 ）》

unmerciful[7] 〔 ʌn'mɝsɪfəl 〕*adj.* 殘酷的；無情的
《*un-*（ not ）+ *merciful*（ 慈悲的 ）》

unmistakable[7] 〔͵ʌnmə'stekəbl̩ 〕*adj.* 不會錯的；不會被誤解的；
明顯的《*un-*（ not ）+ *mistakable*（ 易錯誤的；易誤解的 ）》

un +	mis +	tak +	able
not +	wrongly +	take +	adj.

unnecessary[7] 〔 ʌn'nɛsə͵sɛrɪ 〕*adj.* 不必要的
《*un-*（ not ）+ *necessary*（ 必要的 ）》

unorthodox[7] 〔 ʌn'ɔrθə͵daks 〕*adj.* 非正統的；異端的
《*un-*（ not ）+ *ortho-*（ right ）+ *dox*（ opinion ）》

un +	ortho +	dox
not +	right +	opinion

unparalleled[7] 〔 ʌn'pærə͵lɛld 〕*adj.* 無可比擬的；空前的
《*un-*（ not ）+ *parallel*（ 比較；匹敵 ）+ *-ed*（ 形容詞字尾 ）》

unpopular[7] 〔 ʌn'papjələ˞ 〕*adj.* 不流行的；不受歡迎的
《*un-*（ not ）+ *popular*（ 流行的 ）》

unprecedented[7] 〔 ʌn'prɛsəˌdɛntɪd 〕 *adj.* 空前的；無前例的
《*un-* (not) + *precedented* (有先例的)》

un	+	pre	+	ced	+	ent	+	ed
not	+	*before*	+	*go*	+	*n.*	+	*adj.*

unquestionable[7] 〔 ʌn'kwɛstʃənəbḷ 〕 *adj.* 確定的；無可指責的
《*un-* (not) + *questionable* (可疑的)》

unreasonable[7] 〔 ʌn'riznəbḷ 〕 *adj.* 不合理的；過分的
《*un-* (not) + *reasonable* (合理的)》

unreliable[7] 〔ˌʌnrɪ'laɪəbḷ 〕 *adj.* 不可靠的；不可信賴的
《*un-* (not) + *reliable* (可靠的)》

unrest[7] 〔 ʌn'rɛst 〕 *n.* 騷亂；不安《*un-* (not) + *rest* (安穩)》

unsanitary[7] 〔 ʌn'sænəˌtɛrɪ 〕 *adj.* 不衛生的
《*un-* (not) + *sanit* (health) + *-ary* (形容詞字尾)》

un	+	sanit	+	ary
not	+	*health*	+	*adj.*

unsatisfied[7] 〔 ʌn'sætɪsfaɪd 〕 *adj.* 不滿意的
《*un-* (not) + *satisfied* (滿意的)》

unseasonable[7] 〔 ʌn'siznəbḷ 〕 *adj.* 不合時宜的；不合季節的
《*un-* (not) + *seasonable* (合時的)》

unsophisticated[7] 〔ˌʌnsə'fɪstɪˌketɪd 〕 *adj.* 純眞的；簡單的
《*un-* (not) + *sophisticated* (通世故的)》

unspoken[7] 〔 ʌn'spokən 〕 *adj.* 未說出口的；不說話的
《*un-* (not) + *spoken* (口頭的)》

unsuitable[7] 〔 ʌn'sutəbḷ 〕 *adj.* 不適當的；不相配的
《*un-* (not) + *suitable* (適當的)》

un	+	suit	+	able
not	+	*follow*	+	*adj.*

unsystematic[7] 〔ˌʌnsɪstə'mætɪk 〕 *adj.* 無系統的；不成體系的；
無組織的《*un-* (not) + *systematic* (有系統的)》

untidy[7] 〔 ʌnˈtaɪdɪ 〕 *adj.* 不整潔的《*un-* (not) + *tidy* (整齊的)》

untimely[7] 〔 ʌnˈtaɪmlɪ 〕 *adj.* 不合時宜的；不合時節的；過早的

《*un-* (not) + *timely* (合時的)》

unutterable[7] 〔 ʌnˈʌtərəbḷ 〕 *adj.* 非語言所能表達的；無法形容的；

徹底的《*un-* (not) + *utter* (說出) + *-able* (形容詞字尾)》

unverifiable[7] 〔 ʌnˈvɛrɪfaɪəbḷ 〕 *adj.* 無法證實或證明的；不能確

定的《*un-* (not) + *verifiable* (可證明的)》

```
un  +  ver  +  ifi  +  able
 |       |       |       |
not  +  true  +  make  +  adj.
```

unwarrantable[7] 〔 ʌnˈwɑrəntəbḷ 〕 *adj.* 難保證的

《*un-* (not) + *warrantable* (可保證的)》

unwholesome[7] 〔 ʌnˈholsəm 〕 *adj.* 不健全的

《*un-* (not) + *wholesome* (健康的；健全的)》

```
un  +  whole  +  some
 |        |        |
not  +  healthy  +  like
```

unwilling[7] 〔 ʌnˈwɪlɪŋ 〕 *adj.* 不願意的；不情願的；勉強的

《*un-* (not) + *willing* (願意的)》

unwitting[7] 〔 ʌnˈwɪtɪŋ 〕 *adj.* 不知情的；不知不覺的；不是故意的

《*un-* (not) + *witting* (故意的；知曉的)》

unwonted[7] 〔 ʌnˈwʌntɪd 〕 *adj.* 不尋常的；非普通的；不習慣的

《*un-* (not) + *wonted* (習慣的)》

```
un  +  wonted
 |       |
not  +  accustomed
```

unworldly[7] 〔 ʌnˈwɝldlɪ 〕 *adj.* 脫離世俗的；超俗的；非人世間的

《*un-* (not) + *worldly* (世俗的；塵世的)》

unyielding[7] 〔 ʌnˈjildɪŋ 〕 *adj.* 不屈的；不讓步的

《*un-* (not) + *yielding* (服從的)》

字首 ultra-~with-

132　un- = the reversal of an action

* 接於動詞之前，表示動作的相反。

unarm[7]〔 ʌnˈɑrm 〕 *v.* 解除武器；放下武器
　《*un-* + *arm* (武器；供給武器)》

unbind[7]〔 ʌnˈbaɪnd 〕 *v.* 解開束縛；釋放《*un-* + *bind* (束縛)》

unbosom[7]〔 ʌnˈbʊzəm 〕 *v.* 表白 (情感)；吐露 (機密)
　《*un-* + *bosom* (隱藏在胸中)》

unbuckle[7]〔 ʌnˈbʌkḷ 〕 *v.* 解開帶鈕；解下；放下
　《*un-* + *buckle* (用鈕環扣住)》

unburden[7]〔 ʌnˈbɝdn̩ 〕 *v.* 解除負擔；使輕鬆
　《*un-* + *burden* (使負重擔)》

unbury[7]〔 ʌnˈbɛrɪ 〕 *v.* 挖掘《*un-* + *bury* (埋)》

unbutton[7]〔 ʌnˈbʌtn̩ 〕 *v.* 解開鈕扣《*un-* + *button* (扣鈕扣)》

uncage[7]〔 ʌnˈkedʒ 〕 *v.* 釋放《*un-* + *cage* (監禁)》

```
un  +    cage
 |        |
not + hollow place
```

uncap[7]〔 ʌnˈkæp 〕 *v.* 脫帽；除去蓋子《*un-* + *cap* (戴帽；加蓋)》

uncase[7]〔 ʌnˈkes 〕 *v.* 除去盒蓋；揭示；暴露《*un-* + *case* (裝於盒中)》

unclose[7]〔 ʌnˈkloz 〕 *v.* 打開《*un-* + *close* (關閉)》

uncork[7]〔 ʌnˈkɔrk 〕 *v.* 拔去～的塞子《*un-* + *cork* (用軟木塞塞住)》

```
un + cork
 |     |
not + oak
```

uncover[6]〔 ʌnˈkʌvɚ 〕 *v.* 除去覆蓋物；揭露；暴露
　《*un-* + *cover* (覆蓋)》

undo[6]〔 ʌnˈdu 〕 *v.* 恢復；解開；破壞；取消；解決《*un-* + *do* (做)》

undress[7]〔 ʌnˈdrɛs 〕 *v.* 脫去衣服；除去裝飾；解下繃帶
　《*un-* + *dress* (穿衣服；裝飾；包紮)》

unearth[7]〔 ʌnˈɝθ 〕 *v.* 挖掘；掘出；揭發《*un-* + *earth* (埋入土中)》

unfold[6]〔ʌnˈfold〕*v.* 展開；顯露；表白；說明；開放
《*un-* + *fold* (摺疊)》

ungird[7]〔ʌnˈgɜd〕*v.* 解開～的帶子《*un-* + *gird* (以帶束緊)》

```
un  +  gird
 |      |
not + enclose
```

unhinge[7]〔ʌnˈhɪndʒ〕*v.* 擾亂；使失常；使動搖
《*un-* + *hinge* (裝以鉸鏈)》

unload[7]〔ʌnˈlod〕*v.* 卸貨；解除負擔《*un-* + *load* (裝貨；使負重擔)》

unlock[6]〔ʌnˈlɑk〕*v.* 開鎖；揭開；吐露《*un-* + *lock* (上鎖)》

unmask[7]〔ʌnˈmæsk〕*v.* 拿下面具；露出眞面目
《*un-* + *mask* (戴面具；僞裝)》

unpack[6]〔ʌnˈpæk〕*v.* 開箱取出；吐露《*un-* + *pack* (包裝)》

unroll[7]〔ʌnˈrol〕*v.* 展開；公開；顯露《*un-* + *roll* (捲)》

unseal[7]〔ʌnˈsil〕*v.* 開～之封緘；使開啓《*un-* + *seal* (封印)》

unseam[7]〔ʌnˈsim〕*v.* 自縫合處拆開《*un-* + *seam* (縫合)》

unsettle[7]〔ʌnˈsɛtl̩〕*v.* 使紊亂；使不安定；使失去平靜
《*un-* + *settle* (整頓；使安定)》

```
un  + sett  + le
 |      |      |
not + seat +  v.
```

unshackle[7]〔ʌnˈʃækl̩〕*v.* 除去枷鎖；解除束縛；使重獲自由
《*un-* + *shackle* (戴上手銬腳鐐；束縛)》

untangle[7]〔ʌnˈtæŋgl̩〕*v.* 排解 (糾紛)；解決 (困難)
《*un-* + *tangle* (使纏結)》

```
un  +  tangle
 |       |
not + disarrange
```

untie[7]〔ʌnˈtaɪ〕*v.* 解開；打開《*un-* + *tie* (打結)》

unveil[7]〔ʌnˈvel〕*v.* 取下面紗；顯露眞面目；揭露 (祕密等)
《*un-* + *veil* (罩上面紗；遮掩)》

unwind[7] 〔 ʌn'waɪnd 〕 v. (將捲起的東西) 解開；展開；使放鬆
《*un-* + *wind* (纏繞)》

```
un  +  wind
 |        |
not  +  twist
```

unwrap[7] 〔 ʌn'ræp 〕 v. 打開 (包裹)《*un-* + *wrap* (包)》
unwrinkle[7] 〔 ʌn'rɪŋkl̩ 〕 v. 將～的皺紋弄平《*un-* + *wrinkle* (起皺紋)》

133　**under-** = beneath ; under

* 表示「在～之下」、「低於」。

underachieve[7] 〔 ˌʌndərə'tʃiv 〕 v. 學習成績不良 (低於智力測驗
平均水平)《*under-* (under) + *a-* (to) + *chieve* (chief)》
underage[7] 〔 'ʌndɚ'edʒ 〕 adj. 未成年的
undercurrent[7] 〔 'ʌndɚˌkɝənt 〕 n. 下面的水流或氣流；暗流
adj. 不外露的 (下面的水流)
underdeveloped[7] 〔 ˌʌndɚdɪ'vɛləpt 〕 adj. 發展不全的；低度開發的
underemployment[7] 〔 'ʌndɚɪm'plɔɪmənt 〕 n. 就業率過低；
未充分就業

```
under     + em +  ploy  + ment
  |           |      |       |
insufficiently + in + fold  +  n.
```

underestimate[6] 〔 n. ˌʌndɚ'ɛstəmɪt v. ˌʌndɚ'ɛstəˌmet 〕
n. 評價過低；低估　　n. 低估
undergo[6] 〔 ˌʌndɚ'go 〕 v. 遭受；忍受；經歷 (行走於苦難之下)
undergraduate[5] 〔 ˌʌndɚ'grædʒuɪt , -ˌet 〕 n., adj. 大學生 (的)
(還未從學校畢業)

```
under + gradu +   ate
  |        |        |
under + walk  +  n., adj.
```

underground[7]〔 *adv.* ˌʌndə'ɡraʊnd *adj.* , *n.* 'ʌndə'ɡraʊnd 〕
　adj. 地下的；祕密的　*adv.* 在地下；祕密地
　n.〔英〕地下鐵 (=〔美〕 *subway*)

underlie[7]〔ˌʌndə'laɪ 〕*v.* 位於～之下；為～之基礎 (橫放在下面)

underline[5]〔 *v.* ˌʌndə'laɪn *n.* 'ʌndəˌlaɪn 〕*v.* 為～畫底線；強調
　n. 底線 (在下面畫線)

undermine[6]〔ˌʌndə'maɪn 〕*v.* 在～下面挖掘；破壞～的基礎；
　在無形中損壞 (在下面埋地雷)

undernourishment[7]〔'ʌndə'nɝɪʃmənt 〕*n.* 營養不足

```
under + nour + ish + ment
  |      |      |      |
under + nurse +  v.  +  n.
```

underpass[4]〔'ʌndəˌpæs 〕*n.*〔美〕地下道 (=〔英〕 *subway*)
　cf. **overpass** (〔美〕陸橋；天橋)

underrate[7]〔ˌʌndə'ret 〕= underestimate　*v.* 低估；輕視

understand[1]〔ˌʌndə'stænd 〕*v.* 懂；了解；通曉；認為
　(站在下面 → 深入了解)

undertake[6]〔ˌʌndə'tek 〕*v.* 從事；擔任；許諾；著手
　(向下取得 → 身受)

undertone[7]〔'ʌndəˌton 〕*n.* 小聲；淡色；潛在的因素

134　**uni-** = one

　* 拉丁文 *unus*，表示「單一」。〔變化型〕un-。

unicellular[7]〔ˌjunɪ'sɛljələ 〕*adj.* 單細胞的

unicorn[7]〔'junɪˌkɔrn 〕*n.* 獨角獸《*uni-* (one) + *corn* (horn)》

```
uni + corn
 |      |
one + horn
```

uniform[2]〔'junəˌfɔrm 〕*adj.* 相同的　*n.* 制服　*v.* 使一致
　(一個形式)《*uni-* (one) + *form*》

unilateral[7] 〔͵junɪˈlætərəl 〕 *adj.* 單方面的

union[3] 〔ˈjunjən 〕 *n.* 聯合；結合；合併；一致；
和睦；同盟；工會

unique[4] 〔 juˈnik 〕 *adj.* 唯一的；獨特的；珍奇的
n. 獨一無二之物

```
uni + on
 |     |
one +  n.
```

unison[7] 〔ˈjunəsn̩ 〕 *n.* 和諧；一致

unit[1] 〔ˈjunɪt 〕 *n.* 單位；單元

unite[3] 〔 juˈnaɪt 〕 *v.* 聯合；結合；合併；兼備（各種性質）

unity[3] 〔ˈjunətɪ 〕 *n.* 單一性；統一體；一致；聯合；調和；和諧

universal[4] 〔͵junəˈvɝsl̩ 〕= turned into one　*adj.* 一般的；
宇宙的；全體的；全世界的（變成一體）

《*uni-*（ one ）+ *vers*（ turn ）+ *-al*（ 形容詞字尾 ）》

```
uni + vers  + al
 |     |       |
one +  turn +  adj.
```

unanimous[7] 〔 juˈnænəməs 〕 *adj.* 意見一致的；全體一致的；
異口同聲的（相同心意的）

《*un-* = *uni-*（ one ）+ *anim*（ mind ）+ *-ous*（ 形容詞字尾 ）》

135　**up-** = up；aloft　*表示「向上」、「在上」。

upend[7] 〔 ʌpˈɛnd 〕 *v.* 豎立（把末端朝上）

uphold[6] 〔 ʌpˈhold 〕 *v.* 舉起；支持；鼓勵；擁護；維持
（保持於上面）

upland[7] 〔ˈʌp͵lænd 〕 *n., adj.* 山地（的）；高地（的）（上面的土地）

uplift[7] 〔 *v.* ʌpˈlɪft　*n.* ˈʌp͵lɪft 〕 *v.* 舉起；振奮；提高
n. 舉起；感情激昂；（地面的）隆起（向上舉）

```
up + lift
 |    |
up + raise
```

upright[5] 〔 ˈʌpˌraɪt 〕 *adj.* 直的；正直的；誠實的　　*n.* 直立之物
（筆直的）

uprise[7] 〔 ʌpˈraɪz 〕 *v.* （太陽）升起；站起；起床（向上升）

uproar[7] 〔 ˈʌpˌror 〕 *n.* 喧囂；騷動（吼叫聲沖天）

uproot[7] 〔 ʌpˈrut 〕 *v.* 拔～的根；根除（把根拿上來）

```
up  +  root
 |       |
up  +  tear up
```

upset[3] 〔 *v.* ʌpˈsɛt　*n.* ˈʌpˌsɛt　*adj.* ˈʌpˈsɛt 〕 *v.* 傾覆；擾亂
n. 顛覆；煩惱　　*adj.* 受擾的；混亂的（置於上方）

upstairs[1] 〔 *adv.*, *adj.* ˈʌpˈstɛrz　*n.* ʌpˈstɛrz 〕 *v.* 在樓上；向樓上
adj. 樓上的　　*n.* 樓上　　*cf.* **downstairs**（在樓下；樓下的；樓下）

upsurge[7] 〔 *v.* ʌpˈsɝdʒ　*n.* ˈʌpˌsɝdʒ 〕 *v.* 向上湧；上升
n. 上湧；上升（從下往上湧）

```
up  +  sur  +   ge
 |       |       |
up  + under + direct
```

upswing[7] 〔 *v.* ʌpˈswɪŋ　*n.* ˈʌpˌswɪŋ 〕 *v.* 向上擺動；進步
n. 上揚；進步

uptake[7] 〔 ˈʌpˌtek 〕 *n.* 舉起；拿起；理解；通風管；吸收

upturn[7] 〔 *v.* ʌpˈtɝn　*n.* ˈʌpˌtɝn 〕 = turn up　*v.* 使向上；翻起
n. 上升；好轉

136　**with-** = against；back　　* 表示「反對」、「反抗」。

withdraw[4] 〔 wɪðˈdrɔ 〕 = draw back　*v.* 取回；撤回；取消；
引退；撤退

withhold[7] 〔 wɪðˈhold 〕 = hold back　*v.* 抑制；拒絕

withstand[6] 〔 wɪθˈstænd 〕 = stand against　*v.* 抵抗；對抗

字　尾（Suffix）

　　現代英語中，字尾的數目極為龐大，變化也極為繁複，因此要了解透徹並不是一件簡單的事。但一般學英文的人，一看就知道 employer 是「雇主」，employee 是「雇員」，trial、bravery 是 try、brave 的名詞型，以及 magnate 表示「人」，magnify 是其動詞，magnificent 是形容詞，magnificence 是抽象名詞等等，都是依照字尾來判斷的。因此，熟悉字尾是直接了解這些字義的必備條件。本篇詳細整理出各種類型的字尾，供您參考。

【1】名詞字尾

⑴ 表示「人」的名詞字尾

1　　-ain　　*　法文 aine。*

captain[2]〔'kæptən〕*n.* 首領；船長；隊長；指揮者
《拉丁文 *cap* = head》
chaplain[7]〔'tʃæplɪn〕*n.* 牧師《拉丁文 *chapel* = 禮拜堂》
villain[5]〔'vɪlən〕*n.* 惡棍；惡徒（農夫粗人）
《拉丁文 *villa* = 鄉下的房子》

2　　-aire , -air

billionaire[7]〔ˌbɪljən'ɛr〕*n.* 億萬富翁《*billion*〔英〕兆；〔美〕十億》
corsair〔'kɔrsɛr〕*n.* 海盜；海盜船《拉丁文 *cursus* = course》

legionnaire[7] 〔͵lidʒən'ɛr 〕 *n.* (L-) 法國外籍兵團團員；退伍軍人協會會員《*legion* 軍隊》

millionaire[3] 〔͵mɪljən'ɛr 〕 *n.* 百萬富翁；大富豪《*million* 百萬》

3　-an , -ian , -ean

＊ 此種字尾型也可作爲形容詞使用。

American[7] 〔 ə'mɛrɪkən 〕 *n.* 美國人　*adj.* 美國（人）的

Asian[7] 〔'eʃən 〕 *n.* 亞洲人　*adj.* 亞洲（人）的

barbarian[5] 〔 bɑr'bɛrɪən 〕 *n.* 野蠻人；蠻族

> 【解說】 當時自恃文明甚高的希臘人，輕視希臘語以外的各種語言，認爲外國語的發音聽起來只有 "bar-bar"，因此稱那些外國人爲 barbaros（外國的；無知的；粗野的），其拉丁文是 barbarus，演變成英文則爲 barbarous，barbarian。barbarus 也和法文的 balbus（口吃；結巴）同類，balus 進入西班牙文中，變爲 bobo（笨蛋），在英文中則爲 booby（呆子；蠢蛋）。

German[7] 〔'dʒɝmən 〕 *n.* 德國人；德語　*adj.* 德國（人；語）的

partisan[7] 〔'pɑrtəzn̩ 〕 *n.* 黨人；同類；游擊隊

Mohammedan[7] 〔 mo'hæmədən 〕 *n.* 回教徒

orphan[3] 〔'ɔrfən 〕 *n.* 孤兒

guardian[3] 〔'gɑrdɪən 〕 *n.* 管理人；監護人
　《*guard*（ watch over ）+ *-ian*》

historian[3] 〔 hɪs'torɪən 〕 *n.* 歷史學家《*histor*（ knowing ）+ *-ian*》

```
histor  +  ian
  |         |
knowing + person
```

Indian[7] 〔'ɪndɪən 〕 *n.* 印度人；印第安人；印第安語
　adj. 印度（人）的；印第安（人）的

Italian[7] 〔 ɪ'tæljən 〕 *n.* 義大利人；義大利語
　adj. 義大利（人；語）的

magician[2]〔mə'dʒɪʃən〕*n.* 魔術師《*magic*（魔法）+ *-ian*》

musician[2]〔mju'zɪʃən〕*n.* 音樂家《*music* 音樂》

pedestrian[6]〔pə'dɛstrɪən〕*n.* 行人；步行者《拉丁文 *ped* = 腳》

physician[4]〔fə'zɪʃən〕*n.* 醫生；內科醫生《*physic*（醫學）+ *-ian*》
　cf. **physicist**（物理學家）

utopian[7]〔ju'topɪən〕*n.* 理想家；夢想家
　《*u-*（not）+ *top*（place）+ *-ian*》

　【解説】本字是由 Utopia（烏托邦）衍生而來。「烏托邦」一詞首見於
　　　　柏拉圖的「理想國」。Utopia 的字義即是不存在的地方，而其
　　　　對西方人的意義，正如同中國人的桃花源一樣，令人嚮往。

vegetarian[4]〔ˌvɛdʒə'tɛrɪən〕*n.* 素食者

European[7]〔ˌjʊrə'pɪən〕*n.* 歐洲人　*adj.* 歐洲（人）的

4　-ant

　* 法文 *-ant*，拉丁文 *-antem*。此種字尾也可作為形容詞用。

accountant[4]〔ə'kaʊntənt〕*n.* 會計師

assistant[2]〔ə'sɪstənt〕*n.* 助手；助教《*assist* 幫助》

```
as  +  sist  +  ant
 |       |       |
to  +  stand  + person
```

descendant[6]〔dɪ'sɛndənt〕*n.* 後裔；子孫《*descend* 下降》

emigrant[6]〔'ɛməgrənt〕*n.*（自本國移居他國的）移民
　《*emigrate* 自本國移居到他國》

giant[2]〔'dʒaɪənt〕*n.* 巨人

immigrant[4]〔'ɪməgrənt , -ˌgrænt〕*n.*（自外國移入的）移民
　《*immigrate* 自外國移入》

```
im  +  migr  +  ant
 |       |       |
into  + move  + person
```

inhabitant[6] 〔ɪn'hæbətənt 〕 *n.* 居民；居住者《*inhabit* 居住於》
peasant[5] 〔'pɛznt 〕 *n.* 農夫；無知識的人《法文 *pais* = 鄉村》
servant[2] 〔's̃ɝvənt 〕 *n.* 僕人；服務生《*serve* 服務》
tenant[5] 〔'tɛnənt 〕 *n.* 佃戶；房客 (擁有土地、房屋的人)
  《拉丁文 *ten* = hold》
tyrant[5] 〔'taɪrənt 〕 *n.* 暴君

5 -ar   * 拉丁文 *-aris*，是 -er 的變化型。

beggar[3] 〔'bɛgɚ 〕 *n.* 乞丐《*beg* 乞求》
burglar[3] 〔'b̃ɝglɚ 〕 *n.* 竊賊《*burgle* 竊盜》
friar[7] 〔'fraɪr 〕 *n.* 修道士《拉丁文 *frater* = brother (修士)》
liar[3] 〔'laɪɚ 〕 *n.* 說謊者《*lie* 說謊》
scholar[3] 〔'skɑlɚ 〕 *n.* 學者；享有獎學金的學生《*school* 學校》
Templar 〔'tɛmplɚ 〕 *n.* (基督教) 聖殿騎士；〔美〕共濟會會員
  《*temple* 寺廟》

6 -ard , -art

  * 中世紀的高地德語 *-hart*，通常表示「過於～的人」。

bard[7] 〔 bɑrd 〕 *n.* 吟遊詩人
  【解說】原是指古代凱爾特族的吟遊詩人，他們攜帶豎琴，自編、自
      彈、自唱，內容多半敘述英雄事蹟或愛情故事。
coward[3] 〔'kauɚd 〕 *n.* 膽小者；懦夫 (看到尾巴就逃走)
  《法文 *coart* = *coe* = tail》
drunkard[7] 〔'drʌŋkɚd 〕 *n.* 醉漢
sluggard[7] 〔'slʌgɚd 〕 *n.* 怠惰者；懶人《*slug* 虛擲光陰；慢行》

```
slugg + ard
  |      |
lazy  +  n.
```

Spaniard[7] 〔ˈspænjəd 〕*n.* 西班牙人《*Spain* 西班牙》

　cf. **Spanish**（西班牙語），**the Spanish**（西班牙人）

steward[5] 〔ˈstjuwəd 〕*n.* 管家；執事；管理人

　【解說】 以前被僱來看守豬圈的人稱爲 steward；後來引申爲管理衆
　　　　　人財產的人。

wizard[4] 〔ˈwɪzəd 〕*n.* 巫師（wiz 源自 wise，古時候聰明的人才當巫師）

braggart[7] 〔ˈbrægət 〕*n.* 自誇者《*brag* 誇張》

7 **-ary** ＊拉丁文 *-arius, -aria, -arium*。

adversary[7] 〔ˈædvəˌsɛrɪ 〕*n.* 對手；仇敵《*adverse* 逆的》

contemporary[5] 〔kənˈtɛmpəˌrɛrɪ 〕*n.* 同時代的人

functionary[7] 〔ˈfʌŋʃənˌɛrɪ 〕*n.* 公務員；官吏；職員

　《*function* 功能；職務》

funct	+ ion +	ary
perform +	*n.* +	*person*

lapidary[7] 〔ˈlæpəˌdɛrɪ 〕*n.* 寶石匠《拉丁文 *lapid* = stone》

secretary[2] 〔ˈsɛkrəˌtɛrɪ 〕*n.* 秘書；大臣《*secret* 祕密》

8 **-ast** ＊希臘文 *-astes*。

ecdysiast 〔ɛkˈdɪzɪˌæst 〕*n.* 脫衣舞孃

　《*ec-* = *ex-*（out）+ *dysi*（put on）+ *-ast*》

encomiast 〔ɛnˈkomɪˌæst 〕*n.* 宣讀或寫作頌辭之人；讚頌者

　《*encomium* 讚頌》

enthusiast[7] 〔ɪnˈθjuzɪˌæst 〕*n.* 狂熱者《*enthusiasm* 狂熱》

pederast 〔ˈpɛdəˌræst 〕*n.* 雞姦者；好男色者

　《希臘文 *pais* = child ; boy》

scholiast 〔ˈskolɪˌæst 〕*n.*（經典著作的）評註者

　《希臘文 *skhol* = school》

表「人」的字尾

9 -ate * 拉丁文 *-atus*。

advocate[6] 〔ˈædvəkɪt〕 *n.* 辯護者；提倡者

apostate 〔 əˈpɑstet , -ɪt 〕 *n.* 叛教者；脫黨者；變節者

《拉丁文 *apo-* (off) + *st* (stand) + *-ate*》

candidate[4] 〔ˈkændə͵det , ˈkændədɪt 〕 *n.* 候選人；候補者

《*candid* = white》　☞ 參照 p.629 ambition 的解說。

delegate[5] 〔ˈdɛlə͵get , ˈdɛləgɪt 〕 *n.* 代表者 (被派遣的人)

《拉丁文 *legare* = send》　*cf.* **legate** (使節)

magnate[7] 〔ˈmægnet 〕 *n.* (政界、財界的) 偉人；大企業家

《拉丁文 *magn* = great》

pirate[4] 〔ˈpaɪrət , ˈpaɪrɪt 〕 *n.* 海盜 (船)

《希臘文 *peira* = attack》

10 -ee * 和 -er 相反，表示「被～人」之意。

committee[3] 〔 kəˈmɪtɪ 〕 *n.* 委員會《*commit* 委託》

devotee[7] 〔͵dɛvəˈti 〕 *n.* 獻身者《*devote* 獻身》

employee[3] 〔͵ɛmplɔɪˈi 〕 *n.* 受雇者；員工《*employ* 雇用》

examinee[4] 〔 ɪg͵zæməˈni 〕 *n.* 應試者 (被考的人)

nominee[6] 〔͵nɑməˈni 〕 *n.* 被提名 (任命、推薦) 者

《拉丁文 *nomin* = name》

```
nomin +    ee
  |         |
name  +  person
```

payee[7] 〔 peˈi 〕 *n.* 收款人《*pay* 支付》

referee[5] 〔͵rɛfəˈri 〕 *n.* 裁判；仲裁人《*refer* 託付；委任》

trainee[7] 〔 trenˈi 〕 *n.* 受訓者；新兵 (接受訓練的人)

trustee[7] 〔 trʌsˈti 〕 *n.* 受託人；董事《*trust* 信賴；委託》

表「人」的字尾

11　-eer　* 拉丁文 -arius，重音在此音節上。

auctioneer[7] 〔͵ɔkʃən'ɪr 〕 *n.* 拍賣人；競賽者《*auction* 拍賣》

cannoneer[7] 〔͵kænən'ɪr 〕 *n.* 砲手；砲兵《*cannon* 大砲》

engineer[3] 〔͵ɛndʒə'nɪr 〕 *n.* 工程師；技師《*engine* 引擎》

```
en  +  gin(e)  +  eer
 |       |         |
to  +  produce  +  person
```

mountaineer[7] 〔͵maʊntn̩'ɪr 〕 *n.* 登山者《*mountain* 山》

pioneer[4] 〔͵paɪə'nɪr 〕 *n.* 拓荒者；工兵（軍隊中最前面的兵士）
《法文 *peon* = foot soldier（步兵）》　*cf.* **pawn**（西洋棋的「卒」）

profiteer[7] 〔͵prɑfə'tɪr 〕 *n.* 暴利獲得者；奸商《*profit* 利益》

```
pro  +  fit  +  eer
 |       |       |
forward  +  make  +  person
```

volunteer[4] 〔͵vɑlən'tɪr 〕 *n.* 志願者；義勇兵
《拉丁文 *voluntas* = free will》　*cf.* **voluntary**（自願的）

12　-en　* 古英文 -an。

citizen[2] 〔'sɪtəzn̩ 〕 *n.* 市民；公民《*city* 城市》

heathen[7] 〔'hiðən 〕 *n.* 異教徒；粗人（住在荒野上的人）
《*heath* 石南屬的常青灌木（茂盛的荒野）》

warden[7] 〔'wɔrdn̩ 〕 *n.* 看守人；監護人；校長《*ward* 守護》

13　-ent　* 拉丁文 -ens，表示「動作者」。

agent[4] 〔'edʒənt 〕 *n.* 代理人（店）；動作者；原動力
《拉丁文 *agere* = do ; drive》　*cf.* **agile**（敏捷的）

client[3] 〔'klaɪənt 〕 *n.* 訴訟委託人；客戶《拉丁文 *cliens* = follower》

表「人」的字尾

correspondent[6] 〔͵kɔrə'spɑndənt 〕 *n.* 通信者；通信記者
  《*correspond* 通信》

opponent[5] 〔 ə'ponənt 〕 *n.* 對手；敵手 (反對者)
  《*op-* (against) + *pon* (place) + *-ent*》

```
   op  +  pon  +  ent
   |       |       |
against + place + person
```

president[2] 〔'prɛzədənt 〕 *n.* 董事長；大學校長；總統
  《*preside* 主持》

resident[5] 〔'rɛzədənt 〕 *n.* 居民《*reside* 居住》

student[1] 〔'stjudn̩t 〕 *n.* 學生《*study* 研讀》

14　**-er**　* 古英文 *-ere*，通常表示「從事～職業的人」。

baker[7] 〔'bekɚ 〕 *n.* 麵包師傅《*bake* 烘焙》

barber[1] 〔'bɑrbɚ 〕 *n.* 理髮師《拉丁文 *barba* = beard (鬍鬚)》

commander[4] 〔 kə'mændɚ 〕 *n.* 司令官；領袖《*command* 命令》

```
  com  +  mand  +   er
   |        |        |
together + order + person
```

customer[2] 〔'kʌstəmɚ 〕 *n.* 顧客《*custom* 惠顧》

dancer[1] 〔'dænsɚ 〕 *n.* 舞者；舞蹈家《*dance* 跳舞》

driver[1] 〔'draɪvɚ 〕 *n.* 司機《*drive* 駕駛》

examiner[4] 〔 ɪg'zæmɪnɚ 〕 *n.* 主考官；檢查者《*examine* 考試》

follower[3] 〔'faloɚ 〕 *n.* 追隨者；門徒；夥伴《*follow* 追隨》

foreigner[2] 〔'fɔrɪnɚ 〕 *n.* 外國人《*foreign* 外國的》

```
foreign +   er
   |         |
outside + person
```

gardener[2] 〔'gɑrdn̩ɚ 〕 *n.* 園丁《*garden* 花園》

leader[1] 〔ˈlidɚ〕 *n.* 領導者《*lead* 引導》

lodger[7] 〔ˈlɑdʒɚ〕 *n.* 房客；寄宿者《*lodge* 提供住宿》

Londoner[7] 〔ˈlʌndənɚ〕 *n.* 倫敦人

manufacturer[4] 〔ˌmænjəˈfæktʃərɚ〕 *n.* 製業（造）者
《*manufacture* 製造》

```
manu  +  fact  +  ur(e)  +   er
 |        |        |         |
hand  +  make  +   n.   +  person
```

mariner[7] 〔ˈmærənɚ〕 *n.* 水手；船員《*marine* 海的》

member[2] 〔ˈmɛmbɚ〕 *n.* 成員；會員（團體中的一份子）
《拉丁文 *membrum* = part》

messenger[4] 〔ˈmɛsṇdʒɚ〕 *n.* 報信者；先驅者《*message* 消息》

miller[6] 〔ˈmɪlɚ〕 *n.* 磨坊主人《*mill* 磨坊》

murderer[4] 〔ˈmɝdərɚ〕 *n.* 謀殺者《*murder* 謀殺》

officer[1] 〔ˈɔfəsɚ〕 *n.* 軍官；公務員《*office* 辦公室》　*cf.* **official**（官員）

outsider[5] 〔aʊtˈsaɪdɚ〕 *n.* 局外人；門外漢《*outside* 外面》

owner[2] 〔ˈonɚ〕 *n.* 所有者《*own* 擁有》

payer[7] 〔ˈpeɚ〕 *n.* 付款人《*pay* 支付》

philosopher[4] 〔fəˈlɑsəfɚ〕 *n.* 哲學家；哲人《*philosophy* 哲學》

```
philo  +  soph  +   er
  |         |        |
loving  +  wise  +  person
```

prisoner[2] 〔ˈprɪznɚ〕 *n.* 囚犯；犯人《*prison* 監獄》

producer[2] 〔prəˈdjusɚ〕 *n.* 生產者；製作者《*produce* 製造》

publisher[4] 〔ˈpʌblɪʃɚ〕 *n.* 出版者《*publish* 出版》

reader[7] 〔ˈridɚ〕 *n.* 讀者《*read* 閱讀》

reporter[2] 〔rɪˈportɚ〕 *n.* 記者；採訪員；報告者《*report* 報告》

```
re  +  port  +   er
 |       |        |
back  +  carry  +  person
```

表「人」的字尾

robber[3] 〔'rɑbɚ〕*n.* 強盜《*rob* 搶劫》

ruler[2] 〔'rulɚ〕*n.* 統治者;尺《*rule* 統治》

speaker[2] 〔'spikɚ〕*n.* 說話者;演說者《*speak* 說話》

trainer[7] 〔'trenɚ〕*n.* 訓練者;教練《*train* 訓練》

writer[1] 〔'raɪtɚ〕*n.* 作家《*write* 寫作》

15 -ese

* 放在專有名詞之後,表示「國民」、「國語」,也可做形容詞。

Chinese[7] 〔 tʃaɪ'niz 〕*n.* 中國人;中文 *adj.* 中國(人)的;中文的

Japanese[7] 〔ˌdʒæpə'niz 〕*n.* 日本人;日語 *adj.* 日本(人)的;
日語的

Portuguese[7] 〔'portʃəˌgiz 〕*n.* 葡萄牙人;葡萄牙語
adj. 葡萄牙(人)的;葡萄牙語的《*Portugal* 葡萄牙》

Taiwanese[7] 〔ˌtaɪwɑ'niz 〕*n.* 臺灣人;臺灣話
adj. 臺灣(人)的;臺灣話的

Vietnamese[7] 〔 viˌɛtnɑ'miz 〕*n.* 越南人;越南話
adj. 越南(人)的;越南話的

16 -ess　　* 希臘文 *-issa*,作為女性名詞。

actress[1] 〔'æktrɪs 〕*n.* 女演員《*actor* 演員》

baroness[7] 〔'bærənɪs 〕*n.* 男爵夫人《*baron* 男爵》

empress[7] 〔'ɛmprɪs 〕*n.* 皇后;女皇《*emperor* 皇帝》

em +	pr(e) +	ess
|	|	|
in +	*set in order* +	*person*

goddess[1] 〔'gɑdɪs 〕*n.* 女神《*god* 神》

governess[7] 〔'gʌvənɪs 〕*n.* 女家庭教師;褓姆;女總督;女州長;
總督夫人;州長夫人《*governor* 總督;州長》

表「人」的字尾

hostess[2] 〔'hostɪs 〕 *n.* 女主人；女侍《*host* 主人》
mistress[5] 〔'mɪstrɪs 〕 *n.* 女主人；女教師；情婦《*master* 主人》
princess[2] 〔'prɪnsɪs 〕 *n.* 公主；王妃《*prince* 王子》
stewardess[7] 〔'stjuwɚdɪs 〕 *n.* 女管家；空中小姐《*steward* 管家》

17 -eur   * 表示「人」的法文字尾。

amateur[4] 〔'æmə,tʃur 〕 *n.* 業餘愛好者
　《拉丁文 *amare* = love》 *cf.* **amorous** (多情的)
chauffeur[7] 〔'ʃofɚ 〕 *n.* 私人司機
coiffeur[7] 〔 kwa'fɝ 〕 *n.* (尤指爲女子做頭髮的) 男理髮師
connoisseur[7] 〔,kanə'sɝ 〕 *n.* 鑑定家《拉丁文 *noscere* = know》

```
con  +  noiss  +  eur
 |        |        |
full  +  know  +  person
```

entrepreneur[7] 〔,antrəprə'nɝ 〕 *n.* 企業家《*enterprise* 企業》

18 -herd   * 指管理家畜的人。

cowherd[7] 〔'kau,hɝd 〕 *n.* 牧牛者《*cow* + *herd*》
shepherd[3] 〔'ʃɛpɚd 〕 *n.* 牧羊者《*sheep* + *herd*》
swineherd[7] 〔'swaɪn,hɝd 〕 *n.* 養豬的人《*swine* 豬》

19 -ier   * 法文 *-ier*、拉丁文 *-arius*，表示「與～事物有關」的人。

cashier[6] 〔 kæ'ʃɪr 〕 *n.* 出納員《*cash* 現金》
cavalier[7] 〔,kævə'lɪr 〕 *n.* 騎士《*caval* = *cheval* = horse》
　cf. **chevalier** (騎士)
financier[7] 〔,fɪnən'sɪr , ,faɪnən- 〕 *n.* 金融業者；財政家
　《*finance* 財政》

premier[6] 〔'primɪɚ, prɪ'mɪr〕 *n.* 首相《*prime* 首要的》

soldier[2] 〔'soldʒɚ〕 *n.* 軍人；士兵

《拉丁文 *solidus* = solid → gold coin》

【解說】 因爲史上各時期的傭兵，大部分都是有報酬的，故稱之。

20 -iff

bailiff[7] 〔'belɪf〕 *n.* 法警《*bail* 保釋金》

plaintiff[7] 〔'plentɪf〕 *n.* 原告

《*plain* = complain》 *cf.* **defendant** (被告)

sheriff[5] 〔'ʃɛrɪf〕 *n.* 〔英〕郡長；行政司法官；〔美〕郡保安官

《*shire* 〔英〕郡》

21 -ist　　* 希臘文 *-istes*，表示「～主義者」、「從事～的專家」。

biologist[7] 〔baɪ'ɑlədʒɪst〕 *n.* 生物學家《*biology* 生物學》

communist[5] 〔'kɑmju,nɪst〕 *n.* 共產主義者《*communism* 共產主義》

defeatist[7] 〔dɪ'fitɪst〕 *n.* 失敗主義者《*defeat* 打敗》

dogmatist 〔'dɔgmətɪst〕 *n.* 獨斷者；獨斷論者《*dogma* 獨斷》

```
dogma +  ist
  |         |
belief + person
```

dramatist[7] 〔'dræmətɪst〕 *n.* 劇作家；編劇《*drama* 戲劇》

feminist[7] 〔'fɛmənɪst〕 *n.* 女權主義者《*feminine* 女性的》

florist[7] 〔'flɔrɪst, 'flar-〕 *n.* 花匠；花商《拉丁文 *flor* = flower》

```
flor  +  ist
  |        |
flower + person
```

humanist[7] 〔'hjumənɪst〕 *n.* 人道主義者《*human* 有人性的》

idealist[7] 〔aɪ'dɪəlɪst〕 *n.* 理想主義者《*ideal* 理想》

表「人」的字尾

journalist[5] 〔'dʒɝnḷɪst 〕 *n.* 新聞記者《*journal* 報紙》

militarist[7] 〔'mɪlətərɪst 〕 *n.* 軍國主義者《*military* 軍事的》

modernist[7] 〔'madɚnɪst 〕 *n.* 現代主義者《*modern* 現代的》

naturalist[6] 〔'nætʃərəlɪst 〕 *n.* 自然主義者《*natural* 自然的》

novelist[3] 〔'navḷɪst 〕 *n.* 小說家《*novel* 小說》

oculist[7] 〔'akjəlɪst 〕 *n.* 眼科醫師《拉丁文 *oculus* = eye》

ornithologist 〔ˌɔrnɪ'θalədʒɪst 〕 *n.* 鳥類學家《*ornithology* 鳥類學》

```
ornitho + log  +  ist
   |         |       |
  bird   + study + person
```

romanticist[7] 〔 ro'mæntəsɪst 〕 *n.* 浪漫主義者

sophist 〔'safɪst 〕 *n.* 詭辯家；學者《拉丁文 *sophos* = wise》

specialist[5] 〔'spɛʃəlɪst 〕 *n.* 專家《*special* 特別的》

tourist[3] 〔'tʊrɪst 〕 *n.* 旅行者；觀光客《*tour* 旅行》

typist[4] 〔'taɪpɪst 〕 *n.* 打字員《*type* 打字》

ventriloquist[7] 〔 vɛn'trɪləkwɪst 〕 *n.* 腹語者

```
ventri + loqu +  ist
   |        |       |
 belly + speak + person
```

violinist[5] 〔ˌvaɪə'lɪnɪst 〕 *n.* 小提琴家《*violin* 小提琴》

22 -ite

* 希臘文 *-ites*，表示「和～有關的人」、「屬於～團體的人」。

cosmopolite[7] 〔 kaz'mapəˌlaɪt 〕 *n.* 世界人民
《*cosmopolitism* 世界主義》

Israelite[7] 〔'ɪzrɪəlˌaɪt 〕 *n.* 以色列人；猶太人《*Israel* 以色列》

labo(u)rite[7] 〔'lebɚˌraɪt 〕 *n.* 勞工黨員《*labo(u)r* 勞動》

Tokyoite[7] 〔'tokɪoˌaɪt , -kjo- 〕 *n.* 東京人

23 -ive   * 以形容詞表示名詞的字尾。

captive[6] 〔'kæptɪv〕 *n.* 俘虜（被捉的）

detective[4] 〔dɪ'tɛktɪv〕 *n.* 偵探

fugitive[7] 〔'fjudʒətɪv〕 *n.* 逃亡者；難民

（逃走的）《拉丁文 *fugere* = flee》

```
fugit  +   ive
  |         |
 flee  +  person
```

native[3] 〔'netɪv〕 *n.* 本地人；土著（土著的）

operative[7] 〔'ɑpə,retɪv〕 *n.* 工人；技工（工作的）

relative[4] 〔'rɛlətɪv〕 *n.* 親戚（有關係的）

24 -man , -sman

* -sman 的 s 不是複數，而是表示所有格。

businessman[7] 〔'bɪznɪs,mæn〕 *n.* 生意人；商人《*business* 生意》

chairman[5] 〔'tʃɛrmən〕 *n.* 主席；會長；委員長《*chair* 議長的座位》

fireman[2] 〔'faɪrmən〕 *n.* 救火員；消防員《*fire* 火》

freshman[4] 〔'frɛʃmən〕 *n.* 新生；初學者《*fresh* 新鮮的》

gentleman[2] 〔'dʒɛntḷmən〕 *n.* 紳士《*gentle* 溫柔的》

fisherman[2] 〔'fɪʃəmən〕 *n.* 漁夫《*fish* 魚》

postman[7] 〔'postmən〕 *n.* 郵差《*post* 郵件》

salesman[4] 〔'selzmən〕 *n.* 店員；推銷員《*sale* 出售》

```
sale  +  s  +  man
  |      |      |
selling + of + person
```

seaman[7] 〔'simən〕 *n.* 海員；水手《*sea* 海洋》

spaceman[7] 〔'spes,mæn〕 *n.* 太空人《*space* 太空》

spokesman[7] 〔'spoksmən〕 *n.* 發言人

sportsman[4] 〔'sportsmən〕 *n.* 運動員《*sport* 運動》

statesman[5] 〔'stetsmən〕 *n.* 政治家（主持國事的人）《*state* 國家》

stuntman[7] 〔'stʌntmən〕 *n.*（演員的）特技替身《*stunt* 特技》

表「人」的字尾

25　-nik　*＊俄文 -nik。*

beatnik[7]〔'bitnɪk〕*n.* 披頭族（之成員）；「垮掉的一代」中的一員

【解說】 披頭族（beat generation），指在 1950～1960 年對當時的美國
社會感到失望和不滿，而以奇裝異服和乖張行為表現自我的一群
反社會的年輕人。

nudnik[7]〔'nʊdnɪk〕*n.*〔俚〕討厭的傢伙
《俄文 *nudnyi* = tedious ; boring》

peacenik[7]〔'pisnɪk〕*n.*〔俚〕反戰分子《*peace* 和平》

26　-on

champion[3]〔'tʃæmpɪən〕*n.* 冠軍；勇士；鬥士
《拉丁文 *campus* = 戰場》

companion[4]〔kəm'pænjən〕*n.* 同伴；朋友（一起吃麵包的人）
cf. **pantry**（食品室；餐具室）

```
com + pani +  on
 |      |      |
with + bread + person
```

matron[7]〔'metrən〕*n.* 年長已婚之婦女；褓姆；護士長
《拉丁文 *mater* = mother》　*cf.* **maternal**（母親的），**paternal**（父親的）

patron[5]〔'petrən〕*n.* 保護人；贊助人《拉丁文 *pater* = father》

surgeon[4]〔'sɝdʒən〕*n.* 外科醫生《*surgery* 外科手術》

27　-or , -our　*＊拉丁文 -or , -ator，表示與 -ee 相對的人。*

ambassador[3]〔æm'bæsədɚ〕*n.* 大使；使節《*embassy* 大使館》

conqueror[7]〔'kɑŋkərɚ〕*n.* 征服者《*conquer* 征服》

counsel(l)or[5]〔'kaʊnslɚ〕*n.* 顧問《*counsel* 勸告》

editor[3]〔'ɛdɪtɚ〕*n.* 編者；主筆《*edit* 編輯》

governor[3] 〔'gʌvənə 〕 *n.* 統治者；州長《*govern* 統治》

illustrator[7] 〔 ɪ'lʌstretə 〕 *n.* 插畫家《*illustrate* 以插圖說明》

```
il  +  lustrat  +   or
|        |          |
in  +  light up  +  person
```

inspector[3] 〔 ɪn'spɛktə 〕 *n.* 檢查官；巡官《*inspect* 檢查》

investigator[6] 〔 ɪn'vɛstəˌgetə 〕 *n.* 調查員《*investigate* 調查》

```
in  +  vestigat  +   or
|         |           |
in  +   track   +   person
```

mayor[3] 〔'meə 〕 *n.* 市長《拉丁文 *major* = greater》

narrator[6] 〔 næ'retə 〕 *n.* 敘述者《*narrate* 敘述》

neighbo(u)r[2] 〔'nebə 〕 *n.* 鄰居（住在附近的百姓）

　《*nei*（near）+ *ghbour*（boor 百姓）》

```
nei  +  ghbour
 |        |
near  +  boor
```

pastor[7] 〔'pæstə 〕 *n.* 牧師；精神領袖

savio(u)r[7] 〔'sevjə 〕 *n.* 救濟者；拯救者《*save* 拯救》

sculptor[5] 〔'skʌlptə 〕 *n.* 雕刻家《*sculpt* 雕刻》

successor[6] 〔 sək'sɛsə 〕 *n.* 後繼者；繼承者；繼任者《*succeed* 繼承》

　　cf. **predecessor**（前任者）

tailor[3] 〔'telə 〕 *n.* 裁縫師（剪斷的人）《拉丁文 *taleare* = cut》

tutor[3] 〔'tutə 〕 *n.* 家庭教師；助教（照顧者）

　《拉丁文 *tueri* = look after；guard》

28　　-ster　　* 古英文 *-estre*。

gamester[7] 〔'gemstə 〕 *n.* 賭徒《*game* 比賽》

gangster[4] 〔'gæŋstə 〕 *n.* 歹徒；盜匪《*gang* （做壞事的）一幫》

表「人」的字尾

表「縮小」的字尾

minister[4]〔ˈmɪnɪstɚ〕 *n.* 牧師；部長（神或國民的僕人）
　《拉丁文 *mini* = small》

songster[7]〔ˈsɔŋstɚ〕 *n.* 歌手；詩歌的作者《*song* 歌》

spinster[7]〔ˈspɪnstɚ〕 *n.* 未婚女性；老處女《*spin* 紡線》
　cf. **bachelor**（未婚男性）

　【解說】　以前，未婚女性通常都在家裡紡線織布，所以十七世紀之後，
　　　　　　過了適婚年齡而未結婚的女人都被這麼稱呼。

youngster[3]〔ˈjʌŋstɚ〕 *n.* 青年；少年《*young* 年輕的》

29　-y , -yer

enemy[2]〔ˈɛnəmɪ〕 *n.* 敵人（不是朋友的人）《拉丁文 *amicus* = friend》

> en + em + y
> | 　　 | 　　 |
> *not* + *love* + *person*

lady[1]〔ˈledɪ〕 *n.* 女士；淑女

lawyer[2]〔ˈlɔjɚ〕 *n.* 律師《*law* 法律》

sawyer[7]〔ˈsɔjɚ〕 *n.* 鋸木匠《*saw* 鋸》

(2) 表示「縮小」的名詞字尾

　＊帶有「小的」、「可愛的」、「可親近的」等意味。

1　-cle　＊表示「個體」或「個別」。

article[2,4]〔ˈɑrtɪkḷ〕 *n.* 文章；條款；物品；冠詞

follicle[7]〔ˈfɑlɪkḷ〕 *n.* 小囊；濾泡《拉丁文 *follis* = bag》

icicle[7]〔ˈaɪsɪkḷ〕 *n.* 冰柱；垂冰《*ice* 冰》

miracle[3]〔ˈmɪrəkḷ〕 *n.* 奇蹟；奇事《拉丁文 *mirare* = wonder at》

particle[5]〔ˈpɑrtɪkḷ〕 *n.* 分子；微粒；質點《*part* 部分》

pinnacle[7]〔ˈpɪnəkḷ〕 *n.* 小尖塔；山頂；頂點《拉丁文 *pinna* = 頂點》

speckle[7]〔'spɛkḷ〕*n.* 小點；斑點《*speck* 斑點》

vehicle[3]〔'viɪkḷ〕*n.* 車輛；媒介物（搬運物）《拉丁文 *vehere* = carry》

2　-(c)ule　* 拉丁文 *-culus*。

animalcule〔ˌænə'mælkjul〕*n.* 微生物《*animal* 動物》

corpuscule〔kɔr'pʌskjul〕*n.* 血球；微粒《拉丁文 *corpus* = body》

　　cf. **corpse**（屍體）

globule[7]〔'glabjul〕*n.* 極小的球體或液滴《*globe* 球》

granule[7]〔'grænjul〕*n.* 小粒；微粒《*grain* 穀粒》

minuscule[7]〔mɪ'nʌsˌkjul〕*n.* 小寫字體；小字《拉丁文 *minus* = less》

molecule[5]〔'maləˌkjul〕*n.* 分子；微點

3　-el , -le

damsel[7]〔'dæmzḷ〕*n.* 少女；處女《*dame* 婦女》

　　cf. **maiden**（少女；處女）

model[2]〔'madḷ〕*n.* 模型；模範《*mode* 樣式》

vessel[4]〔'vɛsḷ〕*n.* 船艦；容器；管《拉丁文 *vascellum* = small vase》

bottle[2]〔'batḷ〕*n.* 瓶《拉丁文 *butta* = cask（桶）》

bundle[2]〔'bʌndḷ〕*n.* 捆；束《*bind* 綁》

```
bund  +     le
  |         |
bind  +  small thing
```

pebble[4]〔'pɛbḷ〕*n.* 小圓石《*cobble* 圓石子》

riddle[3]〔'rɪdḷ〕*n.* 謎；謎樣的人（應該能讀的東西）《*read* 閱讀》

4　-en , -in　* 表示「小型的」。

chicken[1]〔'tʃɪkɪn〕*n.* 雞；雞肉

kitten[1] 〔'kɪtn̩ 〕 *n.* 小貓

bulletin[4] 〔'bʊlətɪn 〕 *n.* 佈告；公告；報告（小的印記 → 簡短的告示）

```
bullet  +   in
  |          |
 seal  +  small
```

elfin[7] 〔'ɛlfɪn 〕 *n.* 小精靈；頑童《*elf* 小精靈》

violin[2] 〔ˌvaɪə'lɪn 〕 *n.* 小提琴《*viola* 中提琴》

5 -et , -ette * 拉丁文 *-itus* , *-ita*。

banquet[5] 〔'bæŋkwɪt 〕 *n.* 盛宴；酒宴（排列著菜餚的桌子）

《高地德語 *banc* = bench ; table》 *cf.* **bank**（堤；銀行），**bench**（長凳）

basket[1] 〔'bæskɪt 〕 *n.* 籃子

blanket[3] 〔'blæŋkɪt 〕 *n.* 毯子《法文 *blanc* = white》

cf. **blank**（空白處）

bouquet[7] 〔 bu'ke , bo'ke 〕 *n.* 花束

bucket[3] 〔'bʌkɪt 〕 *n.* 水桶《古英文 *buc* = vessel》

cabinet[4] 〔'kæbənɪt 〕 *n.* 內閣；小房間《*cabin* 小屋》

cigarette[3] 〔ˌsɪgə'rɛt , 'sɪgəˌrɛt 〕 *n.* 香煙《*cigar* 雪茄煙》

gazette[7] 〔 gə'zɛt 〕 *n.* 報紙；政府的公報（為了買報紙所付的小額的錢）

islet[7] 〔'aɪlɪt 〕 *n.* 小島《*isle* 島》

《義大利文 *gazzetta* = small coin》

novelette[7] 〔ˌnɑvl̩'ɛt 〕 *n.* 短篇或中篇小說《*novel* 小說》

planet[2] 〔'plænɪt 〕 *n.* 行星

pocket[1] 〔'pɑkɪt 〕 *n.* 口袋

puppet[2] 〔'pʌpɪt 〕 *n.* 木偶《拉丁文 *pupa* = girl ; doll》

tablet[3] 〔'tæblɪt 〕 *n.* 藥片；錠劑（小而平的東西）

target[2] 〔'tɑrgɪt 〕 *n.* 靶子；目標

ticket[1] 〔'tɪkɪt 〕 *n.* 票；入場券；標籤《法文 *etiquet* = 標籤》

6 **-kin** * 中世紀荷蘭語 *-ken*。

cannikin[7] 〔'kænəkın 〕 *n.* 小罐；小杯《*can* 金屬罐》

lambkin[7] 〔'læmkın 〕 *n.* 小羊《*lamb* 小羊》

manikin[7] 〔'mænəkın 〕 = a little man *n.* 侏儒；人體解剖模型

napkin[2] 〔'næpkın 〕 *n.* 餐巾《拉丁文 *napa* = cloth》 *cf.* **map**（地圖）

pumpkin[2] 〔'pʌmpkın , 'pʌŋkın 〕 *n.* 南瓜

《拉丁文 *peponem* = large melon》

$$
\begin{array}{ccc}
\text{pump} & + & \text{kin} \\
| & & | \\
\textit{large melon} & + & \textit{small}
\end{array}
$$

7 **-let** * 法文 *-el* 和 *-et* 的結合。

booklet[7] 〔'bʊklɪt 〕 *n.* 小冊子

bullet[3] 〔'bʊlɪt 〕 *n.* 子彈（球樣的小東西）《法文 *boule* = ball》

cutlet[7] 〔'kʌtlɪt 〕 *n.* 供燒烤或煎炸的薄肉片（把肉切成小塊的東西）

fillet[7] 〔'fɪlɪt 〕 *n.* 束髮帶；肉片；魚片《拉丁文 *filum* = thread（線）》

hamlet[7] 〔'hæmlɪt 〕 = a small village *n.* 小村

leaflet[7] 〔'liflɪt 〕 *n.* 小葉；傳單《*leaf* 葉》

pamphlet[5] 〔'pæmflɪt 〕 = a small book *n.* 小冊子

rivulet[7] 〔'rɪvjəlɪt 〕 *n.* 小河；溪流《*river* 河》 *cf.* **streamlet**（小河）

8 **-ling**

* 由 -le（小的）、-ing（特定的一類）組合而成；表示「幼小」、
「不重要」。

darling[3] 〔'dɑrlɪŋ 〕 *n.* 親愛的人《*dear*（親愛的）+ *-ling*》

duckling[1] 〔'dʌklɪŋ 〕 *n.* 小鴨《*duck* 鴨》

gosling[7] 〔'gɑzlɪŋ 〕 *n.* 小鵝《*goose* 鵝》

「抽象名詞」字尾

seedling[7]〔ˈsidlɪŋ〕*n.* 幼苗《*seed* 種子》
underling[7]〔ˈʌndəlɪŋ〕*n.* 職位低的人《*under* 在～之下》
yearling[7]〔ˈjɪrlɪŋ〕*n.* 一歲的小動物《*year* 年》

9 -ock * 古英文 -*oc* , -*uc*。

bullock〔ˈbulək〕*n.* 小公牛；（食用的）閹牛《*bull* 公牛》
hillock〔ˈhɪlək〕*n.* 小丘；塚《*hill* 山丘》
paddock[7]〔ˈpædək〕= park *n.* 小塊空地或圍場；賽馬場的圍場
（類似公園的一塊小地方）

10 -ie , -y * 作為專有名詞的暱稱。

auntie；aunty[7]〔ˈænti , ˈɑn-〕= aunt *n.* 姑姑、嬸嬸、阿姨之暱稱
Billy[7]〔ˈbɪlɪ〕*n.* William 之暱稱
birdie[7]〔ˈbɝdɪ〕= bird *n.* 小鳥；鳥（暱稱）
daddy[1]〔ˈdædɪ〕= dad *n.* 爹地（孩童用語）
kitty[7]〔ˈkɪtɪ〕= kitten *n.* 小貓
pony[3]〔ˈponɪ〕*n.* 小馬
Tommy[7]〔ˈtɑmɪ〕*n.* Thomas 之暱稱

(3) 表示「抽象名詞」字尾

1 -ace

grimace[7]〔grɪˈmes〕*n.* 面部的歪扭；鬼臉《*grim* 冷酷的；猙獰的》
menace[5]〔ˈmɛnɪs〕*n.* 威脅；脅迫
《拉丁文 *minere* = jut out（突出；伸出）》 *cf.* **eminent**（卓越的）
solace[7]〔ˈsɑlɪs , -əs〕*n.* 安慰；慰藉《拉丁文 *solari* = console（安慰）》

2 -ade   * 拉丁文 *-atus*；表示「行動」、「行動的人」。

ambuscade 〔͵æmbəs'ked〕 *n.* 埋伏；伏兵

《法文 *embuscade* = place in ambush》

arcade[7] 〔ɑr'ked〕 *n.* 拱廊《*arc* 弧形物》

blockade[7] 〔blɑ'ked〕 *n.* 封鎖；斷絕；障礙（物）

《*block* 封鎖；妨礙》

cannonade 〔͵kænən'ed〕 *n.* （連續）砲擊《*cannon* 大砲》

comrade[5] 〔'kɑmræd〕 *n.* 同伴；同志；同事

crusade[7] 〔kru'sed〕 *n.* 十字軍；改革運動《拉丁文 *cruc* = cross》

```
crus + ade
  |      |
cross +  n.
```

decade[3] 〔'dɛked〕 *n.* 十年；由十所構成的一組《希臘文 *deka* = ten》

escapade[7] 〔'ɛskə͵ped〕 *n.* 逃脫；膽大妄為；惡作劇《*escape* 逃脫》

lemonade[2] 〔͵lɛmən'ed〕 *n.* 檸檬水《*lemon* 檸檬》

masquerade[7] 〔͵mæskə'red〕 *n.* 化裝舞會

《*masquer* = *masker*（戴假面具者）》

orangeade 〔'ɔrɪndʒ'ed〕 *n.* 橘子水；柳橙汁《*orange* 橙；柑橘》

renegade[7] 〔'rɛnɪ͵ged〕 *n.* 變節者；脫黨者《拉丁文 *renegare* = deny》

```
re + neg + ade
 |    |     |
again + deny + n.
```

serenade[7] 〔͵sɛrə'ned〕 *n.* 小夜曲《拉丁文 *sera* = evening》

stockade[7] 〔stak'ed〕 *n.* 柵欄；防禦障礙物《*stock* 樁；圓木》

3 -age   * 拉丁文 *-aticum*。

courage[2] 〔'kɝɪdʒ〕 *n.* 勇氣《拉丁文 *cor* = heart》   *cf.* **cordial**（熱心的）

damage[2] 〔'dæmɪdʒ〕 *n.* 傷害；損失《*damn* 破壞》

lineage[7] 〔'lɪnɪɪdʒ 〕 *n.* 血統；系統《*line* 線》

marriage[2] 〔'mærɪdʒ 〕 *n.* 婚姻《*marry* 結婚》

【解說】 美國法律規定結婚年齡為十八歲以上，結婚前要先取得結婚許可
證（ **marriage license** ），有許多州還規定要做婚前健康檢查。
西方人特別喜歡在六月結婚，因為六月（ **June** ）的名稱，是來自
希臘羅馬神話故事中，婚姻守護神——天后茱諾（ **Juno** ）。

passage[3] 〔'pæsɪdʒ 〕 *n.* 通過；變遷；通道；（文章之）一段
《*pass* 通過》

```
pass + age
 |      |
step  +  n.
```

personage[7] 〔'pɝsn̩ɪdʒ 〕 *n.* 名人；貴人；知名人士《*person* 人》

shortage[5] 〔'ʃɔrtɪdʒ 〕 *n.* 缺乏；不足；缺陷《*short* 短少的》

shrinkage[7] 〔'ʃrɪŋkɪdʒ 〕 *n.* 收縮（量）；縮小《*shrink* 收縮；縮小》

usage[4] 〔'jusɪdʒ 〕 *n.* 使用（法）；慣例；慣用法《*use* 使用》

wreckage[7] 〔'rɛkɪdʒ 〕 *n.* 殘骸；毀滅《*wreck* 弄壞》

4 **-al**　　* 把動詞變成抽象名詞。

approval[4] 〔 ə'pruvl̩ 〕 *n.* 贊成；核准《*approve* 贊成》

arrival[3] 〔 ə'raɪvl̩ 〕 *n.* 到達《*arrive* 到達》

avowal[7] 〔 ə'vauəl 〕 *n.* 坦白承認；公開宣稱
《*a-* (to) + *vow* (call) + *-al*》

```
a + vow + al
|    |     |
to + call + n.
```

betrayal[7] 〔 bɪ'treəl 〕 *n.* 背叛；出賣《*betray* 背叛》

denial[5] 〔 dɪ'naɪəl 〕 *n.* 拒絕；否認《*deny* 否認》

portrayal[7] 〔 por'treəl 〕 *n.* 描繪；肖像《*portray* 描繪》

refusal[4] 〔 rɪ'fjuzl̩ 〕 *n.* 拒絕；取捨權《*refuse* 拒絕》

survival³〔 sə'vaɪv! 〕*n.* 殘存（者）；遺物《*survive* 殘存》

```
sur  +  viv  +  al
 |       |       |
above  + live  +  n.
```

trial²〔'traɪəl 〕*n.* 審判；試驗；考驗《*try* 試驗》

withdrawal⁷〔 wɪð'drɔəl , wɪθ'drɔl 〕*n.* 撤退；提款
　《*withdraw* 撤回》

5　-ance , -ancy　*〔變化型〕-ence , -ency。

absence²〔'æbsn̩s 〕*n.* 缺席；不在《*absent* 缺席的》

allowance⁴〔 ə'lauəns 〕*n.* 允許；零用錢；津貼《*allow* 允許》

appearance²〔 ə'pɪrəns 〕*n.* 出現；外表《*appear* 出現》

attendance⁵〔 ə'tɛndəns 〕*n.* 出席；列席；侍候《*attend* 出席》

```
at  +  tend  + ance
 |      |        |
to  + stretch +  n.
```

confidence⁴〔'kɑnfədəns 〕*n.* 信賴；確信；自信
　《*confident* 確信的》

decency⁷〔'disn̩sɪ 〕*n.* 端莊；莊重《*decent* 高尚的》

excellence³〔'ɛksl̩əns 〕*n.* 優秀；傑出《*excellent* 優秀的》

```
ex  +   cell   + ence
 |       |         |
from + rise high +  n.
```

forbearance⁷〔 fɔr'bɛrəns 〕*n.* 抑制；忍耐；寬容《*forbear* 抑制》

guidance³〔'gaɪdn̩s 〕*n.* 指導；嚮導《*guide* 引導》

hindrance⁷〔'hɪndrəns 〕*n.* 妨礙；阻礙《*hinder* 妨礙》

indulgence⁷〔 ɪn'dʌldʒəns 〕*n.* 放縱；沈溺《*indulgent* 沈溺的》

innocence⁴〔'ɪnəsn̩s 〕*n.* 無罪；清白；天真無邪《*innocent* 天真的》

insolvency[7] 〔ɪnˋsɑlvənsɪ〕 *n.* 無力清還債務；破產
《*insolvent* 破產的》

$$
\begin{array}{ccc}
\text{in} & + \text{ solv } & + \text{ ency} \\
| & | & | \\
\textit{not} & + \textit{ loosen } & + \quad \textit{n.}
\end{array}
$$

obedience[4] 〔əˋbidɪəns〕 *n.* 服從；孝順《*obedient* 服從的》

permanence[7] 〔ˋpɝmənəns〕 *n.* 永久；不變《*permanent* 永久的》

perseverance[6] 〔͵pɝsəˋvɪrəns〕 *n.* 堅持；毅力《*persevere* 堅持》

$$
\begin{array}{ccc}
\text{per} & + \text{ sever } & + \text{ ance} \\
| & | & | \\
\textit{intensive} & + \textit{ severe } & + \quad \textit{n.}
\end{array}
$$

presence[2] 〔ˋprɛzn̩s〕 *n.* 在場；出席《*present* 在場的》

reliance[6] 〔rɪˋlaɪəns〕 *n.* 信賴；信任《*rely* 信賴》

reluctance[7] 〔rɪˋlʌktəns〕 *n.* 勉強；不願《*reluctant* 勉強的》

$$
\begin{array}{ccc}
\text{re} & + \text{ luct } & + \text{ ance} \\
| & | & | \\
\textit{against} & + \textit{ struggle } & + \quad \textit{n.}
\end{array}
$$

silence[2] 〔ˋsaɪləns〕 *n.* 沈默《*silent* 沈默的》

tolerance[4] 〔ˋtɑlərəns〕 *n.* 容忍《*tolerant* 容忍的》

utterance[7] 〔ˋʌtərəns，ˋʌtrəns〕 *n.* 發言；發聲《*utter* 說出》

vacancy[5] 〔ˋvekənsɪ〕 *n.* 空虛；空缺；茫然若失《*vacant* 空的》

violence[3] 〔ˋvaɪələns〕 *n.* 暴力《*violent* 暴力的》

6　-cy

aristocracy[7] 〔͵ærəˋstɑkrəsɪ〕 *n.* 貴族政治；上流社會
《*aristocrat* 貴族》

bankruptcy[7] 〔ˋbæŋkrʌptsɪ，-rəptsɪ〕 *n.* 破產《*bankrupt* 破產的》

fallacy[7] 〔ˋfæləsɪ〕 *n.* 謬見；謬誤《*fallible* 可能犯錯的》

intimacy[6] 〔ˈɪntəməsɪ〕 *n.* 親密；熟悉《*intimate* 親密的》
prophecy[7] 〔ˈprɑfəsɪ〕 *n.* 預言《*prophesy* 〔ˈprɑfəˌsaɪ〕 *v.* 預言》

7 -dom * 表示「狀況」、「權力」、「地位」。

freedom[2] 〔ˈfridəm〕 *n.* 自由；免除《*free* 自由的》
martyrdom[7] 〔ˈmɑrtədəm〕 *n.* 殉教；苦痛《*martyr* 殉教者》
wisdom[3] 〔ˈwɪzdəm〕 *n.* 智慧；學識《*wise* 聰明的》

8 -hood , -head * 表示「時期」、「狀況」、「性質」。

boyhood[5] 〔ˈbɔɪhʊd〕 *n.* 少年時代；童年《*boy* 男孩》
childhood[3] 〔ˈtʃaɪldˌhʊd〕 *n.* 兒童期；童年時代《*child* 兒童》
falsehood[7] 〔ˈfɔlshʊd〕 *n.* 虛偽；謊言《*false* 虛偽的》
likelihood[5] 〔ˈlaɪklɪˌhʊd〕 *n.* 可能性《*likely* 有可能的》

```
likeli  +  hood
  |         |
possible  +  n.
```

livelihood[7] 〔ˈlaɪvlɪˌhʊd〕 *n.* 生活；生計《*live* 活著的》
manhood[7] 〔ˈmænhʊd〕 *n.* 成年；【集合用法】成年男子《*man* 男人》
neighbo(u)rhood[3] 〔ˈnebəˌhʊd〕 *n.* 鄰近地區《*neighbo(u)r* 鄰居》
godhead[7] 〔ˈgɑdhɛd〕 = godhood *n.* 神；神格；神性
maidenhead[7] 〔ˈmednˌhɛd〕 *n.* 處女性；處女膜《*maiden* 處女》

9 -ic(s) * 常用於學術用語的字尾。

aerobatics[7] 〔ˌɛərəˈbætɪks , ˌɛrə-〕 *n.* 特技飛行（術）

```
aero  +  bat  +  ics
  |        |       |
air  +  walk  +  n.
```

aesthetics[7] 〔 ɛsˈθɛtɪks 〕 *n.* 美學

arithmetic[3] 〔 əˈrɪθmə͵tɪk 〕 *n.* 算術 《拉丁文 *arithmos* = number》

classics[7] 〔ˈklæsɪks 〕 *n.* 古典 (學) 《*classic* 古典的》

dynamics[7] 〔 daɪˈnæmɪks 〕 *n.* 動力學《*dynamic* 動力的》

ethics[5] 〔ˈɛθɪks 〕 *n.* 倫理 (學) 《希臘文 *ethos* = custom》

hysteric[7] 〔 hɪsˈtɛrɪk 〕 *n.* 歇斯底里發作《希臘文 *hustera* = womb》

logic[4] 〔ˈlɑdʒɪk 〕 *n.* 邏輯；理則學

lyric[6] 〔ˈlɪrɪk 〕 *n.* 抒情詩；抒情詩人；(*pl.*) 歌詞

　　《*lyre* 里拉，古希臘弦樂器》

magic[2] 〔ˈmædʒɪk 〕 *n.* 魔法；魔術《希臘文 *magos* = 古波斯教士》

mathematics[3] 〔͵mæθəˈmætɪks 〕 *n.* 數學

　　《希臘文 *manthanein* = learn》

```
mathemat + ics
    |        |
  learn   +  n.
```

metaphysics[7] 〔͵mɛtəˈfɪzɪks 〕 *n.* 形而上學；玄學

music[1] 〔ˈmjuzɪk 〕 *n.* 音樂《*Muse* 繆斯，古希臘神話中掌管文藝和
科學的女神》

phonetics[7] 〔 foˈnɛtɪks , fə- 〕 *n.* 語音學《希臘文 *phonein* = utter》

physic[7] 〔ˈfɪzɪk 〕 *n.* 醫術；醫學《希臘文 *physis* = nature》

physics[4] 〔ˈfɪzɪks 〕 *n.* 物理學

poetics[7] 〔 poˈɛtɪks 〕 *n.* 詩學《*poetry* 詩》

rhetoric[6] 〔ˈrɛtərɪk 〕 *n.* 修辭學《希臘文 *rhetor* = orator (演說家)》

```
rhetor + ic
   |      |
 orator +  n.
```

skeptic[7] 〔ˈskɛptɪk 〕 *n.* 懷疑 (論) 者

　　《希臘文 *skeptikos* = inquiring》

stoic[7] 〔ˈstoɪk 〕 *n.* 禁慾主義者；堅忍的人

10 -ice , -ise　*表示「狀態」。

avarice[7]〔'ævərɪs 〕*n.* 貪財；貪婪

caprice[7]〔 kə'pris 〕*n.* 反覆無常；善變《*caper* 跳躍》

cowardice[7]〔'kaʊə·dɪs 〕*n.* 怯懦《*coward* 膽小者》

justice[3]〔'dʒʌstɪs 〕*n.* 正義《*just* 正直的》

service[1]〔's3vɪs 〕*n.* 服務；助益；幫助《*serve* 服務》

treatise[7]〔'tritɪs 〕*n.* 論文（處理某問題的方法）《*treat* 對侍》

11 -ing　*表示「狀態」。

aging[7]〔'edʒɪŋ 〕*n.* 衰老《*age* （使）衰老》

bearing[7]〔'bɛrɪŋ , 'bær- 〕*n.* 意義；關係；態度《*bear* 負荷》

blessing[4]〔'blɛsɪŋ 〕*n.* 祝福；神恩《*bless* 祝福》

calling[7]〔'kɔlɪŋ 〕*n.* 召集；職業《*call* 呼叫》

clothing[2]〔'kloðɪŋ 〕*n.*【集合用法】衣服《*clothe* 穿衣》

thanksgiving[7]〔ˌθæŋks'gɪvɪŋ 〕*n.* 感謝；感恩的表示

12 -ion　*拉丁文 -io，表示「行為」、「過程」。

addition[2]〔 ə'dɪʃən 〕*n.* 附加（物）《*add* 增加》

civilization[4]〔ˌsɪvḷə'zeʃən , ˌsɪvḷaɪ- 〕*n.* 文明；教養《*civilize* 使開化》

coronation[7]〔ˌkɑrə'neʃən 〕*n.* 加冕禮

　　《拉丁文 *corona* = crown（王冠）》

exaggeration[5]〔 ɪgˌzædʒə'reʃən 〕*n.* 誇張《*exaggerate* 誇張》

ex	+	ag	+	ger	+	ation
out	+	to	+	carry	+	*n.*

extension[5]〔 ɪk'stɛnʃən 〕*n.* 延長；擴張；（電話）分機《*extend* 伸張》

invitation[2]〔ˌɪnvə'teʃən 〕*n.* 邀請；請帖《*invite* 邀請》

protection³ 〔 prə'tɛkʃən 〕 *n.* 保護（物）《*protect* 保護》

```
pro  +  tect  +  ion
 |        |       |
before + cover  +  n.
```

quotation⁴ 〔 kwo'teʃən 〕 *n.* 引用（文）《*quote* 引用》

submission⁷ 〔 səb'mɪʃən 〕 *n.* 屈服；服從《*submit* 屈服》

13 -ism , -asm * 表示「主義」、「學說」、「特性」。

antagonism⁷ 〔 æn'tægə,nɪzəm 〕 *n.* 敵對；反對《*antagonist* 敵手》

aphorism⁷ 〔'æfə,rɪzəm 〕 *n.* 格言；箴言；警句

barbarism⁷ 〔'bɑrbə,rɪzəm 〕 *n.* 野蠻；野蠻的行爲

Buddhism⁷ 〔'bʊdɪzəm 〕 *n.* 佛教《*Buddha* 佛》

centralism⁷ 〔'sɛntrəl,ɪzəm 〕 *n.* 中央集權主義《*center* 中央》

commercialism⁷ 〔 kə'mɝʃəlɪ,zəm 〕 *n.* 重商主義《*commerce* 商業》

```
com  +  merc  +  ial  +  ism
 |        |       |        |
together + trade +  adj.  +  n.
```

communism⁵ 〔'kɑmju,nɪzəm 〕 *n.* 共產主義《*communist* 共產主義者》

despotism⁷ 〔'dɛspət,ɪzəm 〕 *n.* 專制政治《*despot* 暴君》

exoticism⁷ 〔 ɪg'zɑtə,sɪzm̩ 〕 *n.* 異國風味《*exotic* 有異國風味的》

hedonism⁷ 〔'hidn̩,ɪzəm 〕 *n.* 享樂主義《*hedonic* 享樂的》

```
hedon  +  ism
  |        |
delight +  n.
```

heroism⁷ 〔'hɛro,ɪzəm 〕 *n.* 英勇；勇敢的事蹟《*hero* 英雄》

imperialism⁷ 〔 ɪm'pɪrɪəl,ɪzəm 〕 *n.* 帝國主義《*imperial* 帝國的》

Marxism⁷ 〔'mɑrksɪzm̩ 〕 *n.* 馬克斯主義

modernism⁷ 〔'mɑdɚn,ɪzəm 〕 *n.* 現代主義；現代思想
《*modern* 現代的》

「抽象名詞」字尾

optimism[5] 〔'ɑptə,mɪzəm 〕 *n.* 樂觀（主義）《*optimum* 最佳條件》

```
optim + ism
  |       |
best  +  n.
```

passivism[7] 〔'pæsə,vɪzm̩ 〕 *n.* 消極主義《*passive* 消極的》

pessimism[5] 〔'pɛsə,mɪzəm 〕 *n.* 悲觀（主義）

　　cf. **pessimist**（悲觀主義者）

skepticism[7] 〔'skɛptə,sɪzəm 〕 *n.* 懷疑論《*skeptical* 懷疑的》

symbolism[7] 〔'sɪmbḷ,ɪzəm 〕 *n.* 象徵主義《*symbol* 象徵》

totalitarianism[7] 〔 to,tælə'tɛrɪənɪzm̩ 〕 *n.* 極權主義《*total* 全體的》

enthusiasm[4] 〔 ɪn'θjuzɪ,æzəm 〕 *n.* 狂熱；熱心

14 -itude 　 * 表示動作或狀態。

altitude[5] 〔'æltə,tjud 〕 *n.* 高度；高處《拉丁文 *altus* = high》

aptitude[6] 〔'æptə,tjud , -,tud 〕 *n.* 性向；才能《*apt* 適合的》

decrepitude 〔 dɪ'krɛpɪ,tjud 〕 *n.* 衰老；破舊《*decrepit* 衰老的》

```
de    + crep + itude
 |        |      |
intensive + crack +  n.
```

fortitude[7] 〔'fɔrtə,tjud 〕 *n.* 剛毅；不屈不撓《拉丁文 *fortis* = strong》

gratitude[4] 〔'grætə,tjud 〕 *n.* 感謝；謝意《拉丁文 *gratus* = pleasing》

　　cf. **grateful**（感謝的）

latitude[5] 〔'lætə,tjud 〕 *n.* 緯度；自由範圍《拉丁文 *latus* = wide》

magnitude[6] 〔'mægnə,tjud 〕 *n.* 大小；長度；重要

　　《拉丁文 *magn* = great》

```
magn + itude
  |       |
great  +  n.
```

multitude[7] 〔'mʌltə,tjud 〕 *n.* 眾多；群眾《拉丁文 *multus* = many》

solitude[6]〔'sɑlə,tjud〕*n.* 孤獨；荒僻之處《*sole* 唯一的》

　cf. **solitary**（孤獨的）

vicissitude[7]〔və'sɪsə,tjud〕*n.* 變遷；變化；盛衰；榮枯

　《拉丁文 *vicis* = change》

```
viciss + itude
  |        |
change +   n.
```

15　-(i)um　*多用於元素的名稱。

aluminum[4]〔ə'lumɪnəm〕*n.* 鋁

ammonium[7]〔ə'monɪəm〕*n.* 銨

barium[7]〔'bɛrɪəm, 'ber-〕*n.* 鋇

magnesium[7]〔mæg'niʃɪəm, -ʒɪəm〕*n.* 鎂

petroleum[6]〔pə'trolɪəm〕*n.* 石油（岩油）

　《*petr*（rock）+ *oleum*（oil）》

16　-ment　*法文 -ment，表示「結果」、「手段」。

achievement[3]〔ə'tʃivmənt〕*n.* 完成；成就《*achieve* 完成》

amendment[7]〔ə'mɛndmənt〕*n.* 修正《*amend* 修正》

amusement[4]〔ə'mjuzmənt〕*n.* 娛樂；消遣《*amuse* 娛樂》

```
a + muse + ment
|    |      |
at + stare + n.
```

arrangement[2]〔ə'rendʒmənt〕*n.* 安排；佈置《*arrange* 安排》

astonishment[5]〔ə'stɑnɪʃmənt〕*n.* 驚奇《*astonish* 使驚奇》

```
as  +  ton  + ish + ment
 |      |      |     |
out + thunder + v. +  n.
```

attachment[4] 〔 əˋtætʃmənt 〕 *n.* 繫；附加；屬於《*attach* 繫》

banishment[7] 〔ˋbænɪʃmənt 〕 *n.* 放逐；驅逐《*banish* 驅逐出境》

bombardment[7] 〔 bamˋbardmənt 〕 *n.* 攻擊

《法文 *bombarde* = 砲擊》

engagement[3] 〔 ɪnˋgedʒmənt 〕 *n.* 預訂；訂婚《*engage* 預訂》

equipment[4] 〔 ɪˋkwɪpmənt 〕 *n.* 裝備《*equip* 裝備》

fulfil(l)ment[4] 〔 fʊlˋfɪlmənt 〕 *n.* 履行；實現《*fulfil(l)* 履行》

government[2] 〔ˋgʌvɚnmənt 〕 *n.* 政府《*govern* 統治》

judg(e)ment[2] 〔ˋdʒʌdʒmənt 〕 *n.* 審判；判斷（力）《*judge* 判斷》

```
judg(e) + ment
   |        |
  law   +   n.
```

lineament[7] 〔ˋlɪnɪəmənt 〕 *n.* 相貌；特徵（線 → 臉的輪廓）

《*line* 線》

merriment[7] 〔ˋmɛrɪmənt 〕 *n.* 歡樂《*merry* 歡樂的》

movement[1] 〔ˋmuvmənt 〕 *n.* 運動；動作；行動；動向《*move* 移動》

ointment[7] 〔ˋɔɪntmənt 〕 *n.* 藥膏

payment[1] 〔ˋpemənt 〕 *n.* 支付；付款《*pay* 支付》

refreshment[6] 〔 rɪˋfrɛʃmənt 〕 *n.* 恢復精神；身心愉快

《*refresh* 使提神》

treatment[5] 〔ˋtritmənt 〕 *n.* 待遇；治療；處理《*treat* 對待》

17 **-mony**   * 是 -ment 的變化型。

ceremony[5] 〔ˋsɛrəˌmonɪ 〕 *n.* 典禮；儀式；有禮貌的行為

harmony[4] 〔ˋharmənɪ 〕 *n.* 和諧；一致；和聲

matrimony[7] 〔ˋmætrəˌmonɪ 〕 *n.* 婚姻；婚姻關係（變成母親）

《拉丁文 *mater* = mother》

testimony[7] 〔ˋtɛstəˌmonɪ 〕 *n.* 證詞；口供；證據

《拉丁文 *testis* = witness》

18 -ness *能將形容詞變成抽象名詞。

abrasiveness [7] (ə'bresɪvnɪs) *n.* 磨損;剝蝕
《*abrasive* 磨損的;剝蝕的》

adhesiveness [7] (əd'hisɪvnɪs) *n.* 黏性《*adhesive* 有黏性的》

attractiveness [7] (ə'træktɪvnɪs) *n.* 魅力;吸引力

```
at + tract + ive + ness
 |     |      |      |
to + draw + adj. +  n.
```

awareness [7] (ə'wɛrnɪs) *n.* 知道;察覺《*aware* 知道的》

boldness [7] ('boldnɪs) *n.* 勇敢;大膽;無禮《*bold* 大膽的》

brightness [7] ('braɪtnɪs) *n.* 光亮;燦爛;快樂
《*bright* 光亮的》

business [2] ('bɪznɪs) *n.* 生意;商業;責任

carelessness [7] ('kɛrlɪsnɪs) *n.* 粗心《*careless* 粗心的》

coldness [7] ('koldnɪs) *n.* 寒冷《*cold* 寒冷的》

consciousness [7] ('kɑnʃəsnɪs) *n.* 知覺;意識;自覺
《*conscious* 有意識的》

```
con + sci + ous + ness
 |    |     |      |
with + know + adj. +  n.
```

darkness [7] ('dɑrknɪs) *n.* 黑暗《*dark* 黑暗的》

emptiness [7] ('ɛmptɪnɪs) *n.* 空位;空虛《*empty* 空的》

forgiveness [7] (fɚ'gɪvnɪs) *n.* 原諒《*forgive* 原諒》

```
for + give + ness
 |     |      |
away + give +  n.
```

friendliness [7] ('frɛndlɪnɪs) *n.* 友誼;友情;親切;親密
《*friendly* 親切的》

goodness [7] ('gʊdnɪs) *n.* 善良;美德《*good* 好的》

「抽象名詞」字尾

happiness[7] 〔'hæpɪnɪs〕 *n.* 幸運;幸福;愉快《*happy* 幸福的》

holiness[7] 〔'holɪnɪs〕 *n.* 神聖《*holy* 神聖的》

illness[7] 〔'ɪlnɪs〕 *n.* 疾病《*ill* 生病的》

indebtedness[7] 〔ɪn'dɛtɪdnɪs〕 *n.* 恩惠《*indebted* 感激的》

```
in + debt + ed + ness
 |     |     |     |
in + owe + adj. +  n.
```

kindness[7] 〔'kaɪndnɪs〕 *n.* 親切;仁慈《*kind* 親切的》

likeness[7] 〔'laɪknɪs〕 *n.* 相似《*like* 相似的》

loneliness[7] 〔'lonlɪnɪs〕 *n.* 寂寞《*lonely* 寂寞的》

loveliness[7] 〔'lʌvlɪnɪs〕 *n.* 可愛《*lovely* 可愛的》

madness[7] 〔'mædnɪs〕 *n.* 瘋狂;憤怒《*mad* 瘋狂的》

mildness[7] 〔'maɪldnɪs〕 *n.* 溫和;溫暖《*mild* 溫和的》

```
mild + ness
 |      |
tender + n.
```

politeness[7] 〔pə'laɪtnɪs〕 *n.* 禮貌《*polite* 有禮貌的》

quickness[7] 〔'kwɪknɪs〕 *n.* 迅速《*quick* 快速的》

rudeness[7] 〔'rudnɪs〕 *n.* 無禮;粗暴《*rude* 無禮的》

sadness[7] 〔'sædnɪs〕 *n.* 悲傷《*sad* 悲傷的》

sickness[7] 〔'sɪknɪs〕 *n.* 疾病;嘔吐;弊病《*sick* 有病的》

stillness[7] 〔'stɪlnɪs〕 *n.* 靜止;安靜《*still* 靜止的》

tenderness[7] 〔'tɛndɚnɪs〕 *n.* 溫柔;柔軟《*tender* 溫柔的》

weakness[7] 〔'wiknɪs〕 *n.* 柔弱;缺點《*weak* 虛弱的》

weariness[7] 〔'wɪrɪnɪs〕 *n.* 疲倦;厭倦《*weary* 疲倦的》

wickedness[7] 〔'wɪkɪdnɪs〕 *n.* 邪惡;邪惡的行為或事物
《*wicked* 邪惡的》

wordiness[7] 〔'wɝdɪnɪs〕 *n.* 冗長《*wordy* 冗長的》

19 -o(u)r *〔英〕-our，〔美〕-or。

ardo(u)r[7] 〔'ɑrdɚ〕 *n.* 熱情；激情；灼熱《*ardent* 熱烈的》

behavio(u)r[4] 〔bɪ'hevjɚ〕 *n.* 行為；態度《*behave* 舉動》

endeavo(u)r[5] 〔ɪn'dɛvɚ〕 *n.* 努力

```
en + deav + o(u)r
|     |       |
in + duty +   n.
```

favo(u)r[2] 〔'fevɚ〕 *n.* 恩寵；同意；偏好；利益

humo(u)r[2] 〔'hjumɚ, 'ju-〕 *n.* 幽默（感）；心情；體液

　　《拉丁文 *humor* = moisture（水分）》 *cf.* **humid**（潮濕的）

　【解說】 以前人們認為，人類的健康與性格決定於 4 種液體（humors）
　　　　　的組合。

　　　　　當「血液」（blood）較多時就變得 **sanguine**「快活的；樂觀的」；
　　　　　若較多「黏液」（phlegm），則為 **phlegmatic**「沒有精神的」；
　　　　　若是「膽汁」（choler）較多，則成為 **choleric**「易怒的；脾氣暴
　　　　　躁的」；「憂鬱液」（melancholy）較多，則為 **melancholic**「有
　　　　　憂鬱症的」。

　　　　　這四種液體決定了人的健康與性格，若不能維持平衡，就變得奇
　　　　　怪。因此，由 humor 衍生出「滑稽；奇怪；幽默」等意思。

odo(u)r[5] 〔'odɚ〕 *n.* 氣味；香氣；名聲

savo(u)r[7] 〔'sevɚ〕 *n.* 風味；滋味

splendo(u)r[5] 〔'splɛndɚ〕 *n.* 光輝；壯麗；卓越《*splendid* 光輝的》

valo(u)r[7] 〔'vælɚ〕 *n.* 勇氣《拉丁文 *valere* = strong》

　　cf. **valiant**（勇敢的）

20 -ry * 字尾 -ery 的縮寫型。

artistry[7] 〔'ɑrtɪstrɪ〕 *n.* 藝術性《*artist* 藝術家》

bravery[3] 〔'brevərɪ〕 *n.* 勇敢《*brave* 勇敢的》

bribery[7] 〔'braɪbərɪ〕 *n.* 行賄或受賄的行為《*bribe* 賄賂》

drudgery[7] 〔'drʌdʒərɪ 〕 *n.* 苦力；沈悶的工作《*drudge* 做苦工》

grocery[3] 〔'grosəɪ 〕 *n.* 雜貨店《*grocer* 雜貨商》

history[1] 〔'hɪstərɪ 〕 *n.* 歷史

husbandry[7] 〔'hʌzbəndrɪ 〕 *n.* 節約；務農；家計
《*hus* (house) + *band* (householder 屋主) + *-ry*》

hus +	band	+ ry
house +	householder +	*n.*

luxury[4] 〔'lʌkʃərɪ 〕 *n.* 奢侈 (品)

misery[3] 〔'mɪzərɪ 〕 *n.* 痛苦；悲慘

mockery[7] 〔'makərɪ 〕 *n.* 嘲弄；挖苦《*mock* 嘲弄》

mystery[3] 〔'mɪstrɪ , 'mɪstərɪ 〕 *n.* 神祕；不可思議的事

pedantry[7] 〔'pɛdṇtrɪ 〕 *n.* 賣弄學問《*pedant* 賣弄學問之人》

penury[7] 〔'pɛnjərɪ 〕 *n.* 貧窮；貧乏
《拉丁文 *penuria* = want 》

penu + ry
want + *n.*

rivalry[6] 〔'raɪvḷrɪ 〕 *n.* 競爭；敵對《*rival* 對手》

robbery[3] 〔'rabərɪ 〕 *n.* 搶劫；盜取《*rob* 搶奪》

slavery[6] 〔'slevərɪ 〕 *n.* 奴隸狀態；苦役；奴隸制度《*slave* 奴隸》

theory[3] 〔'θiərɪ 〕 *n.* 理論《希臘文 *theoria* = contemplation (沉思)》

treachery[7] 〔'trɛtʃərɪ 〕 *n.* 不忠；叛國《*treacherous* 不忠的》

21　-ship

* 和船沒有關係，是古英文中的 *-scipe* (= *shape*) 變來的，表示
「樣子」。

championship[4] 〔'tʃæmpɪənˌʃɪp 〕 *n.* 冠軍 (地位)

citizenship[7] 〔'sɪtəznˌʃɪp 〕 *n.* 公民的身份；公民的職責或權利
(市民的樣子)

craftsmanship[7] 〔'kræftsmənˌʃɪp 〕 *n.* 技巧；技術《*craftsman* 工匠》

fellowship[7] 〔'fɛloˌʃɪp 〕 *n.* 同伴關係；友情《*fellow* 夥伴》

friendship[3]〔'frɛndʃɪp〕*n.* 友誼；友情；友善（朋友的樣子）

hardship[4]〔'hɑrdʃɪp〕*n.* 困苦；辛苦（困難的樣子）

landscape[4]〔'lænskep , 'lændskep〕*n.* 風景；山水（土地的樣子）

leadership[2]〔'lidəʃɪp〕*n.* 領導地位；領導能力《*leader* 領袖》

```
lead +   er   + ship
 |        |       |
lead + person +  n.
```

partnership[4]〔'pɑrtnɚˏʃɪp〕*n.* 合夥；合作；協力《*partner* 夥伴》

relationship[2]〔rɪ'leʃənˏʃɪp〕*n.* 關係《*relation* 關係》

scholarship[3]〔'skɑləˏʃɪp〕*n.* 學識；獎學金《*scholar* 學者》

```
schol +   ar   + ship
  |        |       |
school + person +  n.
```

statesmanship[7]〔'stetsmənʃɪp〕*n.* 政治才能《*statesman* 政治家》

workmanship[7]〔'wɝkmənˏʃɪp〕*n.* 手藝；技巧；工藝
《*workman* 工人》

worship[5]〔'wɝʃəp〕*n.* 崇拜；崇敬（把價值有形化 → 認知價值）

22　-t , -th

flight[12]〔flaɪt〕*n.* 飛行；飛翔《*fly* 飛行》

flight[22]〔flaɪt〕*n.* 逃走；逃逸《*flee* 逃跑》

gift[1]〔gɪft〕*n.* 贈與；禮物《*give* 給予》

restraint[6]〔rɪ'strent〕*n.* 抑制；約束《*restrain* 抑制》

```
re  +   strain   + t
 |        |         |
back + draw tight + n.
```

thrift[6]〔θrɪft〕*n.* 節儉；節約；繁茂（繁榮的根本）《*thrive* 繁榮》

weight[1]〔wet〕*n.* 重量；重要《*weigh* 重》

breadth[5]〔brɛdθ〕*n.* 寬度《*broad* 寬廣的》

death[1] 〔 dɛθ 〕 *n.* 死亡；毀滅《*dead* 死的》

growth[2] 〔 groθ 〕 *n.* 生長；發展；栽培《*grow* 生長》

health[1] 〔 hɛlθ 〕 *n.* 健康《*heal* 治療》

labyrinth[7] 〔'læbə,rɪnθ 〕 *n.* 迷宮（要費很大的力氣才能走出來）

```
labyr + in + th
  |      |    |
labor + into + n.
```

sloth[7] 〔 sloθ 〕 *n.* 怠惰《*slow* 緩慢的》

stealth[7] 〔 stɛlθ 〕 *n.* 祕密行動（悄悄去偷取）《*steal* 盜取》

strength[3] 〔 strɛŋθ , strɛŋkθ 〕 *n.* 力氣；兵力《*strong* 強壯的》

tilth[7] 〔 tɪlθ 〕 *n.* 耕作；耕地《*till* 耕種》

truth[2] 〔 truθ 〕 *n.* 眞實；眞相《*true* 眞實的》

warmth[3] 〔 wɔrmθ 〕 *n.* 溫暖《*warm* 溫暖的》

width[2] 〔 wɪdθ 〕 *n.* 寬；寬度《*wide* 寬的》

youth[2] 〔 juθ 〕 *n.* 青春；青年《*young* 年輕的》

23　　-ty　　*〔變化型〕-ety , -ity。

bounty[7] 〔'baʊntɪ 〕 *n.* 慷慨；獎勵金《*bounteous* 慷慨的》

certainty[6] 〔'sɝtntɪ 〕 *n.* 確實；確信《*certain* 確實的》

cruelty[4] 〔'kruəltɪ 〕 *n.* 殘忍；虐待《*cruel* 殘忍的》

loyalty[4] 〔'lɔɪəltɪ , 'lɔjəltɪ 〕 *n.* 忠貞；忠實《*loyal* 忠實的》

novelty[7] 〔'nɑvḷtɪ 〕 *n.* 新奇；新奇的事或物《*novel* 新奇的》

```
novel + ty
  |      |
 new  + n.
```

poverty[3] 〔'pɑvətɪ 〕 *n.* 貧困；缺乏《*poor* 貧窮的》

safety[2] 〔'seftɪ 〕 *n.* 安全《*safe* 安全的》

anxiety[4] 〔 æŋ'zaɪətɪ 〕 *n.* 焦慮；渴望《*anxious* 焦慮的》

propriety[7] 〔 prə'praɪətɪ 〕 *n.* 適當；禮節《*proper* 適當的》

variety[3] 〔 və'raɪətɪ 〕 *n.* 變化；多樣性；種類《*vary* 改變》

absurdity[7] 〔 əb's3dətɪ 〕 *n.* 愚蠢；荒謬《*absurd* 荒謬的》

ambiguity[6] 〔 ˌæmbɪ'gjuətɪ 〕 *n.* 含糊；模稜兩可《*ambiguous* 含糊的》

austerity[7] 〔 ɔ'stɛrətɪ 〕 *n.* 嚴厲；簡樸《*austere* 嚴厲的》

charity[4] 〔 'tʃærətɪ 〕 *n.* 慈善；施與；寬恕《*charitable* 慈悲的》

chastity[7] 〔 'tʃæstətɪ 〕 *n.* 貞節；節操《*chaste* 貞節的》

elasticity[7] 〔 ɪˌlæs'tɪsətɪ , ˌilæs- 〕 *n.* 彈性；伸縮力《*elastic* 有彈性的》

```
elast + ic + ity
  |      |     |
drive + adj. + n.
```

eternity[6] 〔 ɪ't3nətɪ 〕 *n.* 永恆《*eternal* 永恆的》

familiarity[6] 〔 fəˌmɪlɪ'ærətɪ 〕 *n.* 熟知；精通；親密
《*familiar* 熟悉的》

fixity[7] 〔 'fɪksətɪ 〕 *n.* 固定；不變《*fix* 固定》

futurity[7] 〔 fju't(j)urətɪ 〕 *n.* 未來；後世《*future* 未來（的）》

hilarity[7] 〔 hɪ'lærətɪ , hə- , haɪ- 〕 *n.* 歡樂；熱鬧《*hilarious* 熱鬧的》

```
hilar + ity
  |      |
glad  + n.
```

hospitality[6] 〔 ˌhɑspɪ'tælətɪ 〕 *n.* 好客；款待；慇懃
《*hospitable* 好客的》

hostility[6] 〔 hɑs'tɪlətɪ 〕 *n.* 敵意；敵對《*hostile* 敵對的》

humidity[4] 〔 hju'mɪdətɪ 〕 *n.* 潮溼；溼氣；溼度《*humid* 潮溼的》

immensity[7] 〔 ɪ'mɛnsətɪ 〕 *n.* 廣大；龐大《*immense* 廣大的》

```
im + mens + ity
 |     |      |
not + measure + n.
```

maturity[4] 〔 mə'tjurətɪ , -'tʃu 〕 *n.* 成熟；完成《*mature* 成熟的》

originality[6] 〔 əˌrɪdʒə'nælətɪ 〕 *n.* 獨創力；創意《*original* 原本的》

「抽象名詞」字尾

personality[3] 〔͵pɝsn̩ˈælətɪ〕 *n.* 個性;人格《*person* 人物》

possibility[2] 〔͵pɑsəˈbɪlətɪ〕 *n.* 可能(性)《*possible* 可能的》

proximity[7] 〔prɑkˈsɪmətɪ〕 *n.* 接近《*proximate* 緊鄰的》

quality[2] 〔ˈkwɑlətɪ〕 *n.* 性質;品質《拉丁文 *gualis* = of what kind》

rapidity[7] 〔rəˈpɪdətɪ〕 *n.* 迅速;急促《*rapid* 快的》

reality[2] 〔rɪˈælətɪ〕 *n.* 眞實;實體《*real* 眞實的》

reliability[7] 〔rɪ͵laɪəˈbɪlətɪ〕 *n.* 可靠性《*reliable* 可靠的》

sagacity[7] 〔səˈgæsətɪ〕 *n.* 聰明;睿智《*sagacious* 聰明的》

```
sagac + ity
  |      |
wise  +  n.
```

singularity[7] 〔͵sɪŋgjəˈlærətɪ〕 *n.* 特異性;特徵《*singular* 單一的》

spontaneity[7] 〔͵spɑntəˈniətɪ〕 *n.* 自然《拉丁文 *sponte* = of free will》

stupidity[7] 〔stjuˈpɪdətɪ〕 *n.* 愚蠢;愚笨的行爲《*stupid* 愚笨的》

tranquility[7] 〔trænˈkwɪlətɪ〕 *n.* 平靜;安靜

　　《*tran-*(beyond)+ *quil*(quiet)+ *-ity*》

```
tran  +  quil  + ity
  |        |      |
beyond + quiet +  n.
```

24　　-ure　　* 拉丁文 *-ura*。

censure[7] 〔ˈsɛnʃɚ〕 *n.* 責難;不友善的批評(陳述自己的意見,
　　並責備對方)《拉丁文 *censura* = opinion》

creature[3] 〔ˈkritʃɚ〕 *n.* 人;動物《*create* 創造》

departure[4] 〔dɪˈpartʃɚ〕 *n.* 離開;出發《*depart* 離去》

```
de   +  part  + ure
  |       |      |
apart + divide +  n.
```

disclosure[6] 〔dɪsˈkloʒɚ〕 *n.* 揭露;洩露《*disclose* 揭發》

exposure[4] 〔ɪkˈspoʒɚ〕 *n.* 暴露；接觸；揭發；曝光《*expose* 暴露》

failure[2] 〔ˈfeljɚ〕 *n.* 失敗；怠慢；不足《*fail* 失敗》

furniture[3] 〔ˈfɜnɪtʃɚ〕 *n.* 設備；傢俱《*furnish* 使配備傢俱》

legislature[6] 〔ˈlɛdʒɪsˌletʃɚ〕 *n.* 立法機關《*legislate* 制定法律》

literature[4] 〔ˈlɪtərətʃɚ〕 *n.* 文學；文獻；著作《拉丁文 *littera* = letter》

mixture[3] 〔ˈmɪkstʃɚ〕 *n.* 混合（物）《*mix* 混合》

pressure[3] 〔ˈprɛʃɚ〕 *n.* 壓；壓力；壓迫；困厄《*press* 壓》

seizure[7] 〔ˈsiʒɚ〕 *n.* 捕捉；扣押；強奪；發作《*seize* 捕捉》

「集合名詞」字尾

25　-y　　* 拉丁文 -ia。

agony[5] 〔ˈægənɪ〕 *n.* 極大的痛苦；臨死時的掙扎；鬥爭

delivery[3] 〔dɪˈlɪvərɪ〕 *n.* 遞送；分娩；拯救《*deliver* 遞送》

```
de  +  liver  +  y
 |       |       |
from + set free + n.
```

discovery[3] 〔dɪˈskʌvərɪ〕 *n.* 發現《*discover* 發現》

flattery[7] 〔ˈflætərɪ〕 *n.* 阿諛之詞；諂媚《*flatter* 諂媚》

folly[7] 〔ˈfɑlɪ〕 *n.* 愚笨；愚昧的行為《*fool* 愚人》

honesty[3] 〔ˈɑnɪstɪ〕 *n.* 正直；誠實《*honest* 誠實的》

jealousy[4] 〔ˈdʒɛləsɪ〕 *n.* 嫉妒《*jealous* 嫉妒的》

modesty[4] 〔ˈmɑdəstɪ〕 *n.* 謙虛；羞怯；適度《*modest* 謙遜的》

treaty[5] 〔ˈtritɪ〕 *n.* 條約；談判《*treat* 處理》

tyranny[6] 〔ˈtɪrənɪ〕 *n.* 暴政；暴虐《*tyrant* 暴君》

(4) 表示「集合名詞」的字尾

1　-age　　* 拉丁文 -aticum。

foliage[7] 〔ˈfolɪɪdʒ〕 *n.* 葉子的集合稱《拉丁文 *folium* = leaf》

peerage[7] 〔ˈpɪrɪdʒ〕 *n.* 貴族的集合稱《*peer* 貴族》
plumage[7] 〔ˈplumɪdʒ〕 *n.* (鳥類) 羽毛的集合稱《*plume* 羽毛》

2   -ary

dictionary[2] 〔ˈdɪkʃənˌɛrɪ〕 *n.* 字典;辭典 (語法的集合體)
《*diction* 語法》
vocabulary[2] 〔 vəˈkæbjəˌlɛrɪ , ˈvo- 〕 *n.* 語彙;字彙
《*vocable* 語;單字》

3   -ry   * 字尾 -ery 的縮寫。

cavalry[6] 〔ˈkævl̩rɪ〕 *n.* 騎兵 (隊) 《*caval* = *cheval* = horse》
  cf. **cavalier** (騎士),**chevalier** (騎士)
gentry[7] 〔ˈdʒɛntrɪ〕 *n.* 紳士階段《*gentle* 文雅的》
machinery[4] 〔 məˈʃinərɪ 〕 *n.* 機械類;機器《*machine* 機械》
poultry[4] 〔ˈpoltrɪ〕 *n.*【集合用法】家禽《*poult* 雛》
scenery[4] 〔ˈsinərɪ〕 *n.*【集合用法】風景《*scene* (部分的) 風景》

⑸ 表示「地點」的名詞字尾

1   -ace

furnace[7] 〔ˈfɜnɪs〕 *n.* 火爐;熔爐
terrace[5] 〔ˈtɛrɪs , -əs 〕 *n.* 梯形地之一層;台地
《拉丁文 *terra* = earth》

```
terr  +  ace
 |        |
earth  +  n.
```

2   -age   * 表示「住處」或「場所」。

anchorage[7] 〔ˈæŋkərɪdʒ , -krɪdʒ 〕 *n.* 停泊 (處)《*anchor* 錨》

cottage[4]〔'kɑtɪdʒ〕*n.* 小屋；別墅（有小屋的地方）《*cot* 小屋》

village[2]〔'vɪlɪdʒ〕*n.* 村莊；村落（有鄉下房子的地方）

《*villa* 鄉下的房子 → 別墅》

3 **-ary** *　* 表示「～的處所」。

apothecary[7]〔ə'pɑθəˌkɛrɪ〕*n.* 藥劑師；藥店（有倉庫的地方 → 店）

《拉丁文 *apotheca* = storehouse（倉庫）》

【解說】 起初 apothecary 和藥沒有關係。於十七世紀之前，apothecary
在英國是販賣各種物品的商店。後來，the Apothecaries'
Company of London 和 Company of Grocers 分開，而前者
變成只賣藥品。

granary[7]〔'grænərɪ, 'gren-〕*n.* 穀倉《*grain* 穀類》

library[2]〔'laɪˌbrɛrɪ, -brərɪ〕*n.* 圖書館；文庫；藏書

《拉丁文 *liber* = book》

seminary[7]〔'sɛməˌnɛrɪ〕*n.* 學校；神學院；發源地（苗床 → 培養地）

《拉丁文 *semen* = seed（種子）》　　*cf.* seminal（精液的；種子的）

4 **-dom** *　* 表示「地位」或「領域」。

dukedom[7]〔'djukdəm〕*n.* 公爵管轄的地區；公國《*duke* 公爵》

filmdom[7]〔'fɪlmdəm〕*n.* 電影界《*film* 膠卷；影片》

kingdom[2]〔'kɪŋdəm〕*n.* 王國；領域；神的王國《*king* 王》

stardom[7]〔'stɑrdəm〕*n.*【集合用法】明星；明星的地位

《*star* 星星；明星》

5 **-ery** *　* 法文 *-erie*，表示「場所」。

bakery[2]〔'bekərɪ〕*n.* 麵包店《*bake* 烘焙》

brewery[7]〔'bruərɪ〕*n.* 釀造廠；啤酒廠《*brew* 釀造》

表「地點」的字尾

cemetery[6] (ˈsɛməˌtɛrɪ) *n.* 墓地（安息地）《希臘文 *koiman* = sleep》

```
cemet  +  ery
  |        |
sleep  +   n.
```

【解説】 美國的墓地常整理得像公園一樣漂亮，而且大多有人負責管理。
而華盛頓（Washington, D.C.）郊外的阿靈頓國家公墓
（Arlington National Cemetery），甚至成為著名的觀光勝
地。此外，歐洲有些教堂旁邊也有一片空地作為墓地，那叫作
churchyard。

gallery[4] (ˈgælərɪ , -lrɪ) *n.* 走廊；畫廊
《拉丁文 *galeria* = long portico（長的柱廊）》

表「地點」的字尾

6   -ory   * 源自於法文 *-orie*。

dormitory[4,5] (ˈdɔrməˌtorɪ) *n.* 宿舍（睡覺的地方）
《拉丁文 *dormire* = sleep》   *cf.* **dormant**（睡眠狀態的）

【解説】 學校為學生準備的宿舍稱為 **dormitory**，通常都有大廳（**hall**）、
會客室或交誼廳。美國的大學生通常可以選擇要住學校宿舍，
或是自行租賃校外公寓，或者是選擇住自己的「兄弟會館」
（fraternity house）或「姊妹會館」（sorority house）。

factory[1] (ˈfæktrɪ , -tərɪ) *n.* 工廠（做成產品的地方）
《拉丁文 *facere* = make》

laboratory[4] (ˈlæbrəˌtorɪ , ˈlæbərə-) *n.* 研究室；實驗室
（苦心研究的地方）《*labor* 勞動》

observatory[7] (əbˈzɝvəˌtorɪ) *n.* 天文臺；瞭望臺《*observe* 觀測》

territory[3] (ˈtɛrəˌtorɪ , -tɔrɪ) *n.* 領土；領域《拉丁文 *terra* = earth》

7   -um

aquarium[3] (əˈkwɛrɪəm) *n.* 水族館《拉丁文 *aqua* = water》

auditorium[5]〔͵ɔdəˈtorɪəm〕*n.* 禮堂；聽衆席（聽的地方）

《拉丁文 *audire* = hear》

gymnasium[3]〔dʒɪmˈnezɪəm〕*n.* 健身房；體育館；（德國的）

大學預科學校《*gymnastics* 體操》

museum[2]〔mjuˈziəm, -ˈzɪəm〕*n.* 博物館（藝術之神的殿堂）

《*the Muses* 司文學、藝術、科學等之九女神》

【解說】　在美國，只要有展示物品的地方，就可以稱爲 **museum**。因此

美國到處都有博物館。而眞正展示藝術品的地方，則稱爲「美

術館」（**gallery**）。

sanatorium[7]〔͵sænəˈtorɪəm〕*n.* 療養院

《拉丁文 *sanare* = heal（治療）》

8　-y

abbey[7]〔ˈæbɪ〕*n.* 修道院；僧院《*abbot* 修道院長》

balcony[2]〔ˈbælkənɪ〕*n.* 陽臺；戲院的包廂

《義大利文 *balcone* = 房子較突出的一角》

county[2]〔ˈkaʊntɪ〕*n.*〔英〕郡；〔美〕郡（伯爵的領地）《*count* 伯爵》

treasury[5]〔ˈtrɛʒərɪ〕*n.* 國庫；資金；有價值的人或書《*treasure* 財寶》

【2】形容詞字尾

1　-able, -ible

* 表示「有能力」、「適合」，被修飾的名詞有被動的意思。

adorable[7]〔əˈdorəbl̩〕*adj.* 可愛的；值得崇拜的《*adore* 崇拜》

amenable[7]〔əˈminəbl̩, -ˈmɛn-〕*adj.* 順從的；有順從義務的

《拉丁文 *a-* = *ad-*（to）+ *men*（lead）+ *-able*》

```
a + men + able
|     |     |
to + lead + adj.
```

available[3] 〔 ə'veləbḷ 〕 *adj.* 可利用的；可獲得的《*avail* 有益》

bearable[7] 〔'bɛrəbḷ 〕 *adj.* 能忍受的；支持得住的《*bear* 忍受》

changeable[3] 〔'tʃendʒəbḷ 〕 *adj.* 可改變的；易變的《*change* 變化》

culpable[7] 〔'kʌlpəbḷ 〕 *adj.* 該受譴責的；有過失的

　　《拉丁文 *culpa* = crime》

desirable[3] 〔 dɪ'zaɪrəbḷ 〕 *adj.* 值得要的；讓人喜愛的

　　《*desire* 想要》

favorable[4] 〔'fevərəbḷ 〕 *adj.* 贊成的；適合的《*favor* 贊成》

habitable[7] 〔'hæbɪtəbḷ 〕 *adj.* 適合居住的《*habit* 居住》

hospitable[6] 〔'hɑspɪtəbḷ 〕 *adj.* 好客的《拉丁文 *hospes* = host ; guest》

imaginable[4] 〔 ɪ'mædʒɪnəbḷ 〕 *adj.* 想像得到的《*imagine* 想像》

imponderable[7] 〔 ɪm'pɑndərəbḷ 〕 *adj.* 無重量的；無法衡量的

　　《*im-* = not ; *ponder* 深思；衡量》

```
im + ponder + able
 |     |        |
not + weigh  + adj.
```

innumerable[5] 〔 ɪ'njumərəbḷ , ɪ'nu- 〕 *adj.* 無數的《*in-* = not》

interminable[7] 〔 ɪn'tɝmɪnəbḷ 〕 *adj.* 無終止的

　　《*in-* = not ; *termin* = end》

```
in + termin + able
 |     |       |
not + end   + adj.
```

irritable[6] 〔'ɪrətəbḷ 〕 *adj.* 易怒的；過敏的《*irritate* 激怒》

measurable[2] 〔'mɛʒərəbḷ 〕 *adj.* 可測量的；相當的；不可忽視的

　　《*measure* 測量》

miserable[4] 〔'mɪzərəbḷ 〕 *adj.* 不幸的；可憐的

noticeable[5] 〔'notɪsəbḷ 〕 *adj.* 明顯的；值得注意的《*notice* 注意》

reasonable[3] 〔'riznəbḷ 〕 *adj.* 通人情的；合理的《*reason* 推理》

unforgettable[7] 〔ˌʌnfə'gɛtəbḷ 〕 *adj.* 令人難忘的《*forget* 忘記》

unspeakable[7] 〔 ʌn'spikəbḷ 〕 *adj.* 無法形容的《*speak* 說》

contemptible[7] 〔kən'tɛmptəb!〕*adj.* 卑鄙的《*contempt* 蔑視》

con	+ tempt +	ible
intensive +	*scorn* +	*adj.*

horrible[3] 〔'hɑrəb!〕*adj.* 可怕的《*horror* 恐怖》
incredible[7] 〔ɪn'krɛdəb!〕*adj.* 難以置信的；可疑的《*credit* 信用》
negligible[7] 〔'nɛglədʒəb!〕*adj.* 可忽視的《*neglect* 忽視》

2 -al , -ial   * 表示「有關～」、「有～性質」。

brutal[4] 〔'brut!〕*adj.* 野蠻的；殘忍的《*brute* 禽獸》
confessional[7] 〔kən'fɛʃənəl〕*adj.* 自白的；懺悔的《*confess* 招認》

con	+ fess +	ion +	al
together +	*speak* +	*n.* +	*adj.*

educational[3] 〔ˌɛdʒə'keʃən!〕*adj.* 教育的《*education* 教育》
eternal[5] 〔ɪ't3n!〕*adj.* 永恆的《*eternity* 永恆》
factual[7] 〔'fæktʃʊəl〕*adj.* 事實的《*fact* 事實》
federal[5] 〔'fɛdərəl〕*adj.* 聯邦制的；聯邦政府的（由盟約束縛）
　　《拉丁文 *foedus* = treaty（條約）》
functional[4] 〔'fʌŋkʃən!〕*adj.* 有用的；功能的
　　《*funct*（perform）+ *-ion*（名詞字尾）+ *-al*（形容詞字尾）》

funct	+ ion +	al
perform +	*n.* +	*adj.*

internal[3] 〔ɪn't3n!〕*adj.* 內部的；內在的
　　《拉丁文 *internus* = inward》
literal[6] 〔'lɪtərəl〕*adj.* 逐字的；實實在在的；字面上的
　　《拉丁文 *littera* = letter》
mortal[5] 〔'mɔrt!〕*adj.* 不免一死的；致命的《拉丁文 *mors* = death》

Occidental[7] 〔͵ɑksə'dɛntḷ 〕 *adj.* 西洋的；西方的

《*Occident* 西方》 *cf.* **Oriental**（東方的）

personal[2] 〔'pɝsṇḷ 〕 *adj.* 個人的；私人的；本身的《*person* 人》

punctual[6] 〔'pʌŋktʃʊəl 〕 *adj.* 守時的；準時的；仔細的

（正好在某一時點上）《拉丁文 *punct*（prick）+ *-ual*（形容詞字尾 ）》

cf. **punctuate**（給…加標點符號 ），**puncture**（孔；洞 ）

regal[7] 〔'rigḷ 〕 *adj.* 帝王的；莊嚴的《拉丁文 *rex* = king》

cf. **regent**（攝政 ）

regional[3] 〔'ridʒənḷ 〕 *adj.* 地區的；區域的

traditional[2] 〔 trə'dɪʃənḷ 〕 *adj.* 傳統的《*tradition* 傳統》

```
tra  +  dit  +  ion  +  al
 |        |       |       |
across + give  +  n.  +  adj.
```

aerial[7] 〔 e'ɪrɪəl , 'ɛrɪəl 〕 *adj.* 空氣的；在空中的；幻想的

《拉丁文 *aer* = air》

cordial[6] 〔'kɔrdʒəl 〕 *adj.* 熱心的；眞誠的；興奮的

《拉丁文 *cor* = heart》

genial[7] 〔'dʒinjəl 〕 *adj.* 愉快的；暖和的；天才的

《拉丁文 *genialis* = pleasant》

racial[3] 〔'reʃəl 〕 *adj.* 人種的；種族的《*race* 種族》

3   -an , -ian

* 多接於專有名詞之後，做形容詞使用，也可做「～人」解。

European[7] 〔 jurə'piən 〕 *adj.* 歐洲（人 ）的

republican[5] 〔 rɪ'pʌblɪkən 〕 *adj.* 共和國的；共和政體的（衆人
之事 ）《*republic* 共和國》

```
re   +   public   +  an
 |          |          |
thing + of the people + adj.
```

suburban[6] 〔 sə'bɝbən 〕 *adj.* 郊外的《*suburb* 郊區》

cf. **rural**（田園的）

veteran[6] 〔'vɛtərən 〕 *adj.* 老練的；退伍軍人的

《拉丁文 *vetus* = old》

agrarian[7] 〔 ə'grɛrɪən , ə'grer- 〕 *adj.* 土地的；農民的

《拉丁文 *agrarius* = field》

```
agrar + ian
  |      |
field  + adj.
```

Christian[7] 〔'krɪstʃən 〕 *adj.* 基督（教）的

Egyptian[7] 〔 ɪ'dʒɪpʃən , i- 〕 *adj.* 埃及（人）的

Parisian[7] 〔 pə'rɪʒən , pə'rɪzɪən 〕 *adj.* 巴黎（人）的

4　-ant , -ent　　* 拉丁文 *-ans* , *-ens*。

brilliant[3] 〔'brɪljənt 〕 *adj.* 燦爛的；光輝的

《拉丁文 *berillus* , *beryllus* = gem（寶石）》　cf. **beryl**（綠寶石）

buoyant[7] 〔'bɔɪənt 〕 *adj.* 能漂浮的；快活的；漲勢的

《*buoy* 浮標；救生圈》

defiant[7] 〔 dɪ'faɪənt 〕 *adj.* 大膽反抗的；挑釁的《*defy* 反抗》

indignant[5] 〔 ɪn'dɪgnənt 〕 *adj.* 憤慨的；不平的

《拉丁文 *in-*（not）+ *dign*（worthy）+ *-ant*》　cf. **dignity**（尊嚴）

```
in +  dign  + ant
 |     |       |
not + worthy + adj.
```

luxuriant[7] 〔 lʌg'ʒurɪənt , lʌk'ʃur- 〕 *adj.* 豐富的；繁茂的；華美的

（近乎奢侈的）《*luxury* 奢侈》　cf. **luxurious**（奢侈的）

radiant[6] 〔'redɪənt 〕 *adj.* 閃爍的；洋溢著喜悅的；輻射的

《拉丁文 *radius* = ray（光線）》

tolerant[4] 〔'tɑlərənt 〕 *adj.* 容忍的；寬大的《*tolerate* 容忍》

形容詞字尾

triumphant[6] 〔traɪˈʌmfənt〕 *adj.* 勝利的；成功的；得意洋洋的

《*triumph* 勝利》

ardent[7] 〔ˈɑrdṇt〕 *adj.* 熱情的；激烈的《拉丁文 *ardere* = burn》

cf. **arid**（乾燥的）

decent[6] 〔ˈdisṇt〕 *adj.* 高尚的；端莊的《拉丁文 *decere* = 合宜的》

excellent[2] 〔ˈɛksḷənt〕 *adj.* 優秀的

fluent[4] 〔ˈfluənt〕 *adj.* 流利的；流暢的《拉丁文 *fluere* = flow》

frequent[3] 〔ˈfrikwənt〕 *adj.* 經常的《拉丁文 *frequens* = numerous》

indolent[7] 〔ˈɪndələnt〕 *adj.* 怠惰的《*in-*（not）+ *dol*（feel pain）+ *-ent*》

```
in  +  dol  +  ent
|       |       |
not + feel pain + adj.
```

insolent[7] 〔ˈɪnsələnt〕 *adj.* 粗野的；無禮的（傲慢的）

《拉丁文 *in-*（against）+ *sol*（swell）+ *-ent*》

obedient[4] 〔əˈbidɪənt〕 *adj.* 服從的；順從的《*obey* 服從》

proficient[7] 〔prəˈfɪʃənt〕 *adj.* 精通的；熟練的

《拉丁文 *pro-*（forward）+ *fici*（make）+ *-ent*》　　*cf.* **profit**（利益）

```
pro  +  fici  +  ent
|        |        |
forward + make + adj.
```

prudent[7] 〔ˈprudṇt〕 *adj.* 謹慎的；節儉的

quiescent[7] 〔kwaɪˈɛsṇt〕 *adj.* 靜止的；安靜的

《拉丁文 *quies* = rest ; quiet》

recent[2] 〔ˈrisṇt〕 *adj.* 最近的《拉丁文 *recens* = fresh》

5　**-ar**

circular[4] 〔ˈsɝkjələ〕 *adj.* 圓的；巡迴的《*circle* 圓》

familiar[3] 〔fəˈmɪljə〕 *adj.* 熟悉的；非正式的（像一家人）

《*family* 家族》

muscular[5] 〔'mʌskjələ·〕 *adj.* 肌肉的；強壯的

　《*muscle*〔'mʌsl̩〕*n.* 肌肉》

polar[5] 〔'polə·〕 *adj.* 南北極的；極端相反的《*pole*（地球的）極》

popular[2,3] 〔'pɑpjələ·〕 *adj.* 受歡迎的；普遍的；民衆的《*people* 民衆》

similar[2] 〔'sɪmələ·〕 *adj.* 類似的；同樣的

　《拉丁文 *similis* = like（相似的）》

```
simil + ar
  |      |
like  + adj.
```

vulgar[6] 〔'vʌlgə·〕 *adj.* 粗俗的；平民的；不出色的

　《拉丁文 *vulgus* = common people》

6　-ary

customary[6] 〔'kʌstəm,ɛrɪ〕 *adj.* 習慣的；慣常的《*custom* 習慣》

dilatory[7] 〔'dɪlə,torɪ , -tɔrɪ〕 *adj.* 緩慢的；拖延的

　《拉丁文 *dilatus*（*differre* 的過去分詞）= postpone》

elementary[4] 〔,ɛlə'mɛntərɪ〕 *adj.* 基礎的；初步的《*element* 元素》

exemplary[7] 〔ɪg'zɛmplərɪ , ɛg-〕 *adj.* 模範的；典型的

　《*exemplar* 模範》

imaginary[4] 〔ɪ'mædʒə,nɛrɪ〕 *adj.* 想像的；虛構的

　《*imagine* 想像》

necessary[2] 〔'nɛsə,sɛrɪ〕 *adj.* 必須的；不可缺的

sanitary[7] 〔'sænə,tɛrɪ〕 *adj.* 衛生的

　《拉丁文 *sanus* = of sound mind　　*cf.* **sane**（神智清明的）

secondary[3] 〔'sɛkən,dɛrɪ〕 *adj.* 第二的；從屬的；輔助的

temporary[3] 〔'tɛmpə,rɛrɪ〕 *adj.* 暫時的；一時的；臨時的

　《拉丁文 *tempus* = time》

voluntary[4] 〔'vɑlən,tɛrɪ〕 *adj.* 自願的；故意的

　《拉丁文 *voluntas* = free will》

形容詞字尾

7 -ate，-ete，-ute

* 表示「有～性質的」、「有～味道的」。

accurate[3] 〔'ækjərɪt 〕 *adj.* 正確的；準確的《*accuracy* 正確》

affectionate[6] 〔 ə'fɛkʃənɪt 〕 *adj.* 摯愛的；親切的《*affection* 情愛》

considerate[5] 〔 kən'sɪdərɪt , -'sɪdrɪt 〕 *adj.* 體諒的；顧慮周到的
《*consider* 考慮》

fortunate[4] 〔'fɔrtʃənɪt 〕 *adj.* 幸運的；幸福的《*fortune* 幸運》

obstinate[5] 〔'abstənɪt 〕 *adj.* 頑固的；不屈服的（對～加以反抗）
《拉丁文 *ob-*（against）+ *stin*（cause to stand）+ *-ate*》

```
ob    +    stin    + ate
|           |          |
against + cause to stand + adj.
```

ornate[7] 〔 ɔr'net 〕 *adj.* 裝飾的；華麗的
《拉丁文 *ornatus*（*ornare* 的過去分詞）= furnish》

passionate[5] 〔'pæʃənɪt 〕 *adj.* 熱情的；易動感情的《*passion* 熱情》

temperate[7] 〔'tɛmprɪt 〕 *adj.* 有節制的；適度的；溫和的
（適度地混合）《拉丁文 *temperare* = mix properly》

complete[2] 〔 kəm'plit 〕 *adj.* 完整的；全部的；徹底的
（完全被充滿）《拉丁文 *com-*（fully）+ *ple*（fill）+ *-te*》

```
com + ple + te
|      |      |
fully + fill + adj.
```

obsolete[7] 〔'absə,lit 〕 *adj.* 作廢的；過時的（與習慣相違的）
《拉丁文 *ob-*（against）+ *sol* = *solere*（be accustomed）+ *-ete*》

absolute[4] 〔'æbsə,lut 〕 *adj.* 完全的；純粹的；不受限制的；絕對的
（解開 → 不受約束）《拉丁文 *ab-*（from）+ *solute* = *solvere*（loosen）》

minute[1] 〔 mə'njut , maɪ- 〕 *adj.* 微小的；詳細的《拉丁文 *min* = small》

```
min + ute
|      |
small + adj.
```

形容詞字尾

8　-ed　* 多接於名詞之後，表示「具有～」或「充滿～」。

aged[7]〔'edʒɪd〕*adj.* 年老的《*age* 年齡》
bearded[7]〔'bɪrdɪd〕*adj.* 有鬍鬚的《*beard* 鬍鬚》
crowned[7]〔kraʊnd〕*adj.* 有皇冠的；王室的《*crown* 王冠》
cultured[7]〔'kʌltʃəd〕*adj.* 有修養的《*culture* 教養》

```
cult + ur(e) + ed
 |      |      |
till +   n.  + adj.
```

gifted[4]〔'gɪftɪd〕*adj.* 有天賦才能的《*gift* 天賦》
landed[7]〔'lændɪd〕*adj.* 擁有土地的《*land* 土地》
moneyed[7]〔'mʌnɪd〕*adj.* 金錢上的；有錢的《*money* 錢》
ringed[7]〔rɪŋd〕*adj.* 環狀的；輪狀的；正式結婚的《*ring* 環》
talented[7]〔'tæləntɪd〕*adj.* 有才能的《*talent* 才能》

9　-en　* 多接於物質名詞之後，表示「由～做成」。

brazen[7]〔'brezn̩〕*adj.* 黃銅製的；黃銅色的；堅硬的；厚顏無恥的
《*braze* 以黃銅製造》
earthen[7]〔'ɝθən〕*adj.* 土製的；陶土製的；地球上的
golden[2]〔'goldən〕*adj.* 金的；金製的；金色的
leaden[7]〔'lɛdn̩〕*adj.* 鉛製的；鉛色的；沈悶的

　　【注意】leaden sword 不是「用鉛做成的刀」，而是「鈍刀」之意。

wooden[2]〔'wʊdn̩〕*adj.* 木製的；呆笨的
wool(l)en[7]〔'wʊlɪn , -ən〕*adj.* 羊毛製的

10　-ern　* 主要用於表示「方向」。

eastern[2]〔'istən〕*adj.* 東方的；東方國家的；（風）來自東方的
northern[2]〔'nɔrðən〕*adj.* 北方的；（風）來自北方的

形容詞字尾

southern[2] 〔'sʌðən 〕 *adj.* 南方的；（風）來自南方的
western[2] 〔'wɛstən 〕 *adj.* 西方的；（風）來自西方的
modern[2] 〔'mɑdən 〕 *adj.* 現代的；時髦的（合於樣式）《*mode* 樣式》

11 -ese * 加在國名之後成爲形容詞和名詞。

Chinese[7] 〔 tʃaɪ'niz 〕 *adj.* 中國（人）的；中文的
Japanese[7] 〔ˌdʒæpə'niz 〕 *adj.* 日本（人）的；日文的
Portuguese[7] 〔'portʃəˌgiz , 'pɔr- 〕 *adj.* 葡萄牙（人）的；
葡萄牙語的
Taiwanese[7] 〔ˌtaɪwɑ'niz 〕 *adj.* 臺灣（人）的；臺灣話的
Vietnamese[7] 〔 viˌɛtnɑ'miz 〕 *adj.* 越南（人）的；越南話的

12 -fold

* 加在數字之後表示「～倍的」、「～重的」。原意是重疊或折疊。

manifold[7] 〔'mænəˌfold 〕 *adj.* 多種的；多倍的《*mani-* = many》
twofold[7] 〔'tu'fold 〕 *adj.* 二倍的；二重的
tenfold[7] 〔'tɛn'fold 〕 *adj.* 十倍的
twentyfold[7] 〔'twɛntɪˌfold 〕 *adj.* 二十倍的
hundredfold[7] 〔'hʌndrədˌfold 〕 *adj.* 百倍的
thousandfold[7] 〔'θauznd'fold 〕 *adj.* 千倍的
millionfold[7] 〔'mɪljənˌfold 〕 *adj.* 百萬倍的

13 -ful

* 多加在名詞之後，表示「充滿」的意思，是最常用的形容詞字尾，
相反詞是 -less。

awful[3] 〔'ɔfḷ 〕 *adj.* 可怕的《*awe* 畏懼》
beautiful[1] 〔'bjutəfəl 〕 *adj.* 美麗的《*beauty* 美麗》

形容詞字尾

careful[1] 〔'kɛrfəl 〕 *adj.* 小心的《*care* 小心》

cheerful[3] 〔'tʃɪrfəl 〕 *adj.* 愉快的《*cheer* 高興》

colorful[2] 〔'kʌləfəl 〕 *adj.* 多采多姿的《*color* 顏色》

doubtful[3] 〔'dautfəl 〕 *adj.* 懷疑的《*doubt* 懷疑》

dreadful[5] 〔'drɛdfəl 〕 *adj.* 可怕的《*dread* 恐怖》

fateful[7] 〔'fetfəl 〕 *adj.* 致命的《*fate* 命運》

fearful[2] 〔'fɪrfəl 〕 *adj.* 可怕的《*fear* 恐懼》

forgetful[5] 〔 fə'gɛtfəl 〕 *adj.* 健忘的；遺忘的《*forget* 忘記》

```
for  +  get  +  ful
 |       |       |
away  +  get  +  adj.
```

fruitful[7] 〔'frutfəl 〕 *adj.* 果實很多的；多產的；有收穫的
《*fruit* 果實》

graceful[4] 〔'gresfəl 〕 *adj.* 優雅的；得體的《*grace* 優雅》

harmful[3] 〔'hɑrmfəl 〕 *adj.* 有害的《*harm* 傷害》

hateful[2] 〔'hetfəl 〕 *adj.* 厭惡的；可恨的《*hate* 憎恨》

helpful[2] 〔'hɛlpfəl 〕 *adj.* 有幫助的；有益的《*help* 幫助》

merciful[7] 〔'mɝsɪfəl 〕 *adj.* 仁慈的；慈悲的《*mercy* 慈悲》

```
merci  +  ful
  |        |
reward  +  adj.
```

mournful[6] 〔'mornfḷ , 'mɔr- 〕 *adj.* 悲哀的；悽慘的《*mourn* 悲傷》

painful[2] 〔'penfəl 〕 *adj.* 痛苦的《*pain* 痛苦》

peaceful[2] 〔'pisfəl 〕 *adj.* 和平的《*peace* 和平》

pitiful[7] 〔'pɪtɪfəl 〕 *adj.* 可憐的《*pity* 同情》

powerful[2] 〔'pauəfəl 〕 *adj.* 有力的《*power* 權力》

regretful[7] 〔 rɪ'grɛtfəl 〕 *adj.* 後悔的；遺憾的；哀悼的《*regret* 後悔》

```
re   +  gret  +  ful
 |       |        |
again  +  weep  +  adj.
```

scornful[7] 〔'skɔrnfəl 〕 *adj.* 輕視的《*scorn* 輕蔑》
shameful[4] 〔'ʃemfəl 〕 *adj.* 可恥的《*shame* 羞恥》
thankful[3] 〔'θæŋkfəl 〕 *adj.* 感激的《*thank* 感謝》
thoughtful[4] 〔'θɔtfəl 〕 *adj.* 深思的；體貼的《*thought* 思慮；思想》
watchful[7] 〔'watʃfəl 〕 *adj.* 注意的；警惕的《*watch* 注意》
wonderful[2] 〔'wʌndɚfəl 〕 *adj.* 令人驚嘆的《*wonder* 驚嘆》

14 -iac * 表示「與～有關的」。

cardiac[7] 〔'kardɪ,æk 〕 *adj.* 心臟（病）的
《希臘文 *kardia* = heart》
demoniac[7] 〔 dɪ'monɪ,æk 〕 *adj.* 惡魔的；凶惡的《*demon* 惡魔》
insomniac[7] 〔 ɪn'samnɪæk 〕 *adj.* 失眠症的；令人失眠的
《拉丁文 *in-*（not）+ *somnus*（sleep）》
maniac[7] 〔'menɪ,æk 〕 *adj.* 發狂的；瘋狂的《*mania* 狂熱》

15 -ic * 表示「與～有關的」、「～的」。

形容詞字尾

academic[4] 〔,ækə'dɛmɪk 〕 *adj.* 學院的；學術的；理論性的
《*academy* 學院》
alcoholic[6] 〔,ælkə'hɔlɪk 〕 *adj.* 酒精的《*alcohol* 酒精》
angelic[7] 〔 æn'dʒɛlɪk 〕 *adj.* 天使的《*angel* 天使》
arctic[6] 〔'arktɪk 〕 *adj.* 北極的；北極地方的（大熊座的附近 → 北）
《希臘文 *arktos* = bear（熊））》 *cf.* **antarctic**（南極的）
aristocratic[7] 〔 ə,rɪstə'krætɪk 〕 *adj.* 貴族的《*aristocrat* 貴族》

```
aristo + crat + ic
  |        |      |
 best  +  rule + adj.
```

athletic[4] 〔 æθ'lɛtɪk 〕 *adj.* 運動的；強健的《*athlete* 運動員》
atomic[4] 〔 ə'tamɪk 〕 *adj.* 原子的《*atom* 原子》

automatic[3] 〔͵ɔtə'mætɪk 〕 *adj.* 自動的

《*auto-* (self) + *mat* (think) + *-ic*》

```
auto + mat + ic
 |      |     |
self + think + adj.
```

basic[1] 〔'besɪk 〕 *adj.* 基本的；鹼性的《*base* 基礎》

calorific[7] 〔͵kælə'rɪfɪk 〕 *adj.* 生熱的《拉丁文 *calor* = heat》

carbonic[7] 〔kɑr'bɑnɪk 〕 *adj.* 碳的；碳酸的《*carbon* 碳》

chaotic[7] 〔ke'ɑtɪk 〕 *adj.* 混亂的；無秩序的《*chaos* 混沌》

characteristic[4] 〔͵kærɪktə'rɪstɪk 〕 *adj.* 有特色的；特有的

n. 特性《*character* 性格；特色》

civic[5] 〔'sɪvɪk 〕 *adj.* 市民的；市的《*city* 都市》

diplomatic[5] 〔͵dɪplə'mætɪk 〕 *adj.* 外交的；有外交手腕的

《*diploma* 公文》

domestic[3] 〔də'mɛstɪk 〕 *adj.* 家庭的；國內的；馴服的

《拉丁文 *domus* = house》

dramatic[3] 〔drə'mætɪk 〕 *adj.* 戲劇的；戲劇性的《*drama* 戲劇》

dynamic[4] 〔daɪ'næmɪk 〕 *adj.* 動力的；動態的；活躍的

egoistic[7] 〔͵igo'ɪstɪk 〕 *adj.* 自我中心的；自私自利的《*ego* 自我》

emphatic[6] 〔ɪm'fætɪk 〕 *adj.* 有力的；強調的《*emphasis* 強調》

```
em + phat + ic
 |     |     |
in + show + adj.
```

energetic[3] 〔͵ɛnɚ'dʒɛtɪk 〕 *adj.* 精力充沛的《*energy* 精力》

enigmatic[7] 〔͵ɛnɪg'mætɪk 〕 *adj.* 謎一般的；難解的《*enigma* 謎》

enthusiastic[5] 〔ɪn͵θjuzɪ'æstɪk 〕 *adj.* 熱心的；狂熱的

《*en-* (in) + *thusiast* (god) + *-ic*》

```
en + thusiast + ic
 |      |       |
in +  god    + adj.
```

形
容
詞
字
尾

exotic[6]〔ɪɡ'zɑtɪk〕*adj.* 外來的；外國產的《希臘文 *exo* = outward》

fantastic[4]〔fæn'tæstɪk〕*adj.* 怪異的；幻想的；很棒的
 《*fantasy* 幻想；奇想》

gigantic[4]〔dʒaɪ'ɡæntɪk〕*adj.* 巨大的《*giant* 巨人》

heroic[5]〔hɪ'ro‧ɪk〕*adj.* 英雄的《*hero* 英雄》

idiotic[7]〔ˌɪdɪ'atɪk〕*adj.* 白痴的《*idiot* 白痴》

lunatic[6]〔'lunəˌtɪk〕*adj.* 瘋的；極端愚蠢的（源自瘋病與月亮有關
 的迷信）《拉丁文 *luna* = moon》 *cf.* **lunar**（月的）

magnetic[4]〔mæɡ'nɛtɪk〕*adj.* 有磁性的；有魅力的《*magnet* 磁鐵》

optimistic[3]〔ˌaptə'mɪstɪk〕*adj.* 樂觀的《*optimism* 樂觀主義》

patriotic[6]〔ˌpetrɪ'atɪk〕*adj.* 愛國的；有愛國心的《*patriot* 愛國者》

pessimistic[4]〔ˌpɛsə'mɪstɪk〕*adj.* 悲觀的《*pessimism* 悲觀主義》

poetic[5]〔po'ɛtɪk〕*adj.* 詩的；有詩意的《*poetry* 詩》

problematic[7]〔ˌprablə'mætɪk〕*adj.* 有問題的《*problem* 問題》

pro	+	blem	+	atic
forward	+	*casting*	+	*adj.*

prosaic[7]〔pro'ze‧ɪk〕*adj.* 散文的；平淡的《*prose* 散文》

realistic[4]〔ˌriə'lɪstɪk〕*adj.* 現實的；寫實的《*real* 眞實的》

romantic[3]〔ro'mæntɪk〕*adj.* 浪漫的；傳奇性的；愛幻想的
 《*romance* 浪漫》

rustic[7]〔'rʌstɪk〕*adj.* 鄉村的；質樸的；粗野的
 《拉丁文 *rus* = country（鄉村）》

satiric[7]〔sə'tɪrɪk〕*adj.* 諷刺的《*satire* 諷刺》

scenic[6]〔'sinɪk, 'sɛn-〕*adj.* 背景的；戲劇的；風景的《*scene* 景色》

soporific[7]〔ˌsopə'rɪfɪk, ˌsapə-〕*adj.* 催眠的；想睡的
 《拉丁文 *sopor* = deep sleep》

sudorific[7]〔ˌsudə'rɪfɪk〕*adj.* 使發汗的；促進發汗的
 《拉丁文 *sudor* = sweat》

systematic[4]〔ˌsɪstə'mætɪk〕*adj.* 有系統的《*system* 系統》

形容詞字尾

tragic[4] 〔'trædʒɪk 〕 *adj.* 悲劇的《*tragedy* 悲劇》

volcanic[7] 〔 vɑl'kænɪk 〕 *adj.* 火山的；激烈的《*volcano* 火山》

16 -ical

* 表示「有關～」、「～性的」，重音在 -ical 之前的音節。

biological[6] 〔,baɪə'lɑdʒɪk̩l 〕 *adj.* 生物學的《*biology* 生物學》

```
bio + log  + ical
 |     |      |
life + study + adj.
```

botanical[7] 〔 bo'tænɪk̩l 〕 *adj.* 植物學的《*botany* 植物學》

chemical[2] 〔'kɛmɪk̩l 〕 *adj.* 化學的《*chemistry* 化學》

cynical[7] 〔'sɪnɪk̩l 〕 *adj.* 憤世嫉俗的《*cynic* 憤世嫉俗的人》

identical[4] 〔 aɪ'dɛntɪk̩l 〕 *adj.* 一致的；完全相同的《*identify* 認同》

ironic(al)[6] 〔 aɪ'rɑnɪk(l̩) 〕 *adj.* 反諷的《*irony* 反諷》

methodical[7] 〔 mə'θɑdɪk̩l 〕 *adj.* 有方法的；有條不紊的《*method* 方法》

musical[3] 〔'mjuzɪk̩l 〕 *adj.* 音樂的《*music* 音樂》

mythological[7] 〔,mɪθə'lɑdʒɪk̩l 〕 *adj.* 神話的；想像的
《*mythology* 神話》

```
myth + olog  + ical
 |      |       |
myth + study + adj.
```

physical[4] 〔'fɪzɪk̩l 〕 *adj.* 物質的；自然的；物理學的；身體的
《*physics* 物理學》

practical[3] 〔'præktɪk̩l 〕 *adj.* 實際的；有用的《*practice* 實行》

radical[6] 〔'rædɪk̩l 〕 *adj.* 根本的；激進的；根的《*radix* 根源》

rhetorical[7] 〔 rɪ'tɔrɪk̩l 〕 *adj.* 修辭學的《*rhetoric* 修辭學》

surgical[7] 〔'sɝdʒɪk̩l 〕 *adj.* 外科（用）的《*surgery* 外科手術》

theatrical[7] 〔 θɪ'ætrɪk̩l 〕 *adj.* 戲院的；演戲的；戲劇性的
《*theater* 戲院》

形容詞字尾

tropical[3]〔'trɑpɪkḷ〕*adj.* 回歸線的；熱帶地方的
　《*tropic* 回歸線；熱帶地方》

typical[3]〔'tɪpɪkḷ〕*adj.* 典型的；象徵的《*type* 典型》

zoological[7]〔ˌzoə'lɑdʒɪkḷ〕*adj.* 動物學的《*zoology* 動物學》

```
zoo  +  log  +  ical
 |        |       |
animal + study +  adj.
```

【注意】-ic 和 -ical 兩者，有時在意義上有別，有時則無。以下是有差別
　　　　的例子：
　　　　econom**ic** *adj.* 經濟學的（economics 經濟學）
　　　　econom**ical** *adj.* 節儉的（economy 節約；經濟）
　　　　histor**ic** *adj.* 歷史上有名的　a **historic** spot 是「歷史有名的
　　　　地方」。
　　　　histor**ical** *adj.* 歷史上的；歷史的　a **historical** event 是「歷
　　　　史上的事件」。
　　　　mechan**ic** *n.* 技工；機械工　　mechan**ical** *adj.* 機械的；機械論的
　　　　polit**ic** *adj.* 明智的；狡詐的
　　　　polit**ical** *adj.* 政治的；政治學的；政黨的
　　　　techn**ic** *n.* 工藝；技術　　　　techn**ical** *adj.* 專門的；工藝的

17　-id　　*　拉丁文 -idus。

languid[7]〔'læŋgwɪd〕*adj.* 軟弱無力的；精神不振的；無生氣的
　《拉丁文 *languidus* = languish（失去生氣）》

limpid[7]〔'lɪmpɪd〕*adj.* 清澈的；透明的；清晰的
　《拉丁文 *limpa* = water》

placid[7]〔'plæsɪd〕*adj.* 安靜的；平靜的《拉丁文 *placere* = please》

rapid[2]〔'ræpɪd〕*adj.* 迅速的（快速地搶奪過來）
　《拉丁文 *rapere* = snatch（搶奪）》　*cf.* **rape**（強暴）

```
rap  +  id
 |       |
snatch + adj.
```

solid[3]〔ˈsɑlɪd〕*adj.* 固體的；牢固的；純粹的《拉丁文 *solidus* = firm》

splendid[4]〔ˈsplɛndɪd〕*adj.* 輝煌的；壯麗的

　　《拉丁文 *splendere* = shine》

stupid[1]〔ˈstjupɪd〕*adj.* 愚笨的；魯鈍的；昏迷不醒的

　　《拉丁文 *stupere* = be amazed》　*cf.* **stupendous**（驚人的）

timid[4]〔ˈtɪmɪd〕*adj.* 膽小的；怯懦的

　　《拉丁文 *timere* = fear》　*cf.* **timorous**（畏怯的）

vivid[3]〔ˈvɪvɪd〕*adj.* 鮮明的；生動的；活潑的《拉丁文 *vivere* = live》

18　**-ile**　* 拉丁文 *-ilis*，表示「易於～」、「有～的傾向」。

ductile[7]〔ˈdʌktḷ, -tɪl〕*adj.* 延展性的；可塑性的；易受影響的

　　《拉丁文 *ductus*（*ducere* 的過去分詞）= lead》

facile[7]〔ˈfæsḷ, -sɪl〕*adj.* 易得的；隨和的《拉丁文 *facere* = do》

fertile[4]〔ˈfɝtḷ〕*adj.* 多產的；肥沃的《拉丁文 *ferre* = bear（結實）》

```
fert  +  ile
 |        |
bear  +  adj.
```

fragile[6]〔ˈfrædʒəl〕*adj.* 易碎的《拉丁文 *fragilis* = easily broken》

　　cf. **fragment**（碎片）

gracile[7]〔ˈgræsḷ, -ɪl〕*adj.* 細薄的；纖弱的《拉丁文 *gratus* = pleasing》

hostile[5]〔ˈhɑstɪl〕*adj.* 敵方的；懷敵意的《拉丁文 *hostis* = enemy》

juvenile[5]〔ˈdʒuvənḷ, -ˌnaɪl〕*adj.* 青少年的；不成熟的

　　《拉丁文 *juvenis* = young》

puerile[7]〔ˈpjuəˌrɪl, -əˌrəl〕*adj.* 小孩的；天眞的

　　《拉丁文 *puer* = child》

sterile[7]〔ˈstɛrəl〕*adj.* 不肥沃的；不能生育的；無菌的；枯燥的

　　《拉丁文 *sterilis* = barren（貧瘠的）》

versatile[6]〔ˈvɝsətɪl, -taɪl〕*adj.* 多才多藝的；易變的；多用途的

　　（經常改變方向）《拉丁文 *versare* = turn often》

19 -ine * 表示「具有～性質」。

divine[4]〔dəˈvaɪn〕*adj.* 神的；神聖的；超人的

《拉丁文 *divinus* = 屬於神的》

feminine[5]〔ˈfɛmənɪn〕*adj.* 婦女（似）的；柔弱的

《拉丁文 *femina* = woman》 *cf.* **female**（女性的）

genuine[4]〔ˈdʒɛnjʊɪn〕*adj.* 眞正的；眞實的；純種的

《拉丁文 *genuinus* = innate（生來的）》 *cf.* **genus**（屬）

```
genu  + ine
 |        |
innate + adj.
```

masculine[5]〔ˈmæskjəlɪn〕*adj.* 男人的；雄壯的

《拉丁文 *masculus* = male》

sanguine[7]〔ˈsæŋgwɪn〕*adj.* 血紅的；面色紅潤的；樂天的；自信的

《拉丁文 *sanguis* = blood》

20 -ing * 把動詞變爲形容詞的形式。

abiding[7]〔əˈbaɪdɪŋ〕*adj.* 永久的；持久的《*abide* 忍耐；等候》

```
a     +  bid  + ing
|         |       |
intensive + remain + adj.
```

agonizing[7]〔ˈægəˌnaɪzɪŋ〕*adj.* 使痛苦的《*agonize*（使）痛苦》

alarming[7]〔əˈlɑrmɪŋ〕*adj.* 令人擔憂的；緊迫的《*alarm* 使驚慌》

amazing[7]〔əˈmezɪŋ〕*adj.* 令人吃驚的《*amaze* 使吃驚》

amusing[7]〔əˈmjuzɪŋ〕*adj.* 有趣的《*amuse* 使開心》

astonishing[7]〔əˈstɑnɪʃɪŋ〕*adj.* 令人驚訝的《*astonish* 使驚異》

becoming[7]〔bɪˈkʌmɪŋ〕*adj.* 合適的《*be-*（upon）+ *com*（come）+ *-ing*》

```
be  + com  + ing
|       |      |
upon + come + adj.
```

boiling[7]〔'bɔɪlɪŋ〕*adj.* 沸騰的《*boil* 沸騰》

charming[7]〔'tʃɑrmɪŋ〕*adj.* 迷人的；嬌媚的《*charm* 使迷醉》

corresponding[7]〔,kɔrə'spɑndɪŋ〕*adj.* 相當的；一致的
《*correspond* 符合》

```
cor  +  re  + spond  +  ing
 |       |      |         |
together + back + pledge + adj.
```

crying[7]〔'kraɪɪŋ〕*adj.* 哭泣的；明顯的；緊急的《*cry* 哭泣》

cunning[4]〔'kʌnɪŋ〕*adj.* 狡猾的；熟練的；巧妙的（知道並非是惡
意的）《古英文 *cunnen* = know》

daring[7]〔'dɛrɪŋ〕*adj.* 勇敢的；大膽的《*dare* 敢》

dazzling[7]〔'dæzl̩ɪŋ〕*adj.* 令人目眩的；耀眼的《*dazzle* 使目眩》

discouraging[7]〔dɪs'kɝɪdʒɪŋ〕*adj.* 令人氣餒的《*discourage* 使氣餒》

```
dis + courag(e) + ing
 |       |         |
not  +  heart   + adj.
```

disgusting[7]〔dɪs'gʌstɪŋ〕*adj.* 令人厭惡的《*disgust* 厭惡》

enduring[7]〔ɪn'djurɪŋ〕*adj.* 持久的；持續的《*endure* 忍受》

exciting[7]〔ɪk'saɪtɪŋ〕*adj.* 興奮的；刺激的《*excite* 使興奮》

existing[7]〔ɪg'zɪstɪŋ〕*adj.* 現有的；既存的《*exist* 存在》

flaming[7]〔'flemɪŋ〕*adj.* 燃燒的；火焰般的；閃亮的《*flame* 火焰》

following[2]〔'faləwɪŋ〕*adj.* 其次的；以下的；下列的《*follow* 跟隨》

forbidding[7]〔fɚ'bɪdɪŋ〕*adj.* 討厭的；恐怖的；令人害怕的
《*forbid* 禁止》

forgiving[7]〔fɚ'gɪvɪŋ〕*adj.* 寬大的；慈悲的《*forgive* 原諒》

freezing[7]〔'frizɪŋ〕*adj.* 結冰的；寒冷的《*freeze* 冰凍》

irritating[7]〔'ɪrə,tetɪŋ〕*adj.* 惱人的；刺激的《*irritate* 激怒》

lasting[7]〔'læstɪŋ, 'lɑstɪŋ〕*adj.* 持久的；永恆的《*last* 持續》

longing[7]〔'lɔŋɪŋ〕*adj.* 渴望的《*long* 渴望》

loving[7]〔'lʌvɪŋ〕*adj.* 鍾愛的；親愛的《*love* 喜愛》

形容詞字尾

missing[3]〔'mɪsɪŋ〕*adj.* 失蹤的；缺少的《*miss* 遺漏》

oncoming[7]〔'ɑn͵kʌmɪŋ〕*adj.* 接近的；即將來臨的

outstanding[4]〔'aut'stændɪŋ〕*adj.* 突出的；顯著的

overwhelming[7]〔͵ovɚ'hwɛlmɪŋ〕*adj.* 壓倒性的；無法抵抗的
《*overwhlem* 征服；壓倒》

```
over  +  whelm  +  ing
 |         |        |
above  +  cover  +  adj.
```

rambling[7]〔'ræmblɪŋ〕*adj.* 漫步的；迂迴曲折的；毫無頭緒的
《*ramble* 漫步》

refreshing[7]〔rɪ'frɛʃɪŋ〕*adj.* 提神的；清爽而宜人的《*refresh* 使爽快》

rolling[7]〔'rolɪŋ〕*adj.* 滾動的《*roll* 滾動》

satisfying[7]〔'sætɪs͵faɪɪŋ〕*adj.* 令人滿意的《*satisfy* 使滿足》

```
satis  +  fy  +  ing
  |        |      |
enough +  make  + adj.
```

形容詞字尾

shocking[7]〔'ʃɑkɪŋ〕*adj.* 令人震驚的；令人氣憤的《*shock* 震驚》

sleeping[7]〔'slipɪŋ〕*adj.* 睡著的；睡覺的《*sleep* 睡覺》

sparkling[7]〔'sparklɪŋ〕*adj.* 發出火花的；耀眼的；燦爛的
《*sparkle* 發光》

standing[7]〔'stændɪŋ〕*adj.* 站著的；永久性的；經常的《*stand* 站立》

startling[7]〔'startlɪŋ〕*adj.* 令人吃驚的《*startle* 使吃驚》

striking[7]〔'straɪkɪŋ〕*adj.* 顯著的；引人注意的《*strike* 給人深刻印象》

surprising[7]〔sə'praɪzɪŋ〕*adj.* 令人驚訝的
《*sur-*（above）+ *pris*（seize）+ *-ing*》

```
sur  +  pris  +  ing
 |       |       |
above + seize +  adj.
```

touching[7]〔'tʌtʃɪŋ〕*adj.* 感人的《*touch* 觸摸》

trying[7]〔'traɪɪŋ〕*adj.* 難堪的；使人痛苦的《*try* 考驗》

wanting[7] 〔'wɔntɪŋ 〕 *adj.* 缺乏的；不足的《*want* 欠缺》

willing[2] 〔'wɪlɪŋ 〕 *adj.* 情願的；願意的《*will* 以意志力驅使》

21　-ior　　* 這是拉丁文中用來表示比較級的字尾。

inferior[3] 〔 ɪn'fɪrɪɚ 〕 *adj.* 下級的；較劣的《拉丁文 *inferus* = low》

　　cf. **infernal**（地獄的）

junior[4] 〔'dʒunjɚ 〕 *adj.* 年少的；資淺的《拉丁文 *juvenis* = young》

　　cf. **juvenile**（青少年的）

> jun　+ ior
> ｜　　｜
> *young* + *adj.*

senior[4] 〔'sinjɚ 〕 *adj.* 年長的；前輩的；資淺的《拉丁文 *sen* = old》

　　cf. **senate**（元老院；參議院）

superior[3] 〔 sə'pɪrɪɚ , su- 〕 *adj.* 上級的；較優的

　　《拉丁文 *superus* = high》

22　-ique , -esque　　* 表示「～的風格」。

antique[5] 〔 æn'tik 〕 *adj.* 古代的；過時的　　*n.* 古董（很久以前的）

　　《拉丁文 *ante-* = before》

arabesque[7] 〔ˌærə'bɛsk 〕 *adj.* 阿拉伯式的；奇特的《*Arabia* 阿拉伯》

grotesque[7] 〔 gro'tɛsk 〕 *adj.* 古怪的；可笑的；醜怪的（由古老

　　洞穴中發現的壁畫而來的靈感）《義大利文 *grotta* = grotto（洞穴）》

oblique[7] 〔 ə'blik , ə'blaɪk 〕 *adj.* 歪的；斜的；間接的（向～方向

　　彎曲）《拉丁文 *ob-*（towards）+ *lique*（bent）》

> ob　　+ lique
> ｜　　　｜
> *towards* + *bent*

picturesque[6] 〔ˌpɪktʃə'rɛsk 〕 *adj.* 如畫的；生動的《*picture* 畫》

形容詞字尾

23　-ish　* 表示「帶有～性質」、「有關～的」。

bookish[7]〔ˈbʊkɪʃ〕*adj.* 好讀書的；迂腐的
brownish[7]〔ˈbraʊnɪʃ〕*adj.* 呈棕色的
childish[2]〔ˈtʃaɪldɪʃ〕*adj.* 幼稚的　*cf.* **childlike**（天眞的；單純的）
feverish[7]〔ˈfivərɪʃ〕*adj.* 發熱的；狂熱的；悶熱的
　《*fever* 發燒（與 heat 用法不同）》
selfish[1]〔ˈsɛlfɪʃ〕*adj.* 自私的
yellowish[7]〔ˈjɛloɪʃ〕*adj.* 微黃的；帶點黃色的

　【注意】-ish 大多暗示「**有點不好**」的意味，-ly 是「**好的**」意思，-like
　　　　則多用於這兩者之間的意思。

　　　　mannish（含有責備、嘲弄的語氣）　像男人的；男人特質的
　　　　manly（帶有讚賞的意味）　像男人的；有男人氣概的
　　　　manlike（不帶有任何特殊意味）　像男人的；有男人特質的

24　-ite　* 希臘文 *-ites*。

形容詞字尾

exquisite[6]〔ˈɛkskwɪzɪt , ɪkˈskwɪzɪt〕*adj.* 精美的；極度的；高尚的
（被找出 → 被選出）《拉丁文 *ex-*（out）+ *quis*（seek）+ *-ite*》

```
ex  +  quis  +  ite
|       |       |
out +  seek  +  adj.
```

favo(u)rite[2]〔ˈfevərɪt〕*adj.* 最喜愛的；中意的
　《拉丁文 *favere* = befriend（對～以朋友相待）》
infinite[5]〔ˈɪnfənɪt〕*adj.* 無限的；極大的（沒有結束的）
　《拉丁文 *in-*（not）+ *fin*（end）+ *-ite*》

```
in  +  fin  +  ite
|       |      |
not +  end  +  adj.
```

opposite[3]〔ˈɑpəzɪt〕*adj.* 相對的；相反的《*oppose* 反對》

polite² 〔pə'laɪt〕*adj.* 有禮貌的；文雅的（被琢磨而成的）

《拉丁文 *polire* = polish》

25　-ive　* 拉丁文 *-ivus*。

aggressive⁴ 〔ə'grɛsɪv〕*adj.* 有攻擊性的；積極進取的

《*aggress* 侵略》

constructive⁴ 〔kən'strʌktɪv〕*adj.* 建設性的《*construct* 建設》

defective⁷ 〔dɪ'fɛktɪv〕*adj.* 有缺陷的《*defect* 缺陷》

exclusive⁶ 〔ɪk'sklusɪv〕*adj.* 不許外人加入的；排外的；獨家的

《*exclude* 除外》

exhaustive⁷ 〔ɪg'zɔstɪv〕*adj.* 枯竭的；消耗的《*exhaust* 用盡》

```
ex  +  haust  +  ive
 |       |        |
out  +  draw  +  adj.
```

expansive⁷ 〔ɪk'spænsɪv〕*adj.* 寬廣的；胸襟寬闊的

imaginative⁴ 〔ɪ'mædʒə‚netɪv〕*adj.* 富於想像力的；幻想的；

虛構的《*imagine* 想像》

initiative⁶ 〔ɪ'nɪʃɪ‚etɪv〕*adj.* 初步的；主動的

《拉丁文 *initiare* = begin》

intuitive⁷ 〔ɪn'tuɪtɪv〕*adj.* 直覺的《*intuition* 直覺》

inventive⁷ 〔ɪn'vɛntɪv〕*adj.* 發明的；有創意的《*invention* 發明》

```
in  +  vent  +  ive
 |       |       |
upon + come  +  adj.
```

massive⁵ 〔'mæsɪv〕*adj.* 大量的；宏偉的；塊狀的《*mass* 塊；團》

primitive⁴ 〔'prɪmətɪv〕*adj.* 原始的《*prime* 首要的》

representative³ 〔‚rɛprɪ'zɛntətɪv〕*adj.* 象徵性的；代表性的

n. 代表《*represent* 表示；象徵；代表》

respective⁶ 〔rɪ'spɛktɪv〕*adj.* 個別的　*cf.* **respectable**（可敬的）

形容詞字尾

seductive[7] (sɪ'dʌktɪv) adj. 有魅力的；誘惑的《seduce 誘惑》

```
se  + duct + ive
 |     |      |
apart + lead + adj.
```

selective[6] (sə'lɛktɪv) adj. 選擇性的《select 選擇》
suggestive[7] (sə'dʒɛstɪv) adj. 暗示性的《suggest 暗示》
talkative[2] ('tɔkətɪv) adj. 愛說話的《talk 說話》

26　-less

* 由古英文 *leas* 而來的形式，表示「沒有」的意思，相反詞為 *-ful*。

aimless[7] ('emlɪs) adj. 無目標的《aim 目標》
blameless[7] ('blemlɪs) adj. 無可責備的；無過失的；無罪的
　《blame 責備》
bloodless[7] ('blʌdlɪs) adj. 無血的；貧血的；蒼白的《blood 血》
boundless[7] ('baundlɪs) adj. 無限的；無窮的；無止境的
　《bound 範圍》

```
bound  + less
  |        |
boundary + adj.
```

careless[7] ('kɛrlɪs) adj. 粗心的；不小心的《care 小心》
cloudless[7] ('klaudlɪs) adj. 無雲的；晴朗的《cloud 雲》
countless[7] ('kauntlɪs) adj. 無數的；數不盡的《count 計算》
germless[7] ('dʒɝmlɪs) adj. 無菌的《germ 病菌》
groundless[7] ('graundlɪs) adj. 沒理由的；無根據的《ground 根據》
hapless[7] ('hæplɪs) adj. 不幸的；倒楣的《hap 幸運》
harmless[7] ('hɑrmlɪs) adj. 無害的；無惡意的《harm 傷害》

```
harm + less
 |       |
hurt  + adj.
```

heartless[7] 〔'hɑrtlɪs 〕 adj. 無情的；冷酷的《**heart** 心》

helpless[7] 〔'hɛlplɪs 〕 adj. 無助的；迷惑的《**help** 幫助》

hopeless[7] 〔'hoplɪs 〕 adj. 無希望的；絕望的《**hope** 希望》

lifeless[7] 〔'laɪflɪs 〕 adj. 無生命的；無趣的《**life** 生命》

limitless[7] 〔'lɪmɪtlɪs 〕 adj. 無界限的；無限制的《**limit** 限制》

mindless[7] 〔'maɪndlɪs 〕 adj. 不留意的；愚鈍的《**mind** 留意》

```
mind + less
  |      |
think  + adj.
```

noiseless[7] 〔'nɔɪzlɪs 〕 adj. 無聲的《**noise** 噪音》

nameless[7] 〔'nemlɪs 〕 adj. 無名的；匿名的；不齒的《**name** 命名》

odorless[7] 〔'odɚlɪs 〕 adj. 無臭的；沒有氣味的《**odor** 氣味》

penniless[7] 〔'pɛnɪlɪs 〕 adj. 身無分文的；一文不名的《**penny** 分》

priceless[5] 〔'praɪslɪs 〕 adj. 極貴重的；無價的（無法賦予價值的）
　　《**price** 價格》

reckless[5] 〔'rɛklɪs 〕 adj. 鹵莽的；不顧一切的；不謹慎的《**reck** 注意》

regardless[6] 〔 rɪ'gɑrdlɪs 〕 adj. 不顧《**regard** 考慮》

```
re  +  gard  + less
 |       |       |
again + watch over + adj.
```

restless[7] 〔'rɛstlɪs 〕 adj. 不安靜的；無睡眠的；無休止的；紛擾的；
　　好動的《**rest** 休息》

senseless[7] 〔'sɛnslɪs 〕 adj. 無感覺的；不省人事的；無知的
　　《**sense** 感覺》

shameless[7] 〔'ʃemlɪs 〕 adj. 無恥的《**shame** 羞恥》

shapeless[7] 〔'ʃeplɪs 〕 adj. 無形的；形狀醜陋的《**shape** 形狀》

sleepless[7] 〔'sliplɪs 〕 adj. 失眠的；不休息的《**sleep** 睡覺》

speechless[7] 〔'spitʃlɪs 〕 adj. 不能說話的；無言的《**speech** 說話》

valueless[7] 〔'væljʊlɪs 〕 adj. 沒有價值的《**value** 價值》

voiceless[7] 〔'vɔɪslɪs 〕 adj. 無聲的《**voice** 聲音》

27 -like *表示「像～樣的」或「喜歡～的」。

businesslike[7] (ˈbɪznɪsˌlaɪk) *adj.* 認眞的；實事求是的
《*business* 事務》

```
busi + ness + like
 |      |      |
busy +  n.  + adj.
```

childlike[2] (ˈtʃaɪldˌlaɪk) *adj.* 天眞無邪的；單純的
ladylike[7] (ˈledɪˌlaɪk) *adj.* 如貴婦的；高貴的；優雅的
sportsmanlike[7] (ˈsportsmənˌlaɪk , ˈsports-) *adj.* 有運動家風度
的；光明磊落的《*sportsman* 運動家》
warlike[7] (ˈworˌlaɪk) *adj.* 好戰的；尙武的；戰爭的
womanlike[7] (ˈwumənˌlaɪk) *adj.* 像女人的

28 -ly *加上名詞做形容詞，若加上形容詞則爲副詞。

bodily[5] (ˈbɑdḷɪ , -dɪlɪ) *adj.* 身體上的；具體的
costly[2] (ˈkɔstlɪ) *adj.* 貴重的；昂貴的《*cost* 費用》
cowardly[5] (ˈkaʊɚdlɪ) *adj.* 膽小的《*coward* 膽小者》
earthly[7] (ˈɝθlɪ) *adj.* 大地的；世俗的 *cf.* heavenly (天國的)
fortnightly[7] (ˈfortnaɪtlɪ) *adj.* 兩週一次的；隔週的《*fortnight* 兩週》

```
fort   + night + ly
 |        |       |
fourteen + night + adj.
```

friendly[2] (ˈfrɛndlɪ) *adj.* 友善的；親切的
leisurely[4] (ˈliʒɚlɪ , ˈlɛ-) *adj.* 悠閒的；不慌不忙的 (時間允許的)
《*leisure* 空閒》

```
leisure  + ly
   |       |
be allowed + adj.
```

monthly[4] 〔ˈmʌnθlɪ〕 *adj.* 每月的；每月一次的
stately[7] 〔ˈstetlɪ〕 *adj.* 威嚴的；堂皇的《*state* 威嚴》
timely[7] 〔ˈtaɪmlɪ〕 *adj.* 適時的；適宜的
worldly[7] 〔ˈwɝldlɪ〕 *adj.* 現世的；世俗的

29 -most   * 表示最高級的意思。

almost[1] 〔ˈɔl‚most，ɔlˈmost〕 *adj.*，*adv.* 差不多；幾乎
foremost[7] 〔ˈfor‚most，ˈfɔr-〕 *adj.* 最先的；首要的《*fore* = before》

```
fore  +  most
 |         |
before  +  adj.
```

innermost[7] 〔ˈɪnɚ‚most〕 *adj.* 最深奧的；最內部的
utmost[6] 〔ˈʌt‚most〕 *adj.* 最遠的；極度的《古英文 *ut* = out》

30 -ory   * 表示「帶有～的性質」之意。

compulsory[7] 〔kəmˈpʌlsərɪ〕 *adj.* 強迫的；強制的；必修的
　《*compel* 強迫》
contradictory[7] 〔‚kɑntrəˈdɪktərɪ〕 *adj.* 矛盾的；相反的；對立的
　《*contradict* 矛盾》

```
contra  +  dict  +  ory
  |          |        |
against  +  speak  +  adj.
```

obligatory[7] 〔əˈblɪgə‚torɪ，ˈɑblɪgə‚torɪ〕 *adj.* 義務的；有拘束力的
　《*oblige* 強制》
preparatory[7] 〔prɪˈpærə‚torɪ〕 *adj.* 準備的；初步的
　《*prepare* 準備》
satisfactory[3] 〔‚sætɪsˈfæktərɪ〕 *adj.* 令人滿意的；適合的
　《*satisfy* 使滿意》

形容詞字尾

31 -ous   *表示「充滿了」。

advantageous[7]〔͵ædvən'tedʒəs〕 *adj.* 有利的；有益的
《*advantage* 利益》

avaricious[7]〔͵ævə'rɪʃəs〕 *adj.* 貪心的；貪婪的《*avarice* 貪心》

cautious[5]〔'kɔʃəs〕 *adj.* 細心的；謹慎的《*caution* 小心》

capricious[7]〔kə'prɪʃəs〕 *adj.* 善變的；任性的；反覆無常的
《*caprice* 反覆無常》

```
cap + ric + ious
 |     |      |
head + curl + adj.
```

courteous[4]〔'kɝtɪəs〕 *adj.* 有禮貌的；體諒的《*courtesy* 禮貌》

covetous[7]〔'kʌvɪtəs〕 *adj.* 貪婪的《*covet* 貪求》

dangerous[2]〔'dendʒərəs〕 *adj.* 危險的《*danger* 危險》

delicious[2]〔dɪ'lɪʃəs〕 *adj.* 美味可口的
《*de-*（ intensive ）+ *lic*（ entice 引誘 ）+ *-ious*》

envious[4]〔'ɛnvɪəs〕 *adj.* 嫉妒的；羨慕的《*envy* 羨慕》
cf. **enviable**（ 可羨慕的 ）

frivolous[7]〔'frɪvələs〕 *adj.* 輕浮的；膚淺的《*frivol*（ silly ）+ *-ous*》

furious[4]〔'fjʊrɪəs〕 *adj.* 狂怒的；猛烈的《*fury* 憤怒》

glorious[4]〔'glorɪəs , 'glɔr-〕 *adj.* 光榮的；輝煌的《*glory* 光榮》

gorgeous[5]〔'gɔrdʒəs〕 *adj.* 華麗的；燦爛的（ 志得意滿時放大喉嚨 ）
《法文 *gorge* = throat（ 喉嚨 ）》

```
gorge + ous
  |       |
throat + adj.
```

harmonious[7]〔hɑr'monɪəs〕 *adj.* 和諧的；協調的《*harmony* 和諧》

hideous[7]〔'hɪdɪəs〕 *adj.* 可怕的；非常醜陋的《*hide* 隱藏》

industrious[7]〔ɪn'dʌstrɪəs〕 *adj.* 勤勉的《*industry* 勤勉》
cf. **industrial**（ 工業的 ）

laborious[7] 〔 ləˋborɪəs , -ˋbɔr- 〕 *adj.* 費力的；勤勞的《*labo(u)r* 勞苦》

malicious[7] 〔 məˋlɪʃəs 〕 *adj.* 惡意的；蓄意的《*malice* 惡意》

oblivious[7] 〔 əˋblɪvɪəs 〕 *adj.* 健忘的；不專心的《*oblivion* 遺忘；湮沒》

```
ob  +  livi  +  ous
 |       |       |
over + smooth + adj.
```

odious[7] 〔ˋodɪəs 〕 *adj.* 討厭的；嫌惡的；可恨的《*odium* 討厭》

ominous[7] 〔ˋɑmənəs 〕 *adj.* 不祥的；凶兆的《*omen* 預兆》

outrageous[6] 〔ˋaʊtˋredʒəs 〕 *adj.* 粗暴的；可惡的；無法無天的
《*outrage* 暴行》

```
outr  +  age  +  ous
  |        |       |
beyond  +  n.  +  adj.
```

perilous[7] 〔ˋpɛrələs 〕 *adj.* 危險的；冒險的《*peril* 危險》

poisonous[4] 〔ˋpɔɪznəs 〕 *adj.* 有毒的；有害的；討厭的《*poison* 毒》

pompous[7] 〔ˋpɑmpəs 〕 *adj.* 傲慢的；自負的；誇大的《*pomp* 炫耀》

righteous[7] 〔ˋraɪtʃəs 〕 *adj.* 公正的；正當的；正直的《*right* 正義》

serious[2] 〔ˋsɪrɪəs 〕 *adj.* 認真的；嚴肅的《拉丁文 *serius* = heavy》

spacious[6] 〔ˋspeʃəs 〕 *adj.* 廣大的；廣闊的《*space* 空間》

spontaneous[6] 〔 spɑnˋtenɪəs 〕 *adj.* 自然的；率直的
《拉丁文 *sponta* = of free will》

strenuous[7] 〔ˋstrɛnjʊəs 〕 *adj.* 費力的；艱辛的；努力的
《希臘文 *stereos* = firm (穩固的)》   *cf.* **stereoscope** (實體鏡)

```
stren  +  uous
  |         |
firm   +  adj.
```

studious[7] 〔ˋstjudɪəs 〕 *adj.* 好學的；用功的；用心的《*study* 讀書》

tedious[6] 〔ˋtidɪəs 〕 *adj.* 沈悶的；冗長的《*tedium* 沈悶》

treacherous[7] 〔ˋtrɛtʃərəs 〕 *adj.* 叛逆的；背叛的；靠不住的
《*treachery* 背叛》

tremendous[4]〔trɪˈmɛndəs〕*adj.* 巨大的；恐怖的；了不起的
《*tremble* 震動》

tremulous[7]〔ˈtrɛmjələs〕*adj.* 顫慄的；抖動的；畏縮的；怯懦的
《*tremor* 顫抖》

```
tremul + ous
  |
tremble + adj.
```

various[3]〔ˈvɛrɪəs〕*adj.* 不同的；各式各樣的《*vary* 改變》

vicious[6]〔ˈvɪʃəs〕*adj.* 邪惡的；謬誤的《*vice* 邪惡》

virtuous[7]〔ˈvɝtʃuəs〕*adj.* 有品德的；貞潔的《*virtue* 美德》

zealous[7]〔ˈzɛləs〕*adj.* 熱心的；熱衷的《*zeal* 熱心》

32 -proof　*多加在名詞之後，表示「防～的」。

airproof[7]〔ˈɛrˌpruf〕*adj.* 不通氣的；密不透氣的

bombproof[7]〔ˈbɑmˈpruf〕*adj.* 防空（用）的

bulletproof[7]〔ˈbʊlɪtˌpruf〕*adj.* 防彈的

fireproof[6]〔ˈfaɪrˈpruf〕*adj.* 防火的；耐火的

foolproof[7]〔ˈfulˈpruf〕*adj.* 愚人也會的；極簡單的；安全無比的

germproof[7]〔ˈdʒɝmˌpruf〕*adj.* 抗菌的《*germ* 病菌》

rainproof[7]〔ˈrenˈpruf〕*adj.* 防水的；不漏雨的

soundproof[7]〔ˈsaʊndˌpruf〕*adj.* 隔音的；防音的

waterproof[6]〔ˈwɔtɚˈpruf〕*adj.* 不透水的；防水的

weatherproof[7]〔ˈwɛðɚˌpruf〕*adj.* 能耐風雨的

33 -some

　　*這是 *same* 的變化型，表示「像～樣的」或「有～傾向」。

burdensome[7]〔ˈbɝdn̩səm〕*adj.* 沈重的《*burden* 重擔》

irksome[7]〔ˋɝksəm〕*adj.* 令人煩惱的；令人厭煩的；討厭的
　《*irk* 使苦惱》

meddlesome[7]〔ˋmɛdl̩səm〕*adj.* 愛管閒事的；好干涉的
　《*meddle* 干涉》

```
meddle + some
  |        |
 mix   + adj.
```

quarrelsome[6]〔ˋkwɔrəlsəm , ˋkwɑr-〕*adj.* 愛爭吵的《*quarrel* 爭吵》

tiresome[4]〔ˋtaɪrsəm〕*adj.* 令人厭倦的；吃力的《*tire* 使疲倦》

troublesome[4]〔ˋtrʌbl̩səm〕*adj.* 令人苦惱的；困難的；麻煩的
　《*trouble* 使煩惱》

```
trouble + some
   |        |
 bother + adj.
```

wearisome[7]〔ˋwɪrɪsəm〕*adj.* 使人疲倦的；使人厭煩的；無聊的
　《*weary* 使疲倦》

wholesome[5]〔ˋholsəm〕*adj.* 合乎衛生的；有益健康的；有益的
　《*whole* 完全的》

34　**-ward**　* 古英文 *-weard*，主要用來表示方向。

awkward[4]〔ˋɔkwəd〕*adj.* 笨拙的；無技巧的（不好的方向）
　《古英文 *awk* = wrong》

backward[2]〔ˋbækwəd〕*adj.* 向後的；無進步的；遲鈍的

downward[5]〔ˋdaʊnwəd〕*adj. , adv.* 向下的；向下地

eastward[7]〔ˋistwəd〕*adj. , adv.* 向東的；向東地

homeward[7]〔ˋhomwəd〕*adj. , adv.* 回家（國）的；回家（國）地

onward[7]〔ˋɑnwəd〕*adj. , adv.* 向前的；前進地

seaward[7]〔ˋsiwəd〕*adj. , adv.* 向海的；向海地

wayward[7]〔ˋwewəd〕*adj.* 剛愎的；任性的《*way* 習性》

形容詞字尾

35 **-y** * 表示「充滿～」、「有～性質」、「有～傾向」。

bloody[2] 〔'blʌdɪ〕*adj.* 血的；流血的；殘忍的《*blood* 血液》

bushy[7] 〔'buʃɪ〕*adj.* 灌木叢生的；濃密的《*bush* 灌木》

cloudy[2] 〔'klaudɪ〕*adj.* 多雲的；不明朗的《*cloud* 雲》

clumsy[4] 〔'klʌmzɪ〕*adj.* 笨拙的；樣子不好看的（凍僵的）

　　《古英文 *clumsen* = benumb (使麻木)》

cosy；**-zy**[5] 〔'kozɪ〕*adj.* 溫暖而舒適的；安逸的

　　《挪威文 *kosa* = refresh (使爽快)》

$$\begin{array}{ccc} \text{cos} & + & \text{y} \\ | & & | \\ \textit{refresh} & + & \textit{adj.} \end{array}$$

dreamy[7] 〔'drimɪ〕*adj.* 夢的；幻想的；模糊的《*dream* 夢》

dusky[7] 〔'dʌskɪ〕*adj.* 微暗的；微黑的《*dusk* 黃昏》

foggy[2] 〔'fɔgɪ，'fɑ-〕*adj.* 有濃霧的；多霧的；模糊不清的《*fog* 霧》

greedy[2] 〔'gridɪ〕*adj.* 貪心的《*greed* 貪心》

$$\begin{array}{ccc} \text{greed} & + & \text{y} \\ | & & | \\ \textit{wanting} & + & \textit{adj.} \end{array}$$

greeny[7] 〔'grinɪ〕*adj.* 淺綠色的；帶點綠色的《*green* 綠色》

icy[3] 〔'aɪsɪ〕*adj.* 似冰的；冷淡的《*ice* 冰》

notchy[7] 〔'nɑtʃɪ〕*adj.* 有凹口的；有鋸齒狀的

　　《*notch* 凹口；凹痕》

plumy[7] 〔'plumɪ〕*adj.* 有羽毛的《*plume* 羽毛》

scanty[7] 〔'skæntɪ〕*adj.* 缺乏的；不足的《*scant* 減少》

spicy[4] 〔'spaɪsɪ〕*adj.* 有香味的；活潑的《*spice* 香料》

tardy[7] 〔'tɑrdɪ〕*adj.* 遲延的；緩慢的《拉丁文 *tardus* = slow》

worthy[5] 〔'wɝðɪ〕*adj.* 有價值的；值得的《*worth* 價值》

形容詞字尾

【3】副詞字尾

1　-ence　*表示 *from* 的意思；*-ither* 則表示 *to* 的意思。

hence[5] 〔hɛns 〕= from here　*adv.* 因此；從此時（地）
   cf. **hither**（到此處）
thence[7] 〔ðɛns 〕= from there　*adv.* 由彼處；因而；從那時
   cf. **thither**（到彼處）
whence[7] 〔hwɛns 〕= from there　*adv.* 從何處；何以
   cf. **whither**（向何處）

2　-ling , -long　*表示「在～方向」。

darkling[7] 〔'dɑrklɪŋ 〕*adv.* 在黑暗中
flatling[7] 〔'flætlɪŋ 〕*adv.* 平坦地
sideling[7] 〔'saɪdlɪŋ 〕*adv.* 橫地；斜地
headlong[7] 〔'hɛd,lɔŋ 〕*adv.* 頭向前地
sidelong[7] 〔'saɪd,lɔŋ 〕*adv.* 橫地；斜地

3　-ly　*從古英文 *lic*（= *like*）而來的字根，大多接於形容詞之後。

absolutely[7] 〔'æbsə,lutlɪ 〕*adv.* 絕對地；完全地《*absolute* 絕對的》
actually[7] 〔'æktʃuəlɪ 〕*adv.* 眞實地；實際地《*actual* 眞實的》
barely[3] 〔'bɛrlɪ 〕*adv.* 僅；赤裸裸地《*bare* 赤裸的》
heartily[7] 〔'hɑrtɪlɪ 〕*adv.* 誠懇地；豐盛地《*heart* 心》
invariably[7] 〔 ɪn'vɛrɪəblɪ 〕*adv.* 不變地；一定地；必然地
   《*invariable* 不變的》

```
in  +  vari  +  ab(le)  +  ly
 |      |        |         |
not  +  vary  +  adj.   +  adv.
```

literally[7]〔ˈlɪtərəlɪ〕 *adv.* 逐字地；實在地《*literal* 文字的》

readily[7] 〔ˈrɛdlɪ, ˈrɛdɪlɪ〕 *adv.* 迅速地；容易地

《*ready* 隨時會發生的》

roughly[4] 〔ˈrʌflɪ〕 *adv.* 粗魯地；概略地《*rough* 粗野的》

shortly[3] 〔ˈʃɔrtlɪ〕 *adv.* 不久；簡略地《*short* 短的》

steadily[7] 〔ˈstɛdəlɪ〕 *adv.* 穩定地；不斷地《*steady* 穩定的》

violently[7] 〔ˈvaɪələntlɪ〕 *adv.* 激烈地；熱烈地《*violent* 激烈的》

4　-s

besides[2] 〔bɪˈsaɪdz〕 *adv.* 此外；而且　*cf.* **beside**（在…旁邊）

indoors[3] 〔ˈɪnˈdorz〕 *adv.* 在室內　*cf.* **indoor**（室內的）

needs[7] 〔nidz〕 *adv.* 必要地；一定地

nowadays[4] 〔ˈnaʊəˌdez〕 *adv.* 現今；時下

outdoors[3] 〔ˈaʊtˈdorz〕 *adv.* 在戶外　*cf.* **outdoor**（戶外的）

sometimes[1] 〔ˈsʌmˌtaɪmz〕 *adv.* 有時　*cf.* **sometime**（在某時）

5　-ward(s)　*表示方向。

afterward(s)[3] 〔ˈæftəwəd(z)〕 *adv.* 以後

backward(s)[2] 〔ˈbækwəd(z)〕 *adv.* 向後地

downward(s)[5] 〔ˈdaʊnwəd(z)〕 *adv.* 向下地

homeward(s)[7] 〔ˈhomwəd(z)〕 *adv.* 回家（國）地

inward(s)[5] 〔ˈɪnwəd(z)〕 *adv.* 內部地；向內部

northward(s)[7] 〔ˈnɔrθwəd(z)〕 *adv.* 向北地

outward(s)[5] 〔ˈaʊtwəd(z)〕 *adv.* 向外；在外

southward(s)[7] 〔ˈsaʊθwəd(z)〕 *adv.* 向南地

sunward(s)[7] 〔ˈsʌnwəd(z)〕 *adv.* 向陽地

upward(s)[5] 〔ˈʌpwəd(z)〕 *adv.* 向上地；向上游；超過

副詞字尾

6　-way(s)，-wise　*兩者字源相同，表示「方式」。*

always[1] 〔ˈɔlwez，ˈɔlwɪz 〕*adv.* 永遠；總是；不斷地

anyway[2] 〔ˈɛnɪˌwe 〕= anyhow　*adv.* 無論如何（用什麼方法都）

endways[7] 〔ˈɛndˌwez 〕*adv.* 末端向前地；直立地；兩端相接地

sideways[7] 〔ˈsaɪdˌwez 〕*adv.* 橫向地；從旁邊

someway(s)[7] 〔ˈsʌmˌwe(z) 〕*adv.* 以某種方法

straightway[7] 〔ˈstretˌwe 〕*adv.* 立刻；即刻

crosswise[7] 〔ˈkrɔsˌwaɪz 〕*adv.* 橫地；斜地；交叉地；相反地

likewise[6] 〔ˈlaɪkˌwaɪz 〕*adv.* 同樣地；也

otherwise[4] 〔ˈʌðɚˌwaɪz 〕*adv.* 用不同方法地；在別的方面地；
否則；要不然（用其他的方式）

sidewise[7] 〔ˈsaɪdˌwaɪz 〕*adv.* = sideways

【4】動詞字尾

1　-ate　*源自於拉丁文 -atus，最常作動詞字尾，其名詞是 -ation。*

accommodate[6] 〔 əˈkɑməˌdet 〕*v.* 給方便；容納；供給宿舍；
使適應；調停；調解《拉丁文 *accommodare* = fit；adapt（使適應）》

assassinate[6] 〔 əˈsæsn̩ˌet 〕*v.* 暗殺
《雅典文 *haschisch* 為（大麻的雌花花穗製造的）麻醉劑》

【解說】十三世紀巴基斯坦祕密組織的頭目，為了提高部下士氣，令其喝
麻醉劑，而殺害當時十字軍的領導者。

cf. **hasheesh**，**hashish**（麻醉劑）

celebrate[3] 〔ˈsɛləˌbret 〕*v.* 慶祝；讚美；表揚
《拉丁文 *celeber* = populous》

congratulate[4] 〔 kənˈgrætʃəˌlet 〕*v.* 祝賀（把快樂分享大眾）
《*gratus* = pleasing》　*cf.* **grateful**（感謝的）

動詞字尾

contemplate[5]〔'kɑntəm,plet〕 *v.* 深思；預料

《*con-*（ intensive ）+ *templ(e)*（ temple ）+ *-ate*》

```
con    + templ(e) + ate
 |          |        |
intensive + temple +  v.
```

decorate[2]〔'dɛkə,ret〕 *v.* 裝飾《拉丁文 *decus* = ornament》

deteriorate[6]〔 dɪ'tɪrɪə,ret〕 *v.* 惡化；減低；墮落

《拉丁文 *deterior* = worse》

fascinate[5]〔'fæsn̩,et〕 *v.* 使著迷；蠱惑

《拉丁文 *fascinum* = spell（ 符咒；魔力 ）》

federate[7]〔'fɛdə,ret〕 *v.*（ 使 ）成爲聯盟（ 相信對方而結盟 ）

《*federal* 聯盟的》

```
feder + ate
  |      |
trust +  v.
```

frustrate[3]〔'frʌstret〕 *v.* 使受挫《拉丁文 *frustra* = in vain》

isolate[4]〔'aɪsl̩,et , 'ɪs- 〕 *v.* 隔離；使孤立（ 像島的 ）

《拉丁文 *insula* = island》 *cf.* **insular**（ 島國的 ）

narrate[6]〔 næ'ret〕 *v.* 敘述；說明《拉丁文 *narrare* = tell》

navigate[5]〔'nævə,get〕 *v.* 駕駛；航行；領航；操縱（ 使船前進 ）

《拉丁文 *nav* = *navis*（ ship ）+ *ig*（ drive ）+ *-ate*》 *cf.* **navy**（ 海軍 ）

```
nav + ig + ate
 |     |    |
ship + drive + v.
```

nominate[5]〔'nɑmə,net〕 *v.* 提名；任命；派定

《拉丁文 *nomen* = name》

originate[6]〔 ə'rɪdʒə,net〕 *v.* 起源；創始；發明

《拉丁文 *oriri* = rise ; begin》 *cf.* **Orient**（ 東方國家 ）

penetrate[5]〔'pɛnə,tret〕 *v.* 貫穿；滲入；看透

《*pen*（ food ）+ *etr*（ enter ）+ *-ate*》

perpetuate[7] 〔 pɚˈpɛtʃʊˌet 〕 v. 使永存；使不朽
《**per-** (through) + **petu** (strive) + **-ate**》

```
per  +  petu  +  ate
 |        |        |
through + strive +  v.
```

speculate[6] 〔ˈspɛkjəˌlet 〕 v. 沈思；思索；猜測；投機
《拉丁文 **specere** = see》

vibrate[5] 〔ˈvaɪbret 〕 v. 震動；顫動；擺動；回響
《拉丁文 **vibrare** = shake》

violate[4] 〔ˈvaɪəˌlet 〕 v. 破壞；違反；妨害《**violence** 暴力》

2 -en　* 加上形容詞、名詞，表示「使成～」。

darken[7] 〔ˈdɑrkən 〕 v. 變黑暗；使黑暗

fasten[3] 〔ˈfæsn̩ , ˈfɑ- 〕 v. 裝牢；繫緊；連結 (牢牢地)《**fast** 牢固的》

hasten[4] 〔ˈhesn̩ 〕 v. 催促；促進；趕快《**haste** 急忙》

```
hast(e) + en
   |       |
 quick  +  v.
```

heighten[5] 〔ˈhaɪtn̩ 〕 v. 增高；增強《**height** 高度》

lengthen[3] 〔ˈlɛŋkθən , ˈlɛŋθən 〕 v. (使) 變長；延長

moisten[7] 〔ˈmɔɪsn̩ 〕 v. 使濕潤《**moist** 潮濕的》

sharpen[5] 〔ˈʃɑrpən 〕 v. 使銳利；削 (鉛筆)；使敏銳
《**sharp** 銳利的》

strengthen[4] 〔ˈstrɛŋθən 〕 v. 加強；使堅固；鼓勵；增援
《**strength** 力氣》

```
streng + th + en
  |       |    |
strong +  n. +  v.
```

threaten[3] 〔ˈθrɛtn̩ 〕 v. 威脅；恐嚇；預示～的惡兆《**threat** 威脅》

weaken[3] 〔'wikən 〕 *v.* 使變弱；使稀薄
worsen[7] 〔'wɝsṇ 〕 *v.* （使）惡化；（使）變壞《*worse* 更壞的》

3　-er　　* 表示「反覆」的聲音或動作。

batter[5] 〔'bætə 〕 *v.* 連續敲擊《*bat* 用棒擊打》
chatter[5] 〔'tʃætə 〕 *v.* 喋喋不休；（鳥類的）啁啾《*chat* 閒談》
flicker[6] 〔 'flɪkə 〕 *v.* 搖曳；閃爍不定
flutter[6] 〔'flʌtə 〕 *v.* 擺動；拍動（翅膀）
glitter[5] 〔'glɪtə 〕 *v.* 閃爍；耀眼

> 【解說】 **gl-** 含有「光」的概念，在表「光的移動」、「視線的移動」的
> 字，其字首常為此。相當於中文「閃爍」的意思。
>
> | 例： | **glance**（匆匆地一看） | **glare**（發出強光） |
> |---|---|---|
> | | **glass**（反映） | **gleam**（微光） |
> | | **glimmer**（發微光） | **glimpse**（瞥見） |
> | | **glisten**（閃爍） | **glory**（光榮） |
> | | **gloss**（發光澤） | **glow**（發光） |

loiter[7] 〔'lɔɪtə 〕 *v.* 逍遙；閒蕩
patter[7] 〔'pætə 〕 *v.* 發出急速的輕拍聲
quiver[5] 〔'kwɪvə 〕 *v.* 使振動；顫慄
shiver[5] 〔'ʃɪvə 〕 *v.* 顫抖
totter[7] 〔'tɑtə 〕 *v.* 蹣跚；搖搖欲墜
twitter[7] 〔'twɪtə 〕 *v.* 緊張；興奮；鳥鳴
waver[7] 〔'wevə 〕 *v.* 擺動；搖曳

動詞字尾

4　-esce　　* 表示動作開始或正在進行。

acquiesce[7] 〔,ækwɪ'ɛs 〕 *v.* 默認；默許
　　《拉丁文 *acquiescere* = *ac-*（to）+ *quiescere*（be quiet）》

coalesce[7] 〔͵koə'lɛs〕 *v.* 合併;聯合;攜手合作

《拉丁文 *coalescere* = *co-* (together) + *alescere* (grow)》

```
co    + alesce
|        |
together + grow
```

convalesce[7] 〔͵kɑnvə'lɛs〕 *v.* (病) 有起色;恢復健康

《拉丁文 *convalescere* = *con-* (together) + *valescere* (grow strong)》

deliquesce[7] 〔͵dɛlə'kwɛs〕 *v.* 潮解;液化

《拉丁文 *deliquescere* = *de-* (apart) + *liquescere* (be fluid)》

```
de   + liquesce
|        |
apart + be fluid
```

effloresce[7] 〔͵ɛflo'rɛs, -flɔ-〕 *v.* 開花;繁盛

《拉丁文 *efflorescere* = *ef-* (out) + *florescere* (begin to blossom)》

evanesce[7] 〔͵ɛvə'nɛs〕 *v.* 漸漸消失《拉丁文 *evanescere* = vanish (消失)》

incandesce[7] 〔͵ɪnkən'dɛs, -kæn-〕 *v.* (使) 白熱化

《拉丁文 *incandescere* = become hot》

obsolesce[7] 〔͵ɑbsə'lɛs〕 *v.* 荒廢;廢棄

《拉丁文 *obsolescere* = become disused》

5 -(i)fy

* 是拉丁文 *facere* 的變化型 (= *make*),表示「做成」、「使~化」。

classify[4] 〔'klæsə͵faɪ〕 *v.* 分類 (分成等級)《*class* 等級》

edify[7] 〔'ɛdə͵faɪ〕 *v.* 陶冶;教化 (建築)《拉丁文 *aedes* = building》

    cf. **edifice** (大廈)

fortify[6] 〔'fɔrtə͵faɪ〕 *v.* 加強;設防;證實《拉丁文 *fortis* = strong》

```
forti + fy
|       |
strong + v.
```

動詞字尾

fructify[7] 〔'frʌktə,faɪ〕 v. 結果實；有成果《拉丁文 *fructus* = fruit》

identify[4] 〔 aɪ'dɛntə,faɪ〕 v. 認出；視為同一；使有關係（使相同）
《拉丁文 *idem* = the same》

justify[5] 〔'dʒʌstə,faɪ〕 v. 證明～為正常或應該；證明確有其事
《*just* 公平的》

liquefy[7] 〔'lɪkwə,faɪ〕 v.（使）液化《*liquid* 液體》

mollify[7] 〔'malə,faɪ〕 v. 緩和；使鎮靜；撫慰《拉丁文 *mollis* = soft》

```
moll  +  ify
 |         |
soft  +   v.
```

nullify[7] 〔'nʌlə,faɪ〕 v. 使無效；廢棄；取消《拉丁文 *nullus* = not any》

personify[7] 〔 pə'sanə,faɪ〕 v. 擬人化；賦與人性《*person* 人》

petrify[7] 〔'pɛtrə,faɪ〕 v. 使堅硬；使石化（使成岩石）
《拉丁文 *petra* = rock（岩石）》 *cf.* **petroleum**（石油）

```
petr  +  ify
 |         |
rock  +   v.
```

purify[6] 〔'pjurə,faɪ〕 v. 淨化；精煉《*pure* 純粹的》

qualify[5] 〔'kwalə,faɪ〕 v. 使合格；使勝任；限制；形容《*quality* 品質》

satisfy[2] 〔'sætɪs,faɪ〕 v. 使滿足（使充分）《拉丁文 *satis* = enough》
cf. **sate**（充分滿足），**satiate**（使飽；使滿足）

signify[6] 〔'sɪgnə,faɪ〕 v. 象徵；表示～之意；有重要性（以標幟表示）
《*sign* 記號》

simplify[6] 〔'sɪmplə,faɪ〕 v. 使單純；簡化《*simple* 簡單的》

stupefy[7] 〔'stjupə,faɪ〕 v. 使失去知覺；使發呆；使驚駭
《拉丁文 *stupere* = be astonished》

```
stupe        +  fy
 |               |
be astonished +  v.
```

vilify[7] 〔'vɪlə,faɪ〕 v. 誹謗；中傷（貶低別人）《拉丁文 *vilis* = cheap》

6　-ish　*表示「做～」的意思。*

admonish[7] 〔 əd'mɑnɪʃ 〕 *v.* 警告；勸告《拉丁文 *monere* = advise》
cf. **monition**（警告）

banish[7] 〔'bænɪʃ 〕 *v.* 放逐《*ban* 禁止》

blemish[7] 〔'blɛmɪʃ 〕 *v.* 使有缺點；損傷（打得青一塊紫一塊）
《冰島文 *blar* = bluish（帶青色的）》

```
blem  +  ish
 |        |
bluish +  v.
```

blush[4] 〔 blʌʃ 〕 *v.* 臉紅；慚愧；成為紅色
《古英文 *blyscan* = glow（熾熱）》

cherish[4] 〔'tʃɛrɪʃ 〕 *v.* 珍愛；珍惜；撫育《拉丁文 *carus* = dear》
cf. **caress**（愛撫）

demolish[7] 〔 dɪ'mɑlɪʃ 〕 *v.* 毀壞；推翻；吃光
《拉丁文 *demoliri* = pull down》

```
demol    +  ish
  |          |
pull down +  v.
```

diminish[6] 〔 də'mɪnɪʃ 〕 *v.* 減少；縮小《拉丁文 *minutus* = small》

embellish[7] 〔 ɪm'bɛlɪʃ 〕 *v.* 裝置；布置；修飾；潤色《*bellus* = fine》

famish[7] 〔'fæmɪʃ 〕 *v.* 飢餓；挨餓《拉丁文 *fames* = hunger》
cf. **famine**（饑荒）

flourish[5] 〔'flɝɪʃ 〕 *v.* 繁榮；茂盛；活躍（極度地誇耀）
《拉丁文 *florere* = flower（繁盛）》

```
flour  +  ish
  |        |
flower +  v.
```

furnish[4] 〔'fɝnɪʃ 〕 *v.* 供給；陳設《古代法文 *furnir* = 備有》
cf. **furniture**（傢俱）

garnish[7] 〔'gɑrnɪʃ 〕v. 加裝飾;在食物中加調味料

《法文 *garnir* = defend (保衛)》

languish[7] 〔'læŋgwɪʃ 〕v. 凋萎;憔悴;渴望

《拉丁文 *languere* = be weak》

```
langu  +  ish
  |        |
be weak  +  v.
```

publish[4] 〔'pʌblɪʃ 〕v. 發表;出版;公開;公佈 (公開地做)

《*public* 公開的》

punish[2] 〔'pʌnɪʃ 〕v. 懲罰;處罰;對付

《拉丁文 *poena* = penalty (刑罰)》   *cf.* **pain** (痛苦)

7 -ize , -ise

* 表示「使成～狀態」、「使～化」等意思,英式英語中也使用 *-ise*。

cauterize[7] 〔'kɔtə,raɪz 〕v. 灼燒;腐蝕;使麻木《希臘文 *kaiein* = burn》

civilize[6] 〔'sɪvḷ,aɪz 〕v. 使開化;使文明化;敎化

《拉丁文 *civis* = citizen》

```
civil  +  ize
  |        |
citizen  +  v.
```

dramatize[7] 〔'dræmə,taɪz 〕v. 編爲戲劇;使戲劇化《*drama* 戲劇》

generalize[6] 〔'dʒɛnərəl,aɪz 〕v. 概括;歸納;做結論;使普及

《*general* 一般的》

organize[2] 〔'ɔrgən,aɪz 〕v. 組織;成爲有機體《*organ* 器官;機關》

pulverize[7] 〔'pʌlvə,raɪz 〕v. 將～磨成粉;粉碎

《拉丁文 *pulver* = powder ; dust》

```
pulver  +  ize
  |         |
powder  +   v.
```

動詞字尾

specialize[6] 〔'spɛʃəl,aɪz 〕*v.* 專門研究；使專門；專攻

  《*special* 特殊的》

symbolize[6] 〔'sɪmbl̩,aɪz 〕*v.* 象徵；以符號表示《*symbol* 象徵》

utilize[6] 〔'jutl̩,aɪz 〕*v.* 利用；使用《拉丁文 *uti* = use》

  cf. utensil（用具）

victimize[6] 〔'vɪktɪm,aɪz 〕*v.* 使犧牲；使受害；欺騙

  《*victim* 受害者》

8   -le   *＊表示「反覆」。

chuckle[6] 〔'tʃʌkl̩ 〕*v.* 咯咯笑；低聲輕笑（像勒緊咽喉時發出的

  聲音）《*choke* 窒息》

dazzle[6] 〔'dæzl̩ 〕*v.* 使目眩；使迷惑《*daze* 使暈眩》

dwindle[7] 〔'dwɪndl̩ 〕*v.* 縮減；減少（消瘦而漸漸縮小）

  《冰島文 *dwina* = 消瘦》

scribble[7] 〔'skrɪbl̩ 〕*v.* 潦草書寫；亂寫；胡寫

  《拉丁文 *scribere* = write》

```
scribb  +  le
  |          |
write   +   v.
```

sparkle[4] 〔'spɑrkl̩ 〕*v.* 發出火花；閃爍；閃耀《*spark* 火花》

sprinkle[3] 〔'sprɪŋkl̩ 〕*v.* 散布；撒落；下小雨《*spring* 彈回》

startle[5] 〔'stɑrtl̩ 〕*v.* 使吃驚；使驚愕；驚動

  《*start* 突然跳起；吃驚》

trickle[7] 〔'trɪkl̩ 〕*v.*（淚水等）滴流；細流

  《古英文 *strikelen* = 無止境地流下去》

twinkle[4] 〔'twɪŋkl̩ 〕*v.* 閃爍；閃動；迅速移動

  《古英文 *twinken* = wink（眨眼）》

單字索引・Word Index

索引

索引

利用「字根」記憶，
是增加單字最快速的方法。

碰到背不下來的單字，
可查閱書後的「索引」。

如對字根、字首、字尾已經有概念，
就可直接看書的
頁眉，查閱字根或字首。

長久累積下去，
字根分析能力會愈來愈強，
以後不需要查字典，
也能猜出生字的意義。